PENGUIN BOOKS

A SECOND DALGLIESH TRILOGY

P. D. James was born in Oxford in 1920 and educated at Cambridge High School. From 1949 to 1968 she worked in the National Health Service as an administrator, and the experience she gained from her job helped her with the background for *Shroud for a Nightingale*, *The Black Tower* and *A Mind to Murder*. In 1968 she entered the Home Office as Principal, working first in the Police Department concerned with the forensic science service and later in the Criminal Policy Department. She retired in 1979. She is a Fellow of the Royal Society of Literature and a Fellow of the Royal Society of Arts, a governor of the BBC and a member of the board of the British Council. She served on the Arts Council and was chairman of its Literary Advisory Panel from 1988 to 1992. She has served as a magistrate in Middlesex and London. P. D. James has twice been the winner of the Silver Dagger Award of the Crime Writers' Association and in 1987 was awarded the Diamond Dagger Award for services to crime writing. In 1983 she received the OBE and was created a life peer in 1991. She has been a widow for over twenty-five years and has two children and five grandchildren.

Her other novels include *An Unsuitable Job for a Woman*, *Innocent Blood* and *The Skull Beneath the Skin* (which are also published by Penguin in one volume as *Trilogy of Death*), *Shroud for a Nightingale*, *The Black Tower* and *Death of an Expert Witness* (also published by Penguin as *A Dalgliesh Trilogy*), *Cover Her Face*, *Unnatural Causes* and *The Children of Men*. She is co-author, with T. A. Critchley, of *The Maul and the Pear Tree*.

Devices and Desires was shortlisted for the *Sunday Express* Book of the Year Award in 1989.

P. D. JAMES

A SECOND DALGLIESH TRILOGY

A MIND TO MURDER
A TASTE FOR DEATH
DEVICES AND DESIRES

PENGUIN BOOKS
IN ASSOCIATION WITH FABER & FABER

PENGUIN BOOKS

Published by the Penguin Group
Penguin Books Ltd, 27 Wrights Lane, London w8 5tz, England
Penguin Books USA Inc., 375 Hudson Street, New York, New York 10014, USA
Penguin Books Australia Ltd, Ringwood, Victoria, Australia
Penguin Books Canada Ltd, 10 Alcorn Avenue, Toronto, Ontario, Canada m4v 3b2
Penguin Books (NZ) Ltd, 182–190 Wairau Road, Auckland 10, New Zealand

Penguin Books Ltd, Registered Offices: Harmondsworth, Middlesex, England

A Mind to Murder first published by Faber & Faber 1963
Published by Penguin Books 1974
Published by Penguin Books in association with Faber & Faber 1989
Copyright © P. D. James 1963

A Taste for Death first published by Faber & Faber 1986
Published by Penguin Books in association with Faber & Faber 1989
Copyright © P. D. James 1986

Devices and Desires first published by Faber & Faber 1989
Published by Penguin Books in association with Faber & Faber 1990
Copyright © P. D. James 1989

The moral right of the author has been asserted

This collection first published by Penguin Books in association with Faber & Faber 1993

1 3 5 7 9 10 8 6 4 2

Typeset by Datix International Limited, Bungay, Suffolk
Printed in England

CONTENTS

A Mind to Murder   1

A Taste for Death   209

Devices and Desires   673

A MIND TO MURDER

For Edward Gordon James

AUTHOR'S NOTE

There is only a small number of autonomous psychiatric out-patient clinics in London and it is obvious that these units, dealing as they do with the same medical speciality and organized within a unified National Health Service, must inevitably have some methods of treatment and administrative procedures in common. A number of these they clearly share with the Steen Clinic. It is more important to state clearly that the Steen is an imaginary clinic situated in an imaginary London square, that none of its patients or staff, medical or lay, represent living people, and that the deplorable events which took place in its basement have their origin only in that curious psychological phenomenon – the imagination of the crime novelist.

P. D. J.

CHAPTER ONE

Dr Paul Steiner, consultant psychiatrist at the Steen Clinic, sat in the front ground-floor consulting-room and listened to his patient's highly rationalized explanation of the failure of his third marriage. Mr Burge lay in comfort on a couch the better to expound the complications of his psyche. Dr Steiner sat at his head in a chair of the carefully documented type which the Hospital Management Committee had decreed for the use of consultants. It was functional and not unattractive but it gave no support to the back of the head. From time to time a sharp jerk of his neck muscles recalled Dr Steiner from momentary oblivion to the realities of his Friday evening psychotherapy clinic. The October day had been very warm. After a fortnight of sharp frosts during which the staff of the clinic had shivered and pleaded, the official date for starting the central heating had coincided with one of those perfect autumn days when the city square outside had brimmed with yellow light and the late dahlias in the railed garden, bright as a paint-box, had shone like the gauds of high summer. It was now nearly seven o'clock. Outside, the warmth of the day had long given way, first to mist and then to chilly darkness. But here, inside the clinic, the heat of noon was trapped, the air, heavy and still, seemed spent with the breath of too much talking.

Mr Burge enlarged on the immaturity, coldness and insensitivity of his wives in a querulous falsetto. Dr Steiner's clinical judgement, not uninfluenced by the late effects of a large lunch and the unwise choice of a cream doughnut with his afternoon tea, told him that the time was not yet ripe to point out that the one defect shared by the three mesdames Burge had been a singular lack of judgement in their choice of husband. Mr Burge was not yet ready to face the truth of his own inadequacy.

Dr Steiner felt no moral indignation about his patient's behaviour. It would indeed have been most unethical had any such improper emotion clouded his judgement. There were few things in life which aroused Dr Steiner's moral indignation and most of them affected his own comfort. Many of them were, indeed, concerned with the Steen Clinic and its administration. He disapproved strongly of the administrative officer, Miss Bolam, whose preoccupation with the number of patients he saw in a session and the accuracy of his travelling expense form he saw as part of a systematic policy of persecution. He resented the fact that his Friday evening clinic coincided with Dr James Baguley's electro-convulsive therapy session so that his psychotherapy patients, all of them of high intelligence and sensible of the privilege of being treated by him, had to sit in the waiting-room with the motley crowd of depressed suburban housewives and ill-educated psychotics that Baguley seemed to delight in collecting. Dr Steiner had refused the use of one of the third-floor consulting-rooms. These had been formed by partitioning the large and elegant Georgian rooms and he despised them as badly proportioned and unpleasing cells, ill-suited either to his grade or to the importance of his work. Nor had he found it convenient to change the time of his session. Baguley, therefore, should change his. But Dr Baguley had stood firm and in this, too, Dr Steiner had seen the influence of Miss Bolam. His plea that the ground-floor consulting-rooms should be sound-proofed had been turned down by the Hospital Management Committee on the grounds of expense. There had, however, been no demur over providing Baguley with a new and highly expensive contraption for shocking his patients out of the few wits they still possessed. The matter had, of course, been considered by the Clinic Medical Committee, but Miss Bolam had made no secret of where her sympathies lay. In his diatribes against the administrative officer, Dr Steiner found it convenient to forget that her influence over the Medical Committee was non-existent.

It was difficult to forget the irritations of the E.C.T. session. The clinic building had been put up when men built to last, but even the sturdy oak door of the consulting-room could not muffle the comings and goings of a Friday night. The front door was closed at 6 p.m. and patients at the evening clinics were booked in and out since the time, over five years ago, when a patient had

A MIND TO MURDER

entered unobserved, secreted herself in the basement lavatory
and chosen that insalubrious place in which to kill herself. Dr
Steiner's psychotherapy sessions were punctuated by the ringing
of the front-door bell, the passing of feet as patients came and
went, the hearty voices of relatives and escorts exhorting the
patient or calling good-byes to Sister Ambrose. Dr Steiner wondered why relatives found it necessary to shout at the patients as
if they were deaf as well as psychotic. But possibly after a session
with Baguley and his diabolic machine they were. Worst of all
was the clinic domestic assistant, Mrs Shorthouse. One might
imagine that Amy Shorthouse could do the cleaning early in the
mornings as was surely the normal arrangement. That way there
would be the minimum of disturbance to the clinic staff. But Mrs
Shorthouse maintained that she couldn't get through the work
without an extra two hours in the evenings and Miss Bolam had
agreed. Naturally, she would. It appeared to Dr Steiner that very
little domestic work was done on Friday evenings. Mrs Shorthouse
had a predilection for the E.C.T. patients – indeed, her own
husband had once been treated by Dr Baguley – and she was
usually to be seen hanging around the hall and the ground-floor
general office while the session was being held. Dr Steiner had
mentioned it at the Medical Committee more than once and had
been irritated by his colleagues' general uninterest in the problem.
Mrs Shorthouse should be kept out of sight and encouraged to
get on with her work, not permitted to stand around gossiping
with the patients. Miss Bolam, so unnecessarily strict with other
members of the staff, showed no inclination to discipline Mrs
Shorthouse. Everyone knew that good domestic workers were
hard to get but an administrative officer who knew her job would
recruit them somehow. Weakness solved nothing. But Baguley
could not be persuaded to complain about Mrs Shorthouse and
Bolam would never criticize Baguley. The poor woman was probably in love with him. It was up to Baguley to take a firm line
instead of sloping around the clinic in that ridiculously long white
coat which made him look like a second-rate dentist. Really, the
man had no idea of the dignity with which a consultant clinic
should be conducted.

Clump, clump went someone's boots along the passage. It was

7

probably old Tippett, a chronic schizophrenic patient of Baguley's who for the past nine years had regularly spent Friday evenings carving wood in the art therapy department. The thought of Tippett increased Dr Steiner's petulance. The man was totally unsuitable for the Steen. If he were well enough to be out of hospital, which Dr Steiner doubted, he ought to attend a Day Hospital or one of the County Council's sheltered workshops. It was patients like Tippett who gave the clinic a dubious reputation and obscured its real function as an analytically orientated centre of psychotherapy. Dr Steiner felt positively embarrassed when one of his own carefully selected patients encountered Tippett creeping about the clinic on a Friday evening. Tippett wasn't even safe to be out. One day there would be an incident and Baguley would find himself in trouble.

Dr Steiner's happy contemplation of his own colleague in trouble was punctured by the ring of the front-door bell. Really, it was impossible! This time it was apparently a hospital car service driver calling for a patient. Mrs Shorthouse went to the door to speed them away. Her eldritch screech echoed through the hall. 'Cheerio, ducks. See you next week. If you can't be good be careful.'

Dr Steiner winced and shut his eyes. But his patient, happily engaged in his favourite hobby of talking about himself, seemed not to have heard. Mr Burge's high whine had not, in fact, faltered for the past twenty minutes.

'I don't pretend I'm an easy person. I'm not, I'm a complicated devil. That's something which Theda and Sylvia have never understood. The roots of it go deep of course. You remember that session we had in June? Some pretty basic stuff came out then I thought.'

His therapist did not recall the session in question but was unconcerned. With Mr Burge pretty basic stuff was invariably near the surface and could be trusted to emerge. An unaccountable peace fell. Dr Steiner doodled on his notepad, regarded his doodle with interest and concern, looked at it again with the pad held upside down and became for a moment more preoccupied with his own subconscious than with that of his patient. Suddenly he became aware of another sound from outside, faint at first and then becoming louder. Somewhere a woman was screaming. It was a horrible noise, high, continuous, and completely animal. Its effect on Dr Steiner was peculiarly unpleasant. He was naturally timid and highly strung. Although his job involved him in the occasional emotional crises he was more adept at circumventing than coping with an emergency. Fear gave vent to irritation and he sprang from his chair exclaiming:

'No! Really, this is too bad! What's Miss Bolam doing? Isn't anyone supposed to be in charge here?'

'What's up?' inquired Mr Burge, sitting up like a jack-in-the-box and dropping his voice half an octave to its more normal tone.

'Nothing. Nothing. Some woman having an attack of hysteria that's all. Stay where you are. I'll be back,' commanded Dr Steiner.

Mr Burge collapsed again but with eye and ear cocked for the door. Dr Steiner found himself in the hall.

Immediately a little group swung round to face him. Jennifer Priddy, the junior typist, was clinging to one of the porters, Peter Nagle, who was patting her shoulder in embarrassed pity and looking puzzled. Mrs Shorthouse was with them. The girl's screams were subsiding into whimpers but her whole body was shaking, and she was deathly pale.

'What's the matter?' asked Dr Steiner sharply. 'What's wrong with her?'

Before anyone had a chance to reply the door of the E.C.T. room opened and Dr Baguley came out followed by Sister Ambrose and his anaesthetist, Dr Mary Ingram. The hall seemed suddenly full of people. 'Calm down, that's a good girl,' said Dr Baguley mildly. 'We're trying to run a clinic.' He turned to Peter Nagle and asked in a low voice: 'What's the matter anyway?'

Nagle seemed about to speak when, suddenly, Miss Priddy gained control. Breaking free she turned to Dr Baguley and said with absolute clearness:

'It's Miss Bolam. She's dead. Someone's killed her. She's in the basement record-room and she's murdered. I found her, Enid's been murdered!'

She clung to Nagle and began to cry again but more quietly. The dreadful shaking had ceased. Dr Baguley said to the porter:

'Take her into the treatment-room. Make her lie down. Better give her something to drink. Here's the key. I'll be back.'

He made for the basement stairs and the rest, abandoning the girl to Nagle's ministrations, followed in a jostling bunch. The basement at the Steen was well lit; all its rooms were used by the clinic which, like most psychiatric units, was chronically short of space. Here, below stairs, in addition to the boiler-room, the telephone equipment-room and the porters' quarters, was the art therapy department, a medical records storeroom and, at the front of the building, a treatment-room for the lysergic acid patients. As the little group reached the bottom of the stairs the door of this room opened and Nurse Bolam, Miss Bolam's cousin, looked out briefly – a shadowy wraith in her white uniform against the darkness of the room behind. Her gentle, puzzled voice floated to them down the corridor. 'Is there anything wrong? I thought I heard a scream a few minutes ago.'

Sister Ambrose said with brusque authority:

'There's nothing wrong, Nurse. Get back to your patient.'

The white figure disappeared and the door was shut. Turning to Mrs Shorthouse, Sister Ambrose went on:

'And there's nothing for you to do here, Mrs Shorthouse. Please stay upstairs. Miss Priddy might like a cup of tea.'

Mrs Shorthouse was heard to mutter rebelliously but beat a reluctant retreat. The three doctors, with Sister in tow, pressed on.

The medical record-room was on their right, between the porters' rest-room and the art therapy department. The door was ajar and the light was on.

Dr Steiner, who had become unnaturally aware of every small detail, noticed the key was in the lock. No one was about. The steel racks, with their tight-packed rows of manilla folders, ran ceiling high and at right angles to the door forming a series of narrow aisles, each lit by a fluorescent light. The four high windows were barred and dissected by the racks; it was an airless little room rarely visited and seldom dusted. The little group pushed its way down the first passage and turned left to where there was a small windowless space clear of shelving and furnished with a table and chair where records could be sorted for filing or information copied from the notes without the need to take the file away. Here was chaos. The chair was overturned. The floor was littered with records. Some had their covers wrenched apart and their pages torn, others lay dumped in shifting layers beneath gaps on the shelves which looked too narrow to have held such a weight of paper. And in the middle of this confusion, like a plump and incongruous Ophelia afloat on a tide of paper, was the body of Enid Bolam. On her chest rested a heavy and grotesque image carved in wood, her hands folded about its base so that she looked, horribly, like a parody of motherhood with her creature ritually laid to her breast.

There could be no doubt that she was dead. Even in the midst of his fear and repugnance Dr Steiner could not miss that final diagnosis. Staring at the wooden figure he cried:

'Tippett! That's his fetish! That's the carving he's so proud of. Where is he? Baguley, he's your patient! You'd better handle this!'

He looked round nervously as if expecting Tippett to materialize, arm raised to strike, the very personification of violence.

Dr Baguley was kneeling by the body. He said quietly:

'Tippett isn't here this evening.'

'But he's always here on Fridays! That's his fetish! That's the weapon!' Dr Steiner wailed against such obtuseness.

Dr Baguley gently lifted Miss Bolam's left eyelid with his thumb. Without looking up he said:

'We had a phone call from St Luke's this morning. Tippett's been admitted with pneumonia. Last Monday, I think. Anyway, he wasn't here this evening.' Suddenly he gave an exclamation. The two women bent closer to the body. Dr Steiner, who could not bring himself to watch the examination, heard him say:

'She's been stabbed, too. Through the heart by the look of it and with a black-handled chisel. Isn't this one of Nagle's, Sister?' There was a pause and Dr Steiner heard Sister's voice:

'It looks very like it, Doctor. All his tools have black handles. He keeps them in the porters' rest-room.' She added defensively, 'Anyone could get at them.'

'It looks as if someone has.' There was the sound of Dr Baguley getting to his feet. Still keeping his eyes on the body he said:

'Phone Cully on the door, will you, Sister. Don't alarm him, but tell him that no one is to be admitted or to leave the building. That includes the patients. Then get Dr Etherege and ask him to come down. He'll be in his consulting-room I imagine.'

'Oughtn't we to phone the police?' Dr Ingram spoke nervously and her pink face, so ridiculously like that of an angora rabbit, flushed pinker. It was not only in moments of high drama that one was apt to overlook the presence of Dr Ingram, and Dr Baguley stared blankly at her as if he had momentarily forgotten her existence.

'We'll wait for the medical director,' he said.

Sister Ambrose disappeared with a rustle of starched linen. The nearest telephone was just outside the record-room door but, insulated by tiers of paper from every outside noise, Dr Steiner strained his ears in vain to hear the lift of the receiver or the murmur of Sister's voice. He forced himself to look once more at Miss Bolam's body. In life he had thought of her as graceless and unattractive, and death had lent her no dignity. She lay on her back, her knees raised and parted so that there was an expanse of pink woollen knicker clearly visible, looking far more indecent than naked flesh. Her round, heavy face was quite peaceful. The two thick plaits which she wore wound above her forehead were undisturbed. But then, nothing had ever been known to disturb Miss Bolam's archaic hairstyle. Dr Steiner was reminded of his private fantasy that the thick, lifeless plaits exuded their own mysterious secretion and were fixed for ever, immutably, about that placid brow. Looking at her in the defenceless indignity of death, Dr Steiner tried to feel pity and knew that he felt fear. But he was fully conscious only of repugnance. It was impossible to feel tenderly towards something so ridiculous, so shocking, so obscene. The ugly word spun unbidden to the surface of thought. Obscene! He felt a ridiculous urge to pull down her skirt, to cover that puffy, pathetic face, to replace the spectacles which had slipped from her nose and hung, askew, from her left ear. Her eyes were half closed, her small mouth pursed as if in disapproval of so undignified and unmerited an end. Dr Steiner was not unfamiliar with that look: he had seen it on her face in life. He thought, 'She looks as if she's just confronting me with my travelling expense form.'

Suddenly he was seized with an intolerable need to giggle. Laughter welled up uncontrollably. He recognized that this horrible urge was the result of nervousness and shock but understanding did not bring control. Helplessly, he turned his back on his colleagues and fought for composure, grasping the edge of a filing rack and pressing his forehead for support against the cold metal, his mouth and nostrils choked with the musty smell of old records.

He was not aware of Sister Ambrose's return but, suddenly, he heard her speaking.

'Dr Etherege is on his way down. Cully is on the door and I've told him that no one is to leave. Your patient is making rather a fuss, Dr Steiner.'

'Perhaps I'd better go up to him.' Faced with the need for decision, Dr Steiner regained control. He felt that it was somehow important that he should stay with the others and be there when the medical director arrived; that it would be wise to ensure that nothing important was said or done out of his hearing. On the other hand he was not anxious to stay with the body. The record-room, brightly lit as an operating theatre, claustrophobic and overheated, made him feel like a trapped animal. The heavy close-packed shelves seemed to press upon him, compelling his eyes again and again to that lumpen figure on its paper bier.

'I'll stay here,' he decided. 'Mr Burge must wait like everyone else.'

They stood together without speaking. Dr Steiner saw that Sister Ambrose, white-faced but otherwise apparently unmoved, stood stockily calm with her hands loosely clasped over her apron. So must she have stood time without number in nearly forty years of nursing, waiting at the bedside of a patient, quietly deferential, for the doctor's orders. Dr Baguley pulled out his cigarettes, looked at the packet for a moment as if surprised to find it in his hand, and replaced it in his pocket. Dr Ingram seemed to be silently crying. Once Dr Steiner thought he heard her murmur: 'Poor woman. Poor woman!'

Soon they heard footsteps and the medical director was with them followed by the senior psychologist, Fredrica Saxon. Dr Etherege knelt down beside the body. He did not touch it but put his face close to Miss Bolam's as if he were about to kiss her. Dr Steiner's sharp little eyes did not miss the glance that Miss Saxon gave Dr Baguley, that instinctive move towards each other and the quick withdrawal.

'What happened?' she whispered. 'Is she dead?'

'Yes. Murdered apparently.' Baguley's tone was flat. Miss Saxon made a sudden gesture. For one unbelievable moment Dr Steiner thought that she was going to cross herself.

'Who did it? Not poor old Tippett? That's his fetish, surely.'

'Yes, but he isn't here. He's in St Luke's with pneumonia.'

'Oh, my God! Then who?' This time she moved close to Dr Baguley and they did not draw apart. Dr Etherege scrambled to his feet.

'You're right, of course. She's dead. Stunned first apparently and then stabbed through the heart. I'll go upstairs to phone the police and let the rest of the staff know. We'd better keep people together. Then we three had better search the building. Nothing must be touched of course.'

Dr Steiner dared not meet Dr Baguley's eyes. Dr Etherege in his role of the calm, authoritative administrator had always struck him as slightly ridiculous. He suspected that Baguley felt the same.

Suddenly they heard footsteps and the senior psychiatric social worker Miss Ruth Kettle appeared from behind the filing racks, peering at them short-sightedly.

'Ah, there you are, Director,' said Miss Kettle, in her fluting, breathless voice. (She was the only staff member, thought Dr Steiner, to give Dr Etherege that ridiculous title and God only knew why. It made the place sound like a nature-cure clinic.)

'Cully told me you were down here. Not busy, I hope? I'm so distressed, I don't want to make trouble but it really is too bad! Miss Bolam has booked me a new patient for ten on Monday. I've just seen the appointment in my diary. No consultation with me of course. She knows I always see the Worrikers then. It's quite deliberate, I'm afraid. You know, Director, someone has really got to do something about Miss Bolam.'

Dr Baguley stood aside and said grimly: 'Someone has.'

At the other end of the square Superintendent Adam Dalgliesh

14

of the Criminal Investigation Department was attending the ritual autumn sherry party given by his publishers which had coincided with the third reprint of his first book of verse. He didn't overestimate his talent or the success of his book. The poems, which reflected his detached, ironic and fundamentally restless spirit, had happened to catch a public mood. He did not believe that more than half a dozen would live even in his own affections. Meanwhile he found himself awash on the shallows of an unfamiliar sea in which agents, royalties and reviews were agreeable hazards. And now there was this party. He had thought of it without enthusiasm as something to be endured, but it had proved unexpectedly enjoyable. Messrs Herne and Illingworth were as incapable of providing poor sherry as they were of publishing poor work; Dalgliesh estimated that his publishers' share of his own book's profits had been drunk in the first ten minutes. Old Sir Hubert Illingworth had made his brief appearance in the course of it, had shaken Dalgliesh sadly by the hand, and had shuffled off muttering under his breath as if deploring that yet another writer on the firm's list was exposing himself and his publisher to the doubtful gratifications of success. To him all writers were precocious children; creatures to be tolerated and encouraged but not overexcited in case they cried before bedtime.

There were less welcome diversions than the brief appearance of Sir Hubert. Few of the guests knew that Dalgliesh was a detective and not all of them expected him to talk about his job. But there were inevitably those who thought it inappropriate that a man who caught murderers should also write verse and who said so with varying degrees of tact. Presumably they wanted murderers caught however much they might argue about what should happen to them afterwards; but they displayed a typical ambivalence towards those who did the catching. Dalgliesh was used to this attitude and found it less offensive than the common assumption that there was a particular glamour in being a member of the murder squad. But if there had been the expected quota of furtive curiosity and the inanities common to all such parties, there had also been agreeable people saying agreeable things. No writer, however apparently detached about his talent, is immune to the subtle reassurance of disinterested praise and Dalgliesh, fighting the suspicion that few of those who admired had actually read and fewer still had bought, found that he was quietly enjoying himself and was honest enough to admit why.

The first hour had been hectic but, soon after seven o'clock, he found himself standing alone glass in hand beside the ornate James Wyatt chimney-piece. A thin wood fire was burning, filling the room with a faint country smell. It was one of those inexplicable moments when one is suddenly completely alone in the middle of a crowd, when the noise is muted and the pressing bodies seem to recede and become remote and mysterious as actors on some distant stage. Dalgliesh leaned the back of his head against the mantelpiece, savouring this momentary privacy and noting appreciatively the elegant proportions of the room. Suddenly he saw Deborah Riscoe. She must have come into the room very quietly. He wondered how long she had been there. Immediately his diffuse sense of peace and happiness gave way to a pleasure as keen and painful as that of a boy in love for the first time. She saw him at once and, glass in hand, edged her way across the room to him.

Her appearance was wholly unexpected and he did not deceive himself that she was there on his account. After their last encounter that would hardly be likely.

He said, 'It's very pleasant to see you here.'

'I should have come anyway,' she replied. 'But actually I work here, Felix Herne got me the job after Mummy died. I'm quite useful. I'm the general dogsbody. Shorthand and typing, too. I took a course.'

He smiled.

'You make it sound like a cure.'

'Well, in a way it was.'

He did not pretend not to understand. They were both silent. Dalgliesh knew that he was morbidly sensitive to any allusion to the case which nearly three years ago, had led to their first meeting. That sore could not stand even the gentlest of probes. He had seen the announcement of her mother's death in the paper about six months ago, but it had seemed impossible and impertinent then to send her a message or to speak the customary words of condolence. After all, he was partly responsible for her death. It was no easier now. Instead they talked of his verse and of her job. Taking his share of this casual undemanding small talk he wondered what she would say if he asked her to have dinner with him. If she didn't turn him down flat – and she probably would – it could be for him the beginning of involvement. He didn't deceive himself that he only wanted an agreeable meal with a woman he happened to think beautiful. He had no idea what she thought of him, but, ever since their last meeting, he had known himself to be on the brink of love. If she accepted – for this or for any evening – his solitary life would be threatened. He knew this with complete certainty and the knowledge frightened him. Ever since the death of his wife in childbirth he had insulated himself carefully against pain; sex little more than an exercise in skill; a love affair merely an emotional pavan, formalized, danced according to the rules, committing one to nothing. But, of course, she wouldn't accept. He had absolutely no reason to think that she was interested in him. It was only this certainty that gave him the confidence to indulge his thoughts. But he was tempted to try his luck. As they talked he mentally rehearsed the words, wryly amused to recognize after so many years the uncertainties of adolescence.

The light tap on his shoulder took him by surprise. It was the chairman's secretary to say that he was wanted on the telephone. 'It's the Yard, Mr Dalgliesh,' she said, with well-controlled interest as if Herne and Illingworth's authors were accustomed to calls from the Yard.

He smiled his excuses at Deborah Riscoe and she gave a little resigned shrug of her shoulders.

'I won't be a moment,' he said. But even as he threaded his way through the crush of chatterers he knew that he wouldn't be back.

He took the call in a small office next to the boardroom, struggling to the telephone through chairs heaped with manuscripts, rolled galley proofs and dusty files. Hearne and Illingworth fostered an air of old-fashioned leisureliness and general muddle which concealed – sometimes to their authors' discomfiture – a formidable efficiency and attention to detail.

The familiar voice boomed in his ear.

'That you, Adam? How's the party? Good. Sorry to break it up but I'd be grateful if you'd look in over the way. The Steen Clinic, Number 31. You know the place. Upper class neuroses catered for only. It seems that their secretary or administrative officer or what have you has got herself murdered. Bashed on the head in the basement and then stabbed expertly through the heart. The boys are on their way. I've sent you Martin, of course. He'll have your gear with him.'

'Thank you, sir. When was it reported?'

'Three minutes ago. The medical director rang. He gave me a concise account of practically everyone's alibi for the supposed time of death and explained why it couldn't possibly be one of the patients. He was followed by a doctor called Steiner. He explained that we met about five years ago at a dinner party given by his late brother-in-law. Dr Steiner explained why it couldn't have been him and favoured me with his interpretation of the psychological make-up of the killer. They've read all the best detective fiction. No one has touched the body, they're not letting anyone in or out of the building and they've all collected into one room to keep an eye on each other. You'd better hurry over, Adam, or they'll solve the crime before you arrive.'

'Who is the medical director?' asked Dalgliesh.

'Dr Henry Etherege. You must have seen him on television. He's the establishment psychiatrist, dedicated to making the profession respectable. Distinguished looking, orthodox and earnest.'

'I've seen him in court,' said Dalgliesh.

'Of course. Remember him in the Routledge case? He practically had me weeping into my hankie and I knew Routledge better than most. Etherege is the natural choice of any defence counsel – if he can get him. You know their bleat. Find me a psychiatrist who looks respectable, speaks English and won't shock the jury or antagonize the judge. Answer, Etherege. Ah, well, good luck!'

The A.C. was optimistic in supposing that his message could break up the party. It had long reached the stage when the departure of a solitary guest disconcerted no one. Dalgliesh

18

thanked his host, waved a casual good-bye to the few people who caught his eye and passed almost unnoticed out of the building. He did not see Deborah Riscoe again, and made no effort to find her. His mind was already on the job ahead and he felt that he had been saved, at best from a snub and, at worst, from folly. It had been a brief, tantalizing, inconclusive and unsettling encounter but, already, it was in the past.

Walking across the square to the tall Georgian building that housed the Steen Clinic, Dalgliesh recalled some of the scant items of information about the place that had come his way. It was a well-known witticism that you had to be exceptionally sane to be accepted for treatment at the Steen. Certainly it had a reputation – Dalgliesh thought probably undeserved – for selecting its patients with more regard to their intelligence and social class than their mental condition, subjecting them to diagnostic procedures designed to deter all but the most enthusiastic, and then placing them on a waiting list for treatment long enough to ensure that the curative effects of time could exert their maximum influence before the patient actually attended for his first psychotherapy session. The Steen, Dalgliesh remembered, had a Modigliani. It was not a well-known painting, nor did it represent the artist at his best, but it was, undeniably, a Modigliani. It hung in the first-floor boardroom, the gift of a former grateful patient, and it represented much that the clinic stood for in the public eye. Other National Health Service clinics brightened their walls with reproductions from the Red Cross picture library. The Steen staff made no secret that they preferred a second-rate original to a first-class reproduction any day. And they had a second-rate original to prove it.

The house itself was one of a Georgian terrace. It stood at the south corner of the square, comfortable, unpretentious and wholly pleasing. At the rear a narrow passage ran into Lincoln Square Mews. There was a railed basement; in front of the house the railings curved on each side of the broad steps which led to the door and supported two wrought-iron lamp standards. On the right of the door an unpretentious bronze plaque bore the name of the Hospital Management Committee which administered the unit and, underneath, the words, 'The Steen Clinic'. No other information was given. The Steen did not advertise its function to a vulgar world nor did it wish to invite an influx of the local psychotics seeking treatment or reassurance. There were four cars parked outside but no signs yet of the police. The house looked very quiet. The door was shut but a light shone from the elegant Adam fanlight above the door and between the folds of drawn curtains in the ground-floor rooms.

The door was opened almost before he had taken his finger from the bell. They had been waiting for him. A stockily built young man in porter's uniform opened the door and let him in without speaking. The hall blazed with light and struck very warm after the coolness of the autumn night. To the left of the door was a glass-panelled reception kiosk with a telephone switchboard. A second, and much older, porter sat at the board in an attitude of utter misery. He looked round and glanced briefly at Dalgliesh with rheumy eyes, then returned to his contemplation of the board as if the arrival of the superintendent was the last straw of an intolerable burden which, if ignored, might be lifted from him. In the main body of the hall the reception committee came forward, the medical director with outstretched hand as if welcoming a guest. 'Superintendent Dalgliesh? We're very glad to see you. May I introduce my colleague, Dr James Baguley, and the secretary of the Hospital Management Committee, Mr Lauder.'

'You got here very promptly, sir,' said Dalgliesh to Lauder. The group secretary said:

'I didn't know about the murder until I arrived two minutes ago. Miss Bolam telephoned me at lunchtime today and said she wanted to see me urgently. Something was going on at the clinic and she needed advice. I came as soon as I could and found that she'd been murdered. In the circumstances, I had more reasons than one for deciding to stay around. It looks as if she needed advice more than she knew.'

'Whatever it was, you've come too late, I'm afraid,' said Dr Etherege.

Dalgliesh saw that he was much shorter than his television appearances suggested. His large, high-domed head with its aureole of white hair soft and fine as a baby's looked too weighty for the slight supporting body which seemed to have aged independently giving him an oddly disintegrated appearance. It was difficult to guess his age but Dalgliesh thought that he must be nearer seventy than sixty-five, the normal retiring age for a consultant. He had the face of an indestructible gnome, the cheeks mottled with high colour so that they looked painted, the eyebrows springing above eyes of a piercing blue. Dalgliesh felt that those eyes and the soft, persuasive voice were not the least of the medical director's professional assets.

In contrast, Dr James Baguley was six feet tall, nearly as tall as Dalgliesh, and the immediate impression he gave was of intense weariness. He was wearing a long white coat which hung loosely from his bowed shoulders. Although he was much the younger man he had none of the medical director's vitality. His hair was straight and turning iron-grey. From time to time he swept it out of his eyes with long nicotine-stained fingers. His was a handsome, bony face, but the skin and eyes were dulled as if with permanent tiredness.

The medical director said:

'You will, of course, want to see the body straight away. I'll ask Peter Nagle, our second porter, to come down with us if you've no objection. His chisel was one of the weapons used – not that he could help that, poor fellow – and no doubt you will want to ask him questions.'

'I shall want to question everyone here in due course,' replied Dalgliesh.

It was apparent that the medical director had taken charge. Dr Baguley, who had not yet spoken, seemed glad to accept that position. Lauder had apparently decided to adopt a watching brief. As they moved towards the basement stairs at the back of the hall he caught Dalgliesh's eye. The momentary glance was hard to analyse, but Dalgliesh thought he detected an amused gleam and a certain wry detachment.

They stood in silence as Dalgliesh knelt by the body. He did not touch it except to part the cardigan and blouse, both of which were unbuttoned, and expose the handle of the chisel. It had been driven in up to the hilt. There was very little bruising of the tissues and no blood. The woman's vest had been rolled up above her breasts to expose the flesh for that vicious, calculated thrust. Such deliberation suggested that the killer had a confident knowledge of anatomy. There were easier ways of killing than to pierce the heart with one thrust. But for those with the knowledge and the strength there were few ways so sure.

He got to his feet and turned to Peter Nagle.

'Is that your chisel?'

'Apparently. It looks like it and mine isn't in the box.' Despite the omission of the usual 'sir' the voice, educated and unemphatic, held no trace of insolence or resentment. Dalgliesh asked:

'Any idea how it got here?'

'None at all. But I'd hardly be likely to say if I had, would I?'

The medical director gave Nagle a quick frown of warning or admonition and placed his hand briefly on the porter's shoulder. Without consulting Dalgliesh he said gently:

'That will be all for the present, Nagle. Just wait outside, will you?'

Dalgliesh made no demur as the porter quietly detached himself from the group and left without another word.

'Poor boy! The use of his chisel has naturally shocked him. It looks unpleasantly like an attempt to implicate him. But you will find, Superintendent, that Nagle is one of the few members of the staff with a complete alibi for the presumed time of death.' Dalgliesh did not point out that this was, in itself, highly suspicious.

'Did you make any estimate of the time of death?' he asked.

Dr Etherege replied:

'I thought that it must have been very recent. That is Dr Baguley's view too. The clinic is very warm today — we've just started our central heating — so that the body would cool very slowly. I didn't try for rigor. I am, of course, little more than a layman in such matters. Subsequently I knew that she must have died within the hour. Naturally we have been talking among ourselves while waiting for you and it appears that Sister Ambrose was the last person to see Miss Bolam alive. That was at twenty past six. Cully, our senior porter, tells me that Miss Bolam rang him on the internal phone at about six-fifteen to say that she was going down to the basement and that Mr Lauder should be directed to her office if he arrived. A few minutes later, as far as she can judge, Sister came out of the E.C.T. room on the ground floor and crossed the hall to the patients' waiting-room to let a husband know that his wife was ready to be taken home. Sister saw Miss Bolam going down the hall towards the basement stairs. No one saw her alive again after that.'

'Except her murderer,' said Dalgliesh.

Dr Etherege looked surprised.

'Yes, that would be so, of course. I mean that none of us saw her alive again. I have asked Sister Ambrose about the time and Sister is quite sure . . .'

'I shall be seeing Sister Ambrose and the other porter.'

'Of course. Naturally you will want to see everybody. We expect that. While waiting we telephoned our homes to say that we would be delayed tonight but gave no explanation. We had already searched the building and ascertained that the basement door and the ground-floor rear entrance were both bolted. Nothing has been touched in here naturally. I arranged for the staff to stay together in the front consulting-room except for Sister and Nurse Bolam who were with the remaining patients in the waiting-room. No one but Mr Lauder and you have been allowed in.'

'You seem to have thought of everything, Doctor,' said Dalgliesh. He got up from his knees and stood looking down at the body.

'Who found her?' he asked.

'One of our medical secretaries, Jennifer Priddy. Cully, the senior porter, has been complaining of stomach-ache most of the day and Miss Priddy went to find Miss Bolam to ask if he could go home early. Miss Priddy is very upset but she was able to tell me . . .'

'I think it would be better if I heard it from her direct. Was this door kept locked?'

His tone was perfectly courteous but he felt their surprise. The medical director's tone did not change as he replied:

'Usually it is. The key is kept on a board with other clinic keys in the porters' duty-room here in the basement. The chisel was kept there, too.'

'And this fetish?'

'Taken from the basement art therapy room across the passage. It was carved by one of our patients.'

It was still the medical director who replied. So far Dr Baguley hadn't spoken a word. Suddenly he said:

'She was knocked out with the fetish and then stabbed through the heart by someone who was either knowledgeable or damned lucky. That much is obvious. What isn't obvious is why they had this free-for-all with the medical records. She's lying on them so it must have happened before the murder.'

'The result of a struggle, perhaps,' suggested Dr Etherege.

'It doesn't look like it. They were pulled out of the shelves and deliberately chucked about. There must have been a reason. There wasn't anything impulsive about this murder.'

It was then that Peter Nagle, who had apparently been standing outside the door, came into the room.

'There's been a ring at the door, sir. Would that be the rest of the police?'

Dalgliesh noted that the record-room was almost sound-proof. The front-door bell was strident but he had not heard it.

'Right,' he said. 'We'll go up.'

As they moved together towards the stairs Dr Etherege said:

'I wonder, Superintendent, if you could see the patients fairly soon. We have only two still with us, a male psychotherapy patient of my colleague Dr Steiner, and a woman who has been receiving lysergic acid treatment down here in the basement front treatment-room. Dr Baguley will be able to explain the treatment to you – she is his patient – but you can be assured that she wasn't capable of leaving her bed until a few minutes ago and certainly wouldn't know anything about the murder. These patients become quite disorientated during treatment. Nurse Bolam was with her all the evening.'

'Nurse Bolam? She is a relation of the dead woman?'

'Her cousin,' said Dr Baguley briefly.

'And your disorientated patient, Doctor. Would she know if Nurse Bolam left her alone during treatment?'

Dr Baguley said curtly:

'Nurse Bolam would not have left her.'

24

They mounted the stairs together to meet the murmur of voices in the hall.

That ring at the door brought into the Steen Clinic the paraphernalia and skills of an alien world. Quietly and without fuss the experts in violent death got busy. Dalgliesh disappeared into the record-room with the police surgeon and photographer. The print man, small and plump-cheeked as a hamster, with tiny delicate hands, gave his attention to door handles, locks, the tool case and Tippett's fetish. Plain-clothes men, looking disconcertingly like television actors playing plain-clothes men, made their methodical search of every room and cupboard in the clinic verifying that there was indeed no unauthorized person on the premises and that the back doors both of the ground floor and the basement were securely locked from the inside. The clinic staff, excluded from these activities and congregated in the front ground-floor consulting-room, which had been hastily furnished with additional easy chairs from the patients' waiting-room, felt that their familiar ground had been taken over by strangers and that they were caught up in the inexorable machinery of justice and being ground forward to God knew what embarrassments and disasters. Only the group secretary appeared unperturbed. He had stationed himself in the hall like a watchdog and sat there patient and alone until his turn came to be interviewed.

Dalgliesh took Miss Bolam's office for his use. It was a small room on the ground floor situated between the large general office at the front of the building and the E.C.T. treatment-room and recovery-room at the rear. Opposite it was a suite of two consulting-rooms and the patients' waiting-room. The office had been formed by partitioning the end of a larger room so that it was oddly proportioned and unattractively narrow for its height. It was sparsely furnished and lacked all evidence of personal taste except for a large bowl of chrysanthemums set on one of the filing cabinets. There was an old-fashioned safe against one wall and the other was lined with green metal filing cabinets. The desk was unostentatious and held nothing but a stationery office desk calendar, a jotting pad, and a small stack of manilla folders. Dalgliesh looked through them and said, 'This is odd. These are staff dossiers apparently, but only of the female staff.

Her own isn't here incidentally. I wonder why she got these out?'

'Checking on people's annual leave entitlement or something like that perhaps,' suggested Sergeant Martin.

'Could be, I suppose. But why only the women? Oh well, it's hardly of immediate importance. Let's have a look at that jotter.'

Miss Bolam was apparently one of those administrators who prefer not to trust to memory. The top leaf of the jotter, headed with the date, was well filled with notes in a sloping, rather childish handwriting.

Medical Committee – speak M.D. re proposed Adolescent Dept.

Speak Nagle – broken sash cord Miss Kallinski's room.

Mrs Shorthouse – ? leave.

These notes were at least self-explanatory but the jottings below them – written it appeared in some hurry – were less explicit.

Woman. Here eight years. To arrive 1st Monday.

Dalgliesh said: 'These look like the jottings of a telephone call. It could have been a private call, of course, and nothing to do with the clinic. It could have been a doctor trying to trace a patient, or vice versa. Something, or someone, is apparently expected to arrive on the first Monday or on Monday the first. There are a dozen possible interpretations and none of them relevant to the murder. Still, someone phoned recently about a woman and Miss Bolam was obviously examining the dossiers of every woman on the staff except herself. Why? To check which of them were here eight years ago? It's all pretty far-fetched. We'll leave the pleasures of conjecture for the moment and get down to seeing these people. I'd like that typist in first, the girl who found the body. Etherege said she was upset. Let's hope she's calmed down by now or we'll be here half the night.'

But Jennifer Priddy was perfectly calm. She had obviously been drinking and her grief was overlaid with a barely suppressed excitement. Her face, still swollen from crying, was blotched with high colour and her eyes were unnaturally bright. But the drink had not fuddled her and she told her story well. She had been busy in the ground-floor general office for most of the evening and had last seen Miss Bolam at about five-forty-five when she had gone into the A.O.'s office with a query about a patient's appointment. Miss Bolam had seemed the same as usual to her. She had returned to the general office and had been joined by Peter Nagle at about six-ten. He was wearing his coat and had come to collect the outgoing post. Miss Priddy had registered the last few letters in the post book and handed them to him. At about quarter or twenty past six Mrs Shorthouse had joined them. Mrs Shorthouse had mentioned that she had just come from Miss Bolam's office where she had been settling a query about her annual leave entitlement. Peter Nagle had gone out with the post and she and Mrs Shorthouse had stayed together until his return some ten minutes later. Nagle had then gone down to the basement porters' room to hang up his coat and feed Tigger, the office cat, and she had followed him down almost immediately. She had helped him feed Tigger and they had returned to the general office together. At about seven the senior porter, Cully, complained again about his stomach-ache which had been troubling him all day. Miss Priddy, Mrs Bostock, the other medical secretary, and Peter Nagle had all had to take Cully's place at the switchboard from time to time because of his stomach-ache, but he had refused to go home. Now he was willing to go and Miss Priddy had gone to the A.O.'s office to ask Miss Bolam if he could leave early. Miss Bolam wasn't in her office so she had looked in the nurses' duty-room on the ground floor. Sister Ambrose told her that she had seen the A.O. passing down the hall towards the basement stairs about thirty minutes or so earlier, so Miss Priddy had looked in the basement. The record-room was usually kept locked but the key was in the lock and the door just ajar, so she had looked inside. The light was on. She had found the body – here Miss Priddy's voice faltered – and had rushed upstairs at once to get help. No, she hadn't touched anything. She didn't know why the medical records were strewn around. She didn't know how she had known that Miss Bolam was dead. It was just that Miss Bolam had looked so very dead. She didn't know why she had been so sure it was murder. She thought she had seen a bruise on Miss Bolam's head. And, then, there had been Tippett's fetish laying on the body. She was afraid that Tippett was hiding among the record racks and would jump out at her. Everyone said that he wasn't dangerous –

at least everyone except Dr Steiner – but he had been in a mental hospital and, after all, you couldn't be really sure, could you? No, she hadn't known that Tippett wasn't in the clinic. Peter Nagle had taken the call from the hospital and had told Miss Bolam but he hadn't told her. She hadn't seen the chisel in Miss Bolam's chest but Dr Etherege had told the staff about the stabbing when they were gathered together in the front consulting-room waiting for the police. She thought that most of the staff knew where Peter Nagle kept his tools and also which key opened the door of the basement record-room. It hung on hook number 12 and was shinier than the other keys, but it wasn't labelled. Dalgliesh said:

'I want you to think very hard and very carefully. When you went downstairs to help Mr Nagle feed the cat, was the record-room door ajar and the light on as it was when you went down later and found Miss Bolam?'

The girl pushed back her dank blonde hair and said with sudden weariness:

'I . . . I can't remember. I didn't go past that door you see. I went straight into the porters' room at the bottom of the stairs. Peter was there clearing up Tigger's plate. He hadn't eaten all of his last meal so we scraped it off his plate and washed it at the sink. We didn't go near the record-room.'

'But you could see the door as you came down the stairs. Would you be likely to notice if the door were ajar? The room isn't often used, is it?'

'No, but anyone might go there if they wanted a record. I mean, if the door were open I wouldn't go to see who was there or anything like that. I think I would notice if the door was wide open so I suppose it wasn't, but I can't remember, honestly I can't.'

Dalgliesh ended by asking her about Miss Bolam. It appeared that Miss Priddy knew her outside the clinic, that the Priddy family attended the same church and that Miss Bolam had encouraged her to take the job at the clinic.

'I shouldn't have got this job if it hadn't been for Enid. Of course, I never called her that inside the clinic. She wouldn't have liked it.' Miss Priddy gave the impression that she had only reluctantly brought herself to use the Christian name outside the clinic. She went on: 'I don't mean she actually appointed me. I had to be interviewed by Mr Lauder and by Dr Etherege, but I know she spoke up for me. My shorthand and typing weren't very good then – it was nearly two years ago when I came – and I was lucky to get here. I didn't see very much of Enid at the clinic but she was always very kind and keen for me to get on. She wanted me to take the Institute of Hospital Administration Diploma so that I needn't be a shorthand typist all my life.'

This ambition for Miss Priddy's future career struck Dalgliesh as a little odd. The child gave no impression of being ambitious and she would surely marry in time. It hardly needed the Institute's diploma, whatever that might be, to save her from being a shorthand typist for life. He felt a little sorry for Miss Bolam who could scarcely have picked a less promising protégée. She was pretty, honest and naïve, but not, he thought, particularly intelligent. He had to remind himself that she had given her age as twenty-two not seventeen. She had a shapely and oddly mature body, but her thin face with its frame of long, straight hair was the face of a child.

There was little she could tell him about the administrative officer. She hadn't noticed any change recently in Miss Bolam. She didn't know that the A.O. had sent for Mr Lauder and had no idea what could be worrying Miss Bolam at the clinic. Everything was going on very much as usual. Miss Bolam had no enemies as far as she knew, certainly no one who would wish to kill her.

'She was happy here, then, as far as you know? I was wondering whether she had asked for a move. A psychiatric clinic can't be the easiest unit to administer.'

'Oh, it isn't! I don't know how Enid carried on sometimes. But I'm sure she would never ask for a move. Someone must have given you the wrong impression. She was never one to give up. If she thought people wanted her to go she'd dig her toes in. The clinic was a kind of challenge to her.'

It was probably the most illuminating thing she had said about Miss Bolam. As he thanked her and asked her to wait with the rest of the staff until his preliminary interviews were over, Dalgliesh pondered on the possible nuisance value of an administrator who regarded her job as a challenge, a battleground from which she would never willingly retreat. He asked next to see Peter Nagle.

If the junior porter was worried by the killer's choice of his chisel as a weapon he gave no sign. He answered Dalgliesh's questions calmly and politely, but so dispassionately that they might have been discussing some minor point of clinic procedure which was only doubtfully his concern. He gave his age as twenty-seven and an address in Pimlico and confirmed that he had been employed at the clinic for just over two years and was previously at a provincial art school. His voice was level and educated, his mud-brown eyes were large, almost expressionless. Dalgliesh noticed that he had unusually long arms which, held loosely from his short and powerful body, gave an impression of simian strength. His hair was black, coiling tightly over the scalp. It was an interesting face, withdrawn but intelligent. There could scarcely have been a greater contrast with poor old Cully, long since despatched home to nurse both his stomach-ache and his grievance at being kept late.

Nagle confirmed Miss Priddy's story. He again identified his chisel with no more emotion than a brief moue of distaste and said that he had last seen it at eight o'clock that morning when he had arrived on duty and – for no particular reason – had made a check of his toolbox. Everything was in order then. Dalgliesh asked whether it was generally known where the box was kept. Nagle replied:

'I'd be a fool if I said no, wouldn't I?'

'You'd be a fool to say anything but the truth now or later.'

'I suppose most of the staff knew. Those who didn't could find out easily enough. We don't keep the porters' room locked.'

'Isn't that rather unwise? What about the patients?'

'They don't go down to the basement on their own. The lysergic acid patients are always escorted and the art therapy people usually have someone keeping an eye on them. The department hasn't been down there for long. The light's bad and it isn't really suitable. It's a temporary department.'

'Where used it to be, then?'

'On the third floor. Then the clinic Medical Committee decided they wanted the large room there for the marital problems discussion groups, so Mrs Baumgarten – she's the art therapist – lost it. She's been agitating to get it back, but the M.P.D. patients say it would be psychologically disturbing for them to meet in the basement.'

'Who runs the M.P.D.?'

'Dr Steiner and one of the psychiatric social workers, Miss Kallinski. It's a club where the divorced and the single tell the patients how to be happy though married. I don't see how it can concern the murder.'

'Nor do I. I asked about it to satisfy my curiosity as to why the art therapy department was so unsuitably housed. When did you hear that Tippett wasn't attending today, by the way?'

'At about nine o'clock this morning. The old boy had been worrying St Luke's Hospital to telephone and let us know what had happened. So they did. I told Miss Bolam and Sister.'

'Anyone else?'

'I think I mentioned it to Cully when he came back on the board. He's had a belly-ache for most of the day.'

'So I'm told. What's wrong with him?'

'Cully? Miss Bolam made him go to hospital for an examination but nothing was found. He gets these belly-aches if anyone upsets him. They say here it's psychosomatic.'

'What upset him this morning?'

'I did. He got here before me this morning and started sorting the post. That's my job. I told him to concentrate on his own work.'

Dalgliesh took him patiently over the events of the evening. His story agreed with Miss Priddy's and, like her, he was unable to say whether the door of the basement record-room had been ajar when he returned from posting the letters. He admitted that he had passed the door when he went to ask Nurse Bolam if the laundry was sorted. It was usual for the door to be closed as the room was seldom visited and he thought he would have noticed had it been open. It was frustrating and maddening that this crucial point could not be cleared up, but Nagle stood firm. He hadn't noticed. He couldn't say. He hadn't noticed, either, whether the record-room key was on the board in the porters' rest-room. This was easier to understand. There were twenty-two hooks on the board and most of the keys were in use and missing. Dalgliesh said:

'You realize that Miss Bolam's body was almost certainly lying in the record-room when you and Miss Priddy were together feeding the cat? You realize how important it is to remember whether the door was open or shut?'

'It was ajar when Jenny Priddy went down later. That's what she says and she's no liar. If it was shut when I got back from the post someone must have opened it between six-twenty-five and seven. I don't see what's so impossible about that. It would be better for me if I could remember about the door, but I can't. I hung up my coat in my locker, went straight to ask Nurse Bolam about the clean laundry, and then returned to the rest-room. Jenny met me at the bottom of the stairs.'

He spoke without heat, almost unemotionally. It was as if he said, 'That's what happened. Like it or not, it happened that way.' He was too intelligent not to see that he was in some danger. Perhaps he was also intelligent enough to know that the danger was minimal to an innocent man who kept his head and told the truth.

Dalgliesh told him to let the police know at once if he remembered anything fresh and let him go.

Sister Ambrose was seen next. She strutted into the room, armour-plated in white linen, belligerent as a battleship. The bib of her apron, starched rigid as a board, curved against a formidable bosom on which she wore her nursing badges like medals of war. Grey hair spurted from each side of her cap which she wore low on her forehead above a face of uncompromising plainness. Her colour was high; Dalgliesh thought that she was finding it difficult to control her resentment and distrust. He dealt with her gently, but his questions were answered in an atmosphere of rigid disapproval. She confirmed briefly that she had last seen Miss Bolam walking through the hall towards the basement stairs at about twenty past six. They had not spoken and the administrative officer had looked the same as usual. Sister Ambrose was back in the E.C.T. room before Miss Bolam was out of sight and had been there with Dr Ingram until the body was found. In reply to Dalgliesh's question whether Dr Baguley had also been with them for the whole of that time, Sister Ambrose suggested that he should ask the doctor direct. Dalgliesh replied mildly that this was his intention. He knew that the Sister could give him a great deal of useful information about the clinic if she chose but, apart from a few questions about Miss Bolam's personal relationships from which he gained nothing, he did not press her. He thought that she was probably more shocked by the murder, by the calculated violence of Miss Bolam's death, than anyone he had yet seen. As sometimes happens with unimaginative and inarticulate people, this shock gave vent to ill-temper. She was very cross; with Dalgliesh because his job gave him the right to ask impertinent and embarrassing questions; with herself because she could not conceal her feelings; with the victim, even, who had involved the clinic in this bizarre predicament. It was a reaction Dalgliesh had met before and no good came of trying to force co-operation on such a witness. Later on Sister Ambrose might be induced to talk more freely; at present, it was a waste of time to do more than elicit the facts which she was prepared to give. One fact at least was crucial. Miss Bolam was alive and making her way towards the basement stairs at about twenty past six. At seven o'clock her body was discovered. Those forty minutes were vital and any member of the staff who could produce an alibi covering them could be eliminated from the inquiry. On the face of it the case presented little difficulty. Dalgliesh did not believe that an outsider had somehow gained access to the clinic and lain in wait for Miss Bolam. The killer was almost certainly still in the building. It was now a matter of careful questioning, of the methodical checking of alibis, of the seeking out of a motive. Dalgliesh decided to talk to the one man whose alibi appeared unassailable and who would have the detached, outsider's view of the clinic and its varied personalities. He thanked Sister Ambrose for her valuable co-operation – a flicker of the eyes behind the steel-rimmed spectacles suggested that the irony was not lost on her – and asked the constable at the door to send in Mr Lauder.

CHAPTER TWO

It was the first chance Dalgliesh had had to observe the group secretary closely. He saw a thick-set, chubby-featured man, mild-eyed behind the heavy square spectacles, who looked, in his well-cut tweeds, more like a country doctor or small-town solicitor than a bureaucrat. He was completely at ease and bore himself like a man confident of his powers, unwilling to be hurried, keeping always something in reserve, including, Dalgliesh thought, a keener intelligence than his appearance might suggest.

He seated himself opposite Dalgliesh, drew his chair comfortably forward and, without either apology or excuse, took a pipe from one pocket and sought in the other for his tobacco pouch. Nodding towards Martin and his open notebook he said, in a slow voice with a trace of north-country accent:

'Reginald Iven Lauder. Date of birth, 21st April 1905. Address, 42 Makepeace Avenue, Chigwell, Essex. Occupation, Group Secretary, East Central Hospital Management Committee. And now, Superintendent, what do you want to know?'

'A great deal, I'm afraid,' said Dalgliesh. 'And firstly, have you any idea at all who could have killed Miss Bolam?' The group secretary established his pipe and, leaning his elbows on the desk, regarded its glowing head with satisfaction.

'I wish I had. I'd have been in here to tell you before now, never fear. But, no. I've no help of that kind for you.'

'Miss Bolam had no enemies as far as you were aware?'

'Enemies? Well now, Superintendent, that's a strong word! She had people who didn't much like her, the same as I have. You, too, no doubt. But we don't go in fear of being murdered. No, I wouldn't have said she had enemies. Mind you, I know nothing of her private life. That's not my concern.'

'Could you tell me something about the Steen and the position she held? I know something of the clinic's reputation, of course, but it would be helpful if I could have a clear picture of what goes on here.'

34

'A clear picture of what goes on?' It might have been imagination, but Dalgliesh thought he saw the group secretary's mouth twitch.

'Well, the medical director could tell you more about that than I – on the medical side, that is. But I can give you a gist. The place was founded between the wars by the family of a Mr Hyman Stein. The story goes that the old man suffered from impotence, got himself some psychotherapy and subsequently fathered five children. So far from impoverishing him they all did well and when papa died they put the clinic on a sound financial footing as a memorial to him. After all, they did owe the place something. The sons all changed their name to Steen – for the usual reason I suppose – and the clinic was given the anglicized name. I often wonder what old Hyman would have thought.'

'Is it well endowed?'

'It was. The state got the endowments of course on the Appointed Day following the 1946 Act. A bit has come in since, but not much. People aren't so keen to will money to institutions run by the Government. But the place was quite well off before 1948 as these places go. They did themselves well in the way of equipment and facilities. The Hospital Management Committee's had quite a job providing for them in the way to which they'd become accustomed.'

'Is the clinic difficult to administer? I imagine there may be personality problems.'

'No more difficult than any other small unit. You get personality problems anywhere. I'd rather deal with a difficult psychiatrist than a difficult surgeon any day. They're the real prima donnas.'

'Did you consider Miss Bolam a successful administrative officer?'

'Well . . . she was efficient. I hadn't really any complaints. She was a bit rigid, I suppose. After all, Ministry circulars haven't even the force of law, so there's no sense in treating them as if they are personally dictated by God Almighty. I doubt whether Miss Bolam would have got much further. Mind you, she was a competent, methodical and highly conscientious officer. I don't think she ever sent in an inaccurate return.'

'Poor devil!' thought Dalgliesh, stung by the bleak anonymity of that official epitaph. He asked:

'Was she popular here? With the medical staff, for example?'

'Well, now, Superintendent, you'll have to ask them. I can't think of any reason why she shouldn't be.'

'You were not then under any pressure from the medical committee to remove her from the clinic?'

The mild grey eyes grew suddenly blank. There was a momentary pause before the group secretary calmly replied:

'I have had no official request of that kind made to me.'

'But unofficially?'

'There has been a feeling here from time to time, I believe, that a change of job might be helpful to Miss Bolam. Now that's not such a bad idea, Superintendent! Any officer in a small unit, particularly a psychiatric clinic, can benefit from a change of experience. But I don't transfer my staff at the whim of medical committees. Bless me, no! And, as I said, no official request was made. If Miss Bolam herself had asked for a transfer, that would have been a different matter. Even so, it wouldn't have been easy. She was a general administrative officer and we haven't many posts in that grade.'

Dalgliesh then asked again about Miss Bolam's telephone call and Lauder confirmed that he had spoken to her at about ten to one. He remembered the time because he was just about to go for lunch. Miss Bolam had asked to speak to him personally and had been put through by his secretary. She had asked whether she could see him urgently.

'Can you remember the exact conversation?'

'More or less. She said: "Can I have an appointment to see you as soon as possible? I think there may be something going on here that you ought to know about. I should like your advice. Something that started well before my time here." I said that I couldn't see her this afternoon as I would be in the Finance and General Purposes Committee from two-thirty onwards and had a Joint Consultative Committee immediately afterwards. I asked whether she could give me any idea what it was all about and whether it couldn't wait until Monday. She hesitated, so, before she could reply, I said I'd drop in on my way home this evening. I knew they had a late clinic on Fridays. She said that she would arrange to be alone in her office from six-thirty onwards, thanked me, and rang off. The J.C.C. lasted longer than I expected – that Committee always does – and I got here just before seven-thirty. But you know that. I was still in Committee at the time they found the body, as no doubt you'll be checking in due course.'

'Did you take Miss Bolam's message seriously? Was she the sort of woman who ran to you with trifles or would a request to see you really mean that something serious was wrong?'

The group secretary thought for a moment before replying: 'I took it seriously. That's why I came round tonight.'

'And you have no idea at all what it might be?'

'None, I'm afraid. It must have been something that she learned about since Wednesday. I saw Miss Bolam then at the House Committee meeting in the late afternoon and she told me afterwards that things were pretty quiet here at present. That is the last time I saw her, incidentally. She was looking rather well I thought. Better than for some time.'

Dalgliesh asked the group secretary what, if anything, he knew of Miss Bolam's private life.

'Very little. I believe she has no near relations and lives alone in a flat in Kensington. Nurse Bolam will be able to tell you more about her. They're cousins, and Nurse Bolam is probably the nearest living relative. I've got an idea that she had private means. All the official information about her career will be on her dossier. Knowing Miss Bolam, I expect her file will be as meticulously kept as any other staff dossier. It'll be here no doubt.'

Without moving from his chair he leaned sideways, jerked open the top drawer of the filing cabinet and inserted a chubby hand between the manilla folders.

'Here we are. Bolam, Enid Constance. I see she came to us in October 1949 as a shorthand typist. She spent eighteen months in Group Headquarters, was transferred to one of our chest clinics on 19th April 1951 on Grade B and applied for the vacant post of administrative officer here on 14th May 1957. The post was then Grade D and she was lucky to get it. We hadn't a very strong field, I remember. All administrative and clerical jobs were regraded in 1958 following the Noel Hall report and, after some argument with the Regional Board, we managed to get this one graded as general administrative. It's all down here. Date of birth, 12th December 1922. Address, 37a Ballantyne Mansions, S.W.8. Then come details about her tax code, national insurance number and incremental date. She's only had one week off sick since she came here and that was in 1959 when she had flu. There isn't much more here. Her original application form and letters of appointment will be on her main dossier at Group Headquarters.'

He handed the file to Dalgliesh who looked through it and then said:

'This states that her previous employers were the Botley Research Establishment. Isn't that Sir Mark Etherege's show? They dabble in aeronautical research. He's Dr Etherege's brother, isn't he?'

'I think Miss Bolam did mention to me when she was appointed to this post that she knew Dr Etherege's brother slightly. Mind you now, it can't have been more than that. She was only a shorthand typist at Botley. It's a bit of a coincidence, I suppose, but then she had to come from somewhere. I seem to remember it was Sir Mark who gave her a reference when she applied to us. That will be on her Group dossier, of course.'

'Would you mind telling me, Mr Lauder, what arrangements you propose making here now that she's dead?'

The group secretary replaced the file in the cabinet.

'I don't see why not. I shall have to consult my Committee, of course, as the circumstances are unusual, but I shall recommend that the senior medical stenographer here, Mrs Bostock, takes over in an acting capacity. If she can do the job – and I think she can – she'll be a strong candidate for the vacancy, but the post will be advertised in the usual way.'

Dalgliesh did not comment but he was interested. Such a quick decision on Miss Bolam's successor could only mean that Lauder had earlier given some thought to it. The approaches of the medical staff may have been unofficial, but they had probably been more effective than the group secretary cared to admit. Dalgliesh returned to the telephone call which had brought Mr Lauder to the clinic. He said:

'The words Miss Bolam used strike me as significant. She said that there may be something very serious going on here which you ought to know about and that it started before her time. That suggests, firstly that she wasn't yet certain but only suspicious, and secondly that she wasn't worried about a particular incident but about something of long standing. A systematic policy of thieving, for example, as opposed to one isolated theft.'

'Well now, Superintendent, it's odd you should mention theft. We have had a theft recently, but it was an isolated incident, the first we've had here for years, and I can't see how it could be connected with murder. It was just over a week ago, last Tuesday if I remember rightly. Cully and Nagle were the last to leave the clinic as usual and Cully asked Nagle to have a drink with him at the "Queen's Head". You know it, I expect. It's the pub on the far corner of Beefsteak Street. There are one or two odd things about this story and one of the strangest is that Cully should invite Nagle for a drink. They've never struck me as buddies. Anyway, Nagle accepted and they were in the "Queen's Head" together from about seven. At about half past, a pal of Cully's came in and said he was surprised to see Cully there as he had just passed the clinic and there was a faint light in one of the windows — as if someone was moving around with a torch, he said. Nagle and Cully went off to investigate and found one of the back basement windows broken, or rather, cut out. Quite a clever job it was. Cully didn't feel inclined to investigate further without reinforcements and I'm not sure that I blame him. He's sixty-five, remember, and not strong. After some whispering together, Nagle said that he'd go in and Cully had better telephone the police from the kiosk on the corner. Your people came pretty smartly but they didn't get the intruder. He gave Nagle the slip inside the building, and when Cully got back from telephoning he was just in time to see the man slip out of the mews.'

'I'll check how far our people have got with the investigation,' said Dalgliesh. 'But I agree that a connection between the crimes seems unlikely on the face of it. Was much taken?'

'Fifteen pounds from a drawer in the psychiatric social worker's office. The door was locked but he wrenched it open. The money was in an envelope addressed in green ink to the administrative secretary of the clinic and had been received a week earlier.

There was no letter with it, only a note to say that the money was from a grateful patient. The other contents of the drawer were torn and scattered but nothing else was stolen. Some attempt had been made to force open the cabinets of records in the general office and Miss Bolam's desk drawers had been forced but nothing taken.'

Dalgliesh asked whether the fifteen pounds should have been placed in the wall safe.

'Well now, Superintendent, you're right, of course. It should have been. But there was a little difficulty about using the money. Miss Bolam phoned me about its arrival and said that she thought it should be paid immediately into the clinic's free money account to be used in due course on the authority of the House Committee. That was a very proper course of action, and so I told her. Shortly afterwards the medical director phoned me to ask if he could have authority to spend the money on some new flower vases for the patients' waiting-room. The vases were certainly needed and it seemed a correct use for non-Exchequer funds, so I rang the chairman of the House Committee and got his approval. Apparently Dr Etherege wanted Miss Kettle to choose the vases and asked Miss Bolam to hand over the cash. I had already notified Miss Bolam of the decision so she did so, expecting that the vases would be bought at once. Something happened to change Miss Kettle's plans and, instead of returning the cash to the A.O. for safe custody, she locked it in her drawer.'

'Do you know how many of the staff knew that it was there?'

'That's what the police asked. I suppose most people knew that the vases hadn't been bought or Miss Kettle would have shown them around. They probably guessed that, having been handed the cash, she wouldn't be likely to return it even temporarily. I don't know. The arrival of that fifteen pounds was mysterious. It caused nothing but trouble and its disappearance was equally mysterious. Anyway, Superintendent, no one here stole it. Cully only saw the thief for a second but he was certain that he didn't know the man. He did say, though, that he thought the chap looked like a gentleman. Don't ask me how he knew or what his criteria are. But that's what he said.'

Dalgliesh thought that the whole incident was odd and would

bear further investigation but he could see no apparent connection between the two crimes. It was not even certain that Miss Bolam's call to the group secretary for advice was related to her death, but here the presumption was much stronger. It was very important to discover, if possible, what she had suspected. He asked Mr Lauder once more whether he could help.

'I told you, Superintendent, I haven't an idea what she meant. If I suspected that anything was wrong I shouldn't wait for Miss Bolam to phone me. We're not quite so remote from the units at group offices as some people think and I usually get to know anything I ought to know. If the murder is connected with that phone message something pretty serious must be happening here. After all, you don't kill just to prevent the group secretary knowing that you've fiddled your travelling claim or overspent your annual leave. Not that anyone has as far as I know.'

'Exactly,' said Dalgliesh. He watched the group secretary's face very closely and said, without emphasis:

'It suggests something that might ruin a man professionally. A sexual relationship with a patient perhaps – something as serious as that.' Mr Lauder's face did not change.

'I imagine every doctor knows the seriousness of that, particularly psychiatrists. They must have to be pretty careful with some of the neurotic women they treat. Frankly, I don't believe it. All the doctors here are eminent men, some of them with world-wide reputations. You don't get that sort of reputation if you're a fool, and men of that eminence don't commit murder.'

'And what about the rest of the staff? They may not be eminent, but presumably you consider them honest?'

Unruffled, the group secretary replied:

'Sister Ambrose has been here for nearly twenty years and Nurse Bolam for five. I would trust them both absolutely. All the clerical staff came with good references and so did the two porters, Cully and Nagle.' He added wryly: 'Admittedly I didn't check that they hadn't committed murder but none of them strike me as homicidal maniacs. Cully drinks a bit and is a pathetic fool with only another four months' service to complete. I doubt whether he could kill a mouse without making a hash of it. Nagle is a cut above the usual hospital porter. I understand he's an art student and works here for pocket money. He's only been with us a couple of years so he wasn't here before Miss Bolam's time. Even if he's been seducing all the female staff, which seems unlikely, the worst that could happen to him would be the sack and that wouldn't worry him as things are today. Admittedly she was killed with his chisel but anyone could have got their hands on that.'

'I'm afraid this was an inside job, you know,' said Dalgliesh gently. 'The murderer knew where Tippett's fetish and Nagle's chisel were kept, knew which key opened the old record-room, knew where that key was hung on the board in the porters' duty-room, probably wore one of the rubber aprons from the art therapy room as a protection, certainly had medical knowledge. Above all, of course, the murderer couldn't have left the clinic after the crime. The basement door was bolted and so was the ground-floor back door. Cully was watching the front door.'

'Cully had a belly-ache. He could have missed someone.'

'Do you really believe that's possible?' asked Dalgliesh. And the group secretary did not reply.

At first sight Marion Bolam could be thought beautiful. She had the fair, classical good looks which, enhanced by her nurse's uniform, gave an immediate impression of serene loveliness. Her blonde hair, parted above a broad forehead and twisted into a high roll at the back of her head, was bound by the simple white cap. It was only at second glance that the illusion faded and beauty gave way to prettiness. The features, individually ana-lysed, were unremarkable, the nose a little too long, the lips a little too thin. In ordinary clothes, hurrying home perhaps at the end of the day, she would be undistinguished. It was the combina-tion of the starched formal linen with that fair skin and yellow hair which dazzled the eye. Only in the broad forehead and the sharpness of the nose could Dalgliesh detect any likeness to her dead cousin. But there was nothing ordinary about the large grey eyes which met his fully for a brief second before she lowered her glance and gazed fixedly at the clasped hands in her lap.

'I understand that you are Miss Bolam's next of kin. This must be a terrible shock for you.'

'Yes. Oh, yes, it is! Enid was my cousin.'

'You have the same name. Your fathers were brothers?'

'Yes, they were. Our mothers were sisters, too. Two brothers married two sisters so that we were doubly related.'

'Had she no other relations living?'

'Only Mummy and me.'

'I shall have to see Miss Bolam's solicitor, I expect,' said Dalgliesh, 'but it would be helpful if you would tell me as much as you know about her affairs. I'm afraid I have to ask these personal questions. Usually they have no bearing on the crime, but one must know as much as possible about everyone concerned. Had your cousin any income apart from her salary?'

'Oh, yes. Enid was quite well off. Uncle Sydney left her mother about £25,000 and it all came to Enid. I don't know how much was left, but I think she had about £1,000 a year coming in apart from her salary here. She kept on Auntie's flat in Ballantyne Mansions and she . . . she was always very good to us.'

'In what way, Miss Bolam? Did she make you an allowance?'

'Oh, no! Enid wouldn't want to do that. She gave us presents. Thirty pounds at Christmas and fifty in July for our summer holiday. Mummy has disseminated sclerosis and we couldn't go away to an ordinary hotel.'

'And what happens to Miss Bolam's money now?'

The grey eyes lifted to meet his with no trace of embarrassment. She answered simply:

'It will come to Mummy and me. There wasn't anyone else to leave it to, was there? Enid always said it would come to us if she died first. But, of course, it wasn't likely that she would die first; not while Mummy was alive anyway.'

It was indeed unlikely, in the ordinary course of events, that Mrs Bolam would ever have benefited from that £25,000 or what was left of it, thought Dalgliesh. Here was the obvious motive, so understandable, so universal, so dear to any prosecuting counsel. Every juryman understood the lure of money. Could Nurse Bolam really be unaware of the significance of the information which she was handing him with such unembarrassed candour? Could innocence be so naïve or guilt so confident? He said suddenly:

'Was your cousin popular, Miss Bolam?'

'She hadn't many friends. I don't think she would have called herself popular. She wouldn't want that. She had her church activities and the Guides. She was a very quiet person really.'

'But you know of no enemies?'

'Oh, no! None at all. Enid was very much respected.'

The formal, old-fashioned epithet was almost inaudible. Dalgliesh said:

'Then it looks as if this is a motiveless, unpremeditated crime. Normally that would suggest one of the patients. But it hardly seems possible, and you are all insistent that it isn't likely.'

'Oh, no! It couldn't be a patient! I'm quite sure none of our patients would do a thing like that. They aren't violent.'

'Not even Mr Tippett?'

'But it couldn't have been Mr Tippett. He's in hospital.'

'So I'm told. How many people here knew that Mr Tippett wouldn't be coming to the clinic this Friday?'

'I don't know. Nagle knew because he took the message and he told Enid and Sister. Sister told me. You see, I usually try to keep an eye on Tippett when I'm specialling the LSD patients on Fridays. I can't leave my patient for more than a second, of course, but I do pop out occasionally to see if Tippett is all right. Tonight it wasn't necessary. Poor Tippett, he does love his art therapy! Mrs Baumgarten has been away ill for six months now, but we couldn't stop Tippett from coming. He wouldn't hurt a fly. It's wicked to suggest that Tippett could have anything to do with it. Wicked!'

She spoke with sudden vehemence. Dalgliesh said mildly:

'But no one is suggesting anything of the sort. If Tippett is in hospital – and I haven't the least doubt we shall find that he is – then he couldn't have been here.'

'But someone put his fetish on the body, didn't they? If Tippett had been here you would have suspected him straight away and he would have been so upset and confused. It was a wicked thing to do. Really wicked!'

Her voice broke and she was very near to tears. Dalgliesh watched the thin fingers twisting in her lap. He said gently:

'I don't think we need worry about Mr Tippett. Now I want

44

you to think carefully and tell me everything that you know happened in the clinic from the time you came on duty this evening. Never mind about other people, I just want to know what you did.'

Nurse Bolam remembered very clearly what she had done and, after a second's hesitation, she gave a careful and logical account. It was her job on Friday evenings to 'special' any patient undergoing treatment with lysergic acid. She explained that this was a method of releasing deep-seated inhibitions so that the patient was able to recall and recount the incidents which were being repressed in his subconscious and were responsible for his illness. As she spoke about the treatment Nurse Bolam lost her nervousness and seemed to forget that she was talking to a layman. But Dalgliesh did not interrupt.

'It's a remarkable drug and Dr Baguley uses it quite a lot. Its name is lysergic acid diethylamide and I think it was discovered by a German in 1942. We administer it orally, and the usual dose is 0.25 mg. It's produced in ampoules of 1 mg. and mixed with from 15 to 30 c.c.s of distilled water. The patients are told not to have any breakfast. The first effects are noticed after about half an hour and the more disturbing subjective experiences occur from one to one and a half hours after administration. That's when Dr Baguley comes down to be with the patient. The effects can last for as long as four hours and the patient is flushed and restless and quite withdrawn from reality. They're never left alone, of course, and we use the basement room because it's secluded and quiet and other patients aren't distressed by the noise. We usually give LSD treatments on Friday afternoon and evening, and I always "special" the patient.'

'I suppose that, if any noise, such as a cry, were heard on Fridays in the basement most of the staff would assume that it was the LSD patient?'

Nurse Bolam looked doubtful.

'I suppose they might. Certainly these patients can be very noisy. My patient today was more disturbed than usual which was why I stayed close to her. Usually I spend a little time in the linen-room which adjoins the treatment-room sorting the clean laundry as soon as the patient is over the worst. I keep the door open between the rooms, of course, so that I can watch the patient from time to time.'

Dalgliesh asked what exactly had happened during the evening.

'Well, the treatment began just after three-thirty and Dr Baguley looked in shortly after four to see if all was well. I stayed with the patient until four-thirty when Mrs Shorthouse came to tell me that tea was made. Sister came down while I went upstairs to the nurses' duty-room and drank tea. I came down again at a quarter to five and rang for Dr Baguley at five. He was with the patient for about three-quarters of an hour. Then he left to return to his E.C.T. clinic. I stayed with the patient, and as she was so restless I decided to leave the laundry until later in the evening. At about twenty to seven Peter Nagle knocked on the door and asked for the laundry. I told him that it wasn't sorted and he looked a bit surprised but didn't say anything. A little time after that I thought I heard a scream. I didn't take any notice at first as it didn't seem very close and I thought it was children playing in the square. Then I thought I ought to make sure and I went to the door. I saw Dr Baguley and Dr Steiner coming into the basement with Sister and Dr Ingram. Sister told me that nothing was wrong and to go back to my patient, so I did.'

'Did you leave the treatment-room at all after Dr Baguley left you at about quarter to six?'

'Oh, no! There wasn't any need. If I'd wanted to go to the cloakroom or anything like that (Nurse Bolam blushed faintly) I would have phoned for Sister to come and take my place.'

'Did you make any telephone calls from the treatment-room at all during the evening?'

'Only the one to the E.C.T. room at five to call Dr Baguley.'

'Are you quite sure you didn't telephone Miss Bolam?'

'Enid? Oh, no! There wouldn't be any reason to call Enid. She . . . that is, we, didn't see very much of each other in the clinic. I am responsible to Sister Ambrose, you see, and Enid wasn't concerned with the nursing staff.'

'But you saw quite a lot of her outside the clinic?'

'Oh, no! I didn't mean that. I went to her flat once or twice, to collect the cheque at Christmas and in the summer, but it isn't easy for me to leave Mummy. Besides, Enid had her own life to live. And then she's quite a lot older than me. I didn't really know her very well.'

Her voice broke and Dalgliesh saw that she was crying. Fumbling under her apron for the pocket in her nurse's dress, she sobbed:

'It's so dreadful! Poor Enid! Putting that fetish on her body as if he was making fun of her, making it look as if she was nursing a baby!'

Dalgliesh hadn't realized that she had seen the body and said so.

'Oh, I didn't! Dr Etherege and Sister wouldn't let me go in to her. But we were all told what had happened.'

Miss Bolam had indeed looked as if she were nursing a baby. But he was surprised that someone who hadn't seen the body should say so. The medical director must have given a graphic description of the scene.

Suddenly Nurse Bolam found her handkerchief and drew it out of her pocket. With it came a pair of thin, surgical gloves. They fell at Dalgliesh's feet. Picking them up he asked:

'I didn't realize that you used surgical gloves here.'

Nurse Bolam seemed unsurprised by his interest. Checking her sobs with surprising control she replied:

'We don't use them very often but we keep a few pairs. The whole Group's gone over to disposable gloves now, but there are a few of the old kind about. That's one of them. We use them for odd cleaning jobs.'

'Thank you,' said Dalgliesh. 'I'll keep this pair if I may. And I don't think I need worry you any more at present.'

With a murmured word which could have been 'thank you', Nurse Bolam almost backed out of the room.

The minutes dragged heavily to the clinic staff waiting in the front consulting-room to be interviewed. Fredrica Saxon had fetched some papers from her room on the third floor and was scoring an intelligence test. There had been some discussion about whether she ought to go upstairs alone, but Miss Saxon

had stated firmly that she didn't intend to sit there wasting time
and biting her nails until the police chose to see her, that she
hadn't the murderer hidden upstairs, nor was she proposing to
destroy incriminating evidence and that she had no objection to
any member of the staff accompanying her to satisfy themselves
on this point. This distressing frankness had provoked a murmur
of protests and reassurance, but Mrs Bostock had announced
abruptly that she would like to fetch a book from the medical
library and the two women had left the room and returned
together. Cully had been seen early, having established his right
to be classed as a patient, and had been released to cosset his
stomach-ache at home. The only remaining patient, Mrs King,
had been interviewed and allowed to depart with her husband
in attendance. Mr Burge had also left, protesting loudly at
the interruption of his session and the trauma of the whole
experience.

'Mind you, he's enjoying himself, you can see that,' confided
Mrs Shorthouse to the assembled staff. 'The superintendent had a
job getting rid of him, I can tell you.'

There was a great deal which Mrs Shorthouse seemed able to
tell them. She had been given permission to make coffee and
prepare sandwiches in her small ground-floor kitchen at the rear
of the building, and this gave her an excuse for frequent trips up
and down the hall. The sandwiches were brought in almost
singly. Cups were taken individually to be washed. This coming
and going gave her an opportunity of reporting the latest situation
to the rest of the staff who awaited each instalment with an
anxiety and eagerness which they could only imperfectly conceal.
Mrs Shorthouse was not the emissary they would have chosen
but any news, however obtained and by whomever delivered,
helped to lighten the weight of suspense and she was certainly
unexpectedly knowledgeable about police procedure.

'There's several of them searching the building now and they've
got their own chap on the door. They haven't found anyone, of
course. Well, it stands to reason! We know he couldn't have got out
of the building. Or in for that matter. I said to the sergeant: "This
clinic has had all the cleaning from me that it's getting today, so
tell your chaps to mind where they plant their boots . . ."'

'The police surgeon's seen the body. The fingerprint man is still downstairs and they're taking everyone's prints. I've seen the photographer. He went through the hall with a tripod and a big case, white on top and black at the bottom . . .'

'Here's a funny thing now. They're looking for prints in the basement lift. Measuring it up, too.'

Fredrica Saxon lifted her head, seemed about to say something, then went on with her work. The basement lift, which was about four feet square and operated by a rope pulley, had been used to transport food from the basement kitchen to the first-floor dining-room when the clinic was a private house. It had never been taken out. Occasionally medical records from the basement record-room were hoisted in it to the first- and second-floor consulting-rooms, but it was otherwise little used. No one commented on a possible reason why the police should test it for prints.

Mrs Shorthouse departed with two cups to be washed. She was back within five minutes.

'Mr Lauder's in the general office phoning the chairman. Telling him about the murder, I suppose. This'll give the H.M.C. something to natter about and no mistake. Sister is going through the linen inventory with one of the police. Seems there's a rubber apron from the art therapy room missing. Oh, and another thing. They're letting the boiler out. Want to rake it through, I suppose. Nice for us, I must say. This place'll be bloody cold on Monday . . .'

'The mortuary van's arrived. That's what they call it, the mortuary van. They don't use an ambulance, you see. Not when the victim's dead. You probably heard it arrive. I dare say if you draw the curtains back a bit you'll see her being took in.'

But no one cared to draw back the curtains and as the soft, careful feet of the stretcher-bearers shuffled past the door no one spoke. Fredrica Saxon laid down her pencil and bowed her head as if she were praying. When the front door closed their relief was heard in the soft hiss of breath released. There was a brief silence and then the van drove off. Mrs Shorthouse was the only one to speak.

'Poor little blighter! Mind you I only gave her another six

months here what with one thing and another, but I never thought she'd leave feet first.'

Jennifer Priddy sat apart from the rest of the staff on the edge of the treatment couch. Her interview with the superintendent had been unexpectedly easy. She didn't know quite what she had expected but certainly it wasn't this quiet, gentle, deep-voiced man. He hadn't bothered to commiserate with her on the shock of finding the body. He hadn't smiled at her. He hadn't been paternal or understanding. He gave the impression that he was interested only in finding out the truth as quickly as possible and that he expected everyone else to feel the same. She thought that it would be difficult to tell him a lie and she hadn't tried. It had all been quite easy to remember, quite straightforward. The superintendent had questioned her closely about the ten minutes or so she had spent in the basement with Peter. That was only to be expected. Naturally he was wondering whether Peter could have killed Miss Bolam after he returned from the post and before she joined him. Well, it wasn't possible. She had followed him downstairs almost immediately and Mrs Shorthouse could confirm it. Probably it hadn't taken long to kill Enid – she tried not to think about that sudden, savage, calculated violence – but however quickly it was done, Peter hadn't had time.

She thought about Peter. Thinking about him occupied most of her few solitary hours. Tonight, however, the familiar warm imaginings were needled with anxiety. Was he going to be cross about the way she had behaved? She remembered with shame her delayed scream of terror after finding the body, the way she had thrown herself into his arms. He had been very kind and considerate, of course, but then he always was considerate when he wasn't working and remembered she was there. She knew that he hated fuss and that any demonstration of affection irked him. She had learned to accept that their love, and she dared no longer doubt that it was love, must be taken on his terms. Since their brief time together in the nurses' duty-room after the finding of Miss Bolam she had scarcely spoken to him. She couldn't guess what he felt. She was only sure of one thing. She couldn't possibly pose for him tonight. It hadn't anything to do with shame or guilt; he had long since cut her free of those twin encumbrances. He would expect her to arrive at the studio as planned. After all, her alibi was fixed and her parents would accept that she was at her evening class. He would see no reasonable grounds for altering their arrangements and Peter was a great one for reason. But she couldn't do it! Not tonight. It wasn't so much the posing as what would follow. She wouldn't be able to refuse him. She wouldn't want to refuse him. And tonight, with Enid dead, she felt that she couldn't bear to be touched.

When she returned from her talk with the superintendent, Dr Steiner had come to sit beside her and had been very kind. But then Dr Steiner was kind. It was easy enough to criticize his indolence or laugh at his odd patients. But he did care about people, whereas Dr Baguley, who worked so hard and wore himself out with his heavy clinics, didn't really like people at all, but only wished that he did. Jenny wasn't sure how she knew this so clearly. She hadn't really thought about it before. Tonight, however, now that the first shock of finding the body had passed, her mind was unnaturally clear. And not only her mind. All her perceptions were sharpened. The tangible objects about her, the chintz covering on the couch, the red blanket folded at its foot, the bright varied greens and golds of the chrysanthemums on the desk, were clearer, brighter, more real to her than ever before. She saw the line of Miss Saxon's arm as it rested on the desk curved around the book she was reading and the way in which the small hairs on her forearm were tipped with light from the desk lamp. She wondered whether Peter always saw the life around him with this wonder and clarity as if one were born into an unfamiliar world with all the first bright hues of creation fresh upon it. Perhaps this was what it felt like to be a painter.

'I suppose it's the brandy,' she thought, and giggled a little. She remembered hearing the muttered grumblings of Sister Ambrose half an hour earlier.

'What's Nagle been feeding to Priddy? That child's half drunk.' But she wasn't drunk and she didn't really believe it was the brandy.

Dr Steiner had drawn his chair close to her and had laid his hand briefly on her shoulder. Without thinking, Miss Priddy had said:

'She was kind to me and I didn't like her.'

She no longer felt sad or guilty about it. It was a statement of fact.

'You mustn't worry about it,' he said gently, and patted her knee. She didn't resent the pat. Peter would have said: 'Lecherous old goat! Tell him to keep his paws to himself.' But Peter would have been wrong. Jenny knew that it was a gesture of kindliness. For a moment she was tempted to put her hand over his to show that she understood. He had small and very white hands for a man, so different from Peter's long, bony, paint-stained fingers. She saw how the hairs curled beneath his shirt cuffs, the stubble of black along the knuckles. On his little finger he wore a gold signet ring, heavy as a weapon.

'It's natural to feel as you do,' he said. 'When people die we always wish that we had been kinder to them, had liked them better. There is nothing to be done about it. We shouldn't pretend about our feelings. If we understand them we learn in time to accept them and to live with them.'

But Jenny was no longer listening. For the door had opened quietly and Peter Nagle had come in.

Bored with sitting in the reception desk and exchanging commonplace remarks with the uncommunicative policeman on duty there, Nagle sought diversion in the front consulting-room. Although his formal interview was over he wasn't yet free to leave the clinic. The group secretary obviously expected him to stay until the building could be locked for the night and it would be his job to open it again on Monday morning. The way things were going it looked as if he would be stuck in the place for another couple of hours at least. That morning he had planned to get home early and work on the picture, but it was no use thinking of that now. It might well be after eleven o'clock before the business was settled and he was free to go home. But even if they could go to the Pimlico flat together Jenny wouldn't pose for him tonight. One glance at her face told him that. She did not come across to him as he entered the room and he was grateful for that amount of restraint at least. But she gave him her shy, elliptical glance, half conspiratorial and half pleading. It was her way of asking him to understand, of saying sorry. Well, he was sorry, too. He had hoped to put in a good three hours tonight and time was getting short. But if she was only trying to convey that she wasn't in the mood for making love, well, that suited him all right. It suited him most nights if she only knew. He wished that he could take her – since she was so tiresomely insistent on being taken – as simply and quickly as he took a meal, a means of satisfying an appetite that was nothing to be ashamed of but nothing to fuss about either. But that wasn't Jenny. He hadn't been as clever as he thought and Jenny was in love. She was hopelessly, passionately and insecurely in love, demanding a constant reassurance, facile tenderness and time-consuming technique which left him exhausted and barely satisfied. She was terrified of becoming pregnant so that the preliminaries to love-making were irritatingly clinical, the aftermath, more often than not, her wild sobbing in his arms. As a painter he was obsessed by her body. He couldn't think of changing his model now and he couldn't afford to change. But the price of Jenny was getting too high.

He was almost untouched by Miss Bolam's death. He suspected that she had always known just how little work he did for his money. The rest of the staff, deluded by comparing him with that poor fool, Cully, thought they had a paragon of industry and intelligence. But Bolam had been no fool. It was not that he was lazy. One could have an easy life at the Steen – and most people, including some psychiatrists, did – without risking that imputation. Everything required of him was well within his capabilities and he gave no more than was required. Enid Bolam knew that all right, but it worried neither of them. If he went she could only hope to replace him by a porter who did less and did it less efficiently. And he was educated, personable and polite. That had meant a great deal to Miss Bolam. He smiled as he remembered how much it had meant. No, Bolam had never bothered him. But he was less confident about her successor.

He glanced across the room to where Mrs Bostock sat alone, gracefully relaxed in one of the more comfortable patients' chairs that he had brought in from the waiting-room. Her head was studiously bent over a book, but Nagle had little doubt that her mind was otherwise occupied. Probably working out her incremental date as A.O., he thought. This murder was a break for her all right. You couldn't miss compulsive ambition in a woman. They burnt with it. You could almost smell it sizzling their flesh. Underneath that air of calm unflappability she was as restless and nervous as a cat on heat. He sauntered across the room to her and lounged against the wall beside her chair, his arm just brushing her shoulder.

'Nicely timed for you, isn't it?' he said.

She kept her eyes on the page but he knew that she would have to answer. She could never resist defending herself even when defence only made her more vulnerable. She's like the rest of them, he thought. She can't keep her bloody mouth shut.

'I don't know what you mean, Nagle.'

'Come off it. I've been admiring your performance for the last six months. Yes, Doctor. No, Doctor. Just as you like, Doctor. Of course, I'd like to help, Doctor, but there are certain complications here . . . You bet there were! She wasn't giving up without a struggle. And now she's dead. Very nice for you. They won't have to look far for their new A.O.'

'Don't be impertinent and ridiculous. And why aren't you helping Mrs Shorthouse with the coffee?'

'Because I don't choose to. You're not the A.O. yet, remember.'

'I've no doubt the police will be interested in knowing where you were this evening. After all, it was your chisel.'

'I was out with the post and fetching my evening paper. Disappointing, isn't it? And I wonder where you were at six-twenty-two.'

'How do you know she died at six-twenty-two?'

'I don't. But Sister saw her going down to the basement at six-twenty and there wasn't anything in the basement to keep her as far as I know. Not unless your dear Dr Etherege was there, of course. But surely he wouldn't demean himself cuddling Miss Bolam. Not quite his type I'd have said. But you know his tastes in that direction better than I do, of course.'

Suddenly she was out of her chair and, swinging her right arm, she slapped his cheek with a force that momentarily rocked him. The sharp crack of the blow echoed in the room. Everyone looked at them. Nagle heard Jennifer Priddy's gasp, saw Dr Steiner's worried frown as he looked from one to the other in puzzled inquiry, saw Fredrica Saxon's contemptuous glance at them before her eyes fell again to her book. Mrs Shorthouse, who was piling plates on to a tray at a side table, looked round a second too late. Her sharp little eyes darted from one to the other, frustrated at having missed something worth seeing. Mrs Bostock, her colour heightened, sank back in her chair and picked up her book. Nagle, holding his hand to his cheek, gave a shout of laughter.

'Is anything the matter?' asked Dr Steiner. 'What happened?'

It was then that the door opened and a uniformed policeman put his head in and said:

'The superintendent would like to see Mrs Shorthouse now, please.'

Mrs Amy Shorthouse had seen no reason why she should stay in her working clothes while waiting to be interviewed so that, when called in to Dalgliesh, she was dressed ready to go home. The metamorphosis was striking. Comfortable working slippers had been replaced by a modish pair of high-heeled court shoes, white overall by a fur coat, and head scarf by the latest idiocy in hats. The total effect was curiously old-fashioned. Mrs Shorthouse looked like a relic of the gay twenties, an effect which was heightened by the shortness of her skirt and the careful curls of peroxided hair which lay cunningly arranged on forehead and cheeks. But there was nothing false about her voice and little, Dalgliesh suspected, about her personality. The little grey eyes were shrewd and amused. She was neither frightened nor distressed. He suspected that Amy Shorthouse craved more excitement than her life customarily afforded and was enjoying herself. She would not wish anyone violently dead but, since it had happened, one might as well make the most of it.

When the preliminaries were over and they got down to the events of the evening, Mrs Shorthouse came out with her prize piece of information.

'No good saying I can tell you who did it because I can't. Not that I haven't got my own ideas. But there's one thing I can tell you. I was the last person to talk to her, no doubt about that. No, scrub that out! I was the last person to talk to her, face to face. Excepting the murderer, of course.'

'You mean that she subsequently spoke on the telephone? Hadn't you better tell me about it plainly? I've got enough mystery here for one evening.'

'Smart, aren't you?' said Mrs Shorthouse without rancour. 'Well, it was in this room. I came in at about ten past six to ask how much leave I'd got left on account of wanting a day off next week. Miss Bolam got out my dossier – leastwise it was already out come to think of it – and we fixed that up and had a bit of a chat about the work. I was on my way out really, just standing at the door for a few last words as you might say, when the phone rang.'

'I want you to think very carefully, Mrs Shorthouse,' said Dalgliesh. 'That call may be important. I wonder if you can remember what Miss Bolam said?'

'Think someone was enticing her down to her death, do you?' said Mrs Shorthouse with alliterative relish. 'Well, could be, come to think of it.'

Dalgliesh thought that his witness was far from being a fool. He watched while she screwed up her face in a simulated agony of effort. He had no doubt that she remembered very well what had been said.

After a nicely judged pause for suspense, Mrs Shorthouse said:

'Well, the phone rang like I said. That would be about six-fifteen, I suppose. Miss Bolam picked up the receiver and said, "Administrative Officer speaking." She always answered like that. Very keen on her position she was. Peter Nagle used to say, "Who the hell does she think we're expecting to hear? Khrushchev?" Not that he said it to her. No fear! Anyway, that's what she said. Then there was a little pause and she looked up at me and said: "Yes, I am." Meaning, I suppose, that she was alone, not counting me. Then there was a longer pause while the chap at the other end spoke. Then she said: "All right, stay where you are. I'll be down." Then she asked me to show Mr Lauder into her office if I was about when he arrived, and I said I would and pushed off.'

'You're quite sure about her conversation on the telephone?'

'Sure as I'm sitting here. That's what she said all right.'

'You talked about the chap at the other end. How could you tell it was a man?'

'Never said I could. Just assumed it was a chap, I suppose. Mind you, if I'd been closer I might have known. You can sometimes get an idea who's speaking from the crackly noise the phone makes. But I was standing against the door.'

'And you couldn't hear the other voice at all?'

'That's right. Suggests he was talking low.'

'What happened then, Mrs Shorthouse?'

'I said cheerio and toddled off to do a bit in the general office. Peter Nagle was there taking young Priddy's mind off her work as usual, and Cully was in the reception kiosk, so it wasn't them. Peter went out with the post as soon as I arrived. He always does at about a quarter past six.'

'Did you see Miss Bolam leaving her office?'

'No, I didn't. I told you. I was in with Nagle and Miss Priddy. Sister saw her, though. You ask her. Sister saw her going down the hall.'

'So I understand. I have seen Sister Ambrose. I wondered whether Miss Bolam followed you out of the room.'

'No, she didn't. Not at once anyway. Perhaps she thought it would do the chap good to be kept waiting.'

'Perhaps,' said Dalgliesh. 'But she would have gone down promptly I expect if a doctor had phoned for her.'

Mrs Shorthouse gave a shriek of laughter.

'Maybe. Maybe not. You didn't know Miss Bolam.'

'What was she like, Mrs Shorthouse?'

'All right. We got on. She liked a good worker and I'm a good worker. Well – you can see how the place is kept.'

'I can indeed.'

'Her yea was yea and her nay, nay. I'll say that for her. Nothing unpleasant behind your back. Mind you, quite a bit of unpleasantness in front of your face sometimes if you didn't watch out. Still, I'd rather have it that way. She and me understood each other.'

'Had she any enemies – anyone who bore her a grudge?'

'Must have had, mustn't she? That wasn't no playful tap on the head. Carrying a grudge a bit far, if you ask me.' She planted her feet apart and leaned towards Dalgliesh confidentially.

'Look, ducks,' she said. 'Miss B. put people's backs up. Some people do. You know how it is. They can't make no allowances. Right was right and wrong was wrong and nothing in between. Rigid. That's what she was. Rigid.' Mrs Shorthouse's tone and tightened mouth expressed the ultimate in virtuous inflexibility. 'Take the little matter of the attendance book now. All the consultants are supposed to sign it so that Miss Bolam could make her monthly return to the Board. All very right and proper. Well, the book used to be kept on a table in the doctors' cloakroom and no trouble to anyone. Then Miss B. gets to noticing that Dr Steiner and Dr McBain are coming in late, so she moves the book to her office and they all have to go in there to sign. Mind you, as often as not Dr Steiner won't do it. "She knows I'm here," he says. "And I'm a consultant not a factory hand. If she wants her stupid book signed she can put it back in the medical cloakroom." The doctors have been trying to get rid of her for a year or more, I do know that.'

'How do you know, Mrs Shorthouse?'

'Let's just say that I know. Dr Steiner couldn't stand her. He goes in for psychotherapy. Intensive psychotherapy. Ever heard of it?'

Dalgliesh admitted that he had. Mrs Shorthouse gave him a look in which disbelief fought with suspicion. Then she leaned forward conspiratorially as if about to divulge one of Dr Steiner's less reputable idiosyncrasies.

'He's analytically orientated, that's what he is. Analytically orientated. Know what that means?'

'I've some idea.'

'Then you know that he doesn't see many patients. Two a session, three if you're lucky, and a new patient once every eight weeks. That doesn't push up the figures.'

'The figures?'

'The attendance figures. They go to the Hospital Management Committee and the Regional Board every quarter. Miss Bolam was a great one for pushing up the figures.'

'Then she must have approved thoroughly of Dr Baguley. I understand that his E.C.T. sessions are usually very busy.'

'She approved all right. Not about his divorce, though.'

'How could that affect the figures?' asked Dalgliesh, innocently obtuse. Mrs Shorthouse looked at him pityingly.

'Who said anything about the figures? We were talking about the Baguleys. Getting a divorce, they were, on account of Dr Baguley having an affair with Miss Saxon. It was in all the papers, too. Psychiatrist's wife cites psychologist. Then suddenly Mrs Baguley withdrew the case. Never said why. No one said why. Didn't make any difference here, though. Dr B. and Miss Saxon went on working together easy as you please. Still do.'

'And Dr Baguley and his wife were reconciled?'

'Who said anything about reconciled? They stayed married, that's all I know. Miss Bolam couldn't say a good word for Miss Saxon after that. Not that she ever talked about it; she wasn't one for gossip, I'll give her that. But she let Miss Saxon see what she felt. She was against that sort of thing Miss Bolam was. No carrying on with her, I can tell you!'

Dalgliesh inquired whether anyone had tried. It was a question he usually put with the maximum of tact, but he felt that subtlety would be lost on Mrs Shorthouse. She gave a scream of laughter.

'What do you think? She wasn't one for the men. Not as far as I know, anyway. Mind you, some of the cases they have here would put you off sex for life. Miss Bolam went to the medical director once to complain about some of the reports Miss Priddy was given to type. Said they weren't decent. Of course, she was always a bit odd about Priddy. Tried to fuss round the kid too much if you ask me. Priddy used to be in Miss Bolam's Guide Company or something when she was young, and I suppose Bolam wanted to keep an eye on her in case she forgot what captain had taught her. You could see the kid was embarrassed by it. There wasn't anything wrong, though. Don't you go believing it if they hint that there was. Some of them here have dirty minds and there's no denying it.'

Dalgliesh asked whether Miss Bolam had approved of Miss Priddy's friendship with Nagle.

'Oh, you're on to that, are you? Nothing to approve of, if you ask me. Nagle's a cold fish and as mean as hell. Just try getting his tea money out of him! He and Priddy play around a bit and I dare say Tigger could tell a thing or two if cats could speak. I don't think Bolam noticed though. She kept pretty much to her own office. Anyway, Nagle isn't encouraged in the general office and the medical stenogs are kept pretty busy, so there isn't much time for hanky-panky. Nagle took good care to keep in Miss B.'s good books. Quite the little blue-eyed boy he was. Never absent, never late, that's our Peter. Leastways, he got stuck in the Underground one Monday and wasn't he in a state about it! Spoilt his record, you see. He even came in on May first when he had the flu because we had a visit from the Duke and, naturally, Peter Nagle had to be here to see everything was done proper. Temperature of 103 he had. Sister took it. Miss Bolam sent him home pretty soon, I can tell you. Dr Steiner took him in his car.'

'Is it generally known that Mr Nagle keeps his tools in the porters' duty-room?'

'Of course it is! Stands to reason. People are always wanting him to mend this or that and where else would he keep his tools? A proper old woman he is about them, too. Talk about fussy. Cully isn't allowed to touch them. Mind you they aren't clinic tools. They belong to Nagle. There wasn't half a row about six weeks ago when Dr Steiner borrowed a screwdriver to do something to his car. Being Dr Steiner he mucked up the job and bent the screwdriver. Talk about trouble! Nagle thought it was Cully and they had one hell of a row which brought on Cully's belly-ache again, poor old blighter. Then Nagle found out that someone had seen Dr Steiner coming out of the porters' duty-room with the tool so he complained to Miss Bolam and she spoke to Dr Steiner and made him buy another screwdriver. We do see life here, I can tell you. Never a dull moment. Never had a murder before, though. That's something new. Nice goings-on, I don't think.'

'As you say. If you've any idea who did it, Mrs Shorthouse, now's the time to say so.'

Mrs Shorthouse adjusted one of the curls on her forehead with a licked finger, wriggled more comfortably into her coat and got to her feet, thus indicating that, in her opinion, the interview was over.

'No fear! Catching murderers is your job, mate, and you're

welcome to it. I'll say this much, though. It wasn't one of the doctors. They haven't the guts. These psychiatrists are a timid lot. Say what you like about this killer, the chap has nerve.'

Dalgliesh decided to question the doctors next. He was surprised and interested by their patience, by their ready acceptance of his role. He had kept them waiting because he judged it more important to his inquiry to see other people first, even such an apparently less important witness as the domestic assistant. It looked as if they appreciated that he wasn't trying to irritate them or keep them unnecessarily in suspense. He wouldn't have hesitated to do either if it would have served his purpose, but it was his experience that useful information could most often be obtained when a witness hadn't been given time to think and could be betrayed by shock or fear into garrulity and indiscretion. The doctors had not kept themselves apart. They had waited in the front consulting-room with the others, quietly and without protest. They gave him the credit of knowing his job and let him get on with it. He wondered whether consultant surgeons or physicians would have been so accommodating and felt with the group secretary that there were worse people to deal with than psychiatrists.

Dr Mary Ingram was seen first by request of the medical director. She had three young children at home and it was important that she get back to them as soon as possible. She had been crying spasmodically while waiting, to the embarrassment of her colleagues who had difficulty in comforting a grief which seemed to them unreasonable and ill-timed. Nurse Bolam was bearing up well, after all, and she was a relative. Dr Ingram's tears added to the tension and provoked an irrational guilt in those whose emotions were less uncomplicated. There was a general feeling that she should be allowed to go home to her children without delay. There was little she could tell Dalgliesh. She attended the clinic only twice weekly to help with the E.C.T. sessions and had hardly known Miss Bolam. She had been in the E.C.T. room with Sister Ambrose for the whole of the crucial time from six-twenty until seven. In reply to Dalgliesh's question she admitted that Dr Baguley might have left them for a short time after six-fifteen, but she couldn't remember when exactly or for how long. At the end of the interview she looked at Dalgliesh from reddened eyes and said:

'You will find out who did it, won't you? That poor, poor girl.'

'We shall find out,' replied Dalgliesh.

Dr Etherege was interviewed next. He gave the necessary personal details without waiting to be asked and went on:

'As regards my own movements this evening, I'm afraid I can't be very helpful. I arrived at the clinic just before five and went into Miss Bolam's office to speak to her before going upstairs. We had a little general conversation. She seemed perfectly all right to me and didn't tell me that she had asked to see the group secretary. I rang the general office for Mrs Bostock at about five-fifteen and she was with me taking dictation until about ten to six when she went downstairs with the post. She came back after ten minutes or so and we continued with the dictation until some time before half past six, when she went next door to type material directly from a tape machine. Some of my treatment sessions are recorded and the material subsequently played back and a typescript made either for research purposes or for the medical record. I worked alone in my consulting-room except for one brief visit to the medical library – I can't remember when, but it was very shortly after Mrs Bostock left me – until she returned to consult me on a point. That must have been just before seven because we were together when Sister rang to tell me about Miss Bolam. Miss Saxon came down from her room on the third floor to go home and caught us up on the stairs, so she and I went to the basement. You know what we found and the subsequent steps I took to ensure that no one left the clinic.'

'You seem to have acted with great presence of mind, Doctor,' said Dalgliesh. 'As a result the field of inquiry can be considerably narrowed. It looks, doesn't it, as if the murderer is still in this building?'

'Certainly Cully has assured me that no one got past him after 5 p.m. without being entered in his register. That is our system here. The implication of that locked back door is disturbing, but I'm sure you are too experienced an officer to jump to conclusions. No building is impregnable. The . . . the person responsible could have got in at any time, even early this morning, and lain hidden in the basement.'

'Can you suggest where such a person lay concealed or how he got out of the clinic?'

The medical director did not reply.

'Have you any idea who that person might be?'

Dr Etherege slowly traced the line of his right eyebrow with his middle finger. Dalgliesh had seen him do this on television and reflected, now as then, that it served to draw attention to a fine hand and a well-shaped eyebrow even if as an indication of serious thought the gesture seemed slightly spurious.

'I have no idea at all. The whole tragedy is incomprehensible. I'm not going to claim that Miss Bolam was an altogether easy person to get on with. She sometimes aroused resentment.' He smiled deprecatingly. 'We're not always very easy to get on with ourselves and the most successful administrator of a psychiatric unit is probably someone far more tolerant than Miss Bolam, less obsessional perhaps. But this is murder! I can't think of anyone, patient or staff, who would want to kill her. It's very horrible to me as medical director to think that there might be someone as disturbed as that working at the Steen and I never knew.'

'As disturbed or as wicked,' said Dalgliesh, unable to resist the temptation. Dr Etherege smiled again, patiently explaining a difficult point to an obtuse member of the television panel. 'Wicked? I'm not competent to discuss this in theological terms.'

'Nor am I, Doctor,' replied Dalgliesh. 'But this crime doesn't look like the work of a madman. There's an intelligence behind it.'

'Some psychopaths are highly intelligent, Superintendent. Not that I am knowledgeable about psychopathy. It's a most interesting field but not mine. We have never claimed at the Steen to be able to treat the condition.'

Then the Steen was in good company, thought Dalgliesh. The Mental Health Act, 1959, may have defined psychopathy as a disorder requiring or susceptible to medical treatment, but there appeared little enthusiasm on the part of doctors to treat it. The word seemed little more than a psychiatrist's term of abuse and he said as much. Dr Etherege smiled, indulgent, unprovoked.

'I have never accepted a clinical entity because it is defined in an Act of Parliament. However, psychopathy exists. I'm not convinced at present that it is susceptible to medical treatment. What I am sure is that it is not susceptible to a prison sentence. But we have no certainty that we're looking for a psychopath.'

Dalgliesh asked Dr Etherege whether he knew where Nagle kept his tools and which key opened the door of the record-room.

'I knew about the key. If I'm working late and alone I sometimes need one of the old files and I fetch it myself. I do a certain amount of research and, of course, lecturing and writing, and it's important to have access to the medical records. I last fetched a file about ten days ago. I don't think I've ever seen the box of tools in the porters' room, but I knew that Nagle had his own set and was particular about them. I suppose if I'd wanted a chisel I should have looked in the porters' room. The tools would hardly be kept anywhere else. Obviously, too, I should expect Tippett's fetish to be in the art therapy department. It was a most curious choice of weapons! What I find interesting is the apparent care taken by the murderer to fix suspicion on the clinic staff.'

'Suspicion can hardly rest elsewhere in the face of those locked doors.'

'That's what I meant, Superintendent. If a member of the staff present this evening did kill Miss Bolam surely he would want to divert suspicion from the relatively few people known to be in the building at the time. The easiest way to do that would be to unlock one of the doors. He'd need to wear gloves, of course, but then, I gather that he did wear them.'

'There are no prints on either of the weapons, certainly. They were wiped, but it is probable that he did wear gloves.'

'And yet, those doors were kept locked, the strongest evidence that the murderer was still in the building. Why? It would be risky to unlock the back door on the ground floor. That, as you know, is between the E.C.T. room and the medical staff-room and it leads into a well-lit road. It would be difficult to unlock it without the risk of being seen, and a murderer would hardly make his exit that way. But there are the two fire-escape doors on the second and third floors and the door in the basement. Why not unlock one of those? It can only be, surely, because the murderer hadn't the opportunity between the time of the crime and the finding of the body, or that he deliberately wished to throw suspicion on the clinic staff even at the inevitable cost of increasing his own danger.'

'You talk about "he", Doctor. Do you think, as a psychiatrist, that we should be looking for a man?'

'Oh yes! I would expect this to be the work of a man.'

'Although it didn't require great strength?' asked Dalgliesh.

'I wasn't thinking primarily of the strength required but of the method and the choice of weapon. I can only give my opinion, of course, and I'm not a criminologist. I would expect it to be a man's crime. But, of course, a woman could have done it. Psychologically, it's unlikely. Physically, it's perfectly possible.'

It was indeed, thought Dalgliesh. It required merely knowledge and nerve. He pictured for a moment an intent, pretty face bent over Miss Bolam's body; a thin, girlish hand slipping open the sweater buttons and rolling up the fine cashmere jumper. And then, that clinical selection of exactly the right place to pierce, and the grunt of effort as the blade went home. And, last of all, the sweater drawn lightly back to conceal the chisel handle, the ugly fetish placed in position on the still twitching body in an ultimate gesture of derision and defiance. He told the medical director about Mrs Shorthouse's evidence of the phone call.

'No one has admitted to making that call. It looks very much as if she were tricked down to the basement.'

'That is mere supposition, Superintendent.'

Dalgliesh pointed out mildly that it was also common sense, the basis of all sound police work. The medical director said:

'There is a card hung beside the telephone outside the record-room. Anyone, even a stranger to the clinic, could discover Miss Bolam's number.'

'But what would be her reaction to an internal call from a stranger? She went downstairs without question. She must have recognized the voice.'

'Then it was someone she had no reason to fear, Superintendent. That doesn't tie up with the suggestion that she was in possession of some dangerous knowledge and was killed to prevent her passing it on to Lauder. She went down to her death without fear or suspicion. I can only hope that she died quickly and without pain.'

Dalgliesh said that he would know more when he got the autopsy report but that death was almost certainly instantaneous. He added:

'There must have been one dreadful moment when she looked up and saw her murderer with the fetish raised, but it happened very quickly. She would feel nothing after she was stunned. I doubt whether she even had time to cry out. If she did the sound would be muffled by the tiers of paper and I'm told that Mrs King was being rather noisy during her treatment.' He paused for a moment, then said quietly: 'What made you describe to the staff just how Miss Bolam died? You did tell them?'

'Of course. I called them together in the front consulting-room – the patients were in the waiting-room – and made a brief statement. Are you suggesting that the news could have been kept from them?'

'I am suggesting that they need not have been told the details. It would have been useful to me if you hadn't mentioned the stabbing. The murderer might have given himself away by showing more knowledge than an innocent person could have possessed.'

The medical director smiled.

'I'm a psychiatrist not a detective. Strange as it may seem to you, my reaction to this crime was to assume that the rest of the staff would share my horror and distress, not to lay traps for them. I wanted to break the news to them myself, gently and honestly. They have always had my confidence and I saw no reason for withholding that confidence now.'

That was all very well, thought Dalgliesh, but an intelligent man must surely have seen the importance of saying as little as possible. And the medical director was a very intelligent man. As he thanked his witness and drew the interview to its close, his mind busied itself with the problem. How carefully had Dr Etherege considered the position before he spoke to the staff? Had his disclosure of the stabbing been as thoughtless as it appeared? It would, after all, have been impossible to deceive most of the staff. Dr Steiner, Dr Baguley, Nagle, Dr Ingram and Sister Ambrose had all seen the body. Miss Priddy had seen it but had apparently fled without a second look. That left Nurse Bolam, Mrs Bostock, Mrs Shorthouse, Miss Saxon, Miss Kettle and Cully. Possibly Etherege was satisfied that none of these was the murderer. Cully and Shorthouse both had an alibi. Had the medical director been reluctant to lay a trap for Nurse Bolam, Mrs Bostock or Miss Saxon? Or was he so certain in his own mind that the murderer must be a man that any subterfuge to mislead the women seemed a waste of time, likely to result only in embarrassment and resentment? The medical director had certainly been almost blatant in his hints that anyone working on the second or third floor could be eliminated since they would have had the opportunity of opening one of the fire-escape doors. But then, he himself had been in his consulting-room on the second floor. In any case, the obvious door for the killer to unlock was the one in the basement and it was hard to believe that he had lacked the opportunity. It would be a second's work only to draw back that lock and provide evidence that the murderer could have left the clinic that way. Yet the basement door had been fast bolted. Why?

Dr Steiner came in next, short, dapper, outwardly self-composed. In the light from Miss Bolam's desk lamp his pale smooth skin looked slightly luminous. Despite his calmness he had been sweating heavily. The heavy smell hung about his clothes, about the well-cut, conventional black coat of a consultant. Dalgliesh was surprised when he gave his age as forty-two. He looked older. The smooth skin, the sharp black eyes, the bouncy walk gave a superficial impression of youth but he was already thickening and his dark hair, cunningly sleeked back, could not quite conceal the tonsure-like patch on the crown of the head.

Dr Steiner had apparently decided to treat his encounter with a policeman as a social occasion. Extending a plump, well-kept hand, he smiled a benign 'how d'you do' and inquired whether he was speaking to the writer, Adam Dalgliesh.

'I have read your verse,' he announced complacently. 'I congratulate you. Such a deceptive simplicity. I started at the first poem and read straight through. That is my way of experiencing verse. At the tenth page I began to think that we might have a new poet.'

Dalgliesh admitted to himself that Dr Steiner had not only read the book but showed some critical insight. It was at the tenth page that he, too, sometimes felt they might have a new poet. Dr Steiner inquired whether he had met Ernie Bales, the new young playwright from Nottingham. He looked so hopeful that Dalgliesh felt positively unkind as he disclaimed acquaintance with Mr Bales and steered the conversation from literary criticism back to the purpose of the interview. Dr Steiner at once assumed an air of shocked gravity.

'The whole affair is dreadful, quite dreadful. I was one of the first people to see the body as you may know and it has distressed me greatly. I have always had a horror of violence. It is an appalling business. Dr Etherege, our medical director, is due to retire at the end of the year. This is a most unfortunate thing to happen in his last months here.'

He shook his head sadly, but Dalgliesh fancied that the little black eyes held something very like satisfaction.

Tippett's fetish had yielded its secrets to the fingerprint expert and Dalgliesh had stood it on the desk before him. Dr Steiner put out his hand to touch it then drew back and said:

'I had better not handle it, I suppose, because of fingerprints.' He darted a quick look at Dalgliesh and getting no response went on: 'It's an interesting carving, isn't it? Quite remarkable. Have you ever noticed, Superintendent, what excellent art the mentally ill can produce, even patients without previous training or experience? It raises interesting questions on the nature of artistic achievement. As they recover, their work deteriorates. The power and originality go. By the time they are well again the stuff they produce is valueless. We've got several interesting examples of patients' work in the art therapy department, but this fetish is outstanding. Tippett was very ill when he carved it and went to hospital shortly afterwards. He's a schizophrenic. The fetish has the typical facies of the chronic disease, the frog-like eyes and spreading nostrils. Tippett looked very like that himself at one time.'

'Everyone knew where this thing was kept, I suppose?' said Dalgliesh.

'Oh, yes! It was kept on the shelf in the art therapy department. Tippett was very proud of it and Dr Baguley often showed it to House Committee members when they made visits of inspection. Mrs Baumgarten, the art therapist, likes to keep some of the best work on show. That's why she had the shelves put up. She's on sick leave at the present but you've been shown the department, I expect?'

Dalgliesh said that he had.

'Some of my colleagues feel that the art therapy is a waste of money,' confided Dr Steiner. 'Certainly I never use Mrs Baumgarten. But one must be tolerant. Dr Baguley refers patients now and again, and it probably does them less harm to dabble about down there than to be subjected to E.C.T. But to pretend that the patients' artistic efforts can help towards a diagnosis seems very far-fetched to me. Of course that claim is all part of the effort to get Mrs Baumgarten graded as a lay psychotherapist, quite unwarrantably, I'm afraid. She has no analytical training.'

'And the chisel? Did you know where that was kept, Doctor?'

'Well, not really, Superintendent. I mean, I knew that Nagle had some tools and presumably kept them in the porters' duty-room, but I didn't know exactly where.'

'The toolbox is large and clearly labelled and is kept on the small table in the duty-room. It would be difficult to miss.'

'Oh, I'm sure it would! But then, I have no reason to go into the porters' duty-room. That is true of all the doctors. We must get a key for that box now and see that it's kept somewhere safe. Miss Bolam was very wrong to allow Nagle to keep it unlocked. After all, we do occasionally have disturbed patients and some tools can be lethal.'

'So it appears.'

'This clinic wasn't intended to treat grossly psychotic patients, of course. It was founded to provide a centre for analytically orientated psychotherapy, particularly for middle class and highly intelligent patients. We treat people who would never dream of entering a mental hospital – and who would be just as out of place in the ordinary psychiatric out-patient department. In addition, of course, there is a large research element in our work.'

'What were you doing between six o'clock and seven this evening, Doctor?' inquired Dalgliesh.

Dr Steiner looked pained at this sudden intrusion of sordid curiosity into an interesting discussion but answered, meekly enough, that he had been conducting his Friday night psychotherapy session.

'I arrived at the clinic at five-thirty when my first patient was booked. Unfortunately he defaulted. His treatment has arrived at a stage when poor attendance is to be expected. Mr Burge was booked for six-fifteen and he is usually very prompt. I waited for him in the second consulting-room on the ground floor and joined him in my own room at about ten past six. Mr Burge dislikes waiting with Dr Baguley's patients in the general waiting-room and I really don't blame him. You've heard of Burge, I expect. He wrote that interesting novel *The Souls of the Righteous*, a quite brilliant exposure of the sexual conflicts concealed beneath the conventionality of a respectable English suburb. But I'm forgetting. Naturally you have interviewed Mr Burge.'

Dalgliesh had indeed. The experience had been tedious and not unenlightening. He had also heard of Mr Burge's book, an opus of some two hundred thousand words in which the scabrous episodes are inserted with such meticulous deliberation that it only requires an exercise in simple arithmetic to calculate on what page the next will occur. Dalgliesh did not suspect Burge of any part in the murder. A writer who could produce such a hotchpotch of sex and sadism was probably impotent and certainly timid. But he was not necessarily a liar. Dalgliesh said:

'Are you quite sure of your times, Doctor? Mr Burge says that he arrived at six-fifteen and Cully has booked him in at that time. Burge says he went straight into your own consulting-room, having checked with Cully that you weren't seeing a patient, and that it was a full ten minutes before you joined him. He was getting impatient and was thinking of going to inquire where you were.'

Dr Steiner did not appear either frightened or angry at his patient's perfidy. He did, however, look embarrassed.

'It's interesting Mr Burge should say that. I'm afraid he may be right. I thought he seemed a little put out when we began the session. If he says that I joined him at six-twenty-five I have no doubt he's telling the truth. The poor man has had a very short

and interrupted session this evening. It's very unfortunate at this
particular stage in his treatment.'

'So, if you weren't in the front consulting-room when your
patient arrived, where were you?' persisted Dalgliesh gently.

An astonishing change came over Dr Steiner's face. Suddenly
he looked as shamefaced as a small boy who has been caught in
the middle of mischief. He didn't look frightened but he did look
extremely guilty. The metamorphosis from consultant psychiatrist
to embarrassed delinquent was almost comical.

'But I told you, Superintendent! I was in number two
consulting-room, the one between the front one and the patients'
waiting-room.'

'Doing what, Doctor?'

Really, it was almost laughable! What could Steiner have been
up to to produce this degree of embarrassment? Dalgliesh's mind
toyed with bizarre possibilities. Reading pornography? Smoking
hemp? Seducing Mrs Shorthouse? It surely couldn't be anything
so conventional as planning murder. But the doctor had obviously
decided that the truth must be told. He said with a burst of
shamefaced candour:

'It sounds silly, I know, but . . . well . . . it was rather warm
and I'd had a busy day and the couch was there.' He gave a little
giggle. 'In fact, Superintendent, at the time Miss Bolam is thought
to have died, I was, in the vulgar parlance, having a kip!'

Once this embarrassing confession was off his chest Dr Steiner
became happily voluble and it was difficult to get rid of him. But
at last he was persuaded that he could help no more for the
present and his place was taken by Dr Baguley.

Dr Baguley, like his colleagues, made no complaint of his long wait,
but it had taken its toll. He was still wearing his white coat and he
hugged it around himself as he drew the chair under him. He
seemed to have difficulty in settling comfortably, twitching his lean
shoulders and crossing and recrossing his legs. The clefts from nose
to mouth looked deeper, his hair was dank, his eyes black pools in
the light of the desk lamp. He lit a cigarette and, fumbling in his
coat pocket, produced a slip of paper and passed it to Martin.

'I've written down my personal details. It'll save time.'

'Thank you, sir,' said Martin stolidly.

'I may as well say now that I haven't an alibi for the twenty minutes or so after six-fifteen. I expect you've heard that I left the E.C.T. clinic a few minutes before Sister saw Miss Bolam for the last time. I went into the medical staff cloakroom at the end of the hall and had a cigarette. The place was empty and no one came in. I didn't hurry back to the clinic so I suppose it was about twenty to seven before I rejoined Dr Ingram and Sister. They were together for the whole of that time, of course.'

'So Sister tells me.'

'It's ridiculous even to consider that either of them would be involved but I'm glad they happened to stick together. The more people you can eliminate the better from your point of view, I suppose. I'm sorry not to be able to produce an alibi. I can't help in any other way either, I'm afraid. I heard and saw nothing.'

Dalgliesh asked the doctor how he had spent the evening.

'It was the usual pattern, until seven o'clock that is. I arrived just before four and went into Miss Bolam's office to sign the medical attendance book. It used to be kept in the medical staff cloakroom until recently when she moved it into her office. We talked for a short time – she had some queries about the servicing arrangements for my new E.C.T. machine – and then I went to start my clinic. We were pretty busy until just after six and I also had my lysergic acid patient to visit periodically. She was being specialled by Nurse Bolam in the basement treatment-room. But I'm forgetting. You've seen Mrs King.'

Mrs King and her husband had been sitting in the patients' waiting-room on Dalgliesh's arrival and he had taken very little time to satisfy himself that they could have had nothing to do with the murder. The woman was still weak and a little disorientated and sat holding tightly to her husband's hand. He had not arrived at the clinic to escort her home until a few minutes after Sergeant Martin and his party. Dalgliesh had questioned the woman briefly and gently and had let her go. He had not needed the assurances of the medical director to be satisfied that this patient could not have left her bed to murder anyone. But he was equally sure that she was in no state to give an alibi to anyone else. He asked Dr Baguley when he had last visited his patient.

'I looked in on her shortly after I arrived, before I started the shock treatment actually. The drug had been given at three-thirty and the patient was beginning to react. I ought to say that LSD is given in an effort to make the patient more accessible to psychotherapy by releasing some of the more deep-seated inhibitions. It's only given under close supervision and the patient is never left. I was called down again by Nurse Bolam at five and stayed for about forty minutes. I went back upstairs and gave my last shock treatment at about twenty to six. The last E.C.T. patient actually left the clinic a few minutes after Miss Bolam was last seen. From about six-thirty I was clearing up and writing my notes.'

'Was the door of the medical record-room open when you passed it at five o'clock?'

Dr Baguley thought for a moment or two and then said:

'I think it was shut. It's difficult to be absolutely certain, but I'm pretty sure I should have noticed if it had been open or ajar.'

'And at twenty to six when you left your patient?'

'The same.'

Dalgliesh asked again the usual, the inevitable, the obvious questions. Had Miss Bolam any enemies? Did the doctor know of any reason why someone might wish her dead? Had she seemed worried lately? Had he any idea why she might have sent for the group secretary? Could he decipher the notes on her jotting pad? But Dr Baguley could not help. He said:

'She was a curious woman in some ways, shy, a little aggressive, not really happy with us. But she was perfectly harmless, the last person I'd have said to invite violence. One can't go on saying how shocking it is. Words seem to lose their meaning with repetition. But I suppose we all feel the same. The whole thing is fantastic! Unbelievable!'

'You said she wasn't happy here. Is this a difficult clinic to administer? From what I've heard, Miss Bolam wasn't particularly skilled at dealing with difficult personalities.'

Dr Baguley said easily:

'Oh, you don't want to believe all you hear. We're individual-ists, but we get along with each other pretty well on the whole. Steiner and I scrap a bit but it's all quite amiable. He wants the place to become a psychotherapy training unit with registrars and lay professional staff running around like mice and a bit of research on the side. One of those places where time and money are spent lavishly on anything but actually treating patients – especially psychotics. There's no danger he'll get his way. The Regional Board wouldn't wear it for one thing.'

'And what were Miss Bolam's views, Doctor?'

'Strictly speaking she was hardly competent to hold any, but that didn't inhibit her. She was anti-Freudian and pro-eclectic. Anti-Steiner and pro-me if you like. But that didn't mean anything. Neither Dr Steiner nor I were likely to knock her on the head because of our doctrinal differences. As you see we haven't even taken a knife to each other yet. All this is utterly irrelevant.'

'I'm inclined to agree with you,' said Dalgliesh. 'Miss Bolam was killed with great deliberation and considerable expertise. I think the motive was a great deal more positive and important than a mere difference of opinion or clash of personality. Did you know, by the way, which key opens the record-room?'

'Of course. If I want one of the old records I usually fetch it myself. I also know, if it's any help to you, that Nagle keeps his box of tools in the porters' rest-room. Furthermore, when I arrived this afternoon, Miss Bolam told me about Tippett. But that's hardly relevant, is it? You can't seriously believe that the murderer hoped to implicate Tippett.'

'Perhaps not. Tell me, Doctor. From your knowledge of Miss Bolam what would be her reaction to finding those medical records strewn about the floor?'

Dr Baguley looked surprised for a second then gave a curt laugh.

'Bolam? That's an easy one! She was obsessionally neat. Obviously she'd start to pick them up!'

'She wouldn't be more likely to ring for a porter to do the work or to leave the records where they were as evidence until the culprit was discovered?'

Dr Baguley thought for a moment and seemed to repent of his first categorical opinion.

'One can't possibly know for certain what she'd do. It's all conjecture. Probably you're right and she'd ring for Nagle. She wasn't afraid of work but she was very conscious of her position as A.O. I'm sure of one thing, though. She wouldn't have left the place in a mess like that. She couldn't pass a rug or a picture without straightening it.'

'And her cousin? Are they alike? I understand that Nurse Bolam works for you more than for any other consultant.'

Dalgliesh noticed the quick frown of distaste that this question provoked. Dr Baguley, however co-operative and frank about his own motives, was not disposed to comment on those of anyone else. Or was it that Nurse Bolam's gentle defencelessness had aroused his protective instincts? Dalgliesh waited for a reply. After a minute the doctor said curtly:

'I shouldn't have said the cousins were alike. You will have formed your own impression of Nurse Bolam. I can only say that I have complete trust in her, both as a nurse and a person.'

'She is her cousin's heir. Or perhaps you knew that?'

The inference was too plain to be missed and Dr Baguley too tired to resist the provocation.

'No, I didn't. But I hope for her sake that it's a bloody great sum and that she and her mother will be allowed to enjoy it in peace. And I hope, too, that you won't waste time suspecting innocent people. The sooner this murder is cleared up the better. It's a pretty intolerable position for all of us.'

So Dr Baguley knew about Nurse Bolam's mother. But, then, it was likely that most of the clinic staff knew. He asked his last question:

'You said, Doctor, that you were alone in the medical staff cloakroom from about six-fifteen until twenty to seven. What were you doing?'

'Going to the lavatory. Washing my hands. Smoking a cigarette. Thinking.'

'And that was absolutely all you did during the twenty-five minutes?'

'Yes – that was all, Superintendent.'

Dr Baguley was a poor liar. The hesitation was only momentary; his face did not change colour; the fingers holding his cigarette were quite steady. But his voice was a little too nonchalant, the disinterest a little too carefully controlled. And it was with a palpable effort that he made himself meet Dalgliesh's eyes. He was too intelligent to add to his statement but his eyes held those of the detective as if willing Dalgliesh to repeat his question, and bracing himself to meet it.

'Thank you, Doctor,' said Dalgliesh calmly. 'That will be all for the present.'

CHAPTER THREE

And so it went on; the patient questioning, the meticulous taking of notes, the close watch of suspects' eyes and hands for the revealing flicker of fear, the tensed reaction to an unwelcome change of emphasis. Fredrica Saxon followed Dr Baguley. As they passed each other in the doorway Dalgliesh saw that they were careful not to meet each other's eyes. She was a dark, vital, casually dressed woman of twenty-nine who would do no more than give brief but straightforward answers to his questions and who seemed to take a perverse pleasure in pointing out that she had been alone scoring a psychological test in her own room from six until seven and could neither claim an alibi for herself nor give one to anyone else. He got little help or information from Fredrica Saxon but did not, on that account, assume that she had none to give.

She was followed by a very different witness. Miss Ruth Kettle had apparently decided that the murder was none of her affair and, although she was willing to answer Dalgliesh's questions, it was with a vague lack of interest which suggested that her thoughts were on higher things. There is only a limited number of words to express horror and surprise and the clinic staff had used most of them during the evening. Miss Kettle's reaction was less orthodox. She gave her opinion that the murder was peculiar . . . really very odd indeed, and sat blinking at Dalgliesh through her thick spectacles in gentle bewilderment as if she did indeed find it odd, but hardly sufficiently odd to be worth discussing at length. But at least two pieces of information which she was able to give were interesting. Dalgliesh could only hope that they were reliable.

She had been vague about her own movements during the evening, but Dalgliesh's persistence elicited that she had been interviewing the wife of one of the E.C.T. patients until about twenty to six when Sister had telephoned to say that the patient was ready to be taken home. Miss Kettle had walked downstairs with her client, said 'good night' in the hall, and had then gone straight down to the record-room to fetch a file. She had found the room in perfect order and had locked it after her. Despite her gentle incertitude about most of the evening's activities she was positive about the time. In any case, thought Dalgliesh, it could probably be verified by Sister Ambrose. The second clue was more nebulous and Miss Kettle mentioned it with apparent indifference to its importance. Some half-hour after returning to her room on the second floor she had heard the unmistakable sound of the service lift thumping to a stop.

Dalgliesh was tired now. Despite the central heating he felt spasms of cold and recognized the familiar malaise that preceded an attack of neuralgia. The right side of his face already felt stiff and heavy, and the needling pain was beginning to stab spasmodically behind his eyeball. But his last witness was here.

Mrs Bostock, the senior medical stenographer, had none of the doctors' tolerant acceptance of a long wait. She was angry and her anger came into the room with her like a chill wind. She seated herself without speaking, crossed a pair of long and remarkably shapely legs, and looked at Dalgliesh with frank dislike in her pale eyes. She had a striking and unusual head. Her long hair, golden as a guinea, was coiled in intricate folds above a pale, arrogant, sharp-nosed face. With her long neck, poised, colourful head and slightly protuberant eyes, she looked like some exotic bird. Dalgliesh had difficulty in concealing his shock when he saw her hands. They were as huge, red and raw-boned as the hands of a butcher and looked as if they had been incongruously grafted on to the slim wrists by some malignant fate. It was almost a deformity. She made no attempt to conceal them, but her nails were short and she wore no polish. She had a beautiful figure and was well and expensively dressed, an object lesson in the art of minimizing one's defects and emphasizing one's advantages. She probably lived her life, thought Dalgliesh, on much the same principle.

She gave details of her movements since six o'clock that evening briefly and with no apparent reluctance. She had last seen Miss Bolam at six o'clock when, as was usual, she had taken in the post for the administrative officer to sign. There were only five letters. Most of the post consisted of medical reports and letters to general practitioners from the psychiatrists and Miss Bolam was not, of course, concerned with these. All the outgoing mail was registered in the post book either by Mrs Bostock or Miss Priddy, and was then taken across the road by Nagle to catch the six-thirty from the pillar-box. Miss Bolam had seemed her usual self at six o'clock. She had signed her own letters and Mrs Bostock had returned to the general office, handed them with the doctors' post to Miss Priddy, and had then gone upstairs to take dictation from Dr Etherege for the last hour of the day. It was an under-stood thing that she helped Dr Etherege on Friday evenings for one hour with his research project. She and the medical director had been together except for a few short periods. Sister rang at about seven o'clock with the news of Miss Bolam's death. As she and Dr Etherege left the consulting-room they met Miss Saxon who was just leaving. She went down to the basement with the medical director. Mrs Bostock, at Dr Etherege's request, had gone to join Cully at the front door to ensure that the instructions were followed about no one leaving the building. She had stayed with Cully until the party from the basement appeared and they had then all collected in the waiting-room to await the arrival of the police, except for the two porters who remained on duty in the hall.

'You said that you were with Dr Etherege from just after six onwards except for short periods. What were you both doing?'

'We were both working, naturally.' Mrs Bostock managed to suggest that the question had been both stupid and a little vulgar. 'Dr Etherege is writing a paper on the treatment of twin schizo-phrenic women by psychoanalysis. As I said, it has been agreed that I shall assist him for one hour on Friday evenings. That is quite inadequate for his needs, but Miss Bolam took the view that the work wasn't strictly a clinic concern and that Dr Etherege should do it in his own consulting-room with the help of his private secretary. Naturally that's impossible. All the material, including some on tape, is here. My part of the job is varied. For some of the time I take dictation. Sometimes I work in the little office typing directly from the tape. Sometimes I look up references in the staff library.'

'And what did you do this evening?'

'I took dictation for about thirty minutes. Then I went into the adjoining office and worked from the tape. Dr Etherege rang me to come in at about ten to seven. We were working together when the phone rang.'

'That would mean that you were with Dr Etherege taking dictation until about six-thirty-five.'

'Presumably.'

'And for the whole of that time you were together?'

'I think Dr Etherege went out for a minute or so to verify a reference.'

'Why should you be uncertain, Mrs Bostock? Either he did or he didn't.'

'Naturally, Superintendent. As you say, either he did or he didn't. But there is no reason why I should particularly remember. This evening was in no way remarkable. My impression is that he did go out for a short time but I really couldn't recall exactly when. I expect he may be able to help you.'

Suddenly Dalgliesh changed the course of questioning. He paused for a full half-minute and then asked quietly:

'Did you like Miss Bolam, Mrs Bostock?'

It was not a welcome question. Under the patina of make-up he saw a flush of anger or embarrassment die along her neck.

'She wasn't an easy person to like. I tried to be loyal to her.'

'By loyal you mean, no doubt, that you tried to smooth down rather than exacerbate her difficulties with the medical staff and refrained from any overt criticism of her as an administrator?'

The tinge of sarcasm in his voice awoke, as was intended, all her latent hostility. Behind the mask of hauteur and detachment he glimpsed the insecure schoolgirl. He knew that she would have to justify herself even against an implied criticism. She did not like him but she could not bear to be underrated or ignored.

'Miss Bolam wasn't really a suitable administrator for a psychiatric unit. She hadn't any sympathy with what we're trying to do here.'

'In what way was she unsympathetic?'

'Well, for one thing, she didn't like neurotics.'

Neither do I, God help me, thought Dalgliesh. Neither do I. But he said nothing and Mrs Bostock went on:

'She was difficult, for example, about paying out some of the patients' travelling expenses. They only get them if they're on National Assistance, but we help other cases from the Samaritan Fund. We have one girl, a most intelligent person, who comes here twice a week from Surrey to work in the art therapy department. Miss Bolam thought she ought to get treatment nearer home – or go without. Actually she made it pretty plain that, in her view, the patient ought to be discharged to do a job of work, as she put it.'

'She didn't say this sort of thing to the patient.'

'Oh, no! She was careful enough what she actually said. But I could see that the sensitive ones weren't at ease with her. Then she was very critical of intensive psychotherapy. It's a time-consuming procedure. It has to be. Miss Bolam tended to judge a psychiatrist's worth by the number of patients he saw in a session. But that was less important than her attitude to the patients. There was a reason for it, of course. Her mother was mentally ill and in analysis for years before she died. I understand that she killed herself. Miss Bolam can't have had an easy time. Naturally she couldn't allow herself to hate her mother, so she projected her resentment on to the patients here. She was subconsciously afraid of her own neurosis too. That was pretty obvious.'

Dalgliesh did not feel qualified to comment on these theories. He was prepared to believe that there was truth in them but not that Mrs Bostock had thought them out for herself. Miss Bolam may have irritated the psychiatrists by her lack of sympathy, but here, at least, they had a believer.

'Do you know who treated Mrs Bolam?' he asked.

Mrs Bostock uncrossed her elegant legs and settled herself more comfortably in the chair before deigning to reply.

'I do, as a matter of fact. But I hardly see its relevance to this inquiry.'

'Shall we leave that to me to decide? I can find out quite easily. If you don't know or aren't sure it would save time if you said so.'

'It was Dr Etherege.'

'And who do you think will be appointed to succeed Miss Bolam?'

'As administrative officer? Really,' said Mrs Bostock coolly, 'I've no idea.'

At last the main work of the evening was over for Dalgliesh and Martin. The body had been taken away and the record-room sealed. All the clinic staff had been questioned and most of them had left for their homes. Dr Etherege had been the last doctor to leave and had hung around uneasily for some time after Dalgliesh had said he might go. Mr Lauder and Peter Nagle were still in the clinic and were waiting together in the hall where two uniformed policemen were on duty. The group secretary had said with quiet determination that he preferred to be on the premises while the police were still there, and Nagle could not leave until the front door had been locked and the key handed over since it was his job to open the clinic at eight o'clock on Monday morning.

Dalgliesh and Martin made their last round of the premises together. Watching them at work a casual observer might have been misled into the facile assumption that Martin was merely a foil for the younger, more successful man. Those at the Yard who knew them both judged differently. In appearance they were certainly unalike. Martin was a big man, nearly six feet and broad-shouldered and looking, with his open ruddy face, more like a successful farmer than a detective. Dalgliesh was even taller, dark, lean and easy moving. Beside him Martin seemed ponderous. No one watching Dalgliesh at work could fail to recognize his intelligence. With Martin one was less sure. He was ten years older than his chief and it was unlikely now that he would gain further promotion. But he had qualities that made him an admirable detective. He was never tormented by doubt of his own motives. Right and wrong stood for him as immutable as the two poles. He had never wandered in that twilight country where the nuances of evil and good cast their perplexing shadows. He had great determination and infinite patience. He was kind without being sentimental and meticulous for detail without losing sight of the whole. Looking at his career, no one could have called him brilliant. But if he was incapable of high intelligence he was equally incapable of stupidity. Most police work consists of the boring, repetitive and meticulous checking of detail. Most murders are sordid little crimes bred out of ignorance and despair. It was Martin's job to help solve them and, patiently and uncensoriously, that is what he did. Faced with the murder at the Steen Clinic with its frightening undertones of a trained intelligence at work, he remained unimpressed. Methodical attention to detail had solved other murders and would solve this one. And murderers, intelligent or subnormal, devious or impulsive, had to be caught. He walked, as was usual, a pace or two behind Dalgliesh and said little. But when he spoke it was usually to the point.

They went through the building for the last time that evening, starting on the third floor. Here the eighteenth-century rooms had been divided to provide accommodation for psychiatric social workers, psychologists and lay therapists, together with two larger treatment-rooms for the use of psychiatrists. There was one pleasant and unconverted room at the front of the building furnished comfortably with easy chairs and a number of small tables. This, apparently, was the rendezvous of the marital problem group who could enjoy an agreeable view over the square in the intervals of analysing their domestic and sexual incompatibilities. Dalgliesh could understand the chagrin of the absent Mrs Baumgarten. The room was admirably suited for the art therapy department.

The more important rooms were on the floor below and here there had been little alteration or adaptation so that ceilings, doors and windows could contribute their own graciousness to the atmosphere of elegance and calm. The Modigliani was out of place in the boardroom but not aggressively so. The smaller medical library next door with its antique bookcases, each bearing the name of the donor, could have been an eighteenth-century gentleman's library until one looked at the titles on the books. There were low bowls of flowers set on the bookcases and a number of armchairs which looked right together although they had obviously come originally from half a dozen different houses.

On this floor, too, the medical director had his consulting-room and it was one of the most elegant in the clinic. The treatment couch which stood against the far wall, was the same pattern as that in each of the other psychiatrists' rooms, a low single divan, covered in chintz and with a red blanket folded at its foot and one pillow. But no H.M.C. had provided the rest of the furniture. The eighteenth-century desk was uncluttered by cardboard calendars or stationery office diaries and held merely a leather-bound blotter, a silver inkstand and a tray for papers. There were two leather armchairs and a mahogany corner cupboard. It appeared that the medical director collected old prints and was particularly interested in mezzotints and eighteenth-century engravings. Dalgliesh inspected a collection of works by James McArdell and Valentine Green, arranged on each side of the chimney-piece, and noted that Dr Etherege's patients unburdened their subconscious beneath a couple of fine lithographs by Hullmandel. He reflected that the unknown clinic thief might have been a gentleman if Cully's opinion was to be trusted, but he was certainly no connoisseur. It was more typical of the small-time professional to neglect two Hullmandels for fifteen pounds in cash. It was certainly a pleasant room, proclaiming its owner as a man with taste and the money to indulge it, the room of a man who sees no reason why his working life should be spent in less agreeable surroundings than his leisure. And yet it was not wholly successful. Somewhere there was a lack. The elegance was a little too contrived, the good taste a little too orthodox. Dalgliesh felt that a patient might well be happier in the warm, untidy, oddly shaped cell upstairs where Fredrica Saxon worked in a litter of papers, pot-plants and the paraphernalia of tea-brewing. Despite the engravings the room lacked the nuances of personality. In that it was somehow typical of its owner. Dalgliesh was reminded of a recent conference which he had attended on mental illness and the law at which Dr Etherege had been one of the speakers. At the time his paper had seemed a model of felicitous wisdom; afterwards Dalgliesh was unable accurately to recall a single word.

They went down to the ground floor where the group secretary and Nagle, chatting quietly to the police constables, turned to watch but made no move to join them. The four waiting figures were standing together in a sad group like mourners after a funeral, uncertain and disorganized in the hiatus that follows grief. When they talked together their voices sounded muted in the silence of the hall.

The ground-floor plan was simple. Immediately inside the front door and to the left as one entered was the glass-panelled reception kiosk. Dalgliesh noted again that it commanded a good view of the whole hall, including the great curved staircase at the end. Yet Cully's observations during the evening had been curiously selective. He was positive that everyone entering or leaving the clinic after 5 p.m. had been seen by him and entered in his book, but many of the comings and goings in the hall had passed unnoticed. He had seen Mrs Shorthouse come out of Miss Bolam's office and into the front general office but had not seen the administrative officer passing down the hall to the basement stairs. He had seen Dr Baguley coming out of the medical staff cloakroom but not entering it. Most of the movements of patients and their relations had not escaped him and he was able to confirm the comings and goings of Mrs Bostock. He was certain that Dr Etherege, Miss Saxon and Miss Kettle had not passed through the hall after 6 p.m. If they had, he hadn't noticed. Dalgliesh would have felt more confidence in Cully's evidence if it were not apparent that the pathetic little man was terrified. When they arrived at the clinic he had been merely depressed and a little surly. By the time he was allowed to go home he was in a state of terror. At some stage of the investigation, thought Dalgliesh, he would have to find out why.

Behind the reception kiosk and with windows facing the square was the general office, part of which had been partitioned to form a small filing-room for the current medical records. Next to the general office was Miss Bolam's room and, beyond that, the E.C.T. suite with its treatment-room, nurses' duty-room and male and female recovery bays. This suite was separated by a hallway from the medical staff cloakroom, clerical staff lavatories and the domestic assistant's pantry. At the end of the hallway was the locked side door, seldom used except by members of the staff who had been working late and who did not want to give Nagle the trouble of undoing the more complicated locks, bolts and chains on the front door.

At the opposite side of the main hall were two consulting-rooms and the patients' waiting-room, and lavatories. The front room had been divided to form two fairly large psychotherapy-rooms which were separated from the waiting-room by a passage. Dr Steiner could, therefore, move from one to the other without coming within Cully's view. But he could hardly move down the hall to the basement stairs without risk of being seen. Had he been seen? What was Cully keeping back and why?

Together, Dalgliesh and Martin examined the basement rooms for the last time that night. At the rear was the door which led to the area steps. Dr Etherege had said that this door was bolted when he and Dr Steiner had examined it after finding the body. It was still bolted. It had been tested for fingerprints, but the only decipherable ones had been Peter Nagle's. Nagle had said that he was probably the last person to touch the lock since it was his habit to check that the door was securely bolted before he locked up at night. It was rare for him or for any member of the staff to use the basement exit and the door was usually only opened when the coal or other heavy supplies were delivered. Dalgliesh shot back the bolt. There was a short flight of iron steps leading to the rear railings. Here, again, the wrought-iron door was bolted and fitted with a lock and chain. But an intruder would have no difficulty in getting into the basement area, particularly as the mews at the back was ill lit and unoccupied. The clinic itself would be less easy of access. All the basement windows, except the small lavatory window, were barred. It was through that window the clinic thief had cut his way.

Dalgliesh bolted the door again and they went into the porters' rest-room which occupied most of the back of the building. Nothing was changed since they had first examined it. Two clothes lockers stood against one wall. The centre of the floor was occupied by a heavy square table. There was a small old-fashioned gas cooker in one corner and, beside it, a cupboard containing cups and saucers and tins of tea, sugar and biscuits. Two shabby leather chairs were drawn up one on each side of the gas fire. To the left of the door was a keyboard with the hooks numbered but not named. On this board had hung, among others, the key to the basement record-room. That key was now in the possession of the police.

A large striped cat was curled in a basket before the unlit gas fire. When the light was switched on it stirred and, lifting its heavy barred head, gave the intruders a stare, blank and expressionless, from immense yellow eyes. Dalgliesh knelt beside the basket and stroked the top of its head. The cat shivered then sat immobile under his touch. Suddenly it rolled on its back, and stretched out its legs, rigid as poles, to display a ridge of soft belly hair for Dalgliesh's ministrations. The superintendent stroked and talked while Martin, whose preference was for dogs, looked on in tolerant patience. He said: 'I've heard about him from Mrs Shorthouse. It's Tigger, Miss Bolam's cat.'

'We deduce that Miss Bolam read A. A. Milne as a child. Cats are nocturnal. Why isn't he let out at night?'

'I heard about that, too. Miss Bolam thought he'd keep the mice down if he were shut in. Nagle goes out at lunch time for a beer and a sandwich, but Cully eats his grub here and Miss B. was always on to him about crumbs. The cat is shut in here every night and let out during the day. He's got his food and his scratch tin.'

'So I see. Furnished with cinders from the boiler.'

'Pity he can't talk, sir. He was in here for most of the evening waiting to be fed. He was probably here when the murderer came in for the record-room key.'

'And for the chisel. Oh, yes, Tigger saw it all right. But what makes you think he'd tell you the truth?'

Sergeant Martin didn't reply. People who went for cats in a big way were like that, of course. Childish you might call it. Unusually talkative, he said:

'Miss B. had him doctored at her own expense. Mrs Shorthouse told P. C. Holliday that Dr Steiner was very upset about it. He likes cats seemingly. They had words over it. Dr Steiner told Mrs Bostock that Miss Bolam would like everything male at the clinic doctored if she had her way. He put it rather crudely, I gather. Of course, it wasn't meant to get back to Miss Bolam but Mrs Bostock saw that it did.'

'Yes,' said Dalgliesh shortly. 'She would.'

They continued their inspection.

It was not an uncomfortable room. It smelled of food and

leather and, just perceptibly, of gas. There were a number of pictures which looked as if they had found a home with the porters when their previous owners had seen enough of them. One was of the founder of the Steen surrounded, appropriately enough, by his five sons. It was a faded sepia photograph in a gilt frame more indicative, Dalgliesh thought, of old Hyman's character than the more orthodox commemorative oil which hung upstairs in the hall.

On a smaller table against the rear wall lay Nagle's box of tools. Dalgliesh lifted the lid. The tools, meticulously cared for, lay each in its correct place. There was only one missing and that one was unlikely ever again to find its place in Nagle's toolbox.

'He could have come in through that rear door if he left it unlocked,' said Martin, voicing Dalgliesh's thought.

'Of course. I admit to a perverse disposition to suspect the one person who was apparently not even in the building when the murder was committed. There's little doubt, though, that Nagle was with Miss Priddy in the general office when Mrs Shorthouse left Miss Bolam. Cully confirms that. And Miss Priddy states that she never left the general office except momentarily to fetch a file from the next room. What did you think of Shorthouse by the way?'

'I thought she was telling the truth, sir. I wouldn't put her above a bit of lying when it suited her. She's the sort who likes things to happen and isn't averse to giving them a bit of a shove in the right direction. But she had plenty to tell us without adding any frills.'

'She had, indeed,' agreed Dalgliesh. 'There isn't any reasonable doubt that Miss Bolam came down to the basement as a result of that call which fixes the approximate time of death for us very satisfactorily. It ties up with the police surgeon's view, too, but we shall know more about that when we get the result of the P.M. The call could have been genuine, of course. It's possible that someone phoned from the basement, spoke to Miss Bolam somewhere down here, then left her to go back to his or her own room and is now too afraid to admit making the call. As I say, it's possible, but I don't think it's likely.'

'If the call was genuine it could have been someone calling her down to look at the mess in the record-room. Those files were certainly chucked about before the murder. Some of them were under the body. It looked to me as if she was struck as she crouched to pick them up.'

'That's how it looked to me,' said Dalgliesh. 'Well, let's press on.'

They passed the service lift door without comment and went next into the basement treatment-room at the front of the building. Here Nurse Bolam had sat with her patient through the early hours of the evening. Dalgliesh switched on the lights. The heavy curtains had been drawn back but the windows were hung with thin net, presumably to give privacy during the day. The room was simply furnished. There was a low stretcher bed in one corner with a hospital screen at its foot and a small armchair at its head. Against the front wall was a small table and chair, apparently for the use of the nurse in attendance. The table held a rack of nursing report forms and blank medical record sheets. The left-hand wall was lined with cupboards where the clinic's clean linen was stored. Some attempt had been made to sound-proof the fourth wall. It had been lined with acoustic panels and the door, strong and well built, was hung with a heavy curtain.

Dalgliesh said:

'If her patient were noisy I doubt whether Nurse Bolam would hear much that went on outside. Walk down the passage will you, Martin, and make a call on the telephone, the one just outside the medical record-room.'

Martin closed the door behind him and Dalgliesh was alone with the heavy silence. His hearing was acute and Martin's heavy tread was just audible. He doubted whether he would have heard it against the noise of a distressed patient. He could not hear the faint ring as Martin took off the receiver nor the swing of the dial. In a few seconds he heard the footsteps again and Martin was back. He said:

'There's a card giving the internal numbers so I rang 004. That's Miss Bolam's room. Funny how eerie a telephone bell sounds when there's no one to answer. Then someone did. It gave me quite a shock when the ringing stopped. It was Mr Lauder, of course. He sounded a bit surprised, too. I told him we wouldn't be long now.'

'Nor shall we. I couldn't hear you, by the way. And yet Nurse Bolam did hear the Priddy child scream. Or so she says.'

'She took her time doing anything about it, didn't she, sir? What's more she apparently heard the doctors and Sister when they came down.'

'That's reasonable enough. There were four of them clattering about. She's the obvious suspect, of course. She could have telephoned her cousin from this room, saying perhaps that someone had been creating chaos in the record-room. Her patient would be far too disorientated to hear or understand. I saw her with Dr Baguley and it was obvious that she wasn't capable of giving anyone an alibi. Nurse Bolam could have left the treatment-room and waited for her cousin in the record-room with a fair degree of safety. She had the best opportunity to kill, she has the necessary medical knowledge, she has an obvious motive. If she is the murderer the crime probably had nothing to do with the phone call to Lauder. We shall have to find out what Bolam did think was going on here, but it needn't necessarily have anything to do with her death. If Nurse Bolam knew that the group secretary was coming she might have decided to kill now with the idea of obscuring the real motive.'

'She doesn't strike me as clever enough for that kind of planning, sir.'

'She doesn't strike me as a murderer, Martin, but we've known less likely ones. If she is innocent then her being down here alone was very convenient for the murderer. Then there are those rubber gloves. Of course, she had an explanation for them. There are plenty of pairs about and it's perfectly reasonable for a member of the nursing staff to have a used pair in her apron pocket. But the fact remains that we haven't found any dabs on either of the weapons nor on the door key, not even old prints. Someone wiped them first and handled them with gloves. And what more suitable than thin surgical gloves. Driving that chisel in was practically a surgical operation.'

'If she had the sense to use the gloves, then she'd have the sense to destroy them afterwards. The boiler was alight. What about that missing rubber apron from the art department? If the killer used that as possible protection and disposed of it in the boiler, it would be daft to hang on to the gloves.'

'So daft that we're probably meant to think that no sane person would do it. I'm not sure about that apron, anyway. Apparently there's one missing and it's possible that the killer wore it. But this was a clean death and it was planned that way. Anyway, we'll know tomorrow when the boiler's cold and can be raked out. Those aprons have metal studs on the shoulder straps and, with luck, we might find them.'

They closed the treatment door behind them and went upstairs. Dalgliesh began to be conscious of his tiredness and the stabbing pain behind his eye was now almost continuous. It had not been an easy week and the sherry party, which promised an agreeable relaxing finish to a busy day, had proved an unsettling preliminary to an even busier night. He wondered briefly where Deborah Riscoe had dined, and with whom. Their meeting now seemed part of a different world. Perhaps because he was tired he felt none of the confidence with which he usually began a case. He did not seriously believe that the crime would defeat him. Professionally he had never yet known the taste of failure. It was all the more irritating, therefore, to be visited by this vague sensation of inadequacy and unrest. For the first time he felt unsure of his own mastery, as if he were opposed by an intelligence actively working against him and equal to his own. And he did not think that Nurse Bolam had that intelligence.

The group secretary and Nagle were still waiting in the hall. Dalgliesh handed over the clinic keys and was promised that an additional set, now held at group headquarters, would be delivered to the police next day. Martin and he, with the two constables, waited while Nagle checked that all lights were out. Soon the whole clinic was in darkness and the six men stepped into the foggy chill of the October night and went their separate ways.

CHAPTER FOUR

Dr Baguley knew that he couldn't in decency neglect to offer Miss Kettle a lift home. She lived in Richmond and her house was directly on the route to his Surrey village. Usually he managed to avoid her; her attendance at the clinic was so erratic that they seldom left at the same time and he could usually drive alone without compunction. He enjoyed driving. Even the frustrations of getting through the city in the rush hour were a small price to pay for those few miles of straight road before he reached home when he could feel the power of the car like a physical thrust in his back and the tensions of the day were ripped from him in the singing air. Just before he reached Stalling it was his custom to stop at a quiet pub for a pint of beer. He never drank more nor less. This nightly ritual, the formal division of day from night, had become necessary to him since he had lost Fredrica. The night brought no relief from the strain of coping with neurosis. He was accustoming himself to a life in which the greatest demands on his patience and professional skill were made in his own home. But it was good to sit alone and in peace, savouring the brief interlude between two different but essentially similar worlds.

He drove slowly at first since Miss Kettle was known to dislike speed. She sat beside him, close-wrapped in a heavy tweed coat, her grey cropped head incongruously crowned with a knitted red cap. Like many professional social workers she had little instinctive understanding of people, a lack which had gained her an undeserved reputation for insensitivity. It was, of course, different if they were her clients – and how Baguley hated that word! Once they were securely caged behind the bars of a professional relationship she gave them a dedicated and meticulous attention which left few of their privacies intact. They were understood whether they liked it or not, their weaknesses exposed and condoned, their efforts applauded and encouraged, their sins forgiven.

Apart from her clients the rest of the Steen Clinic hardly existed for Miss Kettle. Baguley did not dislike her. He had long come to the melancholy conclusion that psychiatric social work held a strong attraction for those least suited to it, and Miss Kettle was better than most. The reports she provided for him were over-long and spattered with the peculiar jargon of the job, but at least she provided them. The Steen Clinic had its share of those P.S.W.s who, driven by their irresistible urge to treat patients, were restless until they had trained as lay psychotherapists and left behind such lesser excitements as the writing of social reports and the arranging of recuperative holidays. No, he did not dislike Ruth Kettle, but tonight, of all nights, he would have been happier to drive alone.

She did not speak until they had reached Knightsbridge, then her high breathy voice fluted in his ear.

'Such a very complicated murder, wasn't it? And so oddly timed. What did you think of the superintendent?'

'He's efficient, I suppose,' replied Dr Baguley. 'My attitude to him is a little ambivalent, probably because I haven't an alibi. I was alone in the medical staff cloakroom when Miss Bolam is thought to have died.'

He knew that he was hoping for reassurance, expecting to hear her eager protestations that, naturally, no one could think of suspecting him. Despising himself he added quickly:

'It's a nuisance, of course, but not important. I expect he'll clear the matter up pretty quickly.'

'Oh, do you think so? I wonder. I thought he seemed rather puzzled by the whole thing. I was alone in my room most of the evening so I probably haven't an alibi either. But then I don't know when she's supposed to have died.'

'Probably at about six-twenty,' said Baguley briefly.

'Is that so? Then I most certainly haven't an alibi.' Miss Kettle spoke with the liveliest satisfaction. After a moment she said: 'I shall be able to arrange a country holiday from Free Money for the Worrikers now. Miss Bolam was always so difficult about spending Free Money on patients. Dr Steiner and I feel that if the Worrikers can have a quiet fortnight together in some pleasant country hotel they may be able to sort things out. It may save the marriage.'

Dr Baguley was tempted to say that the Worriker marriage had been in jeopardy for so many years that its salvation or otherwise was hardly likely to be settled in a fortnight, however pleasant the hotel. Being precariously married was the Worrikers' main emotional preoccupation and one they were unlikely to relinquish without a struggle. He asked:

'Isn't Mr Worriker in work then?'

'Oh, yes! He's in work,' replied Miss Kettle, as if that fact could have no relevance to his ability to pay for a holiday. 'But his wife is a poor manager, I'm afraid, although she does her best. They can't really afford to go away unless the clinic pays. Miss Bolam wasn't very sympathetic, I'm sorry to say. There was another matter, too. She would make appointments for me to see patients without telling me. It happened today. When I looked at my diary just before I left there was a new patient booked for ten on Monday. Mrs Bostock had written it in, of course, but she added "on Miss Bolam's instructions". Mrs Bostock would never do a thing like that herself. She's a very pleasant and efficient secretary.'

Dr Baguley thought that Mrs Bostock was an ambitious trouble-maker, but saw no point in saying so. Instead, he asked how Miss Kettle had got on during her interview with Dalgliesh.

'I wasn't able to help him very much, I'm afraid, but he was interested to hear about the lift.'

'What about the lift, Miss Kettle?'

'Someone was using it this evening. You know how it creaks when someone's using it and then bangs when it reaches the second floor? Well, I heard it bang. I don't know exactly when, of course, as it didn't seem important at the time. It wasn't very early in the evening. I suppose it could have been at about six-thirty.'

'Surely Dalgliesh isn't seriously thinking that someone used the lift to get down to the basement. It's large enough, of course, but it would need two people.

'Yes, it would, wouldn't it? No one could hoist himself up in it. It would need an accomplice.' She spoke the word conspiratorially as if it were part of some criminal patois, a naughty expression which she was daring to use. She went on: 'I can't imagine dear

Dr Etherege squatting in the lift like a plump little Buddha while Mrs Bostock heaved on the ropes with her strong red hands, can you?'

'No,' said Dr Baguley curtly. The description had been unexpectedly vivid. To change the image he said:

'It would be interesting to know who was last in the medical record-room. Before the murder, I mean. I can't remember when I last used the place.'

'Oh, can't you? How strange! It's such a dusty claustrophobic room that I can always remember when I have to go down there. I was there at a quarter to six this evening.'

Dr Baguley nearly stopped the car in his surprise.

'At five-forty-five this evening? But that was only thirty-five minutes before the time of death!'

'Yes, it must have been, mustn't it, if she died at about six-twenty? The superintendent didn't tell me that. But he was interested to hear that I'd been in the basement. I fetched one of the old Worriker records. It must have been about five-forty-five when I went down and I didn't stay; I knew just where the record was.'

'And the room was as usual? The records weren't chucked on the floor?'

'Oh, no, everything was perfectly tidy. The room was locked, of course, so I got the key from the porters' rest-room and locked the room again when I'd finished. I put the key back on the board.'

'And you didn't see anyone?'

'No, I don't think so. I could hear your LSD patient, though. She seemed very noisy, I thought. Almost as if she were alone.'

'She wasn't alone. She never is. As a matter of fact I was with her myself up to about five-forty. If you'd been a few minutes earlier we should have seen each other.'

'Only if we'd happened to pass on the basement stairs or if you'd come into the record-room. But I don't think I saw anyone. The superintendent kept asking me. I wonder if he's a capable man. He seemed very puzzled by the whole thing, I thought.'

They did not speak again about the murder although, to Dr

Baguley, the air of the car was heavy with unspoken questions. Twenty minutes later he drew up outside Miss Kettle's flat off Richmond Green and leaned over to open the car door for her with a sense of relief. As soon as she had disappeared from view he got out of the car and, in defiance of the chilly dampness, opened the roof. The next few miles fled in a gold thread of winking cats'-eyes marking the crown of the road, a rush of cold autumnal air. Outside Stalling he turned from the main road to where the dark, uninviting little pub was set well back among its surrounding elms. The bright boys of Stalling Coombe had never discovered it or had rejected it in favour of the smart pubs edging the green belt; their Jaguars were never seen parked against its black brick walls. The saloon bar was empty as usual, but there was a murmur of voices across the wooden partition which separated it from the public bar. He took his seat by the fire which burned summer and winter, evidently stoked with malodorous chunks of the publican's old furniture. It was not a welcoming room. The chimney smoked in an east wind, the stone floor was bare and the wooden benches lining the walls were too hard and narrow for comfort. But the beer was cold and good, the glasses clean, and there was a kind of peace about the place bred out of its bareness and the solitude.

George brought over his pint.

'You're late this evening, Doctor.'

George had called him that since his second visit. Dr Baguley neither knew nor cared how George had discovered what his job was.

'Yes,' he replied. 'I was kept late at the clinic.'

He said no more and the man went back to his bar. Then he wondered whether he had been wise. It would be in all the papers tomorrow. They would probably be talking about it in the public bar. It would be natural for George to say:

'The doctor was in as usual on Friday. He didn't say anything about the murder . . . Looked upset, though.'

Was it suspicious to say nothing? Wasn't it more natural for an innocent man to want to talk about a murder case in which he was involved? Suddenly the little room became unbearably stuffy, the peace dissolved in an uprush of anxiety and pain. He had got to tell Helen somehow, and the sooner she knew the better.

But although he drove fast it was well after ten before he reached home and saw through the tall beech hedge, the light in Helen's bedroom. So she had gone up without waiting for him; that was always a bad sign. Garaging the car he braced himself for whatever lay ahead. Stalling Coombe was very quiet. It was a small private estate of architect-designed houses, built in the traditional manner, and set each in a spacious garden. It had little contact with the neighbouring village of Stalling and was, indeed, an oasis of prosperous suburbia whose inhabitants, bound by ties of common prejudices and snobberies, lived like exiles determinedly preserving the decencies of civilization in the midst of an alien culture. Baguley had bought his house fifteen years ago, soon after his marriage. He had disliked the place then and the past years had taught him the folly of disregarding first impressions. But Helen had liked it; and Helen had been pregnant then so that there was an additional reason for trying to make her happy. To Helen, the house, spacious mock Tudor, had promised much. There was the huge oak in the front lawn ('just the place for the pram on hot days'), the wide entrance hall ('the children will love it for parties later on'), the quiet of the estate ('so peaceful for you, darling, after London and all those dreadful patients').

But the pregnancy had ended in a miscarriage and there had never again been the hope of children. Would it have made any difference if there had? Would the house have been any less an expensive repository of lost hopes? Sitting quietly in the car and watching that ominous square of lighted window, Dr Baguley reflected that all unhappy marriages were fundamentally alike. He and Helen were no different from the Worrikers. They stayed together because they expected to be less miserable together than apart. If the strain and miseries of marriage became greater than the expense, the inconvenience and the trauma of a legal separation, then they would part. No sane person continued to endure the intolerable. For him there had been only one valid and overriding need for a divorce, his hope of marrying Fredrica Saxon. Now that the hope was over for ever he might as well continue to endure a marriage which, for all its strain, at least gave him the comfortable illusion of being needed. He despised his private image, the stock predicament of the psychiatrist unable to manage his own personal relationships. But at least something remained from the marriage; a fugitive surge of tenderness and pity which for most of the time enabled him to be kind.

He locked the garage gates and crossed the wide lawn to the front door. The garden was looking unkempt. It was expensive to maintain and Helen took little interest in it. It would be better in every way if they sold and bought a smaller place. But Helen wouldn't talk of selling. She was as happy at Stalling Coombe as she could hope to be anywhere. Its narrow and undemanding social life gave her at least a semblance of security. This cocktail-and-*canapé* existence, the bright chatter of its smart, lean, acquisitive women, the gossip over the iniquities of foreign maids and *au pair* girls, the lamentations over school fees and school reports and the boorish ingratitude of the young, were preoccupations which she could sympathize with or share. Baguley had long known with pain that it was in her relationship with him that she was least at home.

He wondered how he could best break the news of Miss Bolam's murder. Helen had only met her once, that Wednesday at the clinic, and he had never learned what they had said to each other. But that brief, catalytic encounter had established some kind of intimacy between them. Or was it perhaps an offensive alliance directed against himself? But not on Bolam's part, surely? Her attitude to him had never altered. He could even believe that she approved of him more than of most psychiatrists. He had always found her co-operative, helpful and correct. It was without malice, without vindictiveness, without even disliking him particularly, that she had called Helen into her office that Wednesday afternoon and, in half an hour's conversation, destroyed the greatest happiness he had ever known. It was then that Helen appeared at the top of the stairs.

'Is that you, James?' she called.

For fifteen years he had been greeted every night with that unnecessary question.

'Yes. I'm sorry I'm late. I'm sorry, too, that I couldn't tell you more on the phone. But something pretty dreadful has happened at the Steen and Etherege thought it better to say as little as possible. Enid Bolam has been killed.'

But her mind had seized on the medical director's name.

'Henry Etherege! He would, of course. He lives in Harley Street with an adequate staff and about twice our income. He might consider me a little before keeping you at the clinic until this hour. His wife isn't stuck in the country alone until he chooses to come home.'

'It wasn't Henry's fault that I was kept. I told you. Enid Bolam's been killed. We've had the police at the clinic most of the evening.'

This time she heard. He sensed her sharp intake of breath, saw her eyes narrow as she came down the stairs to him, clutching her dressing-gown around her.

'Miss Bolam killed?'

'Yes, murdered.'

She stood motionless, seeming to consider, then asked calmly: 'How?'

As he told her she still didn't speak. Afterwards they stood facing each other. He wondered uneasily whether he ought to go to her, to make some gesture of comfort or sympathy. But why sympathy? What, after all, had Helen lost? When she spoke her voice was as cold as metal.

'You none of you liked her, did you? Not one of you!'

'That's ridiculous, Helen! Most of us hardly came into touch with her except briefly and in her capacity as A.O.'

'It looks like an inside job, doesn't it?'

He winced at the crude, police-court jargon, but said curtly:

'On the face of it, yes. I don't know what the police think.'

She laughed bitterly.

'Oh, I can guess what the police think!'

Again she stood silent, then suddenly asked:

'Where were you?'

'I told you. In the medical staff cloakroom.'

'And Fredrica Saxon?'

It was hopeless now to wait for that spring of pity or tenderness. It was useless, even, to try to keep control. He said with a deadly calm:

'She was in her room, scoring a Rorschach. If it's any satisfaction to you, neither of us had an alibi. But if you're hoping to pin this murder on Fredrica or me you'll need more intelligence than I give you credit for. The superintendent's hardly likely to listen to a neurotic woman, acting out of spite. He's seen too many of that type. But make an effort! You might be lucky! Why not come and examine my clothes for blood?'

He threw out his hands towards her, his whole body shaking with anger. Terrified, she gave him one glance, then turned and stumbled up the stairs, tripping over her dressing-gown and crying like a child. He gazed after her, his body cold from tiredness, hunger and self-disgust. He must go to her. Somehow it must be put right. But not now, not at once. First, he must find a drink. He leaned for a moment against the banister and said with infinite tiredness:

'Oh, Fredrica. Darling Fredrica. Why did you do it? Why? Why?'

Sister Ambrose lived with an elderly nurse friend who had trained with her thirty-five years ago and who had recently retired. Together they had bought a house in Gidea Park where they had lived together for the last twenty years on their joint income, in comfort and happy accord. Neither of them had married and neither of them regretted it. In the past they had sometimes wished for children, but observation of the family life of their relations had convinced them that marriage, despite a common belief to the contrary, was designed to benefit men at the expense of women, and that even motherhood was not an unmixed blessing. Admittedly this conviction had never been put to the test since neither of them had ever received a proposal. Like any professional worker in a psychiatric clinic, Sister Ambrose was aware of the dangers of sexual repression, but it had never once occurred to her that these might apply to herself and, indeed, it would be difficult to imagine anyone less repressed. It is possible that she would have dismissed most of the psychiatrists' theories as dangerous nonsense if she had ever considered them critically. But Sister Ambrose had been trained to think of consultants as only one degree lower than God. Like God they moved in mysterious ways their wonders to perform but, like God, they were not subject to open criticism. Some, admittedly, were more

mysterious in their ways than others, but it was still the privilege
of a nurse to minister to these lesser deities, to encourage the
patients to have confidence in their treatment, especially when its
success appeared most doubtful, and to practise the cardinal
professional virtue of complete loyalty.

'I've always been loyal to the doctors,' was a remark frequently
heard at Acacia Road, Gidea Park. Sister Ambrose often noted
that the young nurses who occasionally worked at the Steen as
holiday reliefs were trained in a less accommodating tradition,
but she had a poor opinion of most young nurses, and an even
poorer opinion of modern training.

As usual she took the Central Line to Liverpool Street, changed
to an electric train on the eastern suburban line, and twenty
minutes later was letting herself into the neat semi-detached
house which she shared with Miss Beatrice Sharpe. Tonight,
however, she fitted her key in the lock without her customary
inspection of the front garden, without running a critical eye over
the paintwork on the door, and even without reflecting as was
her custom on the generally satisfactory appearance of the property and on the gratifying capital investment that its purchase
had proved to be.

'Is that you, Dot?' called Miss Sharpe from the kitchen. 'You're
late.'

'It's a wonder I'm not later. We've had murder at the clinic
and the police have been with us for most of the evening. As far
as I know they're still there. I've had my fingerprints taken and
so have the rest of the staff.'

Sister Ambrose deliberately kept her voice level but the effect
of the news was gratifying. She had expected no less. It is not
every day one has such excitement to relate and she had spent
some time in the train rehearsing how most effectively to break
the news. The selected sentence expressed concisely the salient
details. Supper was temporarily forgotten. Murmuring that a
casserole could always wait, Miss Sharpe poured her friend and
herself a glass of sherry, specific against shock, and settled down
with it in the sitting-room to hear the full story. Sister Ambrose,
who had a reputation at the clinic for discretion and taciturnity,
was a great deal more forthcoming at home, and it wasn't long

before Miss Sharpe knew as much about the murder as her friend was able to tell.

'But who do you think did it, Dot?' Miss Sharpe refilled their glasses – an unprecedented extravagance – and applied her mind to analysis.

'As I see it the murder must have been done between six-twenty when you saw Miss Bolam going towards the basement stairs and seven o'clock when the body was discovered.'

'Well, that's obvious! That's why the superintendent kept asking me whether I was sure about the time. I was the last person to see her alive, there's no doubt about that. Mrs Belling had finished treatment and was ready to go home at about six-fifteen and I went across to the waiting-room to let her husband know. He's always fussed about time because he's on night duty and has to be fed and at work by eight. So I looked at my watch and saw that it was just six-twenty. As I came out of the E.C.T. room door Miss Bolam passed me and went towards the basement stairs. The superintendent asked me what she looked like and whether we spoke. Well, we didn't and, as far as I could see, she looked the same as usual.'

'What's he like?' asked Miss Sharpe, visions of Maigret and Inspector Barlow crowding her mind.

'The superintendent? Perfectly polite. I must say. One of those lean, bony faces. Very dark. I didn't say a great deal. You could see he's used to smarming things out of people. Mrs Shorthouse was with him for hours and I bet he got plenty out of her. Well, I wasn't playing that game, I've always been loyal to the clinic.'

'All the same, Dot, it is murder.'

'That's all very well, Bea, but you know what the Steen is. There's enough gossip without adding to it. None of the doctors liked her and nor did anyone else as far as I know. But that's no reason for killing her. Anyway, I kept my mouth shut and if the others have any sense they'll do the same.'

'Well, you're all right, anyway. You've got an alibi if you and Dr Ingram were together in the E.C.T. room all the time.'

'Oh, we're all right. So are Shorthouse and Cully and Nagle and Miss Priddy. Nagle was out with the post after six-fifteen and the others were together. I'm not sure about the doctors, though, and it's a pity that Dr Baguley left the E.C.T. room after the Belling treatment. Mind you, no one in their senses could suspect him, but it's unfortunate all the same. While we were waiting for the police, Dr Ingram came over to suggest that we ought not to say anything about it. A nice mess we'd get Dr Baguley into with that kind of hanky-panky! I pretended not to understand. I just gave her one of my looks and said: "I'm sure that if we all tell the truth, Doctor, the innocent will have nothing to fear." That shut her up all right. And that's what I did. I told the truth. But I wasn't going any further. If the police want gossip they can go to Mrs Shorthouse.'

'What about Nurse Bolam?' inquired Miss Sharpe.

'It's Bolam I'm worried about. She was on the spot all right and you can't say an LSD patient is an alibi for anyone. The superintendent was on to her quick enough. He tried to pump me. Were she and her cousin friendly? No doubt they worked at the Steen to be together? You can tell that to the Marines, I thought, but I kept my mouth shut. He didn't get much change out of me. But you could see which way his mind was working. You can't wonder, really. We all know Miss Bolam had money and if she hasn't willed it to a cats' home it will go to her cousin. There's no one else to leave it to after all.'

'I can't see her leaving it to a cats' home,' said Miss Sharpe, who had a literal mind.

'I didn't mean that exactly. As a matter of fact she never took much notice of Tigger although he's supposed to be her cat. I always thought that was typical of Miss Bolam. She found Tigger practically starving in the square and took him into the clinic. Ever since then she's bought three tins of cat meat for him every week. But she never petted him or fed him or let him into any of the upstairs rooms. On the other hand, that fool Priddy is always down in the porters' room with Nagle making a fuss of Tigger, but I've never seen either of them bringing in food for him. I think Miss Bolam just bought the food out of a sense of duty. She didn't really care for animals. But she might leave her money to that church she's so keen on, or to the Guides, for that matter.'

'You'd think she'd leave it to her own flesh and blood,' said Miss Sharpe. She herself had a poor opinion of her own flesh and blood, and found much to criticize in the conduct of her nephews and nieces, but her small and slowly accumulated capital had been carefully willed between them. It was beyond her understanding that money should be left out of the family.

They sipped their sherry in silence. The two bars of the electric fire glowed and the synthetic coals shone and flickered as the little light behind them revolved. Sister Ambrose looked around at the sitting-room and found it good. The standard lamp threw a soft light on the fitted carpet and the comfortable sofa and chairs. In the corner a television set stood, its small twin aerials disguised as two flowers on their stems. The telephone nestled beneath the crinolined skirt of a plastic doll. On the opposite wall, above the piano, hung a cane basket from which an indoor plant, cascading streamers of green, almost concealed the wedding group of Miss Sharpe's eldest niece which had pride of place on the piano. Sister Ambrose took comfort from the unchanged homeliness of these familiar things. They at least were the same. Now that the excitement of telling her news was over she felt very tired. Planting her stout legs apart she bent to loosen the laces of her regulation black shoes, grunting a little with the effort. Usually she changed out of uniform as soon as she got home. Tonight she couldn't be bothered. Suddenly she said:

'It isn't easy to know what to do for the best. The superintendent said that anything, however small, might be important. That's all very well. But suppose it's important in the wrong way? Suppose it gives the police the wrong ideas?'

Miss Sharpe was not imaginative nor sensitive, but she had not lived in the same house as her friend for twenty years without recognizing a plea for help.

'You'd better tell me what you have in mind, Dot.'

'Well, it happened on Wednesday. You know what the ladies' cloakroom is like at the Steen? There's the large outside room with the wash-basin and the lockers and two lavatories. The clinic was rather later than usual. I suppose it was well after seven when I went to wash. Well, I was in the lavatory when Miss Bolam came into the outer room. Nurse Bolam was with her. I thought they'd both gone home, but I suppose Miss Bolam must have wanted something from her locker and Nurse just

followed her in. They must have been in the A.O.'s office together
because they'd obviously been talking and were just carrying on
with the argument. I couldn't help hearing. You know how it is.
I could have coughed or flushed the pan, I suppose, to show I
was there but, by the time I thought of it, it was too late.'

'What were they arguing about?' inquired her friend. 'Money?'
In her experience this was the most frequent cause of family
dissension.

'Well, that's what it sounded like. They weren't talking loudly
and I certainly didn't try to hear. I think they must have been
having words about Nurse Bolam's mother − she's a D.S., you
know, and more or less confined to bed now − because Miss
Bolam said she was sorry, but she was doing as much as she could
and that it would be wiser if Marion accepted the situation and
placed her mother's name on a waiting list for a hospital bed.'

'That's reasonable enough. You can't nurse these cases at
home indefinitely. Not without giving up outside work and
staying at home all the time.'

'I don't suppose Marion Bolam could afford that. Anyway, she
started arguing and saying that her mother would only end up in
a geriatric ward with a lot of senile old women and Enid had a
duty to help them because that's what her mother would have
wanted. Then she said something about the money coming to her
if Enid died and how much better to have some now when it
would make such a difference to them.'

'What did Miss Bolam reply to that?'

'That's what's worrying me,' said Sister Ambrose. 'I can't
remember the actual words, but what it amounted to was that
Marion shouldn't rely on getting any of the money because she
was going to change her will. She said that she meant to tell her
cousin quite openly as soon as she had really made up her mind.
She talked about what a great responsibility the money was and
how she had been praying for guidance to do the right thing.'

Miss Sharpe sniffed. She found it impossible to believe that the
Almighty would ever counsel leaving cash away from the family.
Miss Bolam was either an ineffectual petitioner or had wilfully
misinterpreted the divine instructions. Miss Sharpe was not even
sure that she approved of the praying. There are some things,

surely, which one ought to be able to decide on one's own. But she saw her friend's difficulty.

'It would look bad if it came out,' she admitted. 'No doubt about that.'

'I think I know Bolam pretty well, Bea, and that child wouldn't lay hands on a fly. The idea of her murdering anyone is ridiculous. You know what I think about young nurses generally. Well, I wouldn't mind Bolam taking over when I retire next year and that's saying something. I'd trust her completely.'

'Maybe, but the police wouldn't. Why should they? She's probably their first suspect already. She was on the spot; she hasn't an alibi; she has medical knowledge and would know where the skull is most vulnerable; and where to put that chisel in. She was told that Tippett wouldn't be in the clinic. And now this!'

'And it's not as if it's a small sum.' Sister Ambrose leaned forward and dropped her voice. 'I thought I heard Miss Bolam mention thirty thousand pounds. Thirty thousand, Bea! It would be like winning the pools!'

Miss Sharpe was impressed despite herself, but remarked merely that people who went on working when they had thirty thousand wanted their brains examined.

'What would you do, Bea? Do you think I ought to say anything?'

Sister Ambrose, sturdily independent and used to settling her own affairs, recognized that this decision was beyond her and threw half the burden on her friend. Both of them knew that the moment was unique. Never had two friends made fewer demands on each other. Miss Sharpe sat in silence for a moment or two, then said:

'No. Not yet, anyway. After all she is your colleague and you trust her. It wasn't your fault that you overheard the conversation, but it was only overhearing. It was only chance that you happened to be in the loo. I should try to forget it. The police will find out how Bolam has left her money anyway and whether the will has been changed. Either way Nurse Bolam will be suspected. And if it should come to a trial – I'm only saying "if", remember – well, you don't want to get involved unnecessarily.

Remember those nurses in the Eastbourne case, the hours they spent in the box. You wouldn't want that kind of publicity.'

Indeed she wouldn't, thought Sister Ambrose. Her imagination set the scene only too vividly. Sir Somebody or Other would be prosecuting, tall, beak-nosed, bending his terrifying gaze on her, thumbs hooked in the bands of his gown.

'And now, Sister Ambrose, perhaps you will tell his Lordship and the jury what you were doing when you overheard this conversation between the accused and her cousin.'

Titters in court. The judge, terrifying in scarlet and white wig, leans down from his seat.

'If there is any more of this laughter I shall clear the court.'

Silence. Sir Somebody on the ball again.

'Well, Sister Ambrose . . .?'

No, she certainly wouldn't want that kind of publicity.

'I think you're right, Bea,' she said. 'After all, it's not as if the superintendent actually asked me whether I'd ever overheard them quarrelling.' Certainly he hadn't and, with luck, he never would.

Miss Sharpe felt that it was time to change the subject.

'How did Dr Steiner take it?' she asked. 'You always said that he was working to get Bolam moved to another unit.'

'That's another extraordinary thing! He was terribly upset. You know I told you that he was with us when we first saw the body? D'you know he could hardly control himself? He had to turn his back on us and I could see his shoulders shaking. He was actually crying, I think. I've never seen him so upset. Aren't people extraordinary, Bea?'

It was a vehement cry of resentment and protest. People were extraordinary! You thought you knew them. You worked with them, sometimes for years. You spent more time with them than you would with family or close friends. You knew every line of their faces. And all the time they were private. As private as Dr Steiner who cried over the dead body of a woman he had never liked. As private as Dr Baguley who had been having a love affair with Fredrica Saxon for years with no one knowing until Miss Bolam found out and told his wife. As private as Miss Bolam who had taken God knows what secrets to the grave. Miss Bolam, dull, ordinary, unremarkable Enid Bolam, who had inspired so much hate in someone that she had ended with a chisel in her heart. As private as that unknown member of the staff who would be at the clinic on Monday morning, dressed as usual, looking the same as usual, speaking and smiling as usual and who was a murderer.

'Damned smiling villain!' said Sister Ambrose suddenly. She thought that the phrase was a quotation from some play or other. Shakespeare probably. Most quotations were. But its terse malevolence suited her mood.

'What you need is food,' said Miss Sharpe positively. 'Something light and nourishing. Suppose we leave the casserole until tomorrow night and just have boiled eggs on a tray?'

She was waiting for him at the entrance to St James's Park just as he had expected her to be. As he crossed the Mall and saw the slight figure drooping a little disconsolately by the war memorial Nagle could almost feel sorry for her. It was the hell of a raw night to be standing about. But her first words killed any impulse to pity.

'We should have met somewhere else. This is all right for you, of course. You're on the way home.'

She sounded as peevish as a neglected wife.

'Come back to the flat, then,' he taunted her softly. 'We can get a bus down.'

'No. Not the flat. Not tonight.'

He smiled into the darkness and they moved together into the black shadow of the trees. They walked a little way apart and she made no move towards him. He glanced down at the calm, uplifted profile cleansed now of all traces of crying. She looked desperately tired. Suddenly she said:

'That superintendent is very good-looking, isn't he? Do you think he suspects us?'

So here it was, the grasping at reassurance, the childish need to be protected. And yet she had sounded almost uncaring. He said roughly:

'For God's sake why should he? I was out of the clinic when she died. You know that as well as I do.'

'But I wasn't. I was there.'

'No one's going to suspect you for long. The doctors will see to that. We've had all this out before. Nothing can go wrong if you keep your head and listen to me. Now this is what I want you to do.'

She listened as meekly as a child, but watching that tired, expressionless face he felt that he was in the company of a stranger. He wondered idly whether they would ever get free of each other again. And suddenly he felt that it was not she who was the victim.

As they came to the lake she stopped and gazed out over the water. Out of the darkness came the subdued cry and shuffle of ducks. He could smell the evening breeze, salty as a sea wind, and shivered. Turning to study her face, ravaged now with fatigue, he saw, in his mind's eye, another picture; a broad brow under a white nurse's cap, a swathe of yellow hair, immense grey eyes which gave nothing away. Tentatively he pondered a new idea. It might come to nothing, of course. It might easily come to nothing. But the picture would soon be finished and he could get rid of Jenny. In a month he would be in Paris, but Paris was only an hour's flight away and he would be coming back often. And with Jenny out of the way and a new life in his grasp it would be worth trying. There were worse fates than marrying the heiress to thirty thousand pounds.

Nurse Bolam let herself into the narrow terraced house at 17 Rettinger Street, N.W.1, and was met by the familiar ground-floor smell compounded of frying fat, furniture polish and stale urine. The twins' pram stood behind the door with its stained under-blanket thrown across the handle. The smell of cooking was less strong than usual. She was very late tonight and the ground-floor tenants must long have finished their evening meal. The wail of one of the babies sounded faintly from the back of the house, almost drowned by the noise of the television. She could hear the National Anthem. The B.B.C. service was closing for the day.

She mounted to the first floor. Here the smell of food was fainter and was masked by the tang of a household disinfectant.

The first-floor tenant was addicted to cleanliness as the basement tenant was to drink. There was the usual note on the landing window ledge. Tonight it read: 'Do not stand your dirty milk bottles here. This ledge is private. This means you.' From behind the brown polished door, even at this late hour, came the roar of a vacuum cleaner in full throttle.

Up now to the third floor, to their own flat. She paused on the bottom step of the last flight and saw, as if with a stranger's eyes, the pathetic attempt she had made to improve the look of the place. The walls here were painted with white emulsion paint. The stairs were covered with a grey drugget. The door was painted a bright citrus yellow and sported a brass knocker in the shape of a frog's head. On the wall, carefully disposed one above the other, were the three flower prints she had picked up in Berwick Street market. Until tonight she had been pleased with the result of her work. It really had given the entrance quite an air. There had been times when she had felt that a visitor, Mrs Bostock from the clinic, perhaps, or even Sister Ambrose, might safely be invited home for coffee without the need to apologize or explain. But tonight, freed, gloriously freed for ever, from the self-deceit of poverty, she could see the flat for what it was, sordid, dark, airless, smelly and pathetic. Tonight, for the first time, she could safely recognize how much she hated every brick of 17 Rettinger Street.

She trod very softly, still not ready to go in. There was so little time in which to think, in which to plan. She knew exactly what she would see when she opened the door of her mother's room. The bed stood against the window. In summer evenings Mrs Bolam could lie and watch the sun setting behind a castellation of sloping roofs and twisting chimneys with, in the distance, the turrets of St Pancras Station darkening against a flaming sky. Tonight the curtains would be drawn. The district nurse would have put her mother to bed, would have left the telephone and portable wireless on the bedside table, together with the handbell which could, if necessary, summon aid from the tenant of the flat below. Her mother's bedside lamp would be lit, a small pool of light in the surrounding gloom. At the other end of the room one bar of the electric fire would be burning, one bar only, the nicely calculated allocation of comfort for an October evening. As soon as she opened the door her mother's eyes would meet her, brightened by pleasure and anticipation. There would be the same intolerably bright greeting, the same minute inquiries about the doings of the day.

'Did you have a good day at the clinic, darling? Why were you late? Did anything happen?'

And how did one answer that?

'Nothing of any importance, Mummy, except that someone has stabbed Cousin Enid through the heart and we're going to be rich after all.'

And what did that mean? Dear God, what didn't it mean? No more smell of polish and napkins. No more need to propitiate the second-floor harpy in case she were needed to answer that bell. No more watching the electricity meter and wondering whether it were really cold enough for that extra bar of the fire. No more thanking Cousin Enid for her generous cheque twice a year, the one in December that made such a difference to Christmas, the one late in July that paid for the hired car, the expensive hotel which catered for invalids who could afford to pay for being a nuisance. No longer any need to count the days, to watch the calendar, to wonder whether Enid were going to oblige this year. No need to take the cheque with becoming gratitude to conceal behind lowered eyes the hate and resentment that longed to tear it up and throw it in that smug, plain, condescending face. No need to climb these stairs any more. They could have the house in a suburb which her mother talked about. One of the better-class suburbs, of course, near enough to London for easy travelling to the clinic – it wouldn't be wise to give up the job before she really had to – far enough out for a small garden, perhaps, even for a country view. They might even afford a little car. She could learn to drive. And then, when it was no longer possible for her mother to be left, they could be together. It meant the end of this nagging anxiety about the future. There was no reason now to picture her mother in a chronic sick ward, cared for by over-worked strangers, surrounded by the senile and incontinent, waiting hopelessly for the end. And money could buy less vital but not unimportant pleasures. She would get some clothes. It would no longer be necessary to wait for the biennial sales if she wanted a suit with some evidence of quality. It would be possible to dress well, really well, on half the amount Enid had spent on those unattractive skirts and suits. There must be wardrobes full of them in the Kensington flat. Someone would have the job of sorting them out. And who would want them? Who would want anything that had belonged to Cousin Enid? Except her money. Except her money. Except her money. And suppose she had already written to her solicitor about changing the will. Surely that wasn't possible! Nurse Bolam fought down panic and forced herself once again to consider the possibility rationally. She had thought it out so many times before. Suppose Enid had written on Wednesday night. All right, suppose she had. It would be too late to catch the post that evening so the letter would have been received only this morning. Everyone knew how long solicitors took to do anything. Even if Enid had stressed the urgency, had caught the Wednesday post, the new will couldn't possibly be ready for signature yet. And if it were ready, if it were waiting to be posted in its solid official-looking envelope, what did it matter? Cousin Enid wouldn't sign it now with that round, upright, unadult hand which had always seemed so typical of her. Cousin Enid would never sign anything again.

She thought again about the money. Not about her own share. That was hardly likely to bring her happiness now. But, even if they arrested her for murder they couldn't stop Mummy inheriting her share. No one could stop that. But somehow she must get hold of some cash urgently. Everyone knew that a will took months to prove. Would it look very suspicious or heartless if she went to Enid's solicitor to explain how poor they were and to ask what could be arranged? Or would it be wiser to approach the bank? Perhaps the solicitor would send for her. Yes, of course he would. She and her mother were the next of kin. And as soon as the will was read she could tactfully raise the question of an advance. Surely that would be natural enough? An advance of one hundred pounds wouldn't be much to ask by someone who was going to inherit a share of thirty thousand.

Suddenly she could bear it no longer. The long tension broke. She wasn't conscious of covering those last few stairs, of putting her key in the lock. At once she was in the flat and through to her mother's room. Howling with fear and misery, crying as she had not cried since childhood, she hurled herself on her mother's breast and felt around her the comfort and the unexpected strength of those brittle, shaking arms. The arms rocked her like a baby. The beloved voice cooed its reassurance. Under the cheap nightdress she smelt the soft familiar flesh.

'Hush, my darling. My baby. Hush. What is it? What's happened? Tell me, darling.'

And Nurse Bolam told her.

Since his divorce two years earlier Dr Steiner had shared a house in Hampstead with his widowed sister. He had his own sitting-room and kitchen, an arrangement which enabled Rosa and him to see little of each other, thus fostering the illusion that they got on well together. Rosa was a culture snob. Her house was the centre for a collection of resting actors, one-volume poets, aesthetes posing on the fringe of the ballet world, and writers more anxious to talk about their craft in an atmosphere of sympathetic understanding than to practise it. Dr Steiner did not resent them. He merely ensured that they ate and drank at Rosa's expense, not his. He was aware that his profession had a certain cachet for his sister and that to introduce 'my brother Paul – the famous psychoanalyst' was in some measure a compensation for the low rent which he spasmodically paid and the minor irritations of propinquity. He would hardly have been housed so economically and comfortably had he been a bank manager.

Tonight Rosa was out. It was exasperating and inconsiderate of her to be missing on the one evening when he needed her company, but that was typical of Rosa. The German maid was out, too, presumably illicitly, since Friday was not her half-day. There was soup and salad put ready for him in his kitchen, but even the effort of heating the soup seemed beyond him. The sandwiches he had eaten without relish at the clinic had taken away his appetite but left him hungry for protein, preferably hot and properly cooked. But he did not want to eat alone. Pouring himself a glass of sherry he recognized his need to talk to someone – anyone, about the murder. The need was imperative. He thought of Valda.

His marriage to Valda had been doomed from the start, as any marriage must be when husband and wife have a basic ignorance of each other's needs coupled with the illusion that they understand each other perfectly. Dr Steiner had not been desolated by his divorce, but he had been inconvenienced and distressed, and had been harried afterwards by an irrational sense of failure and guilt. Valda, on the other hand, apparently throve on freedom. When they met he was always struck with her glow of physical well-being. They did not avoid each other, since meeting her ex-husband and discarded lovers with the greatest appearance of friendliness and good humour was what Valda meant when she talked about civilized behaviour. Dr Steiner did not like or admire her. He liked the company of women who were well-informed, well-educated, intelligent and fundamentally serious. But these were not the kind of women he liked to go to bed with. He knew all about this inconvenient dichotomy. Its causes had occupied many expensive hours with his analyst. Unfortunately, knowing is one thing and changing is another, as some of his patients could have told him. And there had been times with Valda (christened Millicent) when he hadn't really wanted to be different.

The telephone rang for about a minute before she answered and he told her about Miss Bolam against a background noise of music and clinking glasses. The flat was apparently full of people. He wasn't even sure she had heard him.

'What is it?' he asked irritably. 'Are you having a party?'

'Just a few chums. Wait while I turn down the gramophone. Now, what did you say?'

Dr Steiner said it again. This time Valda's reaction was entirely satisfactory.

'Murdered! No! Darling, how too frightful for you! Miss Bolam. Isn't she that dreary old A.O. you hated so much? The one who kept trying to do you down over your travelling claims?'

'I didn't hate her, Valda. In some ways I respected her. She had considerable integrity. Of course, she was rather obsessional, frightened of her own subconscious aggressions, possibly sexually frigid . . .'

'That's what I said, darling. I knew you couldn't bear her. Oh, Paulie, they won't think you did it, will they?'

'Of course not,' said Dr Steiner, beginning to regret his impulse to confide.

'But you always did say that someone should get rid of her.'

The conversation was beginning to have a nightmare quality. The gramophone thudded its insistent bass to the treble cacophony of Valda's party and the pulse in Dr Steiner's temple beat in unison. He was going to start one of his headaches.

'I meant that she should be transferred to another clinic, not bashed on the head with a blunt instrument.'

The hackneyed phrase sharpened her curiosity. Violence had always fascinated her. He knew that she saw in imagination a spatter of blood and brains.

'Darling, I must hear all about it. Why not come over?'

'Well, I was thinking of it,' said Dr Steiner. He added cunningly: 'There are one or two details I can't give you over the phone. But if you've got a party it's rather difficult. Frankly, Valda, I'm not capable of being sociable just now. I've got one of my heads starting. This has all been a terrible shock. After all, I did more or less discover the body.'

'You poor sweet. Look, give me half an hour and I'll get rid of the chums.'

The chums sounded to Dr Steiner as if they were well entrenched and he said so.

'Not really. We were all going on to Toni's. They can manage without me. I'll give them a shove and you set off in about half an hour. All right?'

It was certainly all right. Replacing the receiver, Dr Steiner decided that he would just have time to bath and change in comfort. He pondered on a choice of tie. The headache unaccountably seemed to have gone. Just before he left the house the telephone rang. He felt a spasm of apprehension. Perhaps Valda had changed her mind about seeing off the chums and having some time alone together. That, after all, had been a recurring pattern in his marriage. He was irritated to find that the hand reaching for the receiver was not quite steady. But the caller was only Dr Etherege to say that he was calling an emergency meeting of the clinic Medical Committee for 8 p.m. the following evening. In his relief Dr Steiner, momentarily forgetting

Miss Bolam, just saved himself in time from the folly of asking why.

If Ralfe and Sonia Bostock had lived in Clapham their flat would have been called a basement. Since, however, it was in Hampstead, half a mile in fact from Dr Steiner's house, a small wooden notice, lettered with impeccable taste, directed one to the garden flat. Here they paid nearly twelve pounds a week for a socially acceptable address and the privilege of seeing a green sloping lawn from the sitting-room window. They had planted this lawn with crocuses and daffodils and in spring those plants which managed to bloom in the almost complete lack of sun, at least fostered the illusion that the flat had access to a garden. In autumn, however, the view was less agreeable and dampness from the sloping soil seeped into the room. The flat was noisy. There was a nursery school two houses away and a young family in the ground-floor flat. Ralfe Bostock, dispensing drinks to their carefully selected friends and raising his voice against the wail of bath-time tantrums, would say:

'Sorry for the row. I'm afraid the intelligentsia have taken to breeding but not – alas – to controlling their brats.' He was given to malicious remarks, some of which were clever, but he overworked them. His wife lived in constant apprehension that he would make the same witticism twice to the same people. There were few things more fatal to a man's chances than the reputation for repeating his jokes.

Tonight he was out at a political meeting. She approved of the meeting which might be an important one for him and she did not mind being alone. She wanted time to think. She went into the bedroom and took off her suit, shaking it carefully and hanging it in the wardrobe, then put on a housecoat of brown velvet. Next she sat at her dressing-table. Binding a *crêpe* bandage about her brow she began to cream the make-up from her face. She was more tired than she had realized and needed a drink, but nothing would deter her from her evening ritual. There was much to think about, much to plan. The grey-green eyes, ringed with cream, gazed calmly back at her from the glass. Leaning forward she inspected the delicate folds of skin beneath each eye, watching for the first lines of age. She was only twenty-eight after all. There was no need to worry yet. But Ralfe was thirty this year. Time was passing. If they were to achieve anything there was no time to lose.

She considered tactics. The situation would need careful hand-ling and there was no room for mistakes. She had made one already. The temptation to slap Nagle's face had proved irresist-ible, but it was still a mistake and possibly a bad one, too like vulgar exhibitionism to be safe. Aspiring administrative officers did not slap a porter's face, even when under strain, particularly if they wanted to create an impression of calm, authoritative competence. She remembered the look on Miss Saxon's face. Well, Fredrica Saxon was in no position to be censorious. It was a pity that Dr Steiner was there, but it had all happened so quickly that she couldn't be sure that he had really seen. The Priddy child was of no importance.

Nagle would have to go, of course, once she was appointed. Here, too, she would have to be careful. He was an insolent devil, but the clinic could do much worse and the consultants knew it. An efficient porter made quite a difference to their comfort, especially when he was willing and able to carry out the many small repair jobs that were needed. It wouldn't be a popular move if they had to wait for someone to come from the group engineer's department every time a sash cord broke or a fuse needed replacing. Nagle would have to go, but she would put out feelers for a good replacement before taking any action.

The main concern at present must be to get the consultants' support for her appointment. She could be sure of Dr Etherege and his was the most powerful voice. But it wasn't the only one. He would be retiring in six months' time and his influence would be on the wane. If she were offered an acting appointment, and all went well, the Hospital Management Committee might not be in too much of a hurry to advertise the post. Almost certainly they would wait until the murder was either solved or the police shelved the case. It was up to her to consolidate her position in the intervening months. It wouldn't do to take anything for granted. When there had been trouble at a unit, committees tended to make an outside appointment. There was safety in bringing in a stranger uncontaminated by the previous upset. The group secretary would be an influence there. It had been a wise move to see him last month and ask his advice about working for the diploma of the Institute of Hospital Administrators. He liked his staff to qualify and, being a man, he was flattered to be asked for advice. But he wasn't a fool. He didn't have to be. She was as suitable a candidate as the H.M.C. were likely to find, and he knew it.

She lay back, relaxed, on her single bed, her feet raised on a pillow, her mind busy with the images of success. 'My wife is administrative officer of the Steen Clinic.' So much more satisfactory than, 'Actually, my wife is working as a secretary at present. The Steen Clinic, as a matter of fact.'

And less than two miles away, in a mortuary in north London, Miss Bolam's body, tight-packed as a herring in an ice box, stiffened slowly through the autumn night.

CHAPTER FIVE

If there had to be a murder at the Steen, Friday was the most convenient day for it. The clinic did not open on Saturday so that the police were able to work in the building without the complications presented by the presence of patients and staff. The staff, presumably, were glad of two days' grace in which to recover from the shock, determine at leisure what their official reaction should be and seek the comfort and reassurance of their friends.

Dalgliesh's day began early. He had asked for a report from the local C.I.D. about the Steen burglary and this, together with typescripts of the previous day's interviews, was waiting on his desk. The burglary had puzzled the local men. There could be no doubt that someone had broken into the clinic and that the £15 was missing. It was not so certain that these two facts were related. The local sergeant thought it odd that a casual thief had picked the one drawer which held cash while neglecting the safe and leaving untouched the silver inkstand in the medical director's office. On the other hand, Cully had undoubtedly seen a man leaving the clinic and both he and Nagle had alibis for the time of entry. The local C.I.D. were inclined to suspect Nagle of having helped himself to the cash while he was alone in the building, but it had not been found on him and there was no real evidence. Besides, the porter had plenty of opportunities for dishonesty at the Steen if he were so inclined, and nothing was known against him. The whole affair was puzzling. They were still working on it but weren't very hopeful. Dalgliesh asked that any progress should be reported to him at once and set off with Sergeant Martin to examine Miss Bolam's flat.

Miss Bolam had lived on the fifth floor of a solid, red-brick block near Kensington High Street. There was no difficulty over the key. The resident caretaker handed it over with formal and perfunctory expressions of regret at Miss Bolam's death. She seemed to feel that some reference to the murder was necessary, but managed to give the impression that the company's tenants usually had the good taste to quit this life in more orthodox fashion.

'There will be no undesirable publicity, I hope,' she murmured, as she escorted Dalgliesh and Sergeant Martin to the lift. 'These flats are very select and the company are most particular about their tenants. We have never had trouble of this kind before.'

Dalgliesh resisted the temptation to say that Miss Bolam's murderer had obviously not recognized one of the company's tenants.

'The publicity is hardly likely to affect the flats,' he pointed out. 'It's not as if the murder took place here.' The caretaker was heard to murmur that she hoped not indeed!

They ascended to the fifth floor together in the slow, old-fashioned panelled lift. The atmosphere was heavy with disapproval.

'Did you know Miss Bolam at all?' Dalgliesh inquired. 'I believe she had lived here for some years.'

'I knew her to say good morning to, nothing more. She was a very quiet tenant. But then all our tenants are. She has been in residence for fifteen years, I believe. Her mother was the tenant previously and they lived here together. When Mrs Bolam died her daughter took over the tenancy. That was before my time.'

'Did her mother die here?'

The caretaker closed her lips repressively.

'Mrs Bolam died in a nursing home in the country. There was some unpleasantness, I believe.'

'You mean that she killed herself?'

'I was told so. As I said, it happened before I took this job. Naturally I never alluded to the fact either to Miss Bolam or to any of the other tenants. It is not the kind of thing one would wish to talk about. They really do seem a most unfortunate family.'

'What rent did Miss Bolam pay?'

The caretaker paused before replying. This was obviously high on her list of questions that should not properly be asked. Then, as if reluctantly admitting the authority of the police, she replied:

'Our fourth and fifth floor two-bedroom flats are from £490 excluding rates.'

That was about half Miss Bolam's salary, thought Dalgliesh. It was too high a proportion for anyone without private means. He had yet to see the dead woman's solicitor, but it looked as if Nurse Bolam's assessment of her cousin's income was not far wrong.

He dismissed the caretaker at the door of the flat and he and Martin went in together.

This prying among the personal residue of a finished life was a part of his job which Dalgliesh had always found a little distasteful. It was too much like putting the dead at a disadvantage. During his career he had examined with interest and with pity so many petty leavings. The soiled underclothes pushed hurriedly into drawers, personal letters which prudence would have destroyed, half-eaten meals, unpaid bills, old photographs, pictures and books which the dead would not have chosen to represent their taste to a curious or vulgar world, family secrets, stale make-up in greasy jars, the muddle of ill-disciplined or unhappy lives. It was no longer the fashion to dread an unshriven end but most people, if they thought at all, hoped for time to clear away their debris. He remembered from childhood the voice of an old aunt exhorting him to change his vest. 'Suppose you got run over, Adam. What would people think?' The question was less absurd than it had seemed to a ten-year-old. Time had taught him that it expressed one of the major preoccupations of mankind, the dread of losing face.

But Enid Bolam might have lived each day as if expecting sudden death. He had never examined a flat so neat, so obsessively tidy. Even her few cosmetics, the brush and comb on her dressing-table were arranged with patterned precision. The heavy double bed was made. Friday was obviously her day for changing the linen. The used sheets and pillow-cases were folded into a laundry box which lay open on a chair. The bedside table held nothing but a small travelling clock, a carafe of water and a Bible with a booklet beside it appointing the passage to be read each day and expounding the moral. There was nothing in the table drawer but a bottle of aspirin and a folded handkerchief. A hotel room would have held as much individuality.

All the furniture was old and heavy. The ornate mahogany

door of the wardrobe swung open soundlessly to reveal a row of tightly packed clothes. They were expensive but unexciting. Miss Bolam had bought from that store which still caters mainly for country-house dowagers. There were well-cut skirts of indeterminate colour, heavy coats tailored to last through a dozen English winters, woollen dresses which could offend no one. Once the wardrobe was closed it was impossible accurately to recall a single garment. At the back of them all, closeted from the light, were bowls of fibre, planted no doubt with bulbs whose Christmas flowering Miss Bolam would never see.

Dalgliesh and Martin had worked together for too many years to find much talking necessary and they moved about the flat almost in silence. Everywhere was the same heavy, old-fashioned furniture, the same ordered neatness. It was hard to believe that these rooms had been recently lived in, that anyone had cooked a meal in this impersonal kitchen. It was very quiet. At this height and muffled by the solid Victorian walls the clamour of traffic in Kensington High Street was a faint, distant throbbing. Only the insistent ticking of a grandfather clock in the hall stabbed the still silence. The air was cold and almost odourless except for the smell of the flowers. They were everywhere. There was a bowl of chrysanthemums on the hall table and another in the sitting-room. The bedroom mantelpiece held a small jug of anemones. On the kitchen dresser was a taller brass jug of autumn foliage, the gatherings perhaps of some recent country walk. Dalgliesh did not like autumn flowers, the chrysanthemums which obstinately refuse to die, flaunting their shaggy heads even on a rotting stem, scentless dahlias fit only to be planted in neat rows in municipal parks. His wife had died in October and he had long recognized the minor bereavements which follow the death of the heart. Autumn was no longer a good time of the year. For him the flowers in Miss Bolam's flat emphasized the general air of gloom, like wreaths at a funeral.

The sitting-room was the largest room in the flat and here was Miss Bolam's desk. Martin fingered it appreciatively.

'It's all good solid stuff, sir, isn't it? We've got a piece rather like this. The wife's mother left it to us. Mind you, they don't make furniture like it today. You get nothing for it, of course. Too big for modern rooms, I suppose. But it's got quality.'

'You can certainly lean against it without collapsing,' said Dalgliesh.

'That's what I mean, sir. Good solid stuff. No wonder she hung on to it. A sensible young woman on the whole, I'd say, and one who knew how to make herself comfortable.' He drew a second chair up to the desk where Dalgliesh was already seated, planted his heavy thighs in it, and did indeed look comfortable and at home.

The desk was unlocked. The top rolled back without difficulty. Inside was a portable typewriter and a metal box containing files of paper, each file neatly labelled. The drawers and compartments of the desk held writing paper, envelopes, and correspondence. As they expected, everything was in perfect order. They went through the files together. Miss Bolam paid her bills as soon as they were due and kept a running account of all her household expenditure.

There was much to be gone through. Details of her investments were filed under the appropriate heading. At her mother's death the trustee securities had been redeemed and the capital reinvested in equities. The portfolio was skilfully balanced and there could be little doubt that Miss Bolam had been well advised and had increased her assets considerably during the past five years. Dalgliesh noted the name of her stockbroker and solicitor. Both would have to be seen before the investigation was complete.

The dead woman kept few of her personal letters; perhaps there had been few worth keeping. But there was one, filed under P, which was interesting. It was written in a careful hand on cheap lined paper from a Clapham address, and read:

Dear Miss Bolam,

These are just a few lines to thank you for all you done for Jenny. It hasn't turned out as we wished and prayed for but we shall know in His good time what His purpose is. I still feel we did right to let them marry. It wasn't only to stop talk as I think you know. He has gone for good, he writes. Her Dad and me didn't know that things had got that bad between them. She doesn't talk much to us but we shall wait patiently and maybe, one day, she will be our girl again. She seems very quiet and won't talk about it so we don't know whether she grieves. I try not to feel bitterness against him. Dad and I think it would be a good idea if you could get Jenny a post in the health service. It is really good of you to offer and be interested after all that's happened. You know what we think about divorce so she must look to her job now for happiness. Dad and I pray every night that she'll find it.

Thanking you again for all your interest and help. If you do manage to get Jenny the post I'm sure she won't let you down. She's learned her lesson and it's been a bitter one for us all. But His will be done.

Yours respectfully,
EMILY PRIDDY (Mrs)

It was extraordinary, thought Dalgliesh, that people still lived who could write a letter like that, with its archaic mixture of subservience and self-respect, its unashamed yet curiously poign-ant emotionalism. The story it told was ordinary enough, but he felt detached from its reality. The letter could have been written fifty years ago; almost he expected to see the paper curling with age and smell the tentative scent of potpourri. It had no relevance, surely, to that pretty, ineffectual child at the Steen.

'It's unlikely to have any importance,' he said to Martin. 'But I'd like you to go over to Clapham and have a word with these people. We'd better know who the husband is. But, somehow, I don't think he'll prove to be Dr Etherege's mysterious marauder. The man – or woman – who killed Miss Bolam was still in the building when we arrived. And we've talked to him.'

It was then that the telephone rang, sounding ominously strident in the silence of the flat as if it were calling for the dead. Dalgliesh said:

'I'll take it. It will be Dr Keating with the P.M. report. I asked him to ring me here if he got through with it.'

He was back with Martin within two minutes. The report had been brief. Dalgliesh said:

'Nothing surprising. She was a healthy woman. Killed by a stab through the heart after being stunned, which we could see for ourselves, and *virgo intacta* which we had no reason to doubt. What have you got there?'

'It's her photograph album, sir. Pictures of Guide camps

mostly. It looks as if she went away with the girls every year.'

Probably making that her annual holiday, thought Dalgliesh. He had a respect bordering on simple wonder for those who voluntarily gave up their leisure to other people's children. He was not a man who liked children and he found the company of most of them insupportable after a very brief time. He took the album from Sergeant Martin. The photographs were small and technically unremarkable, taken apparently with a small box camera. But they were carefully disposed on the page, each labelled in neat white printing. There were Guides hiking, Guides cooking on primus stoves, erecting tents, blanket-swathed around the camp-fire, lining up for kit inspection. And in many of the photographs there was the figure of their captain, plump, motherly, smiling. It was difficult to connect this buxom, happy extrovert with that pathetic corpse on the record-room floor – or with the obsessional, authoritative administrator described by the staff of the Steen. The comments under some of the photographs were pathetic in their evocation of happiness remembered:

'The Swallows dish up. Shirley keeps an eye on the spotted dick.'

'Valerie "flies up" from the Brownies.'

'The Kingfishers tackle the washing-up. Snap taken by Susan.'

'Captain helps the tide in! Taken by Jean.'

This last showed Miss Bolam's plump shoulders rising from the surf, surrounded by some half-dozen of her girls. Her hair was down and hanging in flat swaths, wet and dank as seaweed, on either side of her laughing face. Together the two detectives looked at the photograph in silence. Then Dalgliesh said:

'There haven't been many tears shed for her yet, have there? Only her cousin's and they were more shock than grief. I wonder whether the Swallows and the Kingfishers will weep for her.'

They closed the album and went back to their search. It disclosed only one further item of interest, but that was very interesting indeed. It was the carbon copy of a letter from Miss Bolam to her solicitor, dated the day before her death, and making an appointment to see him 'in connection with the proposed changes to my will which we discussed briefly on the telephone yesterday night.'

*

After the visit to Ballantyne Mansions there followed a hiatus in the investigation, one of those inevitable delays which Dalgliesh had never found it easy to accept. He had always worked at speed. His reputation rested on the pace as well as the success of his cases. He did not ponder too deeply the implications of this compulsive need to get on with the job. It was enough to know that delay irritated him more than it did most men.

This hold up was, perhaps, to be expected. It was hardly likely that a London solicitor would be in his office after midday on Saturday. It was more dispiriting to learn by telephone that Mr Babcock of Babcock and Honeywell had flown with his wife to Geneva on Friday afternoon to attend the funeral of a friend and would not be back in his City office until the following Tuesday. There was now no Mr Honeywell in the firm, but Mr Babcock's chief clerk would be in the office on Monday morning if he could help the superintendent. It was the caretaker speaking. Dalgliesh was not sure how far the chief clerk could help him. He much preferred to see Mr Babcock. The solicitor was likely to be able to give a great deal of useful information about Miss Bolam's family as well as her financial affairs, but much of it would probably be given with at least a token show of resistance and obtained only by the exercise of tact. It would be folly to jeopardize success by a prior approach to the clerk.

Until the details of the will were available there was little point in seeing Nurse Bolam again. Frustrated in his immediate plans Dalgliesh drove without his sergeant to call on Peter Nagle. He had no clear aim in view but that didn't worry him. The time would be well spent. Some of his most useful work was done in these unplanned, almost casual encounters when he talked, listened, watched, studied a suspect in his own home, or gleaned the thin stalks of unwittingly dropped information about the one personality which is central to any murder investigation – that of the victim.

Nagle lived in Pimlico on the fourth floor of a large, white, stuccoed Victorian house near Eccleston Square. Dalgliesh had last visited this street three years previously when it had seemed irretrievably sunk into shabby decay. But the tide had changed. The wave of fashion and popularity which flows so inexplicably in London, sometimes missing one district while sweeping through its near neighbour, had washed the broad street bringing order and prosperity in its wake. Judging by the number of house agents' boards, the property speculators, first as always to sniff the returning tide, were reaping the usual profits. The house on the corner looked newly painted. The heavy front door stood open. Inside, a board gave the names of the tenants, but there were no bells. Dalgliesh deduced that the flats were self-contained and that, somewhere, there was a resident caretaker who would answer the front-door bell when the house was locked for the night. He could see no lift so set himself to climb the four flights to Nagle's flat.

It was a light, airy house and very quiet. There was no sign of life until the third floor where someone was playing the piano and playing well; perhaps a professional musician, practising. The treble cascade of sound fell over Dalgliesh and receded as he reached the fourth floor. Here there was a plain wooden door with a heavy brass knocker and a card pinned above it on which was lettered the one word – Nagle. He rapped and heard Nagle shout an immediate 'come in'.

The flat was surprising. He hardly knew what he had expected, but it was certainly not this immense, airy, impressive studio. It ran the whole length of the back of the house, the great north window, uncurtained, giving a panoramic view of twisted chimney-pots and irregular sloping roofs. Nagle was not alone. He was sitting, knees apart, on a narrow bed which stood on a raised platform at the east side of the room. Curled against him, clad only in a dressing-gown, was Jennifer Priddy. They were drinking tea from two blue mugs; a tray holding the teapot and a bottle of milk was on a small table beside them. The painting on which Nagle had recently been working stood on an easel in the middle of the room.

The girl showed no embarrassment at seeing Dalgliesh but swung her legs from the bed and gave him a smile which was frankly happy, almost welcoming, certainly without coquetry.

'Would you like some tea?' she asked.

Nagle said:

'The police never drink on duty and that includes tea. Better

get your clothes on, kid. We don't want to shock the superintendent.'

The girl smiled again, gathered up her clothes with one arm
and the tea tray with the other and disappeared through a door
at the far end of the studio. It was difficult to recognize in this
confident sensual figure the tear-stained, diffident child Dalgliesh
had first seen at the Steen. He watched her as she passed. She
was obviously naked except for the dressing-gown of Nagle's; her
hard nipples pointed the thin wool. It came to Dalgliesh that
they had been making love. As she passed from view he turned
to Nagle and saw in his eyes the transitory gleam of amused
speculation. But neither of them spoke.

Dalgliesh moved about the studio, watched by Nagle from the
bed. The room was without clutter. In its almost obsessional
neatness it reminded him of Enid Bolam's flat with which it had
otherwise nothing in common. The dais with its plain wooden
bed, chair and small table obviously served as a bedroom. The
rest of the studio was taken up with the paraphernalia of a
painter, but there was none of that undisciplined muddle which
the uninitiated associate with an artist's life. About a dozen large
oils were stacked against the south wall and Dalgliesh was surprised by their power. Here was no amateur indulging his little
talent. Miss Priddy was apparently Nagle's only model. Her
heavy-busted, adolescent body gleamed at him from a diversity of
poses, here foreshortened, there curiously elongated as if the
painter gloried in his technical competence. The most recent
picture was on the easel. It showed the girl sitting astride a stool
with the childish hands hanging relaxed between her thighs, the
breasts bunched forward. There was something in this flaunting
of technical expertise, in the audacious use of greens and mauve
and in the careful tonal relationships which caught at Dalgliesh's
memory.

'Who teaches you?' he asked. 'Sugg?'

'That's right.' Nagle did not seem surprised. 'Know his work?'

'I have one of his early oils. A nude.'

'You made a good investment. Hang on to it.'

'I've every intention of doing so,' said Dalgliesh mildly. 'I
happen to like it. Have you been with him long?'

'Two years. Part time, of course. In another three years I'll be teaching him. If he's capable of learning, that is. He's getting an old dog now and too fond of his own tricks.'

'You appear to have imitated some of them,' said Dalgliesh.

'You think so? That's interesting.' Nagle did not seem affronted. 'That's why it will be good to get away. I'm off to Paris by the end of the month at the latest. I applied for the Bollinger scholarship. The old man put in a word for me and last week I had a letter to say that it's mine.'

Try as he would he could not entirely keep the note of triumph from his voice. Underneath the assumption of nonchalance there was a spring of joy. And he had reason to be pleased with himself. The Bollinger was no ordinary prize. It meant, as Dalgliesh knew, two years in any European city with a generous allowance and freedom for the student to live and work as he chose. The Bollinger trust had been set up by a manufacturer of patent medicines who had died wealthy and successful, but unsatisfied. His money had come from stomach powders but his heart was in painting. His own talent was small and, to judge by the collection of paintings which he bequeathed to the embarrassed trustees of his local gallery, his taste had been on a par with his performance. But the Bollinger scholarship had ensured that artists should remember him with gratitude. Bollinger did not believe that art flourished in poverty or that artists were stimulated to their best efforts by cold garrets and empty bellies. He had been poor in his youth and had not enjoyed it. He had travelled widely in his old age and been happy abroad. The Bollinger scholarship enabled young artists of promise to enjoy the second without enduring the first and it was well worth winning. If Nagle had been awarded the Bollinger he was hardly likely to be much concerned now with the troubles of the Steen Clinic.

'When are you due to go?' Dalgliesh asked.

'When I like. By the end of the month, anyway. But I may go earlier and without notice. No sense in upsetting anyone.' He jerked his head towards the far door as he spoke and added: 'That's why this murder is such a nuisance. I was afraid it might hold things up. After all, it was my chisel. And that wasn't the only attempt made to implicate me. While I was in the general office waiting for the post someone phoned to ask me to go down for the laundry. It sounded like a woman. I'd got my coat on and was more or less on my way out, so I said I'd collect it when I got back.'

'So that's why you went to see Nurse Bolam on your return from the post and asked her whether the laundry was ready?'

'That's right.'

'Why didn't you tell her about the phone call at the time?'

'I don't know. There didn't seem any point. I wasn't anxious to hang about the LSD room. Those patients give me the creeps with their moaning and muttering. When Bolam said the stuff wasn't ready I thought it was Miss Bolam who had phoned and it wouldn't have done to have said so. She was a bit too apt to interfere with the nursing responsibilities, or so they thought. Anyway, I didn't say anything about the call. I might have done but I didn't.'

'And you didn't tell me either when you were first interviewed.'

'Right again. The truth is that the whole thing struck me as a bit odd and I wanted time to think about it. Well, I've thought, and you're welcome to the story. You can believe it or not, as you like. It's all the same to me.'

'You seem to be taking it pretty calmly if you really believe that someone was trying to involve you in the murder.'

'I'm not worrying. They didn't succeed for one thing, and for another, I happen to believe that the chance of an innocent man getting convicted of murder in this country is practically nil. You ought to find that flattering. On the other hand given the jury system – the chances of the guilty getting off are high. That's why I don't think you're going to solve this murder. Too many suspects. Too many possibilities.'

'We shall see. Tell me more about this call. When exactly did you receive it?'

'I can't remember. About five minutes before Shorthouse came into the general office, I think. It could have been earlier. Jenny may remember.'

'I'll ask her when she gets back. What exactly did the voice say?'

'Just, "The laundry's ready if you'd fetch it now, please." I took it that Nurse Bolam was phoning. I replied that I was just going out with the post and would see to it when I got back. Then I put down the receiver before she had a chance to argue.'

'You were sure it was Nurse Bolam speaking?'

'I'm not sure at all. I naturally thought it was at the time because Nurse Bolam usually does phone about the laundry. As a matter of fact the woman spoke softly and it could have been anyone.'

'But it was a woman's voice?'

'Oh, yes. It was a woman all right.'

'At any rate it was a false message because we know that, in fact, the laundry wasn't sorted.'

'Yes. But what was the point of it? It doesn't add up. If the idea was to lure me down to the basement to frame me, the killer stood the risk that I'd arrive at the wrong moment. Nurse Bolam, for example, wouldn't want me on the spot inquiring for the laundry if she were planning to be in the record-room slugging her cousin. Even if Miss Bolam were dead before the call was made it still doesn't make sense. Suppose I'd nosed around and found the body? The killer couldn't have wanted it discovered that soon! Anyway, I didn't go down until I got back from the post. Lucky for me I was out with it. The box is only just across the road, but I usually go down to Beefsteak Street to buy a *Standard*. The man there probably remembers me.'

Jennifer Priddy had returned during the last few words. She had changed into a plain woollen dress. Clasping a belt round her waist, she said:

'It was the row over your paper that finished poor old Cully. You might have let him have it, darling, when he asked. He only wanted to check on his horses.'

Nagle said without rancour:

'Mean old devil. He'd do anything to save himself three-pence. Why can't he pay for it occasionally? I'm no sooner in the door before he puts out his hand for it.'

'Still, you were rather unkind to him, darling. It isn't as if you wanted it yourself. We only glanced at it downstairs then used it to wrap up Tigger's food. You know what Cully is. The least upset goes to his stomach.'

Nagle expressed his opinion of Cully's stomach with force and originality. Miss Priddy glanced at Dalgliesh as if inviting his shocked admiration of the vagaries of genius and murmured:

'Peter! Really, darling, you are awful!'

She spoke with coy indulgence, the little woman administering a mild rebuke. Dalgliesh looked at Nagle to see how he bore it, but the painter seemed not to have heard. He still sat, immobile, on the bed and looked down at them. Clad now in brown linen trousers, thick blue jersey and sandals, he yet looked as formal and neat as he had in his porter's uniform, his mild eyes unworried, his long, strong arms relaxed.

Under his gaze the girl moved restlessly about the studio, touching with happy possessiveness the frame of a painting, running her fingers along the window ledge, moving a jug of dahlias from one window to the next. It was as if she sought to impose the soft nuances of femininity on this disciplined masculine workshop, to demonstrate that this was her home, her natural place. She was entirely unembarrassed by the pictures of her naked body. It was possible that she gained satisfaction from this vicarious exhibitionism. Suddenly Dalgliesh asked:

'Do you remember, Miss Priddy, whether anyone telephoned Mr Nagle while he was in the office with you?'

The girl looked surprised but said unconcernedly to Nagle:

'Nurse Bolam phoned about the laundry, didn't she? I came in from the record-room – I'd only been gone a second – and heard you say that you were just on your way out and would go down when you came back.' She laughed. 'After you put the receiver down you said something much less polite about the way the nurses expect you to be at their beck and call. Remember?'

'Yes,' said Nagle shortly. He turned to Dalgliesh. 'Any more questions, Superintendent? Jenny'll have to be getting home soon and I usually go part of the way. Her parents don't know she sees me.'

'Only one or two. Have either of you any idea why Miss Bolam should send for the group secretary?'

Miss Priddy shook her head. Nagle said:

'It was nothing to do with us, anyway. She didn't know that Jenny poses for me. Even if she found out she wouldn't send for Lauder. She wasn't a fool. She knew he wouldn't concern himself with anything the staff did in their own time. After all, she found out about Dr Baguley's affair with Miss Saxon, but she wasn't daft enough to tell Lauder.'

Dalgliesh did not ask whom Miss Bolam had told. He said:

'It was obviously something concerned with the administration of the clinic. Had anything unusual happened lately?'

'Nothing but our famous burglary and the missing fifteen quid. But you know about that.'

'That's nothing to do with Peter,' said the girl with quick defensiveness. 'He wasn't even at the clinic when the fifteen pounds arrived.' She turned to Nagle. 'You remember, darling? That was the morning you got stuck in the Underground. You didn't even know about the money!'

She had said something wrong. The flash of irritation in those large mud-brown eyes was momentary, but Dalgliesh did not miss it. There was a pause before Nagle spoke, but his voice was perfectly controlled.

'I knew soon enough. We all did. What with the fuss over who sent it and the row over who was to spend it, the whole damn group must have known.' He looked at Dalgliesh.

'Is that all?'

'No. Do you know who killed Miss Bolam?'

'I'm glad to say I don't. I shouldn't think it was one of the psychiatrists. Those boys are the strongest reason I know for staying sane. But I can't see any of them actually killing. They haven't the nerve.'

Someone very different had said much the same thing.

As he reached the door, Dalgliesh paused and looked back at Nagle. He and the girl were sitting together on the bed as he had first seen them, neither of them made any move to see him out, but Jenny gave him her happy valedictory smile.

Dalgliesh asked his last question:

'Why did you go for a drink with Cully on the night of the burglary?'

'Cully asked me.'

'Wasn't that unusual?'

'So unusual that I went with him out of curiosity to see what was up.'

'And what was?'

'Nothing really. Cully asked me to lend him a quid which I refused, and while the clinic was left empty someone broke in. I don't see how Cully could have foreseen that. Or maybe he did. Anyway, I can't see what it's got to do with the murder.'

Nor, on the face of it, could Dalgliesh. As he passed down the stairs he was vexed by the thought of time passing, time wasted, the drag of hours before Monday morning when the clinic would reopen and his suspects reassemble in the place where they were likely to be most vulnerable. But the last forty minutes had been well spent. He was beginning to trace the dominant thread in this tangled skein. As he passed by the third-floor flat the pianist was playing Bach. Dalgliesh paused for a moment to listen. Contrapuntal music was the only kind he truly enjoyed. But the pianist stopped suddenly with a crash of discordant keys. And then nothing. Dalgliesh passed down the stairs in silence and left the quiet house unseen.

When Dr Baguley arrived at the clinic for the Medical Committee meeting, the parking space reserved for doctors' cars was already occupied. Dr Etherege's Bentley was there parked next to Steiner's Rolls. On the other side of it was the battered Vauxhall which proclaimed that Dr Albertine Maddox had decided to attend.

Upstairs in the first-floor boardroom the curtains were drawn against the blue-black October sky. In the middle of the heavy mahogany table was a bowl of roses. Baguley remembered that Miss Bolam had always supplied flowers for the meetings of the Medical Committee. Someone had decided to continue the practice. The roses were the slim, hothouse buds of autumn, rigid and scentless on their thornless stems. In a couple of days they would open for their brief and barren flowering. In less than a week they would be dead. Baguley thought that so extravagant and evocative a flower was inappropriate to the mood of the meeting. But the empty bowl would have been unbearably poignant and embarrassing.

'Who supplied the roses?' he asked.

'Mrs Bostock, I think,' said Dr Ingram. 'She was up here getting the room ready when I arrived.'

'Remarkable,' said Dr Etherege. He put out a finger and stroked one of the buds so gently that the stem did not even tremble. Baguley wondered whether the comment referred to the quality of the roses or to Mrs Bostock's perspicacity in supplying them.

'Miss Bolam was very fond of flowers, very fond,' said the medical director. He looked round as if challenging his colleagues to disagree.

'Well,' he said. 'Shall we get started?'

Dr Baguley, as honorary secretary, seated himself on the right of Dr Etherege. Dr Steiner took the chair next to him. Dr Maddox sat on Steiner's right. No other consultant was there. Dr McBain and Dr Mason-Giles were in the States attending a conference. The rest of the medical staff, torn between curiosity and a disinclination to interrupt their weekend break, had apparently decided to wait in patience for Monday. Dr Etherege had thought it proper to telephone them all and let them know of the meeting. He gave their apologies formally and they were as gravely received.

Albertine Maddox had been a surgeon and a highly successful one before she qualified as a psychiatrist. It was perhaps typical of her colleagues' ambivalence towards their specialty that Dr Maddox's double qualification enhanced her standing in their eyes. She represented the clinic on the Group Medical Advisory Committee, where she defended the Steen against the occasional snipings of physicians and surgeons with a wit and vigour which made her respected and feared. At the clinic she took no part in the Freudian versus eclectic controversy being, as Baguley observed, equally beastly to both sides. Her patients loved her, but this did not impress her colleagues. They were used to being loved by their patients and merely observed that Albertine was particularly skilful in handling a strong transference situation. Physically she was a plump, grey-haired, unremarkable woman who looked what she was, the comfortable mother of a family. She had five children, the sons intelligent and prosperous, the girls well-married. Her insignificant-looking husband and the children treated her with a tolerant, faintly amused solicitude which never failed to astonish her colleagues at the Steen to whom she was a formidable personality. She sat now with Hector, her old Pekinese, squatting malevolently on her lap looking as comfortably anticipatory as a suburban housewife at a matinée. Dr Steiner said testily:

'Really, Albertine, need you have brought Hector? I don't want to be unkind but that animal is beginning to smell. You should have him put down.'

'Thank you, Paul,' replied Dr Maddox in her deep, beautifully modulated voice. 'Hector will be put down, as you so euphemistically describe it, when he ceases to find life pleasant. I judge that he has not yet reached that state. It is not my habit to kill off living creatures simply because I find certain of their physical characteristics displeasing; nor, I may say, because they have become somewhat of a nuisance.'

Dr Etherege said quickly:

'It was good of you to find time to come tonight, Albertine. I'm sorry that the notice was so short.'

He spoke without irony, although he was as well aware as were his colleagues that Dr Maddox only attended one committee meeting in four on the grounds, which she made no effort to conceal, that her contract with the Regional Board contained no clause compelling her to a monthly session of boredom laced with claptrap, and that the company of more than one psychiatrist at a time made Hector sick. The truth of this last assertion had been demonstrated too often to be safely challenged.

'I am a member of this committee, Henry,' replied Dr Maddox graciously. 'Is there any reason why I should not make the effort to attend?'

Her glance at Dr Ingram implied that not everyone present had an equal right. Mary Ingram was the wife of a suburban general practitioner and attended the Steen twice a week to give the anaesthetic at E.C.T. sessions. Not being either a psychiatrist or a consultant she was not normally present at meetings of the Medical Committee. Dr Etherege interpreted the glance correctly and said firmly:

'Dr Ingram has been good enough to come along tonight at my request. The main business of the meeting is naturally concerned with Miss Bolam's murder, and Dr Ingram was in the clinic on Friday evening.'

'But is not a suspect, so I understand,' replied Dr Maddox. 'I congratulate her. It is gratifying that there is one member of the medical staff who has been able to produce a satisfactory alibi.'

She looked at Dr Ingram severely, her tone implying that an alibi was, in itself, suspicious and hardly becoming to the most junior member of the staff since three senior consultants had been unable to produce one. No one asked how Dr Maddox knew about the alibi. Presumably she had been speaking to Sister Ambrose. Dr Steiner said pettishly:

'It's ridiculous to talk about alibis as if the police could seriously suspect one of us! It's perfectly obvious to me what happened. The murderer was lying in wait for her in the basement. We know that. He may have been hidden down there for hours, perhaps even since the previous day. He could have slipped past Cully with one of the patients or have pretended to be a relative or a hospital-car attendant. He could even have broken in during the night. That has been known, after all. Once in the basement there would be plenty of time to discover which key opened the record-room door and plenty of time to select a weapon. Neither the fetish nor the chisel were hidden.'

'And how do you suggest this unknown murderer left the building?' asked Dr Baguley. 'We searched the place pretty thoroughly before the police arrived and they went over it again. The basement and first-floor doors were both bolted on the inside, remember.'

'Climbed up the lift shaft by the pulley ropes and out through one of the doors leading to the fire-escape,' replied Dr Steiner, playing his trump card with a certain panache. 'I've examined the lift and it's just possible. A small man – or a woman, of course – could squeeze over the top of the box and get into the shaft. The ropes are quite thick enough to support a considerable weight and the climb wouldn't be too difficult for anyone reasonably agile. They'd need to be slim, of course.' He glanced at his own rounding paunch with complacency.

'It's a pleasant theory,' said Baguley. 'Unfortunately all the doors opening on the fire-escape were also bolted on the inside.'

'There is no building in existence which a desperate and experienced man cannot break into or get out of,' proclaimed Dr

Steiner, as if from a plenitude of experience. 'He could have got out of a first-floor window and edged along the sill until he could get a foothold on the fire-escape. All I'm saying is that the murderer isn't necessarily one of the staff who happened to be on duty yesterday evening.'

'It could be I, for example,' said Dr Maddox.

Dr Steiner was undaunted.

'That, of course, is nonsense, Albertine. I make no accusations. I merely point out that the circle of suspects is less restricted than the police seem to think. They should direct their inquiries to Miss Bolam's private life. Obviously she had an enemy.'

But Dr Maddox was not to be diverted.

'Fortunately for me,' she proclaimed, 'I was at the Bach recital at the Royal Festival Hall last night with my husband and dined there before the concert. And while Alasdair's testimony on my behalf might be suspect, I was also with my brother-in-law who happens to be a bishop. A High Church bishop,' she added complacently, as if incense and chasuble set a seal on episcopal virtue and veracity.

Dr Etherege smiled gently and said:

'I should be relieved if I could produce even an evangelical curate to vouch for me between six-fifteen and seven o'clock yesterday evening. But isn't all this theorizing a waste of time? The crime is in the hands of the police and there we must leave it. Our main concern is to discuss its implications for the work of the clinic and, in particular, the suggestion of the chairman and the group secretary that Mrs Bostock should carry on for the present as acting administrative officer. But we'd better proceed in order. Is it your pleasure that I sign the minutes of the last meeting?'

There was the unenthusiastic but acquiescent mumble which this question usually provokes and the medical director drew the minute book towards him and signed. Dr Maddox said suddenly:

'What is he like? This superintendent, I mean.'

Dr Ingram, who hadn't so far spoken, surprisingly replied:

'He's about forty, I should think. Tall and dark. I liked his voice and he has nice hands.' Then she blushed furiously, remembering that, to a psychiatrist, the most innocent remark could be embarrassingly revealing. That comment about nice hands was, perhaps, a mistake. Dr Steiner, ignoring Dalgliesh's physical characteristics, launched into a psychological assessment of the superintendent to which his fellow psychiatrists gave the polite attention of experts interested in a colleague's theories. Dalgliesh, had he been present, would have been surprised and intrigued by the accuracy and percipience of Dr Steiner's diagnosis. The medical director said:

'I agree that he's obsessional and also that he's intelligent. That means that his mistakes will be the mistakes of an intelligent man – always the most dangerous. We must hope for all our sakes that he makes none. The murder, and the inevitable publicity, are bound to have an effect on the patients and on the work of the clinic. And that brings us to this suggestion about Mrs Bostock.'

'I have always preferred Bolam to Bostock,' said Dr Maddox. 'It would be a pity if we lost one unsuitable A.O. – however regrettably and fortuitously – only to be saddled with another.'

'I agree,' said Dr Baguley. 'Of the two I personally always preferred Bolam. But this would only be a temporary arrangement presumably. The job will have to be advertised. In the meantime someone's got to take over and Mrs Bostock does at least know the work.'

Dr Etherege said:

'Lauder made it plain that the H.M.C. wouldn't favour putting in an outsider until the police have finished their investigation, even if they could find anyone willing to come. We don't want any additional upheaval. There will be enough disturbance to cope with. And that brings me to the problem of the press. Lauder suggested, and I have agreed, that all inquiries are referred to group headquarters and that no one here makes any statements. It seems much the best plan. It's important in the interests of the patients that we don't have reporters running all over the clinic. Therapy is likely to suffer enough without that. Have I this Committee's formal confirmation of the decision?'

He had. No one evinced any enthusiasm for coping with the press. Dr Steiner did not contribute to the general murmur of consent. His thoughts were still with the problem of Miss Bolam's successor. He said querulously:

'I can't understand why Dr Maddox and Dr Baguley have this animus against Mrs Bostock. I've noticed it before. It's ridiculous to compare her adversely with Miss Bolam. There's no doubt which of them is – was – is – the more suitable administrator. Mrs Bostock is a highly intelligent woman, psychologically stable, efficient and with a real appreciation of the importance of the work we do here. No one could have said as much of Miss Bolam. Her attitude to the patients was sometimes most unfortunate.'

'I didn't know that she came into contact much with the patients,' said Dr Baguley. 'Anyway, none of mine complained.'

'She made appointments occasionally and paid out travelling expenses. I can quite believe that your patients didn't remark on her attitude. But mine are a rather different class. They're also more sensitive to these things. Mr Burge, for example, mentioned the matter to me.'

Dr Maddox laughed unkindly.

'Oh, Burge! Is he still coming? I see that his new opus is promised for December. It will be interesting to see, Paul, whether your efforts have improved his prose. If so, it's probably public money well spent.'

Dr Steiner burst into pained expostulation. He treated a fair number of writers and artists, some of them protégés of Rosa in search of a little free psychotherapy. Although he was sensitive to the arts his usually keen critical insight failed completely where his patients were concerned. He could not bear to hear them criticized, lived in perpetual hope that their great talents would at last be recognized, and was roused to quick defensive anger on their behalf. Dr Baguley thought that it was one of Steiner's more endearing qualities; in many ways he was touchingly naïve. He launched now into a muddled defence both of his patient's character and his prose style, ending:

'Mr Burge is a most talented and sensitive man, very distressed by his inability to sustain a satisfactory sexual relationship, particularly with his wives.'

This unfortunate solecism seemed likely to provoke Dr Maddox to further unkindness. It was certainly, thought Baguley, her night to be pro-eclectic.

Dr Etherege said mildly:

'Could we forget our professional differences for a moment and concentrate on the matter in hand? Dr Steiner, have you any objection to accepting Mrs Bostock as a temporary administrative officer?'

Dr Steiner said grumpily:

'The question is purely academic. If the group secretary wishes her to be appointed she will be appointed. This farce of appearing to consult us is ridiculous. We have no authority either to approve or disapprove. That was made perfectly clear to me by Lauder when I approached him last month about getting Bolam transferred.'

'I didn't know you had approached him,' said Dr Etherege.

'I spoke to him after the September meeting of the House Committee. It was merely a tentative suggestion.'

'And was met with a pretty positive brush off, no doubt,' said Baguley. 'You would have been wiser to keep your mouth shut.'

'Or to have brought the matter before this Committee,' said Etherege.

'And with what result?' cried Steiner. 'What happened last time I complained about Bolam? Nothing! You all admitted that she was an unsuitable person to hold the post of administrative officer. You all agreed – well, most of you agreed – that Bostock – or even an outsider – would be preferable. But when it came to action not one of you was prepared to put your signature to a letter to the Hospital Management Committee. And you know very well why! You were all terrified of that woman. Yes, terrified!'

Amid the murmur of outraged denial, Dr Maddox said:

'There was something intimidating about her. It may have been that formidable and self-conscious rectitude. You were as affected by it as anyone, Paul.'

'Possibly. But I did try to do something about her. I spoke to Lauder.'

'I spoke to him, too,' said Etherege quietly, 'and possibly with more effect. I made it clear that this Committee realized that we had no control over the administrative staff, but I said that Miss Bolam appeared to me, speaking as a psychiatrist and as chairman of the Medical Committee, to be temperamentally unsuitable for her job. I suggested that a transfer would be in her own interests. There could be no criticism of her efficiency and I made none. Lauder was non-committal, of course, but he knew perfectly well that I was entitled to make the point. And I think he took it.'

Dr Maddox said:

'Allowing for his natural caution, his suspicion of psychiatrists and the usual speed of his administrative decisions, I suppose we should have been rid of Miss Bolam within the next two years. Someone has certainly speeded things up.'

Suddenly Dr Ingram spoke. Her pink, rather stupid face flushed unbecomingly. She sat stiffly upright and her hands, clasped on the table in front of her, were shaking.

'I don't think you ought to say things like that. It . . . it isn't right. Miss Bolam is dead, brutally murdered. You sit here, all of you, and talk as if you didn't care! I know she wasn't very easy to get on with but she's dead, and I don't think this is the time to be unkind about her.'

Dr Maddox looked at Dr Ingram with interest and a kind of wonder as if she were faced by an exceptionally dull child who had somehow succeeded in making an intelligent remark. She said:

'I see that you subscribe to the superstition that one should never tell the truth about the dead. The origins of that atavistic belief have always interested me. We must have a talk about it sometime. I should like to hear your views.'

Dr Ingram, scarlet with embarrassment and close to tears, looked as if the proposed talk were a privilege she would be happy to forgo. Dr Etherege said:

'Unkind about her? I should be sorry to think that anyone here was being unkind. There are some things, surely, which don't need saying. There can't be a member of this Committee who isn't horrified at the senseless brutality of Miss Bolam's death and who wouldn't wish her back with us no matter what her defects as an administrator.'

The bathos was too blatant to be missed. As if conscious of their surprise and discomfiture, he looked up and said challengingly:

'Well, is there? Is there?'

'Of course not,' said Dr Steiner. He spoke soothingly, but the sharp little eyes slewed sideways to meet Baguley's glance. There was embarrassment in that look, but Baguley recognized also the smirk of malicious amusement. The medical director wasn't playing this too cleverly. He had allowed Albertine Maddox to get out of hand and his control over the Committee was less sure than formerly. The pathetic thing about it, thought Baguley, was that Etherege was sincere. He meant every word. He had – and so had they all, come to that – a genuine horror of violence. He was a compassionate man shocked and saddened by the thought of a defenceless woman brutally done to death. But his words sounded false. He was taking refuge in formality, deliberately trying to lower the emotional tone of the meeting to one of platitudinous convention. And he only succeeded in sounding insincere.

After Dr Ingram's outburst the meeting seemed to lose heart. Dr Etherege made only spasmodic attempts to control it and the conversation ranged in a tired, desultory way, from one subject to another but, always and inevitably, returned to the murder. There was a feeling that the Medical Committee should express some common view. Groping from theory to theory the meeting eventually came to accept Dr Steiner's proposition. The killer had obviously entered the clinic earlier in the day when the system of booking people in and out was not in force. He had secreted himself in the basement, selected his weapons at leisure, and called Miss Bolam down by noting the number of her extension from the card hung beside the telephone. He had made his way to the upper floors without being observed and left by one of the windows, managing to close it behind him before edging his way on to the fire-escape. That this procedure argued considerable luck, coupled with unusual and remarkable agility, was not over-emphasized. Under Dr Steiner's leadership the theory was elaborated. Miss Bolam's telephone call to the group secretary was dismissed as irrelevant. She had undoubtedly wished to complain about some trifling misdemeanour, real or imagined, and which was quite unconnected with her subsequent death. The suggestion that the killer had swarmed up the pulley in the lift shaft was generally discounted as somewhat fanciful although, as Dr Maddox pointed out, a man who could shut a heavy window while balancing on the outside sill, then swing himself some five feet through space to reach the fire-escape, would hardly find the lift shaft an insuperable problem.

Dr Baguley, wearying of his part in the fabrication of this mythical killer, half-closed his eyes and gazed from under lowered lids, at the bowl of roses. Their petals had been opening gently and almost visibly in the warmth of the room. Now the red, green and pink swam together in an amorphous pattern of colour which, as his gaze shifted, was reflected in the shining table. Suddenly he opened his eyes fully and saw Dr Etherege looking fixedly at him. There was concern in that sharp, analytic regard; Dr Baguley thought that there was also pity. The medical director said:

'Some of our members have had enough. So, I think, have I. If no one has any urgent business to bring forward I declare the meeting closed.'

Dr Baguley thought that it was not altogether by chance that he and the medical director found themselves alone in the room, the last to leave. As he tested the windows to check that they were locked, Dr Etherege said:

'Well, James, have you come to a decision yet about succeeding me as medical director?'

'It's more a question of deciding whether or not to apply for the job when it's advertised, surely?' said Baguley. He asked: 'What about Mason-Giles or McBain?'

'M.G. isn't interested. It's maximum sessions, of course, and he doesn't want to give up his teaching hospital connection. McBain is tied up with the new regional unit for adolescents.'

It was typical of the medical director's occasional insensitivity that he didn't try to soften the fact that he had tried others first. He's scraping the bottom of the barrel, thought Baguley.

'And Steiner?' he asked. 'He'll be applying, I imagine?'

The medical director smiled.

'Oh, I don't think the Regional Board will appoint Dr Steiner. This is a multi-discipline clinic. We must have someone who can hold the place together. And there may be very great changes. You know my views. If there is to be a closer integration of psychiatry with general medicine a place like this may have to die for the greater good. We ought to have access to beds. The Steen may find its natural home in a general hospital out-patient department. I don't say it's probable. But it's possible.'

So that was the way the Board was thinking? Dr Etherege had his ear well to the ground. A small out-patient unit with no registrars, no training function and no link with a general hospital might well become anachronistic in the eyes of the planners. Dr Baguley said:

'I don't mind where I see my patients as long as I get peace and quiet, a certain tolerance, and not too much of the hierarchical claptrap and starched linen. These proposed psychiatric units in general hospitals are all very well so long as the hospital appreciates what we're going to need in staff and space. I'm too tired to do battle.'

He looked at the medical director.

'Actually, I had more or less decided not to apply. I telephoned your room yesterday evening from the medical staffroom to ask if we could chat about it after the clinic.'

'Indeed? At what time?'

'At about six-twenty or six-twenty-five. There was no reply. Later, of course, we had other things to think about.'

The medical director said:

'I must have been in the library. I'm very glad I was if it means that you've had time to reconsider your decision. And I hope that you will reconsider it, James.'

He turned out the lights and they went downstairs together. Pausing at the foot, the medical director turned to Baguley and said:

'It was at about six-twenty that you telephoned? I find that very interesting, very interesting indeed.'

'Well, about then, I suppose.'

Dr Baguley realized with irritation and surprise, that it was he, not the medical director, who sounded guilty and embarrassed. He was seized by an intense desire to get out of the clinic, to escape from the blue, speculative gaze which was so adept at putting him at a disadvantage. But there was something else which must be said. At the door he forced himself to pause and face Dr Etherege. But despite his attempt at nonchalance his voice sounded forced, even belligerent:

'I'm wondering whether we ought to do something about Nurse Bolam.'

'In what way?' asked the medical director gently. Receiving no reply, he went on: 'All the staff know that they can ask to see me at any time. But I'm not inviting confidences. This is a murder investigation, James, and it's out of my hands. Out of my hands completely. I think you would be wise to take the same attitude. Good night.'

CHAPTER SIX

Early Monday morning, the anniversary of his wife's death, Dalgliesh called in at a small Catholic church behind the Strand to light a candle. His wife had been a Catholic. He had not shared her religion and she had died before he could begin to understand what it meant to her or what importance this fundamental difference between them might have for their marriage. He had lit the first candle on the day she had died out of the need to formalize an intolerable grief and, perhaps, with a childish hope of somehow comforting her spirit. This was the fourteenth candle. He thought of this most private action in his detached and secretive life, not as superstition or piety, but as a habit which he could not now break even if he wished. He dreamed of his wife only seldom, but then with absolute clarity; waking he could no longer accurately recall her face. He pushed his coin through the slot and held his candle's wick to the dying flame of a moist stump. It caught immediately and the flame grew bright and clear. It had always been important to him that the wick should catch at once. He gazed through the flame for a moment feeling nothing, not even anger. Then he turned away.

The church was nearly empty, but it held for him an atmosphere of intense and silent activity which he sensed but could not share. As he walked to the door he recognized a woman, red-coated and with a dark green scarf over her head, who was pausing to dip her fingers in the water stoup. It was Fredrica Saxon, senior psychologist of the Steen Clinic. They reached the outer door together and he forced it open for her against the sudden swirl of an autumn wind. She smiled at him, friendly and unembarrassed.

'Hullo. I haven't seen you here before.'

'I only come once a year,' Dalgliesh replied. He gave no explanation and she asked no questions. Instead she said:

'I wanted to see you. There's something I think you ought to know. Are you off duty? If you aren't could you be unorthodox and talk to a suspect in a coffee bar? I'd rather not come to your office and it isn't easy to ask for an interview at the clinic. I need some coffee anyway. I'm cold.'

'There used to be a place round the corner,' said Dalgliesh. 'The coffee is tolerable and it's pretty quiet.'

The coffee bar had changed in a year. Dalgliesh remembered it as a clean but dull café with a row of deal tables covered with plastic cloths and a long service counter embellished with a tea urn and layers of substantial sandwiches under glass domes. It had risen in the world. The walls had been panelled with imitation old oak against which hung a formidable assortment of rapiers, ancient pistols and cutlasses of uncertain authenticity. The waitresses looked like *avant-garde* débutantes earning their pin money and the lighting was so discreet as to be positively sinister. Miss Saxon led the way to a table in the far corner.

'Just coffee?' asked Dalgliesh.

'Just coffee, please.'

She waited until the order had been given and then said:

'It's about Dr Baguley.'

'I thought it might be.'

'You were bound to hear something, I suppose. I'd rather tell you about it now than wait to be asked and I'd rather you heard it from me than from Amy Shorthouse.'

She spoke without rancour or embarrassment. Dalgliesh replied:

'I haven't asked about it because it doesn't seem relevant, but if you like to tell me it may be helpful.'

'I don't want you to get a wrong idea about it that's all. It would be so easy for you to imagine that we had a grudge against Miss Bolam. We didn't, you know. At one time we even felt grateful to her.'

Dalgliesh had no need to ask who she meant by that 'we'.

The waitress, uninterested, came with their coffee, pale foam served in small transparent cups. Miss Saxon slipped her coat from her shoulders and unknotted her head scarf. Both of them wrapped their fingers round the hot cups. She heaped the sugar into her coffee then pushed the plastic bowl across the table to

Dalgliesh. There was no tension about her, no awkwardness. She had the directness of a schoolchild drinking coffee with a friend. He found her curiously peaceful to be with, perhaps because he did not find her physically attractive. But he liked her. It was difficult to believe that this was only their second meeting and that the matter that had brought them together was murder. She skimmed the froth from her coffee and said, without looking up:

'James Baguley and I fell in love nearly three years ago. There wasn't any great moral struggle about it. We didn't invite love but we certainly didn't fight against it. After all, you don't voluntarily give up happiness unless you're a masochist or a saint, and we aren't either. I knew that James had a neurotic wife in the way one does get to know these things, but he didn't talk much about her. We both accepted that she needed him and that a divorce was out of the question. We convinced ourselves that we weren't doing her any harm and that she need never know. James used to say that loving me made his marriage happier for both of them. Of course, it is easier to be kind and patient when one is happy, so he may have been right. I don't know. It's a rationalization that thousands of lovers must use.

'We couldn't see each other very often, but I had my flat and we usually managed to have two evenings a week together. Once Helen – that's his wife – went to stay with her sister and we had a whole night together. We had to be careful at the clinic, of course, but we don't really see very much of each other there.'

'How did Miss Bolam find out about it?' asked Dalgliesh.

'It was silly, really. We were at the theatre seeing Anouilh and she was sitting alone in the row behind. Who would suppose that Bolam would want to see Anouilh, anyway? I suppose she was sent a free ticket. It was our second anniversary and we held hands all through the play. We may have been a little drunk. Afterwards we left the theatre still hand in hand. Anyone from the clinic, anyone we knew, could have seen us. We were getting careless and someone was bound to see us sooner or later. It was just chance that it happened to be Bolam. Other people would probably have minded their own business.'

'Whereas she told Mrs Baguley? That seems an unusually officious and cruel thing to have done.'

'It wasn't, really. Bolam wouldn't see it that way. She was one of those rare and fortunate people who never for one moment doubt that they know the difference between right and wrong. She wasn't imaginative so she couldn't enter into other people's feelings. If she were a wife whose husband was unfaithful I'm sure that she would want to be told about it. Nothing would be worse than not knowing. She had the kind of strength that relishes a struggle. I expect she thought it was her duty to tell. Anyway, Helen came to the Steen to see her husband unexpectedly one Wednesday afternoon and Miss Bolam invited her into the A.O.'s office and told her. I often wonder what exactly she said. I imagine that she said we were "carrying on". She could make practically anything sound vulgar.'

'She was taking a risk, wasn't she?' said Dalgliesh. 'She had very little evidence, certainly no proof.'

Miss Saxon laughed.

'You're talking like a policeman. She had proof enough. Even Bolam could recognize love when she saw it. Besides, we were enjoying ourselves together without a licence and that was infidelity enough.'

The words were bitter but she did not sound resentful or sarcastic. She was sipping her coffee with evident satisfaction. Dalgliesh thought that she might have been talking about one of the clinic patients, discussing with detached and mild professional interest the vagaries of human nature. Yet he did not believe that she loved easily or that her emotions were superficial. He asked what Mrs Baguley's reaction had been.

'That's the extraordinary thing, or at least it seemed so at the time. She took it wonderfully well. Looking back I wonder whether we weren't all three mad, living in some kind of imaginary world that two minutes' rational thought would have shown us couldn't exist. Helen lives her life in a series of attitudes and the one she decided to adopt was the pose of the brave, understanding wife. She insisted on a divorce. It was going to be one of those friendly divorces. That kind is only possible, I imagine, when people have ceased to care for each other, perhaps never have cared or been capable of caring. But that was the kind we were going to have. There was a great deal of discussion. Everyone's happiness was to be safeguarded. Helen was going to open a dress shop – it's a thing she's talked about for years. We all three got interested in it and looked for suitable premises. It was pathetic really. We actually fooled ourselves that it was all going to come right. That's why I said that James and I felt grateful to Enid Bolam. People at the clinic got to know that there was to be a divorce and that Helen would name me – it was all part of the policy of frankness and honesty – but very little was said to us. Bolam never mentioned the divorce to anyone. She wasn't a gossip and she wasn't malicious, either. Somehow her part in it got about in the way these things do. I think Helen may have told someone, but Miss Bolam and I never talked about it ever.

'Then the inevitable happened. Helen began to crack. James had left her with the Surrey house and was living with me in the flat. He had to see her fairly often. He didn't say very much at first, but I knew what was happening. She was ill, of course, and we both knew it. She had played out the role of the patient, uncomplaining wife and, according to the novels and the films, her husband should, by now, have been returning to her. And James wasn't. He kept most of it from me, but I had some idea what it was doing to him, the scenes, the tears, the entreaties, the threats of suicide. One minute she was going through with the divorce, the next she would never give him his freedom. She couldn't, of course. I see that now. It wasn't hers to give. It's degrading to talk about a husband as if he's a dog chained up in the back yard. All the time that this was happening I was realizing more and more that I couldn't go on. Something that had been a slow process over the years came to a head. There's no point in talking about it or trying to explain. It isn't relevant to your inquiry, is it? Nine months ago I started to receive instruction with the hope of being received into the Catholic Church. When that happened Helen withdrew her petition and James went back to her. I think he no longer cared what happened to him or where he went. But you can see, can't you, that he had no reason to hate Bolam. I was the enemy.'

Dalgliesh thought that there could have been very little struggle. Her rosy, healthy face with the broad and slightly tiptilted nose, the wide cheerful mouth, was ill-suited to tragedy. He recalled how Dr Baguley had looked, seen in the light of Miss Bolam's desk lamp. It was stupid and presumptuous to try to assess suffering by the lines on a face or the look in the eyes. Miss Saxon's mind was probably as tough and resilient as her body. It did not mean that she felt less because she could withstand more. But he felt profoundly sorry for Baguley, rejected by his mistress at the moment of the greatest trial in favour of a private happiness which he could neither share nor understand. Probably no one could fully know the magnitude of that betrayal. Dalgliesh did not pretend to understand Miss Saxon. It wasn't hard to imagine what some people at the clinic would make of it. The facile explanations came easily to mind. But he could not believe that Fredrica Saxon had taken refuge in religion from her own sexuality or had ever refused to face reality.

He thought of some of the things she had said about Enid Bolam.

'Who would suppose that Bolam would want to see Anouilh? I suppose she was sent a free ticket . . . Even Bolam could recognize love when she saw it . . . She could make practically anything sound vulgar.' People did not automatically become kind because they had become religious. Yet there had been no real malice in her words. She spoke what she thought and would be equally detached about her own motives. She was probably the best judge of character in the clinic. Suddenly, and in defiance of orthodoxy, Dalgliesh asked:

'Who do you think killed her, Miss Saxon?'

'Judging by character and the nature of the crime and taking no account of mysterious telephone calls from the basement, creaking lifts, and apparent alibis?'

'Judging by character and the nature of the crime.'

She said without hesitation and with no apparent reluctance:

'I'd have said it was Peter Nagle.'

Dalgliesh felt a stab of disappointment. It was irrational to have thought that she might actually know.

'Why Nagle?' he asked.

'Partly because I think this was a masculine crime. The stabbing is significant. I can't see a woman killing in just that way. Faced with an unconscious victim I think a woman would strangle. Then there's the chisel. To use it with such expertise suggests an identification of the weapon with the killer. Why use it otherwise? He could have struck her again and again with the fetish.'

'Messy, noisy and less sure,' said Dalgliesh.

'But the chisel was only sure in the hands of a man who had confidence in his ability to use it, someone who is literally "good with his hands". I can't see Dr Steiner killing in that way, for instance. He couldn't even knock in a nail without breaking the hammer.'

Dalgliesh was inclined to agree that Dr Steiner was innocent. His clumsiness with tools had been mentioned by more than one member of the clinic staff. Admittedly he had lied in denying that he knew where the chisel was kept, but Dalgliesh judged that he had acted from fear rather than guilt. And his shame-faced confession of falling asleep while awaiting Mr Burge had the ring of truth.

Dalgliesh said:

'The identification of the chisel with Nagle is so certain that I think we were meant to suspect him. And you do?'

'Oh, no! I know he couldn't have done it. I only answered the question as you posed it. I was judging by character and the nature of the crime.'

They had finished their coffee now and Dalgliesh thought that she would want to go. But she seemed in no hurry. After a moment's pause, she said:

'I have one confession to make; on another person's behalf actually. It's Cully. Nothing important but something you ought to know and I promised I'd tell you about it. Poor old Cully is scared out of his wits and they aren't plentiful at the best of times.'

'I knew he was lying about something,' said Dalgliesh. 'He saw someone passing down the hall, I suppose.'

'Oh, no! Nothing as useful as that. It's about the missing rubber apron from the art therapy department. I gather you thought that the murderer might have worn it. Well, Cully borrowed it from the department last Monday to wear while he emulsion-painted his kitchen. You know what a mess paint makes.

He didn't ask Miss Bolam if he could take it because he knew what the answer would be and he couldn't ask Mrs Baumgarten because she's away sick. He meant to bring it back on Friday but when Sister was checking the inventory with your sergeant and they asked him if he'd seen it he lost his head and said "no". He's not very bright and he was terrified that you'd suspect him of the murder if he owned up.'

Dalgliesh asked her when Cully had told her of this.

'I knew he had the apron because it just happened that I saw him take it. I guessed that he'd be in a state about it so I went round to see him yesterday morning. His stomach gets upset when he worries and I thought someone had better keep an eye on him.'

'Where is the apron now?' asked Dalgliesh.

Miss Saxon laughed.

'Disposed about London in half a dozen litter baskets if they haven't been emptied. Poor old Cully daren't put it in his own dustbin in case it was searched by the police and couldn't burn it because he lives in a council flat with electric heating and no stove. So he waited until his wife was in bed, then sat up until eleven cutting it into pieces with the kitchen scissors. He put the pieces into a number of paper bags, shoved the bags into a hold-all, and took a 36 bus up the Harrow Road until he was well away from his home ground. Then he slipped one of the bags into each litter bin he came across and dropped the metal buttons down the gutter grating. It was a formidable undertaking and the poor fellow could hardly creep home what with fear, tiredness – he'd lost the last bus – and the belly-ache. He wasn't in too good a shape when I called next morning, but I did manage to convince him that it wasn't a matter of life and death – particularly death. I told him I'd let you know about it.'

'Thank you,' said Dalgliesh gravely. 'You haven't any other confessions to pass on, I suppose? Or have you a conscientious objection to handing over an unfortunate psychopath to justice?'

She laughed, pulling on her coat and tying the scarf over her dark, springing hair.

'Oh, no! If I knew who did it I'd tell you. I don't like murder and I'm quite law-abiding, really. But I didn't know we were talking about justice. That's your word. Like Portia, I feel that in the course of justice none of us would see salvation. Please, I would much rather pay for my own coffee.'

She doesn't want to feel I bought information from her, thought Dalgliesh, not even a shilling's worth. He resisted the temptation to say that the coffee could come from expenses, wondering a little at this impulse to sarcasm which she aroused in him. He liked her, but there was something about her certainty, her self-sufficiency, which he found irritating. Perhaps what he felt was envy.

As they left the café he asked her whether she was on her way to the Steen.

'Not today. I don't have a session on Monday mornings. But I shall be there tomorrow.'

She thanked him formally for the coffee and they parted. He turned eastwards towards the Steen and she disappeared in the direction of the Strand. As he watched her slim, dark figure swinging out of sight he pictured Cully creeping through the night with his pathetic bundle, half petrified with fright. He was not surprised that the old porter had confided so fully in Fredrica Saxon; in Cully's place, he would probably have done the same. She had, thought Dalgliesh, given him a great deal of interesting information. But what she hadn't been able to give him was an alibi for Dr Baguley or for herself.

Mrs Bostock, shorthand-notebook at the ready, sat beside Dr Etherege's chair, her elegant legs crossed at the knees and her flamingo head lifted to receive, with becoming gravity, the medical director's instructions.

'Superintendent Dalgliesh has telephoned to say that he will be here shortly. He wants to see certain members of the staff again and has asked for an interview with me before lunch.'

'I don't see how you can fit him in before lunch, Doctor,' said Mrs Bostock repressively. 'There's the Professional Staff Committee at two-thirty and you haven't had time to look at the agenda. Dr Talmage from the States is booked for twelve-thirty and I was hoping for an hour's dictation from 11 a.m.'

'That will have to wait. The superintendent will be taking up a great deal of your own time, I'm afraid. He has some questions about the working of the clinic.'

'I'm afraid I don't quite understand, Doctor. Do you mean he's interested in the general administrative arrangements?' Mrs Bostock's tone was a nice blend of surprise and disapproval.

'Apparently so,' replied Dr Etherege. 'He mentioned the appointments diary, the diagnostic index, the arrangements for registering incoming and outgoing post, and the medical record system. You had better deal with him personally. If I want to dictate I'll send for Miss Priddy.'

'I'll do what I can to help, naturally,' said Mrs Bostock. 'It's unfortunate that he should have picked one of our busiest mornings. It would be simpler to arrange a programme for him if I knew what he had in mind.'

'We should all like to know that, I imagine,' replied the medical director. 'I should just answer his questions as fully as you can. And please get Cully to ring me as soon as he wants to come up.'

'Yes, Doctor,' said Mrs Bostock, recognizing defeat. And took her leave.

Downstairs, in the E.C.T. room, Dr Baguley twitched himself into his white coat, helped by Nurse Bolam.

'Mrs King will be here for her LSD treatment on Wednesday as usual. I think it will be best if we give it in one of the P.S.W. rooms on the third floor. Miss Kettle isn't in on Wednesday evenings, is she? Have a word with her. Alternatively we could use Mrs Kallinski's room or one of the small interviewing rooms at the back.'

Nurse Bolam said:

'It won't be so convenient for you, Doctor. It means coming up two flights when I phone.'

'That isn't going to kill me. I may look in my dotage but I still have the use of my legs.'

'There's the question of a bed, Doctor. I suppose we could put up one of the recovery stretchers from the E.C.T. clinic.'

'Get Nagle to see to it. I don't want you alone in that basement.'

'I'm not in the least frightened, really, Dr Baguley.'

Dr Baguley lost his temper.

'For God's sake, use your brain, Nurse. Of course you're frightened! There's a murderer loose somewhere in this clinic and no one – except one person – is going to be happy about staying alone for any length of time in the basement. If you really aren't frightened then have the good sense to conceal the fact, especially from the police. Where's Sister? In the general office?'

He picked up the receiver and dialled jerkily.

'Sister? Baguley here. I've just told Nurse Bolam that I don't feel happy about using the basement room for LSD this week.'

Sister Ambrose's voice came back clearly:

'Just as you like, Doctor, of course. But if the basement is more convenient and we could get a relief nurse from one of the general hospitals in the group for the E.C.T. clinic, I should be quite happy to stay downstairs with Nurse Bolam. We could special Mrs King together.'

Dr Baguley said shortly:

'I want you in the E.C.T. clinic as usual, Sister, and the LSD patient will go upstairs. I hope that's finally understood.'

In the medical director's room two hours later, Dalgliesh placed three black metal boxes on Dr Etherege's desk. The boxes, which had small round holes punched in each of the shorter sides, were packed with buff-coloured cards. It was the clinic diagnostic index. Dalgliesh said:

'Mrs Bostock has explained this to me. If I've understood her correctly, each of these cards represents a patient. The information on the case record is coded and the patient's code punched on the card. The cards are punched with even rows of small holes and the space between each hole is numbered. By punching any number with the hand machine I cut out the card between the two adjacent holes to form an oblong slit. If this metal rod is then inserted through say, hole number 20 on the outside of the box, and pushed right through the cards, and the box is rotated, any card which has been punched through that number will stand out. It is, in fact, one of the simplest of the many punch-card systems on the market.'

'Yes. We use it principally as a diagnostic index and for

research.' If the medical director was surprised at Dalgliesh's interest he made no sign. The superintendent went on:

'Mrs Bostock tells me that you don't code from the case record until the patient has completed treatment and that the system was started in 1952. That means that patients at present attending won't yet have a card – unless, of course, they were treated here earlier – and that patients who completed treatments before 1952 aren't included.'

'Yes. We should like to include the earlier cases, but it's a question of staff time. The coding and punching are time-consuming and it's the kind of job that gets put on one side. At present we're coding the February 1962 discharges, so we're quite a bit behind.'

'But once the patient's card is punched you can select any diagnosis or category of patient at will?'

'Yes, indeed.' The medical director gave his slow sweet smile. 'I won't say that we can pick out immediately all the indigenous depressives with blue-eyed grandmothers who were born in wedlock because we haven't coded information about grandparents. But anything coded can be extracted without trouble.'

Dalgliesh laid a slim manilla file on the desk.

'Mrs Bostock has lent me the coding instructions. I see that you code sex, age, marital status, address by local authority area, diagnosis, consultant who treated the patient, dates of first and subsequent attendances and a considerable amount of detail about symptoms, treatment and progress. You also code social class. I find that interesting.'

'It's unusual, certainly,' replied Dr Etherege. 'Chiefly, I suppose, because it can be a purely subjective assessment. But we wanted it because it's sometimes useful in research. As you see we use the Registrar-General's classes. They're accurate enough for our purposes.'

Dalgliesh ran the thin metal rod through his fingers.

'So I could select, for example, the cards of patients in class one who were treated eight to ten years ago, were married with a family, and were suffering from, say, sexual aberration, kleptomania, or any other socially unacceptable personality disorder.'

'You could,' admitted the medical director quietly. 'But I can't see why you should want to.'

'Blackmail, Doctor. It occurs to me that we have here a neatly contrived apparatus for the pre-selection of a victim. You push through the rod and out pops your card. The card bears a number on the top right-hand corner. And down in the basement record-room the medical record is filed and waiting.'

The medical director said:

'This is nothing but guesswork. There isn't a shred of evidence.'

'There's no proof, certainly, but it's a reasonable possibility. Consider the facts. On Wednesday afternoon Miss Bolam saw the group secretary after the House Committee meeting and told him all was well at the clinic. At twelve-fifteen on Friday morning she telephoned to ask for an urgent visit because "something is going on here that he ought to know about". It was something serious and continuing and something that started before her time here, that is more than three years ago.'

'Whatever it was we've no evidence that it was the reason for her death.'

'No.'

'In fact, if the murderer wanted to prevent Miss Bolam seeing Lauder he left it rather late. There was nothing to stop the group secretary turning up here any time after one o'clock.'

Dalgliesh said:

'She was told over the telephone that he couldn't arrive until after the J.C.C. meeting that evening. That leads us to ask who could have overheard the telephone call. Cully was officially on the board, but he was unwell most of the day and, from time to time, other members of the staff took over, sometimes only for a few minutes. Nagle, Mrs Bostock, Miss Priddy and even Mrs Shorthouse, all say that they helped on the board. Nagle thinks he took over for a short time at midday before he went out for his lunchtime beer, but says that he can't be sure. Nor can Cully. No one admits to having put through this particular call.'

'They might not know if they had,' replied Dr Etherege. 'We're insistent that the operator doesn't listen in to calls. That, after all, is important in our work. Miss Bolam may have merely asked for group offices. She must put through calls fairly often to the finance and supplies departments as well as the group secretary. The operator couldn't know there was anything special about this call. She might even have asked for an outside line and put through the call herself. That is possible, of course, with the P.A.B.X. system.'

'But it could still be overheard by the person on the board.'

'If he plugged in I suppose it could.'

Dalgliesh said: 'Miss Bolam told Cully late in the afternoon that she was expecting Mr Lauder and she may have mentioned the visit to other people. We don't know. No one will admit to having been told except Cully. In the circumstances, that isn't perhaps surprising. We're not going to get much further with it at present. What I must do now is to find out what Miss Bolam wanted to tell Mr Lauder. One of the first possibilities to be considered in a place like this must be blackmail. God knows that's continuing and it's serious enough.'

The medical director did not speak for a moment. Dalgliesh wondered whether he was contemplating a further remonstrance, selecting appropriate words to express concern or disbelief. Then he said quietly:

'Of course it's serious. There's no point in wasting time discussing just how serious. Obviously, having thought up this theory, you have to carry through your investigation. Any other course of action would be most unfair to the members of my staff. What do you want me to do?'

'To help me select a victim. Later, perhaps, to make some telephone calls.'

'You appreciate, Superintendent, that the case records are confidential?'

'I'm not asking to see a single case record. But if I did I don't think either you or the patient need worry. Shall we get started? We can take out our class 1 patients. Perhaps you would call out the codes for me.'

A considerable number of the Steen patients were in class 1. 'Upper-class neuroses catered for only', thought Dalgliesh. He surveyed the field for a moment and then said:

'If I were the blackmailer would I choose a man or a woman? It would depend on my own sex probably. A woman might pick on a woman. But, if it's a question of a regular income a man is probably a better bet. Let's take out the males next. I imagine our victim will live out of London. It would be risky to select an ex-patient who could too easily succumb to the temptation to pop into the clinic and let you know what was going on. I think I'd select my victim from a small town or village.'

The medical director said:

'We only coded the county if it were an out-London address. London patients are coded by borough. Our best plan will be to take out all the London addresses and see what's left.'

This was done. The number of cards still in the survey was now only a few dozen. Most of the Steen patients, as might be expected, came from the county of London. Dalgliesh said:

'Married or single? It's difficult to decide whether one or the other would be most vulnerable. Let's leave it open and start on the diagnosis. This is where I need your help particularly, Doctor. I realize this is highly confidential information. I suggest that you call out the codes for the diagnoses or symptoms which might interest a blackmailer. I don't want details.'

Again the medical director paused. Dalgliesh waited patiently, metal rod in hand, while the doctor sat in silence, the code book open before him. He seemed not to be seeing it. After a minute he roused himself and focused his eyes on the page. He said quietly:

'Try codes 23, 68, 69 and 71.'

There were now only eleven cards remaining. Each of them bore a case record number on the top right-hand margin. Dalgliesh made a note of the numbers, and said:

'This is as far as we can go with the diagnostic index. We must now do what I think our blackmailer did, have a look at the case records, and learn more of our prospective victims. Shall we go down to the basement?'

The medical director got up without a word. As they went down the stairs they passed Miss Kettle on her way up. She nodded to the medical director and gave Dalgliesh a brief, puzzled glance as if wondering whether he were someone she had met and ought to recognize. In the hall Dr Baguley was talking with Sister Ambrose. They broke off and turned to watch with grave, unsmiling faces as Dr Etherege and Dalgliesh made their way to the basement stairs. At the other end of the hall the grey outline of Cully's head could be seen through the glass of the reception kiosk. The head did not turn and Dalgliesh guessed that Cully, absorbed in his contemplation of the front door, had not heard them.

The record-room was locked, but no longer sealed. In the porters' rest-room Nagle was putting on his coat, evidently on his way out to an early lunch. He made no sign as the medical director took the record-room key from its hook, but the flash of interest in his mild, mud-brown eyes was not lost on Dalgliesh. They had been well observed. By early afternoon everyone in the clinic would know that he had examined the diagnostic index with the medical director and then visited the record-room. To one person that information would be of crucial interest. What Dalgliesh hoped was that the murderer would become frightened and desperate; what he feared was that he would become more dangerous.

Dr Etherege switched on the light in the record-room and the fluorescent tubes flickered, yellowed and blazed into whiteness. The room stood revealed. Dalgliesh smelt again its characteristic smell, compounded of mustiness, old paper and the tang of hot metal. He watched without betraying any emotion while the medical director locked the door on the inside and slipped the key in his pocket.

There was no sign now that the room had been the scene of murder. The torn records had been repaired and replaced on the shelves, the chair and table placed upright in their usual position.

The records were tied together with string in bundles of ten. Some of the files had been stored for so long that they seemed to adhere to each other. The string bit into the bulging manilla covers; across their tops was a thin patina of dust. Dalgliesh said:

'It should be possible to tell which of these bundles have been untied since the records were weeded out and brought down for storage. Some of them look as if they haven't been touched for years. I realize that a bundle may have been untied to extract a record for a perfectly innocent purpose, but we may as well make a start with files from those bundles which have obviously been untied within the last year or so. The first two numbers are in the eight thousand range. These seem to be on the top shelf. Have we a ladder?'

The medical director disappeared behind the first row of shelves and reappeared with a small step-ladder which he manoeuvred with great difficulty into the narrow aisle. Looking up at Dalgliesh as the detective mounted, he said:

'Tell me, Superintendent. Does this touching confidence mean that you have eliminated me from your list of suspects? If it does I should like to know by what process of deduction you came to that conclusion. I can't flatter myself that you believe me incapable of murder. No detective would accept that, surely, of any man.'

'And no psychiatrist possibly,' said Dalgliesh. 'I don't ask myself whether a man is capable of murder, but whether he is capable of this particular murder. I don't think you're a petty blackmailer. I can't see how you could have known about Lauder's proposed visit. I doubt whether you've either the strength or skill to kill in that way. Lastly, I think you're probably the one person here whom Miss Bolam wouldn't have kept waiting. Even if I'm wrong you can hardly refuse to co-operate, can you?'

He was deliberately curt. The bright blue eyes were still gazing into his, inviting a confidence which he did not want to give but found it difficult to resist. The medical director went on:

'I have only met three murderers. Two of them are buried in quicklime. One of the two hardly knew what he was doing and the other couldn't have stopped himself. Are you satisfied, Superintendent, with that solution?'

Dalgliesh replied:

'No man in his senses would be. But I don't see how that affects what I'm trying to do now; catch this murderer before he – or she – kills again.'

The medical director said no more. Together they found the eleven case records they sought and took them up to Dr Etherege's room. If Dalgliesh had expected the medical director to make difficulties over the next stage of the investigation he was agreeably surprised. The hint that this killer might not stop at one victim had struck home. When Dalgliesh explained what he wanted the medical director did not protest. Dalgliesh said:

'I'm not asking for the names of these patients. I'm not interested in what was wrong with them. All I want you to do is to telephone each of them and ask tactfully whether they rang the clinic recently, probably on Friday morning. You could explain that someone made a call which it's important to trace. If one of these patients did ring I want the name and address. Not the diagnosis. Just the name and address.'

'I must ask the patient's consent before I give that information.'

'If you must,' said Dalgliesh. 'I leave that to you. All I ask is to get that information.'

The medical director's stipulation was a formality and both of them knew it. The eleven case records were on the desk and nothing but force could keep the addresses from Dalgliesh if he wanted them. He sat at some distance from Dr Etherege in one of the large, leather-covered chairs, and prepared to watch, with professional interest, his unusual collaborator at work. The medical director picked up his receiver and asked for an outside line. The patients' telephone numbers had been noted on the case records and the first two tries at once reduced the eleven possibles to nine. In each case the patient had changed his address since his attendance. Dr Etherege apologized for disturbing the new subscribers to the numbers concerned and dialled for the third time. The third number answered and the medical director asked if he might speak to Mr Caldecote. There was a prolonged crackling from the other end and Dr Etherege made the appropriate response.

'No, he hadn't heard. How very sad. Really? No, it was nothing important. Just an old acquaintance who would be driving through Wiltshire and hoped to meet Mr Caldecote again. No, he wouldn't speak to Mrs Caldecote. He didn't want to distress her.'

'Dead?' asked Dalgliesh, as the receiver was replaced.

'Yes. Three years ago, apparently. Cancer, poor fellow. I must note that on his record.'

He did so while Dalgliesh waited.

The next number was difficult to get and there was much talk with the exchange. When at last the number was rung there was no reply.

'We seem to be having no success, Superintendent. It was a clever theory of yours, but, it appears, more ingenious than true.'

'There are still seven more patients to try,' said Dalgliesh quietly. The medical director murmured something about a Dr Talmage whom he was expecting, but referred to the next file and dialled again. This time the patient was at home and, apparently, not in the least surprised to hear from the medical director of the Steen. He poured out a lengthy account of his present psychological condition to which Dr Etherege listened with patient sympathy and made appropriate replies. Dalgliesh was interested and a little amused at the skill with which the call was conducted. But the patient had not recently telephoned the clinic. The medical director put down the receiver and spent some time noting what the patient had told him on the case record.

'One of our successes, apparently. He wasn't at all surprised that I telephoned. It's rather touching the way patients take it for granted that their doctors are immensely concerned for their welfare and are thinking of them personally at all times of the day and night. But he didn't phone. He wasn't lying, I assure you. This is very time-consuming, Superintendent, but I suppose we must go on.'

'Yes, please. I'm sorry, but we must go on.'

But the next call brought success. At first it sounded like another failure. From the conversation Dalgliesh gathered that the patient had recently been taken to hospital and that it was his wife who had answered. Then he saw the medical director's face change, and heard him say:

'You did? We knew that someone had telephoned and were trying to trace the call. I expect you've heard about the very dreadful tragedy that we've had here recently. Yes, it is in connection with that.' He waited while the voice spoke at some length from the other end. Then he put down the receiver and wrote briefly on his desk jotting pad. Dalgliesh did not speak. The medical director looked up at him with an expression half puzzled, half surprised.

'That was the wife of a Colonel Fenton of Sprigg's Green in Kent. She telephoned Miss Bolam about a very serious matter at about midday last Friday. She didn't want to talk to you on the phone about it and I thought it better not to press her. But she'd like to see you as soon as possible. I've written down the address.'

'Thank you, Doctor,' said Dalgliesh, and took the proffered paper. He showed neither surprise nor relief, but his heart was singing. The medical director shook his head as if the whole thing were beyond his understanding. He said:

'She sounds rather a formidable old lady and very formal. She said that she would be very glad if you would take afternoon tea with her.'

Just after four o'clock Dalgliesh drove slowly into Sprigg's Green. It revealed itself as an undistinguished village lying between the Maidstone and Canterbury roads. He could not remember having passed through it before. There were few people about. The village, thought Dalgliesh, was too far from London to tempt the commuter and had no period charm to attract retired couples or artists and writers in search of country peace with a country cost of living. Most of the cottages were obviously lived in by farm workers, their front gardens clumped with cabbages and brussels sprouts, straggly and stem-scarred from recent pickings, their windows shut close against the treachery of an English autumn. Dalgliesh passed the church, its short flint-and-stone tower and clear glass windows only half-visible behind the surrounding chestnut trees. The churchyard was untidy but not offensively so. The grass had been mown between the graves and some attempt made to weed the gravel paths. Separated from the churchyard by a tall laurel hedge stood the vicarage, a sombre Victorian house built to accommodate a Victorian-size family and its appendages. Next came the green itself, a small square of grass bounded by a row of weather-boarded cottages and faced by a more than usually hideous modern pub and petrol station. Outside the 'King's Head' was a concrete bus shelter where a group of women waited dispiritedly. They gave Dalgliesh a brief and uninterested glance as he passed. In spring, no doubt, the surrounding cherry orchards would lend their charm even to Sprigg's Green. Now, however, there was a chill dampness in the air, the fields looked perpetually sodden, a slow mournful procession of cows being driven to the evening milking churned the road verges to mud. Dalgliesh slowed to a walking pace to pass them, keeping his watch for Sprigg's Acre. He did not want to ask the way.

He was not long in finding it. The house lay a little back from the road and was sheltered from it by a six-foot beech hedge which shone golden in the fading light. There appeared to be no drive and Dalgliesh edged his Cooper Bristol carefully on to the grass verge before letting himself in through the white gates of the garden. The house lay before him, rambling, low built and thatched, with an air of comfort and simplicity. As he turned from latching the gate behind him a woman turned the corner of the house and came down the path to meet him. She was very small. Somehow this surprised Dalgliesh. He had formed a mental picture of a stout, well-corseted colonel's wife condescending to see him, but at her own time and place. The reality was less intimidating and more interesting. There was something gallant and a little pathetic in the way she came down the path towards him. She was wearing a thick skirt and a tweed jacket and was hatless, her thick white hair lifting with the evening breeze. She wore gardening gloves, incongruously large with vast gauntlets which made the trowel she carried look like a child's toy. As they met she pulled off the right glove and held out her hand to him, looking up at him with anxious eyes which lightened, almost imperceptibly, with relief. But when she spoke her voice was unexpectedly firm.

'Good afternoon. You must be Superintendent Dalgliesh. My name is Louise Fenton. Did you come by car? I thought I heard one.'

Dalgliesh explained where he had left it and said that he hoped that it would not be in anyone's way.

'Oh, no! Not at all. Such an unpleasant way to travel. You could have come by train quite easily to Marden and I would have sent the trap for you. We haven't a car. We both dislike them very much. I'm sorry you had to sit in one all the way from London.'

'It was the fastest way,' said Dalgliesh, wondering if he should apologize for living in the twentieth century. 'And I wanted to see you as soon as possible.'

He was careful to keep the urgency from his voice, but he could see the sudden tensing of her shoulders.

'Yes. Yes, of course. Would you like to see the garden before we go in? The light is fading but we might just have time.'

An interest in the garden was apparently expected and Dalgliesh acquiesced. A light east wind, rising as the day died,
whipped uncomfortably around his neck and ankles. But he
never hurried an interview. This one promised to be difficult for
Mrs Fenton and she was entitled to take her time. He wondered
at his own impatience even as he concealed it. For the last two
days he had been irked by a foreboding of tragedy and failure
which was the more disturbing because it was irrational. The
case was young yet. His intelligence told him that he was making
progress. Even at this moment he was within grasp of motive,
and motive, he knew, was crucial to this case. He hadn't failed
yet in his career at the Yard and this case, with its limited
number of suspects and careful contriving, was an unlikely candidate for a first failure. Yet he remained worried, vexed by this
unreasonable fear that time was running out. Perhaps it was the
autumn. Perhaps he was tired. He turned up his coat collar and
prepared himself to look interested and appreciative.

They passed together through a wrought-iron gate at the side
of the house and entered the main garden. Mrs Fenton was
saying:

'I love the garden dearly, but I'm not much good at it. Things
don't grow for me. My husband has the green fingers. He's in
Maidstone Hospital at present having an operation for hernia.
It's all been very successful I'm happy to say. Do you garden,
Superintendent?'

Dalgliesh explained that he lived in a flat high above the
Thames in the City and had recently sold his Essex cottage.

'I really know very little about gardening,' he said.

'Then you will enjoy looking at ours,' replied Mrs Fenton, with
gentle if illogical persistence.

There was, indeed, plenty to see even in the fading light of an
autumn day. The colonel had given his imagination full play,
compensating perhaps for the enforced regimentation of much of
his life by indulgence in a picturesque and undisciplined profu-
sion. There was a small lawn surrounding a fish pond and edged
with crazy paving. There was a succession of trellis archways
leading from one carefully tended plot to another. There was a
rose garden with a sundial where a few last roses still gleamed

white on their leafless stems. There were hedges of beech, yew and hawthorn as gold and green backcloths to the banked chrysanthemums. At the bottom of the garden ran a small stream, crossed every ten yards by wooden bridges which were a monument to the colonel's industry, if not to his taste. The appetite had grown by what it fed on. The colonel, having once successfully bridged his brook, had been unable to resist further efforts. Together they stood for a moment on one of the bridges. Dalgliesh could see the colonel's initials cut into the wood of the handrail. Beneath their feet the little stream, already half choked with the first fallen leaves, made its own sad music. Suddenly, Mrs Fenton said:

'So somebody killed her. I know I ought to feel pity for her whatever she did. But I can't. Not yet. I should have realized that Matthew wouldn't be the only victim. These people never stop at one victim, do they? I suppose someone couldn't stand it any more and took that way out. It's a very terrible thing, but I can understand it. I read about it in the papers, you know, before the medical director telephoned. Do you know, Superintendent, for a moment I was glad? That's a terrible thing to say, but it's true. I was glad she was dead. I thought that now Matthew needn't worry any more.'

Dalgliesh said gently:

'We don't think that Miss Bolam was blackmailing your husband. It's possible that she was, but not likely. We think she was killed because she had found out what was happening and meant to stop it. That's why it's so important that I talk to you.'

Mrs Fenton's knuckles whitened. The hands grasping the bridge began to shake. She said:

'I'm afraid I've been very stupid. I mustn't waste any more of your time. It's getting cold, isn't it? Shall we go indoors?'

They turned towards the house, neither of them speaking. Dalgliesh shortened his stride to the slow pace of the thin, upright figure at his side. He glanced at her anxiously. She was very pale and he thought he saw her lips moving soundlessly. But she walked firmly. She was going to be all right. He told himself that he mustn't hurry things. In half an hour, perhaps less, he would have the motive securely in his hands like a bomb that would blow the whole case wide open. But he must be patient. Once again he was touched by an indefinable unrest as if, even at this moment of imminent triumph, his heart held the sure knowledge of failure. The dusk closed in around them. Somewhere a bonfire smouldered, filling his nostrils with acrid smoke. The lawn was a wet sponge under his feet.

The house welcomed them, blessedly warm and smelling faintly of home-baked bread. Mrs Fenton left him to put her head into a room at the far end of the hall. He guessed that tea was being ordered. Then she led him into the drawing-room to the comfort of a wood fire which threw immense shadow over the chintz-covered chairs and sofa and the faded carpet. She switched on a huge standard lamp at the side of the fireplace and tugged the curtains across the windows, shutting out desolation and decay. Tea arrived, the tray set on a low table by a stolid and aproned maid almost as old as her mistress who carefully avoided looking at Dalgliesh. It was a good tea. Dalgliesh saw with an emotion which was too like compassion to be comfortable, that trouble had been taken on his behalf. There were fresh-baked scones, two kinds of sandwiches, home-made cakes and an iced sponge. There was too much of everything, a schoolboy's tea. It was as if the two women, faced with their unknown and most unwelcome visitor, had sought relief from uncertainty in the provision of this embarrassingly liberal feast. Mrs Fenton herself seemed surprised at the variety which faced her. She manoeuvred cups on the tray like an anxious, inexperienced hostess. It was only when Dalgliesh was provided with his tea and sandwich that she spoke again about the murder.

'My husband attended the Steen Clinic for about four months, nearly ten years ago, soon after he left the army. He was living in London at the time and I was in Nairobi staying with my daughter-in-law who was expecting her first baby. I never knew about my husband's treatment until he told me a week ago.'

She paused and Dalgliesh said:

'I ought to say now that we aren't, of course, interested in what was wrong with Colonel Fenton. That is a confidential medical matter and it isn't the concern of the police. I didn't ask Dr Etherege for any information and he wouldn't have given it to me if I had. The fact that your husband was being blackmailed may have to come out − I don't think that can be avoided − but his reason for going to the clinic and the details of his treatment are no one's business but his and yours.'

Mrs Fenton replaced her cup on the tray with infinite care. She looked into the fire and said:

'I don't think it is my business, really. I wasn't upset because he didn't tell me. It's so easy to say now that I would have understood and would have tried to help, but I wonder. I think he was wise not to speak about it. People make such a fuss about absolute honesty in marriage, but it isn't very sensible to confess hurtful things unless you really mean to hurt. I wish Matthew had told me about the blackmail, though. Then he really needed help. Together I'm sure we could have thought of something.'

Dalgliesh asked how it had started.

'Just two years ago, Matthew says. He had a telephone call. The voice reminded him about his treatment at the Steen and actually quoted some of the very intimate details Matthew had told the psychiatrist. Then the voice suggested that he would like to help other patients who were trying to overcome similar difficulties. There was a lot of talk about the dreadful social consequences of not getting cured. It was all very subtle and clever, but there wasn't the least doubt what the voice was after. Matthew asked what he was expected to do and was told to send fifteen pounds in notes to arrive by the first post on the first day of every month. If the first was a Saturday or Sunday, the letter was to arrive on Monday. He was to address the envelope in green ink to the administrative secretary and enclose with the money a note to say that it was a donation from a grateful patient. The voice said that he could be sure that the cash would go where it could do most good.'

'It was a clever enough plan,' said Dalgliesh. 'Blackmail would be difficult to prove and the amount was nicely calculated. I imagine that your husband would have been forced to take a different line if the demand had been too exorbitant.'

'Oh, he would! Matthew would never let us be ruined. But you see, it was such a small amount really. I don't mean that we could afford to lose fifteen pounds a month, but it was a sum which Matthew could just find by personal economies without making me suspicious. And the demand never rose. That was the extraordinary thing about it. Matthew said that he always understood a blackmailer was never satisfied but kept increasing the demand until the victim couldn't pay another penny. It wasn't like that at all. Matthew sent the money to arrive on the first day of the next month and he had another call. The voice thanked him for his kind donation and made it quite clear that no more than fifteen pounds was expected. And no more ever was. The voice said something about sharing the sacrifice equally. Matthew said he could almost persuade himself that the thing was genuine. About six months ago he decided to miss a month and see what happened. It wasn't very pleasant. There was another call and the menace was unmistakable. The voice talked about the need to save patients from social ostracism and said how distressed the people of Sprigg's Green would be to hear about his lack of generosity. My husband decided to go on. If the village really got to know, it would mean leaving this house. My family have lived here for two hundred years and we both love it. Matthew would be heartbroken to leave the garden. And then there's the village. Of course, you haven't seen it at its best, but we love it. My husband is a churchwarden. Our small son, who was killed in a road accident, is buried here. It isn't easy to pull up your roots at seventy.'

No, it wouldn't be easy. Dalgliesh didn't question her assumption that discovery would mean that they must leave. A younger, tougher, more sophisticated couple would no doubt ride the publicity, ignore the innuendoes and accept the embarrassed sympathy of their friends in the sure knowledge that nothing lasts for ever and that few things in village life are as dead as last year's scandal. Pity was less easy to accept. It was probably the fear of pity that would drive most victims to retreat. He asked what had brought the matter to a head. Mrs Fenton replied:

'Two things, really. The first is that we needed more money. My husband's younger brother died unexpectedly a month ago and left his widow rather badly off. She is an invalid and not likely to live more than a year or two, but she is very happily settled in a nursing-home near Norwich and would like to stay there. It was a question of helping with the fees. She needed about another five pounds a week and I couldn't understand why Matthew seemed so worried about it. It would mean careful planning, but I thought we ought to be able to manage it. But he knew, of course, that we couldn't if he had to go on sending the fifteen pounds to the Steen. Then there was his operation. It wasn't a very serious one I know, but any operation is a risk at seventy and he was afraid that he might die and the whole story come out without his being able to explain. So he told me. I was very glad he did. He went into hospital perfectly happy as a result and the operation went very well. Really very well indeed. Could I give you some more tea, Superintendent?'

Dalgliesh passed her his cup and asked what action she had decided to take. They were now coming to the crux of the story, but he was careful neither to hurry her nor to appear over-anxious. His comments and questions might have been those of any afternoon guest, dutifully taking a polite share in his hostess's conversation. She was an old lady who had been through a severe strain and was faced with one even greater. He guessed a little of what this revelation to a stranger must be costing her. Any formal expression of sympathy would have been a presump-tion, but at least he could help, with patience and understanding.

'What did I decide to do? Well, that was the problem, of course. I was determined that the blackmailing should be stopped, but I wanted to spare us both if I could. I'm not a very intelligent woman – it's no use shaking your head, if I were this murder wouldn't have happened – but I thought it out very carefully. It seemed to me that the best thing was to visit the Steen Clinic and see someone in authority. I could explain what was happening, perhaps even without mentioning my name, and ask them to make their own investigation and put a stop to the blackmail. After all, they would know about my husband, so I wouldn't be confiding his secret to anyone new and they would be just as anxious to avoid publicity as I was. It wouldn't do the clinic any good if this came out, would it? They could probably find out who was responsible without a great deal of difficulty. Psychiatrists are supposed to understand people's characters after all, and it must be someone who was at the clinic when my husband attended. And then, being a woman, would narrow the field.'

'Do you mean the blackmailer was a woman?' asked Dalgliesh, surprised.

'Oh, yes! At least, the voice on the telephone was a woman's voice, my husband says.'

'Is he quite sure of that?'

'He didn't express any doubt to me. It wasn't only the voice, you see. It was some of the things she said. Things like it not being only members of my husband's sex who had these illnesses, and had he ever thought what unhappiness they could cause to women, and so on. There were definite references to her being a woman. My husband remembers the telephone conversations very clearly and he will be able to tell you what the remarks were. I expect you will want to see him as soon as possible, won't you?'

Touched by the obvious anxiety in her voice, he replied:

'If his doctor thinks Colonel Fenton is well enough to have a brief talk to me I should like to see him on my way back to London tonight. There are one or two points – this matter of the blackmailer's sex is one – that only he can help with. I shan't bother him more than necessary.'

'I'm sure he will be able to see you. He has a little room of his own – an amenity bed they call them – and he's doing very well. I told him that you were coming today so he won't be surprised to see you. I don't think I'll come too, if you don't mind. I think he would rather see you alone. I shall write a note for you to take.'

Dalgliesh thanked her and said:

'It's interesting that your husband should say it was a woman. He could be right, of course, but it could be a clever deception on the blackmailer's part and difficult to disprove. Some men are able to mimic a woman's voice very convincingly and the casual references to establish sex would be even more effective than a disguised voice. If the colonel had decided to prosecute and the matter had come to court, it would have been very difficult to convict a man of this particular crime unless the evidence was very strong. And as far as I can see the evidence would be almost non-existent. I think we'll keep a very open mind on the question of the blackmailer's sex. But I'm sorry. I interrupted.'

'It was rather an important point to establish, wasn't it? I hope that my husband will be able to help with it. Well, as I was saying, I decided that the best move was to visit the clinic. I went up to London last Friday morning on an early train. I had to see my chiropodist and there were one or two things Matthew needed in hospital. I decided to shop first. I should have gone direct to the clinic, of course. That was another mistake. It was cowardice, really. I wasn't looking forward to it and I tried to behave as if it were nothing so very special, just a casual visit I could fit in between the shopping and the chiropodist. In the end I didn't go at all. I telephoned instead. You see, I told you I wasn't very intelligent.'

Dalgliesh asked what had led to the change of plan.

'It was Oxford Street. I know that sounds silly, but it happened that way. I hadn't been up to London alone for a very long time and I had forgotten how dreadful it is now. I used to love it when I was a girl. It seemed a gracious city then. Now the skyline has changed and the streets seem full of freaks and foreigners. One shouldn't resent them, I know – the foreigners, I mean. It's just that I felt so alien. And then there were the cars. I tried to cross Oxford Street and was stranded among them on one of the islands. Of course, they weren't killing anyone or knocking anyone down. They couldn't. They couldn't even move. But they smelt so horrible that I had to hold my handkerchief to my nose and I felt so faint and ill. When I reached the pavement I went into one of the stores to find the women's rest-room. It was on the fifth floor and it took me a long time to get to the right lift. The crowds were dreadful and we were all squashed in together. When I got to the rest-room all the chairs were taken. I was standing against the wall wondering whether I could summon enough energy to queue for my lunch when I saw the row of telephone boxes. Suddenly I realized that I could telephone the clinic and save myself the journey and the ordeal of telling my story face to face. It was stupid of me, I see that now, but at the time it seemed a very good idea. It would be easier to conceal my identity on the telephone and I felt that I should be able to explain more fully. I also gained a great deal of comfort from the thought that, if the conversation became too difficult, I could always ring off. You see, I was being very cowardly and my only excuse is that I was very tired, far more tired than I imagined possible. I expect you will say that I ought to have gone straight to the police, to Scotland Yard. But Scotland Yard is a place I associate with detective stories and murders. It hardly seems possible that it actually exists and you can call there and tell your story. Besides, I was still very anxious to avoid publicity. I didn't think the police would welcome someone who wanted help, but wasn't prepared to co-operate by telling the whole story or being willing to prosecute. All I wanted, you see, was to stop the blackmailer. It wasn't very public-spirited of me, was it?'

'It was very understandable,' replied Dalgliesh. 'I thought it very possible that Miss Bolam got the warning by telephone. Can you remember what you said to her?'

'Not very clearly. I'm afraid. When I had found the four pennies for the call and looked up the number in the directory I spent a few minutes deciding what I would say. A man's voice answered and I asked to speak to the administrative secretary. Then there was a woman's voice which said, "Administrative officer speaking." I hadn't expected to hear a woman and I suddenly got it into my mind that I was speaking to the black-mailer. After all, why not? So I said that someone from the clinic, and probably she, had been blackmailing my husband and that I was telephoning to say that she wouldn't get another penny from now on and that if we received any more telephone calls we should go straight to the police. It all came out in a rush. I was shaking rather badly and had to lean against the wall of the telephone box for support. I must have sounded a little hysterical. When she could get a word in she asked me whether I was a patient and who was treating me and said something about asking one of the doctors to have a word with me. I suppose she thought I was out of my mind. I replied that I had never attended the clinic and that, if ever I needed treatment, which God forbid, I should know better than to go to a place where a patient's indiscretions and unhappiness were made an opportunity for blackmail. I think I ended up by saying that there was a woman involved, that she must have been at the clinic for nearly ten years, and that, if the administrative officer wasn't the person concerned, I hoped that she would make it her duty to discover who was. She tried to get me to leave my name or to come to see her, but I rang off.'

'Did you give her any details about how the blackmail was organized?'

'I told her that my husband had sent fifteen pounds a month in an envelope addressed in green ink. That's when she became suddenly very anxious that I should visit the clinic or at least leave my name. It was rude of me to ring off without ending the conversation, but I suddenly became frightened. I don't know why. And I had said all that I meant to say. One of the chairs in the rest-room was vacant by then, so I sat down for half an hour until I felt better. Then I went straight to Charing Cross and had some coffee and sandwiches in the buffet there and waited for my train home. I read about the murder in the paper on Saturday and I'm afraid I took it for granted that one of the other victims – for there must have been others, surely – had taken that way out. I didn't connect the crime with my telephone call, at least, not at first. Then I began to wonder whether it might not be my duty to let the police know what had been going on at that dreadful place. Yesterday I talked to my husband about it and we decided to do nothing in a hurry. We thought it might be best to wait and see whether we received any further calls from the blackmailer. I wasn't very happy about our silence. There haven't been many details of the murder in the papers, so I don't know what exactly happened. But I did realize that the blackmail might be in some way connected with the crime and that the police would wish to know about it. While I was still worrying about what to do, Dr Etherege telephoned. You know the rest. I'm still wondering how you managed to trace me.'

'We found you in the same way as the blackmailer picked out Colonel Fenton, from the clinic diagnostic index and the medical record. You mustn't think that they don't look after their confidential papers at the Steen. They do. Dr Etherege is very distressed indeed about the blackmail. But no system is completely proof against clever and deliberate wickedness.'

'You will find him, won't you?' she asked. 'You will find him?'

'Thanks to you, I think we shall,' Dalgliesh replied. As he held out his hand to say good-bye, she suddenly asked:

'What was she like, Superintendent? I mean the woman who was murdered. Tell me about Miss Bolam.'

Dalgliesh said:

'She was forty-one years old. Not married. I never saw her alive, but she had light brown hair and blue-grey eyes. She was rather stout, wide browed, thin mouthed. She was an only child and both her parents were dead. She lived rather a lonely life, but her church meant a great deal to her and she was a Guide captain. She liked children and flowers. She was conscientious and efficient, but not very good at understanding people. She was kind when they were in trouble but they thought her rigid, humourless and censorious. I think they were probably right. She had a great sense of duty.'

'I am responsible for her death. I have to accept that.'

Dalgliesh said gently:

'That's nonsense, you know. Only one person is responsible and, thanks to you, we shall get him.'

She shook her head.

'If I had come to you in the first place or even had the courage to turn up at the clinic instead of telephoning she would be alive today.'

Dalgliesh thought that Louise Fenton deserved better than to be pacified with easy lies. And they would have brought no comfort. Instead he replied:

'I suppose that could be true. There are so many "ifs". She would be alive today if her group secretary had cancelled a meeting and hurried to the clinic, if she herself had gone at once to see him, if an old porter hadn't had stomach-ache. You did what you thought right and no one can do more.'

'So did she, poor woman,' replied Mrs Fenton. 'And look where it led her.'

She patted Dalgliesh briefly on the shoulder, as if it were he who needed the comfort and reassurance.

'I didn't mean to bore you. Please forgive me. You've been very patient and kind. Might I ask one more question? You said that, thanks to me, you would get this murderer. Do you know now who it is?'

'Yes,' said Dalgliesh. 'I think I now know who it is.'

CHAPTER SEVEN

Back in his office at the Yard just over two hours later, Dalgliesh talked over the case with Sergeant Martin. The file lay open on the desk before him.

'You got corroboration of Mrs Fenton's story all right, sir?'

'Oh, yes. The colonel was quite forthcoming. Now that he's recovered from the twin ordeals of his operation and the confession to his wife, he's inclined to take both experiences rather lightly. He even suggested that the request for money could have been genuine and that it was reasonable to assume that it was. I had to point out that a woman has been murdered before he faced the realities of the situation. Then he gave me the full story. It agreed with what Mrs Fenton had told me except for one interesting addition. I give you three guesses.'

'Would it be about the burglary? It was Fenton I suppose?'

'Damn you Martin, you might make an effort sometimes to look surprised. Yes, it was our colonel. But he didn't take the fifteen pounds. I wouldn't have blamed him if he had. The money was his after all. He admits himself that he would have taken it back if he'd seen it, but, of course, he didn't. He was there for quite another purpose, to get hold of that medical record. He was a bit out of his depth in most things but he did realize that the medical record was the only real evidence of what happened when he was a patient at the Steen. He mucked up his burglary attempt of course despite having practised glass-cutting in his greenhouse, and made an undignified exit when he heard Nagle and Cully arriving. He got nowhere near the record he wanted. He assumed it was in one of the files in the general office and managed to prise those open. When he saw that the records were filed numerically he knew he couldn't succeed. He had long forgotten his clinic number. I expect he put it firmly out of his mind when he felt he was cured.'

'Well, the clinic did that for him, anyway.'

'He doesn't admit it I can tell you. I believe that's not uncommon with psychiatric patients. It must be rather disheartening for psychiatrists. After all, you don't get surgical patients claiming that they could have performed their own operation given half a chance. No, the colonel isn't feeling particularly grateful to the Steen, nor inclined to give the clinic much credit for keeping him out of trouble. I suppose he could be right. I don't imagine that Dr Etherege would claim that you can do a great deal for a psychiatric patient in four months which was the length of time Fenton attended. His cure – if you can call it that – probably had something to do with leaving the army. It's difficult to judge whether he welcomed that or dreaded it. Anyway, we'd better resist the temptation to be amateur psychologists.'

'What sort of man is the colonel, sir?'

'Small. Probably looks smaller because of his illness. Sandy hair; bushy eyebrows. Rather like a small fierce animal glaring out from its hole. A much weaker personality than his wife, I'd say, despite Mrs Fenton's apparent frailty. Admittedly it's difficult to be at one's best lying in a hospital bed wearing a striped bedjacket and with a formidable Sister warning one to be a good boy and not talk too long. He wasn't very helpful about the telephone voice. He says that it sounded like a woman and it never occurred to him that it mightn't be. On the other hand he wasn't surprised when I suggested that the voice could have been disguised. But he's honest, and, obviously, he can't go further than that. He just doesn't know. Still, we've got the motive. This is one of those rare cases in which knowing why is knowing who.'

'Are you applying for a warrant?'

'Not yet. We're not ready. If we don't go carefully now the whole case could come apart in our hands.'

Again he was visited by the chilling presentiment of disaster. He found himself analysing the case as if he had already failed. Where had it gone wrong? He had shown his hand to the murderer when he had taken the clinic diagnostic index so openly into the medical director's room. That fact would be round the clinic quickly enough. He had meant it to be. There came a time when it was useful to frighten your man. But was this killer the kind who could be frightened into betraying himself?

Had it been an error of judgement to move so openly? Suddenly Martin's plain, honest face looked irritatingly bovine as he stood there unhelpfully waiting for instructions. Dalgliesh said:

'You went to the Priddys' place, I suppose. Well, let's have the dirt about that. The girl is married, I suppose?'

'There's no doubt about that, sir. I was there earlier this evening and I had a chat with the parents. Luckily Miss Priddy was out, fetching fish and chips for supper. They're in quite poor circumstances.'

'That's a *non sequitur*. However, go on.'

'There isn't much to report. They live in one of those terrace houses leading down to the southern railway line in Clapham. Everything's very comfortable and neat but there's no television or anything like that. I suppose their religion's against it. Both the Priddys are over sixty I reckon. Jennifer's the only child and her mother must have been more than forty when she was born. It's the usual story about the marriage. I was surprised they told me but they did. The husband's a warehouseman; used to work with the girl at her last job. Then there was a baby on the way so they had to get married.'

'It's almost pitiably common. You'd think that her generation, who think they know all the answers about sex, would make themselves familiar with a few basic facts. However, we're told these little mishaps don't worry anyone these days.'

Dalgliesh was shocked by the bitterness in his own voice. Was it really necessary, he wondered, to protest quite so vehemently about so common a little tragedy? What was happening to him? Martin said stolidly:

'They worry people like the Priddys. These kids get themselves into trouble but it's usually the despised older generation who have to cope. The Priddys did their best. They made the kids marry of course. There isn't much room in the house but they gave up the first floor and made it into a small flat for the young couple. Very nicely done it was too. They showed me.'

Dalgliesh thought how much he disliked the expression 'young couple' with its cosy undertones of dewy-eyed domesticity, its echo of disillusion.

'You seem to have made a hit in your brief visit,' he said.

'I liked them, sir. They're good people. The marriage didn't last of course, and I think that they wonder now whether they did the right thing in forcing it. The chap left Clapham over two years ago and they don't know where he is now. They told me his name and I saw his photograph. He's got nothing to do with the Steen Clinic, sir.'

'I didn't think he had. We hardly expected to discover that Jennifer Priddy was Mrs Henry Etherege. Neither her parents nor her husband have anything to do with this crime.'

Nor had they, except that their lives, like flying tangents, had made brief contact with the circle of death. Every murder case produced such people. Dalgliesh had sat more times than he could remember in sitting-rooms, bedrooms, pubs and police stations talking to people who had come, however briefly, in touch with murder. Violent death was a great releaser of inhibitions, the convulsive kick which spun open the top of so many ant hills. His job, in which he could deceive himself that non-involvement was a duty, had given him glimpses into the secret lives of men and women whom he might never see again except as half-recognized faces in a London crowd. Sometimes he despised his private image, the patient, uninvolved, uncensorious inquisitor of other people's misery and guilt. How long could you stay detached, he wondered, before you lost your own soul?

'What happened to the child?' he asked suddenly.

'She had a miscarriage, sir,' answered Martin.

'Of course,' thought Dalgliesh. 'She would.' Nothing could go right for such as the Priddys. Tonight he felt that he, too, was tainted with their ill luck. He asked what Martin had learned about Miss Bolam.

'Not much that we didn't know already. They went to the same church and Jennifer Priddy used to be a Girl Guide in Bolam's company. The old people spoke of her with a great deal of respect. She was helpful to them when the baby was on the way – I got the impression that she paid to have the house converted – and when the marriage failed she suggested that the Priddy child should work at the Steen. I think the old people were glad to think that someone was keeping an eye on Jenny. They couldn't tell me much about Miss Bolam's private life, at least, nothing that we don't know. There was one odd thing though. It happened when the girl got back with the supper. Mrs Priddy asked me to stay and have a meal with them but I said I'd better be getting back. You know what it is with fish and chips. You just buy the right number of pieces and it isn't easy to fit in an extra. Anyway, they called the girl in to say "good-bye" and she came in from the kitchen looking like death. She only stayed a second or two and the old people didn't seem to notice anything. But I did. Something had scared the kid properly.'

'Finding you there, perhaps. She may have thought that you'd mentioned her friendship with Nagle.'

'I don't think it was that, sir. She looked into the sitting-room when she first got back from the shop and said "good evening" without turning a hair. I explained that I was just having a chat with her parents because they were friends of Miss Bolam and might be able to tell us something useful about her private life. It didn't seem to worry her. It was about five minutes later that she came back looking so odd.'

'No one arrived at the house or telephoned during that time?'

'No. I heard no one anyway. They aren't on the phone. I suppose it was something that occurred to her while she was alone in the kitchen. I couldn't very well ask her. I was on my way out and there wasn't anything you could put tongue to. I just told them all that if they thought of anything that might help they should let us know at once.'

'We've got to see her again, of course, and the sooner the better. That alibi's got to be broken and she's the only one who can do it. I don't think the girl was consciously lying, or even deliberately withholding evidence. The truth simply never occurred to her.'

'Nor to me, sir, until we got the motive. What do you want to do now? Let him sweat a bit?'

'I daren't, Martin. It's too dangerous. We've got to press on. I think we'll go now and have a little chat with Nagle.'

But when they reached the Pimlico house twenty minutes later they found the flat locked and a folded scrap of paper wedged under the knocker. Dalgliesh smoothed it out and read aloud. 'Darling. Sorry I missed you. I must speak to you. If I don't see you tonight I'll be at the clinic early. Love, Jenny.'

'Any point in waiting for him, sir?'

'I doubt it. I think I can guess where he is. Cully was on the board when we did our phoning this morning but I made sure that Nagle, and probably everyone else at the Steen, knew that I was interesting myself in the medical records. I asked Dr Etherege to put them back after I left. Nagle goes into the Steen on one or two evenings in the week to see to the boiler and turn off the art therapy department kiln. I imagine that he's there tonight, taking the opportunity of seeing which records have been moved. We'll look in anyway.'

As the car moved northwards towards the river, Martin said:

'It's easy to see that he needed the cash. You couldn't rent a flat like that on a porter's pay. And then there would be his painting gear.'

'Yes. The studio is pretty impressive: I should like you to have seen it. And there were the lessons from Sugg. Nagle may have got those on the cheap but Sugg doesn't teach for nothing. I don't think the blackmailing was particularly lucrative. That's where he was clever. There was probably more than one victim and the amounts were nicely calculated. But even if he only made fifteen to thirty pounds a month, tax free, it would be enough to carry him over until he won the Bollinger or made his name.'

'Is he any good?' asked Sergeant Martin. There were subjects on which he never expressed an opinion but took it for granted that his super was an expert.

'The trustees of the Bollinger Trust think so apparently.'

'There's not much doubt is there, sir?' And Martin was not referring to Nagle's talent for painting. Dalgliesh said irritably:

'Of course there's doubt. There always is at this stage of an investigation. But consider what we know. The blackmailer instructed that the cash should be sent in a distinctively addressed envelope, presumably so that he could pick it out before the post was opened. Nagle gets to the clinic first and is responsible for sorting and distributing the post. Colonel Fenton was asked to send the money so that it arrived on the first of each month. Nagle came to the clinic on 1st May although he was ill and had to be taken home later. I don't think it was anxiety about the Duke's visit that brought him in. The only time he didn't manage to get first to work was the day he got stuck in the tube and that was the day Miss Bolam received fifteen pounds from an unknown grateful patient.

'And now we come to the murder and theory replaces fact. Nagle was helping on the switchboard that morning because of Cully's belly-ache. He listens to Mrs Fenton's call. He knows what Miss Bolam's reaction will be and, sure enough, he is asked to put through a call to the group offices. He listens again and learns that Mr Lauder will be at the Steen after the J.C.C. meeting. Sometime before then Miss Bolam has got to die. But how? He can't hope to entice her away from the Steen. What excuse could he use and how could he provide himself with an alibi? No, it must be done in the clinic. And perhaps that isn't such a bad plan after all. The A.O. isn't popular. With luck there will be plenty of suspects to keep the police occupied, some of them with pretty good reasons for wishing Miss Bolam dead.

'So he makes his plans. It was obvious, of course, that the phone call to Miss Bolam wasn't necessarily made from the basement. Nearly all the rooms have telephones. But if the murderer wasn't in the record-room waiting for her how could he ensure that she would stay there until he could get down? That's why Nagle chucked the records about. He knew Miss Bolam well enough to be fairly sure that she couldn't bear not to pick them up. Dr Baguley thought that her first reaction might be to phone for Nagle to help. She didn't, of course, because she was expecting him to appear any minute. Instead she made a start on the job herself, giving him the two or three minutes that he needed.

'This is what I think happened. At about ten past six he goes down to the porters' rest-room to put on his outdoor coat. It's then that he unlocks the record-room door and throws the files on the floor. He leaves the light on and shuts the door but doesn't bolt it. Then he unlocks the back door. Next he goes into the general office to collect the outgoing post. Miss Priddy is there but periodically visits the adjoining filing-room. He only needs half a minute to telephone Miss Bolam and to ask her to come down to the record-room as he has something serious to show her. We know how she reacted to that message. Before Nagle has a chance to replace the receiver Jennifer Priddy is back. He keeps his head, depresses the receiver rest, and pretends to be speaking to Nurse Bolam about the laundry. Then, without wasting any more time, he leaves with the post. He has only to take it to the box across the road. Then he darts down the mews, enters the basement by the unlocked back door, slips the chisel in his pocket, collects Tippett's fetish and enters the record-room. Miss Bolam is there as he expects, kneeling to pick up the torn and scattered files. She looks up at him, ready no doubt to ask where he's been. But, before she has time to speak he strikes. Once she's unconscious he can take his time over the stabbing. There mustn't be any mistake, and there isn't. Nagle paints from the nude and his knowledge of anatomy is probably as good as that of most psychiatrists. And he was handy with that chisel. For this most important job he chose a tool he had confidence in and knew how to use.' Martin said:

'He couldn't have got down to the basement in time if he'd walked to the corner of Beefsteak Street for his *Standard*. But the newsboy there couldn't swear that he'd seen him. He was carrying a paper when he returned to the Steen but he could have got that in his lunch hour and kept it in his pocket.'

'I think he did,' said Dalgliesh. 'That's why he wouldn't let Cully see it to check the racing results. Cully would have seen at once that it was the midday edition. Instead Nagle takes it downstairs and later uses it to wrap up the cat's food before burning it in the boiler. He wasn't in the basement alone for long, of course. Jenny Priddy was hard on his heels. But he had time to bolt the back door again and visit Nurse Bolam to ask if the clean laundry was ready to be carried upstairs. If Priddy hadn't come down Nagle would have joined her in the general office. He would take care not to be alone in the basement for more than a minute. The killing had to be fixed for the time when he was out with the post.' Martin said:

'I wondered why he didn't unbolt the basement door after the killing but like as not he couldn't bring himself to draw attention to it. After all, if an outsider could have gained access that way it wouldn't take long for people to start thinking "and so could Nagle". He took that fifteen quid no doubt after Colonel Fenton's break-in. The local boys always did think it odd that the thief knew where to find it. Nagle thought he had a right to it I suppose.'

'More likely he wanted to obscure the reason for the break-in, to make it look like a common burglary. It wouldn't do for the police to start wondering why an unknown intruder should want to get his hands on the medical records. Pinching that fifteen pounds – which only Nagle had the chance to do – confused the issue. So did that business with the lift, of course. That was a nice touch. It would only take a minute to wind it up to the second floor before he slipped out of the basement door and there was a reasonable chance that someone would hear it and remember.'

Sergeant Martin thought that it all hung together very well but that it was going to be the devil to prove and said so.

'That's why I showed my hand at the clinic yesterday. We've got to get him rattled. That's why it's worth looking in at the Steen tonight. If he's there we'll put on the pressure a bit. At least we know now where we're going.'

Half an hour before Dalgliesh and Martin called at the Pimlico flat, Peter Nagle let himself into the Steen by the front door and locked it behind him. He did not put on the lights but made his way to the basement with the aid of his heavy torch. There wasn't much to be done; just the kiln to be turned off, the boiler inspected. Then there was a little matter of his own to be attended to. It would mean entering the record-room but that warm, echoing place of death had no terror for him. The dead were dead, finished, powerless, silenced for ever. In a world of increasing uncertainty that much was certain. A man with the nerve to kill had much that he might reasonably fear. But he had nothing to fear from the dead.

It was then that he heard the front-door bell. It was a hesitant, tentative ring but it sounded unnaturally loud in the silence of the clinic. When he opened the door the figure of Jenny slid through so quickly that she seemed to pass by him like a wraith, a slim ghost born of the darkness and mist of the night. She said breathlessly:

'I'm sorry darling. I had to see you. When you weren't at the studio I thought you might be here.'

'Did anyone see you at the studio?' he asked. He felt that the question was important without knowing why.

She looked up at him surprised.

'No. The house seemed empty. I didn't meet anyone. Why?'

'Nothing. It doesn't matter. Come on downstairs. I'll light the gas stove. You're shivering.'

They went down to the basement together, their footsteps echoing in the eerie, presageful calm of a house which, with tomorrow, will awaken to voices, movement and the ceaseless hum of purposeful activity. She began walking on tiptoe and when she spoke it was in whispers. At the top of the stairs she reached for his hand and he could feel hers trembling. Halfway down there was a sudden faint noise and she started.

'What is it? What's that noise?'

'Nothing. Tigger in his scratch tin I imagine.'

When they were in the rest-room and the fire was lit he threw himself into one of the armchairs and smiled up at her. It was the devil of a nuisance that she should turn up now but somehow he must hide his irritation. With any luck he could get rid of her fairly quickly. She would be out of the clinic well before ten.

'Well?' he asked.

Suddenly she was on the rug at his feet and clasping his thighs. Her pale eyes searched his in passionate entreaty.

'Darling, I've got to know! I don't mind what you've done as long as I know. I love you and I want to help. Darling, you must tell me if you're in any trouble.'

It was worse than he feared. Somehow she had got hold of something. But how, and what? Keeping his voice light he asked:

'What sort of trouble for God's sake? You'll be saying next that I killed her.'

'Oh, Peter, please don't joke! I've been worried. There is something wrong, I know there is. It's the money isn't it? You took that fifteen pounds.'

He could have laughed aloud with relief. In a surge of emotion he put his arms round her and drew her down upon him, his voice muffled in her hair.

'You silly kid. I could have helped myself to the petty cash any time if I wanted to steal. What the hell started you off on this nonsense?'

'That's what I've been telling myself. Why should you take it? Oh, darling, don't be angry with me. I've been so worried. You see, it was the paper.'

'What paper, for God's sake?' It was all he could do not to shake her into coherence. He was glad that she could not see his face. So long as he need not meet her eyes he could fight his anger and the fatal, insidious panic. What in God's name was she trying to say?

'The *Standard*. That sergeant came to see us this evening. I'd been to fetch the fish and chips. When I was unwrapping them in the kitchen I looked at the paper they were wrapped in. It was Friday's *Standard* and it had a large picture of that air crash, all over the front page. Then I remembered that we had used your *Standard* to wrap up Tigger's food and the front page was different. I hadn't seen that picture before.'

He tightened his hold on her and said very quietly:

'Did you say anything about this to the police?'

'Darling, of course I didn't! Suppose it made them suspect you! I didn't say anything to anyone; but I needed to see you. I don't care about the fifteen pounds. I don't care if you did meet her in the basement. I know you didn't kill her. All I want is for you to trust me. I love you and I want to help. I can't bear it if you keep things from me.'

That's what they all said but there wasn't one in a million who really wanted to know the truth about a man. For a second he was tempted to tell her, spit the whole brutal story into her silly pleading face and watch the sudden draining away of pity and love. She could probably bear to know about Bolam. What she couldn't bear would be the knowledge that he hadn't blackmailed for her sake, that he hadn't acted to preserve their love, that there wasn't any love to preserve and never had been. He would have to marry her, of course. He had always known that it might be necessary. Only she could effectively witness against him and there was one sure way to stop her tongue. But time was short. He planned to be in Paris by the end of the week. Now it looked as if he wouldn't be travelling alone. He thought quickly. Shifting her weight to the arm of the chair but still keeping his arms around her, his face resting against her cheek he said softly:

'Listen darling. There's something you've got to know. I didn't tell you before because I didn't want to worry you. I did take the fifteen quid. It was a bloody stupid thing to do but there's no sense in worrying about that now. I suppose Miss Bolam might have guessed. I don't know. She didn't say anything to me and it wasn't I who phoned her. But I was in the basement after she was killed. I left the back door open and came back that way. I get sick of that old fool Cully booking me in and out as if I were as nutty as a patient and asking for the paper as soon as I appear. Why can't he buy his own, the mean old devil? I thought I'd fool him for once. When I came in at the basement door I saw that there was a light in the record-room and the door was ajar, so I went to look. I found her body. I knew that I daren't be found there, particularly if they ever discovered about the fifteen quid, so I said nothing and left again by the back door and came in as usual by the front. I've kept quiet ever since. I must, darling. I've got to take up the Bollinger by the end of this week and the police wouldn't let me go if they started suspecting me. If I don't get away now I'll never have the chance again as long as I live.'

That at least was true. He had to get away now. It had become an obsession. It wasn't only the money, the freedom, the sun and the colours. It was the final vindication of the lean, pallid years of struggle and humiliation. He had to take up the Bollinger. Other painters could fail here and still succeed in the end. But not he.

And, even now, he might fail. It was a thin story. He was struck, as he spoke, by the inconsistencies, the improbabilities. But it hung together – just. He couldn't see how she could prove it false. And she wouldn't want to try. But he was surprised by her reaction.

'By the end of this week! You mean, you're going to Paris almost at once. What about the clinic . . . your job?'

'For God's sake, Jenny, what the hell does that matter? I shall leave without notice and they'll find someone else. They'll have to do without me.'

'And me?'

'You're coming with me of course. I always meant that you should. Surely you knew that?'

'No,' she said, and it seemed to him that her voice held a great sadness. 'No, I never knew that.'

He tried to assume a tone of confidence tinged with slight reproach.

'I never discussed it because I thought there were some things we didn't need to say. I know the time's short but it'll be easier if you don't have to stick around too long at home waiting. They'd only get suspicious. You've got a passport, haven't you? Didn't you go to France with the Guides that Easter? What I suggest is that we marry by special licence as soon as possible – after all we've got the money now – and write to your parents when we get to Paris. You do want to come, don't you, Jenny?'

Suddenly she was shaking in his arms and he felt the warm wetness of her tears stinging his face.

'I thought you meant to go without me. The days went by and you never said anything. Of course, I want to come. I don't care what happens as long as we're together. But we can't get married. I never told you because I was afraid you'd be angry and you've never asked me anything about myself. I can't get married because I'm married already.'

The car had turned into Vauxhall Bridge Road but traffic was heavy and they were making poor time. Dalgliesh sat back in his seat as if all day were before him, but inwardly he was fidgeting with anxiety. He could discover no rational cause for this impatience. The call at the Steen was merely speculative. The chances were that Nagle, if indeed he had called at the clinic, would have left before they arrived. Probably he was even now putting down his evening pint in some Pimlico pub. At the next corner the traffic lights were against them and the car slowed to a halt for the third time in a hundred yards. Suddenly Martin said:

'He couldn't have got away with it for long, even by killing Bolam. Sooner or later Mrs Fenton – or another victim maybe – would have turned up at the Steen.'

Dalgliesh replied:

'But he might well have got away with it for long enough to

take up the Bollinger. And even if the blackmailing came to light before he got away – what could we prove? What can we prove now, come to that? With Bolam dead what jury could be sure beyond reasonable doubt that she wasn't the blackmailer? Nagle's only got to say that he remembers seeing the odd envelope addressed in green ink and that he placed it with the A.O.'s post. Fenton will confirm that he thought the telephone calls came from a woman. And blackmailers do occasionally come to a violent end. Nagle wouldn't go on with it after Mrs Fenton's call. Even that would help his case. Bolam dies and the blackmailing stops. Oh, I know all the arguments against it! But what can anyone prove?'

Martin said stolidly:

'He'll try to be too clever. They always do. The girl's under his thumb of course, poor little devil. If she sticks to her story that he wasn't alone long enough to make that call . . .'

'She'll stick all right, Sergeant.'

'I'm pretty sure he doesn't know about the husband. If she looks dangerous he probably thinks that he can stop her tongue by marrying her.'

Dalgliesh said quietly:

'What we've got to do is to pull him in before he finds out that he can't.'

In the porters' room at the Steen, Nagle was writing a letter. He wrote easily. The glib and lying phrases flowed with unexpected ease. He would have died rather than send such a letter. It would have been unbearable to think that any eyes could see this spate of emotional clap-trap and recognize it as his. But the letter never would be read except by Jenny. Within thirty minutes it would be thrust into the boiler, its purpose served and the oily phrases only an uncomfortable memory. In the meantime he might as well make it convincing. It was easy enough to guess what Jenny would want him to say. He turned over the paper and wrote:

> By the time you read this we shall be in France together. I know that this will cause you very great unhappiness, but please believe me when I say that we can't live without each other. I know that one day we shall be free to marry. Until then Jenny will be safe with me and I

shall spend my life trying to make her happy. Please try to understand and to forgive.

It was a good ending, he thought. It would appeal to Jenny, anyway, and no one else was going to see it. He called to her and pushed the paper across the table.

'Will this do?'

She read it in silence.

'I suppose so.'

'Damn it all kid, what's wrong with it?' He felt a surge of anger that his careful effort should be found inadequate. He had expected, and had braced himself to meet, her astonished gratitude. She said quietly:

'Nothing's wrong with it.'

'You'd better write your bit then. Not on the end. Take a fresh sheet.'

He slid the paper across the table at her, not meeting her eyes. This was taking time, and he could not be sure how much time there was.

'Better make it short,' he said.

She took up the pen but made no effort to write.

'I don't know what to say.'

'There isn't much you need say. I've said it all.'

'Yes,' she said with great sadness. 'You've said it all.'

He kept the rising irritation from his voice and told her:

'Just write that you're sorry to cause them unhappiness, but you can't help yourself. Something like that. Damn it all, you're not going to the end of the world. It's up to them. If they want to see you I shan't stop them. Don't pile the agony on too much. I'm going upstairs to mend that lock in Miss Saxon's room. When I come down we're going to celebrate. There's only beer, but tonight you'll drink beer, my darling, and like it.'

He took a screwdriver from the tool box and went out quickly before she had time to protest. His last glimpse was of her frightened face staring after him. But she didn't call him back.

Upstairs it was a moment's work only to slip on a pair of rubber gloves and prise open the door of the dangerous-drugs cupboard. It gave with a terrifyingly loud crack so that he stood rooted for a moment half expecting to hear her call. But there was no sound. He remembered clearly that scene some six months ago when one of Dr Baguley's patients had become violent and disorientated. Nagle had helped to control him while Baguley had called to Sister for paraldehyde. Nagle recalled the words:

'We'll give it in beer. It's pretty filthy stuff but they can hardly taste it in beer. Odd that. Two drams, Sister, to 2 cc.'

And Jenny, who disliked beer, would taste it even less.

Quickly he put the screwdriver and the small blue bottle of paraldehyde in his jacket pocket and slipped out, lighting his way with the torch. All the clinic curtains were drawn, but it was important to show as little light as possible. He needed at least another undisturbed half-hour.

She looked up in surprise at his quick reappearance. He went over to her and kissed the back of her neck.

'I'm sorry sweetie, I shouldn't have left you. I'd forgotten that you might be nervous. The lock can wait, anyway. How's the letter going?'

She pushed it over to him. He turned his back on her to read the few carefully penned lines deliberately, taking his time. But his luck had held. It was as neat and convincing a suicide note as was ever read in a Coroner's court. He couldn't have dictated anything better. He felt a surge of confidence and excitement as he did when a painting was going well. Nothing could spoil it now. Jenny had written:

I can't say I'm sorry for what I've done. I haven't any choice. I feel so happy and it would all be perfect if I didn't know that I'm making you miserable. But it's the only and best thing for me. Please try to understand. I love you very much. Jenny.

He put the letter back on the table and went to pour out the beer, his actions hidden by the open door of the cupboard. God, the stuff did stink! Quickly he added the foaming light ale and called to her.

'Are you happy?'

'You know I am.'

'Then let's drink to it. To us, darling.'

'To us.'

She grimaced as the liquid met her lips. He laughed.

'You look as if you're drinking poison. Knock it back, girl. Like this!'

He opened his throat and drained his own glass. Laughing, she shuddered slightly and gulped down her ale. He took the empty glass from her and folded her in his arms. She clung to him, her hands like a cold compress on the back of his neck. Releasing himself he drew her down beside him on to the armchair. Then, clasped together they slid to the floor and lay together on the rug in front of the gas fire. He had turned off the light and her face shone in the fierce red glow of the fire as if she lay in the full sun. The hiss of the gas was the only sound in the silence.

He pulled a cushion from one of the armchairs and pushed it under her head. Only one cushion; he had a use for the other. It could rest on the bottom of the gas stove. She would be less likely to wake if he made her comfortable on that last brief slide from unconsciousness to death. He put his left arm around her and they lay tight clasped without speaking. Suddenly she turned her face to his and he felt her tongue, wet and slippery as a fish, infiltrating between his teeth. Her eyes, their pupils black in the gaslight, were heavy with desire. 'Darling,' she whispered. 'Darling.' Christ, he thought, not that. He couldn't make love to her now. It would keep her quiet but it wasn't possible. There wasn't time. And surely the police pathologist could tell how recently that had happened to a woman. He thought for the first time with relief of her obsession with safety and whispered, 'We can't darling. I haven't got anything with me. We can't risk it now.'

She gave a little murmur of acquiescence and nuzzled against him, moving her left leg over his thighs. It lay there, heavy and inert, but he dare not move nor speak in case he broke that insidious drop into unconsciousness. She was breathing more deeply now, hotly and irritatingly into his left ear. God, how much longer was it going to take! Holding his own breath he listened. Suddenly she gave a little snort like a contented animal. Under his arm he sensed a change in the rhythm of her breathing. There was an almost physical release of tension as her body relaxed. She was asleep.

Better give her a few minutes, he thought. There wasn't much time to spare, but he dare not hurry. It was important that there

were no bruises on her body and he knew he couldn't face a
struggle. But there could be no turning back now. If she woke
and resisted it would still have to be done.

So he waited, lying so still that they might both have been
dead bodies stiffening together into a final stylized embrace. After
a little time he raised himself cautiously on his right elbow and
looked at her. Her face was flushed, her mouth with its short
upper lip curved against the white childish teeth was half open.
He could smell the paraldehyde on her breath. He watched her
for a moment, noting the length of the pale lashes against her
cheeks, the upward slant of the eyebrows and the shadows under
the broad cheek bones. Strange that he had never got round to
drawing her face. But it was too late to think of that now.

He murmured to her as he lifted her gently across the room to
the black mouth of the gas oven.

'It's all right, Jenny darling. It's only me. I'm making you
comfortable. It's all right, darling.'

But it was himself that he was reassuring.

There was plenty of room in the large, old-fashioned oven,
even with the cushion. The bottom of the oven was only a few
inches from the ground. Feeling for her shoulder blades he edged
her gently forward. As the cushion took the weight of her head he
looked to make sure that the gas jets were still unimpeded. Her
head rolled gently sideways so that the half-open mouth, moist
and vulnerable as a baby's, hung just above them, poised and
ready to suck up death. As he slid his hands from under her body
she gave a little sigh as if she were comfortable at last.

He gave one last look at her, satisfied with his handiwork.

And now it was time to hurry. Feeling in his pocket for the
rubber gloves, he moved with fantastic speed, treading lightly, his
breath coming in shallow gasps as if he could no longer bear the
sound of his own breathing. The suicide note was on the table.
He took the screwdriver and wrapped her right hand gently
round it, pressing the palm around the shining handle, the right
finger-tip against the base of the blade. Was that how she would
have held it? Near enough. He placed the screwdriver on top of
the suicide note.

Next he washed up his own glass and put it back in the

cupboard, holding the dish-cloth in front of the gas fire for a second until the damp stain had evaporated. He turned off the fire. No need to worry about prints here. There was nothing to show when last it had been lit. He wondered briefly about the paraldehyde bottle and Jenny's glass, but decided to leave them on the table with the note and the screwdriver. The natural thing would surely be for her to drink sitting at the table and then to move to the stove when she felt the first signs of drowsiness. He wiped his own prints from the bottle and clasped her left hand around it, her right-hand index finger and thumb on the stopper. He was almost afraid to touch her, but she was now deeply asleep. Her hand was very warm to his touch and so relaxed that it felt boneless. He was repelled by its limp flaccidity, by this touch which was without communication, without desire. He was glad when he had dealt similarly with the drinking glass and the bottle of beer. It would only be necessary now to touch her once again.

Last of all he took his own letter to the Priddys and the pair of gloves and threw them into the boiler. There was only the gas tap to turn on. It was on the right of the stove and within easy reach of her limp right arm. He lifted the arm, pressed her index finger and thumb against the tap, and turned it on. There was the soft hiss of escaping gas. How long, he wondered, was it likely to take? Not long surely? Perhaps only a matter of minutes. He put out the light and backed out, closing the door behind him.

It was then that he remembered the front-door keys. They must be found on her. His heart struck cold as he realized how fatal that one mistake could have been. He edged into the room again by the light of his torch. Taking the keys from his pocket and holding his breath against the gas, he placed them in her left hand. He had reached the door before he heard Tigger's mew. The cat must have been sleeping under the cupboard. It was moving slowly round the body now, putting out a tentative paw towards the girl's right foot. Nagle found that he could not bear to go near her again.

'Come here Tigger,' he whispered. 'Come here boy.'

The cat turned its great amber eyes on him and seemed to be considering, but without emotion and without haste. Then it came slowly across to the door. Nagle hooked his left foot under the soft belly and lifted the cat through the door in one swift movement.

'Come out of it, you bloody fool. D'you want to lose all nine lives at one go? That stuff's lethal.'

He closed the door, and the cat, suddenly active, shot away into the dark.

Nagle made his way without lights to the back door, felt for the bolts, and let himself out. He paused for a moment, back against the door, to check that the mews was empty. Now that it was over he had time to note the signs of strain. His forehead and hands were wet with sweat and he had difficulty with his breathing. He drew in deep gasps of the damp and blessedly cool night air. The fog wasn't thick, hardly more than a heavy mist, through which the street lamp which marked the end of the mews gleamed like a yellow smudge in the darkness. That gleam, only forty yards away, represented safety. Yet all at once it seemed unattainable. Like an animal in its lair he gazed in horrified fascination at the dangerous beacon and willed his legs to move. But their power had gone. Crouching in the darkness and shelter of the doorway, his back pressed against the wood, he fought off panic. After all, there was no great hurry. In a moment he would leave this spurious sanctuary and put the mews behind him. Then it was only a matter of re-entering the square from the other side and waiting until there was a casual passer-by to witness his vain hammering at the front door. Even the words he would speak were ready. 'It's my girl. I think she's in there, but she won't open up. She was with me earlier this evening and when she'd gone I found the keys were missing. She was in a queer state. Better get a copper. I'm going to smash this window.'

Then the crash of broken glass, the dash to the basement and the chance to lock the back door again before the hurrying footsteps were at his heels. The worst was over. From now on it was all so easy. By ten o'clock the body would have been removed, the clinic empty. In a moment he would move on to the final act. But not yet. Not quite yet.

Along the Embankment the traffic was almost stationary. There seemed to be some kind of function on at the Savoy. Suddenly Dalgliesh said:

'There's no guard at the clinic now, of course?'

'No, sir. You remember I asked you this morning if we need keep a man there and you said no.'

'I remember.'

'After all, sir, it hardly seemed necessary. We'd examined the place thoroughly and there aren't all those men to spare.'

'I know, Martin,' replied Dalgliesh testily. 'Surprisingly enough those were the reasons for my decision.' The car came to a stop once more. Dalgliesh put his head out of the window. 'What the hell does he think he's doing?'

'I think he's doing his best, sir.'

'That's what I find so depressing. Come on, Sergeant. Get out! We'll do the rest on foot. I'm probably being a bloody fool, but when we get to the clinic, we'll cover both exits. You go round to the back.'

If Martin felt surprise it was not his nature to show it. Something seemed to have got into the old man. As like as not Nagle was back in his flat and the clinic locked and deserted. A couple of fools they'd look creeping up on an empty building. Still, they'd know soon enough. He bent his energies to keeping up with the superintendent.

Nagle never knew how long he waited in the doorway, bent almost double and panting like an animal. But after a time, calmness returned and with it the use of his legs. He moved stealthily forward, hoisted himself over the rear railings and set off down the mews. He walked like an automaton, hands stiffly by his sides, his eyes closed. Suddenly he heard the footfall. Opening his eyes, he saw silhouetted against the street lamp, a familiar bulky figure. Slowly, inexorably, it moved towards him through the mist. His heart leapt in his chest then settled into a regular tumultuous throbbing that shook his whole body. His legs felt heavy and cold as death, checking that first fatal impulse to flight. But at least his mind worked. While he could think there was hope. He was cleverer than they. With luck they wouldn't even think of entering the clinic. Why should they? And surely she would be dead by now! With Jenny dead they could suspect what they liked. They'd never prove a thing.

The torch shone full on his face. The slow unemphatic voice spoke: 'Good evening, lad. We were hoping to meet you. Going in or coming out?'

Nagle did not reply. He stretched his mouth into the semblance of a smile. He could only guess how he looked in that fierce light; a death's head, the mouth agape with fright, the eyes staring.

It was then that he felt the tentative rub against his legs. The policeman bent and scooped up the cat, holding it between them. Immediately it began to purr, throbbing its contentment at the warmth of that huge hand.

'So here's Tigger. You let him out, did you? You and the cat came out together.'

Then, instantaneously, they were both aware of it and their eyes met. From the warmth of the cat's fur there rose between them, faint but unmistakable, the smell of gas.

The next half-hour passed for Nagle in a confused whirl of noise and blinding lights out of which a few vivid tableaux sprang into focus with unnatural clarity and stayed fixed in his mind for the rest of his life. He had no memory of the sergeant dragging him back over the iron railings, only of the grip, firm as a tourniquet, numbing his arm and the hot rasp of Martin's breath in his ear. There was a smash and the sad, delayed tinkle of broken glass as someone kicked out the windows of the porters' room, the shrill screech of a whistle, a confusion of running feet on the clinic stairs, a blaze of lights hurting his eyes. In one of the tableaux Dalgliesh was crouched over the girl's body, his mouth wide-stretched as a gargoyle's, clamped over her mouth as he forced his breath into her lungs. The two bodies seemed to be fighting, locked in an obscene embrace like the rape of the dead. Nagle didn't speak. He was almost beyond thought, but instinct warned him that he must say nothing. Pinned against the wall by strong arms and watching fascinated the feverish heave of Dalgliesh's shoulders, he felt tears start in his eyes. Enid Bolam was dead, and Jenny was dead, and he was tired now, desperately tired. He hadn't wanted to kill her. It was Bolam who had forced him into all the trouble and danger of murder. She and Jenny between them had left him no choice. And he had lost Jenny. Jenny was dead. Faced with the enormity, the unfairness of what they had made him do, he felt without surprise the tears of self-pity flow in a warm stream down his face.

The room was suddenly full. There were more uniformed men, one of them burly as a Holbein, pig-eyed, slow-moving. There was the hiss of oxygen, a murmur of consulting voices. Then they were edging something on to a stretcher with gentle, experienced hands, a red-blanketed shape which rolled sideways as the poles were lifted. Why were they carrying it so carefully? It couldn't feel jolting any more.

Dalgliesh didn't speak until Jenny had been taken away. Then, without looking at Nagle, he said:

'Right, Sergeant. Get him down to the station. We can hear his story there.'

Nagle moved his mouth. His lips were so dry that he heard them crack. But it was some seconds before the words would come and then there was no stopping them. The carefully rehearsed story tumbled out in a spate, bald and unconvincing:

'There's nothing to tell. She came to see me at my flat and we spent the evening together. I had to tell her that I was going away without her. She took it pretty badly, and after she'd left I found that the clinic keys were missing. I knew she was in a bit of a state so I thought I'd better come along. There's a note on the table. She's left a note. I could see she was dead and I couldn't help, so I came away. I didn't want to be mixed up in it. I've got the Bollinger to think of. It wouldn't look good getting mixed up with a suicide.'

Dalgliesh said:

'You'd better not say anything else for the present. But you'll have to do better than that. You see, it isn't quite what she has told us. That note on the table isn't the only one she left.'

With slow deliberation he took from his breast pocket a small folded sheet of paper and held it an inch from Nagle's fascinated, fear-glazed eyes:

'If you were together this evening in your flat, how do you explain this note which we found under your door knocker?'

It was then that Nagle realized with sick despair that the dead, so impotent and so despised, could bear witness against him after all. Instinctively he put out his hand for the note, then dropped his arm. Dalgliesh replaced the note in his pocket. Watching Nagle closely, he said:

'So you rushed here tonight because you were concerned for her safety? Very touching! In that case let me put your mind at rest. She's going to live.'

'She's dead,' said Nagle dully. 'She killed herself.'

'She was breathing when we'd finished with her. Tomorrow, if all goes well, she'll be able to tell us what happened. And not only what happened here tonight. We shall have some questions about Miss Bolam's murder.'

Nagle gave a shout of harsh laughter:

'Bolam's murder! You'll never get me for that! And I'll tell you why, you poor boobs. Because I didn't kill her! If you want to make fools of yourselves, go ahead. Don't let me stop you. But I warn you. If I'm arrested for Bolam's murder I'll make your names stink in every newspaper in the country.'

He held out his wrists to Dalgliesh.

'Come on, Superintendent! Go ahead and charge me. What's stopping you? You've worked it all out very cleverly, haven't you? You've been too clever by half, you bloody supercilious copper!'

'I'm not charging you,' said Dalgliesh. 'I'm inviting you to come to headquarters to answer some questions and to make a statement. If you want a solicitor present you're entitled to have one.'

'I'll have one all right. But not just at the moment. I'm in no hurry, Superintendent. You see, I'm expecting a visitor. We arranged to meet here at ten and it's nearly that now. I must say we'd planned to have the place to ourselves and I don't think my visitor will be particularly pleased to see you. But if you want to meet Miss Bolam's killer you'd better stick around. It won't be long. The person I'm expecting has been trained to be on time.'

Suddenly all his fear seemed to have left him. The large brown eyes were expressionless again, muddy pools in which only the black iris burned with life. Martin, still clasping Nagle's arms, could feel the muscles bracing, could sense the physical return of confidence. But before anyone had time to speak their ears caught simultaneously the sound of footsteps. Someone had come in by the basement door and was moving quietly down the passage.

Dalgliesh moved to the door in one silent stride and braced himself against it. The footsteps, timid, hesitant, stopped outside. Three pairs of eyes watched as the door-knob turned, first right, then left. A voice called softly:

'Nagle! Are you there, Nagle! Open the door.'

With a single movement Dalgliesh stepped to one side and crashed open the door. The slight figure moved forward involuntarily under the blaze of the fluorescent lights. The immense grey eyes widened and slewed from face to face, the eyes of an uncomprehending child. Whimpering, she clutched a handbag to her breast in a sudden protective gesture as if she were shielding a baby. Wrenching himself from Martin's grip Nagle snatched it from her and tossed it to Dalgliesh. It fell plumply into the detective's hands, the cheap plastic sticking warmly to his fingers. Nagle tried to keep his voice level, but it cracked with excitement and triumph.

'Take a look inside, Superintendent. It's all there. I'll tell you what you'll find. A signed confession of Enid Bolam's murder and one hundred pounds in notes, a first payment on account to keep my mouth shut.'

He turned to his visitor.

'Sorry, kid. I didn't plan it this way. I was willing enough to keep quiet about what I'd seen, but things have changed since Friday night. I've got troubles of my own to worry about now and no one's going to pin a murder charge on me. Our little arrangement's off.'

But Marion Bolam had fainted.

Two months later a magistrate's court committed Marion Grace Bolam for trial on a charge of her cousin's murder. A capricious autumn had hardened into winter and Dalgliesh walked back alone to headquarters under a grey blanket of sky which sagged with its weight of snow. The first moist flakes were already falling, melting gently against his face. In his chief's office the lights were lit and the curtains drawn, shutting out the glittering river, the necklace of light along the Embankment and all the cold inertia of a winter afternoon. Dalgliesh made his report briefly. The A.C. listened in silence, then said:

'They'll try for diminished responsibility, I suppose. How did the girl seem?'

'Perfectly calm, like a child who knows she's been naughty and is on her best behaviour in the hope that the grown-ups will overlook it. She feels no particular guilt, I suspect, except the usual female guilt at being found out.'

'It was a perfectly straightforward case,' said the A.C. 'The obvious suspect, the obvious motive.'

'Too obvious for me, apparently,' said Dalgliesh bitterly. 'If this case doesn't cure me of conceit, nothing will. If I'd paid more attention to the obvious I might have questioned why she didn't get back to Rettinger Street until after eleven when the television service was closing down. She'd been with Nagle, of course, arranging the blackmail payments. They met in St James's Park, apparently. He saw his chance all right when he went into that record-room and found her bending over her cousin's body. He must have been on her before she heard a sound. He took over from there with his usual efficiency. It was he who put the fetish so carefully on the body, of course. Even that detail misled me. Somehow I couldn't see Marion Bolam making that final contemptuous gesture. But it was an obvious crime, all right. She hardly made an attempt at concealment. The rubber gloves she wore were stuffed back in her uniform pocket. The weapons she chose were the ones nearest to hand. She wasn't trying to incriminate anyone else. She wasn't even trying to be clever. At about six-twelve she telephoned the general office and asked Nagle not to come down yet for the laundry; he couldn't resist lying about that call, incidentally, which gave me another opportunity for being over-subtle. Then she rang for her cousin. She couldn't be absolutely sure that Enid would come alone and the excuse had to be valid so she threw the medical records on the floor. Then she waited in the record-room for her victim, fetish in hand and chisel in her uniform pocket. It was unfortunate for her that Nagle returned secretly to the clinic when he was out with the post. He'd overheard Miss Bolam's call to the group secretary and wanted to get his hands on the Fenton record. It seemed safer to chuck it in the basement furnace. Coming upon the murder forced him to change his plan and he didn't get another chance once the body was discovered and the record-room sealed. Nurse Bolam, of course, had no choice of time. She discovered on Wednesday night that Enid intended to alter her will. Friday was the earliest evening when there was a lysergic acid session and she would have the basement to herself. She couldn't act earlier: she daren't act later.'

'The murder was highly convenient for Nagle,' said his chief. 'You can't blame yourself for concentrating on him. But if you insist on indulging in self-pity don't let me spoil your fun.'

'Convenient, perhaps, but not necessary,' Dalgliesh replied. 'And why should he have killed Bolam? His one aim, apart from making easy money, was to take up the Bollinger and get away to Europe without fuss. He must have known that it would be difficult to pin the Fenton blackmail on him even if the group secretary decided to call in the police. And, in fact, we still haven't enough evidence to charge him. But murder is different. Anyone connected with murder is likely to have his private plans disorganized. Even the innocent can't so easily shake off that contaminating dust. To kill Bolam only increased his danger. But to kill Priddy was a different matter. At one stroke he could safeguard his alibi, get rid of an encumbrance and give himself the hope of marrying the heiress of nearly thirty thousand. He knew he'd have little chance with Marion Bolam if she learned that Priddy had been his mistress. She wasn't Enid Bolam's cousin for nothing.'

The A.C. said:

'At least we've got him as an accessory after the fact and that should put him away for quite a time. I'm not sorry that the Fentons will be spared the ordeal of giving evidence. But I doubt whether the charge of attempted murder will stick – not unless Priddy changes her mind. If she persists in supporting his story we'll get nowhere.'

'She won't change her mind, sir,' said Dalgliesh bitterly. 'Nagle doesn't want to see her, of course, but nothing makes any difference. All she thinks about is planning their life together when he comes out. And God help her when he does.'

The A.C. shifted his immense bulk irritably in his chair, closed the file and pushed it across the table to Dalgliesh. He said:

'There's nothing that you or anyone else can do about that. She's the kind of woman who pursues her own destruction. I've had that artist, Sugg, on to me by the way. Extraordinary ideas about judicial procedure these people have! I told him that it's out of our hands now and referred him to the proper quarter. He wants to pay for Nagle's defence, if you please! Said that if we've made a mistake the world will lose a remarkable talent.'

'It will be lost, anyway,' replied Dalgliesh. Thinking aloud, he added: 'I wonder just how good an artist would have to be before one let him get away with a crime like Nagle's. Michelangelo? Velazquez? Rembrandt?'

'Oh, well,' said the A.C. easily. 'If we had to ask ourselves that question we wouldn't be policemen.'

Back in Dalgliesh's office Sergeant Martin was putting away papers. He took one look at his super's face, pronounced a stolid 'Good night, sir,' and left. There were some situations which his uncomplicated nature found it prudent to avoid. The door had hardly closed behind him when the telephone rang. It was Mrs Shorthouse.

'Hullo!' she yelled. 'Is that you? I had the devil of a job getting through to you. Saw you in court today. Don't suppose you noticed me, though. How are you?'

'Well, thank you, Mrs Shorthouse.'

'Don't suppose we'll be meeting again, so I thought I'd give you a ring to say cheerio and tell you the news. Things have been happening at the clinic, I can tell you. Miss Saxon's leaving for one thing. She's going to work in a home for subnormal kids up north. Run by the R.C.s it is. Fancy going off to work in a convent! No one at the Steen ever did that before.'

Dalgliesh said he could well believe it.

'Miss Priddy's been transferred to one of the group's chest clinics. Mr Lauder thought the change would do her good. She's had a terrible row with her people and she's living alone now in a bed-sitter in Kilburn. But you know all about that, no doubt. Mrs Bolam's gone to an expensive nursing-home near Worthing. All on her share of Cousin Enid's money, of course. Poor sod. I'm surprised she could bring herself to touch a penny of it.'

Dalgliesh wasn't surprised, but did not say so. Mrs Shorthouse went on:

'And then there's Dr Steiner. He's getting married to his wife.'

'What did you say, Mrs Shorthouse?'

'Well, re-married. Fixed it up very sudden they did. They got divorced and now they're getting married again. What d'you think of that?'

Dalgliesh said that it was a question of what Dr Steiner thought of it.

'Oh, he's as pleased as a dog with a new collar. And a collar is just about what he's getting, if you ask me. There's a rumour that the Regional Board may close the clinic and move everyone to a hospital out-patient department. Well, you can't wonder! First a stabbing and then a gassing, and now a murder trial. Not nice really. Dr Etherege says it's upsetting for the patients, but I haven't noticed it to speak of. The numbers haven't half gone up since last October. That would have pleased Miss Bolam. Always worrying about the numbers she was. Mind you, there are those who say we wouldn't have had that trouble with Nagle and Priddy if you'd picked on the right one first go. It was a near thing all right. But what I say is, you did your best and there's no harm done to speak of.'

No harm to speak of! So these, thought Dalgliesh bitterly, as he replaced the receiver, were the concomitants of failure. It was enough to taste his sour, corroding self-pity without enduring the A.C.'s moralizing, Martin's tact, Amy Shorthouse's condolences. If he were to break free from this pervasive gloom he needed a respite from crime and death, needed to walk for one brief evening out of the shadow of blackmail and murder. It came to him that what he wanted was to dine with Deborah Riscoe. At least, he told himself wryly, it would be a change of trouble. He put his hand on the receiver and then paused, checked by the old caution, the old uncertainties. He was not even sure that she would wish to take a call at the office, what exactly her place was at Hearne and Illingworth. Then he remembered how she had looked when last they met and he lifted the receiver. He could surely dine with an attractive woman without this preparatory morbid self-analysis. The invitation would commit him to nothing more crucial than seeing that she had a pleasant evening and paying the bill. And a man was surely entitled to call his own publishers.

A TASTE FOR DEATH

To my daughters,
Clare and Jane
and in memory of their father,
Connor Bantry White

Some can gaze and not be sick,
But I could never learn the trick.
There's this to say for blood and breath,
They give a man a taste for death.

A. E. Housman

CONTENTS

BOOK ONE
Death of a Baronet   215

BOOK TWO
Next of Kin   303

BOOK THREE
Helping with Inquiries   385

BOOK FOUR
Devices and Desires   447

BOOK FIVE
Rhesus Positive   525

BOOK SIX
Mortal Consequences   585

BOOK SEVEN
Aftermath   665

AUTHOR'S NOTE

My apologies are due to the inhabitants of Campden Hill Square for my temerity in erecting a Sir John Soane house to disrupt the symmetry of their terraces and to the Diocese of London for providing, surplus to pastoral requirements, a Sir Arthur Blomfield basilica and its campanile on the banks of the Grand Union Canal. Other places described are recognizably part of London. It is the more important to state, therefore, that all the events described in the novel are fictional and all the characters, living and dead, wholly imaginary.

I am grateful to the Director and staff of the Metropolitan Police Forensic Science Laboratory for their generous help with the scientific details.

BOOK ONE

Death of a Baronet

I

The bodies were discovered at eight forty-five on the morning of Wednesday 18 September by Miss Emily Wharton, a 65-year-old spinster of the parish of St Matthew's in Paddington, London, and Darren Wilkes, aged 10, of no particular parish as far as he knew or cared. This unlikely pair of companions had left Miss Wharton's flat in Crowhurst Gardens just before half past eight to walk the half-mile stretch of the Grand Union Canal to St Matthew's church. Here Miss Wharton, as was her custom each Wednesday and Friday, would weed out the dead flowers from the vase in front of the statue of the Virgin, scrape the wax and candle stubs from the brass holders, dust the two rows of chairs in the Lady Chapel, which would be adequate for the small congregation expected at that morning's early Mass, and make everything ready for the arrival at nine twenty of Father Barnes.

It was on a similar mission seven months earlier that she had first met Darren. He had been playing alone on the towpath, if anything as purposeless as hurling old beer cans into the canal could be described as playing, and she had paused to say good morning to him. Perhaps he had been surprised to be greeted by an adult who didn't either admonish or cross-examine him. For whatever reason, after his initial expressionless stare, he had attached himself to her, at first dawdling behind, then circling round her, as might a stray dog, and finally trotting at her side. When they had reached St Matthew's church he had followed her inside as naturally as if they had set out together that morning.

It was apparent to Miss Wharton, on that first day, that he had never been inside a church before, but neither then nor on any subsequent visit did he evince the least curiosity about its purpose. He had prowled contentedly in and out of the vestry and bellroom while she got on with her chores, had watched critically while she had arranged her six daffodils eked out with foliage in the vase at the foot of the Virgin, and had viewed with the bland indifference of childhood Miss Wharton's frequent genuflections, obviously taking these sudden bobbings to be one more manifestation of the peculiar antics of adults.

But she had met him on the towpath the next week and the one following. After the third visit he had, without invitation, walked home with her and had shared her tin of tomato soup and her fish fingers. The meal, like a ritual communion, had confirmed the curious, unspoken, mutual dependence which bound them. But by then she had known, with a mixture of gratitude and anxiety, that he had become necessary to her. On their visits to St Matthew's he always left the church, mysteriously present one moment and the next gone, when the first members of the congregation began to trickle in. After the service, she would find him loitering on the towpath, and he would join her as if they hadn't parted. Miss Wharton had never mentioned his name to Father Barnes or to anyone else at St Matthew's and, as far as she knew, he had never, in his secretive world of childhood, mentioned hers. She knew as little about him now, his parents, his life, as she had at their first meeting.

But that had been seven months ago, a chill morning in mid-February, when the bushes which screened the canal walk from the neighbouring council estate had been tangled thickets of lifeless thorn; when the branches of the ash trees had been black with buds so tight that it seemed impossible they could ever crack into greenness; and the thin denuded wands of willow, drooping over the canal, had cut delicate feathers on the quickening stream. Now high summer was browning and mellowing into autumn. Miss Wharton, briefly closing her eyes as she trudged through the mush of fallen leaves, thought that she could still scent, above the smell of sluggish water and damp earth, a trace of the heady elderberry flowers of June. It was that smell that on summer mornings most clearly brought back to her the lanes of her Shropshire childhood. She dreaded the onset of winter, and on waking this morning she had thought that she could smell its breath in the air. Although it hadn't rained for a week, the path was slippery with mud, deadening sound. They walked under the leaves in an ominous quietness. Even the tinny clatter of the sparrows was stilled. But to their right the ditch which bordered the canal was still lush with its summer greenness, its grasses thick over the split tyres, discarded mattresses and scraps of clothing rotting in its depths, and the torn and laden boughs of the willows dropped their thin leaves on to a surface which seemed too oily and stagnant to suck them in.

It was eight forty-five and they were nearing the church, passing now into one of the low tunnels that spanned the canal. Darren, who liked best this part of the walk, gave a whoop and rushed into the tunnel, hollering for an echo and running his hands, like pale starfish, along the brick walls. She followed his leaping figure, half-dreading the moment when she would pass through the arch into that claustrophobic, dank, river-smelling darkness and would hear, unnaturally loud, the suck of the canal against the paving stones and the slow drip of water from the low roof. She quickened her pace and within minutes the half moon of brightness at the end of the tunnel had widened to receive them again into the daylight and he was back, shivering at her side.

She said:

'It's very cold, Darren. Oughtn't you to be wearing your parka?' He hunched his thin shoulders and shook his head. She was amazed at how little he wore and how impervious he was to the cold. Sometimes it seemed to her that he preferred to live in a perpetual shiver. Surely wrapping up well on an autumn chill morning wasn't considered unmanly? And he looked so nice in his parka. She had been relieved when he first appeared in it; it was bright blue striped with red, expensive, obviously new, a reassuring sign that the mother she had never met and of whom he never spoke, tried to take good care of him.

Wednesday was her day for replacing the flowers, and this morning she was carrying a small tissue-wrapped bunch of pink roses and one of small white chrysanthemums. The stems were wet and she felt the dampness seeping through her woollen gloves. The flowers were tight budded but one was beginning to open and a transitory evocation of summer came to her, bringing with it an old anxiety. Darren often arrived on their church morning with a gift of flowers. These, he had told her, were from Uncle Frank's stall at Brixton. But could that really be true? And then, there was the smoked salmon, last Friday's gift, brought to her flat just before suppertime. He told her he had been given it by Uncle Joe who kept a café up Kilburn way. But the slivers, so moist, so delicious, had been interleaved with greaseproof paper, and the white tray in which they lay had looked so very like the ones she had looked at with hopeless longing in Marks and Spencer, except that someone had torn off the label. He had sat opposite her, watching her while she ate, making an extravagant moue of distaste when she suggested that he share it, but staring at her with a concentrated, almost angry, satisfaction; rather, she thought, as a mother might watch a convalescent child taking her first mouthful. But she had eaten it, and with the delicious taste still lingering on her palate it had seemed ungrateful to cross-question him. But the presents were getting more frequent. If he brought her any more, then they would have to have a little talk.

Suddenly, he gave a yell, raced furiously ahead and leapt up at an overhanging bough. There he swung, thin legs jerking, the white, thick-soled running shoes looking incongruously heavy for the bony legs. He was given to these sudden spurts of activity, running ahead to hide among the bushes and jump out at her, leaping across puddles, rummaging for broken bottles and cans in the ditch and hurling them with a desperate intensity into the water. She would pretend to be frightened when he jumped out, would call out to him to be careful when he crept along an overhanging branch and hung, skimming the water. But on the whole, she rejoiced in his liveliness. It was less worry than the lethargy which so often seemed to overcome him. Now, watching his grinning monkey face as he swung, arm over arm, the frantic twisting of his body, the silver of the delicate ribcage under the pale flesh where the jacket had parted from his jeans, she felt a surge of love so painful that it was like a thrust to the heart. And with the pain came again the old anxiety. As he dropped beside her she said:

'Darren, are you sure your mother doesn't mind your helping me with St Matthew's?'

'Naw, that's OK, I told ya.'

'You come to the flat so often. It's lovely for me but are you quite sure she doesn't mind?'

'Look, I told ya. It's OK.'

'But wouldn't it be better if I came to see her, just to meet her, so that she knows who you're with?'

'She knows. Anyway, she ain't at home. She's off visiting me Uncle Ron at Romford.'

Another uncle. How could she possibly keep track of them? But a fresh anxiety surfaced.

'Then who is looking after you, Darren? Who is at home?'

'No one. I'm sleepin' with a neighbour till she comes back. I'm OK.'

'And what about school today?'

'I told ya. I don't have to go. It's a holiday, see, it's a holiday! I told ya!'

His voice had become high, almost hysterical. Then, as she didn't speak, he fell in beside her and said more calmly:

'They got Andrex at forty-eight pee a double roll up at Notting Hill. That new supermarket. I could get ya a couple of rolls if you're interested.'

He must, she thought, spend a lot of time in supermarkets, shopping for his mother, perhaps, on his way home from school. He was clever at finding bargains, reporting back to her about the special offers, the cheaper lines. She said:

'I'll try to get up there myself, Darren. That's a very good price.'

'Yeah, that's what I thought. It's a good price. First time I seen 'em under fifty pee.'

For almost the whole of their walk their objective had been in sight: the green copper cupola of the soaring campanile of Arthur Blomfield's extraordinary Romanesque basilica, built in 1870 on the bank of this sluggish urban waterway with as much confidence as if he had erected it on the Venetian Grand Canal. Miss Wharton, on her first visit to St Matthew's, nine years previously, had decided that it was expedient to admire it since it was her parish church and offered what she described as Catholic privileges. She had then put its architecture firmly out of her mind, together with her yearnings for Norman arches, carved reredos and familiar Early English spires. She supposed that she had now got used to it. But she was still slightly surprised when she found Father Barnes showing round groups of visitors, experts interested in Victorian architecture, who enthused over the baldachin, admired the Pre-Raphaelite paintings on the eight panels of the pulpit, or set up their tripods to photograph the apse, and who compared it, in confident, unecclesiastical tones (surely even experts ought to lower their voices in church) with the Cathedral of Torcello near Venice or with Blomfield's similar basilica at Jericho in Oxford.

And now, as always, with dramatic suddenness, it loomed before them. They passed through the turnstile in the canal railings and took the gravel path to the porch of the south door, the one to which Miss Wharton had a key. This led to the Little Vestry where she would hang up her coat and to the kitchen where she would wash out the vases and arrange the fresh flowers. As they reached the door she glanced down at the small flower bed which gardeners in the congregation were trying to cultivate with more optimism than success in the unrewarding soil at the side of the path.

'Oh look, Darren, how pretty. The first dahlias. I never thought they'd flower. No, don't pick them. They look so nice there.' He had bent down, his hand among the grasses but as she spoke he straightened up and thrust a grubby fist into his pocket.

'Don't you want 'em for the BVM?'

'We've got your uncle's roses for Our Lady.' If only they were his uncle's! I shall have to ask him, she thought. I can't go on like this, offering Our Lady stolen flowers, if they were stolen. But suppose they weren't and I accuse him? I shall destroy everything there is between us. I can't lose him now. And it might put the idea of theft into his head. The half-remembered phrases fell into her mind; corrupting innocence, an occasion of sin. She thought, I shall have to think about it. But not now, not yet.

She rummaged in her handbag for the key on its wooden key ring and tried to fit it into the lock. But she couldn't get it in. Puzzled, but not yet worried, she tried the doorknob and the heavy iron bound door swung open. It was already unlocked, a key in place on the other side. The passage was quiet, unlit, the oak door to the Little Vestry on the left tightly closed. So Father Barnes must already be here. But how strange that he should arrive before her. And why hadn't he left on the passage light? As her gloved hand found the switch, Darren scampered past her, up to the wrought iron grille which separated the passage from the nave of the church. He liked to light a candle when they arrived, thrusting thin arms through the grille to reach the candleholder and the coin box. Early in their walk she had handed him the usual tenpenny piece, and now she heard a faint tinkle and watched while he stuck his candle in the socket, and reached for the matches in their brass holder.

And it was then, in that moment, that she felt the first twitch of anxiety. Some premonition alerted her subconscious; earlier disquiets and a vague sense of unease came together and focused into fear. A faint smell, alien yet horribly familiar; the sense of a recent presence; the possible significance of that unlocked outer door; the dark passageway. Suddenly she knew that something was dreadfully wrong. Instinctively she called out:

'Darren!'

He turned and looked at her face. And then, immediately, he was back at her side.

Gently at first, and then with one sharp movement, she opened the door. Her eyes dazzled with light. The long fluorescent tube which disfigured the ceiling was on, its brightness eclipsing the gentle glow from the passageway. And she saw horror itself.

There were two of them and she knew instantly, and with absolute certainty, that they were dead. The room was a shambles. Their throats had been cut and they lay like butchered animals in a waste of blood. Instinctively she thrust Darren behind her. But she was too late. He, too, had seen. He didn't scream but she felt him tremble and he made a small, pathetic groan, like an angry puppy. She pushed him back into the passage, closed the door, and leaned against it. She was aware of a desperate coldness, of the tumultuous thudding of her heart. It seemed to have swollen in her chest, huge and hot, and its painful drumming shook her frail body as if to burst it apart. And the smell, which at first had been tentative, elusive, no more than an

221

alien tincture on the air, now seemed to seep into the passage with the strong effluvium of death.

She pressed her back against the door, grateful for the support of its solid carved oak. But neither its strength nor her tightly closed eyes could shut out horror. Brightly lit as on a stage, she saw the bodies still, more garish, more brightly lit than when they had first met her horrified eyes. One corpse had slipped from the low single bed to the right of the door and lay staring up at her, the mouth open, the head almost cleft from the body. She saw again the severed vessels, sticking like corrugated pipes through the clotted blood. The second was propped, ungainly as a rag doll, against the far wall. His head had dropped forward and over his chest a great mat of blood had spread like a bib. A brown and blue woollen cap was still on his head but askew. His right eye was hidden but the left leered at her with a dreadful knowingness. Thus mutilated, it seemed to her everything human had drained away from them with their blood; life, identity, dignity. They no longer looked like men. And the blood was everywhere. It seemed to her that she herself was drowning in blood. Blood drummed in her ears, blood gurgled like vomit in her throat, blood splashed in bright globules against the retinas of her closed eyes. The images of death she was powerless to shut out swam before her in a swirl of blood, dissolved, reformed, and then dissolved again, but always in blood. And then she heard Darren's voice, felt the tug of his hand on her sleeve.

'We gotta get outer here before the filth arrive. Come on. We ain't seen nothin', nothin'. We ain't been 'ere.'

His voice squeaked with fear. He clutched at her arm. Through the thin tweed, his grubby fingers bit, sharp as teeth. Gently she prised them loose. When she spoke, she was surprised at the calmness of her voice.

'That's nonsense, Darren. Of course they won't suspect us. Running away . . . now that would look suspicious.'

She hustled him along the passage.

'I'll stay here. You go for help. We must lock the door. No one must come in. I'll wait here and you fetch Father Barnes. You know the Vicarage? It's the corner flat in that block on Harrow Road. He'll know what to do. He'll call the police.'

'But you can't stay 'ere on your own. Suppose 'e's still here? In the church, waitin' and watchin'? We gotta keep together. OK?'

The authority in his childish voice disconcerted her.

'But it doesn't seem right, Darren, to leave them. Not both of us. It seems, well, callous, wrong. I ought to stay.'

'That's daft. You can't do nothin'. They're dead, stiff. You saw 'em.'

He made a swift gesture of drawing a knife across his throat, rolled up his eyes and gagged. The sound was horribly realistic, a gush of blood in the throat. She cried out:

'Oh don't, Darren, please don't!'

Immediately he was conciliatory, his voice calmer. He put his hand in hers. 'Better come along with me to Father Barnes.' She looked down at him, piteously, as if she were the child.

'If you think so, Darren.'

He had regained his mastery now. The small body almost swaggered. 'Yeah, that's what I think. Come along with me.' He was excited. She heard it in the raised treble, saw it in the bright eyes. He was no longer shocked and he wasn't really upset. It had been silly to think that she needed to protect him from the horror. That spurt of fear at the thought of the police had passed. Brought up on those bright flickering images of violence, could he distinguish between them and reality, she wondered. Perhaps it was more merciful that, protected by his innocence, he shouldn't be able to. He put a thin arm around her shoulders, helping her to the door and she leaned against him, feeling the sharp bones under her arm.

'How kind he is,' she thought, 'how sweet, this dear, dear child.' She would have to talk to him about the flowers and the salmon. But she needn't think about that now, not now.

They were outside. The air, fresh and cold, smelled to her as sweet as a sea breeze. But when, together, they had pulled shut the heavy door with its iron decorated bands, she found she couldn't fit the key into the lock. Her fingers were jumping rhythmically, as if in spasm. He took the key from her and, stretching high, thrust it into the lock. And then her legs gently folded and she subsided slowly on the step, ungainly as a marionette. He looked at her.

'You all right?'

'I'm afraid I can't walk, Darren. I'll be better soon. But I have to stay here. You fetch Father Barnes. But hurry!'

As he still hesitated, she said:

'The murderer, he can't still be inside. The door was unlocked when we arrived. He must have left after he'd – he wouldn't hang about inside waiting to be caught, would he?'

How odd, she thought, that my mind can reason that out while my body seems to have given up.

But it was true. He couldn't still be there, hiding in the church, knife in hand. Not unless they had died very recently. But the blood hadn't looked fresh ... Or had it? Her bowels suddenly churned. Oh God, she prayed, don't let that happen, not now. I'll never get to the lavatory. I can't make it past that door. She thought of the humiliation, of Father Barnes coming, the police. It was bad enough to be slumped here like a heap of old clothes.

'Hurry,' she said. 'I'll be all right. But hurry!'

He made off, running very fast. When he had gone, she still lay there, fighting the terrible loosening of her bowels, the need to vomit. She tried to pray but, strangely, the words seemed to have got muddled up. 'May the souls of the righteous, in the mercy of Christ, rest in peace.' But perhaps they hadn't been the righteous. There ought to be a prayer that would do for all men, all the murdered bodies all over the world. Perhaps there was. She would have to ask Father Barnes. He would be sure to know.

And then came a new and different terror. What had she done with her key? She looked down at the one clutched in her hand. This was weighted with a large wooden tag charred at the end where Father Barnes had put it down too close to a gas flame. So this was his spare key, the one he kept at the Vicarage. It must be the one they had found in the lock and she had handed it to Darren to relock the door. So what had she done with hers? She rummaged frantically in her handbag as if the key were a vital clue, its loss disastrous, seeing in imagination a phalanx of accusing eyes, the police demanding she account for it, Father Barnes's tired and dispirited face. But her scrabbling fingers found it safe between her purse and the bag lining, and she drew it out with a moan of relief. She must have automatically put it away when she found the door already open. But how odd that she couldn't remember! Everything was a blank between their arrival and the moment in which she had thrust open the Little Vestry door.

She was aware of a dark shadow looming beside her. She looked up and saw Father Barnes. Relief flooded her heart. She said:

'You've rung the police, Father?'

'Not yet. I thought it was better to see for myself, in case the boy was playing tricks.'

So they must have stepped past her, into the church, into that dreadful room. How odd that, huddled in the corner, she hadn't even noticed. Impatience rose like vomit in her throat. She wanted to cry out, 'Well now you've seen!' She had thought that when he arrived everything would be all right. No, not all right but better, made sense of. Somewhere there were the right words and he would speak them. But looking at him, she knew that he brought no comfort. She looked up at his face, unattractively blotched by the morning chill, at the grubby stubble, at the two brittle hairs at the corners of his mouth, at the trace of blackened blood in the left nostril, as if he had had a nose bleed, at the eyes, still gummy with sleep. How silly to think that he would bring his strength, would somehow make the horror bearable. He didn't even know what to do. It had been the same over the Christmas decorations. Mrs Noakes had always done the pulpit, ever since Father Collins's time. And then Lily Moore had suggested that it wasn't fair, that they ought to take turns at the pulpit and the font. He should have made up his mind and stood firm. It was always the same. But what a time to be thinking of Christmas decorations, her mind a tangle of hollyberries and gaudy poinsettias, red as blood. But it hadn't been so very red, more a reddish brown.

Poor Father Barnes, she thought, irritation dissolving into sentimentality. He's a failure like me, both failures. She was aware of Darren shivering beside her. Someone ought to take him home. Oh God, she thought, what will this do to him, to both of us? Father Barnes was still standing beside her, twisting the doorkey in his ungloved hands. She said, gently:

'Father, we have to get the police.'

'The police. Of course. Yes, we must call the police. I'll phone from the Vicarage.'

But still he hesitated. On an impulse she asked:

'Do you know them, Father?'

'Oh yes, yes. The tramp. That's Harry Mack. Poor Harry. He sleeps in the porch sometimes.'

He didn't need to tell her that. She knew that Harry liked to doss down in the porch. She had taken her turn at clearing up after him, the crumbs, the paper bags, the discarded bottles, sometimes even worse things. She ought to have recognized Harry, that woollen hat, the jacket. She tried not to dwell on why it was that she hadn't. She asked, with the same gentleness:

'And the other, Father. Did you recognize him?'

He looked down at her. She saw his fear, his bewilderment, and above all, a kind of astonishment at the enormity of the complications that lay ahead. He said slowly, not looking at her:

'The other is Paul Berowne, Sir Paul Berowne. He is – he was – a Minister of the Crown.'

2

As soon as he had left the Commissioner's office and was back in his own room Commander Adam Dalgliesh rang Chief Inspector John Massingham. The receiver was snatched at the first ring and Massingham's disciplined impatience came across as strongly as his voice. Dalgliesh said:

'The Commissioner has had a word with the Home Office. We're to take this one, John. The new squad will officially be in existence on Monday anyway, so we're only jumping the gun by six days. And Paul Berowne may still technically be the Member for Hertfordshire North East. He wrote to the Chancellor of the Exchequer to apply for the Chiltern Hundreds on Saturday, apparently, and no one seems quite sure whether the resignation dates from the day the letter was received or the date the warrant is signed by the Chancellor. Anyway all that is academic. We take the case.'

But Massingham was uninterested in the procedural details for the resignation of a parliamentary seat. He said:

'Division are sure, sir, that the body is Sir Paul Berowne?'

'One of the bodies. Don't forget the tramp. Yes, it's Berowne. There's evidence of identity at the scene, and the parish priest knew him, apparently. It wasn't the first time Berowne had spent the night in St Matthew's church vestry.'

'An odd place to choose to sleep.'

'Or to die. Have you spoken to Inspector Miskin?'

Once they had begun working together they would both be calling her Kate, but now Dalgliesh gave her her rank. Massingham said:

'She's off today, sir, but I managed to get her at her flat. I've asked Robins to collect her gear and she'll meet us at the scene. I've alerted the rest of the team.'

'Right, John. Get the Rover, will you. I'll meet you outside. Four minutes.'

It crossed his mind that Massingham might not have been too displeased had Kate Miskin already left her flat and been impossible to contact. The new squad had been set up in C1 to investigate serious crimes that, for political or other reasons, needed particularly sensitive handling. It had been so self-evident to Dalgliesh that the squad would need a senior woman detective that he had devoted his energy to choosing the right one, rather than to speculating how well she would fit into the team. He had selected the 27-year-old Kate Miskin on her record and her performance at interview, satisfied that she had the qualities for which he was looking. They were also the ones he most admired in a detective: intelligence, courage, discretion and common sense. What else she might have to contribute remained to be seen. He knew that she and Massingham had worked together before when he had been a newly promoted divisional detective inspector and she a sergeant. It was rumoured that the relationship had at times been stormy. But Massingham had learned to discipline some of his prejudices since then, as he had the notorious Massingham temper. And a fresh, even an iconoclastic, influence, even a little healthy rivalry, could be more effective operationally than the collusive and macho freemasonry which frequently bound together a team of all male officers.

Dalgliesh began rapidly but methodically to clear his desk,

then checked his murder bag. He had told Massingham four minutes, and he would be there. Already he had moved, as if by a conscious act of will, into a world in which time was precisely measured, details obsessively noticed, the senses preternaturally alert to sounds, smell, sight, the flick of an eyelid, the timbre of a voice. He had been called from this office to so many bodies, in such different settings, such different states of dissolution, old, young, pathetic, horrifying, having in common only the one fact, that they were violently dead and by another's hand. But this body was different. For the first time in his career, he had known and liked the victim. He told himself that it was pointless to speculate what difference, if any, this would make to the investigation. Already he knew that the difference was there.

The Commissioner had said:

'His throat is cut, possibly by his own hand. But there's a second body, a tramp. This case is likely to be messy in more ways than one.'

His reaction to the news had been partly predictable and partly complex and more disturbing. There had been the natural initial shock of disbelief at hearing of the unexpected death of any person even casually known. He would have felt no less if he'd been told that Berowne was dead of a coronary or killed in a car smash. But this had been followed by a sense of personal outrage, an emptiness and then a surge of melancholy, not strong enough to be called grief but keener than mere regret, which had surprised him by its intensity. But it hadn't been strong enough to make him say:

'I can't take this case. I'm too involved, too committed.'

Waiting briefly for the lift he told himself that he was no more involved than he would be in any other case. Berowne was dead. It was his business to find out how and why. Commitment was to the job, to the living, not to the dead.

He had hardly passed through the swing doors when Massingham drove up the ramp with the Rover. Getting in beside him Dalgliesh asked:

'Fingerprints and photography, they're on their way?'

'Yes, sir.'

'And the lab?'

'They're sending a senior biologist. She'll meet us there.'

'Did you manage to get Doctor Kynaston?'

'No, sir, only the housekeeper. He's been in New England visiting his daughter. He always goes there in the autumn. He was due back at Heathrow on BA flight 214 arriving at seven twenty-five. It's landed, but he's probably stuck on the Westway.'

'Keep on trying his home until he arrives.'

'Doc Greeley is available, sir. Kynaston will be jet-lagged.'

'I want Kynaston, jet-lagged or not.'

Massingham said:

'Only the best for this cadaver.'

Something in his voice, a tinge of amusement, even contempt, irritated Dalgliesh. He thought, my God, am I getting oversensitive about this death even before I've seen the body? He fastened his seat belt without speaking and the Rover slid gently into Broadway, the road he had crossed less than a fortnight earlier on his way to see Sir Paul Berowne.

Gazing straight ahead, only half-aware of a world outside the claustrophobic comfort of the car, of Massingham's hands stroking the wheel, the almost soundless changing of the gears, the pattern of traffic lights, he deliberately let his mind slip free of the present and of all the conjecture about what lay ahead, and remembered, by an exercise of mental recall, as if something important depended on his getting it right, every moment of that last meeting with the dead man.

3

It was Thursday 5 September and he was about to leave his office to drive to Bramshill Police College to begin a series of lectures to the Senior Command Course when the call came through from the private office. Berowne's private secretary spoke after the manner of his kind. Sir Paul would be grateful if Commander Dalgliesh could spare a few minutes to see him. It would be convenient if he could come at once. Sir Paul would be leaving his office to join a party of his constituents at the House in about an hour.

Dalgliesh liked Berowne, but the summons was inconvenient. He was not expected at Bramshill until after luncheon and had planned to take his time over the journey to north Hampshire, visiting churches at Sherborne St John and Winchfield and lunching at a pub near Stratfield Saye before arriving at Bramshill in time for the usual courtesies with the Commandant before his two-thirty lecture. It occurred to him that he had reached the age when a man looks forward to his pleasures less keenly than in youth but is disproportionately aggrieved when his plans are upset. There had been the usual time-consuming, wearying and slightly acrimonious preliminaries to the setting up of the new squad in C1 and already his mind was reaching out with relief to the solitary contemplation of alabaster effigies, sixteenth-century glass and the awesome decorations of Winchfield. But it looked as if Paul Berowne wasn't proposing to take much time over their meeting. His plans might still be possible. He left his grip in the office, put on his tweed coat against a blustery autumnal morning and cut through St James's Park station to the Department.

As he pushed his way through the swing doors he thought again how much he had preferred the Gothic splendour of the old building in Whitehall. It must, he recognized, have been infuriating and inconvenient to work in. It had, after all, been built at a time when the rooms were heated by coal fires tended by an army of minions and when a score of carefully composed handwritten minutes by the Department's legendary eccentrics were adequate to control events which now required three divisions and a couple of under secretaries. This new building was no doubt excellent of its kind, but if the intention had been to express confident authority tempered by humanity he wasn't sure that the architect had succeeded. It looked more suitable for a multinational corporation than for a great Department of State. He particularly missed the huge oil portraits which had dignified that impressive Whitehall staircase, intrigued always by the techniques by which artists of varying talents had coped with the challenge of dignifying the ordinary and occasionally unprepossessing features of their sitters by the visual exploitation of magnificent robes and by imposing on their pudgy faces the stern consciousness of imperial power. But at least they had removed the studio photograph of a royal princess which until recently had graced the entrance hall. It had looked more suitable for a West End hairdressing salon.

He was smilingly recognized at the reception desk, but his credentials were still carefully scrutinized and he was required to await the escorting messenger, even though he had attended enough meetings in the building to be reasonably familiar with these particular corridors of power. Few of the elderly male messengers now remained, and for some years the Department had recruited women. They shepherded their charges with a cheerful, maternal competence as if to reassure them that the place might look like a prison but was as gently beneficent as a nursing home and that they were only there for their own good.

He was finally shown into the outer office. The House was still in recess for the summer and the room was unnaturally quiet. One of the typewriters was shrouded and a single clerk was collating papers with none of the urgency which normally powered a minister's private office. It would have been a very different scene a few weeks earlier. He thought, not for the first time, that a system which required ministers to run their departments, fulfil their parliamentary responsibilities, and spend the weekend listening to the grievances of their constituents, might have been designed to ensure that major decisions were made by men and women tired to the point of exhaustion. It certainly ensured that they were heavily dependent on their permanent officials. Strong ministers were still their own men; the weaker degenerated into marionettes. Not that this would necessarily worry them. Departmental heads were adept at concealing from their puppets even the gentlest jerk of strings and wire. But Dalgliesh hadn't needed his private source of department gossip to know that there was nothing of this limp subservience about Paul Berowne.

He came forward from behind his desk and held out his hand as if this were a first meeting. His was a face, stern, even a little melancholy in repose, which was transfigured when he smiled. He smiled now. He said:

'I'm sorry to bring you here at short notice. I'm glad we managed to catch you. It isn't particularly important but I think it may become so.'

Dalgliesh could never see him without being reminded of the portrait of his ancestor, Sir Hugo Berowne, in the National Portrait Gallery. Sir Hugo had been undistinguished except for a passionate, if ineffective, allegiance to his king. His only notable recorded act had been to commission Van Dyck to paint his portrait. But it had been enough to ensure him, at least pictorially, a vicarious immortality. The manor house in Hampshire had long since passed from the family, the fortune was diminished; but Sir Hugo's long and melancholy face framed by a collar of exquisite lace still stared with arrogant condescension at the passing crowd, the definitive seventeenth-century Royalist gentleman. The present baronet's likeness to him was almost uncanny. Here was the same long-boned face, the high cheekbones tapering to a pointed chin, the same widely spaced eyes with the droop of the left eyelid, the same long-fingered pale hands, the same steady but slightly ironic gaze.

Dalgliesh saw that his desk top was almost clear. It was a necessary ploy for an overworked man who wanted to stay sane. You dealt with one thing at a time, gave it your whole attention, decided it, then put it aside. At this moment he managed to convey that the one thing requiring attention was comparatively unimportant, a short communication on a sheet of quarto-sized white writing paper. He handed it over. Dalgliesh read:

'The member for Hertfordshire North East, despite his fascist tendencies, is a notable liberal when it comes to women's rights. But perhaps women should beware; proximity to this elegant baronet can be lethal. His first wife was killed in a car accident; he was driving. Theresa Nolan, who nursed his mother and slept in his house, killed herself after an abortion. It was he who knew where to find the body. The naked body of Diana Travers, his domestic servant, was found drowned at his wife's Thames-side birthday party, a party at which he was expected to be present. Once is a private tragedy, twice is bad luck, three times looks like carelessness.'

Dalgliesh said:

'Typed with an electric golfball machine. They're not the easiest to identify. And the paper is from a pad of ordinary commercial bond sold in thousands. Not much help there. Have you any idea who could have sent it?'

'None. One gets used to the usual abusive or pornographic letters. They're part of the job.'

Dalgliesh said:

'But this is close to an accusation of murder. If the sender is traced I imagine your lawyer would advise that it's actionable.'

'Actionable, yes, I imagine so.'

Dalgliesh thought that whoever had composed the message hadn't been uneducated. The punctuation was careful, the prose had a certain rhythm. He or she had taken trouble over the arrangement of the facts and in getting in as much relevant information as possible. It was certainly a cut above the usual filth and drivel which dropped unsigned into a minister's postbag, and it was the more dangerous for that.

He handed it back and said:

'This isn't the original, of course. It's been photocopied. Are you the only person to receive it, Minister, or don't you know?'

'It was sent to the press, at least to one paper, the *Paternoster Review*. This is in today's edition, I've only just seen it.'

He opened his desk drawer, took out the journal and handed it to Dalgliesh. There was a folded marker at page eight. Dalgliesh let his eyes slide down the page. The paper had been running a series of articles on junior members of the Government and it was Berowne's turn. The first part of the article was innocuous, factual, hardly original. It briefly reviewed Berowne's previous career as a barrister, his first unsuccessful attempt to enter Parliament, his success at the 1979 election, his phenomenal rise to junior ministerial rank, his probable standing with the Prime Minister. It mentioned that he lived with his mother, Lady Ursula Berowne, and his second wife in one of the few extant houses built by Sir John Soane and that he had one child by his first marriage, 24-year-old Sarah Berowne, who was active in left-wing politics and who was thought to be estranged from her father. It was unpleasantly snide about the circumstances of his second marriage. His elder brother, Major Sir Hugo Berowne, had been killed in Northern Ireland and Paul Berowne had married his brother's fiancée within five months of the car accident which had killed his wife. 'It was, perhaps, appropriate that the bereaved fiancée and husband should find mutual consolation although no one who has seen the beautiful Barbara Berowne could suppose that the marriage was merely a matter of fraternal duty.' It went on to prognosticate with some insight but little charity about his political future. But much of that was little more than Lobby gossip.

The sting lay in the final paragraph and its origin was unmistakable. 'He is a man who is known to like women; certainly most find him attractive. But those women closest to him have been singularly unlucky. His first wife died in a car smash while he was driving. A young nurse, Theresa Nolan, who nursed his mother, Lady Ursula Berowne, killed herself after an abortion, and it was Berowne who found the body. Four weeks ago a girl who worked for him, Diana Travers, was found drowned following a party given for his wife on her birthday, a party at which he was expected to be present. Bad luck is as lethal for a politician as halitosis. It could yet follow him into his political career. It could be the sour smell of misfortune rather than the suspicion that he doesn't know what he really wants which could mock the prediction that here is the next Conservative Prime Minister but one.'

Berowne said:

'The *Paternoster Review* isn't circulated in the Department. Perhaps it should be. Judging from this we might be missing entertainment if not instruction. I read it occasionally at the club, mainly for the literary reviews. Do you know anything about the paper?'

He could, thought Dalgliesh, have asked the Department's own public relations people. It was interesting that apparently he hadn't chosen to. He said:

'I've known Conrad Ackroyd for some years. He owns and edits the *Paternoster*. His father and grandfather had it before him. In those days it was printed in Paternoster Place in the City. Ackroyd doesn't make money out of it. Papa left him reasonably well provided for through more orthodox investments, but I imagine it just about breaks even. He likes to print gossip occasionally, but the paper isn't a second *Private Eye*. Ackroyd hasn't the guts for one thing. I don't think he has ever risked being sued in the history of the paper. It makes it less audacious and less entertaining than the *Eye*, of course, except for the literary and dramatic reviews. They have an enjoyable perversity.' Only the

Paternoster, he recalled, would have described a revival of Priestley's *An Inspector Calls* as a play about a very tiresome girl who caused a great deal of trouble to a respectable family. He added: 'The facts will be accurate as far as they go. This will have been checked. But it's surprisingly vicious for the *Paternoster*.'

Berowne said:

'Oh yes, the facts are accurate.' He made the statement calmly, almost sadly, without explanation and apparently without the intention of offering any.

Dalgliesh wanted to say 'Which facts? The facts in this journal or the facts in the original communication?' But he decided against the question. This wasn't yet a case for the police, least of all for him. For the present, anyway, the initiative must lie with Berowne. He said:

'I remember the Theresa Nolan inquest. This Diana Travers drowning is new to me.'

Berowne said:

'It didn't make the national press. There was a line or two in the local paper reporting the inquest. It made no mention of my wife. Diana Travers wasn't a member of her birthday party but they did dine at the same restaurant, the Black Swan on the river at Cookham. The authorities seem to have adopted that slogan of the insurance company. Why make a drama out of a crisis?'

So there had been a cover up, of sorts anyway, and Berowne had known it. The death by drowning of a girl who worked for a Minister of the Crown and who died after dining at the restaurant where the Minister's wife was also dining, whether or not he himself was present, would normally have justified at least a brief paragraph in one of the national papers. Dalgliesh asked:

'What do you want me to do, Minister?'

Berowne smiled.

'Do you know, I'm not exactly sure. Keep a watching brief, I suppose. I'm not expecting you to take this on personally. That would obviously be ridiculous. But if it does develop into open scandal I suppose someone eventually will have to deal with it. At this stage I wanted to put you in the picture.'

But that was precisely what he hadn't done. With any other man Dalgliesh would have pointed this out and with some asperity. The fact that he felt no temptation to do so with Berowne interested him. He thought, there'll be reports on both the inquests. I can get most of the facts from official sources. For the rest, if it does blow up into an open accusation, he'll have to come clean. And if that happened, whether it became a matter for him personally and for the proposed new squad would depend on how great the scandal, how real the suspicion and of what precisely. He wondered what Berowne was expecting him to do; find a potential blackmailer or investigate him for double murder? But it seemed likely that a scandal of some sort would eventually break. If the communication had been sent to the *Paternoster Review*, it had almost certainly been sent to other papers or journals, possibly to some of the nationals. They might at present be choosing to hold their fire, but that didn't mean they'd have thrown the communication into their wastepaper baskets. They had probably spiked it while they checked with their lawyers. In the meantime, to wait and watch was probably the wisest option. But there would be no harm in having a word with Conrad Ackroyd. Ackroyd was one of the greatest gossips in London. Half an hour spent in his wife's elegant and comfortable drawing room was usually more productive and a great deal more entertaining than hours spent beavering through official files.

Berowne said:

'I'm meeting a party of constituents at the House. They want to be shown round. Perhaps if you've time you could walk over with me.' Again the request was a command.

But when they left the building he turned without explanation to the left and down the steps to Birdcage Walk. So they were to walk to the House the longest way, along the fringe of St James's Park. Dalgliesh wondered if there were things his companion wished to confide which could more easily be said out of the office. The ninety acres of entrancing if formalized beauty of the park, crossed by paths so convenient that they might have been purposefully designed to lead from one centre of power to another, must, he thought, have heard more secrets than any other part of London.

But if that were Berowne's intention, it was destined to be thwarted. They had hardly crossed Birdcage Walk when they were hailed by a cheerful shout and Jerome Mapleton trotted up beside them, rubicund, sweaty-faced, a little out of breath. He was the member for a South London constituency, a safe seat which he nevertheless hardly ever left, as if fearing that even a week's absence might put it in jeopardy. Twenty years in the House still hadn't dampened his extraordinary enthusiasm for the job and his not unappealing surprise that he should actually be there. Talkative, gregarious and insensitive, he attached himself as if by magnetic force to any group larger or more important than the one he was actually in. Law and order was his chief interest, a concern popular with his prosperous middle-class constituents cowering behind their security locks and decorative window bars. Adapting his subject to his captive audience, he plunged at once into parliamentary small talk about the newly appointed committee, bobbing up and down between Berowne and Dalgliesh like a small craft on bumpy water.

'This committee, "Policing a Free Society: The Next Decade", isn't that what it's called? Or is it "Policing in a Free Society: The Next Decade"? Didn't you spend the first session deciding whether to include that little preposition? So typical. You're looking at policy as well as technical resources aren't you? Isn't that a tall order? It's made the committee larger than is usually thought effective hasn't it? Wasn't the original idea to look again at the application of science and technology to policing? The committee seems to have enlarged its terms of reference.'

Dalgliesh said:

'The difficulty is that technical resources and policy aren't easily separated, not when you get to practical policing.'

'Oh I know, I know. I quite appreciate that, my dear Commander. This proposal to monitor vehicle movements on the motorways, for example. You can do it, of course. The question is, should you do it? Similarly with surveillance. Can you imagine advanced scientific methods divorced from the policy and ethics of their actual use? That's the question, my dear Commander. You know it, we all know it. And, come to that, can we any longer rely on the received doctrine that it's for the Chief Constable to decide on the allocation of resources?'

Berowne said:

'You aren't, of course, about to utter heresy – that we ought to have a national force?' He spoke without apparent interest, his eyes fixed ahead. It was as if he were thinking: Since we're lumbered with this bore, let's throw him a predictable subject and hear his predictable views.

'No. But it might be better to have one by will and intention than by default. De jure, Minister, not de facto. Well, you'll have plenty to keep you busy, Commander, and given the membership of the working party it won't be dull.' He spoke wistfully. Dalgliesh suspected that he had hoped to be a member. He heard him add: 'I suppose that's the attraction of the job for the sort of man you are.'

What sort of man, thought Dalgliesh. The poet who no longer writes poetry. The lover who substitutes technique for commitment. The policeman disillusioned with policing. He doubted whether Mapleton intended his words to be offensive. The man was as insensitive to language as he was to people.

He said:

'I've never been quite sure what the attraction is except that the job isn't boring and it gives me a private life.'

Berowne spoke with sudden bitterness:

'It's a job with less hypocrisy than most. A politician is required to listen to humbug, talk humbug, condone humbug. The most we can hope for is that we don't actually believe it.' The voice rather than the words disconcerted Mapleton. Then he decided to treat it as a joke and giggled. He turned to Dalgliesh.

'So what now for you personally, Commander? Apart from the working party, of course?'

'A week of lectures to the Senior Command Course at Bramshill. Then back here to set up the new squad.'

'Well, that should keep you busy. What happens if I murder the member for Chesterfield West when the working party is actually sitting?' He giggled again at his own audacity.

'I hope you'll resist the temptation, sir.'

'Yes, I must try. The committee is too important to have the senior police detective interest represented on a part-time basis. And by the way, talking of murder, there's a very odd paragraph about you, Berowne, in today's *Paternoster Review*. Not altogether friendly, I thought.'

'Yes,' said Berowne shortly. 'I've seen it.' He increased his pace so that Mapleton, already out of breath, had to choose between talking or using his energy to keep up. When they reached the Treasury, he obviously decided that the reward was no longer worth the effort and with a valedictory wave disappeared up Parliament Street. But if Berowne had been seeking a moment for further confidences it had disappeared. The pedestrian signal had turned to green. No pedestrian, seeing the lights in his favour at Parliament Square, hesitates. Berowne gave him a rueful glance as if to say: 'See how even the lights conspire against me,' and walked briskly across. Dalgliesh watched as he crossed Bridge Street, acknowledged the salute of the policeman on duty and disappeared into New Palace Yard. It had been a brief and unsatisfactory encounter. He had the feeling that Berowne was in some trouble deeper and more subtly disturbing than poison pen messages. He turned back to the Yard telling himself that if Berowne wanted to confide he would do it in his own good time.

But that time had never come. And it had been on his drive back from Bramshill a week later that he had turned on his radio and heard the news of Berowne's resignation of his ministerial post. The details had been sparse. Berowne's only explanation had been that he felt it was time for his life to take a new direction. The Prime Minister's letter, printed in the next day's *Times* had been conventionally appreciative but brief. The great British public, most of whom would have been hard pressed to name three members of the Cabinet of this or any administration, were pre-occupied with chasing the sun in one of the rainiest summers in recent years and took the loss of a junior minister with equanimity. Those parliamentary gossips still in London enduring the boredom of the silly season waited in happy expectation for the scandal to break. Dalgliesh waited with them. But there was, apparently, to be no scandal. Berowne's resignation remained mysterious.

Dalgliesh had already sent while at Bramshill for the reports of the inquests on Theresa Nolan and Diana Travers. On the face of it there was no cause for concern. Theresa Nolan, after having a medical termination on psychiatric grounds, had left a suicide note for her grandparents which they had confirmed was in her handwriting and which made her intention to kill herself plain beyond any doubt. And Diana Travers, after drinking and eating unwisely, had apparently herself dived into the Thames to swim out to her companions who were messing about in a punt. Dalgliesh had been left with an uneasy feeling that neither case was as straightforward as the reports made it appear, but certainly there was no prima facie evidence of foul play in connection with either of the two deaths. He was uncertain how much further he was expected to probe or whether, in the light of Berowne's resignation, there was any point in his probing. He had decided to do nothing further for the present and leave it to Berowne to make the first move.

And now Berowne, the harbinger of death, was himself dead, by his hand or another's. Whatever secret he had been hoping to confide on that short walk to the House would remain for ever unspoken. But if he had, indeed, been murdered then the secrets would be told; through his dead body, through the intimate detritus of his life, through the mouths, truthful, treacherous, faltering, reluctant of his family, his enemies, his friends. Murder was the first destroyer of privacy as it was of so much else. And it seemed to Dalgliesh an ironic twist of fate that it should be he, whom Berowne had shown a disposition to trust, who should now be travelling to begin that inexorable process of violation.

4

They were almost at the church before he wrenched his mind back to the present. Massingham had driven in, for him, an unusual silence as if sensing that his chief was grateful for this small hiatus between knowledge and discovery. And he had no need to inquire the way. As always, he had mapped his route before setting out. They were driving up the Harrow Road and had just passed the complex of St Mary's Hospital when the campanile of St Matthew's came suddenly into view on their left. With its crossed bands of stone, its high arched windows and copper cupola it reminded Dalgliesh of the brick towers he had laboriously erected as a child, brick on precarious brick, until they toppled in noisy disorder on the nursery floor. It held for him some of the same hubristic impermanence and, even as he gazed, he half expected it to bend and sway.

Without speaking, Massingham took the next turning to the left and drove towards it down a narrow road bordered on each side by a terrace of small houses. They were identical with their small upper windows, narrow porches and square bays, but it was obvious that the road was coming up in the world. Some few still showed the tell-tale signs of multiple occupation, dishevelled lawns, peeling paint and drawn secretive curtains. But these were succeeded by bright little bandboxes of social aspiration; newly painted doors, carriage lamps, an occasional hanging basket, the front garden paved to provide standing for the car. At the end of the road the huge bulk of the church with its soaring walls of smoke-blackened brick looked as much out of keeping as it was out of scale with this small domestic self-sufficiency.

The huge north door, large enough for a cathedral, was closed. Beside it a grime encrusted board gave the name and address of the parish priest and the time of services, but there was nothing else to suggest that the door was ever opened. They drove slowly down a narrow asphalt drive between the southern wall of the church and the railing bordering the canal, but still there was no sign of life. It was obvious that the news of a murder hadn't yet spread. There were only two cars parked outside the south porch. One, he guessed, belonged to Detective Sergeant Robins and the red Metro to Kate Miskin. He wasn't surprised that she was there before them. She opened the door before Massingham had time to ring, her handsome shield-shaped face composed under the light brown fringe, and looking in her shirt, slacks and leather jerkin as elegantly informal as if she had just come in from a country walk. She said:

'The DI's compliments, sir, but he had to get back to the station. They've got a homicide at Royal Oak. He left as soon as Sergeant Robins and I arrived. He'll be available from midday if you need him. The bodies are here, sir. They call it the Little Vestry.'

It was typical of Glyn Morgan not to have disturbed the scene. Dalgliesh had a respect for Morgan as a man and a detective but was grateful that either duty, tact or a mixture of both had taken him away. It was a relief not to have to soothe and propitiate an experienced detective who could hardly be expected to welcome a commander from the new C1 squad intruding on his patch.

Kate Miskin pushed open the first door on the left and stood aside for Dalgliesh and Massingham to enter. The Little Vestry was garishly lit like a film set. Under the glare of the fluorescent light the whole bizarre scene, Berowne's sprawled body and severed throat, the clotted blood, the tramp propped like a stringless marionette against the wall, looking for a moment unreal, a Grand Guignol tableau too overdone and too contrived to be convincing. Hardly glancing at Berowne's body Dalgliesh picked his way across the carpet to Harry Mack and squatted beside him. Without turning his head he asked:

'Were the lights on when Miss Wharton found the bodies?'

'Not in the passage, sir. But she says this light was on. The boy confirms it.'

'Where are they now?'

'In the church, sir. Father Barnes is with them.'

'Have a word with them will you, John? Tell them I'll speak to them as soon as I'm free. And try to contact the boy's mother. We ought to get him away from here as soon as possible. Then I want you here.'

Harry looked as derelict in death as he must have done in life. If it hadn't been for the breastplate of blood, he could have been asleep, legs stuck out, head slumped forward, his woollen cap slipped over his right eye. Dalgliesh put his hand under the chin and gently lifted the head. He had the sensation that it would come apart from the body and roll over into his hands. He saw what he had expected to find, the single slash across the throat, apparently from left to right, cutting through the trachea to the vertebrae. Rigor mortis was already well established and the skin was ice cold and goosefleshed as the erector muscles of the hairs contracted with the onset of rigor. Whatever concatenation of chance or desire had brought Harry Mack to this place, there was no mystery about the cause of death.

He was wearing old plaid trousers, over-large and loose as pantaloons, and tied at the ankles with string. Above them, as far as it was possible to see for the blood, he wore a striped knitted pullover over a navy jumper. A malodorous checked jacket, stiff with grime, was unbuttoned, the left flap lying open. Dalgliesh raised it with careful fingers touching only the extreme edge of the cloth and saw underneath a smudge of blood on the carpet about two centimetres long and thicker at the right end than at the left. Peering closer he thought he could see a smear roughly the same length on the jacket pocket, but the cloth was too dirty for him to be sure. But the implication of the smear on the carpet was plain enough. One or more drops of blood must have fallen or been spilt from the weapon before Harry fell and had then been smeared along the carpet as the body was dragged against the wall. But whose blood? If it proved to be Harry's, the discovery was of small significance. But suppose it were Berowne's? Dalgliesh felt impatient for the arrival of the forensic biologist, although he knew he couldn't hope for the answer, not yet. Samples of both victims' blood would be taken from the bodies at the post-mortem, but it would be three days at least before he could expect to get the result of the analysis.

He wasn't sure what impulse had made him go first to Harry Mack's body. But now he trod carefully across the carpet to the bed and stood silently looking down at the body of Berowne. Even as a 15-year-old boy, standing at the side of the bed of his dead mother, he hadn't felt the need to think, far less to utter, the word goodbye. You couldn't speak to someone who was no longer there. He thought: we can vulgarize everything but not this. The body in its stiff ungainliness, beginning already, or so it seemed to his over-sensitive nose, to emit the first sour-sweet stink of decay, yet had an inalienable dignity because it once had been a man. But he knew, none better, how quickly this spurious humanity would drain away. Even before the pathologist had finished at the scene and the head was wrapped, the hands mittened in their plastic bags, even before Doc Kynaston got to work with his scalpels, the corpse would be an exhibit, more important, more cumbersome and more difficult to preserve than other exhibits in the case, but still an exhibit, tagged, documented, dehumanized, invoking only interest, curiosity or disgust. But not yet. He thought: I knew this man, not well but I knew him. I liked him. Surely he deserves better of me than to gaze at him with my policeman's eyes.

He lay head towards the door and at an angle of forty-five degrees from the bed, his shoes touching the end. The left hand was flung out, the right lay closer to the body. The bed had been covered with a blanket of hand-knitted squares of bright wool. It looked as if Berowne had clutched it as he fell, half-pulling it from the bed, so that it lay partly bunched at his right side. An open razor, the blade thick with clotted blood lay on top of it, a few inches from his right hand. It was extraordinary how many details simultaneously impressed themselves on Dalgliesh's mind. A thin wedge of what looked like mud caked between the heel and the sole of the left shoe; the pattern of blood stiffening the fine fawn cashmere of the sweater; the half-open mouth fixed in a rictus between a smile and a sneer; the dead eyes seeming as he watched to shrink into their sockets; the left hand with its long pale fingers, curved and delicate as a girl's; the palm of the right hand thick with blood. But the whole picture struck him as wrong, and he knew why. Berowne couldn't both have held the razor in his right hand and clutched at the blanket as he fell. But if he had first dropped the razor, why should it be lying on top of the blanket and so conveniently close to his hand as if it had slipped from the opening fingers? And why should the palm be so thickly clotted, almost as if another's hand had lifted it and smeared it into the blood at the throat? If Berowne himself had wielded the razor, surely the palm which had clutched it would have been less bloodied.

He was aware of a small noise at his side and looked round to see Detective Inspector Kate Miskin looking, not at the corpse, but at him. She quickly turned her eyes away but not before he had detected, to his discomfort, a look of grave, almost maternal solicitude. He said roughly:

'Well, Inspector?'

'It looks obvious, sir, murder followed by suicide. The classical pattern of self-inflicted wounds – three cuts, two tentative, the third cutting through the trachea.' She added:

'It could be used as an illustration in a textbook of forensic medicine.'

He said:

'There's no difficulty in recognizing the obvious. One should

244

be slower to believe it. I want you to break the news to his family. The address is 62 Campden Hill Square. There is a wife and an elderly mother, Lady Ursula Berowne, and a housekeeper of sorts. Use your discretion about which is best able to take it. And take a DC. When the news breaks they may be pestered and need protection.'

'Yes, sir.'

She showed no resentment at being ordered from the scene. She knew that the job of breaking the news wasn't a routine chore, that she hadn't been chosen merely because she was the only woman in his team and he saw this as a woman's job. She would break the news with tact, discretion, even with compassion. God knew she had had enough practice in ten years of policing. But she would still be a traitor to grief, watching and listening, even as she spoke the formal words of condolence, for the flicker of an eyelid, the tensing of hands and face muscles, for the unwise word, for any sign that for someone in that waiting house in Campden Hill Square this might not be news at all.

5

Before he concentrated on the actual scene of the crime, Dalgliesh always liked to make a cursory survey of the surroundings to orientate himself, and, as it were, to set the scene of murder. The exercise had its practical value, but he recognized that, in some obscure way, it fulfilled a psychological need, just as in boyhood he would explore a country church by first walking slowly round it before, with a frisson of awe and excitement, pushing open the door and beginning his planned progress of discovery to the central mystery. And now, in these few remaining minutes, before the photographer, the fingerprint officers, the forensic biologists arrived at the scene, he had the place almost to himself. Moving into the passage he wondered whether this quiet air tinctured with the scent of incense, candles, and the more solidly Anglican smell of musty prayer books, metal polish and flowers, had held for Berowne also the promise of discovery, of a scene already set, a task inevitable and inescapable.

The brightly lit passage with its floor of encaustic tiles and its white painted walls ran the whole west end of the church. The Little Vestry was the first room on the left. Next to it and with a connecting door, was a small kitchen about ten feet by eight. Then came a narrow lavatory with an old-fashioned bowl of decorated porcelain and a mahogany seat with, above it, a hanging chain set under a single high window. Lastly an open door showed him a high square room, almost certainly set under the campanile, which was obviously both the vestry proper and the bell room. Opposite it the passage was separated from the body of the church by a ten foot long grille in delicate wrought iron which gave a view up the nave to the cavernous glitter of the apse and the Lady Chapel on the right. A central door in the grille topped with figures of two trumpeting angels gave entry to the church for the processing priest and choir. To the right a padlocked wooden box was fixed to the grille. Behind it, but within reach of stretching hands, stood a branching candlestand, also in wrought iron, with a box of matches in a brass holder attached to it with a chain, and a tray containing a few small candles. Presumably this was to enable people who had business in the vestry to light a candle when the grille door to the church was locked. Judging from the cleanness of the candleholders it was a facility of which they seldom, if ever, took advantage. There was only one candle in place, stuck upright like a pale wax finger, and this had never been lit. Two of the brass chandeliers suspended above the nave gave a gentle diffused light but the church looked dimly mysterious compared with the glare of the passage and the figures of Massingham and the detective sergeant quietly conferring, of Miss Wharton and the boy patiently sitting like hump-backed dwarfs on low chairs in what must be the children's corner, seemed as distanced and insubstantial as if they moved in a different dimension of time. As he stood watching Massingham looked up, caught his eye, and moved down the nave towards him.

He returned to the Little Vestry and, standing in the doorway, drew on his latex gloves. It always surprised him a little that it was possible to fix the attention on the room itself, its furniture and objects, even before the bodies had been packaged and taken away, as if in their fixed and silent decrepitude they had for a moment become part of the room's artefacts, as significant as any other physical clue, no more and no less. As he moved into the room he was aware of Massingham behind him, alert, already drawing on his gloves but, for him, unnaturally subservient, pacing quietly behind his chief like a recently qualified houseman deferentially attendant on the consultant. Dalgliesh thought: Why is he behaving as if I need tactful handling, as if I'm suffering from a private grief? This is a job like any other. It promises to be difficult enough without John and Kate treating me as if I'm a sensitive convalescent.

Henry James, he remembered, had said of his approaching death, 'So here it is at last, the distinguished thing!' If Berowne had thought in these terms, then this was an incongruous place in which to receive so honoured a visitation. The room was about twelve foot square and lit by a fluorescent tube running almost the full length of the ceiling. The only natural light came from two high curved windows. They were covered outside by a protective mesh which looked like chicken wire on which the dirt of decades had accumulated, so that the panes were honeycombs of greenish grime. The furniture, too, looked as if it had been gradually acquired over the years; gifts, rejects, the unregarded remnants of long-forgotten jumble sales. Opposite the door and set under the windows was an ancient oak desk with three right-hand drawers, one without handles. On its top was a simple oak cross, a much used blotter in a leather pad, and an old-fashioned black telephone, the receiver off the rest and lying on its side.

Massingham said:

'Looks as if he took it off. Who wants the telephone to ring just when he's concentrating on slitting his jugular?'

'Or his killer was taking no chances on the bodies being discovered too soon. If Father Barnes took it into his head to ring and got no reply he'd probably come round to see if Berowne was all right. If he continued to get the engaged sound he'd probably assume that Berowne was having an evening of telephoning and let it go.'

'We might get a palm print, sir.'

'Unlikely, John. If this is murder, we're not dealing with a fool.'

He continued his exploration. With his gloved hands, he pulled open the top drawer and found a stack of white writing paper, of cheap quality, headed with the name of the church, and a box of envelopes. Apart from these, the desk held nothing of interest. Against the left-hand wall was an assortment of canvas and metal chairs neatly stacked, presumably for the occasional use of the parochial church council. Beside them was a five-drawer metal filing cabinet, and next to it a small glass-fronted bookcase. He slipped the catch and saw that it contained an assortment of old prayer books, missals, devotional pamphlets, and a pile of booklets about the history of the church. There were only two easy chairs, one set on each side of the fireplace; a compact brown chair in torn leather with a patchwork cushion, and a grubby, more modern chair with fitted pads. One of the stacked chairs had been uprighted. A white towel hung over its back and on the seat rested a brown canvas bag, its zip open. Massingham rummaged gently inside and said:

'A pair of pyjamas, a spare pair of socks, and a table napkin wrapped round half a sliced loaf, wholemeal, and a piece of cheese. Roquefort by the look of it. And there's an apple. A Cox if that's relevant.'

'Hardly. Is that all, John?'

'Yes, sir. No wine. Whatever he thought he was doing here, it doesn't look like an assignation, not with a woman anyway. And why choose this place with the whole of London open to him? Bed too narrow. No comfort.'

'Whatever he was looking for, I don't think it was comfort.'

Dalgliesh had moved over to the fireplace, a plain wooden overmantel with an iron surround patterned with grapes and convolvulus set in the middle of the right-hand wall. It must, he thought, have been decades since a fire was lit in it for warmth. In front of the grate was a tall electric fire with artificial coals, a high curved back and a triple set of burners. He moved it gently forward and saw that the grate had, in fact, been recently used; someone had tried to burn a diary. It lay open in the firebasket, its leaves curled and blackened. Some pages had apparently been torn out and separately burnt; the brittle fragments of black ash had floated down to lie on top of the debris under the grate, old

twisted matchends, coal dust, carpet fluff, the accumulated grit of
years. The blue cover of the diary with the year clearly printed
had been more resistant to the flames; one corner only was
slightly scorched. Whoever had burnt it had evidently been in a
hurry, unless, of course, he had been concerned only to destroy
certain pages. Dalgliesh made no attempt to touch it. This was a
job for Ferris, the scene of crime officer, already hovering impatiently in the passage. The Ferret was never happy when anyone
other than himself was examining a scene of crime and it seemed
to Dalgliesh that his impatience to get on with the job came
through the wall as a palpable force. He crouched low and
peered into the debris under the grate. Among the fragments of
blackened paper he saw a used safety match, the unburnt half of
the stem clean and white as if it had only recently been struck.
He said:

'He could have used this to burn the diary. But, if so, where is
the box? Have a look in the jacket pockets will you, John.'

Massingham walked over to Berowne's jacket hanging on a
hook at the back of the door and felt in the two outer and one
inner pockets. He said:

'A wallet, sir, a Parker fountain pen and a set of keys. No
lighter and no matches.'

And there were none, either, visible in the room.

With mounting excitement which neither betrayed they moved
over to the desk and peered intently at the blotter. It, too, must
have been there for years. The pink blotting paper tattered at the
edges was marked with a criss-cross of different inks blodged with
faded blots. It wasn't, thought Dalgliesh, surprising; most people
now used ballpoints rather than ink. But peering more closely he
could see that someone had recently been writing with a fountain
pen. Superimposed on the older markings were more recent
blottings, a pattern of broken lines and half curves in black ink
extending over some six inches of the blotter. Their newness was
obvious. He went over to Berowne's jacket, and brought out the
fountain pen. It was elegantly slim, one of the newest models,
and filled, he saw, with black ink. It should be possible for the lab
to match the ink even if the letters couldn't be deciphered. But if
Berowne had been writing and had blotted the paper at the desk,

where was it now? Had he himself disposed of it, torn it up, flushed it down the lavatory, burnt it among the debris of the diary pages? Or had someone else found it, perhaps even come specifically to find it, and either destroyed it or taken it away?

Lastly, he and Massingham passed through the open door to the right of the fireplace, careful not to brush against Harry's body, and explored the kitchen. There was a gas boiler, comparatively modern, mounted above a deep square porcelain sink much stained and with a clean but crumpled tea towel hanging on a hook beside it. Dalgliesh peeled off his gloves and felt the towel. It was slightly damp not in patches but all over as if it had been soaked in water then wrung out and left to dry through the night. He handed it to Massingham who took off his own gloves and ran it through his hand. He said:

'Even if the murderer were naked, or half-naked he would have needed to wash his hands and arms. He could have used this. Berowne's towel is presumably the one hanging on the chair and that looked dry enough.'

He went out to check while Dalgliesh continued his exploration. On the right was a cupboard with a Formica top, brown with tea stains, on which stood one large kettle, one smaller more modern kettle and two teapots. There was also a chipped enamel mug stained almost black inside and smelling of spirits. Opening the cupboard he saw that it contained a collection of unmatched crockery and two folded clean tea towels, both dry, and on the bottom shelf an assortment of flower vases and a battered cane basket containing folded dusters, and tins of metal and furniture polish. Here presumably Miss Wharton and her fellow helpers would arrange the flowers, wash out their dusters, refresh themselves with tea.

Attached to the pipe of the gas boiler by a brass chain was a box of safety matches in a brass holder, similar to the one chained to the candlestand; hinged at the top to allow the insertion of a fresh box. There had been a similar holder and brass chain in the parish room of his father's Norfolk church but he couldn't remember seeing one since. They were clumsy to use, the striking surface barely adequate. It was difficult to believe that the boxes had been removed, then replaced and even more difficult to credit that a match from either of the chained boxes had been struck, then carried lit and precariously flickering into the Little Vestry and used to burn the diary.

Massingham was back beside him. He said:

'The towel next door is perfectly dry and only slightly dirtied. It looks as if Berowne could have washed his hands when he arrived and that's all. It's odd that he didn't leave it in here, except that there's nowhere convenient to hang it. Odder, though, that the killer, assuming there is a killer, didn't use it to dry himself rather than the smaller tea towel.'

Dalgliesh said:

'If he remembered to take it out with him to the kitchen. If he didn't, he'd hardly want to go back for it. Too much blood, too much risk of leaving a clue. Better to use what he found to hand.'

It was apparent that the kitchen was the only room with water and a sink; hand washing as well as washing up must be done here, if at all. Above the sink was a mirror composed of glass tiles stuck to the wall, and under it a simple glass shelf. Upon this was a sponge bag, its zip open, containing a toothbrush and a tube of paste, a dry face flannel and a used bar of soap. Beside this was a more interesting find, a narrow leather case with the initials PSB stamped on it in faded gold. With his gloved hands Dalgliesh lifted the lid and found what he had expected to see, the twin to the cut-throat razor lying so incriminatingly close to Berowne's right hand. On the satin lining of the lid was a sticker with the maker's name in old-fashioned twirls, P. J. Bellingham, and the Jermyn Street address. Bellingham, the most expensive and prestigious barber in London and supplier still of razors to those clients who had never adjusted to the shaving habits of the twentieth century.

There was nothing of apparent interest in the lavatory and they made their way into the robing vestry. It was obvious that this was where Harry Mack had settled himself for the night. What looked like an old army blanket, frayed at the edges and stiff with dirt, had been loosely spread in a corner, its fumy stink mingling with the smell of incense to produce an incongruous amalgam of piety and squalor. Beside it was an overturned bottle, a length of grubby cord and a sheet of newspaper on which lay a crust of brown loaf, the core of an apple and some crumbs of cheese. Massingham picked them up and rubbed them between his palms and thumbs and sniffed. He said:

'Roquefort, sir. Hardly a cheese which Harry would have provided for himself.'

There was no evidence that Berowne had started his own meal – that in itself might be of some help in deciding on the approximate time of death – but he had apparently either cajoled Harry into the church with the promise of a meal or, more likely, had supplied an obvious and immediate need before he was ready for his own share of the supper.

The vestry itself was so familiar from childhood memories that Dalgliesh could have taken one quick glance, shut his eyes and spoken aloud an inventory of high church piety: the packets of incense on top of the cupboard; the incense holder and censer; the crucifix and, behind the faded red serge curtain, the lace-trimmed vestments and the short starched surplices of the choir. But now his mind was on Harry Mack. What had roused him from his half-drunken sleep; a scream, the sound of a quarrel, a falling body? But could he have heard it from this room? As if echoing his thoughts, Massingham said:

'He could have been roused by thirst, gone to the kitchen for a drink of water and stumbled into the crime. That enamel mug looked as if it might be his. Father Barnes will know whether it belongs to the church and with luck there may be prints. Or he could have gone to the lavatory, but I doubt whether he would have heard anything from there.'

And, thought Dalgliesh, he was unlikely to have gone afterwards into the kitchen to wash. Massingham was probably right. Harry had settled himself for the night and then felt the need for a drink of water. But for that fatal thirst, he might still be quietly sleeping.

Outside in the passage Ferris was prancing gently on his toes like a runner limbering for a race.

Massingham said:

'The blotter, the enamel mug, the tea towel and the diary are all important and there's what looks like a recently struck match in the grate; we need that. But we shall want all the debris in the fireplace and the S-bends in the pipes. The probability is that the murderer washed himself in the kitchen.'

None of it really needed saying, least of all to Charlie Ferris. He was the most expert of the Met's scene of crime officers and the one Dalgliesh always hoped would be available when he began a new case. It was inevitable that he should be nicknamed 'the Ferret', although seldom in his hearing. He was very small, sandy-haired, sharp-featured and with his sense of smell so well developed that it was rumoured that he had sniffed out a suicide in Epping Forest even before the animal predators got to it. In his spare time he sang in one of the most famous of London's amateur choirs. Dalgliesh, who had heard him at a police concert, never ceased to be surprised that so narrow a chest and so slight a frame could produce such a powerful organ-toned bass. He was fanatical about his job and had even designed the most appropriate clothes for searching: white shorts and a sweat shirt, a plastic swimming cap, tight fitting to prevent the spilling of hairs, latex gloves as fine as a surgeon's and rubber bathing shoes over his bare feet. His creed was that no murderer ever left the scene of a crime without leaving some physical evidence of his crime behind him. If it were there, Ferris would find it.

There were voices in the passage. The photographer and fingerprint officers had arrived. Dalgliesh could hear George Matthews's booming voice cursing the traffic in Harrow Road and Sergeant Robins's quieter answer. Someone laughed. They were neither callous nor particularly insensitive, but neither were they undertakers, required to assume a professional reverence in the face of death. The forensic biologist hadn't yet arrived. Some of the most distinguished scientists at the Metropolitan Laboratory were women and Dalgliesh, recognizing in himself an old-fashioned sensitivity which he certainly wouldn't have confessed to them, was always glad when it was possible to remove the more horrific bodies before they arrived to track and photograph the bloodstains and supervise the collection of samples. He left Massingham to greet and brief the new arrivals. It was time to talk to Father Barnes. But first he wanted a word with Darren before the boy was driven home.

6

Sergeant Robins said:

'He'd have been gone by now, sir, but the little devil's been playing us up. We couldn't get an address out of him, and when he did come up with one it was wrong, a non-existent road. Could have been a bloody waste of time. I think he's telling the truth now but I had to threaten him with the Juvenile Bureau, the Welfare and God knows what before he did. And then he tried to give us the slip and run off. I was lucky to grab him.'

Miss Wharton had already been driven back to Crowhurst Gardens by a WPC, there to be solaced no doubt with tea and sympathy. She had made gallant efforts to pull herself together but had still been confused about the precise sequence of events between arriving at the church and the moment when she had pushed open the door of the Little Vestry. The important fact for the police to ascertain was whether she or Darren had actually entered the room with the risk that the scene had been contaminated. Both were adamant that they had not. Beyond this there was little of importance which she could tell and Dalgliesh had briefly heard her story and let her go.

But it was irritating that Darren was still with them. If he needed to be questioned again it was right that it should be at home and with his parents present. Dalgliesh knew that his present insouciance in the face of death was no guarantee that the horror hadn't touched him. It wasn't always an obvious trauma which disturbed a child the most. And it was odd that the boy was so resistant to being driven home. Normally, a ride in a car, even a police car, would be something of a treat for a child particularly now that a gratifying crowd was beginning to collect to witness his notoriety, drawn by the yards of white tape which sealed off the whole of the south part of the church and by the police cars and the unmistakable black and sinister mortuary van parked between the church wall and the canal. Dalgliesh went up to the car and opened the door. He said:

'I'm Commander Dalgliesh. It's time we got you home, Darren. Your mother will be worried.' And surely the boy should be at school. The term must have started. But that, thank God, was hardly his concern.

Darren, looking small and extremely disgruntled, was slumped in the front left-hand seat. He was an odd-looking child with an engaging monkey-like face, pale under the rash of freckles, snub-nosed and bright-eyed beneath the spiked almost colourless lashes. He and Sergeant Robins had obviously tried each other's patience to the limits, but he cheered up at the sight of Dalgliesh and enquired with childish belligerence:

'You the boss man round here?'

A little disconcerted, Dalgliesh replied cautiously:

'You could say that.'

Darren looked round with bright suspicious eyes, then said:

'She never did it, Miss Wharton. She's innercent.'

Dalgliesh said, seriously:

'No, we didn't think she did. You see, it needed more strength than an elderly lady or a boy could have. You're both in the clear.'

'Yeah, that's all right then.'

Dalgliesh said:

'You're fond of her?'

'She's all right. She wants lookin' after, mind you. She's daft. She hasn't got the sense she was born with. I keep an eye on her, like.'

'I think she relies on you. It was lucky you were together when you found the bodies. It must have been horrible for her.'

'Turned her up proper. She don't like blood, you see. That's why she won't have a coloured TV. She makes out she can't afford it. That's daft. She's always buying flowers for that BVM.'

'BVM?' said Dalgliesh, his mind scurrying after some unrecognized make of car.

'That statue in the church. The lady in blue with the candles in front of her. They're called BVMs. She's always puttin' flowers there and lightin' candles. Ten pee, they are. Five pee for the small ones.'

His eyes shifted as if he had been lured on to dangerous ground. He added quickly:

'I reckon she won't have a coloured TV 'cause she don't like the colour of blood.'

Dalgliesh said:

'I think you're probably right. You've been very helpful to us, Darren. And you're quite sure that you didn't go into that room, either of you?'

'Naw, I told yer. I was behind 'er all the time.' But the question had been unwelcome and for the first time some of his cockiness seemed to have drained from him. He slumped back in his seat and stared resentfully through the windscreen.

Dalgliesh went back into the church and found Massingham.

'I want you to go home with Darren. I've a feeling there's something he's keeping back. It might not be important but it would be helpful to have you there when he talks to his parents. You've got brothers, you know about small boys.'

Massingham said, 'You want me to go now, sir?'

'Obviously.'

Dalgliesh knew that the order was unwelcome. Massingham hated to leave a scene of crime even temporarily while the body was still there, and he would go the more unwillingly because Kate Miskin, back now from Campden Hill Square, was to stay. But if he had to go he would go alone. He ordered the police driver out of the car with unusual curtness and drove off at a speed which suggested that Darren was about to enjoy a gratifyingly exciting ride.

Dalgliesh passed through the grille door into the body of the church, turning to close it gently behind him. But even so the soft clang rang sharply in the silence and echoed around him as he made his way down the nave. Behind him out of sight, but always present to the mind, was the apparatus of his trade; lights, cameras, equipment, a busy silence broken only by voices unhushed and confident in the presence of death. But here, guarded by the elegant whorls and bars of wrought iron, was another world as yet uncontaminated. The smell of incense strengthened and he saw ahead a haze of gold where the gleaming mosaics of the apse stained the air and the great figure of Christ in glory, his wounded hands stretched out, glared down the nave with cavernous eyes. Two more of the nave lights had been switched on but the church was still dim compared with the harsh glare of the arc lights trained on the scene and it took him a minute to locate Father Barnes, a dark shape at the end of the first row of chairs under the pulpit. He walked up to him, aware of the ring of his feet on the tiled floor, wondering whether they sounded as portentous to the priest as they did to him.

Father Barnes was sitting bolt upright on his chair, his eyes staring ahead at the gleaming curve of the apse, his body taut and contracted, like that of a patient expecting pain, willing himself to endure. He didn't turn his head as Dalgliesh approached. He had obviously been summoned in a hurry. His face was unshaved and the hands, rigidly clamped together in his lap, were grubby, as if he had gone to bed unwashed. The cassock, whose long black lines etiolated still further his lean body, was old and stained with what looked like gravy. One spot he had tried ineffectively to rub away. His black shoes were unpolished, the leather cracked at the sides, the toes scruffed into greyness. There came from him a smell, half-musty, half disagreeably sweet, of old clothes and incense, overlaid with stale sweat, a smell which was a pitiable amalgam of failure and fear. As Dalgliesh eased his long limbs in the adjoining chair and rested his arm along its back, it seemed to him that his body encompassed and, by its own calm presence, gently eased a core of fear and tension in his companion, so strong that it was almost palpable. He felt a sudden compunction. The man would, of course, have come fasting to the first Mass of the day. He would be craving hot coffee and food. Normally someone at or near the scene would be brewing tea but Dalgliesh had no intention of using the washroom even to boil a kettle until the scene of crime officer had done his work.

He said:

'I won't keep you long, Father. There are just a few questions and we'll let you go back to the Vicarage. This must have been a horrible shock to you.' Father Barnes still didn't look at him. He said in a low voice:

'A shock. Yes, it was a shock. I shouldn't have let him have the key. I don't know really why I did. It isn't easy to explain.' The voice was unexpected. It was low with an agreeable trace of huskiness and with a hint of more power than the frail body would suggest; not an educated voice but one on which education had imposed a discipline which hadn't quite obliterated the provincial, probably East Anglian, accent of childhood. He turned now to Dalgliesh and said again:

'They'll say I'm responsible. I shouldn't have let him have the key. I'm to blame.'

Dalgliesh said:

'You aren't responsible. You know that perfectly well and so will they.' The ubiquitous, frightening, judgemental 'they'. He thought, but did not say, that murder provided its own dreadful excitement for those who neither mourned nor were directly concerned and that people were commonly indulgent to those who helped provide the entertainment. Father Barnes would be surprised – agreeably or otherwise – by the size of next Sunday's congregation. He said:

'Could we start at the beginning? When did you first meet Sir Paul Berowne?'

'Last Monday, just over a week ago. He called at the Vicarage at about half past two and asked if he could see the church. He'd come here first and found he couldn't get in. We'd like to keep the church open all the time but you know how it is today. Vandals, people trying to break open the offertory box, stealing the candles. There's a note in the north porch saying that the key is at the Vicarage.'

'I suppose he didn't say what he was doing in Paddington?'

'Yes, he did, actually. He said that an old friend was in St Mary's Hospital and he'd been to see him. But the patient was having treatment and couldn't see visitors so he had an hour to spare. He said he'd always wanted to see St Matthew's.'

So that was how it had started. Berowne's life, like that of all busy men, was dominated by the clock. He had set aside an hour to visit an old friend. The hour had become unexpectedly available for a private indulgence. He was known to be interested in Victorian architecture. However fantastic the labyrinth into which that impulse had led him, his first visit to St Matthew's at least had had the comforting stamp of normality and reason.

Dalgliesh said:

'Did you offer to accompany him?'

'Yes, I offered but he said not to trouble. I didn't press it. I thought he might want to be alone.' So, Father Barnes was not without sensitivity. Dalgliesh said:

'So you gave him the key. Which key?'

'The spare one. There are only three to the south porch. Miss Wharton has one and I keep the other two at the Vicarage. There are two keys on each ring, one to the south door and a smaller key which opens the door in the grille. If Mr Capstick or Mr Pool want a key – they're our two churchwardens – they come to the Vicarage. It's quite close, you see. There's only one key to the main north door. I always keep that in my study. I never lend it out in case it gets lost. It's too heavy, anyway, for general use. I told Sir Paul that he would find a booklet describing the church in the bookstand. It was written by Father Collins and we've always meant to revise it. It's over there on the table by the north porch. We only charge three pence.' He turned his head painfully, like an arthritic patient, as if inviting Dalgliesh to buy a copy. The gesture was pathetic and rather appealing. He went on:

'I think he must have taken one because two days later I found a five pound note in the box. Most people just put in three pence.'

'Did he tell you who he was?'

'He said his name was Paul Berowne. I'm afraid it didn't mean anything to me at the time. He didn't say he was an MP or a baronet, nothing like that. Of course, after he'd resigned I knew who he was. It was in the papers and on the television.'

Again there was a pause. Dalgliesh waited. After a few seconds the voice began again, stronger now and more resolute.

'I suppose he was away about an hour, perhaps less. Then he returned the key. He said he would like to sleep that night in the Little Vestry. Of course he didn't know it was called that. He said in the small room with the bed. The bed has been there since Father Collins's time, in the war. He used to sleep in the church during air raids so that he could put out the fire bombs. We've never taken it away. It's useful if people feel ill during services or if I want to rest before midnight Mass. It doesn't take up much room. It's only a narrow collapsible bed. Well, you've seen it.'

'Yes. Did he give any reason?'

'No. He made it sound quite an ordinary request and I didn't like to ask why. He wasn't a man you could cross-question. I did ask what about sheets, a pillowcase. He said he'd bring anything he needed.'

He had brought one double sheet and had slept between it, doubled over. Otherwise he had used the existing old army blanket folded beneath him and on top the blanket of multicoloured woollen squares. The pillowcase on what was obviously a chair cushion was also presumably his.

Dalgliesh asked:

'Did he take the key away with him then or call back for it that night?'

'He called back for it. That must have been about eight o'clock or a little earlier. He was standing at the door of the Vicarage carrying a grip. I don't think he came by car. I didn't see one. I gave him the key. I didn't see him again until next morning.'

'Tell me about the next morning.'

'I used the south door as usual. It was locked. The door to the Little Vestry was open and I could see that he wasn't there. The bed was made up very tidily. Everything was tidy. There was a sheet and a pillowcase folded on top. I looked through the grille into the church. The lights weren't on but I could just see him. He was sitting in this row, a little further along. I went into the vestry and robed for the Mass, then through the grille door into the church. When he saw that Mass was to be in the Lady Chapel he moved across and sat in the back row. He didn't speak. No one else was there. It wasn't Miss Wharton's morning and Mr Capstick, who likes to come to the nine thirty Mass, had influenza. There were just the two of us. When I'd finished the first prayer and turned to face him, I saw that he was kneeling. He took Communion. Afterwards, we walked together to the Little Vestry. He handed me back the key, thanked me, picked up his grip and left.'

'And that was all on that first occasion?'

Father Barnes turned and looked at him. In the dimness of the church his face looked lifeless. Dalgliesh saw in his eyes a mixture of entreaty, resolution, and pain. There was something he feared to say yet needed to confide. Dalgliesh waited. He was used to waiting. At last Father Barnes spoke.

'No, there is something. When he lifted his hands and I placed the wafer in his palms – I thought I saw –' he paused then went on, 'there were marks, wounds. I thought I saw stigmata.'

Dalgliesh fixed his eyes on the pulpit. The painted figure of a Pre-Raphaelite angel carrying a single lily, its yellow hair crimped under the wide halo, looked back at him with its bland, uncurious gaze. He asked:

'On his palms?'

'No. On his wrists. He was wearing a shirt and a pull-over. The cuffs were a little loose. They slipped back. That's when I saw.'

'Have you told anyone else about this?'

'No, only you.'

For a full minute neither of them spoke. In all his career as a detective Dalgliesh couldn't remember a piece of information from a witness more unwelcome and – there was no other word – more shocking. His mind busied itself with images of what this news could do to his investigation if it ever became public; the newspaper headlines; the half-amused speculation of the cynics; the crowds of sightseers, the superstitious, the credulous, the genuine believers, thronging the church in search of . . . what? A thrill, a new cult, hope, certainty? But his distaste went deeper than irritation at an unwelcome complication to his inquiry, at the bizarre intrusion of irrationality into a job so firmly rooted in the search for evidence which would stand up in court, documented, demonstrable, real. He was shaken, almost physically, by an emotion far stronger than distaste and one of which he was half-ashamed; it seemed to him both ignoble and in itself hardly more rational than the event itself. What he was feeling was a revulsion amounting almost to outrage. He said:

'I think you should continue to say nothing. It isn't relevant to Sir Paul's death. It isn't even necessary to include it in your statement. If you do feel the need to confide in anyone, tell your bishop.'

Father Barnes said simply:

'I shan't tell anyone else. I think I did have a need to speak about it, to share it. I've told you.'

Dalgliesh said:

'The church was dimly lit. You said the lights weren't on. You were fasting. You could have imagined it. Or it could have been a trick of the light. And you saw the marks only for a couple of seconds when he lifted his palms to receive the Host. You could have been mistaken.'

He thought: Who am I trying to reassure, him or me?

And then came the question which against reason he had to ask:

'How did he look? Different? Changed?'

The priest shook his head then said, with great sadness:

'You don't understand. I wouldn't have recognized it, the difference, even if it had been there.' Then he seemed to recover himself. He went on resolutely:

'Whatever it was I saw, if it was there, it didn't last long. And it's not so very unusual. It has been known before. The mind works on the body in strange ways; an intense experience, a powerful dream. And as you say the light was very dim.'

So Father Barnes didn't want to believe it either. He was arguing it away. Well that, thought Dalgliesh wryly, was better than a note in the parish magazine, a telephone call to the daily papers or a sermon next Sunday on the phenomenon of stigmata and the inscrutable wisdom of providence. He was interested to find that they shared the same distrust, perhaps the same revulsion. Later there would be a time and a place to consider why this was so. But now there were more immediate concerns. Whatever had brought Berowne again to that vestry it had been a human hand, his or another's, which had wielded that razor. He said:

'What about yesterday night? When did he ask you if he could come back?'

'In the morning. He rang shortly after nine. I said I'd be in any time after six that evening and he came for the key precisely on the hour.'

'Are you sure of the time, Father?'

'Oh yes, I was watching the six o'clock news. It had only just started when he rang the bell.'

'And again, no explanation?'

'No. He was carrying the same grip. I think he came by bus or underground or walked. I didn't see a car. I handed him the key at the door, the same key. He thanked me and left. I didn't come to the church that night, I had no reason to. The next I knew was when the boy came for me and told me that there were two dead bodies in the Little Vestry. You know the rest.'

Dalgliesh said:

'Tell me about Harry Mack.'

The change of subject was obviously welcome and Father Barnes was voluble on the subject of Harry. Poor Harry was a problem for St Matthew's. For some reason, no one knew why, he had for the last four months taken to sleeping in the south porch. He usually bedded down on newspapers and covered himself with an old blanket which he sometimes left in the porch, ready for the next night, and sometimes took away, rolled into a long wad and tied around his stomach with string. Father Barnes, when he found the blanket, hadn't liked to remove it. After all, it was Harry's only covering. But it wasn't really convenient to have the porch used as a shelter or as a storage for Harry's odd and rather smelly belongings. The Parochial Church Council had actually discussed whether they ought to install railings and a gate, but that had seemed uncharitable and there were more important things to spend their money on. They had difficulty in meeting their diocesan quota as it was. They had all tried to help Harry, but he wasn't easy. He was known at the Wayfarers' Refuge in Cosway Street in St Marylebone, an excellent place, where he usually got a midday meal and medical attention for minor ailments when he needed it. He was a little too fond of drink and would occasionally get into fights. St Matthew's had liaised with the Refuge about Harry but they hadn't known what to suggest. They had tried to persuade Harry to have a bed in their dormitory but he wouldn't agree. He couldn't bear the intimate contact with other people. He wouldn't even eat his dinner at the Refuge. He'd put it between slabs of bread then take it away to eat in the streets. The porch was his place, snug, south-facing, out of public view.

Dalgliesh said:

'So he's not likely to have knocked on the door yesterday evening and asked Sir Paul to let him in.'

'Oh no, Harry wouldn't have done that.'

But somehow he had got in. Perhaps he'd already settled down under his blanket when Berowne arrived. Berowne had asked him in out of the cold to share his meal. But how had he persuaded Harry? He asked Father Barnes what he thought.

'It must have happened that way, I suppose. Harry could already have been here in the porch. He usually dosses down fairly early. And it was unexpectedly cold last night for September. But it's very odd. There must have been something about Sir Paul that gave him confidence. He wouldn't have done it for most people. Even the warden at the Refuge, so experienced with the city's derelicts, couldn't persuade Harry to spend the night there. But they only have the dormitory, of course. It was sleeping or eating with other people Harry couldn't stand.'

And here, thought Dalgliesh, he had had the larger vestry to himself. It could have been the assurance of that privacy and, perhaps, the promise of food which had persuaded him in from the cold. He asked:

'When were you last here in the church, Father? I'm talking about yesterday.'

'From four thirty till about quarter past five, when I read Evensong in the Lady Chapel.'

'And when you locked up after you, how certain could you be that there was no one here, perhaps hidden? Obviously you didn't search the church. Why should you? But if someone were hiding here, would you have been likely to have seen him?'

'I think so. You see how it is. We've no high pews, only the chairs. There's nowhere he could have hidden.'

Dalgliesh said:

'Perhaps under the altar, the high altar or in the Lady Chapel? Or in the pulpit?'

'Under the altar? It's a horrible thought, sacrilege. But how could he have got in? I found the church locked when I arrived at four thirty.'

'And no one had collected the keys during the day, not even the churchwardens?'

'No one.'

And Miss Wharton had assured the police that her key hadn't left her handbag. He said:

'Could anyone have got in during Evensong? Perhaps while you were praying? Were you alone in the Lady Chapel?'

'Yes. I came in by the south door as usual and locked both it and the door in the grille after me. Then I unlocked the main door. That would be the natural way in for any stranger wanting to attend a service. My people know that I always unlock the main door for Evensong and it's very heavy. It squeaks dreadfully. We're always meaning to oil it. I don't think anyone could have entered without my hearing.'

'Did you tell any other person that Sir Paul was spending the night here yesterday?'

'Oh no. There wasn't anyone to tell. And I wouldn't have said anything. He didn't ask for secrecy; he didn't ask for anything. But I don't think he would have liked another person to know. No one else knew anything about him, not until this morning.'

Dalgliesh went on to question him about the blotter and the spent match. Father Barnes said that the Little Vestry had last been used two days ago on Monday the sixteenth when the Parochial Church Council had met as usual at five thirty, immediately after Evensong. He had presided, sitting at the desk, but hadn't used the blotter. He always wrote with a biro. He hadn't been aware of any recent marks but, then, he wasn't very clever at noticing that kind of detail. He was sure that the match couldn't have been left there by anyone in the PCC. Only George Capstick smoked and he used a pipe which he lit with a lighter. But he hadn't been at the PCC because of recovering, still, from the flu. People had remarked how pleasant it was not to be enveloped in smoke.

Dalgliesh said:

'These are small details and probably of no importance. But I would be grateful if you would keep them to yourself. And I'd like you to have a look at the blotter and see whether you can remember what it looked like on Monday. And we've found a rather dirty enamel mug. It would be helpful to know if that belonged to Harry.'

Seeing Father Barnes's face, he added:

'You won't need to go back into the Little Vestry. When the photographer has finished we'll bring out the items to you. And then I expect you'll be glad to get back to the Vicarage. We shall need a statement later, but that can wait.'

They sat for a minute in silence as if what had passed between them needed to be assimilated in peace. So here, thought Dalgliesh, lay the secret of Berowne's quixotic decision to give up his job. It had been something more profound, less explicable, than disillusionment, mid-life restlessness, the fear of a threatened scandal. Whatever had happened to him on that first night in St Matthew's vestry had led him, the next day, to change the whole direction of his life. Had it also led him to his death?

As they both got up they heard the clang of the grille door. Inspector Miskin was walking down the aisle. When she came up to them she said:

'The pathologist has arrived, sir.'

7

Lady Ursula Berowne sat immobile in her sitting room on the fourth floor of 62 Campden Hill Square and gazed out over the top boughs of the plane trees as if at some far distant unseeable vista. It seemed to her that her mind was like an overfilled glass which only she could hold steady. One jerk, one shudder, one small loss of control and it would spill over into a chaos so terrible that it could only end in death. It was strange, she thought, that her physical response to shock should be the same now as it had been after Hugo was killed, so that to her present grief was added a grief for him as keen, as new as when she had first heard that he was dead. And the physical symptoms had been the same; a raging thirst, her body parched and shrivelled, her mouth dry and sour as if infected with her own breath. Mattie had brewed her pot after pot of strong coffee which she had gulped down scalding hot, black, unaware of its oversweetness. Afterwards she had said:

'I would like something to eat, something salty. Anchovy toast.' She had thought: I'm like a woman pregnant with grief, subject to odd fancies.

But that was over now. Mattie had wanted to put a shawl over her shoulders, but she had shrugged it off and demanded to be left alone. She thought: There is a world outside this body, this pain. I shall take hold of it again. I shall survive. I must survive. Seven years, ten at the most, that's all I need. Now she waited, husbanding strength for the first of many visitors. But this was someone she herself had summoned. There were things which had to be said to him and there might not be much time.

Shortly after eleven she heard the doorbell ring, then the groaning of the lift and a soft clatter as the grille door closed. The door of her sitting room opened and Stephen Lampart came quietly in.

It seemed to her important that she should meet him standing. But she couldn't restrain the grimace of pain as her arthritic hip took the weight and she knew that the hand grasping the knob of her cane was trembling. Immediately he was at her side. He said:

'Oh no. Please, you mustn't.'

With one firm hand on her arm he solicitously helped her back into the chair. She disliked casual touching, the assumption of acquaintances or strangers that her disablement entitled them to handle her, as if her body were a despised encumbrance which it was proper gently to push and pull into place. She wanted to shrug off his firm, proprietorial grasp but managed to resist. But she couldn't prevent the tightening of her muscles at his touch and she knew that he hadn't missed this instinctive revulsion. When he had settled her, gently and with professional competence, he seated himself in the chair opposite. They were separated by a low table. A circle of polished rosewood established his dominance; strength against weakness, youth against age, doctor and subservient patient. Except that she wasn't his patient. He said:

'I believe you're waiting for a hip replacement.' It was Barbara, of course, who had told him, but he wouldn't be the first one to mention her name.

'Yes, I'm on the list of the orthopaedic hospital.'

'Forgive me, but why not go private? Aren't you suffering unnecessarily?'

It was, she thought, an almost indecently incongruous remark with which to begin a visit of condolence; or was this his way of confronting her grief and stoicism by taking refuge on professional

ground, the only one on which he felt confident and could speak
with authority?

She said:

'I prefer to be treated as a National Health patient. I enjoy my
privileges but that is one I don't happen to want.'

He smiled gently, humouring a child.

'It seems a little masochistic.'

'Possibly. But I haven't called you here for a professional
opinion.'

'Which as an obstetrician I wouldn't, in any case, be competent
to give. Lady Ursula, this news about Paul is horrifying, unbelievable. Shouldn't you have sent for your own doctor? Or a friend?
You should have someone with you. It's wrong for you to be
alone at a time like this.'

She said:

'I have Mattie if I need the usual palliatives, coffee, alcohol,
warmth. At 82, the few people one might wish to see are all dead.
I have outlived both my sons. That is the worst thing that can
happen to a human being. I have to endure it. But I don't have
to talk about it.' She could have added: 'least of all with you' and
it seemed to her that the words, unspoken, hung on the air
between them. He was for a moment silent as if considering them,
accepting their justice. Then he said:

'I would, of course, have called on you later even if you hadn't
telephoned. But I wasn't sure that you'd want to see anyone so
soon. You got my letter?'

He must have written it as soon as Barbara had telephoned the
news and had sent it round by one of his nurses who, in a hurry
to get home after night duty, hadn't even stopped to hand it in
but had slipped it through the letter box. He had used all the
obvious adjectives. He hadn't needed a thesaurus to decide on
the appropriate response. Murder, after all, was appalling, terrible, horrific, unbelievable, an outrage. But the letter, a social
obligation too promptly performed, had lacked conviction. And
he should have known better than to have his secretary type it.
But that, she thought, was typical. Scrape away the carefully
acquired patina of professional success, prestige, orthodox good
manners, and the real man was there; ambitious, a little vulgar,

sensitive only when sensitivity paid. But much of this, she knew, was prejudice and prejudice was dangerous. She must be careful to betray it as little as possible if the interview were to go the way she wanted. And it was hardly fair to criticize the letter. Dictating condolences to the mother of a murdered husband whom you've been cuckolding for the last three years would take more than his limited social vocabulary.

She hadn't seen him for nearly three months and she was struck anew by his good looks. He had been an attractive youth, tall, rather ungainly, with a thatch of black hair. But now the gangling figure had been smoothed and tailored by success, he carried his height with easy assurance and the grey eyes – which he knew so well how to use – held a basic wariness. His hair, frosted now with grey, was still thick with an unruliness that expensive cutting still hadn't completely disciplined. It added to his attractiveness, hinting at an untamed individuality which was far removed from the tedium of conventional male good looks.

He leaned forward and looked across at her intently, his grey eyes softened with sympathy. She found herself resenting his easy assumption of professional concern. But he did it very well. She almost expected him to say, 'We did all we could, all that was humanly possible.' Then she told herself that the concern could be genuine. She had to resist the temptation to underrate him, to stereotype him as the handsome, experienced seducer of cheap fiction. Whatever he was, he wasn't as uncomplicated as that. No human being could be. And he was, after all, acknowledged as a fine gynaecologist. He worked hard, he knew his job.

When Hugo was at Balliol, Stephen Lampart had been his closest friend. She had liked him in those days and some of that liking still remained, resented, only half-acknowledged, but bound up with memories of sunlit walks in Port Meadow, luncheon and laughter in Hugo's rooms, with the years of hope and promise. He had been the clever, handsome, ambitious boy from a lower-middle-class home, likeable, amusing, buying himself into the company he wanted by looks and wit, clever at concealing the itch of ambition. Hugo had been the privileged one, his mother an earl's daughter, his father a baronet and a distinguished soldier, possessor of the Berowne name, inheritor of what remained of the Berowne money. For the first time she found herself wondering whether he had resented not only Hugo but all the family, and whether that subsequent betrayal could have had long roots in the soil of an old envy. She said:

'There are two things we have to discuss and there may not be much time or another opportunity. Perhaps I ought to say first that I didn't ask you here to criticize my daughter-in-law for infidelity. I'm not in a position to criticize anyone's sexual life.'

The grey eyes grew cautious. He said:

'How wise of you. Few of us are.'

'But my son was murdered. The police will know that soon if they don't already. And I know it now.'

He said:

'Forgive me, but can you be sure? All Barbara could tell me when she rang this morning was that the police had found Paul's body and that of a tramp,' he paused, 'with injuries to their throats.'

'Their throats were cut. Both their throats. And from the careful tact with which the news was broken, I imagine that the weapon was one of Paul's razors. I suppose Paul could have been capable of killing himself. Most of us are, given sufficient pain. But what he wasn't capable of was killing that tramp. My son was murdered, and that means that there are certain facts the police will make it their business to discover.'

He asked, calmly:

'What facts, Lady Ursula?'

'That you and Barbara are lovers.'

The hands clasped loosely in his lap tightened then relaxed. But he was still able to meet her eyes.

'I see. Was it Paul or Barbara who told you that?'

'Neither. But I've lived in the same house with my daughter-in-law for four years. I'm a woman. I may be crippled but I have the use of my eyes and my intelligence.'

'How is she, Lady Ursula?'

'I don't know. But before you leave I suggest that you make it your business to find out. I've only seen my daughter-in-law for three minutes since I got the news. She is, apparently, too distressed to talk to visitors. It seems that I count as a visitor.'

'Is that quite fair? Sometimes other people's grief is harder to bear, to face, than one's own.'

'Particularly if one's own isn't acute?'

He leaned forward and said quietly:

'I don't think we have any right to assume that. Barbara's feelings may not be intense but Paul was her husband. She cared for him, probably more than either of us understand. This is a horrible business for her, for all of us. Look, do we have to talk now? We're both in shock.'

'We have to talk and there isn't much time. Commander Adam Dalgliesh is coming to see me as soon as they've finished with whatever it is they're doing at the church. Presumably he'll want to interview Barbara, too. In time, probably sooner than later, they'll get round to you. I have to know what you propose to tell them.'

'This Adam Dalgliesh, isn't he some kind of poet? An odd hobby for a policeman.'

'If he's as good a detective as he is a poet, he's a dangerous man. Don't underestimate the police because of what you read in the upmarket papers.'

He said:

'I don't underestimate the police, but I've no reason to fear them. I know that they combine a macho enthusiasm for selective violence with a rigid adherence to middle-class morality, but you aren't seriously suggesting that they'll suspect me of cutting Paul's throat because I go to bed with his wife? They may be out of touch with social reality but, surely, not that much out of touch.'

She thought: This is more like it, this is the real man.

She said calmly:

'I'm not saying they'll suspect you. I've no doubt you'll be able to provide a satisfactory alibi for last evening. But it will cause less trouble if neither of you lies about your relationship. I'd prefer not to have to lie about it myself. Naturally, I shan't volunteer the information. But it is possible that they will ask.'

'And why should they, Lady Ursula?'

'Because Commander Dalgliesh will liaise with Special Branch. My son was a Minister of the Crown, however briefly. Do you suppose there's anything about a minister's private life, particularly a minister in that Department, which isn't known to those people whose business it is to discover and document this kind of potential scandal? What sort of world do you think we're living in?'

He got up and began slowly pacing in front of her. He said:

'I suppose I ought to have thought of that. I would have thought of it given time. Paul's death has been such an appalling shock. I don't think my mind is working properly yet.'

'Then I suggest that it begins working. You and Barbara have to agree on your story. Better still, agree to tell the truth. I take it that Barbara was your mistress when you first introduced her to Hugo and that she remained your mistress after Hugo was killed and she married Paul.'

He stopped and turned to her.

'Believe me, Lady Ursula, it wasn't intended, it wasn't like that.'

'You mean that she and you graciously decided to abstain from your sexual liaison, at least until the honeymoon was over?'

He came and stood in front of her and looked down.

'I think there's something I ought to say but I'm afraid it isn't, well, gentlemanly.' She thought but did not speak: That word is meaningless now. With you it probably always was. Before 1914, one could talk like that without sounding false or ridiculous, but not now. That word and the world it represented have gone for ever, trodden into the mud of Flanders. She said:

'My son's throat was cut. In the light of that brutality, I don't think we need concern ourselves about gentility, spurious or otherwise. It's about Barbara, of course.'

'Yes. There's something you ought to understand if you don't already. I may be her lover but she doesn't love me. She certainly doesn't want to marry me. She's as satisfied with me as she can be with any man. That's because I understand her needs and I don't make demands. Not many demands. We all make some. And, of course, I'm in love with her as far as I'm capable of loving anyone. That's necessary to her. And she feels safe with me. But she wouldn't get rid of a perfectly good husband and a title to marry me. Not by divorce. Certainly not by conniving at murder. You have to believe that if you and she are going to go on living together.'

She said:

'That at least was frank. You seem well suited to each other.'

He accepted the subtle insult behind the irony.

'Oh yes,' he said sadly, 'we suit each other.' He added, 'I suspect she doesn't even feel particularly guilty. Less so than I do, oddly enough. It's difficult to take adultery seriously if you're not getting much pleasure out of it.'

'Your role must be exhausting and hardly satisfying. I admire your self-sacrifice.'

His smile was reminiscent, secretive.

'She's so beautiful. It's absolute, isn't it? It doesn't even depend on whether she's well or happy or not tired or on what she wears. It's always there. You can't blame me for trying.'

'Oh yes,' she said, 'I can, and I do.'

But she knew that she was being less than honest. All her life she had been beguiled by physical beauty in men and in women. It was what she had lived by. When, in 1918, with her brother and fiancé both killed, she, an earl's daughter, had gone on the stage in defiance of tradition, what else had she to offer? Not, she thought with wry honesty, any great dramatic talent. She had, almost casually and instinctively, demanded physical beauty in her lovers and had been unjealous and over-indulgent of it in her women friends. They had been the more surprised when, at the age of 32, she had married Sir Henry Berowne, apparently for less obvious qualities, and had given him two sons. She thought now of her daughter-in-law as she had watched her many times, standing motionless in front of the glass in the hall. Barbara was incapable of passing a mirror without that moment of narcissistic stillness, that calm reflective gaze. What had she been watching for? That first droop from the corner of the eyes, the fading blue, the dry fold of skin, the first crêping of the neck which would show how transitory it was, this over-prized perfection.

He was still restlessly pacing, still talking.

'Barbara likes to feel that attention is being paid to her. You have to admit that about the sexual act. Attention, specific and intense, is certainly being paid. She needs men to desire her. She doesn't much want them actually to touch her. If she thought I had a hand in killing Paul she wouldn't thank me. I don't think she'd forgive me. And she certainly wouldn't protect me. I'm sorry. I've been too frank. But I think it had to be said.'

'Yes, it had to be said. Who would she protect?'

'Her brother, possibly, but not, I should have thought for long and certainly not at any risk to herself. They've never been particularly close.'

She said dryly:

'No sibling loyalty will be demanded of her. Dominic Swayne was here in this house with Mattie for the whole of yesterday evening.'

'Is that his story or hers?'

'Are you accusing him of having a hand in my son's death?'

'Of course not. The idea is ridiculous. And if Mattie says he was with her, I've no doubt he was. We all know that Mattie is a model of rectitude. You asked me if there was anyone Barbara would protect, I can think of no one else.'

He had stopped his pacing now and sat down again opposite to her.

He said:

'Your reasons for telephoning me. You said there were two things we needed to discuss.'

'Yes. I should like to be sure that the child Barbara is carrying is my grandchild, not your bastard.'

His shoulders stiffened. For a moment, it could have been a second only, he sat rigidly gazing down at his clasped hands. In the silence she heard the ticking of the carriage clock. Then he looked up. He was still calm but she thought that his face was paler.

'Oh, there's no doubt about that. No possible doubt. I had a vasectomy three years ago. I'm not suited to fatherhood and I hadn't any wish to be made ridiculous by paternity suits. I can give you the name of my surgeon if you want proof. That's probably simpler than relying on blood tests once he's born.'

'He?'

'Oh yes, it's a boy. Barbara had an amniocentesis. Your son wanted an heir and he's going to get an heir. Didn't you know?'

She sat for a moment in silence. Then she said:

'Isn't that a risky procedure for the foetus, particularly so early in the pregnancy?'

'Not with the new techniques and in expert hands. And I saw that she was in expert hands. No, not mine. I'm not that kind of fool.'

She asked:

'Did Paul know about the child before he died?'

'Barbara hasn't said. I imagine not. After all, she's only just heard of it herself.'

'The pregnancy? Surely not.'

'No, the sex of the child. I rang and told her first thing yesterday morning. But Paul may have suspected that there was a child on the way. After all, he did go back to that church, presumably to ask his God for further and better instructions.'

She was seized by an anger so intense that, for a moment, she couldn't speak. And when her voice did come it quavered like the voice of an old, impotent woman. But at least her words could sting. She said:

'You never could resist it, even as a boy, the temptation to combine vulgarity with what you imagined was wit. Whatever happened to my son in that church, and I don't pretend to understand it, in the end he died because of it. When next you're tempted to indulge in a cheap witticism you might remember that.'

His own voice was low and as cold as steel.

'I'm sorry. I thought from the beginning that this conversation was a mistake. We're both too shocked to be rational. And now, if you'll excuse me, I'll go down to see Barbara before the police descend on her. She's alone I take it?'

'As far as I know she is. Anthony Farrell should be arriving soon. I sent for him to his private address as soon as I got the news but he has to get up from Winchester.'

'The family lawyer? Having him here when the police arrive – won't that look suspicious? Too like a necessary precaution?'

'He's a family friend as well as a lawyer. It's natural for both of us to want him here. But I'm glad you're seeing her before he arrives. Tell her to answer Dalgliesh's questions but not to volunteer information, any information. I've no reason to suppose the police will take an unnecessarily dramatic view of what, after all, was common adultery. But it isn't something they'll expect her to confide even if they know about it. Too much candour looks as suspicious as too little.'

He asked:

'Were you with her when the police broke the news?'

'The police didn't break the news. I did. It seemed to me advisable in all the circumstances. A competent woman officer told me first, then I went down alone to see Barbara. She behaved very prettily. Barbara has always known what emotion it is appropriate for her to feel. And she's a good actress. She should be. She's had plenty of practice. Oh, and another thing. Tell her to say nothing about the child. That's important.'

'If it's what you want, what you think is wise. But it could be helpful to mention the pregnancy. They'd be particularly gentle with her.'

'They'll be gentle. They won't be sending a fool.'

They were speaking like confederates, precariously allied in a conspiracy which neither would acknowledge. She felt a cold disgust as physical as nausea and with it there swept over her a weakness which shrivelled her in her chair. Immediately, she was aware of him at her side, of his fingers, gentle, firm, pressing her wrist. She knew that she should have resented his touch, but now it comforted her. She lay back, her eyes closed, and her pulse strengthened under his fingers. He said:

'Lady Ursula, you really should see your doctor. Malcolm Hancock, isn't it? Let me ring him.' She shook her head.

'I'm all right. I can't cope with another person yet. Until the police arrive I need to be alone.' It was a confession of weakness which she hadn't expected to make, not to him and not at such a moment. He walked to the door. When his hand was on the knob she said:

'There's one more thing. What do you know about Theresa Nolan?'

'No more than you, I imagine, probably less. She only worked at Pembroke Lodge for four weeks and I hardly set eyes on her. She nursed you, lived in this house, for over six. And when she came to me she was already pregnant.'

'And Diana Travers?'

'Nothing, except that she was unwise enough to overeat, drink too much and then dive into the Thames. As you must know, Barbara and I had left the Black Swan before she drowned.' He was silent for a moment and then said, gravely:

'I know what you're thinking about, that ludicrous article in the *Paternoster Review*. Lady Ursula, may I give you some advice? Paul's murder, if it is murder, is perfectly simple. He let someone into that church, a thief, another derelict, a psychopath, and that person killed him. Don't complicate his death which, God knows, is horrible enough, with old, irrelevant tragedies. The police will have enough to get their teeth into without that.'

'Are they both irrelevant?'

He didn't answer. Instead he said:

'Has Sarah been told?'

'Not yet. I tried to telephone her this morning at the flat but there was no reply. She was probably out getting a paper. I'll try again as soon as you leave.'

'Would you like me to go round? She is Paul's daughter, after all. This will be a terrible shock to her. She oughtn't to learn it from the police or the television news.'

'She won't. If necessary, I'll go round myself.'

'But who will drive you? Isn't Wednesday Halliwell's day off?'

'There are taxis.'

She resented the way in which he seemed to be taking over, insinuating himself into the family as cunningly as he once had in Oxford. And then, again, she reproached herself for unfairness. He had never lacked his measure of kindness. He said:

'She ought to have time for preparation before the police burst in on her.'

Time for what? she wondered. To make a decent pretence that she cared? She didn't reply. Suddenly she wanted him gone so urgently that it was all she could do not to order him to get out. Instead she held out her hand. Bending, he took it in his and then raised it to his lips. The gesture, theatrical and ludicrously inappropriate disconcerted but did not disgust her. After he had left, she found herself looking down at her thin, ring-encrusted fingers, at the age-mottled knuckles against which, briefly, his lips had rested. Was the gesture a tribute to an old woman facing with dignity and courage a last tragedy? Or had it been something more subtle, a pledge that, despite everything, they were allies, that he understood her priorities and would make them his?

8

Dalgliesh remembered a surgeon once telling him that Miles Kynaston had shown promise of becoming a brilliant diagnostician, but had given up general medicine for pathology at registrar level because he could no longer bear to watch human suffering. The surgeon had sounded a note of amused condescension as though he were betraying a colleague's unfortunate weakness, wryly observed, which a more prudent man would have detected before beginning his medical training, or at least would have come to terms with before his second year. It could, Dalgliesh thought, have been true. Kynaston had fulfilled his promise, but now he applied his diagnostic skills to the unrepining dead, whose eyes couldn't implore him to offer hope, whose mouths could no longer cry out. Certainly he had a taste for death. Nothing about it disconcerted him; its messiness, its smell, the most bizarre of its trappings. Unlike most doctors, he saw it, not as the final enemy, but as a fascinating enigma, each cadaver, which he would gaze at with the same intent look as he must once have fixed on his living patients, a new piece of evidence which might, if rightly interpreted, bring him closer to its central mystery.

Dalgliesh respected him more than any other pathologist with whom he had worked. He came promptly when called, and was equally prompt reporting on a post-mortem. He didn't indulge in the crude autopsy humour which some of his colleagues found necessary to bolster their social self-esteem; dinner guests could know themselves safe from distasteful anecdotes about carving knives or missing kidneys. Above all he was good in the witness box, too good for some people. Dalgliesh remembered the sour comment of a defending counsel after a verdict of guilty: 'Kynaston's getting dangerously infallible with juries. We don't want another Spilsbury.'

He never wasted time. Even as he greeted Dalgliesh he was taking off his jacket and was drawing his fine latex gloves over stubby-fingered hands which looked unnaturally white, almost bloodless. He was tall and stolidly built, giving an impression of shambling clumsiness until one saw him working in a confined space when he would seem physically to contract and become compact, even graceful, moving about the body with the lightness and precision of a cat. His face was fleshy, the dark hair receding from a high speckled forehead, the long upper lip as precisely curved as an arrowhead, and the full, heavily lidded eyes dark and very bright, giving his face a look of sardonic, humorous intelligence. Now he squatted, toad-like, by Berowne's body, his hands hanging loosely in front of him, palely disembodied. He gazed at the throat wounds with extraordinary concentration, but made no move to touch the body except to run his hand lightly over the back of the head, like a caress. Then he said:

'Who are they?'

'Sir Paul Berowne, late MP and junior minister, and a tramp, Harry Mack.'

'On the face of it, murder followed by suicide. The cuts are textbook; two fairly superficial from left to right, then one above, swift, deep, severing the artery. And the razor neatly to hand. As I say, on the face of it obvious. A little too obvious?'

Dalgliesh said:

'I thought so.'

Kynaston stepped gingerly over the carpet to Harry, prancing on tiptoe like an inexpert dancer.

'One cut. Enough. Again from left to right. Which means that Berowne, if it were Berowne, stood behind him.'

'So why isn't Berowne's right shirt-sleeve soaked with blood? All right, it's heavily bloodstained, his own or Harry's blood or both. But if he killed Harry, wouldn't you expect a greater amount of soaking?'

'Not if he turned up his shirt-sleeve first and took him from behind.'

'And turned it down again before slitting his own throat? Unlikely, surely.'

Kynaston said:

'Forensic should be able to identify Harry's blood, or what could be Harry's blood, on the shirt-sleeve as well as Berowne's own. There seem to be no visible stains between the bodies.'

Dalgliesh said:

'Forensic have been over the carpet with the fibre-optic lamp. They may get something. And there is one discernible smudge under Harry's jacket and a trace of what looks like blood on the jacket lining immediately above it.'

He lifted the corner. Both of them looked at the stain on the carpet in silence. Dalgliesh said:

'It was under the jacket when we found it. That means it was there before Harry fell. And if it proves to be Berowne's blood, then he died first, unless, of course, he staggered across to Harry after making one or more of the superficial cuts in his own throat. As a theory, it strikes me as ludicrous. If he were in the very act of cutting his own throat, how could Harry have stopped him? So why bother to kill him? But is it possible, medically possible?'

Kynaston looked at him. Both knew the importance of the question. He said:

'After the first superficial cut, I'd say that it was.'

'But would he still have had the strength to kill Harry?'

'With his own throat partly cut? Again, after that first superficial cut, I don't think one can rule it out. He'd be in a state of high excitement, remember. It's amazing what strength people do find. After all, we're supposing that he was interrupted in the act of suicide. Hardly the moment when a man is at his most rational. But I can't be certain. No one can. You're asking the impossible, Adam.'

'I was afraid so. But it's too neat.'

'Or you want to believe it's too neat. How do you see it?'

'From the position of the body I think he could have been sitting on the edge of the bed. Assuming he was murdered, assuming that the murderer went first into the kitchen, then he could have crept back silently and attacked Berowne from behind. A blow, a cord round the throat. Or he grabs him by the hair, drags back the head, makes the first deep cut. The others, the ones designed to look tentative, could have come afterwards. So we look for any mark under the cuts, or for a bump on the back of the head.'

Kynaston said:

'There is a bump but it's small. It could have been caused by the body falling. But we'll know more at the PM.'

'An alternative theory is that the killer knocked him out first, then went into the washroom to strip and came back for the final throat-cutting before Berowne had a chance to come round. But that raises obvious objections. He'd have to judge the force of the blow very carefully and you'd expect it to leave more than a slight bump.'

Kynaston said:

'But it raises fewer objections than the first theory, that he came in half-naked and armed with a razor and yet there are no obvious signs that Berowne put up any resistance.'

'He could have been taken by surprise. He would expect his visitor to come back through the door to the kitchen. It's possible that he tiptoed down the passage and came in by the main door. That's the most likely theory, given the position of the body.'

Kynaston said:

'You're assuming premeditation then? That the killer knew he'd find a razor to hand?'

'Oh yes. If Berowne were murdered then the killing was premeditated. But I'm theorizing in advance of the facts, the unforgivable sin. All the same, there's something contrived about it, Miles. It's too obvious, too neat.'

Kynaston said:

'I'll finish the preliminary examination and then you can take them away. I would normally do the PM first thing tomorrow but they aren't expecting me back at the hospital until Monday and the PM room is tied up until the afternoon. Three thirty is the earliest. Is that all right for your people?'

'I don't know about the lab. The sooner the better for us.'

Something in his voice alerted Kynaston. He said:

'Did you know him?'

Dalgliesh thought: This is going to come up again and again. You knew him. You're emotionally involved. You don't want to see him as mad, a suicide, a killer. He said:

'Yes, I knew him slightly, mostly across a committee table.'

The words seemed to him grudging, almost a small treachery. He said again:

'Yes, I knew him.'

'What was he doing here?'

'He had some kind of religious quasi-mystical experience here in this room. He may have been hoping to recapture it. He'd arranged with the parish priest to stay the night here. He gave no explanation.'

'And Harry?'

'It looks as if Berowne let him in. He may have found him sleeping in the porch. Apparently Harry couldn't tolerate being with other people. There's evidence that he was proposing to sleep further along the passage in the larger vestry.'

Kynaston nodded and got down to his familiar routine. Dalgliesh left him to it and went out into the passage. Watching this violation of the body's orifices, preliminaries to the scientific brutality to follow, had always made him feel uncomfortably like a voyeur. He had often wondered why he found it more offensive and ghoulish than the autopsy itself. Was it, perhaps, because the body was so recently dead, sometimes hardly cold. A superstitious man might fear that the spirit, so recently released, hovered around to be outraged at this insult to the discarded, still vulnerable, flesh. There was nothing for him to do now until Kynaston had finished. He was surprised to find himself tired. He expected to be exhausted later in an investigation when he would be working a sixteen-hour day, but this early heaviness, the feeling that he was already spent in mind and body was new to him. He wondered whether it was the beginning of age, or one more sign that this case was going to be different.

He went back into the church, sat down in a chair in front of a statue of the Virgin. The huge nave was empty now. Father Barnes had gone, escorted home by a police constable. He had been readily helpful about the mug, identifying it as one Harry had often had with him when he was found sleeping in the porch. And he had tried to be helpful about the blotter, staring at it with almost painful intensity before saying that he thought that the black markings hadn't been there when he had last seen the blotter on Monday evening. But he couldn't be sure. He had taken a sheet of writing paper from the desk and used it to make notes during the meeting. This had covered the blotter so that he had really only seen it for a short time. But, as far as his memory went, the black markings were new.

Dalgliesh was grateful for these minutes of quiet contemplation. The scent of incense seemed to have intensified, but it smelled to him overlaid with a sickly, more sinister smell, and the silence wasn't absolute. At his back he could hear the ring of footsteps, an occasional raised voice, calm, confident and unhurried, as the unseen professionals went about their work behind the grille. The sounds seemed very far off and yet distinct and he had the sensation of a secret, sinister busy-ness, like the scrabbling of mice behind the wainscot. Soon, he knew, the two bodies would be neatly parcelled in plastic sheeting. The rug would be carefully folded to preserve bloodstains, and in particular, that one significant stain of dried blood. The scene of crime exhibits, packed and tagged, would be carried to the police car; the razor, the crumbs of bread and cheese from the larger room, the fibres from Harry's clothing, that single burnt matchhead. For the moment he would keep possession of the diary. He needed to have it with him when he went to Campden Hill Square.

At the foot of the statue of the Virgin and Child stood a wrought-iron candleholder bearing its triple row of clotted sockets, the tips of burnt wick deep in their rims of wax. On impulse he felt in his pocket for a tenpenny piece and dropped it in the box. The clatter was unnaturally loud. He half-expected to hear Kate or Massingham moving up beside him to watch, unspeaking but with interested eyes, his untypical act of sentimental folly. There was a box of matches in a brass holder chained to the candlerack, similar to the one at the back of the church. He took one of the smaller candles and, striking a match, held it to the wick. It seemed to take an unduly long time before it took hold. Then the flame burnt steadily, a limpid, unflickering glow. He stuck the candle upright in a socket then sat and gazed at the flame, letting it mesmerize him into memory.

9

It was over a year ago but it seemed even longer. They had both been attending a seminar on judicial sentencing at a northern university, Berowne to open it formally with a brief speech, Dalgliesh to represent the police interest; and they had travelled by rail in the same first class compartment. For the first hour Berowne, with his private secretary, had dealt with official papers while Dalgliesh, after a final perusal of the agenda, had settled down to reread Trollope's *The Way We Live Now*. When the last file had been placed in the briefcase, Berowne had looked across at him and had seemed to want to talk. The young Principal, with a tact that would help ensure he remained a 'high flyer', had suggested that he should take first luncheon if that were agreeable to the Minister, and had disappeared. And for a couple of hours they had talked.

Looking back on it, Dalgliesh was still amazed that Berowne should have been so frank. It was as if the train journey itself, the old-fashioned intimate compartment in which they had found themselves, the freedom from interruptions and the tyranny of the telephone, the sense of time visibly flying, annihilated under the pounding wheels, not to be accounted for, had released both of them from a carefulness which had become so much a part of living that they were no longer aware of its weight until they let it slip from their shoulders. Both were very private men. Neither needed the masculine camaraderie of club or golf course, pub or grouse moor which so many of their colleagues found necessary to solace or sustain their over-busy lives.

Berowne had spoken at first spasmodically, then easily, and finally intimately. From the ordinary subjects of casual conversation – books, recent plays, acquaintances they had in common – he had gone on to talk about himself. Both had leaned forward, hands loosely clasped. To a casual passenger, glancing in as he lurched down the corridor, they must, thought Dalgliesh, have looked like two penitents in a private confessional absolving each other. Berowne had seemed not to expect a reciprocal confidence, indiscretion traded for indiscretion. He spoke; Dalgliesh listened. Dalgliesh knew that no politician would have talked with such freedom unless he had had absolute confidence in his listener's discretion. It was impossible not to feel flattered. He had always respected Berowne; now he warmed to him and was honest enough about his own reactions to know why Berowne had spoken of his family:

'We're not a distinguished family, merely an old one. My great grandfather lost a fortune because he was fascinated by a subject for which he had absolutely no talent – finance. Someone told him that the way to make money was to buy when the shares were low and sell when they were high. A simple enough rule which struck his rather undeveloped mind with the force of divine inspiration. He had absolutely no difficulty in following the first precept. The problem was that he never had the opportunity to follow the second. He had a positive genius for picking losers. So had his father. In his case the losers were on four legs. But I feel grateful to great grandfather nevertheless. Before he lost his money he had the good sense to commission John Soane to design the Campden Hill Square house. You're interested in architecture, aren't you? I'd like you to see it when you can spare a couple of hours. It needs at least that. In my view it's even more interesting than the Soane museum in Lincoln's Inn Fields; a perverse neo-classicism I suppose you'd call it. I find it satisfying, architecturally anyway. But I'm not sure that it isn't a house to admire rather than to live in.'

Dalgliesh had wondered how Berowne knew about his fondness for architecture. It could only have been because he read his poetry. A poet may heartily dislike having to talk about his verse but the knowledge that someone has actually read it is never unwelcome.

And now, sitting legs stretched, on a chair too low comfortably to accommodate his six feet two inches, eyes fixed on that single taper, unflickering in the incense-heavy stillness, he could hear again the tone, taut with self-disgust, in which Berowne had explained why he had given up the law:

'Such odd things determine why and when one makes that kind of decision. I suppose I had persuaded myself that sending men to prison wasn't something I cared to do for the rest of my life. And appearing only for the defence has always seemed too easy an option. I was never really good at pretending that I could assume my client to be innocent because I or my instructing solicitor had been careful to ensure that he didn't actually confess. By the time you've seen your third rapist walk free because you've been cleverer than the prosecuting counsel, you lose the

taste for that particular victory. But that's just the easy explanation. I suspect it wouldn't have happened if I hadn't lost an
important case, important to me anyway. You won't remember it
– Percy Matlock. He killed his wife's lover. It wasn't a particularly
difficult case and we were confident we'd get it reduced to
manslaughter. Even with that lesser verdict there was plenty of
mitigation. But I didn't prepare carefully enough. I suppose I
thought I didn't need to. I was pretty arrogant in those days. But
it wasn't only that. At the time I was very much in love, one of
those adventures which seem of overwhelming importance at the
time but, afterwards, leave one wondering if it wasn't a kind of
sickness. But I just wasn't giving the case what it needed. Matlock
was convicted of murder and died in prison. He had one child, a
daughter. Her father's conviction unhinged what precarious stability she'd managed to maintain and after she came out of the
psychiatric hospital she got in touch with me and I gave her a
job. She still keeps house for my mother. I don't think she's
otherwise employable, poor girl. So I live with a constant and
uncomely reminder of folly and failure, and no doubt it does me
good. The fact that she's actually grateful to me, devoted is the
word people use, doesn't make it easier.'

He had gone on to talk of his brother, killed five years earlier
in Northern Ireland:

'The title came to me through his death. Most of the things I
expected to value in life have come to me through death.'

Not, Dalgliesh remembered, the 'things I value'. The 'things I
expected to value'.

He could smell above the all-pervading redolence of incense,
the faint acrid smoke of the candle. Getting up from his chair, he
left it burning, the pale flame staining the air, and moved down
the nave through the grille and into the back of the church.

In the bell room Ferris had set up his metal exhibits table and
had neatly laid out his spoils, each tagged and shrouded in its
plastic envelope. Now he was standing back regarding them with
the faintly anxious proprietorial air of a stallholder at a church
bazaar wondering whether he has set out his wares to best
advantage. And indeed, thus dignified and labelled, these diverse
and ordinary objects had assumed an almost ritualistic signific-

ance; the shoes, one with its wedge of mud behind the heel, the stained beaker, the blotter with its criss-cross of dead marks made by dead hands, the diary, the remains of Harry Mack's last meal, the closed razor case and, occupying the centre of the table, the prize exhibit, the open cut-throat razor, its blade and bone handle gummy with blood. Dalgliesh asked:

'Anything interesting?'

'The diary, sir.' He made a move as if to take it out of its packet. Dalgliesh said:

'Leave it. Just tell me.'

'It's the last page. It looks as if he tore out the entries for the last two months and burned those pages separately, then chucked the book open on the flames. The cover is only singed. The last page is the one which sets out the summary of the calendars for last year and next. There's no sign even of singeing, but the top half is missing. Someone has torn the page in two.' He added:

'I suppose he could have folded it and used it as a spill to get a light from the pilot on the gas water heater.'

Dalgliesh picked up the bag containing the shoes. He said:

'It's possible.'

But it struck him as unlikely. For a murderer in a hurry, and this murderer had been in a hurry, it would have been a tedious and uncertain way to get a light. If he'd come without a lighter or matches, surely the obvious thing would have been to remove the box from the chained brass holder attached to the heater. He turned the shoes over in his hands and said:

'Handmade. There are some extravagances it's difficult to forgo. The toes are still polished, the sides and heels dull and slightly smeared. It looks as if they've been washed. And there are still traces of mud at the sides as well as under the left heel. The lab will probably find scrape marks.'

They were hardly, he thought, the shoes you'd expect to find on a man who had spent the day in London unless he had walked in the parks or along the towpath of the canal. But he could hardly have walked to St Matthew's that way; there were no signs that he had cleaned his shoes anywhere in the church. But this, again, was theorizing in advance of the facts. They could hope to learn later where Berowne had spent his last day on earth.

Kate Miskin appeared in the doorway. She said:

'Doc Kynaston has finished, sir. They're ready to remove the bodies.'

IO

Massingham had expected that Darren would live in one of the high rise local authority housing estates in Paddington. Instead the address which he had at last been persuaded to give was in a short and narrow street off the Edgware Road, an enclave of cheap, unsmart cafés chiefly Goan and Greek. As they turned into it Massingham realized that it wasn't strange to him, he had been here before. It was surely in this street that he and old George Percival had picked up two excellent vegetarian take-aways when they were both detective-sergeants on Division. Even the names, exotic, until now almost forgotten, came back to him: Alu Ghobi, Sag Bhajee. It had changed little since then, a street where people minded their own business, principally that of supplying their own kind with meals remarkable for value and cheapness. Although it was morning and the quietest time of the day the air was already pungent with the smell of curry and spices, reminding Massingham that it was some hours since breakfast and that there was no certainty when he would get his lunch.

There was only one pub, a high narrow Victorian building squeezed between a Chinese take-away and a Tandoori café, darkly uninviting, with a painted scrawl on the window advert-ising with defiant Englishness: 'Bangers and mash', 'Bangers and bubble-and-squeak' and 'Toad-in-the-hole'. Between the pub and the café was a small door with a single bell and a card with the one name 'Arlene'. Darren stooped, took a key from the side of his canvas trainer shoes, then tiptoeing, inserted it in the lock. Massingham followed him up the narrow uncarpeted stairs. At the top he said:

'Where's your ma?'

Still without speaking, the boy pointed to the door on the left. Massingham knocked gently, then, getting no reply, pushed it open.

The curtains were drawn but they were thin and unlined and even in the subdued light he could see that the room was spectacularly untidy. There was a woman lying on the bed. He moved over and putting out his hand found the switch of the bedside light. As it clicked on she gave a small grunt but didn't move. She was lying on her back, naked except for a short wrapover dressing gown from which one blue-veined breast had escaped and lay like a quivering jellyfish against the pink satin. A thin line of lipstick outlined the moistly open mouth from which a bleb of mucus ballooned and fell. She was snorting gently, small guttural sounds as if there were phlegm in her throat. Her eyebrows had been plucked in the manner of the thirties, thin arches high above the natural line of the brow. They gave the face, even in sleep, a look of clownish surprise, enhanced by the circles of rouge on both cheeks. On a chair beside the bed was a large jar of Vaseline, the lid open, a single fly gummed to the rim. The back of the chair and the floor were strewn with clothes and the top of a chest of drawers which served as a dressing table under an oval mirror was crowded with bottles, dirty glasses, jars of make-up and packets of tissues. Set incongruously among the mess was a jam jar with a bunch of freesias still bound with a rubber band, whose delicate sweetness was lost in the stink of sex, scent and whisky. He said:

'Is this your ma?'

He wanted to ask 'Is she often like this?', but instead, he drew the boy out and closed the door. He had never liked questioning a child about its parents and he didn't propose to do it now. It was a common enough tragedy, but it was a job for the Juvenile Bureau not for him and the sooner one of their officers arrived the better. He was fretted by the thought of Kate, back at the scene of crime by now, and he felt a spurt of resentment against Dalgliesh who had involved him in this irrelevant mess. He asked:

'Where do you sleep, Darren?'

The boy pointed to a back bedroom and Massingham pushed him gently before him.

It was very small, hardly more than a box room, with a single high window. Under it was a narrow bed covered with a brown army blanket and beside it a chair with a collection of objects neatly arranged. There was a model of a fire engine; a glass dome which shaken would produce a miniature snow storm; two models of racing cars; three large veined marbles; and another jam jar, this one holding a bunch of roses, whose heads were already bending on their high thornless stems. An old chest of drawers, the only other furniture, was piled with an incongruous collection of objects, shirts still in their transparent packets, women's underwear, silk scarves, tins of salmon, baked beans, soup, a packet of ham and one of tongue, three model kits for making boats, a couple of lipsticks, a box of model soldiers, three packets of cheap scent.

Massingham had been a policeman too long to be easily moved. Some offences, cruelty to children or animals, violent crime against the vulnerable old, could still produce a flare of the spectacular Massingham temper which had resulted in more than one of his forebears facing a duel or a court martial. But even this he had learned to discipline. But now, viewing with angry eyes this childish room with its pathetic neatness, its evidence of small self-sufficiency, the single jar of flowers which he guessed the boy himself had arranged, he was seized with an impotent anger against the drunken slut next door. He said:

'Did you steal these things, Darren?'

Darren didn't reply, then he nodded.

'Matey, you're in trouble.'

The boy sat on the edge of the bed. Two tears rolled down his cheeks, followed by sniffs and heaves of the narrow chest. Suddenly he shouted:

'I ain't going to one of them council homes, I ain't! I ain't!'

'Stop crying,' said Massingham urgently, hating the tears, wanting to get away. Christ, why had AD let him in for this? What was he supposed to be, a childminder? Torn between pity, anger and his impatience to be back on his proper job, he said more roughly:

'Stop crying!'

There must have been something urgent in his voice. Darren's gulps were immediately checked although the tears flowed on. Massingham said more gently:

'Who said anything about a home? Look, I'm going to ring the Juvenile Bureau. Someone will come to look after you. It will probably be a WPC, you'll like her.' Darren's face expressed an immediate and lively scepticism which in other circumstances, Massingham would have found amusing. The boy looked up and asked:

'Why can't I go 'ome with Miss Wharton?'

Why not, indeed, thought Massingham. The poor little bugger seemed to be attached to her. Two waifs supporting each other. He said:

'I don't really think that's on. Wait here, I'll be back.'

He looked at his watch. He would have to stay, of course, until the WPC arrived but she shouldn't be too long and at least AD would have an answer to his question. He knew now what had been worrying Darren, what he had been concealing. One small mystery, at least, was solved. AD could relax and get on with the inquiry. And so, with luck, could he.

II

Even Father Barnes's predecessor, Father Kendrick, hadn't been able to do much with St Matthew's Vicarage. It occupied the corner of St Matthew's Court, an undistinguished three-storey, red brick block of flats bordering the Harrow Road. After the war, the Church Commissioners had finally decided that the existing huge Victorian house was unmanageable and uneconomic, and had sold the site to a developer on the understanding that a maisonette on the ground and first floor should be made over, in perpetuity, to house the parish priest. It was the only maisonette in the block but was otherwise indistinguishable from the flats, with their mean windows and small, badly proportioned rooms. At first the flats had been let to carefully chosen tenants and an attempt made to preserve the modest amenities; the square of lawn bordering the road, the two rose beds, the hanging windowboxes on each of the balconies. But the block, like most of its kind, had had a chequered history. The first property company had gone into liquidation and it had been sold to a second and then a third. The rents were raised, to general dissatisfaction, but were still inadequate to cover the maintenance costs of a poorly constructed building and there were the usual acrimonious disputes between the tenants and the landlords. Only the church maisonette was well maintained, its two storeys of white windows an incongruous badge of respectability among the peeling paint and disintegrating windowboxes.

The original tenants had been replaced by the transients of the city, the peripatetic young, sharing three to a room, unmarried mothers on social security, foreign students; a racial mix which, like some human kaleidoscope, was continually being shaken into new and brighter colours. Those few who did attend church found a congenial home with Father Donovan at St Anthony's with its steel bands, carnival processions, and general interracial bonhomie. None of them ever knocked on Father Barnes's door. They saw, with watchful and expressionless eyes, his almost furtive comings and goings. But he was as much an anachronism at St Matthew's Court as was the church he represented.

He had been escorted back to the Vicarage by a plainclothes officer, not the one who had been working most closely with Commander Dalgliesh, but an older man, broad-shouldered, stolid, reassuringly calm, who had spoken to him in a soft country accent which he couldn't recognize but was most certainly not local. He said he was from the Harrow Road Station but had only recently been transferred there from West End Central. He waited while Father Barnes unlocked the front door, then followed him in and offered to make a cup of tea, the British specific against disaster, grief and shock. If he was surprised by the grubbiness of the ill-equipped Vicarage kitchen he concealed it. He had made tea in worse places. When Father Barnes reiterated that he was perfectly all right and that Mrs McBride who did for him was due at ten thirty, he didn't persist. Before he left he handed Father Barnes a card with a number on it.

'That's the number Commander Dalgliesh said you were to ring if you need anything. If you're worried like. Or if anything new occurs to you. Just give a ring. It'll be no trouble. And when the press come bothering, just tell them as little as you need. No speculating. No use in speculating, is there? Just tell it how it was. A lady from your congregation and a boy found the bodies and the boy fetched you. Better not give any names unless you have to. You saw that they were dead and rang for the police. No need to say more. That's all there is to it.'

The statement, stupendous in its over-simplification, opened a new abyss before Father Barnes's horrified eyes. He had forgotten about the press. How soon would they arrive? Would they want to take photographs? Ought he to call an emergency meeting of the PCC? What would the Bishop say? Ought he to ring the Archdeacon at once and leave it to him? Yes, that would be the best plan. The Archdeacon would know what ought to be done. The Archdeacon was capable of coping with the press, the Bishop, the police and the Parochial Church Council. Even so, he feared that St Matthew's was fated to be the centre of a dreadful attention.

He always went to Mass fasting and, for the first time that morning, he was aware of feeling weak, even paradoxically a little sick. He sank down on to one of the two wooden chairs at the kitchen table and looked rather helplessly at the card with its seven clearly written digits, then glanced round as if seeking inspiration where to put it for safe keeping. Finally, he dug in his cassock pocket for his wallet and slipped it in with his bank card and single credit card. He let his eyes roam round the kitchen, seeing it as that pleasant policeman must have seen it, in all its sad decrepitude. The plate from which he had eaten his hamburgers and frozen green beans, which had been last night's supper, still unrinsed in the sink; the splatter of grease marks above the ancient gas stove; the viscous mess of grime gumming the narrow gap between stove and cupboard; the soiled and smelly teacloth hanging from its hook at the side of the sink; last year's calendar askew on its nail; the two open shelves jammed with a conglomeration of half-used cereal packets, jars of stale jam, cracked mugs, packets of detergent; the cheap, unstable table with its two chairs, their backs grubby from numerous clutching hands; the linoleum curving at the wall where it had become unstuck; the general air of discomfort, uncaring, negligence, dirt. And the rest of the flat wasn't much better. Mrs McBride took no pride in it because there was nothing to take a pride in. She didn't care because he didn't. Like him, she had probably ceased to notice the slow accretion of dirt over their lives.

After thirty years of marriage to Tom McBride, Beryl McBride sounded more Irish than did her husband. Sometimes, indeed, Father Barnes suspected that the brogue was less acquired than assumed, a music hall stereotype of Irishness adopted either out of marital togetherness or from some less recognizable need. He had noticed that in rare moments of stress she was apt to revert to her original Cockney. She was employed by the parish for twelve hours a week and her nominal duties were to come in on Mondays, Wednesdays and Fridays, clean the flat, wash and spin dry any linen or articles in the soiled linen basket, and prepare and leave for him a simple lunch on a tray. On the other weekdays and at weekends, Father Barnes was expected to look after himself. There had never been a job description. Mrs McBride and the current incumbent were expected to work out a mutually agreed arrangement of hours and duties.

Twelve hours a week had been an adequate, even generous allocation of time when young Father Kendrick had been priest-in-charge. He was married to the prototype of an ideal parson's wife, a capable and buxom physiotherapist, well able to run her part-time hospital job and the parish simultaneously and to pound Mrs McBride into shape as vigorously as, no doubt, she did her patients. No one, of course, had expected Father Kendrick to stay. He had only been a stop-gap, to fill in after Father Collins's long, thirty-five-year ministry and the appointment of a permanent successor, if there were to be a successor. St Matthew's, as the Archdeacon was never tired of pointing out, was surplus to the Church's pastoral ministry in inner London. With two other Anglican churches within a three-mile radius, both with vigorous young clergy and enough parochial organizations to provide serious competition for the social services department, St Matthew's, with its small and ageing population, was an uncomfortable reminder of the declining authority of the established church in the inner cities. But as the Archdeacon said, 'Your people are remarkably loyal. It's a pity they aren't also rich. The parish is a drain on resources, no doubt about it. But we can hardly sell it. The building is supposed to be of some importance, architecturally. I can never see it myself. That extraordinary campanile. Hardly English, is it? One isn't, after all, on the Venetian Lido, whatever the architect thought.' For the Archdeacon, who had, in fact, never seen the Venetian Lido, had been reared in the Close at Salisbury and, making some allowance for scale, had known from childhood exactly what a church should look like.

Before Father Kendrick had set off for his new city parish – racial mix, boys' club, mothers' union, young people's fellowship; the proper challenge for a mildly high-church, ambitious young priest with one eye on a mitre – he had had a brief word about Beryl McBride.

'Frankly, she terrifies me. I keep well out of her way. But Susan seems able to manage her. Better have a word with her about the domestic arrangements. I wish Mrs McBride had taken her husband's religion instead of his accent. That way St Anthony's would have had the benefit of her cooking. I did hint to Father Donovan that here was a brand ready for plucking, but Michael knows when to leave well alone. Now, if you can seduce his housekeeper Mrs Kelly into Anglicanism, you'll be in clover.'

Susan Kendrick, expertly wrapping china in newspaper and ankle-deep in shavings from her packing cases, had been briskly informative but hardly more reassuring.

'She needs watching. Her plain cooking is quite good although the repertoire is a bit limited. But she isn't so dependable when it comes to housework. You need to begin as you mean to go on. If you set the right standards and she knows that she can't fool you, you'll be all right. She's been here a long time, of course, from Father Collins's days. She wouldn't be easy to dislodge. And she's a very loyal member of the congregation. St Matthew's seems to suit her for some reason. As I said, just begin as you mean to go on. Oh, and watch the sherry. There's no real dishonesty. You can leave anything out, money, your watch, food. It's just that she likes the odd nip. Better offer her one occasionally. That way there's less temptation. You can hardly lock the stuff up.'

'No, of course not,' he had said. 'No, I quite see that.'

But it had been Mrs McBride who had started as she meant to go on. It had been hopeless from the start. He still recalled, with a flush of shame, that first, all-important interview. He had sat in front of her, in the square little room which was used as a study, as if he were the suppliant, and had seen her sharp little eyes, black as currants, move round the room, noting the gaps in the shelves where Father Kendrick's leatherbound volumes had been stacked, the meagre rug in front of the gas fire, his few prints stacked against the wall. And that wasn't all she had taken in. She had had him summed up, all right. She had seen his timidity, his ignorance of housekeeping, his lack of authority as a man or a priest. And he suspected that she had known more intimate secrets. His virginity, his half-shameful fear of her close, warm-smelling, overwhelming femaleness, his social insecurity, born in that small, terraced house near the river at Ely, where he had lived with his widowed mother, nurtured by the desperate contrivings, the small deceptions of respectable poverty, the deprivation that was so much more humiliating than the real poverty of the inner cities. He could imagine the words in which she would later report to her husband.

'He's not really a gentleman, not like Father Kendrick. You can see that. Father Kendrick's father was a bishop, after all, and Mrs Kendrick is the niece of Lady Nichols, when all's said and done. There's no knowing where this one comes from.' Sometimes he suspected that she had even known how diminished was his remaining store of faith, that it was this essential lack and not his general inadequacy which was at the core of her disdain.

His most recent library book had been a Barbara Pym. He had read with envious disbelief the gentle and ironic story of a village parish where the curates were entertained, fed, and generally spoilt by the female members of the congregation. Mrs McBride, he thought, would soon put a stop to anything like that at St Matthew's. Indeed, she had put a stop to it. During his first week, Mrs Jordan had visited him with a homemade fruitcake. She had seen it on the table on her Wednesday visit and had said:

'One of Ethel Jordan's, is it? You want to watch her, Father, an unmarried priest like you.' The words had hung on the air, heavy with innuendo, and an act of simple kindness had been spoiled. Eating the cake, he had felt it like tasteless dough in his mouth, every mouthful an act of shared indecency.

She arrived on time. Whatever her other negligences, Mrs McBride was a stickler for punctuality. He heard her key in the door and a minute later she was in the kitchen. She didn't seem surprised to see him sitting there still in his cloak and obviously only just returned from Mass, and he knew at once that she had been told about the murders. He watched while she carefully removed her headscarf to reveal the upswept waves of unnaturally dark hair, hung up her coat in the hall cupboard, donned her overall from its hook behind the kitchen door, took off her outdoor shoes and eased her feet into her house slippers. It wasn't until she had put on the kettle for their morning coffee that she spoke.

'Well, here's a nice thing for the parish, Father. Two of 'em dead, so Billy Crawford was saying in the newsagent's. And one of 'em old Harry Mack.'

'I'm afraid so, Mrs McBride. One of them was Harry.'

'And who would the other be? Or aren't the police knowing yet?'

'I think we'll have to wait until they notify the next of kin before they release that information.'

'But you saw him, Father. Wasn't it with your own eyes now? And were you not recognizing him?'

'You really mustn't ask me that, Mrs McBride. We must wait for the police.'

'And who'd be wantin' to kill Harry? Sure, he wouldn't be killed for anything he had on him, the poor soul. It wasn't suicide, was it, Father? One of those suicide pacts? Or do the police think Harry did it?'

'They don't know what happened yet. We really ought not to speculate.'

'Well, I don't believe it. Harry Mack's no murderer. As well believe that the other chap, the one you're keeping so quiet about, the one you're not telling about, did in Harry. Harry was a nasty, thieving, foul-mouthed old devil, God rest him, but he was harmless enough. The police have no call to be pinning it on Harry.'

'I'm sure they won't try to. It could have been anyone, someone who broke in to steal. Or someone Sir Paul Berowne himself let in. Anyone. The door of the vestry was open when Miss Wharton arrived this morning.'

He turned towards the stove so that she shouldn't see the flush of shame and dismay that he had let slip Berowne's name. And she hadn't missed it, not she. And why had he told her about that unlocked door? Was he trying to reassure her, or himself? But what did it matter? The details would be out soon enough and it would look odd if he were too reticent, odd and suspicious. But why suspicious? Surely no one, not even Mrs McBride, was going to suspect him. He recognized, with a familiar confusion of self-disgust and hopelessness, that he was telling more than he ought in his usual attempt to propitiate her, to get her on his side. It had never worked and it wouldn't now. She didn't pick up the name Berowne although he knew that it was safely stowed in her mind. Sitting across from her, he saw the triumph in her cunning little eyes, heard in her voice the note of ghoulish relish.

'Bloody murder, is it then? That's a nice thing for the parish. You'll be needing to get the church fumigated, Father.'

'Fumigated?'

'Well, sprinkled with holy water, that sort of thing. Maybe my Tom had better speak to Father Donovan. He could let us have some from St Anthony's.'

'We have our own holy water, Mrs McBride.'

'In a case like this, you can't take chances. Better get some from Father Donovan. Be on the safe side. My Tom can bring it along after Mass on Sunday. Here's your coffee, Father. I've made it extra strong. You've had a nasty shock and that's the truth of it.'

The coffee, as always, was the cheapest kind of bottled grains. It was even less palatable now that its strength made the taste discernible. On the brown surface a few globules of half-sour milk swam and coalesced. There was a smear of what looked like lipstick on the brim of the cup and he turned it away from him slowly, so that she shouldn't notice. He knew that he could have carried the coffee into the comparative serenity of his study but he hadn't the courage to get to his feet. And to leave before both cups had been drained would only offend her. She had said, on her first morning with him, 'Mrs Kendrick and me always had a cup of coffee together before I got started, nice and friendly like.' He had had no way of knowing whether this was the truth, but the pattern of spurious intimacy had been established.

'That Paul Berowne, he was an MP wasn't he? Resigned or something. I remember reading about him in the *Standard*.'

'Yes, he was an MP.'

'And a Sir, too, didn't you say?'

'A baronet, Mrs McBride.'

'What was he doing in the Little Vestry, then? I never knew we had any baronets attending St Matthew's.'

It was too late now to take refuge in discretion.

'He didn't. He was just someone I knew. I gave him the key. He wanted to spend some time quietly in the church,' he added in a vain hope that a confidence so dangerously close to intimacy, to his job as priest, might flatter her, might even silence curiosity. 'He wanted somewhere quiet to think, to pray.'

'In the Little Vestry? A funny place to choose. Why wasn't he on his knees in a pew? Why wasn't he in the Lady Chapel in front of the Blessed Sacrament? That's the proper place to be praying for them who can't wait till Sunday.' Her voice with its note of aggrieved disapproval suggested that both the place and the praying were equally reprehensible.

'He could hardly sleep in the church, Mrs McBride.'

'And why should he want to be sleeping? Hadn't he his own bed to be going home to?'

Father Barnes's hands had begun to shake again. The coffee cup lurched in his fingers and he felt two scalding drops on his hand. Carefully, he replaced the cup in its saucer, willing the dreadful shaking to stop. He almost lost her next words.

'Well, if he did kill himself, he died clean, I'll say that for him.'

'Died clean, Mrs McBride?'

'Wasn't he washing himself when Tom and I passed by last night just after eight o'clock? Him or Harry Mack? And you can't be telling me that Harry went near running water if he could help it. Fairly gushing out of the drainpipe it was. 'Course we thought you were there. "Father Barnes is having a stripwash in the vestry wash-room." That's what I said to Tom. "Perhaps he's saving on the gas bill back at the Vicarage." We had a laugh about it.'

'When exactly was this, Mrs McBride?'

'I told you, Father, just after eight. We were on our way to the

Three Feathers. We wouldn't have been passing the church except that we called in to collect Maggie Sullivan and it's a shortcut from her place to the Feathers.'

'But the police ought to know. This could be important information. They'll be interested in anyone who was near St Matthew's last night.'

'Interested? Is that what they'll be? And what are you getting at then, Father? You're saying that Tom and old Maggie Sullivan and I cut his throat for him?'

'Of course not, Mrs McBride. That's ridiculous. But you could be important witnesses. That gushing water. It means that Sir Paul was alive at eight o'clock.'

'Someone was alive in there at eight and that's for sure. And a fine rush of water he was using.'

Father Barnes was struck with a terrible possibility and, without thinking, gave it voice:

'Did you notice what colour it was?'

'And what would I be doing peering down drains? Of course I didn't notice what colour it was. What colour would it be? But it was running away, fast and furious, that's for sure.'

Suddenly, she pushed her face over the table towards him. Her huge breasts, so much at odds with the thin face and the bony arms, were pushed into great half moons by the table edge. Her coffee cup clattered in the saucer. The sharp little eyes widened. She whispered with alliterative relish:

'Father, are you saying that it would be running red?'

He said, weakly:

'I suppose it's possible.'

'You think he was in there do you, Father, washing his bloody hands? Oh my God! Suppose he had come out and seen us. We could have been murdered on the spot, Tom and Maggie and me. He could have slit our throats for us then and there and thrown us in the canal, likely as not. Holy Mother of God!'

The conversation had become bizarre, unreal, totally uncontrollable. He had been told by the police to say as little as possible to anyone. He had meant to say nothing. But now she knew the names of the victims, she knew who had found them, she knew that the door had been unlocked, she knew how they had died, although surely he hadn't mentioned the slitting of throats. But that could have been guesswork. A knife was, after all, a more likely weapon in London than a gun. She knew all that and, more, she had actually been passing at the time. He gazed back at her across the stained table with appalled eyes, linked to her by that bloodstained gurgle of water which was gushing through both their minds, sharing the same dreadful imagining of that silently emerging figure, the raised and bloody knife. And he was aware of something else. Horrible as was the deed that bound them in a fascinated confederacy of blood they were, for the first time, having a conversation. The eyes which met his across the table top were bright with horror and with an excitement which was too close to relish to be comfortable. But the familiar glance of insolence and contempt had gone. He could almost deceive himself that she was confiding in him. The relief was so great that he found that his hand was creeping across the table towards hers in some gesture of mutual comfort. Ashamed, he quickly drew it back.

She said:

'Father, what shall we do?' It was the first time she had ever asked him that question. He was surprised at the confidence in his voice.

'The police have given me a special telephone number. I think we ought to ring now, at once. They'll send someone round, either here or to your house. After all, you and Tom and Maggie are very important witnesses. And then when we've done that, I shall need to be undisturbed in the study. I wasn't able to say Mass. I shall read Morning Prayer.'

'Yes, Father,' she said, her voice almost meek. And there was something else he ought to do. Strange that thought hadn't occurred to him before. Surely it must be his duty to call in the next day or so on Paul Berowne's wife and his family. Now that he knew what had to be done, it was remarkable how different he felt. A biblical phrase dropped into his mind, 'Doing evil that good may come'. But he quickly put it away from him. It was too close to blasphemy to be comfortable.

BOOK TWO

Next of Kin

I

After leaving the church Dalgliesh went briefly back to the Yard to
pick up his files on Theresa Nolan and Diana Travers and it was
after midday before he arrived at 62 Campden Hill Square. He had
brought Kate with him, leaving Massingham to supervise what
remained to be done at the church. Kate had told him that at
present there were only women in the house and it seemed sensible
that he should have a woman with him, particularly as it was Kate
who had first broken the news. It was not a decision he had expected
Massingham to welcome, and nor had he. These first interviews
with the next of kin were crucial and Massingham wanted to be
there. He would work with Kate Miskin loyally and conscientiously
because he respected her as a detective and that was what he was
required to do. But Dalgliesh knew that Massingham still half-
regretted the days when women police officers were content to find
lost children, search female prisoners, reform prostitutes, comfort
the bereaved and, if they hankered for the excitement of criminal
investigation, were suitably occupied coping with the peccadilloes
of juvenile delinquents. And, as Dalgliesh had heard him argue, for
all their demands for equality of status and opportunity, putting
them in the front line behind the riot shields, taking the petrol
bombs, the hurled stones and now the bullets, only made the job of
their male colleagues even more onerous. In Massingham's view the
instinct to protect a woman in moments of high danger was deep-
seated and ineradicable, and the world would be a worse place if it
wasn't. He had, as Dalgliesh knew, grudgingly respected Kate's
ability to look down at the butchered bodies in St Matthew's vestry
and not be sick, but he hadn't liked her the better for it.

He knew that he would find no police officer at the house.
Lady Ursula had gently but firmly rejected the suggestion that
someone should stay. Kate had reported her words:

'You are not, presumably, expecting this murderer, if he exists, to turn his attention to the rest of the family. That being so, I hardly see the need for police protection. You, I am sure, have a better use for your manpower and I would prefer not to have an officer sitting in the hall like a bailiff.'

She had, too, insisted on herself breaking the news to her daughter-in-law and the housekeeper. Kate was given no opportunity to observe the reaction of anyone other than Lady Ursula to Paul Berowne's death.

Campden Hill Square lay in its midday calm, an urban oasis of greenery and Georgian elegance rising from the ceaseless grind and roar of Holland Park Avenue. An early morning mist had cleared and a fugitive sun glinted on leaves which were only now beginning to yellow and which hung in heavy swathes, almost motionless in the still air. Dalgliesh couldn't remember when he had last seen the Berowne house. Living as he did high above the Thames on the fringe of the city, this wasn't his part of London. But the house, one of the rare examples of Sir John Soane's domestic architecture, was pictured in so many books on the capital's buildings that its elegant eccentricity was as familiar to him as if he commonly walked these streets and squares. The conventional Georgian houses each side of it were as high, but its neo-classical façade in Portland stone and brick dominated the terrace and the whole square, inalienably a part of them, yet looking almost arrogantly unique.

He stood for a minute looking up at it, Kate unspeaking at his side. On the second floor rose three very high, curved windows, originally, he suspected, an open loggia but now glazed and fronted with a low stone balustrade. Between the windows, mounted on incongruous corbels which looked more Gothic than neo-classical, were stone caryatids, whose flowing lines, reinforced by the typically Soanian pilasters at the corners of the house, drew the eye upwards, past the square windows of the third storey to a fourth storey faced in brick and, finally, to the stone balustrade with its row of curved shells echoing the curve of the lower windows. As he stood contemplating it, as if hesitating to violate its calm, there was a moment of extraordinary silence in which even the muted roar of the traffic in the avenue was stilled and in which it seemed to him that two images, the shining façade of the house and that dusty blood-boltered room in Paddington, were held suspended out of time, then fused so that the stones were blood splattered, the caryatids dripped red. And then the traffic lights released the stream of cars, time moved on, the house lay uncontaminated in its pale pristine silence. But he had no sense that they were being watched, that somewhere between these walls and the windows glinting in the transitory sun there were people waiting for him in anxiety, grief, perhaps in fear. Even when he rang the doorbell it was a full two minutes before the door was opened and he faced a woman who he knew must be Evelyn Matlock.

She was, he guessed, in her late thirties, and was uncompromisingly plain in a way it struck him few women nowadays were. A small sharp nose was imbedded between pudgy cheeks on which the threads of broken veins were emphasized rather than disguised by a thin crust of make-up. She had a primly censorious mouth above a slightly receding chin already showing the first slackness of a dewlap. Her hair, which looked as if it had been inexpertly permed, was pulled back at the sides but frizzed over the high forehead in the poodle-like fashion of an Edwardian. But as she stood aside to let them enter he saw that her wrists and ankles were slim and delicate, curiously at odds with the sturdy body, heavy-busted, almost voluptuous under the high-necked blouse. He remembered what Paul Berowne had said of her. Here was the woman whose father he had unsuccessfully defended, to whom he had given a home and a job, who was supposed to be devoted to him. If that were true, she was concealing her grief at his death with remarkable stoicism. A police officer, he thought, is like a visiting doctor. One is greeted with no ordinary emotions. He was used to seeing relief, apprehension, dislike, even hatred; but now, for a moment, he saw in her eyes naked fear. It passed almost at once and gave place to what seemed to him an assumed and slightly truculent indifference, but it had been there. She turned her back on them, saying:

'Lady Ursula is expecting you, Commander. Will you please follow me.'

The words, spoken in a high, rather forced voice, had the

repressive authority of a nurse-receptionist greeting a patient from whom she expects nothing but trouble. They passed through the outer vestibule then under the fluted dome of the inner hall. To their left, the finely wrought balustrade of a stone cantilevered staircase rose like a border of black lace. Miss Matlock opened the double door to the right and stood back to let them enter. She said:

'If you will wait in here I will let Lady Ursula know that you have arrived.'

The room in which they found themselves ran the whole length of the house and was obviously both the formal dining-room and library. It was full of light. At the front, two high curved windows gave a view of the square garden while at the rear one huge expanse of glass looked out over a stone wall with three niches, each containing a marble statue; Venus, naked, one hand delicately shielding the mons Veneris, one pointing at her left nipple, a second female figure, half robed and wearing a wreath of flowers and, between them, Apollo with his lyre, laurel-crowned. The two sections of the room were divided by projecting piers formed of mahogany glass-fronted bookcases from which sprang a canopy of three semi-circular arches decorated and painted in green and gold. High bookcases lined the library walls and stood between the windows, each topped with a marble bust. The volumes, bound in green leather and tooled in gold, were identical in size and fitted the bookshelves so precisely that the effect was more of an artist's *trompe-l'œil* than of a working library. Between the shelves and in the recesses over them were mirrors so that the rich splendour of the room seemed to be endlessly reflected, a vista of painted ceilings, leather books, of marble, gleaming mahogany and glass. It was difficult to imagine the room being used for dining, or indeed, for any purpose other than the admiring contemplation of the architect's romantic obsession with spatial surprise. The oval dining table stood before the rear window, but it held in the middle a model of the house on a low plinth as if it were a museum exhibit, and the eight high-backed dining chairs had been set back against the walls. Over the marble fireplace was a portrait, presumably of the baronet who had commissioned the house. Here the delicate fastidiousness of the painting in the National Portrait Gallery was metamorphosed into a sturdier nineteenth-century elegance, but with the unmistakable Berowne features still arrogantly confident above the faultlessly tied cravat. Looking up at it, Dalgliesh said:

'Lady Ursula Berowne, remind me of what she said, Kate.'

'She said: "After the first death there is no other." It sounded like a quotation.'

'It is a quotation.' He added without explanation, 'Her elder son was killed in Northern Ireland. Do you like this room?'

'If I wanted to settle down for a quiet read I'd prefer the Kensington public library. It's for show rather than use, isn't it? Odd idea, having a library and dining room in one.' She added: 'But I suppose it's splendid in its way. Not exactly cosy, though. I wonder if anyone has ever been murdered for a house.'

It was a long speech for Kate.

Dalgliesh said:

'I can't say that I remember a case. It might be a more rational motive than murdering for a person; less risk of subsequent disenchantment.'

'Less chance of betrayal, too, sir.'

Miss Matlock appeared in the doorway; she said with cold formality:

'Lady Ursula is ready to see you now. Her sitting room is on the fourth floor, but there is a lift. Would you please follow me.'

They could have been a couple of unpromising applicants for a minor domestic job. The lift was an elegant gilded birdcage in which they were borne slowly upwards in a repressive silence. When it jerked to a stop they were led out into a narrow carpeted passage. Miss Matlock opened a door immediately opposite and announced:

'Commander Dalgliesh and Miss Miskin are here, Lady Ursula.' Then without waiting for them to step into the room, she turned and left.

And now, as he entered Lady Ursula Berowne's sitting room, Dalgliesh felt for the first time that he was in a private house, that this was a room which the owner had made peculiarly her own. The two high beautifully proportioned windows with their twelve panes gave a view of sky delicately laced with the top boughs of the trees and the long narrow room was full of light. Lady Ursula was sitting very upright to the right of the fireplace, her back to the window.

There was an ebony cane with a gold knob leaning against her chair. She did not rise when they came in but held out her hand as Kate introduced Dalgliesh. Her clasp, quickly released, was surprisingly strong but it was still like holding briefly a disconnected set of bones loosely enclosed in dry suede. She gave Kate a quick appraising glance and a nod which could have been acknowledgement or approval and said:

'Please sit down. If Inspector Miskin is required to make notes, then she may find that chair by the window convenient. Perhaps you will sit opposite me, Commander.'

The voice, with its timbre of upper-class arrogance, an arrogance of which its owner so often seems unaware, was exactly as he would have expected. It seemed artificially produced, as if in an attempt to control any quavering she had had to gather both breath and energy to produce the measured cadences. But it was still a beautiful voice. As she sat facing him, rigidly upright, he saw that her chair was one designed for the disabled with a button in the armrest to raise the seat when she wanted help in rising. Its functional modernity struck a discordant note in a room which was otherwise cluttered with eighteenth-century furniture; two chairs with embroidered seats, a Pembroke table, a bureau, each a fine example of its period, were strategically placed to provide an island of support if she needed to make her painful progress to the door, so that the room looked rather like an antique shop with its treasures ineptly displayed. It was an old woman's room, and above the smell of beeswax and the faint summer scent from a bowl of pot-pourri on the Pembroke table, his sensitive nose could detect a whiff of the sour smell of old age. Their eyes met and held. Hers were still remarkable, immense, well-spaced and heavily lidded. They must once have been the focus of her beauty, and although they were sunken now, he could still see the glint of intelligence behind them. Her skin was cleft with deep lines running from the jaw to the high jutting cheekbones. It was as if two palms had been placed against the frail skin and forced it upwards so that he saw with a shock of premonitory recognition the shine of the skull beneath the skin. The scrolls of the ears flat against the side of the skull were so large that they looked like abnormal excrescences. In youth she would have dressed her hair to cover them. Her face was devoid of make-up and with the hair drawn back tightly and twisted into a high roll it looked naked, a face stripped for action. She was wearing black trousers topped with a belted tunic in thin grey wool, high-buttoned almost to the chin, and deep-cuffed. Her feet were lodged in wide black-barred shoes and in their immobility gave the impression of being clamped to the carpet. There was a paperback on the round table to the right of her chair. Dalgliesh saw that it was Philip Larkin's *Required Writing*. She put out her hand and laid it on the book, then said:

'Mr Larkin writes here that it is always true that the idea for a poem and a snatch or line of it come simultaneously. Do you agree, Commander?'

'Yes, Lady Ursula, I think I do. A poem begins with poetry, not with an idea for poetry.'

He betrayed no surprise at the question. He knew that shock, grief, trauma took people in different ways, and if this bizarre opening was helping her, he could conceal his impatience. She said:

'To be a poet and a librarian, even if unusual, has a certain appropriateness, but to be a poet and a policeman seems to me eccentric, even perverse.'

Dalgliesh said:

'Do you see the poetry as inimical to the detection, or the detection to the poetry?'

'Oh, the latter, surely. What happens if the muse strikes – no, that is hardly the appropriate word – if the muse visits you in the middle of a case? Although if I remember, Commander, your muse in recent years has been somewhat fugitive.' She added with a note of delicate irony: 'to our great loss.'

Dalgliesh said:

'It hasn't so far happened. Perhaps the human mind can deal with only one intense experience at a time.'

'And poetry is, of course, an intense experience.'

'One of the most intense there is.'

Suddenly she smiled at him. It lit up her face with the intimacy of a shared confidence, as if they were old sparring partners.

'You must excuse me. Being interrogated by a detective is a new experience for me. If there is an appropriate dialogue for this occasion, I haven't yet found it. Thank you, anyway, for not burdening me with your condolences. I have received too many official condolences in my time. They have always seemed to me either embarrassing or insincere.'

Dalgliesh wondered what she would reply if he had said: 'I knew your son. Not well, but I did know him. I accept that you don't want my condolences, but if I had been able to speak the right words, they would not have been insincere.'

She said:

'Inspector Miskin broke the news to me with tact and consideration. I am grateful. But she was, of course, unable or unwilling to tell me much more than that my son was dead, and that there were certain wounds. How did he die, Commander?'

'His throat was cut, Lady Ursula.'

There was no way of softening that brutal reality. He added:

'The tramp with him, Harry Mack, died the same way.'

He wondered why he had felt it important to speak Harry's name. Poor Harry, so incongruously yoked in the forced democracy of death, whose stiffening body would receive far more attention in its dissolution than it had ever received in life. She said:

'And the weapon?'

'A bloodstained razor, his apparently, was close to your son's right hand. There are a number of forensic tests to be carried out but I expect to find that the razor was the weapon.'

'And the door to the church – the vestry, or wherever he was – that was open?'

'Miss Wharton, who with a young boy discovered the bodies, says that she found it unlocked.'

'Are you treating this as suicide?'

'The tramp, Harry Mack, didn't kill himself. My preliminary view is that neither did your son. It's too early to say more until we get the results of the post-mortem examination and the forensic tests. Meantime I am treating it as a double murder.'

'I see. Thank you for being so frank.'

Dalgliesh said:

'There are questions I need to ask. If you would rather wait I could come back later, but it is, of course, important to lose as little time as possible.'

'I would prefer to lose none, Commander. And two of your questions I can anticipate. I have no reason to believe that my son was contemplating ending his life and he had to my knowledge no enemies.'

'As a politician that makes him unusual, surely.'

'He had political enemies, obviously. Some few from his own party, no doubt. But none as far as I know is a homicidal maniac. And terrorists, surely, use bombs and guns not their victim's razor. Forgive me, Commander, if I'm stating the obvious, but isn't it most likely that someone unknown to him, a tramp, a psychopath, a casual thief, killed both him and this Harry Mack?'

'It is one of the theories we have to consider, Lady Ursula.' He asked: 'When did you last see your son?'

'At eight o'clock yesterday morning when he carried up my breakfast tray. That was his usual practice. He wished to reassure himself, no doubt, that I had survived the night.'

'Did he tell you then or at any time that he intended returning to St Matthew's?'

'No. We didn't discuss his plans for the day, only mine, and those I presume are hardly of interest to you.'

Dalgliesh said:

'It could be important to know who was here in the house during the day and at what time. Your own timetable could help us to that.'

He gave no further explanation and she asked for none.

'My chiropodist, Mrs Beamish, arrived at ten thirty. She always comes to the house. I was with her for about an hour. Then I was driven to a luncheon engagement with Mrs Charles Blaney at her club, the University Women's. After luncheon we went to look at some watercolours in which she is interested at Agnew's, in Bond Street. We had tea at the Savoy together and I dropped Mrs Blaney at her Chelsea house before returning here at about half past five. I asked Miss Matlock to bring me up a thermos of soup and a plate of smoked salmon sandwiches at six o'clock. She did so and I told her I preferred not to be disturbed again that evening. The luncheon and exhibition had been more tiring than I had expected. I spent the evening reading, and rang for Miss Matlock to help me to bed shortly before eleven.'

'Did you see any other member of the household during the day apart from your son, Miss Matlock and the chauffeur?'

'I saw my daughter-in-law briefly when I had occasion to go into the library. That was some time during the early part of the morning. I presume that this is relevant, Commander?'

'Until we know how your son died it is difficult to be sure what is or is not relevant. Did any other member of the household know that Sir Paul intended revisiting St Matthew's yesterday evening?'

'I have had no opportunity to ask them. I can't believe it likely that they did. No doubt you will inquire. We have only a small staff. Evelyn Matlock, whom you have met, is the housekeeper. Then there is Gordon Halliwell. He is an ex-sergeant in the Guards, who served with my elder son. He, I suppose, would describe himself as a chauffeur-handyman. He came here just over five years ago, before Hugo was killed, and has stayed on.'

'He drove your son?'

'Rarely. Paul, of course, had the use of his ministerial car before he resigned; otherwise he drove himself. Halliwell drives me almost daily, and occasionally my daughter-in-law. He has a flat over the garage. You will have to wait, Commander, to hear anything he may disclose. Today is his day off.'

'When did he leave, Lady Ursula?'

'Either very late last night or early this morning. That is his usual practice. I have no idea where he is. I don't question my servants about their private lives. If the news of my son's death is broadcast this evening, as I expect it will be, no doubt he will return early. In any case he is normally back before eleven. Incidentally, I spoke to him by house telephone yesterday evening shortly after eight o'clock and, again, at about nine fifteen. Apart from Halliwell, there is now only one other member of the staff, Mrs Iris Minns, who comes here four days a week to do general housework. Miss Matlock can give you her address.'

Dalgliesh asked:

'This experience of your son's in the vestry of St Matthew's, did he talk to you about it?'

'No. It was not a subject with which he would expect me to sympathize. I have not since 1918 been a religious woman. I doubt if I ever was in any real sense. Mysticism, in particular, is as meaningless to me as music must be to the tone deaf. I accept, of course, that people do have these experiences. I would expect the causes to be physical and psychological; overwork, the *ennui* of middle age, or a need to find some meaning to existence. That to me has always been a fruitless quest.'

'Did your son find it fruitless?'

'Until this happened, I would have described him as a conventional Anglican. I suspect that he used the offices of his religion as a reminder of fundamental decencies, an affirmation of identity, a brief breathing space when he could think without fear of interruption. Like most upper-class Anglicans he would have found the incarnation more understandable if God had chosen to visit His creation as an eighteenth-century English gentleman. But like most of his class, he got over that little difficulty by more or less refashioning Him in the guise of an eighteenth-century English gentleman. His experience – his alleged experience – in that church is inexplicable, and to do him justice, he didn't attempt to explain it, at least not to me. I hope you won't expect me to discuss it. The subject is unwelcome, and it can surely have had nothing to do with his death.'

It was a long speech and he could see that it had tired her. And she could not, thought Dalgliesh, be as naive as that; he was surprised that she could expect him to believe that she was. He said:

'When a man changes the whole direction of his life and is dead – possibly murdered – within a week of that decision, it must be relevant, at least to our investigation.'

'Oh yes, it's relevant to that I've no doubt. There will be very few privacies in this family which won't be relevant to your investigation, Commander.'

He saw that in the last few seconds, she had been overcome with exhaustion. Her body looked diminished, almost shrivelled, in the huge chair, and the gnarled hands on the arms began very gently to shake. But he controlled his compassion as she was controlling her grief. There were questions he still needed to ask and it wouldn't be the first time that he had taken advantage of tiredness or grief. He bent and took from his case the half-burnt diary still in its protective transparent wrapping. He said:

'It's been examined for fingerprints. We shall need in time to check which belong to people who had a right to handle the diary; Sir Paul, yourself, members of the household. I wanted you to confirm that it is in fact his. It would be helpful if you could do that without unwrapping it.'

She took the package and it lay for a moment in her lap while she stared down at it. He had a sense that she was unwilling to meet his eyes. She sat with extraordinary stillness, then she said:

'Yes, this is his. But it's unimportant surely. A mere record of engagements. He wasn't a diarist.'

'It's odd, in that case, that he should wish to burn it – if he did burn it. And there's another oddity; the top half of the last page has been torn away. It's the page setting out last year's calendar and the calendar for 1986. Can you recall what else, if anything, was on that page, Lady Ursula?'

'I can't remember that I ever saw that page.'

'Can you recall when and where you last saw the diary?'

'I'm afraid that's the kind of detail it's impossible for me to remember. Is there anything else, Commander? If there is, and it isn't urgent, perhaps it could wait until you are sure that you are, in fact, investigating murder.'

Dalgliesh said:

'We know that already, Lady Ursula. Harry Mack was murdered.'

She didn't reply, and for about a minute they sat in silence, facing each other. Then she lifted her great eyes to his and he thought he detected a mixture of fleeting emotions: resolution, appeal, defiance. He said:

'I am afraid I've kept you too long and tired you. There is really only one more matter. Is there anything you can tell me about the two young women who died after they had been working in this house, Theresa Nolan and Diana Travers?'

The production of the half-burnt diary had shocked her deeply, but this question she took in her stride. She said calmly:

'Very little, I'm afraid. I've no doubt you know most of it already. Theresa Nolan was a gentle, considerate nurse and a competent, but not, I think, very intelligent, young woman. She came as night-nurse on the second of May when I had a bad attack of sciatica and left on the fourteenth of June. She had a room in this house but was on duty only at night. She went, as I expect you know, to a maternity nursing home in Hampstead. I accept that she probably became pregnant while she was working here, but I can assure you that no one in this house was responsible. Pregnancy is not an occupational hazard of nursing an 82-year-old arthritic woman. I know even less of Diana Travers. She was, apparently, an unemployed actress who was doing domestic work while she was "resting" – I think that's the euphemism they use. She came to the house in response to a card Miss Matlock had placed in a local newsagent's window and Miss Matlock took her on to replace a cleaning woman who had recently left.'

'After consulting you, Lady Ursula?'

'It was hardly a matter on which she needed to consult me and, in fact, she did not. I know, of course, why you are inquiring about both women. One or two of my friends made it their business to send me the cutting from the *Paternoster Review*. I'm surprised that the police should trouble themselves with what is surely no more than cheap journalistic spite. It can hardly be relevant to my son's murder. If that is all, Commander, perhaps you would like to see my daughter-in-law now. No, don't bother to ring. I prefer to take you down myself. And I can manage perfectly well without your help.'

She pressed the knob in the arm of her chair and the seat slowly rose. It took her a moment to establish her balance. Then she said:

'Before you meet my daughter-in-law there is something I should, perhaps, say. You may find her less apparently distressed than you expect. That is because she has no imagination. Had she found my son's body she would have been disconsolate, certainly too shocked and distressed to talk to you now. But what her eyes don't actually see she finds it difficult to imagine. I say this only in justice to both of you.'

Dalgliesh nodded but didn't reply. It was, he thought, the first mistake she had made. The implication of her words was obvious, but it would have been wiser of her to have left them unspoken.

2

He watched while she braced herself for the first step, steeling herself for the expected gripe of pain. He made no move to help her; he knew that the gesture would be as presumptuous as it was unwelcome and Kate, sensitive as always to unspoken commands, closed her notebook then waited in watchful silence. Slowly Lady Ursula made her way to the door, steadying herself with her cane. Her hand shook on the gold knob, the veins starting out like blue cords. They followed her slowly down the carpeted corridor and into the lift. There was barely room in its elegantly curved interior for three and Dalgliesh's arm was against hers. Even through the tweed of his sleeve he could sense its brittleness and could feel its gentle, perpetual shaking. He was aware that she was under intense strain and he wondered how much it would take to break her and whether it would be his job to see that she did break. As the lift ground slowly down the two floors he knew that she was as aware of him as he was of her, and that she saw him as the enemy.

They followed her into the drawing room. This room, too, Paul Berowne would have shown him, and for a moment he had the illusion that it was the dead man, not his mother, who stood at his side. Three tall curved windows, ornately curtained, gave a view of the garden trees. They looked unreal, a one-dimensional woven tapestry in an infinite variety of green and gold. Under the elaborately enriched ceiling with its curious mixture of the Classic and Gothic, the room was sparsely furnished and the air had the melancholy, unbreathed atmosphere of a seldom-visited country house drawing room, an amalgam of pot-pourri and wax polish. Almost he expected to see a white looped cord marking off the area where tourists' feet were forbidden to tread.

The bereaved mother had received him alone, presumably by choice. The widow had thought it prudent to be solaced and protected by her doctor and her lawyer. Lady Ursula briefly introduced them then immediately went out and Dalgliesh and Kate were left to walk alone across the carpet to a scene which looked as contrived as a tableau. Barbara Berowne was sitting in a high-backed armchair to the right of the fire. Opposite her, and leaning forward in his chair was her lawyer, Anthony Farrell. Standing beside her with his hand on her wrist was her doctor. It was he who spoke first:

'I'll leave you now, Lady Berowne, but I'll look in again this evening, about six o'clock if that is convenient, and we'll try to do something to help you sleep tonight. If you need me earlier, get Miss Matlock to ring. Try to eat a little supper if you can. Get her to make you something light. You won't feel like food, I know, but I want you to try. Will you?'

She nodded and held out her hand. He held it for a moment, then turned his gaze on Dalgliesh, shifted his eyes and muttered:

'Appalling, appalling.'

As Dalgliesh made no response, he said:

'I think Lady Berowne is strong enough to talk to you now, Commander, but I hope it won't take long.'

He spoke like an amateur actor in a murder play, predictable dialogue predictably delivered. It surprised Dalgliesh that a doctor, presumably not unused to tragedy, should be more ill at ease than his patient. When he reached the door, Dalgliesh asked quietly:

'Were you also Sir Paul's physician?'

'Yes, but only recently. He was a private patient of Dr Gillespie who died last year. Sir Paul and Lady Berowne then registered with me under the National Health Service. I now have his medical records but he has never consulted me professionally. He was a very healthy man.'

So part of the unease was explained. Here was no old and valued family physician but an overworked local general practitioner, understandably anxious to get back to a crowded surgery, or his round of visits, perhaps unhappily aware that the situation required a social skill and concentrated attention which he hadn't the time to give, but trying, not very convincingly, to play the part of a family friend in a drawing room which he probably had not entered until that moment. Dalgliesh wondered whether Paul

Berowne's decision to register as a National Health patient had been a matter of political expediency, conviction or economy, or of all three. There was a rectangle of faded wallpaper above the carved marble fireplace. It was half-obscured by a not particularly distinguished family portrait, but Dalgliesh suspected that a more valuable oil had once hung there. Barbara Berowne said:

'Please sit down, Commander.'

She waved vaguely towards a sofa set against the wall. It was inconveniently placed and looked too insubstantial for use, but Kate went over to it, sat down and unobtrusively took out her notebook. Dalgliesh walked over to one of the upright chairs, carried it across to the fireplace and set it down to the right of Anthony Farrell. He said:

'We are sorry to have to bother you at a time like this, Lady Berowne, but I'm sure you'll understand that it is necessary.'

But Barbara Berowne was gazing after Dr Piggott. She said resentfully:

'What a funny little man! Paul and I only registered with him last June. His hands are sweaty.'

She gave a little moue of distaste and rubbed her fingers stiffly together. Dalgliesh said:

'Do you feel able to answer some questions?'

She looked across at Farrell rather like a child expecting guidance. He said in his smooth professional voice:

'I'm afraid, my dear Barbara, that in a murder investigation the usual civilized conventions have to go. Delay is a luxury the police can't afford. I know that the Commander will make it as short as possible, and you'll be brave and make it as easy for him as you can.'

Before she had a chance to reply, he said to Dalgliesh:

'I'm here as Lady Berowne's friend as well as her lawyer. The firm has looked after the family for three generations. I had a great personal regard for Sir Paul. I've lost a friend as well as a client. That's partly why I'm here. Lady Berowne is very much alone. Her mother and stepfather are both in California.'

Dalgliesh wondered what Farrell would say if he replied: 'But her mother-in-law is only a couple of floors away.' He wondered if the implication of their separateness at a time when the family would naturally seek support, if not comfort, from each other, was lost on them, or on Farrell, or whether they were so used to living their lives under one roof but apart that even in a moment of high tragedy neither could cross the psychological barrier represented by that caged lift, those two floors.

Barbara Berowne turned her remarkable violet-blue eyes on Dalgliesh and he was for a second disconcerted. After the first fleeting glimmer of curiosity the glance was deadened, almost lifeless, as if he were looking into coloured contact lenses. Perhaps after a lifetime of seeing the effect of her gaze she no longer needed to animate it with any expression other than a casual interest. He had known that she was beautiful, how he couldn't remember, probably it was an accumulation of casually dropped comments when her husband was talked of, of press photographs. But it wasn't a beauty to stir his heart. It would have given him pleasure to sit unnoticed and look at her as he might at a picture, to note with dispassionate admiration the delicate, perfectly curved arch above the slanting eyes, at the curve of the upper lip, the shadowed hollow between the cheekbone and the jaw, the rise of the slim throat. He could look and admire and leave without regret. For him this blonde loveliness was too exquisite, too orthodox, too perfect. What he loved was a more individual and eccentric beauty, vulnerability allied to intelligence. He doubted whether Barbara Berowne was intelligent, but he didn't underrate her. Nothing in police work was more dangerous than to make superficial judgements about human beings. But he wondered briefly whether here now was a woman for whom a man would kill. He had known three such women in his career; none would have been described as beautiful.

She was sitting in her chair with a still, relaxed elegance. Above her skirt of light grey, finely-pleated wool, she wore a silk shirt of pale blue with a grey cashmere cardigan slung loosely over her shoulders. Her only jewellery was a couple of gold chains and small gold stud earrings. Her hair, with its strands of pale and darker corn yellow, was drawn back and hung over her shoulder in a single thick pleat fastened at the end with a tortoiseshell clamp. Nothing, he thought, could have been more discreetly fitting. Black, particularly in so recent a widow, would have been ostentatious, theatrical, even vulgar. This gentle arrangement of grey and blue was entirely appropriate. Kate had, he knew, arrived with her news before Lady Berowne had dressed. She had been told that her husband was dead with his throat cut, and she had still been able to take trouble with her dressing. And why not? He was too old a hand to assume grief wasn't genuine because it was appropriately clad. There were women whose self-respect demanded perpetual attention to detail no matter how violent events, others for whom it was a matter of confidence, of routine, or of defiance. In a man such punctiliousness was normally regarded as commendable. Why not, then, in a woman? Or was it merely that her appearance had for over twenty years been the major preoccupation of her life and she couldn't change that habit merely because someone had slit her husband's throat? But he couldn't help noticing the details, the intricate buckle at the side of the shoes, the lipstick meticulously applied and precisely matching the pink of her nail varnish, the trace of eye-shadow. Her hands at least had been steady. When she spoke her voice was high and, to him, unpleasing. It would, he thought, easily degenerate into a childish whine. She said:

'Of course I want to help, but I don't know I can. I mean it's all so incredible. Who could have wanted to kill Paul? He hadn't any enemies. Everyone liked him. He was very popular.'

The banal, inadequate tribute in that high, slightly jarring tone must have struck even her as gauche. There was a short silence which Farrell thought it prudent to break; he said:

'Lady Berowne is, of course, deeply shocked. We were hoping, Commander, that you would be able to give us more information than we have at present. We gather that the weapon was some kind of knife and that there were injuries to the throat.'

And that, thought Dalgliesh, was as tactful a way of saying that Sir Paul's throat had been slit as even the most skilled lawyer could devise. He said:

'Both Sir Paul and the tramp were apparently killed in the same way.'

'Was the weapon at the scene?'

'A possible weapon was at the scene. They may both have been killed with Sir Paul's razor.'

'And that was left by the murderer in the room?'

'We found it there, yes.'

The implication of his careful words wasn't lost on Farrell. For his part he wouldn't use the word 'suicide', but it lay between them with all its implications. He went on:

'And the church door. Had that been forced?'

'It was unlocked when Miss Wharton, the church worker, found the bodies this morning.'

'So anyone could have got in and someone, presumably, did?'

'Certainly. You will understand that the investigation is still in its early stages. We can be sure of nothing until we have the result of the autopsy and the forensic reports.'

'Of course. I ask because Lady Berowne prefers to know the facts, or as many of them as are available. And she has a right, of course, to be kept fully informed.'

Dalgliesh made no reply, nor did he need to; they understood each other perfectly. Farrell would be polite, studiously so, but not affable. His carefully controlled demeanour, so much a part of his professional life that it no longer seemed assumed, was saying: 'We're both professionals with something of a reputation in our jobs. We both know what we're about. You will excuse a certain lack of amiability but we may be required to be on different sides.'

The truth was that they were already on different sides and both knew it. It was as if Farrell emanated an ambiguous ecto-plasm which folded Barbara Berowne in its comforting aura saying: 'Here I am, I'm on your side, leave this to me. There's nothing to worry about.' It came to Dalgliesh as a subtle, masculine understanding, close to conspiracy, from which she was excluded. He did it very well.

His city firm of Torrington, Farrell and Penge, with its many ramifications, had enjoyed an unsullied legal reputation for over two hundred years. Its criminal department had represented some of the most ingenious villains in London. Some were holiday-ing in their Riviera villas, some on their yachts. Very few were behind bars. Dalgliesh had a sudden picture of a prison van which two days previously he had driven past on his way to the Yard, of the row of anonymous, hostile eyes gazing out through the slots as if they were expecting to see nothing more. The ability to pay for a couple of hours of Farrell's time at a crucial stage of their misfortunes would have made all the difference. Barbara Berowne said peevishly:

'I don't see why I have to be bothered. Paul didn't even tell me he was going to spend the night in that church. Dossing down with a tramp. I mean, it was all so silly.'

Dalgliesh said:

'When did you last see him?'

'At about nine fifteen yesterday morning. He came up to see me just before Mattie brought up my breakfast tray. He didn't stay long. About fifteen minutes.'

'How did he seem, Lady Berowne?'

'He seemed himself. He didn't say very much. He never did. I think I told him how I was going to spend the day.'

'And how was that?'

'I had a hair appointment at Michael and John in Bond Street at eleven. Then I lunched in Knightsbridge with an old school friend and we did some shopping in Harvey Nichols. I got home here at teatime and by then he'd left. I never saw him after nine fifteen.'

'And, as far as you know, he didn't return to the house?'

'I don't think so, but I wouldn't have seen him anyway. After I got back I changed and then took a taxi to Pembroke Lodge. That's my cousin's nursing home in Hampstead. He's an obstetrician, Mr Stephen Lampart. I was with him until midnight when he brought me home. We drove to Cookham to have dinner at the Black Swan. We left Pembroke Lodge at seven forty and drove straight to the Black Swan. I mean, we didn't stop on the way.'

It was, he thought, remarkably pat. He had expected her to come out with an alibi sooner or later, but hardly so soon and in such detail. He asked:

'And when you last saw Sir Paul at breakfast time, he didn't tell you how he proposed to spend the day?'

'No. But couldn't you look in his diary? He keeps it in his desk drawer in the study.'

'We found part of his diary in the vestry. It had been burnt.'

He was watching her face closely as he spoke. The blue eyes flickered, grew wary, but he could have sworn that this was news to her. She turned again to Farrell:

'But this is extraordinary! Why should Paul burn his diary?'

Dalgliesh said:

'We don't know that he did. But the diary was there in the grate. A number of the pages were burnt and the final page torn in half.'

Farrell's eyes met Dalgliesh's. Neither spoke. Then Dalgliesh said:

'So we need to try to establish his movements some other way. I had hoped you might be able to help.'

'But does it matter? I mean, if someone broke in and killed him, how does it help to know that he went to the estate agent a few hours earlier?'

'And did he?'

'He said he had an appointment.'

'Did he say with which one?'

'No, and I didn't ask. I suppose God told him to sell the house. I don't think He told him which estate agent to use.'

The words were as shocking as an indecency. Dalgliesh felt Farrell's dismayed surprise as clearly as if the man had gasped. He could detect neither bitterness nor irony in that high, slightly petulant voice. She could have been a mischievous child, daring in the presence of adults to say the unpardonable thing and half-surprised by her own temerity. Anthony Farrell decided that the time had come to intervene. He said smoothly:

'I myself was expecting to see Sir Paul yesterday afternoon. He had made an appointment at two thirty with me and two of my colleagues on the financial side of the firm to discuss certain arrangements made necessary, I understand, by his decision to give up his parliamentary career. But he rang yesterday shortly before ten to cancel the appointment and to make a new appointment for the same time today. I hadn't myself arrived at the office when he telephoned, but he left a message with my clerk. If you are able to prove that his death was murder, then I naturally accept that every detail of his affairs will properly come under scrutiny. Both Lady Ursula and Lady Berowne would wish that they should.'

He might be a pompous ass, thought Dalgliesh, but he was no fool. He knew or guessed, that most of these questions were premature. He was prepared to allow them, but he could stop them when he chose. Barbara Berowne turned on him her remarkable eyes.

'But there isn't anything to discuss. Paul left everything to me. He told me he had after we were married. The house too. It's quite straightforward. I'm his widow. It's all mine, well nearly all.'

Farrell said smoothly:

'Perfectly straightforward, my dear. But it's hardly necessary to discuss it now.'

Dalgliesh took from his wallet a copy of the poison pen letter and handed it to her.

He said:

'I expect you saw this.'

She shook her head and gave it to Farrell, who read it, taking his time, his face expressionless. If he had seen it before, he certainly wasn't admitting to the knowledge.

He said:

'That on the face of it is a malicious and possibly actionable attack on Sir Paul's character.'

'It may have nothing to do with his death but, obviously, we should like to clear it out of the way.'

He turned again to Barbara Berowne.

'Are you sure that your husband didn't show it to you?'

'No, why should he? Paul didn't believe in worrying me with things I couldn't do anything about. Isn't it the usual kind of poison pen letter? I mean, politicians get them all the time.'

'You mean, this wasn't unusual, that your husband had received similar communications?'

'No, I don't know, I don't think he did. He never said so. I meant that anyone in public . . .'

Farrell broke in, smoothly professional:

'Lady Berowne means, of course, that anyone in public life and particularly in politics has to expect a certain amount of this kind of malice and unpleasantness.'

Dalgliesh said:

'But not quite as specific as this, surely. There was a subsequent article, obviously based on this, in the *Paternoster Review*. Did you see that, Lady Berowne?'

She shook her head.

Farrell said:

'I suppose this has to be relevant, but do we need to talk about it now?'

Dalgliesh said:

'Not if Lady Berowne finds it too distressing.'

The implication was plain and Farrell didn't like it. His client helped him. She turned to him with a look in which appeal, surprise and distress were beautifully mingled.

'But I don't understand. I've told the Commander all I know. I've tried to help, but how can I? I don't know anything about Diana Travers. Miss Matlock, Mattie, looks after the house. I think this girl answered an advertisement and Mattie took her on.'

Dalgliesh said:

'Wasn't that rather unusual for these days? Young people don't often want to do housework.'

'Mattie said that she was an actress who only wanted to work a few hours each week. It suited her.'

'Did Miss Matlock consult you before taking on the girl?'

'No. I expect she asked my mother-in-law. They look after the house between them. They don't bother me with it.'

'And the other dead girl, Theresa Nolan. Did you have anything to do with her?'

'She was my mother-in-law's nurse, nothing to do with me. I hardly saw her.'

She turned to Anthony Farrell:

'Do I have to answer all these questions? I want to help but how can I? If Paul did have enemies, I don't know about them. We didn't really talk about politics, things like that.'

The sudden blaze of blue conveyed that no man would wish to burden her with matters so irrelevant to the essential fact about her.

She added:

'It's too dreadful. Paul dead, murdered – I can't believe it. I haven't really taken it in. I don't want to go on talking about it. I just want to be left alone and to go to my room. I want Mattie.'

The words were a piteous appeal for sympathy, for understanding, but the voice was that of a querulous child.

Farrell went over to the fireplace and pulled on the bell cord. He said:

'I'm afraid that one of the dreadful facts about murder is that the police are obliged to intrude on grief. It's their job. They have to be sure that there is nothing your husband said to you which could give them a clue to suggest that he had an enemy. Someone who might know that he would be in St Matthew's Church that night, someone who had a grudge against him, might want him out of the way. It seems most likely that Paul was killed by a casual intruder but the police have to exclude other possibilities.'

If Anthony Farrell thought that he was going to conduct the interview on his terms, he was mistaken. But before Dalgliesh could speak, the door burst open and a young man flung himself across the room to Barbara Berowne. He cried:

'Barbie darling! Mattie rang me with the news. It's awful, unbelievable. I'd have come earlier only she couldn't reach me until eleven. Darling, how are you? Are you all right?'

She said rather faintly:

'This is my brother, Dominic Swayne.'

He nodded at them as if their presence were an intrusion and turned again to his sister.

'But what happened, Barbie? Who did it? D'you know?'

Dalgliesh thought, this isn't genuine, he's acting. And then he told himself that the judgement was certainly premature and possibly unjust. One thing policing taught you was that in moments of shock and grief, even the most articulate could sound platitudinous. If Swayne were over-acting the part of a devoted consoling brother, that didn't necessarily mean that he wasn't both genuinely devoted and anxious to console. But Dalgliesh hadn't missed Barbara Berowne's small shudder as his arms went round her shoulders. It could, of course, have been a small manifestation of shock, but Dalgliesh wondered if it hadn't also been one of mild revulsion.

He wouldn't have known at first that they were brother and sister. True Swayne had the same corn-yellow hair, but his, either by nature or art, was tightly curled above a round pale forehead. The eyes, too, were alike, the same remarkable violet blue under the curved brows. But there the resemblance ended. He had none of his sister's classical heart-catching beauty. But his face, delicately featured, wasn't without a certain puckish charm with its well-formed rather petulant mouth, ears as tiny as a child's, milk-white and slightly jutting like incipient wings. He was short, little more than five foot three, but broad shouldered and with long arms. This simian strength grafted on to the delicate head and face were so discordant that the first impression was of a minor physical deformity.

But Miss Matlock had answered the bell and was standing in the doorway. Without saying goodbye and with a little moan Barbara Berowne half-stumbled over to her. The woman gazed first at her, then at the men in the room impassively, then, placing an arm across her shoulder, guided her out. There was a moment of silence, then Dalgliesh turned to Dominic Swayne:

'As you are here, perhaps you would answer one or two questions. It's possible you may be able to help us. When did you last see Sir Paul?'

'My revered brother-in-law? Do you know, I can't remember. Not for some weeks anyway. Actually I was in this house all yesterday evening, but we didn't meet. Evelyn, Miss Matlock, wasn't expecting him back for dinner. She said that he had left after breakfast and no one knew where he had gone.'

Kate asked from her seat by the wall:

'When did you arrive, sir?'

He turned to look at her, the blue eyes amused, frankly appraising, as if signalling a sexual invitation.

'Just before seven. The neighbour was coming out of his door and saw me arrive so he'll be able to confirm the time if it's important. I can't see why it should be. Miss Matlock too, of course. I stayed until just before ten thirty then went over to the local pub, the Raj, for a last drink. They'll remember me there. I was one of the last to leave.'

Kate asked:

'And you were here the whole time?'

'Yes. But what's it got to do with Paul's death? I mean is it important?'

He couldn't, thought Dalgliesh, be as naive as that. He said:

'It could be helpful in tracing Sir Paul's movements yesterday. Could he have returned to the house while you were here?'

'I suppose so, but it doesn't seem likely. I was having a bath for about an hour, that's principally why I came, and he might have come back then, but I think that Miss Matlock would have mentioned it. I'm an actor, out of work at present. Just auditioning. They call it resting, God knows why. It seems more like feverish activity to me. I lodged here for a week or two in May, but Paul wasn't all that welcoming, so I moved in with Bruno Packard. He's a theatre designer. He has a small flat, a conversion, at Shepherd's Bush. But what with his model sets and gear there's not a lot of room. On top of that there isn't a bath, only a shower, and that's in the loo, so it isn't exactly convenient for anyone reasonably fastidious. I've taken to turning up here for an occasional bath and meal.'

It was, thought Dalgliesh, almost suspiciously pat as if the whole speech had been rehearsed. And he was certainly being unusually confiding for a man who hadn't even been asked to explain his movements, who could have no reason to suppose that this was a case of murder. But if the times were confirmed, it looked as if Swayne could be in the clear. Swayne said:

'Look, if there's nothing else you want I'll go up to Barbie. This is an appalling shock for her. Mattie will give you Bruno's address if you want it.'

After he had left, no one spoke for a moment, then Dalgliesh said:

'I am interested that Lady Berowne inherits the house. I would have expected it to be entailed.'

Farrell took the question with professional calm:

'Yes, the situation is unusual. I have, of course, authority from both Lady Ursula and Lady Berowne to give you any information you need. The old Berowne property, the one in Hampshire, was entailed, but that has long since gone, together with most of the fortune. This house has always been willed from one baronet to the next. Sir Paul inherited it from his brother, but he had absolute discretion about its disposal. After his marriage he made a new will and left it to his wife absolutely. The will is quite straightforward. Lady Ursula has her own money but there is a small bequest to her and a larger one to his only child, Miss Sarah Berowne. Halliwell and Miss Matlock get £10,000 each and he has left an oil painting, an Arthur Devis if I remember rightly, to the chairman of his local party. There are other minor bequests. But the house, its contents, and an adequate provision goes to his wife.'

And the house alone, thought Dalgliesh, must be worth at least three-quarters of a million, probably considerably more given its position and unique architectural interest. He recalled as he so often did the words of an old detective sergeant when he, Dalgliesh, had been a newly appointed DC. 'Love, Lust, Loathing, Lucre, the four Ls of murder, laddie. And the greatest of these is lucre.'

3

Their last interview that afternoon at Campden Hill Square was with Miss Matlock. Dalgliesh had asked to be shown where Berowne had kept his diary and she had led them into the ground floor study. It was, he knew, architecturally one of the most eccentric rooms in the house, and the one, perhaps, most typical of Soane's style. It was octagonal, each wall fitted from floor to ceiling with glass fronted bookcases between which fluted pilasters rose to a dome topped by an octagonal lantern decorated with richly coloured glass. It was, he thought, an exercise in the clever organization of limited space, an eminently successful example of the architect's peculiar genius. But it was still a room to wonder at rather than to live in, to work in, or to enjoy.

Solidly placed in the centre of the room was Berowne's mahogany desk. Dalgliesh and Kate moved over to it while Miss Matlock stood in the doorway and watched them, her eyes fixed on Dalgliesh's face, as if a momentary lapse of concentration might cause him to spring at her. Dalgliesh said:

'Could you show me, please, exactly where the diary was kept?'

She moved forward and, without speaking, pulled open the top right hand drawer. It was empty now except for a box of writing paper and one of envelopes. He asked:

'Did Sir Paul work here?'

'He wrote letters. He kept his parliamentary papers in his office at the House and everything to do with his constituency at his office at Wrentham Green.' She added:

'He liked things separate.'

Dalgliesh thought: Separate, impersonal, under control. Again he had the sense that he was in a museum, that Berowne had sat in this richly ornamented cell like a stranger. He said:

'What about his private papers? Do you know where those are kept?'

'I suppose in the safe. It's concealed behind the books in the case to the right of the door.'

If Berowne had, indeed, been murdered the safe and its contents would have to be examined. But that, like much else, could wait.

He moved over to the bookcase. It was, of course, popular wisdom that personality could be diagnosed from the shelves of a private library. These revealed that Berowne had read more biography, history and poetry than he had fiction, and yet, scanning the shelves, it struck Dalgliesh that he could have been browsing in the library of a private club, or a luxury cruise ship, although admittedly one where the object of the voyage was cultural enrichment rather than popular entertainment, and the fares high. Here, tidily shelved, was essentially the predictable, unexceptional choice of a well-educated, cultured Englishman who knew what it was proper to read. But he couldn't believe that Berowne was a man whose idea of choosing fiction was to order routinely the Booker shortlist. Again he had the sense of a personality escaping him, of even the room and its objects conspiring to hide from him the essential man. He asked:

'How many people had access to this room yesterday?'

The formal impersonality of the library must have affected him. The question sounded oddly phrased even to his own ears, and she made no attempt to hide the tone of contempt.

'Access? The study is part of a private house. We don't keep it locked. All the family and their friends have what you call access.'

'And who did, in fact, come in here yesterday?'

'I can't be sure. I suppose Sir Paul must have done if you found his diary with him in the church. Mrs Minns would have come in to dust. Mr Frank Musgrave, who is chairman of the constituency party was shown in here at lunchtime, but he didn't wait. Miss Sarah Berowne called in during the afternoon to see her grandmother, but I think she waited in the drawing room. She left before Lady Ursula returned.'

Dalgliesh asked:

'Mr Musgrave and Miss Berowne were let in by you?'

'I opened the door to them. There's no one else to do it.' She paused, then added:

'Miss Berowne used to have her own keys to the front door, but she didn't take them with her when she left home.'

'And when did you last see the diary?'

'I can't remember. I think it was about two weeks ago when Sir Paul rang from his office in the Department and asked me to check on a dinner engagement.'

'And when did you last see Sir Paul?'

'Just before ten o'clock yesterday. He came into the kitchen to collect some food for a picnic lunch.'

'Then perhaps we could go to the kitchen now.'

She led him along the tiled passage, down a couple of steps, then through a baize-covered door to the back of the house. Then she stood aside to let him in, and again stood at the door, hands clasped, the parody of a cook awaiting judgement on the cleanliness of the kitchen. And indeed there would be nothing to fault. Like the study it was curiously impersonal, lacking cosiness without being actually uncomfortable or poorly equipped. There was a central table in well-scrubbed pine with four chairs and a large and very old gas-cooker in addition to a more modern solid-fuel stove. It was obvious that little money had been spent on the kitchen in recent years. From the low window he could see the back of the wall dividing the house from the mews garages, and the feet only of the marble statues in their niches. Thus truncated, a row of delicately carved toes, they seemed to emphasize the room's colourless deprivation. The only individual note was a pink geranium in a pot on the shelf over the sink, and beside it a second pot with a couple of cuttings. He said:

'You told me that Sir Paul collected his lunch. Did he do that himself or did you get it for him?'

'He did. He knew where things were kept. He was often in the kitchen when I prepared Lady Ursula's breakfast tray. He used to take it up to her.'

'And what did he take away with him yesterday?'

'Half a loaf of bread which he sliced ready to eat, a piece of Roquefort cheese, two apples.' She added:

'He seemed preoccupied. I don't think he much minded what he was taking.'

It was the first time she had volunteered any information, but when he went on to question her gently about Berowne's mood, what, if anything he had said, she seemed to regret the moment of confidence and became almost surly. Sir Paul had told her that he wouldn't be in to luncheon, but nothing else. She hadn't known that he was going to St Matthew's church, nor whether he would be back for dinner. Dalgliesh said:

'So you prepared dinner in the usual way and at the usual time?'

The question disconcerted her. She flushed and the clasped hands tightened. Then she said:

'No. No, not in the usual way. Lady Ursula asked me when she got back after her tea engagement to bring up a tray with a flask of soup and a plate of smoked salmon sandwiches on brown bread. She didn't want to be disturbed again that evening. I took it up shortly after six. And I knew that Lady Berowne was dining out. I decided to wait and see if Sir Paul actually came back. There were things I could cook quickly if he did. I had soup I could warm up. I could make him an omelette. There's always something.' She sounded as defensive as if he had accused her of dereliction of duty.

He said:

'But it was, perhaps, a little inconsiderate of him not to let you know whether he would be in to dinner.'

'Sir Paul was never inconsiderate.'

'And to stay out all night without a word was surely unusual? It must have been worrying for all the household?'

'Not for me. It isn't my business what the family choose to do.

He could have been staying in the constituency. At eleven o'clock I asked Lady Ursula if it was all right to go to bed and leave the front door unbolted. She said that I should. Lady Berowne knew that it was necessary to bolt it after her when she came in.'

Dalgliesh changed the tack of his questions.

'Did Sir Paul take matches with him yesterday morning?'

Her surprise was obvious and, he thought, unfeigned.

'Matches? He didn't need matches. Sir Paul doesn't – he didn't – smoke. I didn't see him with any matches.'

'If he had taken them, where would he have got them?'

'From here at the side of the stove. It isn't self-lighting. Or there is a packet of four boxes in the cupboard above.'

She opened and showed him. The paper wrapping round the four boxes had been torn and one box taken, presumably that now lying at the side of the stove. She was gazing at him now with a fixed attention, her eyes very bright, her face a little flushed, as if she had a slight fever. His questions about the matches, which had first surprised her, now seemed to disconcert her. She was more on her guard, warier, much more tense. He was too experienced and she too poor an actress for him to be deceived. Up to now she had answered his questions in the tone of a woman performing a necessary if disagreeable duty. But now the interview had become an ordeal. She wanted him gone. He said:

'We would like to see your sitting room, if you have no objection?'

'If you think it necessary. Lady Ursula said that you were to be given every facility.'

Dalgliesh thought it unlikely that Lady Ursula had said any such thing, and certainly not in those words. He and Kate followed her across the passage and into the opposite room. It must, Dalgliesh thought, once have been the butler's or house-keeper's sanctum. As with the kitchen there was no view except of the courtyard and the door leading through to the mews garages. But the furniture was comfortable enough; a chintz-covered sofa for two, a matching armchair, a gate-legged table and two dining chairs set against the wall, a bookcase filled with volumes of an identical size, obviously from a book club. The fireplace was of marble with a wide over-mantel on which was crowded, with no attempt at arrangement, a collection of modern and prettily sentimental figurines, women in crinolines, a child hugging a puppy, shepherds and shepherdesses, a ballet dancer. These presumably belonged to Miss Matlock. The pictures were prints in modern frames, one of Constable's *Hay Wain* and, more surprising, Monet's *Women in a Field*. They and the furniture were innocuous, predictable, as if someone had said, 'We need to employ a housekeeper, furnish a room for her.' Even rejects from the rest of the house would have had more character than these impersonal objects. What again was missing was the sense that someone had impressed on this place her own personality. He thought: They live here their separate cabined lives. But only Lady Ursula is at home in this house. The rest are no more than squatters.

He asked her where she had spent the previous evening. She said:

'I was here or in the kitchen. Mr Dominic Swayne came for a meal and a bath, and afterwards we played Scrabble. He arrived shortly before seven and left before eleven. Our neighbour, Mr Swinglehurst, was garaging his car and saw Mr Swayne arrive.'

'Did anyone else in the house see him while he was here?'

'No, but he did take a telephone call at about twenty to nine. It was from Mrs Hurrell, the wife of the last agent at the constituency. She wanted to try and contact Sir Paul. I told her that no one knew where he was.'

'And Mr Swayne, where did he bath?'

'Upstairs, in the main bathroom. Lady Ursula has her own bathroom, and there is a shower room down here, but Mr Swayne wanted a proper bath.'

'So you were either in this room or the kitchen and Mr Swayne was upstairs for at least part of the evening. The back door, was it locked?'

'Locked and bolted. It always is after tea. The key is here on the keyboard in that cupboard.'

She opened it and showed him the wall-mounted board with its rows of hooks and tagged keys. He asked:

'Could anyone have gone out without your noticing, perhaps while you were in the kitchen?'

'No. I usually keep the door to the passage open. I should have seen or heard. No one left the house last night by that door.' She seemed to rouse herself then said with sudden vigour:

'All these questions. What was I doing? Who was here? Who could have left without being seen? Anyone would think he was murdered.'

Dalgliesh said:

'It is possible that Sir Paul was murdered.'

She gazed at him, appalled, then sank down on to the chair. He saw that she was shaking. She said in a low voice:

'Murdered. No one said anything about murder. I thought . . .'

Kate moved over to her, glanced at Dalgliesh, then placed her hand on Miss Matlock's shoulder. Dalgliesh asked:

'What did you think, Miss Matlock?'

She looked up at him and whispered so quietly that he had to bend his head to hear.

'I thought he might have done it himself.'

'Had you any reason to suppose that?'

'No. No reason. Of course not. How could I? And Lady Berowne said . . . There was something about his razor. But murder . . . I don't want to answer any more questions, not tonight. I don't feel well. I don't want to be badgered. He's dead. That's terrible enough. But murder! I can't believe it's murder. I want to be left alone.'

Looking down at her, Dalgliesh thought: The shock is real enough, but part of this is acting, and not very convincing acting at that. He said coolly:

'We're not allowed to badger a witness, Miss Matlock, and I don't think you really believe that we have been badgering you. You've been very helpful. I'm afraid we shall have to talk again, to ask you more questions, but it needn't be now. We can see ourselves out.'

She got out of the chair as clumsily as an old woman and said:

'No one sees themselves out of this house. That's my job.'

In the Rover Dalgliesh rang the Yard. He said to Massingham:

'We'll see Mr Lampart as early as we can tomorrow. It would be helpful if we could fit that in before the PM at three thirty. Is there any news of Sarah Berowne?'

'Yes sir. She's a professional photographer, apparently, and has had sessions all today. She's got another booked for tomorrow afternoon, a writer who's due to leave for the States in the evening. It's rather important so she hopes it won't be necessary to cancel. I told her we'd come along in the evening at six thirty. And Press Office want an urgent word. The news will break at six o'clock and they want to set up a press conference first thing tomorrow.'

'That's premature. What on earth do they expect us to be able to say at this stage? Try to get it postponed, John.'

If he could prove that Berowne had been murdered the whole investigation would take place against a background of feverish media interest. He knew that, although he didn't welcome it, but there was no reason why it should start yet. As Kate manoeuvred the Rover out of its restricted parking place and began to move slowly down the Square he looked back at the elegant façade of the house, at the windows like dead eyes. And then, on the top floor, he saw the twitch of a curtain and knew that Lady Ursula was watching them leave.

4

It was six twenty before Sarah Berowne managed to reach Ivor Garrod by telephone. She had been in her flat for most of the early part of the afternoon but hadn't dared ring from there. It was an absolute rule of his, born, she had sometimes felt, from his obsession with secrecy, that nothing important should ever be told over her own telephone. So the whole afternoon from the time her grandmother had left her had been dominated by the need to find a convenient public kiosk, to have sufficient coins ready. But he had always been unavailable and she hadn't liked to risk leaving a message, not even her name.

Her only appointment of the day had been to photograph a visiting writer staying with friends in Hertfordshire. She always worked with the minimum of equipment and had travelled by train. She couldn't remember very much of the short session. She had worked like an automaton choosing the best setting, testing the light, fitting the lenses. She supposed it had gone reasonably well, the woman had seemed satisfied, but even as she worked she had been impatient to get away to find a public telephone, to try once again to reach Ivor.

She had jumped down from the train almost before it drew to a stop at King's Cross and had looked round with desperate eyes for the arrows pointing to the telephones. They were open instruments banked each side of a malodorous passageway leading from the main concourse, its walls scribbled with numbers and graffiti. The rush hour was in progress and it was a couple of minutes before an instrument was free. She almost snatched it, still warm, from the relinquishing hand. And this time she was lucky; he was in his office, it was his voice that answered. She gave a small sob of relief:

'It's Sarah. I've been trying to reach you all day. Can you talk?'

'Briefly. Where are you?'

'At King's Cross. You've heard?'

'Only now, on the six o'clock news. It hasn't made the evening papers.'

'Ivor, I have to see you.'

He said calmly:

'Naturally. There are things we need to talk about, but not tonight. That isn't possible. Have the police been in touch with you?'

'They've been trying to get me, but I told them that I was tied up all today and wouldn't be free until six thirty tomorrow.'

'And are you?'

What does that matter, she thought. She said:

'I've got two appointments in the afternoon.'

'Hardly being tied up all day. Never lie to the police unless you can be sure that they have no way of finding out. They only have to check with your diary.'

'But I couldn't let them come until we'd spoken. There are things they might ask. About Theresa Nolan, about Diana. Ivor, we have to meet.'

'We shall. And they won't ask about Theresa. Your father killed himself, his final and most embarrassing folly. His life was a mess. The family will want it decently buried, not dragged out stinking into the daylight. How did you learn the news, by the way?'

'Grandmama. She rang me, then came round by taxi after the police had left her. She didn't tell me very much. I don't think she knew all the details. She doesn't believe that Daddy killed himself.'

'Naturally. The Berownes are expected to put on uniform and kill other people, not themselves. But that, come to it, was apparently what he did, kill another person. I wonder how much sympathy Ursula Berowne will waste on that dead tramp.'

A small burr of doubt caught at her mind. Could they possibly have said on the news that the second victim was a tramp? She said:

'But it isn't only Grandmama. The police, a Commander Dalgliesh, he doesn't seem to think that Daddy killed himself either.'

The level of noise had risen. The narrow hallway was crowded with people needing to telephone before catching their trains. She felt their bodies thrusting against her. The air was a jabber of voices against the background tramp of feet, the raucous, unintelligible litany of the station announcer. She bent her head more closely over the mouthpiece. She said:

'The police don't seem to think it was suicide.'

There was a silence. She dared to speak more loudly against the noise.

'Ivor, the police don't think . . .'

He cut in:

'I heard you. Look, stay where you are. I'll come now. We can only have half an hour but you're right, we ought to talk. And don't worry, I'll be with you in the flat when they arrive tomorrow. It's important you don't see them alone. And, Sarah . . .'

'Yes, I'm here.'

'We were together the whole of yesterday evening. We were together from six o'clock when I arrived from work. We stayed together all night. We ate in the flat. Get that into your mind. Start concentrating on it now. And stay where you are. I'll be there in about forty minutes.'

She replaced the receiver and stood for a moment motionless, her head against the cold metal of the instrument. A furious female voice said: 'Do you mind. Some of us have trains to catch', and she felt herself pushed aside. She fought her way out of the hall and leaned against the wall. Small waves of faintness and nausea flowed over her, each leaving her more desolate, but there was nowhere to sit, no privacy, no peace. She could go to the coffee bar but he might get there early. Suppose she became disorientated, lost track of time. He had said 'stay where you are', and obeying him had become a habit. She leaned back and closed her eyes. She had to obey him now, rely on his strength, rely on him to tell her what to do. She had no one else.

He hadn't once said he was sorry that her father was dead, but he wasn't sorry and he didn't expect her to be. He had always been brutally unsentimental; that was what he meant by honesty. She wondered what he would do if she said: 'He was my father and he's dead. I loved him once. I need to mourn for him, for myself. I need to be comforted. I'm lost, I'm frightened. I need to feel your arms around me. I need to be told that it wasn't my fault.'

The marching horde flowed past her, a phalanx of grey intent faces, eyes staring ahead. They were like a flood of refugees from a stricken city, or a retreating army, still disciplined, but dangerously on the edge of panic. She closed her eyes and let the tramp of their feet engulf her. And, suddenly, she was in another station, another crowd. But then she had been six years old and the station had been Victoria. What were they doing there, she and her father? Probably meeting her grandmother, returning by overland and by boat from her house rising out of the Seine at Les Andelys. For one moment she and her father had been parted. He had paused to greet an acquaintance and she had momentarily slipped his hand and run to look at the brightly coloured poster of a seaside town. Looking round she saw with panic that he was no longer there. She was alone, menaced by a moving forest of endless, tramping, terrifying legs. They could have been parted only for seconds, but the terror had been so dreadful that, recalling it now, eighteen years later, she felt the same loss, the same engulfing terror, the same absolute despair. But suddenly he had been there, striding towards her, his long tweed coat flapping open, smiling, her father, her safety, her god. Not crying, but shuddering with terror and relief, she had run into his outstretched arms and felt herself lifted high, had heard his voice: 'It's all right, my darling, it's all right, it's all right.' And she had felt the dreadful shaking dissolving in his strong clasp.

She opened her eyes and blinking away the smarting tears she saw the drab blacks and greys of the marching army fudge, dissolve, then whirl into a kaleidoscope shot through with flashes of bright colour. It seemed to her that the moving feet were pounding over and through her, that she had become invisible, a brittle, empty shell. But suddenly the mass parted and he was there, still in that long tweed coat, moving towards her, smiling, so that she had to restrain herself from crying 'Daddy, Daddy', and running into his arms. But the hallucination passed. This wasn't he, this was a hurrying stranger with a briefcase who glanced with momentary curiosity at her eager face and out-stretched arms, then looked through her and passed on. She shrank back, wedging herself more firmly against the wall, and began her long, patient wait for Ivor.

5

It was just before ten o'clock and they were thinking of locking up their papers for the night when Lady Ursula rang. Gordon Halliwell had returned and she would be grateful if the police could see him now. He himself would prefer it. Tomorrow was going to be a busy day for both of them, and she couldn't say when they would be available. Dalgliesh knew that Massingham, if in charge, would have said firmly that they would arrive next morning, if only to demonstrate that they worked at their own convenience, not that of Lady Ursula. Dalgliesh, who was anxious to question Gordon Halliwell and who had never felt the need to bolster either his own authority or his self-esteem, said that they would arrive as soon as possible.

The door of number sixty-two was opened by Miss Matlock who gazed at them for a couple of seconds with tired, resentful eyes before standing to one side to let them in. Dalgliesh could see that her skin was grey with weariness, the set of her shoulders a little too rigid to be natural. She was wearing a long dressing gown in flowered nylon, strained across the breast, the belt double-knotted as if she were afraid they would tear it off. She made a clumsy flutter of her hands towards it and said peevishly:

'I'm not dressed for visitors. We were hoping to get to bed early. I wasn't expecting you to come back tonight.'

Dalgliesh said:

'I'm sorry to have to disturb you again. If you want to go to bed, perhaps Mr Halliwell could let us out.'

'It isn't his job. He's only the chauffeur. Locking up the house is my responsibility. Lady Ursula has asked him to take the telephone calls tomorrow, but it isn't suitable, it isn't right. We've had no peace since the six o'clock news. This will kill her if it goes on.'

It was, thought Dalgliesh, likely to go on for a very long time but he doubted whether it would kill Lady Ursula.

Their footsteps rang on the marble floor as Miss Matlock led them down the passage past the octagonal study then through the baize door to the back of the house and finally down three stairs to the outside door. The house was very quiet but portentously expectant like an empty theatre. He had the sense, as he often did in the houses of the recently murdered, of a thin denuded air, a voiceless presence. She drew the locks and they found themselves in the rear courtyard. The three statues in their niches were subtly lit with concealed lighting and seemed to float, gently gleaming, in the still air. The night was surprisingly balmy for autumn, and there came from some nearby garden the transitory smell of cypress so that he felt for a moment displaced, disorientated as if transported to Italy. It seemed to him inappropriate that the statues should be lit, the beauty of the house still celebrated when Berowne lay frozen like a carcass of meat in his plastic shroud, and he found himself instinctively putting out his hand for a switch before following Miss Matlock through a second door which led to the old mews and the garages.

The rear of the wall with the statues was unadorned; the spoils of the eighteenth-century grand tour were not for the eyes of the footmen or coachmen who once must have inhabited the mews.

The yard was cobbled and led to two large garages. The double doors of the left were open and in the glare of two long tubes of fluorescent light they saw that the entrance to the flat was by way of a wrought-iron staircase leading up the side of the garage wall. Miss Matlock merely pointed to the door at the top and said:

'You'll find Mr Halliwell there.' And then, as if to justify the formal use of his name, she said: 'He used to be a sergeant in the late Sir Hugo's regiment. He's been decorated for bravery, the Military Medal. I expect Lady Ursula told you. He isn't the usual kind of chauffeur-handyman.'

And what in these egalitarian, servantless days, thought Dalgliesh, did she suppose the usual kind of chauffeur-handyman to be?

The garage was large enough comfortably to hold the black Rover with its A registration and a white Golf, both of which were neatly parked with room for a third car. Making their way down the side of the Rover through a strong smell of petrol they saw that the garage was obviously also used as a workshop. Under a high, long window at the rear was a wooden bench with fitted drawers, and on the wall above, a pegboard on which tools were neatly displayed. Propped against the right-hand wall was a man's bicycle.

They had hardly set foot on the bottom step of the staircase when the door above opened and the figure of a man stood stockily silhouetted against the light. As they came up to him Dalgliesh saw that he was both older and shorter than he had expected, surely only just the statutory height for a soldier, but broad shouldered and giving an immediate impression of disciplined strength. He was very dark, almost swarthy, and the straight hair, longer than it would have been in his Army days, fell across his forehead almost touching eyebrows straight as black gashes above the deep-set eyes. His nose was short with slightly flared nostrils, the mouth uncompromising above a square chin. He was wearing well-cut fawn slacks and a woollen checked shirt, open-necked, and gave no sign of tiredness, seeming as fresh as if this were a morning visit. He looked at them with keen but untroubled eyes; eyes that had seen worse things than a couple of CID officers arriving at night. Standing aside to let them in, he said in a voice which held only a trace of roughness:

'I'm just making coffee, or there's whisky if you'd prefer it.'

They accepted the coffee and he went through a door at the back of the room from which presently they heard the noise of running water, the clatter of a kettle lid. The sitting room was long but narrow, its low windows looking out on the blank rear of the wall. Soane, as a good architect, would have ensured that the privacy of the family was protected; the mews would be unseen from all but the top windows of the house. At the far end of the room a door stood open and Dalgliesh could glimpse the end of a single bed. At the back was a small, delicately wrought Victorian fireplace with a carved wooden surround and an elegant fire-basket reminding him of the grate in St Matthew's church. A modern three-bar electric fire was plugged in to a socket at its side.

A pine table with four chairs occupied the middle of the room and two rather battered armchairs stood each side of the fireplace. Between the windows was a worktop with, above it, a pegboard of tools, smaller and more delicate than those in the garage. They saw that Halliwell's hobby was wood carving and that he was working on a Noah's Ark with a set of animals. The ark was beautifully constructed with dove-tail joints and an elegant clap-board roof; the completed animals, a pair of lions, tigers and giraffes were more crudely carved but instantly recognizable and with a certain vigorous life.

The far wall was fitted with a bookshelf from floor to ceiling. Dalgliesh moved across to it and saw with interest that Halliwell owned what looked like a complete set of the *Notable British Trials*. And there was one other volume even more interesting: he drew out and leafed through the eighth edition of Keith Simpson's *Textbook on Forensic Medicine*. Replacing it, and glancing round the room he was struck with its tidiness, with its self-containment. It was the room of a man who had organized his living space and probably his life to fulfil his needs, who knew his own nature and was at peace with it. Unlike Paul Berowne's study, this was the room of a man who felt he had a right to be there.

Halliwell came in carrying a tray with three stoneware mugs, a bottle of milk and one of Bell's whisky. He motioned towards the whisky and when Dalgliesh and Massingham shook their heads added a generous measure to his own black coffee. They sat round the table.

Dalgliesh said:

'I see you've got what looks like a complete set of the *Notable British Trials*. That must be comparatively rare.'

Halliwell said:

'It's an interest of mine. I could have fancied being a criminal lawyer if things had been different.'

He spoke without resentment. It was a statement of fact; but there was no need to ask which things. The law was still a privileged profession. It was rare for a working-class boy to end up eating his dinners in the Inns of Court.

He added:

'It's the trials I find interesting, not the defendants. Most murderers seem pretty stupid and commonplace when you see them in the dock. Same will be true of this chap, no doubt, when you get your hands on him. But maybe a caged animal is always less interesting than one running wild, especially when you've glimpsed his spoor.'

Massingham said:

'So you're assuming it's murder.'

'I'm assuming that a Commander and Chief Inspector of the CID wouldn't come here after ten at night to discuss why Sir Paul Berowne should want to slit his throat.'

Massingham leaned across to reach the milk bottle. Stirring his coffee he asked:

'When did you hear of Sir Paul's death?'

'On the six o'clock news. I rang Lady Ursula and said I'd drive back at once. She said I wasn't to hurry. There was nothing I could do here and she wouldn't be wanting the car. She said the police had asked to see me, but that you'd have plenty to occupy yourselves until I got back.'

Massingham asked:

'How much has Lady Ursula told you?'

'As much as she knows, which isn't a great deal. She said that their throats were cut and that Sir Paul's razor had been the weapon.'

Dalgliesh had asked Massingham to do most of the questioning.

This apparent reversal of role and status was often disconcerting to a suspect, but not to this one. Halliwell was either too confident or too unworried to be troubled by such niceties. Dalgliesh had the impression that, of the two, it was Massingham who was, unaccountably, the less at ease. Halliwell, who answered his questions with what seemed deliberate slowness, had an odd and disconcerting trick of fixing his dark eyes intently on the questioner as if it were he who was the interrogator, he who was seeking to fathom an unknown, elusive personality.

He admitted that he had known that Sir Paul used a cut-thoat razor; anyone in the house would know that. He knew that the diary was kept in the top right-hand drawer. It wasn't private. Sir Paul might ring and ask whoever answered the telephone to check on the time of an engagement. There was a key to the drawer, kept usually in the lock or in the drawer itself. Occasionally Sir Paul had been known to lock the drawer and take the key with him, but that wasn't usual. These were the sort of details you got to know if you lived or worked in a house. But he couldn't remember when he had last seen the razor or the diary, and he hadn't been told that Sir Paul would be visiting the church that previous evening. He couldn't say whether anyone else in the house had known; no one had mentioned the matter to him.

Asked for his movements during the day, he said that he had got up at about half-past six and had gone for a half-hour jog in Holland Park before boiling an egg for his breakfast. At eight thirty he had gone over to the house to see if there were any odd jobs which Miss Matlock had needed doing. She had given him a table lamp to mend and an electric kettle. He had then driven to collect Mrs Beamish, Lady Ursula's chiropodist who lived in Parsons Green and who no longer ran a car. That was a regular arrangement on the third Tuesday in the month. Mrs Beamish was over seventy and Lady Ursula was the only patient she now saw. The session was over by eleven thirty and he had then driven Mrs Beamish home and returned to take Lady Ursula to a luncheon engagement with a friend, Mrs Charles Blaney, at the University Women's Club. He had parked the car near the club, gone for a solitary pub lunch and returned at two forty-five to drive both ladies to an exhibition of watercolours at Agnew's. Afterwards he had driven them to the Savoy for afternoon tea, then returned to Campden Hill Square by way of Chelsea where he had dropped Mrs Blaney at her house. He and Lady Ursula were back at number sixty-two by five thirty-three. He could remember the time exactly because he had looked at the car clock. He was used to organizing his life by time. He had helped Lady Ursula into the house, had then garaged the Rover and had spent the rest of the evening in his flat until leaving for the country just after ten o'clock. Massingham said:

'I believe Lady Ursula telephoned you twice during the evening. Can you remember when that was?'

'Yes. Once at about eight, and again at nine fifteen. She wanted to discuss next week's arrangements and to remind me that she had said I could take the Rover. I drive one of the early Cortinas but it's having its MOT test.'

Massingham asked:

'When the cars are garaged, the Rover, your own and the Golf, is the garage kept locked?'

'It's kept locked whether or not the cars are garaged. The outer gate is, of course, always secure so there isn't much risk of theft, but it's possible that kids from the comprehensive school could climb over the wall, perhaps as a dare. There are dangerous tools in the larger garage and Lady Ursula thinks it wiser always to keep it locked. I didn't bother to lock it tonight because I knew you were coming.'

'And yesterday evening?'

'It was locked after five forty.'

'Who has the keys except yourself?'

'Sir Paul and Lady Berowne both have a set and there's a spare bunch on the keyboard in Miss Matlock's sitting room. Lady Ursula wouldn't need them. She relies on me to drive her.'

'And were you here in this flat all yesterday evening?'

'From five forty. That's right.'

'Is there any chance that someone from the house or from outside could have taken out a car or the bicycle without your knowing?'

Halliwell paused, then said:

'I don't see how that would be possible.'

Dalgliesh interposed quietly:

'I'd like you to be more definite than that, Mr Halliwell, if you can be. Could they or couldn't they?'

Halliwell looked at him.

'No, sir, they couldn't. I must have heard the garage being unlocked. I've got sharp ears.'

Dalgliesh went on:

'So last night from about five forty until you left for the country shortly after ten you were here alone in this flat and the garage door was bolted?'

'Yes, sir.'

'Is it usual for you to keep the doors bolted when you're in the flat?'

'If I know I'm not going out, it is. I rely on the garage door for my security. The flat lock is only a Yale. It's become a habit to bolt the doors.'

Massingham asked:

'And where did you go when you left here?'

'Into the country. To Suffolk, to see a friend. It's a two-hour drive. I arrived about midnight. It's the widow of one of my mates killed in the Falklands. There's a boy. He doesn't miss his dad, he was killed before he was born, but his mother reckons that it's good for him to have a man about the place occasionally.'

Massingham asked:

'So you went to see the boy?'

The smouldering eyes were fixed on him. Halliwell answered simply:

'No. I went to see his mother.'

Massingham said:

'Your private life is your affair, but we need confirmation about when you arrived at your friend's house. That means we need to know her address.'

'Maybe, sir, but I don't see why I need to give it. She's had enough to put up with in the last three years without the police bothering her. I left here just after ten. If Sir Paul was dead before then, what I did later that night isn't relevant. Maybe you know when he died, maybe not. But when you get the autopsy report you'll get a clearer idea. If I need to give you her name and address then, OK, I'll give it. But I'll wait until you convince me that it's necessary.'

Massingham said:

'We shan't bother her. She merely has to answer one simple question.'

'A question about murder. She's had enough of death and dying. Look, I left here shortly after ten and I arrived almost exactly at midnight. If you do ask her, she'll say the same, and if it's relevant, if I had anything to do with Sir Paul's death, then I'll have fixed a time with her anyway, won't I?'

Massingham asked:

'Why did you start out so late? Today was your day off. Why hang about until ten before starting on a two-hour journey?'

'I prefer driving when the worst of the traffic is over, and I had some jobs I wanted to get finished first, a plug to fix on the table lamp, the electric kettle to mend. They're on the side if you want to check on the work. Then I bathed, changed, cooked myself a meal.'

The words, if not the voice, were on the edge of insolence, but Massingham held his temper. Dalgliesh, his own well under control, thought he knew why. Halliwell was a soldier, decorated, a hero. Massingham would have dealt less gently with any man for whom he felt less instinctive respect. If Halliwell had murdered Paul Berowne then the Victoria Cross wouldn't save him, but Dalgliesh knew that Massingham would prefer almost any other suspect to be guilty. Massingham asked:

'Are you married?'

'I had a wife and a daughter. They're both dead.'

He turned and looked directly at Dalgliesh. He said:

'What about you, sir? Are you married?'

Dalgliesh had reached out behind him and taken up one of the carved lions. Now he turned it gently in his hands. He said:

'I had a wife and a son. They, too, are dead.'

Halliwell turned again to Massingham and bent on him his dark unsmiling eyes.

'And if that question was none of my business, neither are my wife and daughter any of yours.'

Massingham said:

'Nothing is irrelevant when it comes to murder. This lady you visited yesterday night, are you engaged to her?'

'No. She's not ready for that. After what happened to her husband I don't know that she ever will be. That's why I don't want to give you her address. She's not ready for that kind of question from the police, or for any other question.'

Massingham rarely made that kind of mistake and he didn't compound it by explanation or excuse. Dalgliesh didn't press the matter. The important hour was eight o'clock. If Halliwell had an alibi for the hours until ten he was in the clear and was entitled to his privacy for the following day. If he were trying with difficulty to build up a relationship with a bereaved and vulnerable woman it was understandable that he didn't want the police arriving with unnecessary questions however tactful. He said:

'How long have you been working here?'

'Five years three months, sir. I took the job when Major Hugo was alive. After he was killed Lady Ursula asked me to stay on. I stayed. The money suits, the place suits, you could say Lady Ursula suits. Apparently I suit her. I like living in London and I haven't decided yet what to do with my gratuity.'

'Who pays your wages? Who actually employs you?'

'Lady Ursula. It's my job to drive her mostly. Sir Paul used to drive himself or use the ministerial car. Occasionally I'd drive him and her young ladyship if they were out in the evening. There wasn't much of that. They weren't a social couple.'

'What sort of couple were they?' Massingham's voice was carefully uninterested.

'They didn't hold hands in the back of the car, if that's what you mean.' He paused, then added: 'I think that she was a bit afraid of him.'

'With reason?'

'Not that I could see, but I wouldn't describe him as an easy man. Nor a happy one, come to that. If you can't cope with guilt, best avoid doing things that make you feel guilty.'

'Guilt?'

'He killed his first wife didn't he? All right it was an accident;

349

wet road, bad visibility, a notorious bend. That all came out at the inquest. But he was the one driving. I've seen it before. They never quite forgive themselves. Something here' – he gave his chest a gentle thump – 'keeps asking them whether it really was an accident.'

'There's no evidence that it wasn't, and he was as likely to kill himself as his wife.'

'Maybe that wouldn't have worried him that much. Still he didn't die, did he? She did. And then, five months later, he married again. He got his brother's fiancée, his brother's house, his brother's money, his brother's title.'

'But not his brother's chauffeur?'

'No. He didn't take over me.'

Dalgliesh asked:

'Did the title matter to him? I shouldn't have thought so.'

'Oh it mattered all right, sir. It wasn't much, I suppose, a baronetcy, but it was old. 1642. He liked it all right, the sense of continuity, his little bit of vicarious immortality.'

Massingham said:

'Well, we can all hope for that. You don't sound as if you much liked him.'

'Liking didn't come into it between him and me. I drove his mother, she paid me. And if he disliked me he didn't show it. But I reckon I reminded him of things he'd rather forget.'

Massingham said:

'And now it's all gone, ended with him, even the title.'

'Maybe. Time will show. I think I'd wait nine months before I was sure of that.'

It was a hint of a possibility Dalgliesh had already suspected, but he didn't pursue it. Instead he asked:

'When Sir Paul gave up his ministerial job and then his parliamentary seat, what was the feeling in the house among the staff?'

'Miss Matlock didn't discuss it. This isn't the sort of house where the staff sit in the kitchen drinking tea and gossiping about the family. We leave upstairs, downstairs to the telly. Mrs Minns and I thought we might be in for a scandal.'

'What sort of a scandal?'

'Sexual, I suppose. That's the kind it usually is.'

'Had you any reason to suspect that?'

'None, except that bit of dirt in the *Paternoster Review*. I've no evidence. You asked me what I thought, sir. That was what I thought most likely. Turns out I was wrong. It was more complicated apparently. But then he was a complicated man.'

Massingham went on to ask him about the two dead women. Halliwell said:

'I hardly saw Theresa Nolan. She had a room here but she either stayed in it most of the time, or went out. Kept herself to herself. She was employed as a night-nurse and wasn't supposed to be on duty until seven. Miss Matlock nursed Lady Ursula during the day. She seemed a quiet, rather shy girl. A bit timid for a nurse, I thought. Lady Ursula had no complaints as far as I know. You'd better ask her.'

'You know that she got pregnant while she was working here?'

'Maybe, but she didn't get pregnant in this flat, nor in the house for all I know. There's no law which says you can only have sex between seven at night and seven next morning.'

'And Diana Travers?'

Halliwell smiled:

'A different girl altogether. Lively. Very bright, I'd say. I saw more of her although she only worked the two days, Monday and Friday. Odd sort of job for a girl like that to take, I thought. And a bit of a coincidence seeing Miss Matlock's advert just when she was looking for a part-time job. Those cards usually stick in the windows until they get too brown and faded to be read.'

Massingham said:

'Apparently Lady Berowne's brother, Mr Swayne, was here last evening. Did you see him?'

'No.'

'Is he often here?'

'More often than Sir Paul liked. Or other people for that matter.'

'Including you?'

'Me and his sister, I reckon. He has a habit of turning up for a bath or a meal when it suits him, but he's harmless. Spiteful, but about as dangerous as a wasp.'

It was, Dalgliesh thought, too facile a judgement.

Suddenly all three men, keen-eared, raised their heads and listened. Someone was coming through the garage. There was a rush of footfalls, soft soled, on the iron staircase, the door was almost flung open and Dominic Swayne stood in the entrance. Halliwell must have left the latch of the Yale up. It was, thought Dalgliesh, a curious oversight unless, of course, he had been half-expecting this sudden intrusion. But he made no sign, merely fixing on Swayne his dark unwelcoming gaze before turning again to his mug of coffee. Swayne must have known that they were there since, presumably, Miss Matlock had let him into the house, but his start of surprise and the tentative embarrassed smile were nicely judged.

'Oh my God! Sorry, sorry! I seem to have an unlucky habit of bursting in when the police are doing their stuff. Well, I'll leave you to the third degree.'

Halliwell said coldly:

'Why not try knocking first?'

But it was to Dalgliesh that Swayne turned:

'I only wanted to tell Halliwell that my sister says I can borrow the Golf tomorrow.'

Halliwell said without moving from his seat:

'You can borrow the Golf without prior notice. You usually do.'

Swayne kept his eyes on Dalgliesh.

'That's OK then. Look, I'm here. Is there anything you want to ask me? If so, go ahead.'

Massingham had got up from the table and had picked up one of the carved elephants. His voice was carefully devoid of emphasis.

'Just to confirm again that you were here in the house the whole of last evening from the time you arrived, just before seven, till you left for the Raj at half past ten?'

'That's right, Inspector. Clever of you to remember.'

'And during that time you didn't leave number sixty-two?'

'Right again. Look, I'm hardly everyone's favourite brother-in-law, I admit, but I had nothing to do with Paul's death. And I don't see why Paul should have resented me so much unless I reminded him of someone he'd rather not be reminded of. I mean I don't drug unless someone else is paying which they so rarely do. I'm comparatively sober. I work when there's work to be had. I admit I bath and eat at his expense occasionally, but I don't see why he should resent that – he's hardly on the bread line – or my having a game of Scrabble with poor Evelyn. No one else bothers to. And I didn't slit his throat for him. I'm not in the least bloodthirsty. I don't think I've got the nerve. I'm not like Halliwell, trained to creep about among the rocks with my face blacked and a knife between my teeth. That's not my idea of amusement.'

Massingham put the elephant down. It was like a rejection.

He said:

'You prefer an evening's Scrabble with your lady friend? Who won?'

'Oh, Evelyn won, she usually does. Yesterday she got "zephyr" on a treble, clever girl. Three hundred and eighty-two points to my two hundred. It's extraordinary how often she picks the high numbers. If she weren't so depressingly honest, I'd suspect her of cheating.'

Massingham said:

' "Zig-zag" would have scored even higher.'

'Ah, but there aren't two Zs in Scrabble. I can see that you aren't an addict. You should try it sometime, Inspector. It's excellent for sharpening the wits. Well, if that's all I'll be off.'

Dalgliesh said:

'Not quite all. Tell us about Diana Travers.'

Swayne stood for a couple of seconds very still, the bright eyes rapidly blinking. But the shock, if it were shock, was quickly mastered. Dalgliesh could see the muscles of his hands and shoulders relaxing. He said:

'What about her? She's dead.'

'We know that. She drowned after a dinner party given by you at the Black Swan. You were there when she died. Tell us about it.'

'There's nothing to tell. I mean, you must have read the report of the inquest. And I don't see what it's got to do with Paul. She wasn't his girl or anything like that.'

353

'We didn't suppose that she was.'

He shrugged and held out his palms in a parody of resigned reasonableness.

'Well, what do you want to know?'

'Why not begin by telling us why you invited her to the Black Swan.'

'No particular reason. Call it a generous impulse. I knew my dear sister was having what she would describe as an intimate dinner party for her birthday, too intimate to invite me apparently. So I thought I'd organize a little celebration of my own. I was here bringing Barbara my birthday present, and I saw Diana dusting the hall as I left. So I asked her to come along. I picked her up outside Holland Park tube at six thirty and drove her to meet the gang at the Black Swan.'

'Where you had dinner.'

'Where we had dinner. Do you want the details of the menu?'

'Not unless it's relevant. Suppose you go on from there.'

'After dinner we went out to the river bank and found this punt moored upstream. The rest of the party thought it would be amusing to mess about on the river. Diana and I decided that it would be even more amusing to mess about on the bank. She was pretty high. Drink not drugs. Then we thought it would be fun to swim out to the punt and bob up beside them.'

'Having first taken off your clothes.'

'They were already off. Sorry if I shock you.'

'And you dived in first.'

'Not dived, waded. I never dive into unknown water. Anyway, I struck out with my usual elegant crawl and reached the punt. Then I looked back for Diana. I couldn't see her on the bank, but then, there are quite a few bushes at the spot, Jean Paul trying to make some sort of a garden I suppose, and I thought she might have changed her mind and be dressing. I was a bit worried, but not frantically worried, if you see what I mean. But I thought I'd better go back and check. And the whole idea of the swim was losing its charm. The water was icy cold and very dark and the chums hadn't greeted me with quite the enthusiasm I expected. So I let go of the punt and struck back towards the bank. She wasn't there, but her clothes were. So then I really was scared. I called out to the party in the punt but they were rocking about, giggling, and I don't think they heard me. And then they found her. They struck the body with the punt pole just as she surfaced. Pretty ghastly for the girls. They managed to hold her head above water and paddled to the bank, nearly upsetting the punt in the process. I helped drag her out and we tried the usual mouth to mouth. It was a god awful mess. The girls crying and trying to get some clothes on her. Me dripping wet and shivering. Tony forcing his breath into her mouth as if he were pumping up a balloon. Diana lying there, eyes staring, with the water running off her hair and the weeds wrapped round her neck like a green scarf . . . They made her look decapitated. Erotic in a horrible way. And then one of the girls ran to the restaurant for help and that chef chap came out and took over. He seemed to know what he was doing. But no good. End of Diana. End of a jolly evening. End of story.'

There was a scrape of wood as Halliwell violently pushed himself up from the table and disappeared swiftly into the kitchen. Swayne looked after him.

'What's he upset about? I was the one who had to look at her. You'd think he'd heard worse things than that.'

Neither Dalgliesh nor Massingham spoke and almost immediately Halliwell was back. He was carrying another half bottle of Scotch and set it down. It seemed to Dalgliesh that his face was paler but he poured himself another tot of whisky with a perfectly steady hand. Swayne glanced at the bottle as if wondering why he wasn't invited to drink then turned again to Dalgliesh.

'I'll tell you one thing about Diana Travers. She wasn't an actress. I found that out on our drive to the Black Swan. No Equity card. No drama school. No theatrical jargon. No agents. No parts.'

'Did she say what her job really was?'

'She said she wanted to be a writer and was collecting material. It was easier to tell people you were on the stage. That way, they never asked why you wanted a temporary job. I can't say I cared one way or the other. I mean, I was taking the girl out to dinner, I wasn't proposing to shack up with her.'

'And during the time you were with her on the river bank,

before the swim and when you went back to find her, did you see or hear any other person?'

The blue eyes widened and became so like his sister's that the resemblance was uncanny. He said:

'I don't think so. We were a bit preoccupied, if you get me. You mean, a peeping Tom, someone spying on us? The thought didn't occur to me.'

'Let it occur to you now. Were you absolutely alone?'

'We must have been, mustn't we? I mean, who else would be there?'

'Think back. Did you see or hear anything suspicious?'

'I can't say that I did, but then there was all the jolly girlish screaming from the punt. And I don't think I would have seen or heard anything very clearly once I'd waded in and begun swimming. I do seem to remember that I heard Diana diving in after me, but that's what I expected her to do so maybe I imagined it. And there could have been someone watching us I suppose. In the bushes, maybe. But I didn't see him. Sorry, if that's the wrong answer. And sorry for barging in. Oh, by the way, I'll be staying here in the house if you want me. Brotherly consolation for the widow.'

He gave a shrug and a smile which seemed bestowed on the room generally rather than anyone in it. Then he was gone. They heard the soft thud of his descending footsteps on the iron staircase. No one made any comment. As they rose to go, Massingham asked his last question. He said:

'We can't be certain yet how Sir Paul and Harry Mack died, but we think the probability is that both were murdered. Have you seen or heard anything in this house or outside it which would give you a suspicion of who might be responsible?'

It was the question they always asked, expected, formal, almost crudely direct. Because of this, it was often the one least likely to elicit the truth.

Halliwell poured himself another whisky. It looked as if he were settling in for a night's hard drinking. Without looking up he said:

'I didn't slit his throat for him. If I knew who had, I'd probably tell you.'

Massingham persevered:

'Sir Paul had no enemies as far as you are aware?'

'Enemies?'

Halliwell's smile was nearer a grin. It transformed his swarthy good looks into a mask at once sinister and sardonic, giving force to Swayne's description of him creeping black-faced among the rocks.

'He must have had, mustn't he, sir, being a politician? But that's all over now. Done with. Finished. Like the Major, he's moved out of their gunshot now.'

And with that echo of Bunyan, which Dalgliesh suspected might have been a deliberate half-quotation, the interview was at an end.

Halliwell went down with them through the garage and dragged the heavy doors shut behind them. They heard the rasp of the two bolts. The lights in the niches had been switched off and the cobbled yard was in darkness except for twin wall mounted lights at each end of the garage wall. In the half-darkness the smell of cypress had strengthened, but was overlaid with a scent sicklier and funereal as if somewhere close was a dustbin of dead and rotting flowers. As they approached the back door to the house the figure of Miss Matlock stepped noiselessly out of the shadows. In the folds of the long dressing gown she seemed taller, hierarchic, almost graceful in her watching stillness. Dalgliesh wondered how long she had stood silently waiting for them.

He and Massingham followed her in silence through the quiet house. As she turned the key and drew back the bolts of the front door Massingham said:

'That game of Scrabble you played last night with Mr Swayne. Who won?'

The ploy was deliberately naive, the trap obvious. But her reaction was surprising. In the subdued light of the hall they watched the flush mottle her throat then flare up to crimson her face.

'I did. I got three hundred and eighty-two points in case you should be interested. That game was played, Inspector. You may be used to talking to liars. I'm not one of them.'

Her body was rigid with fury but the clasped hands shook as if they were palsied. Dalgliesh said gently:

'No one is suggesting that you are, Miss Matlock. Thank you for waiting up for us. Goodnight.'

Outside as he unlocked the Rover, Massingham said:

'Now why should that simple question shake her? Literally.'

Dalgliesh had met with it before, the clumsy aggression of women who were both shy and insecure. He wished that he could feel more sorry for her. He said:

'It wasn't particularly subtle, John.'

'No sir, it wasn't meant to be. She played that game of Scrabble all right. The question is, when?'

Dalgliesh took the wheel. He drove away from the house then drew into a vacant space half-way down Campden Hill Square and rang the Yard. Kate Miskin's answering voice sounded as strong and lively as it had in the early hours of the inquiry.

'I've traced and seen Mrs Hurrell, sir. She confirms that she did ring the Campden Hill Square house just before eight forty-five to ask for Sir Paul. A man answered. He said: "Swayne speaking". Then when she told him what she wanted he handed her over to Miss Matlock. Miss Matlock said that she didn't know where Sir Paul was, and nor did anyone else in the house.'

It was, thought Dalgliesh, an odd way for Swayne to answer the telephone when in someone else's house. One might almost believe that he wanted to establish that he was there. He asked:

'Anything from the door-to-door inquiries?'

'Nothing yet, sir, but I've spoken again to the McBrides and Maggie Sullivan. All three are definite about the gush of water from the church drain. Someone was using the sink in the washroom just after eight o'clock. They all agree about the time.'

'And the lab?'

'I've had a word with the senior biologist. If they can get the blood samples immediately after the PM, say by late afternoon, they'll set up the electrophoresis overnight. The director has agreed that they can work over the weekend. We should know about the bloodstains by Monday morning.'

'No news from the document examiner yet, I suppose. And what about the match end?'

'The document examiner hasn't been able to start on the blotter yet, but he'll give it priority. The usual problems with the match, sir. They'll do an analysis with the S.E.M. and look for print marks, but they're unlikely to be able to say more than that the wood is the usual poplar. They couldn't possibly say that it was from a particular box, and it's too short for a length comparison.'

'Right, Kate. We'll call it a day. Better get home. Goodnight.'

'Goodnight, sir.'

As the car slid down Campden Hill Square and turned into Holland Park Avenue Dalgliesh said:

'Halliwell has expensive tastes. That set of the *Notable British Trials* must have cost close on a thousand pounds, unless he collected them volume by volume over the years.'

'Not as expensive as Swayne's though, sir. That's a Fellucini jacket he was wearing, silk and linen, silvercrested buttons. They sell for four fifty.'

'I'll take your word for it. I wonder why he burst in like that. It was an unconvincing performance. Probably hoping to find out how much Halliwell was telling. It's significant, though, that he did burst in and as if he made a habit of it. And when Halliwell isn't there, he'd have no problem in getting hold of a key or even manipulating the Yale if necessary.'

'Is it important, sir, whether he could get into the mews flat?'

'I think so. This murderer was aiming at verisimilitude. There's a copy of Simpson's *Textbook on Forensic Medicine* in Halliwell's bookcase. It's all set out there in Chapter Five with the writer's usual clarity, a table showing the distinction between suicidal and homicidal cuts of the throat. Swayne could have seen it at any time, browsed through it, remembered it. So, too, could anyone else at Campden Hill Square with access to the garage flat, and most easily, of course, Halliwell himself. Whoever slit Berowne's throat knew exactly what effect he was aiming to produce.'

Massingham asked:

'If other people knew of its existence, to destroy it would be more incriminating than to leave it on the shelf. But Halliwell has to be in the clear if Lady Ursula is telling the truth about those two telephone calls, and I can't see her giving Halliwell an alibi for the murder of her son. Or any other suspect for that matter.'

Massingham said:

'Or Halliwell giving Swayne an alibi unless he had to. There's no love lost there. He despises the man. Incidentally, I knew I'd seen Swayne somewhere before. I've remembered now. He was in that play at the Coningsby Theatre in Camden Town a year ago. *The Garage*. The cast actually constructed a garage on the stage. In the first act they put it up, in the second they knocked it down.'

'I thought it was a wedding tent.'

'Wrong play, sir. Swayne played the local psychopath, one of the gang who pulled it down. So he must have an Equity card.'

'How did he strike you as an actor?'

'Energetic but unsubtle. Not that I'm much of a judge. I prefer films. I only went because Emma was going through her cultural stage. The play was highly symbolic. The garage was supposed to represent Britain, or capitalism, or imperialism, or, maybe, the class struggle. I'm not sure the author knew. You could tell that it was going to be a great critical success. No one spoke a literate line and a week later I couldn't remember a word of the dialogue. There was some fairly energetic fighting in the second act. Swayne knows how to handle himself. Still, kicking in a garage wall isn't the most suitable training for slitting a throat. I can't see Swayne as a killer, not this killer, anyway.'

They were both experienced detectives, they knew the importance at this stage of keeping the detection rational, of concentrating on the physical, ascertainable facts. Which of the suspects has the means, the opportunity, the knowledge, the physical strength, the motive? It was unproductive so early in the investigation to begin asking: has this man the ruthlessness, the nerve, the desperation, the psychological make-up to commit this particular crime? And yet, seduced by the fascination of human personality, they nearly always did.

6

In the small back bedroom on the second floor of 49 Crowhurst Gardens, Miss Wharton lay rigidly awake and stared into the darkness. Her body, pressed into the hard mattress, felt unnaturally hot and heavy as if weighted with lead. Even to turn in search of greater comfort was too great an effort. She hadn't expected to sleep soundly, but she had gone through her nightly routine with a dogged hope that adhering to these small and comforting rituals would deceive her body into slumber, or at least into quietude; the chapter of scripture prescribed in her book of devotions, the hot milk, the one digestive biscuit, final indulgence of the day. None had worked. The passage from St Luke's Gospel had been the parable of the good shepherd. It was one of her favourites, but tonight she had read it with a sharpened, perversely questioning mind. What, after all, was a shepherd's job? Only to care for the sheep, to make sure they didn't escape so that they could be branded, sheared and then slaughtered. Without the need for their wool, their flesh, there would be no job for the shepherd.

Long after she had closed her Bible she lay rigid for what seemed an endless night, her mind burrowing and scurrying like a tormented animal. Where was Darren? How was he? Who was making sure that he wasn't lying uncomforted or distressed? He hadn't seemed too affected by the horror of that awful scene, but with a child one never knew. And it was her fault that they were cut off from each other. She should have insisted on knowing where he lived, meeting his mother. He had never spoken of his mother and when she had asked him he had shrugged and not replied. She hadn't liked to press it. Perhaps she could reach him through the police. But ought she to worry Commander Dalgliesh when he had two murders to solve?

And the word 'murder' brought on a new anxiety. There was something she ought to remember but couldn't; something she ought to have told Commander Dalgliesh. He had questioned her briefly, gently, sitting beside her on one of the small chairs in the children's corner of the church, as if uncaring, even unaware, how oddly it suited his tall figure. She had tried to be calm, accurate, matter-of-fact, but she knew there were gaps in her memory, that there was something the horror of the scene had blotted out. Yet what could it be? It was something small, possibly insignificant, but he had said she must tell him every detail, however trivial.

But now another and more immediate worry surfaced. She needed to go to the lavatory. She switched on her bedside light, fumbled for her spectacles and peered at the carriage clock ticking gently on her bedside table. It was only ten past two. There was no hope of waiting until morning. Although she had her own sitting room, bedroom and kitchen, Miss Wharton shared the bathroom with the McGraths in the flat below. The plumbing was old-fashioned and if she had to use the lavatory in the night, Mrs McGrath would complain next morning. The alternative was to use her chamberpot but that had to be emptied and the whole morning would be dominated by her anxious listenings to know when it would be safe to carry it down to the lavatory without meeting Mrs McGrath's bold, contemptuous eyes. Once she had bumped into Billy McGrath on the stairs with the covered pot in her hand. The memory of it still burned her cheeks. But she would have to use it. The night was still so quiet she couldn't face creeping down to shatter its peace with cascades of swirling water, those long drawn-out shakes and grumbles of the pipe.

Miss Wharton didn't know why the McGraths disliked her so much, why her inoffensive gentility should be so provocative to them. She tried to keep out of their way, although this wasn't easy when they shared the same front door, the same narrow entrance passage. She had explained Darren to them on his first visit to her room by telling them that his mother worked at St Matthew's. The lie, blurted out in panic, had seemed to satisfy them and she had subsequently put it resolutely out of her mind since she could hardly include it in her weekly confession and Darren was so swift in his comings and goings that there was little risk they would question him. It was as if he sensed that the McGraths were enemies, better avoided than encountered. She attempted to propitiate Mrs McGrath with a desperate overpoliteness and even by small acts of kindness; taking her milk bottles in out of the sun in summer, leaving a jar of homemade jam or chutney on her doorstep when she came home from St Matthew's Christmas Fair. But these signs of weakness seemed only to increase their enmity, and she knew in her heart that there was nothing to be done about it. People, like countries, needed someone weaker and more vulnerable than themselves to bully and despise. This was what the world was like. As she gently dragged the chamberpot from under the bed and crouched over it, muscles tense, trying to regulate and quieten the flow, she thought again how much she would have liked to have a cat. But the garden, twenty yards of unmown grass, hummocky as a field, surrounded by an almost obliterated border of overgrown rose bushes, and torn, unflowering shrubs, belonged to the bottom flat. The McGraths would never let her have use of it and it wouldn't be fair to keep a cat cooped up all night and day in her own two small rooms.

Miss Wharton had been taught to fear in her childhood and it isn't a lesson children can ever unlearn. Her father, a schoolmaster in an elementary school, had managed to maintain a precarious tolerance in the classroom by a compensating tyranny in his own home. His wife and three children were all afraid of him. But shared fear hadn't brought the children closer. When, with his usual irrationality, he would single out one child for his displeasure, the siblings would see in each other's shamed eyes their relief at this reprieve. They learned to lie to protect themselves, and were beaten for lying. They learned to be afraid, and were punished for cowardice. And yet, Miss Wharton kept on her side table a silver framed photograph of both her parents. She never blamed her father for past or present unhappiness. She had learned her lesson well. She blamed herself.

She was now virtually alone in the world. Her younger brother, John, to whom she had been closest, more psychologically robust than his siblings, had fared best. But John had been burnt alive in the rear gun turret of his Lancaster bomber the day before his nineteenth birthday. Miss Wharton, mercifully ignorant of the steel-bound inferno in which John had screamed away his life, had been able to prettify his death into the peaceful picture of the single German bullet finding the heart, the young, pale-faced warrior being gently wafted earthwards, his hand still resting on his gun. Her older brother, Edmund, had emigrated to Canada after the war and now, divorced and childless, worked as a clerk in some small northern town whose name she could never remember since he so seldom wrote.

She slid the chamberpot back under the bed, then put on her dressing gown and padded on naked feet across the narrow hall and into her front sitting room to the single window. The house was very quiet. Under the lights the street shone ebony black between the banks of parked cars. Even with her window closed she could hear the muted roar of night traffic along the Harrow Road. It was a night of low cloud, stained red with the glare of the restless city. Sometimes it seemed to Miss Wharton, looking out into that eerie half-darkness, that London was built on coal and was perpetually smouldering, that Hell, unrecognized, was all around her. To the right, silhouetted against the hectic glow, was the campanile of St Matthew's. Usually it gave her comfort. Here was a place where she was known, valued for the small services she could give, kept busily occupied, solaced, shriven and at home. But now the thin, alien tower, stark against the ruddy sky was a symbol of horror and death. And her twice-weekly walk to St Matthew's along the towpath; how could she face that now? The path had seemed to her mysteriously exempt from the terrors of the city streets, except for those brief stretches under the bridges. Even on the darkest morning she had walked there in blessed freedom from fear. And in recent months she had had Darren. But now Darren was gone, safety was gone, the towpath would always be slippery with imagined blood. Creeping back to bed her mind journeyed across the roofs to the Little Vestry. It would be empty now, of course. The police would have taken the bodies away. The black windowless van had been parked there ready even before she had left. There would be nothing now but the bloodstains browning on the carpet – or would that, too, have been taken away? Nothing but emptiness and darkness and the smell of death, except in the Lady Chapel where the sanctuary light would still be gleaming. Was she to lose even this, she wondered? Was this what murder did to the innocent? Took away the people they loved, loaded their minds with terror, left them bereft and unfriended under a smouldering sky.

7

It was after eleven thirty when Kate Miskin clanged the lift door behind her and unlocked the security lock of her flat. She had wanted to wait at the Yard until Dalgliesh and Massingham had returned from seeing Halliwell. But AD had suggested that it was time she called it a day and there was little more that she or anyone could do until the morning. If AD was right, and Berowne and Harry Mack had both been murdered, she and Massingham could be regularly working a sixteen-hour day, sometimes longer. It wasn't a possibility she feared; she had done it before. As she switched on the light and double-locked the door behind her it struck her as odd, perhaps even reprehensible, that she should be hoping that AD was right. Then almost immediately she absolved herself with the universal and comforting platitude. Both Berowne and Harry were dead; nothing could bring them back. And if Sir Paul Berowne hadn't slit his own throat, then the case promised to be fascinating as well as important, and not only to her personally, to her chance of promotion. There had been a certain amount of opposition to the setting-up in C1 of a special squad to investigate serious crimes which were thought to be politically or socially sensitive and she could name a number of senior officers who wouldn't be sorry if this, their first case, collapsed into a commonplace tragedy of murder followed by suicide.

She entered her flat, as always, with a sense of satisfaction, of coming home. She had lived in Charles Shannon House for just over two years. Buying the flat on a carefully calculated mortgage had been the first step in a planned upward progress; even eventually to one of the converted warehouses on the Thames, wide windows overlooking the river, huge rooms with their bare rafters, a distant view of Tower Bridge. But this was a beginning. She rejoiced in it, and sometimes had to prevent herself from prowling round, touching the walls, the furniture, to reassure herself of its reality.

The flat, a long sitting room with a narrow iron balcony running its whole width, two small bedrooms, a kitchen and a bathroom and separate lavatory, was on the top floor of a Victorian block just off Holland Park Avenue. It had been built in the early 1860s to provide studios for artists and designers in the growing arts and crafts movement, and a couple of blue commemorative plaques over the door testified to its historic interest. But architecturally it was without merit, an aberration of yellowish London brick set amidst the surrounding Regency elegance, immensely tall, castellated and incongruous as a Victorian castle. The soaring walls, broken by numerous carved and oddly proportioned windows and criss-crossed with iron fire escapes, rose to a roof topped with rows of chimney pots between which sprouted a variety of television aerials, some long defunct.

It was the only place she had ever thought of as home. She was illegitimate and had been brought up by her maternal grandmother who had been nearly sixty when she was born. Her mother had died within days of her birth and was known to her only as a thin serious face in the front row of a school photograph, a face in which she could recognize none of her own strong features. Her grandmother had never spoken of her father and she had assumed that her mother had never divulged his identity. She was fatherless even in name, but it had long ceased to worry her, if it ever had. Apart from the inevitable fantasies of early childhood when she had pictured her father seeking her out, she hadn't known any urgent need to discover her roots. Two half-remembered lines of Shakespeare which had met her eyes when she had casually opened the book in the school library had become for her the philosophy by which she intended to live.

'What matters it what went before or after
Now with myself I will begin and end.'

She hadn't chosen to furnish her flat in a period style. She had little feeling for the past; all her life had been a striving to struggle free of it, to make a future fashioned to her own need for order, security, success. So she had lived for a couple of months with nothing but a folding table, one chair and a mattress on the floor, until she had saved the money to buy the austere, well-designed modern furniture she liked; the sofa and two easy chairs in real leather, the dining table and four chairs in polished elm, the fitted bookcase completely covering one wall, the sleek, professionally designed kitchen which held the minimum of necessary utensils and crockery but nothing superfluous. The flat was her private world kept inviolate from colleagues in the police. Only her lover was admitted, and when Alan had first stepped through the door, uncurious, unthreatening, carrying as always his plastic bag of books, even his gentle presence had seemed for a moment a dangerous intrusion.

She poured herself an inch of whisky, mixed it with water, then unlocked the security lock of the narrow door which led from the sitting room to the iron balcony. The air rushed in, fresh and clean. She closed the door then stood, glass in hand, leaning back against the brickwork and staring out eastward over London. A low bank of heavy cloud had absorbed the glare of the city's lights and lay, palely crimson, like a colour-wash carefully laid against the richer blue-black of night. There was a light breeze just strong enough to stir the branches of the great limes lining Holland Park Avenue, and to twitch the television aerials which sprouted like frail exotic fetishes from the patterned roofs fifty feet below. To the south the trees of Holland Park were a black curdle against the sky, and ahead the spire of St John's church gleamed like some distant mirage. It was one of the pleasures of these moments, seeing how the spire appeared to move, sometimes so close that she felt that she would only have to stretch out a hand to feel its harshly textured stones, sometimes, like tonight, as distant and insubstantial as a vision. Far below to her right under the high arc lights the avenue ran due west, greasy as a molten river, bearing its unending cargo of cars, trucks and red buses. This, she knew, had once been the old Roman road leading westward straight out of Londinium; its constant grinding roar came to her only faintly like the surge of a distant sea.

Whatever the time of year, except in the worst of winter weather, this was her nightly routine. She would pour herself a whisky, Bell's, and take out the glass for these minutes of contemplation, rather, she thought, like a caged prisoner reassuring herself that the city was still there. But her small flat was no prison, rather the physical affirmation of a freedom hard won and jealously maintained. She had escaped from the estate, from her grandmother, from that meanly proportioned, dirty, noisy flat on the seventh floor of a post-war tower block, Ellison Fairweather Buildings, monument to a local councillor passionately dedicated, like most of his kind, to the destruction of small neighbourhood streets and the erection of twelve-storey monuments to civic pride and sociological theory. She had escaped from the shouting, the graffiti, the broken lifts, the stink of urine. She remembered the first evening of her escape, the eighth of June over two years ago. She had stood where she stood now and poured her whisky like a libation, seeing the momentary arc of liquid light as it fell between the grating, saying aloud 'Sod you, Councillor Bloody Fairweather. Welcome freedom.'

And now she was really on her way. If she made a success of this new job anything, well almost anything, was possible. It was perhaps not surprising that AD would choose at least one woman for his squad. But he wasn't the man to make routine gestures to feminism, or to any other fashionable cause come to that. He had selected her because he needed a woman in the squad and because he knew her record, knew that he could rely on her to do a good job. Looking out over London she felt confidence surge through her veins strong and sweet as the first conscious breath of morning. The world stretched out below her was one she was at home in, part of that dense, exciting conglomerate of urban villages which made up the Metropolitan Police district. She pictured it stretching away over Notting Hill Gate, over Hyde Park and the curve of the river, past the towers of Westminster and Big Ben, briefly over that anomaly, the patch of the City of London Police, then on through the eastern suburbs to the boundary with the Essex Constabulary. She knew almost to a yard where that boundary lay. This was how she saw the capital, patterned in police areas, districts, divisions and sub-divisions. And immediately below her lay Notting Hill, that tough, diverse, richly cosmopolitan village where she had been posted after leaving the preliminary training school. She could remember every sound, colour, smell as strongly as on that torrid August night eight years ago when it had happened, the moment when she knew that her choice had been right and that this was her job.

She had been on foot patrol in Notting Hill with Terry Read on the hottest August night in living memory. A boy, almost squealing with excitement, had rushed at them and, gibbering, had pointed to a nearby tenement. She saw it again; the huddle of frightened neighbours at the foot of the stairs, faces gleaming with sweat, stained shirts stuck to steaming bodies, a smell of hot, unwashed humanity. And above the whispers a raucous voice from upstairs shouting its unintelligible protest. The boy said:

'He's got a knife, miss. George tried to get in but he threatened him. That's right, ain't it, George?'

George, white, small, weasel-like in the corner:

'Yeah, that's right.'

'And he's got Mabelle in with him, Mabelle and the kid.'

A woman whispered:

'Blessed Jesus, he's got the kid in there.'

They had fallen back to let her through, her and Terry.

She asked:

'What's his name?'

'Leroy.'

'His other name?'

'Price. Leroy Price.'

The hallway was dark, the room itself, unlocked since the lock was smashed, was even darker. The harsh glare filtered through a torn piece of carpet nailed over the window. She could see dimly the stained double mattress on the floor, a folding table, two chairs, one on its side. There was a smell of vomit, of sweat, of beer overlaid with the strong oily smell of fish and chips. Against the wall cowered a woman, a child in her arms.

She said gently:

'It's all right, Mr Price. I'll have that knife. You don't mean to hurt them. She's your kid. You wouldn't want to hurt either of them. I know what it is, it's too hot, and you've had enough. We all have.'

She had seen it before, on the estate as well as on the beat, that moment when the burden of frustration, hopelessness and misery suddenly became too heavy and the mind exploded into an anarchy of protest. He had indeed had too much. Too many unpaid, unpayable bills, too much worry, too many demands, too much frustration and, of course, too much drink. She had walked up to him not speaking, calmly meeting his eyes, holding out her hand for the knife. She wasn't aware of fear, only the fear that

Terry might come crashing in. There was no sound; the group at the foot of the stairs was frozen into silence, the street outside stilled in one of those strange moments of quietness which sometimes fall on even the rowdiest quarters of London. She could hear only her own quiet breathing and his harsh grating breaths. Then with a wild sob he had dropped the knife and flung himself towards her. She had held him, murmuring as she might to a child, and it was over.

She had overplayed Terry's part in the affair, and he had let her. But old Moll Green, never absent when there was a chance of excitement and the hope of bloodshed, had been one of those waiting, bright-eyed, at the foot of the stairs. The following Tuesday Terry had busted her for carrying hash, admittedly with small provocation, but he was behind with his self-imposed weekly quota of arrests. Moll, motivated either by an unexpected surge of female solidarity, or a revulsion against men in general and Terry in particular, had given her own version of the incident to the station sergeant. Little was subsequently said to Kate, but enough to make it plain that the truth was known, and that her reticence had done her no harm. Now she wondered briefly what had happened to that man, to Mabelle, to the child. For the first time it struck her as odd that, the incident over, her report made, she had never given any of them another thought.

She came in, closed the door and drew the heavy linen curtains, then went to telephone Alan. They had planned to see a film the following night but this would no longer be possible. It was pointless to make any plans until the case was finished. He took the news calmly as he always did when she had to break a date. One of the many things she liked about him was that he never fussed.

He said:

'It looks then as if dinner next Thursday may not be possible either.'

'We may be through by then, but it's unlikely. Still, keep it free and if I have to I'll ring and cancel.'

'Well, good luck with the case. I hope it won't be love's labour's lost.'

'What?'

'Sorry. Berowne is the name of an attendant lord in Shakespeare. It's an unusual and interesting name.'

'It was an unusual and interesting death. See you next Thursday at about eight.'

'Unless you find it necessary to cancel. Goodbye, Kate.'

She thought that she detected a trace of irony in his voice, then decided that tiredness had made her imaginative. It was the first time he had wished her good luck with a case, but he had still asked no questions. He was, she thought, as punctiliously discreet about her job as she was herself. Or was it merely that he didn't care? Before he put the receiver down she said quickly:

'That attendant lord, what happened to him?'

'He loved a woman called Rosaline, but she told him to go and nurse the sick. So he went off to jest a twelvemonth in a hospital.'

There was hardly, she thought, much inspiration to be gained from that. She smiled as she put down the receiver. It was a pity about next Thursday's dinner. But there would be other dinners, other evenings. He would come when she rang and asked him. He always did.

She suspected that she had met Alan Scully just in time. Her early sexual education in the concrete underpasses of the high-rise flats and behind the bicycle sheds of her north London comprehensive, the mixture of excitement, danger and disgust, had been a good preparation for life but a poor preparation for loving. Most of the boys had been less intelligent than herself. This might not have mattered to her if they had had looks or some wit. She was amused, but also a little dismayed, to realize by the time she was eighteen that she was thinking of men as they were alleged so often to regard women, an occasional sexual or social diversion, but too unimportant to be allowed to interfere with the serious business of life; passing her A-levels, planning her career, getting away from Ellison Fairweather Buildings. She found that she could enjoy sex while despising the source of her pleasure. It wasn't, she knew, an honest basis for any relationship. And then, two years ago, she had met Alan. His flat in a narrow street behind the British Museum had been burgled and it was she who had arrived with the fingerprint and scene of crime officers. He told her that he worked in a theological library in

Bloomsbury and that he was an amateur collector of books of early Victorian sermons – it seemed to her an extraordinary choice – and that two of the most valuable volumes had been taken. They had never been recovered and she sensed from the calm resignation with which he answered her questions that he had hardly expected that they would be. His flat, small, cluttered, a repository for books rather than a space for living, was unlike any place she had ever seen, as he was unlike any man. She had had to make a return visit and they had spent about an hour chatting over coffee. He had then asked her, simply, to go with him to see a Shakespearian production at the National Theatre.

It was less than a month after that evening that they first went to bed together and he had demolished one of her firmly held assumptions, that intellectuals weren't interested in sex. He was both interested in and very good at it. They had settled into a comfortable, apparently mutually satisfactory, loving friendship in which each saw the other's job, without resentment or envy, as foreign territory, its speech and mores so far removed from any possibility of comprehension that they rarely spoke of it. Kate knew that he was intrigued, not so much by her lack of religious faith as by the fact that she apparently had no intellectual curiosity about its diverse and fascinating manifestations. She sensed, too, although he never said so, that he thought that her literary education had been neglected. She could, if challenged, quote angry modern verse about unemployed youth in the inner cities and the subjection of the blacks in South Africa, but this he saw as a poor substitute for Donne, Shakespeare, Keats or Eliot. She, for her part, saw him as an innocent, so deficient in the skills necessary for survival in the urban jungle that it amazed her that he should walk with such apparent indifference through its perils. Apart from the burglary, which remained mysterious, nothing untoward ever seemed to happen to him or, if it did, he failed to notice. It amused her to ask him to recommend books and she persevered with those which, diffidently, he produced for her. At present her bedtime reading was Elizabeth Bowen. The life of her heroines, their private incomes, their charming houses in St John's Wood, their uniformed parlourmaids and formidable aunts, above all the delicate sensitivity of their emotions amazed her. 'Not enough washing-up, that's their trouble,' she told Alan, having in mind the author as well as her characters. But it interested her that she needed to go on reading.

And now it was close to midnight. She was both too excited and too tired to feel much hunger, but she supposed that she ought to cook something light, perhaps an omelette, before she went to bed. But first she switched on the answerphone. And with the first sound of the familiar voice euphoria died to be replaced by a confusion of guilt, resentment and depression. It was her grandmother's social worker. There were three messages, each at two hourly intervals, controlled professional patience gradually giving way to frustration and, finally, an irritation that was close to hostility. Her grandmother, weary of incarceration in her seventh-floor flat, had gone out to the post office to collect her pension and had come back to find that the window had been smashed and an attempt made to force the door. It was the third such incident in less than a month. Mrs Miskin was now too apprehensive to go out. Would Kate please ring the local authority social services department as soon as she got in, or, if it were after five thirty, ring her grandmother direct. It was urgent.

It always was, she thought wearily. And this was a ridiculously late hour at which to ring. But it couldn't wait until morning. Her grandmother wouldn't sleep until she had rung. Her call was answered after the first burr and she guessed that the old lady had been sitting waiting by the telephone.

'Oh, there you are. Fine time to ring. Nearly bloody midnight. Mrs Mason's been trying to get you.'

'I know. Are you all right, Gran?'

'Course I'm not all right. Bloody hell, I'm not. When are you coming round?'

'I'll try to look in sometime tomorrow but it won't be easy. I'm in the middle of a case.'

'Better come at three o'clock. Mrs Mason said she'll look in at three. She wants to see you 'specially. Three o'clock, mind.'

'Gran, that's not possible.'

'How'm I goin' to get my shopping, then? I'm not leaving this flat alone, I tell you that.'

'There should be enough in the freezer for at least another four days.'

'I don't fancy that made-up muck. I told you before.'

'Can't you ask Mrs Khan? She's always so helpful.'

'No I can't. She don't go out now, not unless her husband's with her, not since that lot from the National Front were up this way. Besides, it's not fair. More than enough trouble luggin' up her own stuff. The kids have broken the bloody lift again in case you didn't know.'

'Gran, is the window mended?'

'Oh, they've been and mended the window.' Her grandmother's voice suggested that this was no more than an unimportant detail.

She added:

'You gotta get me out of this place.'

'I'm trying, Gran. You're on the waiting list for a one-person flat in one of those blocks with a warden, sheltered housing. You know that.'

'I don't need any bloody warden. I ought to be with my own kith and kin. See you tomorrow then at three o'clock. Mind you come. Mrs Mason wants to see you.'

She put down the receiver.

Kate thought: Oh God, I can't cope with this again, not now, not just at the beginning of a new case.

She told herself with angry self-justification, that she wasn't irresponsible, that she did what she could. She had bought her grandmother a new refrigerator topped with a small freezer and visited every Sunday to stock it with meals for the week ahead only, more often than not, to be met with the familiar complaint:

'I can't eat that fancy stuff. I want to do my own shopping. I want to get out of here.'

She had paid for a telephone to be installed and had taught her grandmother not to be afraid of it. She had liaised with the local authority and arranged for a weekly visit from a home help to clean the flat. She would willingly have cleaned it herself if her grandmother would have tolerated the interference. She would take any trouble, spend any money, to avoid taking her grandmother to live with her in Charles Shannon House. But that, she knew, was what the old lady, in alliance with her social worker, was inexorably pressing her to accept. And she couldn't do it.

She couldn't give up her freedom, Alan's visits, the spare room where she did her painting, her privacy and peace at the end of the day for an old woman's impedimenta, the ceaseless noise of her television, the mess, the smell of old age, of failure, the smell of Ellison Fairweather Buildings, of childhood, of the past. And now, more than ever, it was impossible. Now, with her first case with the new squad, she needed to be free.

She was seized with a spurt of envy and resentment against Massingham. Even if he had a dozen difficult and demanding relatives no one would expect him to have to cope. And if she did have to take time off from the job he would be the first to point out that, when the going got really tough, you couldn't rely on a woman.

8

In her bedroom on the second floor Barbara Berowne lay back on her bank of pillows and stared ahead at the television screen mounted on the wall opposite her uncurtained four-poster. She was waiting for the late-night movie, but had switched on the set as soon as she had got into bed, and was now tuned to the last ten minutes of a political discussion. She had turned down the sound so low that she could hear nothing, but she still gazed intently at the restless mouths as if she were lip-reading. She remembered how Paul's mouth had tightened with disapproval when he had first seen the television set, mounted on its swivel, obtrusively over-large, spoiling the wall and dwarfing into insignificance the two Cotman watercolours of Norwich Cathedral each side of it. But he had said nothing, and she had told herself defiantly that she didn't care. But now she could watch the late film without being uneasily aware that he was there in the next room, perhaps lying sleepless in rigid disapproval, hearing the muted screams and gunfire like the noisy manifestations of their own subtler, undeclared warfare.

He had disliked, too, her untidiness, an unconscious protest against the impersonality, the obsessive neatness of the rest of the house. In the light of her bedside lamp she gazed untroubled over the muddle in the room; the clothes strewn where she had dropped them; the sheen of her satin dressing-gown thrown across the foot of the bed, the grey skirt splayed fan-like over a chair, her pants lying like a pale shadow on the carpet, her brassière hanging by one strap from the dressing table. What an indecent, silly garment it looked, thus casually discarded; so precisely shaped and moulded and looking surgical for all its lace and delicacy. But Mattie would tidy up her things in the morning, gather up her underclothes for washing, hang jackets and skirts in the wardrobe. And she would lie with the breakfast tray on her knees, and watch; then get up, bath, dress and face the world, as always immaculate.

It had been Anne Berowne's room and she had moved into it after their marriage. Paul had suggested that they might change bedrooms but she hadn't seen why she should sleep in a smaller inferior room, deprived of the view of the Square garden, simply because this had been Anne's bed. First it had been Anne's room, then it was Paul's and hers, then it was hers alone, but always with the knowledge that he was sleeping next door. And now it was hers absolutely. She remembered the afternoon when they had first stood in the bedroom together after their marriage, his voice so formal that she had hardly recognized it. He could have been showing round a prospective purchaser.

'You may care to choose different pictures; there are some in the small salon. Anne liked watercolours and the light here is good for them, but you don't have to keep them.'

She hadn't cared about the pictures which had seemed to her rather dull, insignificant English landscapes by painters Paul seemed to think she ought to recognize. She still didn't care, not even enough to change them. But the bedroom had, from her first possession, taken on a different personality; softer, more luxurious, scented and feminine. And gradually it had become as cluttered as an indiscriminately stocked antique shop. She had gone round the house and moved up to her room the items of furniture, the oddly assorted objects which had taken her fancy, as if obsessively raping the house, leaving no space for those rejected but insidious ghosts. A Regency two-handed vase under a glass dome filled with multi-coloured flowers intricately devised from shells, a gilt-bronze Tudor wood cabinet decorated with porcelain ovals of shepherds and shepherdesses, a bust of John Soane on a marble pedestal, a collection of eighteenth-century snuff boxes, taken from their showcase and now casually littering her dressing table. But there were still ghosts, living ghosts, voices on the air which no object, however desired, had power to exorcise. Propped against the scented pillows she was back in her childhood bed, a 12-year-old lying rigid and sleepless, hands clutching the bedclothes. Snatches of endless argument half-heard over weeks and months, then only partly understood, had come together into a coherent whole, refined by her imagination and now unforgettable. First her mother's voice:

'I thought you'd want custody of the children. You're their father.'

'And leave you free of responsibility to enjoy yourself in California? Oh no, my dear, you were the one who wanted children, you take them. I suppose Frank didn't bargain for two stepchildren? Well, he's got them. I hope he likes them.'

'They're English. Their place is here.'

'What did you tell him? That you were coming without encumbrances? A little shop-soiled, darling, but unencumbered? Their place is with their mother. Even a bitch has some maternal instincts. You take them or I fight the divorce.'

'My God, they're your children. Don't you care? Don't you love them?'

'I might have done if you'd let me and if they'd been less like you. As it is, I'm frankly indifferent. You want freedom, so do I.'

'All right, we'll share. I'll take Barbie, you have Dicco. A boy's place is with his father.'

'Then we're in a difficulty. You'd better consult the father, that is if you know which one it was. By all means let him have Dicco. I won't stand in his way. If there was anything of me in that boy I'd have recognized it. He's grotesque.'

'My God, Donald, you bastard!'

'Oh no, my dear, I'm not the bastard in this family.'

She thought: I won't listen, I won't remember, I won't think about it, and pressed the volume button, letting the rancorous voices batter at her ears. She didn't hear the door open, but suddenly there was an oblong of pale light and Dicco stood there,

wrapped in his knee-length dressing gown, his springing hair a
tangled halo. He stood watching her in silence, then moved
barefooted across the room and the bedsprings bounced as he
settled himself close against her. He said:

'Can't you sleep?'

She turned off the set, feeling the familiar guilt.

'I was thinking about Sylvia and father.'

'Which one? We've had so many.'

'The first. Our proper father.'

'Our proper father? Our improper father. I wonder if he's dead
yet. Cancer was too good for him. Don't think about them, think
about the money. That's always a comfort. Think about being
free, your own person. Think how well you always look in black.
You aren't frightened, are you?'

'No, of course not. There's nothing to be frightened about.
Dicco, go back to bed.'

'His bed. You knew that, didn't you? You know where I'm
sleeping. In his bed.'

'Mattie won't like that, nor will Lady Ursula. Why couldn't
you sleep in the spare room? Or go back to Bruno?'

'Bruno doesn't want me in the flat. He never did. There isn't
room. And I wasn't comfortable. You want me to be comfortable,
surely? And I'm getting a little tired of Bruno. My place is here.
I'm your brother. This is your house now. You're not being very
welcoming, Barbie. I thought you'd want me near you, in case
you wanted to talk in the night, confide, confess. Come on,
Barbie, confess. Who do you think killed him?'

'How do I know? Someone broke in, I suppose, a thief, another
tramp, someone who wanted to steal the church collection. I
don't want to talk about it.'

'Is that what the police think?'

'I suppose so. I don't know what they think.'

'Then I can tell you. They think it was an odd church for a
thief to choose. I mean, what was there worth stealing?'

'There are things on the altar, aren't there? Candlesticks, a
cross. There were in the church where I married.'

'I wasn't there when you were married, Barbie. You didn't
invite me, remember?'

'Paul wanted a quiet wedding, Dicco. What does it matter?'

And that, she thought, was another thing Paul had cheated her out of. She had imagined a grand wedding, herself floating up the aisle of St Margaret's Westminster, the sheen of white satin, a veil like a cloud, the flowers, the crowds, the photographers. Instead he had suggested a registrar's office and when she had protested had insisted on their local parish church and the quietest of ceremonies, almost as if the wedding were something to be ashamed of, something furtive and indecent.

Dicco's voice came to her in a low insinuating whisper:

'But they don't keep them on the altar any more, not at night. Crosses and candlesticks, they lock them away. Churches are dark, empty. No silver, no gold, no lights. Nothing. Do you suppose that's when their God comes down from his cross and walks about, goes up to the altar and finds that it's only a wooden table with a piece of fancy cloth pinned round it?'

She wriggled under the bedclothes.

'Don't be silly, Dicco. Go to bed.'

He leaned forward, and the face so like hers and yet so different gleamed within inches of her eyes, so that she could actually see the sheen of sweat on his brow, and smell the wine on his breath.

'That nurse, Theresa Nolan, the one who killed herself. Was Paul the father of her baby?'

'Of course not. Why does everyone go on about Theresa Nolan?'

'Who goes on about her? Did the police ask about her?'

'I can't remember. I think they asked why she left. Something like that. I don't want to think about it.'

His soft, indulgent laugh was like a conspiracy.

'Barbie, you've got to think. You can't go through life not thinking about things just because they're inconvenient or unpleasant. It was his child, wasn't it? That's what your husband was up to while you were cavorting with your lover, fucking his mother's nurse. And that other girl, Diana Travers, the one who drowned. What was she doing in this house?'

'You know what she was doing. Helping Mattie.'

'A dangerous occupation, though, isn't it, working for your

husband? Look, if someone did murder Paul it was someone very clever and cunning; someone who knew he was there in that church; someone who knew he would find a cut-throat razor ready to hand; someone with the nerve to take one enormous risk; someone used to cutting human flesh. Do you know someone like that, Barbie? Do you? It's lucky, isn't it, that you and Stephen have an alibi.'

'You have an alibi, too?'

'And Mattie, of course. And Lady Ursula. And Halliwell. It's a bit suspicious, all these iron-clad alibis. What about Sarah?'

'I haven't spoken to her.'

'Well let's hope she hasn't an alibi too, otherwise the police will begin to scent conspiracy. When you rang to tell me that he was going to chuck you, I said that it would be all right. Well, it is all right. I said not to worry about the money. Well, you don't have to worry. It's all yours.'

'Not so very much.'

'Come off it, Barbie, enough. The house to begin with, that must be worth a cool million. And he was insured, wasn't he? Was there a suicide clause? That would be awkward.'

'Mr Farrell said that there wasn't. I asked.'

Again that soft inward laugh, something between a grunt and a giggle:

'So you actually got round to asking about the insurance! You don't waste time, do you? And that's what the lawyers think, is it? That Paul killed himself?'

'Lawyers never say. Mr Farrell told me not to talk to the police unless he was there.'

'The family won't want it to be suicide; they'd rather he was murdered. And perhaps he was. If he'd wanted to kill himself, why didn't he use the gun? His brother's gun. A man doesn't cut his throat if he's got a gun. And he had ammo, too, didn't he?'

'Ammo?'

'Bullets. Where is the gun? Still in his safe?'

'No. I don't know where it is.'

'What do you mean you don't know? Have you looked?'

'Yesterday after he'd left. Not for the gun, I wanted to look for some papers, his will. I opened the safe and it wasn't there.'

'Are you sure?'

'Of course I'm sure. It's a very small safe.'

'And you didn't tell the police, naturally. It wouldn't be easy to explain why you wanted to take a look at your husband's will just a few hours before he so conveniently died.'

'I haven't told anyone. How did you know about the gun, anyway?'

'My God, Barbie, you are extraordinary! Your husband has his throat slit, his gun is missing and you tell no one.'

'I expect he got rid of it. Anyway, what does it matter? He didn't shoot himself. Dicco, go to bed. I'm tired.'

'But you aren't frightened about the gun, are you? Barbie, why aren't you frightened? It's because you know who's taken it, don't you? You know, or you suspect. Who was it, Lady Ursula, Halliwell, Sarah, your lover?'

'Of course I don't know! Dicco, leave me alone. I'm tired. I don't want to talk any more. I want to sleep.'

Her eyes brimmed with tears. It was unfair of him to upset her like this. She felt an immense sorrow for herself, widowed, alone, vulnerable. And pregnant. Lady Ursula didn't want her to tell anyone about the baby yet, not the police, not Dicco. But he would have to know some time. Everyone would. And they ought to know so that they could look after her, see that she wasn't worried. Paul would have looked after her, but Paul wasn't here. And she had only told him about the baby yesterday morning. Yesterday. But she wouldn't think about yesterday, not now, not ever again. And the film was due to begin, a Hitchcock repeat, and she had always liked Hitchcock. It wasn't fair of Dicco to come in, badgering her, making her remember.

He smiled and patted her on the head as he would a dog, and then he was gone. She waited until the door was closed and she could be certain he wouldn't reappear, then she pressed on the TV button. The screen glowed into light and the credits for the previous programme began to roll. She was in time. She settled more comfortably against her pillows, keeping the sound low so that he shouldn't hear.

9

Massingham had hung about at the Yard longer than was strictly necessary and it was a minute to midnight by the time he drove up to the villa in St Petersburgh Place. But the downstairs light was still on; his father hadn't yet gone up to bed. He turned the key in the lock as quietly as possible and pushed open the door as stealthily as if he were making an illegal entrance. But it was no good. His father must have been waiting for the noise of the car. Almost at once the door of the small front sitting room opened and Lord Dungannon shuffled out. The words 'slippered pantaloon' fell into Massingham's mind bringing with them the familiar dragging weight of pity, irritation and guilt.

His father said:

'Oh, here you are then, my dear boy. Purves has just brought in the grog tray. Would you care to join me?'

His father never used to call him my dear boy. The words sounded false, over-rehearsed, ridiculous. And his answering voice struck the same note of embarrassed insincerity.

'No thank you, Father. I'd better get up. It's been a tiring day. We're working on the Berowne case.'

'Of course. Berowne. She was Lady Ursula Stollard before she married. Your Aunt Margaret was presented in the same year. But she must be over eighty. It can't have been unexpected.'

'It's not Lady Ursula who's dead, Father. It's her son.'

'But I thought Hugo Berowne was killed in Northern Ireland.'

'Not Hugo, Father. Paul.'

'Paul.' His father seemed to contemplate the word then said:

'Then I must, of course, write to Lady Ursula. Poor woman. If you're sure you won't come in . . .' His voice, which since April had become the quaver of an old man, broke off. But Massingham was already bounding up the stairs. Half-way along the landing he paused and glanced down over the banisters expecting to see his father shuffling back into the sitting room to his solitude and his whisky. But the old man was still there, gazing up at him with what seemed almost indecent longing. In the strong light from the hall lamp he saw clearly what the last five months had done to the craggy Massingham features. The flesh seemed to have slipped from the bones so that the beaked nose cleft the skin sharp as a knife edge while the jowls hung in slack mottled pouches like the flesh of a plucked fowl. The flaming Massingham hair was bleached and faded now to the colour and texture of straw. He thought: He looks as archaic as a Rowlandson drawing. Old age makes caricatures of us all. No wonder we dread it.

Mounting the short flight of stairs to his flat he was caught in the same old muddle. It really was becoming intolerable. He had to get away and soon. But how? Apart from a brief spell in the Section House he had lived in his separate rooms in his parents' house ever since he had joined the police. While his mother had been alive, the arrangement had suited him admirably. His parents, absorbed in each other as they had been ever since his father's late marriage in his mid-forties, had left him alone, hardly noticing whether he was in or out. The shared front door had been an inconvenience but nothing more. He had lived comfortably, paid a nominal rent, saved money, told himself that he would buy his own flat when he was ready. He had even found it possible to conduct his love affairs in privacy, while at the same time being able to call on his mother's depleted staff if he wanted a meal cooked, his clothes washed, his rooms cleaned, his parcels taken in.

But with his mother's death in April, all that had changed. While the House of Lords was sitting his father managed to get through his days, padding out with his bus pass to catch the number 12 or the 88 to Westminster, lunching at the House, occasionally sleeping through the evening debates. But at the weekends, even more in the Parliamentary recess, he had become as clinging as a possessive woman, watching his son's comings and goings with almost obsessive interest, listening for his key in the lock, making his quiet but desperate pleas for companionship. Massingham's two youngest brothers were still at school and escaped from their father's grief during the holidays by staying with friends. His only sister was married to a diplomat and lived in Rome. His younger brother was at Sandhurst. The burden fell almost entirely on him. And now he knew that even the rent he paid had become a necessary contribution, almost as important to his father's dwindling resources as the daily attendance payment at the Lords.

Suddenly repentant he thought: I could have spared him ten minutes. Ten minutes of embarrassing non-communication, of small talk about his job which, until now, his father had never thought worthy of interest. Ten minutes of boredom only partly alleviated by alcohol, and setting a precedent for nights of boredom to come.

Closing the door of his flat behind him he thought of Kate Miskin, less than a couple of miles to the west, relaxing in her flat, pouring herself a drink, free of responsibility, free of guilt, and felt a surge of envy and irrational resentment so strong that he could almost persuade himself that it was all her fault.

BOOK THREE

Helping with Inquiries

I

The message from Pembroke Lodge was polite but unambiguous. Mr Lampart would be operating all morning but would be happy to see Commander Dalgliesh when he was free. That would be at about one o'clock or a little later, depending on the length of his list. Translated, this meant that Mr Lampart was a busy man concerned with saving life and alleviating pain, who could legitimately claim that these benign activities took precedence over the sordid preoccupations of a policeman, however distinguished. And the time of the appointment was nicely judged, too. Dalgliesh could hardly complain about going without his lunch since Mr Lampart, more importantly occupied, was obviously unconcerned about his.

He took Kate with him and asked her to drive. She slid into the right-hand seat without fuss and drove as she always did, competently and strictly according to the book, with none of Massingham's occasional impatience or sudden spurts of speed. When they had climbed Haverstock Hill and were passing the Round Pond he said:

'Pembroke Lodge is about a half mile after the Spaniards. The entrance could be easy to miss.' She slowed down, but even so they saw it only just in time, a wide, white painted gate, set well back from the road and screened with horse chestnuts. A wide gravel drive curved to the left, then divided to circle an immaculate lawn fronting the house. They saw a low elegant Edwardian villa set on the edge of the heath, obviously built when a rich man could indulge his fancy for fresh air, an open view, and convenient proximity to London without being thwarted by planning authorities or conservationists concerned about encroachment on public land. As the Rover crunched slowly over the gravel Dalgliesh saw that the former stables to the right of the house had been converted to garages, but little other architectural change was apparent, at least outwardly. He wondered how many beds the nursing home could accommodate. Probably not more than thirty at most. But Stephen Lampart's activities wouldn't be restricted to his private facilities here. He was, as Dalgliesh had already checked, on the staff of two major London teaching hospitals, and no doubt operated at private clinics other than Pembroke Lodge. But this was his personal domain and Dalgliesh had no doubt that it was a highly profitable one.

The outer door was open. It led into an oval and elegant vestibule with a pair of ornate doors and a notice inviting visitors to enter. They found themselves in an entrance hall, square and very light. The staircase, with its delicate carved balustrade, was lit by a huge stained glass window. To the left was a carved fireplace in veined marble. Above it hung an oil painting in the manner of a late Gainsborough, a young mother, serious faced, her white arms encircling her two daughters in folds of blue satin and lace. To the right was a desk in polished mahogany, decorative rather than utilitarian, complete with its bowl of roses and presided over by a white-coated receptionist.

The smell of disinfectant was discernible, but overlaid with a heavier scent of flowers. It was apparent that a consignment had recently been delivered. Great sheaves of roses and gladioli, formal arrangements in beribboned baskets and more outré examples of the florist's ingenuity were piled by the door awaiting distribution. The aura of pampered femininity was almost overwhelming. It was not a place in which a man could feel at home, yet Dalgliesh sensed that it was Kate who felt the more ill at ease. He saw her give a glance of fascinated disgust at one of the more bizarre offerings of conjugal congratulations: a baby's cot, over two feet long, tightly covered with the wired heads of rosebuds, dyed blue, and with a pillow and coverlet of white carnations similarly decapitated, the whole monstrosity embellished with a huge blue bow. As they moved to the reception desk across a carpet thick enough to drag at their feet, a trolley of coloured bottles, nail varnishes and assorted jars, was pushed across the hall by an elegant older woman in a pale pink trousersuit, obviously the beautician. Dalgliesh was reminded of a conversation overheard at a dinner party some months earlier. 'But darling, the place is divine. One is pampered from the moment one arrives. Hairdresser, facials, cordon bleu menu, champagne instead of Valium for the blues. The lot. The thing is, though, that I'm not sure they don't overdo it. One feels absolutely outraged when labour starts and one realizes that there are some humiliations and discomforts that even dear Stephen can't do much about.' Dalgliesh wondered suddenly and irrelevantly whether Lampart's patients ever died on him. Probably not, not here anyway. Those at risk would be admitted elsewhere. The place had its own subtle aura of bad taste, but the ultimate bad taste of death and failure would be rigorously excluded.

The receptionist, like the decor, had been carefully chosen to reassure, not to threaten. She was middle-aged, pleasant looking rather than beautiful, well-groomed, immaculately coiffured. They were, of course, expected. Mr Lampart wouldn't keep the Commander more than a few minutes. Would they care for some coffee? No? Then perhaps they wouldn't mind waiting in the drawing room.

Dalgliesh looked at his watch. He estimated that Lampart would arrive in about five minutes, a nicely calculated delay long enough to demonstrate lack of anxiety, but short enough not to antagonize a man who was, after all, a senior officer of the Yard.

The drawing room into which they were shown was large and high-ceilinged with a central bay window and two flanking smaller ones overlooking the lawn and giving a distant view of the heath. Something of its Edwardian formality and plush comfort remained in the Axminster carpet, the heavy sofas set at right angles to the fire, and the open fire itself in which synthetic nuggets were roasting under the carved overmantel. Stephen Lampart had resisted any temptation to combine the room's domesticity with a consulting room. There was no couch tactfully secreted behind screens, no washbasin. This was a room where clinical realities could be, for a moment, forgotten. Only the mahogany desk reminded the visitor that it was also a room for business.

Dalgliesh glanced at the pictures. There was a Frith over the fireplace and he walked over to study more closely its meticulous romanticizing of Victorian life. It showed a London railway terminus; uniformed heroes returning from some colonial adventure. The first class carriages were in the foreground. Richly mantled and beribboned ladies, with their decorously pantalooned daughters, decorously greeted their returning menfolk while the more unrestrained welcomes of the common soldiery occupied the periphery of the canvas. On the opposite wall was a bank of stage designs, drawings and costumes for what looked like Shakespearian productions. Dalgliesh supposed that the stage provided some of Lampart's most notable patients and that these were a thank-offering for services rendered. A side table was covered with signed photographs in silver frames. Two, flamboyantly signed, were from minor European ex-royalty. The rest were of impeccably groomed mothers, wistful, sentimental, triumphant, or reluctant, who displayed their babies in unpractised arms. There was the unmistakable aura of nanny in the background. This phalanx of maternity in a room which otherwise was essentially male, struck an incongruous note. But at least, thought Dalgliesh, the man hadn't displayed his medical diplomas over the sideboard.

Dalgliesh left Kate studying the Frith and walked over to the windows. The huge horse chestnut in the middle of the lawn was still heavy with its summer foliage, but the screen of beech trees which partly hid the heath were already showing the first bronze of autumn. The morning light was diffused through a sky which had at first been as opaque as thin milk but which had now lightened into silver. There was no sun but he was aware that it shone above the gauze of clouds and the air was light. Along the path two figures were slowly walking, a nurse wearing a white cap and cloak and a woman with a helmet of yellow hair and a ponderous fur coat which looked far too heavy for a day in early autumn.

It was six minutes precisely before Stephen Lampart arrived. He came in without hurry, apologized for the delay, and greeted them with calm courtesy as if this were a social call. If he was surprised to find Dalgliesh accompanied by a woman detective, he concealed it admirably. But, as Dalgliesh introduced them and they shook hands, he caught Lampart's sharp appraising glance. He could have been greeting a prospective patient, assessing from long experience, in this their first meeting, whether he was likely to have trouble with her.

He was expensively but not formally dressed. The dark grey tweed with its almost invisible stripe and the immaculate blue shirt were, no doubt, designed to distance him from the more intimidating orthodoxy of the successful consultant. He could, thought Dalgliesh, have been a merchant banker, an academic, a politician. But whatever the job, he would have been good at it. His face, his clothes, the confident gaze, all bore the unmistakable imprint of success.

Dalgliesh had expected him to seat himself at the desk with the advantage of dominance which this would give. Instead, he motioned them to the low sofa and sat opposite them in a higher and straight-backed armchair. It gave him a more subtle advantage while reducing the interview to the level of an intimate, even cosy, discussion of a mutual problem. He said:

'I know, of course, why you're here. This is an appalling business. I still find it difficult to believe. I suppose relations and friends all tell you that. Brutal murder is the sort of thing that happens to strangers, not to the people one knows.'

Dalgliesh said:

'How did you learn about it?'

'Lady Berowne telephoned me soon after your people brought the news, and as soon as I was free I called in at the house. I wanted to offer any help I could to her and Lady Ursula. I still don't have any details. Are you any clearer yet what exactly happened?'

'Both their throats were cut. We don't yet know why or by whom.'

'I understood that much from the press and television, but the reports seemed almost wilfully uncommunicative. I take it you're treating it as murder.'

Dalgliesh said, drily:

'There's no evidence to suggest that it was a suicide pact.'

'And the church door, the one leading to this vestry or wherever it was where the bodies were found, may I ask whether you found it open or is that the sort of question that you're not supposed to answer?'

'It was unlocked.'

He said:

'Well, that at least will reassure Lady Ursula.' He didn't elucidate. But then, he didn't need to. After a pause he asked:

'What do you want of me, Commander?'

'I'd like you to talk to us about him. This murder could be what at first sight it appears. He let someone in and that person, a stranger, killed them both. But if it isn't as simple as that, then we need to know as much about him as we can get.'

Lampart said:

'Including who could have known where he was yesterday night and who hated him enough to cut his throat.'

'Including anything you can tell us which could be even remotely relevant.'

Lampart paused as if to collect and marshal his thoughts. It was unnecessary. Both of them knew that his thoughts had been marshalled long before. Then he said:

'I don't think I can give much help. Nothing I know or could guess about Paul Berowne is remotely relevant to his death. If you ask about his enemies, I suppose he must have had them, political enemies. But I should suppose that Paul had fewer than most people in government and, anyway, they're not the sort to go in for murder. The idea that this could be a political crime is absurd. Unless, of course' – again he paused and Dalgliesh waited – 'unless someone on the extreme Left had a personal animosity. But it seems unlikely. More than unlikely, ridiculous. Sarah, his daughter, strongly disliked his politics. But I've no reason to suppose that the set she's mixed up with or even her Marxist boyfriend go in for razor slashing.'

'What set is that?'

'Oh, some minor revolutionary outfit on the extreme Left. I don't suppose Labour would have them. I'd have thought you would already have known. Don't Special Branch make it their business to keep track of these people?' His gaze was open and mildly inquiring but Dalgliesh caught the bite of contempt and dislike in the careful voice and wondered if Kate had heard it too. He asked:

'Who is the boyfriend?'

'Oh really, Commander, I'm not accusing him, I'm not accusing anyone.' Dalgliesh didn't speak. He wondered what length of silence Lampart would think convincing before he came across with the information. After a pause he said: 'He's Ivor Garrod. Banner carrier for all the fashionable shibboleths. I've only met him once. Sarah brought him to dinner at Campden Hill Square about five months ago, principally, I imagine, to annoy Papa. It was a meal I prefer to forget. From the talk then, the violence he advocates is on a somewhat grander scale than merely cutting the throat of a single Tory ex-minister.'

Dalgliesh asked quietly:

'When did you last see Sir Paul Berowne?' The change of questioning almost disconcerted Lampart but he answered calmly enough:

'About six weeks ago. We're not as friendly as we used to be. Actually I was proposing to telephone him today and ask if he could have dinner with me tonight or tomorrow, unless, of course, religious conversion had destroyed his taste for good food and wine.'

'Why did you want to see him?'

'I wanted to ask him what he intended to do about his wife. You know, of course, that he'd recently resigned his seat as well as his job as junior minister and you probably know as much as I do why. He was proposing apparently to drop out of public life. I wanted to know if that included dropping out of his marriage. There was the question of financial provision for Lady Berowne, for Barbara. She is my cousin, I've known her since childhood. I have an interest.'

'How strong an interest?'

Lampart looked sideways over his shoulder at the fair-haired woman and her nurse, still patiently circling the lawn. He seemed momentarily to transfer his interest to them then recollected himself, a little too obviously, and turned again to Dalgliesh.

'I'm sorry. How strong an interest? I don't want to marry her if that's what you're implying, but I am concerned about her. For the past three years I've been her lover as well as her cousin. You could call that a strong interest, I suppose.'

'Did her husband know that you and she were lovers?'

'I've no idea. Husbands usually do get to know these things. Paul and I didn't see each other often enough to make it an embarrassment. We're both busy men with little in common now. Except Barbara, of course. Anyway, he was hardly in a position to object, morally speaking. He had a mistress as I've no doubt you've discovered. Or haven't you grubbed out that piece of dirt yet?'

Dalgliesh said:

'I'm interested in knowing how you managed to grub it out.'

'Barbara told me. She guessed, or rather she knew. She employed a private detective about eighteen months ago and had him followed. To be accurate, she told me of her suspicions and I got hold of a suitably discreet man on her behalf. I don't think it bothered her particularly, the infidelity. It was just that she liked to know. I don't think she saw the woman as a serious rival. Actually, I suspect she was quite pleased. It amused her and it gave her something to hold over Paul if the need arose. And, of course, freed her from the disagreeable necessity of sleeping with him, at least on an inconveniently regular basis. But she didn't lock her door. Barbara liked an occasional assurance that he was still suitably enthralled.'

He was, thought Dalgliesh, being remarkably candid, unnecessarily so. He wondered whether this apparently naive willingness to confide his own and other people's more intimate emotions arose from over-confidence, arrogance and vanity, or whether there was a more sinister motive. Lampart wouldn't be the first murderer to argue that if you told the police details they had no particular right to demand they would be less likely to suspect other more dangerous secrets.

He asked:

'And was he still suitably enthralled?'

'I imagine so. What a pity he isn't here to be asked.' With a quick and surprisingly clumsy gesture he got up and walked to the window as if seized by restlessness. Dalgliesh turned in his chair and watched him. Suddenly he strode over to the desk, picked up the telephone and dialled. He said:

'Sister, I think Mrs Steiner has had enough outdoor exercise. It's too cold this morning for slow walking. Tell her I'll be along to see her again in,' he glanced at his watch, 'in about fifteen minutes. Thank you.' He put down the receiver, came back to his chair and said almost roughly: 'Let's get down to it, shall we? What you want from me, I suppose, is some sort of statement. Where was I, what was I doing, who was I with when Paul got himself killed? If it was murder, I'm not naive enough to deceive myself that I'm not a suspect.'

'It isn't a question of suspicion. We have to ask those questions of anyone who was closely connected with Sir Paul.'

He laughed, a sudden explosion of sound, harsh and mirthless.

'Closely connected! You could say that I suppose. And it's all just a matter of routine. Isn't that what you usually tell your victims?' Dalgliesh didn't reply. The silence seemed to irritate Lampart. He said: 'Where do I make it, this statement? Here, or at the local police station? Or are you operating from the Yard?'

'You could make it there, in my office, if that's convenient for you. Perhaps you could come in this evening. Or it could be taken at the local station if that would save time. But it would be helpful to have the gist of it now.'

Lampart said:

'You've noticed, I suppose, that I haven't asked to have my solicitor present. That shows rather a touching confidence in the police, wouldn't you say?'

'If you want him to be present that, of course, is your right.'

'I don't want him. I don't need him. I hope you won't be disappointed, Commander, but I think I have an alibi. That is if Berowne died between seven and midnight.' Still Dalgliesh didn't speak. Lampart went on: 'I was with Barbara for the whole of that time as, no doubt, you already know. You must have seen her. Earlier, from two o'clock until five I was here operating. The list is available and theatre sister and the anaesthetist can corroborate. I know I was gloved, gowned and masked, but I can assure you that my staff recognize my work even if they don't actually see my face. But, of course, they did see it, before I gowned up. I mention that in case you had some fanciful idea that I might have persuaded a colleague to stand in for me.'

Dalgliesh said:

'That might work in fiction but hardly in real life.'

'And afterwards, Barbara and I had tea in this room then spent some time in my private flat, upstairs. Then I changed and we left here together at about seven forty. The night porter saw us go and can probably confirm the time. We drove to the Black Swan at Cookham where we had dinner together. I wasn't particularly noticing the time but I suppose we got there at about eight thirty. I drive a red Porsche, in case that's significant. The table was booked for eight forty-five. Jean Paul Higgins is the manager. He'll be able to confirm it. No doubt he'll also confirm that it was after eleven when we left. But I'd be grateful for a little tact. I'm not over-sensitive about reputation, but I can't afford to have half of fashionable London gossiping about my private life. And while some of my patients have their little foibles like giving birth under water or squatting on the drawing room carpet, being delivered by a murder suspect isn't everyone's fancy.'

'We'll be discreet. When did Lady Berowne arrive here? Or did you call for her earlier at Campden Hill Square?'

'No. I haven't been inside number sixty-two for weeks. Barbara came by cab. She dislikes driving in London. She arrived about four, I suppose. She was in the theatre watching me operate from about four fifteen until I finished. Did I mention that?'

'She was with you the whole time?'

'Most of the time. I think she slipped out for a few minutes after I'd completed the third Caesarean.'

'And she was masked and gowned too?'

'Of course. But what possible relevance is that? He couldn't have died, surely, before the evening.'

'Is that something she often does? Watch you operate?'

'It isn't uncommon. It's a fancy she has,' he paused and added, 'from time to time.'

They were both silent. There were some things, thought Dalgliesh, that even Stephen Lampart, with his pose of ironic detachment and contempt for reticence, couldn't bring himself actually to say. So that was how she got her kicks. That was what turned her on; watching, masked and gowned, while his hands cut into another woman's body. The erotic charge of the medical priesthood. The attendant nurses moving in patterned ceremony about him. The grey eyes meeting the blue above the mask. And afterwards, watching, while he peeled off his gloves, held out his arms in a parody of benediction while an acolyte lifted the gown from his shoulders. The heady mixture of power, mystery, ruthlessness. The rituals of knife and blood. Where, he wondered, had they made love. His bedroom, a private sitting room? It was surprising that they didn't couple on the operating table. Perhaps they did.

The telephone on the desk rang. With a muttered apology, Lampart picked up the receiver. The conversation, apparently with a colleague, was highly clinical and onesided with Lampart doing most of the listening. But he made no attempt to cut it short. Dalgliesh gazed out over the garden while his mind busied itself with its preliminary assessment. If they had left Pembroke Lodge at seven forty it would need fast driving to get to the Black Swan by eight thirty. Time to take in a murder on the way? It was feasible provided he could make an excuse to leave her in the car. No man in his senses would take her with him into the church on such a bloody mission even if she knew or guessed what he had in mind. So there would have to be an excuse. Someone he had briefly to see. Some business to be transacted. The car would have to be parked close to the church. That in itself would be risky. A red Porsche was conspicuous. And then what? The knock on the church door. Berowne letting him in. The rehearsed excuse for calling. How long for these preliminaries? Less than a minute perhaps. The sudden blow to knock Berowne out. Then to the washroom for the razor which he could be sure he would find, the quick stripping off of jacket and shirt and back to the vestry, razor in hand. The careful tentative cuts followed by the final slash to the bone. He must have done some forensic medicine when a student, if not since. He would know better than any other suspect how to simulate a suicide.

And then the disaster. Harry appears, stumbling, probably half-drunk, half-asleep, but not so asleep that he couldn't see, couldn't remember. And now, there would be no time for finesse and none needed. And afterwards: the quick wash; the razor placed near Berowne's hand; the rapid glance to left and right; the covering darkness; the door left unlocked since he couldn't take away the key; the unhurried return to the car. He would have to depend on her silence, of course. He would need to be certain that she would stick to their story and say that they had driven straight to the Black Swan. But it was an easy lie, no complicated fabrication, no difficult details of timing to remember. She would say what in fact she had in effect already said. 'We drove straight there. No, I can't remember the route. I wasn't noticing. But we didn't stop.' He would have to fabricate a good reason for asking her to lie. 'I needed to see one of my patients, a woman.' But why not tell the police that? There's nothing wrong about a quick professional visit. The need to stop would have to be faintly disreputable. Either that or something he had suddenly remembered. A telephone call which had been unanswered. Too quick. He would need longer than that. And why not wait and make it from the Black Swan? But, of course, there was the obvious ploy. He would say he had called at the church, spoken to Berowne, left him alive and well. That way, she would back up his alibi in her own interest as well as his. And if, in the end, she didn't, he would still have his story. 'I called to talk to Berowne about his wife. I only stayed for ten minutes at the most. The discussion was perfectly amicable. I saw no one but Berowne and I left him alive and well.'

Lampart replaced the receiver. He said:

'Sorry about that. Where were we, Commander? At the Black Swan?'

But Dalgliesh changed the tack of the questioning. He said:

'You knew Sir Paul Berowne intimately once, even if you weren't particularly close at the end. No two men share a woman without being interested in each other.' He could have added, 'sometimes obsessed with each other'. He went on: 'You're a doctor. I'm wondering what you make of it, this experience he had in the vestry at St Matthew's.' The flattery was hardly subtle and Lampart was too clever a man to miss it. But he wouldn't be able to resist it. He was used to being asked his opinion, to being listened to with deference. It was partly what he lived by. He said:

'I'm an obstetrician, not a psychiatrist. But I shouldn't have thought the psychology of it was particularly complicated. The usual story. It's only the manifestations that are a little bizarre. Call it the mid-life crisis. I don't like the expression "male menopause". It's inaccurate anyway. The two things are fundamentally different. I think he looked at his life, what he'd achieved, what he could hope for, and didn't much care for it. He'd tried law and politics and neither satisfied him. He had a wife he lusted after but didn't love. A daughter who didn't love him. A job which constrained any hope he might have of breaking out into spectacular or exuberant protest. All right; he'd got himself a mistress. That's the easy expedient. I haven't seen the lady but from what Barbara told me it's more a question of comfort and cocoa, a bit of mild office gossip on the side rather than any breaking of the straitjacket he got himself strapped into. So he needed an excuse for chucking it all. What better one than proclaiming that God himself has told you you're on the wrong tack? I don't think it would be my way out. But you can argue that it's preferable to a nervous breakdown, alcoholism or cancer.'

When Dalgliesh didn't speak he went on quickly, with a kind of nervous sincerity which was almost convincing.

'I see it all the time. The husbands. They sit where you're sitting now. Ostensibly, they come to talk to me about their wives. But they're the ones with the problem. They can't win. It's the tyranny of success. They spend most of their youth working to qualify, most of their young manhood building up success – the right wife, the right house, the right schools for the children, the right clubs. For what? For more money, more comfort, a bigger house, a faster car, more taxation. And they don't even get much of a kick out of it. And there's another twenty years to be got through. And it isn't much better for those who aren't disillusioned, who find their niche, who actually enjoy what they do. Their fear is the prospect of retirement. Overnight you're nobody. The walking dead. Haven't you seen those dreadful old men, trawling for a committee, angling for a royal commission, a job, any kind of a job, as long as it gives them the illusion that they're still important.'

Dalgliesh said:

'Yes, I've seen them.'

'Christ, they practically go down on their knees and slaver for it.'

'I think that's true enough, but it didn't apply to him. He was still only a junior minister. His success was ahead. He was still at the striving stage.'

'Oh yes, I know. The next Tory Prime Minister but one. Do you think that was a serious possibility? I don't. He hadn't the fire in the belly, not for politics anyway. Not even one little smouldering coal.'

He spoke with a kind of triumphant bitterness. He said:

'I'm all right, Jack. I'm one of the lucky ones. No hostages to fortune. The job gives me what I need. And when I'm all ready for the scrapheap, I've got the *Mayflower*, a sloop, fifty feet. She's berthed at Chichester. I don't get much time for her now. But once retired, I'll provision her and be off. And you, Commander? No *Mayflower*?'

'No *Mayflower*.'

'But you've your poetry, of course. I was forgetting.' He spoke the word as if it were an insult. As if he were saying, 'you've got your woodwork, your stamp collection, your embroidery'. Worse, he spoke it as if he knew there hadn't been a poem for four years, that there might never be one again. Dalgliesh said:

'For someone who wasn't intimate, you know a lot about him.'

'He interested me. And at Oxford his elder brother and I were friends. I dined at Campden Hill Square fairly often when he was alive and the three of us used to sail together. To Cherbourg specifically, in 1978. You get to know a man when you've survived a force ten gale together. Actually, Paul saved my life. I went overboard and he got me back.'

'But isn't yours a rather superficial assessment, the obvious explanation?'

'It's surprising how often the obvious explanation is the correct one. If you were a diagnostician, you'd know that.'

Dalgliesh turned to Kate:

'Is there anything you wanted to ask, Inspector?' Lampart wasn't quite quick enough to restrain his momentary frown of surprise and discomfiture that a woman he had taken to be no more than Dalgliesh's helot, whose role was to take unobtrusive

398

notes and sit as a meek and silent witness, was apparently licensed to question him. He turned on her a half-smiling over-attentive gaze but his eyes were wary.

Kate said:

'This dinner at the Black Swan, is that a favourite place of yours? Do you and Lady Berowne go there often?'

'Fairly often in summer. Less so in winter. The ambience is agreeable. It's a convenient distance from London and now that Higgins has changed his chef the food is good. If you're asking for a recommendation for a quiet dinner, yes, I can recommend it.' The sarcasm was unsubtle and he had made his resentment too obvious. The question, innocuous enough, if apparently irrel-evant, had rattled him. Kate said:

'And you were there, both of you, on the evening of the seventh of August, when Diana Travers was drowned?'

He said dryly:

'You obviously already know that we were there so there seems little point in asking. It was Lady Berowne's twenty-seventh birthday party. She was born on the seventh of August.'

'And you escorted her, not her husband?'

'Sir Paul Berowne was otherwise engaged. I gave the party for Lady Berowne. He was expected to join us later but rang to say that he couldn't make it. Since you know that we were there, you obviously know, too, that we left before the tragedy.'

'And the other tragedy, sir, Theresa Nolan? You were not, of course, present when that happened either?' Careful, Kate, thought Dalgliesh. But he didn't interfere, and he wasn't anxious.

'If you mean did I sit by her side in Holland Park when she swallowed a bottle of Distalgesic tablets and washed them down with cooking sherry, no I wasn't. If I had been, obviously I should have stopped her.'

'She left a note making it plain that she'd killed herself because of guilt over her abortion. A perfectly legal abortion. She was one of your nurses here. I wonder why she didn't have the operation at Pembroke Lodge?'

'She didn't ask. And if she had, I wouldn't have done it. I prefer not to operate on my own staff. If there appear to be medical reasons for termination, I refer them to a fellow gynaecologist or a psychiatrist. Actually, I can't see how her death or that of Diana Travers has anything to do with the business that brings you here this morning. Ought we to be wasting time with irrelevant questions?'

Dalgliesh said:

'Not irrelevant. Sir Paul received letters suggesting, obliquely but fairly unmistakably, that he was somehow connected with those two deaths. Anything that happened to him during the last weeks of his life has to be relevant. The letters were probably the usual malicious nonsense that politicians expose themselves to but it's as well to clear them out of the way.'

Lampart turned his gaze from Kate to Dalgliesh.

'I see. I'm sorry if I sounded uncooperative but I know absolutely nothing of the Travers girl except that she worked at Campden Hill Square as a part-time domestic and that she was at the Black Swan on the night of the birthday party. Theresa Nolan came here from Campden Hill Square where she'd been nursing Lady Ursula who was laid low with sciatica. I understand they got her from a nursing agency. When Lady Ursula no longer needed a night nurse, she suggested to the girl that she apply here. She had a midwifery qualification. She was perfectly satisfactory. She must have got pregnant when she was working at Campden Hill Square. But I didn't ask by whom and I don't think she ever said.'

Dalgliesh said:

'Did it occur to you that the child could have been Sir Paul Berowne's?'

'Yes. It occurred to me. I imagine it occurred to quite a number of people.' He said no more and Dalgliesh didn't press him. He asked:

'What happened when she discovered she was pregnant?'

'She came to me and said that she couldn't face having a baby and wanted a termination. I referred her to a psychiatrist and left him to make the necessary arrangements.'

'Did you think that the girl's condition at the time, I mean her mental condition, was such that she was likely to qualify legally for an abortion?'

'I didn't examine her. I didn't discuss it with her. And it

wasn't a medical decision I was qualified to make. As I said, I referred her to a psychiatric colleague. I told her that she could have leave with pay until a decision was made. She only came back here for a week after the operation. And the rest you know.'

Suddenly he got to his feet and began restlessly pacing. Then he turned to Dalgliesh.

'I've given some thought to this business of Paul Berowne. Man is an animal and he lives most at ease with himself and the world when he remembers that. Admittedly he's the cleverest and most dangerous of animals, but he's still an animal. The philosophers, and poets too, for all I know, make it all too complicated. It isn't. Our basic needs are pretty straightforward – food, shelter, warmth, sex, prestige, in that order. The happiest people go after them and are satisfied with them. Berowne wasn't. God knows what unattainable intangibles he thought he'd a right to. Eternal life, probably.'

Dalgliesh said:

'So you believe the probability is that he killed himself?'

'I haven't enough evidence. But let's say that if you finally decide it was suicide, then I for one won't be surprised.'

'And the tramp? There were two deaths.'

'That's more difficult. Did he kill Paul or did Paul kill him? Obviously the family won't want to believe the latter. Lady Ursula will never accept that explanation, whatever the final verdict.'

'But you . . .'

'Oh, I feel that if a man has sufficient violence in him to slit his own throat, he's certainly capable of slitting another's. And now, perhaps you'll excuse me,' he glanced at Kate, 'both of you. I have a patient waiting. I'll call in at the Yard between eight and nine thirty and sign my statement.' He added, rising: 'Perhaps by then I shall manage to think of something else to help you. But don't be too sanguine.' He made it sound like a threat.

2

There was an almost unbroken stream of traffic past the front gate and Kate had to wait for over a minute before it was safe to filter in. She thought: I wonder just how he does it. The interview was all there in her notebook in her neat, unorthodox shorthand but she had the gift of almost perfect verbal recall and she could have typed most of it out without reference to the hieroglyphics. She let her mind slide over each question and response and she still couldn't see where AD had been so clever.

He had said very little, his questions short and sometimes apparently unrelated to the line of inquiry. But Lampart, and that after all was the intention, had been seduced into saying a great deal too much. And all that guff about the male mid-life crisis, popular psychology which you could have sent to you in a plain envelope if you wrote to the agony aunties inquiring what was wrong with your old man. He could be right, of course. But, after all, medically speaking, varieties of the male menopause weren't Stephen Lampart's field. He'd been asked for his opinion and he'd given it, but you'd expect a man as fond of his own voice as he was to be even more forthcoming about the psychological problems of pregnancy and abortion. But when it came to Theresa Nolan, what had they got? A brush off, the keep off signs clearly posted. He hadn't even wanted to think about her, let alone talk about her. And it wasn't just because she, Kate, had been the one to do the questioning and had done it with that undeferential over-politeness which she had known would be more offensive to his vanity than rudeness or open antagonism. She had hoped that, with luck, it might goad him into an indiscretion, but it wouldn't have worked if there had been nothing to conceal. She heard AD's voice:

'That touching detail, about Sir Paul saving his life. Did you believe it?'

'No, sir. Not as he told it. I think something of the sort probably happened. He went overboard and his friend yanked him back. He wouldn't have mentioned it if there weren't some corroboration. But I think he was really saying, "Look, I might have pinched his wife but I wouldn't have killed him, would I? He saved my life."' She added: 'It wasn't very subtle the way he fingered Garrod.' She glanced at him quickly. He smiled with wry distaste as he sometimes did when a colleague used an Americanism. But he let it pass, merely saying:

'Nothing about him was subtle.'

Suddenly she felt a surge of optimism, heady, intoxicating and dangerously close to the euphoria which always came when a case was going well but which she had learned to distrust and subdue. If this goes all right, if we get him, whoever he is, and we will, then I'm on my way. I'm really on my way. But the elation went deeper than mere ambition or the satisfaction of a test passed, a job well done. She had enjoyed herself. Every minute of her brief confrontation with that self-satisfied poseur had been deeply pleasurable. She thought of her first months with the CID, the plugging, conscientious, door-to-door inquiries which had made up her day, the pathetic victims, the even more pathetic villains. How much more satisfying was this sophisticated manhunt; the knowledge that they were up against a killer with the intelligence to think and plan, who wasn't an ignorant, feckless victim of circumstance or passion. She had learned facial control long before she had joined the police. She drove carefully, her face calmly set on the road ahead. But something of what she was feeling must have communicated itself to her companion. He said:

'Did you enjoy yourself, Inspector?' The question and the rare use of her rank jolted her but she decided to answer it honestly, knowing that she had no option. She had done her homework. She knew his reputation, and when colleagues had spoken about him she had made it her business to listen. They had said: 'He's a bastard, but a just bastard.' She knew that there were some inadequacies he could forgive and some foibles he could tolerate. But dishonesty wasn't among them. She said:

'Yes, sir. I liked the sense of being in control, that we were getting somewhere.' Then she added, knowing as she spoke that this was dangerous territory, but hell, she thought, why should he get away with it:

'Was the question meant as a criticism, sir?'

'No. No one joins the police without getting some enjoyment out of exercising power. No one joins the murder squad who hasn't a taste for death. The danger begins when the pleasure becomes an end in itself. That's when it's time to think about another job.'

She wanted to ask: 'Have you ever thought of another job, sir?'

But she knew the temptation was illusory. There were some senior officers of whom one could ask that question after a couple of whiskies in the senior officers' mess, but he wasn't among them. She remembered the moment when she had told Alan that Dalgliesh had chosen her for the new squad. He had said, smiling: 'So isn't it about time you tried reading his verse?' and she had replied: 'I'd better come to terms with the man before I try coming to terms with his poetry.' She wasn't sure that she had succeeded. Now she said:

'Mr Lampart spoke about razor slashing. We deliberately didn't tell him how Sir Paul died. So why should he have mentioned a razor?'

Dalgliesh said:

'Reasonably enough. He was an old friend, one of the people who would know how Berowne shaved. He must have guessed what weapon was used. It's interesting that he couldn't bring himself to ask us outright if it was. Incidentally, we'll have to check that timing fairly quickly. It's a job for Saunders, I think. He'd better make three runs, the same time, the same make of car, the same night of the week, and, with luck, the same weather conditions. And we'll need to know everything possible about Pembroke Lodge. Who owns the freehold, who holds shares, how the business operates, what its reputation is.' She couldn't make a written note of his instructions. But then, she didn't need to.

She said:

'Yes, sir.'

Dalgliesh went on:

'He had the means, he had the knowledge, he had the motive. I don't think he wanted marriage with the lady but he certainly didn't want an impoverished mistress who might begin thinking in terms of divorce. But if he wanted Berowne dead, and dead before he threw away his money on some half-baked scheme for housing derelicts, he didn't need to slit his throat. He's a doctor. There are more subtle methods. This murderer didn't kill merely from expediency. There had been hatred in that room. Hate isn't an easy emotion to hide. I didn't see it in Stephen Lampart. Arrogance, aggression, sexual jealousy of the man in possession. But not hate.'

Kate had never lacked courage and she didn't now. After all, he'd selected her for the team. Presumably he thought her opinion worth having. He wasn't looking for a female subordinate to massage his ego. She said:

'But couldn't it have been expediency rather than hate, sir? Killing without arousing suspicion isn't easy even for a doctor. He wasn't Sir Paul's general practitioner. And this, if he could pull it off, would be the perfect murder, one that isn't even suspected as murder. It was Harry Mack who did for him. Without that second killing, wouldn't we have taken it at its face value . . . suicide?'

Dalgliesh said:

'Followed by the usual euphemistic verdict "while the balance of his mind was disturbed". Perhaps. If he hadn't made the mistake of taking away the matches and of half-burning the diary. That was an unnecessary refinement. In some ways, the clue of that half-burned match is the most interesting in the case.'

Suddenly she felt at ease with him, almost companionable. She was no longer thinking of the impression she might be making but of the case. She did what she would have done with Massingham. With her eyes fixed on the road ahead, she thought it through aloud:

'Once the killer decided to burn the diary, he'd know he needed to take the matches with him to the church. Berowne didn't smoke so there wouldn't be a lighter on the body. Obviously, he'd be unwise to risk using his own lighter if he had one, and he couldn't be sure he'd find matches in the vestry. And when he did, they were chained and it was easier and quicker to use the box he'd brought with him. Time was vital. So we get back to someone who knew Sir Paul, knew his habits, knew where he was on Tuesday night but who wasn't familiar with the church. But he'd hardly be carrying the diary in his hand when he arrived. So he was wearing a jacket or coat with largish pockets. Or he had a bag of some kind, a carrier, a tote bag, a briefcase, a medical bag.'

Dalgliesh said:

'Or he could have carried it folded inside an evening paper.'

Kate went on:

'He rings. Sir Paul lets him in. He asks to go to the washroom. He leaves his bag there together with the matches and the diary. He strips. Perhaps he strips naked. Then it's back to the Little Vestry. But this is getting bizarre, sir. His victim isn't going to sit there quietly waiting for it. Not confronted by a man, stark naked with an open razor in his hand. Paul Berowne wasn't old or sick or weak. He would have defended himself. It couldn't have happened that way.'

'Concentrate on the matches.'

'But he must have been naked when he killed. Naked to the waist anyway. He must have known that it would be a bloody business. He couldn't have risked getting his clothes splashed. But of course! He knocks out his victim first. Then he goes for the razor, strips, does the fancy bit. Then back to the washroom. He has a quick but thorough sluice down and gets back into his clothes. Then, last of all, he burns the diary. That way he can be sure there's no blood on the cover or in the grate. It must have happened in that order. Finally, perhaps a matter of habit, he slips the matchbox in his jacket pocket. That suggests he was used to carrying matches. A smoker, perhaps. It must have given him a shock when he put his hands in his pocket later and found them and realized that he should have left them at the scene. Why didn't he go back? Too late, perhaps. Or perhaps he couldn't face the shambles.'

Dalgliesh said:

'Or he knew that a second visit would add to the risk of being seen, of leaving some trace of himself in the vestry. But let's assume that the killer took his own box away on purpose. What does that suggest?'

'That the box he used could be traced to him. But that's unlikely, surely. He'd use an ordinary brand, one of a million similar boxes. And he couldn't have known that we'd find that half-burned match. Perhaps he took it away because it was a box someone might miss. Perhaps he always planned to return it. And that means he didn't go to the church from his own home. Logically, he came from Campden Hill Square, where he'd helped himself both to the diary and to the box of matches. But if so, if the matchbox came from Berowne's own home, why not leave it at the scene? Even if the box were traced, it would only lead us back to Berowne himself. So we get back to a simple mistake. A matter of habit. He slipped the box into his pocket.'

Dalgliesh said:

'If he did it might not have worried him too much after the first shock of discovery. He'd tell himself that we'd assume Berowne used the matches from the chained box, or that we'd think that the matches had been burned with the diary. Or perhaps we'd argue that he could have used a match from one of those packets you can pick up in hotels and restaurants, small enough to burn away without a trace. Admittedly, Berowne wasn't a man likely to collect restaurant matches but defence counsel could argue that it happened that way. This isn't exactly a propitious time to ask for a conviction on forensic evidence alone, certainly not on one inch of a half-burned match.'

Kate asked:

'How do you think it happened, sir?'

'Possibly much as you've described. If Sir Paul had been faced with a naked and armed assailant, I doubt if we'd have found what we did find at the scene. There was no sign of a struggle. That suggests that he must have been knocked out first. That done, the killer got to work swiftly, expertly, knowing just what he was about. And he didn't need much time. A couple of minutes to strip and lay his hands on the razor. Less than ten seconds to do the killing. So the knockout blow need not have been heavy. In fact, it would have had to be nicely judged if it weren't to leave a suspiciously large bruise. But there's another possibility. He could have slipped something over Berowne's head and dragged him down. Something soft, a scarf, a towel, his own shirt. Or a noose, a cord, a handkerchief.'

Kate said:

'But he'd have to be careful not to pull it too tight, not to throttle his victim. The cause of death had to be the slit throat. And wouldn't a scarf or handkerchief leave a mark?'

Dalgliesh said:

'Not necessarily. Not when he'd finished his butchery. But we may get something from this afternoon's PM.'

And suddenly, she was back in the Little Vestry, looking down again at that half-severed head, seeing the whole picture, vivid, clear-edged, bright as a coloured print. And this time there was no blessed moment of preparation, no chance to compose her mind and muscles for what she knew she would have to face. Her hands, white knuckled, tightened on the wheel. For a moment she imagined the car had stalled, that she had stepped on the brake. But they were still riding smoothly, down the Finchley Road. How strange, she thought, that the horror, briefly recalled, should be more terrible than reality. But her companion was speaking. She must have lost a few seconds of what he was saying. But now she heard him talking about the time of the post-mortem, saying that she might like to watch. Normally the suggestion, which she translated as an order, would have pleased her. She would have welcomed it as one more affirmation that she was really part of his team. But now for the first time she felt a spasm of distaste, almost a revulsion. She would be there, of course. This wouldn't be her first autopsy. She had no fear of disgracing herself. She could gaze and not be sick. In detective training school, she had seen her male colleagues topple in the PM room while she had stood firm. It was important to be present at the PM if the pathologist would allow it. You could learn a lot, and she was eager to learn. Her grandmother and the social worker would be waiting for her at three o'clock but they would have to wait. She had tried, but not too hard, to find a moment in the day to ring and say that she couldn't be there. But she told herself that it wasn't necessary; her grandmother knew that already. She would try to drop in at the end of the day if it wasn't too late. But for her, now at this moment, the dead had to take priority over the living. But for the first time since she had joined the CID, a small treacherous voice, whispering in self-distrust, asked her what exactly it was that her job was doing to her.

She had chosen to be a police officer deliberately, knowing that the job was right for her. But she had never, even from the first, had any illusions about it. It was a job where people when they needed you demanded that you should be there at once, unques-tionably, effectively, and when they didn't preferred to forget you existed. It was a job where you were sometimes required to work with people you'd rather not work with and show respect for senior officers for whom you felt little or none; where you could find yourself allied to men you despised and against some for whom, more often than you'd bargained for, more often than was comfortable, you felt sympathy, even pity. She knew the comfortable orthodoxies, that law and order were the norms, crime the aberration, that policing in a free society could only be done with the consent of the policed, even presumably in those areas where the police had always been seen as the enemy and had now been elevated into convenient stereotypes of oppression. But she had her own credo. You kept sane by knowing that hypocrisy might be politically necessary but that you didn't have to believe it. You kept honest; there was no point in the job otherwise. You did the job so that your male colleagues had to respect you even if it was too much to expect that they would like you. You kept your private life private, unmessy. There were men enough in the world without being trapped by propinquity into sexual entanglement with your colleagues. You didn't fall into the easy habit of obscenity; you had heard enough of that in Ellison Fairweather Buildings. You knew how far you could reasonably hope to rise and how you proposed to get there. You made no unnecessary enemies; it was hard enough for a woman to climb without getting kicked in the ankles on the way up. Every job, after all, had its disadvantages. Nurses got used to the smell of dressings and bedpans, unwashed bodies, other people's pain, the smell of death. She had made her choice. And now, more than ever, she had no regrets.

3

The hospital where Miles Kynaston held his appointment as consultant pathologist had needed a new PM room for years but facilities for the living patients had taken priority over accommodation for the dead. Kynaston grumbled but Dalgliesh suspected that he didn't really care. He had the equipment he needed and the PM room in which he worked was sparse familiar territory in which he felt as comfortably at home as he might in an old dressing gown. He had no real wish to be banished to some larger, more remote and more impersonal quarters, and his occasional complaints were no more than ritual noises made to remind the medical committee that the Forensic Pathology Department existed.

But there was, inevitably, always something of a squash. Dalgliesh and his officers were there primarily from interest rather than necessity, but the exhibits sergeant, the fingerprint officer, the scene of crime and exhibit officers with their envelopes, bottles and tubes, took up necessary room. Kynaston's secretary, a plump, middle-aged woman, cheerfully efficient as a president of the Women's Institute, sat in her twin-set and tweeds, squashed in the corner with a bulging bag at her feet. Dalgliesh always expected her to take out her knitting. Kynaston had always disliked using a tape-recorder and from time to time he turned towards her and dictated his findings in low, staccato sentences which she seemed to understand. He always worked to music, usually baroque and often a string quartet, Mozart, Vivaldi, Haydn. This afternoon's recording was one Dalgliesh immediately recognized since he, too, owned it, Neville Marriner conducting Telemann's Viola Concerto in G. Dalgliesh wondered if its enigmatic, richly melancholic tone provided Kynaston with a necessary catharsis; whether it was his way of attempting to dramatize the routine indignities of death; or whether, like house painters or others less singularly employed, he simply liked music while he worked.

Dalgliesh noted with a mixture of interest and irritation that Massingham and Kate kept their eyes fixed on Kynaston's hands with an attention which suggested that they were afraid to shift their gaze in case inadvertently they should happen to meet his eyes. He wondered how they could possibly suppose that he saw this ritual disembowelment as having anything to do with Berowne. The detachment, which had become second nature to him, was helped by the matter-of-fact efficiency with which the organs were drawn out, examined, bottled and labelled. He felt exactly as he had when, as a young probationer, he had watched his first autopsy; a surprise at the bright colours of the coils and pouches dangling in the pathologist's gloved and bloody hands, and an almost childish wonder that so small a cavity should be capable of accommodating such a large and diverse collection of organs.

Afterwards, as they scrubbed their hands in the wash-room, Kynaston from necessity, Dalgliesh from a fastidiousness which he would have found difficult to explain, he asked:

'What about the time of death?'

'No reason to alter the estimate I made at the scene. Seven o'clock would be the earliest. Say between seven and nine. I may be able to be a little more precise when the stomach contents have been analysed. There were no signs of a struggle. And if Berowne was attacked he made no attempt to protect himself. There are no cuts across the gripping aspect of his palm. Well, you saw that for yourself. The blood on his right palm came from the razor not from defensive cuts.'

Dalgliesh said:

'From the razor or from the blood on his throat?'

'That's possible. The palm was certainly more thickly coated than one might expect. Nothing complicated about the cause of death in either case. In both, it's a classical fine cut, through the thyro-hyoid ligament, severing everything from the skin to the spine. Berowne was healthy, no reason why he shouldn't have lived to a good old age if someone hadn't cut his throat for him. And Harry Mack was in better shape, medically speaking, than I expected. Liver not too good but it could have stood a few more years' abuse before it actually gave out on him. The lab will get the throat tissue under the microscope, but I don't think you'll get any joy. There is no obvious sign of a ligature at the edge of the wound. The bump on the back of Berowne's head is superficial, probably made when he fell.'

Dalgliesh said:

'Or was pulled down.'

'Or was pulled down. You'll have to wait for the lab report on the blood smear before you can go much further, Adam.'

Dalgliesh said:

'And even if that smear isn't Harry Mack's blood you still aren't prepared to say that Berowne wasn't capable of stumbling across to Harry even with those two superficial cuts in his throat.'

Kynaston said:

'I could say it was improbable. I couldn't say that it was impossible. And we're not just talking about the superficial cuts. Remember that case quoted by Simpson? The suicide practically severed his head yet remained conscious long enough to kick the ambulance man downstairs.'

'But if Berowne killed Harry why move back to the bed to finish himself off?'

'A natural association, bed, sleep, death. If he had decided to die on his bed, why should he change his mind because it was necessary to kill Harry first?'

'It wasn't necessary. I doubt whether Harry could have reached him in time to stop that final cut. It offends against common sense.'

'Or it offends against your idea of Paul Berowne.'

'Both. This was double murder, Miles.'

'I believe you, but it's going to be the devil to prove and I don't think my report will be much help. Suicide is the most private and mysterious of acts, inexplicable because the chief actor is never there to explain it.'

Dalgliesh said:

'Unless, of course, he leaves his testimony behind. If Berowne did decide to kill himself I'd have expected to find some kind of note, an attempt at explanation.'

Kynaston said enigmatically:

'The fact that you didn't find it doesn't necessarily mean that he didn't write it.'

He drew on a fresh pair of gloves and pulled his face mask over his mouth and nose. Already a new cadaver was being wheeled in. Dalgliesh looked at his watch. Massingham and Kate could drive back to the Yard and get on with the paperwork. He had another appointment. After the frustrations of the day he needed a little light relief, even a little cosseting. He proposed to extract information by more agreeable ways than a police interrogation. He had earlier that morning telephoned Conrad Ackroyd and had been invited to take a civilized afternoon tea with the owner and editor of the *Paternoster Review*.

4

Conrad and Nellie Ackroyd lived in a gleamingly neat stucco Edwardian villa in St John's Wood with a garden running down to the canal, a house reputedly built by Edward the Seventh for one of his mistresses and inherited by Nellie Ackroyd from a bachelor uncle. Ackroyd had moved into it from his city flat above the *Paternoster* office three years previously following his marriage and had happily accommodated his books, his belongings and his life to Nellie's taste for comfort and domesticity. Now, although they had a servant, he himself welcomed Dalgliesh at the door, his black eyes as brightly expectant as a child's.

'Come in, come in. We know what you're here for, dear boy. It's about my little piece in the *Review*. I'm glad you haven't felt it necessary to come in pairs. We're quite prepared to help the police with their inquiries, as you so tactfully put it, when you've caught your man and he's having his arms twisted in a little backroom, but I draw the line at giving afternoon tea to some oversized minion who wears out the springs in my sofa and eats my cucumber sandwiches with one hand while taking down everything I say with the other.'

Dalgliesh said:

'Be serious, Conrad. We're talking about murder.'

'Are we? There was a rumour – just a rumour, of course – that Paul Berowne could have made his own quietus. I'm glad it isn't true. Murder is more interesting and far less depressing. It's inconsiderate of one's friends to commit suicide; too like setting a good example. But all that can wait. Tea first.'

He called up the stairs:

'Nellie, darling, Adam is here.' Looking at him as he led the way into the drawing room, Dalgliesh thought that he never seemed a day older than when they had first met. He gave the impression of plumpness, perhaps because of his almost round face and the chubbiness of his marsupial cheeks. But he was firm fleshed, active, moving with the nimble grace of a dancer. His eyes were small and upward-slanting. When he was amused he would narrow them into twin creases of flesh. The most remarkable thing about his face was the restless mobility of his small, delicately formed mouth which he used as a moist focus of emotion. He would press it in disapproval, turn it down like a child's in disappointment or disgust, lengthen and curve it when he smiled. It seemed never still, never the same shape. Even in repose he would munch with it as if relishing the taste of his tongue.

Nellie Ackroyd, in contrast, was slim where he was plumpish, fair where he was dark, and out-topped him by three inches. She wore her long blonde hair twined in a plait round her head in the fashion of the twenties. Her tweed skirts were well cut but longer than had been fashionable for half a century and topped invariably by a loose cardigan. Her shoes were pointed and laced. Dalgliesh remembered one of his father's Sunday-school teachers who could have been her double. As she came into the room, he was for a moment back in that village church hall, sitting in a circle with the other children on the low wooden chairs and waiting for Miss Mainwaring to hand out that Sunday's stamp, a coloured biblical picture which he would lick with infinite care on that week's space on his card. He had liked Miss Mainwaring – dead now for over twenty years, of cancer, and buried in that distant Norfolk churchyard – and he liked Nellie Ackroyd.

The Ackroyds' marriage had astounded their friends and been a source of prurient speculation to their few enemies. But whenever he was with them Dalgliesh never doubted that they were genuinely happy together and he marvelled anew at the infinite variety of marriage, that relationship at once so private and public, so hedged with convention and yet so anarchical. In his private life Ackroyd was reputed to be one of the kindest men in London. His victims pointed out that he could afford to be: one issue of the *Paternoster Review* commonly contained sufficient spleen to satisfy a normal lifespan. The reviews of new books and plays were always clever and entertaining, sometimes perceptive and occasionally cruel and were a form of fortnightly entertainment cherished by all except the victims. Even when the *Times Literary Supplement* changed its practice, the *Paternoster* continued to preserve the anonymity of its reviewers. Ackroyd took the view that no reviewer, not even the most scrupulous or disinterested, could be completely honest if his copy were signed and he preserved the confidence of his contributors with all the high-minded zeal of an editor who knows that he is hardly likely to be presented with a court injunction. Dalgliesh suspected that the most vicious reviews were written by Ackroyd himself, abetted by his wife, and indulged a private picture of Conrad and Nellie sitting up in their separate beds and calling their happier inspirations through the open communicating door.

Whenever he was with them he was struck anew by the self-sufficiency amounting to conspiracy of their connubial felicity. If ever there were a marriage of convenience, this was it. She was a superb cook. He loved food. She liked nursing, and he suffered each winter from a mild recurrent bronchitis and from attacks of sinus headache which exacerbated his mild hypochondria and which kept her happily busy with chest rubs and inhalations. Dalgliesh, although the least prurient of men about the sex lives of his friends, couldn't resist wondering occasionally whether the marriage had ever been consummated. On the whole he thought that it had. Ackroyd was a stickler for legality and on one honeymoon night at least he must have closed his eyes and thought of England. After which necessary sacrifice to legal and theological requirements they had both settled down to the more important aspects of matrimony, the decoration of their house and the state of Conrad's bronchial tubes.

He hadn't come empty-handed. His hostess was a passionate collector of 1920s and 1930s girls' school stories, her series of early Angela Brazil being particularly notable. The shelves of her sitting room were witness to her addiction to this potent nostalgia; stories in which a succession of sloping-bosomed heroines, bloused and booted, called Dorothy or Madge, Marjorie or Elspeth, whacked hockey sticks with vigour, exposed the cheat in the upper fourth or were instrumental in unmasking German spies. Dalgliesh had found his first edition some months earlier in a second-hand bookshop in Marylebone. The fact that he couldn't recall precisely when or where reminded him how long it had been since he had last seen the Ackroyds. He suspected that they were most often visited by people who, like himself, wanted something, usually information. Dalgliesh reflected again on the oddness of human relationships in which people could describe themselves as friends who were content not to see each other for years, yet when they did meet could resume their intimacy as if there had been no interval of neglect. But their mutual liking was genuine enough. Dalgliesh might only call when there was something he needed, but he was never less than glad to sit in Nellie Ackroyd's elegant sitting room and gaze out through the Edwardian conservatory to the shimmer of the canal. Resting his eyes on it now, it was difficult to believe that this light-dappled water seen through hanging baskets of variegated ivy and pink geraniums was the same which, a couple of miles upstream, slid like a liquid menace through the dark tunnels and flowed sluggishly past the south door of St Matthew's Church.

He handed over his offering with the customary chaste kiss which seemed to have become a social convention even among comparatively recent acquaintances.

'For you,' he said. 'I think it's called *Dulcy on the Game*.'

Nellie Ackroyd unwrapped it with a little squeak of pleasure.

'Don't be naughty, Adam. *Dulcy Plays the Game*. How lovely! And it's in perfect condition. Where did you find it?'

'In Church Street, I think. I'm glad you haven't got it already.'

'I've been looking for it for years. This completes my pre-1930 Brazils. Conrad, darling, look what Adam has brought.'

'Very civil of you, dear boy. Ah, here comes tea.'

It was brought in by an elderly maid and set down in front of Nellie Ackroyd with almost ritual care. The tea was substantial. Thin crustless bread and butter, a plate of cucumber sandwiches, homemade scones with cream and jam, a fruitcake. It reminded him of childhood rectory teas, of visiting clergy and parish workers balancing their wide-brimmed cups in his mother's shabby but comfortable drawing room, of himself, carefully schooled, handing round plates. It was odd, he thought, that the sight of a coloured plate of thinly cut bread and butter could still evoke a momentary but sharp pain of grief and nostalgia. Watching Nellie as she carefully aligned the handles, he guessed that all their life was governed by small diurnal rituals; early morning tea, the cocoa or milk last thing at night, beds carefully turned down, nightdress and pyjamas laid out. And now it was five fifteen, the autumn day would soon be darkening into evening and this small, very English tea ceremony was designed to propitiate the afternoon furies. Order, routine, habit, imposed on a disorderly world. He wasn't sure that he would like to live with it, but as a visitor he found it soothing and he didn't despise it. He had, after all, his own contrivances for keeping reality at bay. He said:

'This piece in the *Review*. I hope you're not thinking of turning the paper into a new gossip magazine.'

'Not at all, dear boy. But people like an occasional titbit. I'm thinking of including you in our new column, "What They Find to Talk About". Incongruous people seen dining together. Adam Dalgliesh, poet-detective, with Cordelia Gray at Mon Plaisir, for example.'

'Your readers must lead very dull lives if they can find vicarious excitement in a young woman and myself virtuously eating duck à l'orange.'

'A beautiful young woman dining with a man over twenty years her senior is always interesting to our readers. It gives them hope. And you're looking very well, Adam. The new adventure obviously suits you. All right, I meant the new job, of course. Aren't you in charge of the sensitive crime squad?'

'It doesn't exist.'

'No, that's my name for it. The Met probably call it C3A or something equally boring. But we know about it. If the Prime Minister and the leader of the Social Democrats imbibe arsenic while secretly dining together to plan a coalition and the Cardinal Archbishop of Westminster and His Grace of Canterbury are seen tiptoeing mysteriously from the scene we don't want the local CID charging in to dirty the carpets with their size twelves. Isn't that rather the idea?'

'A fascinating if unlikely scenario. What about the editor of a literary review found battered to death and a senior detective observed tiptoeing from the scene? Your piece about Paul Berowne, Conrad, what started it off?'

'An anonymous communication. And you needn't assume a look of pained disgust. We all know that your people sit in pubs paying out taxpayers' money to the most sordid ex-cons for information received, most of it no doubt of highly dubious accuracy. I know all about snouts. And I didn't even have to pay for this. It came through the post, free and gratis.'

'Who else had it, do you know?'

'It went to three of the dailies, to the gossip writers. They decided to wait and see before using it.'

'Very prudent. You checked it.'

'Naturally I checked it. At least Winifred did.'

Winifred Forsythe was nominally Ackroyd's editorial assistant but there were few jobs connected with the *Review* that she couldn't turn her hand to and there were those who claimed that it was Winifred's financial nous that kept the journal afloat. She had the appearance, dress and voice of a Victorian governess, an intimidating woman who was accustomed to getting her own way. Perhaps because of some atavistic fear of female authority, few people stood up to her and when Winifred asked a question she expected to get an answer. There were times when Dalgliesh wished that he had her on his staff.

Ackroyd said:

'She began by telephoning the Campden Hill Square house and asking for Diana Travers. A woman answered, not Lady Berowne or Lady Ursula. Either a servant or housekeeper, Winifred said she didn't sound like a secretary, not authoritative enough, not that competent kind of voice. Anyway, Berowne never had a living-in secretary. It was probably the housekeeper. When she heard the question there was a silence and she gave a kind of gasp. Then she said: "Miss Travers isn't here, she's left." Winifred asked if they had an address and she said: "No" and put down the receiver rather sharply. It wasn't well handled. If they wanted to conceal the fact that Travers had worked there they should have schooled the woman more efficiently. There was no mention at the inquest that the girl had worked for Berowne and no one else seems to have caught on to it. But it looked as if our poison pen was right in at least one of his facts. Travers was certainly known at Campden Hill Square.'

Dalgliesh asked:

'And after that?'

'Winifred went down to the Black Swan. I have to admit her

cover story wasn't particularly convincing. She told them that we were thinking of doing an article on drowning accidents in the Thames. We could confidently expect that no one would have heard of the *Paternoster Review* so that the essential incongruity of it wouldn't be apparent. Even so, everyone was remarkably cagey. The proprietor – what's his name, some Frenchman? – wasn't there when Winifred called but the people she did talk to had been well rehearsed. After all, no restaurant owner wants a death on the premises. In the midst of life we are in death, but not, one hopes, in the midst of dinner. Dropping unfortunate live lobsters into boiling water is one thing – really, how can people believe that they don't feel it? – but a drowned customer on the premises is quite another. Not that the Thames exactly counts as his premises, but the general theory holds. Much too close to be comfortable. From the moment one of the party she was with came dripping in to say the girl was dead, he and his staff took up their defensive positions and I must say they seemed to have carried it off very neatly.'

Dalgliesh didn't say that he had already studied the local police reports. He asked:

'What happened exactly? Did Winifred find out?'

'The girl, Diana Travers, came with a party of five friends. I gather they were mostly theatrical people, on the fringe anyway. No one well known. They got a little noisy after dinner and went out to the riverbank where there was a certain amount of larking about. That isn't encouraged at the Black Swan, tolerated if you're a young viscount with the right connections no doubt, but this particular lot weren't rich enough, aristocratic enough, or famous enough for that kind of licence. The owner was wondering whether to send someone out to remonstrate when the party moved further downstream and more or less out of earshot.'

Dalgliesh said:

'Presumably they'd paid their bill by then.'

'Oh yes, everything settled.'

'Who paid?'

'Now this may surprise you. Dominic Swayne, Barbara Berowne's brother. It was his party. He booked the table, he paid.'

Dalgliesh said:

'The young man must have plenty of money if he could settle a bill for six at the Black Swan. Why wasn't he a member of his sister's birthday party?'

'Now that wasn't a question Winifred thought it would be productive to ask. But it did occur to her that he might have held his own party on the same night to embarrass his sister or, of course, her escort.'

It had also occurred to Dalgliesh. He recalled the police report. There had been six in the party; Diana Travers, Dominic Swayne, two female drama students whose names he couldn't recall, Anthony Baldwin, a stage designer, and Liza Galloway, who was taking a course in stage management at the City College. None had a criminal record, and it would have been a matter of mild surprise if they had. None had been investigated by the Thames Valley Police and that wasn't surprising either. There had been nothing suspicious, at least on the surface, about the Travers death. She had dived naked into the Thames and drowned with unspectacular efficiency, in twelve feet of reed-infested water on a warm summer night.

Ackroyd went on with his story:

'Apparently the party had the good sense, from the restaurant's point of view, not to carry a dead and weed-wrapped body straight through the french windows into the dining room. Luckily the side door which leads to the kitchen quarters was the one closest. The girls rushed in bleating that one of their party had drowned, while Baldwin, who seems to have behaved with more good sense than the rest of them, was trying to give the girl the "kiss of life", not very efficiently. The chef ran out and took over with rather more expertise and worked on her until the ambulance arrived. By then she was dead by any criteria. She probably had been from the moment they brought her out. But you know all this. Don't tell me that you haven't studied the inquest report.'

Dalgliesh said:

'Did Winifred ask whether Paul Berowne had been there that evening?'

'Yes, she did, with as much tact as she's capable of. Apparently he was expected. He had some business that prevented him joining the party for dinner but he said that he would try to get there in time for coffee. Just before ten there was a telephone call to say that he had been delayed and couldn't make it. The interesting thing is that he was there . . . at least his car was.'

'How did Winifred discover that?'

'Well, I must say, by a great deal of cleverness and even more good luck. You know the car park at the Black Swan presumably?'

Dalgliesh said:

'No, I've never been there. It's a pleasure to come. Tell me.'

'Well, the proprietor dislikes the sound of cars arriving and leaving and I don't blame him, so the park is about fifty yards from the restaurant and surrounded by a high beech hedge. They haven't got valet parking, presumably that would be too expensive. People just have to walk the fifty yards and if it's raining they drop their guests at the door first. So the car park is secluded and reasonably private. Even so, the doorman does keep an eye on it from time to time and it occurred to Winifred that Berowne would hardly leave his car there if he were actually telephoning to say that he couldn't arrive. After all, any of the party might have taken it into their heads to leave soon afterwards and would have recognized it. So she made some further inquiries further down the lane. There's a kind of lay-by just before you reach the A3 opposite a farm cottage lying a little back from the road. She inquired there.'

Dalgliesh asked:

'On what pretext?'

'Oh she just said that she was a private inquiry agent trying to trace a stolen car. People will answer almost anything as long as you ask with sufficient assurance. You should know that, my dear Adam.'

Dalgliesh said:

'And she struck lucky.'

'Indeed she did. A boy, he's fourteen, was doing his homework upstairs in his front bedroom in the cottage and saw a black Rover parked. Being a boy he was naturally interested. He was quite definite about the make. It was there from about ten o'clock and was still there when he went to bed.'

'Did he get the number?'

'No, that would have meant going out of the house, of course, and he wasn't sufficiently intrigued to take that kind of trouble. What interested him was that there was only one man in the car. He parked it, locked it, and walked off towards the Black Swan. It's not unusual to have cars parked there, but they're usually courting couples and they stay in the car.'

'Was he able to give a description?'

'Only a very general one, but as far as it went it corresponded more or less with Berowne. I'm satisfied myself that it was his car and that he was there. But I admit there's no proof. It was ten at night when the boy glimpsed him and there are no lights in the lane. I couldn't be certain that he was at the Black Swan when Diana Travers drowned and as you'll have noticed from my piece, I very carefully didn't say that he was.'

'Did you check it with your lawyers before you printed it?'

'Indeed I did. They weren't exactly happy but they had to admit that it wasn't libellous. After all, it was purely factual. Our gossip always is.'

And gossip, thought Dalgliesh, was like any other commodity in the marketplace. You only received it if you had something of value to give. And Ackroyd, one of London's most notorious gossips, had a reputation for accuracy and value. He collected small titbits of information as other men hoarded screws and nails. They might not be wanted for the job on hand but sooner or later they would come in useful. And he liked the sense of power which gossip gave him. Perhaps it reduced for him the vast amorphous city to manageable proportions, a few hundred people who counted in his world and who gave him the illusion of living in a private village, intimate but diverse and not unexciting. And he wasn't vicious. He liked people and he enjoyed pleasing his friends. Ackroyd crouched spider-like in his study and spun his web of mild intrigue. It was important to him that at least one thread connected him to a senior police officer as others, rather stronger, did to the parliamentary lobby, the theatre, Harley Street, the Bar. Almost certainly he would have tapped his sources, ready to offer Dalgliesh a small bonus of information. Dalgliesh thought it was time he fished for it. He said:

'What do you know of Stephen Lampart?'

'Not a great deal, since nature has mercifully spared me the experience of childbirth. Two dear friends had their babies at his place in Hampstead, Pembroke Lodge. Everything went very well; an heir to a dukedom and a future merchant banker, both safely delivered and both boys, which, after a succession of girls, was what was wanted. He's reputedly a good gynaecologist.'

'What about women?'

'Dear Adam, how prurient you are. Being a gynaecologist must present particular temptations. Women after all are so ready to show their gratitude in the only way some of the poor dears know. But he protects himself, and not only where his sex life is concerned. There was a libel case eight years ago. You may remember it. A journalist, Mickey Case, was so ill-advised as to suggest that Lampart had carried out an illegal abortion at Pembroke Lodge. Things were a little less liberal in those days. Lampart sued and got exemplary damages. It ruined Mickey. There's not been a hint of scandal since. There's nothing like a reputation for being litigious to save you from slander. It is occasionally rumoured that he and Barbara Berowne are rather more than cousins but I don't think anyone has actual proof. They've been remarkably discreet, and Barbara Berowne, of course, played the part of the MP's adoring and beautiful wife to perfection when called upon to do so, which wasn't very often. Berowne was never a social chap. A small dinner party occasionally, the usual mild constituency beanfeasts, fund raising and so on. But otherwise, she wasn't required to exhibit herself in that particular role inconveniently often. The odd thing about Lampart is that he spends his life delivering babies but he dislikes children intensely. But then I rather agree with him. Up to four weeks they're quite enchanting. After that all one can say in favour of children is that they eventually grow up. He took his own precautions against procreation. He's had a vasectomy.'

'How on earth did you get to know that, Conrad?'

'My dear boy, it isn't a secret. People used to boast about it. When he first had it done he used to wear one of those revolting ties advertising the fact. A little vulgar, I admit, but then there is a streak of vulgarity in Lampart. He keeps it under better control now, the vulgarity I mean. The tie is folded away in a drawer along, no doubt, with other mementos from his past.'

And this indeed was a bonus, thought Dalgliesh If Barbara Berowne were pregnant and Lampart wasn't the father, then who was? If it were Berowne himself and he had known of the fact, would he have been more or less likely to have killed himself? A jury would probably think less likely. To Dalgliesh, who had never believed the suicide theory, this wasn't particularly relevant. But it would be highly relevant to the prosecution if he caught his man and the case came to trial.

Ackroyd said:

'How did you get on with the formidable Lady Ursula? Had you met her before?'

'No. In my life, I don't often meet the daughter of an earl. Until now I haven't met one in my job either. What should I think of her? You tell me.'

'What everyone wants to know about her – everyone of her generation, anyway – is why she married Sir Henry. Now I happen to know the answer. I've thought it out all on my own. You may think my theory is obvious but it's none the worse for that. It explains why so many beautiful women choose such ordinary men. It's because a beautiful woman – and I'm talking about beauty, not just prettiness – is so ambivalent about her beauty. With part of her mind she knows it's the most important thing about her. Well, of course, it is. But with another part she distrusts it. After all, she knows how transitory it is. She has to watch it fading. She wants to be loved for some other quality, usually one she doesn't possess. So when Lady Ursula got tired of all the importunate young men badgering and praising her she chose dear old Henry who had loved her devotedly for years, would obviously continue to love her until he died, and seemed not to notice that he'd got himself the most admired beauty in England. Apparently it worked out very well. She gave him two sons and was faithful to him, well, more or less. And now, poor dear, she's left with nothing. Her father's title became extinct when her only brother was killed in 1917. And now this. Unless, of course, Barbara Berowne is pregnant with an heir which, on the face of it, seems unlikely.'

Dalgliesh asked:

'Isn't that the least important part of the tragedy, the extinction of the baronetcy?'

'Not necessarily. A title, particularly an old one, confers a comforting sense of family continuity, almost a kind of personal immortality. Lose it and you really begin to understand that all flesh is grass. I'll give you a word of advice, my dear Adam. Never underestimate Lady Ursula Berowne.'

Dalgliesh said:

'I'm in no danger of that. Did you ever meet Paul Berowne?'

'Never. I knew his brother, but not well. We met when he was first engaged to Barbara Swayne. Hugo was an anachronism, more like a First World War hero than a modern soldier. You half-expected to see him slapping his cane against khaki breeches, carrying a sword. You expect his kind to get killed. They're born for it. If they didn't, what on earth would they do with themselves in old age? He was very much the favourite son, of course. He was the kind of man his mother understood, was brought up with, that mixture of physical beauty, recklessness and charm. I began to get interested in Paul Berowne when we decided to do that short feature, but I admit that most of my information about him is second hand. Part of Paul Berowne's private tragedy, admittedly a small one viewed sub specie aeternitatis, was neatly summed up by Jane Austen. "His temper might, perhaps, be a little soured by finding, like many others of his sex, that through some unaccountable bias in favour of beauty he was the husband of a very silly woman." *Pride and Prejudice*, Mr Bennet.'

'*Sense and Sensibility*, Mr Palmer. And when one meets Barbara Berowne the bias doesn't seem so very unaccountable.'

'*Sense and Sensibility*? Are you sure? Anyway, I'm glad that I'm immune to that particular enthralment and the urge for possession that seems inseparable from it. Beauty suborns the critical faculty. God knows what Berowne thought he was getting, apart from a load of guilt. Probably the Holy Grail.'

All in all, thought Dalgliesh, the visit to St John's Wood had been even more fruitful than he had hoped. He took his time over finishing his tea. He owed his hostess at least the appearance of a decent civility and he had no particular wish to hurry away.

Soothed by Nellie Ackroyd's solicitous attention, comfortably ensconced in a gently rocking button-backed armchair whose arms and headrest seemed precisely designed to suit his body, and with his eyes soothed by the distant sheen of the canal seen through the light-filled conservatory, he had to make an effort to rouse himself to make his farewells and set off to drive back to the Yard, pick up Kate Miskin and take her with him to interview Berowne's only child.

5

Melvin Johns hadn't intended to make love. He had met Tracy at their usual place, the gate leading to the towpath, and they had walked together, her arm tucked under his, her thin body hugging against him until they came to their secret place, the patch of flattened grass behind the thick elderberries, the straight, dead stump of tree. And it had happened, as he knew it would. The brief, unsatisfactory spasm and what went before were no different than they had always been. The potent smell of loam and dead leaves, the soft earth under his feet, her eager body straining under his, the smell of her armpits, her fingers scratching at his scalp, the scrape of the bark of the tree against his cheek, the gleam of the canal seen through a thicket of leaves. All over. But afterwards the depression that always followed was worse than he had ever known. He wanted to sink into the earth and groan aloud. She whispered:

'Darling, we have to go to the police. We must tell them what we saw.'

'It wasn't anything. Just a car parked outside the church.'

'Outside the vestry door. Outside where it happened. The same night. And we know the time, about seven o'clock. It could be the murderer's car.'

'It isn't likely he'd be driving a black Rover, and it isn't as if we noticed the number, even.'

'But we have to tell. If they never find who did it, if he kills again, we'd never forgive ourselves.'

The note of unctuous self-righteousness nauseated him. How was it, he wondered, that he'd never noticed before that perpetual whine in her voice. He said hopelessly:

'You said your dad would kill us if he knew we'd been meeting. The lies, telling him you were at evening classes. You said he'd kill us.'

'But, darling, it's different now. He'll understand that. And we can get engaged. We'll tell them all that we were engaged.'

Of course, he thought, suddenly enlightened. Dad, that respectable lay preacher, wouldn't mind as long as there was no scandal. Dad would enjoy the publicity, the sense of importance. They would have to marry. Dad, Mum, Tracy herself, would ensure that. It was as if his life was suddenly revealed to him in a slow unwinding reel of hopelessness, picture succeeding picture down the inescapable years. Moving into her parents' small house; where else could they afford to live? Waiting for a council flat. The first baby crying in the night. Her whining, accusing voice. The slow death, even of desire. A man was dead, an ex-minister, a man he had never known, never seen, whose life and his had never until this moment touched. Someone, his murderer or an innocent motorist, had parked his Rover outside the church. The police would catch the killer, if there was a killer, and he would go to prison for life and in ten years he would be let out, free again. But he was only 21 and his life sentence would end only with his death. And what had he done to deserve his punishment? Such a little sin compared with murder. He almost groaned aloud with the injustice of it.

'All right,' he said with dull resignation. 'We'll go to the Harrow Road police station. We'll tell them about the car.'

6

Sarah Berowne's flat was in a gaunt Victorian terrace of five-storey houses whose over-ornate and grimy façade was set back some thirty feet from the Cromwell Road behind a hedge of dusty laurel and spiky, almost leafless privet. Next to the entry-phone was a bank of nine bells, the top one bearing only the single word 'Berowne'. The door opened to their push as soon as they rang and Dalgliesh and Kate passed through a vestibule into a narrow hall, the floor linoleum-covered, the walls painted the ubiquitous glossy cream, the only furniture a table for letters.

The caged box of a lift was only large enough for two passengers. Its back wall was almost completely mirrored, but as it groaned slowly upwards, the image of their two figures standing so close that he could smell the clean sweet scent of her hair, could almost imagine that he could hear her heart beat, did nothing to dispel his incipient claustrophobia. They stopped with a jerk. As they stepped out into the corridor and Kate turned to close the lift grille he saw that Sarah Berowne was standing waiting for them at her open door.

The family resemblance was almost uncanny. She stood framed against the light from her flat like a frail feminine shadow of her father. Here were the same wide spaced grey eyes, the same droop of the eyelid, the same finely boned distinction but devoid of the patina of masculine confidence and success. The fair hair, not layered in gold like Barbara Berowne's but darker, almost ginger, already showed its first grey and hung in dry lifeless strands framing the tapering Berowne face. She was, he knew, only in her early twenties but she looked much older, the honey-coloured skin drained with weariness. She didn't even bother to glance at his warrant card and he wondered whether she didn't care or was making a small gesture of contempt. She gave only a nod of acknowledgement as he introduced Kate, then stood aside and motioned them across the hall into the sitting room. A familiar figure rose to meet them and they found themselves facing Ivor Garrod.

Sarah Berowne introduced them but didn't explain his presence. But then there was no reason why she should; this was her flat, she could invite in whom she wished. It was Kate and he who were the interlopers, there at best by invitation or on sufferance, tolerated, seldom welcome.

After the dimness of the hall and the claustrophobic lift they had walked into emptiness and light. The flat was a conversion from the mansard roof, the low sitting room running almost the whole length of the house, its northern wall composed entirely of glass with sliding doors opening on to a narrow balustraded balcony. There was a door at the far end, presumably leading to the kitchen. The bedroom and bathroom would, he assumed, open from the entrance-hall at the front of the house. Dalgliesh had developed a knack of taking in the salient features of a room without that preliminary frank appraisal which he himself would have found offensive from any stranger, let alone a policeman. It was odd, he sometimes thought, that a man morbidly sensitive about his own privacy should have chosen a job that required him to invade almost daily the privacy of others. But people's living-space, and the personal possessions with which they surrounded themselves, were inevitably fascinating to a detective, an affirmation of identity, intriguing both in themselves and as a betrayal of character, interests, obsessions.

This room was obviously both her living room and her studio. It was sparsely but comfortably furnished. Two large and battered sofas sat against opposite walls with shelves over them for books, stereo and a drinks cupboard. Before the window there was a small round table with four dining chairs. The wall facing the window was covered with a cork board on which was pinned a collection of photographs. To the right were pictures of London and Londoners obviously designed to make a political point; couples over-dressed for a Palace garden party drifting across the grass of St James's Park against the background of the bandstand; a group of blacks in Brixton staring resentfully into the lens; the Queen's Scholars of Westminster School filing decorously into the Abbey; an over-crowded Victorian playground with a thin wistful-eyed child grasping the railings like an imprisoned waif; a woman with a face like a fox choosing a fur in Harrods; a couple of pensioners, gnarled hands curled in their laps sitting stiff as Staffordshire figures one each side of their single-bar electric fire. The political message was, he thought, too facile to carry much weight but, as far as he was capable of judging, the pictures were technically clever; they were certainly well composed. The left of the board displayed what had probably been a more lucrative commission: a line of portraits of well-known writers. Some of the photographer's concern with social deprivation seemed to have infected even her work here. The men, unshaven, fashionably under-dressed in their tieless open-necked shirts, looked as if they had either just taken part in a literary discussion on Channel Four, or were on their way to a 1930s labour exchange, while the women looked either haunted or defensive, except for a buxom grandmother noted for her detective stories, who gazed mournfully at the camera as if deploring either the bloodiness of her craft or the size of her advance.

Sarah Berowne motioned them to the sofa at the right of the door and seated herself on the one opposite. It was hardly, thought Dalgliesh, a convenient arrangement for other than shouted conversation. Garrod perched himself on the arm of the sofa further from her as if deliberately distancing himself from all three of them. In the last year he had, it seemed deliberately, moved out of the political limelight and was now less often heard propounding the views of the Workers' Revolutionary Campaign, concentrating apparently, on his job as a community social worker, whatever that might mean. But he was immediately recognizable, a man who even in repose held himself as if well aware of the power of his physical presence but with that power under conscious control. He was wearing denim jeans with a white open-necked shirt and contrived to look both casual and elegant. He could, thought Dalgliesh, have stepped down from a portrait in the Uffizi with his long arrogant Florentine face, the generously curved mouth under the short upper lip, the high arched nose and tumble of dark hair, the eyes which gave nothing away. He said:

'Would you like something to drink? Wine, whisky or coffee?'

His tone was almost studiously polite, but neither sardonic nor provocatively obsequious. Dalgliesh knew his opinion of the Metropolitan Police; he had proclaimed it often enough. But he was playing this very carefully. They were all to be on the same side, at least for the present. Dalgliesh and Kate refused his offer of a drink and there was a small silence broken by Sarah Berowne. She said:

'You're here about my father's death, of course. I don't think there's very much I can say to help. I haven't seen or spoken to him for over three months.'

Dalgliesh said:

'But you were at 62 Campden Hill Square on Tuesday afternoon.'

'Yes, to see my grandmother. I had an hour to spare between appointments and I wanted to try to find out what was happening, my father's resignation, the rumour about his experience in that church. There was no one else to ask, to talk to. But she was out to tea. I didn't wait. I left at about four thirty.'

'Did you go into the study?'

'The study?'

She looked surprised, then asked:

'I suppose you're thinking of his diary. Grandmama told me that you'd found it half-burned in the church. I was in the study but I didn't see it.'

Dalgliesh said:

'But you knew where he kept it?'

'Of course. In the desk drawer. We all knew that. Why do you ask?'

Dalgliesh said:

'Just in the hope that you might have seen it. It would have been useful to know if the diary was there at four thirty. We can't trace your father's movements after he left the office of an estate agent in Kensington High Street at half past eleven. If you had happened to look in the drawer and seen the diary then there is the possibility that he came back to the house unnoticed sometime during the afternoon.'

That was only one possibility and Dalgliesh didn't deceive himself that Garrod, for one, was ignorant of the others. Now he said:

'We don't even know what happened except what Sarah has learned from her grandmother, that Sir Paul and the tramp had their throats cut and that it looks as if his razor was the weapon. We were hoping you would be able to tell us more. Are you suggesting that it was murder?'

Dalgliesh said:

'Oh, I don't think there can be any doubt that this was murder.'

He watched as the two bodies opposite seemed visibly to stiffen, then added calmly:

'The tramp, Harry Mack, certainly didn't slit his own throat. His death may not be of shattering social significance but no doubt his life had some importance, at least to him.'

He thought: If that doesn't provoke Garrod then I wonder what would. But Garrod merely said:

'If you're asking us to provide an alibi for Harry Mack's murder, then we were here together from six o'clock on Tuesday until nine o'clock Wednesday morning. We had supper here. I bought a mushroom flan from Marks and Spencer's in Kensington High Street and we ate that. I could tell you what wine we drank with it but I don't suppose that's relevant.'

It was the first sign of irritation but his voice was still mild, the gaze clear and unflustered. Sarah Berowne said:

'But Daddy! What happened to Daddy?'

Suddenly she sounded as frightened and helpless as a lost child. Dalgliesh said:

'We're treating it as a suspicious death. We can't say much more until we get the result of the post-mortem and the forensic tests.'

Suddenly she got up and moved over to the window staring out over the thirty yards of dishevelled autumnal garden. Garrod slid down from the arm of the sofa and went to the drinks cupboard, then poured a couple of glasses of red wine. He took one over to her and offered it silently, but she shook her head. He moved back to the sofa and sat holding his own glass, not drinking. He said:

'Look, Commander, this isn't exactly a visit of condolence, is it? And although it's reassuring to hear of your concern for Harry Mack, you're not here because of a dead tramp. If Harry's body had been the only one in that church vestry it would have ranked a detective sergeant at best. I would have thought Miss Berowne had a right to know whether she's being questioned in a murder investigation or whether you're just curious to know why Paul Berowne should have slit his own throat. I mean, either he did or he didn't. Criminal investigation is your job, not mine, but I should have thought that, by now, it ought to be pretty clear cut one way or the other.'

Dalgliesh wondered whether the dreadful pun had been intentional. Either way, Garrod saw no reason to apologize for it. Watching that still figure by the window Dalgliesh saw Sarah Berowne give a little shudder. Then, as if by an act of will, she turned from the window and faced him. He ignored Garrod and spoke directly to her.

'I should like to be more positive but, at the moment, that just isn't possible. Suicide is obviously one possibility. I was hoping that you might have seen your father recently and been able to say how he seemed to you, whether he said anything that could be relevant to his death. I know this is painful for you. I'm sorry that we have to ask these questions, that we have to be here.'

She said:

'He did speak to me once about suicide, but not in the way you mean.'

'Recently, Miss Berowne?'

'Oh no, we haven't spoken for years. Not really spoken, really talked to each other as opposed to making sounds with our mouths. No, this was when I was home from Cambridge after my first term. One of my friends had killed himself and my father and I talked about his death, about suicide generally. I've always remembered it. He said that some people thought of suicide as one of the options open to them. It wasn't. It was the end of all options. He quoted Schopenhauer: "Suicide may be regarded as an experiment, a question which man puts to nature trying to force her to an answer. It is a clumsy experiment to make; for it involves the destruction of the very consciousness which puts the question and awaits the answer." Daddy said that while we live there is always the possibility, the certainty of change. The only rational time for a man to kill himself is not when life is intolerable but when he would prefer not to live it even if it became tolerable, even pleasant.'

Dalgliesh said:

'That sounds like the ultimate despair.'

'Yes. I suppose that's what he could have felt, ultimate despair.'

Suddenly Garrod spoke. He said:

'He could more reasonably have quoted Nietzsche. "The thought of suicide is a great consolation: by means of it one gets successfully through many a bad night."'

Ignoring him, Dalgliesh still spoke directly to Sarah Berowne. He said:

'So your father didn't see you or write to you? He didn't explain what had happened in that church, why he was giving up his job, his parliamentary seat?'

433

He almost expected her to say: 'What has that to do with this inquiry and what has it to do with you?' Instead she said:

'Oh no! I don't suppose he thought that I cared one way or the other. I only learned about it when his wife telephoned me. That was when he gave up his ministerial job. She seemed to think I might have some influence over him. It showed how little she understood either of us. If she hadn't telephoned, I should have had to learn about his resignation from the newspapers.' Then she suddenly broke out:

'My God! He couldn't even get converted like an ordinary man. He had to be granted his own personal beatific vision. He couldn't even resign his job with decent reticence.'

Dalgliesh said mildly:

'He seems to have acted with considerable reticence. He obviously felt that it was a private experience to be acted upon rather than discussed.'

'Well, he could hardly splash it on the front pages of the Sunday heavies. Perhaps he realized that he'd only make himself ridiculous. Himself and the family.'

Dalgliesh asked:

'Would that have mattered?'

'Not to me, but Grandmama would have minded – will mind now, I suppose. And his wife, of course. She thought she was marrying the next prime minister but one. She wouldn't relish being tied to a religious crank. Well, she's free of him now. And he's free of us, all of us.'

She was silent for a moment, then said with sudden vehemence:

'I'm not going to pretend. Anyway you know perfectly well that my father and I were, well, estranged. There's no secret about it. I didn't like his politics, I didn't like the way he treated my mother, I didn't like the way he treated me. I'm a Marxist, there's no secret about that either. Your people will have me on one of their little lists somewhere. And I care about my political beliefs. I don't believe he really did. He expected me to discuss politics as if we were chatting about a recent play we'd both seen, or a book we'd read, as if it were an intellectual diversion, something you could have what he would call a civilized argument about. He said that was one of the things he deplored about the loss of religion, it meant that people elevated politics into a religious faith and that was dangerous. Well that's what politics are for me, a faith.'

Dalgliesh said:

'Feeling as you do about him, his bequest to you must present you with a dilemma of conscience.'

'Is that your tactful way of asking me if I killed my father for his money?'

'No, Miss Berowne. It's a not particularly tactful way of finding out what you feel about a not uncommon moral dilemma.'

'I feel fine, just fine. There's no dilemma as far as I'm concerned. Anything I get will be put to good use for a change. It won't be much. Twenty thousand, isn't it? It's going to need more than twenty thousand pounds to change this world.'

Suddenly she went back to the sofa, sat down, and they saw that she was crying. She said:

'I'm sorry, I'm sorry. This is ridiculous. It's only shock. And tiredness. I didn't sleep much last night. And I've had a busy day, things I couldn't cancel. Why should I cancel them, anyway? There's nothing I can do for him.'

The phenomenon wasn't new to him. Other people's tears, other people's grief were inseparable from a murder inquiry. He had learned not to show surprise or embarrassment. The response varied, of course. A cup of hot, sweet tea if there was someone around to make it, a glass of sherry if the bottle was to hand, a slug of whisky. He had never been good at the comforting hand on the shoulder, and here, he knew, it wouldn't be welcome. He felt Kate stiffen at his side as if to make an instinctive move towards the girl. Then she looked at Garrod, but Garrod didn't move. They waited silently. The sobbing was quickly checked and Sarah Berowne again raised her face to them. She said:

'I'm sorry, I'm sorry. Please don't mind me. I'll be all right in a minute.'

Garrod said:

'I don't think there's anything else we can usefully tell you but if there is, perhaps it could wait until another time. Miss Berowne is upset.'

Dalgliesh said:

'I can see that. If she wants us to go, of course we shall.'

She looked up and said to Garrod:

'You go. I'm all right. You've said what you came to say. You were here with me on Tuesday night, all night. We were together. And there's nothing you can say about my father. You never knew him. So why don't you go?'

Dalgliesh was surprised by the sudden venom in her voice. Garrod could have hardly welcomed this curt dismissal, but he was too controlled and too astute to protest. He looked at her with what seemed detached interest rather than resentment and said:

'If you need me, just ring.'

Dalgliesh waited until he was at the door then said quietly:

'One moment. Diana Travers and Theresa Nolan. What do you know about them?'

Garrod was motionless for a second then swung slowly round. He said:

'Only that they're both dead. I do occasionally see the *Paternoster Review*.'

Dalgliesh said:

'The recent article about Sir Paul in the *Review* was partly based on a scurrilous communication sent to him and to a number of papers. This communication.'

He took it from his briefcase and handed it to Garrod. There was a silence while he read it. Then, his face devoid of expression, he handed it to Sarah Berowne. He said:

'You aren't, surely, suggesting that Berowne cut his throat because someone sent him an unkind letter? Wouldn't that be a little over-sensitive for a politician? And he was a barrister. If he thought it was actionable, he had his remedy.'

Dalgliesh said:

'I'm not suggesting that it provides a motive for suicide. I was wondering whether you or Miss Berowne had any idea who could have sent it?'

The girl handed it back, merely shaking her head. But Dalgliesh saw that its production had been unwelcome. She was neither a good actress nor a good liar. Garrod said:

'I admit that I took it for granted that the child Theresa Nolan aborted was Berowne's, but I didn't feel called upon to do anything about it. If I had, I'd have done something more effective than this farrago of unsubstantiated spite. I only met the girl once, at an unfortunate dinner party at Campden Hill Square. Lady Ursula was convalescent; it was her first night down. The poor girl certainly didn't look happy. But then, Lady Ursula was brought up to know what room people are entitled to dine in, and, of course, their proper placement at table. Nurse Nolan, poor child, was eating out of her station and was made to feel it.'

Sarah Berowne said softly:

'Not intentionally.'

'Oh, I didn't say it was intentional. Women like your grandmother are offensive merely by existing. Intention doesn't come into it.'

Then without touching Sarah Berowne, without even a glance at her, he said his goodbyes to Kate and Dalgliesh as formally as if they had been fellow guests at a dinner party, and the door closed behind him. The girl tried to control herself, then broke into open sobbing. Kate got up, went through the opposite door and after what seemed to Dalgliesh an unnecessarily long time, came back with a glass of water, then sat down beside Sarah Berowne and silently offered it. The girl drank it thirstily, then said:

'Thank you. This is silly. It's just that I can't believe he's dead, that I'll never see him again. I suppose I always thought that sometime, somehow, things would be right between us. I suppose I thought that there was plenty of time. All the time in the world. They've all gone now, Mummy, Daddy, Uncle Hugo. Oh God, I feel so hopeless.'

There were things that he would have liked to have asked but now wasn't the time. They waited until she was calm again and then asked if she was sure she was all right before they left. The question struck him as insincere, a formal hypocrisy. She was as right as she would ever be when they were there.

As they drove away Kate was for a time silent, then she said:

'It's an all-electric kitchen, sir. There's one wrapped packet of four boxes of Bryant and May matches in the cupboard, that's all. But that doesn't prove anything. They could have bought a single box and chucked it away afterwards.'

Dalgliesh thought: She was fetching the glass of water showing genuine sympathy, genuine concern. But her mind was still on the evidence. And some of my officers think women are more sentimental than men. He said:

'We shan't get much joy trying to trace a single box of matches. A safety match is the easiest thing to lay hands on, the most difficult to identify.'

'There's another thing, though, sir. I looked in the waste bin. I found the cardboard packet from the Marks and Spencer mushroom flan. They ate it all right, but it was two days past its last marked date of sale on Tuesday. He couldn't have bought it then. Since when have Marks and Spencer sold stale food? I wasn't sure whether you'd want the package or not.'

Dalgliesh said:

'We haven't yet a right to take anything out of that flat. It's too early. You could argue that it's a clue in their favour. If they'd planned this crime I suspect Garrod would have bought the food on Tuesday morning and have made sure that the girl at the desk remembered him. And there's another thing, they've produced an alibi for the whole night. That suggests that they may not know the relevant time.'

'But isn't Garrod too clever to fall into that trap?'

'Oh, he wouldn't produce an alibi neatly timed for eight o'clock, but the somewhat over-generous one he has produced to cover every hour from six to nine the next morning does suggest that he's playing safe.'

And like the other alibis it wouldn't be an easy one to break. They had briefed themselves before this visit as they did before every interview. They knew that Garrod lived alone in a single-bedroom mansion flat in Bloomsbury, a large, anonymous block, without a porter. If he claimed to have spent the night elsewhere it was difficult to see who could prove otherwise. Like everyone else concerned with the case whom they had interviewed to date, Sarah Berowne and her lover had produced an alibi. The police might not consider it a particularly convincing one, but Dalgliesh had too high an opinion of Garrod's intelligence to suppose that it could be easily broken and certainly not by a date stamp on the carton of a mushroom flan.

Back at the Yard, Dalgliesh had hardly entered his office before Massingham came in. He prided himself on his ability to control his excitement and his voice was carefully nonchalant.

'Harrow Road have just been on the phone, sir. There's an interesting development. A couple walked into the station ten minutes ago, a 21-year-old and his girl. They say they were on the towpath on Tuesday evening, courting apparently. They passed through the turnstile by St Matthew's just before seven There was a large black Rover parked outside the south door.'

'Did they get the number?'

'No such luck. They can't even be sure of the make. But they are definite about the time. The girl was expected home by seven thirty and they looked at their watches just before leaving the towpath. And the boy, Melvin Johns, thinks that it could have been an A registration. Harrow Road think he's telling the truth. The poor kid seems petrified. He's certainly not a nutcase looking for publicity. They've asked the couple to wait until I get over.' He added:

'That parking lot by the church could be useful for anyone who knew it. But the local people obviously prefer to park their cars where they can keep an eye on them. And it isn't as if the area has a theatre, fashionable restaurants. For my money, there's only one black Rover one might expect to see parked outside that church.'

Dalgliesh said:

'That's premature, John. It was dusk, they were in a hurry. They can't even be sure of the make.'

'You're depressing me, sir. I'd better get over there. It'll be just my luck to discover it was the local undertaker's hearse!'

7

She knew that Ivor would come back that night. He wouldn't telephone first, partly out of excessive caution, partly because he always expected her to be there waiting when she knew he was likely to arrive. For the first time since they had become lovers she found herself dreading his signal, the one long ring of the entry-phone followed by the three short. Why couldn't he tele-phone, she thought resentfully, let her know when to expect him? She tried to settle to work on her newest project, the montage of two black-and-white photographs taken last winter in Richmond Park of the naked boughs of huge oak trees under a sky of tumbling clouds, and which she now planned to mount, one reversed under the other, so that the tangled boughs looked like roots reflected in water. But it seemed to her as she shifted the prints with increasing dissatisfaction that the device was meaningless, a cheap derivative effect; that this, like all her work, was symbolic of her life, thin, insubstantial, second-hand, pilfered from other people's experience, other people's ideas. Even the London pictures, cleverly composed, were without conviction, stereotypes seen through Ivor's eyes not her own. She thought: I must learn to be my own person, however late, however much it hurts, I have to do it. And it seemed to her strange that it should have taken her father's death to show her what she was.

At eight o'clock she was aware of hunger and cooked herself scrambled eggs, stirring them carefully over the low burner, taking as much trouble as if Ivor had been there to share them. If he did arrive while she was eating he could cook his own. She washed up and he still hadn't arrived. Walking out to the balcony she gazed over the garden to the darkening bulk of the opposite terrace whose windows were beginning to light up like signals from space. Those unknown people would be able to see her window too, the huge expanse of lighted glass. Would the police call on them, ask them whether they had seen a light here on Tuesday night? Had Ivor, for all his cleverness, thought of that?

Gazing out over the darkness she made herself think of her father. She could recall the precise moment at which things had changed between them. They had been living then in the Chelsea house, just her parents, herself and Mattie. It had been seven o'clock on a misty August morning and she had been alone in the dining room, pouring her first cup of coffee, when the call came. She had answered the telephone from the hall and had been given the news just as her father came down the stairs. He had seen her face, stopped, his hand on the banister and she had looked up at him.

'It's Uncle Hugo's Colonel. He wanted to ring himself. Daddy, Hugo's dead.' And then their eyes had met, had for a moment held, and she had seen it clearly; the mixture of exultation and wild hope, the knowledge that now he could have Barbara. It had lasted only a second. Time had moved on. And then he had taken the receiver from her and, without speaking, she had walked back into the dining room, through the french windows and into the enclosing greenness of the garden shaking with the horror of it.

Nothing afterwards could ever be right between them. Everything that followed, the car accident, her mother's death, his marriage to Barbara less than five months later, had seemed only the inevitable consequence of that moment of realization, not willed by him, not even connived at, but accepted as inescapable. And even before the marriage the enormity of that mutual knowledge made it impossible for them to meet each other's eyes. He was ashamed that she knew. She was ashamed of knowing. And it seemed to her that when they moved into Hugo's house, the house which from their first moment of possession had seemed to resent and reject them, she carried her knowledge like a secret infection, that if Halliwell, Mattie, her grandmother knew, they had caught the knowledge from her.

At Campden Hill Square she and her father had been like fellow guests at a hotel who had met by chance, aware of a shared and shameful history, creeping down the passages in case the other should suddenly appear, planning to take meals at different times, harassed by the knowledge of the other's presence, the footstep in the hall, the key in the door. Ivor had been her escape and her revenge. She had been desperate for a cause, for an excuse to distance herself from her family, for love; but most of all for revenge. Ivor, whom she had met when he had commissioned a series of photographs, had provided them all. Before her father's marriage to Barbara she had moved out, borrowing against her modest legacy from her mother's will to put down a deposit on the Cromwell Road flat. She had tried, by embracing with passion everything he most disliked or despised, to free herself of her father. But now he was gone and she would never be free of him, never again.

One of the dining chairs was still pulled out from the table. Here, only yesterday, her grandmother had painfully seated herself and told her the news in brutal monosyllables, the taximeter ticking away outside. She had said:

'No one expects you to show much grief but try, when the police arrive, as they will, to behave with reasonable discretion. If you have any influence over him, persuade your lover to do the same. And now perhaps you could help me with the lift door.'

She had always been a little afraid of her grandmother, knowing from childhood that she was a disappointment, that she should have been a son. And she had none of the qualities her grandmother admired; beauty, intelligence, wit, not even courage. There was no comfort for her in that cluttered top-floor sitting room at Campden Hill Square where the old lady had sat since Hugo's death like some archaic prophetess awaiting the inevitable doom. It was her father who had always come first with her, in her childhood and afterwards. It was her father who had been the more supportive when she had left Cambridge at the end of her first year and had gone to a London polytechnic to study photography. How much had she really cared about her mother's anguish when the infatuation with Barbara became obvious? Wasn't it just that she had hated the threat to her comfortable, ordered, conventional life, resented the fact that, entranced, her father no longer seemed even to notice her? Perhaps, she thought, the belated acknowledgement of that old jealousy was one small step towards becoming her own person.

It was after eleven before he arrived, and she was very tired. He made no excuses and wasted no time on preliminaries. Throwing himself down on the sofa, he said:

'It wasn't very clever, was it? The idea of my being here was to have a witness. You let yourself be left alone with probably the most dangerous detective of the Yard and a female sidekick brought along to reassure you that he wasn't going to stop behaving like a gentleman.'

She said:

'Don't worry. I didn't reveal the Boy Scout password. And they're human, I suppose. Inspector Miskin was rather kind.'

'Don't be ridiculous. The girl's a fascist.'

'Ivor, how can you say that? How can you know?'

'I make it my business to know. I suppose she held your hand, made you a nice cup of tea.'

'She fetched me a drink of water.'

'Which gave her an excuse to ferret around in the kitchen without the trouble of getting a search warrant.'

She cried:

'It wasn't like that! She wasn't like that!'

'You haven't an idea what any of the police are like. The trouble with you middle-class liberals is that you're conditioned to see them as allies. You never accept the truth about them. You can't. To you they're always the avuncular Sergeant Dixon tugging his forelock and telling the kids the time. It's what you're brought up on. "If you're ever in difficulty, darling, if a nasty man approaches you and wiggles his johnny at you, always find a policeman." Look, Dalgliesh knows your politics, he knows about the legacy, he knows you've got a lover who's a committed Marxist and who might like to get his hands on the cash for the best or worst of reasons. So he's got a motive and a suspect, a very satisfactory suspect from his point of view, just what the Establishment are hoping for. Then he can get down to the business of fabricating the evidence.'

'You don't really believe that.'

'For Christ's sake, Sarah, there are precedents. You can't have lived for over twenty years with your eyes shut. Your grandmother prefers to believe that her son wasn't a murderer or a suicide. Fair enough. She may even persuade the police to play along with her fantasy. She's nearly in her dotage but these old women still have extraordinary influence. But she's not making me the sacrificial victim to Berowne family pride. There's only one way to treat the police. Tell them nothing, nothing. Let the bastards find out the hard way. Make them do some work for their index-linked pensions.'

She said:

'I suppose if it really comes to it you'll let me tell them where I was Tuesday night?'

443

'If it comes to what? What are you talking about?'

'If they actually arrest me.'

'For cutting your father's throat? Is it likely? Come to think of it, a woman could have done it. Given a razor it wouldn't need much strength, only immense nerve. But it would have to be a woman he trusted, one who could get close to him. That could explain why there wasn't a struggle.'

She said:

'How do you know that there wasn't a struggle, Ivor?'

'If there had been, the press and the police would have said so. It would have been one of the strongest indications that it wasn't suicide. You must have read the sort of thing they print: "Sir Paul put up a desperate struggle for life. There were considerable signs of disorder in the room." Your father killed himself, but that doesn't mean that the police won't use his death to make nuisances of themselves.'

She said:

'Suppose I decide to tell?'

'Tell what? Give them the code names of eleven people whose addresses, whose real names you don't even know? Give them the address of a suburban terraced house where they'll find nothing incriminating? The moment a police officer sets foot in the safe house the cell is disbanded, reformed, rehoused. We're not fools. There is a procedure for treachery.'

'What procedure? Throwing me in the Thames? Slitting my throat?'

She saw the surprise in his eyes. Was it her imagination that it was tinged with respect? But he only said:

'Don't be ridiculous.'

He unwound himself from the sofa and made for the door. But there was something she needed to ask. Once she would have been afraid, she was still a little afraid, but perhaps it was time to take a small step towards courage. She said:

'Ivor, where were you on Tuesday night? You've never been late for a cell meeting before, you've always been there before the rest of us. But it was after ten past nine before you arrived.'

'I was with Cora at the bookshop and there was a hold-up on the tube. I explained at the time. I wasn't at St Matthew's

Church cutting your father's throat, if that's what you're implying. And until the police are forced to accept that he killed
himself we'd better not meet. If it's necessary I'll be in touch in
the usual way.'

'And the police? Suppose they come back?'

'They'll come back. Stick to the alibi and don't try to be
clever. Don't embroider. We were here together from six o'clock
all night. We ate a mushroom flan, we drank a bottle of Riesling.
All you have to do is to remember what we did on Sunday night
and transpose it to Tuesday. Don't think you're doing me any
great favour, it's yourself you need to protect.'

And without touching her he was gone. So that, she thought
wearily, was how love ended, with the slam of a grille door, the
grind of the lift bearing him slowly downwards out of her life.

BOOK FOUR

Devices and Desires

I

The Black Swan, despite its name, didn't derive from a riverside pub but from an elegant two-storey villa built at the turn of the century by a prosperous Kensington painter seeking a weekend retreat with country quiet and a river view. After his death it had suffered the usual vicissitudes of a private residence too damp and inconveniently situated to be suitable as a permanent home and too large for a weekend cottage. It had been a restaurant of sorts for twenty years under its original name, but hadn't flourished until Jean Paul Higgins took it over in 1980, renamed it, built on a new dining room with wide windows overlooking the river and the far water meadows, employed a French chef, Italian waiters, and an English doorman, and set out to win his first modest mention in *The Good Food Guide*. Higgins's mother had been a Frenchwoman and he had obviously decided that, as a restaurateur, it was that half of his parentage he had better emphasize. His staff and customers called him Monsieur Jean Paul and it was only his bank manager who, to his chagrin, insisted on greeting him with cheerful exuberance as Mr Higgins. He and his bank manager were on excellent terms and for the best of reasons: Mr Higgins was doing very well. In the summer it was necessary to book a table for luncheon or dinner at least three days in advance. In autumn and winter the place was less busy and the luncheon menu offered only three main dishes but the standard of cooking and service never varied. The Black Swan was close enough to London to attract a number of city regulars willing to drive twenty odd miles for the Black Swan's peculiar advantages; an attractive ambience, tables spaced at a reasonable distance, a low noise level, no piped music, unostentatious service, discretion and excellent food.

Monsieur Jean Paul was small and dark with melancholy eyes

and a thin moustache which made him look like a stage Frenchman, an impression strengthened when he spoke. He himself
greeted Dalgliesh and Kate at the door with unflurried courtesy
as if there were nothing he had been looking forward to more
than a visit from the police. But Dalgliesh noticed that despite
the early hour and the quietness of the house, they were shown
into his private office at the rear of the building with the minimum
of delay. Higgins was of the school which believes, not without
reason, that even when the police come visiting in plainclothes
and don't actually kick down the door, they are always unmistakably the police. Dalgliesh didn't miss his quick glance of appraisal
at Kate Miskin, the quickly suppressed look of surprise changing
to modified approval. She was wearing slacks in fawn gaberdine
with a well-cut, unobtrusive checked jacket over a rollneck cashmere jumper and with her hair bound back in a short, thick
plait. Dalgliesh wondered what Higgins expected a plain-clothes
policewoman to look like, an over-made-up harpy in black satin
and a trenchcoat?

He offered refreshment, at first carefully ambiguous about the
kind, and then more specific. Dalgliesh and Kate accepted coffee.
It came quickly, served by a young waiter in a short white jacket,
and it was excellent. When Dalgliesh had swallowed his first sip,
Higgins gave a small sigh of relief as if his guest, now irrevocably
compromised, had lost some of his power.

Dalgliesh said:

'As I expect you know, we are investigating the death of Sir
Paul Berowne. You may have information which can help fill in
some of the background.'

Jean Paul spread his palms and launched into his voluble
Frenchman act. But the melancholy eyes were wary.

'The death of Sir Paul, so terrible, so tragic. I ask myself what
the world is coming to when such violence is possible. But how
can I help the Commander? He was murdered in London, not
here, thank God. If it was murder. There's a rumour that,
maybe, Sir Paul himself . . . But that, too, would be terrible,
more terrible for his wife than murder, perhaps.'

'He came here regularly?'

'From time to time, not regularly. He was a busy man, of course.'

'But Lady Berowne was here more often, usually with her cousin, I understand?'

'A delightful lady. She adorned my dining room. But, of course, one does not always notice who is dining with whom. We concentrate on the food and the service. We are not gossip writers, you understand.'

'But presumably you can remember whether she was dining with her cousin, Mr Stephen Lampart, on the Tuesday of this week, just three days ago?'

'On the seventeenth. That was so. They were seated at twenty minutes to nine. It is a little foible of mine, to note the time the customer is actually seated. The booking was for eight forty-five but they were a little early. Monsieur may wish to inspect the book.'

He opened his desk drawer and produced it. Obviously, thought Dalgliesh, he had been expecting a visit from the police and had placed the evidence to hand. The time against the name Lampart was written clearly and there was no sign that the figures had been altered.

He asked:

'When was the table booked?'

'That morning. At ten thirty, I believe. I cannot, I regret, be more precise.'

'Then he was fortunate to get it.'

'We can always find a table for an old and valued customer, but it is, of course, easier if a booking is made. The notice was sufficient.'

'How did Mr Lampart and Lady Berowne seem when they arrived?'

The dark eyes lifted reproachfully to his as if in silent protest at so tactless a question.

'How should they seem, Commander? Hungry.' Then he added as if fearing the answer had been imprudent:

'They were as usual. The lady is always gracious, most friendly. They were content that I was able to give them their usual table, in the corner by the window.'

'What time did they leave?'

'At eleven or a little after. One does not hurry a good dinner.'

'And during dinner? They talked presumably.'

'They talked, monsieur. It is a pleasure of dining, to share good food, good wine and good talk with a friend. But as for what they said, we are not eavesdroppers, Commander. We are not the police. These are good customers you understand.'

'Unlike some of the customers you had here on the night Diana Travers drowned. You had time to notice them, I suppose?'

Higgins showed no surprise at the sudden change in questioning. He spread his hands in a Gallic gesture of resignation.

'Alas, who could overlook them? They were not the kind of client we usually attract. At dinner they were quiet enough but afterwards, well, it was not agreeable. I was relieved when they left the dining room.'

'Sir Paul Berowne wasn't with his wife's party, I understand.'

'That is so. When they arrived, Mr Lampart said that Sir Paul hoped to join them later, in time for coffee. But as you may know, he telephoned at ten o'clock or a little later maybe and said that it would not, after all, be possible.'

'Who took the call?'

'My doorman, Henry. Sir Paul asked to speak to me and I was called to the telephone.'

'Did you recognize his voice?'

'As I have said, he was not here so very often, but I knew his voice. It was a voice, how you say, a distinctive voice, surprisingly like your own, Commander, if I may be permitted to say so. I cannot swear to these things, but I had no doubt at the time who was speaking.'

'Have you any doubt now?'

'No, Commander, I cannot say that I have.'

'The two parties for dinner, Mr Lampart's and the young people, did they mix, greet each other?'

'They may have done, on arrival, but the tables were not close.' He would have seen to that, thought Dalgliesh. If there had been the slightest sign of embarrassment on Barbara Berowne's part, or of insolence on her brother's, Higgins would have noticed it.

'And the members of Diana Travers's party, had you ever seen them here before?'

'Not that I remember, except for Mr Dominic Swayne. He has dined here once or twice with his sister, but the last time was some months ago. But for the others, I cannot be sure.'

'It was strange, surely, that Mr Swayne wasn't included in Lady Berowne's birthday party?'

'Monsieur, it is not for me to dictate which guests my customers should invite. No doubt there were reasons. There were four only in the birthday group, an intimate party. The table was balanced.'

'But would have become unbalanced if Sir Paul had arrived?'

'That is so, but then he was expected only for coffee and he was, after all, the lady's husband.'

Dalgliesh went on to ask Higgins about the events leading up to the drowning.

'As I have said, I was glad when the young people left the dining room and went out through the conservatory to the garden. They took two bottles of wine with them. It was not the best claret but for them it was good enough. I do not like to see my wine swung about as if it were beer. There was much laughter and I was wondering whether to send Henry or Barry to deal with them, but they moved along the bank out of earshot. It was there that they found the punt. It was tied up, wedged you might say, in a small inlet about eighty yards upstream. Now, of course, it has been removed. Perhaps it should not have been there, but how can I blame myself? They were not children although they behaved like children. I cannot control what my patrons do when they are off the premises, nor indeed when they are here.'

He used the word blame but the regret was perfunctory. No voice could have held less concern. Dalgliesh suspected that the only thing Higgins ever blamed himself for was a spoilt dinner or poor service. He went on:

'The next thing I know is the chef beckoning me from the door of the dining room. That was unusual, you understand. Immediately I could see something is wrong. I go quickly out. In the kitchen is one of the girls crying and saying that this other girl, Diana, is dead, drowned. We go out to the riverbank. The night is dark, you understand, the stars high and the moon not full. But there is some light from the car park which is always brightly lit, and some from the kitchen wing of the house. But I take with me a torch. Monsieur may imagine the distress. The girls crying, one of the young men working on the body, Mr Swayne standing there with his clothes dripping. Marcel takes over the respiration – he has many talents, that one – but it is of no use. I could see she was dead. The dead are not like the living, monsieur, never, never, never.'

'And the girl was naked?'

'As you no doubt have been told. She had taken off all her clothes and dived in for a swim. It was a great folly.'

There was a silence while he contemplated the folly. Then Dalgliesh put down his coffee cup. He said:

'It was convenient that Mr Lampart should have been dining that night. It was natural, of course, to call on him for help.'

The dark eyes, carefully expressionless, looked straight into his.

'That was my first thought, Commander. But it was too late. When I reached the dining room, I was told that Mr Lampart's party had only that moment left. I myself saw the Porsche as it turned out of the drive.'

'So Mr Lampart could have been fetching his car from the park shortly before you learned of the tragedy?'

'That is possible, certainly. I understand that the rest of his party waited at the door.'

'Surely an early, and somewhat hurried, end to the evening?'

'As to hurried, that I cannot say. But the party had been seated early, shortly after seven. If Sir Paul had been able to join them, no doubt they would have stayed later.'

Dalgliesh said:

'There has been a suggestion that Sir Paul may have arrived here that night after all.'

'I have heard that, Commander. There was a woman who came to question my staff. It was not agreeable. I was not here at the time but I would have dealt with her. No one saw Sir Paul on that night I assure you. And his car was not seen in the parking lot. It may have been there but it was not seen. And how can this concern his death I ask myself.' Dalgliesh could usually tell when he wasn't getting the truth or was getting only part of it. It was less a matter of instinct than of experience. And Higgins was lying. Now he decided to take a chance. He said:

'But someone did see Sir Paul Berowne that night. Who was it?'

'Monsieur, I assure you . . .'

'I need to know and I'm quite prepared to hang around until I do. If you want to get rid of us, a perfectly reasonable wish on your part, you'll succeed most quickly by answering my questions. The verdict at the inquest was accidental death. No one, to my knowledge, has suggested that it was anything else. She had eaten too much, drunk too much, she got caught in the reeds and panicked. It is of academic interest whether she died of shock or was drowned. So what are you hiding and why?'

'We are hiding nothing, Commander, nothing. But as you have just said, the death was an accident. Why then make trouble? Why add to distress? And one cannot be sure. A figure quickly walking, glimpsed in the darkness, in the shadow of the hedge, who can tell who it was?'

'So who was it saw him? Henry?'

It was less a lucky guess than a reasonable assumption. Berowne almost certainly hadn't shown himself on the premises and the doorman was the member of staff most likely to have been outside.

'It was Henry, yes.' Higgins admitted the fact with a sad defeatism. The mournful eyes gazed reproachfully at Dalgliesh as if to say: 'I have been helpful, I have given you information and coffee, and look where it has led me.'

'Then perhaps you'll send for him. And I'd like to speak to him alone.'

Higgins lifted the telephone receiver and dialled a single digit. It connected him to the front entrance. Henry answered it and was summoned. When he appeared, Higgins said:

'This is Commander Dalgliesh. Please tell him what you thought you saw the night that girl was drowned.' Then he gave him a half-rueful glance, shrugged his shoulders and left. Henry, unruffled, stood at attention. Dalgliesh saw that he was older than his confident, upright figure would suggest. Certainly nearer seventy than sixty.

He said:

'You're ex-Army, aren't you?'

'That's right, sir, the Gloucesters.'

'How long have you been working here for Mr Higgins, for Monsieur Jean Paul?'

'Five years, sir.'

'You live in?'

'No, sir. The wife and I, we live at Cookham. This place is handy as places go.' He added, as if hoping that a personal touch would demonstrate his willingness to co-operate frankly: 'I've got my Army pension but a little extra never hurts.'

And it wouldn't be so little, thought Dalgliesh. The tips would be good and most of them, given human frailty about the depredations of the Inland Revenue, would be tax free. Henry would want to keep his job.

He said:

'We're investigating the death of Sir Paul Berowne. We're interested in anything that happened to him during the last weeks of his life, however unimportant and irrelevant it might seem. Apparently he was here on the night of the seventh of August and you saw him.'

'Yes, sir, crossing the car park. One of our guests that night was leaving and I was fetching his Rolls. We haven't valet parking, sir, it would take me off the door too often. But occasionally guests like to have their cars parked and they hand me their keys on arrival. Antonio, he's one of the waiters, gave me the word that my party was ready to leave and I went for the car. I was standing there putting the key in the lock when I saw Sir Paul cross the car park walking along the line of the hedge and out through the gate leading to the river.'

'How certain are you it was Sir Paul Berowne?'

'Pretty certain, sir. He isn't here often but I've a good eye for faces.'

'Do you know what car he drives?'

'A black Rover, I think. An A registration. I can't remember the number.' Couldn't or wouldn't, thought Dalgliesh. A black Rover would be difficult to identify; a registration number was irrefutable evidence. He asked:

'And there was no black Rover parked that night?'

'Not that I noticed, sir, and I think I would have noticed.'

'And you said he was walking briskly?'

'Very briskly, sir, purposefully you might say.'

'When did you tell Monsieur Jean Paul about this?'

'The next morning, sir. He said that there was no need to tell the police. Sir Paul had a right to walk by the river if he chose. He said we had better wait until the inquest. If there had been marks on the body, any suggestion of foul play, that would be different. The police would want to know the names of anyone who had been here that night. But it was accidental death. The coroner was satisfied that the young lady had herself dived into the river. After that, Monsieur Jean Paul decided we should say nothing.'

'Even after Sir Paul's death?'

'I don't think Monsieur thought the information would be helpful, sir. Sir Paul Berowne was dead. How could it matter if he'd taken a walk by the river six weeks earlier?'

'Have you told this story to anyone else? Anyone at all? Your wife, a member of the staff here?'

'To no one, sir. There was a lady came inquiring. I was off sick that day. But even if I'd been here, I would have said nothing, not unless Monsieur had told me it was all right.'

'And about ten minutes after you saw him walking across the car park, Sir Paul rang to say he wouldn't be arriving after all?'

'Yes, sir.'

'Did he say where he was ringing from?'

'No, sir. It couldn't have been from here. The only public telephone we have is in the hall. There's a telephone kiosk in Mapleton, that's the nearest village, but I happen to know that it was out of order that night. My sister lives there and wanted to ring me. There's no box nearer, not that I know of. That call was a proper mystery, sir.'

'When you mentioned the matter next day, what did you and Monsieur think Sir Paul might have been doing here? I take it you discussed it.'

Henry paused, then he said:

'Monsieur thought Sir Paul might have been keeping an eye on his wife.'

455

'Spying on her?'

'I suppose it was possible, sir.'

'By walking along the riverbank?'

'It doesn't seem very likely, not put like that.'

'And why should he have wished to spy on his wife?'

'I can't say, I'm sure, sir. I don't think Monsieur was serious. He just said: "It is none of our business, Henry. Maybe he is keeping an eye on her Ladyship."'

'And that's all you can tell me?'

Henry hesitated. Dalgliesh waited. Then he said:

'Well, there is something else, sir. But it seems daft when I come to think about it. The car park is well lit, sir, but he was walking quickly and in the shadow of the hedge at the far side. But there was something about the way his jacket was clinging, his trousers, too. I think, sir, he'd been in the river, and that's why I say it was daft. He wasn't walking away from the river, sir, he was walking towards it.'

He looked from Dalgliesh to Kate, his eyes puzzled as if the full peculiarity of it had only now struck him.

'I'll swear he was wet, sir, soaking wet. But like I said, he was walking towards the river, not away from it.'

Dalgliesh and Kate had driven separately to the Black Swan. She was returning directly to the Yard and he driving north-east to Wrentham Green to lunch with the Chairman and Vice-Chairman of Berowne's constituency party. They would meet at the Yard in the mid-afternoon to attend the brief formalities of the preliminary inquest before going on to what promised to be a more interesting appointment, to interview Paul Berowne's mistress. As Kate unlocked the door of her Metro he said:

'We'd better have a word with the couple who were dining here with Mr Lampart and Lady Berowne on August the seventh. They might be able to say when exactly Lampart left the table to fetch the car, how long he was away. Get their names and addresses, will you, Kate? I suggest from the lady, rather than Lampart. And it would be useful to know more about the mysterious Diana Travers. According to the police report on the drowning she emigrated with her parents to Australia in 1963. They stayed, she came back. Neither of them came over for the inquest or the funeral. Thames Valley had some difficulty in finding someone to identify her. They dug up an aunt and she made the funeral arrangements. She hadn't seen her niece for over a year but she had absolutely no doubt about the identification. And while you're at number sixty-two, see if you can get anything more out of Miss Matlock about the girl.'

Kate said:

'Mrs Minns might be able to tell us something, sir. We're seeing her first thing tomorrow.' She added:

'There was one thing Higgins said about the Travers drowning which struck me as odd. It doesn't tie up.'

So she had noticed the anomaly. Dalgliesh said:

'It seems to have been an evening for river sports. It was almost as odd as Henry's story. Paul Berowne with his wet clothes clinging to him, but walking towards the river, not away from it.'

Kate still lingered, her hand on the car door. Dalgliesh gazed out over the high beech hedge which separated the car park from the river. The day was changing. The early morning air had held a brittle and transitory brightness, but now the storm clouds, forecast for the afternoon, were rolling in from the west. But it was still warm for early autumn and there came to him as he stood in the almost deserted car park, cleansed of the smell of hot metal and petrol, the scent of river water and sun-warmed grasses. He stood for a moment savouring it like a truant, feeling the pull of the water, wishing that there were time to follow the wraith of that dripping figure through the gateway to the peace of the riverbank. Kate, coming out of her momentary trance, opened the car door and slid in. But she seemed to have shared his mood. She said:

'It all seems so far away from that dingy Paddington vestry.' He wondered if she was implying, not daring to say:

'It's Berowne's murder we're supposed to be investigating, not the coincidental drowning of a girl he may hardly have seen.'

But now, more than ever, he was convinced that the three deaths were linked, Travers, Nolan, Berowne. And the main purpose of their visit to the Black Swan had been achieved. Lampart's alibi held. Even driving a Porsche it was hard to see how he could have killed Berowne and still been seated by eight forty.

2

With the electrification of the north-east suburban line, Wrentham Green had increasingly become a commuter town despite the protestations of its older inhabitants that it was a county town of character not a dormitory suburb of London. The town had woken up sooner than some of its less vigilant neighbours to the post-war despoliation of England's heritage by developers and local authorities, and had checked the worst excesses of that unholy alliance just in time. The broad eighteenth-century high street, although desecrated by two modern multiple stores, was essentially intact, and the small close of Georgian houses facing the river was still regularly photographed for Christmas calendars even if it required some contortions on the part of the photographer to exclude the end of the car park and the municipal lavatories. It was in one of the smaller houses of the close that the Constituency Conservative Party had its headquarters. Passing through the porticoed door with its gleaming brass plate, Dalgliesh was met by the Chairman, Frank Musgrave, and the Vice-Chairman, General Mark Nollinge.

As always he had prepared himself for the visit. He knew more about both of them than he suspected either would have thought necessary. Together in amicable harness they had for the last twenty years run the local Party. Frank Musgrave was an estate agent who ran a family business, still independent of the large conglomerates, which he had originally inherited from his father. From the number of house boards Dalgliesh had noticed on his drive through the town and the neighbouring villages, the business was flourishing. The single word, 'Musgrave', bold black lettering on white, had met him at every turn. Its reiteration had become an irritating, almost premonitory, reminder of his destination.

He and the General were an incongruous pair. It was Musgrave who at first sight looked like a soldier, indeed his resemblance to the late Field-Marshal Montgomery was so marked that Dalgliesh wasn't surprised to hear him speak in a parody of that formidable warrior's staccato bark. The General barely came up to his shoulder. He held his slight body so rigidly that it seemed as if his vertebrae were fused, and his tonsured head, the crown ringed with fine white hair, was speckled as a thrush's egg. As Musgrave made the introductions he looked up at Dalgliesh with eyes as innocently candid as a child's, but strained and puzzled as if he had looked too long on unattainable horizons. In contrast to Musgrave's formal business suit and black tie, the General was wearing an ancient tweed jacket cut according to some personal whim with two oblong patches of suede on each elbow. His shirt and regimental tie were immaculate. With his shining face he had the polished vulnerability of a well-tended child. Even in the first minutes of casual conversation the mutual respect of the two men was immediately apparent. Whenever the General spoke, Musgrave would gaze from him to Dalgliesh with the slightly anxious frown of a parent, worried lest his offspring's brilliance should be underrated.

Musgrave led the way through the wide hall, down a short passage to the room at the back of the house which Berowne had used as his office. He said:

'Kept it locked since Berowne's death. Your people rang, but we'd have locked it anyway. The General and I thought it the right thing to do. Not that there's anything here to shed light. Shouldn't think so, anyway. Welcome to look, of course.'

The air smelt stale and dusty, almost sour, as if the room had been locked for months rather than days. Musgrave switched on the light, then strode over to the window and vigorously tugged back the curtains with a rattle of rings. A thin northern light filtered through the plain nylon curtains beyond which Dalgliesh could see a small walled car park. He had seldom, he thought, been in a more depressing room, and yet it was difficult to explain why he should feel this sudden weight of dejection. The room was no worse than any of its kind, functional, uncluttered, impersonal, and yet he felt that the very air he breathed was infected by melancholy.

He said:

'Did he stay in this house when he was in the constituency?'

'No. Just used this room here as an office. He always stayed at the Courtney Arms. Mrs Powell kept a bed for him. It was cheaper and less trouble than having a flat in the constituency. Talked occasionally about asking me to find one, but it never came to anything. I don't think his wife was keen.'

Dalgliesh asked casually:

'Did you see very much of Lady Berowne?'

'Not a lot. Did her bit, of course. Annual fête, appearances at the local elections, that sort of thing. Decorative and gracious all round. Not much interested in politics, would you say, General?'

'Lady Berowne? No, not greatly. The first Lady Berowne was different, of course. But then, the Manstons have been a political family for four generations. I used to wonder sometimes whether Berowne entered politics to please his wife. I don't think he felt the same commitment after she was killed.'

Musgrave gave him a sharp glance as if this were a heresy, previously unacknowledged, which even now was better left unspoken. He said quickly:

'Yes, well, water under the bridge. A sad business. He was driving at the time. I expect you've heard.'

Dalgliesh said:

'Yes. I had heard.'

There was a short, uncomfortable pause during which it seemed to him that the golden image of Barbara Berowne glimmered, unacknowledged and disturbing, in the still air.

He began his examination of the room, aware of the General's anxious, hopeful gaze, of Musgrave's sharp eyes on him as if watching a trainee clerk taking his first inventory. Set in the middle of the floor and facing the window was a solid Victorian desk and a button-backed swivel chair. In front of it were two smaller leather armchairs. There was a modern desk with a heavy old-fashioned typewriter to one side and two more chairs and a low coffee table in front of the fireplace. The only memorable piece of furniture was a bureau-bookcase with brass bound panes which occupied the recess to the right of the fireplace. Dalgliesh wondered if his companions knew its value. Then he guessed that respect for tradition would forbid its sale. Like the desk, it was part of the room, inviolate, not to be disposed of for a quick profit. Strolling over to it, he saw that it held an oddly assorted collection of reference books, local guides, biographies of notable Tory politicians, *Who's Who*, parliamentary reports, Stationery Office publications, even a few classical novels, apparently gummed together by immutable time.

On the wall behind the desk was a copy of a well-known oil portrait of Winston Churchill with a large colour photograph of Mrs Thatcher hung to its right. But it was the picture above the fireplace which immediately caught the eye. Moving to it from the bookcase, Dalgliesh saw that it was an eighteenth-century oil painting by Arthur Devis of the Harrison family. The young Harrison, legs elegantly crossed in their satin breeches, stood with proprietorial arrogance beside a garden seat on which sat his thin-faced wife, her arm round a young child. A small girl sat demurely beside her holding a basket of flowers, while to the left her brother's arm was raised to the string of a kite, luminous in the summer sky. Behind the group stretched a gentle English landscape in high summer, smooth lawns, a lake, a distant manor house. Dalgliesh recalled from his interview with Anthony Farrell that Musgrave had been left a Devis. This, presumably, was it. The General said:

'Berowne brought it here from Campden Hill Square. He moved the Churchill portrait and hung it here instead. There was some feeling about it at the time. The Churchill had always hung over the mantelpiece.'

Musgrave had moved up beside Dalgliesh. He said:

'I'll miss that picture. Never tired of looking at it. It was painted in Hertfordshire, only six miles from here. You can still see that landscape. The same oak tree, same lake. And the house. It's a school now. My grandfather was agent when it was sold. It couldn't be anywhere else but England. I never knew that painter's work till Berowne brought it here. Rather like a Gainsborough, isn't it? But I'm not sure I don't like it better than that one in the National Gallery – Mr and Mrs Robert Andrews. The women are a bit alike, though, aren't they? Thin-faced, arrogant, wouldn't care to be married to either of them. But it's lovely, lovely.'

The General said quietly:

'I'll be relieved when the family send for it. It's a responsibility.'

So neither of them knew about the legacy, unless they were

better actors than he thought likely. Dalgliesh kept a prudent silence, but he would have given much to have seen Musgrave's face when he learned of his good luck. He wondered what spurt of quixotic generosity had prompted the gift. It was surely an exceptionally generous way of rewarding political loyalty. And it was an irritating complication. Common sense and imagination protested at the thought of Musgrave slitting a friend's throat to possess a picture, however obsessively desired, which there was no evidence he even knew had been willed to him. But in the normal course of human life he would have been lucky to have outlived Berowne. He had been at the Campden Hill Square house on the afternoon of Berowne's death. He could have taken the diary. He almost certainly knew that Berowne used a cut-throat razor. Like everyone else who benefited from the death, he would have to be tactfully investigated. It was almost certainly a waste of effort; it would take time; it complicated the main thrust of the inquiry; but it still had to be done.

They were, he knew, waiting for him to talk about the murder. Instead he walked over to the desk and seated himself in Berowne's chair. That, at least, was comfortable, fitting his long limbs as if made for him. There was a thin film of dust on the desk surface. He pulled open the right-hand drawer and found nothing but a box of writing paper and envelopes, and a diary similar to the one found by the body. Opening it, he saw that it contained only engagements and an *aide-mémoire* for the days he spent in his constituency. Here, too, his life had been ordered, compartmentalized.

Outside, a thin drizzle was beginning to fall, misting the window, so that he saw the brick wall of the car park and the bright curved roofs of the cars as if in a pointillist oil painting. What burden, he wondered, had Berowne brought with him into this sunless and depressing office? Disenchantment with the second job to which he had committed himself? Guilt over his dead wife, his failed marriage? Guilt over the mistress whose bed he had so recently left? Guilt over his neglect of his only child, over the baronetcy which had been rightly his brother's? Guilt because that better loved elder son was dead and he was still alive? 'Most of the things I expected to value in life have come to me through death.' And had there been, perhaps, a more recent guilt, Theresa Nolan, who had killed herself because she had aborted a child? His child? And what was there for him here amid these files and papers, mocking in their meticulous order his disordered life, but the Catch 22 of the well-intentioned? The miserable batten on their victims. If you provide them what they crave, open your heart and mind to them, listen with sympathy, they come in ever increasing numbers, draining you emotionally and physically until you have nothing left to give. If you repel them they don't come back and you're left despising yourself for your inhumanity. He said:

'I suppose this room is the place of last resort.'

It was Musgrave who understood him the quicker.

'Nine times out of ten that's what it is. They've exhausted the patience of their families, DHSS staff, local authorities, friends. Then it's here. "I voted for you. Do something." Some Members like it, of course. Find it the most fascinating part of the job. They're the social workers *manqué*. I suspect he didn't. What he tried to do, seemed almost obsessed with at times, was explaining to people the limits of government power, any government. Remember the last debate on the inner cities? I was in the public gallery. There was a lot of suppressed anger in his irony. "If I understand the Honourable Member's somewhat confused argument the Government are asked to ensure equality of intelligence, talent, health, energy and wealth while, at the same time, abolishing original sin as from the beginning of the next financial year. What divine providence has singularly failed to do, Her Majesty's Government are to achieve by Statutory Order." The House didn't much like it. Not their kind of humour.'

He added:

'It was a lost battle anyway, educating the electorate in the limits of executive power. No one wants to believe it. And anyway, in a democracy there's always an opposition to tell them that anything is possible.'

The General said:

'He was a conscientious constituency MP, but it took a lot out of him, more than we realized. I think he was sometimes torn between compassion and irritation.'

Musgrave jerked open the drawer of a filing cabinet, and pulled out a file at random:

'Take this one, spinster, aged 52. In the middle of the change and feeling like hell. Dad dead. Mum at home and virtually bedridden, demanding, incontinent, getting senile. No hospital bed, and Mum wouldn't go voluntarily even if there were. Or this one. Two kids, both of them 19. She gets pregnant, they marry. Neither set of parents like it. Now they're living with the in-laws in a small terraced house. No privacy. Can't make love. Mum will hear through the walls. Baby squalling. Family saying "I told you so". No hope of a council house for another three years, maybe longer. And that's typical of what he got every Saturday. Find me a hospital bed, a house, work. Give me money, give me hope, give me love. It's partly what the job is all about, but I think he found it frustrating. I'm not saying he wasn't sympathetic to the genuine cases.'

The General said quietly:

'All the cases are genuine. Misery always is.'

He gazed out of the window to where the drizzle had now strengthened to steady rain, and then said:

'Perhaps we should have found him a more cheerful room.'

Musgrave expostulated:

'But the Member has always used this room for his surgery, General, and it's only once a week.'

The General said quietly:

'Nevertheless, when we get the new Member he should have something better.'

Musgrave capitulated without rancour.

'We could oust George. Or use that front room on the top floor for the surgery. But then the elderly would have to manage the stairs. I don't see how we could rehouse the bar.'

Dalgliesh half-expected him to call at once for plans and begin the reallocation, his own concerns half-forgotten. He said:

'Did his resignation come as a surprise?'

It was Musgrave who answered:

'Absolutely. A complete shock. A shock and a betrayal. It's no good beating about the bush, General. It's a bad time for a by-election, and he must have known.'

The General said:

'Hardly a betrayal. We've never seen ourselves as a marginal seat.'

'Anything under fifteen thousand is marginal these days. He should have soldiered on until the election.'

Dalgliesh asked:

'Did he explain his reasons? I take it that he did see you both, he didn't merely write.'

Again it was Musgrave who answered:

'Oh, he saw us all right. Actually deferred writing to the Chancellor until he'd told us. I was on holiday – my usual short autumn break – and he had the decency to wait until I was back. Came up here late last Friday, Friday the thirteenth appropriately enough. He said that it wouldn't be right for him to continue as our Member. It was time that his life took a different turn. Naturally I asked what he meant by a different turn. "You're a Member of Parliament," I said. "You're not driving a bloody bus." He said that he didn't know yet. He hadn't been shown. "Hadn't been shown by whom?" I asked. He said "God". Well, there's not much a man can say to that. Nothing like an answer like that for putting a stopper on rational discussion.'

'How did he seem?'

'Oh, perfectly calm, perfectly normal. Too calm. That's what was so odd about it. A bit eerie really, wouldn't you say, General?'

The General said very quietly:

'He looked to me like a man released from pain, physical pain. Pale, drawn, but very peaceful. You can't mistake the look.'

'Oh, he was peaceful enough. Obstinate too. You couldn't argue. His decision had nothing to do with politics, though. We did at least establish that. I asked him outright. "Are you disillusioned with policy, with the Party, with the PM, with us?" He said it was nothing like that. He said: "It's nothing to do with the Party. It's myself I have to change." He seemed surprised by the question, almost amused as if it were irrelevant. Well, it wasn't irrelevant to me. The General and I have given a lifetime of service to the Party. It matters to us. It's not some kind of game, a trivial pursuit that you can pick up and put down when you're bored. We deserved a better explanation and a bloody sight more consideration than we got. He seemed almost to resent having to talk about it. We could have been discussing arrangements for the summer fête.'

He began pacing the narrow room, his outrage a palpable force. The General said mildly:

'I'm afraid we were no help to him. None at all.'

'He wasn't asking for help, was he? Or for advice. He'd gone to a higher power for that. It's a pity he ever set foot in that church. Why did he, anyway? D'you know?' He shot the question at Dalgliesh like an accusation. Dalgliesh said mildly:

'Out of an interest in Victorian church architecture apparently.'

'Pity he didn't take up fishing or stamp collecting. Oh well, he's dead, poor devil. No point in feeling bitter now.'

Dalgliesh said: 'You saw that article in the *Paternoster Review*, of course?'

Musgrave had got himself under control. He said:

'I don't read that kind of journal. If I want book reviews I get them from the Sunday papers.' His tone suggested that he was occasionally given to such odd indulgences.

'But someone read it and cut it out; it was round the constituency pretty sharply. The General's view was that it was actionable.'

General Nollinge said:

'I thought that it might be. I advised him to consult his lawyer. He said he'd think about it.'

Dalgliesh said:

'He did more than that. He showed it to me.'

'Asked you to investigate, did he?' Musgrave's tone was sharp.

'Not really. He wasn't specific.'

'Exactly. He wasn't specific about anything in those last few weeks.'

He added:

'Of course, when he first told us that he'd written to the PM and was applying for the Chiltern Hundreds, we remembered that *Review* article and braced ourselves for the scandal. Quite wrong, of course. Nothing as human or understandable. There's one odd thing, though, which we thought we'd better mention. Now that he's dead it can't do any harm. It happened on the night that girl was drowned. Diana Something-or-other.'

Dalgliesh said:

'Diana Travers.'

'That's right. He turned up here that night, well, early morning really. He didn't arrive until well after midnight but I was still here working on some papers. Something or someone had scratched his face. It was superficial, but deep enough to have bled. The scab had just formed. It could have been a cat, I suppose, or he may have fallen into a rosebush. Equally the claws could have been a woman's.'

'Did he give you any explanation?'

'No. He didn't mention it and neither did I, either then or later. Berowne had a way of making it impossible for you to ask unwelcome questions. It couldn't have had anything to do with the girl, of course. Apparently, he wasn't dining at the Black Swan that night. But afterwards when we read that article, it struck me as an odd coincidence.'

It was indeed, thought Dalgliesh. He asked, because the question was necessary, not because he expected any useful information, whether anyone in the constituency could have known that Berowne would be in St Matthew's Church on the night of his death. Catching Musgrave's sharp, suspicious glance and the General's pained frown, he added:

'We have to consider the possibility that this was a planned murder, that the killer knew he would be there. If Sir Paul told someone in the constituency – telephoned perhaps – there has to be the chance that the conversation was overheard or passed on unwittingly.'

Musgrave said:

'You're not suggesting that he was killed by an aggrieved constituent? A bit far-fetched, surely.'

'But not impossible.'

'Aggrieved constituents write to the local press, cancel their subs and threaten to vote SDP next time. Can't see this as political in any sense. Damn it, man, he'd resigned his seat. He was out, finished, spent, no danger to anyone. After that nonsense in the church no one was going to take him seriously any more.'

The General's soft voice broke in:

'Not even the family knew where he was that night. It would be strange if he told someone here when he hadn't told them.'

'How do you know, General?'

'Mrs Hurrell rang Campden Hill Square shortly after eight thirty and spoke to the housekeeper, Miss Matlock. At least, I understand that it was a young man who answered the telephone but he handed her over to Miss Matlock. Wilfred Hurrell was the agent here. He died at three o'clock the next morning in St Mary's Hospital, Paddington. Cancer, poor devil. He was devoted to Berowne and Mrs Hurrell rang Campden Hill Square because he was asking for him. Berowne had told her to ring at any time. He'd see that he could always be reached. That's what I find so odd. He knew that Wilfred hadn't long to go, yet he didn't leave a number or an address. That wasn't like him.'

Musgrave said:

'Betty Hurrell rang me afterwards to see if he were in the constituency. I wasn't at home. I hadn't got back from London by then, but she spoke to my wife. She couldn't help her, of course. A bad business.'

Dalgliesh gave no sign that the call wasn't news to him. He asked:

'Did Miss Matlock say that she'd ask any of the family whether they knew how to contact Sir Paul?'

'She just told Mrs Hurrell that he wasn't at home and that no one in the house knew where he was. Mrs Hurrell could hardly press the matter. Apparently he left home shortly after ten thirty and never returned. I called at the house just before lunch hoping to catch him, but he never came back. I expect they told you I was there.'

The General said:

'I tried to reach him later, just before six o'clock, to make an appointment for the next day. I thought it might be helpful if we could have a quiet talk. He wasn't at home then. Lady Ursula answered the telephone. She said she'd look at his diary and ring back.'

'Are you sure, General?'

'That I spoke to Lady Ursula? Oh yes. Usually Miss Matlock answers, but sometimes one gets Lady Ursula.'

'Are you sure that she said she'd consult the diary?'

'She may have said that she'd see if he were free and ring back. Something like that. Naturally I assumed that meant she would consult his diary. I said not to worry if it was any trouble. She's crippled with arthritis, you know.'

'Did she ring back?'

'Yes, about ten minutes later. She said that Wednesday morning seemed all right, but she'd ask Berowne to ring me and confirm next morning.'

Next morning. That suggested that she knew that her son wouldn't be back that night. More importantly, if she had, indeed, gone down to the study and had consulted the diary, then it had been there in the study drawer shortly after six on the day of Berowne's death. And at six o'clock, according to Father Barnes, he had arrived at the Vicarage. Here at last could be the vital clue linking the murder with Campden Hill Square. This had been a carefully planned killing. The murderer had known where to find the diary, had taken it with him to the church, had partly burned it in an attempt to add verisimilitude to the suicide theory. And that placed the heart of the murder firmly in Berowne's household. But wasn't that where he had always known that it lay?

He recalled that moment in Lady Ursula's sitting room when he had revealed the diary. The clawed hands shrivelled with age tightening on the plastic. The frail body frozen into immobility. So she had known. Shocked as she was, her mind had still been working. But would any mother shield her son's murderer? Under one circumstance he thought it possible that this mother might. But the truth was probably less complicated and less sinister. She couldn't believe that anyone she personally knew had been capable of this particular crime. She could accept only two possibilities. Either her son had killed himself or, more likely and more acceptably, his murder had been the work of casual unpremeditated violence. If Lady Ursula could bring herself to believe this, then she would see any connection with Campden Hill Square as irrelevant, a potential source of scandal and, worse, a damaging diversion of police energies from their job of finding the real killer. But he would have to question her about that telephone call. He had never in his professional life been afraid of a witness or a suspect. But this was one interview to which he wasn't looking forward. But if the diary had been in the desk at six o'clock, then at least Frank Musgrave was in the clear. He had left Campden Hill Square before two. But his suspicion of Musgrave had immediately struck him as an irrelevance. And then another thought, possibly equally irrelevant, fell into his mind. What was it that Wilfred Hurrell, lying on his deathbed, had been so anxious to say to Paul Berowne? And was it possible that someone had been determined that he shouldn't have the opportunity to say it?

Afterwards the three of them lunched together in the elegant first-floor dining room overlooking the river, now running thick and turbulent under the driving rain. As they were seated, Musgrave said:

'My great-grandfather once dined with Disraeli at this table. They looked out over much the same view.'

The words confirmed what Dalgliesh had suspected, that it was Musgrave whose family had always voted Tory and who would find any other allegiance unthinkable, the General who had come to his political philosophy by a process of thought and intellectual commitment.

It was an agreeable meal, stuffed shoulder of lamb, fresh vegetables beautifully cooked, a gooseberry tart with cream. He guessed that both his companions had tacitly agreed not to pester him with inquiries about the progress of the police investigation. They had earlier asked the obvious questions and had met his reticence with tactful silence. He was inclined to put this restraint down to a wish that he should enjoy a meal over which they had obviously taken trouble, rather than to any reluctance to discuss a painful subject, or any fear that they might let slip things best left unspoken. They were served by an elderly black-coated waiter with the face of an anxiously amiable toad, who poured an excellent Niersteiner with shaky hands, but without spilling a drop. The dining room was almost empty – there were only two couples and they were at distant tables. Dalgliesh suspected that his hosts had tactfully ensured that he should enjoy his luncheon in peace. But both men found an opportunity to give him their opinion. When, after coffee, the General remembered the need to make a telephone call, Musgrave leaned confidingly across the table:

'The General can't believe it was suicide. It isn't something he'd do himself so he can't imagine it in his friends. I'd have said the same myself once, about Berowne, I mean. Not so sure now. There's a madness in the air. Nothing's certain any more, least of all people. You think you know them, know how they'd behave. But you don't, you can't. We're all strangers. That girl now, the nurse, the one who killed herself. If it was Berowne's child she aborted, that couldn't have been easy for him to live with. Not trying to interfere, you understand. Your job, of course, not mine. But the case seems pretty straightforward to me.'

And it was in the car park when Musgrave had left them to go to his car that the General said:

'I know that Frank thinks that Berowne killed himself, but he's wrong. Not malicious, or disloyal or unkind; just wrong. Berowne wasn't the kind of man to kill himself.'

Dalgliesh said:

'I don't know whether he was or wasn't. What I am reasonably sure of is that he didn't.'

They watched in silence while Musgrave, with a final wave, negotiated the gate and accelerated out of sight. It seemed to Dalgliesh an additional perversity of fate that he should be driving a black Rover with an A registration.

Half an hour later Frank Musgrave turned into the drive of his house. It was a small but elegant red-bricked country house designed by Lutyens and bought by his father forty years earlier. Musgrave had inherited it with the family business and regarded it with as much obsessional pride as if it had been a two-hundred-year-old family seat. He maintained it with jealous care as he looked after everything that was his, his wife, his son, his business, his car. Usually he drove up to it with no more than customary satisfaction at the old man's good eye for a house, but every six months, as if in obedience to some unstated law, he would halt the car and make a deliberate revaluation of its market price. He did that now.

He had hardly entered the hall when his wife, anxious faced, came out to meet him. Taking the coat from his shoulders, she said:

'How did it go, dear?'

'All right. He's an odd man. Not altogether friendly but perfectly civil. Seemed to enjoy his lunch.' He paused and added:

'He knows that it was murder.'

'Oh Frank, no! Not that! What are you going to do?'

'What everyone else concerned with Berowne will do, try to limit the damage. Has Betty Hurrell rung?'

'About twenty minutes ago. I told her that you'd be coming to see her.'

'Yes,' he said heavily, 'I must do that.'

He laid his hand momentarily on his wife's shoulder. Her family hadn't wanted her to marry him, hadn't thought him good enough for the only child of a previous Lord Lieutenant of the County. But he had married her and they had been happy, were still happy. He thought with sudden anger: He's done enough damage, but this is where it stops. I'm not going to risk everything I've worked for, everything I've achieved and my father before me, just because Paul Berowne goes off his head in a church vestry.

3

Scarsdale Lodge was a large, L-shaped, modern block of flats, brick-built, its front disfigured rather than enhanced by a series of irregular, jutting balconies. A path of stone blocks led between twin lawns to the canopied entrance porch. In the middle of each lawn, a small circular flower bed closely packed with dwarf dahlias ranging in circles through white to yellow and, finally, red glared upwards like a bloodshot eye. To the left a driveway brought them to the rear garage block and to a marked parking lot with a notice warning that it was strictly for the use of visitors to Scarsdale Lodge. It was overlooked by the smaller windows at the back of the building and Dalgliesh, knowing how paranoid flat residents became over unlicensed parking, guessed that a watch would be kept on it for alien cars. Almost certainly

Berowne would have judged it safer to leave his car in the public park at Stanmore Station and would have walked the last quarter of a mile uphill, an anonymous commuter with the ubiquitous briefcase, the carrier bag of wine, the offering of flowers probably bought from a stall near Baker Street or Westminster Underground. And Stanmore wasn't so very far out of his way. It was, in fact, conveniently on the route to his Hertfordshire constituency. He would be able to snatch the odd hour on a Friday night, that hiatus between his London life and his Saturday morning constituency surgery.

He and Kate walked in silence to the front door. It was fitted with an intercom; hardly the most effective security but better than none, and with the advantage that there was no porter to watch comings and goings. Kate's ring and her careful announcement of their names through the grille was answered only by the burr of the released door and they passed through a hall that was typical of a thousand in similar apartment blocks in suburban London. The floor was of checkered vinyl, polished to mirror brightness. On the left wall was a cork board with notices from the managing agents about the date of lift maintenance and the cleaning contract. To the right an immense cheese plant in a green plastic pot, inadequately supported, drooped its bifurcated leaves. Ahead of them were the twin lifts. The silence was absolute. Somewhere up there, people must be living their cabined lives, but the air, sharp with the tang of floor polish, was as silent as if this were an apartment house of the dead. The tenants would be Londoners, transients most of them, young professionals on their way up, secretaries sharing with each other, retired couples living their self-contained lives. And a visitor could be coming to any one of the forty-odd flats. If Berowne were sensible he would have taken the lift to a different floor each time and walked up. But the risk would be small. Stanmore, for all its high leafiness, was no longer a village. There would be no peeping eyes behind the curtains to watch when he came or went. If Berowne had bought it for his mistress, as a convenient, anonymous meeting place he had chosen well.

Number forty-six was the corner flat on the top floor. They trod silently along a carpeted corridor to the white unnamed door. When Kate rang he wondered whether an eye was regarding them through the peephole, but the door was opened at once as if she had been standing there waiting for them. She stood aside and motioned them in. Then she turned to Dalgliesh and said:

'I've been expecting you. I knew you'd come sooner or later. And at least I'll know now what happened. I can hear someone speak his name, even if it's only a policeman.'

She was ready for them. She had done her crying; not all the crying she would do for her lover, but that dreadful howling anguish that tears the body apart was over now, at least for a time. He had had to witness its effects too often to miss the signs; the puffy eyelids, the skin dulled by grief's despoiling power, the lips swollen and unnaturally red, as if the lightest blow would burst them open. It was difficult to know how she normally looked. He thought that she had a pleasant, intelligent face, long-nosed but with high cheekbones and a firm jaw and a good skin. Her hair, mid-brown, strong and straight, was drawn back from her face and tied with a tag of crumpled ribbon. A few hairs lay damply across her forehead. Her voice was cracked and strained with recent crying but she had it well under control. He felt a respect for her. If grief was the criterion, she was the widow. As they followed her into the sitting room, he said:

'I'm very sorry to have to trouble you, and so soon. You know why we're here, of course. Do you feel able to talk about him? I need to know him better than I do if I'm to get anywhere.' She seemed to understand what he meant, that the victim was central to his death. He died because of what he was, what he knew, what he did, what he planned to do. He died because he was uniquely himself. Murder destroyed privacy, laid bare with brutal thoroughness all the petty contrivances of the dead life. Dalgliesh would rummage through Berowne's past as thoroughly as he rummaged through a victim's cupboards and files. The victim's privacy was the first to go, but no one intimately concerned with murder was left unscathed. The victim had at least escaped beyond earthbound considerations of dignity, embarrassment, reputation. But for the living, to be part of a murder investigation was to be contaminated by a process which would leave few of their lives unchanged. But at least, he thought, it had the merit of democracy. Murder remained the unique crime. Peer and pauper stood equal before it. The rich were, of course, advantaged in this as in everything. They could afford the best lawyers. But in a free society there was little else they could buy. She asked:

'Would you like some coffee?'

'Very much please, if it's not too much trouble.' Kate asked:

'Can I help?'

'It won't take long.'

Kate apparently took the words as an acceptance and followed the girl into the kitchen leaving the door ajar. It was typical of her, thought Dalgliesh, this unsentimental, practical response to people and their immediate concerns. Without hectoring or presumption, she could reduce the most embarrassing situation to something approaching normality. It was one of her strengths. Now, above the tinkle of kettle lid and crockery, he could hear their voices, conversational, almost ordinary. From the few phrases he could catch, they seemed to be discussing the merits of a make of electric kettle which both possessed. Suddenly he felt that he shouldn't be there, that he was redundant as a detective and a man. They would both get on better without his male, destructive presence. Even the room seemed inimical to him, and he could almost persuade himself that the low broken sibilants of female voices were in conspiracy.

There was the grinding roar of a coffee mill. So, she used fresh ground beans. But of course. She would take trouble over the coffee. It was the drink she and her lover must most often have shared. He looked around the sitting room with its long window giving a distant view of the London skyline. The furniture represented a rather orthodox good taste. The sofa, covered with fawn linen, uncrumpled, still pristine, looked expensive and was probably Scandinavian in the austerity of the design. On each side of the fireplace were matching armchairs, the covers more worn than that on the sofa. The fireplace itself was modern, a simple shelf of white wood above a plain surround. And the fire, he saw, was one of the newest gas models which gave an illusion of burning coals and a living flame. She would have been able to turn it on as soon as she heard his ring; instant comfort, instant warmth. And if he didn't come, if there was business at the House or at home or in the constituency which kept him from her, there would be no cold ash the next morning to mock her with its easy symbolism.

Above the sofa was a line of watercolours; gentle English landscapes, their quality unmistakable. He thought he recognized a Lear and a Cotman. He wondered if these had been Berowne's gifts, a way perhaps of transferring to her something of value which both could enjoy and which her pride could accept. The wall opposite the fireplace was covered with wooden adjustable units reaching from floor to ceiling. These held a simple stereo system, racks for records, a television set, and her books. Walking over to inspect them and flicking them open, he saw she had read history at Reading University. Take away the books and substitute popular prints for the watercolours and the room could have been a showroom in a newly built block of flats, seducing the prospective buyer with a depressingly orthodox good taste. He thought: There are rooms designed to be got away from, bleak anterooms where the armour is buckled on to confront the real world outside. There are rooms to come back to, claustrophobic refuges from the arduous business of work and striving. This room was a world in itself, a still centre provisioned with economy and care but containing everything necessary to its owner's life; the flat itself an investment in more than property. All her capital had been tied up here, monetary and emotional. He looked at the row of plants, varied, well-tended, glossily healthy, which were ranged on the window sill. But then, why shouldn't they be healthy? She was always there to tend them.

The two women came back into the room, Miss Washburn carrying a tray with a percolator, three large white cups, a jug of hot milk, and sugar crystals. She set it down on the coffee table. Dalgliesh and Kate seated themselves on the sofa. Miss Washburn poured the coffee, including a cup for herself, then carried it over to her seat by the fire. As Dalgliesh had expected, the coffee was excellent, but she didn't drink. She gazed across at them and said:

'The television newsreader said knife wounds. What wounds?'

'Is that how you heard, on the television news?'

476

She said with great bitterness:

'Of course. How else would I hear?'

Dalgliesh was shaken by a pity so unexpected and so acute that for a moment he dared not speak. And with the pity came a resentment against Berowne which frightened him with its intensity. Surely the man had faced the possibility of sudden death. He was a public figure; he must have known there was always a risk. Hadn't there been someone that he could trust with his secret? Someone who could have broken the news to her, visited her, brought her at least the comfort that he had thought about saving her pain. Couldn't he have found time in his over-busy life to write a letter which could have been privately taken to her if he died unexpectedly? Or had he been arrogant enough to think himself immune from the risks of lesser mortals; a coronary, a car accident, an IRA bomb? The tide of anger ebbed, leaving a slough of self-disgust. It had been directed against himself. He thought: Isn't that how I might have behaved? We're alike even in this. If he had a splinter of ice in the heart, then so have I.

She repeated stubbornly:

'What knife wounds?'

There was no way of telling it gently.

'His throat was cut. His and the tramp's who was with him, Harry Mack.' He didn't know why telling her Harry's name should be important as it had been important to speak it to Lady Ursula. It was as if he were determined that none of them should forget Harry.

She asked:

'With Paul's razor?'

'It's probable.'

'And the razor was still there, by the body?'

She had said body, not bodies. There was only one which concerned her. He said:

'Yes, by his outstretched hand.'

'And the outside door, was it unlocked?'

'Yes.'

She said:

'So he let in his murderer just as he let in the tramp. Or did the tramp kill him?'

'No, the tramp didn't kill him. Harry was a victim, not a killer.'

'Then it was an outsider. Paul couldn't have killed anyone, and I don't believe he killed himself.'

Dalgliesh said:

'We don't believe it either. We're treating it as murder. That's why we need your help. We need you to talk about him. You probably knew him better than any other person.'

She said, so low that he could only just catch the whisper: 'I thought I did. I thought I did.'

She took up her cup and tried to lift it to her lips, but couldn't control it. Dalgliesh felt Kate stiffen at his side and wondered whether she was controlling an impulse to put her arms round the girl's shoulder and raise the cup to her lips. But she didn't move and, at the second attempt, Miss Washburn managed to get her mouth to the brim. She gulped in the coffee, noisily, like a thirsty child.

Watching her, Dalgliesh knew what he was doing and the more fastidious part of his mind was repelled by it. She was alone, unacknowledged, denied the simple human need to share her grief, to talk about her lover. And it was that need which he was about to exploit. He sometimes thought bitterly that exploitation was at the heart of successful detection, particularly with murder. You exploited the suspect's fear, his vanity, his need to confide, the insecurity that tempted him to say that one vital sentence too many. Exploiting grief and loneliness was only another version of the same technique.

She looked at him and said:

'Can I see where it happened? I mean without making a fuss about it or being noticed. I should like to sit there alone when they have the funeral. It would be better than sitting at the back of the congregation trying not to make a fool of myself.'

He said:

'At the moment the back of the church is being kept locked. But I'm sure it could be arranged once we've finally finished with the place. Father Barnes, he's the parish priest, would let you in. It's a very ordinary room. Just a vestry, dusty, rather cluttered, smelling of hymn books and incense, but a very peaceful place.' He added, 'I think it happened very quickly. I don't think he felt any pain.'

'But he must have felt fear.'

'Perhaps not even that.'

She said:

'It's such an unlikely thing to have happened, that conversion, divine revelation, whatever it was. That sounds foolish. Of course it's unlikely. I meant that it's an unlikely thing to have happened to Paul. He was, well, worldly. Oh I don't mean in the sense that he only cared about success, money, prestige. But he was so in the world, of the world. He wasn't a mystic. He wasn't even particularly religious. He usually went to church on Sundays and on the major feast days because he enjoyed the liturgy – he wouldn't attend if they used the new Bible or Prayer Book. And he said he liked an hour when he could think without interruptions, without the telephone ringing. He once said that formal religious observance confirmed identity, reminded one of the limits of behaviour, something like that. Belief wasn't meant to be a burden. Nor was disbelief. Does any of this make sense?'

'Yes.'

'He liked food, wine, architecture, women. I don't mean that he was promiscuous. But he loved the beauty of women. I couldn't give him that. But I could give him something no one else could, peace, honesty, total trust.'

It was odd, he thought. It was the religious experience not the murder that she needed most to talk about. Her lover was dead and even the enormity of that final, irrevocable loss couldn't blot out the pain of that earlier betrayal. But they would get round to the murder in time. There was no hurry. He wouldn't get what he wanted by rushing her now. He asked:

'Did he explain it to you, that experience in the vestry?'

'He came round the following night. He'd had a meeting in the House and it was late. He couldn't stay long. He told me that he had had an experience of God. That's all. An experience of God. He made it sound perfectly matter-of-fact. But it wasn't, of course. Then he left. I knew then I'd lost him. Not as a friend, perhaps, but then I didn't want him as a friend. I'd lost him as a lover. I'd lost him for ever. He didn't need to tell me that.'

There were, he knew, women to whom secrecy, risk, treachery, conspiracy, gave a love affair that extra erotic charge. They were women as uncommitted as their men, as fond of personal privacy, who wanted an intense relationship but not at the price of their careers, women to whom sexual passion and domesticity were irreconcilable. But she, he thought, had not been one of them. He recalled word for word his conversation with Higginson of Special Branch. Higginson, in his carefully tailored tweeds, straight-backed, clear-eyed, firm-jawed under the cropped moustache, so like the conventional image of an army officer that, for Dalgliesh, he walked in an aura of bogus respectability; a conman deferential on suburban doorways, a second-hand car salesman loitering at Warren Street Underground. Even his cynicism seemed as carefully calculated as his accent. Yet the accent was perfectly genuine and so was the cynicism. The worst you could say of Higginson was that he liked his job too well.

'It's the usual thing, my dear Adam. A decorative wife for show, the devoted little woman on the side for use. Only in this case I'm not sure what use precisely. The choice is a little surprising. You'll see. But there's no security problem, never has been. They've both been remarkably discreet. Berowne has always made it plain that he accepted any necessary security precautions but that he was entitled to take some risks where his private life was concerned. She has never made trouble. I'd be surprised if she makes it now. There'll be no embarrassing little bundle in eight months' time.'

Could she, he wondered, have really shut her eyes to the reality, that the affair was documented, every step of its progress noted with almost clinical detachment by those cynical watchers who had decided, no doubt after the normal bureaucratic processes, that she could be classified as a harmless diversion, that Berowne could enjoy his weekly entertainment without official harassment. Surely she couldn't have deceived herself, and neither could he. She was, after all, herself a bureaucrat, a Principal. She must know how the system worked. She was still comparatively junior, but it was her world. One sign that she was a security risk and he would have been warned off. And he would have taken the warning. You didn't become a Minister of State if you hadn't enough ambition, egotism, and ruthlessness to know where your priorities had to lie.

He asked:

'How did you meet?'

'How do you expect? At work. I was a Principal in his private office.'

So it had been as he had expected.

'And then when you became lovers, you asked for a transfer?'

'No, I was due for a transfer. You don't stay long in private office.'

'Did you ever meet his family?'

'He didn't take me home, if that's what you mean. He didn't introduce me to his wife or Lady Ursula and say, "Meet Carole Washburn. Meet my mistress."'

'How often did you see him?'

'As often as he could get away. Sometimes we had a half-day. Sometimes a couple of hours. He tried to drop in on his way to his constituency if he were alone. Sometimes we couldn't meet for weeks.'

'And he never suggested marriage? Forgive me, this question could be important.'

'If you mean that someone could have slit his throat to prevent him asking for a divorce to marry me, you're wasting your time. The answer to your question, Commander, is no, he never suggested marriage. And neither did I.'

'Would you describe him as happy?'

She didn't seem surprised by the apparent irrelevance of the question nor did she need to give it much thought. She had known the answer for a long time. 'No, not really. What happened to him – I don't mean the murder – what happened to him in that church, whatever it was, I don't think it would have happened if he'd been satisfied with his life, if our love had been enough for him. It was enough for me; all I wanted, all I needed. It wasn't enough for him. I've always known that. Nothing was enough for Paul, nothing.'

'Did he tell you that he'd had a poison pen letter about Theresa Nolan and Diana Travers?'

'Yes, he told me. He didn't take it seriously.'

'He took it seriously enough to show it to me.'

She said:

'Theresa Nolan's child, the one she aborted, it wasn't his if that's what you're thinking. It couldn't have been. He would have told me. Look, it was just a poison pen letter. Politicians get them all the time. They're used to them. Why worry about it now?'

'Because anything that happened during the last weeks of his life could be important. You must see that.'

'What does it matter, the scandal or the lies. They can't touch him now. They can't hurt him. Nothing can. Not any more.'

He asked, gently:

'Were there things that hurt him?'

'He was human, wasn't he? Of course there were things that hurt him.'

'What things? His wife's infidelity?'

She didn't reply.

He said:

'Miss Washburn, my priority is catching his murderer, not preserving his reputation. They needn't be incompatible. I'll try to see that they aren't. But I'm clear which has to come first. Shouldn't you be?'

She spoke with sudden fierceness:

'No. I've preserved his privacy – not reputation, privacy – for three years. It's cost me a lot. I haven't complained to him. I'm not complaining now. I knew the rules. But I'm going to go on preserving his privacy. It was important to him. If I don't, all those years of discretion, never being seen together, never being able to say "This is my man, we're lovers", always taking second place to his job, his wife, his constituents, his mother, what has been the point of it? You can't bring him back.'

That was always the cry when the going got rough, 'You can't bring them back.' He remembered his second child murderer; the hidden cache of pornographic photographs the police had uncovered in the killer's flat, indecent poses of his victims, pathetic childish bodies violated and exposed. It had been his job as a newly promoted detective inspector to ask a mother to identify her daughter. The woman's eyes had glanced at the photograph once only and then stared ahead, denying knowledge, denying truth. There were some realities which the mind refused to accept even in the cause of retribution, of justice. You can't bring them back. It was the cry of the whole defeated, anguished, grieving world.

But she was speaking.

'There were a lot of things I couldn't give him. But I could give him secrecy, discretion. I've heard about you. There was that business down in the Fens, the forensic scientist who was murdered. Paul told me about it. It was quite a triumph for you, wasn't it? You say, "What about the victim?" But what about your victims? I expect you'll catch Paul's murderer. You usually do, don't you? Does it ever occur to you to count the cost?'

Dalgliesh felt Kate stiffen at the clear note of dislike and contempt. The girl went on:

'But you'll have to do it without me. You don't really need my help. I'm not going to break Paul's confidences just so that you can notch up another success.'

He said:

'There's the matter of the dead tramp, Harry Mack.'

'I'm sorry, but I've nothing left over to spare for Harry Mack, not even sympathy. I'm leaving Harry Mack out of my calculations.'

'I can't leave him out of mine.'

'Of course not, that's your job. Look, I know nothing that can help solve this murder for you. If Paul had enemies I don't know about them. I've told you about him and me. You knew anyway. But I'm not getting involved any deeper. I'm not ending up in the witness box, photographed on my way into court, pictured on the front page "Paul Berowne's Little Bit On The Side".'

She got to her feet. It was the sign for them to go. When they reached the door, she said:

'I want to get away, just for a couple of weeks. I've plenty of leave in hand. If the papers find out about me then I don't want to be here when it happens. I couldn't bear that. I want to get out of London, out of England. You can't stop me.'

Dalgliesh said:

'No. But we'll still be here when you come back.'

'And if I don't come back?' She spoke with the weary accept-ance of defeat. How could she live abroad, dependent as she was on her job, her salary? This flat might have lost its meaning for her but London was still her home and the job would be important to her for more reasons than money. A young woman didn't become a Principal without intelligence, hard work, ambition. But he answered her question as if it had reality.

'Then I should have to come to you.'

Outside in the car, buckling on his seatbelt, he said:

'I wonder if we would have got more out of her if you'd seen her alone. She might have spoken more freely if I hadn't been there.'

Kate said:

'Possibly, sir, but only if I'd promised to keep it confidential, and I don't see how I could have done that.'

Massingham, he suspected, would have promised secrecy and then had no compunction in telling. That was one of the differences between them.

'No,' he said, 'you couldn't have done that.'

4

Back in New Scotland Yard, Kate burst into Massingham's office. She found him alone, surrounded by paper, and had pleasure in interrupting his conscientious but unenthusiastic perusal of the door-to-door inquiry reports with a vehement account of the interview. She had controlled her sense of outrage with difficulty on the drive back to the Yard and was in the mood for a confrontation, preferably with a male.

'The man was a shit!'

'Oh, I don't know. Aren't you being a bit hard?'

'It's the same old story. He basks in his success; she's tucked away in the equivalent of a Victorian love-nest to serve his purpose when he has an odd moment to spare for her. We could be back in the nineteenth century.'

'But we aren't. It's her choice. Come off it, Kate! She has a good job, her own flat, a good salary, a career with a pension. She could have chucked him any day she chose. He wasn't coercing her.'

'Not physically, perhaps.'

'Don't start singing a variation of the old song "It's the Man What Gets the Pleasure, It's the Girl What Gets the Blame". Recent history is against you anyway. There was nothing to stop her having it out with him. She could have given him an ultimatum. "You've got to choose, it's her or me".'

'Knowing what his choice would be?'

'Well that's the risk isn't it? She might have struck lucky. This isn't the nineteenth century. And he's not Parnell. Divorce wouldn't have harmed his career, not for long, not much.'

'It wouldn't have helped it.'

'OK. Take your chap, whoever he is. Or any chap you might fancy. If you had to choose between him and your job, would that be so easy? When you're feeling censorious, better ask yourself which you'd choose.'

The question disconcerted her. He probably either knew or had guessed about Alan. You didn't keep many secrets in the CID and her very reticence about her private life would have stimulated curiosity. But she hadn't expected such perception from him or such frankness and she wasn't sure she liked it. She said:

'Well, it hasn't made me respect him.'

'We don't have to respect him. We're not asked to respect him or like him or admire his politics, his ties or his taste in women. Our job is to catch his murderer.'

She sat down opposite him, suddenly weary, and let her shoulder bag slip to the floor, then watched him as he began putting his papers together. She liked his office, intrigued by the difference between its sparse masculinity and the murder squad room down the corridor. There the atmosphere was heavily masculine, reminiscent, she thought, of an officers' mess, but as she had once overheard Massingham say to Dalgliesh with the sly malice which his subordinates found offensive and which reminded them of his old nickname of the Honjohn ... 'Not altogether a first class regiment would you say, sir?' The squad were called in to investigate crime at sea and were usually rewarded with a framed photograph of the ship concerned. These were mounted in regular lines along the walls together with signed portraits of chiefs of police from Commonwealth countries, emblems and badges, signed testimonials, even the occasional photograph of a celebratory dinner. Massingham's walls were decorated only with colour prints of early cricket matches borrowed, she guessed, from his home. These gentle evocations of long dead summers, the oddly shaped bats, the top hats of the players, the familiar cathedral spires piercing an English sky, the shadowed grass, and the crinolined ladies with their parasols, had at first been a source of mild interest to his colleagues but were now hardly noticed. Kate thought his choice showed a nice compromise between masculine conformity and personal taste. And he could hardly have mounted his school photographs. Eton wasn't exactly unacceptable to the Met but it wasn't a school to boast about. She asked:

'How is the house-to-house going?'

'As you'd expect. No one saw or heard anything. They were all sitting glued to the box, down at the Dog and Duck, or at bingo. No big fish, but we've netted the usual minnows. Pity we can't throw them back. Still, it'll keep Division busy.'

'And the cab drivers?'

'No luck. One chap remembered driving a middle-aged gent to within forty yards of the church at the relevant time. We traced the fare. He was visiting his lady friend.'

'What? In a love-nest off the Harrow Road?'

'He had somewhat specific requirements. Remember Fatima?'

'Good God, is she still on the job?'

'Very much so. She's also taken to doing a little snouting for Chalkey White. The lady's none too pleased with us at present. And neither is Chalkey.'

'And the fare?'

'Well, he's putting in an official complaint. Harassment, interference with personal liberty, the usual. And we've had six confessions to the murder.'

'Six. So soon?'

'Three of them we've met before. All certifiable. One did it to protest against Tory policy on immigration, one because Berowne had seduced his granddaughter, and one because the Archangel Gabriel told him to. They've all got the time wrong. They all used a knife not a razor and you won't be surprised to hear that none of them can produce it. With a singular lack of originality, they all claim to have chucked it in the canal.'

She said:

'Do you ever wonder how much of our job is really cost effective?'

'From time to time. What do you expect us to do about it?'

'Waste less time on the minnows to begin with.'

'Come off it, Kate. We can't pick and choose. Only within strict limits anyway. And it's no different with a doctor. He can't make the whole society healthy, he can't heal the world. He'd go crazy if he tried. He just treats what comes his way. Sometimes he wins, sometimes he loses.'

She said:

'But he doesn't spend all his time cauterizing warts while the cancers go untreated.'

He said:

'Hell, if bloody murder isn't a cancer, what is? Actually, it's probably a murder investigation, not common crime, which isn't cost effective. Think what it cost to put the Yorkshire Ripper behind bars. Think what this killer will cost the taxpayer before we get him.'

'If we get him.' And for the first time she was tempted to add: 'And if he exists.'

Massingham got up from the desk.

'You need a drink. I'll buy you one.'

Suddenly she almost liked him.

'OK,' she said, 'thanks.' She picked up her shoulder bag and they went out together to the senior officers' mess.

5

Mrs Iris Minns lived in a council flat on the second floor of a block off the Portobello Road. To park anywhere close on a Saturday, the day of the street market, was impossible, so Massingham and Kate left the car at the Notting Hill police station and walked. The Saturday market was, as always, a carnival; a cosmopolitan, peaceable if noisy celebration of human gregariousness, curiosity, gullibility and greed. It brought back to Kate memories of her early days in the division. She always walked through the cluttered street with pleasure, although she seldom bought; she had never shared the popular obsession with the trivia of the past. And for all its air of cheerful camaraderie, the market was, she knew, less innocent than it looked. Not all the bundles of notes in various currencies changing hands would find their way into tax returns. Not all the trading was in the harmless artefacts of the past. The usual number of unwary visitors would be relieved of their wallets or purses before they reached the bottom of the road. But few London markets were as gentle, as entertaining or as good-humoured. This morning, as always, she entered the narrow, raucous thoroughfare with a lifting of the spirits.

Iris Minns lived in flat twenty-six of Block Two, a building separated from the main block and from the road by a wide courtway. As they crossed it, watched by several pairs of carefully incurious but wary eyes, Massingham said:

'I'll do the talking.' She felt the familiar spurt of resentment but said nothing.

The appointment had been made by telephone for nine thirty, and from the speed with which the front door was opened to their ring, Mrs Minns must have been among those watching their arrival from behind their curtains. They found themselves facing a small compact figure with a square face, a round determined chin, a long mouth which twitched into a brief smile which seemed less one of welcome than of satisfaction that they were on time, and a pair of dark, almost black, eyes which gave them a quick, appraising glance as if inspecting them for dust. She took the trouble to examine Massingham's warrant card with some care, then stood aside and motioned them in, saying:

'Well, you're on time, I'll say that for you. There's tea or coffee if you fancy it.'

Massingham quickly refused it for both of them. Kate's first instinct was to say quickly that she would like coffee, but she resisted the temptation. This could be an important interview; there was no point in jeopardizing its success out of personal pique. And Mrs Minns wouldn't miss any overt antagonism between them. She couldn't have been mistaken in the flash of intelligence in those dark eyes.

The sitting room into which they were shown was so remarkable that she hoped that her surprise didn't show too clearly on
her face. Provided by local bureaucracy with an oblong box
fifteen feet by ten, a single window and a door opening to a
balcony too small for any purpose but giving air to a few pot
plants, Mrs Minns had created a small Victorian sitting room,
dark, cluttered, claustrophobic. The wallpaper was a dark olive-
green patterned with ivy and lilies, the carpet a faded but
serviceable Wilton, while occupying almost the whole of the
middle of the room was an oblong table of polished mahogany
with curved legs, its surface mirror-bright, and four high-backed
carved chairs. A smaller octagonal table was set against one wall
holding an aspidistra in a brass pot while the walls were hung
with sentimental prints in maple frames; the *Sailor's Farewell* and
Sailor's Return, a child reaching for a flower above a brook, its
heedless steps protected by a winged angel wearing an expression
of pious imbecility. In front of the window stood a long plant-
holder of wrought iron painted white, filled with pots of geraniums, and outside on the balcony they could glimpse terracotta
pots holding ivy and climbing plants whose variegated leaves
were entwined with the railings.

The focus of the room was a seventeen-inch television set, but
this was less of an anachronism than might first appear since it
was placed against a background of green ferns whose fronds
curled against the screen like an ornate but living frame. The
window-ledge was covered with small tubs of African violets,
deep purple and a freckled paler mauve. Kate thought that they
were planted in yoghurt tubs, but it was difficult to be sure since
each was decorated with a plaited paper doily. A sideboard with
an elaborately carved back was covered with china animals, dogs
discordant in size and breed, a spotted fawn, and half a dozen
china cats in unconvincing feline attitudes, each one on a starched
linen mat, presumably to protect the polished mahogany.

The whole room was spotlessly clean, the pungent smell of
polish overwhelming. When in winter the heavy red velvet curtains were drawn it would be possible to believe oneself in
another setting, another age. And Mrs Minns could have been
part of it. She was wearing a black skirt and a white blouse

buttoned to the neck and fastened with a cameo brooch and with her greying hair dressed high at the front and coiled in a small bun at the nape of the neck, she looked, thought Kate, like an ageing actress dressed for the part of a Victorian housekeeper. The only criticism one could make was that the rouge and eye-shadow had been over-lavishly applied. She seated herself in the right-hand armchair and motioned Kate to the other, leaving Massingham to seat himself by turning round one of the dining chairs. In it he looked uncomfortably high and, thought Kate, somewhat at a disadvantage, a male intruder into comfortable female domesticity. In the autumn light, filtered through lace curtains and the green of the balcony plants, his face under the thatch of red hair looked almost sickly, the freckles over the forehead standing out like a splutter of pale blood. He said:

'Can't we have the door closed? I can't hear myself speak.'

The door on to the balcony was ajar. Kate got up and went over to close it. To the right she could glimpse the huge blue and white teapot hanging outside the Portobello Pottery and the painted wall panel of the porcelain market. The noise of the street came up to her like the clatter of shingle on a seashore. Then she closed the door and the sound was deadened. Mrs Minns said:

'It's only on a Saturday. Mr Smith and I don't much mind it. You get used to it. I always say it's a bit of life.' She turned to Kate:

'You live in these parts, don't you? I'm sure I've seen you shopping up at the Gate.'

'Very possibly, Mrs Minns. I'm not far away.'

'Oh well, it's a village, isn't it? You see everyone up at the Gate sooner or later.'

Massingham said impatiently:

'You mentioned a Mr Smith.'

'He lives here, but you can't see him. Not that he'd be able to tell you anything. But he's off roamin'.'

'Roaming? Where?'

'How do I know. On his bicycle. His folk used to live in Hillgate Village in the old days. Proper little slum it was when his grandad was alive. A hundred and sixty thousand they're asking for the houses now. I reckon he's got gypsy blood, has Mr Smith. There was a lot of gypsies settled round here after they pulled down the Hippodrome racecourse. He's always roamin'. It's easier for him now that British Rail let his bike go free. Lucky for you he isn't here. He's not too keen on the police. Too many of your chaps pick him up for nothing only sleeping under a hedge. That's what's wrong with this country, too much pickin' on decent people. And other things I could mention what we're not allowed to say.'

Kate could sense Massingham's anxiety to get on with the matter in hand. As if she too had sensed it, Mrs Minns said:

'It was a proper shock for me, I don't mind telling you. Lady Ursula rang me up just before nine o'clock that night. She told me you'd be sure to be along sooner or later.'

'So that was the first you'd heard of Sir Paul's death, when his mother rang to warn you?'

'Warn me? No call to warn me. I didn t slit his throat for him, poor gentleman, nor I don't know who did. You'd have thought Miss Matlock might have taken the trouble to phone earlier. That would have been better for me than hearing it on the six o'clock news. I wondered whether to ring the house, find out if there was anything I could do, but I reckoned they'd be bothered with enough calls without me on the line. Better wait, I thought, until someone rings.'

Massingham said:

'And that was Lady Ursula, just before nine?'

'That's right. Nice of her to trouble. But then we've always got on well, me and Lady Ursula. You call her Lady Ursula Berowne because she's the daughter of an earl. Lady Berowne is only the wife of a baronet.'

Massingham said impatiently:

'Yes, we do know that.'

'Oh you do, do you? Millions don't, nor don't care neither. Still, it's as well to get it right if you're thinking of hanging about Campden Hill Square.'

Massingham asked:

'How did she sound when she rang you?'

'Lady Ursula? How do you expect? She wasn't laughing, was

she? Wasn't crying neither. That's not her way. She was calm like she always is. Couldn't tell me much, though. What happened? Suicide was it?'

'We can't be sure, Mrs Minns, until we know more, get the results of some tests. We have to treat this as a suspicious death. When did you last see Sir Paul?'

'Just before he went out on Tuesday, about half past ten that would be. We was in the library. I'd gone in to polish the desk and there he was, sitting there. So I said I'd come back later, and he said "No, come in, Mrs Minns, I won't be long."'

'What was he doing?'

'Like I said, he was sitting at the desk. He had his diary open.'

Massingham said sharply:

'Are you sure?'

'Of course I'm sure. He had it open in front of him and he was looking through it.'

'How can you be certain that it was his diary?'

'Look, it was open in front of him and I could see it was a diary. It had different days on the page, it had dates in it and he'd written in it. Think I don't know a diary when I see one? Afterwards he closed it up and put it in the top right-hand drawer where it's usually kept.'

Massingham asked:

'How do you know where it's usually kept?'

'Look. I've worked in that house nine years. I was taken on by her Ladyship when Sir Hugo was baronet. You get to know things.'

'What else happened between you?'

'Nothing much. I asked him if I could borrow one of his books.'

'Borrow one of his books?' Massingham frowned his surprise.

'That's right. I'd seen it on the bottom shelf when I'd been dusting and I fancied reading it. It's there, under the television set, if you're interested. *A Rose by Twilight* by Millicent Gentle. I haven't seen a book by her for years.'

She reached for it and handed it to Massingham. It was a slim book still in its dust cover, a picture of an egregiously handsome dark-haired hero holding a blonde girl half-swooning in his arms against a background riot of roses. Massingham flicked through it and said with a note of amused contempt:

'Hardly his kind of reading, I should have thought. Sent to him, I imagine, by one of his constituents. It's signed by the author. I wonder why he bothered to keep it.'

Mrs Minns said sharply:

'Why shouldn't he keep it? She's a good writer is Millicent Gentle. Not that she's been doing much lately. I'm very partial to a good romantic novel. Better than all those horrible murders. I can't be doing with them. So I asked if I could borrow it and he said I could.'

Kate took the book and opened it. On the flyleaf was written: 'To Paul Berowne, with every good wish from the author'. Underneath was the signature, Millicent Gentle and the date, the seventh of August. It was the date of Diana Travers' drowning, but apparently Massingham hadn't noticed. She closed the book and said:

'We'll take this book back to Campden Hill Square if you've finished with it, Mrs Minns.'

'Please yourself. I wasn't thinking of pinchin' it if that's what you're thinking.'

Massingham asked:

'What else happened after he'd said you could borrow the book?'

'He asked me how long I'd been working at Campden Hill Square. I said nine years. Then he said "Have they been good years for you?" I said, as good for me as they have for most.'

Massingham smiled. He said:

'I don't think that's what he meant.'

'I know what he meant all right. But what did he expect me to say? I do the work, they pay me; four pounds an hour which is above the going rate, and a taxi home if I'm there after dark. I wouldn't stay if the job didn't suit. But what do they expect for their money? Love? If he'd wanted me to say that I'd spent the best years of my life at Campden Hill Square then he was disappointed. Mind you, it was different when the first Lady Berowne was alive.'

'How do you mean, different?'

'Just different. The house seemed more alive then. I liked the first Lady Berowne. She was a very pleasant lady. Not that she lasted long, poor soul.'

Kate asked:

'Why did you continue to work at number sixty-two, Mrs Minns?'

Mrs Minns turned her bright little eyes on Kate and said simply:

'I like polishing furniture.'

Kate guessed that Massingham was tempted to ask what she thought of the second Lady Berowne, but he decided to keep to his main line of questioning.

'And what then?' he asked.

'He went out, didn't he?'

'Out of the house?'

'That's right.'

'Can you be sure?'

'Look, he had his jacket on, he picked up that hold-all he had, he went through the hall and I heard the front door open and shut. If it wasn't him going out then who was it?'

'But you didn't actually see him go?'

'I never followed him to the door to kiss him goodbye, if that's what you mean. I have my work to do. But that's the last time I saw him in this world, and I've no expectations of seeing him in the next, that's for sure.'

Perhaps prudently Massingham did not pursue this thought. He said:

'And you're certain that he put the diary back in the drawer?'

'He didn't take it with him. Look, what is it about the diary? Are you saying I stole it or something?'

Kate broke in:

'It isn't in the drawer now, Mrs Minns. Of course, we don't suspect anyone of taking it. It hasn't any value. But it does seem to be missing, and it could be important. You see, if he did make an appointment for the next day, then it wouldn't be very likely that he set out from home meaning to kill himself.'

Mrs Minns, mollified, said:

'Well, he didn't take it with him. I saw him put it back with my own eyes. And if he did come back for it later, it wasn't while I was in the house.'

Massingham asked:

'That's possible, of course. When did you leave?'

'Five o'clock. My usual time. I wash up the lunch things and I have my special afternoon job. Some days it might be the silver, some days the linen cupboard. On Tuesday it was dusting the books in the library. I was there from half past two until four, when I went to help Miss Matlock with the tea. He certainly didn't come back then. I'd have heard anyone if they'd come through the hall.'

Suddenly Kate asked:

'Would you say it was a happy marriage, Mrs Minns?'

'Hardly ever saw them together to tell. When I did they seemed all right. They never shared a bedroom, though.'

Massingham said:

'That's not so very unusual.'

'Maybe. But there's not sharing and not sharing if you get my meaning. I make the beds, you see. That may be your idea of a marriage but it's not mine.'

Massingham said:

'Hardly the way to produce the next baronet.'

'Well, I did wonder about that a few weeks ago. Off her breakfast she was and that isn't like her. But not much chance I reckon. Too worried about her figure. Mind you, she's not bad when she's in a good mood. Too gushing though. "Oh Mrs Minns be a darling and fetch my dressing gown." "Mrs Minns, be an angel and run a bath for me." "Be a dear and make a cup of tea." Sweet as sugar as long as she gets her own way. Well, she more or less has to be. Same with Lady Ursula. She doesn't much care for Miss Matlock helping her to bath and dress. I can see that even if Matlock can't. But there it is. If you get used to having your bath run and your breakfast in bed and your clothes hung up, you have to put up with some inconvenience in return. Different when Lady Ursula was a girl, of course. Servants were seen and not heard then. Pressed back against the wall when the gentry go by in case they have to look at you. Hand the post with a glove so as not to contaminate it. Think yourself lucky to have a good place. My gran was in service; I know.'

Massingham said:

'There were no quarrels, then, as far as you know?'

'It would have been better, maybe, if there had been. He was too polite, formal you could say. Now that's not natural in a marriage. No, there were no quarrels, not till Tuesday morning anyway. And then you could hardly call it a quarrel. Takes two to quarrel. She was screeching fit to reach the whole house, but I didn't hear much from him.'

'When was this, Mrs Minns?'

'When I took up her breakfast tray at half past eight. I do that every morning. Sir Paul used to take up Lady Ursula's. She only has orange juice, two slices of wholemeal bread, toasted, marmalade and coffee, but Lady Berowne has the whole hog. Orange juice, cereal, scrambled egg, toast, the lot. Never puts on an ounce though.'

'Tell me about the quarrel, Mrs Minns. What did you hear?'

'I got to the bedroom door when I heard her screeching: "You're going to that whore. You can't, not now. We need you, we both need you. I won't let you go." Something like that. And then I could hear his voice, very low. I couldn't hear what he was saying. I stood outside the door and wondered what to do. I put the tray down on the table by the door. I usually do that while I knock. But it didn't seem right to go barging in. On the other hand I couldn't stand there like a daft thing. Then the door opened and he came out. White as paper he was. He saw me and said: "I'll take the tray, Mrs Minns." So I gave it to him. The way he looked it was a wonder he didn't drop it there and then.'

Massingham said:

'But he took it into the bedroom?'

'That's right, and shut the door. And I went back to the kitchen.'

Massingham changed the direction of his questions. He asked:

'Did anyone else enter the library that Tuesday as far as you know?'

'That Mr Musgrave from the constituency did. He waited from about half past twelve to nearly two o'clock hoping Sir Paul would be back for lunch. Then he gave up and went away. Miss

Sarah was there about four o'clock. She'd come to see her grandmother. I told her Lady Ursula wasn't expected back to tea, but she said she'd wait. Then she got fed up too, seemingly. Must have let herself out. I didn't see the going of her.'

Massingham went on to ask her about Diana Travers. Kate sensed that he had less faith than she had in AD's belief that the deaths of both girls were somehow connected with Paul Berowne's murder, but he dutifully did what was expected of him. The result proved a great deal more interesting than either of them had thought possible. Mrs Minns said:

'I was there when Diana arrived. We'd just lost Maria. She was Spanish, her husband worked as a cook in Soho, then she got pregnant with her third and the doctor said to cut down on her outside jobs. She was a good worker, was Maria. Those Spanish girls know how to house-clean, I'll say that for them. Anyway, Miss Matlock put a card in the newsagent's window at the end of Ladbroke Grove and Diana turned up. The card couldn't have been there more than an hour. A bit of luck, really, I never thought she'd get any answers. Good cleaning ladies don't have to look in newsagents for jobs these days.'

'And was she a good cleaner?'.

'Never done it in her life before, you could see that. But she was willing enough. Of course Miss Matlock never let her touch the best china or polish in the drawing room. She took over the bathrooms, bedrooms, prepared vegetables, did a bit of shopping. She was all right.'

'A strange job for her to choose, though, a girl like that.'

Mrs Minns understood what he meant.

'Oh, she was educated all right, you could see that. Well it wasn't badly paid, four pounds an hour, a good midday meal if you're there for it and no tax unless you're daft enough to pay it. She said she was an actress looking for work and wanted a job she could chuck at once if something turned up. What's so interesting about Diana Travers anyway?'

Massingham ignored the question. He said:

'Did you and she get on well together?'

'No reason why we shouldn't. I told you, she was all right. A bit nosey. Found her one day looking in the drawer of Sir Paul's desk. Didn't hear me till I was on top of her. Bold as brass about it. Just laughed. Asked a lot about the family, too. She didn't get much out of me, nor from Miss Matlock either. No harm in her though, just a bit too keen on chat. I liked her all right. If I hadn't I wouldn't have let her come here.'

'You mean she lived here? We weren't told that at Campden Hill Square.'

'Well, they didn't know, did they? No reason why they should. She was buying herself a flat in Ridgmount Gardens and there was a hold-up. The owners weren't ready to move into their new place. You know how it is. Anyway, she had to leave her old place and find somewhere for a month. Well, I've got the two bedrooms so I told her she could move in here. Twenty-five pounds a week including a good breakfast. Not bad. I don't know that Mr Smith was all that keen but he was due to be off roamin' anyway.'

And there were the two bedrooms, thought Kate. Mrs Minns' black eyes stared at Massingham, defying him to inquire about the usual sleeping arrangements. And then she said:

'My gran said every woman should marry once, she owes it to herself. But no point in making a habit of it.'

Kate said:

'A flat in Ridgmount Gardens? Isn't that a bit upmarket for an out-of-work actress?'

'That's what I thought, but she said Daddy was helping. Maybe he was, maybe he wasn't. Maybe it was Daddy, maybe someone else. Anyway, he was in Australia, or so she told me. No business of mine.'

Massingham said:

'So she moved in here. When did she leave?'

'Just ten days before she was drowned, poor kid. And you're not telling me there was anything suspicious about that death. I was at the inquest. Natural interest you might say. Never a mention of where she worked though, was there? You'd have thought they might have sent a wreath to the funeral. Didn't want to know, did they?'

Massingham asked:

'What did she do with herself while she was living here with you?'

'I hardly saw her. No business of mine, was it? Two mornings a week she worked at Campden Hill Square. The rest of the time she said she was off for auditions. She went out a good bit at night, but she never brought anyone here. She was no trouble, neat and tidy always. Well, I wouldn't have had her here if I hadn't known that. Then, the evening after she drowned, before the inquest even, she hadn't been dead twenty-four hours, these two chaps turn up.'

'Here?'

'That's right. Just when I got back from Campden Hill Square. Sitting in their car watching out for me if you ask me. Said they were from her solicitors, come to collect any of her things she might have left here.'

'Did they show you any identity, any authority?'

'A letter from the firm. Posh writing paper. And they had a card, so I let them in. I stayed by the door and watched them, mind you. They didn't like it, but I wanted to see what they were up to. "There's nothing here," I told them. "Look for yourselves. She left nearly a fortnight ago." They properly turned the place over, even turned the mattress up. Found nothing, of course. Funny business, I thought, but nothing came of it so I let it go. No point in making trouble.'

'Who do you think they were?'

Mrs Minns gave a sudden shout of laughter.

'You tell me! Come off it! They were two of your lot. Fuzz. Think I don't know a policeman when I see one?'

Even in the room's dim arboreal light Kate saw the faint flush of excitement on Massingham's face. But he was too experienced to press further. Instead he asked a few harmless questions about the domestic arrangements at Campden Hill Square and prepared to bring the interview to a close. But Mrs Minns had her own ideas. Kate sensed that she had something private to communicate. Getting up she said:

'D'you mind if I use your lavatory, Mrs Minns?'

She doubted whether Massingham was deceived, but he could hardly follow them. Waiting for her outside the door of the bathroom Mrs Minns almost hissed:

'You saw the date in that book?'

'Yes, Mrs Minns. The day Diana Travers was drowned.'

The sharp little eyes gleamed with satisfaction.

'I thought as how you'd noticed. He didn't though, did he?'

'I expect so. He just didn't mention it.'

'He never noticed. I know his sort. Too sharp for their own good and then miss what's under their noses.'

'When did you first see the book, Mrs Minns?'

'The next day, August the eighth. In the afternoon it was, after he came home from the constituency. Must have brought it with him.'

'So she may have given it to him then.'

'Maybe. Maybe not. Interesting though, isn't it? I thought as how you'd noticed. Keep it to yourself, that's my advice. He thinks too much of himself, that Massingham fellow.'

They had turned out of Portobello Road and were walking down Ladbroke Grove before Massingham spoke, then he laughed.

'My God, that room! I pity the mysterious Mr Smith. If I had to live there and with her, I'd go roaming.'

Kate flared:

'What's wrong with it or with her? At least it's got character, not like the bloody building, designed by some bureaucrat with a brief to fit in so many living units with the least possible public expenditure. Just because you've never had to live in one doesn't mean that the people who do like it.' She added with fierce defensiveness: 'Sir.'

He laughed again. She was always punctilious about acknowledging his rank when she was angry.

'All right, all right, I admit the character. They've both got character, she and her room. And what's so wrong with the block? I thought it was rather decent. If the council offered me a flat there I'd take it quickly enough.'

And he would, she thought. He was probably less concerned about the details of his life, where he ate, where he lived, even what he wore, than she was herself. And it was irritating to discover, once more, how easily in his company she was trapped into insincerity. She had never believed that buildings were all that important. It was people, not architects, who made slums.

Even Ellison Fairweather Buildings would have been all right if it had been put up in a different place and filled with different people. He went on:

'And she was useful, wasn't she? If she's right and he did put the diary back in the drawer, and if we can prove that he didn't return . . .'

She broke in:

'That won't be easy, though. It'll mean accounting for every minute of his time. And so far we haven't a clue where he went after he left the estate agent's. He had a key. He could have let himself in and been out again in a minute.'

'Yes, but the probability is that he didn't. After all he went out with his bag, he obviously intended to stay out all day and go straight to the church. And if Lady Ursula did consult the diary before six o'clock when General Nollinge rang, then we know who has to be our chief suspect don't we? Dominic Swayne.'

None of it needed saying. She had seen the importance of the diary as soon as he had. She said:

'Who do you think those men were, the ones who did the search? Special Branch?'

'That's my guess. Either she worked for them and they planted her in Campden Hill Square or she worked for someone or something a great deal more sinister and they rumbled her. Of course they could have been who they said they were, men from a solicitor's firm looking perhaps for papers, a will.'

'Under the mattress? It was a pretty professional search.'

If it were Special Branch, she thought, there was going to be trouble. She said:

'They did tell us about Berowne's mistress.'

'Knowing that we'd have discovered that for ourselves quickly enough. That's typical of Special Branch. Their idea of co-operation is like a minister answering a PQ in the House; keep it short, keep it accurate, make sure you don't tell them anything they don't know already. God, if she was tied up with Special Branch there's going to be trouble.'

She said:

'Between Miles Gilmartin and AD?'

'Between everyone.'

They walked in silence for a moment, then he said:

'Why did you bring away that novel?'

She was for a moment tempted to prevaricate. She knew that when the significance of the date had first struck her she had planned to keep quiet about it, to do a little private detection, trace the writer, see if there was anything in it. Then prudence had prevailed. If it proved important, AD would have to know and she could imagine what his response would be to that particular kind of personal initiative. It was hypocritical to complain about the lack of interdepartmental cooperation while trying to run her own show within the squad. She said:

'The signature is dated the seventh of August, the day Diana Travers died.'

'So what? She signed and posted it on the seventh.'

'Mrs Minns saw it the following afternoon. Since when has the London post arrived that promptly?'

'It's perfectly possible if she sent it first class.'

She persisted:

'It's far more likely that he met Millicent Gentle that day and she gave it to him personally. I thought it would be interesting to know when and why.'

He looked at her and said:

'Could be. It's just as likely that she signed it on the seventh then left it for him at his constituency office.' Then he smiled.

'That's what you and Mrs Minns were having your girlish gossip about.'

He gave a slow, secret smile and she knew, with a spurt of irritation, that he had guessed about her temptation to conceal the evidence and was amused by it.

6

Once back in the Rover and on their way to the Yard she suddenly said:

'I don't understand it, religious experience.'

'You mean you don't know how to categorize it.'

'You were brought up in it, I suppose. They indoctrinated you from the cradle: nursery prayers, school chapel, that sort of thing.'

She had seen the school chapel once on an outing to Windsor. It had impressed her. That, after all, was its purpose. She had felt interest, admiration, even awe, walking under that soaring fan vaulting. But it had still remained a building in which she had felt herself an alien, speaking to her of history, privilege, tradition, an affirmation that the rich, having inherited the earth, could hope to ensure similar privileges in heaven. Someone had been playing the organ and she had sat listening with pleasure to what she thought must have been a Bach cantata, but for her there had been no secret harmonies.

He said, his eyes on the road:

'I'm reasonably familiar with the external forms. Not as much as my father. Compulsory chapel every day for him or so he claims.'

'I don't even feel the need of it, religion, praying.'

'That's perfectly natural. A lot of people don't. You're probably in the respectable majority. It's a matter of temperament. What's worrying you?'

'Nothing's worrying me. But it's odd about praying. Most people do pray apparently. Someone did a survey about it. They pray even if they're not sure who to. What about AD?'

'I don't know what he feels the need of except his poetry, his job and his privacy. And probably in that order.'

'But you've worked with him before, I haven't. Don't you think that there's something about this case that's got under his skin?'

He looked at her as if he were sharing the car with a stranger, wondering just how much he could prudently confide. Then he said:

'Yes, yes I do.'

Something, Kate felt, had been achieved, a confidence, a trust established. She pressed further.

'What's bugging him then?'

'What happened to Berowne in that church, I suppose. AD likes life to be rational. Odd for a poet, but there it is. This case isn't, not altogether.'

'Have you talked to him about it, what happened in that church I mean?'

503

'No. I did try once but all I could get out of him was: "The real world is difficult enough, John. Let's try to stay in it." So I shut my mouth, not being a fool.'

The light changed. She slipped out the clutch, the Rover moved quickly and smoothly away. They were meticulous in taking turns to drive. He yielded up the seat readily enough but like all good drivers he disliked being a passenger and it was a matter of pride for her to match his fast competence. She knew that she was tolerated by him, respected even, but they didn't really like each other. He accepted that the team needed a woman but without being overtly chauvinistic, he would have preferred a man as partner. Her feeling towards him was more positive, compounded of resentment and antipathy. Some of it she knew was class resentment. But at heart there was a dislike more instinctive and fundamental. She found red-haired men physically unattractive. Whatever there was between them it certainly wasn't the antagonism of an unacknowledged sexuality. Dalgliesh, of course, knew that perfectly well. He made use of it as he made use of so much. For a moment she felt a spurt of active dislike of all men. I'm an oddity, she thought. How much would I care, really care, if Alan chucked me? Suppose I had the choice, promotion or Alan, my flat or Alan? She was given to these awkward self-examinations, imaginary choices, ethical dilemmas, none the less intriguing because she knew she would never have to confront them in real life.

She said:

'Do you believe that something really did happen to Berowne in that vestry?'

'It must have, mustn't it? A man doesn't chuck his job and change the direction of his whole life for nothing.'

'But was it real? OK, don't ask me what I mean by real. Real in the sense this car is real, you're real, I'm real. Was he deluded, drunk, drugged? Or did he really have, well, some kind of supernatural experience, I suppose?'

'It seems unlikely for a practising member of the good old C of E, which is what he's supposed to have been. That's the sort of thing you expect of characters in a Graham Greene novel.'

She said:

'You make it sound as if it were in poor taste, eccentric, a bit presumptuous.' She was silent for a moment and then asked:

'If you have a kid will you have him christened?'

'Yes. Why do you ask?'

'So you believe in it, God, the Church, religion.'

'I didn't say so.'

'Then why?'

'My family have been christened for 400 years, longer I suppose. Yours too, I imagine. It doesn't seem to have done us any harm. I don't see why I should be the first to break the tradition, not without some positive feelings against it which I don't happen to have.'

And wasn't that, she thought, one of the things which Sarah Berowne had resented in her father, the ironic detachment which is too arrogant even to care. She said:

'So it's a matter of class.'

He laughed:

'Everything with you is a matter of class. No, it's a matter of family, of family piety if you like.'

She said, carefully not looking at him:

'I'm hardly the person to talk to about family piety. I'm illegitimate, if you didn't know.'

'No, I didn't know.'

'Well, thank you for not telling me it isn't important.'

He said:

'It only concerns one person. You. If you think it's important then OK, it has to be important.'

Suddenly she almost liked him. She glanced at the freckled face under a shock of red hair and tried to see him against the background of that college chapel. Then she thought of her own school. Ancroft Comprehensive had certainly had a religion all right, fashionable and, in a school with twenty different nationalities, expedient. It was anti-racism. You soon learned that you could get away with any amount of insubordination, indolence or stupidity if you were sound on this essential doctrine. It struck her that it was like any other religion; it meant what you wanted it to mean; it was easy to learn, a few platitudes, myths and slogans; it was intolerant, it gave you the excuse for occasional selective aggression, and you could make a moral virtue out of despising the people you disliked. Best of all, it cost nothing. She liked to pretend that this early indoctrination had absolutely nothing to do with the cold fury which seized her when she met its opposite, the obscene graffiti, the shouted insults, the terror of Asian families afraid to leave their barricaded homes. If you had to have a school ethos to give the illusion of togetherness then for her money anti-racism was as good as any. And whatever she might think about its more absurd manifestations, it wasn't likely to lead you to see visions in a dusty church.

7

Dalgliesh had decided to drive alone on the Saturday afternoon to see the Nolans in their Surrey cottage. It was the kind of chore he would normally have entrusted to Massingham and Kate, or even to a detective sergeant and DC, and he could see the surprise in Massingham's eyes when he told him that he had no need of a witness nor of anyone to take notes. The journey itself wasn't unnecessary. If Berowne's murder were linked to Theresa Nolan's suicide, anything he could discover about the girl, who was at present no more than a photograph in a police file, a pale, childish face under a nurse's cap, could be important. He needed to clothe that shadowy ghost with the living girl. But in intruding on her grandparents' grief he could at least make it as easy as possible for them. One police officer must surely be more tolerable than two.

But there was, he knew, another reason for going himself and alone. He needed an hour or two of solitude and quietness, an excuse to get away from London, from his office, from the insistent telephone, from Massingham and the squad. He needed to escape from the AC's carefully unspoken criticism that he was making a mystery out of a tragic but unremarkable suicide and murder, that they were all wasting time on a manhunt without a quarry. He needed to escape, however briefly, from the clutter of his desk and the pressure of personalities, to see the case with clearer, unprejudiced eyes.

It was a warm, blustery day. Torn shreds of clouds dragged

across a sky of clear azure blue and cast their frail shadows over the shorn, autumnal fields. He was travelling via Cobham and Effingham, and once off the A3 he drove the Jaguar XJS into a layby and thrust open the car roof. After Cobham, with the wind tearing at his hair, he thought he could smell in its fitful gusts the rich, pine-scented woodsmoke of autumn. The narrow country roads, bleached white between the grass verges, wound through the Surrey woodlands which would suddenly clear to give him a wide view to the South Downs and Sussex. He found himself wishing that the road would straighten before his wheels and run empty, unsignposted, for ever, that he could press down the accelerator and lose all his frustrations in the surge of power, that this rush of autumn-scented air screaming in his ears could cleanse his mind as well as his eyes of the colour of blood for ever.

He half-dreaded his journey's end, and it came unexpectedly quickly. He passed through Shere and found himself climbing a short hill; and there on the left-hand side of the road, bounded by oaks and silver birch, and separated from the road by a short garden, was an unremarkable Victorian cottage with its name, 'Weaver's Cottage', painted on the white gate. About twenty yards beyond it the road straightened and he drove the Jaguar gently on to the sandy verge. When he had turned off the engine the silence was absolute, birdless, and he sat for a moment, motionless and exhausted, as if he had come through some self-imposed ordeal.

He had telephoned, so he knew that they must be expecting him. But all the windows were fastened, there was no woodsmoke from the stack and the cottage had the secretive, oppressive air of a place not deserted but deliberately closed against the world. The front garden was untended with none of the haphazard exuberance of the normal cottage garden. All the plants were in rows, chrysanthemums, Michaelmas daisies, dahlias, with between them half-denuded rows of vegetables. But the ground was unweeded and the small patch of lawn on each side of the door unmown and shaggy. There was an iron knocker in the form of a horse-shoe, but no bell. He let it fall gently, guessing that they must have heard the car, must surely be expecting the knock, but it was a full minute before the door opened.

He said:

'Mrs Nolan?' and took out his card, feeling as he always did, like an importunate door-to-door salesman. She barely looked at it, but stood aside to let him in. She must, he thought, be nearer seventy than sixty, a small-boned woman with a sharp, anxious face. The exophthalmic eyes, so like her granddaughter's, gazed into his with a look with which he was only too familiar: a mixture of apprehension, curiosity and then relief that at least he looked human. She was wearing a suit in blue and grey crimplene, ill-fitting at the shoulders and puckered where she had shortened it at the hem. In her lapel was a round brooch of coloured stones in silver. It dragged at the thin crimplene. He guessed that this wasn't her usual wear for a Saturday afternoon, that she had dressed up for his visit. Perhaps she was a woman who dressed up to meet all life's ordeals and tragedies; a small gesture of pride and defiance in the face of the unknown.

The square sitting room with its single window looked to him more typical of a London suburb rather than these deep country woods. It was neat, very clean, but characterless and rather dark. The original fireplace had been replaced by one of mock marble with a wooden overmantel and was furnished with an electric fire, one bar of which was burning. Two walls had been papered in a lurid mixture of roses and violets, and two with a plain paper in blue stripes. The thin, unlined curtains were hung with the patterned side towards the road so that the afternoon sunshine was filtered through a pattern of bulbous pink roses and ivy clad latticework. There were two modern armchairs, one each side of the fireplace, and a square central table with four chairs. Against the far wall was a large television set, high on a trolley. Except for a copy of both the *Radio Times* and *TV Times*, there were no magazines and no books. The only picture was a garish print of the Sacred Heart over the fireplace.

Mrs Nolan introduced her husband. He was sitting in the right-hand armchair, facing the window, a huge, gaunt man, who responded to Dalgliesh's greeting with a stiff nod, but didn't get up. His face was rigid. In the shaft of sunlight between the curtains its planes and angles looked as if they had been carved in oak. His left hand, crossed in his lap, was beating a ceaseless, involuntary tattoo.

Mrs Nolan said:

'You'd like some tea, I dare say?'

He said:

'Very much, thank you, if it isn't too much trouble,' and thought: I seem to have heard that question and spoken those words all my life.

She smiled and nodded as if satisfied, and bustled out. Dalgliesh thought: I say the conventional insincerities and she responds as if I were the one doing the favour. What is it about this job that makes people grateful that I can act like a human being?

The two men waited in silence, but the tea came very quickly. So that, he thought, accounted for the delay in opening the door. She had hurried at his knock to put on the kettle. They sat at the table in stiff formality waiting while Albert Nolan raised himself stiffly from his chair and edged his way painfully into his seat. The effort set up a new spasm of shaking. Without speaking his wife poured his tea and set the cup before him. He didn't grasp it, but bent his head and slurped his tea noisily from the side. His wife didn't even look at him. There was a half-cut cake which she said was walnut and marmalade and she smiled again when Dalgliesh accepted a slice. It was dry and rather tasteless, rolling into a soft dough in his mouth. Small pellets of walnut lodged in his teeth and the occasional sliver of orange-peel was sour to the tongue. He washed it down with a mouthful of strong, over-milked tea. Somewhere in the room a fly was making a loud intermittent buzz.

He said:

'I'm sorry that I have to trouble you, and I'm afraid it may be painful for you. As I explained on the telephone, I'm investigating the death of Sir Paul Berowne. A short time before he died he had an anonymous letter. It suggested that he might have had something to do with your granddaughter's death. That's why I'm here.'

Mrs Nolan's cup rattled in her saucer. She put both hands under the table like a well-behaved child at a party. Then she glanced at her husband. She said:

'Theresa took her own life. I thought you'd know that, sir.'

'We did know it. But anything which happened to Sir Paul in the last weeks of his life could be important, and one thing that happened was the arrival of that anonymous letter. We should like to know who sent it. You see, we think it probable that he was murdered.'

Mrs Nolan said:

'Murdered? That letter wasn't sent from this cottage, sir. God help us, we've no call to do such a thing.'

'I know that. We never for a moment thought that it was. But I wondered whether your granddaughter ever talked to you about anyone, a close friend perhaps, someone who might have blamed Sir Paul for her death.'

Mrs Nolan shook her head. She said:

'You mean, someone who might have killed him?'

'It's a possibility we have to consider.'

'Who could there be? It doesn't make sense. She hadn't anyone else, only us, and we never laid hands on him, though God knows we were bitter enough.'

'Bitter against him?'

Suddenly her husband spoke:

'She got pregnant while she was in his house. And he knew where to find her body. How did he know? You tell me that.'

His voice was harsh, almost expressionless, but the words came out with such force that his body shook. Dalgliesh said:

'Sir Paul said at the inquest that your granddaughter spoke to him one night about her love of the woods. He thought that if she had decided to end her life, she might choose the only piece of wild woodland in central London.'

Mrs Nolan said:

'We never sent that letter to him, sir. I did see him at the inquest. Dad didn't go but I thought one of us ought to be there. He just spoke to me, Sir Paul. He was kind really. Said he was sorry. Well, what else can people say?'

Mr Nolan said:

'Sorry. Ay, I dare say.'

She turned to him:

'Dad, there's no proof. And he was a married man. Theresa wouldn't . . . Not with a married man.'

'There's no knowing what she might have done. Or him. What does it matter? She killed herself, didn't she? First getting the baby, then the abortion, then suicide. What's one more sin when you've got that on your conscience?'

Dalgliesh said gently:

'Can you tell me something about her? You brought her up, didn't you?'

'That's right. She hadn't anyone else. We only had the one child, her dad. Her mum died ten days after Theresa was born. She had appendicitis and the operation went wrong. A chance in a million, the doctor said.'

Dalgliesh thought: I don't want to hear this. I don't want to listen to their pain. That was what the consultant obstetrician had said to him when he had gone to take a last look at his dead wife with her newborn son in the crook of her arm, both of them composed in the secret nothingness of death. A chance in a million. As if there could be comfort, almost pride, in the know-ledge that chance had singled out your family to demonstrate the arbitrary statistics of human fallibility. Suddenly the buzzing of the fly was intolerable. He said:

'Excuse me,' and seized the copy of the *Radio Times*. He swiped at it violently, but missed. It took another two vehement slaps against the glass before the buzzing finally stopped and it dropped out of sight leaving only a faint smear. He said:

'And your son?'

'Well, he couldn't look after the baby. It wasn't to be expected. He was only 21. And I think he wanted to get away from the house, from us, even from the baby. In a funny way I think he blamed us. You see, we didn't really want the marriage. Shirley, his wife, she wasn't the girl we would have chosen. We told him no good would come of it.'

And when no good had come of it, it was them he had blamed, as if their disapproval, their resentment, had hovered over his wife like a curse. He asked:

'Where is he now?'

'We don't know. We think he went to Canada, but he never writes. He had a good trade, mechanic. He understood cars. And he was always clever with his hands. He said he'd have no trouble finding a job.'

'So he doesn't know that his daughter is dead?'

Albert Nolan said:

'He hardly knew she was alive. Why should he care now she's dead?'

His wife bent her head as if to let his bitterness wash over her. Then she said:

'I think she always felt guilty, poor Theresa. She thought she'd killed her mum. It was nonsense, of course. And then her dad leaving her, that didn't help. She grew up like an orphan and I think she resented it. When bad things happen to a child, she always thinks it's her fault.'

Dalgliesh said:

'But she must have been happy here with you. She loved the woodlands, didn't she?'

'Maybe. But I think she was lonely. She had to go to school by bus and couldn't stay for after-school activities. And there weren't other girls of her age anywhere near. She used to love walking in the woods, but we didn't encourage that, not on her own. These days you never know. Nobody's safe any more. We hoped that she'd make friends when she started nursing.'

'And did she?'

'She never brought them home. But then there wasn't much here for young people. Not really.'

'And you found nothing among her papers, among things she left, to give you any idea who the father of her child could have been?'

'She didn't leave anything, not even her nursing books. She was living in a hostel near Oxford Street after she left Campden Hill Square and she cleared the whole room, threw everything out. All we had from the police was the letter, her watch, the clothes she was wearing. We threw the letter away. No point in keeping it. You can see her room if you like, sir. It's the one she had since she was a little girl. There's nothing there, just an empty room. We gave everything here, her clothes and her books, to Oxfam. We thought that was what she would have wanted.'

It was, he thought, what they had wanted. She led him up the narrow staircase, showed him the room and then left. It was at the back of the cottage, small, narrow, north-facing, with one latticed window. Outside the pine trees and silver birch were so close that the leaves almost trembled against the panes. The room held a green luminosity as if it were under water. A branch of climbing rose with drooping leaves and one tight cankered bud, tapped at the window. It was, as she had said, only an empty room. The air was very still and held a faint smell of disinfectant as if the walls and floor had been scrubbed. It reminded him of a hospital room from which a dead body had been removed, impersonal, functional, a calculated space between four walls, waiting for the next patient to bring his apprehension, his pain, his hope to give it meaning. They had even stripped the bed. A white coverlet was spread over the bare mattress and the single pillow. The shelves of the wall-hung bookcase were empty; surely they were too fragile ever to have held many books. Nothing else remained except for a crucifix over the bed. Having nothing to remember but grief they had divested the room even of her personality and had closed the door.

Looking down at the stripped and narrow bed he recalled the words of the girl's suicide note. He had read it only twice when studying the report of the inquest but he had no difficulty in remembering it word for word.

'Please forgive me. I can't go on in so much pain. I killed my baby and I know that I shall never see her or you again. I suppose I'm damned but I can't believe in hell any more. I can't believe in anything. You were good to me but I was no use to you, ever. I thought when I became a nurse that everything would be different but the world was never friendly. Now I know that I don't have to live in it. I hope that it won't be children who find my body. Forgive me.'

It was not, he thought, a spontaneous letter. He had read so many suicide notes since he was a young DC. Sometimes they were written out of a pain and anger which produced its own unselfconscious poetry of despair. But this, despite its pathos and seeming simplicity, was more contrived, the tone of self-regard subdued but unmistakable. She may, he thought, have been one of those dangerously innocent young women, often more dangerous and less innocent than they seem, who are the catalysts of tragedy. She stood on the periphery of his investigation like a pale wraith in her nurse's uniform, unknown and now unknowable and yet, he was convinced, central to the mystery of Berowne's death.

He had no hope now of learning anything useful at Weaver's Cottage, but his instinct to search made him pull open the drawer of the bedside cabinet, and he saw that something of her remained: her missal. He picked it up and leafed casually through it. A small square of paper torn from a notebook fell out. He picked it up and found himself looking at three columns of figures and letters:

R	D3	S
B	D2	S
P	D1	S
S-N	S2	D

Downstairs the Nolans were still sitting at the table. He showed them the paper. Mrs Nolan thought that the figures and letters were in Theresa's handwriting, but said she couldn't be sure. Neither of them had any explanation to offer. Neither showed any interest. But they made no difficulty when he said that he would like to take the paper away.

Mrs Nolan went with him to the front door and, somewhat to his surprise, walked with him down the path to the gate. When they reached it she looked across at the dark shadows of the wood and said with barely suppressed passion:

'This cottage is tied to Albert's job. We ought to have been out three years ago when he got really bad, but they've been very kind to us. But we'll be leaving as soon as the local authority finds us a flat, and I won't be sorry. I hate these woods, hate them, hate them. Nothing but the wind forever whistling, sodden earth, darkness pressing in on you, small animals screaming in the night.'

And then as she closed the gate behind him she looked up into his face:

'Why didn't she tell me about the baby? I'd have understood. I'd have looked after her. I could have made Dad understand. That's what hurts. Why didn't she tell me?'

Dalgliesh said:

'I expect she wanted to save you pain. That's what we all try to do, save those we love from pain.'

'Dad's so bitter. He thinks she's damned. But I've forgiven her. God can't be less merciful than I am. I can't believe that.'

'No,' he said, 'I don't think we need believe that.'

She stood at the gate watching him. But when he had got into the car and fastened his seatbelt he looked back at her and found that, almost mysteriously, she had gone. The cottage had returned to its secret reticence. He thought: There's too much pain in this job. To think I used to congratulate myself, to think it useful, God help me, that people found it easy to confide in me. And what has today's brush with reality brought me? A scrap of paper torn from a notebook with a few jottings, letters and digits which she may not even have written. He felt himself contaminated by the Nolans' bitterness and pain. He thought: And if I tell myself that enough is enough, twenty years of using people's weakness against them, twenty years of careful non-involvement, if I resign, what then? Whatever Berowne found in that dingy vestry, it isn't open to me even to look for it. As the Jaguar bumped gently back on to the road he felt a spurt of irrational envy and anger against Berowne who had found so easy a way out.

8

It was six fifteen on Sunday evening and Carole Washburn stood gripping the rail of the balcony and looking down over the panorama of North London. She had never needed to draw the curtains when Paul had been with her, even late at night. They could gaze out together over the city and know themselves unwatched, inviolate. Then it had been good to step outside, feeling the warmth of his arm through his sleeve, and stand there together, secure, private, gazing down at the busy preoccupations of a world patterned in light. Then she had been a privileged spectator; but now she felt like an outcast, yearning for this distant unattainable paradise from which she was for ever excluded. Each night since his death she had stood watching as the lights had come on, block by block, house by house, squares of light, oblongs of light, light glimmering through curtains of rooms where people were living their shared, or secret, lives.

And now what seemed the longest Sunday she had ever endured was drawing to its close. In the afternoon, desperate to get out of the cage of the flat, she had driven to the nearest open supermarket. There was nothing she needed, but she had taken a trolley and pushed it aimlessly between the shelves, automatically reaching out for tins, packages, rolls of toilet paper, piling the trolley high, oblivious of the glances of her fellow shoppers. But then the tears had started to flow again, splashing over her hand, dropping in an unstoppable stream, splodging the packets of cereal, wrinkling the toilet rolls. She had abandoned her trolley laden with unwanted, unsuitable goods and had walked out to the car park and driven home again, slowly and carefully like a novice driver, seeing the world blurred and disorientated, the people jerking like puppets, as if reality were dissolving in perpetual rain.

By evening she had been seized by a desperate need for human companionship. It wasn't the need to begin some sort of life for herself, to plan some sort of future, to cast out her unpractised net into the void she had made around her secret life and begin to draw other people close. Perhaps that would come in time, impossible as it now seemed. It had been a simple uncontrollable longing to be with another human being, to hear a human voice making ordinary, unremarkable human sounds. She had telephoned Emma, who had come into the Civil Service with her from Reading, and who was now a Principal in the Department of Health and Social Security. Before she became Paul's mistress she had spent a fair proportion of her spare time with Emma, quick lunches at a pub or café convenient for both their offices, films, the occasional theatre, even a weekend together in Amsterdam to visit the Rijksmuseum. It had been an undemanding, unconfiding friendship. She had known that Emma would never give up the chance of a date with a man to spend an evening with her; and Emma had been the first victim of her obsessional need for privacy, the reluctance to commit even an hour of time which could be given to Paul. She looked at her watch. It was six forty-two. Unless Emma was spending the weekend out of town she would probably be at home.

She had to look up the number. The familiar digits sprang from the page at her like the key to an earlier, half-forgotten existence. She hadn't spoken to a human being since the police had left, and she wondered if her voice sounded as gruff and false to Emma as it did to her own ears.

'Hello? Emma? You won't believe it. This is Carole, Carole Washburn.'

There was the sound of music, joyous, contrapuntal. It could have been Mozart or Vivaldi. Emma called:

'Turn it down, darling,' and then to Carole:

'Good God! How are you?'

'Fine. It's ages since we met. I wondered if you'd like to see a film or something. Tonight perhaps.'

There was a small silence, and then Emma's voice, carefully uncommitted, surprise and perhaps a small note of resentment carefully controlled.

'Sorry, we've got people coming in for dinner.'

Emma had always said dinner rather than supper even when they were proposing to eat a take-away Chinese meal at the kitchen table. It had been one of those minor snobberies which Carole had found irritating. She said:

'Next weekend perhaps?'

'Not possible, I'm afraid. Alistair and I are driving down to Wiltshire. Visiting his parents, actually. Another time perhaps. Lovely to hear from you. I must fly, the guests are due at seven thirty. I'll give you a ring sometime.'

It was all she could do not to cry out: 'Include me, include me! Please, I need to come.' The receiver was replaced, voice, music, communication cut off. Alistair. But of course, she had forgotten that Emma was engaged. A Principal at the Treasury. So he had moved into the flat. She could imagine what they were saying now.

'Three years without a word and she suddenly rings and wants to see a film. And on Sunday evening for God's sake.'

And Emma wouldn't ring back. She had Alistair; a shared life, shared friends. You couldn't cut people out of your life and expect to find them complaisant, readily available, just because you needed to feel human again.

There were two more days of her leave to get through before she was due back in the office. She could go home, of course, except that this flat was home. And it was hardly worth the drive to Clacton, to the square, high-roofed bungalow outside the town where her widowed mother had lived since her father's death twelve years earlier. She hadn't been home for fourteen months. Friday night was sacrosanct; she could hope for a couple of hours with Paul on his way to his constituency. Sunday she had always kept free for him. Her mother, used to her neglect, seemed no longer to be particularly worried by it. Her mother's sister had the bungalow next door and the two widows, early acrimonies forgotten, had settled into a cosy routine of mutual support, their brick-boxed lives measured out by small treats: shopping, morning coffee at their favourite café, returning their library books, the evening television programmes, supper on a trolley. Carole had almost given up wondering about their lives, why they had chosen to live by the sea when they never went near it, what they talked about. She could telephone now and her mother would be grudgingly acquiescent, resenting the chore of making up the spare bed, the interruption to the weekend programme, the problem of stretching the food. She told herself that she had trained her mother over the past three years to expect neglect, had been grateful that her time with Paul hadn't been threatened by demands from Clacton. It seemed to her ignoble to telephone now, to rush home in search of a comfort for which she couldn't ask and which her mother, even if she had known the truth, wouldn't be able to give.

Six forty-five. If this were a Friday he would have arrived by now, timing his entrance to ensure that there was no one in the hall to see him. There would be the one long ring, the two short peals on the bell which were his signal. And then the bell rang, one long insistent peal. She thought she heard a second and then a third, but that might have been her imagination. For one miraculous second, no more, she thought that he had come, that it had all been an idiotic mistake. She called: 'Paul, Paul my darling!' and almost flung herself against the door. And then her mind took hold of reality and she knew the truth. The receiver slid through her moist hands and almost fell and her lips were so dry that she could hear them cracking. She whispered:

'Who is it?' The answering voice was high, a female voice. It said:

'Could I come up? I'm Barbara Berowne.'

She pressed the button almost without thinking and heard the burr of the released lock, the click of the door as it closed. It was too late now to change her mind, but she knew that there had been no choice. In her present desperate loneliness she would have sent no one away. And this encounter had been inevitable. Ever since her affair with Paul had started she had wanted to see his wife, and now she was going to see her. She opened the door and stood waiting, listening for the whine of the lift, the muted footfalls on the carpet, as she had once waited for his.

She came down the corridor, light-footed, casually elegant, golden, her scent, subtle and elusive, seeming to precede her and then waste itself on the air. She was wearing a coat of cream broadcloth, its wide arms and shoulders pleated, the sleeves fashioned in some finer and differently textured cloth. Her black leather boots looked as soft as her black gloves and she carried a shoulder bag on a slim strap. She was hatless, the corn coloured hair with its streaks of paler gold twisted at the back into a long roll. It surprised Carole that she could notice the details, could actually wonder about the material of the coat sleeves, speculate where it had been bought, how much it had cost.

As she came in it seemed to Carole that the blue eyes looked round the room with a frank, faintly contemptuous appraisal. She said in a voice which she knew must sound forced and ungracious:

'Please sit down. Would you like something to drink? Coffee, sherry, some wine?'

She, herself, moved over to Paul's chair. It seemed to her impossible that his wife should sit where she had been used to seeing him. They faced each other a few yards apart. Barbara Berowne looked down at the carpet as if satisfying herself that it was clean before placing her bag at her feet. She said:

'No thank you. I can't stay long. I have to get back. We've got some people coming, some of Paul's colleagues. They want to talk about the memorial service. We shan't have it until the police discover who killed him, but these things have to be settled weeks in advance if one wants St Margaret's. Apparently they don't think he really qualifies for the Abbey, poor darling. You'll come, of course; to the memorial service I mean. There will be so many people there that you won't be noticed. I mean you needn't feel embarrassed about me.'

'No, I've never felt embarrassed about you.'

'I think it's all rather gruesome actually. I don't think Paul would have wanted all that fuss. But the constituency seemed to feel that we ought to have a memorial service. After all, he was a Minister. The cremation will be private. I don't think you ought to go to that anyway, do you? It will be just the family and really intimate friends.'

Intimate friends. Suddenly she wanted to laugh aloud. She said:

'Is that why you're here? To tell me about the funeral arrangements?'

'I thought Paul would want you to know. After all, we both loved him in our different ways. We're both concerned to safeguard his reputation.'

She said:

'There's nothing you can teach me about safeguarding his reputation. How did you know where to find me?'

'Oh I've known where to find you for months. A cousin of mine employed a private detective. It wasn't very difficult, just a matter of following Paul's car on a Friday evening. And then he eliminated all the couples in this block, all the old women and all the single men. That left you.'

She had drawn off her black gloves and had lain them on her knee. Now she was smoothing them out, finger by finger, with pink tipped hands. She said without looking up:

'I'm not here to make trouble for you. After all we're in this together. I'm here to help.'

'We aren't in anything together. We never have been. And what do you mean by help? Are you offering me money?'

The eyes looked up, and Carole thought she detected a flicker of anxiety, as if the question needed to be taken seriously.

'Not really. I mean, I didn't think you were actually in need. Did Paul buy this flat for you? It's rather cramped, isn't it? Still, it's quite pleasant if you don't mind living in a suburb. I'm afraid he hasn't mentioned you in his will. That's another thing I thought you ought to know, in case you were wondering.'

Carole said, her voice over-loud and harsh even to her own ears:

'This flat is mine. The deposit was paid by me, the mortgage is paid with my money. Not that it's any of your business. But if you have a conscience about me, forget it. There's nothing I want from you or from anyone else connected with Paul. Women who prefer to be kept by men all their lives can never get it into their heads that some of us like to pay our own way.'

'Did you have any choice?'

Speechless, she heard the high, childish voice continuing:

'After all, you've always been discreet. I admire you for that. It can't have been easy only seeing him when he hadn't anything better to do.'

The amazing thing was that the insult wasn't deliberate. She was capable of being intentionally offensive, of course, but this had been a casual remark born of an egotism so insensitive that she spoke what she thought, not wanting particularly to wound, but incapable of caring whether she wounded or not. Carole thought: Paul, how could you have married her? How could you have been taken in? She's stupid, third-rate, spiteful, insensitive, mean minded. Is beauty really so important?

She said:

'If that's all you've come to say, perhaps you'll go. You've seen me. You know what I look like. You've seen the flat. This is the chair he used to sit in. That's the table he used for his drink. If you want I can show you the bed we made love on.'

'I know what he came for.'

She wanted to cry out 'Oh no you don't. You know nothing about him. I was as happy lying with him on that bed as I've ever been or ever shall be. But that wasn't what he came for.' She had believed, still believed, that only with her had he been wholly at peace. He had lived his over-busy life neatly compartmentalized; the Campden Hill Square house, the House of Commons, his ministerial suite at the department, his constituency headquarters. Only in this high, ordinary, suburban flat did the disparate elements fuse together and he could be a whole person, uniquely himself. When he had come in and sat opposite her, had dropped his briefcase at his feet and smiled at her she had watched with joy, time and time again, the taut face soften and relax, become already smooth as if they had just made love.

There were things about his private life which she knew he had held back from her, not consciously or out of lack of trust, but because, when they were together, they had no longer seemed important. But he had never held back himself.

Barbara Berowne was admiring her engagement ring, holding out her hand and moving it slowly in front of her face; the huge diamond in its setting of sapphires twinkled and flashed. She gave a secretive reminiscent smile then looked across at Carole and said:

'There's one other thing which you might as well know. I'm having a baby.'

Carole cried:

'It isn't true! You're lying! You can't be!'

The blue eyes widened.

'Of course it's true. It isn't something you can lie about, not for long anyway. I mean the truth will be obvious to the whole world in a couple of months.'

'It isn't his child!'

She thought: I'm shouting, screaming at her. I must keep calm. O God, help me not to believe.

And now Barbara Berowne actually laughed.

'Of course it's his child. He always wanted an heir, didn't you know that? Look, you may as well accept it. The only other man I've slept with since my marriage is sterile. He's had a vasectomy. I'm going to have Paul's son.'

'He wouldn't have done it. You couldn't have made him do it.'

'But he did. There is one thing you can always make a man do. That is if he likes women at all. Haven't you found that out? You're not pregnant, too, are you?'

Carole buried her face in her hands. She whispered:

'No.'

'I thought I ought to be sure.' She giggled. 'That would have been a complication, wouldn't it?'

Suddenly all control was gone. There was nothing left but naked anger, naked shame. She heard herself bawling like a shrew.

'Get out! Get out of my flat!'

Even in the middle of her anguish and fury she didn't miss the sudden flicker of fear in the blue eyes. She saw it with a spurt of pleasure and triumph. So she wasn't inviolate after all, she could be frightened. But the knowledge was vaguely unwelcome; it made Barbara Berowne vulnerable, more human. Now she got up almost gracelessly, bent to pick up her shoulder bag by the strap, then scampered to the door ungainly as a child. Only when Carole had opened it and stood aside to let her out did she turn and speak.

'I'm sorry you've taken it like this. I think you're being rather silly. After all, I was his wife, I'm the injured party.'

And then she was hurrying down the corridor. Carole called after her:

'The injured party! My God that's good. The injured party!'

She closed the door and leaned against it. Sickness heaved at her stomach. She rushed to the bathroom, spewed into the basin grasping the taps for support. And then came anger, cleansing, almost exhilarating. Between fury and grief she wanted to fling her head back and howl like an animal. She groped her way back into the sitting room and felt for her own chair like a blind woman, then sat gazing at his empty seat, willing herself to calm. When she had herself under control, she fetched her handbag and took out the card with the Scotland Yard extension she had been asked to telephone.

It was Sunday, but someone would be on duty. Even if she couldn't speak to Inspector Miskin now, she could leave a message, ask that she be rung back. It couldn't wait until tomorrow. She had to commit herself irrevocably, and now.

A male voice answered, one she didn't recognize. She gave her name and asked for Inspector Miskin.

She said:

'It's urgent. It's about the Berowne murder.'

There was a delay of only seconds before the Inspector answered. Although she had only heard the voice once before, it came to her with a shock of recognition. She said:

'This is Carole Washburn. I want to see you. There's something I've decided to tell you.'

'We'll come round now.'

'Not here. I don't want you to come here, not ever again. I'll meet you tomorrow morning. Nine o'clock. The formal garden in Holland Park, the one near the orangery. Do you know it?'

'Yes, I know it. We'll be there.'

'I don't want Commander Dalgliesh. I don't want any male officer. Just you. I won't talk to anyone else.'

There was a pause, then the voice spoke again, unsurprised, accepting:

'Nine o'clock tomorrow. The garden, Holland Park. I'll be on my own. Can you give me any idea what it's about?'

'It's about the death of Theresa Nolan. Goodbye.'

Then she replaced the receiver and leaned her forehead against the cold stickiness of the metal. She felt empty, light-headed, shaken by her heartbeats. She wondered what she would feel, how she could go on living when she was capable of knowing what she had done. She wanted to cry aloud: 'My darling, I'm sorry, I'm sorry. I'm sorry.' But she had made her decision. There was no going back now. And it seemed to her that there still hung in the room the fugitive scent of Barbara Berowne's perfume, like the taint of betrayal, and that the air of her flat would never be free of it.

BOOK FIVE

Rhesus Positive

I

Miles Gilmartin of Special Branch was protected from the importunities of casual visitors and the attention of the ill-intentioned by a series of checks and counterchecks which to Dalgliesh, waiting in thwarted anger and impatience while each was negotiated, seemed more childishly ingenious than necessary or effective. It wasn't a game he was in the mood to play. By the time he was finally ushered into Gilmartin's office by a PA who irritatingly combined exceptional beauty with an obvious consciousness of her unique privilege in serving the great man, Dalgliesh was beyond considerations of prudence or discretion. Bill Duxbury was with Gilmartin and they hardly got beyond the few preliminary courtesies before anger found its relief in words.

'We're supposed to be on the same side, if you people acknowledge any side but your own. Paul Berowne was murdered. If I can't get cooperation from you, where can I expect to get it?'

Gilmartin said:

'I can understand a certain resentment that we didn't tell you earlier that Travers was one of our operatives . . .'

'Operatives. You make it sound as if she were on a production line. And you didn't tell me. I had to discover it for myself. Oh, I can see the fascination of your world. It reminds me of my prep school. We had our little secrets, our code words, initiation ceremonies. But when the hell are you people going to grow up? All right, I know it's necessary, some of it anyway, and for some of the time. But you make it into an obsession. Secrecy for its own sake, the whole vast paper-ridden bureaucracy of spying. No wonder your kind of organization breeds its own traitors. In the meantime I'm investigating an actual murder and it would help if you stopped playing games and joined the real world.'

Gilmartin said mildly:

'I'm not sure that speech wouldn't have been more appropriately made to MI5. There's something in what you say. One
ought to guard more against over-enthusiasm, and we're certainly
over-bureaucratized. But then what organization isn't? We deal
in information after all and information is valueless if it isn't
properly documented and easily available. Still, pound for pound,
I think we give the taxpayers value for money.'

Dalgliesh looked at him.

'You really haven't understood a word I've been saying.'

'Oh yes I have, Adam. But it's all so unlike you. Such vehemence! You've been reading too many of those espionage novels.'

Three years ago, thought Dalgliesh bitterly, Gilmartin might
have thought even if he hadn't dared to speak it: It's all that
poetry you write. But he couldn't say that now. Gilmartin went
on:

'Are you sure this Berowne murder isn't getting under your
skin? You knew him, didn't you?'

'For God's sake, if another person suggests I can't handle the
case because I knew the victim, I'll resign.' For the first time, a
look of concern like a brief spasm of pain passed over Gilmartin's
bland, almost colourless face.

'Oh, I shouldn't do that. Not over a small sin of omission on
our part. I suppose that Berowne was murdered, by the way.
There's a rumour that it could have been suicide. After all, he
was hardly normal at the time. This habit he'd developed of
sleeping in church vestries. And isn't he supposed to have had
some kind of divine revelation? Listening to his voices when he
should have been listening to the Prime Minister. And such a
very curious church to choose. I can understand an enthusiasm
for English Perpendicular but a Romanesque basilica in Paddington is surely an improbable choice for a good night's sleep let
alone one's personal road to Damascus.'

Dalgliesh was tempted to ask him whether he would have
found St Margaret's Westminster a more acceptable choice. Gilmartin, having neatly demonstrated at least a superficial knowledge of church architecture and scripture to his own evident
satisfaction, got up from his desk and began to pace between the
windows as if suddenly aware that he was the only one sitting

down at a desk and that this lower status might put him at a disadvantage. He could afford a good tailor and dressed with a careful formality which, in a less confident man, might suggest that he was aware of the slightly ambiguous reputation of the security service and was anxious not to reinforce it by any slovenliness in manner or appearance. But Gilmartin dressed to please himself as he did everything. Today he was elegant in grey. Above the formal suit with its almost invisible darker stripe, the square almost bloodless face and the sleek hair, prematurely white and brushed straight back from the high forehead, reinforced both image and colour scheme; a carefully composed arrangement in grey and silver against which his old school tie, despite its comparative sobriety, hung like a garish flag of defiance.

In contrast Bill Duxbury, stocky, ruddy-faced and loud-voiced, looked like a gentleman farmer whose farming is more successful than his gentility. He stood half looking out of the window like a child ordered to distance himself from the adults and their concerns. Dalgliesh saw that he had recently got rid of his moustache. Without it his face looked incomplete and naked, as if he had been forcibly shaved. He was wearing a tweed checked suit, rather too heavy for the comparatively mild autumn, the jacket cut with a back flap which strained over his large, rather feminine buttocks. When Gilmartin looked at him, which was infrequently, it was with a pained, slightly surprised expression as though deploring both his subordinate's figure and his tailor.

It had early been apparent that Gilmartin was to do the talking. Duxbury would have briefed him but Duxbury would remain silent unless invited to speak. Dalgliesh was suddenly reminded of a dinner party conversation some years previously. He had found himself sitting with a woman on one of those three-person sofas which can only comfortably hold two. It had been a Georgian drawing room in a north Islington square but he couldn't now remember the name of his hostess and God knew what he thought he had been doing there. His companion had been slightly drunk, not offensively so but enough to make her flirtatious, merry, and then confiding. Memory refused to come up with her name and it didn't matter. They had sat together for half an hour before their hostess, with practised tact, had separated them. He could remember only part of their conversation. She and her husband had a penthouse overlooking a street which was commonly used for student demonstrations and the police – she was sure they were Special Branch – had asked if they could use their front sitting room to take photographs from the window.

'We said they could, of course, and they were really very sweet about it. But part of me wasn't really happy. I wanted to say: "They're British subjects. They've got the right to march if they want to. If you want to photograph them, can't you do it openly, in the street?" But I didn't. After all, it was rather fun in a way. The sense of conspiracy, being in the know. And it wasn't up to us to make a stand. They know what they're doing. And it never does to antagonize these people.'

It had seemed to him then, and it did now, to sum up the attitude of decent liberals all over the world: 'They know what they're doing. It isn't up to us to make a stand. It never does to antagonize these people.'

He said bitterly:

'I'm surprised that you and MI5 don't encourage regular secondments to the KGB. You've more in common with them than you have with any outsider. It might be instructive to see how they deal with their paperwork.'

Gilmartin lifted an eyelid at Duxbury as if inviting solidarity in the face of unreason. He said mildly:

'As far as paperwork is concerned, Adam, it would help us if your people were a little more conscientious. Massingham, when requesting information about Ivor Garrod, should have put in an IR49.'

'In quadruplicate, of course.'

'Well, registry need a copy and so, presumably, do you. We're supposed to keep MI5 in the picture. We could look at the procedure again, of course, but I would say that four copies were the minimum.'

Dalgliesh said:

'This girl, Diana Travers. Was she the most suitable person you could find to spy on a Minister of State? Even for Special Branch, it seems an odd choice.'

'But we weren't spying on a Minister of State, she wasn't assigned to Berowne. As we told you when you inquired about his mistress, Berowne never was a risk. No IR49 submitted there either, incidentally.'

'I see. You infiltrated Travers into Garrod's group or cell, whatever he calls it, and conveniently forgot to mention the fact when we inquired about him. You must have known that he was a suspect. He still is.'

'It hardly seemed relevant. We all operate, after all, on the "need to know" principle. And we didn't infiltrate her into Campden Hill Square. Garrod did. Travers's little job for us had nothing to do with Berowne's death.'

'But Travers's death might have.'

'There was nothing suspicious about her death. You must have studied the autopsy report.'

'Which wasn't, I noticed, carried out by the usual Home Office pathologist for Thames Valley.'

'We like to use our own people. He's perfectly competent, I assure you. She died from natural causes, more or less. It could have happened to anyone. She had eaten too much, drunk too much, and she plunged into cold water, got tangled in the reeds, gasped and drowned. There were no suspicious marks on the body. She had had, as you no doubt remember from the PM report, a sexual connection just before death.' He hesitated a little before the phrase. It was the only time Dalgliesh had seen him even slightly discomposed. It was as if he felt the words 'making love' were inappropriate and couldn't bring himself to use a coarser soubriquet.

Dalgliesh was silent. Anger had led him into a protest that now seemed to him humiliatingly childish as well as ineffectual. He had achieved nothing except possibly to exacerbate the simmering professional rivalry between C Division, the Special Branch and MI5 whose uneasy relationship could so easily spill over into high politics. Next time Gilmartin might say: 'And for God's sake, put AD in the picture. He's apt to get his knickers in a twist if he doesn't get his share of the lollipops.' But what depressed him most and left him with a sour taste of self-disgust, was how close he had come to losing his control. He realized how important it had become to him, his reputation for coolness, detachment, uninvolvement. Well, he was involved now. Perhaps they were right. You shouldn't take on a case if you knew the victim. But how could he claim to have known Berowne? What time had they spent together, except for a three-hour train journey, a brief ten-minute spell in his office, an interrupted walk in St James's Park? And yet he knew that he had never felt so great an empathy with any other victim. That impulse to connect his fist with Gilmartin's jaw, to see blood spurting over that immaculate shirtfront, that old school tie; well, fifteen years ago he might have done it and it would have cost him his job. For a moment he almost yearned for the lost uncomplicated spontaneity of youth.

He said:

'I'm surprised that you thought Garrod worth the trouble. He was a left-wing activist at university. It hardly needs an under-cover agent to discover that Garrod doesn't vote Tory. He's never made any secret of his beliefs.'

'Not of his beliefs, but he has of his activities. His group are rather more than the usual middle-class malcontents looking for an ethically acceptable outlet for aggression and some kind of cause, preferably one that gives them the illusion of commitment. Oh yes, he's worth it.'

Gilmartin signalled a glance at Duxbury who said:

'It's only a small group – cell he calls it. At present four are women. Thirteen of them altogether. He never recruits more nor less. A nice touch of counter-superstition, and, of course, it adds to the mystique of conspiracy. The magic number, the closed circle.'

Dalgliesh thought that the number also had a certain opera-tional logic. Garrod could organize three groups of four or two of six for field work and still free himself as coordinator, director, recognized leader. Duxbury went on:

'They're all from the privileged middle class which makes for cohesion and obviates class tensions. The comrades, after all, aren't notable for brotherly love. This lot speak the same language including, of course, the usual Marxist jargon, and they're all intelligent. Silly, maybe, but intelligent. A potentially dangerous bunch. None is a member of the Labour Party, incidentally. Not that the Party would have them. Six of them, including Garrod, are paid up members of the Workers' Revolutionary Campaign but they don't hold office. My guess is that the WRC is little more than a front. Garrod prefers to run his own show. A natural fascination with conspiracy, I suppose.'

Dalgliesh said:

'He should have joined Special Branch. And Sarah Berowne is a member?'

'For the last two years. A member and Garrod's mistress, which gives her a peculiar prestige in the group. In some ways the comrades are remarkably old-fashioned.'

'And what did you get from Travers? All right, let me guess. Garrod introduced her into the Campden Hill Square house. That wouldn't be difficult given the shortage of reliable domestic help. Sarah Berowne would have tipped them off about the advertisement, if she didn't actually suggest it. Anyone willing to do housework and turning up with good references – and you'd have seen to that – would be pretty sure of a job. That was his cell's function presumably, to discredit selected MPs.'

It was Gilmartin who answered:

'One of their functions. They mostly went for the moderate socialists. Dig up the muck, an illicit love affair, preferably homosexual, an ill-advised friendship, a half-forgotten sponsored trip to South Africa, a suggestion of sticky fingers in the party funds. Then when the poor devil goes up for re-selection, spread the manure around judiciously and draw delicate attention to the smell. Discrediting members of the present administration is probably more a matter of occasional duty than enjoyment. I imagine Garrod chose Paul Berowne for personal rather than political reasons. Sarah Berowne dislikes more than her Papa's party.'

So it had been Garrod who had sent the poison pen message to Ackroyd and the gossip writers of the nationals. Well, he had always been Dalgliesh's most likely suspect for that particular mischief. As if hearing his thoughts, Gilmartin said:

'I doubt whether you'll be able to prove he sent that message to the press. They do it very cleverly. A member of the group visits one of those shops where they sell new and second-hand typewriters and let you try out the machines. You know the scene, rows of chained typewriters for the customers to bang away on. The chance of a single prospective customer being recognized is almost nil. We can't keep perpetual watch on all the cell members. They don't warrant that intensity of effort and I'm not sure, anyway, what particular section or subsection of the criminal law they'd be infringing. The information they use is accurate. It's no use to them if it isn't. How did you get on to Travers by the way?'

'Through the woman she lodged with before she moved into her flat. Women have a profound contempt for masculine secret societies and a knack of seeing through them.'

Gilmartin said:

'The whole sex is one secret society. We wanted Travers to live alone. We should have insisted. But I'm surprised that she talked.'

'She didn't. Her landlady didn't altogether believe in an unemployed actress who could yet afford to buy a flat. But it was your men turning up to search her room that confirmed her suspicions. Incidentally, what was your real interest in Garrod, apart from getting some additional names in your activist files?'

Gilmartin pursed his lips.

'There could have been an IRA connection.'

'And was there?'

For a moment Dalgliesh thought that he would refuse to answer. Then he glanced at Duxbury and said:

'Not as far as we've been able to discover. Do you think Garrod is your man?'

'He could be.'

'Well, good hunting.' He seemed suddenly ill at ease as if uncertain how to bring the interview to an end. Then he said:

'It has been useful talking to you, Adam. We've taken notes of the points you've raised. And you'll watch the procedures, won't you? The IR49. A modest little form but it has its uses.'

As the lift bore him down to his own floor it seemed to Dalgliesh that he had been closeted with Special Branch for days rather than less than an hour. He felt contaminated by a kind of sick hopelessness. He knew that he would shake off its symptoms soon enough; he always did. But the infection would still be there in his blood-stream, part of that sickness of the spirit which he was beginning to think he must learn to endure.

But the interview, humiliatingly fractious as it had been, had served its purpose, clearing away a tangle of extraneous brush-wood from the main path of his inquiry. He knew now the identity and motive of the poison pen writer. He knew what Diana Travers had been doing at Campden Hill Square, who had put her there, and why, after the drowning, her room had been searched. Two young women were dead, one by her own hand, one by accident. There was no mystery about why and how they had died and little now about how they had lived. Why then was he still obstinately convinced that these two deaths were not only linked but central to the mystery of Paul Berowne's murder?

2

When he got back from that secretive and self-sufficient world on the eighteenth and nineteenth floors, Dalgliesh found that his own corridor was unusually silent. He put his head in his secretary's office but Susie's typewriter was shrouded, her desk cleared, and he remembered that she had a dental appointment that morning. Kate was meeting Carole Washburn in Holland Park. Irked by his own bad temper he had hardly given a thought to the possibilities of that encounter. Massingham was, he knew, visiting the Wayfarers' Refuge in Cosway Street to talk to the warden there about Harry Mack before going on to interview two of the girls who had been in the punt on the Thames when Diana Travers had drowned. According to their evidence at the inquest neither of them had seen the girl dive into the river. They and the rest of the party had left her with Dominic Swayne on the bank when they pushed out the punt and had seen and heard nothing of her until that awful moment when the punt pole had struck her body. Both had admitted at the inquest that they had been half-drunk at the time. Dalgliesh doubted whether they would have anything more useful to say now that they were sober but, if they had, Massingham was the one best suited to get it out of them.

But Massingham had left a message. As he entered his room, Dalgliesh saw a single sheet of white paper pinned to his blotter with Massingham's paper knife, a long and remarkably sharp dagger which he claimed to have won at a fairground when a child. The dramatic gesture and the few lines of letters and figures in a stark black upright hand said it all. The forensic science laboratory had telephoned the result of the blood analyses. Without pulling out the dagger, Dalgliesh stood silently and looked down at the evidence which, more than any other, was vital to his theory that Berowne had been murdered.

Berowne	Mack	Smears on carpet and jacket pocket
Rhesus Pos	Pos	Pos
ABO A	A	A
AK 2 − 1 (7.6%) (enzymes)	1 (92.3%)	2 − 1
PGM 1 + (40%) (enzymes)	2 + 1 − (4.8%)	1 +
Razor blade:		
AK 2 − 1		
PGM 2 +, 1 −, 1 +		

The PGM system was, he knew, a strong one. There would have been no need to set up a control reaction with the dirty carpet. But the lab must have worked over the weekend despite their heavy load and the fact that, as yet, there was no suspect in custody, and he was grateful. There was blood of two different types on the razor, but that was hardly surprising, the analysis a mere formality. But, more important, the smear on the carpet under Harry's coat wasn't his blood. Dalgliesh had another interview booked for late in the afternoon which promised, in its different way, to be as irritating as the session with Gilmartin. It was helpful that this important piece of scientific evidence had arrived in time.

3

Holland Park was only a few minutes' walk from Charles Shannon House. Kate had woken early shortly after six and by seven had breakfasted and was impatient to get away. After prowling restlessly round an already immaculate flat trying to find jobs to occupy the time she stuffed a paper bag of crumbs for the birds in her jacket pocket and left three-quarters of an hour early, telling herself that it would be less frustrating to walk in the park than to stay cooped up wondering whether Carole Washburn would actually turn up, whether she might already be regretting her promise.

Dalgliesh had accepted that the agreement with the girl must be kept; she would meet Carole Washburn alone. He had given her no instructions and offered no advice. Other senior officers would have been tempted to remind her of the importance of the meeting, but this wasn't his way. She respected him for it, but it increased her burden of responsibility. Everything might depend on how she handled their encounter.

Just before nine she made her way to the terrace above the formal gardens. When she had last visited the park the beds had been richly patterned with the summer display of geraniums, fuchsias, heliotropes and begonias. But now the time had come for the autumn stripping. Half the beds were already bare; expanses of soft loam littered with broken stems, petals like blobs of blood and a scatter of dying leaves. A council cart, like the dread tumbrel of winter, stood ready for the new strippings. And now, as the minute finger of her watch clicked to the hour the squeals and shouts from the grounds of Holland Park School were suddenly hushed and the park lay in its early morning calm. An old woman, bent as a witch, with a team of six small discouraged dogs on a lead shuffled along the side path, then paused to pull and sniff at the last flowers of the lavender. A solitary jogger loped down the steps and disappeared through the arches leading to the orangery.

And suddenly Carole Washburn was there. Almost precisely on the hour a solitary female figure appeared at the far end of the garden. She was wearing a short grey jacket over a matching skirt, her head covered by a voluminous blue and white scarf which almost obscured her face. But Kate knew immediately and with a lift of the heart, who it was. They stood for a moment regarding each other, then advanced between the denuded flower beds in measured, almost ceremonial, paces. Kate was reminded of spy thrillers, the exchange of defectors at some border crossing, a sense of unseen watchers, ears pricked for the crack of a rifle. When they met the girl nodded but did not speak. Kate said simply:

'Thank you for coming.' Then she turned and together they passed up the steps out of the garden, across the spongy turf of the wide lawn and into the path between the rose gardens. Here the freshness of the morning air was tinged with the remembered scent of summer. Roses, thought Kate, were never finished. There was something irritating about a flower which couldn't recognize that its season was over. Even in December there would be tight and browning buds destined to wither before they opened, a few anaemic heavy heads drooping towards the petal-strewn earth. Pacing slowly between the spiked bushes, aware of Carole's shoulder almost brushing hers, she thought: I must have patience. I must wait for her to speak first. She has to be the one to choose the time and place.

They came up to the statue of Lord Holland, seated on his pedestal, gazing benignly towards his house. Still without speaking, they walked on down the mushy path between the woodlands. Then her companion paused. She looked into the wilderness and said:

'That's where he found her, over there, under that slanting silver birch, the one by the holly bush. We came here together a week later. I think he needed to show me.'

Kate waited. It was extraordinary that this wilderness of trees could be close to the centre of a great city. Once over the low palisade it would be possible to believe oneself deep in the countryside. No wonder that Theresa Nolan, reared among the Surrey woodlands, should have chosen this quiet leafy place in which to die. It must have been like a return to early childhood; the smell of leaf loam, the rough bark of the tree against her back, the scurry of small birds and squirrels in the undergrowth, the softness of the earth making death as natural and friendly as falling asleep. For one extraordinary moment it seemed to her that she entered into that death, was mysteriously one with that lonely dying girl under the far tree. She shivered. The moment of empathy was quickly over but its power astonished and a little disturbed her. She had seen enough suicides in her first five years of policing to have learnt detachment, and, for her, it had never been a difficult lesson. She had always been able to distance emotion, to think: This is a dead body. Not: This was a living woman. So why should an imagined death be more distressing than a body actually seen? Perhaps, she thought, I can afford a little involvement, a little pity. But it was strange that it should begin now. What was it, she wondered, about the Berowne case which seemed to be changing even her perception of her job? She turned her eyes again to the path and heard Carole Washburn's voice:

'When Paul learned that she was missing, when the nursing home rang to ask if anyone at Campden Hill Square had seen her or knew where she was, he guessed that she might be here. Before he became a minister and security became a nuisance he often walked through the park to work. He could cross Kensington Church Street, get into Hyde Park and then into Green Park at Hyde Park Corner, walking nearly all the way to the House on grass and under trees. So it was natural to come and look – I mean, he didn't have to go much out of his way. He wasn't putting himself to any great trouble.'

The sudden bitterness in her voice was shocking. Still Kate didn't speak. She dug in her jacket pocket for the small bag of crumbs and held them out on her palm. A sparrow, tame as only London sparrows are, hopped on her fingers with a delicate scrape of claws. His head jerked, and she felt the beak like a pin-prick, and then he was gone.

She said:

'He must have known Theresa Nolan very well.'

'Perhaps. She used to talk to him in the night hours when Lady Ursula was asleep; tell him about herself, her family. He was easy for women to talk to, some women.'

Both of them were for a moment silent. But there was one question which she had to ask. She said:

'The child Theresa Nolan was carrying, could it have been his?' To her relief the question was taken calmly, almost as if it were expected. The girl said:

'Once I would have said no and been absolutely certain. I'm not certain of anything any more. There were things he didn't tell me, I always knew that. I know it even better now. But I think he would have told me that. It wasn't his child. But he did blame himself for what happened to her. He felt responsible.'

'Why?'

'She tried to see him the day before she killed herself. She went to his office, to the department. It was tactless – the kind of thing only an innocent would do – and she couldn't have chosen a worse time. He was just due to go into an important meeting. He could have made five minutes to see her, but it wouldn't have been convenient and it wouldn't have been prudent. When the young HEO in his private office brought in the news that a Miss Theresa Nolan was in the front hall asking to see him urgently, he said that she was probably one of his constituents and sent down a message asking her to leave her address and he'd get in touch. She went away without saying a word. He never heard from her again. I think he would have got in touch, given time. But he wasn't given time. The next day she was dead.'

It was interesting, thought Kate, that this piece of news hadn't come out when Dalgliesh was interviewing Sir Paul's civil servants. Those careful men, by training and instinct, protected their Minister. Were they extending this protection beyond death? They had spoken of Paul Berowne's speed and skill in mastering a complicated submission, but there had been no mention of the inconvenient arrival of an importunate young woman. But perhaps it wasn't surprising. The officer who had taken the message had been comparatively junior. It was another example of the man who had the interesting information not even being questioned. But even if he had been, he might not have thought it important, unless he had read the inquest report and recognized the girl and, perhaps, not even then.

Carole Washburn still stood gazing into the woodlands, hands deep in her jacket pockets, her shoulders hunched as if there blew from the tangled wilderness the first chill wind of winter. She said:

'She was slumped against the trunk – that trunk. You can barely see it now and in high summer it's invisible. She could have been there for days.'

Not for long, thought Kate. The smell would soon have alerted the park-keepers. Holland Park might be a small paradise in the middle of the city, but it was no different from any other Eden. There were still predators on four legs prowling in the undergrowth and predators on two walking the paths. Death was still death. Bodies still stank when they rotted. She glanced at her companion. Carole Washburn was still staring into the woodland with a painful intensity as if conjuring up that slumped figure at the foot of the silver birch. Then she said:

'Paul told the truth about what happened, but not the whole truth. There were two letters in her jacket pocket, one addressed to her grandparents asking forgiveness, the one read out at the inquest. But there was another, marked confidential and addressed to Paul. That's what I've come to tell you.'

'Did you see it? Did he show it to you?' Kate tried to keep the eagerness out of her voice. Could this, she thought, be physical evidence at last?

'No. He brought it to the flat but he didn't give it to me to read. He told me what was in it. Apparently while Theresa was nursing at Pembroke Lodge she was transferred to night duty. One of the patients had been brought some bottles of champagne by her husband and they'd had a party. It's that kind of place. Anyway she was a little tipsy. She was gloating over the baby, a son after three girls, and said "thanks to darling Stephen". Then she let out that if patients wanted a child of a particular sex Lampart would do an early amniocentesis and abort an unwanted foetus. Women who hated childbirth and weren't prepared to go through with it just to get a child of the wrong sex knew where to go.'

Kate said:

'But he was – he is – taking a terrible risk.'

'Not really. Not if there's never anything on paper, never anything specifically said. Paul wondered if some of the pathological reports were falsified to show an abnormality in the foetus. Most of his lab work is done on the premises. Afterwards Theresa

539

tried to get some evidence, but it wasn't easy. When she questioned the patient the next day she laughed and said that she was joking. But she was obviously terrified. That afternoon she discharged herself.'

So this was the explanation of those mysterious jottings which AD had found in Theresa's missal. She had been trying to collect evidence about the sex of the patients' previous children. Kate asked:

'Did Theresa speak to anyone at Pembroke Lodge?'

'She didn't dare. She knew that someone had libelled Lampart once, and been made bankrupt as a result. He was – he is – notoriously litigious. What could she hope to do, a young nurse, poor, without powerful friends, against a man like that? Who would believe her? And then she found that she was pregnant and had her own problems to think about. How could she speak against what she saw as his sin when she was about to commit mortal sin herself? But when she was preparing to die she felt that she had to do something to put a stop to it. She thought about Paul. He wasn't weak, he had nothing to fear. He was a Minister, a powerful man. He would see that it was stopped.'

'And did he?'

'How could he? She hadn't any idea what kind of burden she was putting on him. As I said, she was an innocent. They're always the ones who do the most harm. Lampart is his wife's lover. If he tackled him it would look like blackmail or, worse, revenge. And his own guilt over her death, the lie about her being a constituent, his failure to help her, that must have seemed morally worse than anything Lampart was doing.'

'What did he decide?'

'He tore up the letter while he was with me and flushed it down the lavatory.'

'But he was a lawyer. Wasn't his instinct to preserve evidence?'

'Not that evidence. He said: "If I haven't the courage to use it, then I must get rid of it. There's no compromise. Either I do what Theresa wanted or I destroy the evidence." I suppose he thought that hoarding it might be degrading, might smack of potential blackmail, carefully preserving evidence against your enemy in case you needed it in future.'

'Did he ask your advice?'

'No. Not advice. He needed to think it through and I was there to listen. That's what he usually needed me for, to listen. I realize that now. And he knew what I would say, what I wanted. I would say: "Divorce Barbara and use that letter to make sure that she and her lover make no trouble over it. Use it to get your freedom." I don't know whether I would have said it so brutally, but he knew that's what I wanted him to do. Before he destroyed it he made me promise to say nothing.'

Kate said:

'He took absolutely no action, you're sure of that?'

'I think he may have spoken to Lampart. He told me that he would, but we never discussed it again. He was going to tell Lampart what he knew and admit that he had no evidence. And he took his money out of Pembroke Lodge. There was quite a bit, I think, originally invested by his brother.'

They began walking slowly down the path. Kate thought: Suppose Paul Berowne had spoken to Lampart. With the evidence destroyed, and pathetically inadequate evidence at that, the doctor would have little to fear. A scandal could hurt Paul Berowne as much as it harmed Lampart. But after Sir Paul's experience in that vestry things might be very different. Perhaps the changed Berowne, his own career thrown away, would see it as his moral duty to expose and ruin Lampart, evidence or no evidence. And what of Barbara Berowne, faced on one hand with a husband who had chucked away both job and prospects, and was even proposing to sell their home, and on the other with a lover who might be facing ruin. Kate decided on a blunt question which, in other circumstances, she might have felt unwise:

'Do you think Stephen Lampart killed him, with or without her connivance?'

'No. He'd be a fool to involve her in anything like that. And she hasn't the courage or the wit to plan it alone. She's the kind of woman who gets a man to do her dirty work for her and then persuades herself that she knows nothing about it. But I've given you a motive, a motive for both of them. It ought to be enough to make life uncomfortable for her.'

'Is that what you want?'

The girl turned round on her and said with sudden passion:

'No, that's not what I want. I want her to be harried and grilled and frightened. I want her disgraced. I want her arrested, imprisoned for life. I want her dead. It won't happen, none of it will happen. And the awful thing is that I've hurt myself more than I can ever hurt her. Once I'd made that call to you, once I'd said I'd be here, then I knew I had to come. But he told me in confidence, he trusted me, he always trusted me. Now there's nothing left, nothing I can remember about our loving that will ever be free of pain and guilt.'

Kate looked at her and saw that she was crying. She was making no sound, not even a sob, but from eyes fixed and staring as if in terror the tears ran in a steady stream over the drained face and the half-open quivering mouth. There was something frightening about this steady, silent grief. Kate thought: There isn't a man, any man in the world who is worth this agony. She felt a mixture of sympathy, helplessness and irritation which she recognized was tinged with slight contempt. But the pity won. There was nothing she could find to say which might comfort, but at least she could make some practical response, ask Carole back to the flat for coffee before they parted. She was opening her mouth to speak, then checked herself. The girl wasn't a suspect. Even if it were reasonable to think of her in those terms, she had an alibi, a late meeting out of London for the time of death. But suppose Carole were required to give evidence in court, then any suggestion of friendship, of an understanding between them could be prejudicial to the prosecution. And more than to the prosecution; it could be prejudicial to her own career. It was the kind of sentimental error of judgement which wouldn't exactly displease Massingham if he came to hear of it. And then she heard herself saying:

'My flat is very close, just across the avenue. Come and have coffee before you go.'

In the flat Carole Washburn moved over to the window like an automaton and gazed out without speaking. Then she moved over to the sofa and stood regarding the oil painting on the wall above, three triangles, partly superimposed, in a browny-red, clear green and white. She asked, but not as if she greatly cared:

'Do you like modern art?'

'I like experimenting with shapes and different colours laid against each other. I don't like reproductions and I can't afford originals so I paint my own. I don't suppose they're art, but I enjoy them.'

'Where did you learn to paint?'

'I just bought the canvas and oils and taught myself. The small bedroom is a kind of studio. I haven't had time to do much lately.'

'It's clever. I like the texture of the background.'

'Done by pressing a tissue over the paint just before it dried. Texture's the easy part, it's applying the oil smoothly that I find tricky.'

She went into the kitchen to grind coffee beans. Carole followed and stood listlessly watching from the doorway. She waited until the grinder had been switched off then suddenly asked:

'What made you choose the police?'

Kate was tempted to reply: For much the same reasons that you chose the Civil Service. I thought I could do the job. I was ambitious. I prefer order and hierarchy to muddle. Then she wondered whether Carole needed to ask, not answer, questions, to reach out, however tentatively, to another's life. She said:

'I didn't want an office job. I wanted a career where I could earn well from the start, hope for promotion. I suppose I like pitting myself against men. And they were rather against the idea at the school I went to. That was an added inducement.'

Carole Washburn made no response but watched her for a moment then drifted back into the sitting room. Kate, hands busy with percolator, mug and saucers, tray and biscuits, found herself recalling that last interview with Miss Shepherd, the careers adviser:

'We had rather hoped that you would set your sights higher, university, for example. You're safe, I'd say, for two As and a B at A-level.'

'I want to start earning.'

'That's understandable, Kate, but you'll get a full grant, remember. You can manage.'

'I don't want to have to manage. I want a job, a place of my own. University would be three wasted years.'

543

'Education is never wasted, Kate.'

'I'm not giving up education. I can go on educating myself.'

'But a policewoman ... We had rather hoped that you would choose something more, well, socially significant.'

'You mean more useful.'

'More concerned, perhaps, with basic human problems.'

'I can't think of anything more basic than helping to make sure that people can walk safely in their own city.'

'I'm afraid, Kate, that recent research shows that walking in safety has little to do with the level of policing. Why not read that pamphlet in the library, "Policing the Inner City: A Socialist Solution"? But if this is your choice, naturally we shall do what we can to help. How do you see yourself? In the Juvenile Bureau?'

'No. I see myself as a senior detective.' She had been tempted to add mischievously: 'and as the first woman Chief Constable.' But that, she had known, was as unrealistic as a recruit to the WRAC seeing herself as commanding the Household Cavalry. Ambition, if it were to be savoured, let alone achieved, had to be rooted in possibility. Even her childhood fantasies had been anchored to reality. The lost father would reappear, loving, prosperous, repentant, but she had never expected him to descend from a Rolls-Royce. And in the end he hadn't come, and she had known that she had never really expected him.

There were no sounds from the sitting room and when she carried in the tray of coffee she saw that Carole was sitting on a chair, stiffly upright, gazing down at her clasped hands. Kate set down the tray and at once Carole slopped milk into her mug, then clasped both hands round it and gulped avidly, hunched in her chair like an old starved woman.

It was strange, thought Kate, that the girl seemed more distraught, less under control, than at their first meeting when they had briefly chatted in her own kitchen. What, she wondered, had happened since then to prompt her betrayal of Berowne's confidence, to produce this bitterness and resentment? Had she somehow learned that there was no mention of her in his will? But that, surely, was what she must have expected. But perhaps it mattered more than she had ever thought possible, the public and final confirmation that she had always been on the periphery of his life, officially non-existent after death as she had been in their years together. She thought that she had been indispensable to him, that he had found with her in that ordinary, seldom visited flat, a still centre of fulfilment and peace. Maybe he had, at least for a few snatched hours. But she hadn't been indispensable to him; no one had. He had compartmentalized people as he had the rest of his over-organized life, filing them away in the recesses of his mind until he needed what they had to offer. But then, she asked herself, is that so very different from what I do with Alan?

She knew that she wouldn't be able to bring herself to ask what had brought the girl to this meeting, and it wasn't really important to the inquiry. What was important was that Berowne's confidence had been broken and Lampart's motive immensely strengthened. But how far did that really get them? One piece of hard physical evidence was worth a dozen motives. They were back to the old question, could Lampart and Barbara Berowne really have had the time? Someone, Berowne or his killer, had been using the washroom at St Matthew's at eight o'clock. Three people had seen the gush of water, none of them could be shaken. So either Berowne was alive at eight or the murderer was still on the premises. Either way it was difficult to see how Lampart could have driven to the Black Swan by eight thirty.

When she had finished her coffee Carole managed a weak smile and said:

'Thank you. I'd better go now. I suppose you want all this on paper.'

'We'd like a statement. You could call in at the Harrow Road station, there's an incident room there, or come to the Yard.'

'I'll call in at Harrow Road. There won't be any more questions will there?'

'There could be, but I don't think we'll want you for long.'

At the door they stood for a moment facing each other. Suddenly Kate thought that Carole was going to step forward and fall into her arms, and knew that her unpractised arms might even know how to hold and comfort, that she might even be able to find the right words. But the moment passed and she told herself that the thought had been embarrassing and ridiculous. As soon as she was alone she rang Dalgliesh, careful to keep any note of triumph out of her voice.

'She came, sir. There's no new physical evidence but she has strengthened one of the suspect's motives. I think you'll want to go to Hampstead.'

He said:

'Where are you ringing from? Your flat?'

'Yes, sir.'

'I'll be there in about half an hour.'

But it was less than that when the bell of the entryphone rang. He said:

'I'm parked further up Lansdowne Road. Could you come down now?'

He didn't suggest that he should come up, and she hadn't expected it. No senior officer was more scrupulous in respecting the privacy of his subordinates. She told herself that in him it hardly counted for virtue. He was too scrupulously careful to protect his own. Going down in the lift it occurred to her that the more she learned of Berowne the more alike he seemed to Dalgliesh. She felt a spurt of irritation against both of them. Here waiting for her was a man who might also cause that extremity of grief for a woman unwise enough to love him. She told herself that she was glad that she had that temptation at least well under control.

4

Stephen Lampart said:

'It isn't true. Theresa Nolan was psychologically disturbed; or, if you prefer bluntness, mad enough to kill herself. Nothing she wrote before that act counts as reliable evidence, even if you have this alleged letter, which I assume you haven't. I mean, if it were actually in your possession you'd be flourishing it in my face, surely. What you're relying on is third-hand information. We both know what that's worth in a court of law, or anywhere else for that matter.'

Dalgliesh said:

'Are you telling me that the girl's story is untrue?'

'Let's be charitable and say mistaken. She was lonely, guilt-ridden, particularly about sex, depressed, losing touch with reality. There's a psychiatrist's report on her medical file which, stripped of its jargon, says precisely that. Or you can argue that she was deliberately lying, she or Berowne. Neither was a particularly reliable witness. Both, as it happens, are dead. If this is meant to give me a motive, it's absurd. It's also close to slander and I know how to deal with that.'

Dalgliesh said:

'As you knew how to deal with libel. A police officer, carrying out a murder investigation, isn't so easily ruined.'

'Not financially, perhaps. The courts are so ridiculously indulgent to the police.'

The nurse who had received them at Pembroke Lodge had said, 'Mr Lampart has just finished operating, if you would come this way,' and they had been shown into a room adjacent to the theatre. Lampart had joined them almost at once, pulling off his green operating cap, peeling off his gloves. The room was small, clinical, seeming full of rushing water and the sound of feet passing in the room next door, of confident voices above the unconscious body of the patient. It was a temporary place, a room for quick clinical exchanges not for confidences. Dalgliesh wondered if the ploy had been deliberate, a way of demonstrating the subtle power of his professional status, of reminding the police that there was more than one kind of authority. Dalgliesh didn't think that Lampart had dreaded the interview, even if he had thought it prudent to face it on his own territory. He hadn't shown the least sign of apprehension. After all, he had enjoyed power, one kind of power, long enough to have acquired the self-assertive hubris of success. A man who had developed the confidence of a successful obstetrician certainly had the confidence to confront an investigating officer of the Metropolitan Police.

Now he said:

'I didn't kill Berowne. Even if I were capable of a particularly brutal and bloody murder, I certainly wouldn't take Berowne's wife with me and expect her to wait in the car while I slit her husband's throat. As for this other nonsense, even if it were true that

547

I aborted healthy foetuses because they weren't the sex the mother wanted, how do you propose to prove it? The operations were done here. The pathological reports are on the medical records. There's nothing incriminating on any file in this building. And even if there were, you wouldn't have access to it, not without a great deal of trouble. I have strong feelings about the sanctity of medical records. So what can you do? Start interviewing a succession of patients in the hope of tricking or bullying one of them into an indiscretion? And how would you track them down without my cooperation? Your allegation is ridiculous, Commander.'

Dalgliesh said:

'But Paul Berowne believed it. He got rid of his shares in Pembroke Lodge after Theresa Nolan's death. I think he spoke to you. I don't know what he said to you but I can guess. You could trust him to keep silent at that time, but after his experience in that church, his conversion, whatever it was, could you trust his silence then?'

He wondered whether he had been wise to show his hand so soon and so clearly. But the doubt was momentary. Lampart had to be confronted by the new evidence, tenuous as it might be. He had to be given the right to reply. And if it were irrelevant, the sooner it was cleared out of the way, the better.

Lampart said:

'It wasn't like that. We never spoke. And, assuming that he did believe it, he would have been in a somewhat invidious position, rather more invidious than you realize. He wanted a son but he certainly didn't want another daughter. Nor, incidentally, did Barbara. Barbara might be willing to bear him an heir, if only to consolidate her position. She saw that as part of the bargain. But nine months' discomfort to produce another daughter for him to resent, despise and ignore was asking rather too much of a woman, particularly one who dislikes and fears the thought of childbirth. Assuming the story is true, you could say that Berowne found himself in a curious position, morally anyway. He couldn't stomach the means but I suspect he wasn't entirely displeased with the ends. That has never been a particularly dignified moral stance, not in my book. Barbara had one miscarriage – a female – eight months after their marriage. Do you suppose he grieved over that? No wonder the poor devil was in a mess psychologically. No wonder he took a razor to his throat. What you've discovered, Commander, if true, is an added reason for suicide, not a motive for murder.'

Lampart took down his jacket from a peg, then opened the door for Dalgliesh and Kate with a smiling courtesy that was almost insulting. Then he led the way to his private drawing room, shut the door and motioned them towards the easy chairs before the fire. Sitting opposite he leaned forward, legs apart, and almost thrust his face at Dalgliesh. Dalgliesh could see the handsome features magnified, the pores of the skin glistening with sweat as if he were still in the heat of the theatre, the taut muscles straining at the neck, the smudge of tiredness under the eyes and the threads of scarlet around the irises, the flecks of dandruff at the roots of the undisciplined forelock. It was still a comparatively young face, but the signs of ageing were there and he could suddenly see how Lampart would look in another thirty years; the skin speckled and bleached, the bones less firmly fleshed, the macho confidence soured into the cynicism of old age. But now his voice was strong and harsh and the aggression came over to Dalgliesh, powerful as a force.

'I'll be frank with you, Commander, more frank than I would probably think prudent if what you're saying were true. If I had aborted those unwanted foetuses, it wouldn't be giving me a single pang of what you would probably call conscience. Two hundred years ago, anaesthesia in childbirth was regarded as immoral. Less than a hundred years ago birth control was virtually illegal. A woman has a right to choose whether she bears a child. I happen to think she also has a right to choose which sex. An unwanted child is usually a nuisance to itself, to society, to its parents. And a two-month foetus isn't a human being, it's a complicated collection of tissue. You probably don't personally believe that the child has a soul before birth, at birth, or after birth. Poet or no poet, you're not the kind of man who sees visions and hears voices in church vestries. I'm not a religious man. I was born with my share of neuroses, but not that one. But what surprises me about those who claim to have faith is that they seem to think that we can find out scientific facts behind

God's back. That first myth, the Garden of Eden, is remarkably persistent. We always feel we haven't a right to knowledge or that, when we get it, we haven't the right to use it. In my book we've the right to do anything we can to make human life more agreeable, safer, less full of pain.'

His voice grated and there was a gleam in the grey eyes uncomfortably close to fanaticism. He could, thought Dalgliesh, have been a seventeenth-century religious mercenary reciting his credo with drawn sword.

Dalgliesh said, mildly:

'Provided, presumably, we don't hurt other people and the act isn't illegal.'

'Provided we don't hurt other people. Yes, I'd accept that. Getting rid of an unwanted foetus hurts no one. Either abortion is never justified or it's justified on grounds which the mother happens to think important. The wrong sex is as good a reason as any. I've more respect for those Christians who oppose abortion on any grounds than for those ingenious compromisers who want life on their own terms and a good conscience at the same time. At least the former are consistent.'

Dalgliesh said:

'The law is consistent. Indiscriminate abortion is unlawful.'

'Oh, but this would have been highly discriminatory. All right, I know what you mean. But the law has no place when it comes to private morality, sexual or otherwise.'

Dalgliesh said:

'Where else is it supposed to operate?'

He got up and Lampart saw them out, deferential, smiling, confident. Except for perfunctory courtesies, neither spoke another word.

In the car Kate said:

'It was practically a confession, sir. He didn't even bother to deny it.'

'No. But it isn't one he'd ever make on paper or which we could use in court. And it was a confession to medical malpractice, not murder. And he's right, of course. It would be the devil to prove.'

'But it gives him a double motive. His affair with Lady Berowne and the fact that Berowne might have felt he had a duty to expose him. Under all that bluff and arrogance, he must know that he's as vulnerable to scandal as any other doctor. Even a rumour wouldn't have done him any good. And coming from someone of Berowne's standing, it would have been taken seriously.'

Dalgliesh said:

'Oh, yes, Lampart has got it all – means, motive, opportunity, knowledge, and the arrogance to think he can get away with it. But I accept one thing he told us. He wouldn't have taken Barbara Berowne with him into that vestry and I can't see her agreeing to be left alone in a car parked in a not particularly salubrious area of Paddington whatever the excuse. And, always, we get back to the timing. The night porter saw them leaving Pembroke Lodge together. Higgins saw them arriving at the Black Swan. Unless one or both are lying Lampart has to be in the clear.'

And then he thought: Unless we've been misled by that gush of water from the waste pipe. Unless we've got the time of death totally wrong. If Berowne had died at the earliest time Dr Kynaston had thought possible, say seven o'clock, what happened to Lampart's alibi then? He had claimed to be at Pembroke Lodge with his mistress, but there had to be more ways than one of leaving the Lodge and returning unseen. But someone had been in the church kitchen at eight o'clock; unless, of course, the water had been left deliberately running. But by whom? Someone who had come earlier, at seven o'clock, someone who had arrived in a black Rover? If Berowne had died at seven o'clock, there were suspects other than Stephen Lampart. But what possible purpose would be served by leaving the tap running? There was, of course, always the possibility that it had been left on by accident. But if that were the case, then how and when had it been turned off?

5

Lady Ursula's friends had expressed their condolences with flowers and her sitting room was incongruously festive with long stemmed thornless roses, carnations and imported boughs of white lilac which looked like plastic artefacts sprayed with scent. The flowers had been less arranged than stuck into a variety of vases placed around the room for convenience rather than effect. By her side on the rosewood table was a small cut glass bowl of freesias. Their scent, sweet and unmistakable, came up to Dalgliesh as he neared her chair. She made no attempt to rise, but held out her hand and he took it. It felt cold and dry and there was no responsive pressure. She was sitting, as always, bolt upright, wearing an ankle-length black wrapover skirt with above it a high-necked blouse in fine grey wool. Her only jewellery was a double chain in old gold and her rings; the long fingers resting on the arms of her chair were laden with great flashing stones so that the blue-corded hands with their parchment skin seemed almost too frail to hold the weight of gold.

She motioned Dalgliesh to the opposite chair. When he had seated himself and Massingham had found a place on a small sofa set against the wall, she said:

'Father Barnes called here this morning. Perhaps he thought he had a duty to bring me spiritual comfort. Or was he apologizing for the use made of his vestry? He could hardly suppose I thought it was his fault. If he intended to offer spiritual consolation I'm afraid he found me a disappointing mourner. He's a curious man. I found him rather unintelligent, commonplace. Was that your opinion?'

Dalgliesh said:

'I wouldn't describe him as commonplace, but it's difficult to see him influencing your son.'

'He seemed to me a man who had long ago given up the expectation of influencing anyone. Perhaps he has lost his faith. Isn't that fashionable in the Church today? But why should that distress him? The world is full of people who have lost faith; politicians who have lost faith in politics, social workers who have lost faith in social work, schoolteachers who have lost faith in teaching and, for all I know, policemen who have lost faith in policing and poets who have lost faith in poetry. It's a condition of faith that it gets lost from time to time, or at least mislaid. And why doesn't he get his cassock cleaned? It is a cassock, isn't it?

There were what I assumed were egg stains on the right cuff and the front looked as if he'd dribbled on it.'

Dalgliesh said:

'It's a garment he practically lives in, Lady Ursula.'

'He could buy a spare, surely.'

'If he could afford one. And he had made an attempt to sponge off the stain.'

'Had he? Not very effectively. Well, that's the sort of thing you're trained to notice, of course.'

It did not surprise him that they were discussing ecclesiastical garb while what remained of her son lay headless and disembowelled in a mortuary ice box. Unlike herself and Father Barnes, they had been able to communicate from their first meeting. She shifted a little in her chair, then she said:

'But you are not, of course, here to discuss Father Barnes's spiritual problems. What are you here to say, Commander?'

'I'm here to ask you again, Lady Ursula, whether or not you saw your son's diary in the desk drawer when General Nollinge rang this house at six o'clock last Tuesday.'

The remarkable eyes looked straight into his.

'You have asked that question twice before. I am, of course, always happy to talk to the poet who wrote "Rhesus Negative" but your visits are becoming rather frequent and your conversation predictable. I've nothing to add to what I told you before. I find this reiteration rather offensive.'

'You do understand the implication of what you're saying?'

'Naturally I understand it. Is there anything else you need to ask?'

'I should like you to confirm that you did, in fact, speak to Halliwell twice on the evening your son died and that, to your knowledge, the Rover was not taken out that night before ten o'clock.'

'I've already told you, Commander. I spoke to him at about eight o'clock and then at nine fifteen. That must have been about forty-five minutes before he left for Suffolk. And I think you can safely assume that, if anyone had taken the Rover, Halliwell would have known. Anything else?'

'Yes, I should like to see Miss Matlock again.'

'In that case I would prefer that you see her here and that I remain. Perhaps you will ring the bell.'

He tugged at the bell-cord. Miss Matlock didn't hurry. But three minutes later she stood in the doorway wearing again the long grey skirt with its gaping pleat, the same ill-fitting blouse.

Lady Ursula said:

'Sit down will you, Mattie. The Commander has some questions for you.'

The woman took one of the chairs against the wall and brought it over, placing it beside Lady Ursula's chair. She looked stolidly at Dalgliesh. This time she seemed almost without anxiety. He thought, she's beginning to get confidence. She knows how little we're able to do if she sticks to her story. She's beginning to think that it could be easy after all. He went through her account again. She answered his questions about the Tuesday evening in almost the same words she had previously used. At the end he said:

'It wasn't, of course, unusual for Mr Dominic Swayne to call here for a bath, perhaps a meal?'

'I've told you. He did it from time to time. He's Lady Berowne's brother.'

'But Sir Paul wasn't necessarily aware of these visits?'

'Sometimes he was, sometimes not. It wasn't my place to tell him.'

'What about the time before last, not Tuesday but the time before? What did you do then?'

'He had a bath as usual, then I cooked him supper. He doesn't always have supper here when he comes for his bath but that night he did. I cooked him a pork chop with mustard sauce, sauté potatoes and green beans.'

A more substantial meal, thought Dalgliesh, than the omelette she had cooked on the night of Berowne's death. But on that night he had arrived at shorter notice. Why? Because his sister had telephoned him after her quarrel with her husband? Because she had told him where Berowne would be that night? Because his plan of murder was beginning to take shape?

He asked:

'And after that?'

554

'He had apple tart and cheese.'

'I mean, what did you do after the meal?'

'After that we played Scrabble.'

'You and he seem extraordinarily fond of Scrabble.'

'I like it. I think he plays to please me. There's no one here to give me a game.'

'And who won that time, Miss Matlock?'

'I think I did. I can't remember by how much, but I think I won.'

'You think you won? It was only ten days ago, can't you be sure?'

Two pairs of eyes looked into his, hers and Lady Ursula's. They were not, he thought, natural allies, but now they sat side by side rigidly upright, motionless as if held in a field of force which both sustained and linked them. Lady Ursula was, he sensed, almost at the end of her endurance, but he thought he saw in Evelyn Matlock's defiant gaze a glint of triumph. She said:

'I can remember perfectly. I won.'

It was, he knew, the most effective way of fabricating an alibi. You described events which had, in fact, happened, but on a different occasion. It was the most difficult of all alibis to break since, apart from the alteration in time, the parties concerned were speaking the truth. He thought she was lying, but he couldn't be sure. She was, he knew, a neurotic, and the fact that she was now beginning to enjoy pitting her wits against his might be no more than the self-dramatization of a woman whose life had afforded few such heady excitements. He heard Lady Ursula's voice:

'Miss Matlock has answered all your inquiries, Commander. Should you propose to continue badgering her, then I think we shall have to arrange for my solicitor to be present.'

He said coldly:

'That, of course, is her right, Lady Ursula. And we're not here to badger either you or her.'

'In that case, Mattie, perhaps you will show the Commander and Chief Inspector Massingham out.'

They were driving down Victoria Street when the telephone

rang. Massingham answered it, listened, then handed the receiver to Dalgliesh.

'It's Kate, sir. I detect a note of girlish enthusiasm. Can't wait until we get back apparently. But I think she'd like to tell you herself.'

Kate's voice, like her enthusiasm, was under control but Dalgliesh, too, couldn't miss the note of heady optimism. She said:

'Something interesting has turned up, sir. Hearne and Collingwood rang ten minutes ago with Millicent Gentle's address. She's moved since they last published her and hadn't told them where so it took a little time to trace her. She's at Riverside Cottage, Coldham Lane, near Cookham. I've looked at the ordnance survey. Coldham Lane runs almost opposite the Black Swan. Sir, she must have handed Sir Paul her book on August the seventh.'

'It seems likely. Have you a telephone number?'

'Yes, sir. The firm wouldn't give me either the address or the number until they'd rung her and checked that she agreed.'

'Ring her then, Kate. Ask if she'll see us as early as possible tomorrow morning.'

He replaced the receiver. Massingham said:

'The clue of the romantic novelist. I can't wait to meet the author of *A Rose by Twilight*. Do you want me to go to Cookham, sir?'

'No, John, I'll go.'

At the Yard entrance he got out of the Rover, leaving Massingham to garage it, then hesitated and strode off vigorously to St James's Park. The office was too claustrophobic to contain this sudden surge of irrational optimism. He needed to walk free and alone. It had been a hellish day, beginning in Gilmartin's office with peevish ill-temper, ending in Campden Hill Square with unprovable lies. But now the vexations and frustrations fell from his shoulders. He thought:

Tomorrow I shall know exactly what happened at the Black Swan on the night of the seventh of August. And when I know that, I shall know why Paul Berowne had to die. I may not yet be able to prove it. But I shall know.

6

Brian Nichols, recently promoted Assistant Commissioner, resented Dalgliesh and found this dislike the more irritating because he wasn't sure that it was justified. After twenty-five years of policing he regarded even his antipathies with a judicial eye; he liked to be confident that the case against the accused would stand up in court. With Dalgliesh he wasn't sure. Nichols was the senior in rank but this gave him small satisfaction when he knew that Dalgliesh could have outstripped him had he chosen. This lack of concern about promotion, which Dalgliesh never condescended to justify, he saw as a subtle criticism of his own more ambitious preoccupations. He deplored the poetry, not on principle, but because it had conferred prestige and, therefore, couldn't be regarded as a harmless hobby like fishing, gardening or woodwork. A policeman, in his view, should be satisfied with policing. An added grievance was that Dalgliesh chose most of his friends from outside the force and those fellow officers he consorted with weren't always of an appropriate rank. In a junior officer that would have been regarded as a dangerous idiosyncrasy and in a senior it had a taint of disloyalty. And to compound these delinquencies, he dressed too well. He was standing now with easy assurance looking out of the window wearing a suit in a subtle brown tweed which Nichols had seen him wearing for the last four years. It bore the unmistakable stamp of an excellent tailor, probably, thought Nichols, the firm his grandfather had patronized. Nichols, who enjoyed buying clothes, sometimes with more enthusiasm than discrimination, felt that it was becoming in a man to own rather more suits and those not so well tailored. Finally, whenever he was with Dalgliesh, he felt inexplicably that he ought perhaps to shave off his moustache and would find his hand moving involuntarily to his upper lip as if to reassure himself that the moustache was still a respectable appendage. This impulse, irrational, almost neurotic, irritated him profoundly.

Both men knew that Dalgliesh needn't be here in Nichols's tenth-floor office, that the casual suggestion that the AC should be put in the picture was no more than an invitation, not a command. The new squad was now formally set up; but Berowne's murder had happened six days too soon. In future, Dalgliesh would report directly to the Commissioner. But for now Nichols could claim a legitimate interest. It was his department, after all, which had provided most of the men for Dalgliesh's supporting team. And with the Commissioner temporarily away at a conference, he could argue that he had a right at least to a brief progress report. But, irrationally, part of him wished that Dalgliesh had objected, had given him the excuse for one of those departmental wrangles which he provoked when the job offered less excitement than his restless spirit craved and which he was adept at winning.

While Nichols looked through the file on the case Dalgliesh gazed out eastward over the city. He had seen many capitals from a similar height, all different. When he looked down on Manhattan from his hotel bedroom its spectacular soaring beauty always seemed to him precarious, even doomed. Images would rise from films seen in his boyhood, prehistoric monsters towering above the skyscrapers to claw them down, a vast tidal wave from the Atlantic obliterating the skyline, the light-spangled city darkening into the final holocaust. But London, laid out beneath him under a low ceiling of silver-grey cloud, looked eternal, rooted, domestic. He saw the panorama, of which he never tired, in terms of painting. Sometimes it had the softness and immediacy of watercolour; sometimes, in high summer, when the park burgeoned with greenness, it had the rich texture of oil. This morning it was a steel engraving, hard-edged, grey, one-dimensional.

He turned away from the window with reluctance. Nichols had closed the file but was swivelling his chair and moving his body restlessly as if to emphasize the comparative informality of the proceedings. Dalgliesh moved over and took a seat opposite him. He gave a concise summary of his investigation as far as it had gone and Nichols listened with a show of disciplined patience, still swivelling, his eyes on the ceiling. Then he said:

'All right, Adam, you've convinced me that Berowne was murdered. But then I'm not the one who has to be convinced. But what have you got by way of direct evidence? One small smudge of blood under a fold of Harry Mack's jacket.'

'And a matching stain on the pocket. Berowne's blood. He died first. There's no room for doubt. We can prove that the smear is identical with his blood.'

'But not how it got there. You know what defending counsel will argue if it ever gets to court. One of your chaps carried it there on his shoes. Or the boy did, the one who found the body. Or that spinster – what's her name – Edith Wharton.'

'Emily Wharton. We examined their shoes and I'm confident neither went into the Little Vestry. And, even if they had, it's difficult to see how they could have left a smudge of Berowne's blood under Harry's jacket.'

'It's a very convenient smudge from your point of view. From the family's too, I suppose. But without it there's nothing to suggest that this isn't exactly what it first appeared – murder followed by suicide. A politician, prominent, successful, has some kind of religious conversion, quasi-mystical experience, call it what you will. He throws over his job, his career, possibly his family. Then, don't ask me how or why, he discovers that it's all a chimera.' Nichols repeated the word as if to reassure himself of the pronunciation. Dalgliesh wondered where he had come across it. Then he went on:

'Why did Berowne go back to that church, incidentally? Do you know?'

'Possibly because of a new complication to do with his marriage. I think his wife told him that morning that she was pregnant.'

'There you are then. He was already having doubts. He goes back, faces the reality of what he's given up. There's nothing ahead but failure, humiliation, ridicule. He decides to end it then and there. He has the means to hand. While he's making his preparations, burning his diary, Harry comes in and tries to stop him. Result? Two bodies instead of one.'

'That assumes he didn't know Harry Mack was there. I think he did, he let him in. That's hardly the action of a man contemplating suicide.'

'You've no proof that he let him in. None that would satisfy a jury.'

'Berowne gave Harry part of his supper, wholemeal bread, Roquefort cheese, an apple. It's on the file. You aren't suggesting that Harry Mack bought his own Roquefort? He couldn't have surprised Berowne. He'd been in the church for some time before Berowne died. He was bedded down in the larger vestry. There's physical evidence, hair, fibres from his coat, apart from the crumbs of food. And he wasn't in the vestry or in the church when Father Barnes locked up after Evensong.'

Nichols said:

'He thinks he locked up. Would he swear in the witness box that he turned the key in the south door, that he'd searched every pew? And why should he search? He wasn't expecting a murder. There are plenty of places where Harry, or a murderer for that matter, could have concealed himself. The church was dark presumably; a dim religious light.'

The AC had this habit of spattering his conversation with the odd half-quotation. Dalgliesh could never decide whether he knew that he was doing it or whether the words swam into his consciousness from some half-forgotten pool of schoolroom lore. Now he heard him say:

'How well did you know Berowne personally?'

'I saw him a couple of times across a committee room table. We travelled together to the conference on sentencing. He asked to see me once in his office. We walked through St James's Park to the House together. I liked him but I'm not obsessed with him. I don't identify with him more than anyone does with any victim. This isn't a personal crusade. But I admit to a perfectly reasonable objection to seeing him branded as the brutal murderer of a man who died after he did.'

Nichols said:

'On the evidence of one small smudge of blood?'

'What evidence do we need?'

'To the fact of murder, none. As I said, you don't have to convince me. But I don't see how you're going to get any further unless you find one irrefutable piece of evidence linking one of your suspects to the scene of the crime.' Nichols added, 'Sooner rather than later.'

'The Commissioner is getting complaints, I suppose.'

'The usual thing, two dead bodies, two throats severed, a murderer at large. Why aren't we arresting this dangerous lunatic instead of examining the cars, clothes and houses of respectable citizens? Did you find any trace on the suspects' clothes by the way?'

It was ironic, thought Dalgliesh, but not surprising; the new division set up to investigate serious crimes with sensitive undertones already accused of crass insensitivity. And he knew where the criticisms would have come from. He said:

'No, but I didn't expect any. This killer was naked or nearly naked. He had the means of washing himself to hand. Three passers-by heard the water gushing away shortly after eight.'

'Berowne washing his own hands before supper?'

'If so he was doing it very thoroughly.'

'But his hands were clean when you found him?'

'The left hand was. The right was heavily bloodied.'

'There you are then.'

Dalgliesh said:

'Berowne's towel was hanging over a chair in the vestry, I think his murderer dried himself with the tea towel in the kitchen. It was still slightly damp, not in places but all over, when I touched it. And he was killed with one of his own razors. Berowne had two, Bellinghams, in a case by the washbasin. A casual intruder, or Harry Mack for that matter, wouldn't have known they were there, probably wouldn't even have recognized the case for what it was.'

'And what's a Bellingham for God's sake? Why couldn't the man use a Gillette or an electric razor like the rest of us? OK, so it was someone who knew he shaved with a cut-throat, knew he'd be at the church that night, had access to the Campden Hill Square house to collect the matches and the diary. You know who best fits that list of requirements? Berowne himself. And all you've got against the suicide theory is one smudge of blood.'

Dalgliesh was beginning to think that those four monosyllables would haunt him to the end of the case. He said:

'You're not suggesting, I suppose, that Berowne half-cut his throat, staggered over to Harry to murder him, dripping blood in the act, then staggered back again to the other end of the room to make the third and final cut in his own throat?'

'No, but defence counsel might. And Doc Kynaston hasn't

A SECOND DALGLIESH TRILOGY

entirely ruled it out. You and I have known more ingenious defences succeed.'

Dalgliesh said:

'He wrote something while he was in that vestry. The lab can't identify the words although they think it possible that he signed his name. The ink on the blotter is the same as the ink in his pen.'

'So he wrote a suicide note?'

'Possibly, but where is it now?'

The AC said:

'He burned it with the diary. All right, I know what you're going to say, Adam. Is it likely a suicide would burn a note once written? Well it's not impossible. He could have been dissatisfied with what he'd said. Inadequate words, too trite, let it go. After all, the action speaks for itself. Not every suicide goes documented into that good night.'

A flicker of pleased surprise passed over his face as if he were gratified at the aptness of the allusion but would rather like to be able to remember where it came from. Dalgliesh said:

'There's one thing he could have written which it's unlikely he would have blotted immediately, and that is something that another person might well wish to destroy.'

Nichols was sometimes a little slow in grasping the point, but he was never afraid to take his time. He took it now. Then he said:

'That would need three signatures, of course. It's an interesting theory and it would certainly strengthen the motive for at least two of your suspects. But, again, there's no proof. We get back to that all the time. It's an ingenious edifice you've built up, Adam, I'm half-convinced by it. But what we need is solid, physical evidence.' He added: 'You could say it's like the church, an ingenious edifice erected on an unproved supposition, logical within its terms, but only valid if one can accept the basic premise, the existence of God.'

He seemed pleased with the analogy. Dalgliesh doubted if it were his own. He watched while the AC skimmed over the remaining pages of the file almost dismissively. Closing the file, he said:

'Pity that you haven't been able to trace Berowne's movements after he left 62 Campden Hill Square. He seems to have walked into thin air.'

'Not altogether. We know that he went to Westertons, the estate agents, in Kensington High Street and saw one of their negotiators, Simon Follett-Biggs. He asked someone from the firm to visit the next day to inspect and value the house. Again, hardly the action of a man contemplating suicide. Follett-Biggs says that he was as unconcerned as if he were giving them instructions to sell a forty-thousand one-bedroom basement flat. He did tactfully express his regrets that the family should be selling a house they'd lived in since it was first built. Berowne replied that they'd had it for a hundred and fifty years; it was time someone else had a turn. He didn't want to discuss it, only to ensure that someone came next morning to carry out the valuation. It was a short interview. He was away by eleven thirty. After that, we haven't been able to trace him. But he could have walked in one of the parks or by the river. His shoes were muddied and subsequently washed and scraped clean.'

'Cleaned where?'

'Exactly. It suggests that he could have returned home, but no one admits to having seen him. He might escape notice if he slipped quickly in and out but hardly if he stopped long enough to clean his shoes. And Father Barnes is certain that he arrived at the church by six. We've seven hours to account for.'

'You saw this Follett-Briggs? Extraordinary names these fellows have. He must be feeling pretty sick. That would have been quite a commission. He might get it yet, I suppose, if the widow decides to sell.'

Dalgliesh didn't reply.

'Did Follett-Briggs say what he expected it to fetch?'

He could, thought Dalgliesh, have been speaking of a second-hand car.

'He wouldn't commit himself, of course. He hasn't inspected the house and he took the view that Berowne's instructions no longer held. But under a little tactful pressure he did murmur that he would expect to get in excess of a million. That's excluding the contents, of course.'

'And it all goes to the widow.'

'It goes to the widow.'

'But the widow has an alibi. So has the widow's lover. So, as far as I can see, has every other suspect in the case.'

As he picked up his file and moved to the door, the AC's voice pursued him like a plea.

'Just one piece of physical evidence, Adam. That's what we need. And for God's sake try to get it before we have to call the next press conference.'

7

Sarah Berowne found the postcard on the hall table on Monday morning. It was a card from the British Museum of a bronze cat wearing earrings with Ivor's message written in his cramped upright hand. 'Have tried to ring you but no luck. Hope you're feeling better. Any chance of dinner next Tuesday?'

So he was still using their code. He kept ready a small collection of postcards from the main London museums and galleries. Any mention of telephoning meant a proposal to meet, and this message deciphered, asked her to be near the postcard gallery of the British Museum on Tuesday next. The time varied with the day. On Tuesdays the assignation was always for three o'clock. Like similar messages, this assumed that she could make it. If not she was expected to ring back to say that dinner was impossible. But he had always taken it for granted that she would cancel all other engagements when the cards arrived. A message sent in this way was always urgent.

It was, she thought, hardly a code that would defeat the ingenuity of the police let alone the security forces if they became interested, but perhaps its very openness and simplicity was a safeguard. There was, after all, no law against friends spending an hour looking round museums together, and the rendezvous was a sensible one. They could pore over the same guidebook, talk in the almost obligatory whispers, move about at will to find the deserted galleries.

In those first heady months after he had recruited her to the Cell of Thirteen, when she was beginning to fall in love with him, she had looked for these cards as she might for a love letter, lurking in the hall for the post to fall through the letter box, seizing on the card and poring over its message as if these cramped letters could say everything that she needed so desperately to be told but which she knew he would never write still less speak. But now, for the first time, she read the summons with a mixture of depression and irritation. The notice was ridiculously short; it wouldn't be easy to get to Bloomsbury by three. And why on earth couldn't he telephone? Tearing up the card she felt as she never had before, that the code was a childish and unnecessary device born of his obsessional need to manipulate and conspire. It made them both ridiculous.

He was, as usual, there on time, selecting cards from the stand. She waited while he paid and, without speaking, they moved out of the gallery together. He was fascinated by the Egyptian antiquities and, almost instinctively, they made their way first to the ground-floor galleries and stood together while he contemplated the huge granite torso of Rameses the Second. It had seemed to her once that these dead eyes, this finely chiselled half-smiling mouth above the jutting beard, had been a powerfully erotic symbol of their love. So much had been whispered between them in sly elliptical phrases while they had stood regarding it as if seeing the Pharaoh for the first time, shoulders touching, and she had fought the need to stretch out her hand, to feel his fingers in hers. But now all its power had drained away. It was an interesting artefact, a huge slab of cracked granite, no more. He said:

'Shelley is supposed to have used these features as a model when he wrote "Ozymandias".'

'I know.'

A couple of Japanese tourists, their scrutiny completed, drifted away. With no change in the level or tone of his voice, he said:

'The police seem more certain now that your father was murdered. I imagine they've got the PM and forensic reports. They've been to see me.'

A sliver of fear slid down her spine like iced water.

'Why?'

'In the hope of breaking our alibi. They didn't, and of course they can't. Not unless they break you. Have they been back?'

'Once. Not Commander Dalgliesh, the woman detective and a

younger man, a Chief Inspector Massingham. They asked about Theresa Nolan and Diana Travers.'

'What did you tell them?'

'That I'd seen Theresa Nolan twice, once when I'd called to see Grandmama when she was ill, and once at that dinner party and that I'd never seen Diana. Wasn't that what you expected me to say?'

He answered:

'Let's go and visit Ginger.'

Ginger, named from the colour of the remnants of his hair, was the body of a pre-dynastic man, mummified by the hot desert sands three thousand years before Christ. Ivor had always been intrigued by him and they never left the museum without this almost ritual visit. Now she gazed down at the emaciated body curled on its left side, the pathetic collection of pots to hold the food and drink which would nourish his spirit on its long journey through the underworld, the spear with which he would defend himself against its ghostly terrors until he reached his Egyptian heaven. Perhaps, she thought, if that spirit could awake now and see the bright lights, the huge room, the moving forms of twentieth-century man, he would think that he had attained it. But she had never been able to share Ivor's pleasure in this *memento mori*; the body's emaciation, even its attitude, evoked too strongly a modern horror; the pictures and newsreels of the dead at Belsen. She thought: Even when we're here he never asks what I think, what I feel, what I'd like most to see. She said:

'Let's go to the Duveen Gallery. I want to look at the Parthenon screen.'

They moved slowly away. As they paced, their eyes on the open guidebook, she said:

'Diana Travers. You told me that she wasn't put into Campden Hill Square to spy on Daddy's private life. You said it was only his job you were interested in, finding out what was in the new Police Tactical Options Manual. I must have been naive. I can't think why I believed you. But that's what you told me.'

'I don't need to have a cell member polishing the Berowne family silver to discover what's in the Tactical Options Manual. And she wasn't put there to spy on his private life, not primarily.

I put her there to make her think she had a job to do, that she was trusted. It kept her occupied while I decided what to do about her.'

'What do you mean, do about her? She was a member of the cell. She replaced Rose when Rose went back to Ireland.'

'She thought she was a member, but she wasn't. There's no reason why you shouldn't know. After all, she's dead. Diana Travers was a Special Branch spy.'

He had trained her not to look at him when they were talking but to keep her eyes on the exhibits, the guidebook or straight ahead. She gazed straight ahead now. She said:

'Why didn't you tell us?'

'Four of you were told, not the whole cell. I don't tell the cell everything.'

She had, of course, known that his membership of the Workers' Revolutionary Campaign was a cover for the Cell of Thirteen. But even the cell, apparently, had only been a cover for his private inner cabinet. Like a Russian doll, you unscrewed one deceit to find another nestling within it. There were only four people whom he trusted completely, confided in, consulted, and she hadn't been among them. Had he ever trusted her, she wondered, even from the beginning? She said:

'That first time, when you rang me nearly four years ago and asked me to take photographs of Brixton, was that all part of a plan to recruit me, to get the daughter of a Tory MP into the WRC?'

'Partly. I knew where your political sympathies lay. I guessed you wouldn't exactly welcome your father's second marriage. It seemed a propitious time to make an approach. Afterwards, my interest became, well, more personal.'

'But was there ever love?'

He frowned. She knew how much he hated any intrusion of the personal, the sentimental. He said:

'There was, there still is, great liking, respect, physical attraction. You can call that love if you want to use the word.'

'What do you call it, Ivor?'

'I call it liking, respect, physical attraction.'

They had moved into the Duveen Gallery. Above them pranced

the horses on the Parthenon frieze, the naked riders with their flying cloaks, the chariots, the musicians, the elders and maidens approaching the seated gods and goddesses. But she looked up at this marvel with unseeing eyes. She thought: I need to know, I need to know everything. I have to face the truth. She said:

'And it was you who sent that poison pen note to Daddy and to the *Paternoster Review*? Doesn't it seem rather petty even to you, the people's revolutionary, the great campaigner against oppression, prophet of the new Jerusalem, reduced to gossip, slander, to childish spite? What did you think you were doing?'

He said:

'Making a little mild mischief.'

'Is that what you call it – helping to discredit decent men? And not only my father. Most of them on your own side, men who've given years to the Labour movement, a cause you're supposed to support.'

'Decency doesn't come into it. This is a war. Wars may be fought by decent men but they're not won by them.'

A small group of visitors had drifted up. They moved away and walked slowly down the side of the gallery. He said:

'If you're in the job of organizing a revolutionary group, even a small one, and they're going to have to wait for real action, real power, then you must keep them occupied, keen, give them the illusion that they're achieving something. Talk isn't enough. There has to be action. It's partly a matter of training for the future, partly of keeping up morale.'

She said:

'From now on you're going to have to do it without me.'

'I realize that. I knew that after Dalgliesh had seen you. But I expect you to stay on, at least nominally, until this murder inquiry is over. I don't want to say anything to the others while Dalgliesh is nosing around. Then you can join the Labour Party. You'll be happier there. Or the SDP, of course. Take your choice, there's no difference. By the time you're forty you'll be a Tory anyway.'

She said:

'And you still trust me? You've told me all this knowing that I want to get out?'

'Of course. I know you. You've inherited your father's pride. You wouldn't want people saying that your lover chucked you so you took your revenge by betraying him. You wouldn't want your friends, your grandmother even, to know that you've conspired against your father. You can say I rely on your bourgeois decencies. But there isn't much of a risk. The cell will be dissolved, re-formed, meet elsewhere. That's necessary now anyway.'

She thought: That's another aspect of the revolutionary struggle, getting to know people's decencies and using them against them. She said:

'Daddy, there's something I've learned about him, something I didn't realize until he died. He tried to be good. I suppose those words don't mean anything to you.'

'They mean something. I'm not sure what exactly you expect them to mean. I suppose he tried to behave so that he wasn't made uncomfortable by too much guilt. We all do. Given his politics and lifestyle that can't have been easy. Perhaps in the end he gave up trying.'

She said:

'I wasn't talking about politics. It had nothing to do with politics. I know you think everything has, but there is another view. There is a world elsewhere.'

'I hope you'll be happy in it.'

They were moving out of the gallery now and she knew that this was the last time they would be there together. It surprised her how little she cared. She said:

'But Diana Travers; you said you put her into Campden Hill Square until you decided what to do with her. What did you do? Drown her?'

And now for the first time she saw that he was angry.

'Don't be melodramatic.'

'But it was convenient for you, wasn't it?'

'Oh yes, and not only for me. There's someone else who had a much stronger motive for getting rid of her. Your father.'

Forgetting the need for secrecy, she almost cried:

'Daddy? But he wasn't there! He was expected, but he never arrived.'

'Oh, but he was there. I followed him that night. You could

call it an exercise in surveillance. I drove behind him all the way to the Black Swan and watched him turn into the drive. And if you should decide to talk to Dalgliesh, who seems for some reason to induce in you the need for sentimental girlish confidences, then that is one piece of information that I shall feel it necessary to pass on.'

'But you can't, can you? Not without admitting that you were there, too. If it's a question of motive, Dalgliesh might think there's not a lot to choose between you. And you're alive; he's dead.'

'But unlike your father, I have an alibi. A genuine one this time. I drove straight back to London, to a meeting of senior social workers at the town hall. I'm in the clear. But is he? His memory is unsavoury enough as it is. D'you want another scandal linked to his name? Isn't poor Harry Mack enough for you? Think about that if you're tempted to make an anonymous call to Special Branch.'

8

Tuesday morning couldn't have heralded a better day for a drive out of London. The sunlight was fitful but surprisingly strong and the sky was a high ethereal blue above the scudding clouds. Dalgliesh drove fast, but almost in silence. Kate had expected that they would drive straight to Riverside Cottage but the road passed the Black Swan and when they reached it Dalgliesh stopped the car, appeared to think, then turned into the drive. He said:

'We'll have a beer. I'd like to walk along the river, view the cottage from this bank. It's Higgins's property, most of it anyway. We'd better let him know we're here.'

They left the Rover in the car park, which was empty except for a Jaguar, a BMW, and a couple of Fords, and made their way to the entrance hall. Henry greeted them with impassive courtesy as if unsure whether he was expected to recognize them and, in reply to Dalgliesh's question, told them that Monsieur was in London. The bar was empty except for a quartet of businessmen conspiratorially bent over their whiskies. The barman, baby-faced above his white starched jacket and bow tie, served them with a notable brew of real ale which the Black Swan took some pride in obtaining, then began industriously washing glasses and rearranging his bar as if hoping that a show of busyness might inhibit Dalgliesh from asking any questions. Dalgliesh wondered by what extraordinary alchemy Henry had managed to signal their identities. They carried their beer to the chairs each side of the log fire, drank in companionable silence, then returned to the car park and passed through the gate in the hedge to the riverbank.

It was one of those perfect English autumnal days which occur more frequently in memory than in life. The rich colours of grass and earth were intensified by the mellow light of a sun almost warm enough for spring and the air was a sweet evocation of all Dalgliesh's boyhood autumns; woodsmoke, ripe apples, the last sheaves of harvest, and the strong sea-smelling breeze of flowing water. The Thames was running strongly, under a quickening breeze. It flattened the grasses fringing the river edge and eddied the stream into the little gullies which fretted the bank. Under a surface iridescent in blues and greens, on which the light moved and changed as if on coloured glass, the blade-like weeds streamed and undulated. Beyond the clumps of willows on the far bank, a herd of Friesians were peacefully grazing.

Opposite and about twenty yards downstream he could see a bungalow, little more than a large white shack on stilts, which he guessed must be their destination. And he knew too, as he had known walking under the trees of St James's Park, that here he would find the clue he sought. But he was in no hurry. Like a child postponing the moment of assured satisfaction he was glad that they were early, grateful for this small hiatus of calm. And suddenly he experienced a minute of tingling happiness so unexpected and so keen that he almost held his breath as if he could halt time. They came to him so rarely now, these moments of intense physical joy, and he had never before experienced one in the middle of a murder investigation. The moment passed and he heard his own sigh. Breaking the mood with a commonplace, he said:

'I suppose that must be Riverside Cottage.'

'I think so, sir. Shall I get the map?'

'No. We shall find out soon enough. We'd better get on.'

But he still lingered feeling the wind lift his hair and grateful for another minute of peace. He was grateful, too, that Kate Miskin could share it with him without the need to speak and without making him feel that her silence was a conscious discipline. He had chosen her because he needed a woman in his team and she was the best available. The choice had been partly rational, partly instinctive, and he was beginning to realize just how well his instinct had served him. It would have been dishonest to say that there was no hint of sexuality between them. In his experience there nearly always was, however repudiated or unacknowledged, between any reasonably attractive heterosexual couple who worked closely together. He wouldn't have chosen her if he had found her disturbingly attractive, but the attraction was there and he wasn't immune to it. But despite this pinprick of sexuality, perhaps because of it, he found her surprisingly restful to work with. She had an instinctive knowledge of what he wanted; she knew when to be silent; she wasn't over-deferential. He suspected that with part of her mind she saw his vulnerabilities more clearly, understood him better, and was more judgemental than were any of his male subordinates. She had none of Massingham's ruthlessness, but she wasn't in the least sentimental. But then in his experience, women police officers seldom were.

He took a final look at the bungalow. If he had walked along the riverbank on that first visit to the Black Swan, as he had been tempted to do, he would have viewed its pathetic pretensions with an incurious and disparaging eye. But now as its fragile walls seemed to shimmer in the slight haze from the river it held for him an infinite and disturbing promise. It was built about thirty yards from the water's edge with a wide veranda, a central stack and to the left, upstream, a small landing stage. He thought he could see a patch of broken earth with clumps of mauve and white, perhaps a patch of Michaelmas daisies. Some attempt had been made at a garden. From a distance the bungalow looked well-maintained, the white paintwork gleaming. But even so, it had a summer look; temporary, a little ramshackle. Higgins, he thought, would hardly relish having it in full view of his lawns.

As they looked, the dumpy figure of a woman came out of the

side door and made her way to the landing stage, a large dog trotting at her heels. She lowered herself into a dinghy, leaned over to cast off and began rowing purposefully across the river towards the Black Swan, humpbacked over the oars, the dog sitting bolt-upright in the prow. As the dinghy crawled closer they could see that he was a cross between a poodle and some kind of terrier with a woolly body and an anxious, amiable face almost entirely obscured by hair. They watched as the woman bent and rose over the dipping oars, making slow progress against a current that was bearing her downstream away from them. When the dinghy finally bumped the bank, Dalgliesh and Kate walked up to her. Bending down, he caught the bow of the dinghy and held it steady. He saw that her landing place had not been fortuitous. There was a steel stake driven deep into the grass at the water's edge. He slipped the painter over it and held out his hand. She grasped it and almost hopped ashore, one-footed, and he saw that she wore a surgical boot on her left foot. The dog leapt out after her, sniffed at Dalgliesh's trousers, then flopped, discouraged, on the grass as if the physical effort of the journey had all been his. Dalgliesh said:

'I think you must be Miss Millicent Gentle. If so, we're on our way to see you. We telephoned from Scotland Yard this morning. This is Inspector Kate Miskin and my name is Adam Dalgliesh.'

He looked down at a face round and crumpled like an over-stored apple. The striped russet cheeks were hard balls under small eyes which, when she smiled up at him, creased into narrow slits, then opened to reveal irises as brightly brown as polished pebbles. She was wearing a shapeless pair of brown Terylene slacks and a padded sleeveless jerkin in faded red over a jumper matted with age. Drawn well down over her head was a pixie cap in knitted green and red stripes and with earflaps each ending in a pigtail of plaited wool, decorated with a red bobble. She had an air of slightly battered puckishness like an elderly garden gnome which has weathered too many winters. But when she spoke her voice, deep and resonant, was one of the most beautiful female voices he had ever heard.

'I am expecting you, of course, Commander, but not for another half an hour. How pleasant to meet you so unexpectedly.

I would row you across but with Makepeace it would mean one at a time and that would be rather slow. I'm afraid it's five miles by road, but perhaps you have a car.'

'We have a car.'

'Of course, you would have, being police officers. How silly of me. Then I'll be waiting for you. I've just rowed across with my letters. Mr Higgins lets me put them on the hall table to be posted with his. My postbox is a two-mile walk. It's very kind of him considering that he doesn't really like my cottage. I'm afraid he considers it rather an eyesore. You can't miss the road. Take the first left marked Frolight, then over the hump-backed bridge, then left again at Mr Roland's farm – there's a sign with a Friesian cow on it – then you'll see a track leading to the river and my cottage. As you can see, you can't really miss it. Oh, and you'll have some coffee, I hope.'

'Thank you, we should like that.'

'I thought you might. That's partly why I rowed over. Mr Higgins is kind about selling me an extra pint of milk. It's about Sir Paul Berowne, isn't it?'

'Yes, Miss Gentle, it's about Sir Paul.'

'I thought it might be when you telephoned and said you were police. That dear good man. I shall see you both then in about ten minutes.'

They watched her for a moment as she limped briskly towards the Black Swan, the dog lurching at her heels, then turned and made their way slowly back to the car park. They followed her instructions without difficulty but Dalgliesh drove slowly knowing them to be still ahead of their appointment and wanting to give Miss Gentle time to row back and be waiting for them. Gentle was, apparently, her real name not a pseudonym; it had seemed almost too appropriate for a romantic novelist. Driving with irritating slowness, he was aware of Kate's controlled impatience at his side. But ten minutes later they left the side road and turned up the rough track to the cottage.

It ran across an unhedged field and would, thought Dalgliesh, be little more than an impassable quagmire in the worst of the winter. The bungalow looked more substantial than it had from a distance. A flowerbed, now in its shaggy autumnal decrepitude, bordered the cinder path to the side steps beneath which he could glimpse cans, presumably of paraffin, stacked under a tarpaulin. Behind the bungalow was a vegetable patch; stunted cabbages, and the scarred stems of Brussels sprouts, bulbous onions, broken-leaved, and the last of the runner beans whose dying swathes hung from their poles like rags. The river smell was stronger here and he could picture the scene in winter, the cold mist rising from the water, the soggy fields, the single mud track to a desolate country road.

But when Miss Gentle opened the door to them and smilingly stepped aside they walked into cheerfulness and light. From the wide sitting-room windows it was possible to imagine oneself on a ship with nothing in view but the white veranda rail and the sheen of the river. Despite an ancient wrought iron stove, the room was indeed more typical of a cottage than a riverside shack. One wall, incongruously papered with rosebuds and robins, was almost covered with pictures; dated watercolours of country scenes, twin engravings of Winchester and Wells Cathedrals, four early-Victorian fashion plates mounted in one frame, an embroidered picture in wool and silk of the Angel greeting the Apostles at the empty tomb, a couple of rather good miniature portraits in oval frames. The far wall was covered with books, some of them, Dalgliesh noticed, were Miss Gentle's own, still pristine in their jackets. On each side of the stove was an easy chair and between them a gate-legged table on which a jug of milk and three flowered cups and saucers had already been placed. Miss Gentle, helped by Kate, drew up a small rocking chair for her second guest. Makepeace, having ambled with his mistress to greet them, slumped down in front of the empty stove and heaved a malodorous sigh.

Miss Gentle brought in the coffee almost immediately. The kettle had been on the boil, she had only to pour the water over the grains. Taking his first sip, Dalgliesh had a moment's compunction. He had forgotten how inconvenient it was for the solitary to be faced with unexpected visitors. That row across to the Black Swan had, he suspected, been more for the milk than to get the letters posted. He said, gently:

'You know, of course, that Sir Paul Berowne is dead.'

'Yes, I know. He was murdered, and that's why you're here. How did you find me?'

Dalgliesh explained about the finding of her book. He said:

'Anything that happened to him during the last weeks of his life is important to us. That's why we'd like you to tell us exactly what happened on the night of August the seventh. You did see him?'

'Oh, yes, I saw him.' She put down her cup and gave a little shiver as if she was suddenly cold. Then she settled down to tell her story as if they were children round the nursery fire.

'I really get on very well with Mr Higgins. Of course, he would like to buy the cottage and pull it down, but I've said that he can have first refusal from my executors when I'm dead. We have our little joke about it. And the Black Swan is really very respectably run. A nice type of customer, very quiet. But on that night they weren't. I was trying to work and it got very irritating. Young people shouting and screaming. So I went out to the bank and I could see that there were four of them in a punt. They were rocking very dangerously and two of them were standing up and trying to change places. Apart from the noise they were behaving very foolishly. I tried to ring Mr Higgins but I couldn't get through. So Makepeace and I rowed across. I made for my usual spot – it would have been most imprudent to row up to them and remonstrate, I'm not as strong as I used to be. As I turned the boat to draw up to the bank, I saw the other two men.'

'Did you know who they were?'

'Not at the time. It was, of course, dark by then. There was only the reflected light coming over the hedge from the car park. Afterwards I knew one of them, Sir Paul Berowne.'

'What were they doing?'

'Fighting.' Miss Gentle spoke the word without the least disapproval, almost, Dalgliesh thought, with a note of surprise that he should have needed to ask. Her tone implied that fighting on the riverbank and partly in the dark was an activity to be expected of two gentlemen who had nothing better to do. She said:

'They didn't notice me, of course. Only my head was above the level of the bank. I was afraid Makepeace would bark but I told him not to and he was really very controlled although I could see that he wanted to jump out and join in. I rather wondered if I ought to intervene myself but I decided it would be undignified and really quite ineffective. And it was obviously a private fight. I mean, it didn't look like an unprovoked attack which I feel one has a duty to try to put a stop to. The second man looked much shorter than Sir Paul, which made it rather unfair in a way. But then he was the younger so that redressed the balance. They were getting on very well without me or Makepeace.'

Dalgliesh couldn't resist a glance at Makepeace, steaming in somnolent calm. It seemed unlikely that he could have raised the energy for a bark let alone a bite. He asked:

'Who won?'

'Oh, Sir Paul. He landed what I think is called a hook to the jaw. It looked very satisfying. The younger man fell, then Sir Paul picked him up by the collar of his coat and his trousers, very like a puppy, and threw him into the river. He made quite a splash. "My goodness," I said to Makepeace, "what an extraordinary evening we're having!"'

Dalgliesh thought that the scene was beginning to resemble a chapter from one of Miss Gentle's own genre. He said:

'What happened next?'

'Sir Paul waded into the river and fished him out. I expect he didn't actually want him to drown. Perhaps he didn't know whether he could swim. Then he threw him down on the grass, said something which I couldn't hear and walked upstream towards me. As he drew alongside, I popped up my head. I said: "Good evening. I don't suppose you remember me but we met last June at the Hertfordshire Conservative fête. I was visiting a niece. I'm Millicent Gentle."'

'What did he do?'

'He came over, squatted down by the dinghy, and shook hands. He was quite unflustered, not in the least disconcerted. He was dripping wet, of course, and his cheek was bleeding. It looked like a scratch. But he was as self-possessed as he had been when we'd met at the Conservative fête. I said: "I saw the fight. You haven't killed him, have you?" He said: "No, I haven't killed him. I only wanted to." Then he apologized and I said there was really no need. He was beginning to shiver – it really wasn't warm enough to be standing around in wet clothes – so I suggested he should come back to the cottage and dry off. He said: "That's very kind of you but I think I ought first to move the car." I knew what he meant, of course. It would be better if he left the Black Swan before anyone saw him or knew that he was there. Politicians have to be so careful. I suggested that he park it somewhere at the side of the road and I'd wait for him a little further upstream until he came back. He could have driven round, of course, but it would have been five miles or more and he really was very cold. He disappeared and I waited. It wasn't long. He was back in less than five minutes.'

'And what happened to the other man?'

'I didn't wait to see. I knew he'd be all right. He wasn't alone, you see. He had a girl with him.'

'A girl? Are you sure?'

'Oh yes, quite sure. She came out of the bushes and watched when Sir Paul threw him into the river. I couldn't have missed her. She was quite naked.'

'Could you recognize her?' Without being asked, Kate opened her shoulder bag and handed over the photograph.

Miss Gentle said:

'Isn't that the girl who was drowned? It's possible it was the same one, but I didn't see her face clearly. The light was very poor, as I've said, and they must have been forty yards away.'

'What did she do?'

'She laughed. It was most extraordinary. Peal on peal of laughter. When Sir Paul waded in to help him out, she sat on the bank, quite naked and roared with laughter. One ought not to laugh at another's misfortune, but he really did look funny. The scene was quite bizarre. Two men stumbling out of the river and a naked girl sitting on the bank and laughing. She had rather an infectious laugh, full-throated, joyous. Ringing across the water, it didn't sound malicious. But I suppose it must have been.'

'And what was happening to the party in the punt?'

'They were paddling downstream towards the Black Swan. Perhaps they were beginning to feel a little frightened. The river is so black at night and so strange, almost sinister. I'm used to it

578

now, I feel at home with it. But I think they wanted to get back to the lights and the warmth.'

'So the last you saw of the man and the girl they were together on the bank and you began rowing quietly upstream without being noticed?'

'Yes. The river bends just slightly there and the rushes are taller at the water edge. They were quickly out of sight. I sat quietly and waited until Sir Paul appeared.'

'From what direction?'

'From further upstream, the same direction as I had been rowing. He'd come through the car park, you see.'

'Still out of earshot and sight of the boy and girl?'

'Well, out of sight, but I could still hear her laughing as we rowed across. I had to go carefully. With Makepeace and a passenger we were very low in the water.'

The picture of the two of them in that bucket of a dinghy with Makepeace rigid at the prow was ridiculous but endearing. Dalgliesh wanted to laugh. It wasn't an impulse he had expected to feel in the middle of any murder investigation, least of all this one, and he was grateful. He asked:

'The girl, for how long was she laughing?'

'Until we were almost on the opposite bank. And then, suddenly, the laughing stopped.'

'Did you hear anything at that moment, a cry, a splash?'

'Nothing. But then, if she had dived cleanly in there wouldn't have been much of a splash. And I don't think I would have heard it above the noise of the oars.'

'What happened then, Miss Gentle?'

'First Sir Paul asked if he could use the telephone to make a local call. He didn't say to where and, naturally, I didn't ask. I left him here and went into the kitchen so that he could feel quite private. Then I suggested that he ought to have a hot bath. I switched on the electric wall heater in the bathroom and lit all my paraffin stoves. It didn't seem a time for economy. And I gave him some disinfectant for his face. I don't think I mentioned that the boy had scratched him quite badly on his cheek. Not a very masculine way to fight I thought. Then, while he was in the bathroom, I dried his clothes in the spin-dryer. I haven't got a washing machine. Well, I don't really need one, just being on my own. I can even manage the sheets now that we have drip-dry. But I don't think I could manage without my spin-dryer. Oh, and I handed him my father's old dressing gown to wear while the clothes were drying. It's all wool and beautifully warm. They don't make that quality now. When he came out of the bathroom I thought how handsome he looked in it. We settled down in front of the fire and I made some hot cocoa. Being a gentleman I thought he might prefer something stronger and I offered my elderberry wine. He said he'd rather have the cocoa. Well, he didn't actually say he preferred the cocoa. He would have liked to taste the wine, he was sure it was excellent, but he thought a hot drink might be better. I quite agreed. There's really nothing quite as comforting as good strong cocoa when one is famished with cold. I made it with all milk. I had ordered an extra pint because I planned to have cauliflower cheese for supper. Wasn't that lucky?'

Dalgliesh said:

'Very lucky. Have you spoken of this to any other person?'

'No one. I wouldn't have spoken to you if you hadn't telephoned and he hadn't been dead.'

'Did he ask for your silence?'

'Oh, no, he wouldn't have done that. He wasn't that kind of man, and he knew that I wouldn't tell. You know when you can trust a person about something like that, don't you find? If you can, why ask? If you can't, there's no point in asking.'

'Please continue to say nothing, Miss Gentle. It could be important.'

She nodded but didn't speak. He asked, wondering why it should matter so, why he needed so urgently to know:

'What did you talk about?'

'Not about the fight, at least not very much. I said: "I expect it was about a woman, wasn't it?" And he said it was.'

'The woman who laughed, the naked girl?'

'I don't think so. I'm not sure why, but I don't think so. I've a feeling it was rather more complicated than that. And I don't think he would have fought in front of her, not if he'd known she was there. But then, I don't suppose he did know. She must have concealed herself in the bushes when she saw him coming.'

He thought he knew why Berowne had been on the riverbank. He had arrived to join the dinner party, to greet his wife and his wife's lover, to take part in a civilized charade, the complaisant husband, stock figure of farce. And then he had heard the murmur of running water, had smelt, as had Dalgliesh, that strong nostalgic river smell with its promise of a few moments of solitude and peace. So he had hesitated, then walked through the gate in the hedge from the car park to the riverbank. Such a small thing, a simple impulse obeyed, and it had led him to that blood-boltered vestry.

And it must have been then that Swayne, perhaps pulling his shirt over his head, had stepped out of the bushes to confront him like the personification of everything he despised in his own life, in himself. Had he challenged Swayne about Theresa Nolan, or did he already know? Was that one other secret that the girl had confided to him in that final letter, the name of her lover?

Dalgliesh asked again, gently insistent:

'What *did* you talk about, Miss Gentle?'

'Mainly about my work, my books. He was really very interested in how I started writing, where I got my ideas. Of course, I haven't published anything for six years now. My kind of fiction isn't very fashionable. Dear Mr Hearne, always so kind, so helpful, explained it to me. Romantic fiction is more realistic now. I'm afraid I'm too old-fashioned. But I can't change. People are sometimes a little unkind about romantic novelists, I know, but we're just like other writers. You can only write what you need to write. And I'm very lucky. I have my health, my old-age pension, my home, and Makepeace for company. And I still keep writing. The next book may be the lucky one.'

Dalgliesh asked:

'How long did Sir Paul stay?'

'Oh, for hours, until nearly midnight. But I don't think that he was being polite. I think he was happy here. We sat and talked and I made scrambled eggs when we got hungry. There was enough milk for that but not, of course, for the cauliflower cheese. At one point he said: "No one in the world knows where I am at this moment, not a single soul. No one can get at me." He said it as if I had given him something precious. He sat in that chair, the one you're in now and he looked so comfortable in father's old dressing gown and so at home. You're very like him, Commander. I don't mean your features. He was fair and you're so dark. But you are like him; the way you sit, your hands, the way you walk, even your voice a little.'

Dalgliesh put down his cup and got up. Kate looked at him, surprised, then rose too and picked up her shoulder bag. Dalgliesh heard himself thanking Miss Gentle for the coffee, emphasizing the need for silence, explaining that they would like a written statement and that a police car would call and take her to New Scotland Yard, if that were convenient. They had reached the door when Kate asked, on impulse:

'And when he left you that night, that was the last time you saw him?'

'Oh no. I saw him on the afternoon of his death. I thought you knew.'

Dalgliesh said gently:

'But Miss Gentle, how could we have known?'

'I thought he would have told someone where he was going. Is it important?'

'Very important, Miss Gentle. We've been trying to trace his movements that afternoon. Tell us what happened.'

'There isn't much to tell. He arrived, quite unexpectedly, just before three o'clock. I remember that I was listening to Woman's Hour on Radio Four. He was on foot and he was carrying a bag. He must have walked the four miles from the station but he seemed surprised when I pointed out how far it was. He said he had felt like a walk along the river. I asked him if he'd had any lunch and he said he had some cheese in his bag and that would do. He must have been famished. Luckily I'd made myself a beef stew for lunch and there was some over so I made him come in and he ate that and then we had coffee together. He didn't talk very much. I don't think he'd come to talk. Then he left his bag with me and set off for his walk. He came back about four-thirty and I made tea. His shoes were very dirty – the river meadows have been so waterlogged this summer – so I gave him my shoe cleaning box and he sat outside on the steps and cleaned them. Then he took up his bag, said goodbye and was on his way. It was as simple as that.'

As simple as that, thought Dalgliesh. The lost hours accounted for, the wedge of mud on his shoe explained. He had gone, not to his mistress but to a woman whom he had seen only once before in his life, who asked no questions, made no demands, who had given him those remembered moments of peace. He had wanted to spend those few hours where no one in the world knew where to find him. And he must have gone straight from Paddington to St Matthew's Church. They would have to check the times of the trains, how long the whole journey was likely to have taken. But whether or not Lady Ursula was lying, it seemed highly unlikely that Berowne could have called in at his house, collected his diary, and still arrived at the church by six.

Looking back at the closing door, Kate said:

'I know an old lady who, in her place, would say: "No one wants my books, I'm poor, I'm lame, and I live in a damp cottage with only a dog for company." She says: "I've got my health, my pension, my home, Makepeace for company, and I go on writing." '

Dalgliesh wondered who it was she had in mind. There was a bitterness in her voice which was new to him. Then he remembered that there was an elderly grandmother somewhere in the picture, and wondered. It was the first time that she had ever hinted at a private life. Before he could answer she went on:

'So that explains why Higgins said that Swayne's clothes were dripping wet. It was a night in August, after all. If he'd been swimming naked and then pulled on his clothes after the drowning, why should they be dripping?' She added:

'It's a new motive, sir, a double motive. Swayne must have hated him. The thrashing, the humiliation, thrown into the river and dragged out like a dog, and in front of the girl.'

Dalgliesh said:

'Oh, yes, Swayne must have hated him.'

So he had it at last, the motive not only for murder but for this particular murder with its mixture of planning and impulse, its brutality, its over-ingenuity, the cleverness which hadn't quite been clever enough. It was there before him in its pettiness, its arrogance, its essential inadequacy, but in all its terrible strength. He recognized the mind behind it. He had met it before, the mind of a killer who isn't content merely to take a life, who avenges humiliation with humiliation, who cannot bear the searing knowledge that his enemy breathes the same air, who wants his victim not only dead but disgraced, the mind of a man who has felt despised and inferior all his life but who will never feel inferior again. And if his instinct were right and Dominic Swayne were his man, then to get him he would have to break a vulnerable, lonely and obstinate woman. He shivered and turned up the collar of his coat. The sunlight was fading over the meadows but the wind was freshening and there came from the river a smell, dank and ominous, like the first breath of winter. He heard Kate's voice:

'Do you think we'll be able to break his alibi, sir, by any method we're allowed to use?'

Dalgliesh roused himself and strode to the car.

'We must try, Inspector, we must try.'

I

When Father Barnes had first told Miss Wharton of Susan
Kendrick's suggestion that she might like to spend a day or so
with them in the Nottingham vicarage until the fuss had died
down, she had accepted with gratitude and relief. It was agreed
that she would travel to Nottingham immediately after the inquest
and that Father Barnes would himself go by tube with her to
King's Cross to carry her one case and see her off. The whole
plan had seemed like an answer to a prayer. The half-lubricous
respect with which she was now treated by the McGraths who
seemed to regard her as a prize exhibit, bolstering their esteem in
the road, she found more terrifying than their previous antagonism. It would be a relief to get away from their avid eyes and
endless questions.

The inquest had been less of an ordeal than she had feared.
Only evidence of identity and of the finding of the bodies had
been briefly taken, before, at the request of the police, the
proceedings were adjourned. The coroner had treated Miss Wharton with grave consideration and her time in the witness box had
been so brief that she was hardly aware of standing there before
she was released. Her anxiously searching eyes had failed to see
Darren. She had a confused recollection of being introduced to a
number of strangers including a fair-haired young man who said
that he was Sir Paul's brother-in-law. No one else from the family
was present, although there were a number of sombre-suited men
who Father Barnes told her were lawyers. He himself, resplendent
in a new cassock and biretta, had been extraordinarily at ease.
He had shepherded her with a proprietorial arm, past the photographers, had greeted members of the congregation with an
assurance she had never before seen in him, and had seemed
quite at ease with the police. Miss Wharton, for one appalled

moment, found herself thinking that the murders seemed to have done him good.

She had known after the first day at St Crispin's that the visit wasn't going to be a success. Susan Kendrick was heavily pregnant with her first child but her energy was undiminished and every minute of her day seemed occupied either with parish or domestic concerns or with her part-time physiotherapy clinic at the local hospital. The rambling inner-city vicarage was never empty and, except for Father Kendrick's study, never peaceful. Miss Wharton was constantly introduced to people whose names she couldn't quite catch, and whose functions in the parish she never divined. Where the murders were concerned, her hostess was dutifully sympathetic but obviously took the view that it was unreasonable for anyone to be lastingly distressed by dead bodies, however unpleasant their ends, and that dwelling on the experience was at best self-indulgent and at worst morbid. But Miss Wharton had reached the stage when it would have been helpful to talk, and she was missing Darren with a need which was becoming desperate, wondering where he was, what was happening to him, whether he was happy.

She had expressed her pleasure at the coming baby but nervousness had made her sound coy and her words had sounded gushingly sentimental even to her own ears. Confronted with Susan's robust common sense about her pregnancy she had been made to feel an absurd old maid. She had offered to help in the parish, but her hostess's inability to find a job suitable to her abilities had drained her confidence further. She had begun to creep about the vicarage like the church mouse they probably thought she resembled. After a couple of days she had nervously suggested that she ought to be thinking of home, and no one had made any attempt to dissuade her.

But on the morning of departure she had brought herself to confide in Susan her worries about Darren, and here her hostess had been helpful. Local bureaucracy held no terrors for her. She had known whom to ring, how to discover the number, and had spoken to the unknown voice at the end of the line in the accents of conspiratorial, mutually acknowledged authority. She had made the call from her husband's study with Miss Wharton seated in the chair conveniently placed for those seeking the vicar's counsel. During the telephone conversation, she had felt like the unworthy recipient of patient professional concern, vaguely conscious that she would have done better had she been an unmarried mother or a delinquent, preferably both, and had been black.

Afterwards Susan Kendrick had given her the verdict. She couldn't see Darren at present; his social worker felt that it wasn't at all desirable. He had been taken before the Juvenile Court and a supervision order made. They were hoping to arrange a programme of intermediate treatment for him, but until this was satisfactorily under way they didn't think it wise for him to see Miss Wharton. It might only provoke unfortunate memories. He had been very reluctant to talk about the murders, and his social worker felt that when he was ready to do so it should be with someone suitably qualified in social work skills who could work through the trauma with him. He'll hate it all, thought Miss Wharton. He never did like interference.

Lying in bed on her first night at home, wakeful, as she so often was now, she came to a decision. She would go to Scotland Yard and ask the police to help. Surely they would have some authority, or at least some influence, over Darren's social worker. They had always been kind and helpful to her. They would be able to reassure the local authority that she could be trusted with Darren. The decision brought a measure of peace to her troubled mind and she fell asleep.

The next morning found her less confident, but with her resolution unshaken. She would set out after ten o'clock; there was no point in getting caught up in the rush hour. She dressed carefully for the excursion; first impressions were always important. Before setting out she knelt to pray briefly that the visit might be a success, that she would be met with understanding, that Scotland Yard wouldn't be the terrifying place of her imagination, that Commander Dalgliesh or Inspector Miskin would be willing to talk to the local authority, to explain that she wouldn't even mention the murders to Darren if his social worker thought it unwise. She walked to Paddington underground station and took the Circle Line. At St James's Park station she came out of the wrong exit, was for a few minutes lost and had to inquire the way to the Yard. And suddenly across the road, she saw the revolving sign, and the great glass oblong building so familiar from television news pictures.

The entrance hall surprised her. She wasn't sure what she had imagined; a uniformed officer on duty, perhaps a steel grille, even a succession of manacled prisoners being escorted to the cells. Instead she found herself facing an ordinary reception desk with a couple of young women on duty. The hall was very busy with an air of purposeful but relaxed activity. Men and women showed their passes, and passed happily gossiping through to the lifts. Except for the flame of remembrance burning on its plinth it could, she thought, be almost any office. She asked for Inspector Miskin, having decided that this was a matter on which a woman might be more sympathetic than a man and that she could hardly worry Commander Dalgliesh with something so unimportant, except to her. No, she admitted, she hadn't an appointment. She was asked to sit down on one of the chairs set against the left-hand wall, and watched while the girl telephoned. Her confidence grew, and the hands clutching her handbag gradually relaxed. She was able to take an interest in the busy comings and goings, to feel that she had a right to be there.

And suddenly Inspector Miskin was standing beside her. She hadn't expected her to appear. Somehow she had thought that she would be taken by messengers to the Inspector's office. She thought: She's saving time. If she thinks it's important then she'll take me up. And Inspector Miskin obviously didn't think it important. When Miss Wharton had explained her purpose she sat down beside her and was for a moment silent. Miss Wharton thought: She's disappointed. She hoped I was bringing her some news about the murders, that I'd remembered something new and important. Then the Inspector said:

'I'm sorry, but I don't see how we can help. The Juvenile Court has made a supervision order to the local authority. It's their concern now.'

'I know. That's what Mrs Kendrick told me, but I thought you might be able to use your influence. After all, the police . . .'

'We have no influence, not in this.'

The words sounded dreadfully final. Miss Wharton found herself pleading:

'I wouldn't talk to him about the murder, although I sometimes think that boys are tougher than we are in some ways. But I'd be very careful. I'd feel so much better if only I could see him again, even if briefly, just to know that he's all right.'

'Why can't you? Did they say?'

'They think he ought not to talk about the murders until he can work through the trauma with someone experienced in social work skills.'

'Yes, that sounds like the jargon.'

Miss Wharton was surprised by the sudden bitterness in the Inspector's voice. She sensed that she had an ally. She opened her mouth to make an appeal and decided against it. If anything could be done, Inspector Miskin would do it. The Inspector seemed to be thinking, then she said:

'I can't give you his address; anyway I can't remember it. I'd have to consult the file. I'm not even sure if they've left him at home with his mother, although I suppose they'd have gone for a care order if they'd wanted to remove him. But I can remember the name of his school, Bollington Road Junior. Do you know it?'

Miss Wharton said eagerly:

'Oh yes, I know where Bollington Road is. I can get there.'

'They still come out at about three thirty, don't they? You could try passing at the right time. If you met him accidentally I don't see how they could object to that.'

'Thank you, thank you.'

Miss Wharton, her perceptions sharpened by anxiety and now relief, guessed that Inspector Miskin was wondering whether to ask her again about the murders; but she said nothing. As they got up and the Inspector walked with her to the door, she looked up at her and said:

'You've been very kind. If I remember anything new about the murders, anything I haven't told you, I'll get in touch at once.'

Sitting in the tube on her way to St James's Park station she had planned that, if all went well, she would treat herself afterwards to coffee in the Army and Navy Stores. But her visit to the Yard seemed to have taken more out of her than she had expected, and even the thought of negotiating the traffic of Victoria Street depressed and discouraged her. Perhaps it would be less exhausting to go without the coffee and make for home. While she was hesitating at the edge of the pavement she felt a shoulder brush against hers. A male voice, young, pleasant, said:

'Excuse me, but aren't you Miss Wharton? I met you at the Berowne inquest. I'm Dominic Swayne, Sir Paul's brother-in-law.'

She blinked, confused for a second, and then recognized him. He said:

'We're blocking the pavement,' and she felt his hand on her arm, firmly guiding her across the street. Then, without releasing her, he said:

'You must have been to the Yard. So have I. I feel in need of a drink. Please have one with me. I was thinking of the St Ermin's Hotel.'

Miss Wharton said:

'You're very kind, but I'm not sure . . .'

'Please. I need someone to talk to. You'd be doing me a kindness.'

It really was impossible to refuse. His voice, smile, the press of his arm were persuasive. He was steering her gently but firmly forward through the station and into Caxton Street. And, suddenly here was the hotel, looking so solidly welcoming, its wide courtyard flanked by heraldic beasts. It would be good to have a quiet sit before she started the journey home. He guided her through the left-hand door and into the foyer.

It was, she thought, all very grand; the branching staircase leading to a curved balcony, the glittering chandeliers, the mirrored walls and elegantly carved pillars. Yet she felt strangely at home. There was something reassuring about this Edwardian elegance, this atmosphere of assured, respectable comfort. She followed her companion over the blue and fawn carpet to a couple of high-backed chairs before the fireplace. After they had seated themselves he asked:

'What would you like? There's coffee, but I think you should have something stronger. Sherry?'

'Yes, that would be very nice, thank you.'

'Dry?'

'Well, not too dry, perhaps.'

Mrs Kendrick had brought out the sherry decanter before dinner every evening at St Crispin's vicarage. It had invariably been dry, a pale sour sharpness not really to her taste. But she had missed the evening ritual on her return home. There was no doubt one did get quickly used to these little luxuries. He lifted his finger and the waiter came, swiftly deferential. The sherry arrived, a rich amber, half-sweet. immediately reviving. There was a little bowl of nuts and one of small dry biscuits. How elegant, how soothing it all was. The raucous life of Victoria Street could have been miles away. She sat back, glass at her lips. and looked with tremulous wonder at the ornately carved ceiling. the twin wall-lights with their fringed shades, the huge urns of flowers at the foot of the stair. And suddenly she knew why she felt so at home. Sight, sound, sensation, even the young man's face bent smiling towards her, all fused into a long-forgotten picture. She was in a hotel lounge, surely this same hotel, this very place, sitting with her brother on his first leave after he had gained his sergeant's stripes. And then she remembered. He had been stationed at Bassingbourn in East Anglia. They must have met at a hotel near Liverpool Street, not Victoria. But it had been so very similar. She remembered her pride in the smartness of his uniform, the one winged badge of an air-gunner on his breast, the pristine brightness of his three stripes, her sense of importance at being escorted by him, how she had revelled in the unaccustomed luxury, in the assured way in which he had summoned the waiter; ordered sherry for her, beer for himself. And her present companion reminded her a little of John. Like John, he was barely her own height. 'They like us small, we tail-end Charlies,' John had said. But he had John's fairness, something of John in the blue eyes and the high curve of the eyebrows, and all of John in his kindness and courtesy. Almost she could imagine that she saw the single-winged emblem of the air-gunner on his chest. He said:

'They've been questioning you again about the murders, I suppose. Did they give you a bad time?'

'Oh no, it wasn't at all like that.'

She explained the purpose of her visit, finding it easy to talk to him about Darren, their walks along the towpath, their visits to the church, her need to see him. She said:

'Inspector Miskin couldn't do anything about the local authority, but she has told me where Darren goes to school. She was really very kind.'

'The police are never kind, only when it suits them. They weren't kind to me. You see, they think I know something. They've got a theory. They think my sister might have done it, she and her lover together.' Miss Wharton cried:

'Oh no! But that's a terrible idea. Surely not a woman – and his own wife! A woman couldn't have done it, not this murder. Surely they can't think that.'

'Perhaps not. Perhaps they're only pretending to think it. But they're trying to make me say that she confided in me, confessed even. We're very close, you see; we always have been. We only have each other. They know she'd tell me if she were in any trouble.'

'But that's awful for you. I can't believe that Commander Dalgliesh really believes that.'

'He needs to make an arrest, and the wife or husband is always the obvious suspect. I've had a couple of bad hours.'

Miss Wharton had finished her sherry, and, miraculously it seemed. another was in its place. She took a sip and thought: You poor dear. You poor young man. He, too, was drinking, a paler liquid in a tumbler, mixed with water. Perhaps it was whisky. Now he put down the glass and leaned across the table towards her. She could smell the spirit on his breath, masculine, sour, a little disquieting. He said:

'Talk to me about the murders. Tell me what you saw, what it was like.'

She could feel his need, strong as a force; and her own need rose to meet it. She, too, needed to talk. She had spent too many sleepless nights fighting off horror, willing herself not to think about it, not to remember. It was better to open that vestry door again and confront reality. So she told him, whispering it across the table. She was back again in that slaughterhouse. She described it all; the wounds like flaccid mouths, Harry Mack with his rigid breastplate of dried blood, the stench, more insistent in imagination than it had been in reality, the pale lifeless hands, drooping like flowers. He leaned over the table towards her, mouth to mouth. Then she said:

'And that's all I can remember. Nothing that happened before, nothing afterwards, only the dead bodies. And afterwards, when I dream about them, they're always naked, quite naked. Isn't that extraordinary?'

She gave a little giggle, and lifted her glass carefully to her lips.

She heard him sigh as if the dreadful recital had released something in him. He leaned back in his chair, breathing heavily as if he had been running. Then he said:

'And you didn't go into the room, the vestry where they were found?'

'That's what the Commander kept asking us. He even looked at the soles of our shoes. That wasn't at first, he did that just before we left. And then next day a policeman came and took the shoes away. Wasn't that strange?'

'They were looking for blood.'

'Oh yes,' she said sadly, 'there was so much blood.'

Again, he leaned across the table towards her, his face pale and intent. She could see a small blob of mucus at the corner of the left eye, a dewing of moisture along the upper lip. She took another gulp of the sherry. How warming, how comforting it was. He said:

'Whoever did that, whoever it was, he can't be an ordinary, common intruder. This murder was carefully planned, brilliantly planned too. You're looking for someone with intelligence and nerve. To come back into that room, naked, razor in hand. To confront him, and then to kill. My God, it must have taken courage!' He leaned towards her even closer. 'You must see that. You do see it, don't you?'

Courage, she thought. But courage was a virtue. Could a man be as evil as this and yet show courage? She would have to ask Father Barnes, except that it wasn't so easy to talk to Father Barnes nowadays. But it was easy to talk to this young man looking at her with John's eyes.

She said:

'I had a feeling while Darren and I were sitting there in the church waiting to be interviewed, that there was something he knew, something he was keeping back, something he was feeling, well, perhaps a little guilty about.'

'You've told the police about this?'

'Oh, no, I haven't told them. It would sound so stupid. There isn't anything he could be keeping back, not really. We were together the whole time.'

'But he might have noticed something, something you didn't see.'

'But then the police would have seen it too. It's just a feeling I had. You see, I really know Darren quite well. I know when he's feeling . . . well, a little ashamed. But this time I must be wrong. Perhaps I shall know more when I'm able to see him.'

'What are you planning to do? Meet him outside the school?'

'I thought so. The Inspector said they come out at three thirty.'

'But he'll be with other boys. You know what they are, shouting and rushing home. He might not want to leave the gang. He might be embarrassed to see you waiting there.'

Miss Wharton thought: Perhaps he'll be ashamed of me. Boys are so odd. It will be terrible if I see him and he won't stop, won't acknowledge me.

Her companion said:

'Why not write him a note and ask him to meet you at the usual place? He'll know that means the towpath. I could take it to him if you like.'

'Oh could you? But you won't know him.'

'I'll give it to one of the other kids to deliver. Give him a tip and tell him it's secret. Or I'll ask one of them to point him out. Darren will get it, I promise. Look, let me write it for you. He can read, can't he?'

'Oh yes, I'm sure he can. He can read the notices in church. He's really an intelligent little boy. His social worker told Mrs Kendrick that Darren hasn't been going to school. Apparently his mother moved with him to Newcastle but she didn't find the same opportunities there for her job so they moved back. But she never told the school and I'm afraid it was all too easy for Darren to truant. It was naughty of him. But I'm sure he can read.'

He crooked his finger. The waiter came on silent feet. A few minutes later he was back with a sheet of headed paper and an envelope. Miss Wharton's glass was taken away and a filled one put in place of it.

He said:

'I'll print the message and your name. That'll make it easier for him. And we'd better say to meet you after school. That will be simpler for him than slipping out in the early morning. I may not be able to contact him today but I shall by tomorrow. Suppose we make it Friday at four o'clock on the towpath. Will that be all right for you?'

'Oh yes, yes, perfectly. And I won't let him be too late home.'

He wrote quickly, folded the paper then, without showing it to her, put it in the envelope. 'What is his name?' he asked. 'His surname.'

'Wilkes. He's Darren Wilkes. And the school is Bollington Road Junior, near Lisson Grove.'

She watched while he printed it on the envelope and slipped it into his jacket pocket. He smiled across at her.

'Drink up your sherry,' he said, 'and don't worry. It's going to be all right. He'll be there. You'll see him, I promise.'

As they left the hotel and stepped into the wan sunlight it seemed to Miss Wharton that she was floating in an ecstasy of gratitude and relief. She was hardly aware of giving him her address, of being handed into a taxi, of the five-pound note being slipped into the cabbie's hand. His face, unnaturally large, blocked the cab window.

'Don't worry,' he said again. 'I've paid the cabbie. There'll be a little change. And don't forget. It's Friday at four o'clock.'

Tears of gratitude sprang to her eyes. She held out her hand, seeking for words, but none came. And then the cab moved forward jerking her back in her seat and he was gone. For the whole of the journey home she sat bolt upright, hugging her handbag to her chest as if it symbolized this new found intoxicating happiness. Friday she said aloud. Friday at four.

After the taxi was out of sight, Swayne took out and read the message again, his face expressionless. Then he licked the flap and sealed the envelope. The time and place were exactly as he had said. But the date was the following afternoon, Thursday not Friday. And it was he, not Miss Wharton, who would be waiting on the towpath.

2

Ten minutes after Kate got back to her office, Massingham came in. He and Dalgliesh had been interviewing Swayne. She had concealed her disappointment at being excluded from this first important encounter after the finding of the new evidence, telling herself that her time would come. Unless they broke Swayne quickly, the interrogations, carefully structured, conducted within judges' rules and Force regulations, but planned, varied, persistent, would continue inexorably day after day until that moment when they would either have to charge him or, for the time being at least, leave him in peace. From the look on Massingham's face she would get her chance. He almost threw the file on the desk, then walked over to the window as if the spectacular view of Westminster's towers and the curve of the river could help soothe his frustration.

She said:

'How did it go?'

'It didn't. He sits there with his brief at his side smiling, saying less and less. Or rather, saying the same thing over and over. "Yes, Berowne and I did meet on the riverbank. Yes, we did have a scuffle. He accused me of seducing Theresa Nolan and I resented him trying to father his bastard on me. He went for me as if he were crazy. He was crazy. But he didn't throw me in the river. Berowne had left before I swam out to the punt. And I didn't kill him. I was with Miss Matlock all that evening. I was seen arriving at Campden Hill Square. I took Mrs Hurrell's telephone call at eight forty. I was there until I left for the pub. I was seen there from ten forty-five to closing time. If you think otherwise, prove it."'

'And his brief, who has he got? Someone from Torrington, Farrell and Penge?'

'No. No one from the Berowne connection. I have a feeling Barbara Berowne is distancing herself from her slightly disreputable brother. He's dredged up a bright young pin-stripe from Maurice and Sheldon, perfectly competent and already calculating his fees. There's nothing like a notorious case for getting your name before the public. His strength is that he really believes his client; that must be a rare pleasure for a brief from that firm. You could see how his mind was working. He doesn't think that Swayne has the guts for this particular murder; he can't believe that the motive is strong enough; he can't see how Swayne could have left Campden Hill Square for long enough to commit the murder and returned without Matlock knowing; and he certainly can't see why she should lie. But mainly, of course, he makes it plain that he doesn't believe that Berowne was murdered, and in that he's getting to be one of the majority. He and the AC should get together.'

And so, thought Kate, we try again to break Evelyn Matlock. And she will sit there, chaperoned by Lady Ursula and advised by the family lawyers, half-obstinate, half-triumphant, with that look of dedicated virtue, enjoying her self-imposed martyrdom. In what cause, she wondered. Hatred, revenge, self-glorification, love? For the first time she faced the realization that the case, the first undertaken by the new squad, could end without an arrest in ignominious failure. Massingham turned from the window:

'There still isn't a single piece of physical evidence linking him to the scene. OK, so he had a motive. So did half a dozen others.'

'But if he killed out of hate, surely he couldn't conceal it even now?'

'Oh yes he could, well enough, anyway. He's purged it, hasn't he, the worst of his hatred? He's rid himself of its power. He can sit there smiling, the arrogant bastard, because he's free of his enemy for ever. He had himself well under control, but he was exulting like a man in love.'

She said:

'He killed him and we know he killed him. But we've got to break that alibi. And more than that, we've got to find some physical evidence.'

'Oh, Swayne knows that, none better. He's confident that the evidence doesn't exist. It's all circumstantial. If we'd got anything stronger, we'd have produced it by now. And he's actually saying what other people are thinking, that Berowne got Theresa Nolan pregnant, rejected her, and killed himself, partly out of remorse and partly because the dirt in the *Paternoster Review* warned him that the scandal was going to break. My God, Kate, if the old man's got this wrong it'll be one hell of a fuck-up.'

She glanced at him in surprise. It was rare to hear him use an obscenity. And she guessed that he wasn't only thinking of the success of the new squad, or of those colleagues in C1, and not the most junior, who wouldn't be unhappy to see the maverick Dalgliesh taken down a peg. He had planned his career as carefully as she had hers and the last thing he wanted was a spectacular failure chalked up against him. But he should worry, she thought bitterly. He was hardly likely to find himself back in Division.

She said:

'They'll hardly hold it against you. You'll be off to the Senior Command Course in January anyway, the next step towards the chairmanship of ACPO.'

He spoke almost as if he had forgotten she was there:

'It's not going to be so easy when my father dies.'

'He's not ill, is he?'

'Not ill, but he's over seventy, and a lot of life seems to have gone out of him since my mother died last April. I'd like to move out, buy a flat, but it's difficult just now.'

It was the first time he had ever spoken of his family. The confidence surprised her. The fact that he had made it must, she supposed, say something about their changing relationship, but she sensed that it would be imprudent to probe.

She said:

'I shouldn't lose any sleep over the title. You can always disclaim it. Anyway, the police'll find it easier to accommodate Chief Constable the Lord Dungannon than they would Chief Constable Kate Miskin.'

He grinned.

'Oh well,' he said easily, 'You could have chosen to join the Wrens but you'd hardly expect to end up First Sea Lord. It will come in time; the first Woman Chief Constable: about a decade after the first female Archbishop of Canterbury, I'd say. Not in my time, thank God.'

She didn't respond to the provocation. She was aware of his sudden glance, then he said:

'What's the matter? Something worrying you?'

Is it so obvious, she thought, not altogether pleased at his unusual perception. There was little point in never inviting him to the flat if her mind had become so accessible. She said:

'Miss Wharton turned up while you were with Swayne. She wants to see Darren.'

'Well, what's to stop her?'

'His social worker, apparently, in the interests of good social work practice. Miss Wharton's fond of the boy. She obviously understands him. They get on well together. He likes her. D'you wonder his social worker is determined to keep them apart?'

He smiled, amused, a little indulgent, a man in whose privileged life the word welfare had meant its dictionary definition, nothing more.

'You really hate them, don't you?'

'Anyway, I told her the name of his school. I suggested she could loiter outside and meet him coming out.'

'And you're wondering whether the social services will like it?'

'I know damn well they won't like it. I'm wondering if it was wise.' She added, as if to reassure herself: 'All right, so she'll hang around the school, and with luck get the chance to walk home with him. I can't see what possible harm it can do.'

'None I should think,' he said easily. 'No possible harm in the world. Come and have a drink.'

But before they could reach the door his telephone rang. He went to answer it then held out the receiver to Kate.

'It's for you.'

Kate took it from him, listened in silence for a minute then said briefly:

'All right, I'll come now.'

Watching her face as she put down the receiver Massingham asked:

'What's the matter?'

'It's my grandmother. She's been mugged. That was the hospital. They want me to collect her.'

He said with easy sympathy:

'That's tough. Is it serious? Is she all right?'

'Of course she's not all right! She's over eighty and the bastards have mugged her. She's not seriously hurt if that's what you're asking. But she's not fit to be alone. I'll have to take the rest of today off. Probably tomorrow, too, by the sound of it.'

'Can't they get someone else to cope?'

'If there was anyone else they wouldn't be ringing me.' Then she added more calmly:

'She brought me up. There is no one else.'

'Then you'd better go. I'll tell AD. Sorry about the drink.' He added, his eyes still on her face: 'It's not going to be convenient.'

She said fiercely:

'Of course it's not bloody convenient. You don't have to tell me. When would it ever be?'

Walking beside him down the corridor to her room she suddenly asked:

'What would happen if your father fell ill?'

'I hadn't thought. I suppose my sister would fly home from Rome.'

Of course, she thought. Who else? The resentment against him which she had begun to think was fading spurted into angry life. The case was at last beginning to break and she wouldn't be there. She might be away only for a day and a half but it couldn't be at a worse time. And it could be longer, much longer. Looking up at Massingham's carefully controlled face as they parted at her door she thought: He and AD are on their own now. It'll be like the old days. He might be sorry about our missed drink. But that's all he's sorry about.

3

Thursday was one of the most frustrating days that Dalgliesh could remember. They had decided to give Swayne a rest and there was no further interrogation, but a press conference called for the early afternoon had been particularly difficult. The media were getting impatient, not so much with the lack of progress as with the lack of information. Either Sir Paul Berowne had been murdered or he had killed himself. If the latter, then the family

and the police should admit the fact; if the former it was time for
the new squad to be more forthcoming about their progress in
bringing the murderer to book. Both within and outside the Yard
there were snide comments about the squad being more noted for
its sensitivity than for its effectiveness. As a super in C1 muttered
to Massingham in the bar:

'It'll be a nasty one to leave unsolved, the sort that breeds its
own mythology. Lucky that Berowne was on the Right, not the
Left, or someone would be writing a book by now to prove that
MI5 slit his throat for him.'

Even the tidying of loose ends, although satisfying, hadn't
lifted his depression. Massingham had reported on a visit to Mrs
Hurrell. He must have been persuasive; Mrs Hurrell had admitted
that her husband, in the hours before his death, had confided in
her. There had been a small bill for posters overlooked when the
final accounts were prepared after the last General Election. It
would have put the Party's expenses over the statutory limit and
invalidated Berowne's victory. Hurrell had himself covered the
discrepancy and had decided to say nothing, but it had been on
his conscience and he had wanted to confess to Berowne before he
died. What purpose he thought would be served by the confession
was difficult to envisage. Mrs Hurrell wasn't a good liar and
Massingham reported that she had been rather unconvincingly
insistent that her husband hadn't at any time confided in Frank
Musgrave. But it wasn't a path they needed to explore. They
were investigating murder not malpractice and Dalgliesh was
convinced that he knew his man.

And Stephen Lampart had been cleared of any possible part in
Diana Travers's death. His two guests on the night of the drowning, a fashionable plastic surgeon and his young wife, had been
seen by Massingham. They apparently knew him slightly, and
between pressing drink on him and the gratifying discovery of
shared acquaintances, had confirmed that Stephen Lampart
hadn't left the table during the meal and had spent less than a
couple of minutes fetching the Porsche while they waited chatting
with Barbara Berowne at the door of the Black Swan.

But it was useful to clear this detail out of the way as it was
useful to know from Sergeant Robins's inquiries that Gordon

Halliwell's wife and daughter had been drowned while on holiday in Cornwall. Dalgliesh had briefly wondered whether Halliwell could have been Theresa Nolan's father. It had never seemed very likely but the possibility had had to be explored. These were all loose ends neatly tied up but the main line of the inquiry was still blocked. The words of the AC rang in his brain as insistent and irritating as a television jingle: 'Find me the physical evidence'.

Strangely, it was a relief rather than an additional irritation to hear that Father Barnes had telephoned while he was in the press conference and would like to see him. The message was somewhat confused but hardly more so than Father Barnes himself. Apparently the priest wanted to know whether the Little Vestry could not be unsealed and brought into use and when, if at all, the church was likely to get back the carpet. Would the police arrange for it to be cleaned, or was that a matter for him? Would they have to wait until it had been produced at the trial? Was there a chance that the Criminal Injuries Compensation Board might pay for a new carpet? It seemed odd that even someone as unworldly as Father Barnes should seriously expect the statutory powers of the CICB to include supplying carpets, but, for a man beginning seriously to fear that a murder case might never be brought to trial, this innocent preoccupation with trivia was reassuring, almost touching. He decided on impulse that he might as well call on Father Barnes.

There was no answer at the vicarage and all the windows were dark. And then he remembered from his first visit to the church that the noticeboard had shown Evensong at four on Thursdays. Father Barnes would presumably be in church. And so it proved. The great north door was unbolted and when he turned the heavy iron handle and pushed it open he was met by the expected waft of incense and saw that the lights were on in the Lady Chapel and that Father Barnes, robed only in his surplice and stole, was leading the responses. The congregation was larger than Dalgliesh had expected and the mutter of voices came to him clearly in a gentle, disjointed murmur. He seated himself in the front row just inside the door and sat to listen in patience to Evensong, that most neglected and aesthetically satisfying portion of the Anglican liturgy. For the first time since he had known it the church was being used for the purpose for which it had been built. But it seemed to him subtly changed. In the branched candleholder where, only last Wednesday, his single light had burned, there was now a double row of candles, some newly lit, others flickering with their last tremulous flame. He felt no impulse to add to the glitter. In their light the Pre-Raphaelite face of the Madonna with her flare of crimped and yellow hair under the high crown shone glossily as if newly painted and the distant voices came to him like the ominous premonitory mutterings of success.

The service was short; there was no address and no singing and within minutes Father Barnes's voice, as if from a far distance but very clear, perhaps because the words were so familiar, was speaking the Third Collect for aid against all perils: 'Lighten our darkness we beseech Thee, O Lord; And by Thy great mercy defend us from all perils and dangers of this night for the love of Thine only Son, our saviour Jesus Christ.'

The congregation murmured their amens, got to their feet and began to disperse. Dalgliesh stood up and moved forward. Father Barnes came briskly up to him in a flutter of white linen. He had certainly gained in confidence, almost, Dalgliesh could believe, in physical stature since their first meeting. Now he looked cleaner, more tidily dressed, even plumper as if a little and a not unwelcome notoriety had put flesh on his bones.

He said:

'How kind of you to come, Commander. I'll be with you in a moment. I just have to clear the offertory boxes. My churchwardens like me to keep to schedule. Not that we expect to find much.'

He took a key from his trouser pocket and unlocked the box attached to the votive candlestand in front of the statue of the Virgin, and began counting the coins into a small leather drawstring bag. He said:

'Over three pounds in small change and six one-pound coins. We've never done as well as that before. And the ordinary collections are well up too since the murders.' His face might make an attempt at solemnity but his voice was as happy as a child's.

Dalgliesh moved with him down the nave to the second candle-stand in front of the grille. Miss Wharton, who had finished hanging up the kneelers and straightening the chairs in the Lady Chapel, bustled up beside him. As Father Barnes unlocked the box, she said:

'I don't expect there will be more than eighty pence. I used to give Darren a tenpenny piece to light a candle, but really no one else uses this box. He loved stretching his hands out through the grille and striking the match. He could just reach. It's funny, but I'd forgotten about that until now. I suppose it was because he didn't have time to light the candle that dreadful morning. There it is, you see, still unlit.'

Father Barnes's hands were busy in the box.

'Only seven coins this time, and a button – rather an unusual one. It looks like silver. I thought at first it was a foreign coin.'

Miss Wharton peered closer. She said:

'That must have been Darren. How naughty of him. I remember now, he bent down by the path and I thought he was picking a flower. It really was very wrong of him to steal from the church. Poor child, it must have weighed on his conscience. No wonder I thought he was feeling guilty about something. I'm hoping to see him tomorrow. I'll have a little word about it. But perhaps we should light the candle now, Commander, and say a prayer for the success of your investigation. I think I have ten-pence.'

She began rummaging in her bag.

Dalgliesh said quietly to Father Barnes:

'May I see the button, Father.'

And there at last it was, resting on his palm, the piece of physical evidence they had been seeking. He had seen such a button before, on Dominic Swayne's Italian jacket. A single button. So small a thing, so commonplace, but so vital. And he had two witnesses to its finding. He stood looking at it and there came over him a feeling not of excitement or of triumph, but of immense weariness, of completion.

He said:

'When was this box last cleared, Father?'

'Last Tuesday, it must have been the seventeenth, after morning Mass. As I said, I should have cleared it this Tuesday but I'm afraid in all the excitement I forgot.'

So it had been cleared the morning of the day Berowne was murdered. Dalgliesh said:

'And it wasn't in the box then? Could you have missed it?'

'Oh no, that really wouldn't have been possible. It certainly wasn't there then.'

And the whole west end of the church had been closed after the finding of the bodies until today. In theory, of course, someone in the church itself, a member of the congregation or a visitor, could have put the button in the box. But why should they? The obvious box to use, even for a practical joke, was the one in front of the statue of the Virgin. Why walk the length of the nave to the back of the church? And it couldn't have been put in the box by mistake for a coin. No candle had been lit in this stand. But all this was academic. He was countering arguments like a defence counsel. There was surely only one jacket from which this button could have come. It was too great a coincidence to suppose that someone connected with St Matthew's Church other than Swayne should have dropped it outside the south door.

He said:

'I'm going to place this in one of the envelopes from the Little Vestry and I shall then seal it and ask both of you to sign across the flap. We can unseal the room now, Father.'

'You mean this button is important? It's a clue?'

'Oh yes,' he said, 'It's a clue.'

Miss Wharton said nervously:

'But the owner, do you suppose he'll come looking for it?'

'I don't think for one moment that he's missed it yet. But, even if he has, no one will be in any danger once he knows that the police have it. But I'll send a man round to stay in the church, Father, until we pick him up.'

Neither of them asked whose button it was and he saw no reason to tell them. He went outside to the car and rang Massingham. Massingham said:

'We'd better pick up the boy now.'

'Yes, at once. That's the first priority. Then Swayne. And we shall need the jacket. Check the lab report on it will you, John?

There were no buttons missing when we saw Swayne at Campden Hill Square. This is probably the spare. The lab will have noticed if there was a tag on the hem. And see if you can get proof of sale to Swayne. We need the name of the importers and the retailers. But that will probably have to wait now until tomorrow.'

'I'll put it in hand, sir.'

'But we need a duplicate button now. I'm going to get this one sealed and certified and I haven't a transparent envelope. You recognized the jacket. I suppose it's too much to hope you've got one.'

'Much too much. Three hundred-odd quid too much. My cousin has one. I can get hold of a button.' He added:

'Do you think there's any danger to Miss Wharton or Father Barnes?'

'Obviously Swayne either hasn't missed the button or has no idea when he lost it. But I'd like someone here in the church until we lay hands on him. But first get hold of Darren and quickly. I'm coming straight back and then I'd like you to come with me to 62 Campden Hill Square.'

'Yes, sir. There's a lot to do. It's a pity we haven't Kate. This tends to happen with women officers, the inconvenient domestic emergency.'

Dalgliesh said coldly:

'Not noticeably, John, particularly not with that officer. In twenty minutes then.'

<h2 style="text-align:center">4</h2>

It was only the second time since her father's murder that Sarah had called at 62 Campden Hill Square. The first had been on the morning after the news broke. Then there had been a small group of photographers outside the railings and she had turned instinctively as they had called her name. Next morning she had seen a newspaper picture of herself scurrying furtively up the steps like a delinquent housemaid sneaking in at the wrong door under the caption 'Miss Sarah Berowne was among the callers today at Campden Hill Square'. But now the Square was empty of people. The great elms waited in sodden acquiescence for winter, their boughs moving sluggishly in the rain-drenched air. Although the storm was over the evening was so dark that lights shone palely from first-floor drawing rooms as if it were already night. She supposed that, behind those windows, people lived their secretive, separate even desperate lives, yet the lights seemed to shine out with the promise of unattainable security.

She had no key. Her father had offered her one when she had walked out with, or so it had seemed to her at the time, the stiff formality of a Victorian father reluctant to have her under his roof but recognizing that, as an unmarried daughter, she was entitled to his protection and to a room in his house should she need it. Looking up at the famous façade, at the high elegantly curved windows, she knew that it never had been and that it never could be her home. How much, she wondered, had it really mattered to her father? It had always seemed to her that he lodged in it but had never made it his own any more than it was hers. But had he in boyhood envied his elder brother these dead prestigious stones? Had he lusted after the house as he had lusted after his brother's fiancée? What had he been thinking of when, her mother at his side, he had jammed down his foot at that dangerous corner? What was it out of his past which had finally confronted him in that dingy vestry at St Matthew's Church?

Waiting for Mattie to answer the door she wondered how to greet her. It seemed natural to ask 'How are you, Mattie?' but the question was meaningless. When had she ever cared how Mattie felt? What possible answer other than an equally meaningless courtesy could she expect? The door opened. Gazing at her with a stranger's eyes, Mattie said her quiet 'Good evening'. There was something different about her; but then, hadn't they all changed since that awful morning? She had the drained look which Sarah had seen on a friend's face who had recently given birth, bright eyed, flushed, but bloated and somehow diminished. as if virtue had gone out of her.

She said:

'How are you, Mattie?'

'I am well thank you, Miss Sarah. Lady Ursula and Lady Berowne are in the dining room.'

The oval dining table was spread with correspondence. Her grandmother sat stiffly upright, her back to the window. In front of her was a large blotter and to her left boxes of writing paper and envelopes. She was folding a handwritten letter as Sarah came up to her. The girl was intrigued, as always, that her grandmother should be so meticulous over the niceties of social behaviour, having all her life flouted its sexual and religious conventions. Her stepmother apparently either had no letters of condolence to answer or was leaving the chore to someone else. Now she sat at the end of the table preparing to varnish her nails, her hands hesitating over the ranked bottles. Sarah thought: Surely not blood red? But no, it was to be a soft pink, entirely innocuous, entirely suitable. She ignored Barbara Berowne and said to her grandmother:

'I've come in answer to your letter. The memorial service, it isn't possible. I am sorry but I shan't be there.'

Lady Ursula gave her a long speculative gaze, rather, thought Sarah, as if she were a new lady's maid arriving with somewhat suspect references. She said:

'It is not my wish particularly that there should be a memorial service, but his colleagues expect it and his friends seem to want it. I shall be there and I expect his widow and his daughter to be there with me.'

Sarah Berowne said:

'I told you, it's not possible. I'll come to the cremation, of course, but that will be private and for the family only. But I'm not going to display myself suitably clad in black in St Margaret's, Westminster.'

Lady Ursula drew a stamp across the dampened pad and stuck it precisely in the right-hand corner of the envelope.

'You remind me of a girl I knew in childhood, the daughter of a bishop. She caused something of a scandal in the diocese when she resolutely refused to be confirmed. What struck me as strange even at thirteen was that she hadn't the wit to see that her scruples had nothing to do with religion. She merely wanted to embarrass her father. That, of course, is perfectly understandable, particularly given the bishop in question. But why not be honest about it?'

Sarah Berowne thought: I shouldn't have come. It was stupid to believe that she would understand or even want to try. She said:

'I suppose, Grandmama, you would have wanted her to conform even if the scruples had been genuine.'

'Oh yes, I think so. I would put kindness above what you would call conviction. After all, if the whole ceremony were a charade, which as you know is my opinion, then it could do her no possible harm to let the episcopal hands rest momentarily upon her head.'

Sarah said quietly:

'I'm not sure I'd want to live in a world that put kindness before conviction.'

'No? But it might be more agreeable than the one we have and considerably safer.'

'Well this is one charade which I prefer not to have any part in. His politics weren't mine. They still aren't. I should be making a public statement. I shan't be there and I hope that people will know why.'

Her grandmother said drily:

'Those who notice will; but I shouldn't expect too much propaganda value from it. The old will be watching their contemporaries and wondering how long it will be before their turn comes, hoping their bladders will hold out, and the young will be watching the old. But I dare say enough of them will notice your absence to get the message that you hated your father and are pursuing your political vendetta beyond the grave.'

The girl almost cried:

'I didn't hate him! Most of my life I loved him, I could have gone on loving him if he had let me. And he wouldn't want me to be there, he wouldn't expect it. He would have hated it himself. Oh, it will all be very tasteful, carefully chosen words and music, the right clothes, the right people, but you won't be celebrating him, not the person, you will be celebrating a class, a political philosophy, a privileged club. You can't get it into your head, you and your kind, that the world you grew up in is dead, it's dead.'

Lady Ursula said:

'I know that, my child. I was there in 1914 when it died.'

She took the next letter from the top of a pile and without looking up, went on:

'I've never been a political woman and I can understand the poor and the stupid voting for Marxism or one of its fashionable variants. If you've no hope of being other than a slave, you may as well opt for the most efficient form of slavery. But I must say that I have an objection to your lover, a man who has enjoyed privilege all his life, working to promote a political system which will ensure that no one else gets a chance of what he has so singularly enjoyed. It would be excusable if he were physically ugly; that misfortune tends to breed envy and aggression in a man. But he isn't. I can understand the sexual attraction even if I am fifty years too old to feel it. But you could have gone to bed with him, surely, without taking on all the fashionable baggage.'

Sarah Berowne turned wearily away, walked over to the window and looked out over the square. She thought: My life with Ivor and the cell is over, but it was never honest, it never had any reality, I never belonged. But I don't belong here. I'm lonely and I'm afraid. But I have to find my own place. I can't run back to Grandmama, to an old creed, a spurious safety. And she still dislikes and despises me, almost as much as I despise myself. That makes it easier. I'm not going to stand beside her in St Margaret's like a prodigal daughter.

Then she was aware of her grandmother's voice. Lady Ursula had stopped writing and was leaning both hands on the table. She said:

'Now that you are both here, there is something that I need to ask. Hugo's gun and the bullets are missing from the safe. Does either of you know who has taken them?'

Barbara Berowne's head was buried over her tray of bottles. She glanced up but didn't reply. Sarah, startled, turned quickly round.

'Are you sure, Grandmama?'

Her surprise must have been obvious. Lady Ursula looked at her.

'So you haven't taken it, and presumably, you don't know who has?'

A TASTE FOR DEATH

'Of course I haven't taken it. When did you find it was missing?'

'Last Wednesday morning, shortly before the police arrived. I thought then that it was possible that Paul had killed himself and that there might be a letter to me with his papers. So I opened the safe. There was nothing new. But the gun had gone.' Sarah asked:

'When was it taken, do you know?'

'I haven't had occasion to look in the safe for some months. That is one reason why I have said nothing to the police. It could have been missing for weeks. It could have had nothing to do with Paul's death, and there was no point in concentrating their attention on this house. Later I had another reason for silence.'

Sarah asked:

'What possible other reason could you have had?'

'I thought his murderer might have taken it to use on himself if the police got too close to the truth. That would seem an eminently sensible thing for him to do. I saw no reason to prevent it. Now I think it is time for me to tell the police.'

'Obviously you must tell them.' Sarah frowned, then she said:

'I suppose Halliwell wouldn't have taken it as a sort of memento. You know how devoted he was to Uncle Hugo. He might not like the idea of it getting into someone else's hands.'

Lady Ursula said drily:

'Very probably. I share his concern. But whose hands?'

Barbara Berowne looked up and said in her little girl voice:

'Paul threw it away weeks ago. He told me that it wasn't safe to keep it.'

Sarah looked at her:

'Nor particularly safe, I should have thought, to throw it away. He could have handed it to the police, I suppose. But why? He has a licence and it was perfectly safe where it was.'

Barbara Berowne shrugged:

'Well, that is what he said. And it doesn't matter, does it? He wasn't shot.'

Before either of the other women could reply, they heard the ring of the front door bell. Lady Ursula said:

'That may well be the police. If so, they're back rather sooner

611

than expected. I have a feeling that they may be getting to the end of their inquiries.'

Sarah Berowne said roughly:

'You know, don't you? You have always known.'

'I don't know and I have no real evidence. But I am beginning to guess.'

They listened in silence for Mattie's footfalls on the marble hall, but she seemed not to have heard the bell. Sarah Berowne said impatiently:

'I'll go. And I hope to God that it is the police; it's time that we faced the truth, all of us.'

5

He went first to the Shepherd's Bush flat to collect the gun. He wasn't sure why he needed it, any more than he was sure why he had stolen it from the safe. But it couldn't be left at Shepherd's Bush; it was time he found a new hiding place for it. And to have the gun with him reinforced his sense of power, of being inviolate. The fact that it had once been Paul Berowne's and was now his made it a talisman as well as a weapon. When he held it, pointed it, stroked the barrel, something of that first triumph returned. He needed to feel it again. It was strange how quickly it faded, so that he was sometimes tempted to tell Barbie what he had done for her, tell her now, long before it was safe or wise to confide, seeing in imagination the blue eyes widening with terror, with admiration, with gratitude and, at last, with love.

Bruno was in his workroom, busy with his latest model. Swayne thought how disgusting he was with his huge half-naked chest on which a lucky charm, a silver goat's head on a chain, moved repulsively among the hairs, his pudgy fingers on which the delicate pieces of cardboard seemed to stick while he edged them with infinite care into place. Without looking up, he said:

'I thought you'd moved out for good.'

'I have. I'm just collecting the last of my gear.'

'I'd like the key, then.'

Without speaking, Swayne placed it on the table.

'What shall I say if the police turn up?'

'They won't. They know I've moved out. Anyway, I'm off to Edinburgh for a week. You can tell them that if they come snooping around.'

In the small back room, its walls covered with shelves, which was both Bruno's spare bedroom and a repository for his old models, nothing was ever moved, nothing ever tidied. He stood on the bed to reach the topmost high cluttered shelf, felt under the stage of a model of Dunsinane Castle and drew out the Smith and Wesson and the ammunition. He slipped them into a small canvas bag together with the last of his socks and a couple of shirts. Then, without a final word to Bruno, he left. It had been a mistake to come in the first place. Bruno had never really wanted him. And the place was a hovel, he wondered how he had stuck it for so long. Paul's bedroom at Campden Hill Square was much more suitable. He ran lightly down the stairs to the front door, rejoicing that he need never enter it again.

He was on the canal path too early, just after three thirty, but it wasn't because he was anxious. He knew that the boy would come. Since the meeting with Miss Wharton, he had had the sensation of being carried along by events, not a mere passenger of fate, but triumphantly borne forward on a crest of luck and euphoria. He had never felt stronger, more confident, more in control. He knew that the boy would come, just as he knew that the meeting would be important in ways that he couldn't at present begin to guess.

Even getting the message to Darren had been easier than he had dared to hope. The school was a two storey building of grimy Victorian brick set behind railings. He had loitered close but not directly outside, anxious not to attract the attention of the little group of waiting mothers, and hadn't moved up to the gate until he heard the first squeals of the released children. He had chosen a boy as his messenger. A girl, he felt, might be more curious, more noticing, more likely to question Darren about the message. He picked on one of the younger boys and asked:

'Do you know Darren Wilkes?'

'Yeah. He's over there.'

'Give him this, will you? It's from his mum. It's important.'

He handed over the envelope with a fifty-pence piece. The boy had taken it with hardly a glance at him, snatching the coin as if afraid that he would change his mind. He had run across the playground to where a boy was kicking a football against the wall. Swayne had watched until he saw the envelope change hands and then had turned and walked quickly away.

He had chosen the meeting place with care; a tangled hawthorn growing close to the canal in whose shelter he could stand and watch the long stretch of path to his right and the forty yards which led to the mouth of the tunnel to his left. Behind him, a few yards to the right, was one of the iron gates to the canal path. His brief exploration had shown that it led to a narrow road bounded by lock-up garages, padlocked yards, the blank faces of anonymous industrial buildings. It wasn't a road to tempt the canal walker on a dark autumn afternoon, and it would give him an escape route from the towpath in case of need. But he wasn't seriously worried. He had been standing here for over twenty minutes and had seen no one.

And the boy, too, was early. Just before ten to four the small figure came into sight, loitering along the canal bank. He looked unnaturally tidy in his obviously new jeans topped with a brown and white zipped jacket. Swayne stepped a little back against the bark of a tree and watched his approach through a shield of leaves. Suddenly he wasn't there and Swayne felt a wild apprehension until he saw that the boy had climbed down into the ditch and was now reappearing, his hands stretched round the rim of an old cycle wheel. He began bowling it along the towpath. The wheel lurched and bounded. Swayne stepped out of his hiding place and caught it. The boy, no more than twelve yards away, stopped short, looked at him, wary as an animal, seemed about to turn and run. At once Swayne smiled and bowled the wheel back. The boy caught it, still fixing on him his steady, unsmiling gaze. Then he swung it round, clumsily twirling, staggered and let it go. It rose out over the water, then fell with a splash which seemed to Swayne so loud that he half-expected the canal path to be suddenly alive with people. But there was no one, no calling voices, no running feet.

The ripples widened, then died. He strolled up to the boy and said easily:

'It made a good splash. Do you find many of those in the ditch?'

The boy shifted his glance. Looking out over the canal, he said:
'One or two. Depends.'

'You're Darren Wilkes, aren't you? Miss Wharton told me I'd
find you here. I was looking for you. I'm an Inspector of Special
Branch. Do you know what that means?'

He took out his wallet with its credit cards and his old university
identity card. How lucky that he'd never given that in after his
first and last disastrous semester. It bore his photograph and he
flashed it at the boy, not giving him a chance to see more.

'Where is she then, Miss Wharton?'

The question was carefully casual. He didn't want to betray his
need, if he had a need. But he had bothered to come. He was
here.

Swayne said:

'She can't come. She told me to say that she's sorry but she
isn't feeling very well. Did you bring the note she sent you?'

'What's wrong with 'er then?'

'Only a cold. It's nothing to worry about. Did you bring the
note, Darren?'

'Yeah. I've got it.'

He thrust a small fist into his jeans pocket and brought it out.
Swayne took the crumpled page, glanced at it, then tore it
deliberately into small pieces. The boy watched silently as he
threw them into the water. They lay on the surface like frail
spring petals, then moved sluggishly, darkened, and were lost.

He said:

'Better take no chances. You see I had to be certain that you
really are Darren Wilkes. That's why the note was so important.
We have to have a talk.'

'What about?'

'The murder.'

'I don't know nothin' about the murder. I've talked to the
cops.'

'The ordinary police, yes I know. But they're a bit out of their
depth. There's more to this than they understand. Much more.'

They were moving together slowly upstream towards the entrance to the tunnel. The bushes were thicker here, in one place
so thick that even with their summer greenness dropping away

they still provided a safe screen from the path. He drew the boy with him into the semi-darkness and said:

'I'm going to trust you, Darren. That's because I need your help. You see, we in the Special Branch think that this wasn't an ordinary murder. Sir Paul was killed by a gang, a terrorist gang. You know what I mean by the Special Branch, don't you?'

'Yeah. Somethin' to do with spying.'

'That's right. It's our job to catch the enemies of the state. It's called special because that's what it is. Special and secret. Can you keep secrets?'

'Yeah. I keep plenty.'

The small body seemed to swagger. He looked up at Swayne, the face so like an intelligent monkey, suddenly sharp and knowing.

'Is that why you was there then? Watching 'im?'

The shock was like a physical punch on the chest, painful, disabling. When he could speak Swayne was surprised how calm his voice sounded.

'What makes you think I was there?'

'Them fancy buttons on yer jacket. I found one.'

His heart leaped, then for a second seemed to stop, a dead thing in his chest, dragging him down. But then he felt again its regular thudding, pulsing back warmth and life and confidence. He knew now why he was here, why both of them were here. He said:

'Where, Darren? Where did you find it?'

'On the path by the church. I picked it up. Miss Wharton thought I were picking a flower. She never seed me. She give me ten pee for a candle, see, same as always. I always have ten pee for the BVM.'

For a moment Swayne's mind seemed to whirl out of control. The boy's words no longer made sense. He saw the peaked face, a sickly green in the gloom of the bush, look up at him with something like contempt.

'The BVM. The statue of the lady in blue. Miss Wharton always give me ten pee for the box. Then I lit a candle, see? For the BVM. Only this time I kept the ten pee and I never 'ad time to light the candle 'cos she called me.'

'And what did you do with the button, Darren?'

He had to clench his fists to keep his hands from the boy's neck.

'Put it in the box, didn't I? Only she never knowed. I never tell 'er.'

'And you've told no one else?'

'No one arsed me.'

He looked up again, suddenly sly:

'I don't reckon Miss Wharton would like it.'

'No. Nor would the police – the ordinary police. They'd call it stealing, taking the money for your own use. You know what they do to boys who steal, don't you? They're trying to get you put away, Darren. They want an excuse to put you in a home. You know that too, don't you? You could be in real trouble. But you keep my secret and I'll keep yours. We'll both swear on my gun.'

'You got a gun then?'

For all the childish assumption of nonchalance he couldn't keep the excitement out of his voice.

'Of course. The Special Branch always go armed.'

He drew the Smith and Wesson out of his shoulder bag and held it out in his palm. The boy's eyes fastened on it fascinated. Swayne said:

'Put your hand on it and swear to tell no one about the button, about me, about this meeting.'

The small hand was stretched out eagerly. Swayne watched as it was laid on the barrel. The boy said:

'I swear.'

Swayne put his own hand over Darren's and pressed it down. It felt small and very soft and curiously detached from the boy's body as if it had a separate life like a young animal.

He said solemnly:

'And I swear not to reveal anything that passes between us.'

He was aware of the boy's longing. He said:

'Would you like to hold it?'

'Is it loaded?'

'No. I'm carrying the bullets but it isn't loaded.'

The boy took it and began to point it, first at the canal, then with a grin at Swayne, then again over the canal. He held it as he must have seen it held by cops on the television, straight out, grasping it with both hands. Swayne said:

'You've got the right idea. We could do with you in the Branch when you're older.'

Suddenly they were aware of the swish of bicycle wheels. Both drew back instinctively into the deeper shelter of the bushes. They had a brief glimpse of a middle-aged man in a cloth cap slowly pedalling against the squelch of the mud, his eyes fixed on the towpath. They stood motionless, hardly breathing, until he had disappeared. But he had reminded Swayne that there wasn't very much time. The canal path would become busier. There could be people taking a short cut home. He must do what he had to do quickly and silently. He said:

'You want to be careful, playing by the canal. Can you swim?'

The boy shrugged.

'Didn't they teach you how to swim at school?'

'Naw. I ain't been to school that much.'

It was almost too easy. He fought back a sudden impulse to laugh aloud. He wanted to lie back there on the mushy earth and gaze upwards through the knotted boughs and shout his triumph. He was invincible, out of their reach, protected by luck and cleverness, and something which had nothing to do with either, but which was now part of him for ever. The police couldn't have found the button; if they had they would have confronted him with it, would have taken back the jacket with its tell-tale tag of knotted cotton on the hemline. They must have seen that tag, must have known the spare button was missing when they examined the jacket. But a serious-faced young constable had returned it without comment, and he had worn it almost daily since, feeling superstitiously ill at ease without it. Getting the button wouldn't be difficult. He would first deal with the boy, then go at once to the church. No, not at once. He'd need a chisel to break open the offertory box. He could fetch one from Campden Hill Square, or better, buy one from the nearest Woolworth's. One purchase among so many wouldn't be noticed. And he wouldn't buy the chisel only. It would be safer to collect a number of small items before queuing at the cash point, that way the cashier would be less likely to remember the chisel. And breaking open the offertory box would look like a simple burglary. It was always happening. He doubted whether anyone would bother to inform the police, and if they did why should anyone connect it with the murder? And then it struck him that the box might have been emptied. The thought sobered his triumph, but for a moment only. If it had, the button would either have been given to the police or thrown away as useless. And it couldn't have been given to the police, they would have produced it. And even if by ill-chance it was still in someone's possession, only the boy knew where it had been found. And the boy would be dead, accidentally drowned, one more child unwisely playing on the canal bank.

He moved out of the shelter of the bushes and the boy followed. On either side the path stretched in empty desolation, the canal sliding thick and brown as sludge between the fretted banks. He shivered. For a second he had been seized with the illusion that no one was coming because there was no one left to come, that he and Darren were the last survivors of a dead, deserted world. Even the silence was eerie, and it struck him that since arriving on the path he hadn't heard the rustle of a single animal, nor the note of a bird.

He was aware that Darren had moved from his side and was squatting beside the water. Pausing beside him, Swayne saw that there was a dead rat caught in the crook of a broken twig; the sleek body, elongated, rippled the surface, its snout pointing like a prow. He squatted beside the boy and they contemplated it in silence. The rat, he thought, looked curiously human in death with its glazed eye and the small paws raised as if in a last despairing supplication. He said 'Lucky rat', and then it struck him how senseless was that casual statement. The rat, no longer rat, was neither lucky nor unlucky. It didn't exist. No statement about it had any meaning.

He watched while the boy grasped the end of the twig and began moving the body under the water. Then he lifted it. Small eddies broke over its head, and it rose glistening, hump-backed from the suck of the stinking water. He said sharply:

'Don't do that, Darren.'

The boy let go of the twig and the rat plopped back and began drifting sluggishly downstream.

They walked on. And then suddenly his heart lurched. Darren darted from his side, and with a high shout ran leaping into the tunnel mouth. For one appalled second Swayne thought that his victim must have divined his purpose and was dashing to escape. He rushed after him in the semi-darkness; and then he breathed easily again. Darren, whooping and hollering, was running his hands along the tunnel wall, then leaping, arms outflung, in a vain attempt to touch the roof. In his relief Swayne almost leaped with him.

And this, of course, was the place, none better. He would need only a minute, perhaps only seconds. It would have to be swift and sure. Nothing must be left to chance; he would have to do more than merely throw him in. He would need to kneel and hold the head under the water. The boy might struggle, but it would only be brief. He looked too frail to put up much of a struggle. He slipped his arms out of his jacket and folded it over his shoulder; there was no sense in getting an expensive jacket splashed. But the edge of the towpath was concrete here, not earth. He would be able to kneel if necessary without the risk of getting tell-tale mud on his trousers.

He called quietly:

'Darren.'

The boy, still leaping at the roof, took no notice. Swayne had drawn breath to call again when suddenly the small figure in front of him swayed, crumpled, fell silently as a leaf, and lay still. His first thought was that Darren was playing games; but when he came up to him he saw that the boy had fainted. He lay sprawled, so close to the canal that one thin arm was flung out over it, the small half-clenched fist almost touching the water. He was so motionless that he could have been dead; but Swayne knew that he would have recognized death when he saw it. He squatted and gazed intently into the still face. The boy's mouth was moistly open and he thought he could hear the gentle sigh of the breath. In the half-light the freckles stood out against the whiteness of the skin like splashes of gold paint and he could just see the sparse lashes spiked against the cheek. He thought: There must be something wrong with him. He's sick. Boys don't faint for no reason. And then he was visited by a sensation which was half-pity, half-anger. Poor little bastard. They drag him before the Juvenile Court, put him under supervision and they can't even look after him. They can't even see he's sick. Sod them. Sod the whole fucking lot of them.

But now that what he had to do was made easier than ever, no more than a gentle nudge away, it had suddenly become difficult. He put his foot under the boy and lifted him gently. The body rose on his shoe, seemingly weightless so that he could hardly feel it. But Darren didn't stir. One tip, he thought, one small thrust. If he had believed in a god, he would have said to him: 'You shouldn't have made it this easy. Nothing should be this easy.' It was very quiet in the tunnel. He could hear the slow drip of moisture from the roof, the faint slap of the canal against the pavement edge, the clicking of his digital watch, loud as a time-bomb. The smell of the water came up to him, strong and sour. The two half-moons gleaming at the tunnel ends seemed suddenly very far away. He could imagine them receding and shrinking into thin curves of light, and then fading completely, leaving him and the quietly breathing boy sealed up together in black, damp-smelling nothingness.

And then he thought: Do I need to do it? He hasn't done me any harm. Berowne deserved to die, but he doesn't. And he won't talk. The police have lost interest in him, anyway. And once I have the button it won't matter if he does talk. It will be his word against mine. And without the button, what can they prove? He plucked the jacket from his shoulder and knew as he felt the slip of the lining against his arms that this was the decisive action. The boy would be allowed to live. He savoured for one extra-ordinary moment a new sensation of power, and it seemed to him sweeter, more exhilarating than even the moment when he had finally turned to gaze down on Berowne's body. This was what it felt like to be a god. He had the power to take life or to bestow it. And this time he had chosen to be merciful. He was giving the boy the greatest gift in his power, and the boy wouldn't even know that it was he who had given it. But he would tell Barbie. Some day, when it was safe, he would tell Barbie, about the life he had taken, the life he had graciously spared. He pulled the body a little further from the water's edge and heard the boy moan. The eyelids flickered. As if afraid to meet the opening gaze, Swayne sprang to his feet then almost ran to the tunnel end suddenly desperate to gain that half-moon of light before the darkness closed in on him for ever.

6

It was Sarah Berowne who let them in. Without speaking, she led them across the hall to the library. Lady Ursula was seated at the dining-room table on which were stacked letters and documents in three neat piles. Some of the writing paper was edged with black as if the family had rummaged in their drawers for the mourning paper which must have been fashionable in her youth. As Dalgliesh entered she looked up and gave him a nod then inserted her silver paper knife in yet one more envelope and he heard the faint rasp as the paper slit open. Sarah Berowne walked over to the window and stood looking out, her shoulders hunched. Beyond the rain-washed panes the heavy swathes of the sycamores drooped dankly in the drenched air, the dead leaves torn by the storm hanging like brown dusters among the green. It was very quiet. Even the hiss of the traffic on the avenue was muted like a spent tide on a far distant shore. But inside the room some of the heaviness of the day seemed still to linger and the diffused frontal headache which had plagued him since the morning intensified and focused behind his right eye, a stabbing needle of pain.

He had never felt in this house an atmosphere of peace or ease but now the tension quivered on the air. Barbara Berowne alone seemed impervious to it. She, too, was sitting at the table. She was painting her nails; small gleaming bottles and tufts of cotton wool were set out before her on a tray. As he entered the brush was for a moment poised, its bright tip motionless in the air.

Without looking round, Sarah Berowne said:

'My grandmother is concerned, among other matters, with the arrangements for the memorial service. I suppose you have no views, Commander, on the relative appropriateness of "Fight the Good Fight" and "O Lord and Master of Mankind"?'

Dalgliesh walked across to Lady Ursula and held out the button on the palm of his hand. He said:

622

'Have you seen a button like this, Lady Ursula?'

She beckoned him nearer, then bent her head close to his fingers as if about to smell the button. Then she looked up at him expressionlessly and said:

'Not to my knowledge. It looks as if it came from a man's jacket, probably an expensive one. I can offer no other help.'

'And you, Miss Berowne?'

She came over from the window, looked at it briefly, and said:

'No, it isn't mine.'

'That wasn't my question. I asked if you'd seen it, or one like it.'

'If I have, I can't remember. But then, I'm not very interested in clothes or in trivia. Why not ask my stepmother?'

Barbara Berowne was holding up her left hand and blowing gently on her nails. Only the thumbnail remained unpainted. It looked like a dead deformity among the four pink tips. As Dalgliesh came up to her she took up the brush and began to draw careful sweeps of pink along the thumbnail. This done, she glanced at the button, then turned quickly away and said:

'It isn't off anything of mine. I don't think it belonged to Paul either. I haven't seen it before. Is it important?'

She was, he knew, lying, but not, he thought, through fear or any sense of danger. For her, to lie when in doubt was the easiest, even the most natural, response, a way of buying time, fending off unpleasantness, postponing trouble. He turned to Lady Ursula:

'I should like to speak to Miss Matlock, too, please.'

It was Sarah Berowne who went across to the fireplace and tugged at the bell.

When Evelyn Matlock came in, all three Berowne women turned as one and gazed at her. She stood for a moment her eyes fixed on Lady Ursula, then marched across to Dalgliesh stiff as a soldier on a charge. He said:

'Miss Matlock, I'm going to ask you a question. Don't answer it in a hurry. Think carefully before you speak and then tell me the truth.'

She glared at him. It was the look of a recalcitrant child, obstinate, malicious. He couldn't remember when he had seen so much hate in a face. Again he took his hand from his pocket and held out on his palm the silver-crested button. He said:

'Have you ever seen this button or one like it?'

He knew that Massingham's eyes as well as his own would be fixed on her face. It was easy to speak a lie, one short syllable. To act a lie was more difficult. She could just about control the tone of her voice, could make herself look up and gaze resolutely into his eyes, but the damage was already done. He hadn't missed that instantaneous flicker of recognition, the small start, the quick flush across the forehead; that, most of all, was beyond her control. As she paused, he said:

'Come closer, look at it carefully. It's a distinctive button, probably from a man's jacket. Not the kind you find on ordinary jackets. When did you last see one like it?'

But now her mind was working. He could almost hear the process of thought.

'I can't remember.'

'Are you saying that you can't remember seeing a button like this, or that you can't remember when you saw it last?'

'You're muddling me.'

She turned her face to Lady Ursula who said:

'If you want a lawyer before you answer, you're entitled to one. I can ring Mr Farrell.'

She said:

'I don't want a lawyer. Why should I want a lawyer? And if I did, I wouldn't choose Anthony Farrell. He looks at me as if I'm dirt.'

'Then I suggest you answer the Commander's question. It seems a plain enough one to me.'

'I've seen something like it. I can't remember where. There must be hundreds of similar buttons.'

Dalgliesh said:

'Try to remember. You think you've seen something like it. Where? In this house?'

Massingham, carefully avoiding Dalgliesh's eyes, must have been waiting his moment. His voice was a careful balance of brutality, contempt and amusement.

'Are you his mistress, Miss Matlock? Is that why you're shielding him? Because you are shielding him, aren't you? Is that how he paid you, a quick half hour on your bed between his bath and his supper? He was getting it cheap, wasn't he, his alibi for murder.'

No one did it better than Massingham. Every word was a calculated insult. Dalgliesh thought: My God, why do I always let him do my dirty work for me?

The woman's face flared. Lady Ursula laughed, a tiny cackle of derision. She spoke to Dalgliesh:

'Really, Commander, apart from being offensive, I find that suggestion ridiculous. It's grotesque.'

Evelyn Matlock turned on her, hands clenched, her body quivering with resentment:

'Why is it ridiculous, why is it grotesque? You can't bear to believe it, can you? You've had lovers enough in your time, everyone knows that. You're notorious. Well, you're old now, crippled and ugly and no one wants you, man or woman, and you can't bear to think that someone might want me. Well he did and he does. He loves me. We love each other. He cares. He knows what my life is like in this house. I'm tired, I'm overworked and I hate you all. You didn't know that, did you? You thought I was grateful. Grateful for the job of washing you like a baby, grateful for waiting on a woman too idle to pick up her own underclothes from the floor, grateful for the worst bedroom in the house, grateful for a home, a bed, a roof, the next meal. This place isn't a home. It's a museum. It's dead. It's been dead for years. And you think of no one but yourselves. Do this, Mattie, fetch that, Mattie, run my bath, Mattie. I do have a name. He calls me Evelyn. Evelyn, that's my name. I'm not a cat or a dog, I'm not a household pet.' She turned on Barbara Berowne: 'And what about you? There are things I could tell the police about that cousin of yours. You planned to get Sir Paul even before your fiancé was buried, before his own wife was dead. You didn't sleep with him. Oh no, you were too cunning for that. And what about you, his daughter? How much did you care about him? Or that lover of yours? You only used him to hurt your father. Not one of you knows what caring is, what love is.' She turned again on Lady Ursula: 'And then there's Daddy. I'm supposed to be grateful for what your son did. But what did he do? He couldn't even keep Daddy out of prison. And prison was torture for him. He was claustrophobic. He couldn't take it. He was tortured to death. And how much do you care, any of you? Sir Paul thought that giving me a job, a home, what you call a home, was enough. He thought he was paying for his mistake. He never did pay. I did all the paying.'

Lady Ursula said:

'I didn't know that you felt like this. I should have known. I blame myself.'

'Oh no you don't! Those are just words. You never have blamed yourself. Not ever. Not for anything. Not all your life. Yes, I did sleep with him. And I shall again. You can't stop me. It's no affair of yours. You don't own me body and soul, you only think you do. He loves me and I love him.'

Lady Ursula said:

'Don't be ridiculous. He was using you. He used you to get a free meal, a hot bath, his clothes washed and ironed. And in the end he used you to get an alibi for murder.'

Barbara Berowne had finished her manicure. Now she surveyed her finished nails with the pleased complacency of a child. Then she looked up.

'I know that Dicco made love to her, he told me. Of course he didn't murder Paul, that's silly. That's what he was doing when Paul died. He was making love to her on Paul's bed.'

Evelyn Matlock swung round on her. She cried:

'It's a lie! He couldn't have told you! He wouldn't have told you.'

'Well he did. He thought it would amuse me. He thought it was funny.'

She looked at Lady Ursula, a conspiratorial glance of mingled amusement and contempt, as if inviting her to share a private joke. Barbara Berowne's high, childish voice went on:

'I asked him how he could bear to touch her, but he said he could make love to any woman if he shut his eyes and imagined it was someone else. He said he kept his mind on the hot bathwater and a free meal. Actually, he didn't mind the love-making. He said she hasn't a bad figure and he could quite enjoy it as long as he kept the light off. It was all the sloppy talk, all that messing over him afterwards that he couldn't bear.'

Evelyn Matlock had sunk down on one of the chairs against the wall. She put her face in her hands, then looked up into Dalgliesh's face and said in a voice so low that he had to bend his head to hear:

'He did go out that night, but he told me he wanted to talk to Sir Paul. He wanted to find out what was going to happen to Lady Berowne. He told me they were dead when he arrived. The door was open and they were dead. They were both dead. He loved me. He trusted me. Oh God, I wish he'd killed me too.'

Suddenly she began crying, great retching sobs which seemed to tear her chest apart and rose to a whooping crescendo of agony. Sarah Berowne moved swiftly over to her and awkwardly cradled her head. Lady Ursula said:

'This noise is appalling. Take her to her room.'

As if the half-heard words were a threat, Evelyn Matlock made some attempt to control herself. Sarah Berowne looked across to Dalgliesh and said:

'But surely he couldn't have done it. There wouldn't have been time to commit the murders, clean up afterwards. Not unless he went by car or by bicycle. He'd never have risked a cab. And if he took the cycle, Halliwell must have seen or heard him.'

Lady Ursula said: 'Halliwell wasn't there to hear him.'

She lifted the receiver and dialled a number. They heard her say:

'Could you please come over, Halliwell.'

No one spoke. The only sound in the room was Miss Matlock's muted sobbing. Lady Ursula looked at her with a calmly speculative gaze, without pity, almost, it seemed to Dalgliesh, without interest.

And then they heard footsteps on the marble floor of the hall and Halliwell's stocky figure stood in the doorway. He was wearing jeans and a short-sleeved, open-necked shirt, and stood there completely at ease. The dark eyes flicked briefly from the police to the three Berownes, then to the sobbing, huddled figure in Sarah Berowne's arms. Then he closed the door and looked calmly at Lady Ursula, undeferential, relaxed, wary, shorter than the other two men, but seeming in his calm self-confidence momentarily to dominate the room.

Lady Ursula said:

'Halliwell drove me to St Matthew's Church on the night my son died. Describe to the Commander what happened, Halliwell.'

'Everything, my Lady?'

'Of course.'

He spoke directly to Dalgliesh:

'Lady Ursula rang me at ten to six and asked me to have the car ready. She said that she would come out to the garage and we were to leave as quietly as possible by the back door. When she was seated in the car she said that I was to drive to St Matthew's Church, Paddington. It was necessary for me to consult the road map and I did so.'

So they had left, thought Dalgliesh, nearly an hour before Dominic Swayne arrived. The flat over the garage would have been empty. Swayne would have assumed that Halliwell had already left for his next day's leave. The chauffeur went on:

'We arrived at the church and Lady Ursula asked me to park outside the south door at the back. Her Ladyship rang the bell and Sir Paul answered it. She went inside. About half an hour later she returned and asked me to join them. That must have been about seven o'clock. Sir Paul was there with another man, a tramp. There was a sheet of paper on the table covered with about eight lines of handwriting. Sir Paul said he was about to sign his name and wanted me to witness his signature. Then he signed and I wrote my name underneath. The tramp did the same.'

Lady Ursula said:

'It was fortunate that Harry could write. But then he was an old man. He was at a state school when the young were taught these skills.'

Dalgliesh asked:

'Was he sober?'

It was Halliwell who answered.

'His breath smelt, but he was steady enough on his feet, and he could write his name. He wasn't so drunk that he didn't know what he was doing.'

'Did you read what was written on the paper?'

'No sir. It wasn't my business to read it and I didn't.'

'How was it written?'

'Apparently with Sir Paul's fountain pen. He used the pen to sign his name and then handed it to me and to the tramp. When we had signed, he blotted the paper. Then the tramp went out through the door to the right of the fireplace and Lady Ursula and I left. Sir Paul stayed in the vestry. He didn't see us to the door. Lady Ursula then said that she would like to be taken for a drive before returning home. We drove to Parliament Hill Fields and then to Hampstead Heath. She sat in the car on the edge of the heath for about twenty minutes. Then I drove her home and we arrived back about half past nine. Lady Ursula asked me to drop her at the front door so that she could enter the house unobserved. She told me to park the car in Campden Hill Square and I did so.'

So they had been able to leave and return unobserved. And she had asked for her supper to be brought up on a tray, the thermos of soup, the smoked salmon. No one would disturb her until Miss Matlock came to put her to bed.

He said to Halliwell:

'After you had signed that paper, did Sir Paul say anything?'

Halliwell looked at Lady Ursula but, this time, he got no help. Dalgliesh asked again:

'Did he say anything, to you, to Harry Mack, to his mother?'

'Harry wasn't there. Like I said, he signed and stumbled off. Not much of a man, I'd say, for company or conversation. Sir Paul did speak, to her Ladyship. Only the three words. He said: "Look after him."'

Dalgliesh looked across at Lady Ursula. She was sitting very still, her hands in her lap, looking out across the room beyond the green tapestry of the trees to some imagined future, and he thought he saw the trace of a smile on her lips. He turned again to Halliwell:

'So you now admit that you lied when I asked if a car or the bicycle could have been taken out that night? You lied about being in your flat the whole of that evening?'

Halliwell said, calmly:

'Yes sir, I lied.'

Lady Ursula broke in:

'I asked him to lie. What had happened between me and my son in that vestry wasn't relevant to his death, whether or not he killed himself. It seemed to me important that you should spend your time and effort finding his killer, not meddling in the private affairs of the family. My son was alive when I left him. I asked Halliwell to say nothing about our visit. He is a man accustomed to obeying orders.'

Halliwell said:

'Some orders, my Lady.'

He looked across at her and gave her a grim fleeting smile. She answered his glance with a small self-satisfied nod. It seemed to Dalgliesh that they were for a moment oblivious of anyone else in the room, united in their private conspiratorial world which had its own compulsions. They stood together now as they had from the first. And he had no doubt what it was that bound them. Hugo Berowne had been his commanding officer; she was Sir Hugo's mother. He would have done a great deal more than lie for her.

They had almost forgotten Barbara Berowne. But now she sprang up from the table and almost threw herself at Dalgliesh. The pink fingers scrabbled at his jacket. The spurious sophistication dropped away and he was being clutched by a frightened child. She cried:

'It isn't true, he didn't do it! Dicco didn't leave the house. Can't you see? Mattie is jealous because he never really cared for her. How could he? Look at her. And the family have always hated him, him and me.' She turned to Lady Ursula. 'You never wanted him to marry me. You never thought I was good enough for your precious sons, either of them. Well, this house is mine now, and I think it would be better if you left.'

Lady Ursula said quietly:

'I'm afraid it isn't.'

With difficulty she turned and lifted the strap of her handbag from the back of her chair. They watched as the distorted fingers fumbled at the clip. Then she took out a folded sheet of paper. She said:

'What my son signed was his will. You are adequately, but not extravagantly, provided for. This house and the rest of his property is left to me in trust for his unborn child. If that child does not survive, then it comes to me.'

Barbara Berowne had tears brimming her eyes, a frustrated child. She cried:

'Why did he do it? How did you make him?'

But it was to Dalgliesh that Lady Ursula turned as if it were he who was owed the answer. She said:

'I had gone there to remonstrate with him, to make sure that he knew about the child, knew whether it was his, to ask what he intended. It was the presence of the tramp that gave me the idea. You see, I had the necessary two witnesses. I told him: "If she's carrying your child, I want to ensure that he's born safely. I want to safeguard his future. If you should die tonight, she'll inherit everything and your child will have Lampart as a stepfather. Is that what you want?" He didn't reply. He sat down at the table. I took a sheet of paper from the top drawer of the desk and placed it in front of him. Without speaking he wrote out the will, just the eight lines. A reasonable annual income for his wife and everything else in trust for the child. He may have wanted to get rid of me; I think he did. He may have been beyond caring; that is possible. He may have taken it for granted that he would be alive to make more formal arrangements next day. Most of us make that assumption. Or he may, somehow, have known that he wouldn't survive the night. But that, of course, is ridiculous.'

Dalgliesh said:

'You lied about speaking to Halliwell later that evening. Once the bodies were discovered you knew that he could be at risk. He would lie at your request. You felt you owed him at least an alibi. And you lied about your son's diary. You knew that it was in this house at six o'clock that evening. You went down to the study and took it from the desk drawer when the General telephoned.'

She said:

'At my age the memory is bound to be a little defective.' She added, with what sounded like grim satisfaction: 'I don't think I've ever lied to the police before. My class seldom has the need to. But if we do, then I can assure you that we're quite as ready to and just as good at it, probably better, than other people. But then I don't think you've ever doubted that.'

Dalgliesh said:

'You were waiting, of course, to see how much we had discovered, to be sure that your grandchild's mother wasn't a murderess or the accomplice of a murderer. You knew that you were concealing vital information, information which could have helped your son's butcher to go free. But that wouldn't have mattered, would it? Not if the family line continued, not if your daughter-in-law produced an heir.'

She corrected him gently:

'A legitimate heir. It may not seem very important to you, Commander, but I am over eighty and we have different priorities. She isn't an intelligent woman, not even an admirable one, but she'll be an adequate mother, I'll see to that. He'll do all right. He'll survive. But to grow up knowing that your mother was her lover's accomplice in the brutal murder of your father, that's not a heritage any child could cope with. I didn't intend that my grandson should have to cope with it. Paul asked me to look after his son. That is what I have been doing. There is a peculiar authority about the last wishes of the recently dead. In this case they coincided with my own.'

'That is all you care about?'

She said:

'I am 82, Commander. The men I have loved are all dead. What on earth else is left for me to care about?'

Dalgliesh said:

'We shall want new statements, of course, from all of you.'

'Naturally, you people always want statements. Aren't you sometimes in danger of believing that everything important in life can be put down in words, signed and admitted in evidence? I suppose that's the attraction of the job. All the messy, incomprehensible muddle reduced to words on a sheet of paper, exhibits with tags and numbers. But you're a poet – or were once. You can't possibly believe that what you deal in is the truth.'

Dalgliesh said:

'Dominic Swayne is living here now, isn't he? Do any of you know where he is?' There was no reply. 'Then we shall leave a police officer here until he returns.'

It was then that the telephone began ringing. Barbara Berowne gave a gasp and glanced from the instrument to Dalgliesh with something very like fear. Lady Ursula and Sarah Berowne ignored it as if neither the room nor anything in it was any longer their concern. Massingham moved over to it and lifted the receiver. He gave his name, listened in silence for a couple of minutes during which no one moved, then spoke so quietly that the words were unintelligible and replaced the receiver. Dalgliesh moved over to him. Massingham said very quietly:

'Darren has arrived home, sir. He won't say where he's been and Robins says it's obvious he's hiding something. His mother isn't back yet and no one knows where she is. They're trying her usual pubs and clubs. Two officers are staying with Darren until we pick up Swayne and they've rung the social services to try to contact his supervisor. No luck there. It's after office hours.'

'And Swayne?'

'No trace yet. That designer he shared a flat with says that he looked in at Shepherd's Bush earlier to collect his gear. Said he was off to Edinburgh.'

'Edinburgh?'

'He has friends there, apparently, people he met when he was doing a fringe show at this year's festival. Robins is in touch with Edinburgh. They may be able to pull him off the train.'

'If he took it.'

He walked over to Evelyn Matlock. She lifted to him a face devastated by grief and he saw in her eyes something so like trust that it turned his heart over. He said:

'He used your affection for him to make you lie for him; that was a betrayal. But what he felt for you and what you felt for him is your business and his, no one else's, and no one but you can know the truth about it.'

She said, looking up at him, willing him to understand:

'He did need me. He never had anyone else. It was love. It was love.'

Dalgliesh didn't reply.

Then she said in a voice so low that he could hardly catch the words:

'He did take a box of matches with him when he left. I

wouldn't have known only the electric kettle in the kitchen was broken. Halliwell was mending it for me. I had to light the gas with a match and I needed a new box. The one by the stove was missing.'

She began to cry again, but now almost soundlessly, a stream of silent tears washing down her face as if she wept out of a weariness and hopelessness that had gone beyond pain.

But there were still questions that he needed to ask and to ask now while she had passed beyond the extremity of misery and loss into an acceptance of defeat. He said:

'When Mr Swayne arrived, did he go alone into any part of the house other than your sitting room and the kitchen?'

'Only to take his toilet bag to the bathroom.'

So he would have had the chance to enter the study. He asked:

'And when he came back, was he carrying anything?'

'Only his evening paper. He had it with him when he arrived.'

But why not leave it in the back of the house? Why carry a newspaper with him to the bathroom unless he proposed to use it to conceal something, a book, a file, private letters? Suicides commonly destroyed their papers; he would find something in the house to take with him and burn. It had probably been fortuitous that he had opened the drawer and found the diary ready to hand.

He turned to Sarah Berowne and said:

'Miss Matlock is obviously distressed. I think she would like a cup of tea. Perhaps one of you could go to the trouble of making it for her.'

She said:

'You despise us, don't you? Every one of us.'

He said:

'Miss Berowne, I am in this house as an investigating officer. I have no other right here and no other function.'

He and Massingham had reached the door before Lady Ursula spoke, her voice high, unwavering.

'Before you leave, Commander, I think you should know that a gun is missing from the study safe. It belonged to my elder son, a Smith and Wesson .08. My daughter-in-law tells me that Paul got rid of it, but I think it would be safer to assume that she is —'

She paused and then added with delicate irony, 'that she is mistaken.'

Dalgliesh turned to Barbara Berowne.

'Could your brother have got hold of it? Did he know the combination of the safe?'

'Of course he didn't. Why should Dicco want it? Paul got rid of it. He told me. He thought it was dangerous. He threw it away. He threw it in the river.'

Lady Ursula spoke as if her daughter-in-law were not present.

'I think you can assume that Dominic Swayne knows the combination of the safe. My son changed it three days before he died. He had the habit of noting the new combination in pencil on the last page of his diary until he was sure that he and I had memorized it. His practice was to circle the digits on next year's calendar. That was the page which I think you showed me, Commander, had been torn out.'

7

It was nearly five o'clock by the time he had bought the chisel, the strongest the shop had on display. There hadn't in the end been time to get to a Woolworth's, but he had told himself that it didn't matter and had bought the chisel in a hardware shop off the Harrow Road. The assistant might remember him, but then, who was going to ask? The theft would be seen as an unimportant break-in. And afterwards he would throw the chisel in the canal. Without the chisel to match with the marks on the edge of the box, how could they possibly link him with the crime? It was too long for his jacket pocket, so he placed it with the gun in the canvas bag. It amused him to carry over his shoulder that innocuous commonplace bag, to feel the weight of the gun and the chisel bumping against his side. He had no fear of being stopped. Who would want to stop him, a respectably dressed young man walking quietly home at the end of the day? But the assurance was more deeply rooted. He walked the drab streets head high, invincible, and could have laughed aloud at the grey, stupid faces, staring ahead as they passed him, or bent to the ground as if instinctively searching the pavement in the hope of finding a dropped coin. They were corralled in their hopeless lives, endlessly trudging the same bare perimeters, slaves of routine and convention. He alone had had the courage to break free. He was a king among men, a free spirit. And in a few hours he would be on his way to Spain to the sun. No one could stop him. The police had nothing to justify holding him, and now the only physical evidence linking him with the scene of crime was within his reach. He had enough money to last for the next two months and then he would write to Barbie. The time wasn't ripe to tell her yet, but one day he would tell her and it had to be soon. The need to tell someone was becoming an obsession. He had nearly confided in that pathetic spinster over drinks at the St Ermin's Hotel. Afterwards he had been almost frightened by that urge to confess, to have someone marvel at his brilliance, his courage. Most of all he needed to tell Barbie who had a right to know. He would tell her that she owed her money, her freedom, her future to him. She would know how to be grateful.

The afternoon was so dark now that it could have been night, the sky thick and furred as a blanket, the air heavy to breathe and with the sharp metallic taste of the coming storm. Just as he turned the corner of the road and saw the church, it broke. The air and sky glittered with the first flash of lightning, then almost at once there came the crack of thunder. Two large drops stained the pavement in front of him and the rain sheeted down. He ran into the shelter of the church porch, laughing aloud. Even the weather was on his side; the main approach road to the church had been empty, and now he looked out from the porch into a wash of rain. Already the terraced houses seemed to shiver behind a curtain of water. From the glistening road spurts rose like fountains and the gutters ran and gurgled in torrents.

Gently he turned the great iron handle of the door. It was unlocked, slightly ajar. But he had expected to find it open. With part of his mind he believed that churches, buildings of sanctuary and superstition, were always left open for their worshippers. But nothing could surprise him, nothing could go wrong. The door squeaked as he closed it behind him and stepped into the sweet-smelling quietness.

The church was larger than he had imagined, so cold that he

shuddered and so still that he thought for a second that he heard an animal panting before he realized that it was his own breath. There was no artificial light except for a single chandelier and a lamp in a small side chapel where a crimson glow stained the air. Two rows of candles burning before the statue of the Madonna gusted in the draught from the closing door. There was a locked box attached to the branching candleholder but he knew that it wasn't this that he sought. He had questioned the boy carefully. The box containing the button was at the west end of the church in front of the iron ornamental grille. But he didn't hurry. He moved into the middle of the nave facing the altar and spread his arms wide as if to take possession of the vast emptiness, the holiness, the sweet-smelling air. In front of him the mosaics of the apse gleamed richly gold and turning to look up at the clerestory he could see in the half-light the ranks of painted figures, one-dimensional, harmlessly sentimental as cut-outs from a child's picture book. The rainwater ran down his hair to wash over his face, and he laughed as he tasted its sweetness on his tongue. A small pool gathered at his feet. Then slowly, almost ceremoniously, he paced down the nave to the candleholder in front of the grille.

There was a padlock on the box, but it was only small, and the box itself more fragile than he had expected. He inserted the chisel under the lid and heaved. At first it resisted, and then he could hear the gentle splinter of the wood and the gap widened. He gave one more heave and suddenly the padlock sprang apart with a crack so loud that it echoed through the church like a pistol shot. Almost at once it was answered by a crack of thunder. The gods, he thought, are applauding me.

And then he was aware of a dark shadow moving up to him and heard a voice, quietly untroubled, gently authoritative.

'If you're looking for the button, my son, you've come too late. The police have found it.'

8

Last night Father Barnes had dreamed again the same dream which had visited him on the night of the murder. It had been terrible; terrible on first waking and no less terrible when he thought about it later, and like all nightmares it had left him feeling that it had been no aberration but was firmly lodged in his subconscious, powered with its own terrible reality, crouched ready to return. The dream had been a Technicolor horror. He had been watching a procession, not part of it but standing on the edge of the pavement, alone, disregarded. At its head was Father Donovan in his richest chasuble, prancing in front of the processional cross while the congregation streamed out of his church behind him; laughing faces, bodies leaping and steaming, the clash of the steel drums. David, he thought, leaping about before the Ark of the Lord. And then came the sacrament borne high under a canopy. But when he drew close, he saw that it wasn't a proper canopy but the faded, grubby carpet from the Little Vestry of St Matthew's, its fringe swaying as the poles lurched, and what they were carrying wasn't the sacrament but Berowne's body, pink and naked like a stuck pig with its gaping throat.

He had woken up calling out, fumbling for the bedside lamp. Night after night the nightmare had returned and then, last Sunday, mysteriously, he had been free of it and for several nights his sleep had been deep and undisturbed. As he turned to lock the dark and empty church after Dalgliesh and Miss Wharton had left he found himself praying that it wouldn't revisit him tonight.

He glanced at his wristwatch. It was only quarter past five, but the evening was as dark as midnight. And when he reached the edge of the porch the rain began falling. First came a flash of thunder, so loud that it seemed to shake the church. He thought how unmistakable and how eerie it was, that unearthly sound, something between a growl and an explosion. No wonder, he thought, men have always feared it, like the anger of God. And then, immediately, came the rain spilling from the porch roof in a solid wall of water. It would be ridiculous to set out for the Vicarage through such a storm. He would be soaking wet in seconds. If he hadn't insisted on staying on for a few minutes after Dalgliesh had left to enter the candle money in his petty cash register he could probably have had a lift home. The

Commander was dropping Miss Wharton at her flat on his way to the Yard. But now there was nothing for it but to wait.

And then he remembered Bert Poulson's umbrella. Bert, who sang tenor in the choir, had left it in the bellroom after Sunday's Mass. He could borrow it. He went back into the church leaving the north door ajar, unlocked the door in the grille and made his way into the bellroom. The umbrella was still there. Then it occurred to him that he ought, perhaps, to leave a note on the peg. Bert might turn up early on Sunday and begin agitating when he found it was missing; he was that sort of man. Father Barnes went into the Little Vestry and taking a sheet of paper from the desk drawer wrote: 'Mr Poulson's umbrella is at the Vicarage.'

He had hardly finished writing, and was putting his biro back in his pocket when he heard the sound. It was a loud crack and it was very close. Instinctively he moved out of the Little Vestry and into the passage. Behind the grille was a young man, fair-haired, chisel in hand, and the collection box gaped open.

And then Father Barnes knew. He knew both who it was and why he was here. He remembered Dalgliesh's words: 'No one will be at risk once he knows that we've found the button.' But for one second, no more, he felt fear, an overwhelming, incapacitating terror which rendered him speechless. And then it passed, leaving him cold and faint but perfectly clear-headed. What he felt now was an immense calm, a sense that there was nothing he could do and nothing he need fear. Everything was taken care of. He walked forward as firmly as if he were greeting a new member of his congregation and knew that his face showed the same conscious, sentimental concern. His voice was perfectly steady. He said:

'If you're looking for the button, my son, you've come too late. The police have found it.'

The blue eyes blazed into his. Water was flowing like tears over the young face. It looked suddenly like the face of a desolate and terrified child, the mouth, half-open, gaped at him, speechless. And then he heard a groan and saw with disbelieving eyes the two hands stretched towards him, shaking; and in the hands was a gun. He heard himself say: 'No, oh no, please!' and he knew that he wasn't pleading for pity because there was none. It was a last impotent cry against the inescapable. And even as he made it he felt a thud and his body leaped. It was only seconds later as he hit the ground that he heard the gunshot.

Someone was bleeding over the tiles of the nave. He wondered where it was coming from, this steadily spreading stain. Extra cleaning, he thought. Difficult to get off. Miss Wharton and her ladies wouldn't be pleased. The red stream crept, viscous as oil, between the tiles. Like that TV advert, liquid engineering. Somewhere someone was groaning. It was a horrible noise, very loud. They really ought to stop. And then he thought: This is my blood, this is me bleeding. I'm going to die. There was no fear, but only a moment of dreadful weakness, followed by a nausea more terrible than any physical sensation he had ever experienced. But then that, too, passed. He thought: If this is dying, it is not so very difficult. He knew there were words he ought to say, but he wasn't sure he could remember them and it didn't matter. He thought: I must let go, just let go. After that thought there was no other.

He was unconscious when at last the blood stopped flowing. He was beyond hearing when almost an hour later the door was pushed slowly open and the heavy footsteps of a police officer moved down the nave towards him.

9

From the moment she walked into the casualty department and saw her grandmother, Kate had known that there was no longer any choice. The old lady had been sitting on a chair against the wall, a red hospital blanket around her shoulders, and had a pad of gauze taped to her forehead. She had looked very small and frightened, her face greyer and more wizened than ever before, her anxious eyes fixed on the entrance door. Kate was reminded of a stray dog brought into the Notting Hill nick and awaiting transfer to the Battersea Dogs' Home which, tied by a string to a bench, had gazed quivering at the door with just such an intensity of longing. Walking up to her, it seemed that she was seeing her grandmother with shocked eyes as if they had been parted for months. The tell-tale signs of deterioration, of the draining away of strength and self-respect that she had either ignored or pretended not to see, were suddenly all too plain. The hair, which her grandmother had always tried to dye back to its original red, now hanging in vertical stripes of white, grey and a curious orange each side of the sunken cheeks; the blotched hands thin as talons; the ridged nails on which the remnants of polish, months old, clung like dried blood; the eyes still sharp, but glittering now with the first glint of paranoia; the sour smell of unwashed clothes, unwashed flesh.

Without touching her, Kate sat beside her on the vacant chair. She thought: I mustn't make her ask, not now, not when it has become so important. At least I can spare her that humiliation. Where did I get my own pride if not from her? She said:

'It's all right, Gran. You're coming home with me.' There had been no hesitation and no choice. She couldn't look into those eyes and see for the first time real fear, real despair and still say no. She had left her side only for a few minutes to speak to the staff nurse and confirm that it was all right for her to leave. Then she had led her, docile as a child, to the car, driven her to the flat, and put her to bed. After all the scheming and agonizing, the self-justification, the determination that she and her grandmother would never again live under the same roof, it had been as simple and inevitable as that.

The next day had been hectic for both of them. By the time Kate had seen the local CID, driven her grandmother back to her flat and packed a case with Mrs Miskin's clothes and the odd collection of possessions from which she couldn't bear to be parted, left notes for the neighbours to explain what had happened, and spoken to the social service department and the housing office it was mid-afternoon. Then on their arrival back at Charles Shannon House there had been tea to make, drawers and a cupboard to clear for her grandmother's things, her own painting gear to be stowed away in the corner. God knows, she thought, when I'll be able to use that again.

It was after six before she was free to set off to the Notting Hill Gate supermarket to shop for enough food to leave ready for the next few days. She only hoped that she would be able to get back to work the next morning, that her grandmother would be well enough to leave. She had insisted on accompanying Kate and had stood up well to the day's exertions. But now she was looking tired and Kate was filled with a desperate worry that she might refuse to be left next morning. She had struck her head and bruised her right arm when the youths had jumped on her. But they had been content to grab her purse without kicking in her teeth and the physical damage was superficial. Her head and arm had been X-rayed; the hospital were satisfied that she was fit to be at home if there was someone to keep an eye on her. Well, there was someone to keep an eye on her, the only person in the world she had left.

Pushing her trolley along the aisles at the supermarket, Kate marvelled at the amount of additional food which one other person made necessary. She needed no list. These were the familiar items demanded by her grandmother which she had shopped for every week. As she placed them in the basket she could still hear the echo of that old, confident, disgruntled voice in her ears. Ginger biscuits ('not those soft ones, I like them hard for dipping'), tinned salmon ('red, mind you, I can't be doing with that pink muck'), tinned pears ('at least you can get your teeth into them'), custard powder, packets of cut ham ('keeps fresher that way and you can see what you're getting'), the strongest tasting teabags ('I wouldn't bath a newt in that stuff you bought last week'). But this afternoon had been different. Since coming to the flat she had sat without complaint, a pitiable, tired, docile old woman. Even her expected criticism of Kate's latest painting – 'I don't know why you want to stick that thing on the wall, looks like a kid's drawing' – had sounded more like a ritual objection, an attempt to revive her old bravado, than genuine outrage. She had let Kate set off for the shops with nothing but a sudden deepening of fear in the faded eyes and an anxious:

'You'll not be long then?'

'Not long, Gran. Just off to the supermarket at Notting Hill Gate.'

Then, as Kate reached the door, she called her back and raised her small gallant pennant of pride:

'I'm not asking to be kept. I've got me pension.'

'I know, Gran. There's no problem.'

Manoeuvring her trolley down the aisles stacked with tinned fruit, she thought: I don't seem to need a supernatural religion. Whatever happened to Paul Berowne in that church vestry, it's as closed to me as painting is to the blind. Nothing is more important to me than my job. But I can't make the law the basis of my personal morality. There has to be something more if I'm to live at ease with myself.

And it seemed to her that she had made a discovery about herself and about her job which was of immense importance, and she smiled that it should have happened while she was hesitating between two brands of tinned pears in a Notting Hill Gate supermarket. Odd, too, that it should have happened during this particular case. If she was still with the squad at the end of the inquiry she would like to say to AD: 'Thank you for having me on the case, for choosing me. I've learnt something about the job and myself.' But immediately she realized that it wouldn't be possible. The words would be too revealing, too confiding, the sort of girlish enthusiasm she wouldn't be able to recall afterwards without a flush of shame. And then she thought: For God's sake why not? He's not going to demote me, and it's the truth. I shouldn't be saying it to embarrass him, or impress him or for any other reason except that it's true and I need to say it. She knew that she was overdefensive, probably she always would be. Those early years couldn't be wiped out and they couldn't be forgotten. But surely she could let down one small drawbridge without yielding the whole fortress. And would it matter so much if it were yielded?

She was too clearsighted to expect this mood of exaltation to last long but it depressed her how quickly it drained away. A wind was blustering around Notting Hill Gate, shaking out the sodden litter from the raised flowerbeds and swirling it damply against her ankles. On the parapet an old man, corded in rags and surrounded by bulging plastic bags, lifted his querulous voice and ranted feebly against the world. She hadn't brought the car. It was hopeless to try to park near Notting Hill. But the two bags were heavier than she had expected and their weight began to

drag on her spirits as well as her shoulder muscles. It was all v̱ ,
well to indulge in self-congratulations, to muse on the imperatives
of duty. but now the reality of the situation struck her like a
physical blow, filling her with a misery close to despair. She and
her grandmother would be locked together now until the old lady
died. She was getting too old to cope with independence and
soon she would compensate for its loss by persuading herself that
she didn't really want it. And who now would give her priority
for a single-person flat or a place in an old people's home, even if
she would accept it, with so many more urgent cases on the
waiting list? And when she was too old to be left during the day,
what then? How could she, Kate, carry on her job and at the
same time nurse a geriatric patient? She knew what officialdom
would say. 'Can't you ask for three months' compassionate leave,
or find a part-time job?' And the three months would become a
year, the year might be two or three, her career would be
finished. No hope now of a place on the Bramshill course, of
planning for a senior command. What hope even of staying on in
the special squad with its long unpredictable hours, its demand
for total commitment.

The storm was over now but the great plane trees in Holland
Park Avenue still shook down heavy drops of rain which seeped,
disagreeably cold, under the collar of her coat. The evening rush
hour was in full spate and her ears were battered by the grind
and roar of traffic, a noise which normally she hardly noticed. As
she waited to cross Ladbroke Grove, a van hissing too fast
through the running gutters splashed her ankles with dirt. She
shouted her protest, unheard above the thunder of the road. The
storm had brought down the first autumn fall of leaves. They
drifted sluggishly against the barks of the trees and lay, delicately
veined skeletons, on the tacky pavement. As she trudged past
Campden Hill Square she gazed up towards the Berowne house.
It was hidden by the trees of the square garden but she could
picture its secret life and had to resist the temptation to cross the
road and walk up to it to see if the police Rover was parked
outside. She seemed to have been away from the squad for weeks
rather than a single day.

She was glad to turn from the roar of the avenue into the

comparative quiet of her own road. Her grandmother didn't speak when she rang the bell and called her own name into the entry-phone. But there was a burr and the door was released with surprising speed. The old lady must have been near the door. She humped her carrier bags into the lift and was borne upwards past floor after floor of empty and silent corridors.

She let herself into the flat and, as she always did, turned her key in the security lock. Then she hauled the bags of groceries on to the kitchen table and turned to walk the three yards across the hall to the sitting room door. The flat was silent, unnaturally so. Surely her grandmother would have turned on the television? Small facts, unregarded in her self-obsessed mood of resentment and misery, suddenly came together; the sitting room door tight closed when she had left it open, the swift but voiceless response to her ring at the street door, the unnatural silence. Even as her hand touched the knob and she pushed open the sitting room door, she knew with absolute certainty that something was wrong. But by then it was too late.

He had gagged her grandmother and tied her to one of the dining chairs with strips of white cloth, probably, she thought, a ripped sheet. He himself stood behind her, eyes blazing above the smiling mouth like a bizarre tableau of triumphant youth and age. He was holding the gun with both hands, steadying the barrel, his arms stretched rigid. She wondered if he were used to firearms or whether this was how he had seen a gun held in TV crime series. Her mind was curiously detached. She had often wondered how she would feel if faced with this kind of emergency and it interested her that her reactions were so predictable. Disbelief, shock, fear. And then the surge of adrenalin, the gears of the mind taking hold.

As their eyes met he slowly lowered his arms, then placed the nozzle of the gun against her grandmother's head. Her eyes above the mouth gag were immense, great black pools of terror. It was extraordinary that those restless eyes could be filled with such an intensity of pleading. Kate was seized with such pity and such anger that, for a moment, she dared not speak. Then she said:

'Take off that gag. Her mouth's bleeding. She's had one shock already. D'you want to kill her with pain and fright?'

'Oh, she won't die. They don't, these old bitches. They live for ever.'

'She isn't strong and a dead hostage isn't much use to you.'

'Ah, but I'll still have you. A policewoman, rather more valuable.'

'Will you? D'you think I care a damn except for her? Look, if you want any cooperation from me take off that gag.'

'And have her hollering like a stuck pig? Not that I know what a stuck pig sounds like, but I know the kind of noise she'd make. I'm in a particularly sensitive mood and I never could stand noise.'

'If she does then you can gag her again, can't you? But she won't. I'll see to that.'

'All right. Come and take it off yourself. But be careful. Remember I've got this gun against her head.'

She moved across, knelt and put her hand against her grand-mother's cheek.

'I'm going to take off the gag. Now you mustn't make a noise. Not a sound. If you do, he'll put it on again. Promise?' There was no response, nothing but terror in the glazed eyes. But then her head jerked twice.

Kate said:

'Don't worry, Gran. I'm here. It's going to be all right.'

The stiff hands with their parched swollen knuckles clasped the chair ends as if fastened to the wood. She put her own hands over them. They felt like dry crêpe, cold and lifeless. She pressed down her warm palms and felt the physical transfer of life, of hope. Gently she put her right hand against her grandmother's cheek and wondered how she could ever have found this crumpled flesh repulsive. She thought: We haven't touched each other for fifteen years. And now I am touching her, and with love.

When the gag dropped off, he waved her back and said:

'Stand over there against the wall. Now.' She did as she was ordered. His eyes followed her.

Bound in her chair, her grandmother was rhythmically opening and shutting her mouth like a fish gasping for air. A thin dribble of bloodstained mucus dripped over her chin. Kate waited until she could control her voice. Then she said coolly:

'Why this panic? We've got no real evidence. You must know that.'

'Ah, but now you have.'

Without moving the gun he turned up the corner of his jacket with his left hand.

'My spare button. Your people at the lab won't have missed this broken twist of thread. Pity the buttons are so distinctive. This comes of having expensive taste in clothes. Papa always said it would be my undoing.'

His voice was high, brittle, the eyes large and bright as if he were on drugs. She thought: He's not really as calm as he wants to sound. And he's been drinking. Probably got at my whisky while he was waiting. But that made him more dangerous not less. She said:

'That's not enough, a single button. Look, don't be a fool. Stop play-acting. Hand over the gun. Go home and call your lawyer.'

'Ah, but I don't think I can do that, not now. You see there's this damned officious priest. Or rather, there was this damned officious priest. He had a taste for martyrdom, poor sod. I hope he's enjoying it.'

'You've killed him? Father Barnes?'

'Shot him. So you see I haven't anything to lose. If I'm aiming for Broadmoor rather than a high-security jail, you could say the more the merrier.'

There was, she remembered, a mass murderer who had said just that. Who was it? Haigh?

She said:

'How did you find me?'

'The telephone directory, how else? Rather a coy and uncommunicative entry, but I guessed it was you. No difficulty in getting the old woman to open the door, incidentally. I just said I was Chief Inspector Massingham.'

'All right, so what's the plan?'

'I'm getting out. Spain. There's a boat at Chichester harbour which I can handle. The *Mayflower*. I've sailed on her. She belongs to my sister's lover in case you're interested. You're going to drive me there.'

'Not now I'm not. Not till the roads are clear. Look, I'm as anxious to live as you are. I'm not Father Barnes, I'm no martyr. The police pay me well, but not that well. I'll get you to Chichester but we have to wait until the A3 is clear if we're going to get through. For God's sake, it's the rush hour! You know what the traffic's like getting out of London. I don't fancy getting stuck in a traffic jam with a gun at my back and every other motorist peering into the car.'

'Why should they? The police will be looking for a single man, not a man, wife and his dear old grandma.'

She said:

'They won't be looking for anyone yet, button or no button. Not unless they've found the priest or know that you've got the gun. As far as the police know, there's no hurry. They don't even know that you've found out about the button. If we're to get well away fast and unnoticed we have to have a clear drive to Chichester. And there's no point in carting along my grandmother. She'll only be a hindrance.'

'Possibly, but she's coming. I need her.'

Of course he needed her. His plan was plain enough. She would be expected to drive, he would sit at the back, the gun against the old lady's head. And when they reached the harbour she would be expected to help with the boat, at least until they got out to sea. And what then? Two gun shots, two bodies bundled over the side? He seemed to be considering, then he said:

'All right, we'll wait. Just for an hour. How much food is there?'

'Are you hungry?'

'I shall be, and we'll need provisions. Everything portable that you've got.'

This she knew could be important. Hunger, shared need, shared food, a natural human want satisfied. It was one way of establishing that empathy on which their survival might depend. She remembered what she had been taught about sieges. The prisoners identified with their captors. It was those sinister watching eyes outside, those unseen intelligences, their guns, their listening devices leeched to the walls, their false insinuating voices which became the enemy. She wouldn't identify with him or with his kind if they were together until they starved, but there were things she could do. Use 'we' not 'you'. Try not to provoke him. Try to ease the tension and, if necessary, cook for him. She said:

'I could go and see what we've got. I don't keep much fresh food but there'll be eggs, tins, pasta, and I could cook what I had planned for tonight: spaghetti bolognese.'

He said:

'No knives.'

'You can't do much cooking without a knife of some sort. I'll need to chop onions and the liver. My recipe uses chopped liver.'

'Then do without them.'

Spaghetti bolognese. Strong tasting. Was there anything that she could put into the sauce which would incapacitate him? Her thoughts ranged over the contents of her medicine chest. But she rejected the idea as nonsensical. There would be no opportunity. He wasn't a fool. He'd see to that. And he wouldn't eat anything which she didn't share. Her grandmother began muttering. Kate said:

'I've got to speak to her.'

'All right. But keep your hands behind your back and be careful.'

She had to get hold of the gun, but now wasn't the time. It was pressed hard against her grandmother's skull. One suspicious move on her part and he would press the trigger. She went up again to the chair and bent her head. Her grandmother whispered. Kate said:

'She wants to go to the lavatory.'

'That's too bad. She's staying where she is.'

Kate said angrily:

'Look, d'you want a stink in the room for the next hour? And in the car come to that. I'm fastidious if you're not. Let me take her. What possible danger can she be?'

Again there was a moment's silence while he thought:

'All right. Untie her. But leave the door open. And remember I'll be watching you.'

It took her a full minute to undo the clumsy knots, but at last the linen dropped away and her grandmother fell forward into her arms. She drew her up, marvelling at the lightness of her body, brittle as a bird's. Holding her gently and murmuring encouragement as she might to a child, Kate half-carried her into the lavatory. Supporting her with one arm, she pulled down her knickers and lowered her on to the seat, aware of him standing braced against the passage wall less than two yards away, the gun pointed at her head. Her grandmother whispered:

'He's going to kill us.'

'Nonsense, Gran. Of course he won't kill us.'

The old lady directed a look of venomous hatred across Kate's shoulder. She hissed:

'He's been at your whisky. Bloody cheek.'

'I know, Gran. It doesn't matter. Better not talk, not now.'

'He's going to shoot us. I know.' Then she said: 'Your dad was a copper.'

A policeman! Kate could have laughed aloud. It was extraordinary to learn that now, in this place, at this moment, astonishing to learn it at all. Still shielding her grandmother's body with her own she said:

'Why didn't you tell me?'

'You never asked. No point in telling anyway. He was killed before you were born, in a car smash, chasing a villain. And he had a wife and two kids. Little enough for them on a police pension without letting on about you.'

'So he never knew?'

'That's right. And no point in telling his wife. Nothing she could do about it. More grief, more trouble.'

'So you were landed with me. Poor Gran. I haven't been much use.'

'You've been all right. No worse than any other kid. I never felt right about you. I always felt guilty.'

'Guilty! You! Why on earth?'

'When she died, your ma, I wished it had been you.'

So that had been at the root of all the estrangement. She felt a spring of joy. Here crouching by a lavatory seat, a gun at her head with death perhaps seconds away she could have laughed. She put her arm round the old lady, helping her to her feet, then let her rest against her while she drew up her knickers. She said:

'But of course you did. It was natural. It was right. She was your daughter. You loved her. Of course you wish it had been me who died if one of us had to go.' But she couldn't make herself say: it would have been better if it had been me. Her grandmother muttered:

'I've felt bad about it all these years.'

'Well stop feeling bad about it. We've got a lot of years ahead.'

And then she heard his step as he moved into the doorway, felt his breath on the back of her neck. He said:

'Get her out of here and start cooking that meal.'

But there was something she needed to ask. For over twenty years she hadn't asked, hadn't even cared. But now amazingly, it had become important. Ignoring him she said to her grandmother:

'Was she glad about me? My mother?'

'Seemingly. Before she died she said "my sweet Kate". So that's what I called you.'

So it had been as simple as that, as wonderful as that.

His voice rasped with impatience:

'I said, get her out of here. Take her into the kitchen. Tie her to one of the chairs, against the wall, by the door. I want my gun against her head while you're cooking.'

She did as she was told, fetching the strips of sheeting from the sitting room, drawing her grandmother's wrists gently behind her back, tying them as loosely as she dared, careful not to hurt her. Keeping her eyes on the knots, she said:

'Look, there's something I must do. I've got to ring my boyfriend. He's coming to supper at eight.'

'It doesn't matter. Let him come. We'll be gone by then.'

'It does matter. If he finds the flat empty he'll know something is wrong. He'll check the car. Then he'll ring the Yard. We've got to put him off.'

'How do I know he's expected?'

'You'll find his initials on that wall diary behind you on the clipboard.' She was grateful now that, absorbed with the business of settling in her grandmother, she had telephoned Alan to cancel their date but hadn't rubbed out those faint pencilled initials and the time. She said:

'Look, we've got to get to Chichester before anyone knows we've gone. He won't be altogether surprised to be chucked. We had one hell of a row last time he was here.'

He was silent considering. Then he said:

'All right. What's his name and the number?'

'Alan Scully and he works at the Hoskyns Theological Library. He won't have left yet. He stays late on Thursday.'

He said:

'I'll ring from the sitting room. You stand back against the wall. Don't come to the telephone till I tell you. What's the number?'

She followed him into the sitting room. He motioned her back against the wall to the left of the door then moved over to where the telephone stood on a shelf of the wall unit, the answering machine beside it, the directories neatly stacked beneath. She wondered if he would remember the risk of leaving his palm print. As if the thought had communicated itself to him, he took a handkerchief from his pocket and draped it over the receiver. He said:

'Who will answer, this man Scully or a secretary?'

'At this hour, he will. He'll be alone in his office.'

'Let's hope he is. And don't try anything. If you do I'll shoot you first and then the old witch. And maybe she won't die quickly. You will, but not her. I might have a little fun with her first, switch on the electric stove, clamp down her hand on the hot plate. Think about that if you're tempted to be clever.'

She couldn't believe that, even now, he'd bring himself to do it. He was a killer but not a torturer. But the words, the horror of the picture they evoked, made her shudder. And the threat of death was real enough. He had already killed three men. What had he got to lose? He would prefer a live hostage, prefer to let her do the driving, to have an extra pair of hands on the boat. But if he needed to kill he would, trusting that he could get well on his way before their bodies were found.

He said:

'Right, what's the number?'

She gave it and watched, heart pounding, while he dialled. The call must have been quickly answered. He didn't speak but after less than four seconds he held out the receiver and she moved across and took it from his hand. She began speaking loudly and very fast, desperate to drown any questions, any response.

'Alan? It's Kate. Tonight's off. Look I'm tired, I've had one
hell of a day and I'm fed up with cooking for you every bloody
time we meet. And don't ring back. Just come tomorrow if you
feel like it. Maybe you'll take me out for a change. Aι.d Alan,
remember to bring me that book you promised. The Shakespeare
Love's Labour's Lost for Christ's sake. See you tomorrow. And
remember the Shakespeare.' She banged down the receiver. She
found that she was holding her breath, and let it out gently and
silently, afraid that he would notice the release of tension. Had
her words sounded even remotely credible? The message seemed
to her so obviously false. Could he possibly have been deceived?
But after all, he didn't know Alan, he didn't know her. That
might be typical of the way they spoke to each other. She said:

'That's OK. He'll keep away.'

'He'd better.'

He motioned her back to the kitchen and took up his stance
beside her grandmother, the gun again to her head.

He said:

'You've got wine, I suppose?'

'You should know. You've been at the drinks cupboard.'

'So I have. We'll have the Beaujolais. And we'll take the
whisky and a half-dozen bottles of the claret with us. I've
a feeling I'm going to need alcohol before I get across the
Channel.'

How experienced a sailor was he? she wondered. And what
kind of boat was the *Mayflower*? Stephen Lampart had described
it but she couldn't now remember. And how could he be sure
that the craft would be fuelled and ready for sea, that the tides
would be right? Or had he passed beyond the borders of reason,
of precarious sanity, into a fantasy in which even the tides would
run to his bidding?

He asked:

'Well, aren't you going to get on with it? We haven't much
time.'

She knew that every action must be slow, deliberate, unfrightening, that any sudden movement might be fatal. She said:

'I'm going to reach up and take a frying pan from that top
cupboard. Then I'll need the minced beef and the liver from the

653

refrigerator and a tube of tomato paste and the herbs from this cupboard on my right. OK?'

'I don't need a cookery lesson. And remember, no knives.'

As she started her preparations she thought of Alan. What was he doing? What was he thinking? Would he stand still for a moment, consider, come to the conclusion that she was drunk, hysterical or mad, then go back to his books? But he couldn't! He must know that she was none of these things, that if she did go mad, it wouldn't be in that way. But it was impossible to picture him actually taking action, ringing the Yard, asking for Commander Dalgliesh. It seemed to her that she was expecting him to act a part as out of character as it would be for her to take over his job, catalogue his library. But surely that reference to *Love's Labour's Lost* had been unmistakable. He must know that she was trying to convey an urgent message, that she was under duress. He couldn't have forgotten their talk about Berowne, the attendant lord. She thought: He reads the newspapers, he must know that these things happen. He can't not know what sort of world we live in. And she would never normally speak to him in those terms, in that tone of voice. He knew her well enough to be sure of that. Or did he? They had been happily making love for over two years. There wasn't anything about her body that wasn't familiar to him as his was to her. Since when did that mean that two people knew each other?

Standing back against the wall, the gun still pressed to her grandmother's head, Swayne kept his eyes fixed on her while she took the package of minced steak and the one of liver out of the refrigerator for the frying pan. He said:

'Ever been to California?'

'No.'

'It's the only place to live. Sun. Ocean. Brightness. People who aren't grey and frightened and half-dead. You wouldn't like it. Not your kind of place.'

She asked:

'Why don't you go back?'

'I can't afford to.'

'The air fare or the expense of living there?'

'Neither. My stepfather pays me to stay away. I'll lose my allowance if I go back.'

'Couldn't you get a job?'

'Ah, but then I might lose something else. There is a little matter of step-papa's Seurat.'

'That's a painting, isn't it? What did you do to it?'

'Clever. How did you know that? The history of art isn't in the police curriculum, is it?'

'What did you do to it?'

'Stuck a knife through it several times. I wanted to spoil something he cared about. Actually he didn't much care about it. But he cared about what it cost. Well, it wouldn't have been much good sticking a knife in Mama, would it?'

'What about your mother?'

'Oh, she keeps in with my stepfather. She more or less has to. He's the one with the money. Anyway, she's never much cared for children, not her own, anyway. Barbara's too beautiful for her. She doesn't really like her. That's because she's afraid my step-papa does, too much.'

'And you?'

'They don't want to know about me, either of them. They never have. Not this stepfather, nor the one before. But they will. They will.'

She tipped the mince from the paper into the frying pan and began moving it around with a spatula. Keeping her voice calm as if this were an ordinary dinner and he an ordinary guest, she said above the hiss of singeing meat:

'This really ought to have onions in it.'

'Forget about the onions. What about your mother?'

'My mother's dead and I never knew my father. I'm a bastard.' She thought, I might as well tell him. It could evoke some emotion, curiosity, pity, contempt. No, not pity. But even contempt would be something. Contempt was a human response. If they were to survive she had to get some relationship established that was other than fear, hatred, conflict. But when he spoke his voice held nothing but an amused tolerance.

'One of those, are you? They've all got chips on their shoulders, bastards. I should know. I'll tell you something about my father. When I was eleven he made me have a blood test. A doctor came and stuck a needle in my arm. I could see my own blood flowing out into the syringe. I was terrified. He did it to try and prove that I wasn't his son.'

She said, and meant it:

'That was a terrible thing to do to a child.'

'He was a terrible man. But I got my own back. Is that why you're a policewoman, getting your own back on the rest of us?'

'No, just earning a living.'

'There are other ways. You could have been a decent whore. There aren't enough of those around.'

'Are those the women you fancy, whores?'

'No, what I fancy isn't so easily come by. Innocence.'

'Like Theresa Nolan?'

'So you know about that? I didn't kill her. She killed herself.'

'Because you made her abort your child?'

'Well, she could hardly expect to have it, could she? And how are you so sure that it was mine? You never can be sure, any of you. If Berowne didn't sleep with her he wanted to. By God he wanted to. Why else should he have thrown me into that river? I could have done a lot for him, helped him if he'd let me. He couldn't be bothered even to talk to me. Who did he think he was? He was going to leave my sister, my sister, for his dreary whore or for his God. Who the hell cares which? He was going to sell his house, make us poor and despised. He humiliated me in front of Diana. Well, he chose the wrong man.'

His voice was still low but it seemed to her that it rang out filling the room, charged with anger and triumph.

She thought:

I might as well ask him about it. He'll want to talk. They always do. She spoke almost casually, squeezing the tomato paste into the pan, reaching up for the jar of mixed herbs.

'You knew that he'd be in that vestry. He wouldn't have left home without saying where he could be found, not when there was a risk that a dying man would send for him. You told Miss Matlock to lie to us, but she knew where he was and she told you.'

'He gave her a telephone number. I guessed it was the number of the church but I rang directory enquiries. The number they gave me for St Matthew's was the one he'd given Evelyn.'

'How did you get from Campden Hill Square to the church? Cab? Car?'

'By bicycle, his bicycle. I took the key to the garage from Evelyn's cupboard. Halliwell had left by then, whatever he told the police. His lights were out and the Rover had gone. I didn't take Barbie's Golf. Too conspicuous. A bicycle was just as quick and I could wait in the shadows until the road was clear and pedal quickly away. And I didn't leave it outside the church where it might have been seen. I asked Paul if I could bring it in, leave it in the passage. It was a fine night so I didn't have to worry about muddy tyre marks on the floor. I thought of everything, you see.'

'Not everything. You took away the matches.'

'But I put them back. The matches prove nothing.'

She said:

'And he let you in, you and the bicycle. That's what I find odd. That he actually let you in.'

'It's odder than you think. Much odder. I didn't realize at the time, but I do now. He knew I was coming. He was expecting me.'

She felt a frisson of almost superstitious horror. She wanted to cry out: But he couldn't have known! It isn't possible!

She said:

'And Harry Mack. Did you really have to kill Harry?'

'Of course. It was his bad luck that he came blundering in. But he was better dead, poor sod. Don't worry about Harry. I did him a favour.'

Turning to face him Kate asked:

'And Diana Travers. Did you kill her too?'

He gave a sly smile and seemed to gaze straight through her as if reliving a secret pleasure.

'I didn't need to. The weeds did it for me. I trod water and watched as she dived in. There was a flash of whiteness cleaving the surface. And then it settled and there was nothing, only that liquid darkness. So I waited, counting the seconds. And then quite close to me, a hand rose out of the water. Just a hand, pale, disembodied. It was uncanny. Like this. See, like this.'

He shot up his left hand, the fingers tautly splayed. She could see the stretched sinews under the milk white flesh. She didn't speak. Gently he relaxed his fingers and let his arm fall. He said:

'And then that, too, disappeared. And I waited, still counting the seconds. But there was nothing, not even a ripple.'

'And you swam on, leaving her to drown?'

His eyes focused on her as if with an effort and she heard again in his voice the charge of hatred and triumph.

'She laughed at me. No one does that. No one will, ever again.'

'What did you feel like afterwards, knowing what you'd done in that vestry, the butchery, the blood?'

'You need a woman and I had one handy. Not the one I would have chosen but you have to take what you can get. It was clever too. I knew she'd never break after that.'

'Miss Matlock. You used her in more ways than one.'

'No more than the Berownes did. They think she's devoted to them. Do you know why? Because they never bother to ask themselves what she really thinks. So efficient, so devoted. Almost one of the family, except, of course, that she isn't, is she? She never was. She hates them. She doesn't know it, not really, not yet, but she hates them and one day she'll wake up to it. Like me. That dreadful old bitch, Lady Ursula. I've seen her trying not to cringe when Evelyn touches her.'

'Evelyn?'

'Mattie. She does have a name of her own, you know. They found a pet name for her as they might for a cat or a dog.'

'If they've been overworking her for years why didn't she leave?'

'Too scared. She went off her head. Once you've had one spell in the funny farm and your dad's a murderer people get wary. They're not sure you're safe looking after their precious kids or let loose in the kitchen. Oh, the Berownes had her where they wanted her all right. Why should they think she got a kick out of it, fussing over that selfish old woman, washing under her droopy old tits? Christ, I hope I never get old.'

She said:

'You will. Where you're going, they take good care of you. Healthy diet, daily exercise, locked up safely at night. You'll grow old all right.'

He laughed.

'But they won't kill me, will they? They can't. And I'll be out again. Cured. You'll be surprised how quickly they'll cure me.'

'Not if you kill a police officer.'

'Let's hope I don't have to then. When is that stuff going to be ready? I want to get on.'

She said:

'Soon. It won't be long now.'

Already the kitchen was beginning to fill with the savoury smell of the sauce. She reached up for her pasta jar and tipped out a handful of spaghetti, breaking it. The thin cracks sounded unnaturally loud. She thought: If Alan has telephoned the police they could be outside already, boring through the wall, looking, watching, listening. How would they play it, she wondered. Telephone and begin the long process of negotiation? Crash in? Probably neither. As long as he was ignorant of their presence they would watch and listen, knowing that sooner or later he would leave the flat with his hostages. That would give them their best chance to disable him. If they were there. If Alan had acted.

Suddenly he said:

'My God, this place is bloody pathetic. You can't see it, can you? You think it's all right. No, you think it's better than all right. You think it's really something. You're proud of it, aren't you? Dull, orthodox, ghastly, conventional good taste. Six bloody awful mugs hanging on their little hooks. You don't need any more, do you? Six people are quite enough. No one else can drop in because there isn't a mug for him. And the same in the cupboard. I've had a look. I know. Six of everything. Nothing broken. Nothing chipped. Everything neatly arranged. Six dinner plates, side plates, soup bowls. Christ, I've only got to open this cupboard behind me to know what you're like. Don't you ever want to stop counting the crockery and start living?'

'If by living you mean mess and violence, no I don't. I had enough of that when I was a kid.'

Without moving the gun he reached up his left hand and slipped the catch on the cupboard. Then he took out the dinner plates one by one and placed them on the table. He said:

'They don't look real, do they? They don't look as if they'd break.' He took one of the plates and smashed it down against the side of the table. It cracked neatly into two. Then he took the next. She went quietly on with her cooking and heard as plate after plate was carefully smashed, the two pieces neatly arranged on the table. The pyramid grew. Each crack was like the small report of a gun. She thought: If the police are actually here, if they've got their listening devices on, they'll pick that up, try to identify it. The thought must have occurred to him. He said:

'Lucky for you the fuzz aren't outside. They'd wonder what I'm doing. It would be a shame for the old bitch if they broke in. Plates don't make a mess, but blood and brains, you can't stack those up neatly on the table.'

She said:

'How did you do it? How did you manage to surprise him? I mean you must have burst in on him half-naked, razor in hand.' She had asked the question to propitiate him, flatter him. What she hadn't expected was his reply. It almost burst out of him as if they were lovers and he had been longing to confide. He said:

'But you don't understand! He wanted to die, God rot him, he wanted it! He practically asked for it. He could have tried to stop me, pleaded, argued, put up a fight. He could have begged for mercy. "No, please don't do it. Please!" That's all I wanted from him. Please. Just that one word. The priest could say it, but not Paul Berowne. He looked at me with such contempt. And then he turned his back. I tell you he turned his back on me! When I came in half-naked, his razor in my hand, we stood and looked at each other. He knew then. Of course he knew. And I wouldn't have done it, not if he'd spoken to me as if I were even half-human. I spared the boy. I can be merciful. And that boy is sick. If you get out of here alive, do something about it for Christ's sake. Or don't you bloody care?'

The blue eyes were suddenly luminous. She thought: He's crying. He's actually crying. And he was crying soundlessly, without a twitch of the face. And now her blood ran cold because she knew that anything was possible. She felt no pity, only a detached curiosity. She hardly dared breathe, terrified that his hand would shake, that the gun pressed again against her grandmother's head would go off. She could see the old lady's eyes wide and glazed as if she were already dead, her figure rigid with terror, not daring even to wince at the hurt of the metal hard against the defenceless skull. He took control of himself. With a sound between a sob and a laugh he said:

'Christ, I must have looked daft. Naked, or practically. Just my pants. And the razor. He must have seen the razor. I mean I wasn't hiding it or anything. So why didn't he stop me? He didn't even look surprised. He was supposed to be terrified. He was supposed to prevent it happening. But he knew what I'd come for. He just looked at me as if he were saying "So it's you. How strange that it has to be you." As if I had no choice. Just an instrument. Mindless. But I did have a choice. And so did he. Christ, he could have stopped me. Why didn't he stop me?'

She said:

'I don't know. I don't know why he didn't stop you.' And then she asked: 'You said you spared the boy. What boy? Have you spoken to Darren?'

He didn't reply. He stood staring at her but as if he wasn't seeing her, suddenly remote as if he'd entered a private world. Then he said in a voice so cold, so full of menace, that she could hardly recognize it:

'That message about the Shakespeare: *Love's Labour's Lost*. That was a code, wasn't it?'

He smiled a grim self-satisfied smile and she thought: Oh God he knows and he's glad that he knows. Now he's got the excuse he wants, the excuse to kill us. Her heart began thumping, a leaping animal hurling itself against her chest. But she managed to keep her voice steady:

'Of course not. How could it be? What on earth gave you that idea?'

'Your bookcase. I had a look at it while I was exploring the flat before you came back. Quite a little self-improver, aren't you? All the usual boring stuff people think they ought to have when they are trying to make an impression. Or is the boyfriend trying to educate you? Some job. Anyway, you've got a Shakespeare.'

She said solidly through lips that seemed to have grown dry and huge:

'It wasn't a code. What possible code could it be?'

'I hope for your sake that it wasn't. I'm not going to get myself banged up in this hole with the police outside waiting for an excuse to burst in and kill me. That would be tidy. No awkward questions. I know how they operate. No death penalty any more, so they set up their own execution squads. Well, it isn't going to work with me. So you'd better pray that we get away from here safely before they arrive. Look, you can leave that stuff. We're going now.'

Oh God, she thought, he means it. It would have been better to have done nothing, not to have telephoned Alan, to have got away from the flat as soon as possible, to trust to the hope of crashing the car. And then her heart seemed for a moment literally to stop and she was seized with a dreadful coldness. There was a difference in the room, in the flat. Something had changed. And then she knew what it was. The ceaseless background roar of the traffic along the avenue, faint but continuous, had stopped and nothing was moving down Ladbroke Road. The police were diverting the traffic. Both roads were closed. They weren't risking a shoot out. The siege had begun. And any minute he, too, would realize it.

She thought: I can't bear it. He'll never be able to stand a siege. Neither of us will. He meant what he said. As soon as he realizes the police are outside, as soon as they ring, then he'll shoot us. I've got to get that gun. I've got to get it now.

She said:

'Look, this is ready now. I've cooked it. We may as well eat it. It'll only take a few minutes and it's not as if we can stop on the road.'

There was a silence and then he spoke again in a voice like ice.

'I want to see the Shakespeare. Go and fetch it.'

She forked a strand of spaghetti from the saucepan and tested it with trembling fingers. Without looking round, she said:

'It's about ready. Look, I'm busy. Can't you fetch it? You know where it is.'

'Go and fetch it, unless you want to rid yourself of this old bag.'

'All right.'

It had to be now.

She willed her hands into stillness. With her left fingers she slipped undone the two buttons at the top of her shirt as if the kitchen had suddenly become too hot. The slab of liver lay on the draining board in front of her, bleeding into its wrapping. She plunged her hands into it, tearing at it, squeezing it, smearing her hands until they were thick with blood. It was the work of seconds, no more. Then with an instantaneous gesture she drew her bloody hand fiercely across her throat and swung round, wide-eyed, head thrown back and thrust out at him the blood-clotted hands. Without even waiting for the terror in his eyes, his gasp like a sob, she flung herself at him and they crashed down together. She heard the clatter of the gun as it spun out of his hand and then a thud as it ricocheted against the door.

He had been trained. He was as good at combat as she was and as desperate. And he was strong, far stronger than she had expected. With a sudden convulsive jerk, he was on top of her, mouth to mouth, fierce as a rapist, his harsh breath rasping down her throat. She ground her knee into his groin, heard his yelp of pain, prised his hands from her throat and slid her bloody hands over the floor, feeling for the gun. Then she almost screamed with agony as he jammed his thumbs into her eyes. With their bodies locked, both were reaching desperately for the gun. But she couldn't see. Her eyes were dancing stars of coloured pain, and it was his right hand which found the weapon.

The shot shattered the air like an explosion. Then there was a second explosion and the door of the flat burst open. She had a bizarre sensation of male bodies leaping through the air, then standing arms stretched, guns rigid, their bodies towering over her like dark colossi. Someone was pulling her up. There were shouts, commands, a cry of pain. And then she saw Dalgliesh in the doorway and he was moving towards her, deliberately, gently, like a film in slow motion, speaking her name and, as it seemed, willing her to fix her eyes only on him. But she turned and looked at her grandmother. The sunken eyes were still fixed in that glazed extremity of fear. The hair still hung in its multi-coloured strands. The pad of gauze was still taped to the forehead. But nothing else was there. Nothing. The bottom of her face had been shot away. And strapped to her execution chair by the linen bands which Kate herself had fixed she couldn't even fall. In that second in which she could bear to look it seemed to Kate that the rigid figure fixed on her a glance of sad, reproachful astonishment. Then she was sobbing wildly, burying her head against Dalgliesh's jacket, smearing it with her bloody hands. She could hear him whispering:

'It's all right, Kate. It's all right. It's all right.' But it wasn't. It never had been. It never would be.

He stood there, holding her in his strong clasp among the loud masculine voices, the commands, the sounds of scuffling. And then she pulled away from him, fighting for control and saw over his shoulder Swayne's blue eyes blazing, triumphant. He was handcuffed. An officer she didn't know was dragging him out. But he looked back at her as if she were the only person in the room. Then he jerked his head at her grandmother's body and said:

'Well, you're free of her now. Aren't you going to thank me?'

BOOK SEVEN

Aftermath

Massingham had never been able to understand why it was traditional for police officers to attend the funeral of a murder victim. When the crime was still unsolved there might be some justification for it although he had never himself believed in the theory that a killer was likely to expose himself to the public gaze merely for the satisfaction of watching his victim's corpse go underground or into the fire. He had, too, an unreasonable aversion to cremation – his family had for generations preferred to know where the bones of their forebears lay – and disliked canned religious music, a liturgy denuded of grace and meaning and the hypocrisy of attempting to dignify a simple act of hygienic disposal with a spurious significance.

Mrs Miskin's funeral enabled him to indulge all these prejudices. He was further disgusted when it came to the ritual of examining the wreaths, a pathetically small line of floral contrivances set out along the crematorium wall, to find that a particularly florid example was from the squad. He wondered who had been given the job of buying it and whether the somewhat fulsome message of sympathy was directed at Mrs Miskin who wouldn't see it or Kate who wouldn't want it. But at least the affair had been brief and, by luck, had coincided with the extravagant vulgarity of a pop star's funeral in the neighbouring chapel, so that public and press interest in their more subdued entertainment had been mercifully small.

They were to go back to the Lansdowne Road flat. Waiting for Dalgliesh in the car he only hoped that Kate had provided an adequate amount of refreshment; he badly needed a drink. The experience, too, seemed to have soured his chief's temper. On the drive south into London he was more than usually uncommunicative. Massingham said:

'Did you read that article by Father Barnes in one of the Sunday heavies, sir? Apparently he's claiming that some kind of miracle happened at St Matthew's, that Paul Berowne had stigmata on his wrists after his first night in that vestry.'

Dalgliesh's eyes were fixed on the road ahead.

'I read it.'

'Do you think it's true?'

'Enough people will want it to be to fill the church for the foreseeable future. They should be able to afford a new carpet for the Little Vestry.'

Massingham said:

'I wonder why he did it? Father Barnes, I mean. It won't exactly please Lady Ursula. And Berowne would have hated it, I imagine.'

Dalgliesh said:

'Yes, he'd have hated it. Or perhaps it would have amused him. How can I possibly know? As for why he did it, even a priest, apparently, isn't immune to the temptations of becoming a hero.'

They were driving down the Finchley Road before Massingham spoke again.

'About Darren, sir. Apparently his mum has finally taken off. The council are applying to the Juvenile Court to convert the supervision order into a care order. Poor little sod, he's fallen into the clutches of the Welfare State with a vengeance.'

Dalgliesh said, his eyes still on the road:

'Yes I heard, the Social Service Director found time to ring me. And it's just as well. They think he has leukaemia.'

'That's tough.'

'There's an excellent chance of a cure. They've got it early. They admitted him to Great Ormond Street yesterday.'

Massingham smiled, Dalgliesh glanced at him:

'What's amusing you, John?'

'Nothing, sir. I was thinking about Kate. She'll probably ask me if I seriously suppose that God would kill off Berowne and Harry to get young Darren cured of his leukaemia. It was Swayne, after all, who first pointed out that the kid was sick.'

It had been a mistake, his chief's voice was cold:

'It would argue a certain extravagant use of human resources, wouldn't you say? Watch your speed, John, you're over the limit.'

'Sorry, sir.'

He eased his foot from the accelerator, and drove on in silence.

2

An hour later, balancing a plate of cucumber sandwiches on his knee, Dalgliesh thought that all the funeral teas he had attended had been curiously alike in their mixture of relief, embarrassment and unreality. But this one evoked a stronger and more personal memory. He had been thirteen at the time and had returned with his parents to a Norfolk farmhouse after his father had conducted the funeral service of a local tenant farmer. Then, watching the young widow in new black clothes which she couldn't afford, passing round the home-made sausage rolls and sandwiches, pressing on him the fruit cake which she knew was his favourite, he had felt for the first time an adult and almost overwhelming sense of the sadness at the heart of life and had marvelled at the grace with which the poor and the humble could meet it. He had never thought of humility in connection with Kate Miskin and she had nothing in common with that country widow and her desolate and uncertain future. But when he saw the food brought in, the sandwiches made before she left for the crematorium, then covered with foil to keep them fresh, the fruit cake, he saw that it was almost exactly the same food and it evoked the same surge of pity. It had, he guessed, been difficult for her to decide what should suitably be offered, alcohol or tea. She had decided on tea and she was right; as far as he was concerned it was tea they needed.

It was a small and curiously assorted party; a Pakistani who had been her grandmother's neighbour and his very beautiful wife, both of them more at ease at this funeral than he guessed they might have been at a festivity, sat together in gentle dignity. Alan Scully helped hand round the teacups with a vague self-effacement. Dalgliesh wondered whether he were anxious not to give the impression that he had a right to treat the flat as his own, then decided that this interpretation was over-subtle. Here, surely, was a man supremely unworried about what other people might think. Watching Scully handing round plates with the air of a man unsure what exactly he was holding, or what he was expected to do with it, Dalgliesh recalled that surprising telephone conversation, the persistence with which he had ensured that he spoke only to himself, the clarity of the message, the extraordinary calmness of his voice, and not least, those perceptive last words.

'And there's another thing. There was a pause after I lifted the receiver before she spoke, and then she spoke very fast. I think someone else actually dialled the number and then handed over the receiver. I've given it some thought, and there's only one interpretation which fits all the facts. She's under some kind of duress.'

Watching Scully's gangling six-foot-two body, the mild eyes behind the horn-rimmed spectacles, the lean, rather handsome face, the long strands of fair untidy hair, he thought how unlikely a lover for Kate he seemed, if lover he were. And then he caught Scully's glance at Kate as she was talking to Massingham, speculative, intense, for a moment vulnerable in its open longing, and thought: 'He's in love with her.' And he wondered whether Kate knew, and if she did, how much she cared.

It was Alan Scully who was the first to leave, fading gently away rather than making a definite exit. When the two Khans had also said their goodbyes, Kate carried the tea things into her kitchen. There was a sense of anticlimax, the usual uncomfortable hiatus at the end of a vaguely social occasion. Both men wondered if they should offer to help wash up, or whether Kate wanted them out of the way. And then, suddenly, she said that she would like to go back to the Yard with them and, indeed, there seemed no good reason why she should stay at home.

But Dalgliesh was a little surprised when she followed him into his office and stood in front of the desk as rigid as if she had been summoned for a reprimand. He looked up and saw her face flushed and almost bloated with embarrassment, then she said gruffly:

'Thank you for choosing me for the squad. I've learnt a lot.' The words came out with a harsh ungraciousness which made him realize what it had cost her to say them. He said gently:

'One always does. That's what so often makes it painful.'

She nodded as if it were she dismissing him, then turned and walked stiffly to the door. Suddenly she swung round and cried:

'I shall never know whether I wanted it to happen like that. Her death. Whether I caused it. Whether I meant it. I shall never know. You heard what Swayne called out to me. "Aren't you going to thank me?" He knew. You heard him. How shall I ever be sure?'

He said what it was possible to say:

'Of course you didn't want it to happen. When you think about it calmly and sensibly you know that. You're bound to feel partly responsible. We all do when we lose someone we love. It's a natural guilt, but it isn't rational. You did what you thought was right at the time. We can't any of us do more. You didn't kill your grandmother. Swayne did, his final victim.'

But with murder there never was a final victim. No one touched by Berowne's death would remain unchanged, himself, Massingham, Father Barnes, Darren, even that pathetic spinster, Miss Wharton. Kate knew that perfectly well. Why should she suppose that she was different? The well-worn reassuring phrases sounded false and glib even as he spoke them. And some things were beyond his reassurance. Berowne's foot, hard on the accelerator at that dangerous corner; her bloodstained hands thrust out to the killer. There was action and there was consequence. But she was tough, she would cope. Unlike Berowne, she would learn to accept and carry her personal load of guilt, as he himself had learnt to carry his.

3

Miss Wharton's only experience of a children's hospital was fifty years ago when she had been admitted to her local cottage hospital to have her tonsils out. Great Ormond Street could hardly have been more different from her traumatic memories of that ordeal. It was like walking into a children's party, the ward so full of light, of toys, of mothers and happy activity that it was difficult to believe that this was a hospital until she saw the pale faces and the thin limbs of the children. Then she told herself:

But they're ill, they're all ill, and some of them will die. Nothing can prevent it.

Darren was one of those in bed but sitting up, lively and occupied with a jigsaw on a tray. He said with happy self-importance:

'You can die with what I've got. One of the kids told me.'

Miss Wharton almost cried out her protest.

'Oh Darren, no, no! You aren't going to die!'

'I reckon I won't. But I could. I've gone to foster parents now. Did they tell you?'

'Yes, Darren; that's lovely. I'm so glad for you. Are you happy with them?'

'They're all right. Uncle's going to take me fishing when I get out of here. They're coming in later on. And I got a bicycle – a Chopper.'

Already his eyes were on the door. He had hardly looked at her since she had arrived and when she had walked up to the bed she had glimpsed in his face a curiously adult embarrassment and had suddenly seen herself as he saw her, as all the children must see her, a pathetic, rather silly old woman carrying her gift of an African violet in a small pot. She said:

'I miss you at St Matthew's, Darren.'

'Yeah. Well I reckon I won't have time for that now.'

'Of course not. You'll be with your foster family. I quite understand.'

She wanted to add: But we did have happy times together, didn't we? Then stopped herself. It was too like a humiliating plea for something she knew he couldn't give.

She had brought him the violet because it had seemed more manageable than a bunch of flowers. But he had seemed hardly to look at it and now gazing round the toy-filled ward, she wondered how she could possibly have imagined that it was a suitable gift. He didn't need it, and he didn't need her. She thought: He's ashamed of me. He wants to get rid of me before this new Uncle arrives. He hardly seemed to notice when she said goodbye and slipped away, handing the violet to one of the nurses on her way out.

She took the bus to the Harrow Road and walked to the

church. There was plenty for her to do. Father Barnes, refusing a period of convalescence, had only been back two days but the number of services, and the size of the congregations, had increased since that article in the paper about a miracle and there would be a long line of penitents waiting for confession after this afternoon's Evensong. St Matthew's would never be the same again. She wondered how long there would be a place in it for her.

This was the first time she had gone alone to the church since the murder, but in her misery and loneliness she was hardly aware of apprehension until she tried to fit her key in the lock and found, as she had on that dreadful morning, that she couldn't get it in. The door, as then, was unlocked. She pushed it open, her heart pounding, and called:

'Father, are you there? Father?'

A young woman came out of the Little Vestry. She was an ordinary, respectable, unfrightening girl, wearing a jacket and a blue headscarf. Seeing Miss Wharton's white face, she said:

'I'm sorry. Did I startle you?'

Miss Wharton managed a faint smile:

'It's all right. It's just that I wasn't expecting anyone. Was there anything you wanted? Father Barnes won't be here for another half hour.'

The girl said:

'No, there's nothing. I was a friend of Paul Berowne. It's just that I wanted to visit the Little Vestry, to be alone here. I wanted to see where it happened, where he died. I'm going now. Father Barnes said to return the key to the vicarage but perhaps I could leave it with you as you're here.'

She held it out and Miss Wharton took it. Then she watched as the girl went to the door. When she reached it, she turned and said:

'He was right, Commander Dalgliesh. It's just a room, a perfectly ordinary room. There was nothing there, nothing to see.'

And then she was gone. Miss Wharton, still trembling, locked the outside door, went along the passage to the grille and gazed up through the church to the red glow of the sanctuary lamp.

She thought: and that, too, is only an ordinary lamp made of polished brass with a red glass. You can take it apart, clean it, fill it with ordinary oil. And the consecrated wafers behind the drawn curtain, what are they? Only thin transparent discs of flour and water which come neatly packed in little boxes, ready for Father Barnes to take them in his hands and say the words over them which will change them into God. But they weren't really changed. God wasn't there in that small recess behind the brass lamp. He wasn't any longer in the church. Like Darren, he had gone away. Then she remembered what Father Collins had once said in a sermon when she first came to St Matthew's: 'If you find that you no longer believe, act as if you still do. If you feel that you can't pray, go on saying the words.' She knelt down on the hard floor, supporting herself with her hands grasping the iron grille and said the words with which she always began her private prayers: 'Lord I am not worthy that thou shouldest come under my roof, but speak but the word and my soul shall be healed.'

DEVICES AND DESIRES

CONTENTS

BOOK ONE
Friday 16 September to Tuesday 20 September   677

BOOK TWO
Thursday 22 September to Friday 23 September   741

BOOK THREE
Sunday 25 September   799

BOOK FOUR
Monday 26 September   849

BOOK FIVE
Tuesday 27 September to Thursday 29 September   917

BOOK SIX
Saturday 1 October to Thursday 6 October   995

EPILOGUE
Wednesday 18 January   1077

AUTHOR'S NOTE

This story is set on an imaginary headland on the north-east coast of Norfolk. Lovers of this remote and fascinating part of East Anglia will place it between Cromer and Great Yarmouth but they must not expect to recognize its topography nor to find Larksoken Nuclear Power Station, Lydsett village or Larksoken Mill. Other place names are genuine, but this is merely the novelist's cunning device to add authenticity to fictitious characters and events. In this novel only the past and the future are real; the present, like the people and the setting, exists only in the imagination of the writer and her readers.

I

The Whistler's fourth victim was his youngest, Valerie Mitchell, aged fifteen years, eight months and four days, and she died because she missed the 9.40 bus from Easthaven to Cobb's Marsh. As always she had left it until the last minute to leave the disco and the floor was still a packed, gyrating mass of bodies under the makeshift strobe lights when she broke free of Wayne's clutching hands, shouted instructions to Shirl about their plans for next week above the raucous beat of the music and left the dance floor. Her last glimpse of Wayne was of his serious, bobbing face bizarrely striped with red, yellow and blue under the turning lights. Without waiting to change her shoes, she snatched up her jacket from the cloakroom peg and raced up the road past the darkened shops towards the bus station, her cumbersome shoulder bag flapping against her ribs. But when she turned the corner into the station she saw with horror that the lights on their high poles shone down on a bleached and silent emptiness and dashing to the corner was in time to see the bus already half-way up the hill. There was still a chance if the lights were against it and she began desperately chasing after it, hampered by her fragile, high-heeled shoes. But the lights were green and she watched helplessly, gasping and bent double with a sudden cramp, as it lumbered over the brow of a hill and like a brightly lit ship sank out of sight. 'Oh no!' she screamed after it, 'Oh God! Oh no!' and felt the tears of anger and dismay smarting her eyes.

This was the end. It was her father who laid down the rules in her family and there was never any appeal, any second chance. After protracted discussion and her repeated pleas she had been allowed this weekly visit on Friday evenings to the disco run by the church youth club, provided she caught the 9.40 bus without fail. It put her down at the Crown and Anchor at Cobb's Marsh, only fifty yards from her cottage. From 10.15 her father would begin watching for the bus to pass the front room where he and her mother would sit half watching the television, the curtains drawn back. Whatever the programme or weather, he would then put on his coat and come out to walk the fifty yards to meet her, keeping her always in sight. Since the Norfolk Whistler had begun his killings her father had had an added justification for the mild domestic tyranny which, she half realized, he both thought right in dealing with his only child and rather enjoyed. The concordat had been early established: 'You do right by me, my girl, and I'll do right by you.' She both loved him and slightly feared him and she dreaded his anger. Now there would be one of those awful rows in which she knew she couldn't hope to look to her mother for support. It would be the end of her Friday evenings with Wayne and Shirl and the gang. Already they teased and pitied her because she was treated as a child. Now it would be total humiliation.

Her first desperate thought was to hire a taxi and to chase the bus, but she didn't know where the cab rank was and she hadn't enough money; she was sure of that. She could go back to the disco and see if Wayne and Shirl and the gang between them could lend her enough. But Wayne was always skint and Shirl too mean and by the time she had argued and cajoled it would be too late.

And then came salvation. The lights had changed again to red and a car at the end of a tail of four others was just drawing slowly to a stop. She found herself opposite the open left-hand window and looking directly at two elderly women. She clutched at the lowered glass and said breathlessly: 'Can you give me a lift? Anywhere Cobb's Marsh direction. I've missed the bus. Please.'

The final desperate plea left the driver unmoved. She stared ahead, frowned, then shook her head and let in the clutch. Her companion hesitated, looked at her, then leaned back and released the rear door.

'Get in. Quickly! We're going as far as Holt. We could drop you at the crossroads.'

Valerie scrambled in and the car moved forward. At least they were going in the right direction and it took her only a couple of seconds to think of her plan. From the crossroads outside Holt it would be less than half a mile to the junction with the bus route. She could walk it and pick it up at the stop before the Crown and Anchor. There would be plenty of time; the bus took at least twenty minutes meandering round the villages.

The woman who was driving spoke for the first time. She said: 'You shouldn't be cadging lifts like this. Does your mother know that you're out, what you're doing? Parents seem to have no control over children these days.'

Silly old cow, she thought, what business is it of hers what I do? She wouldn't have stood the cheek from any of the teachers at school. But she bit back the impulse to rudeness, which was her adolescent response to adult criticism. She had to ride with the two old wrinklies. Better keep them sweet. She said: 'I'm supposed to catch the 9.40 bus. My dad'ud kill me if he thought I'd cadged a lift. I wouldn't if you was a man.'

'I hope not. And your father's perfectly right to be strict about it. These are dangerous times for young women, quite apart from the Whistler. Where exactly do you live?'

'At Cobb's Marsh. But I've got an aunt and uncle at Holt. If you put me down at the crossroads he'll be able to give me a lift. They live right close. I'll be safe enough if you drop me there, honest.'

The lie came easily to her and was as easily accepted. Nothing more was said by any of them. She sat looking at the backs of the two grey, cropped heads, watching the driver's age-speckled hands on the wheel. Sisters, she thought, by the look of them. Her first glimpse had shown her the same square heads, the same strong chins, the same curved eyebrows above anxious, angry eyes. They've had a row, she thought. She could sense the tension quivering between them. She was glad when, still without a word, the driver drew up at the crossroads and she was able to scramble out with muttered thanks and watch while they drove out of sight. They were the last human beings, but one, to see her alive.

She crouched to change into the sensible shoes which her parents insisted she wear to school, grateful that the shoulder bag was now lighter, then began trudging away from the town towards the junction where she would wait for the bus. The road was narrow and unlit, bordered on the right by a row of trees, black cut-outs pasted against the star-studded sky and on the left, where she walked, by a narrow fringe of scrub and bushes at times dense and close enough to overshadow the path. Up till now she had felt only an overwhelming relief that all would be well. She would be on that bus. But now, as she walked in an eerie silence, her soft footfalls sounding unnaturally loud, a different, more insidious anxiety took over and she felt the first prickings of fear. Once recognized, its treacherous power acknowledged, the fear took over and grew inexorably into terror.

A car was approaching, at once a symbol of safety and normality and an added threat. Everyone knew that the Whistler must have a car. How else could he kill in such widely spaced parts of the county, how else make his getaway when his dreadful work was done? She stood back into the shelter of the bushes, exchanging one fear for another. There was a surge of sound and the cat's-eyes momentarily gleamed before, in a rush of wind, the car passed. And now she was alone again in the darkness and the silence. But was she? The thought of the Whistler took hold of her mind, rumours, half-truths fusing into a terrible reality. He strangled women, three so far. And then he cut off their hair and stuffed it in their mouths, like straw spilling out of a Guy on 5 November. The boys at school laughed about him, whistling in the bicycle sheds as he was said to whistle over the bodies of his victims. 'The Whistler will get you,' they called after her. He could be anywhere. He always stalked by night. He could be here. She had an impulse to throw herself down and press her body into the soft, rich-smelling earth, to cover her ears and lie there rigid until the dawn. But she managed to control her panic. She had to get to the crossroads and catch the bus. She forced herself to step out of the shadows and begin again her almost silent walk.

She wanted to break into a run but managed to resist. The creature, man or beast, crouching in the undergrowth was already sniffing her fear, waiting until her panic broke. Then she would hear the crash of the breaking bushes, his pounding feet, feel his panting breath hot on her neck. She must keep walking, swiftly but silently, holding her bag tightly against her side, hardly breathing, eyes fixed ahead. And as she walked she prayed: 'Please God, let me get safely home and I'll never lie again. I'll always leave in time. Help me to get to the crossroads safely. Make the bus come quickly. Oh God, please help me.'

And then, miraculously, her prayer was answered. Suddenly, about thirty yards ahead of her, there was a woman. She didn't question how, so mysteriously, this slim, slow-walking figure had materialized. It was sufficient that she was there. As she drew nearer with quickening step she could see the swathe of long, blonde hair under a tight-fitting beret, and what looked like a belted trenchcoat. And at the girl's side, trotting obediently, most reassuring of all, was a small black and white dog, bandy-legged. They could walk together to the crossroads. Perhaps the girl might herself be catching the same bus. She almost cried aloud, 'I'm coming. I'm coming,' and, breaking into a run, rushed towards safety and protection as a child might to her mother's arms.

And now the woman bent down and released the dog. As if in obedience to some command, he slipped into the bushes. The woman took one swift backward glance and then stood quietly waiting, her back half turned to Valerie, the dog's lead held drooping in her right hand. Valerie almost flung herself at the waiting back. And then, slowly, the woman turned. It was a second of total, paralysing horror. She saw the pale, taut face which had never been a woman's face, the simple, inviting, almost apologetic smile, the blazing and merciless eyes. She opened her mouth to scream, but there was no chance and terror had made her dumb. With one movement the noose of the lead was swung over her head and jerked tight and she was pulled from the road into the shadow of the bushes. She felt herself falling through time, through space, through an eternity of horror. And now the face was hot over hers and she could smell drink and sweat and a terror matching her own. Her arms jerked upwards, impotently flailing. And now her brain was bursting and the pain in her chest, growing like a great red flower, exploded in a silent, wordless scream of 'Mummy! Mummy!' And then there was no more terror, no more pain, only the merciful, obliterating dark.

2

Four days later Commander Adam Dalgliesh of New Scotland Yard dictated a final note to his secretary, cleared his in-tray, locked his desk drawer, set the combination of his security cupboard and prepared to leave for a two-week holiday on the Norfolk coast. The break was overdue and he was ready for it. But the holiday wasn't entirely therapeutic; there were affairs in Norfolk that needed his attention. His aunt, his last surviving relative, had died two months earlier leaving him both her fortune and a converted windmill at Larksoken on the north-east coast of Norfolk. The fortune was unexpectedly large and had brought its own, as yet unresolved, dilemmas. The mill was a less onerous bequest but was not without its minor problems. He needed, he felt, to live in it alone for a week or two before finally making up his mind whether to keep it for occasional holidays, sell, or pass it over at a nominal price to the Norfolk Windmill Trust who were, he knew, always anxious to restore old windmills to working order. And then there were family papers and his aunt's books, particularly her comprehensive library of ornithology, to be looked at and sorted and their disposal decided upon. These were pleasurable tasks. Even in boyhood he had disliked taking a holiday totally without purpose. He didn't know from what roots of childhood guilt or imagined responsibility had grown this curious masochism which, in his middle years, had returned with added authority. But he was glad that there was a job to be done in Norfolk, not least because he knew that the journey had an element of flight. After four years of silence, his new book of poetry, *A Case to Answer and Other Poems*, had been published to considerable critical acclaim which was surprisingly gratifying, and to even wider public interest which, less surprisingly, he was finding more difficult to take. After his more notorious murder cases, the efforts of the Metropolitan Police press office had been directed to shielding him from egregious publicity. His publisher's rather different priorities took some getting used to and he was frankly glad of an excuse to escape from them, at least for a couple of weeks.

He had earlier said his goodbye to Inspector Kate Miskin and she was now out on a case. Chief Inspector Massingham had been seconded to the Intermediate Command Course at Bramshill Police College, one more step on his planned progress to a chief constable's braid, and Kate had temporarily taken over his place as Dalgliesh's second in command of the Special Squad. He went into her office to leave a note of his holiday address. It was, as always, impressively tidy, sparsely efficient and yet feminine, its wall enlivened by a single picture, one of her own abstract oils, a study in swirling browns heightened with a single streak of acid green, which Dalgliesh was growing to like more each time he studied it. On the uncluttered desktop was a small glass vase of freesias. Their scent, at first fugitive, suddenly wafted up to him, reinforcing the odd impression he always got that the office was more full of her physical presence empty than it was when she was seated there working. He laid his note exactly in the middle of the clean blotter, and smiled as he closed the door after him with what seemed unnecessary gentleness. It remained only to put his head round the AC's door for a final word and he was on his way to the lift.

The door was already closing when he heard running footsteps, a cheerful shout and Manny Cummings leapt in, just avoiding the bite of the closing steel. As always he seemed to whirl in a vortex of almost oppressive energy, too powerful to be contained by the lift's four walls. He was brandishing a large brown envelope. 'Glad I caught you, Adam. It is Norfolk you're escaping to, isn't it? If the Norfolk CID do lay their hands on the Whistler, take a look at him for me, will you, check he isn't our chap in Battersea.'

'The Battersea Strangler? Is that likely, given the timing and the MO? Surely it isn't a serious possibility?'

'Highly unlikely, but Uncle is never happy unless every stone is explored and every avenue thoroughly upturned. I've put together some details and the Identikit just in case. As you know, we've had a couple of sightings. And I've let Rickards know that you'll be on his patch. Remember Terry Rickards?'

'I remember.'

'Chief Inspector now, apparently. Done all right for himself in Norfolk. Better than he would have done if he'd stayed with us. And they tell me he's married, which might have softened him a bit. Awkward cuss.'

Dalgliesh said: 'I shall be on his patch but not, thank God, on his team. And if they do lay hands on the Whistler, why should I do you out of a day in the country?'

'I hate the country and I particularly loathe flat country. Think of the public money you'll be saving. I'll come down – or is it up? – if he's worth looking at. Decent of you, Adam. Have a good leave.'

Only Cummings would have had the cheek. But the request was not unreasonable made, as it was, to a colleague his senior only by a matter of months and one who had always preached co-operation and the common-sense use of resources. And it was unlikely that his holiday would be interrupted by the need to take even a cursory glance at the Whistler, Norfolk's notorious serial killer, dead or alive. He had been at his work for fifteen months now and the latest victim – Valerie Mitchell wasn't it? – was his fourth. These cases were invariably difficult, time-consuming and frustrating, depending as they often did more on good luck than good detection. As he made his way down the ramp to the underground car park he glanced at his watch. In three-quarters of an hour he would be on his way. But first there was unfulfilled business at his publishers.

3

The lift at Messrs Herne & Illingworth in Bedford Square was almost as ancient as the house itself, a monument both to the firm's obstinate adherence to a bygone elegance and to a slightly eccentric inefficiency behind which a more thrustful policy was taking shape. As he was borne upwards in a series of disconcerting jerks Dalgliesh reflected that success, although admittedly more agreeable than failure, has its concomitant disadvantages. One of them, in the person of Bill Costello, Publicity Director, was waiting for him in the claustrophobic fourth-floor office above.

The change in his own poetic fortunes had coincided with changes in the firm. Herne & Illingworth still existed in so far as their names were printed or embossed on book covers under the firm's ancient and elegant colophon, but the house was now part of a multinational corporation which had recently added books to canned goods, sugar and textiles. Old Sebastian Herne had sold one of London's few remaining individual publishing houses for eight and a half million and had promptly married an extremely pretty publicity assistant who was only waiting for the deal to be concluded before, with some misgivings but a prudent regard for her future, relinquishing the status of newly acquired mistress for that of wife. Herne had died within three months, provoking much ribald comment but few regrets. Throughout his life Sebastian Herne had been a cautious, conventional man who reserved eccentricity, imagination and occasional risk-taking for his publishing. For thirty years he had lived as a faithful, if unimaginative husband and Dalgliesh reflected that if a man lives for nearly seventy years in comparatively blameless conventionality that is probably what his nature requires. Herne had died less of sexual exhaustion, assuming that to be as medically credible as puritans would like to believe, than from a fatal exposure to the contagion of fashionable sexual morality.

The new management promoted their poets vigorously, perhaps seeing the poetry list as a valuable balance to the vulgarity and soft pornography of their best-selling novelists whom they packaged with immense care and some distinction as if the elegance of the jacket and the quality of the print could elevate highly commercial banality into literature. Bill Costello, appointed the previous year as Publicity Director, didn't see why Faber & Faber should have a monopoly when it came to the imaginative publicizing of poetry, and was successful in promoting the poetry list despite the rumour that he never himself read a line of modern verse. His only known interest in verse was his presidency of the McGonagall Club whose members met on the first Tuesday of every month at a City pub to eat the landlady's famous steak and kidney pudding, put down an impressive amount of drink and recite to each other the more risible efforts of arguably Britain's worst poet ever. A fellow poet had once given Dalgliesh his own explanation: 'The poor devil has to read so much incomprehensible modern verse that you can't wonder that he needs an occasional dose of comprehensible nonsense. It's like a faithful husband occasionally taking therapeutic relief at the local cat-house.' Dalgliesh thought the theory ingenious but unlikely. There was no evidence that Costello read any of the verse he so assiduously promoted. He greeted his newest candidate for media fame with a mixture of dogged optimism and slight apprehension, as if knowing that he was faced with a hard nut to crack.

His small, rather wistful and childish face was curiously at odds with his Billy Bunter figure. His main problem was, apparently, whether to wear his belt above or below his paunch. Above was rumoured to indicate optimism, below a sign of depression. Today it was slung only just above the scrotum, proclaiming a pessimism which the subsequent conversation served only to justify.

Eventually Dalgliesh said firmly: 'No, Bill, I shall not parachute into Wembley Stadium holding the book in one hand and a microphone in the other. Nor shall I compete with the station announcer by bawling my verses at the Waterloo commuters. The poor devils are only trying to catch their trains.'

'That's been done. It's old hat. And it's nonsense about Wembley. Can't think how you got hold of that. No, listen, this is really exciting. I've spoken to Colin McKay and he's very enthusiastic. We're hiring a red double-decker bus, touring the country. Well, as much of the country as we can in ten days. I'll get Clare to show you the rough-out and the schedule.'

Dalgliesh said gravely: 'Like a political campaign bus; posters, slogans, loudspeakers, balloons.'

'No point in having it if we don't let people know it's coming.'

'They'll know that all right with Colin on board. How are you going to keep him sober?'

'A fine poet, Adam. He's a great admirer of yours.'

'Which doesn't mean he'd welcome me as a travelling companion. What are you thinking of calling it? Poets' Progress? The Chaucer Touch? Verse on Wheels – or is that too like the WI? The Poetry Bus? That has the merit of simplicity.'

'We'll think of something. I rather like Poets' Progress.'

'Stopping where?'

'Precincts, village halls, schools, pubs, motorway cafés, anywhere where there's an audience. It's an exciting prospect. We were thinking of hiring a train but the bus has more flexibility.'

'And it's cheaper.'

Costello ignored the innuendo. He said: 'Poets upstairs, drinks, refreshments downstairs. Readings from the platform. National publicity, radio and TV. We start from the Embankment. There's a chance of Channel Four and, of course, *Kaleidoscope*. We're counting on you, Adam.'

'No,' said Dalgliesh firmly. 'Not even for the balloons.'

'For God's sake, Adam, you write the stuff. Presumably you want people to read it – well, buy it anyway. There's tremendous public interest in you, particularly after that last case, the Berowne murder.'

'They're interested in a poet who catches murderers, or a policeman who writes poetry, not in the verse.'

'What does it matter as long as they're interested? And don't tell me that the Commissioner wouldn't like it. That's an old cop-out.'

'All right, I won't, but he wouldn't.'

And there was, after all, nothing new to be said. He had heard the questions innumerable times and he had done his best to answer them, with honesty if not with enthusiasm. 'Why does a sensitive poet like you spend his time catching murderers?' 'Which is the more important to you, the poetry or the policing?' 'Does it hinder or help being a detective?' 'Why does a successful detective write poetry?' 'What was your most interesting case, Commander? Do you ever feel like writing a poem about it?' 'The love poems, is the woman you've written them to alive or dead?' Dalgliesh wondered whether Philip Larkin had been badgered about what it felt like to be both poet and librarian, or Roy Fuller on how he managed to combine poetry with law.

He said: 'All the questions are predictable. It would save everyone a great deal of trouble if I answered them on tape, then you could broadcast them from the bus.'

'It wouldn't be at all the same thing. It's you personally they want to hear. Anyone would think you didn't want to be read.'

And did he want to be read? Certainly he wanted some people

to read him, one person in particular, and having read the poems he wanted her to approve. Humiliating but true. As for the others; well, he supposed that the truth was that he wanted people to read the poems but not be coerced into buying them, an over-fastidiousness which he could hardly expect Herne & Illingworth to share. He was aware of Bill's anxious, supplicating eyes, like a small boy who sees the bowl of sweets rapidly disappearing from his reach. His reluctance to co-operate seemed to him typical of much in himself that he disliked. There was a certain illogicality, surely, in wanting to be published but not caring particularly whether he was bought. The fact that he found the more public manifestations of fame distasteful didn't mean that he was free of vanity, only that he was better at controlling it and that in him it took a more reticent form. After all, he had a job, an assured pension and now his aunt's considerable fortune. He didn't have to care. He saw himself as unreasonably privileged compared with Colin McKay who probably saw him – and who could blame Colin? – as a snobbish, oversensitive dilettante.

He was grateful when the door opened and Nora Gurney, the firm's cookery editor, came briskly in, reminding him as she always did of an intelligent insect, an impression reinforced by the bright exophthalmic eyes behind huge round spectacles, familiar fawn jumper in circular ribbing and flat pointed shoes. She had looked exactly the same since Dalgliesh had first known her.

Nora Gurney had become a power in British publishing by the expedience of longevity (no one could remember when she had first come to Herne & Illingworth) and a firm conviction that power was her due. It was likely that she would continue to exercise it under the new dispensation. Dalgliesh had last met her three months previously at one of the firm's periodic parties given for no particular reason so far as he could remember, unless to reassure the authors by the familiarity of the wine and canapés that they were still in business and basically the same lovable old firm. The guest list had chiefly comprised their most prestigious writers in the main categories, a ploy which had added to the general atmosphere of inadvertence and fractionized unease; the poets had drunk too much and had become lachrymose or amorous as their natures dictated, the novelists had herded together in a corner like recalcitrant dogs commanded not to bite, the academics, ignoring their hosts and fellow guests, had argued volubly among themselves and the cooks had ostentatiously rejected their half-bitten canapés on the nearest available hard surface with expressions of disgust, pained surprise or mild, speculative interest. Dalgliesh had been pinned in a corner by Nora Gurney who had wanted to discuss the practicality of the theory she had developed: since every set of fingerprints was unique, could not the whole country be printed, the data stored on a computer and research carried out to discover whether certain combinations of lines and whorls were indicative of criminal tendencies? That way crime could be prevented rather than cured. Dalgliesh had pointed out that, since criminal tendencies were universal, to judge from the places where his fellow guests had parked their cars, the data would be unmanageable, apart from the logistical and ethical problems of mass fingerprinting and the discouraging fact that crime, even supposing the comparison with disease to be valid, was, like disease, easier to diagnose than to cure. It had almost been a relief when a formidable female novelist, vigorously corseted in a florid cretonne two-piece which made her look like a walking sofa, had borne him off to pull out a crumple of parking-tickets from her voluminous handbag and angrily demand what he was proposing to do about them.

The Herne & Illingworth cookery list was small but strong, its best writers having a solid reputation for reliability, originality and good writing. Miss Gurney was passionately committed to her job and her writers, seeing the novels and verse as irritating if necessary adjuncts to the main business of the house which was to nourish and publish her darlings. It was rumoured that she herself was an indifferent cook, one more indication of the firm British conviction, not uncommon in more elevated if less useful spheres of human activity, that there is nothing so fatal to success as knowing your subject. It didn't surprise Dalgliesh that she had seen his arrival as fortuitous and the chore of delivering Alice Mair's proofs as a near-sacred privilege. She said: 'I suppose they've called you in to help catch the Whistler.'

'No, that, I'm thankful to say, is a job for the Norfolk CID. Calling in the Yard happens more often in fiction than real life.'

'It's convenient that you're driving to Norfolk, whatever the reason. I wouldn't really wish to trust these proofs to the post. But I thought your aunt lived in Suffolk? And surely someone said that Miss Dalgliesh had died.'

'She did live in Suffolk until five years ago when she moved to Norfolk. And yes, my aunt has died.'

'Oh well, Suffolk or Norfolk, there's not a lot of difference. But I'm sorry she's dead.' She seemed for a moment to contemplate human mortality and to compare the two counties to the dis- advantage of both, then said: 'If Miss Mair isn't at home you won't leave this at the door, will you? I know that people are extraordinarily trusting in country districts but it would be quite disastrous if these proofs were lost. If Alice isn't at home her brother, Dr Alex Mair, may be. He's the Director of the nuclear power station at Larksoken. But perhaps, on second thoughts, you'd better not hand it to him either. Men can be extremely unreliable.'

Dalgliesh was tempted to point out that one of the country's foremost physicists who was responsible for an atomic power station and, if the papers were to be believed, was strongly tipped for the new post of nuclear power supremo, could presumably be trusted with a parcel of proofs. He said: 'If she's at home, I'll hand it to Miss Mair personally. If she isn't, I'll keep it until she is.'

'I've telephoned to say that it's on its way, so she'll be expecting you. I've printed the address very clearly. Martyr's Cottage. I expect you know how to get there.'

Costello said sourly: 'He can map-read. He's a policeman, re- member.'

Dalgliesh said that he knew Martyr's Cottage and had briefly met Alexander Mair but not his sister. His aunt had lived very quietly but neighbours sharing the same remote district inevitably do get to know each other and, although Alice Mair had been away from home at the time, her brother had made a formal visit of condolence to the mill after Miss Dalgliesh's death.

He took possession of the parcel, which was surprisingly large and heavy and crisscrossed with an intimidating pattern of Sello-tape, and was slowly borne downwards to the basement which gave access to the firm's small car park and his waiting Jaguar.

4

Once free of the knotted tentacles of the eastern suburbs, Dalgliesh made good time and by three he was driving through Lydsett village. Here a right turn took him off the coastal road on to what was little more than a smoothly macadamed track bordered by water-filled ditches and fringed by a golden haze of reeds, their lumbered heads straining in the wind. And now, for the first time, he thought that he could smell the North Sea, that potent but half-illusory tang evoking nostalgic memories of childhood holidays, of solitary adolescent walks as he struggled with his first poems, of his aunt's tall figure at his side, binoculars round her neck, striding towards the haunts of her beloved birds. And here, barring the road, was the familiar old farm gate still in place. Its continued presence always surprised him since it served no pur-pose that he could see except symbolically to cut off the headland and to give travellers pause to consider whether they really wanted to continue. It swung open at his touch but closing it, as always, was more difficult and he lugged and half lifted it into place and slipped the circle of wire over the gatepost with a familiar sensation of having turned his back on the workaday world and entered country which, no matter how frequent his visits, would always be alien territory.

He was driving now across the open headland towards the fringe of pine trees which bordered the North Sea. The only house to his left was the old Victorian rectory, a square, red-brick building, incongruous behind its struggling hedge of rhododen-dron and laurel. To his right the ground rose gently towards the southern cliffs and he could see the dark mouth of a concrete pillbox, undemolished since the war, and as seemingly indestruct-ible as the great hulks of wave-battered concrete, remnants of the old fortifications which lay half-submerged in the sand along part of the beach. To the north the broken arches and stumps of the ruined Benedictine abbey gleamed golden in the afternoon sun against the crinkled blue of the sea and, breasting a small ridge, he glimpsed for the first time the topsail of Larksoken Mill and beyond it, against the skyline, the great grey bulk of Larksoken Nuclear Power Station. The road he was on, veering left, would lead eventually to the station but was, he knew, seldom used since normal traffic and all heavy vehicles used the new access road to the north. The headland was empty and almost bare, the few straggling trees, distorted by the wind, struggled to keep their precarious hold in the uncompromising soil. And now he was passing a second and more dilapidated pillbox and it struck him that the whole headland had the desolate look of an old battlefield, the corpses long since carted away but the air vibrating still with the gunfire of long-lost battles, while the power station loomed over it like a grandiose modern monument to the unknown dead.

On his previous visits to Larksoken he had seen Martyr's Cottage spread out beneath him when he and his aunt had stood surveying the headland from the small top room under the cone of the mill. But he had never been closer to it than the road and now, driving up to it, it struck him again that the description 'cottage' was hardly appropriate. It was a substantial, two-storey, L-shaped house standing to the east of the track with walls partly flint and partly rendered, enclosing at the rear a courtyard of York stone which gave an uninterrupted view over fifty yards of scrub to the grassy dunes and the sea. No one appeared as he drew up and, before lifting his hand to the bell, he paused to read the words of a stone plaque embedded in the flints to the right of the door.

In a cottage on this site lived Agnes Poley, Protestant martyr, burned at Ipswich, 15th August 1557, aged 32 years. Ecclesiastes chapter 3, verse 15.

The plaque was unadorned, the letters deeply carved in an elegant script reminiscent of Eric Gill, and Dalgliesh remembered his aunt telling him that it had been placed there by previous owners in the late twenties, when the cottage was originally extended. One of the advantages of a religious education is the ability to identify at least the better-known texts of scripture and this was one which it needed no effort of memory to recall. As a delinquent nine-year-old at his prep school, he had once been required by the headmaster to write out in his best handwriting the whole of the third chapter of Ecclesiastes, old Gumboil, economical in this as in all matters, believing that writing lines should combine punishment with literary and religious education. The words, in that round childish script, had remained with him. It was, he thought, an interesting choice of text.

> *That which hath been is now; and that which is to be hath already been; and God requireth that which is past.*

He rang and there was only a short delay before Alice Mair opened the door. He saw a tall, handsome woman dressed with careful and expensive informality in a black cashmere sweater with a silk scarf at the throat and fawn trousers. He would have recognized her from her strong resemblance to her brother, although she looked the elder by some years. She took it for granted that each knew who the other was, and standing aside to motion him in she said: 'It's good of you to be so accommodating, Mr Dalgliesh. I'm afraid Nora Gurney is implacable. Once she knew you were on your way to Norfolk you were a predestined victim. Perhaps you would bring the proofs through to the kitchen.'

It was a distinguished face with the deep-set, widely spaced eyes beneath straight brows, a well-shaped, rather secretive mouth and strong greying hair swept upwards and curled into a chignon. In her publicity photographs she could, he recalled, look beautiful in a somewhat intimidating, intellectual and very English mould. But seen face to face, even in the informality of her own house, the absence of a spark of sexuality and, he sensed, a deep-seated reserve, made her seem less feminine and more formidable than he had expected, and she held herself stiffly as if repelling invaders of her personal space. The handshake with which she had greeted him had been cool and firm and her brief smile was surprisingly attractive. He knew that he was oversensitive to the timbre of the human voice and hers, although not jarring or unpleasant, sounded a little forced as if she were deliberately speaking at an unnatural pitch.

He followed her down the hall to the kitchen at the back of the house. It was, he judged, almost twenty feet long and obviously served the triple purpose of sitting room, working place and office. The right-hand half of the room was a well-equipped kitchen with a large gas stove and an Aga, a butcher's chopping block, a dresser to the right of the door holding an assortment of gleaming pots, and a long working surface with a wooden triangle sheathing her assortment of knives. In the centre of the room was a large wooden table holding a stoneware jar of dried flowers. On the left-hand wall was a working fireplace, the two recesses fitted with wall-to-ceiling bookshelves. To each side of the hearth was a high-backed wicker armchair in an intricate closely woven design fitted with patchwork cushions. There was an open roll-top desk facing one of the wide windows and, to its right, a stable door, the top half open, gave a view of the paved courtyard. Dalgliesh could glimpse what was obviously her herb garden planted in elegant terracotta pots carefully disposed to catch the sun. The room, which contained nothing superfluous, nothing pretentious, was both pleasing and extraordinarily comforting and, for a moment, he wondered why. Was it the faint smell of herbs and newly baked dough, the soft ticking of the wall-mounted clock which seemed both to mark the passing seconds and yet to hold time in thrall, the rhythmic moaning of the sea through the half-open door, the sense of well-fed ease conveyed by the two cushioned armchairs, the open hearth? Or was it that the kitchen reminded Dalgliesh of that rectory kitchen where the lonely only child had found warmth and undemanding, uncensorious companionship, been given hot dripping toast and small forbidden treats?

He placed the proofs on the desk, refused Alice Mair's offer of coffee and followed her back to the front door. She walked out with him to the car and said: 'I was sorry about your aunt – sorry for you, I mean. I expect that for an ornithologist death ceases to be terrible once sight and hearing begin to go. And to die in one's sleep without distress to oneself or inconvenience to others is an enviable end. But you had known her for so long that she must have seemed immortal.'

Formal condolences, he thought, were never easy to speak or accept and usually sounded either banal or insincere. Hers had been perceptive. Jane Dalgliesh had indeed seemed to him immortal. The very old, he thought, make our past. Once they go it seems for a moment that neither it nor we have any real existence. He said: 'I don't think death was ever terrible to her. I'm not sure that I really knew her and I'm left wishing I'd tried harder. But I shall miss her.'

Alice Mair said: 'I didn't know her either. Perhaps I should have tried harder too. She was a very private woman, I suspect one of those fortunate people who find no other company more agreeable than their own. It always seems presumptuous to encroach on that self-sufficiency. Perhaps you share it. But if you can tolerate company, I'm having a few people, mostly colleagues of Alex from the power station, to dinner on Thursday night. Would you care to join us? Seven thirty for eight.'

It sounded, he thought, more like a challenge than an invitation. Somewhat to his surprise, Dalgliesh found himself accepting. But then the whole encounter had been a little surprising. She stood regarding him with a serious intensity as he let in the clutch and turned the car and he had the impression that she was watching critically to see how he handled it. But at least, he thought as he gave a final wave, she hadn't asked him whether he had come to Norfolk to help catch the Whistler.

5

Three minutes later he raised his foot from the accelerator. Ahead of him, trudging along on the left of the path, was a little group of children, the eldest girl wheeling a pushchair with two smaller children, one each side of her, clutching the bars. Hearing the noise of the car she turned and he saw a peaked, delicate face framed with red-gold hair. He recognized the Blaney children, met once before with their mother walking along the beach. Obviously the eldest girl had been shopping: the folding pushchair had a shelf under the seat lumped high with plastic bags. Instinctively he slowed down. They were unlikely to be in real danger, the Whistler stalked at night, not in broad daylight, and no vehicle had passed him since he left the coastal road. But the child looked grossly overburdened and ought not to be so far from home. Though he had never seen their cottage he seemed to remember that his aunt had told him that it lay about two miles to the south. He recalled what he knew about them, that their father earned a precarious living as a painter whose innocuous, prettified water-colours were sold in cafés and tourist shops along the coast and that their mother had been desperately ill with cancer. He wondered whether Mrs Blaney was still alive. His instinct was to pile the children into the car and drive them home but that, he knew, was hardly sensible. Almost certainly the eldest child – Theresa, wasn't it? – had been taught not to accept lifts from strangers, particularly men, and he was virtually a stranger. On an impulse he reversed the Jaguar and drove quickly back to Martyr's Cottage. This time the front door was open and a swathe of sunlight lay across the red-tiled floor. Alice Mair had heard the car and came out to him from the kitchen, wiping her hands.

He said: 'The Blaney children are walking home. Theresa is wheeling a pushchair and trying to cope with the twins. I thought I could offer a lift if I had a woman with me, someone they know.'

She said briefly: 'They know me.'

Without another word she went back into the kitchen then came out to him, closed the front door after her without locking it and got into the car. Putting it into gear, his arm brushed her knee. He was aware of an almost imperceptible withdrawing, more emotional than physical, a small delicate gesture of self-containment. Dalgliesh doubted whether that half-imagined recoil had anything to do with him personally, nor did he find her silence disconcerting. Their conversation, when they did speak, was brief. He asked: 'Is Mrs Blaney still alive?'

'No. She died six weeks ago.'

'How are they managing?'

'Not particularly well, I imagine. But Ryan Blaney doesn't welcome interference. I sympathize. Once he lets down his defences half the social workers in Norfolk, amateur and professional, will move in on him.'

When they drew up beside the little band it was Alice Mair who opened the car door and spoke.

'Theresa, here is Mr Dalgliesh to give you all a lift. He's Miss Dalgliesh's nephew from Larksoken Mill. One of the twins had better sit on my lap. The rest of you and the pushchair can fit into the back.'

Theresa looked at Dalgliesh without smiling and said a grave thank you. She reminded him of pictures of the young Elizabeth Tudor, the same red-gold hair framing a curiously adult face both secretive and self-composed, the same sharp nose and wary eyes. The faces of the twins, softer editions of her own, turned towards her questioningly then broke into shy smiles. They looked as if they had been dressed in a hurry and not very suitably for a long walk on the headland, even in a warm autumn. One wore a tattered summer dress in pink spotted cotton with double flounces, the other a pinafore over a checked blouse. Their pathetically thin legs were unprotected. Theresa was wearing jeans and a grubby sweat shirt with a map of London's Underground across the front. Dalgliesh found himself wondering if it had been brought back from a school trip to the capital. It was too large for her and the wide sleeves of limp cotton hung from her freckled arms like rags thrown over a stick. In contrast to his sisters, Anthony was over-clad, a bundle of leggings, jumper and a padded jacket topped with a woollen helmet with a bobble pulled well down over his forehead, beneath which he surveyed their busyness, unsmiling, like a stout imperious Caesar.

Dalgliesh got out of the Jaguar and tried to extricate him from the pushchair, but the anatomy of the chair momentarily defeated him. There was a bar beneath which the child's rigid legs were obstinately stuck. The solid uncooperative bundle was surprisingly heavy; it was like trying to manoeuvre a firm and rather smelly poultice. Theresa gave him a brief, pitying smile, dragged the plastic bags from beneath the seat then expertly freed her brother and settled him on her left hip while, with the other hand, she collapsed the pushchair, with a single vigorous shake. Dalgliesh took the baby from her while Theresa helped the children into the Jaguar and commanded with sudden fierceness, 'Sit still.' Anthony, recognizing incompetence, grasped Dalgliesh's hair firmly with a sticky hand and he felt the momentary touch of a cheek, so soft that it was like the fall of a petal. Throughout these manoeuvrings Alice Mair sat quietly watching from the car but made no move to help. It was impossible to know what she was thinking.

But once the Jaguar had moved away she turned to Theresa and said in a voice of surprising gentleness: 'Does your father know that you're out alone?'

'Daddy has taken the van to Mr Sparks. It's due for its MOT test. Mr Sparks doesn't think it's going to pass. And I found we'd run out of milk for Anthony. We have to have milk. And we wanted some more disposable nappies.'

Alice Mair said: 'I'm giving a dinner party on Thursday evening. If your father agrees, would you like to come and help with the table like you did last month?'

'What are you going to cook, Miss Mair?'

'Put your head close so that I can whisper. Mr Dalgliesh is going to be one of the guests. I want it to be a surprise.'

The pale golden head leaned forward towards the grey and Miss Mair whispered. Theresa smiled and then nodded with serious satisfaction in a moment of grave feminine conspiracy.

It was Alice Mair who directed him to the cottage. After about a mile they turned seaward and the Jaguar lurched and bounced down a narrow track between high, untended hedges of bramble and elderberry. The track led only to Scudder's Cottage, the name crudely painted on a board nailed to the gate. Beyond the cottage it widened to provide a rough, gravelled turning, backed by a forty-foot bank of shingle behind which Dalgliesh could hear the crash and suck of the tide. Scudder's Cottage, small-windowed, picturesque under its tiled, dipping roof, was fronted by a flowering wilderness which had once been a garden. Theresa led the way, between grass almost knee-high bordered by a riot of unpruned roses, to the porch, then reached for a key hung high on a nail, less, Dalgliesh supposed, for security reasons than to ensure that it wasn't lost. With Dalgliesh carrying Anthony they passed into the cottage.

It was much lighter than he had expected, largely because of a rear door, now open, which led to a glass extension giving a view of the headland. He was aware of the room's clutter, the central wooden table still covered with the remains of their midday meal,

an assortment of plates smeared with tomato sauce, a half-eaten
sausage, a large bottle of orangeade uncapped; the children's
clothes thrown over the back of a low nursing chair before the
fireplace, of the smell of milk and bodies and wood smoke. But
what held his attention was a large oil painting propped on a
chair and fronting the door. It was a three-quarter portrait in oils
of a woman, painted with remarkable power. It dominated the
room so that he and Alice Mair stood for a moment, silently
regarding it. The painter had avoided caricature, if only just, but
the portrait was, he felt, intended less as a physical likeness than
an allegory. Behind the wide, full mouth, the arrogant stare of
the eyes, the dark, crimped, Pre-Raphaelite hair streaming in the
wind, was a careful delineation of the headland, its objects
disposed and painted with the meticulous attention to detail of a
sixteenth-century primitive; the Victorian rectory, the ruined
abbey, the half-demolished pillbox, the crippled trees, the small
white mill like a child's toy and, gaunt against a flaming evening
sky, the stark outline of the power station. But it was the woman,
painted more freely, who dominated the landscape, arms
stretched, the palms facing outwards in a parody of blessing.
Dalgliesh's private verdict was that it was technically brilliant,
but overwrought and painted, he felt, in hatred. Blaney's intention to produce a study of evil was as clear as if the portrait had
been labelled. It was so different from the artist's usual work that
without the bold signature, the single surname, Dalgliesh might
have wondered if it was, in fact, his work. He recalled Blaney's
pallid and innocuous watercolours of the better-known beauty
spots of Norfolk: Blakeney, St Peter Mancroft and the cathedral
at Norwich, which he produced for the local shops. They could
have been painted from picture postcards and probably were.
And he could recall seeing one or two small oils hung in local
restaurants and pubs, slap-dash in technique and economical of
paint, but so different from the prettified watercolours that it was
hard to believe that they too were by the same hand. But this
portrait was different from either; the wonder was that the artist
who could produce this disciplined splurge of colour, this technical artistry and imagination, had been content to churn out
meretricious souvenirs for the tourist trade.

'You didn't know I could do it, did you?'

Absorbed in the painting, their ears hadn't caught his almost silent approach through the open door. He moved round and joined them and stared intently at the portrait as if seeing it for the first time. His daughters, as though obedient to some unspoken command, grouped themselves around him in what in older children could have been a conscious gesture of family solidarity. Dalgliesh had last seen Blaney six months earlier splashing alone along the edge of the beach, painting gear slung over his shoulder, and was shocked by the change in the man. He stood a gaunt six foot three in his torn jeans, the checked, woollen shirt open almost to the waist, his long grubby feet in the open sandals looking like dry, brown bones. His face was a picture of red ferocity, the straggling red hair and beard, the bloodshot eyes, the gaunt-featured face burnt red by wind and sun, which yet showed on the cheekbones and under the eyes the bruising stain of tiredness. Dalgliesh saw Theresa slip her hand into his while one of the twins moved closer to him and clasped both arms firmly round one of his legs. Dalgliesh thought that however ferocious he might appear to the outside world his children had no fear of him.

Alice Mair said calmly: 'Good afternoon, Ryan,' but did not appear to expect an answer. She nodded towards the portrait and went on: 'It's remarkable, certainly. What are you proposing to do with it? I can hardly suppose that she sat for you or that it was commissioned.'

'She didn't need to sit. I know that face. I'm showing it at the Norwich Contemporary Arts Exhibition on October the third if I can get it there. The van is out of use.'

Alice Mair said: 'I'll be driving to London within the next week. I could collect it and deliver it if you let me have the address.'

He said: 'If you like.' The response was ungracious but Dalgliesh thought he detected relief. Then he added: 'I'll leave it packed and labelled to the left of the door in the painting shed. The light is just above it. You can collect it whenever it suits you. No need to knock.' The last words had the force of a command, almost of a warning.

Miss Mair said: 'I'll telephone you when I know when I'm going. By the way, I don't think you've met Mr Dalgliesh. He saw the children on the road and thought of giving them a lift.'

Blaney didn't say thank you, but after a moment's hesitation held out his hand which Dalgliesh grasped. Then he said gruffly, 'I liked your aunt. She telephoned offering to help when my wife was ill and when I said there was nothing she or anyone could do, she didn't keep fussing. Some people can't keep away from a deathbed. Like the Whistler, they get their kicks from watching people die.'

'No,' said Dalgliesh, 'she never fussed. I shall miss her. I'm sorry about your wife.'

Blaney didn't reply, but stared hard at Dalgliesh as if assessing the sincerity of that simple statement, and then said curtly, 'Thank you for helping the children,' and lifted his son from Dalgliesh's shoulder. It was a clear gesture of dismissal.

Neither of them spoke as Dalgliesh negotiated the track and finally turned on to the higher road. It was as if the cottage had exerted some spell which it was important to throw off before they talked. Then he asked: 'Who is that woman in the portrait?'

'I hadn't realized that you didn't know. Hilary Robarts. She's Acting Administrative Officer at the power station. Actually you'll meet her at dinner on Thursday night. She bought Scudder's Cottage when she first arrived here three years ago. She's been trying to get the Blaneys out for some time. There's been a certain amount of feeling about it locally.'

Dalgliesh asked: 'Why does she want to gain possession? Does she propose to live there?'

'I don't imagine so. I think she bought it as an investment and wants to sell. Even a remote cottage – particularly a remote cottage – has value on this coast. And she has some justice on her side. Blaney did say that his tenancy would be short-term. I think she feels a certain resentment that he used his wife's illness, her death, and now uses the children as an excuse for reneging on his undertaking to leave when she wanted the cottage back.'

Dalgliesh was interested that Alice Mair apparently knew so much about local affairs. He had thought of her as essentially a private woman who would be very little concerned with her neighbours·or their problems. And what about himself? In his deliberations whether to sell or keep on the mill as a holiday home he had seen it as a refuge from London, eccentric and remote, providing a temporary escape from the demands of his job and the pressures of success. But how far, even as an occasional visitor, could he isolate himself from the community, from their private tragedies no less than their dinner parties? It would be simple enough to avoid their hospitality given sufficient ruthlessness and he had never lacked that when it came to safeguarding his privacy. But the less tangible demands of neighbourliness might be less easily shrugged away. It was in London that you could live anonymously, could create your own ambience, could deliberately fabricate the persona which you chose to present to the world. In the country you lived as a social being and at the valuation of others. So he had lived in childhood and adolescence in the same country rectory, taking part each Sunday in a familiar liturgy which reflected, interpreted, and sanctified the changing seasons of the farming year. It was a world he had relinquished with small regret and he had not expected to find it again on Larksoken headland. But some of its obligations were here, deep-rooted even in this arid and unfertile earth. His aunt had lived as privately as any woman he knew, but even she had visited and tried to help the Blaneys. He thought of the man, bereft and incarcerated in that cluttered cottage behind the great dyke of shingle, listening night after night to the never-ceasing moaning of the tide, and brooding on the wrongs, real or imaginary, which could inspire that hate-filled portrait. It could hardly be healthy for him or for his children. Come to that, he thought grimly, it could hardly be healthy for Hilary Robarts. He asked: 'Does he get much official help with the children? It can't be easy.'

'As much as he's prepared to tolerate. The local authority has arranged for the twins to attend some kind of daycare centre. They get collected most days. And Theresa, of course, is at school. She catches the bus at the end of the lane. She and Ryan between them cope with the baby. Meg Dennison – she housekeeps for the Reverend and Mrs Copley at the Old Rectory – thinks we ought to do more for them but it's difficult to see precisely what. As an ex-schoolmistress I should have thought she'd had her fill of children and I make no pretence at understanding them.' Dalgliesh remembered her whispered confidence to Theresa in the car, the child's intent face and brief transforming smile, and thought that she understood one child at least far better than she would probably claim.

But his thoughts returned to the portrait. He said: 'It must be uncomfortable, particularly in a small community, to be the object of so much malevolence.'

She understood at once what he meant. 'Hatred rather than malevolence, wouldn't you say? Uncomfortable and rather frightening. Not that Hilary Robarts is easily frightened. But she's becoming something of an obsession with Ryan, particularly since his wife's death. He chooses to believe that Hilary practically badgered her into her grave. It's understandable, I suppose. Human beings need to find someone to blame both for their misery and for their guilt. Hilary Robarts makes a convenient scapegoat.'

It was a disagreeable story and coming as it did after the impact of the portrait it provoked in Dalgliesh a mixture of depression and foreboding which he tried to shake off as irrational. He was glad to let the subject drop and they drove in silence until he left her at the gate of Martyr's Cottage. To his surprise she held out her hand and gave him, once again, that extraordinary, attractive smile.

'I'm glad you stopped for the children. I'll see you, then, on Thursday night. You will be able to make your own assessment of Hilary Robarts and compare the portrait with the woman.'

6

As the Jaguar crested the headland Neil Pascoe was dumping rubbish into one of the two dustbins outside the caravan, two plastic bags of empty tins of soup and baby food, soiled disposable napkins, vegetable peelings and squashed cartons, already malodorous despite his careful sealing of the bags. Firmly replacing the lid he marvelled, as he always did, at the difference one girl and an eighteen-month-old baby could make to the volume of household waste. Climbing back into the caravan, he said: 'A Jag has just passed. It looks as if Miss Dalgliesh's nephew is back.'

Amy, fitting a recalcitrant new ribbon to the ancient type-writer, didn't bother to look up.

'The detective. Perhaps he's come to help catch the Whistler.'

'That isn't his job. The Whistler is nothing to do with the Met Police. It's probably just a holiday. Or perhaps he's here to decide what to do with the mill. He can hardly live here and work in London.'

'So why don't you ask him if we can have it? Rent-free, of course. We could caretake, see that no one squats. You're always saying it's antisocial for people to have second homes or leave property empty. Go on, have a word with him. I dare you. Or I will if you're too scared.'

It was, he knew, less a suggestion than a half-serious threat. But for a moment, gladdened by her easy assumption that they were a couple, that she wasn't thinking of leaving him, he actually entertained the idea as a feasible solution to all their problems. Well, almost all. But a glance round the caravan restored him to reality. It was becoming difficult to remember how it had looked fifteen months ago, before Amy and Timmy had entered his life; the home-made shelves of orange boxes ranged against the wall which had held his books, the two mugs, two plates and one soup bowl, which had been adequate for his needs, neatly stacked in the cupboard, the excessive cleanliness of the small kitchen and lavatory, his bed smooth under the coverlet of knitted woollen squares, the single hanging cupboard which had been sufficient for his meagre wardrobe, his other possessions boxed and tidily stowed in the chest under the seat. It wasn't that Amy was dirty; she was continually washing herself, her hair, her few clothes. He spent hours carrying water from the tap outside Cliff Cottage to which they had access. He was continually having to fetch new Calor-gas cylinders from the general store in Lydsett village and steam from the almost constantly boiling kettle made the caravan a damp mist. But she was chronically untidy; her clothes lying where she had dropped them, shoes kicked under the table, knickers and bras stuffed beneath cushions and Timmy's toys littering the floor and table top. The make-up, which seemed to be her sole extravagance, cluttered the single shelf in the cramped shower and he would find half-empty, opened jars and bottles in the food cupboard. He smiled as he pictured Commander Adam Dalgliesh, that no doubt fastidious widower, making his way through the accumulated mess to discuss their suitability as caretakers at Larksoken Mill.

And then there were the animals. She was incurably sentimental about wildlife and they were seldom without some maimed, deserted or starving creatures. Seagulls, their wings covered with oil, were cleansed, caged and then let free. There had been a stray mongrel whom they had named Herbert, with a large uncoordinated body and look of lugubrious disapproval who had attached himself to them for a few weeks and whose voracious appetite for dog-meat and biscuits had had a ruinous effect on the housekeeping. Happily Herbert had eventually trotted off and to Amy's distress had been seen no more, although his lead still hung on the caravan door, a limp reminder of her bereavement. And now there were the two black and white kittens found abandoned on the grass verge of the coast road as they came back in the van from Ipswich. Amy had screamed for him to stop and, scooping up the kittens, had thrown back her head and howled obscenities at the cruelty of human beings. They slept on Amy's bed, drank indiscriminately from any saucer of milk or tea put down for them, were remarkably docile under Timmy's boisterous caresses and, happily, seemed content with the cheapest kind of tinned cat food. But he was glad to have them because they too seemed to offer some assurance that Amy would stay.

He had found her – and he used the word much as he might of finding a particularly beautiful sea-washed stone – one late June afternoon the previous year. She had been sitting on the shingle staring out to sea, her arms clasped round her knees, Timmy lying asleep on the small rug beside her. He was wearing a blue fleecy sleeping suit embroidered with ducks from which his round face seemed to have spilled over, still and pink as a porcelain, painted doll, the delicate lashes brush-tipped on the plump cheeks. And she, too, had something of the precision and contrived charm of a doll with an almost round head poised on a long delicate neck, a snub nose with a splatter of freckles, a small mouth with a full upper lip beautifully curved and a bristle of cropped hair, originally fair but with bright orange tips which caught the sun and trembled in the breeze so that the whole head seemed for a moment to have a vivid life separated from the rest of her body and, the image changing, he had seen her as a bright exotic flower. He could remember every detail of that first meeting. She had been wearing blue faded jeans, and a white sweat shirt flattened against the pointed nipples and the upturned breasts; the cotton seeming too thin a protection against the freshening onshore breeze. As he approached tentatively, wanting to seem friendly but not to alarm her, she had turned on him a long and curious glance from remarkable, slanted, violet-blue eyes.

Standing over her, he had said: 'My name's Neil Pascoe. I live in that caravan on the edge of the cliff. I'm just going to make some tea. I wondered if you'd like a mug.'

'I don't mind, if you're making it.' She had turned away at once and gazed again out to sea.

Five minutes later he had slithered down the sandy cliffs, a mug of tea slopping in each hand. He heard himself say: 'May I sit down?'

'Please yourself. The beach is free.'

So he had lowered himself to sit beside her and together they had stared wordlessly towards the horizon. Looking back on it he was amazed both at his boldness and at the seeming inevitability and naturalness of that first encounter. It was several minutes before he had found the courage to ask her how she had got to the beach. She had shrugged.

'By bus to the village and then I walked.'

'It was a long way carrying the baby.'

'I'm used to walking a long way carrying the baby.'

And then, under his hesitant questioning, the story had come out, told by her without self-pity, almost, it had seemed, without particular interest, as if the events had happened to someone else. It was not, he supposed, an unusual tale. She was living in one of the small private hotels in Cromer on Social Security. She had been in a squat in London but had thought it would be pleasant to have some sea air for the baby for the summer. Only it wasn't working out. The woman at the hotel didn't really want kids and with summer holidays approaching could get a better rate for her rooms. She didn't think she could be turned out, but she wasn't going to stay, not with that bitch.

He asked: 'Couldn't the baby's father help?'

'He hasn't got a father. He did have a father – I mean, he isn't Jesus Christ. But he hasn't got one now.'

'Do you mean that he's dead or that he's gone away?'

'Could be either, couldn't it? Look, if I knew who he was I might know where he was, OK?'

Then there had been another silence during which she took periodical gulps of her tea and the sleeping baby stirred and gave small pig-like grunts. After a few minutes he had spoken again.

'Look, if you can't find anywhere else in Cromer you can share the caravan for a time.' He had added hastily: 'I mean, there is a second bedroom. It's very small, only just room for the bunk, but it would do for a time. I know it's isolated here but it's close to the beach which would be nice for the baby.'

She had turned on him again that remarkable glance in which for the first time he had detected to his discomfiture a brief flash of intelligence and of calculation.

'All right,' she said. 'If I can't find anywhere else I'll come back tomorrow.'

And he had lain awake late that night half hoping, half dreading that she would return. And she had returned the following afternoon, carrying Timmy on her hip and the rest of her possessions in a backpack. She had taken over the caravan and his life. He didn't know whether what he felt for her was love, affection or pity, or a mixture of all three. He only knew that in his anxious and over-concerned life his second greatest fear was that she might leave.

He had lived in the caravan now for just over two years, supported by a research grant from his northern university to study the effect of the Industrial Revolution on the rural industries of East Anglia. His dissertation was nearly finished but for the last six months he had almost stopped work on it and had devoted himself entirely to his passion, a crusade against nuclear power. From the caravan on the very edge of the sea he could see Larksoken Power Station stark against the skyline, as uncompromising as his own will to oppose it, a symbol and a threat. It was from the caravan that he ran People Against Nuclear Power, with its acronym PANUP, the small organization of which he was both founder and president. The caravan had been a stroke of luck. The owner of Cliff Cottage was a Canadian who, returning to his roots and seduced by nostalgia, had bought it on impulse as a possible holiday home. About fifty years earlier there had been a murder at Cliff Cottage. It had been a fairly commonplace murder, a henpecked husband at the end of his tether who had taken a hatchet to his virago of a wife. But if it had been neither particularly interesting nor mysterious, it had certainly been bloody. After the cottage had been bought the Canadian's wife had heard graphic accounts of spilt brains and blood-spattered walls and had declared that she had no intention of living there in summer or at any other time. Its very isolation, once attractive, now appeared both sinister and repellent. And to compound the problem, the local planning authority had shown themselves unsympathetic to the owner's over-ambitious plans for rebuilding. Disillusioned with the cottage and its problems, he had boarded up the windows and returned to Toronto, meaning eventually to come back and make a final decision about his ill-advised purchase. The previous owner had parked a large, old-fashioned caravan at the back and the Canadian had made no difficulty about letting this to Neil for two pounds a week, seeing it as a useful way of having someone to keep an eye on the property. And it was the caravan, at once his home and his office, from which Neil conducted his campaign. He tried not to think about the time, six months ahead, when his grant would finish and he would need to find work. He knew that he had somehow to stay here on the headland, to keep always in view that monstrous building which dominated his imagination as it did his view.

But now, to the uncertainty about his future funding, was added a new and more terrifying threat. About five months earlier he had attended an open day at the power station during which the Acting Administrative Officer, Hilary Robarts, had

given a short preliminary talk. He had challenged almost everything she had said and what was meant as an informative
introduction to a public relations exercise had developed into
something close to a public brawl. In the next issue of his news-
sheet he had reported on the incident in terms which he now
realized had been unwise. She had sued him for libel. The action
was due to be heard in four weeks' time and he knew that,
successful or not, he was faced with ruin. Unless she died in the
next few weeks – and why should she die? – it could be the end of
his life on the headland, the end of his organization, the end of all
he had planned and hoped to do.

Amy was typing envelopes, sending out the final copies of the
newsletter. A pile was already to hand and he began folding the
pamphlets and inserting them into the envelopes. The job wasn't
easy. He had tried to economize with the size and quality and the
envelopes were in danger of splitting. He now had a mailing list
of 250, only a small minority of whom were active supporters of
PANUP. Most never paid any dues towards the organization and
the majority of the pamphlets went unsolicited to public authorities, local firms and industry in the vicinity of Larksoken and
Sizewell. He wondered how many of the 250 were read and
thought, with a sudden spasm of anxiety and depression, of the
total cost of even this small enterprise. And this month's newsletter
wasn't his best. Rereading one before he put it in the envelope, it
seemed to him to be ill-organized, to have no coherent theme.
The principal aim now was to refute the growing argument that
nuclear power could avoid the damage to the environment
through the greenhouse effect, but the mixture of suggestions
ranging from solar power to replacing light bulbs with those
which consumed seventy-five per cent less energy seemed naïve
and hardly convincing. His article argued that nuclear-generated
electricity couldn't realistically replace oil and fossil fuels unless
all nations built sixteen new reactors a week in the five years from
1995, a programme impossible to achieve and one which, if
practicable, would add intolerably to the nuclear threat. But the
statistics, like all his figures, were culled from a variety of sources
and lacked authority. Nothing he produced seemed to him genuinely his own work. And the rest of the newsletter was a jumble of

the usual scare stories, most of which he had used before; allegations of safety breaches which had been covered up, doubts about
the safety of the ageing Magnox stations, the unsolved problem of
storing and transporting nuclear waste. And this issue he had
been hard put to it to find a couple of intelligent letters for the
correspondence page; sometimes it seemed that every crackbrain
in north-east Norfolk read the PANUP newsletter but that no
one else did.

Amy was picking at the letters of the typewriter which had a
persistent tendency to stick. She said: 'Neil, this is a bloody awful
machine. It would be quicker to write the addresses by hand.'

'It's better since you cleaned it and the new ribbon looks fine.'

'It's still diabolical. Why don't you buy a new one? It would
save time in the end.'

'I can't afford it.'

'You can't afford a new typewriter and you think you're going
to save the world.'

'You don't need possessions to save the world, Amy. Jesus
Christ had nothing; no home, no money, no property.'

'I thought you said when I came here that you weren't
religious.'

It always surprised him that, apparently taking no account of
him, she could yet recall comments he had made months earlier.
He said: 'I don't believe Christ was God. I don't believe there is a
God. But I believe in what He taught.'

'If He wasn't a God, I don't see that it matters much what He
taught. Anyway, all I can remember is something about turning
the other cheek which I don't believe in. I mean, that's daft. If
someone slaps your left cheek then you slap his right, only
harder. Anyway, I do know they hung Him up on the cross so it
didn't do Him a lot of good. That's what turning the other cheek
does for you.'

He said: 'I've got a Bible here somewhere. You could read
about Him if you wanted to. Make a start with St Mark's
Gospel.'

'No thanks. I had enough of that in the home.'

'What home?'

'Just a home, before the baby was born.'

'How long were you there?'

'Two weeks. Two weeks too bloody many. Then I ran away and found a squat.'

'Where was that, the squat?'

'Islington, Camden, King's Cross, Stoke Newington. Does it matter? I'm here now, OK?'

'It's OK by me, Amy.'

Lost in his thoughts, he hardly realized that he had given up folding the pamphlets.

Amy said: 'Look, if you're not going to help with these envelopes you might as well go and put a new washer on that tap. It's been dripping for weeks and Timmy's always falling about in the mud.'

'All right,' he said, 'I'll do it now.'

He took down his tool kit from the high cupboard where it was kept well out of Timmy's reach. He was glad to be out of the caravan. It had become increasingly claustrophobic in the last few weeks. Outside he bent to talk to Timmy, caged in his playpen. He and Amy had collected large stones from the beach, looking for those with holes in them – and he had strung them on to strong cord and tied them along one side of the playpen. Timmy would spend hours happily banging them together or against the bars or, as now, slobbering against one of the stones in an attempt to get it into his mouth. Sometimes he would communicate with individual flints, a continuous admonitory prattle broken by sudden triumphant squeals. Kneeling down Neil clutched the bars, rubbed his nose against Timmy's, and was rewarded by his huge, heart-tugging smile. He looked very like his mother with the same round head on a delicate neck, the same beautifully shaped mouth. Only his eyes, widely spaced, were differently shaped, large blue spheres with, above them, straight bushy eyebrows which reminded Neil of pale and delicate caterpillars. The tenderness he felt for the child was equal to, if different from, the tenderness he felt for his mother. He could not now imagine life on the headland without either of them.

But the tap defeated him. Despite his tuggings with the wrench he couldn't get the screw to shift. Even this minor domestic task was apparently beyond his powers. He could hear Amy's derisive voice. 'You want to change the world and you can't change a washer.' After a couple of minutes he gave up the attempt, left the tool box by the cottage wall and walked to the edge of the cliff then slithered down to the beach. Crunching over the ridges of stones, he went down to the edge of the sea and almost violently wrenched off his shoes. It was thus, when the weight of anxiety about his failed ambitions, his uncertain future, became too heavy that he would find his peace, standing motionless to watch the veined curve of the poised wave, the tumult of crashing foam breaking over his feet, the wide intersecting arches washing over the smooth sand as the wave retreated to leave its tenuous lip of foam. But today even this wonder, continually repeated, failed to comfort his spirit. He gazed out to the horizon with unseeing eyes and thought about his present life, the hopelessness of the future, about Amy, about his family. Thrusting his hand in his pocket, he felt the crumpled envelope of his mother's last letter.

He knew that his parents were disappointed in him, although they never said so openly since oblique hints were just as effective: 'Mrs Reilly keeps on asking me, what is Neil doing? I don't like to say that you're living in a caravan with no proper job.' She certainly didn't like to say that he was living there with a girl. He had written to tell them about Amy since his parents constantly threatened to visit and, unlikely as this was actually to happen, the prospect had added an intolerable anxiety to his already anxiety-ridden life.

'I'm giving a temporary home to an unmarried mother in return for typing help. Don't worry, I shan't suddenly present you with a bastard grandchild.'

After the letter had been posted he had felt ashamed. The cheap attempt at humour had been too like a treacherous repudiation of Timmy whom he loved. And his mother hadn't found it either funny or reassuring. His letter had produced an almost incoherent farrago of warnings, pained reproaches and veiled references to the possible reaction of Mrs Reilly if she ever got to know. Only his two brothers surreptitiously welcomed his way of life. They hadn't made university and the difference between their comfortable life style – houses on an executive estate, en suite bathrooms, artificial coal fires in what they called the lounge, working wives, a new car every two years and timeshares in Majorca – provided both with agreeable hours of self-satisfied comparisons which he knew would always end with the same conclusion, that he ought to pull himself together, that it wasn't right, not after all the sacrifices Mum and Dad had made to send him to college and a fine waste of money that had proved.

He had told Amy none of this but would have happily confided had she shown the least interest. But she asked no questions about his past life and told him nothing about hers. Her voice, her body, her smell were as familiar to him as his own, but essentially he knew no more about her now than when she had arrived. She refused to collect any welfare benefits, saying that she wasn't going to have DHSS snoopers visiting the caravan to see if she and Neil were sleeping together. He sympathized. He didn't want them either, but he felt that for Timmy's sake she should take what was on offer. He had given her no money but he did feed both of them, and this was difficult enough on his grant. No one visited her and no one telephoned. Occasionally she would receive a postcard, coloured views usually of London with nondescript, meaningless messages, but as far as he knew she never replied.

They had so little in common. She helped spasmodically with PANUP but he was never sure how far she was actually committed. And he knew that she found his pacifism stupid. He could recall a conversation only this morning.

'Look, if I live next door to an enemy and he has a knife, a gun and a machine gun and I've got the same, I'm not going to chuck mine before he chucks his. I'll say, OK, let the knife go, then the gun maybe, then the machine gun. Him and me at the same time. Why should I throw mine away and leave him with his?'

'But one of you has to make a start, Amy. There has to be a beginning of trust. Whether it's people or nations, we have to find the faith to open our hearts and hands and say, "Look, I've nothing. I've only my humanity. We inhabit the same planet. The world is full of pain but we needn't add to it. There has to be an end of fear."'

She had said obstinately: 'I don't see why he should chuck his weapons once he knows I've got nothing.'

'Why should he keep them? He's got nothing to fear from you any more.'

'He'd keep them because he liked the feeling of having them and because he might like to use them some day. He'd like the power and he'd like knowing he had me where he wanted me. Honestly, Neil, you're so naïve sometimes. That's how people are.'

'But we can't argue like that any more, Amy. We aren't talking about knives and guns and machine guns. We're talking about weapons neither of us could use without destroying ourselves and probably our whole planet. But it's good of you to help with PANUP when you don't sympathize.'

She had said: 'PANUP's different. And I sympathize all right. I just think that you're wasting your time writing letters, making speeches, sending out all those pamphlets. It won't do any good. You've got to fight people their way.'

'But it's done good already. All over the world ordinary people are marching, demonstrating, making their voices heard, letting the people in power know that what they want is a peaceful world for themselves and their children. Ordinary people like you.'

And then she had almost shouted at him: 'I'm not ordinary! Don't you call me ordinary! If there are ordinary people, I'm not one of them.'

'I'm sorry, Amy. I didn't mean it like that.'

'Then don't say it.'

The only cause they had in common was a refusal to eat meat. Soon after she arrived at the caravan he had said: 'I'm vegetarian but I don't expect you to be, or Timmy.' He had wondered as he spoke whether Timmy was old enough to eat meat. He had added: 'You can buy a chop occasionally in Norwich if you feel like it.'

'What you have is all right by me. Animals don't eat me, and I don't eat them.'

'And Timmy?'

'Timmy has what I give him. He's not fussy.'

714

Nor was he. Neil couldn't imagine a more accommodating child nor, for most of the time, a more contented one. He had found the second-hand playpen advertised on a newsagent's board in Norwich and had brought it back on the top of the van. In it Timmy would crawl for hours or pull himself up and stand precariously balancing, his napkin invariably falling about his knees. When thwarted he would rage, shutting his eyes tight, opening his mouth and holding his breath before letting out a bellow of such terrifying power that Neil half expected the whole of Lydsett to come running to see which of them was tormenting the child. Amy never smacked him but would jerk him on to her hip and dump him on her bed saying: 'Bloody awful noise.'

'Shouldn't you stay with him? Holding his breath like that, he could kill himself.'

'You daft? He won't kill himself. They never do.'

And he knew now that he wanted her, wanted her when it was obvious that she didn't want him and would never again risk rejection. On the second night at the caravan she had slid back the partition between his bed and hers and had walked quietly up to his bed and had stood gravely looking down at him. She had been completely naked. He had said: 'Look, Amy, you don't have to pay me.'

'I never pay for anything, at least not like that. But have it your own way.' After a pause she had said: 'You gay or something?'

'No, it's just that I don't like casual affairs.'

'You mean you don't like them, or you don't think you ought to have them?'

'I suppose I mean that I don't think I ought to have them.'

'You religious, then?'

'No, I'm not religious, not in the ordinary way. It's just that I think sex is too important to be casual about. You see, if we slept together and I − if I disappointed you − we might quarrel and then you'd walk out. You'd feel that you had to. You'd leave, you and Timmy.'

'So what, I walk out.'

'I wouldn't want you to do that, not because of anything I'd done.'

715

'Or hadn't done. OK, I expect you're right.' Another pause, and then she had added: 'You'd mind then, if I walked out?'

'Yes,' he said, 'I'd mind.'

She had turned away. 'I always do walk out in the end. No one has ever minded before.'

It was the only sexual advance she had ever made to him and he knew it would be the last. Now they slept with Timmy's co. wedged between the partition and his bed. Sometimes in the night, wakeful because the child had stirred, he would put out his hands and clasp the bars and long to shake this frail barrier that symbolized the unbridgeable gulf between them. She lay there, sleek and curved as a fish or a gull, so close that he could hear the rise and fall of her breath faintly echoing the suspiration of the sea. His body ached for her and he would press his face into the lumpy pillow groaning with the hopelessness of his need. What could she possibly see in him to make her want him, except, as on that one night, out of gratitude, pity, curiosity or boredom? He hated his body, the scrawny legs on which the kneecaps protruded like deformities, the small blinking eyes too closely set, the sparse beard which couldn't disguise the weakness of the mouth and chin. Sometimes, too, he was tormented by jealousy. Without proof, he had convinced himself that there was someone else. She would say that she wanted to walk alone on the headland. And he would watch her go with the certainty that she was meeting a lover. And when she returned he would imagine that he could see the glow of the skin, the satisfied smile of remembered happiness, could almost smell that she had been making love.

He had already heard from the university that his research grant would not be extended. The decision wasn't surprising; he had been warned to expect it. He had been saving as much as possible from the grant in the hope of amassing a small sum which would tide him over until he could find a local job. It hardly mattered what. Anything that would pay enough to live and allow him to remain on the headland to carry on the campaign. In theory he supposed he could organize PANUP from anywhere in the UK, but he knew that it was irrevocably bound to Larksoken headland, to the caravan, to that concrete mass five miles to the north which had power, apparently, to dominate his will as it did his imagination. He had already put out feelers with local employers but they hadn't been too keen on employing a well-known agitator; even those who seemed sympathetic to the anti-nuclear cause didn't actually have work on offer. Perhaps they feared that too many of his energies would be diverted to the campaign. And his small capital was draining away with the extra expense of Amy, Timmy and even the cats. And now there was the threat of this libel action, less of a threat than a certainty.

When, ten minutes later, he returned to the caravan Amy, too, had given up working. She was lying on her bed, looking up at the ceiling, Smudge and Whisky curled on her stomach.

Looking down at her, he said abruptly: 'If the Robarts legal action goes ahead I'll need money. We're not going to be able to go on as we are. We've got to make plans.'

She sat up smartly and stared at him. The kittens, affronted, squealed their protest and fled. 'You mean we might have to leave here?'

The 'we' would normally have lifted his heart, now he hardly noticed it. 'It's possible.'

'But why? I mean, you aren't going to find anything cheaper than the caravan. Try getting a single room for two pounds a week. We're bloody lucky to have this place.'

'But there's no work here, Amy. If I have huge damages to pay, I'll have to get a job. That means London.'

'What sort of a job?'

'Any sort. I've got my degree.'

'Well, I can't see the sense of leaving here, even if there isn't any work. You can go to the DHSS. Draw the dole.'

'That isn't going to pay damages.'

'Well, if you have to go, maybe I'll stay on. I can pay the rent here. After all, what's the difference to the owner? He'll get his two quid whoever pays it.'

'You couldn't live here alone.'

'Why not? I've lived in worse places.'

'On what? What would you do for money?'

'Well, with you gone I could go to the DHSS, couldn't I? They could send their snoopers round and it wouldn't matter. They wouldn't be able to say I was having sex with you then, not if you weren't here. Anyway, I've got a bit in my post office account.'

The casual cruelty of the suggestion struck at his heart. He heard with heavy disgust the note of self-pity which he was unable to suppress. He said: 'Is that what you really want, Amy, for me not to be here?'

'Don't be daft, I was only teasing. Honestly Neil, you should see yourself. Talk about misery. Anyway, it might not happen – the libel action, I mean.'

'It's bound to happen unless she withdraws it. They've set a date for the hearing.'

'She might withdraw it, or else she might die. She might drown on one of those night swims she takes after the headlines on the nine o'clock news, regular as clockwork, right up to December.'

'Who told you that? How do you know that she swims at night?'

'You did.'

'I can't remember telling you.'

'Then someone else did, one of the regulars in the Local Hero, maybe. I mean, it's no secret, is it?'

He said: 'She won't drown. She's a strong swimmer. She wouldn't take foolish risks. And I can't wish her dead. You can't preach love and practise hatred.'

'I can – wish her dead, I mean. Maybe the Whistler will get her. Or you might win the action and then she'll have to pay you. That'd be a laugh.'

'That's not very likely. I consulted a lawyer at the Citizens Advice Bureau when I was in Norwich last Friday. I could see he thought it was serious, that she did have a case. He said I ought to get myself a lawyer.'

'Well, get one.'

'How? Lawyers cost money.'

'Get legal aid. Put a note in the newsletter asking for contributions.'

'I can't do that. It's difficult enough keeping the newsletter going, what with the cost of paper and postage.'

Amy said, suddenly serious: 'I'll think of something. There's still four weeks to go. Anything can happen in four weeks. Stop worrying. It's going to be all right. Look, Neil, I promise you that libel action will never come to court.' And illogically, he was, for the moment, reassured and comforted.

7

It was six o'clock and at Larksoken Power Station, the weekly interdepartmental meeting was drawing to a close. It had lasted thirty minutes longer than usual; Dr Alex Mair took the view, which he could normally enforce by brisk chairmanship, that little original thought was contributed to a discussion after three hours of talking. But it had been a heavy agenda: the revised safety plan still in draft; the rationalization of the internal structure from the present seven departments to three under engineering, production and resources; the report of the district survey laboratory on their monitoring of the environment; the preliminary agenda for the local liaison committee. This annual jamboree was an unwieldy but useful public relations exercise which needed careful preparation, including as it did representatives from the interested government departments, local authorities, police, fire and water authorities, the National Farmers Union and the Country Landowners' Association. Mair sometimes grudged the work and time it involved but he knew its importance.

The weekly meeting was held in his office at the conference table set in front of the south window. Darkness was falling and the huge pane of glass was a black rectangle in which he could see their faces reflected, like the gaunt, disembodied heads of night travellers in a lighted railway carriage. He suspected that some of his departmental heads, particularly Bill Morgan, the Works Office Engineer, and Stephen Mansell, the Maintenance Superintendent, would have preferred a more relaxed setting in his private sitting room next door, the low, comfortable chairs, a few hours of chat with no set agenda, perhaps a drink together afterwards in a local pub. Well, that was one management style, but it wasn't his.

Now he closed the stiff cover of his folder in which his PA had meticulously tagged all the papers and cross-references, and said dismissively: 'Any other business.'

But he was not allowed to get away so easily. On his right, as usual, sat Miles Lessingham, the Operations Superintendent, whose reflection, staring back into the room, looked like a hydrocephalic death's head. Glancing from the image to the face, Mair could see little difference. The stark overhead lights threw deep shadows under the deep-set eyes and the sweat glistened on the wide, rather knobbly forehead with its swathe of fair undisciplined hair. Now he stretched back in his chair and said: 'This proposed job – rumoured job, I should say – I suppose we're entitled to ask whether it has been formally offered to you yet? Or aren't we?'

Mair said calmly: 'The answer is that it hasn't; the publicity was premature. The press got hold of it somehow, as they usually do, but there's nothing official yet. One unfortunate result of our present habit of leaking any information of interest is that the people most concerned become the last to know. If and when it is official you seven will be the first to be told.'

Lessingham said: 'It will have serious implications here, Alex, if you do go. The contract already signed for the new PWR reactor, the internal reorganization which is bound to create disruption, electricity privatization. It's a bad time for a change at the top.'

Mair said: 'Is there ever a good time? But until it happens, if it does happen, there's little point in discussing it.'

John Standing, the station chemist, said: 'But the internal reorganization will go ahead presumably?'

'I hope so, considering the time and energy we've spent planning it. I should be surprised if a change at the top alters a necessary reorganization which is already under way.'

Lessingham asked: 'Who will they appoint, a director or a station manager?' The question was less innocent than it sounded.

'I imagine a station manager.'

'You mean that the research will go?'

Mair said: 'When I go, now or later, the research will go. You've always known that. I brought it with me and I wouldn't have taken the job if I couldn't have continued it here. I asked for certain research facilities and I got them. But research at Larksoken has always been somewhat of an anomaly. We've done good work, are still doing good work, but logically it should be done elsewhere, at Harwell or Winfrith. Is there any other business?'

But Lessingham was not to be discouraged. He said: 'Who will you be responsible to? The Secretary of State for Energy directly or the AEA?'

Mair knew the answer but had no intention of giving it. He said quietly: 'That is still under discussion.'

'Along, no doubt, with such minor matters as pay, rations, scope of your responsibilities and what you are going to be called. Controller of Nuclear Power has a certain cachet. I like it. But what precisely will you control?'

There was a silence. Mair said: 'If the answer to that question were known, no doubt the appointment would have been made by now. I don't want to stifle discussion, but hadn't we better confine it to matters within the competence of this committee? Right, is there any other business?' and this time there was no reply.

Hilary Robarts, the Acting Administrative Officer, had already closed her file. She hadn't taken part in the questioning but the others, Mair knew, would assume that that was because he had already told her the answers.

Even before they had left, his PA, Caroline Amphlett, had come in to take away the tea cups and clear the table. Lessingham made it a habit to leave his agenda behind, a small personal protest against the amount of paper which the formal weekly meeting generated. Dr Martin Goss, head of the medical physics department, had, as always, doodled obsessively. His jotting pad was covered with hot-air balloons, intricately patterned and decorated; part of his mind had obviously been with his private passion. Caroline Amphlett moved, as always, with a quiet, efficient grace. Neither spoke. She had worked for Mair as his PA for the last three years and he knew her now no better than on that morning when she had sat in this same office being interviewed for the job. She was a tall, blonde girl, smooth-skinned with wide-spaced, rather small eyes of an extraordinary deep blue, who would have been thought beautiful if she had shown more animation. Mair suspected that she used her confidential job as his PA to preserve a deliberately intimidating reserve. She was the most efficient secretary he had ever had and it irked him that she had made it clear that, if and when he moved, she would wish to stay at Larksoken. She had told him that her reasons were personal. That, of course, meant Jonathan Reeves, a junior engineer in the workshop. He had been as surprised and chagrined at her choice as he had at the prospect of taking up a new job with an unknown PA, but there had been an additional and more disturbing reaction. Hers was not a type of female beauty which attracted him and he had always assumed that she was physically cold. It was disconcerting to think that an acned nonentity had discovered and perhaps explored depths which he, in their daily intimacy, hadn't even suspected. He had sometimes wondered, although with little real curiosity, whether she might not be less compliant, more complicated than he had supposed, had occasionally had a disconcerting sense that the façade she presented to the power station of dedicated, humourless efficiency had been carefully constructed to conceal a less accommodating, more complex personality. But if the real Caroline was accessible to Jonathan Reeves, if she really liked and wanted that unprepossessing wimp, then she hardly merited the tribute even of his curiosity.

8

He gave his departmental heads time to get back to their offices before he rang for Hilary Robarts and asked her to come back. It would have been more usual to have asked her with careful casualness to wait behind after the meeting but what he had to say was private and he had been trying for some weeks now to cut down the number of times when they were known to be alone together. He wasn't looking forward to the interview. She would see what he had to say as personal criticism and that was something which in his experience few women could take. He thought: She was my mistress once. I was in love with her, as much in love as I thought I was capable of being. And if it wasn't love, whatever that word means, at least I wanted her. Will that make what I have to say easier or more difficult? He told himself that all men were cowards when it came to a showdown with a woman. That first post-natal subservience, bred of physical dependence, was too ingrained ever to be totally eradicated. He wasn't more cowardly than the rest of his sex. What was it he had overheard that woman in the Lydsett stores saying? 'George would do anything to avoid a scene.' Of course he would, poor sod. Women with their womb-smelling warmth, their talcum powder and milky breasts had seen to that in the first four weeks of life.

He stood up when she came in and waited until she had taken the chair on the other side of the desk. Then he opened the right-hand drawer and took out a duplicated news-sheet which he slid across the desk towards her.

'Have you seen this? It's Neil Pascoe's latest news-sheet from PANUP.'

She said: 'People Against Nuclear Power. That means Pascoe and a few dozen other ill-informed hysterics. Of course I've seen it, I'm on his mailing list. He takes good care that I see it.'

She gave it a brief glance, then pushed it back across the desk. He took it up and read: 'Many readers will probably have learned by now that I am being sued by Miss Hilary Robarts, the Acting Administrative Officer at Larksoken Power Station, for alleged libel arising from what I wrote in the May issue of the news-sheet. I shall, of course, strenuously defend the action and, as I have no money to pay for a lawyer, will present my own defence. This is just the latest example of the threat to free information and even free speech presented by the nuclear energy lobby. Apparently now even the mildest criticism is to be followed by the threat of legal action. But there is a positive side. This action by Hilary Robarts shows that we, the ordinary people of this county, are making our impact. Would they bother with our small news-sheet if they weren't running scared? And the libel action, if it comes to trial, will give us valuable national publicity if properly handled. We are stronger than we know. Meanwhile I give below the dates of the next open days at Larksoken so that as many of us as possible can attend and strenuously put our case against nuclear power during the question time which normally precedes the actual tour of the station.'

She said: 'I told you, I've seen it. I don't know why you wasted your time reading it out. He seems determined to aggravate his offence. If he had any sense he'd get himself a good lawyer and keep his mouth shut.'

'He can't afford a lawyer. And he won't be able to pay damages.' He paused, and then said quietly: 'In the interests of the station I think you should drop it.'

'Is that an order?'

'I've no power to compel you and you know that. I'm asking you. You'll get nothing out of him, the man's practically penniless, and he isn't worth the trouble.'

'He is to me. What he describes as mild criticism was a serious libel and it was widely disseminated. There's no defence. Remember the actual words? "A woman whose response to Chernobyl is that only thirty-one people were killed, who can dismiss as unimportant one of the world's greatest nuclear disasters which put thousands in hospital, exposed a hundred thousand or more to dangerous radioactivity, devastated vast areas of land, and may result in deaths from cancer amounting to fifty thousand over the next fifty years, is totally unsuitable to be trusted to work in an atomic power station. While she remains there, in any capacity, we must have the gravest doubts whether safety will ever be taken seriously at Larksoken." That's a clear allegation of professional incompetence. If he's allowed to get away with that, we'll never get rid of him.'

'I wasn't aware that we were in the business of getting rid of inconvenient critics. What method had you in mind?' He paused, detecting in his voice the first trace of that reedy mixture of sarcasm and pomposity which he knew occasionally affected him and to which he was morbidly sensitive. He went on: 'He's a free citizen living where he chooses. He's entitled to his views. Hilary, he's not a worthy opponent. Bring him to court and he'll attract publicity for his cause and do your own no good at all. We're trying to win over the locals, not antagonize them. Let it go before someone starts a fund to pay for his defence. One martyr on Larksoken headland is enough.'

While he was speaking she got up and began pacing to and fro across the wide office. Then she paused and turned to him. 'This is what it's all about, isn't it? The reputation of the station, your reputation. What about my reputation? If I drop the action now it will be a clear admission that he was right, that I'm not fit to work here.'

'What he wrote hasn't hurt your reputation with anyone who matters. And suing him isn't going to help it. It's unwise to let policy be influenced, let alone jeopardized, by outraged personal pride. The reasonable course is quietly to drop the action. What do feelings matter?' He found that he couldn't remain seated while she was striding to and fro across the office. He got to his feet and walked over to the window hearing the angry voice but no longer having to face her, watching the reflection of her pacing figure, the swirling hair. He said again: 'What do feelings matter? It's the work that is important.'

'They matter to me. And that's something you've never understood, have you? Life is about feeling. Loving is about feeling. It was the same with the abortion. You forced me to have it. Did you ever ask yourself what I felt then, what I needed?'

Oh God, he thought, not this, not again, not now. He said, still with his back to her: 'It's ridiculous to say that I forced you. How could I? And I thought you felt as I did, that it was impossible for you to have a child.'

'Oh no, it wasn't. If you're so bloody keen on accuracy, let's be accurate about this. It would have been inconvenient, embarrassing, awkward, expensive. But it wasn't impossible. It still isn't impossible. And, for God's sake, turn around. Look at me. I'm talking to you. What I'm saying is important.'

He turned and walked back to the desk. He said calmly: 'All right, my phrasing was inaccurate. Have a child by all means if that's what you want. I'll be happy for you as long as you don't expect me to father it. But what we're talking about now is Neil Pascoe and PANUP. We've gone to a lot of trouble here to promote good relations with the local community and I'm not going to have all that good work vitiated by a totally unnecessary legal action, particularly not now when work will soon begin on the new reactor.'

'Then try to prevent it. And since we're talking about public relations, I'm surprised you haven't mentioned Ryan Blaney and Scudder's Cottage. My cottage, in case you've forgotten. What am I expected to do about that? Hand over my property to him and his kids rent-free in the interests of good public relations?'

'That's a different matter. It's not my concern as Director. But if you want my opinion, I think you're ill-advised to try and force him out simply because you've got a legal case. He's paying the rent regularly, isn't he? And it isn't as if you want the cottage.'

'I do want the cottage. It's mine. I bought it and now I want to sell it.'

She slumped back into the chair and he, too, sat. He made himself stare into the eyes in which, to his discomfort, he saw more pain than anger. He said: 'Presumably he knows that and he'll get out when he can, but it won't be easy. He's recently widowed and he's got four children. There's a certain amount of local feeling about it, I understand.'

'I've no doubt there is, particularly in the Local Hero where Ryan Blaney spends most of his time and money. I'm not prepared to wait. If we're moving to London in the next three months there's not much time to get the question of the cottage settled. I don't want to leave that kind of unfinished business. I want to get it on the market as soon as possible.'

He knew that this was the moment when he should have said firmly: 'I may be moving to London, but not with you.' But he found it impossible. He told himself that it was late, the end of a busy day, the worst possible time for rational argument. She was already overwrought. One thing at a time. He had tackled her about Pascoe and, although she had reacted much as he'd expected, perhaps she would think it over and do what he advised. And she was right about Ryan Blaney; it was none of his business. The interview had left him with two clear intentions more firmly fixed than ever in his mind. She wasn't coming to London with him and nor would he recommend her as Administrative Officer at Larksoken. For all her efficiency, her intelligence, her appropriate education, she wasn't the right person for the job. For a moment it crossed his mind that here was his bargaining card. 'I'm not offering you marriage but I am offering you the most senior job you could possibly aspire to.' But he knew there was no real temptation. He wouldn't leave the administration of Larksoken in her hands. Sooner or later she was going to have to realize that there would be no marriage and no promotion. But now was the wrong moment and he found himself wondering wryly when the right moment might be.

Instead he said: 'Look, we're here to run a power station efficiently and safely. We're doing a necessary and important job. Of course we're committed to it, we wouldn't be here otherwise. But we're scientists and technicians, not evangelists. We're not running a religious campaign.'

'They are, the other side. He is. You see him as an insignificant twit. He isn't. He's dishonest and he's dangerous. Look how he scrubs around in the records to turn up individual cases of leukaemia which he thinks he can ascribe to nuclear energy. And now he's got the latest Comare report to fuel his spurious concern. And what about last month's newsletter, that emotive nonsense about the midnight trains of death trundling silently through the northern suburbs of London? Anyone would think they were carrying open trucks of radioactive waste. Doesn't he care that nuclear energy has so far saved the world from burning five hundred million tons of coal? Hasn't he heard about the greenhouse effect? I mean, is the fool totally ignorant? Hasn't he any conception of the devastation caused to this planet by burning fossil fuels? Has no one told him about acid rain or the carcinogens in coal waste? And when it comes to danger, what about the fifty-seven miners buried alive in the Borken disaster only this year? Don't their lives matter? Think of the outcry if that had been a nuclear accident.'

He said: 'He's only one voice and a pathetically uneducated and ignorant one.'

'But he's having his effect and you know it. We've got to match passion with passion.'

His mind fastened on the word. We're not, he thought, talking about nuclear energy, we're talking about passion. Would we be having this conversation if we were still lovers? She's demanding from me a commitment to something more personal than atomic power. Turning to face her, he was visited suddenly, not by desire, but by a memory, inconveniently intense, of the desire he had once felt for her. And with memory came a sudden vivid picture of them together in her cottage, the heavy breasts bent over him, her hair falling across his face, her lips, her hands, her thighs.

He said roughly: 'If you want a religion, if you need a religion, then find one. There are plenty to choose from. All right the abbey is in ruins and I doubt whether that impotent old priest up at the Old Rectory has much on offer. But find something or someone; give up fish on Friday, don't eat meat, count beads, put ashes on your head, meditate four times a day, bow down towards your own personal Mecca. But don't, for God's sake, assuming He exists, ever make science into a religion.'

The telephone on his desk rang. Caroline Amphlett had left and it was switched through to an outside line. As he lifted the receiver he saw that Hilary was standing at the door. She gave him a last long look and went out, shutting it with unnecessary firmness behind her.

The caller was his sister. She said: 'I hoped I'd catch you. I forgot to remind you to call at Bollard's farm for the ducks for Thursday. He'll have them ready. We'll be six, incidentally. I've invited Adam Dalgliesh. He's back on the headland.'

He was able to answer her as calmly as she had spoken.

'Congratulations. He and his aunt have contrived with some skill to avoid their neighbours' cutlets for the last five years. How did you manage it?'

'By the expedient of asking. I imagine he may be thinking of keeping on the mill as a holiday home and feels it's time to acknowledge that he does have neighbours. Or he may be planning to sell, in which case he can risk a dinner party without being trapped into intimacy. But why not give him credit for a simple human weakness; the attraction of eating a good dinner which he hasn't had to cook?'

And it would balance her table, thought Mair, although that was hardly likely to have been a consideration. She despised the Noah's Ark convention which decreed that a superfluous man, however unattractive or stupid, was acceptable; a superfluous woman, however witty and well-informed, a social embarrassment.

He said: 'Am I expected to talk about his poetry?'

'I imagine he's come to Larksoken to get away from people who want to talk about his poetry. But it wouldn't hurt you to take a look at it. I've got the most recent volume. And it is poetry, not prose rearranged on the page.'

'With modern verse, can one tell the difference?'

'Oh yes,' she said. 'If it can be read as prose, then it is prose. It's an infallible test.'

'But not one, I imagine, that the English faculties would support. I'll be leaving in ten minutes. I won't forget the ducks.' He smiled as he replaced the receiver. His sister invariably had the power to restore him to good humour.

9

Before leaving he stood for a moment at the door and let his eyes range round the room as if he were seeing it for the first time. He was ambitious for the new job, had cleverly planned and schemed to get it. And now, when it was almost his, he realized how much he would miss Larksoken, its remoteness, its bleak uncompromising strength. Nothing had been done to prettify the site as at Sizewell, on the Suffolk coast, or to produce the pleasantly laid-out grounds of smooth lawn, flowering trees and shrubs which so agreeably impressed him on his periodic visits to Winfrith in Dorset. A low, curving wall faced with flint had been built on the seaward boundary behind whose shelter every spring a bright ribbon of daffodils strained and tossed in the March winds. Little else had been done to harmonize or soften the concrete's grey immensity. But this was what he liked, the wide expanse of turbulent sea, browny-grey, white-laced under a limitless sky, windows which he could open so that, at a touch of his hand, the faint continuous boom like distant thunder would instantaneously pour into his office in a roar of crashing billows. He liked best the stormy winter evenings when, working late, he could see the lights of shipping prinking the horizon as they made their way down the coast to the Yarmouth lanes, and see the flashing lightships and the beam from Happisburgh Lighthouse, which for generations had warned mariners of the treacherous offshore sands. Even on the darkest night, by the light which the sea seemed mysteriously to absorb and reflect, he could make out the splendid fifteenth-century west tower of Happisburgh Church, that embattled symbol of man's precarious defences against this most dangerous of seas. And it was a symbol of more than that. The tower must have been the last sight of land for hundreds of drowning mariners in peace and war. His mind, always tenacious of facts, could recall the details at will. The crew of HMS *Peggy*, driven ashore on 19 December 1770, the 119 members of HMS *Invincible* wrecked on the sands on 13 March 1801 when on her way to join Nelson's fleet at Copenhagen, the crew of HMS *Hunter*, the revenue cutter, lost in 1804, many of their crews buried under the grassy mounds in Happisburgh Churchyard. Built in an age of faith, the tower had stood as a symbol, too, of that final unquenchable hope that even the sea would yield up her dead and that their God was God of the waters as he was of the land. But now mariners could see, dwarfing the tower, the huge rectangular bulk of Larksoken Power Station. For those who sought symbols in inanimate objects its message was both simple and expedient, that man, by his own intelligence and his own efforts, could understand and master his world, could make his transitory life more agreeable, more comfortable, more free of pain. For him this was challenging enough, and if he had needed a faith to live by it would have been starkly sufficient. But sometimes, on the darkest nights, when the waves pounded the shingle like bursts of distant gunfire, both the science and the symbol would seem to him as transitory as those drowned lives and he would find himself wondering if this great hulk would one day yield to the sea, like the wave-smashed concrete from the last war defences, and like them become a broken symbol of man's long history on this desolate coast. Or would it resist even time and the North Sea and still be standing when the final darkness fell over the planet? In his more pessimistic moments some rogue part of his mind knew this darkness to be inevitable, although he did not expect it to come in his time, maybe not even in his son's. He would sometimes smile wryly, telling himself that he and Neil Pascoe, on different sides, would understand each other well. The only difference was that one of them had hope.

10

Jane Dalgliesh had bought Larksoken Mill five years earlier when she had moved from her previous home on the Suffolk coast. The mill, which was built in 1825, was a picturesque brick tower, four storeys high with an octagonal dome cap and skeleton fantail. It had been converted some years before Miss Dalgliesh had bought it by the addition of a flint-faced, two-storey building with a large sitting room, smaller study and a kitchen on the ground floor and three bedrooms, two of them with their own bathrooms, on the floor above. Dalgliesh had never asked her why she had moved to Norfolk but he guessed that the mill's main attraction had been its remoteness, its closeness to notable bird sanctuaries and the impressive view of headland, sky and sea from the top storey. Perhaps she had intended to restore it to working order but with increasing age hadn't been able to summon the energy or enthusiasm to cope with the disturbance. He had inherited it as an agreeable but mildly onerous responsibility, together with her considerable fortune. The origin of that had only become plain after her death. It had originally been left to her by a noted amateur ornithologist and eccentric with whom she had been friendly for many years. Whether the relationship had gone beyond friendship Dalgliesh would now never know. She had, apparently, spent little of the money on herself, had been a dependable benefactress of the few eccentric charities of which she approved, had remembered them in her will, but without egregious generosity, and had left the residue of her estate to him without explanation, admonition or peculiar protestations of affection, although he had no doubt that the words 'my dearly beloved nephew' meant exactly what they said. He had liked her, respected her, had always been at ease in her company, but he had never thought that he really knew her, and now he never would. He was a little surprised how much he minded.

The only change she had made to the property was to build a garage, and after he had unloaded and put away the Jaguar he decided to climb to the top chamber of the mill while it was still light. The bottom room, with its two huge grinding-wheels of burr-granite propped against the wall and its lingering smell of flour, still held an air of mystery, of time held in abeyance, of a place bereft of its purpose and meaning, so that he never entered it without a slight sense of desolation. There were only ladders between the floors and, as he grasped the rungs, he saw again his aunt's long trousered legs ahead of him disappearing into the chamber above. She had used only the top room of the mill which she had furnished simply with a small writing table and chair facing the North Sea, a telephone and her binoculars. Entering it he could imagine her sitting there in the summer days and evenings, working on the papers which she occasionally contributed to ornithological journals and looking up from time to time to gaze out over the headland to the sea and the far horizon, could see again that carved, weather-browned Aztec face with its hooded eyes under the grey-black hair, drawn back into a bun, could hear again a voice which, for him, had been one of the most beautiful female voices he had ever heard.

Now it was late afternoon and the headland lay enriched by the mellow afternoon light, the sea a wide expanse of wrinkled blue with a painter's stroke of purple laid on the horizon. The colours and shapes were intensified by the sun's last strong rays so that the ruins of the abbey looked unreal, a golden fantasy against the blue of the sea, and the dry grass gleamed as richly as a lush water meadow. There was a window at each of the compass points, and, binoculars in hand, he made his slow perambulation. To the west his eyes could travel along the narrow road between the reed beds and the dykes to the flint-walled and Dutch-gabled cottages and the pantiled roofs of Lydsett village and the round tower of St Andrew's Church. To the north the view was dominated by the huge bulk of the power station, the low-roofed administration block with, behind it, the reactor building and the great steel, aluminium-clad building of the turbine house. Four hundred metres out to sea were the rigs and platforms of the intake structures through which the cooling sea water passed to the pump house and the circulating water pumps. He moved again to the eastern window and looked out over the cottages of the headland. Far to the south he could just glimpse the roof of Scudder's Cottage. Directly to his left the flint walls of Martyr's Cottage glistened like marbles in the afternoon sun and less than half a mile to the north, set back among the Californian pines which fringed that part of the coast, was the dull square cottage rented by Hilary Robarts, a neatly proportional suburban villa incongruously set down on this bleak headland and facing inland as if resolutely ignoring the sea. Further inland, and only just visible from the southern window was the Old Rectory, set like a Victorian dolls' house in its large, overgrown garden which, at this distance, looked as neatly green and formal as a municipal park.

The telephone rang. The strident peal was unwelcome. It was to get away from such intrusions that he had come to Larksoken. But the call was not unexpected. It was Terry Rickards saying that he would like to drop in for a chat with Mr Dalgliesh if it wouldn't be too much bother and would nine be convenient? Dalgliesh was unable to think of a single excuse why it shouldn't be. Ten minutes later he left the tower, locking the door after him. This precaution was a small act of piety. His aunt had always kept the door locked, fearing that children might venture into the mill and hurt themselves by tumbling down the ladders. Leaving the tower to its darkness and its solitude, he went into Mill Cottage to unpack and get his supper.

The huge sitting room with its York stone floor, rugs and open fireplace was a comfortable and nostalgic mixture of the old and the new. Most of the furniture was familiar to him from boyhood visits to his grandparents, inherited by his aunt as the last of her generation. Only the music centre and the television set were comparatively new. Music had been important to her and the shelves held a catholic collection of records with which he could refresh or console himself during the two weeks' holiday. And next door, the kitchen contained nothing superfluous but everything necessary to a woman who enjoyed food but preferred to cook it with a minimum of fuss. He put a couple of lamb chops under the grill, made a green salad and prepared to enjoy a few hours of solitude before the intrusion of Rickards and his preoccupations.

It still surprised him a little that his aunt had finally bought a television set. Had she been seduced into conformity by the excellence of the natural history programmes and then, like other late converts he had known, sat captive to virtually every offering as if making up for lost time? That at least seemed unlikely. He switched on to see if the set was still working. A jerking pop star was wielding his guitar as the credits rolled, his parodic sexual gyrations so grotesque that it was difficult to see that even the besotted young could find them erotic. Switching off, Dalgliesh looked up at the oil portrait of his maternal great-grandfather, the Victorian bishop, robed but unmitred, his arms in their billowing lawn sleeves confidently resting on the arms of the chair. He had an impulse to say, 'This is the music of 1988; these are our heroes; that building on the headland is our architecture and I dare not stop my car to help children home because they've been taught with good reason that a strange man might abduct and rape them.' He could have added, 'And out there somewhere is a mass murderer who enjoys strangling women and stuffing their mouths with their hair.' But that aberration, at least, was independent of changing fashions and his great-grandfather would have had his scrupulous but uncompromising answer to it. And with reason. After all, hadn't he been conse-crated bishop in 1888, the year of Jack the Ripper? And probably he would have found the Whistler more understandable than the pop star whose gyrations would surely have convinced him that man was in the grip of his final, manic St Vitus's dance.

Rickards came promptly on time. It was precisely nine when Dalgliesh heard his car and, opening the door on the darkness of the night, saw his tall figure striding towards him. Dalgliesh hadn't seen him for more than ten years when he had been a newly appointed inspector in the Metropolitan CID and was surprised to see how little he had changed; time, marriage, removal from London, promotion, had left no apparent mark on him. His rangy, graceless figure, over six feet high, still looked as incongruous in a formal suit as it always had. The rugged, weatherbeaten face, with its look of dependable fortitude, would have looked more appropriate above a seaman's guernsey, prefer-ably with RNLI woven across the chest. In profile his face, with the long, slightly hooked nose and jutting eyebrows, was impres-sive. In full face the nose was revealed as a little too wide and flattened at the base and the dark eyes, which when he was animated took on a fierce, almost manic gleam, in repose were pools of puzzled endurance. Dalgliesh thought of him as a type of police officer less common than formerly but still not rare; the conscientious and incorruptible detective of limited imagination and somewhat greater intelligence who had never supposed that the evil of the world should be condoned because it was frequently inexplicable and its perpetrators unfortunate.

He gazed round the sitting room at the long wall of books, the crackling wood fire, the oil of the Victorian prelate above the mantelshelf as if deliberately impressing each item on his mind, then sank into his chair and stretched out his long legs with a small grunt of satisfaction. Dalgliesh remembered that he had always drunk beer; now he accepted whisky but said he could do with coffee first. One habit at least had changed. He said: 'I'm sorry that you won't be meeting Susie, my wife, while you're here, Mr Dalgliesh. She's having our first baby in a couple of weeks and she's gone to stay with her mother in York. Ma-in-law didn't like the idea of her being in Norfolk with the Whistler on the prowl, not with me working the hours I do.'

It was said with a kind of embarrassed formality as if he, not Dalgliesh, were the host and he was apologizing for the unexpected absence of the hostess. He added: 'I suppose it's natural for an only daughter to want to be with her mother at a time like this, particularly with a first baby.'

Dalgliesh's wife hadn't wanted to be with her mother, she had wanted to be with him, had wanted it with such intensity that he had wondered afterwards whether she might have felt a premonition. He could remember that, although he could no longer recall her face. His memory of her, which for years, a traitor to grief and to their love, he had resolutely tried to suppress because the pain had seemed unbearable, had gradually been replaced by a boyish, romantic dream of gentleness and beauty now fixed for ever beyond the depredation of time. His newborn son's face he could still recall vividly and sometimes did in his dreams, that white unsullied look of sweet knowledgeable contentment, as if, in a brief moment of life, he had seen and known all there was to know, seen it and rejected it. He told himself that he was the last man who could reasonably be expected to advise or reassure on the problems of pregnancy and he sensed that Rickards's unhappiness at his wife's absence went deeper than missing her company. He made the usual inquiries about her health and escaped into the kitchen to make the coffee.

Whatever mysterious spirit had unlocked the verse, it had freed him for other human satisfactions, for love; or was it the other way around? Had love unlocked the verse? It seemed even to have affected his job. Grinding the coffee beans he pondered life's smaller ambiguities. When the poetry hadn't come, the job too had seemed not only irksome but occasionally repellent. Now he was happy enough to let Rickards impose on his solitude to use him as a sounding board. This new benignity and tolerance a little disconcerted him. Success in moderation was no doubt better for the character than failure but too much of it and he would lose his cutting edge. And five minutes later, carrying in the two mugs and settling back in his chair, he could relish the contrast between Rickards's preoccupation with psychopathic violence and the peace of the mill. The wood fire, now past its crackling stage, had settled into a comfortable glow and the wind, seldom absent from the headland, moved like a benign, gently hissing spirit through the still and soaring clappers of the mill. He was glad that it wasn't his job to catch the Whistler. Of all murders serial killings were the most frustrating, the most difficult and the chanciest to solve, the investigation carried on under the strain of vociferous public demand that the terrifying unknown devil be caught and exorcized for ever. But this wasn't his case; he could discuss it with the detachment of a man who has a professional interest but no responsibility. And he could understand what Rickards needed; not advice – he knew his job – but someone he could trust, someone who understood the language, someone who would afterwards be gone, who wouldn't remain as a perpetual reminder of his uncertainties, a fellow professional to whom he could comfortably think aloud. He had his team and he was too punctilious not to share his thinking with them. But he was a man who needed to articulate his theories and here he could put them forward, embroider, reject, explore without the uncomfortable suspicion that his detective sergeant, deferentially listening, his face carefully expressionless, would be thinking, For God's sake, what's the old man dreaming up now? Or, The old man's getting fanciful.

Rickards said: 'We're not using Holmes. The Met say the system is fully committed at present, and anyway we've got our own computer. Not that there's much data to feed in. The press and public know about Holmes, of course. I get that at every press conference. "Are you using the Home Office special computer, the one named after Sherlock Holmes?" "No," I say, "but we're using our own." Unspoken question: "Then why the hell haven't you caught him?" They think that you've only got to feed in your data and out pops an Identikit of sonny complete with prints, collar-size and taste in pop music.'

'Yes,' said Dalgliesh, 'we're so sated now with scientific wonders that it's a bit disconcerting when we find that technology can do everything except what we want it to.'

'Four women so far and Valerie Mitchell won't be the last if we don't catch him soon. He started fifteen months ago. The first victim was found just after midnight in a shelter at the end of the Easthaven promenade, the local tart, incidentally, although he may not have known or cared. It was eight months before he struck again. Struck lucky, I suppose he'd say. This time a thirty-year-old schoolteacher cycling home to Hunstanton who had a puncture on a lonely stretch of road. Then another gap, just six months, before he got a barmaid from Ipswich who'd been visiting her granny and was daft enough to wait alone for the late bus. When it arrived there was no one at the stop. A couple of local youths got off. They'd had a skinful so weren't in a particularly noticing mood but they saw and heard nothing, nothing except what they described as a kind of mournful whistling coming from deep in the wood.'

He took a gulp of his coffee, then went on: 'We've got a personality assessment from the trick-cyclist. I don't know why we bother. I could have written it myself. He tells us to look for a loner, probably from a disturbed family background, may have a dominant mother, doesn't relate easily to people, particularly women, could be impotent, unmarried, separated or divorced, with a resentment and hatred of the opposite sex. Well, we hardly expect him to be a successful, happily married bank manager with four lovely kids just coming up to GCE or whatever they call it now. They're the devil, these serial murders. No motive – no motive that a sane man can understand anyway – and he could come from anywhere, Norwich, Ipswich, even London. It's dangerous to assume that he's necessarily working in his own territory. Looks like it, though. He obviously knows the locality well. And he seems to be sticking now to the same MO. He chooses a road intersection, drives the car or van into the side of one road, cuts across and waits at the other. Then he drags his victim into the bushes or the trees, kills and cuts back to the other road and the car and makes his getaway. With the last three murders it seems to have been pure chance that a suitable victim did, in fact, come along.'

Dalgliesh felt that it was time he contributed something to the speculation. He said: 'If he doesn't select and stalk his victim, and obviously he didn't in the last three cases, he'd normally have to expect a long wait. That suggests he's routinely out after dark, a night worker, mole-catcher, woodman, gamekeeper, that kind of job. And he goes prepared; on the watch for a quick kill, in more ways than one.'

Rickards said: 'That's how I see it. Four victims so far and three fortuitous, but he's probably been on the prowl for three years or more. That could be part of the thrill. "Tonight I could make a strike, tonight I could be lucky." And, by God, he is getting lucky. Two victims in the last six weeks.'

'And what about his trademark, the whistle?'

'That was heard by the three people who came quickly on the scene after the Easthaven murder. One just heard a whistle, one said it sounded like a hymn and the third, who was a church woman, claimed she could identify it precisely, "Now the Day is Over". We kept quiet about that. It could be useful when we get the usual clutch of nutters claiming they're the Whistler. But there seems no doubt that he does whistle.'

Dalgliesh said: '"Now the day is over / Night is drawing nigh / Shadows of the evening / Fall across the sky". It's a Sunday-school hymn, hardly the kind that gets requested on *Songs of Praise*, I should have thought.'

He remembered it from childhood, a lugubrious, undistinguished tune which, as a ten-year-old, he could pick out on the drawing-room piano. Did anyone sing that hymn now, he wondered? It had been a favourite choice of Miss Barnett on those long dark afternoons in winter before the Sunday school was released, when the outside light was fading and the small Adam Dalgliesh was already dreading those last twenty yards of his walk home where the rectory drive curved and the bushes grew thickest. Night was different from bright day, smelt different, sounded different; ordinary things assumed different shapes; an alien and more sinister power ruled the night. Those twenty yards of crunching gravel where the lights of the house were momentarily screened were a weekly horror. Once through the gate to the drive he would walk fast, but not too fast since the power that ruled the night could smell out fear as dogs smell out terror. His mother, he knew, would never have expected him to walk those yards alone had she known that he suffered such atavistic panic, but she hadn't known and he would have died before telling her. And his father? His father would have expected him to be brave, would have told him that God was God of the darkness as He was of the light. There were after all a dozen appropriate texts he could have quoted. 'Darkness and light are both alike to Thee.' But they were not alike to a sensitive ten-year-old boy. It was on those lonely walks that he had first had intimations of an essentially adult truth, that it is those who most love us who cause us the most pain. He said: 'So you're looking for a local man, a loner, someone who has a night job, the use of a car or van and a knowledge of *Hymns Ancient and Modern*. That should make it easier.'

Rickards said: 'You'd think so, wouldn't you.'

He sat in silence for a minute then said: 'I think I'd like just a small whisky now, Mr Dalgliesh, if it's all the same to you.'

It was after midnight when he finally left. Dalgliesh walked out with him to the car. Looking out across the headland Rickards said: 'He's out there somewhere, watching, waiting. There's hardly a waking moment when I don't think of him, imagine what he looks like, where he is, what he's thinking. Susie's ma is right. I haven't had much to give her recently. And when he's caught, that'll be the end. It's finished. You move on. He doesn't, but you do. And by the end you know everything, or think you do. Where, when, who, how? You might even know why if you're lucky. And yet, essentially, you know nothing. All that wickedness, and you don't have to explain it or understand it or do a bloody thing about it except put a stop to it. Involvement without responsibility. No responsibility for what he did or for what happens to him afterwards. That's for the judge and the jury. You're involved, and yet you're not involved. Is that what appeals to you about the job, Mr Dalgliesh?'

It was not a question Dalgliesh would have expected, even from a friend, and Rickards was not a friend. He said: 'Can any of us answer that question?'

'You remember why I left the Met, Mr Dalgliesh.'

'The two corruption cases? Yes, I remember why you left the Met.'

'And you stayed. You didn't like it any more than I did. You wouldn't have touched the pitch. But you stayed. You were detached about it all, weren't you? It interested you.'

Dalgliesh said: 'It's always interesting when men you thought you knew behave out of character.'

And Rickards had fled from London. In search of what? Dalgliesh wondered. Some romantic dream of country peace, an England which had vanished, a gentler method of policing, total honesty? He wondered whether he had found it.

BOOK TWO

Thursday 22 September to Friday 23 September

11

It was ten past seven and the saloon bar of the Duke of Clarence pub was already smoke-filled, the noise level rising and the crowd at the bar three feet deep. Christine Baldwin, the Whistler's fifth victim, had exactly twenty minutes to live. She sat on the banquette against the wall, sipping her second medium sherry of the evening, deliberately making it last, knowing that Colin was impatient to order the next round. Catching Norman's eye, she raised her left wrist and nodded significantly at her watch. Already, it was ten minutes past their deadline and he knew it. Their agreement was that this was to be a pre-supper drink with Colin and Yvonne, the limit both of time and alcohol consumption clearly understood between her and Norman before they left home. The arrangement was typical of their nine-month-old marriage, sustained less by compatible interests than by a carefully negotiated series of concessions. Tonight it had been her turn to give way, but agreeing to spend an hour in the Clarence with Colin and Yvonne didn't extend to any pretence that she actually enjoyed their company.

She had disliked Colin since their first meeting; the relationship, at a glance, had been fixed in the stereotyped antagonism between newly acquired fiancée and slightly disreputable old schoolmate and drinking partner. He had been best man at their wedding – a formidable pre-nuptial agreement had been necessary for that capitulation – and had carried out his duties with a mixture of incompetence, vulgarity and irreverence which, as she occasionally enjoyed telling Norman, had spoilt for her the memory of her big day. It was typical of him to choose this pub. God knew, it was vulgar enough. But at least she could be certain of one thing: it wasn't a place where there was a risk of meeting anyone from the power station, at least not anyone who mattered. She disliked everything about the Clarence, the rough scrape of the moquette against her legs, the synthetic velvet which covered the walls, the baskets of ivy spiked with artificial flowers above the bar, the gaudiness of the carpet. Twenty years ago, it had been a cosy Victorian hostelry, seldom visited except by its regulars, with an open fire in winter and horse brasses polished to whiteness hung against the black beams. The lugubrious publican had seen it as his job to repel strangers and had employed to that end an impressive armoury of taciturnity, malevolent glances, warm beer and poor service. But the old pub had burnt down in the 1960s and been replaced by a more profitable and thrusting enterprise. Nothing of the old building remained and the long extension to the bar, dignified by the name Banqueting Hall, provided for the undiscriminating a venue for weddings and local functions and on other nights served a predictable menu of prawns or soup, steak or chicken, and fruit salad with ice-cream. Well, at least she had put her foot down over dinner. They had worked out their monthly budget to the last pound, and if Norman thought she was going to eat this overpriced muck with a perfectly good cold supper waiting in the refrigerator at home and a decent pro- gramme on the telly he could forget it. And they had better uses for their money than to sit here drinking with Colin and his latest tart who had opened her legs to half Norwich, if rumour were to be believed. There were the hire purchase repayments on the sitting-room furniture and the car, not to mention the mortgage. She tried again to meet Norman's eye but he was rather desper- ately keeping his attention on that slut Yvonne. And that wasn't proving difficult. Colin leaned over to her, his bold treacle-brown eyes half mocking, half inviting, Colin Lomas, who thought every woman would swoon when he beckoned.

'Relax, darling. Your old man's enjoying himself. It's your round, Norm.'

Ignoring Colin she spoke to Norman: 'Look, it's time we were going. We agreed we'd leave at seven.'

'Oh, come on, Chrissie, give the lad a break. One more round.'

Without meeting her eyes, Norman said: 'What'll you have, Yvonne? The same again? Medium sherry?'

Colin said: 'Let's get on to spirits. I'll have a Johnny Walker.'

He was doing it on purpose. She knew that he didn't even like whisky. She said: 'Look, I've had enough of this bloody place. The noise has given me a head.'

'A headache? Nine months married and she's started the headaches. No point in hurrying home tonight, Norm.'

Yvonne giggled.

Christine said, her face burning, 'You were always vulgar, Colin Lomas, but now you're not even funny with it. You three can do what you like. I'm going home. Give me the car keys.'

Colin leaned back and smiled. 'You heard what your lady wife said. She wants the car keys.'

Without a word, shamefaced, Norman took them out of his pocket and slid them over the table. She snatched them up, pushed back the table, struggled past Yvonne and rushed to the door. She was almost crying with rage. It took her a minute to unlock the car and then she sat shaking behind the wheel, waiting until her hands were steady enough to switch on the ignition. She heard her mother's voice on the day when she had announced her engagement: 'Well, you're thirty-two and if he's what you want I suppose you know your own mind. But you'll never make anything of him. Weak as water, if you ask me.' But she had thought that she could make something of him and that small semi-detached house outside Norwich represented nine months of hard work and achievement. Next year he was due for promotion at the insurance office. She would be able to give up her job as secretary in the medical physics department at Larksoken Power Station and start the first of the two children she had planned. She would be thirty-four by then. Everyone knew that you shouldn't wait too long.

She had only passed her driving test after her marriage and this was the first time that she had driven unaccompanied by night. She drove slowly and carefully, her anxious eyes peering ahead, glad that at least the route home was familiar. She wondered what Norman would do when he saw that the car had gone. Almost certainly he would expect to find her sitting there, fuming but ready to be driven home. Now he'd have to rely for a lift on Colin who wouldn't be so keen on coming out of his way. And if they thought that she was going to invite Colin and

Yvonne in for a drink when they arrived they would get a shock. The thought of Norman's discomfiture at finding her gone cheered her a little and she pressed her foot down on the accelerator, anxious to distance herself from the three of them, to reach the safety of home. But suddenly the car gave a stutter and the engine died. She must have been driving more erratically than she thought for she found herself half skewed across the road. It was a bad place to be stranded, a lonely stretch of country lane with a thin band of trees on either side and it was deserted. And then she remembered. Norman had mentioned that they needed to fill up with petrol and must be sure to call at the all-night garage after they left the Clarence. It was ridiculous to have let the tank get so low but they had had an argument only three days earlier on whose turn it was to call at the garage and pay for the petrol. All her anger and frustration returned. For a moment she sat there, beating her hands impotently on the wheel, desperately turning the key in the ignition, willing the engine to start. But there was no response. And then irritation began to give way to the first tricklings of fear. The road was deserted and even if a motorist came by and drew up, could she be certain that he wasn't a kidnapper, a rapist, even the Whistler? There had been that horrible murder on the A3 only this year. Nowadays you could trust no one. And she could hardly leave the car where it was, slewed across the road. She tried to recall when she had last passed a house, an AA box, a public telephone, but it seemed to her that she had been driving through deserted countryside for at least ten minutes. Even if she left the dubious sanctuary of the car she had no clue to the best direction in which to seek help. Suddenly a wave of total panic swept across her like nausea and she had to resist the urge to dash from the car and hide herself among the trees. But what good would that do? He might be lurking even there.

And then, miraculously, she heard footsteps and, looking round, saw a woman approaching. She was dressed in trousers and a trenchcoat and had a mane of fair hair beneath a tight-fitting beret. At her side on a leash trotted a small, smooth-haired dog. Immediately all her anxiety vanished. Here was someone who would help her push the car into the side of the road, who would know in which direction lay the nearest house, who would be a companion on her walk. Without even troubling to slam the door of the car she called out happily and ran smiling towards the horror of her death.

12

The dinner had been excellent and the wine, a Château Potensac '78, an interesting choice with the main course. Although Dalgliesh knew of Alice Mair's reputation as a cookery writer he had never read any of her books and had no idea to what culinary school, if any, she belonged. He had hardly feared being presented with the usual artistic creation swimming in a pool of sauce and accompanied by one or two undercooked carrots and mange-tout elegantly arranged on a side plate. But the wild ducks carved by Alex Mair had been recognizably ducks, the piquant sauce, new to him, enhanced rather than dominated the taste of the birds, and the small mounds of creamed turnip and parsnip were an agreeable addition to green peas. Afterwards they had eaten orange sorbet followed by cheese and fruit. It was a conventional menu but one intended, he felt, to please the guests rather than to demonstrate the ingenuity of the cook.

The expected fourth guest, Miles Lessingham, had unaccountably failed to arrive, but Alice Mair hadn't rearranged her table and the empty chair and unfilled wineglass were uncomfortably evocative of Banquo's ghost. Dalgliesh was seated opposite Hilary Robarts. The portrait, he thought, must have been even more powerful than he realized if it could so dominate his physical reaction to the living woman. It was the first time they had met although he had known of her existence as he had of all the handful of people who lived, as the Lydsett villagers said, 't'other side of the gate'. And it was a little strange that this was their first meeting; her red Golf was a frequent sight on the headland, her cottage had frequently met his eyes from the top storey of the mill. Now, physically close for the first time, he found it difficult to keep his eyes off her, living flesh and remembered image seeming to fuse into a presence both potent and disturbing. It was a handsome face, a model's face, he thought, with its high cheekbones, long, slightly concave nose, wide, full lips and dark, angry eyes deeply set under the strong brows. Her crimped, springing hair, held back with two combs, fell over her shoulders. He could imagine her posed, mouth moistly open, hips jutting and staring at the cameras with that apparently obligatory look of arrogant resentment. As she leaned forward to twitch another grape from the bunch and almost toss it into her mouth he could see the faint freckles which smudged the dark forehead, the glisten of hairs above a carved upper lip.

On the other side of their host sat Meg Dennison, delicately but unfussily peeling her grapes with pink-tipped fingers. Hilary Robarts's sultry handsomeness emphasized her own very different look, an old-fashioned, carefully tended but unselfconscious prettiness which reminded him of photographs of the late thirties. Their clothes emphasized the contrast. Hilary wore a shirtwaister dress in multicoloured Indian cotton, three buttons at the neck undone. Meg Dennison was in a long black skirt and a blue patterned silk blouse with a bow at the neck. But it was their hostess who was the most elegant. The long shift in fine dark brown wool worn with a heavy necklace of silver and amber hid her angularity and emphasized the strength and regularity of the strong features. Beside her Meg Dennison's prettiness was diminished almost to insipidity and Hilary Robarts's strong-coloured cotton looked tawdry.

The room in which they were dining must, he thought, have been part of the original cottage. From these smoke-blackened beams Agnes Poley had hung her sides of bacon, her bundles of dried herbs. In a pot slung over that huge hearth she had cooked her family's meals and, perhaps, at the end had heard in its roaring flames the crackling faggots of her dreadful martyrdom. Outside the long window had passed the helmets of marching men. But only in the name of the cottage was there a memory of the past. The oval dining table and the chairs were modern as were the Wedgwood dinner service and the elegant glasses. In the drawing room, where they had drunk their pre-dinner sherry, Dalgliesh had a sense of a room which deliberately rejected the past, containing nothing which could violate the owner's essential privacy; no family history in photograph or portrait, no shabby heirlooms given room out of nostalgia, sentimentality or family piety, no antiques collected over the years. Even the few pictures, three recognizably by John Piper, were modern. The furniture was expensive, comfortable, well designed, too elegantly simple to be offensively out of place. But the heart of the cottage wasn't there. It was in that large, warm-smelling and welcoming kitchen.

He had only been half listening to the conversation but now he forced himself to be a more accommodating guest. The talk was general, candlelit faces leaned across the table and the hands which peeled the fruit or fidgeted with the glasses were as individual as the faces. Alice Mair's strong but elegant hands with their short nails, Hilary Robarts's long, knobbled fingers, the delicacy of Meg Dennison's pink-tipped fingers, a little reddened with housework. Alex Mair was saying: 'All right, let's take a modern dilemma. We know that we can use human tissue from aborted foetuses to treat Parkinson's disease and probably Alzheimer's. Presumably you'd find that ethically acceptable if the abortion were natural or legal but not if it were induced for the purpose of providing the tissue. But you can argue that a woman has a right to the use that she makes of her own body. If she's particularly fond of someone who has Alzheimer's and wants to help him by producing a foetus, who has the right to say no? A foetus isn't a child.'

Hilary Robarts said: 'I notice that you assume the sufferer to be helped is a man. I suppose he'd feel entitled to use a woman's body for this purpose as he would any other. But why the hell should he? I can't imagine that a woman who's actually had an abortion wants to go through that again for any man's convenience.'

The words were spoken with extreme bitterness. There was a pause then Mair said quietly: 'Alzheimer's is rather more than an inconvenience. But I'm not advocating it. In any case, under present law, it would be illegal.'

'Would that worry you?'

He looked into her angry eyes. 'Naturally it would worry me. Happily it isn't a decision that I shall ever be required to make. But we're not talking about legality, we're talking about morality.'

His sister asked: 'Are they different?'

'That's the question, isn't it? Are they, Adam?'

It was the first time he had used Dalgliesh's Christian name. Dalgliesh said: 'You're assuming there's an absolute morality independent of time or circumstance.'

'Wouldn't you make that assumption?'

'Yes, I think I would, but I'm not a moral philosopher.'

Mrs Dennison looked up from her plate a little flushed and said: 'I'm always suspicious of the excuse that a sin is justified if it's done to benefit someone we love. We may think so, but it's usually to benefit ourselves. I might dread the thought of having to look after an Alzheimer patient. When we advocate euthanasia is it to stop pain or to prevent our own distress at having to watch it? To conceive a child deliberately in order to kill it to make use of its tissue, the idea is absolutely repugnant.'

Alex Mair said: 'I could argue that what you are killing isn't a child and that repugnance at an act isn't evidence of its immorality.'

Dalgliesh said: 'But isn't it? Doesn't Mrs Dennison's natural repugnance tell us something about the morality of the act?'

She gave him a brief, grateful smile and went on: 'And isn't this use of a foetus particularly dangerous? It could lead to the poor of the world conceiving children and selling the foetuses to help the rich. Already I believe there's a black market in human organs. Do you think a multi-millionaire who needs a heart-lung transplant ever goes without?'

Alex Mair smiled. 'As long as you aren't arguing that we should deliberately suppress knowledge or reject scientific progress just because the discoveries can be abused. If there are abuses, legislate against them.'

Meg protested: 'But you make it sound so easy. If all we had to do was to legislate against social evils Mr Dalgliesh for one would be out of work.'

'It isn't easy but it has to be attempted. That's what being human means, surely, using our intelligence to make choices.'

Alice Mair got up from the table. She said: 'Well, it's time to make a choice now on a somewhat different level. Which of you would like coffee and what kind? There's a table and chairs in the courtyard. I thought we could switch on the yard lights and have it outside.'

They moved through to the drawing room and Alice Mair opened the french windows leading to the patio. Immediately the sonorous booming of the sea flowed into and took possession of the room like a vibrating and irresistible force. But once they had stepped out into the cool air, paradoxically, the noise seemed muted, the sea no more than a distant roar. The patio was bounded on the road side by a high flint wall which, to the south and east, curved to little more than four feet to give an unimpeded view across the headland to the sea.

The coffee tray was carried out by Alex Mair within minutes and, cups in hand, the little party wandered aimlessly among the terracotta pots like strangers reluctant to be introduced or like actors on a stage set, self-absorbed, pondering their lines, waiting for the rehearsal to begin.

They were without coats and the warmth of the night had proved illusory. They had turned as if by common consent to go back into the cottage when the lights of a car, driven fast, came over the southern rise of the road. As it approached its speed slackened.

Mair said: 'Lessingham's Porsche.'

No one spoke. They watched silently as the car was driven at speed off the road to brake violently on the turf of the headland. As if conforming to some prearranged ceremony they grouped themselves into a semicircle with Alex Mair a little to the front, like a formal welcoming party but one bracing itself for trouble rather than expecting pleasure from the approaching guest. Dalgliesh was aware of the heightening tension: small individual tremors of anxiety which shivered on the still, sea-scented air, unified and focused on the car door and on the tall figure which unwound from the driver's seat, leapt easily over the low stone wall and walked deliberately across the courtyard towards them. Lessingham ignored Mair and moved straight to Alice. He took her hand and gently kissed it, a theatrical gesture which Dalgliesh felt had taken her by surprise and which the others had watched with an unnaturally critical attention.

Lessingham said gently: 'My apologies, Alice. Too late for

dinner, I know, but not, I hope, for a drink. And God, do I need one.'

'Where have you been? We waited dinner for forty minutes.' It was Hilary Robarts who asked the obvious question, sounding as accusatory as a peevish wife.

Lessingham kept his eye on Alice. He said: 'I've been considering how best to answer that question for the last twenty minutes. There are a number of interesting and dramatic possibilities. I could say that I've been helping the police with their inquiries. Or that I've been involved in a murder. Or that there was a little unpleasantness on the road. Actually it was all three. The Whistler has killed again. I found the body.'

Hilary Robarts said sharply: 'How do you mean, "found"? Where?'

Again Lessingham ignored her. He said to Alice Mair: 'Could I have that drink? Then I'll give you all the gory details. After unsettling your seating plan and delaying dinner for forty minutes that's the least I owe you.'

As they moved back into the drawing room Alex Mair introduced Dalgliesh. Lessingham gave him one sharp glance. They shook hands. The palm which momentarily touched his was moist and very cold.

Alex Mair said easily: 'Why didn't you ring? We would have kept some food for you.'

The question, conventionally domestic, sounded irrelevant, but Lessingham answered it. 'Do you know, I actually forgot. Not all the time, of course, but it honestly didn't cross my mind until the police had finished questioning me and then the moment didn't seem opportune. They were perfectly civil but I sensed that my private engagements had a pretty low priority. Incidentally, you get absolutely no credit from the police for finding a body for them. Their attitude is rather, "Thank you very much, sir, very nasty, I'm sure. Sorry you've been troubled. But we'll take over now. Just go home and try to forget all about it." I have a feeling that that isn't going to be so easy.'

Back in the drawing room, Alex Mair threw a couple of thin logs on to the glowing embers and went to get the drinks. Lessingham had refused whisky but had asked for wine. 'But don't waste your best claret on me, Alex. This is purely medicinal.' Almost imperceptibly they edged their chairs closer. Lessingham began his story deliberately, pausing at times to take gulps of the wine. It seemed to Dalgliesh that he was subtly altered since his arrival, had become charged with a power both mysterious and oddly familiar. He thought: He has acquired the mystique of the story-teller and, glancing at the ring of fire-lit and intent faces, he was suddenly reminded of his first village school, of the children clustered round Miss Douglas at three o'clock on a Friday afternoon for the half hour of story-time, and felt a pang of pain and regret for those lost days of innocence and love. He was surprised that the memory should have come back so keenly and at such a moment. But this was to be a very different story and one unsuited to the ears of children.

Lessingham said: 'I had an appointment with my dentist in Norwich at five o'clock and then briefly visited a friend in the Close. So I drove here from Norwich, not from my cottage. I'd just turned right off the B1150 at Fairstead when I nearly crashed into the back of this unlit car skewed across the road. I thought it was a damn silly place to park if someone wanted to take a leak in the bushes. Then it crossed my mind that there could have been an accident. And the right-hand door was open, that seemed a bit odd. So I drew into the side and went to take a look. There was no one about. I'm not sure why I walked into the trees. A kind of instinct I suppose. It was too dark to see anything and I wondered whether to call out. Then I felt a fool and decided to leave it and mind my own business. And it was then that I almost tripped over her.'

He took another gulp of the wine. 'I still couldn't see anything, of course, but I knelt down and groped about with my hands. And it was then that I touched flesh. I think I touched her thigh, I can't be sure. But flesh, even dead flesh, is unmistakable. So I went back to the car and got my torch. I shone it on her feet and then slowly up her body to her face. And then, of course, I saw. I knew it was the Whistler.'

Meg Dennison asked gently: 'Was it very terrible?'

He must have heard in her voice what she obviously felt, not prurience but sympathy, an understanding that he needed to talk. He looked at her for a moment as if seeing her for the first time then paused, giving the question serious thought.

'More shocking than terrible. Looking back my emotions were complicated, a mixture of horror, disbelief and, well, shame. I felt like a voyeur. The dead, after all, are at such a disadvantage. She looked grotesque, a little ridiculous, with thin clumps of hair sticking out of her mouth as if she was munching. Horrible, of course, but silly at the same time. I had an almost irresistible impulse to giggle. I know it was only a reaction to shock but it was hardly admirable. And the whole scene was so, well, banal. If you had asked me to describe one of the Whistler's victims that's exactly how I should have seen her. You expect reality to be different from imaginings.'

Alice Mair said: 'Perhaps because the imaginings are usually worse.'

Meg Dennison said gently: 'You must have been terrified. I know I should have been. Alone and in darkness with such horror.'

He shifted his body towards her and spoke as if it were important that she, of all those present, should understand.

'No, not terrified, that was the surprising part. I was frightened, of course, but only for a second or two. After all, I didn't imagine he'd wait around. He'd had his kicks. He isn't interested in men anyway. I found myself thinking the ordinary, commonplace thoughts. I mustn't touch anything. I mustn't destroy the evidence. I've got to get the police. Then, walking back to the car, I started rehearsing what I'd say to them, almost as if I were concocting my story. I tried to explain why it was that I went into the bushes, tried to make it sound reasonable.'

Alex Mair said: 'What was there to justify? You did what you did. It sounds reasonable enough to me. The car was a danger slewed across the road. It would have been irresponsible just to drive on.'

'It seemed to need a lot of explaining, then and later. Perhaps because all the subsequent police sentences began with "why". You get morbidly sensitive to your own motives. It's almost as if you have to convince yourself that you didn't do it.'

Hilary Robarts said impatiently: 'But the body, when you first went back for the torch and saw her, you were certain she was dead?'

'Oh yes, I knew she was dead.'

'How could you have known? It could have been very recent. Why didn't you at least try to resuscitate her, give her the kiss of life? It would have been worth overcoming your natural repugnance.'

Dalgliesh heard Meg Dennison make a small sound between a gasp and a groan. Lessingham looked at Hilary and said coolly: 'It would have been if there had been the slightest point in it. I knew she was dead, let's leave it at that. But don't worry, if I ever find you *in extremis* I'll endeavour to overcome my natural repugnance.'

Hilary relaxed and gave a little self-satisfied smile, as if gratified to have stung him into a cheap retort. Her voice was more natural as she said: 'I'm surprised you weren't treated as a suspect. After all, you were the first on the scene, and this is the second time you've been, well almost, in at the death. It's becoming a habit.'

The last words were spoken almost under her breath but her eyes were fixed on Lessingham's face. He met her glance and said, with equal quietness: 'But there's a difference, isn't there? I had to watch Toby die, remember? And this time no one will even try to pretend that it isn't murder.'

The fire gave a sudden crackle and the top log rolled over and fell into the hearth. Mair, his face flushed, kicked it viciously back.

Hilary Robarts, perfectly calm, turned to Dalgliesh. 'But I'm right, aren't I? Don't the police usually suspect the person who finds the body?'

He said quietly: 'Not necessarily.'

Lessingham had placed the bottle of claret on the hearth. Now he leaned down and carefully refilled his glass. He said: 'They might have suspected me, I suppose, but for a number of lucky circumstances. I was obviously out on my lawful occasions. I have an alibi for at least two of the previous killings. From their point of view I was depressingly free of blood. I suppose they could see I was in a mild state of shock. And there was no sign of the ligature which strangled her, nor of the knife.'

Hilary said sharply: 'What knife? The Whistler's a strangler. Everyone knows that's how he kills.'

'Oh, I didn't mention that, did I? She was strangled all right, or I suppose she was. I didn't keep the torchlight on her face longer than was necessary. But he marks his victims, apart from stuffing their mouths with hair. Pubic hair, incidentally. I saw that all right. There was the letter L cut into her forehead. Quite unmistakable. A detective-constable who was talking to me later told me that it's one of the Whistler's trademarks. He thought that the L could stand for Larksoken and that the Whistler might be making some kind of statement about nuclear power, a protest perhaps.'

Alex Mair said sharply: 'That's nonsense.' Then added more calmly: 'There's been nothing on television or in the papers about any cut on the victims' foreheads.'

'The police are keeping it quiet, or trying to. It's the kind of detail they can use to sort out the false confessions. There have been half a dozen of those already apparently. There's been nothing in the media about the hair either, but that piece of unpleasantness seems to be generally known. After all, I'm not the only one to have found a body. People do talk.'

Hilary Robarts said: 'Nothing has been written or said, as far as I know, about it being pubic hair.'

'No, the police are keeping that quiet too, and it's hardly the sort of detail you print in a family newspaper. Not that it's so very surprising. He isn't a rapist but there was bound to be some sexual element.'

It was one of the details which Rickards had told Dalgliesh the previous evening but one, he felt, which Lessingham could well have kept to himself, particularly at a mixed dinner party. He was a little surprised at his sudden sensitivity. Perhaps it was his glance at Meg Dennison's ravaged face. And then his ears caught a faint sound. He looked across to the open door of the dining room and glimpsed the slim figure of Theresa Blaney standing in the shadows. He wondered how much of Lessingham's account she had heard. However little, it would have been too much. He said, hardly aware of the severity in his voice: 'Didn't Chief Inspector Rickards ask you to keep this information confidential?'

There was an embarrassed silence. He thought, They had forgotten for a moment that I'm a policeman.

Lessingham turned to him. 'I intend to keep it confidential. Rickards didn't want it to become public knowledge and it won't. No one here will pass it on.'

But that single question, reminding them of who he was and what he represented, chilled the room and changed their mood from fascinated and horrified interest to a slightly embarrassed unease. And when, a minute later, he got up to say his goodbyes and thank his hostess, there was an almost visible sense of relief. He knew that the embarrassment had nothing to do with the fear that he would question, criticize, move like a spy among them. It wasn't his case and they weren't suspects, and they must have known that he was no cheerful extrovert, flattered to be the centre of attraction while they bombarded him with questions about Chief Inspector Rickards's likely methods, the chance of catching the Whistler, his theories about psychopathic killers, his own experience of serial murder. But merely by being there he increased their awakening fear and repugnance at this latest horror. On each of their minds was imprinted the mental image of that violated face, the half-open mouth stuffed with hair, those staring, sightless eyes, and his presence intensified the picture, brought it into sharper focus. Horror and death were his trade and, like an undertaker, he carried with him the contagion of his craft.

He was at the front door when, on impulse, he turned back and said to Meg Dennison: 'I think you mentioned that you walked from the Old Rectory, Mrs Dennison. Could I walk home with you, that is if it's not too early for you?'

Alex Mair was beginning to say that he, of course, would drive her but Meg extricated herself clumsily from her chair and said, a little too eagerly: 'I'd be grateful if you would. I would like the walk and it would save Alex getting out the car.'

Alice Mair said: 'And it's time Theresa was on her way. We should have driven her home an hour ago. I'll give her father a ring. Where is she, by the way?'

Meg said: 'I think she was next door clearing the table a minute ago.'

'Well, I'll find her and Alex can drive her home.'

The party was breaking up. Hilary Robarts had been slumped back in her chair, her eyes fixed on Lessingham. Now she got to her feet and said: 'I'll get back to my cottage. There's no need for anyone to come with me. As Miles has said, the Whistler's had his kicks for tonight.'

Alex Mair said: 'I'd rather you waited. I'll walk with you once I've taken Theresa home.'

She shrugged and, without looking at him, said: 'All right, if you insist. I'll wait.'

She moved over to the window, staring out into the darkness. Only Lessingham stayed in his chair, reaching again to fill his glass. Dalgliesh saw that Alex Mair had silently placed another opened bottle in the hearth. He wondered whether Alice Mair would invite Lessingham to stay the night at Martyr's Cottage or whether he would be driven home later by her or her brother. He would certainly be in no state to drive himself.

Dalgliesh was helping Meg Dennison into her jacket when the telephone rang, sounding unnaturally strident in the quiet room. He felt her sudden shock of fear and for a moment, almost involuntarily, his hands strengthened on her shoulders. They heard Alex Mair's voice.

'Yes, we've heard. Miles Lessingham is here and gave us the details. Yes, I see. Yes. Thank you for letting me know.' Then there was a longer silence, then Mair's voice again. 'Completely fortuitous, I should say, wouldn't you? After all, we have a staff of five hundred and thirty. But naturally everyone at Larksoken will find the news deeply shocking, the women particularly. Yes, I shall be in my office tomorrow if there's any help I can give. Her family have been told, I suppose? Yes, I see. Goodnight, Chief Inspector.'

He put down the receiver and said: 'That was Chief Inspector Rickards. They've identified the victim. Christine Baldwin. She is – she was – a typist at the station. You didn't recognize her then, Miles?'

Lessingham took his time refilling his glass. He said: 'The police didn't tell me who she was. Even if they had, I wouldn't have remembered the name. And no, Alex, I didn't recognize her. I suppose I must have seen Christine Baldwin at Larksoken, probably in the canteen. But what I saw earlier tonight wasn't Christine Baldwin. And I can assure you that I didn't shine the torch on her longer than I needed to satisfy myself that she was beyond any help that I could give.'

Without looking round from the window Hilary Robarts said: 'Christine Baldwin. Aged thirty-three. Actually, she's only been with us for eleven months. Married last year. Just transferred to the medical physics department. I can give you her typing and shorthand speeds if you're interested.' Then she turned round and looked Alex Mair in the face. 'It looks as if the Whistler's getting closer, doesn't it, in more ways than one.'

13

The final goodbyes were said and they stepped out from the smell of wood smoke, food and wine from a room which Dalgliesh was beginning to find uncomfortably warm into the fresh, sea-scented air. It took a few minutes before his eyes had adjusted to semi-darkness and the great sweep of the headland became visible, its shapes and forms mysteriously altered under the high stars. To the north the power station was a glittering galaxy of white lights, its stark geometric bulk subsumed in the blue-black of the sky.

They stood for a moment regarding it, then Meg Dennison said: 'When I first came here from London it almost frightened me, the sheer size of it, the way it dominates the headland. But I'm getting used to it. It's still disturbing but it does have a certain grandeur. Alex tries to demystify it, says its function is just to produce electricity for the National Grid efficiently and cleanly, that the main difference between this and any other power station is that you don't have beside it a huge pyramid of polluting coal dust. But atomic power to my generation always means that mushroom cloud. And now it means Chernobyl. But if it were an ancient castle standing there against the skyline, if what we looked out at tomorrow morning was a row of turrets, we'd probably be saying how magnificent it is.'

Dalgliesh said: 'If it had a row of turrets it would be a rather different shape. But I know what you mean. I should prefer the headland without it but it's beginning to look as if it had a right to be there.'

They turned simultaneously from contemplating the glittering lights and looked south to the decaying symbol of a very different power. Before them, at the edge of the cliff, crumbling against the skyline like a child's sandcastle rendered amorphous by the advancing tide, was the ruined Benedictine abbey. He could just make out the great empty arch of the east window and beyond it the shimmer of the North Sea while above, seeming to move through and over it like a censer, swung the smudged yellow disc of the moon. Almost without conscious will they took their first steps from the track on to the rough headland towards it. Dalgliesh said: 'Shall we? Can you spare the time? And what about your shoes?'

'Reasonably sensible. Yes, I'd like to, it looks so wonderful at night. And I don't really need to hurry. The Copleys won't have waited up for me. Tomorrow, when I have to tell them how close the Whistler is getting, I may not like to leave them alone after dark. This may be my last free night for some time.'

'I don't think they'd be in any real danger as long as you lock up securely. So far all his victims have been young women and he kills out of doors.'

'I tell myself that. And I don't think they'd be seriously frightened. Sometimes the very old seem to have moved beyond that kind of fear. The trivial upsets of daily living assume importance but the big tragedies they take in their stride. But their daughter is constantly ringing up to suggest they go to her in Wiltshire until he's caught. They don't want to but she's a strong-minded woman and very insistent, and if she telephones after dusk and I'm not there it will increase the pressure on them.' She paused and then said: 'It was a horrible end to an interesting but rather strange dinner party. I wish Mr Lessingham had kept the details to himself, but I suppose it helped him to talk about it, especially as he lives alone.'

Dalgliesh said: 'It would have needed superhuman control not to have talked about it. But I wish he'd omitted the more salacious details.'

'It will make a difference to Alex, too. Already some of the women staff demand to be escorted home after the evening shifts. Alice has told me that that isn't going to be easy for Alex to organize. They'll only accept a male escort if he has an unbreakable alibi for one of the Whistler murders. People cease to be rational even when they've known and worked with someone for the last ten years.'

Dalgliesh said: 'Murder does that, particularly this kind of murder. Miles Lessingham mentioned another death: Toby. Was that the young man who killed himself at the station? I seem to remember a paragraph in one of the papers.'

'It was an appalling tragedy. Toby Gledhill was one of Alex's most brilliant young scientists. He broke his neck by throwing himself down on top of the reactor.'

'So there was no mystery about it?'

'Oh no, absolutely none, except why he did it. Mr Lessingham saw it happen. I'm surprised you remember it. There was very little about it in the national press. Alex tried to minimize the publicity to protect his parents.'

And to protect the power station, thought Dalgliesh. He wondered why Lessingham had described Gledhill's death as murder but he didn't question his companion further. The allegation had been spoken so quietly that he doubted whether she had in fact heard it. Instead he asked: 'Are you happy living on the headland?'

The question did not appear to surprise her but it did surprise him, as did the very fact that they were walking so companionably together. She was curiously restful to be with. He liked her quiet gentleness with its suggestion of underlying strength. Her voice was pleasant and voices were important to him. But six months ago none of this would have been enough to make him invite her company for longer than was politely necessary. He would have escorted her back to the Old Rectory and then, a minor social obligation performed, turned with relief to walk alone to the abbey, drawing his solitude around him like a cloak. That solitude was still essential to him. He couldn't tolerate twenty-four hours in which the greater part wasn't spent entirely alone. But some change in himself, the inexorable years, success, the return of his poetry, perhaps the tentative beginning of love, seemed to be making him sociable. He wasn't sure whether this was something to be welcomed or resisted.

He was aware that she was giving his question careful thought.

'Yes, I think that I am. Sometimes very happy. I came here to escape from the problems of my life in London and, without really meaning to, I came as far east as I could get.'

'And found yourself confronting two different forms of menace, the power station and the Whistler.'

'Both frightening because both mysterious, both rooted in a horror of the unknown. But the menace isn't personal, isn't directed specifically against me. But I did run away and, I suppose, all refugees carry with them a small burden of guilt. And I miss the children. Perhaps I should have stayed and fought on. But it was becoming a very public war. I'm not suited to the role of popular heroine of the more reactionary press. All I wanted was to be left alone to get on with the job I'd been trained for and loved. But every book I used, every word I spoke was scrutinized. You can't teach in an atmosphere of rancorous suspicion. In the end I found I couldn't even live in it.'

She was taking it for granted that he knew who she was; but then anyone who had read the papers must know that.

He said: 'It's possible to fight intolerance, stupidity and fanaticism when they come separately. When you get all three together it's probably wiser to get out, if only to preserve one's sanity.'

They were approaching the abbey now and the grass of the headland was becoming more hillocky. She stumbled and he put out his hand to steady her. She said: 'In the end it came down to just two letters. They insisted that the blackboard should be called the chalkboard. Black or chalk. I didn't believe, I still don't believe that any sensible person, whatever his colour, objects to the word blackboard. It's black and it's a board. The word black in itself can't be offensive. I'd called it that all my life so why should they try to force me to change the way I speak my own language? And yet, at this moment, on this headland, under this sky, this immensity, it all seems so petty. Perhaps all I did was to elevate trivia into a principle.'

Dalgliesh said: 'Agnes Poley would have understood. My aunt

looked up the records and told me about her. She went to the stake, apparently, for an obstinate adherence to her own uncompromising view of the universe. She couldn't accept that Christ's body could be present in the sacrament and at the same time physically in heaven at God's right hand. It was, she said, against common sense. Perhaps Alex Mair should take her as patron of his power station, a quasi-saint of rationality.'

'But that was different. She believed her immortal soul was in jeopardy.'

Dalgliesh said: 'Who knows what she believed? I think she was probably activated by a divine obstinacy. I find that rather admirable.'

Meg said: 'I think Mr Copley would argue that she was wrong, not the obstinacy, but her earthbound view of the sacrament. I'm not really competent to argue about that. But to die horribly for your own common-sense view of the universe is rather splendid. I never visit Alice without standing and reading that plaque. It's my small act of homage. And yet I don't feel her presence in Martyr's Cottage. Do you?'

'Not in the slightest. I suspect that central heating and modern furniture are inimical to ghosts. Did you know Alice Mair before you came here?'

'I knew no one. I answered an advertisement by the Copleys in *The Lady*. They were offering free accommodation and food to someone who would do what they described as a little gentle housework. It's a euphemism for dusting, but of course it never works out like that. Alice has made a great difference. I hadn't realized how much I was missing female friendship. At school we only had alliances, offensive or defensive. Nothing ever cut across political divisions.'

Dalgliesh said: 'Agnes Poley would have understood that atmosphere too. It was the one she breathed.'

For a minute they walked in silence hearing the rustle of the long grasses over their shoes. Dalgliesh wondered why it was that, when walking towards the sea, there came a moment when its roar suddenly increased as if a menace, quiescent and benign, had suddenly realized and gathered up its power. Looking up at the sky, at the myriad pinpricks of light, it seemed to him that he could feel the turning earth beneath his feet and that time had mysteriously come to a stop, fusing into one moment the past, the present and the future; the ruined abbey, the obstinately enduring artefacts of the last war, the crumbling cliff defences, the windmill and the power station. And he wondered whether it was in such a disorientating limbo of time, listening to the ever-restless sea, that the previous owners of Martyr's Cottage had chosen their text. Suddenly his companion stopped and said: 'There's a light in the ruins. Two small flashes, like a torch.'

They stood still and watched in silence. Nothing appeared. She said, almost apologetically: 'I'm sure I saw it. And there was a shadow, something or somebody moving against the eastern window. You didn't see it?'

'I was looking at the sky.'

She said, almost with a note of regret: 'Well, it's gone now. I suppose I could have imagined it.'

And when, five minutes later, they made their way cautiously over the humpy grass into the heart of the ruins there was no one and nothing to be seen. Without speaking they walked through the gap of the east window and on to the edge of the cliff and saw only the moon-bleached beach stretching north and south, the thin fringe of white foam. If anyone had been there, thought Dalgliesh, there was plenty of opportunity for concealment behind the hunks of concrete or in the crevices of the sandy cliff. There was little point and no real justification in attempting to give chase, even if they had known the direction in which he had disappeared. People were entitled to walk alone at night. Meg said again: 'I suppose I could have imagined it, but I don't think so. Anyway, she's gone now.'

'She?'

'Oh yes. Didn't I say? I had the distinct impression it was a woman.'

14

By four o'clock in the morning, when Alice Mair woke with a small despairing cry from her nightmare, the wind was rising. She stretched out her hand to click on the bedside light, checked her watch, then lay back, panic subsiding, her eyes staring at the ceiling while the terrible immediacy of the dream began to fade, recognized for what it was, an old spectre returning after all these years, conjured up by the events of the night and by the reiteration of the word 'murder' which, since the Whistler had begun his work, seemed to murmur sonorously on the very air. Gradually she re-entered the real world, manifested in the small noises of the night, the moan of the wind in the chimneys, the smoothness of the sheet in her clutching hands, the unnaturally loud ticking of her watch and, above all, in that oblong of pale light, the open casement and the drawn curtains which gave her a view of the faintly luminous star-studded sky.

The nightmare needed no interpretation. It was merely a new version of an old horror, less terrible than the dreams of childhood, a more rational, more adult terror. She and Alex were children again, the whole family living with the Copleys at the Old Rectory. That, in a dream, wasn't so surprising. The Old Rectory was only a larger, less pretentious version of Sunnybank — ridiculously named since it had stood on level ground and no sun ever seemed to penetrate its windows. Both were late Victorian, built in solid red brick, both had a strong, curved door under a high, peaked porch, both were isolated, each in its own garden. In the dream she and her father were walking together through the shrubbery. He was carrying his billhook and was dressed as he was on that last dreadful autumn afternoon, a singlet stained with his sweat, the shorts high cut, showing as he walked the bulge of the scrotum, the white legs, matted with black hair from the knees down. She was worried because she knew that the Copleys were waiting for her to cook lunch. Mr Copley, robed in cassock and billowing surplice, was impatiently pacing the back lawn seeming oblivious to their presence. Her father was explaining something to her in that over-loud, careful voice which he used to her mother, the voice which said: 'I know you are too stupid to understand this but I will talk slowly and loudly and hope that you won't try my patience too far.'

He said: 'Alex won't get the job now. I'll see that he doesn't. They won't appoint a man who's murdered his own father.'

And as he spoke he swung the billhook and she saw that its tip was red with blood. Then suddenly he turned towards her, eyes blazing, lifted it, and she felt its point pierce the skin of her forehead, and the sudden spurt of blood gushing into her eyes. Now wide awake, and breathing as if she had been running, she put her hand up to her brow and knew that the cold wetness she felt was sweat not blood.

There was little hope of falling asleep again; there never was when she woke in the early hours. She could get up, put on her dressing gown, go downstairs and make tea, correct her proofs, read, listen to the BBC World Service. Or she could take one of her sleeping tablets. God knew they were powerful enough to knock her into oblivion. But she was trying to wean herself off them and to give in now would be to acknowledge the potency of the nightmare. She would get up and make tea. She had no fear of waking Alex. He slept soundly, even through the winter gales. But first there was a small act of exorcism to be performed. If the dream were to lose its power, if she were somehow to prevent it recurring, she must face again the memory of that afternoon nearly thirty years ago.

It had been a warm autumnal day in early October and she, Alex and her father were working in the garden. He was clearing a thick hedge of brambles and overgrown shrubs at the bottom of the shrubbery and out of sight of the house, slashing at them with a billhook while Alex and she dragged the freed branches clear ready to build a bonfire. Her father was under-clad for the time of year but was sweating heavily. She saw the arm lifting and falling, heard the crack of twigs, felt again the thorns cutting her fingers, heard his high commands. And then, suddenly, he gave a cry. Either the branch had been rotten or he had missed his aim. The billhook had sliced into his naked thigh and, turning, she saw the great curve of red blood begin to bubble in the air, saw him slowly sink like a wounded animal, his hands plucking the air. His right hand dropped the billhook and he held it out to her, shaking, palm upward, and looked at her beseechingly, like a child. He tried to speak but she couldn't make out the words. She was moving towards him, fascinated, when suddenly she felt a clutch on her arm and Alex was dragging her with him down the path between the laurels towards the orchard.

She cried: 'Alex, stop! He's bleeding. He's dying. We've got to get help.'

She couldn't remember whether she actually said the words. All she later remembered was the strength of his hands on her shoulders as he forced her back against the bark of an apple tree and held her there, imprisoned. And he spoke a single word.

'No.'

Shaking with terror, her heart pounding, she couldn't have broken free even if she had wanted. And she knew now that this powerlessness was important to him. It had been his act and his alone. Compelled, absolved, she had been given no choice. Now, thirty years later, lying rigid, her eyes fixed on the sky, she remembered that single word, his eyes looking into hers, his hands on her shoulders, the bark of the tree scraping her back through her Aertex shirt. Time seemed to stop. She couldn't remember now how long he had held her imprisoned, only that it seemed an eternity of immeasurable time.

And then, at last, he gave a sigh and said: 'All right. We can go now.'

And that, too, amazed her, that he should have been thinking so clearly, calculating how long it would take. He dragged her after him until they stood over her father's body. And, looking down at the still-outstretched arm, the glazed and open eyes, the great scarlet pool soaking into the earth, she knew that it was a body, that he had gone for ever, that there was nothing she need fear from him ever again. Alex turned to her and spoke each word loudly and clearly as if she were a subnormal child.

'Whatever he's been doing to you, he won't do it again. Ever. Listen to me and I'll tell you what happened. We left him and went down to climb the apple trees. Then we decided that we'd better get back. Then we found him. That's all there is, it's as simple as that. You don't need to say anything else. Just leave the talking to me. Look at me, look at me, Alice. You understand?'

Her voice, when it came, sounded like an old woman's voice, cracked and tremulous, and the words strained her throat. 'Yes, I understand.'

And then he was dragging her by the hands, racing across the lawn, nearly pulling her arm from its socket, crashing through the kitchen door, crying aloud so that it sounded like a whoop of triumph. She saw her mother's face draining as if she too were bleeding to death, heard his panting voice.

'It's Father. He's had an accident. Get a doctor quick.'

And then she was alone in the kitchen. It was very cold. There were cold tiles under her feet. The surface of the wooden table on which she rested her head was cold to her cheeks. No one came. She was aware of a voice telephoning from the hall, and other voices, other steps. Someone was crying. Now there were more footsteps and the crunch of car wheels on gravel.

And Alex had been right. It had all been very simple. No one had questioned her, no one had been suspicious. Their story had been accepted. She didn't go to the inquest but Alex did, although he never told her what happened there. Afterwards some of the people concerned, their family doctor, the solicitor, a few of her mother's friends, came back and there was a curious tea party with sandwiches and home-made fruitcake. They were kind to her and Alex. Someone actually patted her head. A voice said, 'It was tragic that there was no one there. Common sense and a rudimentary knowledge of first aid would have saved him.'

But now the memory deliberately evoked had completed its exorcism. The nightmare had been robbed of its terror. With luck it might not return for months. She swung her legs out of bed and reached for her dressing gown.

She had just poured the boiling water on the tea and was standing waiting for it to brew when she heard Alex's footsteps on the stairs and, turning, she saw his tall figure blocking the kitchen door. He looked boyish, almost vulnerable, in the familiar corded dressing gown. He pushed both hands through his sleep-tousled hair. Surprised, because he was usually a sound sleeper, she said: 'Did I disturb you? Sorry.'

'No, I woke earlier and couldn't get off again. Holding dinner for Lessingham made it too late for comfortable digestion. Is this fresh?'

'About ready to pour.'

He took down a second mug from the dresser and poured tea for them both. She seated herself in a wicker chair and took her mug without speaking.

He said: 'The wind's rising.'

'Yes, it has been for the last hour.'

He went over to the door and unbolted the top wooden panel, pushing it open. There was a sensation of rushing white coldness, scentless, but obliterating the faint tang of the tea and she heard the low growling roar of the sea. As she listened it seemed to rise in intensity so that she could imagine, with an agreeable *frisson* of simulated terror, that the low friable cliffs had finally crumbled and that the white foaming turbulence was rolling towards them across the headland, would crash against the door and throw its spume on Alex's face. Looking at him as he stared into the night, she felt a surge of affection as pure and as uncomplicated as the flow of cold air against her face. Its fleeting intensity surprised her. He was so much a part of her that she never needed nor wanted to examine too closely the nature of her feeling for him. She knew that she was always quietly satisfied to have him in the cottage, to hear his footfalls on the floor above, to share with him the meal she had cooked for herself at the end of the day. And yet neither made demands of the other. Even his marriage had made no difference. She had been unsurprised at the marriage since she had rather liked Elizabeth, but equally unsurprised when it ended. She thought it unlikely that he would marry again, but nothing between them would change, however many wives entered, or attempted to enter, his life. Sometimes as now she would smile wryly, knowing how outsiders saw their relationship. Those who assumed that the cottage was owned by him, not her, saw her as the unmarried sister, dependent on him for house-room, companionship, a purpose in life. Others, more perceptive but still nowhere near the truth, were intrigued by their apparent independence of each other, their casual comings and goings, their non-involvement. She remembered Elizabeth saying in the first weeks of her engagement to Alex, 'Do you know, you're a rather intimidating couple?' and she had been tempted to reply, 'Oh, we are, we are.'

She had bought Martyr's Cottage before his appointment as Director of the power station and he had moved in by an unspoken agreement that this was a temporary expedient while he decided what to do, keep on the Barbican flat as his main home or sell the flat and buy a house in Norwich and a smaller *pied-à-terre* in London. He was essentially an urban creature; she didn't see him settling permanently other than in a city. If, with the new job, he moved back to London she wouldn't follow him, and nor, she knew, would he expect her to. Here on this sea-scoured coast she had at last found a place which she was content to call home. That he could walk in and out of it unannounced never made it less than her own.

It must, she thought sipping her tea, have been after one o'clock when he returned from seeing Hilary Robarts home. She wondered what had kept him. Sleeping lightly as always in the early hours, she had heard his key in the lock, his foot on the stairs, before drifting again into sleep. Now it was getting on for five o'clock. He couldn't have had more than a few hours' sleep. Now, as if suddenly aware of the morning chill, he closed the top half of the door, drove home the bolt, then came and stretched himself out in the armchair opposite her. Leaning back, he cradled his mug in his hands.

He said: 'It's a nuisance that Caroline Amphlett doesn't want to leave Larksoken. I don't relish beginning a new job, particularly this job, with an unknown PA. Caroline knows the way I work. I'd rather taken it for granted that she'd come to London with me. It's inconvenient.'

And it was, she suspected, rather more than inconvenient. Pride, even personal prestige, were also at stake. Other senior men took their personal assistants with them when changing jobs. The reluctance of a secretary to be parted from her boss was a flattering affirmation of personal dedication. She could sympathize with his chagrin but it was hardly enough to keep him awake at night.

He added: 'Personal reasons, or so she says. That means Jonathan Reeves, presumably. God knows what she sees in him. The man isn't even a good technician.'

Alice Mair controlled her smile. She said: 'I doubt whether her interest in him is technical.'

'Well, if it's sexual she has less discrimination than I gave her credit for.'

He wasn't, she told herself, a poor judge of men or women. He rarely made fundamental mistakes and never, she suspected, about a man's scientific ability. But he had no understanding of the extraordinary complexities and irrationalities of human motives, human behaviour. He knew that the universe was complex but that it obeyed certain rules, although, she supposed, he wouldn't have used the word 'obey' with its implication of conscious choice. This, he would say, is how the physical world behaves. It is open to human reason and, to a limited extent, to human control. People disconcerted him because they could surprise him. Most disconcerting of all was the fact that he occasionally surprised himself. He would have been at home as a sixteenth-century Elizabethan, categorizing people according to their essential natures; choleric, melancholic, mercurial, saturnine, qualities mirroring the planets that governed their birth. That basic fact established, then you knew where you were. And yet it could still surprise him that a man could be a sensible and reliable scientist in his work and a fool with women, could show judgement in one area of his life and act like an irrational child in another. Now he was peeved because his secretary, whom he had categorized as intelligent, sensible, dedicated, preferred to stay in Norfolk with her lover, a man he despised, rather than follow him to London.

She said: 'I thought you said once that you found Caroline sexually cold.'

'Did I? Surely not. That would suggest a degree of personal experience. I think I said I couldn't imagine ever finding her physically attractive. A PA who is personable and highly efficient but not sexually tempting is the ideal.'

She said drily: 'I imagine that a man's idea of the ideal secretary is a woman who manages to imply that she would like to go to bed with her boss but nobly restrains herself in the interests of office efficiency. What will happen to her?'

'Oh, her job's secure. If she wants to stay at Larksoken there will be plenty of competition to get her. She's intelligent as well as tactful and efficient.'

'But presumably not ambitious, else why should she be content to remain at Larksoken?' She added: 'Caroline may have another reason for wanting to stay in the area. I saw her in Norwich

Cathedral about three weeks ago. She met a man in the Lady Chapel. They were very discreet but it looked to me like an assignation.'

He asked, but without real curiosity: 'What kind of man?'

'Middle-aged. Nondescript. Difficult to describe. But he was too old to be Jonathan Reeves.'

She said no more, knowing that he wasn't particularly interested, that his mind had moved elsewhere. And yet, looking back, it had been an odd encounter. Caroline's blonde hair had been bundled under a large beret and she was wearing spectacles. But the disguise, if it were meant as a disguise, had been ineffective. She herself had moved on swiftly, anxious not to be recognized or to seem a spy. A minute later she had seen the girl slowly walking along the aisle, guidebook in hand, the man strolling behind her carefully distanced. They had moved together and had stood in front of a monument, seemingly absorbed. And when, ten minutes later, Alice was leaving the cathedral she had glimpsed him again. This time it was he who was carrying the guidebook.

He made no further comment about Caroline but after a minute's silence he said: 'Not a particularly successful dinner party.'

'An understatement. Beta-minus, except, of course, for the food. What's the matter with Hilary? Is she actually trying to be disagreeable or is she merely unhappy?'

'People usually are when they can't get what they want.'

'In her case, you.'

He smiled into the empty fire grate but didn't reply.

After a moment she said: 'Is she likely to be a nuisance?'

'Rather more than a nuisance. She's likely to be dangerous.'

'Dangerous? How dangerous? You mean dangerous to you personally?'

'To rather more than me.'

'But nothing you can't cope with?'

'Nothing I can't cope with. But not by making her Administrative Officer. She'd be a disaster. I should never have appointed her in an acting capacity.'

'When are you making the appointment?'

'In ten days' time. There's a good field.'

'So you've got ten days to decide what to do about her.'

'Rather less than that. She wants a decision by Sunday.'

A decision about what? she wondered. Her job, a possible promotion, her future life with Alex? But surely the woman could see that she had no future with Alex.

She asked, knowing the importance of the question, knowing, too, that only she would dare ask it, 'Will you be very disappointed if you don't get the job?'

'I'll be aggrieved, which is rather more destructive of one's peace of mind. I want it, I need it and I'm the right person for it. I suppose that's what every candidate thinks but in my case it happens to be true. It's an important job, Alice. One of the most important there is. The future lies with nuclear power, if we're going to save this planet, but we've got to manage it better, nationally and internationally.'

'I imagine you're the only serious candidate. Surely this is the kind of appointment which they only decide to make when they know they've got the right man available. It's a new job. They've managed perfectly well without a nuclear supremo up to now. I can see that, given the right man, the job has immense possibilities. But in the wrong hands it's just another public relations job, a waste of public money.'

He was too intelligent not to know that she was reassuring him. She was the only person from whom he ever needed reassurance or would ever take it.

He said: 'There's a suspicion that we could be getting into a mess. They want someone to get us out of it. Minor matters like his precise powers, who he'll be responsible to and how much he'll be paid have yet to be decided. That's why they're taking so long over the job specification.'

She said: 'You don't need a written job specification to know what they're looking for. A respected scientist, a proven administrator and a good public relations expert. They'll probably ask you to take a TV test. Looking good on the box seems to be the prerequisite for anything these days.'

'Only for future presidents or prime ministers. I don't think they'll go that far.'

He glanced at the clock. 'It's already dawn. I think I'll get a couple of hours' sleep.' But it was an hour later before they finally parted and went to their rooms.

15

Dalgliesh waited until Meg had unlocked the front door and stepped inside before saying his final goodnight, and she stood for a moment watching his tall figure striding down the gravel path and into the darkness. Then she passed into the square, tessellated hall with its stone fireplace, the hall which, on winter nights, seemed to echo faintly with the childish voices of Victorian rectors' children and which, for Meg, had always held a faintly ecclesiastical smell. Folding her coat over the ornate wooden newel post at the foot of the stairs, she went through to the kitchen and the last task of the day, setting out the Copleys' early-morning tray. It was a large, square room at the back of the house, archaic when the Copleys had bought the Old Rectory and unaltered since. Against the left-hand wall stood an old-fashioned gas stove so heavy that Meg was unable to move it to clean behind it and preferred not to think of the accumulated grease of decades gumming it to the wall. Under the window was a deep porcelain sink stained with the detritus of seventy years' washing-up and impossible to clean adequately. The floor was of ancient stone slabs, hard on the feet, from which in winter there seemed to rise a damp, foot-numbing miasma. The wall opposite the sink and the window was covered with an oak dresser, very old and probably valuable, if it had been possible to remove it from the wall without its collapse, and the original row of bells still hung over the door each with its Gothic script; drawing room, dining room, study, nursery. It was a kitchen to challenge rather than enhance the skills of any cook ambitious beyond the boiling of eggs. But now Meg hardly noticed its deficiencies. Like the rest of the Old Rectory it had become home.

After the stridency and aggression of the school, the hate-mail, she was happy to find her temporary asylum in this gentle household where voices were never raised, where no one obsessively analysed her every sentence in the hope of detecting racist, sexist or fascist undertones, where words meant what they had meant for generations, where obscenities were unknown or at least unspoken, where there was the grace of good order symbolized for her in Mr Copley's reading of the Church's daily offices, Morning Prayer and Evensong. Sometimes she saw the three of them as expatriates, stranded in some remote colony, obstinately adhering to old customs, a lost way of life, as they did to old forms of worship. And she had grown to like both her employers. She would have respected Simon Copley more if he had been less prone to venial selfishness, less preoccupied with his physical comfort, but this she told herself was probably the result of fifty years of spoiling by a devoted wife. And he loved his wife. He relied on her. He respected her judgement. How lucky they were, she thought; secure in each other's affection and presumably fortified in increasing age by the certainty that if they weren't granted the grace of death on the same day there would be no lasting separation. But did they really believe this? She would like to have asked them, but knew that it would have been impossibly presumptuous. Surely they must have some doubts, made some mental reservations to the creed they so confidently recited morning and night. But perhaps what mattered at eighty was habit, the body no longer interested in sex, the mind no longer interested in speculation, the smaller things in life mattering more than the large and, in the end, the slow realization that nothing really mattered at all.

The job wasn't arduous, but she knew that gradually she was taking on much more than the advertisement had suggested and she sensed that the main anxiety of their life was whether she would stay. Their daughter had provided all the labour-saving devices: dishwasher, washing machine, spin-dryer, all housed in a disused still room near the back door, although until she came the Copleys had been reluctant to use them in case they couldn't turn them off, visualizing the machines whirling away all night, overheating, blowing up, the whole rectory pulsating with an uncontrollable power.

Their only child lived in a manor house in Wiltshire and rarely visited, although she telephoned frequently, usually at inconvenient times. It was she who had interviewed Meg for the Old Rectory and Meg now found it difficult to connect that confident, tweeded, slightly aggressive woman with the two gentle old people she knew. And she knew, although they would never have dreamt of telling her, perhaps didn't even admit it to themselves, that they were afraid of her. She bullied them, as she would have claimed, for their own good. Their second greatest fear was that they might be forced to comply with her frequently telephoned suggestion, made purely from a sense of duty, that they should go to stay with her until the Whistler was caught.

Unlike their daughter, Meg could understand why, after retirement, they had used all their savings to buy the rectory and had in old age burdened themselves with a mortgage. Mr Copley had in youth been a curate at Larksoken when the Victorian church was still standing. It was in that ugly repository of polished pine, acoustic tiles and garish, sentimental stained glass that he and his wife had been married, and in a flat in the rectory, living above the parish priest, that they had made their first home. The church had been partly demolished by a devastating gale in the 1930s, to the secret relief of the Church Commissioners who had been considering what to do with a building of absolutely no architectural merit serving a congregation at the major festivals of six at the most. So the church had been finally demolished and the Old Rectory, sheltering behind it and proving more durable, had been sold. Rosemary Duncan-Smith had made her views plain when driving Meg back to Norwich station after her interview.

'It's ridiculous for them to be living there at all, of course. They should have looked for a two-bedded, well-equipped flat in Norwich or in a convenient village close to the shops and post office, and to a church, of course. But Father can be remarkably obstinate when he thinks he knows what he wants and Mother is putty in his hands. I hope you aren't seeing this job as a temporary expedient.'

Meg had replied: 'Temporary, but not short-term. I can't promise that I'll stay permanently, but I need time and peace to decide on my future. And I may not suit your parents.'

'Time and peace. We'd all be glad of that. Well, I suppose it's better than nothing, but I'd be grateful for a month or two's notice when you do decide to go. And I shouldn't worry about suiting. With an inconvenient house and stuck out on that head-land with nothing to look at but a ruined abbey and that atomic power station they'll have to put up with what they can get.'

But that had been sixteen months ago and she was still here.

But it was in that beautifully designed and equipped, but comfortable and homely kitchen at Martyr's Cottage that she had found her healing. Early in their friendship, when Alice had to spend a week in London and Alex was away, she had given Meg one of her spare keys to the cottage so that she could go in to collect and forward her post. On her return, when Meg offered it back, she had said: 'Better keep it. You may need it again.' Meg had never again used it. The door was usually open in summer and, when shut, she would always ring. But its possession, the sight and weight of it on her key ring, had come to symbolize for her the certainty and the trust of their friendship. She had been so long without a woman friend. She had forgotten, some-times she told herself, that she had never before known the comfort of a close, undemanding, asexual companionship with another woman.

Before the accidental drowning of her husband four years earlier, she and Martin had needed only the occasional compan-ionship of friendly acquaintances to affirm their self-sufficiency. Theirs had been one of those childless, self-absorbing marriages which unconsciously repel attempts at intimacy. The occasional dinner party was a social duty; they could hardly wait to get back to the seclusion of their own small house. And after his death it seemed to her that she had walked in darkness like an automaton through a deep and narrow canyon of grief in which all her energies, all her physical strength, had been husbanded to get through each day. She thought and worked and grieved only for a day at a time. To allow herself even to think of the days, the weeks, the months or years stretching ahead would have been to precipitate disaster. For two years she had hardly been sane. Even her Christianity was of little help. She didn't reject it, but it had become irrelevant, its comfort only a candle which served fitfully to illumine the dark. But when, after those two years, the valley had almost imperceptibly widened and there was for the first time, not those black enclosing cliffs, but the vista of a normal life, even of happiness, a landscape over which it was possible to believe the sun might shine, she had become unwittingly embroiled in the racial politics of her school. The older members of staff had moved or retired, and the new headmistress, specifically appointed to enforce the fashionable orthodoxies, had moved in with crusading zeal to smell out and eradicate heresy. Meg realized now that she had, from the first, been the obvious, the predestined victim.

She had fled to this new life on the headland and to a different solitude. And here she had found Alice Mair. They had met a fortnight after Meg's arrival when Alice had called at the Old Rectory with a suitcase of jumble for the annual sale in aid of St Andrew's Church in Lydsett.

There was an unused scullery leading off a passage between the kitchen and the back door which was used as a collecting point for unwanted items from the headland; clothes, bric-à-brac, books and old magazines. Mr Copley took an occasional service at St Andrew's when Mr Smollett, the vicar, was on holiday, an involvement in church and village life which, Meg suspected, was as important to him as it was to the church. Normally, little jumble could be expected from the few cottages on the headland, but Alex Mair, anxious to associate the power station with the community, had put up a notice on the staff board and the two tea chests were usually fairly full by the time the October sale came round. The back door of the Old Rectory, giving access to the scullery, was normally left open during daylight hours and an inner door to the house locked, but Alice Mair had knocked at the front door and made herself known. The two women, close in age, both reserved, both independent, neither deliberately seeking a friend, had liked each other. The next week Meg had received an invitation to dinner at Martyr's Cottage. And now there was rarely a day when she didn't walk the half mile over the headland to sit in Alice's kitchen and talk and watch while she worked.

Her colleagues at school would, she knew, have found their friendship incomprehensible. Friendship there, or what passed for friendship, never crossed the great divide of political allegiance and in the acrimonious clamour of the staffroom could swiftly deteriorate into gossip, rumours, recriminations and betrayal.

This peaceable friendship, asking nothing, was as devoid of intensity as it was of anxiety. It was not a demonstrative friendship; they had never kissed, had never indeed touched hands except at that first meeting. Meg wasn't sure what it was that Alice valued in her, but she knew what she valued in Alice. Intelligent, well-read, unsentimental, unshockable, she had become the focus of Meg's life on the headland.

She seldom saw Alex Mair. During the day he was at the power station and at weekends, reversing the normal peregrination, he was at his London flat, frequently staying there for part of the week if he had a meeting in town. She had never felt that Alice had deliberately kept them apart, fearing that her brother would be bored by her friend. In spite of all the traumas of the last four years Meg's inner self was too confidently rooted to be prone to that kind of sexual or social self-abasement. But she had never felt at home with him, perhaps because, with his confident good looks and the air of arrogance in his bearing, he seemed both to represent and to have absorbed something of the mystery and potency of the power he operated. He was perfectly amiable to her on the few occasions when they did meet; sometimes she even felt that he liked her. But their only common ground was in the kitchen of Martyr's Cottage and even there she was always more at home when he was away. Alice never spoke of him except casually but on the few occasions, like last night's dinner party, when she had seen them together they seemed to have the intuitive mutual awareness, an instinctive response to the other's needs, more typical of a long-standing successful marriage than of an apparently casual fraternal relationship.

And for the first time in nearly three years she had been able to talk about Martin. She remembered that July day, the kitchen door open to the patio, the scent of herbs and sea stronger even than the spicy, buttery smell of newly baked biscuits. She and Alice had sat opposite each other, across the kitchen table, the teapot between them. She could remember every word.

'He didn't get many thanks. Oh, they said how heroic he was and the headmaster said all the right things at the school memorial service. But they thought that the boys shouldn't have been swimming there anyway. The school disclaimed any responsibility for his death. They were more anxious to escape criticism than to honour Martin. And the boy he saved hasn't turned out very well. I suppose I'm silly to worry about that.'

'It would be perfectly natural to hope that your husband hadn't died for someone second-rate, but I suppose the boy has a point of view. It could be an awesome responsibility knowing that someone has died for you.'

Meg said: 'I tried to tell myself that. For a time I was – well, almost obsessed with that boy. I used to hang about the school waiting for him to come out. Sometimes I had the need almost to touch him. It was as if some part of Martin had passed into him. But he was only embarrassed, of course. He didn't want to see me or talk to me, he or his parents. He wasn't, in fact, a very nice boy, a bully and rather stupid. I don't think Martin even liked him although he never said so. He was spotty, too – oh dear, that wasn't his fault, I don't know why I even mentioned it.'

And she had wondered how it was she was speaking of him at all. For the first time after all these years. And that business about her obsession with him; she had never mentioned that to a living soul.

Alice had said: 'It's a pity your husband didn't leave him to drown and save himself, but I suppose that on the spur of the moment he didn't weigh up the relative value of a useful teaching career and pimpled stupidity.'

'Leave him to drown? Deliberately? Oh Alice, you know you couldn't do that yourself.'

'Perhaps not. I'm perfectly capable of irrational folly. I'd probably pull him out if I could do it without too much danger to myself.'

'Of course you would. It's human instinct, surely, to save others, particularly a child.'

'It's human instinct, and a thoroughly healthy one in my view, to save oneself. That's why, when people don't, we call them heroes and give them medals. We know they're acting against nature. I can't understand how you can have such an extraordinarily benign view of the universe.'

'Have I? I suppose I have. Except for the two years after Martin drowned I've always been able to believe that at the heart of the universe there is love.'

'At the heart of the universe there is cruelty. We are predators and are preyed upon, every living thing. Did you know that wasps lay their eggs in ladybirds, piercing the weak spot in their armour? Then the grub grows and feeds on the living ladybird and eats its way out, tying the ladybird's legs together. Whoever thought of that has, you have to admit, a peculiar sense of humour. And don't quote Tennyson at me.'

'Perhaps it doesn't feel anything, the ladybird.'

'Well, it's a comforting thought but I wouldn't bet on it. You must have had an extraordinarily happy childhood.'

'Oh, I did, I did! I was lucky. I would have liked brothers and sisters but I don't remember that I was ever lonely. There wasn't much money but there was a great deal of love.'

'Love. Is that so very important? You were a teacher, you ought to know. Is it?'

'It's vital. If a child has it for the first ten years hardly anything else matters. If he hasn't, then nothing does.'

There had been a moment's silence and then Alice had said: 'My father died, killed in an accident when I was fifteen.'

'How terrible. What kind of accident? Were you there? Did you see it?'

'He cut an artery with a billhook. He bled to death. No, we didn't see it, but we were on the scene soon afterwards. Too late, of course.'

'Alex too, and he was even younger. How awful for you both.'

'It had its effect on our lives undoubtedly, particularly mine. Why don't you try one of those biscuits? It's a new recipe but I'm not sure that it's entirely successful. A little too sweet, and I may have overdone the spice. Tell me what you think.'

Recalled to the present by the cold of the flagstones numbing her feet and automatically aligning the cup handles, she suddenly realized why she had remembered that summer teatime in Martyr's Cottage. The biscuits she would add to the tray next morning were a later batch of the same recipe provided by Alice. But she wouldn't take them from the tin until tomorrow. There was nothing more to do tonight except to fill her hot-water bottle. There was no central heating in the Old Rectory and she seldom switched on the two-bar electric fire in her bedroom, knowing how worried the Copleys were by their fuel bills. Finally, hugging the bottle's warmth to her chest, she checked on the bolts of the front and back doors and made her way up the uncarpeted stairs to bed. On the landing she met Mrs Copley, dressing-gowned, scurrying furtively to the bathroom. Although there was a cloakroom on the ground floor the Old Rectory had only one bathroom, a defect which necessitated embarrassed, low-voiced inquiries before anyone upset their carefully worked out rota by taking an unexpected bath. Meg waited until she heard the main bedroom door shut before going herself to the bathroom.

Fifteen minutes later she was in bed. She knew rather than felt that she was very tired and recognized the symptoms of an overstimulated brain in an exhausted body, the restless limbs and inability to get comfortable. The Old Rectory was too far inland for her to hear the crash of the waves but the smell and the throb of the sea were always present. In summer the headland would vibrate with a gentle rhythmic humming which, on stormy nights or at the spring tides would rise to an angry moan. She slept always with her window open and would drift into sleep soothed by that distant murmur. But tonight it had no power to lull her into unconsciousness. Her bedside book, often reread, was Anthony Trollope's *The Small House at Allington* but tonight it could no longer translate her to the reassuring, comfortable, nostalgic world of Barsetshire, to croquet on Mrs Dale's lawn and dinner at the squire's table. The memories of the evening were too traumatic, too exciting, too recent to be easily assuaged by sleep. She opened her eyes to the darkness, a darkness too often populated before sleep by those familiar, reproachful, childish faces, brown, black and white, bending over her, asking why she had deserted them when they loved her and thought that she had loved them. Usually it was a relief to be free of those gentle and accusing ghosts, which in the last few months had visited her less often. And sometimes they were replaced by a more traumatic memory. The headmistress had tried to insist that she go on a racial awareness course, she who had taught children of different races for over twenty years. There was one scene which for months she had tried resolutely to put out of her mind, that last meeting in the staffroom, the circle of implacable faces, brown, black and white, the accusing eyes, the insistent questions. And in the end, worn down by bullying, she had found herself helplessly weeping. No nervous breakdown, that useful euphemism, had been more humiliating.

But tonight even that shameful memory was replaced by more recent and more disquieting visions. She glimpsed again that girlish figure momentarily outlined against the walls of the abbey only to slip away like a wraith and be lost among the shadows of the beach. She sat again at the dinner table and saw in the candlelight Hilary Robarts's dark, discontented eyes staring intently at Alex Mair; watched the planes of Miles Lessingham's face fitfully lit by the leaping flames of the fire, saw his long-fingered hands reaching down for the bottle of claret, heard again that measured rather high voice speaking the unspeakable. And then, on the verge of sleep, she was crashing with him through the bushes of that dreadful wood, feeling the briars scratching her legs, the low twigs whipping against her cheeks, staring with him as the pool of light from the torch shone down on that grotesque and mutilated face. And in that twilight world between waking and sleeping she saw that it was a face she knew, her own. She jerked back to consciousness with a little cry of terror, switched on the bedside lamp, reached out for her book and began resolutely to read. Half an hour later, the book slipped out of her hand and she fell into the first of the night's uneasy periods of slumber.

16

It took only two minutes of lying stretched and rigid on his bed for Alex Mair to realize that sleep was unlikely to come. To lie in bed wakeful had always been intolerable to him. He could manage with little sleep but that was invariably sound. Now he swung his legs out of bed, reached for his dressing gown and walked over to the window. He would watch the sun rise over the North Sea. He thought back over the last few hours, the acknowledged relief of talking to Alice, the knowledge that nothing shocked her, nothing surprised her, that everything he did, if not right in her eyes, was judged by a different standard from the one she rigorously applied to the rest of her life.

The secret that lay between them, those minutes when he had held her shaking body against the tree trunk and stared into her eyes, compelling obedience, had bound them with a cord so strong that it couldn't be frayed, either by the enormity of their shared guilty secret, or by the small rubs of living together. And yet they had never spoken of their father's death. He didn't know whether Alice ever thought of it, or whether the trauma had erased it from her mind so that she now believed the version he had formulated, had taken the lie into her unconscious and made it her truth. When, quite soon after the funeral, seeing how calm she was, he had imagined that possibility he had been surprised at his reluctance to believe it. He didn't want her gratitude. It was degrading even to contemplate that she would feel an obligation towards him. Obligation and gratitude were words they had never needed to use. But he did want her to know and to remember. The deed was to him so monstrous, so surprising, that it would have been intolerable not to have shared it with a living soul. In those early months he had wanted her to know the magnitude of what he had done and that he had done it for her.

And then, six weeks after the funeral, he had suddenly found himself able to believe that it hadn't happened, not in that way, and that the whole horror was a childhood fantasy. He would lie awake at night and see his father's crumbling figure, the leap of blood like a scarlet fountain, would hear the harshly whispered words. In this revised and comforting version there had been a second of delay, no more, and then he had raced for the house shouting for help. And there was a second and even more admirable fantasy in which he had knelt at his father's side, had pressed his clenched fist hard into the groin, quenching the spurting blood, had whispered reassurance into those dying eyes. It had been too late, of course; but he had tried. He had done his best. The coroner had praised him, that precise little man with his half-moon spectacles, his face like a querulous parrot. 'I congratulate the deceased's son who acted with commendable promptness and courage and did everything possible to try to save his father's life.'

The relief of being able to believe in his innocence was at first so great that temporarily it overwhelmed him. He had lain in bed night after night drifting into sleep on a tide of euphoria. But he had known, even then, that this self-administered absolution was like a drug in the bloodstream. It was comforting and easy, but it wasn't for him. That way lay a danger more destructive even than guilt. He had told himself: 'I must never believe that a lie is the truth. I may tell lies all my life if it's expedient but I must know them for what they are and I must never tell them to myself. Facts are facts. I have to accept them and face them and then I can learn how to deal with them. I can look for reasons for what I did and call those reasons excuses; what he did to Alice, how he bullied Mother, how I hated him. I can attempt to justify his death at least to myself. But I did what I did and he died as he died.'

And with that acceptance came a kind of peace. After a few years he was able to believe that guilt itself was an indulgence, that he didn't need to suffer it unless he chose. And then there came a time when he felt a pride in the deed, in the courage, the audacity, the resolution which had made it possible. But that, too, he knew was dangerous. And for years afterwards he hardly thought of his father. Neither his mother nor Alice ever spoke of him except in the company of casual acquaintances who felt the need to utter embarrassed condolences from which there was no escape. But in the family only once was his name mentioned.

A year after the death his mother had married Edmund Morgan, a widowed church organist of mind-numbing dullness, and had retired with him to Bognor Regis where they lived on his father's insurance money in a spacious bungalow in sight of the sea, in an obsessive mutual devotion which mirrored the meticulous order and tidiness of their world. His mother always spoke of her new husband as Mr Morgan. 'If I don't talk to you about your father, Alex, it isn't that I've forgotten him, but Mr Morgan wouldn't like it.' The phrase had become a catchword between him and Alice. The conjunction of Morgan's job and his instrument offered endless possibilities of adolescent jokes, particularly when he and their mother were on honeymoon. 'I expect Mr Morgan is pulling out all his stops.' 'Do you suppose Mr Morgan is changing his combinations?' 'Poor Mr Morgan, labouring away. I hope he doesn't run out of wind.' They were wary, reticent children, yet this joke would reduce them to screams of helpless laughter. Mr Morgan and his organ releasing them into hysterical laughter had anaesthetized the horror of the past.

And then, when he was about eighteen, reality of another kind intruded itself and he said aloud, 'I didn't do it for Alice, I did it for myself', and thought how extraordinary it was that it had taken four years to discover that fact. And yet was it a fact, was it the truth, or was it merely a psychological speculation which in certain moods he found it interesting to contemplate?

Now, looking out over the headland to the eastern sky already flushed with the first faint gold of dawn, he said aloud: 'I let my father die deliberately. That is a fact. All the rest is pointless speculation.' In fiction, he thought, Alice and I should have been tormented by our joint knowledge, distrustful, guilt-ridden, unable to live apart yet miserable together. Yet since his father's death there had been nothing between him and his sister but companionship, affection, peace.

But now, nearly thirty years later, when he thought he had long come to terms with the deed and his own reaction to it, memory had begun to stir again. It had started with the first Whistler murder. The word 'murder' itself constantly on some-one's lips, like a sonorous curse, seemed to have the power to evoke those half-suppressed images of his father's face which had become as unclear, as devoid of any life, as an old photograph. But in the last six months his father's image had begun to intrude on his consciousness at odd moments, in the middle of a meeting, across a boardroom table, in a gesture, the droop of an eyelid, the tone of a voice, the line of a speaker's mouth, the shape of fingers splayed to an open fire. His father's ghost had returned in the tangle of late-summer foliage, the first fall of the leaves, the tentative autumn smells. He wondered if the same thing was happening to Alice. For all their mutual sympathy, for all the sense he had of their being irrevocably bound together, this was the one question he knew he would never ask.

And there were other questions, one question in particular, which he had no need to fear from her. She wasn't in the least curious about his sexual life. He knew enough psychology to have at least some insight into what those early shaming and terrifying experiences had done to her. Sometimes he thought that she regarded his affairs with a casual, slightly amused indulgence as if, herself immune to a childish weakness, she was nevertheless indisposed to criticize it in others. Once, after his divorce, she had said: 'I find it extraordinary that a straightforward if inelegant device for ensuring the survival of the species should involve human beings in such emotional turmoil. Does sex have to be taken so seriously?' And now he found himself wondering whether she knew or guessed about Amy. And then, as the flaming ball rose from the sea, the gears of time slipped, went into reverse and he was back only five days ago lying with Amy in the deep hollow of the dunes, smelling again the scent of sand and grasses and the salt tang of the sea as the late afternoon warmth drained out of the autumn air. He could recall every sentence, every gesture, the timbre of her voice, could feel again the hairs rising on his arms at her touch.

17

She turned towards him, her head propped on her hand, and he saw the strong afternoon light shafting with gold the cropped brightly dyed hair. Already the warmth was draining from the air and he knew that it was time they were moving. But lying there beside her, listening to the susurration of the tide and looking up at the sky through a haze of grasses he was filled, not with post-coital sadness, but with an agreeable languor as if the long-committed Sunday afternoon still stretched ahead of them.

It was Amy who said: 'Look, I'd better be getting back. I told Neil I wouldn't be more than an hour and he gets fussy if I'm late because of the Whistler.'

'The Whistler kills at night not in daylight. And he'd hardly venture on the headland. Too little cover. But Pascoe's right to be concerned. There isn't much danger, but you shouldn't be out alone at night. No woman should until he's caught.'

She said: 'I wish they would catch him. It'd be one thing less for Neil to worry about.'

Making his voice carefully casual, he asked: 'Doesn't he ever ask where you're going when you sneak out on Sunday afternoons leaving him to look after the child?'

'No, he doesn't. And the child is called Timmy. And I don't sneak. I say I'm going and I go.'

'But he must wonder.'

'Oh, he wonders all right. But he thinks people are entitled to their privacy. He'd like to ask but he never will. Sometimes I say to him, "OK, I'm off now to fuck my lover in the sand dunes." But he never says a word, just looks miserable because he doesn't like me saying "fuck".'

'Then why do you? I mean, why torment him? He's probably fond of you.'

'No, he isn't, not very fond. It's Timmy he likes. And what other word is there? You can't call it going to bed. I've only been in your bed with you once and then you were as jumpy as a cat thinking that sister of yours might come back unexpectedly. And you can't say we sleep together.'

He said: 'We make love. Or, if you prefer it, we copulate.'

'Honestly, Alex, that's disgusting. I think that word is really disgusting.'

'And do you do it with him? Sleep, go to bed, make love, copulate?'

'No, I don't. Not that it's any business of yours. He thinks it would be wrong. That means he doesn't really want to. If men want to they usually do.'

He said: 'That has been my experience, certainly.'

They lay side by side like effigies, both staring at the sky. She seemed content not to talk. So the question had at last been put and answered. It had been with shame and some irritation that he had recognized in himself for the first time the nagging of jealousy. More shaming had been his reluctance to put it to the test. And there were those other questions he wanted to ask but daren't. 'What do I mean to you?', 'Is this important?', 'What do you expect of me?' And most important of all, but unanswerable, 'Do you love me?' With his wife he had known precisely where he was. No marriage had begun with a more definite understanding of what each required of the other. Their unwritten, unspoken, only half-acknowledged pre-nuptial agreement had needed no formal ratification. He would earn most of the money, she would work if and when she chose. She had never been particularly enthusiastic about her job as interior designer. In return his home would be run with efficiency and reasonable economy. They would take separate holidays at least once every two years; they would have at most two children and at a time of her choosing; neither would publicly humiliate the other; the spectrum of marital offences under this heading ranging from spoiling the other's dinner-party stories to a too-public infidelity. It had been a success. They had liked each other, got on with remarkably little rancour and he had been genuinely upset, if principally in his pride, when she had left him. Fortunately marital failure had been mitigated by the public knowledge of her lover's wealth. He realized that to a materialistic society losing a wife to a millionaire hardly counted as failure. In their friends' eyes it would have been unreasonably proprietorial of him not to have released her with a minimum of fuss. But to do her justice, Liz had loved Gregory, would have followed him to California money or no money. He saw again in memory that transformed laughing face, heard her ruefully apologetic voice.

'It's the real thing this time, darling. I never expected it and I can still hardly believe it. Try not to feel too badly, it isn't your fault. There's nothing to be done.'

The real thing. So there was this mysterious real thing before which everything went down, obligations, habit, responsibility, duty. And now, lying in the dunes, seeing the sky through the rigid stalks of marram grasses, he thought about it almost with terror. Surely he hadn't found it at last and with a girl less than half his age, intelligent but uneducated, promiscuous and burdened with an illegitimate child. And he didn't deceive himself about the nature of her hold on him. No lovemaking had ever been as erotic or as liberating as their half-illicit couplings on unyielding sand within yards of the crashing tide.

Sometimes he would find himself indulging in fantasy, would picture them together in London in his new flat. The flat, as yet unsought, no more than a vague possibility among others, would assume dimensions, location, a horribly plausible reality in which he found himself arranging his pictures carefully on a non-existent wall, thinking over the disposal of his household goods, the exact location of his stereo system. The flat overlooked the Thames. He could see the wide windows giving a view over the river as far as Tower Bridge, the huge bed, Amy's curved body striped with bands of sunlight from the slatted wooden blinds. Then the sweet, deluding pictures would dissolve into bleak reality. There was the child. She would want the child with her. Of course she would. Anyway, who else could look after it? He could see the indulgent amusement on the faces of his friends, the pleasure of his enemies, the child lurching, sticky-fingered, about the flat. He could smell in imagination what Liz had never let him know in actuality – the smell of sour milk and dirty nappies, could picture the dreadful lack of peace and privacy. He needed these realities, deliberately emphasized, to bring him back to sanity. He was horrified that even for a few minutes he could seriously have contemplated such destructive stupidity. He thought: I'm obsessed by her. All right, just for these last few weeks I'll enjoy my obsession. This late summer would be brief enough, the warm unseasonable days of mellow sunshine couldn't last. Already the evenings were darkening. Soon he would smell the first sour tang of winter on the sea breezes. There would be no more lying in the warm sand dunes. She couldn't visit Martyr's Cottage again, that would be recklessly stupid. It was easy to convince himself that with care, when Alice was in London and no visitors expected, they could be together in his bedroom perhaps even for a whole night, but he knew that he would never risk it. Little on the headland was private for long. This was his St Martin's summer, an autumnal madness, nothing that the first cold of winter couldn't wither.

But now she said, as if there had been no period of silence between them, 'Neil's my friend, OK? Why do you want to talk about him anyway?'

'I don't. But I wish he'd civilize his living arrangements. That caravan is in direct line of my bedroom windows. It's an eyesore.'

'You'd need binoculars to see it from your windows. And so is your bloody great power station an eyesore. That's in everyone's direct line; we all have to look at that.'

He put out his hand to her shoulder, warm under the gritty film of sand and said with mock pomposity: 'It's generally agreed that, given the constraints imposed by its function and the site, the power station is rather successful architecturally.'

'Agreed by whom?'

'I think so for one.'

'Well, you would, wouldn't you? Anyway, you ought to be grateful to Neil. If he didn't look after Timmy I wouldn't be here.'

He said: 'That whole thing is primitive. He's got a wood stove in there, hasn't he? If that blows up you won't last a minute, all three of you, particularly if the door jams.'

'We don't lock it. Don't be daft. And we let the fire go out at night. And suppose your place blows up. It won't be just the three of us, will it? Bloody hell it won't. Not only humans either. What about Smudge and Whisky? They've got a point of view.'

'It won't blow up. You've been listening to his scaremongering nonsense. If you're worried about nuclear power ask me. I'll tell you what you want to know.'

'You mean while you're poking me you'll explain all about nuclear power? Oh boy, I'll certainly be able to take it in.'

And then she turned to him again. The pattern of sand on her shoulder glistened and he felt her mouth moving over his upper lip, his nipples, his belly. And then she knelt over him and the round childish face with its bush of bright hair shut out the sky.

Five minutes later she rolled apart from him and began shaking the sand from her shirt and jeans. Tugging the jeans over her thighs, she said: 'Why don't you do something about that bitch at Larksoken, the one suing Neil? You could stop her. You're the boss.'

The question – or was it a demand – shocked him out of his fantasy as crudely as if, unprovoked, she had suddenly slapped his face. In their four meetings she had never questioned him about his job, had seldom mentioned the power station except, as on this afternoon, to complain half seriously that it spoilt the view. He hadn't made a deliberate decision to keep her out of his private and professional life. When they were together that life hardly entered into his own consciousness. The man who lay with

Amy in the dunes had nothing to do with that burdened, ambitious, calculating scientist who ran Larksoken, nothing to do with Alice's brother, with Elizabeth's ex-husband, with Hilary's ex-lover. Now he wondered, with a mixture of irritation and dismay, whether she had deliberately chosen to ignore those invisible keep-out signs. And if he had been unconfiding, then so had she. He knew little more about her now than when they had first encountered each other in the abbey ruins on a blustery August evening less than six weeks earlier, had for a minute stood and gazed and had then moved silently towards each other in a wordless, amazed recognition. Later that evening she had told him that she came from Newcastle, that her widowed father had remarried and that she and her stepmother couldn't get on. She had moved down to London and lived in squats. It had sounded commonplace enough but he hadn't quite believed it and nor, he suspected, did she care whether or not he did. Her accent was more Cockney than Geordie. He had never asked about the child, partly from a kind of delicacy but mainly because he preferred not to think of her as a mother, and she had volunteered no information about Timmy or his father.

She said: 'Well, why don't you? Like I said, you're the boss.'

'Not over my staff's private lives. If Hilary Robarts thinks she has been libelled and seeks redress I can't prevent her from going to law.'

'You could if you wanted to. And Neil only wrote what was true.'

'That is a dangerous defence to a libel action. Pascoe would be ill advised to rely on it.'

'She won't get any money. He hasn't got any. And if he has to pay costs it will ruin him.'

'He should have thought of that earlier.'

She lay back with a little thud and for a few minutes they were both silent. Then she said as casually as if the previous conversation had been trivial small talk which was already half forgotten: 'What about next Sunday? I could get away late afternoon. OK by you?'

So she bore no grudge. It wasn't important to her, or if it was, she had decided to drop it, at least for now. And he could put from him the treacherous suspicion that their first meeting had been contrived, part of a plan devised by her and Pascoe to exploit his influence with Hilary. But that, surely, was ridiculous. He had only to recall the inevitability of their first coming together, her passionate, uncomplicated, animal gusto in their lovemaking to know that the thought was paranoid. He would be here on Sunday afternoon. It might be their last time together. Already he had half decided that it had to be. He would free himself from this enslavement, sweet as it was, as he had freed himself from Hilary. And he knew, with a regret which was almost as strong as grief, that with this parting there would be no protests, no appeals, no desperate clinging to the past. Amy would accept his leaving as she had accepted his arrival.

He said: 'OK. About 4.30 then. Sunday the twenty-fifth.'

And now time, which in the last ten minutes seemed mysteriously to have halted, flowed again and he was standing at his bedroom window five days later watching the great ball of the sun rise out of the sea to stain the horizon and spread over the eastern sky the veins and arteries of the new day. Sunday the twenty-fifth. He had made that appointment five days ago and it was one that he would keep. But lying there in the dunes he hadn't known what he knew now, that he had another and very different appointment to keep on Sunday, September the twenty-fifth.

18

Shortly after lunch Meg walked across the headland to Martyr's Cottage. The Copleys had gone upstairs to take their afternoon rest and for a moment she wondered whether to tell them to lock their bedroom door. But she told herself that the precaution was surely unnecessary and ridiculous. She would bolt the back door and lock the front door after her as she left and she wouldn't be gone for long. And they were perfectly happy to be left. Sometimes it seemed to her that old age reduced anxiety. They could look at the power station without the slightest premonition of disaster and the horror of the Whistler seemed as much beyond their interest as it was their comprehension. The greatest excitement in their lives, which had to be planned with meticulous care and some anxiety, was a drive into Norwich or Ipswich to shop.

It was a beautiful afternoon, warmer than most in the past disappointing summer. There was a gentle breeze and from time to time Meg paused and lifted her head to feel the warmth of the sun and the sweet-smelling air moving against her cheeks. The turf was springy beneath her feet and to the south the abbey stones, no longer mysterious or sinister, gleamed golden against the blue untroubled sea.

She did not need to ring. The door at Martyr's Cottage stood open as it often did in sunny weather, and she called out to Alice before, in response to her answering voice, moving down the corridor to the kitchen. The cottage was redolent with the zesty smell of lemon overlaying the more familiar tang of polish, wine and wood smoke. It was a smell so keen that it momentarily brought back the holiday she and Martin had spent in Amalfi, the trudge hand-in-hand up the winding road to the mountain-top, the pile of lemons and oranges by the roadside, putting their noses to those golden, pitted skins, the laughter and the happiness. The image experienced in a flash of gold, a flush of warmth to her face, was so vivid that for a second she hesitated at the kitchen door as if disorientated. Then her vision cleared and she saw the familiar objects, the Aga and the gas stove with the nearby working surfaces, the table of polished oak in the middle of the room with its four elegantly crafted chairs, and at the far end Alice's office with the walls covered with bookshelves and her desk piled with proofs. Alice was standing working at the table, wearing her long fawn smock.

She said: 'As you can see, I'm making lemon curd. Alex and I enjoy it occasionally and I enjoy making it, which I suppose is sufficient justification for the trouble.'

'We hardly ever had it – Martin and I, that is. I don't think I've eaten it since childhood. Mother bought it occasionally as a treat for Sunday tea.'

'If she bought it, then you don't know what it ought to taste like.'

Meg laughed and settled into the wicker chair to the left of the fireplace. She never asked if she could help in the kitchen since she knew Alice would be irritated by an offer which she knew to be impractical and insincere. Help was neither needed nor welcomed. But Meg loved to sit quietly and watch. Was it perhaps a memory of childhood, she wondered, that made watching a woman cooking in her own kitchen so extraordinarily reassuring and satisfying. If so, modern children were being deprived of yet one more source of comfort in their increasingly disordered and frightening world.

She said: 'Mother didn't make lemon curd but she did enjoy cooking. It was all very simple, though.'

'That's the difficult kind. And I suppose you helped her. I can picture you in your pinafore making gingerbread men.'

'She used to give me a piece of the dough when she was making pastry. By the time I'd finished pounding it, rolling it and shaping it, it was dun-coloured. And I used to cut out shaped biscuits. And yes, I did make gingerbread men with currants for their eyes, didn't you?'

'No. My mother didn't spend much time in the kitchen. She wasn't a good cook and my father's criticism destroyed what little confidence she had. He paid for a local woman to come in daily to cook the evening meal, virtually the only one he ate at home except on Sundays. She wouldn't come at weekends so that family meals then tended to be acrimonious. It was an odd arrangement and Mrs Watkins was an odd woman. She was a good cook but worked in a perpetual lather of bad temper and she certainly didn't welcome children in her kitchen. I only became interested in cookery when I was taking my degree in modern languages in London and spent a term in France. That's how it began. I found my necessary passion. I realized that I didn't have to teach or translate or become some man's over-qualified secretary.'

Meg didn't reply. Alice had only once before spoken of her family or her past life and she felt that to comment or question might cause her friend to regret the moment of rare confidence. She leaned comfortably back and watched as the deft, familiar, long-fingered hands moved confidently about their business. Before Alice on the table were eight large eggs in a blue shallow bowl and, beside it, a plate with a slab of butter and another with four lemons. She was rubbing the lemons with lumps of sugar until the lumps crumbled into a bowl, when she would pick up another and again begin patiently working away.

She said: 'This will make two pounds. I'll give you a jar to take to the Copleys if you think they'd like it.'

'I'm sure they would, but I'll be eating it alone. That's what I've come to tell you. I can't stay long. Their daughter is insisting that they go to her until the Whistler is caught. She rang again early this morning as soon as she heard the news of the latest murder.'

Alice said: 'The Whistler's getting uncomfortably close, certainly, but they're hardly at risk. He only stalks at night and all the victims have been young women. And the Copleys don't even go out, do they, unless you drive them?'

'They sometimes walk by the sea, but usually they take their exercise in the garden. I've tried to persuade Rosemary Duncan-Smith that they're not in danger and that none of us is frightened. But I think her friends are criticizing her for not getting them away.'

'I see. She doesn't want to have them, they don't want to go, but the friends, so-called, must be propitiated.'

'I think she's one of those masterful, efficient women who can't tolerate criticism. To be fair to her, I think she's genuinely worried.'

'So when are they going?'

'Sunday night. I'm driving them to Norwich to catch the eight thirty getting into Liverpool Street at 10.58. Their daughter will meet them.'

'That's not very convenient, is it? Sunday travel is always difficult. Why can't they wait till Monday morning?'

'Because Mrs Duncan-Smith is staying at her club in Audley Square for the weekend and has taken a room for them there. Then they can all drive down to Wiltshire first thing on Monday morning.'

'And what about you? Will you mind being left alone?'

'Not in the least. Oh, I expect I'll miss them when they've gone, but at present I keep thinking of all the work I'll be able to catch up on. And I'll be able to spend more time here, helping with the proofs. I don't think I'll be afraid. I can understand the fear and sometimes I find myself almost playing at being frightened, deliberately dwelling on the horror as if I'm testing my own nerve. It's all right in the daytime. But when night falls and we're sitting there by the fire, I can imagine him out there in the darkness, watching and waiting. It's that sense of the unseen, unknowable menace which is so disquieting. It's rather like the feeling I get from the power station, that there's a dangerous unpredictable power out on the headland which I can't control or even begin to understand.'

Alice said: 'The Whistler isn't in the least like the power station. Nuclear power can be understood and it can be controlled. But this latest murder is certainly a nuisance for Alex. Some of the secretaries live locally and bus or cycle home. He's arranging for the staff with cars to take them and pick them up in the morning, but with shift work that means more organizing than you'd expect. And some of the girls are beginning to panic and say they'll only be driven by another woman.'

'But they can't seriously think it's a colleague, someone from the power station?'

'They don't seriously think, that's the trouble. Instinct takes over and their instinct is to suspect every man, particularly if he hasn't an alibi for the last two murders. And then there's Hilary Robarts. She swims almost every evening until the end of October, and sometimes through the winter. She still intends to swim. The chances of her getting murdered may be a million to one but it's an act of bravado which sets a bad example. I'm sorry about yesterday evening, by the way. Not a very successful dinner party. I owed a meal to Miles and Hilary but I hadn't realized just how much they dislike each other. I don't know why. Alex probably does, but I'm not really interested enough to ask. How did you get on with our resident poet?'

Meg said: 'I liked him. I thought he'd be rather intimidating but he isn't, is he? We walked together to the abbey ruins. They look so wonderful by moonlight.'

Alice said: 'Appropriately romantic for a poet. I'm glad you didn't find his company disappointing. But I can never look at the moon without visualizing that litter of hardware. Man leaves his polluting mess behind him like metal turds. But it will be full moon on Sunday night. Why not come here for a quiet supper when you get back from the station and we'll walk to the ruins together. I'll expect you at 9.30. It will probably just be the two of us. Alex usually goes into the station after a weekend in town.'

Meg said regretfully: 'I'd love to, Alice, but I'd better not. The final packing and getting them off will be a formidable business and by the time I get back from Norwich I'll be ready for bed. And I shan't be hungry. I need to make a high tea for them before we leave. I could only stay for an hour, anyway. Mrs Duncan-Smith says that she'll ring from Liverpool Street to say that they've arrived safely.'

Uncharacteristically Alice dried her hands and walked with her to the door. Meg wondered why in chatting about the dinner party and her walk with Adam Dalgliesh, she hadn't mentioned that mysterious female figure glimpsed among the ruins. It wasn't just that she feared to make too much of it; without Adam Dalgliesh's corroboration she could so easily have been mistaken. Something else, a reluctance she could neither explain nor under-stand, held her back. As they reached the door and Meg gazed out over the curve of the sunlit headland she experienced a moment of extraordinary perception in which it seemed to her that she was aware of another time, a different reality, existing simultaneously with the moment in which she stood. The external world was still the same. She saw every detail with a keener eye; the motes of dust dancing in the swathe of sunlight which fell across the stone floor, the hardness of each time-worn slab beneath her feet, every nail mark pitting the great oak door, each indi-vidual grass of the tussock at the fringe of the heath. But it was the other world which possessed her mind. And here there was no sunlight, only an everlasting darkness loud with the sound of horses' hoofs and tramping feet, of rough male voices, of an incoherent babble as if the tide were sucking back the shingle on all the beaches of the world. And then there was a hiss and crackling of faggots, an explosion of fire, and then a second of dreadful silence broken by the high, long-drawn-out scream of a woman.

She heard Alice's voice: 'Are you all right, Meg?'

'I felt strange for a moment. It's over now. I'm perfectly all right.'

'You've been overworking. There's too much for you to do in that house. And last night was hardly restful. It was probably delayed shock.'

Meg said: 'I told Mr Dalgliesh that I never felt Agnes Poley's presence in this house. But I was wrong. She is here. Something of her remains.'

There was a pause before her friend replied. 'I suppose it depends on your understanding of time. If, as some scientists tell us, it can go backwards, then perhaps she is still here, still alive, burning in an everlasting bonfire. But I'm never aware of her. She doesn't appear to me. Perhaps she finds me unsympathetic. For me, the dead remain dead. If I couldn't believe that I don't think I could go on living.'

Meg said her final goodbye and walked out resolutely over the headland. The Copleys, facing the formidable decisions of what to pack for an indeterminate visit, would be getting anxious. When she reached the crest of the headland she turned and saw Alice still standing at the open doorway. She raised her hand in a gesture more like a blessing than a wave and disappeared into the cottage.

BOOK THREE

Sunday 25 September

19

By a quarter past eight on Sunday night Theresa had finished the last of her long-deferred homework and thought she could safely put away her arithmetic book and tell her father that she was tired and ready for bed. He had earlier helped her wash up after supper, the last of the Irish stew to which she had added extra carrots from a tin, and had settled as he always did in front of the television, slumped back in the battered armchair by the empty fire grate with his bottle of whisky on the floor by his side. Here, she knew, he would sit until the last programme had ended, staring fixedly at the screen but not, she felt, really watching those black and white flickering images. Sometimes it was almost dawn when, awake, she would hear his heavy feet on the stairs.

Mr Jago had rung just after half-past seven and she had answered the telephone and taken a message saying that Daddy was in his painting shed and couldn't be disturbed. It wasn't true. He had been in the privy at the bottom of the garden. But she hadn't liked to tell that to Mr Jago and she wouldn't have dreamed of fetching her father, of knocking on the privy door. Sometimes she thought, with a curiously adult perception, that he took his torch and went there when he didn't really need to, that the ramshackle hut with its cracked door and wide comfortable seat was a refuge for him from the cottage, from the mess and muddle, Anthony's crying, her own ineffectual efforts to take her mother's place. But he must have been on his way back. His ears had caught the ring and, coming in, he had asked her who had telephoned.

'It was a wrong number, Daddy,' she had lied, and from habit made a quick act of contrition. She was glad that he hadn't spoken to Mr Jago. Daddy might have been tempted to meet him at the Local Hero knowing that it would be safe to leave her in charge for an hour or two, and tonight it was vitally important that he didn't leave the cottage. He had only half a bottle of whisky left, she had checked on that. She would be gone for only forty minutes or so and if there were a fire, the secret fear which she had inherited from her mother, he wouldn't be too drunk to save Anthony and the twins.

She kissed him briefly on a cheek which was prickly to her lips and smelt the familiar smell of whisky, turpentine and sweat. As always, he put up his hand and gently ruffled her hair. It was the only gesture of affection which he now made to her. His eyes were still on the old black and white screen where the familiar Sunday faces could be glimpsed through an intermittent snowstorm. He wouldn't, she knew, disturb her once the door to the back bedroom she shared with Anthony was closed. Since her mother's death he had never entered her bedroom when she was there, either by night or day. And she had noticed the difference in his attitude towards her, almost a formality, as if in a few short weeks she had grown into womanhood. He would consult her as if she were an adult about the shopping, the next meal, the twins' clothes, even the problem with the van. But there was one subject he never mentioned: her mother's death.

Her narrow bed was directly under the window. Kneeling on it, she gently drew back the curtains letting moonlight stream into the room, seeking out the corners, laying its swathes of cold, mysterious light on the bed and across the wooden floor. The door to the small box room at the front of the cottage where the twins slept was open and she passed through and stood for a moment looking down at the small humps closely curved together under the bedclothes, then, bending low, listened for the regular hiss of their breath. They wouldn't wake now until the morning. She closed the door and went back into her own room. Anthony lay, as he always did, on his back, his legs splayed like a frog, his head to one side and both arms stretched high as if trying to seize the bars of the cot. He had wriggled free of his blanket and she drew it up gently over his sleeping suit. The impulse to snatch him into her arms was so strong that it was almost a pain. But, instead, she carefully let down the side of the cot and, for a moment, laid her head beside his. He lay as if drugged, his mouth pursed, his eyelids delicately veined films under which she could imagine the upturned, unseeing eyes.

Returning to her own bed, she pushed the two pillows down under the blankets and moulded them to the semblance of her body. Her father was very unlikely to look in, but if the unexpected should happen at least he wouldn't see in the moonlight an obviously empty bed. She felt beneath it for the small canvas shoulder bag in which she had placed ready what she knew she would need; the box of matches, the single white household candle, the sharp penknife, the pocket torch. Then she climbed on the bed and opened wide the casement window.

The whole headland was bathed in the silver light which she and her mother loved. Everything was transformed into magic; the outcrops of rock floated like islands of crumpled foil above the still grasses and the broken ill-kept hedge at the bottom of the garden was a mystic thicket woven from thin shafts of light. And beyond it, like a silken scarf, lay the wide untrammelled sea. She stood for a moment transfixed, breathing quickly, gathering up her strength, then climbed out on to the flat roof over the extension. It was covered with shingles and she crept forward with infinite care, feeling the grittiness of the stones through the soles of her plimsolls. It was a drop of only six feet and, with the help of the drainpipe, she made it easily, then scurried down the garden, stooping low, to the rotting wooden lean-to at the rear of her father's painting shed where she and her father kept their bicycles. In the moonlight streaming through the open door she disentangled hers, then wheeled it across the grass and lifted it through a gap in the hedge to avoid using the front gate. It was not until she reached the safety of the sunken lane where the old coastal railway had once run that she dared mount, and began bumping over the humpy grass northwards, towards the fringe of pine trees and the ruined abbey.

The old railway track ran behind the wood of pines which fringed the shore, but here it was less sunken, no more than a gentle depression in the headland. Soon, that too would flatten and there would be nothing, not even the rotting planks of old sleepers, to show where the coastal railway had once run, taking Victorian families with their spades and buckets, their nursemaids, their great portmanteaux, for their summer holiday by the sea. Less than ten minutes later she was in the open headland. She switched off the bicycle lamp, dismounted to check that there was no one in sight, and began bumping across the tough turf towards the sea.

And now the five broken arches of the abbey ruins came into sight, gleaming in the moonlight. She stood for a moment and stared in silence. It looked unreal, ethereal, an insubstantial edifice of light which would dissolve at a touch. Sometimes when, as now, she came to it by moon or starlight, the feeling was so strong that she would put out a hand and touch the stones and feel a physical shock at their rough hardness. Propping her bicycle against the low stone wall, she walked into the space where the great west door must once have been and into the body of the abbey.

It was on calm moonlit nights like this when she and her mother would make their little expeditions together. Her mother would say, 'Let's go and talk to the monks', and they would cycle here together and walk in companionable silence among the ruined arches or stand hand in hand where the altar must once have stood, hearing what those long-dead monks had once heard, but more remotely: the melancholy booming of the sea. It was here, she knew, where her mother liked best to pray, feeling more at home on this rough age-hallowed earth than in that ugly red-brick building outside the village where Father McKee visited every Sunday to say Mass.

She missed seeing Father McKee, missed his jokes, his praise, his funny Irish accent. But since her mother's death he visited only rarely and was never made welcome.

She remembered the last time, the briefness of the visit, her father seeing him out of the door, Father McKee's parting words: 'Her dear mother, God rest her, would want Theresa to be regular at Mass and confession. Mrs Stoddard-Clark would be glad to call for her in the car next Sunday and she could go back to the Grange afterwards for lunch. Now wouldn't that be nice for the child?'

And her father's voice: 'Her mother isn't here. Your God has chosen to deprive her of her mother. Tess is on her own now.

When she feels like going to Mass, she'll go, and she'll go to confession when she has something to confess.'

The grass had grown high here, spiked with tall weeds and dried flowerheads, the ground so humpy that she had to walk with care. She moved up under the highest arch of all where the great eastern window had once shone in an imagined miracle of coloured glass. Now it was an empty eye through which she could see the gleam of the sea and above it the sailing moon. And now, by the light of her torch and very quietly, she began her task. She went over to the wall, knife in hand, and began searching for a large, flat-surfaced stone which would form the basis of her altar. Within minutes she had found one and had prised it loose with her penknife. But there was something hidden in the crevice behind it, a thin piece of cardboard pushed deep into the crevice. She took it out and unfolded it. It was half of a coloured postcard of the west front of Westminster Abbey. Even with the right-hand side cut away she recognized the familiar twin towers. She turned it over and saw that there were a few lines of message which she couldn't read by moonlight and felt no particular curiosity to decipher. It seemed quite new, but with the date stamp unreadable there was no way of knowing how long it had lain there. Perhaps it had been hidden during the summer season as part of a family game. It didn't worry her, indeed, preoccupied as she was, it hardly interested her. This was the kind of secret message her friends left for each other at school, hidden in the bicycle shed, slipped into a blazer pocket. She hesitated for a moment, started to tear it, then smoothed it out and put it carefully back.

Working her way along the wall, she found another suitable stone and the few smaller ones she needed to prop up the single candle. The altar was soon complete. She lit the candle, the hiss of the match sounding unnaturally loud and the sudden flare of the light almost too bright for her eyes. She let the first blobs of wax fall on the stone, then wedged the candle into it, propping it up with pebbles. Then she sat cross-legged before it and gazed into the candle's steady glow. She knew that her mother would come, unseen but known to be present, silent but speaking clearly. She had only to wait in patience and gaze steadily into the candle's unflickering light.

She tried to empty her mind of everything except the questions which she was here to ask. But her mother's death was too recent, the memory too painful to be shut out of her thoughts.

Mummy hadn't wanted to die in hospital and Daddy had promised that she wouldn't. She had heard his whispered assurances. She knew that Dr Entwhistle and the district nurse had opposed them both. There were snatches of conversation she wasn't supposed to overhear but which, standing silently in the darkness of the stairs behind the oak door which led to the sitting room, came to her clearly as if she was standing by her mother's bed.

'You really need twenty-four-hour nursing, Mrs Blaney, more care than I can give. And you'd be more comfortable in hospital.'

'I am comfortable. I have Ryan and Theresa. I have you. You're all so good to me. I don't need anyone else.'

'I do what I can, but twice a day isn't enough. It's a lot to expect of Mr Blaney and Theresa. It's all right saying you've got her, but she's only fifteen.'

'I want to be with them. We want to be together.'

'But if they're frightened . . . it's difficult for children.'

Then that gentle implacable voice, thin and unbreakable as a reed, carrying the obstinate selfishness of the dying. 'They won't be frightened. Do you think we'd let them be frightened? There isn't anything frightening about birth or death if they've been properly taught.'

'There are things you can't teach children, Mrs Blaney, things you can only experience.'

And she, Theresa, had done her best to convince everyone that they were all right, that they could manage. There had been small subterfuges. Before Nurse Pollard and the doctor arrived she would wash the twins, put on clean dresses, change Anthony's nappy. It was important that everything looked under control, so that Dr Entwhistle and the nurse couldn't say that Daddy couldn't cope. One Saturday she cooked buns and handed them gravely round on a plate, the best plate, her mother's favourite, with the delicately painted roses and the holes in the border where you could thread a ribbon. She remembered the doctor's embarrassed gaze as he said, 'No thank you, Theresa, not just now.'

'Please have one. Daddy made them.'

And as he left he had said to her father: 'You may be able to bear this, Blaney, I'm not sure that I can.'

Only Father McKee seemed to notice her efforts. Father McKee, who spoke so like an Irishman on the telly that Theresa thought he was doing it on purpose as a joke and tried always to reward him with a laugh.

'My and isn't it grand the way you have this cottage shining. Couldn't the blessed Virgin herself eat off that floor now? Made by your dad, are they? And very nice too. See, I'm putting one in my pocket for later. Now you be making a nice cup of tea, that's a good girl, while I chat to your ma.'

She tried not to think about the night when they had taken her mother away; waking to hear those awful groaning noises which had made her think that there was an animal in agony snuffling round the cottage; realizing that the noise wasn't outside at all; the sudden terror; her father's figure in the bedroom doorway commanding her to stay there, not to come out, to keep the children quiet. Watching at the window of the little front bedroom with the twins' frightened faces staring from the bed and seeing the ambulance arrive; the two men with the stretcher; that blanket-shrouded figure, quiet now, being carried down the garden path. It was then that she had rushed down the stairs and almost hurled herself at her father's restraining arms.

'Better not, better not. Get her inside.'

She wasn't sure who had spoken the words. Then she was breaking free and running after the ambulance as it turned at the bottom of the lane, beating her hands against the closed doors. She remembered her father lifting her in his arms, carrying her back into the cottage. She remembered the strength of him, the smell and roughness of his shirt, her impotently flailing arms. She had never seen her mother again. It was how God had answered her prayers, her mother's prayers, to be able to stay at home, her mother who asked for so little. And nothing Father McKee could say would make her forgive God.

The chill of the September night was seeping through her jeans and jumper and the small of her back was beginning to ache. For the first time she felt a prick of doubt. And then, in a tremble of the candle flame, her mother was with her. Everything was all right.

There were so many things she needed to ask. Anthony's nappies. The disposable ones were so expensive and so bulky to carry, and Daddy didn't seem to realize how much they cost. Her mother said she should use the terries and rinse them out. Then the twins didn't really like Mrs Hunter who came and collected them to take them to the playgroup. The twins must be polite to Mrs Hunter and not mind. She was doing her best. It was important that they kept going to the playgroup for Daddy's sake. Theresa must tell them that. And then there was Daddy. There was so much to say about him. He didn't go to the pub often because he didn't like to leave them, but there was always whisky in the house. Her mother said that she was not to worry about the whisky. He needed it now, but soon he would begin painting again and then he wouldn't need it so much. But if he really became drunk and there was another bottle in the house she had better pour it away. She needn't be frightened that it would make him angry. He would never be angry with her.

The silent communication went on. She sat as if in a trance, watching while the wax of the candle slowly burned down. And then there was nothing. Her mother had gone away. Before blowing out the candle she scraped away the traces of wax from the stone with her knife. It was important that no evidence remained. Then she replaced the stones in the wall. The ruins held nothing for her now but a cold emptiness. It was time to go home.

Suddenly she was overcome with tiredness. It seemed impossible that her legs would carry her as far as the bicycle and she couldn't face the thought of the bumpy ride across the headland. She didn't know what impulse led her through the great east window to stand on the edge of the cliff. Perhaps it was the need to gather her strength, to look out over the moonlit sea and recapture for a moment that lost communion with her mother. But instead her mind was seized with a very different memory, as recent as that afternoon, and one that was still so frightening that she hadn't spoken of it, even to her mother. She saw again the red car, moving at speed down the lane towards Scudder's Cottage, called the children from the garden, bundled them upstairs and shut the sitting-room door. But later she had stood behind it and listened. It seemed to her that no word of that conversation would ever be forgotten.

First Hilary Robarts's voice: 'This place was totally unsuitable for a sick woman who had to undergo long journeys for radiotherapy. You must have known she was ill when you took it. She couldn't manage.'

And then her father: 'And I suppose you thought that after she'd gone I wouldn't be able to manage either. How many months did you give her? You used to pretend that you were concerned but she knew what you were at. Watching how much weight she was losing each week, more bone showing through, wrists like sticks, the cancer skin. Not much longer now, you thought. You made a bloody good investment in this cottage. You invested in her death and you made her life a bloody misery for her last weeks.'

'That isn't true. Don't load your guilt on me. I had to come here, there were things I had to see. That patch of damp in the kitchen, the problem with rain coming in the roof. You wanted them seen to, presumably. You were the first to point out that I had obligations as a landlady. And if you won't get out I shall have to apply for a rise in the rent. What you pay is derisory. It doesn't even cover repairs.'

'Try. Go to the Rent Tribunal. Let them come and see for themselves. The freehold may be yours but I'm the man in possession. And I pay the rent regularly. You can't get me out, I'm not that daft.'

'You pay the rent, but for how long? You could get by when you had that part-time teaching job, but I can't see you managing now. I suppose you call yourself an artist, but what you are is a cheap hack painter turning out rubbish for undiscriminating tourists who think any fourth-rate original is better than a first-rate print. But they aren't selling as well now, are they? Those four watercolours Ackworth has in his window have been there for weeks. They're beginning to brown. Even tourists are getting a little particular these days. Junk doesn't sell just because it's cheap.'

But the twins, tired of incarceration, began quarrelling and she had to hurry upstairs to tell them it wouldn't be long now, that they mustn't come out until the witch had gone. Then she crept down again. But it wasn't necessary to descend further than the fourth step. The voices were shouting now.

'I want to know if you sent that woman here, that bloody social worker from the local authority who came to spy on me and question my children about me. Did you send her?'

The witch's voice was cool, but she could hear every word: 'I'm not required to answer that. If I did alert them, then it was about time someone did.'

'My God, you're evil, aren't you? You'd do anything to get me and my children out of this cottage. They used to burn people like you four hundred years ago. If it wasn't for the children I'd kill you. But I'm not having them taken into so-called care just for the satisfaction of putting my hands round your throat. But, by God, don't tempt me, don't tempt me. So get out. Get out of my cottage and off my ground. Take your rent and be thankful you're alive to take it. And don't ever interfere with my life again. Not ever, not ever.'

The witch said: 'Don't be hysterical. That's all you're good for, threats and violence. If the local authority took those children into care it would be the best thing for them. Oh, I dare say you'd like to kill me. Your sort always react to reason with threats and violence. Kill me and expect the state to support your children for the next fifteen years. You're ridiculous and pathetic.'

And then her father's voice, not shouting any more but so quiet that she could only just catch the words: 'If I do kill you, no one will lay their hands on me or my children. No one.'

With the reliving of that last awful encounter came anger and the anger flowing into her legs seemed to give them strength. She could cope now with the ride home. And it was time she was leaving. And then she saw that the beach was no longer empty. Suddenly she began shaking like a young puppy and then backed into the shelter of the arch. To the north, running down from the pine trees towards the sea, was a woman, her dark hair streaming, her white body almost naked. And she was shouting, shouting in triumph. It was the witch, Hilary Robarts.

20

Hilary ate an early supper. She wasn't hungry but she took a French roll from the freezer and heated it in the oven, then made herself a herb omelette. She washed up and left the kitchen tidy, then took papers from her briefcase and settled down at the sitting-room table to work. There was a paper to be written about the implications of the reorganization for her department, figures to be collated and presented, an argument for the redeployment of staff logically and elegantly presented. The task was important to her and normally she would have enjoyed it. She knew that she could be faulted when it came to personnel management but no one had been able to criticize her as organizer and administrator. Shuffling the papers she wondered how much, if at all, she would miss it when she and Alex were married and in London. She was surprised how little she cared. This part of her life was over and she would relinquish it without regret, this over-tidy cottage which had never been her own and never could be, the power station, even her job. And now there would be a different life, Alex's job, her status as his wife, entertaining the right people in the right way, some carefully chosen voluntary work, travel. And there would be a child, his child.

This overpowering need for a child had strengthened in the last year, growing in intensity as his physical need for her decreased. She tried to persuade herself that a love affair, like a marriage, couldn't always be maintained at the same pitch of sexual or emotional excitement, that essentially nothing had changed between them and nothing really could. How much commitment, physical or emotional, had there been at the start of the relationship? Well, that had suited her all right at the time; she hadn't wanted any more than he was prepared to give, a mutually satisfactory exchange of pleasure, the kudos of being his half-acknowledged mistress, the careful dissimulation when they were in company together which was hardly necessary or successful and wasn't seriously meant to be but which, for her part at least, had held a powerful erotic charge. It was a game they played; their almost formal greeting before meetings or in the presence of strangers, his twice weekly visits to her cottage. When she had first come to Larksoken she had looked for a modern flat in Norwich and had, for a time, rented one close to the city centre. But once the affair began it was necessary to be near him and she had found a holiday cottage less than a quarter of a mile from Martyr's Cottage. He was, she knew, both too proud and too arrogant to visit her surreptitiously, sneaking out at night like a randy schoolboy. But no degrading pretence was necessary; the headland was invariably deserted. And he never stayed the night. The careful rationing of her company seemed almost a necessary part of the relationship. And in public they behaved as colleagues. He had always discouraged informality, too many first names, except to his immediate colleagues, too much easy camaraderie. The station was as disciplined as a tightly run ship in wartime.

But the affair, begun with such discipline, such emotional and social propriety, had deteriorated into messiness and longing and pain. She thought she knew the moment when the need for a child had begun to grow into an obsession. It was when the theatre sister at that expensive and discreet nursing home, only half concealing her disapproval and disgust, had taken away the kidney-shaped bowl with that quivering mass of tissue which had been the foetus. It was as if her womb, so clinically robbed, was taking its revenge. She hadn't been able to conceal her longing from Alex even though she knew that it repelled him. She could hear again her own voice, truculent, whining, an importunate child, and could see his look, half laughing, of simulated dismay which she knew concealed a genuine repugnance.

'I want a child.'

'Don't look at me, darling. That's one experiment I'm not prepared to repeat.'

'You have a child, healthy, living, successful. Your name, your genes will go on.'

'I've never set store on that. Charles exists in his own right.'

She had tried to argue herself out of the obsession, forcing the unwelcome images on her unreceptive mind, the broken nights, the smell, the constant demands, the lessening of freedom, the lack of privacy, the effect on her career. It was no good. She was making an intellectual response to a need where intellect was powerless. Sometimes she wondered if she was going mad. And she couldn't control her dreams, one in particular. The smiling nurse, gowned and masked, placing the newborn baby in her arms, herself looking down at the gentle, self-contained face bruised with the trauma of birth. And then the sister, grim-visaged, rushing in, snatching the bundle away. 'That isn't your baby, Miss Robarts. Don't you remember? We flushed yours down the lavatory.'

Alex didn't need another child. He had his son, his living hope, however precarious, of vicarious immortality. He might have been an inadequate and scarcely known parent, but he was a parent. He had held in his arms his own child. That wasn't unimportant to him, whatever he might pretend. Charles had visited his father last summer, a golden-bronzed, hefty-legged, sun-bleached giant who had seemed in retrospect to blaze through the station like a meteor, captivating the female staff with his American accent, his hedonistic charm. And Alex, she saw, had been surprised and slightly disconcerted by his pride in the boy, attempting unsuccessfully to conceal it with heavy-handed banter.

'Where is the young barbarian, swimming? He'll find the North Sea an unwelcome change from Laguna Beach.'

'He tells me he proposes to read law at Berkeley. There's a place waiting for him in step-papa's firm, apparently, once he qualifies. Next thing Liz will be writing to say that he's engaged to some socially acceptable sophomore, or do I mean preppy?'

'I'm managing to feed him, by the way. Alice has left me a recipe for hamburgers. Every shelf of the refrigerator is stuffed with ground beef. His vitamin C requirements seem abnormally high even for a boy of his height and weight. I press oranges constantly.'

She had squirmed in a mixture of embarrassment and resentment, the pride and the juvenile humour had both seemed so out of character, almost demeaning. It was as if he, as much as the typists, had been captivated by his son's physical presence. Alice

Mair had left for London two days after Charles had arrived. Hilary wondered whether this had been perhaps a ploy to give father and son some time alone together or whether, and more likely from what she knew or guessed of Alice Mair, it had been a reluctance both to spend time cooking for the boy and to witness his father's embarrassing excess of paternalism.

She thought again of his last visit when he had walked home with her after the dinner party. She had deliberately sounded reluctant to be escorted, but he had come and she had meant that he should. After she had finished speaking he had said quietly: 'That sounds like an ultimatum.'

'I wouldn't call it that.'

'What would you call it then, blackmail?'

'After what's happened between us, I'd call it justice.'

'Let's stick to ultimatum. Justice is too grandiose a concept for the commerce between us two. And like every ultimatum it will have to be considered. It's usual to set a time limit. What's yours?'

She had said: 'I love you. In this new job you're going to need a wife. I'm the right wife for you. It could work. I'd make it work. I could make you happy.'

'I'm not sure how much happiness I'm capable of. Probably more than I've any right to. But it isn't in anyone's gift, not Alice's, not Charles's, not Elizabeth's, not yours. It never has been.'

Then he had come over to her and kissed her on the cheek. She had turned to cling to him but he had put her gently aside. 'I'll think about it.'

'I'd like to announce it soon, the engagement.'

'You're not thinking of a church wedding, I suppose. Orange blossom, bridesmaids, Mendelssohn's "Wedding March", "The voice that breathed o'er Eden".'

She had said: 'I'm not thinking of making either of us ridiculous, now or after marriage. You know me better than that.'

'I see, just a quick, painless turning-off at the local registrar's office. I'll give you my decision next Sunday night after I get back from London.'

She had said: 'You make it sound so formal.'

And he had replied: 'But it has to be formal, doesn't it, the response to an ultimatum?'

He would marry her and, within three months, he would know that she had been right. She would win because, in this, her will was stronger than his. She remembered the words of her father. 'There's only this one life, girlie, but you can live it on your own terms. Only the stupid and the weak need to live like slaves. You've got health, looks, brains. You can take what you want. All you need is the courage and the will.' The bastards had nearly got him in the end, but he had lived life on his own terms and so would she.

Now she tried to put thoughts of Alex, of their future, on one side and concentrate on the task in hand. But she couldn't settle. Restless, she went through the kitchen into the small back parlour which held her wine store and brought out a bottle of claret. She took down a glass from the dresser and poured. Taking her first mouthful, she felt on the corner of her lip the minute scrape of a chip. It was intolerable to her to drink from a chipped glass. Instinctively she took down another and emptied the first glass into it. She was about to throw the defective glass away when she hesitated, her foot on the pedal of the refuse bin. It was one of a set of six that Alex had given her. The defect, unnoticed before, was slight, little more than a roughness on the brim. The glass could be used to hold flowers. She had a picture of them, snowdrops, primroses, small sprigs of rosemary. When she had finished drinking she washed up both glasses and turned them over to drain. The bottle of claret she left uncorked on the table. It had really been too cold to drink, but in another hour it would be about right.

It was time for her swim, just after nine, and tonight she wouldn't bother with the news. Upstairs in her bedroom she stripped naked, put on the bottom half of a black bikini and over it her blue and white tracksuit. On her feet she wore old sandals, the leather stained and toughened by sea water. From the hall peg she took down a small steel locket on a leather thong just large enough to hold her Yale key, which she wore round her neck when swimming. It had been Alex's gift for her last birthday. Touching it, she smiled and felt, strong as the metal against her fingers, the certainty of hope. Then she took a torch from the drawer in the hall table and, closing the door carefully behind her, set off for the beach, her towel slung over her shoulder.

She smelt the resin of the pines before she passed between their slim, spiky trunks. There were only fifty yards of sandy path, thick with their fallen needles, between her and the shore. It was dimmer here, the moon glimpsed fitfully, sailing in majestic splendour above the high spires of the trees, now seen and now obscured, so that for a few seconds she had to switch on her torch. And now she passed out of the shadows and saw before her the white moon-bleached sand and the tremble of the North Sea. Dropping her towel in her usual place, a small hollow on the fringe of the wood, she slipped off her tracksuit and stretched her arms high above her head.

Then she kicked off her sandals and began running, over the narrow band of shingle, over the dusty sand above the watermark, over the smooth, sea-washed eddies of the foam, splashing through the small waves which seemed to be falling without a sound, to hurl herself at last into cleansing peace. She gasped at the coldness of it, fierce as a pain. But almost at once that passed, as it always did, and it seemed to her that the water gliding over her shoulders had taken on her own body warmth and that she swam cocooned in self-sufficiency. With her strong rhythmic crawl she struck out from the shore. She knew how long she could safely stay in; just five minutes before the cold struck again and it was time to return.

And now she stopped swimming and lay for a moment on her back, floating, looking up at the moon. The magic worked again as it always did. The frustrations, the fears, the anger of the day fell away and she was filled instead with a happiness which she would have called ecstasy, except that ecstasy was too ostentatious a word for this gentle peace. And with the happiness came optimism. Everything was going to be all right. She would let Pascoe sweat for another week then withdraw her action. He was too unimportant even to hate. And her solicitor was right, possession of Scudder's Cottage could wait. It was increasing in value every month. The rent was being paid, she was losing nothing. And the daily irritations of the job, the professional jealousies, the resentments, what did they matter now? That part of her life was coming to an end. She loved Alex, Alex loved her. He would see the sense of everything she had said. They would be married. She would have his child. Everything was possible. And then, for a moment, there came a deeper peace in which even none of this mattered. It was as if all the petty preoccupations of the flesh were washed away and she was a disembodied spirit floating free, looking down at her body spreadeagled under the moon, and could feel a gentle, undemanding sorrow for this earth-grounded creature who could find only in an alien element this sweet but transitory peace.

But it was time to get back. She gave a vigorous kick, twisted herself over and began her powerful crawl towards the shore, towards that silent watcher waiting for her in the shadow of the trees.

21

Dalgliesh had spent Sunday morning revisiting Norwich Cathedral and St Peter Mancroft before lunching at a restaurant on the outskirts of the city where he and his aunt two years previously had eaten an unpretentious but excellently cooked meal. But here, too, time had wrought its changes. The exterior and the décor were deceivingly the same but it was quickly apparent that both proprietor and chef had changed. The meal, arriving with suspicious promptness, had obviously been cooked elsewhere and heated up, the grilled liver a grainy slab of indistinguishable grey meat blanketed with a synthetic, glutinous sauce and accompanied by potatoes which were underdone and cauliflower which was a mush. It was not a luncheon to deserve a wine, but he fortified himself with Cheddar and biscuits before setting out on the afternoon's programme, a visit to the fifteenth-century church of St Peter and St Paul at Salle.

During the last four years it had been rare for him to visit his aunt without driving with her to Salle, and she had left with her will a request that her ashes should be strewn in the churchyard there without ceremony and by him on his own. He knew that the church had exerted a powerful influence on her but she had not, as far as he knew, been a religious woman and the request had a little surprised him. It had seemed so much more likely that she would have wanted her physical remains thrown to the winds on the headland, or that she would have left no instructions, regarding this as a simple matter of expedient disposal requiring neither thought on her part nor ceremony on his. But now he had a task to perform and one of surprising importance to him. In recent weeks he had been visited by the nagging guilt of a duty unfulfilled, almost a spirit unpropitiated. He found himself wondering, as he had before in his life, at man's insistent need for ritual, for the formal acknowledgement of each rite of passage. Perhaps this was something his aunt had understood and in her quiet way had made provision for.

He turned off the B1149 at Felthorpe to take the country roads across the flat country. It was unnecessary to consult the map. The magnificent fifteenth-century tower with its four pinnacles was an unmistakable landmark and he drove towards it along the almost deserted roads with the familiar sense of coming home. It seemed strange that his aunt's angular figure wasn't beside him, that all that remained of that secretive but powerful personality was a plastic package, curiously heavy, of white grit. When he reached Salle he parked the Jaguar a little down the lane and made his way into the churchyard. As always, he was struck that a church as magnificent as a cathedral could be so isolated yet seem utterly right among these quiet fields where its effect was less of grandeur and majesty than of an unpretentious and reassuring peace. For a few minutes he stood quietly listening and heard nothing, not even a bird song or the rustle of an insect in the tall grasses. In the frail sunlight the surrounding trees were flushed with the first gold of autumn. The ploughing was over and the brown crust of the crumbled fields stretched in their Sunday calm towards the far horizon. He walked slowly round the church feeling the weight of the package dragging at his jacket pocket, glad that he had chosen a time between services and wondering whether it might not have been courteous, perhaps even necessary, to obtain the consent of the parish priest before carrying out his aunt's wishes. But he told himself that it was too late to think of that now, glad to be spared explanations or complications.

Making his way to the eastern fringe of the churchyard he opened the package and tipped out the ground bones like a libation. There was a flash of silver and all that remained of Jane Dalgliesh sparkled among the brittle autumn stalks and the tall grasses. He knew the customary words for such an occasion; he had heard them often enough on his father's lips. But the ones which came unbidden to his mind were the verses from Ecclesiastes carved on the stone outside Martyr's Cottage and in this timeless place beside the dignity of the great church it seemed to him that they were not inappropriate.

The west door was unlocked and before leaving Salle he spent fifteen minutes in the church revisiting old pleasures: the carvings on the oak stalls, peasants, a priest, animals and birds, a dragon, a pelican feeding its young; the medieval wineglass pulpit, which after five hundred years still showed traces of its original colouring; the chancel screen; the great east window which once had glowed in the glory of red, green and blue medieval glass but which now let in only the clear Norfolk light. As the west door clanged gently behind him he wondered when he would return, or if he would return at all.

It was early evening before he got home. What he had eaten of lunch had been stodgily filling so that he was less hungry than he had expected. He heated up the last of yesterday's home-made soup and followed it with biscuits and cheese and fruit and then kindled the fire and sat on the low chair before it, listening to Elgar's Cello Concerto and making a start on the job of sorting out his aunt's photographs. Tipping them out of their faded envelopes he sorted them with his long fingers on the low mahogany table. It was a task which induced a gentle melancholy from which an occasional scribbled identification on the back of a print, a remembered face or incident, would stab him into pain. And the Elgar was an appropriate accompaniment, the plaintive notes evoking those long, hot Edwardian summers known to him only from novels and poetry, the peace, the certainty, the optimism of the England into which his aunt had been born. And here was her fiancé, looking ridiculously young in his captain's uniform. The photograph was dated 4 May 1918, only a week before he was killed. He gazed for a moment intently at that handsome, debonair young face which, God knew, must by then have seen enough of horror, but it told him nothing. Turning it over Dalgliesh saw that it bore a pencilled message written in Greek. The young man was to have read Classics at Oxford and his aunt had studied Greek with her father. But he knew no Greek; their secret was safe enough with him and soon would be safe for ever. The hand which had formed these fading characters had been dead now for seventy years, the mind that had first created them for nearly two thousand. And here, in the same envelope, was one of his aunt herself at about the same age. It must have been one she had sent to her fiancé at the Front or given to him before he left for war. One corner was stained browny-red with what must be his blood; perhaps the photograph had been returned to her with the rest of his effects. She stood in her long skirt with the high-buttoned blouse, laughing, her hair in two wings on either side and bound above the temples. Over the years her face had always had distinction, but he saw, almost with a shock of surprise, that once she had been beautiful. And now her death had freed him for a voyeurism which in her life would have been repugnant to them both. And yet she hadn't destroyed the photographs. She must have known, realist that she was, that other eyes than hers would eventually see them. Or did extreme old age free one from all such petty considerations of vanity or self-esteem, as the mind gradually distanced itself from the devices and desires of the flesh? It was with a sense of irrational reluctance, almost of betrayal, that eventually he threw both photographs into the fire and watched them curl, blacken and finally flare into ash.

And what was he to do with all these undocumented strangers, the women, sloping-bosomed, under immense hats piled with ribbons and flowers, the cycling parties, the men knickerbockered, the women with their long, bell-shaped skirts and their straw boaters; the wedding parties, bride and bridesmaids almost hidden behind their immense bouquets, the chief participants grouped in recognized hierarchy and staring into the lens as if the click of the shutter could for a second halt time, hold it in thrall, proclaiming that this rite of passage at least had importance, binding the ineluctable past to the unseeable future? As an adolescent boy he had been obsessed with time. For weeks before the summer holidays he would feel a sense of triumph that now he had time by the forelock and could say, 'Go as quickly as you like and the holiday will be here. Or if you must, go slowly, and the summer days will last longer.' Now, in middle age, he knew of no contrivance and no promised pleasure which could halt the inexorable thudding of those chariot wheels. And here was a photograph of himself in his prep-school uniform, taken in the rectory garden by his father, a stranger ridiculously over-clad in cap and striped blazer standing almost to attention, facing the lens as if defying the terror of leaving home. That, too, he was glad to see the end of.

When the concerto was finished, the half-bottle of claret empty, he shuffled the remaining photographs together, placed them in the bureau drawer and decided to shake off melancholy with a brisk walk by the sea before bed. The night was too calm and beautiful to be wasted in nostalgia and futile regrets. The air was extraordinarily still and even the sound of the sea was muted as it stretched, pale and mysterious, under the full moon and the bright pattern of stars. He stood for a moment under the soaring wings of the mill then began walking vigorously over the headland towards the north, past the fringe of pines, until, three-quarters of an hour later, he decided to make for the beach. He half slid down the sandy decline and saw before him the great square hunks of concrete half buried in the sand, the curls of rotting iron springing from them like bizarre antennae. Moonlight, strong as the last light of the setting sun, had changed the texture of the beach so that each grain of sand seemed separately illuminated, every pebble mysteriously unique. Suddenly he had a childish impulse to feel the sea washing over his feet and, taking off his shoes and socks, he stuffed the socks in his jacket pocket and, tying the laces, slung the shoes round his neck. The water, after the first sting of cold, was almost blood-warm and he splashed vigorously along the fringe of the waves, pausing from time to time to look back at his footprints as he had as a child. Now he had reached the narrow strip of pine trees. There was, he knew, a narrow path which cut inland through them past Hilary Robarts's cottage to the road. It was the simplest way of regaining the headland without having to scramble up the friable cliffs to the south. Sitting on a ridge of shingle, he tackled the familiar problem of the paddler: how, with an inadequate handkerchief, to rid the spaces between his toes of the gritty dusting of tenacious sand. That achieved, socks and shoes replaced, he trudged through the pebbles to the shore line.

When he reached the powdery sand on the upper reaches of the beach he saw that someone had been here before him; to his left was a double line of naked footprints, the mark of running feet. These, of course, would be Hilary Robarts's. She must, as usual, have taken her nightly swim. Subconsciously he noticed how distinct they were. She must have left the beach nearly an hour and a half ago, yet on this windless night the indentations were as plain in the dry sand as if they had just been made. The path through the trees lay in front of him leading out of moonlight into the enclosing shadows of the pine wood. And the night was suddenly darker. A low blue-black cloud had momentarily covered the moon, its ragged edges silvered with light.

He switched on his torch and played it over the path. It caught the gleam of something white to his left, a sheet of newspaper, perhaps, a handkerchief, a discarded paper bag. Feeling no more than mild curiosity he stepped from the path to investigate. And then he saw her. Her distorted face seemed to leap up at him and hang suspended in the bright glare of the torchlight like a vision from a nightmare. Staring down, and for a moment transfixed, he felt a shock in which incredulity, recognition and horror fused into a second which made his heart leap. She was lying in a shallow depression of flattened marram grass, hardly a hollow but deep enough for the grasses on each verge to shield her body until he was almost on top of her. To her right, and partly beneath her, was a crumpled beach towel, striped in red and blue, and above it, placed precisely side by side, a pair of open sandals and a torch. Beside them, neatly folded, was what looked like a blue and white tracksuit. It must have been the edge of this which had first caught his eye. She lay on her back, the head towards him, the dead eyes upturned as if they had been fixed on him in a last mute appeal. The small bush of hair had been pushed under the upper lip, exposing the teeth, and giving the impression of a snarling rabbit. A single black hair lay across her cheek and he had an almost irresistible impulse to kneel and pluck it away. She was wearing only the bottom half of a black bikini and that had been pulled down over her thighs. He could clearly see where the hair had been sliced away. The letter L precisely in the centre of the forehead looked as if it had been cut with deliberation, the two thin lines precisely at right angles. Between the splayed and flattened breasts with their dark areolas and pointed nipples, milk-white against the brown skin of her arms, rested a key-shaped metal locket on a chain. And as he gazed down, slowly moving the torchlight over her body, the cloud moved from the face of the moon and she lay stretched out before him clearly, the naked limbs pale and bloodless as the bleached sands and as clearly visible as if it were day.

He was inured to horror; few manifestations of human cruelty, violence or desperation were unfamiliar to his practised eye. He was too sensitive ever to view a violated body with crude indifference but only in one recent case, his last, had this sensitivity caused him more than momentary inconvenience. And with Paul Berowne at least he had been warned. This was the first time he had almost stumbled over a murdered woman. Now, as he looked down on her, his mind analysed the difference between the reaction of an expert summoned to the scene of crime knowing what to expect and this sudden exposure to ultimate violence. He was interested both in the difference and in the detachment which could so coolly analyse it.

Kneeling, he touched her thigh. It felt icy cold and as synthetic as inflated rubber. If he prodded it the mark of his fingers would surely remain. Gently he ran them through her hair. It was still slightly damp at the roots but the ends were dry. The night was warm for September. He looked at his watch: ten thirty-three. He remembered being told, he couldn't recall when or by whom, that it was her practice to take her nightly swim shortly after nine o'clock. The physical signs confirmed what he thought most likely, that she had been dead for less than two hours.

He had seen no footprints on the sand but his and hers. But the tide was ebbing; it must have been high at about nine, although the dustiness of the upper reaches of the beach suggested that it didn't reach the hollow where she lay. But the most likely path for the murderer to have taken was the one through the wood which she herself must have used. He would have had the protection of the trees and a place in their shadow where he could watch and wait unseen. The ground with its mat of pine needles on the sand was unlikely to yield footprints but it was important that it shouldn't be disturbed. Moving carefully, he backed away from the body then walked about twenty yards to the south along a ridge of fine shingle. By the light of his torch, half crouching, he tracked his way through the densely planted pine trees, snapping off the brittle lower twigs as he passed. At least he could be certain that no one had recently passed this way. Within minutes he had gained the road; another ten of brisk walking and he would be at the mill. But the nearest telephone would be at Hilary Robarts's cottage. The probability was that the cottage was locked and he had no intention of breaking in. It was almost as important to leave the victim's house undisturbed as it was not to violate the scene of the crime. There had been no handbag beside her body, nothing but the shoes and torch neatly placed at the head of the hollow, the tracksuit and the brightly striped red and blue beach towel on which she partly lay. Perhaps she had left the key at home, the cottage unlocked. On the headland, after dark, few people would worry if they left a cottage unlocked for half an hour. It was worth taking five minutes to look.

Thyme Cottage, seen from the windows of the mill, had always struck him as the least interesting house on the headland. It faced inland, a square, uncompromising building with a cobbled yard instead of a front garden and picture windows in modern glass which destroyed any period charm it once might have had and made it look like a modern aberration more appropriate to a rural housing estate than to this sea-scarred and remote headland. On three sides the pines grew so closely that they almost touched the walls. He had wondered from time to time why Hilary Robarts should have chosen to live here despite its convenient distance from the power station. After Alice Mair's dinner party he thought he knew why. Now all the lights were blazing in the ground-floor rooms, the large rectangle of the picture window to the left reaching almost to the ground and the smaller square to the right which he thought was probably the kitchen. Normally they would have been a reassuring signal of life, normality and welcome, of a refuge from the atavistic fears of the enclosing wood, the empty moonlit headland. But now those bright, uncurtained windows added to his mounting unease and as he approached the cottage it seemed to him that there floated between him and those bright windows, like a half-developed print, the mental picture of that dead and violated face.

Someone had been here before him. He vaulted over the low stone wall and saw that the pane of the picture window had been almost completely smashed. Small slivers of glass gleamed like jewels on the cobbled yard. He stood and gazed between the jagged edges of the broken glass into the brightness of the sitting room. The carpet was littered with glass fragments like winking beads of silver light. It was obvious that the force of the blow had come from outside the cottage and he saw at once what had been used. Below him, face upwards on the carpet, was the portrait of Hilary Robarts. It had been slashed almost to the frame with two right-angled cuts forming the letter L.

He didn't try the door to see if it was unlocked. It was more important not to contaminate the scene than to save ten or fifteen minutes in ringing the police. She was dead. Speed was important, but it was not vital. Regaining the road he set off towards the mill, half running, half walking. And then he heard the noise of a car and, turning, saw the lights coming at him fast from the north. It was Alex Mair's BMW. Dalgliesh stood in the middle of the road and waved his torch. The car slowed and stopped. Looking up to the open right-side window he saw Mair, his face bleached by moonlight, regarding him for a moment with an unsmiling intensity as if this encounter were an assignation.

Dalgliesh said: 'I'm afraid I have shocking news for you. Hilary Robarts has been murdered. I've just found the body. I need to get to a telephone.'

The hand lying casually on the wheel tightened then relaxed. The eyes fixed on his grew wary. But when Mair spoke his voice was controlled. Only in that involuntary spasm of the hand had he betrayed emotion. He said: 'The Whistler?'

'It looks like it.'

'There's a telephone in the car.'

Without another word he opened the door, got out and stood silently aside while Dalgliesh spent an irritating two minutes getting through to Rickards's headquarters. Rickards wasn't there but the message given, he rang off. Mair had moved about thirty yards from the car and was staring back at the glitter of the power station as if dissociating himself from the whole procedure.

Now, walking back, he said: 'We all warned her not to swim alone but she wouldn't listen. But I didn't really believe there was any danger. I suppose all the victims thought that until it was too late. "It can't happen to me." But it can and it does. But it's still extraordinary, almost unbelievable. The second victim from Larksoken. Where is she?'

'On the fringe of the pines, where she usually swam, I imagine.' As Mair made a move towards the sea, Dalgliesh said: 'There's nothing you can do. I'll go back and wait for the police.'

'I know there's nothing I can do. I want to see her.'

'Better not. The fewer people who disturb the scene the better.'

Suddenly Mair turned on him. 'My God, Dalgliesh, don't you ever stop thinking like a policeman? I said I wanted to see her.'

Dalgliesh thought, this isn't my case and I can't stop him by force. But at least he could ensure that the direct path to the body lay undisturbed. Without another word he led the way and Mair followed. Why this insistence, he wondered, on seeing the body? To satisfy himself that she was, in fact, dead, the scientist's need to verify and confirm? Or was he trying to exorcize a horror which he knew could be more terrible in imagination than in reality? Or was there, perhaps, a deeper compulsion, the need to pay her the tribute of standing over her body in the quietness and loneliness of the night before the police arrived with all the official paraphernalia of a murder investigation to violate for ever the intimacies they had shared.

Mair made no comment when Dalgliesh led him to the south of the well-beaten path to the beach and still without speaking followed him as he plunged into the darkness and began tracking his way between the shafts of the pines. The pool of light from his torch shone on the brittle spars snapped by his previous breakthrough, on the carpet of pine needles dusted with sand, on dried pine cones and the glint of an old battered tin. In the darkness the strong resinous smell seemed to intensify and came up to them like a drug, making the air as heavy to breathe as if it were a sultry night in high summer.

Minutes later they stepped out of stultifying darkness into the white coolness of the beach and saw before them like a curved shield of beaten silver the moonlit splendour of the sea. They stood for a moment side by side, breathing hard as if they had come through some ordeal. Dalgliesh's footprints were still visible in the dry sand above the last ridge of pebbles and they followed them until they stood at the foot of the body.

Dalgliesh thought, I don't want to be here, not with him, not like this, both of us staring down unrebuked at her nakedness. It seemed to him that all his perceptions were preternaturally sharpened in this cold, debilitating light. The blanched limbs, the aureole of dark hair, the gaudy red and blue of the beach towel, the clumps of marram grass, all had the one-dimensional clarity of a colour print. This necessary guard on the body until the police could arrive would have been perfectly tolerable; he was used to the undemanding companionship of the recently dead. But with Mair at his side he felt like a voyeur. It was this revulsion, rather than delicacy, which made him move a little apart and stand looking into the darkness of the pines while remaining aware of every slight move and breath of the tall, rigid figure looking down at her with the concentrated attention of a surgeon.

Then Mair said: 'That locket round her neck, I gave it to her on August the twenty-ninth for her birthday. It's just the right size to hold her Yale key. One of the metal workers in the workshop at Larksoken made it for me. It's remarkable the delicacy of the work they do there.'

Dalgliesh was not inexperienced in the various manifestations of shock. He said nothing. Mair's voice was suddenly harsh.

'For God's sake, Dalgliesh, can't we cover her up?'

With what? thought Dalgliesh. Does he expect me to jerk the towel from under her? He said: 'No, I'm sorry. We mustn't disturb her.'

'But it's the Whistler's work. Dear God, man, it's obvious. You said so yourself.'

'The Whistler is a murderer like any other. He brings something to the scene and leaves something behind him. That something could be evidence. He's a man, not a force of nature.'

'When will the police arrive?'

'They shouldn't be long. I wasn't able to speak to Rickards but they'll be in touch with him. I'll wait if you want to leave. There's nothing you can do here.'

'I can stay until they take her away.'

'That might mean a long wait unless they're able to get the pathologist quickly.'

'Then I'll have a long wait.'

Without another word he turned and walked down to the edge of the sea, his footprints parallel with Dalgliesh's own. Dalgliesh moved down to the shingle and sat there, his arms round his knees, and watched while the tall figure paced endlessly, backwards and forwards, along the fringes of the tide. Whatever evidence he had on his shoes, it wouldn't be there now. But the thought was ridiculous. No murderer had ever left his imprint more clearly on a victim than had the Whistler. Why then did he feel this unease, the sense that it was less straightforward than it seemed?

He wriggled his heels and buttocks more comfortably into the shingle and prepared to wait. The cold moonlight, the constant falling of the waves and the sense of that stiffening body behind him induced a gentle melancholy, a contemplation of mortality including his own. *Timor mortis conturbat me.* He thought: In youth we take egregious risks because death has no reality for us. Youth goes caparisoned in immortality. It is only in middle age that we are shadowed by the awareness of the transitoriness of life. And the fear of death, however irrational, was surely natural whether one thought of it as annihilation or as a rite of passage. Every cell in the body was programmed for life; all healthy creatures clung to life until their last breath. How hard to accept, and yet how comforting, was the gradual realization that the universal enemy might come at last as a friend. Perhaps this was part of the attraction of his job, that the process of detection dignified the individual death, even the death of the least attractive, the most unworthy, mirroring in its excessive interest in clues and motives man's perennial fascination with the mystery of his mortality, providing, too, a comforting illusion of a moral universe in which innocence could be avenged, right vindicated, order restored. But nothing was restored, certainly not life, and the only justice vindicated was the uncertain justice of men. The job certainly had a fascination for him which went beyond its intellectual challenge, or the excuse it gave for his rigorously enforced privacy. But now he had inherited enough money to make it redundant. Was this what his aunt had intended by that uncompromising will? Was she in fact saying, here is enough money to make any job other than poetry unnecessary? Isn't it time that you made a choice?

It wasn't his case. It would never be his case. But by force of habit he timed the arrival of the police and it was thirty-five minutes before his ears caught the first rustle of movement in the pine wood. They were coming the way he had directed and they were making a great deal of noise about it. It was Rickards who appeared first with a younger but stolidly built man at his shoulders and four heavily laden officers in a straggle behind them. It seemed to Dalgliesh, rising to meet them, that they were immense, huge moon men, their features square and blanched in this alien light, bearing with them their bulky and polluting paraphernalia. Rickards nodded but didn't speak other than briefly to introduce his sergeant, Stuart Oliphant.

Together they approached the body and stood looking down at what had been Hilary Robarts. Rickards was breathing heavily, as if he had been running, and it seemed to Dalgliesh that there emanated from him a powerful surge of energy and excitement. Oliphant and the four other officers dumped their equipment and stood silently, a little apart. Dalgliesh had a sense that they were all actors in a film, waiting for the director to give the command to shoot, or that a voice would suddenly shout 'cut' and the little group would break up, the victim stretch herself and sit up and begin rubbing her arms and legs and complaining of stiffness and the cold.

Then, still gazing down at the body, Rickards asked: 'Do you know her, Mr Dalgliesh?'

'Hilary Robarts, Acting Administrative Officer at Larksoken Power Station. I met her first last Thursday, at a dinner party given by Miss Mair.'

Rickards turned and gazed towards the figure of Mair. He was standing motionless with his back to the sea but so close to the surf that it seemed to Dalgliesh that the waves must be washing over his shoes. He made no move towards them, almost as if he were waiting for an invitation or for Rickards to join him.

Dalgliesh said: 'Dr Alex Mair. He's the Director of Larksoken. I used the telephone in his car to call you. He says he'll stay here until the body is removed.'

'Then he's in for a long wait. So that's Dr Alex Mair. I've read about him. Who found her?'

'I did. I thought I made that plain when I telephoned.'

Either Rickards was deliberately extracting information he already knew or his men were singularly inefficient at passing on a simple message.

Rickards turned to Oliphant. 'Go and explain to him that we'll be taking our time. There's nothing he can do here except to get in the way. Persuade him to go home to bed. If you can't persuade, try ordering. I'll talk to him tomorrow.' He waited until Oliphant had started scrunching over the ridge of shingle then called: 'Oliphant. If he won't move, tell him to keep his distance. I don't want him any closer. Then get the screens round her. That'll spoil his fun.'

It was the kind of casual cruelty which Dalgliesh didn't expect from him. Something was wrong with the man, something that went deeper than professional stress at having to view yet another of the Whistler's victims. It was as if some half-acknowledged and imperfectly suppressed personal anxiety had been violently released by the sight of the body, triumphing over caution and discipline.

But Dalgliesh, too, felt a sense of outrage. He said: 'The man isn't a voyeur. He's probably not altogether rational at present. After all, he knew the woman. Hilary Robarts was one of his senior officers.'

'He can't do her any good now, even if she was his mistress.' Then, as if acknowledging the implied rebuke, he said: 'All right, I'll have a word with him.'

He began running clumsily over the shingle. Hearing him, Oliphant turned and together they went up to that silent, waiting figure on the fringe of the sea. Dalgliesh watched as they conferred together, then they turned and began walking up the beach, Alex Mair between the two police officers as if he were a prisoner under escort. Rickards returned to the body but it was obvious that Oliphant was going to accompany Alex Mair back to his car. He switched on his torch and plunged into the wood. Mair hesitated. He had ignored the body as if it were no longer there but now he looked over at Dalgliesh as if there were unfinished business between them. Then he said a quick 'Goodnight' and followed Oliphant.

Rickards didn't comment on Mair's change of mind or on his methods of persuasion. He said: 'No handbag.'

'Her house key is in that locket round her neck.'

'Did you touch the body, Mr Dalgliesh?'

'Only her thigh and the hair to test its wetness. The locket was a gift from Mair. He told me.'

'Lives close, does she?'

'You'll have seen her cottage when you drove up. It's just the other side of the pine wood. I went there after I found the body, thinking it might be open and I could telephone. There's been an act of vandalism, her portrait thrown through the window. The Whistler and criminal damage on the same night; an odd coincidence.'

Rickards turned and looked full at him. 'Maybe. But this wasn't the Whistler. The Whistler's dead. Killed himself in a hotel at Easthaven, sometime around six o'clock. I've been trying to reach you to let you know.'

He squatted by the body and touched the girl's face, then lifted the head and let it drop. 'No rigor. Not even the beginning of it. Within the last few hours, by the look of her. The Whistler died with enough sins on his conscience but this . . . this,' he stabbed his finger violently at the dead body, 'this, Mr Dalgliesh, is something different.'

Rickards rolled on his search gloves. The latex sliding over his huge fingers made them look almost obscene, like the udders of a great animal. Kneeling, he fiddled with the locket. It sprang open and Dalgliesh could see the Yale key nestling inside it, a perfect fit. Rickards extracted it, then said: 'Right, Mr Dalgliesh. Let's go and take a look at that criminal damage.'

Two minutes later he followed Rickards up the path to the front door of the cottage. Rickards unlocked it and they passed into a passage running to the stairs and with doors on either side. Rickards opened the door to the left and stepped into the sitting room with Dalgliesh behind him. It was a large room running the whole length of the cottage with windows at each end and a fireplace facing the door. The portrait lay about three feet from the window surrounded by jagged slivers of glass. Both men stood just inside the door and surveyed the scene.

Dalgliesh said: 'It was painted by Ryan Blaney who lives at Scudder's Cottage further south on the headland. I saw it first on the afternoon I arrived.'

Rickards said: 'A funny way of delivering it. Sat for him, did she?'

'I don't think so. It was painted to please himself, not her.'

He was going to add that Ryan Blaney would, in his view, be the last person to destroy his work. But then he reflected that it hadn't, in fact, been destroyed. Two single cuts in the form of an L wouldn't be too difficult to repair. And the damage had been as precise and deliberate as those cuts on Hilary Robarts's forehead. The picture hadn't been slashed in fury.

Rickards seemed for a moment to lose interest in it. He said: 'So this is where she lived. She must have been fond of solitude. That is if she lived alone.'

Dalgliesh said: 'As far as I know she lived alone.'

It was, he thought, a depressing room. It was not that the place was uncomfortable; it held the necessary furniture but the pieces looked as though they were rejects from someone else's house, not the conscious choice of the occupant. Beside the fireplace with its fitted gas fire were two armchairs in synthetic brown leather. In the centre of the room was an oval dining table with four discordant chairs. On either side of the front window were fitted bookshelves, holding what looked like a collection of textbooks and assorted novels. Two of the lower and taller shelves were packed with box files. Only on the longest wall facing the door was there any sign that someone had made this room a home. She had obviously been fond of watercolours and the wall was as closely hung with them as if it had been part of a gallery. There were one or two which he thought he could recognize and he wished he could walk over to examine them more closely. But it was possible that someone other than Hilary Robarts herself had been in this room before them and it was important to leave the scene undisturbed.

Rickards closed the door and opened the opposite one on the right of the passage. This led to the kitchen, a purely functional, rather uninteresting room, well enough equipped but in stark contrast to the kitchen at Martyr's Cottage.

Set in the middle of the room was a small wooden table, vinyl-covered, with four matching chairs all pushed well in. On the table was an uncorked bottle of wine with the cork and the metal opener beside it. Two plain wineglasses, clean and upturned, were on the draining board.

Rickards said: 'Two glasses, both washed, by her or her killer. We'll get no prints there. And an open bottle. Someone was drinking with her here tonight.'

Dalgliesh said: 'If so he was abstemious. Or she was.'

Rickards with his gloved hand lifted the bottle by its neck and slowly turned it. 'About one glass poured. Maybe they planned to finish it after her swim.' He looked at Dalgliesh and said: 'You didn't come earlier into the cottage, Mr Dalgliesh? I have to ask everyone she knew.'

'Of course. No, I didn't come earlier into the cottage. I was drinking claret tonight, but not with her.'

'Pity you hadn't been. She'd be alive now.'

'Not necessarily. I might have left when she went to change for her swim. And if she did have someone with her here tonight that's probably what he did.' He paused, wondered whether to speak, then said: 'The left-hand glass is slightly cracked at the rim.'

Rickards lifted it to the central light and turned it slowly.

'I wish I had your eyesight. It's hardly significant, surely.'

'Some people strongly dislike drinking from a cracked glass. I do myself.'

'In which case why didn't she break it and chuck it away? There's no point in keeping a glass you aren't prepared to drink from. When I'm faced with two alternatives I start by taking the more likely. Two glasses, two drinkers. That's the common-sense explanation.'

It was, thought Dalgliesh, the basis of most police work. Only when the obvious proved untenable was it necessary to explore less likely explanations. But it could also be the first fatally easy step into a labyrinth of misconceptions. He wondered why his instinct insisted that she had been drinking alone. Perhaps because the bottle was in the kitchen not in the sitting room. The wine was a '79 Château Talbot, hardly an all-purpose tipple. Why not carry it into the sitting room and do it justice in comfort? On the other hand, if she were alone and had needed only a quick swig before her swim she might hardly have bothered. And if two people had been drinking in the kitchen she had been meticulous in pushing back the chairs. But it was the level of the wine that seemed to him almost conclusive. Why uncork a fresh bottle to pour only two half-glasses? Which didn't, of course, mean that she wasn't later expecting a visitor to help finish it.

Rickards seemed to be taking an unnatural interest in the bottle and its label. Suddenly he said gruffly:

'What time did you leave the mill, Mr Dalgliesh?'

'At 9.15. I looked at the carriage clock on the mantelpiece and checked my watch.'

'And you saw no one during your walk?'

'No one, and no footprints other than hers and mine.'

'What were you actually doing on the headland, Mr Dalgliesh?'

'Walking, thinking.' He was about to add: 'And paddling like a boy,' but checked himself.

Rickards said consideringly: 'Walking and thinking.'

To Dalgliesh's oversensitive ears he made the activities sound both eccentric and suspicious. Dalgliesh wondered what his companion would say if he had decided to confide. 'I was thinking about my aunt and the men who loved her, the fiancé who was killed in 1918 and the man whose mistress she might or might not have been. I was thinking of the thousands of people who have walked along that shore and who are now dead, my aunt among them, and how, as a boy, I hated the false romanticism of that stupid poem about great men leaving their footprints on the sands of time, since that was essentially all that most of us could hope to leave, transitory marks which the next tide would obliterate. I was thinking how little I had known my aunt and whether it was ever possible to know another human being except on the most superficial level, even the women I have loved. I was thinking about the clash of ignorant armies by night, since no poet walks by the sea at moonlight without silently reciting Matthew Arnold's marvellous poem. I was considering whether I would have been a better poet, or even a poet at all, if I hadn't also decided to be a policeman. More prosaically, I was, from time to time, wondering how my life would be changed for better or worse by the unmerited acquisition of three-quarters of a million.'

The fact that he had no intention of revealing even the most mundane of these private musings, the childish secrecy about the paddling, induced an irrational guilt, as if he were deliberately withholding information of importance. After all, he told himself, no man could have been more innocently employed. And it was not as if he were a serious suspect. The idea would probably have struck Rickards as too ridiculous even for consideration, although with logic he would have had to admit that no one who lived on the headland and had known Hilary Robarts could be excluded from the inquiry, least of all because he was a senior police officer. But Dalgliesh was a witness. He had information to give or withhold, and the knowledge that he would have no intention of withholding it didn't alter the fact that there was a difference now in their relationship. He was involved, whether he liked it or not, and he didn't need Rickards to point out that uncomfortable reality. Professionally it was none of his business, but it was his business as a man and a human being.

He was surprised and a little disconcerted to discover how

much he had resented the interrogation, mild as it had been. A man was surely entitled to walk along the beach at night without having to explain his reasons to a police officer. It was salutary for him personally to experience this sense of privacy violated, of virtuous outrage which the most innocent of suspects must feel when faced with police interrogation. And he realized anew how much, even from childhood, he had disliked being questioned. 'What are you doing? Where have you been? What are you reading? Where are you going?' He had been the much-wanted only child of elderly parents, burdened by their almost possessive parental concern and over-conscientiousness, living in a village where little the rector's son did was safe from scrutiny. And suddenly, standing here in this anonymous, over-tidy kitchen, he recalled vividly and with heart-stopping pain the moment when his most precious privacy had been violated. He remembered that secluded place, deep in the laurels and elderberries, at the bottom of the shrubbery, the green tunnel of leaves leading to his own three square yards of moist, mould-rich sanctuary, remembered that August afternoon, the crackle of bushes, the cook's great face thrust between the leaves. 'Your ma thought you'd be in here, Master Adam. Rector wants you. What do you do in there, hiding yourself away in all those mucky bushes? Better be playing out in the sunshine.' So the last refuge, the one he had thought totally secret, had been discovered. They had known about it all the time.

He said: 'Oh God from You that I could private be.'

Rickards looked at him. 'What was that, Mr Dalgliesh?'

'Just a quotation that came into my mind.'

Rickards didn't reply. He was probably thinking: 'Well, you're supposed to be a poet. You're entitled.' He gave a last searching look around the kitchen as if by the intensity of his gaze he could somehow compel that unremarkable table and four chairs, the opened bottle of wine, the two washed glasses to yield up their secret.

Then he said: 'I'll lock up here and set someone on guard until tomorrow. I'm due to meet the pathologist, Dr Maitland-Brown, over at Easthaven. He'll take a look at the Whistler and then come straight on here. The forensic biologist should have arrived from the lab by then. You wanted to see the Whistler yourself, didn't you, Mr Dalgliesh? This seems as good a time as any.'

It seemed to Dalgliesh a particularly bad time. One violent death was enough in one night and he was seized with a sudden longing for the peace and solitude of the mill. But there seemed no prospect of sleep for him until the early hours of the morning and there was little point in objecting. Rickards said: 'I could drive you over and bring you back.'

Dalgliesh felt an immediate revulsion at the thought of a car journey tête-à-tête with Rickards. He said: 'If you'll drop me at the mill I'll take my own car. There won't be any reason for me to linger at Easthaven and you may have to wait.'

It surprised him a little that Rickards was willing to leave the beach. Admittedly he had Oliphant and his minions; procedures at the scene of a murder were well established, they would be competent to do what was necessary, and until the forensic pathologist arrived the body couldn't be moved. But he sensed that it was important to Rickards that he and Dalgliesh should see the Whistler's body together and he wondered what forgotten incident in their joint pasts had led to that compulsion.

23

Balmoral Private Hotel was the last house of an undistinguished nineteenth-century terrace at the unfashionable end of the long promenade. The summer lights were still strung between the Victorian lampposts but they had been turned off and now swung in uneven loops like a tawdry necklace which might scatter its blackened beads at the first strong wind. The season was officially over. Dalgliesh drew up behind the police Rover on the left-hand side of the promenade. Between the road and glittering sea was a children's playground, wire-enclosed, the gate padlocked, the shuttered kiosk pasted with fading and half-torn posters of summer shows, bizarrely shaped ice-creams, a clown's head. The swings had been looped high and one of the metal seats, caught by the strengthening breeze, rapped out a regular tattoo against the iron frame. The hotel stood out from its drabber neighbours, sprucely painted in a bright blue which even the dull street lighting could hardly soften. The porch light shone down on a large card with the words 'Under new management. Bill and Joy Carter welcome you to Balmoral'. A separate card underneath said simply 'Vacancies'.

As they waited to cross the road while a couple of cars cruised slowly past, the drivers peering for a parking space, Rickards said: 'Their first season. Done quite well up to now, so they say, despite the bloody awful summer. This won't help. They'll get the ghouls, of course, but parents will think twice before booking in with the kiddies for happy family hols. Luckily the place is half-empty at present. Two cancellations this morning, so they've only got three couples and they were all out when Mr Carter found the body and, so far, we've managed to keep them in happy ignorance. They're in bed now, presumably asleep. Let's hope they stay that way.'

The earlier arrival of the police must have alerted some of the locals but the plainclothes officer unobtrusively on duty inside the porch had dispersed any curious bystanders and now the road was empty except for a little group of four or five people about fifty yards down on the seaward side. They seemed to be muttering together and as Dalgliesh glanced at them they began moving aimlessly as if stirred by the breeze.

He asked: 'Why here, for God's sake?'

'We know why. There's a hell of a lot we don't know but at least we know that. They've got a part-time barman here, Albert Upcraft, seventy-five if he's a day. He remembers. He's a bit vague about what happened yesterday but there's nothing wrong with his long-term memory. The Whistler came here as a kid, apparently. His auntie – his dad's sister – was manager here twenty years ago. Used to take him off his mum's hands for a free holiday when the place was quiet. Mainly when mum had a new man and the new uncle didn't want the kid around. Sometimes he was here for weeks at a time. No trouble to anyone. Helped with the guests, picked up the odd tip, actually went to Sunday school.'

Dalgliesh said: 'Now the Day is Over.'

'Well, his day's over, all right. He booked in at 2.30 this afternoon. Asked for the same room, apparently. Single at the back. Cheapest in the house. The Carters should be grateful for small mercies. He might have chosen to go out in style, best double bedroom, private bathroom, view of the sea, the lot.'

The constable at the door saluted and they passed through the lobby into the hall, and into a smell of paint and polish overlaid with the faint tang of lavender disinfectant. The cleanliness was almost oppressive. The lurid flowered carpet was covered with a narrow strip of perspex. The wallpaper was obviously new, a different pattern on each wall and a glimpse through the open door of the dining room showed tables set for four with shining white cloths and small vases of artificial flowers, daffodils, narcissi and bulbous roses. The couple who came from the back to meet them were as spruce as their hotel. Bill Carter was a dapper little man who looked as if he came fresh from the ironing board, the creases down his white shirt sleeves and the front of his trousers knife sharp, his tie neatly knotted. His wife was wearing a summer dress in a flowered crimplene under a knitted white sweater. She had obviously been crying. Her plump, rather childish face under the carefully set blonde hair was bloated and bruised red as if she had been struck. Her disappointment at seeing just the two of them was pathetically obvious.

She said: 'I thought you'd come to take him away. Why can't you take him away?'

Rickards didn't introduce Dalgliesh. He said soothingly: 'We will, Mrs Carter, as soon as the pathologist has seen him. He shouldn't be long now. He's on his way.'

'Pathologist? That's a doctor, isn't it? Why do you want a doctor? He's dead, isn't he? Bill found him. His throat's cut. How much deader can you get?'

'He won't be with you much longer, Mrs Carter.'

'The sheet's covered with blood, Bill says. He wouldn't let me in. Not that I want to see. And the carpet, ruined. Blood's terrible to get out, everyone knows that. Who's going to pay for the carpet and the bed? Oh God, I thought things were really coming right for us at last. Why did he come back here to do it? Not very nice, was it, not very considerate?'

'He wasn't a considerate man, Mrs Carter.'

Her husband put his arm round her shoulders and led her

away. Less than half a minute later he reappeared and said: 'It's the shock, naturally. She's upset. Well, who wouldn't be? You know the way up, Mr Rickards. Your officer is still there. I won't come up with you if you don't mind.'

'That's all right, Mr Carter, I know the way.'

Suddenly he turned and said: 'Get him out soon, sir, for God's sake.'

For a moment Dalgliesh thought that he, too, was crying.

There was no lift. Dalgliesh followed Rickards up three flights of stairs, down a narrow passage towards the back and a short turn to the right. A young detective constable got up from his chair outside the door and with his left hand opened it then flattened himself against the wall. The smell seemed to gust out of the room at them, a strong effluvium of blood and death.

The light was on and the main bulb in its cheap pink shade hung low and shone full on the horror on the bed. It was a very small room, little more than a box room, with a single window too high to give a view of more than the sky and enough space only for the single bed, a chair, a bedside cabinet and a low chest of drawers with a mirror hung above it which served as a dressing table. But this room, too, was obsessively clean, making that unclean thing on the bed even more horrible. Both the gaping throat with its white corrugated vessels and the sagging mouth above it seemed to be stretched in protest or outrage at this violence to decency and order. There were no preliminary cuts visible and that single act of annihilating violence must surely, Dalgliesh thought, have taken more strength than was possible from the childish hand lying, fingers curved, on the sheet and fixed now in its blackening carapace of dried blood. The knife, six inches of bloodied steel, lay close beside it. For some reason he had undressed himself for death and lay now wearing only a vest and pants and a pair of short blue nylon socks which looked like the onset of putrefaction. On the chair beside the bed a dark grey striped suit was neatly folded. A blue-striped drip-dry shirt was hung from the back of the chair with the tie folded over it. Under the chair his shoes, well worn but polished to mirror brightness, were precisely placed side by side. They looked small enough for a girl.

Rickards said: 'Neville Potter, aged thirty-six. Scrawny little sod. You wouldn't believe he'd got the strength in those arms to throttle a chicken. And he came properly dressed in his Sunday best to meet his Maker, but then thought better of it. Probably remembered that his ma wouldn't like him getting blood on his best suit. You should meet Ma, Mr Dalgliesh. She's a real education, that one. She explains a lot. But he's left the evidence. It's all there, all laid out for us. Neat little devil, wasn't he?'

Dalgliesh edged himself round the end of the bed, being careful not to tread in the blood. On the top of the chest of drawers were the Whistler's weapons and his trophies; a leather dog lead, neatly curled, a blond wig and blue beret, a clasp knife, a lamp with a battery ingeniously fixed to the centre of a metal headband Beside these was a pyramid of tangled bushy hair: blond, dark brown, red. In front of the careful arrangement was a page of paper torn from a notebook with the single written message in biro, printed like a child's. 'It was getting worse. This is the only way I know to stop myself. Please look after Pongo.' The 'Please' was underlined.

Rickards said: 'His dog. Pongo, for God's sake.'

'What did you expect him to be called, Cerberus?'

Rickards opened the door and stood with his back to the gap breathing deeply as if hungry for fresh air. He said: 'He and his ma lived on one of the caravan sites outside Cromer. Been there for twelve years. He was a general handyman, did any easy repairs, kept an eye on the place at night, dealt with complaints. The boss has another site outside Yarmouth and he would go there some nights to relieve the permanent chap. A bit of a loner. Had a small van and the dog. Married a girl he picked up on the site there years ago but it only lasted four months. She walked out on him. Driven out by Ma or by the smell of the caravan. God knows how she stuck it for four months.'

Dalgliesh said: 'He was an obvious suspect. You must have checked him.'

'His ma gave him an alibi for two of the murders. Either she was drunk and didn't know whether he was there or not, or she was covering up for him. Or, of course, she couldn't give a bloody damn one way or the other.' He said with sudden violence,

'I thought we'd learned by now not to take that kind of alibi at its face value. I'm having a word with the DC who interviewed them, but you know how it is. Thousands of interviews, checks, the stuff all put on the computer. I'd give a dozen computers for a DC who can sense when a witness is lying. My God, haven't we learned anything from the Yorkshire Ripper fiasco?'

'Didn't your man search the van?'

'Oh, they searched the van, all right. They showed a modicum of initiative. It was clean. He cached his stuff elsewhere. Probably picked it up every evening, watched, waited, chose his moment.' He gazed down at the head contraption and said: 'Ingenious, isn't it? As his ma says, he was always clever with his hands.'

The small rectangle of sky outside the single high window was blue-black pricked with a single star. It seemed to Dalgliesh that he had experienced half a lifetime of sensations since he had woken that morning to the cool sea-scented autumnal dawn, to the beginning of a day which had included that calm meditative walk under the soaring roof of St Peter Mancroft, the nostalgic self-indulgent pain induced by those faded photographs of the long dead; the rush and pull of the tide over his naked feet, the mingled shock and recognition as his torch shone on Hilary Robarts's body. It was a day which, stretching interminably, seemed to have embraced all seasons. So this was one way of stretching time, time which for the Whistler had stopped with that great gush of blood. And now at the end of the day he had come to this neat box of an execution shed, imposing on his mind as if it were a memory the picture of a skinny child lying supine on that same bed and watching through the high window the same single star while arranged on the chest of drawers with careful art were the trophies of his day: the tips in pennies and sixpences, the shells and coloured stones from the beach, the dried swathe of pustulated seaweed.

And he himself was here because Rickards had willed it, had wanted him here in this room and at this time. He could have viewed the Whistler's body tomorrow in the mortuary, or, since he could hardly claim that he hadn't the stomach for it, on the autopsy table, to confirm what hardly needed confirmation, that this scrawny killer wasn't the once-glimpsed, six-foot, Battersea strangler. But Rickards had needed an audience, had needed him, Dalgliesh, against whose dreadfully experienced and unshockable calm he could hurl the bitterness and frustrations of failure. Five women dead, and the murderer a suspect they had interviewed and cleared early in the inquiry. The smell of that failure would linger at least in his own nostrils long after the media interest, the official inquiries had run their course. And now there was this sixth death, Hilary Robarts who might not have died and certainly wouldn't have died as she had if the Whistler had been stopped in his tracks earlier. But Dalgliesh sensed that something more keenly personal even than professional failure was fuelling Rickards's anger with its uncharacteristic spurts of verbal brutality and he wondered whether it had something to do with his wife and the coming child. He asked: 'What will happen to the dog?'

Rickards seemed not to notice the irrelevance of the question.

'What do you think? Who's going to take on an animal that has been where he's been, seen what he's seen?' He looked down at the stiffening corpse and, turning to Dalgliesh, said harshly: 'You pity him, I suppose.'

Dalgliesh didn't reply. He could have said: 'Yes, I pity him. And his victims. And you. And myself occasionally, come to that.' He thought: Yesterday I was reading *The Anatomy of Melancholy*. Odd. Robert Burton, that seventeenth-century Leicestershire rector, had said all that could be said at such a moment and the words came to him as clearly as if he had spoken them aloud. 'Of their goods and bodies we can dispose; but what shall become of their souls God alone can tell; His mercy may come *inter pontem et fontem, inter gladium et jugulum*, betwixt the bridge and the brook, the knife and the throat.'

Rickards shook himself violently as if suddenly seized with cold. It was an odd gesture. Then he said: 'At least he's saved the country his keep for the next twenty years. One argument for keeping his kind alive instead of putting them down is that we can learn from them, stop it happening again. But can we? We've got Straffen banged up, Brady, Nilson. How much have we learned from them?'

Dalgliesh said: 'You wouldn't hang a madman, presumably?'

'I wouldn't hang anyone, I'd find a less barbaric method. But they aren't mad, are they? Not until they're caught. Until then they cope with life like most other people. Then we discover that they're monsters and decide, surprise, surprise, to classify them as mad. Makes it seem more comprehensible. We don't have to think of them as human any more. We don't have to use the word evil. Everyone feels better. Do you want to see the mother, Mr Dalgliesh?'

'There's no point in it. He obviously isn't our man. I didn't for a moment suppose that he would be.'

'You should see the mother. She's a right bitch, that one. And do you know what her name is? Lillian. L for Lillian. That's something for the trick-cyclist to chew over. She made him what he was. But we can't check on people and decide who's fit to have kids, let alone fit to bring them up. And I suppose that when he was born she must have felt something for him, had some hopes for him. She could hardly know what she'd brought forth. You never had a child, did you, Mr Dalgliesh.'

'I had a son. Briefly.'

Rickards kicked the door gently, looking away. He said: 'Bloody hell, I'd forgotten. Sorry. Wrong time to ask, for both of us.'

There were confident footsteps mounting the stairs and now they had reached the passage. Dalgliesh said: 'It sounds as if the pathologist has arrived.'

Rickards made no reply. He had moved over to the chest of drawers and, with his forefinger, gently urged the tangle of hairs across the polished wood.

He said: 'There's one sample which we won't find here. Hilary Robarts. Forensic will look to make doubly sure, but it won't be here. And now I start looking for a very different murderer. And, by God, Mr Dalgliesh, this time I'm going to get him.'

24

Forty-five minutes later Rickards was back at the scene of the murder. He seemed to have passed beyond conscious tiredness and to be operating in a different dimension of time and space in which his mind worked with unnatural clarity while his body had become almost weightless, a creature of light and air, as insubstantial as the bizarre scene in which he moved and spoke and gave his orders. The pale transparent disc of the moon was eclipsed by the glare of the mounted lights which illumined and solidified the hard outlines of trees and men and equipment, yet paradoxically robbed them of form and essence so that they were, at one and the same time, revealed and clarified and transformed into something alien and strange. And always, beyond the masculine voices, the scrunch of feet on pebbles, the sudden flap of canvas in a tentative breeze, was the continual fall and suck of the tide.

Dr Anthony Maitland-Brown had driven from Easthaven to the scene in his Mercedes and had arrived first. He was already gowned and gloved and crouching by the body by the time Rickards caught up with him. Wisely he left him to it. M-B strongly disliked being watched while he made his preliminary examination at the scene and was apt to protest with a peevish 'Do we really need all these people standing around?' if anyone came within ten feet of him, as if the police photographer, scene-of-crime officer and forensic biologist were all so many snap-happy sightseers. He was an elegant and extraordinarily handsome man, over six feet tall, who had once in youth – so it was rumoured – been told that he looked like Leslie Howard and had spent subsequent years sedulously promoting the image. He was amicably divorced, comfortably well-off – his mother had bequeathed him a private income – and well able to indulge his twin passions of clothes and the opera. In his free time he escorted a succession of young and extremely pretty actresses to Covent Garden and Glyndebourne, where they were apparently content to endure three hours of boredom for the prestige of his company or, perhaps, the *frisson* of knowing that the elegant hands which poured their wine or helped them out of the Mercedes were commonly engaged with more bizarre activities. Rickards had never found him an easy colleague but recognized that he was a first-class forensic pathologist, and God knew they were rare enough. Reading M-B's lucid and comprehensive autopsy reports he could forgive him even his aftershave.

Now, moving away from the body, he stirred himself to greet

the recent arrivals, photographer, cameraman, forensic biologist. The stretch of beach fifty yards each side of the murder scene had been efficiently roped off and plastic sheeting laid over the path now lit by a string of overhead lights. He was aware of his sergeant's disciplined excitement at his side.

Stuart Oliphant said: 'We've found a print, sir. About forty yards into the copse.'

'On grass and pine needles?'

'No, sir, on sand. Someone, a kid perhaps, must have tipped it from a bucket. The print's a good one, sir.'

Rickards followed him into the wood. The whole of the path had been protected but at one place a marker had been driven into the soft ground at the right-hand side. Sergeant Oliphant drew back the plastic then lifted the box covering the print. In the glow of the overhead lights slung along the path it showed clearly, a dusting of moist sand over the pine needles and flattened grass, covering no more than six inches by four, and printed on it the intricate pattern of the sole of a right shoe.

Oliphant said: 'We found it soon after you left, sir. Only the one, but it's pretty clear. The photographs have been taken and the measurements will be at the lab this morning. Size ten by the look of it. They'll be able to give us confirmation pretty quickly, but it's hardly necessary. It's a trainer shoe, sir. A Bumble. You know the make, the one that has a picture of a bee on the heel. And it has the outline of a bee on the sole. You can see the curve of the wing here, sir. It's quite unmistakable.'

A Bumble trainer. If you wanted a print you could hardly hope for anything more distinctive. Oliphant voiced his thoughts: 'Common enough, of course, but not all that common. Bumbles are the most expensive on the market, the Porsche of trainers. Most of the kids with money like to have them. It's a bloody silly name. Part of the firm is actually owned by a man called Bumble and they've only been on the market for a couple of years, but he promotes them fairly vigorously. I suppose he hopes that the name will catch on, that people will start yelling for their Bumbles as they do for their wellie-boots.'

Rickards said: 'It looks fresh enough. When did we last get rain? Late on Saturday night, wasn't it?'

'About eleven. It was over by midnight but it was a heavy shower.'

'And there's no tree cover on this part of the path. The print's perfectly smooth. If it were made before midnight on Saturday I'd expect some spotting. Interesting that there's only the one and that it's pointing away from the sea. If someone wearing Bumble trainers came along this path any time on Sunday you'd expect to find at least one similar print on the upper reaches of the beach.'

'Not necessarily, sir. The shingle comes up almost as high as the path in places. We'd get no prints if he stayed on the pebbles. But if it was made on Sunday before she died would it still be here? She must have come along this path.'

'No reason why she would have trodden on it. It's well to the right of the path. It's odd, though. Too plain, too distinctive, too opportune. You could almost believe it's been deliberately made to deceive us.'

'They sell Bumble trainers at the sports shop in Blakeney, sir. I could send a chap to buy a pair of size ten as soon as they open.'

'See that he's in plain clothes and buys them as an ordinary purchaser. I need confirmation of the pattern before we start asking people to turn out their shoe cupboards. We're going to be dealing with intelligent suspects. I don't want a balls-up at the beginning of the case.'

'Pity to waste time, sir. My brother owns a pair of Bumbles. The print's unmistakable.'

Rickards said obstinately: 'I need confirmation, and I want it fast.'

Oliphant replaced the box and the plastic cover then followed him back to the beach. Rickards was uncomfortably aware of the almost physical weight of resentment, antagonism and slight contempt which seemed to flow from the sergeant. But he was lumbered with the man. Oliphant had been part of the team bearing the brunt of the Whistler investigation and, although this admittedly was a different inquiry, it would be difficult to replace him without causing personal or logistical problems which Rickards was anxious to avoid. During the fifteen-month hunt for the Whistler his mild dislike of the sergeant had grown into an antipathy which he knew to be not wholly reasonable and which he had tried to discipline both in the interests of the investigation and of his own self-regard. A serial murder was difficult enough without personal complications.

He had no real evidence that Oliphant was a bully; he only looked like one. He was six feet of disciplined flesh and muscle, dark and conventionally handsome with rather pudgy features, full-lipped and hard-eyed, with a fleshy chin like a doughnut, dented in the middle with a deep dimple. Rickards found it difficult to keep his eyes off it. His repugnance to the man had elevated it to a deformity. Oliphant drank too much but that was an occupational hazard for a policeman. The fact that Rickards had never seen him actually drunk only increased the offence. A man shouldn't be able to put away that amount of alcohol and still stand firmly on his feet.

He was meticulous in his attitude to senior officers, respectful without being servile, but subtly managed to give Rickards the impression that he wasn't quite measuring up to the standards Oliphant had privately set for him. He was popular enough with the less sensitive probationers; the others wisely kept clear of him. Rickards told himself that if he were ever in trouble, Oliphant was the last police officer he would wish to see on his doorstep. Oliphant would probably regard that sentiment as a compliment. And there had never been from the public even the whisper of a complaint against him. That too, unreasonably, made Rickards suspicious. It suggested that where his interests were at stake the man was devious enough to act against his essential nature. He was unmarried but managed, without the crudity of actual boasting, to give the impression that women found him irresistible. Probably a number did, but at least he kept clear of his colleagues' wives. In all, he represented most of the qualities in a young detective which Rickards disliked: aggression, only controlled because control was prudent, a frank relish for power, too much sexual assurance and an inflated opinion of his own capabilities. But those capabilities weren't negligible. Oliphant would make Chief Inspector at least and might go higher. Rickards had never managed to bring himself to use his sergeant's nickname of Jumbo. Oliphant, so far from resenting a sobriquet both childish and basically unsuitable, seemed to tolerate, even to like it, at least in those colleagues he had privately authorized to use it. Less favoured mortals only used it once.

Maitland-Brown was ready to make his preliminary report. Drawing himself up to his full six feet three inches he peeled off his gloves and tossed them to a DC, rather like an actor casually divesting himself of part of his costume. It wasn't his custom to discuss his findings at the scene. He did, however, condescend to announce them.

'I'll do the autopsy tomorrow and let you have a report by Wednesday. I doubt whether there will be any surprises. On a preliminary examination it's clear enough. Death by strangulation. The implement was smooth and two centimetres in width, perhaps a belt, a strap or a dog lead. She was a tall, well-muscled woman. It would have taken strength but not inordinate strength given the advantage of surprise. He probably stood in the shelter of the pines then stepped out and slung the strap over her head as soon as she got back from the swim. She had just time to pick up her towel. She made one or two convulsive movements with the feet, you can see where the grass is marked. I estimate on the present evidence that she died between 8.30 and ten.'

Maitland-Brown had pronounced and clearly expected no questions. Nor was there need for any. He put out a hand for his coat which was obligingly handed to him by a DC, then took his leave. Rickards almost expected him to bow.

Rickards looked down at the corpse. Now with the head, hands and feet covered with plastic she looked for a second like a gift-wrapped toy, a plaything for someone with expensive and peculiar tastes, an artifice of latex and synthetic hair, glass eyes, a mere simulation of a living woman. Oliphant's voice seemed to come from a far distance.

'Commander Dalgliesh didn't come back with you then, sir?'

'Why should he? This isn't his pigeon. He's probably in bed.'

He thought, And I wish to God I were too. Already the day was crowding in on him as if physical weight were being piled on exhausted body; the press conference about the Whistler's suicide, the Chief Constable, the press officer, this new investigation, suspects to be interviewed, facts established, the whole cumbersome business of a murder investigation set in motion with the knowledge of his previous failure dragging like a stone on his heart. And somehow or other he had to find time to ring Susie.

He said: 'Mr Dalgliesh is a witness, not the investigating officer.'

'A witness, but hardly a suspect.'

'Why not? He lives on the headland, he knew the girl, he knew how the Whistler killed. He may not be a serious suspect in our eyes but he makes his statement like everyone else.'

Oliphant looked at him stolidly. He said: 'That'll be a new experience for him. Let's hope he enjoys it.'

BOOK FOUR

Monday 26 September

25

Anthony woke her, as he usually did, just after 6.30. Theresa wrenched her mind through clogging layers of sleep to the familiar morning sounds, the creak and rock of the cot and the sniffs and grunts as Anthony grasped the rails and pulled himself up. She smelt the familiar nursery smell compounded of baby talc, stale milk and a sodden nappy. She felt for the switch of the bedside light under the grubby shade with its fringe of dancing Bambis and, opening her eyes, stared into Anthony's and was rewarded by his wide, gummy smile and his ritual small bounces of pleasure which shook the cot. Gently opening the door of the twins' room she could see that they were still asleep, Elizabeth a curled lump on the far end of the bed, Marie on her back one arm flung out. If she could change and feed Anthony before he became fretful they would sleep for another half hour, thirty more minutes of peace for her father.

She would look after Elizabeth and Marie for her mother's sake as long as they needed her and with all her strength, but it was Anthony whom she loved. For a moment she lay still regarding him, enjoying this moment of their quiet, mutual pleasure in each other. Then he let go of the cot rail with one hand, raised one leg in a parody of a clumsy ballet dancer, collapsed on to his mattress, then rolled over on to his back, stuffed his fist into his mouth and began noisily sucking. Soon he would tire of this substitute comfort. She swung her legs out of bed, waited for a moment until she felt the physical flow of strength into arms and legs, then went over to the cot, let down the side and gathered him into her arms. She would change him downstairs on newspaper spread on the kitchen table, then strap him into his chair so that he could watch her while she heated his milk. By the time he was fed the twins would be awake and she would be free to help dress them ready for Mrs Hunter from the welfare to collect them and drive them to the playgroup. Then there would be breakfast for her father and herself before it was time to set out with her father and Anthony to walk to the crossroads where she would pick up the school bus.

She had just turned out the gas under the saucepan of milk when the telephone rang. Her heart lurched, then settled into a rhythmic pounding. She snatched at the receiver, hoping that she had been quick enough to stop it waking her father. George Jago's voice came over strongly, conspiratorial, husky with excitement.

'Theresa? Is your dad up yet?'

'No, not yet, Mr Jago. He's still asleep.'

There was a pause as if he were thinking, then he said: 'OK, don't disturb him. When he wakes tell him Hilary Robarts is dead. Last night. Murdered. Found on the beach.'

'You mean the Whistler got her?'

'Looked like that, meant to look like that if you ask me. But it couldn't have been. The Whistler was dead, been dead three hours or more. Like I told you last night. Remember?'

'Yes, I remember, Mr Jago.'

'Good thing I rang last night, isn't it? You told him, your dad? You told your dad about the Whistler?'

She heard under the excitement the insistent note of anxiety. 'Yes,' she said, 'I told him.'

'That's all right then. Now you tell him about Miss Robarts. Ask him to give me a ring. I've got a call to take a party to Ipswich but I'll be back about twelve. Or I could have a word with him now if he's quick.'

'He wouldn't be quick, Mr Jago. He's sound asleep. And I'm trying to feed Anthony.'

'All right. But you tell him, mind.'

'Yes, I'll tell him.'

He said: 'Good thing I rang last night. He'll know why.'

She put down the receiver. Her hands were wet. She wiped them on her nightdress and went over to the stove. But when she picked up the pan of milk her hands were shaking so violently that she knew she wouldn't be able to pour it into the narrow neck of the bottle. She took it over to the sink and, very carefully, managed to half fill it. Then she unstrapped Anthony and seated herself in the low nursing chair before the empty fireplace. His mouth opened and she plugged in the teat of the bottle and watched as he began his vigorous chomping, his eyes, suddenly vacant, fixed on hers, his two chubby hands raised, palms down like the paws of an animal.

It was then that she heard the creak of the stairs, and her father came in. He never appeared in front of her in the mornings without what he used as a dressing gown, an old raincoat buttoned to the neck. Above it his face under the sleep-tousled hair was grey and swollen, the lips unnaturally red.

He said: 'Was that the phone?'

'Yes, Daddy, Mr Jago.'

'What did he want, then, at this hour?'

'He rang to say that Hilary Robarts is dead. She's been murdered.'

Surely he would notice how different her voice sounded. It seemed to her that her lips were so dry that they would look bloated and deformed, and she bent her head low over the baby so that he shouldn't see. But her father didn't look at her and he didn't speak. With his back to her he said: 'The Whistler then, was it? Got her, did he? Well, she was asking for it.'

'No, Daddy, it couldn't have been the Whistler. Remember Mr Jago phoned us last night at half-past seven to say that the Whistler was dead. He said this morning he was glad he rang to tell us and that you would know why.'

Still he didn't speak. She heard the hiss of water from the tap into the kettle and watched him as he took it slowly back to the table and plugged it in, then took down a mug from the shelf. She was aware of the thudding of her heart, of Anthony's warm body against her arm, of her chin gently resting on his downy head. She said: 'What did Mr Jago mean by that, Daddy?'

'He meant that whoever killed Miss Robarts meant to blame it on the Whistler. That means the police will only suspect people who didn't know that the Whistler was dead.'

'But you knew, Daddy, because I told you.'

Then he turned and said without looking at her. 'Your mother wouldn't like you to tell lies.'

But he wasn't cross and he wasn't rebuking her. She heard nothing in his voice but a great weariness. She said quietly: 'But it isn't a lie, Daddy. Mr Jago telephoned when you were out in the privy. When you came back I told you.'

And then he turned and their eyes met. She had never seen him look more hopeless, more defeated. He said: 'That's right, you told me. And that's what you'll tell the police when they ask you.'

'Of course, Daddy. I'll tell them what happened. Mr Jago told me about the Whistler and I told you.'

'And do you remember what I said?'

The teat of the bottle had flattened. She took it from Anthony's mouth and shook the bottle to let in the air. He gave an immediate wail of fury which she plugged with the teat.

She said: 'I think you said that you were glad. We would all be safe now.'

'Yes,' he said, 'we're all safe now.'

'Does that mean that we won't have to leave the cottage?'

'It depends. We shan't have to leave at once anyway.'

'Who will it belong to now, Daddy?'

'I don't know. Whoever she leaves it to in her will, I suppose. They might want to sell it.'

'Could we buy it, Daddy? It would be nice if we could buy it.'

'That would depend on how much they want. There's no point in thinking about that yet. We're all right for the moment anyway.'

She said: 'Will the police be coming here?'

'Sure to. Today, most likely.'

'Why will they be coming here, Daddy?'

'To find out whether I knew if the Whistler was dead. To ask you if I left the cottage last night. They'll be here, most likely, when you get back from school.'

But she wasn't going to school. Today, it was important that she didn't leave her father's side. And she had an excuse ready, a stomach cramp. And that, at least, was true, or partly true. Crouched over the lavatory she had seen that first pink evidence of her monthly period almost with joy.

She said: 'But you didn't leave the cottage, did you, Daddy? I was here until I went to bed at a quarter past eight. I could hear you moving down here. I could hear the television.'

He said: 'The television isn't an alibi.'

'But I came down, Daddy. You remember. I went to bed early at 8.15 but I couldn't sleep and I was thirsty. I came down just before nine o'clock for a drink of water. I sat in Mummy's chair reading. You must remember, Daddy? It was half-past nine before I went back to bed.'

He gave a groan. He said: 'Yes, I remember.'

Suddenly Theresa was aware that the twins had entered the kitchen and were standing silently side by side by the doorway regarding their father expressionlessly. She said sharply: 'Go back and get dressed. You shouldn't be down here undressed like that, you'll catch cold.'

Obediently they turned and padded up the stairs.

The kettle was spouting steam. Her father turned it off but made no move to make the tea. Instead he sat at the table, his head bowed. She thought she heard him whisper: 'I'm no good for you, I'm no good for you.' She couldn't see his face but for one terrible moment she thought that he was crying. Still holding the bottle and feeding Anthony, she got up and moved across to him. She had no free hand but she stood very close. She said: 'It's all right, Daddy. There's nothing to worry about. It's going to be all right.'

26

On Monday 26 September Jonathan Reeves was working the 8.15 to 14.45 shift and, as usual, he was early at his bench. But it was 8.55 before the telephone rang and he heard the expected voice. Caroline sounded perfectly calm; only the words were urgent.

'I have to see you. Now. Can you get away?'

'I think so. Mr Hammond isn't in yet.'

'Then I'll meet you in the library. At once. It's important, Jonathan.'

She had no need to tell him that. She wouldn't be making an assignation during working hours if it weren't important.

The library was housed in the administration block next to the registry. It was part staff sitting room, part library, with three walls covered with shelves, two free-standing racks, and eight comfortable chairs ranged round low tables. Caroline was already waiting when he arrived, standing at the publications display stand and glancing through the latest copy of *Nature*. No one else was there. He moved up to her wondering if she expected him to kiss her, but then she turned and looked at him and he saw that it would be a mistake. And yet this was their first meeting since Friday night, the night that had changed everything for him. Surely, when they were alone like this, they needn't meet as strangers.

He said humbly: 'There's something you want to say.'

'In a minute. It's just on nine o'clock. Pray silence for the voice of God.'

His head jerked up at her. He was as surprised at her tone as if she had uttered an obscenity. They had never talked about Dr Mair except on the most superficial level, but he had always taken it for granted that she admired the Director and was happy to be his PA. He recalled overhearing the whispered words of Hilary Robarts when Caroline had walked into a public meeting at Mair's elbow: 'Behold, the handmaid of the Lord.' That was how they had all seen her, the intelligent, discreet, beautiful but subservient handmaid to a man she was content to serve because she found him worthy of service.

The intercom crackled. There was a background, indecipherable voice and then Mair's measured, serious tones.

'There cannot be anyone on the station who doesn't now know that Hilary Robarts was found dead on the beach last night. She had been murdered. It appeared at first that she was the second Larksoken victim of the Norfolk Whistler, but it now seems almost certain that the Whistler himself died before Hilary. We shall in time find a way of expressing our corporate grief at her loss as we shall at Christine Baldwin's. In the meantime her death is a matter for police investigation and Chief Inspector Rickards of the Norfolk CID, who has been responsible for the investigation into the Whistler murders, has taken charge of the case. He will be on the station later in the morning and may ask to interview those of you who knew Hilary best and may be able to help with details of her life. If any of you has any information, however slight, which may assist the police, please get in touch with Chief Inspector Rickards, either when he is here or at the incident room at Hoveton. The telephone number is 499 623.'

The intercom crackled and was silent. She said: 'I wonder how many drafts it took before he got that right. Innocuous, non-committal, nothing crudely stated but everything understood. And he didn't irritate us by saying that he could rely on us all to get on with the job, as if we were a bunch of excitable sixth-formers. He never wastes time and words on inessentials. He'll make a good senior civil servant all right.'

Jonathan said: 'This Chief Inspector Rickards, do you think he'll want to interview all of us?'

'Anyone who knew Hilary. And that will include us. And that's what I want to talk about. When he sees me I propose telling him that you and I spent the whole of last evening together from six o'clock until about half-past ten. Obviously I'll need you to back me up. And it depends, of course, on whether anyone can disprove it. That's what we have to discuss.'

He stood for a moment appalled. 'But we weren't! You're asking me to lie. This is a murder investigation. It's terribly dangerous to lie to the police, they always find out.'

He knew what he must sound like, a frightened child, petulant, reluctant to take part in a dangerous game. He looked straight ahead, not wanting to meet her eyes, fearful of what he might see there, entreaty, anger, contempt.

She said: 'You told me on Friday that your parents were going to spend Sunday night at Ipswich with your married sister. They went, didn't they?'

He said miserably: 'Yes, they went.'

It was because he knew that they wouldn't be at home that he had hoped, had half expected, that Caroline would suggest that they should be together again in the bungalow. He remembered her words: 'Look, there are times when a woman needs to be on her own. Can't you understand that? What happened yesterday doesn't mean that we have to spend every second of our time together. I've told you that I love you. God knows, I've shown it. Isn't that enough?'

She said: 'So you were alone in the flat yesterday evening. Or weren't you? If anyone called or telephoned, then obviously I've got to think of something else.'

'No one called. I was on my own until after lunch. Then I went for a drive.'

'What time did you get back? Did anyone see you garaging the car? It's not a large block of flats, is it? Did you meet anyone when you got home? And what about lights from the windows?'

'I left the lights on. We always do when the flat is empty. Mother thinks it's safer, makes it look occupied. And I didn't get back until after dark. I wanted to be alone, to think. I drove to Blakeney and walked on the marshes. I wasn't home until 10.45.'

She gave a small contented sigh. 'Then it looks all right. Did you meet anyone on the walk?'

'Only in the distance. A couple with a dog. I don't think they could recognize me even if they knew me.'

'Where did you eat?' Her voice was sharp, the interrogation relentless.

'I didn't. Not until I got home. I wasn't hungry.'

'Well, that's all right then. We're safe. And no one spied on me in the bungalow. And no one would ring or call. No one ever does.'

Spy. It was, he thought, a strange word to use. But she was right. The bungalow, as uninspired as its name, Field View, stood totally isolated on a dull country road outside Hoveton. He had never been inside it, never even been allowed to escort her home before they had arrived together on Friday evening, and it had surprised and a little shocked him. She had told him that it was rented furnished from the owners who had gone to Australia for a year to stay with a married daughter and had decided to stay on. But why had she stayed on, he wondered? Surely there was a more attractive house or cottage somewhere she could have rented, a small flat in Norwich she could have afforded to buy. And following her inside the front door he had been struck by the contrast between its meanness, its vulgarity and her serene loveliness. He could picture it now, the dun-coloured carpet in the hall, the sitting room with two walls papered in pink stripes, the other two with huge clusters of roses, the hard sofa and two chairs with their grubby covers, the small reproduction of Constable's *Hay Wain*, hung too high to be comfortably seen and placed in incongruous proximity to the ubiquitous print of a yellow-faced Chinese girl, the old-fashioned, wall-mounted gas fire. And she had done nothing to change it, nothing to impress on it her own personality. It was as if she hardly noticed its deficiencies, its ugliness. It served its purpose. She asked no more of it. And it had served theirs. But even the hall had struck him chill. He had wanted to cry out, 'This is our first time together, my first time ever. Can't we go somewhere else? Does it have to be here?'

He said miserably: 'I don't think I can do it, not convincingly. Chief Inspector Rickards will know I'm lying. I'll look guilty, embarrassed.'

But she had decided to be gentle with him, reassuring. She said patiently: 'He'll expect you to be embarrassed. You'll be telling him we spent the evening alone making love. That's convincing enough. That's natural enough. He'd find it more suspicious if you didn't look guilty. Don't you see the guilt and embarrassment will make your story more convincing.'

So even his inexperience, his insecurity, yes, even his shame was to be used for her ends.

She said: 'Look, all we need to do is to transpose the two nights. Friday night becomes yesterday. Don't fabricate, don't invent. Tell them what we did, what we ate, the food, the wine, what we talked about. It will sound true because it will be true. And they can't catch us out by asking about the TV programmes we didn't watch.'

'But what happened was private. It was for us alone.'

'Not any more. Murder destroys privacy. We made love. No doubt the police will use a coarser word. If they don't speak it, then they'll think it. But we made love in my bedroom, on my bed. You do remember?'

Remember. Oh yes, he remembered. His face flamed. He felt as if his whole body was burning. The tears that welled up despite his desperate will to hold them back were scalding tears. He squeezed his eyes shut so that he need not have to wipe them away. Of course, he remembered. That dull, square little back room, anonymous as a room in some cheap hotel, the mixture of excitement and terror which half paralysed him, his incompetent fumblings, the whispered endearments which had become commands. She had been patient, experienced and in the end she had taken charge. Well, he had never been naïve enough to suppose that for her it was the first time. For him, but not for her. But what had happened was, he knew, irrevocable. It was she who had possessed him not he her, and that possession was more than physical. For a moment he couldn't speak. It was difficult to believe that those grotesque but controlled writhings had anything to do with the Caroline who stood now so close to him, yet so distanced. He noticed with sharpened perception the pristine cleanness of the grey and white striped shirt, cut like a man's, the sway of the long grey skirt, the black patent court shoes, the simple gold chain and the matching gold cufflinks, the corn-coloured hair sculpted back into the single thick plait. Was this what he had loved, still loved, a boy's romantic ideal, the cold remote perfection of her? And he knew with an almost audible groan that their first coupling had destroyed more than it had affirmed, that what he had yearned for, still yearned for, and had lost for ever, was an unattainable beauty. But he knew, too, that she would only have to stretch out a hand and he would follow her again to that bungalow, to that bed.

He said miserably: 'But why? Why? They won't suspect you, they can't. It's ridiculous even to think it. You got on well with Hilary. You get on well with everyone in the station. You're the last person the police will be interested in. You haven't even a motive.'

'But I have. I've always disliked her and I hated her father. He ruined Mummy, forced her to spend her last years in poverty. And I lost the chance of a decent education. I'm a secretary, essentially a shorthand-typist, and that's all I'll ever be.'

'I've always thought you could be anything you chose.'

'Not without education. All right, I know you can get a grant, but I had to leave school and earn as quickly as possible. And it's not only me, it's what Peter Robarts did to Mummy. She trusted him. She put every penny she'd got, every penny Daddy left, into his plastics company. I've hated him all my life and I hated her because of him. Once the police discover that I'll get no peace.

But if I can produce an alibi, that will be the end. They'll leave us alone, both of us. We only need to say that we were together and there will be the end of it.'

'But they can't see what Hilary's father did to your mother as a motive for murder. It's unreasonable. And it was all so long ago.'

'No motive for killing another human being is ever reasonable. People kill for the strangest reasons. And I've got a thing about the police. It's irrational, I know, but I've always had it. That's why I'm so careful when I'm driving. I know I couldn't stand up to a real interrogation. I'm frightened of the police.'

And she was, he remembered, seizing on this demonstrable truth as if it made the whole request legitimate, reasonable. She was obsessive about the speed limit even when the road was clear, obsessive about wearing her seat belt, the state of her car. And he remembered that time three weeks ago, when she had had her handbag snatched while shopping in Norwich and, despite his protest, hadn't even reported it. He remembered her words. 'It's no use, they'll never get it back. We'll only waste their time at the police station. Let it go, there wasn't much in it.' And then he thought, I'm checking up on what she's telling me, verifying it. And he felt an overpowering shame mixed with pity. He heard her voice.

'All right, I'm asking too much. I know how you feel about truth, honesty, your boy scout Christianity. I'm asking you to sacrifice your good opinion of yourself. No one likes doing that. We all need our self-esteem. I suppose yours is knowing that you're morally better than the rest of us. But aren't you a bit of a hypocrite? You say you love me, but you won't lie for me. It's not an important lie. It won't hurt anyone. But you can't do it. It's against your religion. Your precious religion didn't stop you going to bed with me, did it? I thought Christians were supposed to be too pure for casual fornication.'

Casual fornication. Each word was like a blow, not a fierce stabbing pain but a continuous thud like regular deliberate blows on the same bruised flesh. He had never, even in those first marvellous days together, been able to talk to her about his faith. She had made it plain from the beginning that this was a part of his life with which she had neither sympathy nor understanding.

And how could he begin to explain that he had followed her into the bedroom without guilt because his need of her was stronger than his love for God, stronger than guilt, stronger than faith, needing no rationalization, no justification other than itself. How, he had told himself, could anything be wrong which every nerve and sinew told him was natural and right, even holy.

She said: 'All right, let it go. I'm asking too much.'

Stung by the contempt in her voice, he said miserably: 'It's not that. I'm not better, I'm not. And you could never ask too much. If it's important to you, of course I'll do it.'

She looked at him sharply as if judging his sincerity, his will. He heard the relief in her voice. She said: 'Look, there's no danger. We're both innocent, we know that. And what we tell the police could so easily have been true.'

But that was a mistake, and he saw the realization of it in her eyes. He said: 'It could have been true, but it isn't.'

'And that's what's important to you, more important than my peace of mind, more important than what I thought we felt for each other.'

He wanted to ask why her peace of mind needed to be built on a lie. He wanted to ask what they did, in fact, feel for each other, what she felt for him.

She said, looking at her watch: 'And after all it will be an alibi for you too. That's even more important. After all, everyone knows how unkind she's been to you since that local radio programme. God's little nuclear crusader. You haven't forgotten that?'

The crudity of the implication, the note of impatience in her voice, all repelled him. He said: 'But suppose they don't believe us.'

'Don't let's go over all that again. Why shouldn't they believe us? And it hardly matters if they don't. They can't ever prove we're lying, that's what's important. And after all it's natural that we should have been together. It isn't as if we've just started seeing each other. Look, I've got to get back to the office now. I'll be in touch, but we'd better not see each other tonight.'

He hadn't expected to see her that night. The news of this latest murder would have been broadcast on local radio, passed from mouth to mouth. His mother would be waiting anxiously for his return from work, avid for news.

But there was something he had to tell her before she left and somehow he found the courage. He said: 'I rang you last night. While I was driving around thinking. I stopped at a phone box and telephoned. You weren't in.'

There was a small silence. He glanced nervously at her face but it was expressionless. She said: 'What time was that?'

'About twenty to ten, perhaps a bit later.'

'Why? Why did you telephone?'

'The need to talk to you. Loneliness. I suppose I half hoped that you might change your mind and ask me to come round '

'All right. You might as well know. I was on the headland last night. I took Remus for a run. I left the car down a cart track just outside the village and walked as far as the ruined abbey. I suppose I was there just after ten.'

He said in horrified wonder: 'You were there! And all the time she must have been lying dead within a few yards of you.'

She said sharply: 'Not a few yards, more like a hundred. There was never any chance that I'd find her, and I didn't see her killer if that's what you're thinking. And I stayed on the cliffs. I didn't go down to the beach. If I had, the police would have found my footprints, mine and Remus's.'

'But someone might have seen you. It was bright moonlight.'

'The headland was empty. And if the murderer was lurking in the trees and saw me, he's hardly likely to come forward. But it's not the happiest position to be in. That's why I need an alibi. I wasn't going to tell you, but now you know. I didn't kill her. But I was there and I've got a motive. That's why I'm asking you to help.'

For the first time Jonathan detected in her voice a note of tenderness, almost of pleading. She moved as if to touch him and then drew back and the tentative gesture, the withdrawal, was as endearing as if she had laid her hand against his face. The hurt and misery of the last ten minutes were swept away in a rush of tenderness. His lips seemed to have thickened so that speech was difficult, but he found the words. He said: 'Of course, I'll help. I love you. I won't let you down. You can depend on me.'

27

Rickards had arranged with Alex Mair to be at the power station by nine that morning but had planned to call first at Scudder's Cottage to see Ryan Blaney. The visit was one of some delicacy. He knew that Blaney had children and it would be necessary to question at least the eldest. But this couldn't be done until he had with him a woman police constable and there had been some delay in arranging this. It was one of those comparatively minor irritations which he found difficult to accept, but he knew that it would be unwise to pay more than a brief visit to the Blaneys without a WPC. Whether or not the man proved to be a serious suspect, he couldn't risk a later allegation that information had been extracted from a juvenile without the observance of proper procedures. At the same time Blaney had a right to know what had happened to his picture, and if the police didn't tell him someone else speedily would. And it was important that he was there to see the man's face when he heard the news, both of the slashed portrait and of Hilary Robarts's murder.

He thought that he had seldom seen a more depressing place than Scudder's Cottage. A thin drizzle was falling and he saw the cottage and the neglected garden through a shimmering mist which seemed to absorb shapes and colours so that the whole scene was one damp amorphous grey. Leaving DC Gary Price in the car, Rickards and Oliphant made their way up the weed-infested path to the porch. There was no bell and when Oliphant thudded on the iron knocker the door almost immediately opened. Ryan Blaney stood before them, six foot tall, lank, bleary-eyed and gave them a long unwelcoming stare. The colour seemed to have drained even from his ruddy hair and Rickards thought he had never seen a man look so exhausted and yet still be on his feet. Blaney didn't invite them in and Rickards didn't suggest it. That intrusion had better wait until he was accompanied by a WPC. And Blaney could wait. He was anxious now to get to Larksoken Power Station. He gave the news that the portrait of Hilary Robarts had been slashed and found at Thyme Cottage, but offered no other details. There was no response. He said: 'Did you hear me, Mr Blaney?'

'Yes, I heard you. I knew that the portrait was missing.'

'When?'

'Last night, at about 9.45. Miss Mair called for it. She was going to take it to Norwich with her this morning. She'll tell you. Where is it now?'

'We have it, what remains of it. We shall need it for forensic examination. We'll give you a receipt, naturally.'

'What good will that do? You can keep it, the picture and your receipt. Slashed to pieces, did you say?'

'Not to pieces, in two clean slashes. Perhaps it can be repaired. We'll bring it with us when we come so that you can identify it.'

'I don't want to see it again. You can keep it.'

'We'll need the identification, Mr Blaney. But we'll talk about it when we see you later today. When, incidentally, did you last see the portrait?'

'Thursday evening when I wrapped it and left it in the painting shed. I haven't been in the shed since. And what's the good of talking? It was the best thing I've ever done and that bitch destroyed it. Get Alice Mair or Adam Dalgliesh to identify it. They've both seen it.'

'Are you saying you know who's responsible?' Again there was a silence. Rickards broke it by saying: 'We'll be with you late this afternoon, probably between four and five if that's convenient. And we shall have to talk to the children. We'll have a WPC with us. They're at school, I suppose, the children?'

'The twins are at playgroup, Theresa is here. She isn't well. Look, you're not going to all this trouble about a slashed portrait. Since when have the police cared about pictures?'

'We care about criminal damage. But there is something more. I have to tell you that Hilary Robarts was murdered last night.'

He stared intently at Blaney's face as he spoke. This was the moment of revelation, perhaps the moment of truth. It was surely impossible for Blaney to hear the news without betraying some emotion: shock, fear, surprise, real or simulated. Instead he said calmly: 'You don't have to tell me that either. I knew. George Jago phoned early this morning from the Local Hero.'

Did he indeed, thought Rickards, and mentally added George Jago to his list of people to be questioned as soon as possible. He asked: 'Will Theresa be in and well enough to speak to us this afternoon?'

'She'll be here and she'll be well enough.'

And then the door was closed firmly in their faces.

Oliphant said: 'God knows why Robarts wanted to buy that slum in the first place. And she's been trying to force him and the kids out for months. There's been a great deal of feeling about it in Lydsett as well as on the headland.'

'So you told me on the way here. But if Blaney killed her he'd hardly draw attention to himself by hurling that portrait through the window of Thyme Cottage. And two unrelated criminal acts, murder and malicious damage on the same night, is too great a coincidence to swallow.'

It had been a bad start to the day. The drizzle, seeping coldly under the collar of his coat, added to his mild dejection. He hadn't noticed that it was raining on the rest of the headland and could almost believe that Scudder's Lane and that picturesque but sour little hovel generated their own depressing climate. He had a lot to get through before he returned for a more rigorous confrontation with Ryan Blaney, and he wasn't looking forward to any of it. Forcing the gate shut over a clump of weeds on the path, he took a last look at the cottage. There was no smoke from the chimney and the windows, hazed with salt, were tightly closed. It was difficult to believe that a family lived here, that the cottage hadn't long been abandoned to damp and decay. And then, at the right-hand window, he glimpsed a pale face framed with red-gold hair. Theresa Blaney was looking down at them.

28

Twenty minutes later the three police officers were at Larksoken Power Station. A place had been reserved for them in the car park outside the perimeter fence close to the guard house. As soon as they approached the gate it was unlocked and one of the security police came out and removed the cones. The preliminaries took only a little time. They were received with almost impassive civility by the uniformed security guard on duty, signed the book and were issued with their lapel badges. The guard telephoned the news of their arrival, reported that the Director's PA, Miss Amphlett, would be with them very shortly and then appeared to lose interest in them. His companion, who had opened the gates and removed the cones, stood casually chatting to a stocky man dressed as a diver and carrying his helmet under his arm, who had apparently been working on one of the water towers. Neither of them seemed particularly interested in the arrival of the police. If Dr Mair had instructed that they were to be received with courtesy but the minimum of fuss, his staff couldn't have done it better.

Through the window of the guard house they saw a woman, obviously Miss Amphlett, walking unhurriedly down the concrete path. She was a cool, self-possessed blonde who, on arrival, ignored Oliphant's bold stare as if he weren't present and gravely greeted Rickards. But she didn't respond to his smile, either because she thought a smile inappropriate to the occasion or, more likely, because in her view few visitors to Larksoken merited such a personal welcome and a police officer wasn't among them.

She said: 'Dr Mair is ready for you, Chief Inspector,' and turned to lead the way. It made him feel like a patient being shown into the presence of a consultant. You could tell a lot about a man from his PA and what she told him about Dr Alex Mair reinforced his private imaginings. He thought of his own secretary, tousled-haired, nineteen-year-old Kim, who dressed in the more bizarre extreme of contemporary youth fashion, whose shorthand was as unreliable as her timekeeping, but who never greeted even the lowliest visitor without a wide smile and the offer, which they were ill advised to accept, of office coffee and biscuits.

They followed Miss Amphlett between the wide lawns to the administration building. She was a woman who induced unease and Oliphant, obviously feeling the need to assert himself, began to prattle.

'That's the turbine house to our right, sir, and the reactor building and the cooling plant behind it. The workshop is to the left. It's a Magnox thermal reactor, sir, a type first commissioned in 1956. We had it all explained to us when we went round. The fuel is uranium metal. To conserve the neutrons and to allow natural uranium to be used the fuel is clad in a magnesium alloy called Magnox with a low neutron absorption. That's where the reactor gets its name. They extract the heat by passing carbon dioxide gas over the fuel in the reactor core. That transfers its heat to water in a steam generator and the steam drives a turbine coupled to an electric generator.'

Rickards wished that Oliphant didn't feel the need to demonstrate his superficial knowledge of nuclear power in the presence of Miss Amphlett, and only hoped that it was accurate. Oliphant went on: 'Of course this type of reactor is out of date now. It's being replaced by a PWR, pressurized water reactor, like the one being built at Sizewell. I've been shown over Sizewell as well as Larksoken, sir. I thought I might as well learn what's going on in these places.'

Rickards thought, And if you've learned that, Elephant Boy, you're even cleverer than you think you are.

The room on the second floor of the administration block into which they were shown struck Rickards as immense. It was almost empty, an arrangement of space and light deliberately deployed to make a statement about the man who now rose to his feet behind the huge black modern desk and stood gravely waiting while they walked across what seemed endless yards of carpet. Even as their hands touched, and Alex Mair's grasp was firm and disconcertingly cold, Rickards's eyes and mind took in the salient features of the office. Two of the walls were painted a smooth light grey, but to the east and south sheets of plate glass reached from ceiling to floor giving a panorama of sky, sea and headland. It was a sunless morning but the air was suffused with a pale ambiguous light, the horizon blurred so that sea and sky were one shimmering grey. Rickards had for a moment the sensation of being weightlessly suspended in outer space in some bizarre and futuristic capsule. And then another image supervened. He could almost hear the throb of the engines and feel the ship shudder as the great surge of ocean divided under the prow.

There was very little furniture. Alex Mair's uncluttered desk, with a high but comfortable armchair for visitors, faced the southern window before which stood a conference table set with eight chairs. In front of the east window was a display table holding a model of what Rickards presumed was the new pressurized water reactor shortly to be constructed on the site. Even at a glance he could see that it was beautifully made, a marvel in glass and steel and perspex, as intricately crafted as if it were a decorative object in its own right. On the north wall hung the only picture; a large oil showing a man with a rifle on a skinny horse, posed in a bleak landscape of sand and scrubland with, in the background, a range of distant mountains. But the man had no head. Instead he was wearing a huge square helmet of black metal with a slit for the eyes. Rickards found the picture disturbingly intimidating. He had a faint memory that he had seen a copy of it, or of something very like it, before, and that the artist was Australian. He was irritated to find himself thinking that Adam Dalgliesh would have known what it was and who had painted it.

Mair went over to the conference table and lifting one of the chairs, swung it lightly and placed it by the desk. They were to sit facing him. After a moment's hesitation, Gary Price took a chair for himself, placed it behind Mair, and unobtrusively took out his notebook.

Looking into the grey sardonic eyes Rickards wondered how Alex Mair saw him, and a snatch of conversation, overheard some years ago in the mess at New Scotland Yard, came unbidden into his mind. 'Oh, Ricky's nobody's fool. He's a bloody sight more intelligent than he looks.' 'He'd better be. He reminds me of one of those characters you get in every war film. The poor honest son-of-a-bitch who always ends up with his face in the mud and a bullet in his chest.'

Well, he wasn't going to end with his face in the mud in this inquiry. The room might look as if it were specifically designed to intimidate him, but it was only a working office. Alex Mair, for all his assurance, his rumoured brilliance, was only a man and if he had killed Hilary Robarts he would end up, as better men than he had done, looking at the sky through iron bars and watching the changing face of the sea only in his dreams.

As they seated themselves, Mair said: 'I expect you'll need somewhere to interview people. I've made arrangements for a small room in the medical physics department to be made available when you're finished here. Miss Amphlett will show you the way. I don't know how long you'll need it, but we've moved in a small refrigerator and there are facilities for making tea or coffee or, if you prefer, tea and coffee can be brought to you from the canteen. And the canteen staff can, of course, provide you with simple meals. Miss Amphlett will let you have today's menu.'

Rickards said: 'Thank you. We'll make our own coffee.'

He felt at a disadvantage and wondered if this was intended. They would need an interview room and he could hardly complain if this need had been anticipated. But it would have been a better start if he could have taken the initiative and he felt, perhaps illogically, that there was something demeaning to his job in this careful reassurance that he would get his food and drink. The look bent on him across the desktop was unworried, speculative, almost, he could imagine, slightly judgemental. He knew that he was in the company of power and the kind of power with which he was unfamiliar; confident, intellectual authority. A clutch of chief constables would have been less formidable.

Alex Mair said: 'Your Chief Constable has already liaised with the Atomic Energy Authority Constabulary. Inspector Johnston would like a word with you this morning, probably before you begin your general interview. He realizes that the Norfolk Constabulary have the principal responsibility here, but naturally he has an interest.'

Rickards said: 'We recognize that and we shall be glad of his co-operation.'

And it would be co-operation not interference. He had already made himself familiar with the duties of the AEAC and he was aware that there was a potential risk of dissension and overlapping of powers. But this was essentially a matter for the Norfolk CID and was seen as an extension of the Whistler inquiries. If Inspector Johnston was prepared to be reasonable, then so was he, but it was not a problem which he proposed to discuss with Dr Mair.

Mair opened the right-hand drawer of his desk and took out a manila folder. He said: 'This is Hilary Robarts's personnel file. There's no objection to your seeing it, but it merely gives the background information; age, places of education, degrees, career before she came to us in 1984 as deputy to the Administrative

Officer. A curriculum vitae from which the vitae is, unusually, conspicuously absent. The dry bones of a life.'

Mair slid it across the desk. The action had a curious finality. A life closed, finished with. Taking it Rickards said: 'Thank you, sir. It will be helpful to have it. Perhaps you could flesh out some of the dry bones for us. You knew her well?'

'Very well. Indeed, for a time we were lovers. That doesn't, I admit, necessarily imply more than physical intimacy but I probably did know her as well as anyone here on the station.'

He spoke calmly and totally without embarrassment, as if it were as unimportant as stating that he and Robarts had shared the same university. Rickards wondered if Mair expected him to seize on the admission. Instead he asked: 'Was she popular?'

'She was highly efficient. The two, I find, do not invariably go together. But she was respected and, I think, generally liked by those staff who had dealings with her. She will be greatly missed, probably more deeply than would be more egregiously popular colleagues.'

'And missed by you?'

'By all of us.'

'When did your affair end, Dr Mair?'

'About three or four months ago.'

'Without rancour?'

'With neither a bang nor a whimper. We had been seeing less of each other for some time before then. My personal future is at present rather unsettled but I am unlikely to continue as Director for very much longer. One comes to the end of a love affair as to the end of a job: a natural feeling that a stage of life has run its course.'

'And she felt the same?'

'I imagine so. We both had some regrets at the break but I don't think either of us ever imagined that we were indulging in a grand passion, or indeed expected our relationship to be lasting.'

'There was no other man?'

'None that I know of, but then there's no reason why I should know.'

Rickards said: 'So you would be surprised to learn that she

wrote to her solicitor in Norwich on Sunday morning to make an appointment to discuss her will and that she told him she was expecting shortly to be married? We found the unposted letter among her papers.'

Mair blinked rapidly but otherwise showed no sign of discomposure. He said evenly: 'Yes, it would surprise me, but I'm not sure why. I suppose because she seemed to live rather a solitary life here and it's difficult to see how she could have found time or opportunity to enter into a new relationship. Of course, it's perfectly possible that some man from her past had re-emerged and they had come to an arrangement. I'm afraid I can't help you.'

Rickards changed the tack of his questioning. He said: 'There seems to be a feeling locally that she wasn't much help to you during the public inquiry into the second reactor here. She didn't give evidence to the official inquiry, did she? I can't quite see how she was involved.'

'Officially she wasn't. But at one or two public meetings, unwisely, she got embroiled with hecklers, and on one of our open days the scientist who normally escorts the public was off sick and she took his place. She was, perhaps, less tactful than she should have been with some of the questioners. After that I arranged that she wasn't directly involved with the public.'

Rickards said: 'So she was a woman who provoked antagonism?'

'Not enough, I should have thought, to provoke murder. She was dedicated to the work here and found it difficult to tolerate what she saw as wilful obscurantism. She hadn't a scientific training but she did acquire considerable knowledge of the science done here and perhaps undue respect for what she saw as expert scientific opinion. I pointed out that it was unreasonable to expect this to be shared by the general public. After all they've probably been told by experts in recent years that high-rise flats don't collapse, that the London Underground is safe from fire and that cross-channel ferries can't keel over.'

Oliphant, who had until now remained silent, suddenly said: 'I was one of the visitors on that open day. Someone asked her about Chernobyl. She made a remark, didn't she, about "only thirty dead, so what were people worrying about?" Isn't that what she said? It rather begged the question: how many dead would Miss Robarts agree was an acceptable figure?'

Alex Mair looked at him as if surprised that he could actually speak and, after a moment's contemplation, said: 'In comparing the Chernobyl death toll with fatalities in industry and in mining fossil fuels she was making a perfectly reasonable point, although she could have done it with more tact. Chernobyl is a sensitive subject. We get rather tired of explaining to the public that the Russian RBMK-type of reactor had a number of design weaknesses, notably that it had a fast-acting positive power coefficient when the reactor was at low power. The Magnox, AGR and PWR designs don't have this characteristic at any power level so that a similar accident here is physically impossible. I'm sorry if that sounds over-technical. What I'm saying is: it won't happen here, it can't happen here and, in fact, it didn't happen here.'

Oliphant said stolidly: 'It hardly matters whether it happens here or not, sir, if we get the results of it. Wasn't Hilary Robarts suing someone in the community for alleged libel arising out of the meeting I attended?'

Alex Mair ignored him and spoke to Rickards. 'I think that's generally known. It was a mistake, I think. She had a legitimate case but she wasn't likely to get satisfaction by going to law.'

Rickards asked: 'You tried to persuade her not to in the interests of the station?'

'And in her own. Yes, I tried.'

The telephone on the desk rang. Mair pressed the button. He said: 'This shouldn't take much longer. Tell him I'll ring back in twenty minutes.' Rickards wondered whether he had arranged for the call to be put through. As if in confirmation of the suspicion, Mair said: 'In view of my past relationship with Miss Robarts you'll need to know my movements on Sunday. Perhaps I could give them to you now. Both of us have a busy day ahead, I imagine.' It was a less than subtle reminder that it was time they got down to business.

Rickards kept his voice steady. 'That would be helpful, sir.' Gary Price bent his head over his notebook as assiduously as if he had just been reprimanded for inattention.

'They're hardly relevant until Sunday evening, but I may as well cover the whole of the weekend. I left here just after 10.45 on Friday and drove to London, lunched with an old university friend at the Reform Club and went on at 2.30 to a meeting with the Permanent Secretary at the Department of Energy. I then went to my flat in the Barbican and in the evening attended a performance of *The Taming of the Shrew* at the Barbican Theatre with a party of three friends. If you later need their corroboration, which seems unlikely, I can of course give you their names. I drove back to Larksoken on Sunday morning, lunched at a pub *en route* and arrived home at about four. I had a cup of tea and then went for a walk on the headland and got back to Martyr's Cottage about an hour later. I had a quick supper with my sister at about seven and left for the station at 7.30, or soon afterwards. I was working here in the computer room alone until 10.30 when I left for home. I was driving along the coast road when I was stopped by Commander Dalgliesh with the news that Hilary Robarts had been murdered. The rest you know.'

Rickards said: 'Not altogether, Dr Mair. There was some delay before we arrived. You didn't touch the body?'

'I stood and looked down at her but I didn't touch her. Dalgliesh was rather conscientiously doing his job, or should I say yours. He very rightly reminded me that nothing should be touched and that the scene should be left undisturbed. I went down and walked by the sea until you arrived.'

Rickards asked: 'Do you usually come in to work on Sunday evenings?'

'Invariably if I have had to spend the Friday in London. There is a very heavy pressure of work at present which it is impossible to fit into a five-day week. Actually I stayed for less than three hours, but they were valuable hours.'

'And you were alone in the computer room. Doing what, sir?'

If Mair found the inquiry irrelevant he didn't say so. 'I was engaged on my research which is concerned with the study of reactor behaviour in hypothesized loss-of-coolant accidents. I'm not, of course, the only person working in what is one of the most important areas of research in nuclear reactor design. There's a great deal of international co-operation in these studies. Essentially what I'm doing is evaluating the possible effects of loss of coolant by mathematical models which are then evaluated by numerical analysis and advanced computer programmes.'

Rickards said: 'And you're working here at Larksoken alone?'

'At this station I am. Similar studies are being carried out at Winfrith and in a number of other countries including the USA. As I have said, there's a considerable amount of international co-operation.'

Oliphant asked suddenly: 'Is that the worst thing that can happen, a loss of the coolant?'

Alex Mair looked at him for a moment as if deciding whether the question coming from such a source warranted an answer, then he said: 'The loss of coolant is potentially extremely dangerous. There are, of course, emergency procedures if the normal cooling arrangements fail. The incident at Three Mile Island in the United States has emphasized the need to know more about the extent and nature of the threat posed by that kind of incident. The phenomenon to be analysed is in three main groups: severe fuel damage and core melting, migration of released fission products and aerosols through the primary coolant circuit, and the behaviour of fission products in released fuel and steam in the reactor container building. If you have a genuine interest in the research and enough knowledge to understand it I can provide you with some references, but this hardly seems the time and place for scientific education.'

Oliphant smiled as if gratified by the rebuke. He asked: 'Wasn't the scientist who killed himself, Dr Toby Gledhill, working on the research side here with you? I thought I read something about that in one of the local papers.'

'Yes. He was my assistant here. Tobias Gledhill was a physicist who was also an exceptionally talented computer expert. He is very much missed as a colleague and a man.'

And that, thought Rickards, disposes of Toby Gledhill. From another man the tribute could have been moving in its simplicity. From Mair it sounded like a bleak dismissal. But then, suicide was messy and embarrassing. He would find repugnant its intrusion into his neatly organized world.

Mair turned to Rickards. 'I have a great deal to do this

morning, Chief Inspector, and no doubt you have too. Is this really relevant?'

Rickards said stolidly: 'It helps fill in the picture. I suppose you booked in when you arrived here yesterday night and subsequently booked out?'

'You saw something of the system when you arrived. Every member of the staff has a signed identity badge with a photograph and a personal number which is confidential. The number is electronically registered when the man or woman enters the site and there is, in addition, a visual check of the badge by the gate staff. I have a total staff of five hundred and thirty people working in three shifts covering the twenty-four hours. At the weekend there are two shifts, the day staff coming on from 8.15 until 20.15 and the night from 20.15 until 8.15.'

'And no one could enter or leave undetected, not even the Director?'

'No one, least of all, I imagine, the Director. My check-in time will be recorded and I was seen arriving and leaving by the gate officer on duty.'

'There is no other way into the station except through the guard house?'

'Not unless you emulate the heroes of old war films and tunnel deep under the wire. No one was tunnelling here on Sunday night.'

Rickards said: 'We shall need to know the movements of every member of the staff on Sunday from early evening until 10.30 when Commander Dalgliesh discovered the body.'

'Isn't that an unnecessarily large spread of time? Surely she was killed shortly after nine?'

'That seems the most likely time of death and we expect to get a more accurate estimate from the post-mortem report. At present I prefer to make no assumptions. We have copies of the forms which were distributed in connection with the Whistler inquiry which we would like to issue to all the staff. I imagine that the great majority can be easily eliminated. Most people who have any family or social life can provide an alibi for Sunday evening. Perhaps you could suggest how the forms can be distributed with as little disturbance to the work here as possible.'

Mair said: 'The simplest and most effective way would be to leave them in the guard house. Each member of staff could be given one when he or she checks in. Those staff who are off sick or on leave today will have to receive them at home. I can supply their names and addresses.' He paused and then added: 'It seems to me highly unlikely that this murder has anything to do with Larksoken Power Station, but as Hilary Robarts worked here and you will be interviewing members of staff, it might be helpful if you have some idea of the layout and organization. My PA has put up a file for you with a diagram of the site, a booklet describing the operation of the reactor which will help to give you some idea of the different functions carried out, a list of staff by name and grade and a copy of the existing managerial structure and the operations staff shift rota. If you want to see any particular department I can arrange for you to be escorted. Certain areas cannot, of course, be entered without protective clothing and a subsequent radiological check.'

The file was ready in his right-hand drawer and he handed it over. Rickards took it and studied the organization chart. After a moment he said: 'You have seven divisions, each with a head of department; Medical Physicist, Station Chemist, Operations Superintendent, Maintenance Superintendent, Reactor Physicist, Works Office Engineer and the station Administrative Officer, the post held by Hilary Robarts.'

'Temporarily held. The station Administrative Officer died of cancer three months ago and the post has not yet been filled. We are also about to reorganize the internal administration into three main divisions as at Sizewell where they have what I think is a more effective and rational system. But the future here is uncertain, as you've probably heard, and there may be a case for waiting until a new Director or Station Manager is in post.'

Rickards said: 'And at present the station Administrative Officer is responsible to you through the Deputy Director?'

'Through Dr James Macintosh, that is right. Dr Macintosh is at present in the States studying their nuclear installations and has been for the past month.'

'And the Operations Superintendent – Op. Super. as it says here – is Miles Lessingham, who was one of the guests at Miss Mair's dinner party on Thursday.'

Alex Mair didn't reply.

Rickards went on: 'You've been unfortunate, Dr Mair. Three violent deaths of members of your staff within the space of two months. First Dr Gledhill's suicide, then Christine Baldwin's murder by the Whistler, and now Hilary Robarts.'

Mair asked: 'Have you any doubts that Christine Baldwin was killed by the Whistler?'

'None at all. Her hair was found with that of other victims when he killed himself, and her husband, who would normally be the obvious first suspect, has an alibi. He was driven home by his friends.'

'And Toby Gledhill's death was the subject of an inquest, "death while the balance of his mind was disturbed", that convenient sop to convention and religious orthodoxy.'

Oliphant asked: 'And was the balance of his mind disturbed, sir?'

Mair turned on him his ironic and speculative gaze. 'I have no way of knowing the state of his mind, Sergeant. What I am sure of is that he killed himself and that he did it unaided. No doubt at the time he felt he had sufficient reason. Dr Gledhill was a manic depressive. He coped courageously with his disability and it rarely interfered with his work. But with that psychological make-up, suicide is always an above-average risk. And if you agree that the three deaths are unrelated, then we needn't waste time on the first two. Or was your statement, Chief Inspector, intended as a general commiseration?'

Rickards said: 'Just a comment, sir.' He went on: 'One of your staff, Miles Lessingham, found Christine Baldwin's body. He told us then that he was on his way to have dinner with you and Miss Mair. I suppose he gave you all a graphic description of his experience. Natural I'd say. Difficult thing to keep to yourself.'

Mair said calmly: 'Virtually impossible, wouldn't you say?' He added: 'Among friends.'

'Which he was, of course. All friends together, including Miss Robarts. So you got all the gory details fresh from the scene. Including the ones he'd been specifically told to keep to himself.'

'Which were they, Chief Inspector?'

Rickards didn't reply. Instead he asked: 'Could I have the

names of everyone who was present in Martyr's Cottage when Mr Lessingham arrived?'

'My sister and I, Hilary Robarts, Mrs Dennison, the house-keeper from the Old Rectory, and Commander Adam Dalgliesh of the Metropolitan Police. And the Blaney child – Theresa, I think she's called – was helping my sister with the meal.' He paused and then added: 'These inquiry forms which you're propos-ing to issue to all members of staff; I suppose it is necessary to take up their time in this way. Isn't it fairly plain what happened here? Surely this is what your people call a copycat murder.'

Rickards said: 'It was that all right, sir. All the details correct. Very clever, very convincing. Just the two differences. This murderer knew his victim and this murderer is sane.'

Five minutes later, following Miss Amphlett down the corridor to the interviewing room, Rickards thought, And you're a cool customer, mate. No embarrassing expressions of horror and grief which always sounded insincere. No protestations of innocence. The assumption that no one in his rational mind could suspect you of murder. He hadn't asked for his solicitor to be present, but then he didn't need one. But he was far too intelligent to have missed the significance of those questions about the dinner party. Whoever had killed Hilary Robarts had known that she would be swimming by moonlight sometime after nine o'clock yesterday, had known, too, precisely how the Whistler killed his victims. There were quite a number of people who knew one of these facts, but the number who knew both was limited. And six of them had been present at that dinner party at Martyr's Cottage last Thursday night.

29

The interview room which had been assigned to them was a featureless little office with a view to the west dominated by the great bulk of the turbine house. It was adequately furnished for their purpose, but only just; entirely appropriate, thought Rick-ards sourly, to visitors whose presence was tolerated but hardly welcomed. There was a modern pedestal desk, obviously brought in from someone's office, three upright chairs and one rather more comfortable one with arms, a small side table with an electric kettle on a tray, four cups and saucers (did Mair expect them to make coffee for the suspects?), a bowl full of wrapped sugar lumps and three caddies.

Rickards said: 'What have they given us, Gary?'

Gary Price busied himself with the tins. 'Coffee bags and tea bags, sir. And there's a tin of biscuits.'

Oliphant asked: 'What kind of biscuits?'

'Digestive, Sarge.'

'Chocolate?'

'No, Sarge, just plain digestives.'

'Well, let's hope they're not radioactive. Better get the kettle on; we may as well start with the coffee. Where do they expect us to get water?'

'Miss Amphlett said there was a tap in the cloakroom at the end of the passage, Sarge. The kettle's filled, anyway.'

Oliphant tried one of the upright chairs, stretching in it as if to assess its comfort. The wood creaked. He said: 'Cold fish, wasn't he? And clever with it. Not much out of him, sir.'

'I wouldn't say that, Sergeant. We've learned more about the victim than he probably realizes. Efficient but not much liked, prone to interfere with matters outside her scope of responsibility, probably because she secretly yearned to be a scientist rather than an administrator. Aggressive, uncompromising, intolerant of criticism. Antagonized the locals and from time to time did the station a bit of no good. And, of course, the Director's mistress, for what that was worth.'

Oliphant said: 'Until three or four months ago. A natural end with no hard feelings on either side. His version.'

'And we're never going to get hers, are we? But one thing was odd. When Mair met Mr Dalgliesh he was on his way home from here. His sister presumably was expecting him, yet apparently he didn't telephone her. It never seems to have occurred to him.'

'Shocked, sir, something else on his mind. He's just discovered that his ex-girlfriend is the victim of a particularly vicious psychopathic killer. Tends to eclipse brotherly feelings and thoughts of your bedtime cocoa.'

'Maybe. I wonder whether Miss Mair rang here to find out why he was delayed. We'll ask.'

Oliphant said: 'If she didn't ring, I can think of one reason why. She expected him to be late. She thought he was at Thyme Cottage with Hilary Robarts.'

'If she didn't ring because she thought that, then she can't have known that Robarts was dead. Right, Sergeant, let's get started. First of all we'll have a word with Miss Amphlett. The boss's PA usually knows more about the organization than anyone, including her boss.'

But any information of interest that Caroline Amphlett might have she was adept at concealing. She seated herself in the armchair with the calm assurance of an applicant for a job which she has every confidence of getting, and answered Rickards's questions calmly and without emotion except when he attempted to probe into Hilary Robarts's relationship with the Director. Then she permitted herself a moue of distaste that anyone could be so vulgarly inquisitive about matters which were not his concern and answered repressively that Dr Mair had never confided in her about his private life. She admitted that she knew Hilary Robarts made a habit of swimming at night and kept this up well into the autumn months and sometimes later. She thought the fact was generally known at Larksoken. Miss Robarts had been a strong and enthusiastic swimmer. She was not particularly interested in the Whistler except to take reasonable precautions and avoid walking alone at night, and she knew nothing about his methods except what she had read in the newspapers, that he strangled his victims. She had known about the dinner party at Martyr's Cottage on Thursday, she thought Miles Lessingham might have mentioned it, but no one had discussed with her the events of the evening and she saw no reason why they should.

As for her own movements on Sunday, she had spent the whole of the evening from six o'clock at her bungalow with her boy-friend, Jonathan Reeves. They had been together continually until he had left at about 10.30. Her cool glance at Oliphant challenged him to ask her what they had been doing and he resisted the temptation except to ask what they had drunk and eaten. Asked about her relationship with Hilary Robarts, she said that she had greatly respected her but hadn't particularly liked or disliked her. Their professional relationship had been perfectly friendly but as far as she could remember they had never met outside the power station. As far as she knew, Miss Robarts had no enemies and she had no idea who could have wished her dead. When the door had closed after her Rickards said: 'We'll check her alibi, of course, but there's no hurry. Let young Reeves sweat for an hour or so. I want to check first on the staff who actually worked for Robarts.'

But the next hour was unproductive. The people who had worked directly for Hilary Robarts were more shocked than distressed and their evidence strengthened the image of a woman more respected than liked. But none had an obvious motive, none admitted to knowing precisely how the Whistler had killed and, more to the point, all could produce an alibi for Sunday night. Rickards had hardly expected otherwise.

At the end of the sixty minutes he sent for Jonathan Reeves. He came into the room white-faced and as stiffly controlled as if it were an execution shed and Rickards's first reaction was surprise that a woman as attractive as Caroline Amphlett should have chosen such an unlikely mate. It wasn't that Reeves had a particularly unprepossessing face. You couldn't even describe him as plain if you discounted the acne. And his features, taken individually, were good enough. It was the whole face which was somehow unremarkable, ordinary, the kind of face which defeated any attempt at an Identikit image. Rickards decided that it was best described in terms of movement rather than features; the almost continual blinking behind the horn-rimmed spectacles, the nervous sucking of the lips, his habit of suddenly stretching his neck like a TV comedian. He knew from the list Alex Mair had provided that the staff at Larksoken was predominantly male. Was this the best Amphlett could do for herself? But sexual attraction was irrational anyway. Look at him and Susie. Seeing them together, her friends probably felt an equal surprise.

He left most of the detailed questioning to Oliphant, which was a mistake. Oliphant was always at his worst with a frightened suspect and he took his time extracting, not without pleasure, a straightforward story which confirmed Caroline Amphlett's account.

Afterwards, when Reeves had been finally released, Oliphant

said: 'He was as jumpy as a cat, sir. That's why I took my time over him. I think he's lying.'

It was, thought Rickards, typical of Oliphant both to assume and hope for the worst. He said curtly: 'Not lying necessarily, Sergeant; just frightened and embarrassed. Tough luck when your first night of passion ends in a not particularly subtle police interrogation. But the alibi seems firm enough and neither of them has an obvious motive. And there's no evidence that either knew the details of the Whistler's little habits. Let's get on to someone who did. Miles Lessingham.'

Rickards had last seen Lessingham at the scene of Christine Baldwin's murder, since he hadn't himself been at the incident room when Lessingham had called in next morning to sign his statement. He realized that the sardonic attempt at humour, the controlled detachment the man had shown at the scene were mainly due to shock and distaste, but he had sensed, too, that Lessingham had a wariness of the police amounting to dislike. It was not an uncommon phenomenon nowadays, even among the middle classes, and no doubt he had his reasons. But it hadn't made him easy to deal with then and it didn't now. After the usual preliminaries Rickards asked: 'Were you aware of the relationship between Dr Mair and Miss Robarts?'

'He's the Director, she was Acting Administrator.'

'I meant the sexual relationship.'

'No one told me. But not being entirely insensitive to my fellow mortals I thought it likely that they were lovers.'

'And you knew that it had ended?'

'I assumed so. They didn't confide in me when it began and they didn't confide in me when it ended. You'd better ask Dr Mair if you want details of his personal life. I have enough trouble managing my own.'

'But you weren't aware of any difficulties caused by the relationship: resentment, accusations of favouritism, jealousy perhaps?'

'Not from me, I assure you. My interests lie elsewhere.'

'And what about Miss Robarts? Did you get the impression that the affair ended without rancour? Did she seem upset, for example?'

'If she was she didn't weep on my shoulder. But then mine is hardly the shoulder she would have chosen.'

'And you have no idea who killed her?'

'None.'

There was a pause, then Rickards asked: 'Did you like her?'

'No.'

For a moment Rickards was nonplussed. It was a question which he frequently asked in murder investigations and usually to some effect. Few suspects would admit to disliking the victim without blundering into an attempt at explanation or justification. After a moment's silence, during which it was obvious that Lessingham had no intention of amplifying his statement, he asked: 'Why not, Mr Lessingham?'

'There aren't many people I actually like as opposed to tolerate and she didn't happen to be one of them. There was no particular reason. Does there have to be? You and your sergeant may not like each other for all I know. It doesn't mean that either of you is planning murder. And talking about murder, which is why I assume I'm here, I have an alibi for Sunday night. Perhaps I had better give it to you now. I have a thirty-foot sailing boat berthed at Blakeney. I went out with her on the morning tide and stayed out until nearly ten at night. I have a witness to my departure, Ed Wilkinson who berths his fishing smack next to my boat, but no witness to my return. There was enough wind in the morning to sail and then I anchored, caught a couple of cod and some whiting and cooked them for lunch. I had food, wine, books and my radio. There was nothing else I needed. It may not be the most satisfactory of alibis but it has the merit of simplicity and truth.'

Oliphant asked: 'You had a dinghy with you?'

'I had my inflatable dinghy on the cabin roof. And at the risk of exciting you, I have to say that I also carried my collapsible bicycle. But I didn't put ashore either at Larksoken headland or anywhere else, not even for the purpose of murdering Hilary Robarts.'

Rickards asked: 'Did you see Miss Robarts at any time during your trip? Were you in sight of the beach where she died?'

'I didn't go that far south. And I saw no one, dead or alive.'

Oliphant asked: 'Do you make a habit of sailing alone at the weekend?'

'I don't make a habit of anything. I used to sail with a friend. Now I sail alone.'

Rickards asked him next about Blaney's portrait of Miss Robarts. He admitted that he had seen it. George Jago, the publican of the Local Hero at Lydsett, had put it up for a week in the bar, apparently at Blaney's request. He had no idea where Blaney normally kept it and he had neither stolen it nor destroyed it. If anyone had, he thought it was probably Robarts herself.

Oliphant said: 'And thrown it through her own window?'

Lessingham said: 'You think she would have been more likely to slash it and chuck it through Blaney's? I agree. But whoever slashed it, it wasn't Blaney.'

Oliphant asked: 'How can you be so sure?'

'Because a creative artist, whether he's a painter or a scientist, doesn't destroy his best work.'

Oliphant said: 'Miss Mair's dinner party; you gave your fellow guests a description of the Whistler's methods including information we had specifically asked you not to divulge.'

Lessingham said coolly: 'One could hardly arrive two hours late for a dinner party without some explanation, and mine was, after all, unusual. I thought they were entitled to a vicarious thrill. Apart from that, to keep silent would have needed more self-control than I was capable of at the time. Murdered and mutilated bodies are your trade, of course. Those of us who have chosen less exciting jobs tend to find them distressing. I knew I could trust my fellow guests not to talk to the press and as far as I know none of them did. Anyway, why ask me what happened on the Thursday night? Adam Dalgliesh was a guest at the dinner party so you have a more experienced and no doubt, from your point of view, a more reliable witness. I won't say a police spy: that would be unfair.'

Rickards spoke for the first time in minutes. He said: 'It would also be inaccurate and offensive.'

Lessingham turned on him with a cool 'Exactly. That's why I haven't used the word. And now, if you've no more questions, I have a power station to run.'

30

It was after midday before the interviews at the power station were completed and Rickards and Oliphant were ready to leave for Martyr's Cottage. They left Gary Price to cope with the inquiry forms and arranged to pick him up after the interview with Alice Mair which Rickards felt might be more fruitful with two officers rather than three. Alice Mair received them calmly at the door with no apparent sign either of anxiety or of curiosity, glanced perfunctorily at their identity cards and invited them in. They might, Rickards thought, have been technicians arriving later than expected to repair the television set. And they were, he saw, expected to interview her in the kitchen. At first it struck him as an odd choice but then, looking round, he supposed you could hardly call it a kitchen; more like an office, sitting room and kitchen combined. Its size surprised him and he found himself wondering irrelevantly whether she had knocked down a wall to provide such over-generous working space. He wondered, too, what Susie would think of it and decided that she would find it unsettling. Susie liked her house to be clearly defined by functions; the kitchen was for working, the dining room for eating, the lounge for watching television and the bedroom for sleeping and, once a week, for making love. He and Oliphant sat in two cushioned, high-backed wicker chairs on each side of the fireplace. His was extremely comfortable, gently containing his long limbs. Miss Mair took the chair at her desk and swivelled it round to face him.

'My brother, of course, gave me the news of the murder as soon as he got home last night. I can't help you about Hilary Robarts's death, I'm afraid. I was at home the whole of yesterday evening and saw and heard nothing. But I can tell you a little about her portrait. Would you and Sergeant Oliphant care for coffee?'

Rickards would have cared; he found himself unexpectedly thirsty; but he declined for both of them. The invitation had sounded perfunctory and he hadn't missed her quick glance towards the desktop stacked with orderly piles of printed pages and a typewritten manuscript. It looked as if they had interrupted her in the business of proofreading. Well, if she was busy, so was he.

And he found himself irritated, unreasonably, he felt, by her self-possession. He hadn't expected to find her in hysterics or under sedation for grief. The victim wasn't her next of kin. But the woman had worked closely with Alex Mair, had been a guest at Martyr's Cottage, had, according to Dalgliesh, dined there only four days ago. It was disconcerting to find that Alice Mair could sit quietly correcting proofs, a job which surely required concentrated attention. The killing of Robarts had taken considerable nerve. His suspicion of her was hardly serious; he didn't really see this as a woman's crime. But he let suspicion enter his mind like a barb and lodge there. A remarkable woman, he thought. Perhaps this interview was going to be more productive than he had expected.

He asked: 'You keep house for your brother, Miss Mair?'

'No, I keep house for myself. My brother happens to live here when he is in Norfolk, which naturally is for most of the week. He could hardly administer Larksoken Power Station from his flat in London. If I'm at home and cook dinner he usually shares it. I take the view that it would be unreasonable to demand that he make himself an omelette merely to affirm the principle of shared domestic responsibilities. But I don't see what relevance my house-keeping arrangements have to Hilary Robarts's murder. Could we, perhaps, get on to what happened last night?'

They were interrupted. There was a knock at the door and, without an apology, Alice Mair got up and went through to the hall. They heard a lighter, feminine voice and a woman followed her into the kitchen. Miss Mair introduced her as Mrs Dennison from the Old Rectory. She was a pretty, gentle-looking woman, conventionally dressed in a tweed skirt and twinset, and was obviously distressed. Rickards approved both of her appearance and of the distress. This was how he expected a woman to look and behave after a particularly brutal murder. The two men had got up at her entrance and she took Oliphant's chair while he moved one for himself from the kitchen table.

She turned to Rickards impulsively: 'I'm sorry, I'm interrupting, but I felt I had to get out of the house. This is appalling news, Inspector. Are you absolutely certain that it couldn't have been the Whistler?'

Rickards said: 'Not this time, madam.'

Alice Mair said: 'The timing's wrong. I told you that when I rang early this morning, Meg. The police wouldn't be here now if it wasn't. It couldn't have been the Whistler.'

'I know that's what you said. But I couldn't help hoping that there'd been a mistake, that he'd killed her and then himself, that Hilary Robarts was his last victim.'

Rickards said: 'In a sense she was, Mrs Dennison.'

Alice Mair said calmly: 'I think it's called a copycat murder. There's more than one psychopath in the world and that kind of madness can be infectious, apparently.'

'Of course, but how horrible! Having started, will he too go on, like the Whistler did, death after death, no one feeling safe?'

Rickards said: 'I shouldn't let that worry you, Mrs Dennison.'

She turned to him almost fiercely. 'But of course it worries me! It must worry us all. We've lived so long with the horror of the Whistler. It's appalling to think that it's started all over again.'

Alice Mair got up. 'You need coffee, Meg. Chief Inspector Rickards and Sergeant Oliphant have declined but I think we need it.'

Rickards wasn't going to let her get away with that. He said firmly: 'If you're making it, Miss Mair, I think I'll change my mind. I'd be glad of a coffee. You too no doubt, Sergeant.'

And now, he thought, there'll be a further delay while she grinds beans and no one can talk above the noise. Why can't she just pour boiling water on coffee grains like everyone else?

But the coffee, when it did come, was excellent and he found it unexpectedly comforting. Mrs Dennison took her mug in her hands and cradled it like a child at bedtime. Then she put it down on the hearth and turned to Rickards.

'Look, perhaps you'd rather I went. I'll just have my coffee and then go back to the rectory. If you want to talk to me I'll be there for the rest of the day.'

Miss Mair said: 'You may as well stay and hear what happened last night. It has its points of interest.' She turned to Rickards. 'As I told you, I was here the whole of the evening from half-past five. My brother left for the power station shortly after 7.30 and I settled down to work on my proofs. I switched on the answerphone to avoid interruptions.'

Rickards asked: 'And you didn't leave the cottage for any purpose during the whole of the evening?'

'Not until after half-past nine when I left for the Blaneys'. But perhaps I could tell the story in sequence, Chief Inspector. At about ten past eight I switched off the machine thinking that there might be an important call for my brother. It was then I heard George Jago's message that the Whistler was dead.'

'You didn't ring anyone else to let them know?'

'I knew that wasn't necessary. Jago runs his own information service. He'd make sure that everyone knew. I came back into the kitchen and worked on my proofs until about half-past nine. Then I thought that I'd collect Hilary Robarts's portrait from Ryan Blaney. I'd promised to drop it in at the gallery in Norwich on my way to London and I wanted to make an early start next morning. I tend to be a little obsessive about time and didn't want to go even a short distance out of my way. I rang Scudder's Cottage to let him know that I was collecting the portrait but the number was engaged. I tried several times and then got out the car and drove over. I'd written a note to him to slip through the door telling him that I'd taken the picture as arranged.'

'Wasn't that a little unusual, Miss Mair? Why not knock at the cottage and collect it from him personally?'

'Because he had taken the trouble to tell me, when I first saw it, precisely where it was kept and where I could find the light switch to the left of the door. I took that as a reasonable indication that he didn't expect, or indeed want, to be disturbed by a call at the cottage. Mr Dalgliesh was with me at the time.'

'But that was odd, wasn't it? He must have thought it was a good portrait. He wouldn't wish to exhibit it otherwise. You'd think he'd want to hand it over personally.'

'Would you? It didn't strike me that way. He's an extremely private man, more so since the death of his wife. He doesn't welcome visitors, particularly not women who might cast a critical eye on the tidiness of the cottage and the state of the children. I could understand that. I wouldn't have welcomed it myself.'

'So you went straight to his painting shed? Where is that?'

'About thirty yards to the left of the cottage. It's a small wooden shack. I imagine that it was originally a washhouse or a smoking shed. I shone my torch on the path to the door, although that was hardly necessary. The moonlight was exceptionally bright. It was unlocked. And if you're now about to say that that, too, was odd, you don't understand life on the headland. We're very remote here and we get into the habit of leaving doors unlocked. I don't think it would ever occur to him to lock his painting shed. I switched on the light to the left of the door and saw that the picture wasn't where I expected.'

'Could you describe exactly what happened? The details, please, as far as you can recall them.'

'We're talking about last night, Chief Inspector. It would be difficult not to recall them. I left the light on in the shed and knocked on the front door of the cottage. There were lights on, downstairs only, but the curtains were drawn. I had to wait for about a minute before he came. He half opened the door but didn't invite me in. I said, "Good evening, Ryan." He just nodded, but didn't reply. There was a strong smell of whisky. Then I said, "I've come to collect the portrait but it isn't in the shed, or if it is I haven't found it." Then he said, his speech rather slurred, "It's to the left of the door, wrapped in cardboard and brown paper. A brown paper parcel, Sellotaped." I said, "Not now." He didn't reply but came out to me leaving the door open. We went to the shed together.'

'Was he walking steadily?'

'He was very far from steady, but he could certainly keep on his feet. When I said he smelt of drink and his voice was slurred I didn't mean that he was totally incapable. But I got the impression that he had spent the evening in fairly continuous drinking. He stood in the doorway of the shed with me at his shoulder. He didn't speak for about half a minute. Then all he said was, "Yes, it's gone."'

'How did he sound?' As she didn't reply he asked patiently, 'Was he shocked? Angry? Surprised? Or too drunk to care?'

'I heard the question, Chief Inspector. Hadn't you better ask him how he felt? I'm only competent to describe what he looked like, what he said, and what he did.'

'What did he do?'

'He turned and beat his clenched hands against the lintel of the door. Then he rested his head against the wood for a minute. It seemed at the time a histrionic gesture but I imagine that it was perfectly genuine.'

'And then?'

'I said to him, "Hadn't we better telephone the police? We could do it from here if your telephone is working. I've been trying to get through to you but it's always engaged." He didn't reply and I followed him back to the cottage. He didn't invite me in, but I stood in the doorway. He went over to the recess under the stairs and then said: "The receiver isn't properly on. That's why you couldn't get through." I said again, "Why not telephone the police now? The sooner the theft is reported the better." He turned to me and just said "Tomorrow. Tomorrow." Then he went back to his chair. I persisted. I said, "Shall I ring, Ryan, or will you? This really is important." He said, "I will. Tomorrow. Goodnight." That seemed a clear indication to me that he wanted to be alone, so I left.'

'And during this visit you saw no one other than Mr Blaney. The children weren't up, for example?'

'I took it the children were in bed. I neither saw nor heard them.'

'And you didn't discuss the Whistler's death?'

'I assumed George Jago had telephoned Mr Blaney, probably before he rang me. And what was there to discuss? Neither Ryan nor I were in a mood for doorstep chatting.'

But it was, thought Rickards, a curious reticence on both their parts. Had she been so anxious to get away and he to see her go? Or, for one of them, had an event more traumatic than a missing portrait driven even the Whistler temporarily out of mind?

There was a vital question Rickards needed to ask. The implications were obvious and she was far too intelligent a woman not to see them.

'Miss Mair, from what you saw of Mr Blaney that night, do you think he could have driven a car?'

'Impossible. And he hadn't a car to drive. He has a small van but it has just failed its MOT.'

'Or ridden a bicycle?'

'I suppose he could have tried but he'd have been in the ditch within minutes.'

Rickards's mind was already busy with calculations. He wouldn't get the results of the autopsy until Wednesday but if Hilary Robarts had taken her swim, as was her custom, immediately after the headlines to the main news which, on Sunday, was at 9.10, then she must have died at about half-past nine. At 9.45 or a little later, according to Alice Mair, Ryan Blaney was in his cottage and drunk. By no stretch of the imagination could he have committed a singularly ingenious murder, requiring a steady hand, nerves and the capacity to plan, and been back in his cottage by 9.45. If Alice Mair were telling the truth she had given Blaney an alibi. He, on the other hand, would certainly be unable to give one to her.

Rickards had almost forgotten Meg Dennison, but now he looked across to where she sat like a distressed child, hands in her lap, her untasted coffee still standing in the hearth.

'Mrs Dennison, did you know last night that the Whistler was dead?'

'Oh yes. Mr Jago telephoned me too, about a quarter to ten.'

Alice Mair said: 'He probably tried to get you earlier but you were on the way to Norwich station with the Copleys.'

Meg Dennison spoke directly to Rickards: 'I should have been, but the car broke down. I had to get Sparks and his taxi in a hurry. Luckily he could just do it but he had to go straight on to a job in Ipswich, so he couldn't bring me back. He saw the Copleys safely on the train for me.'

'Did you leave the Old Rectory at any time during the evening?'

Mrs Dennison looked up and met his eyes. 'No,' she said, 'no, after I'd seen them off I didn't leave the house.' Then she paused and said, 'I'm sorry, I did go out into the garden very briefly. It would be more accurate to say that I didn't leave the grounds. And now, if you'll all excuse me, please, I'd like to go home.'

She got up, then turned again to Rickards: 'If you want to question me, Chief Inspector, I'll be at the Old Rectory.'

She was gone before the two men could get to their feet, almost stumbling from the room. Miss Mair made no move to follow her and, seconds later, they heard the front door close.

There was a moment's silence, broken by Oliphant. Nodding

towards the hearth he said: 'Funny. She hasn't even touched her coffee.'

But Rickards had a final question for Alice Mair. He said: 'It must have been getting on for midnight when Dr Mair got home yesterday night. Did you ring the power station to find out if he'd left or why he was delayed?'

She said coolly: 'It didn't occur to me, Chief Inspector. Since Alex is neither my child nor my husband I am spared the compulsion of checking on his movements. I am not my brother's keeper.'

Oliphant had been staring at her with his sombre, suspicious eyes. Now he said: 'But he lives with you, doesn't he? You do talk, don't you? You must have known about his relationship with Hilary Robarts, for example. Did you approve?'

Alice Mair's colour didn't change, but her voice was like steel.

'Either to approve or disapprove would have been as presumptuously impertinent as was that question. If you wish to discuss my brother's private life, I suggest that you do so with him.'

Rickards said quietly: 'Miss Mair, a woman has been brutally done to death and her body mutilated. She was a woman you knew. In the light of that outrage, I hope you won't feel the need to be oversensitive to questions which are bound to seem at times both presumptuous and impertinent.'

Anger had made him articulate. Their eyes met and held. He knew that his were hard with fury, both with Oliphant's tactlessness and her response. But the grey eyes which met his were less easy to read. He thought he could detect surprise, followed by wariness, reluctant respect, an almost speculative interest.

And when, fifteen minutes later, she escorted her visitors to the door he was a little surprised when she held out her hand. As he shook it, she said: 'Please forgive me, Chief Inspector, if I was ungracious. Yours is a disagreeable but necessary job and you are entitled to co-operation. As far as I'm concerned, you will get it.'

31

Even without the garishly painted sign no one from Norfolk would have been in any doubt about the identity of the local hero after whom the Lydsett pub was named, nor could a stranger fail to recognize the admiral's hat with the star, the much-decorated chest, the black patch over one eye, the pinned-up, empty sleeve. Rickards reflected that he had seen worse paintings of Lord Nelson but not many. This made him look like the Princess Royal in drag.

George Jago had obviously decided that the interview should take place in the saloon bar wrapped now in the dim quietness of the late afternoon doldrums. He and his wife led Rickards and Oliphant to a small pub table, wooden-topped and with ornate cast-iron legs, set close to the huge and empty fireplace. They settled themselves round it rather, thought Rickards, like four ill-assorted people proposing to conduct a seance in appropriately ill-lit seclusion. Mrs Jago was an angular, bright-eyed, sharp-featured woman who looked at Oliphant as if she had seen his type before and was prepared to stand no nonsense. She was heavily made up. Two moons of bright rouge adorned each cheek, her long mouth was painted with a matching lipstick and her fingers, blood-tipped talons, were heavy with a variety of rings. Her hair was so glossily black that it looked unnatural and was piled high in the front in three rows of tight curls and swept upwards and secured with combs at the back and sides. She was wearing a pleated skirt topped with a blouse in some shiny material striped in red, white and blue, buttoned high at the neck and hung about with gold chains in which she looked like a bit-part actress auditioning for the part of a barmaid in an Ealing comedy. No woman could have been less suitably dressed for a country pub, yet both she and her husband, seated side by side with the brightly expectant look of children on their best behaviour, looked perfectly at home in the bar and with each other. Oliphant had made it his business to find out something of their past and had relayed the information to Rickards as they drove to the pub. George Jago had previously been the licensee of a pub in Catford but the couple had moved to Lydsett four years ago partly because Mrs Jago's brother, Charlie Sparks, owned a garage and car-hire business on the edge of the village and was looking for part-time help. George Jago occasionally drove for him leaving Mrs Jago in charge of the bar. They had settled happily in the village, took a lively part in community activities and appeared not to miss the raucous life of the city. Rickards reflected that East Anglia had accepted and absorbed more eccentric couples. Come to that, it had absorbed him.

George Jago looked more the part of a country publican, a stocky, cheerful-faced man with bright, blinking eyes and an air of suppressed energy. He had certainly expended it on the interior of the pub. The low, oak-beamed saloon bar was a cluttered and ill-arranged museum devoted to Nelson's memory. Jago must have scoured East Anglia in his search for objects with even a tenuous relationship with the Admiral. Above the open fireplace was a huge lithograph of the scene in the cockpit of the *Victory* with Nelson romantically dying in Hardy's arms. The remaining walls were covered with paintings and prints, including the principal sea battles, the Nile, Copenhagen, Trafalgar; one or two of Lady Hamilton including a lurid reproduction of Romney's famous portrait, while commemorative plates were ranged each side of the doors and the blackened oak beams were festooned with rows of decorated memorial mugs, few of them original to judge from the brightness of the decoration. Along the top of one wall a row of pennants spelled out what was presumably the famous signal and a fishing net had been slung across the ceiling to enhance the general nautical atmosphere. And suddenly, looking up into the brown tar-tangled netting, Rickards remembered. He had been here before. He and Susie had stopped here for a drink when they had been exploring the coast one weekend in the first winter of their marriage. They hadn't stayed for long; Susie had complained that the bar was too crowded and smoke-filled. He could recall the bench at which they had sat, the one against the wall to the left of the door. He had drunk half a pint of bitter, Susie a medium sherry. Then, with the fire blazing, the flames leaping from the crackling logs and the bar loud with cheerful Norfolk voices the pub had seemed interestingly nostalgic and cosy. But now, in the dim light of an autumn afternoon, the clutter of artefacts, so few of them either genuine or of particular merit, seemed to Rickards to trivialize and diminish both the building's own long history and the Admiral's achievements. He felt a sudden onrush of claustrophobia and had to resist an impulse to throw open the door and let in fresh air and the twentieth century.

As Oliphant said afterwards, it was a pleasure to interview George Jago. He didn't greet you as if you were a necessary but unwelcome technician of doubtful competence who was taking up your valuable time. He didn't use words as if they were secret signals to conceal thoughts rather than express them, nor subtly intimidate you with his superior intelligence. He didn't see an interview with the police as a battle of wits in which he necessarily had the advantage, nor react to perfectly ordinary questions with a disconcerting mixture of fear and endurance as if you were secret police from a totalitarian dictatorship. All in all, he pointed out, it made a pleasant change.

Jago admitted cheerfully that he had telephoned the Blaneys and Miss Mair shortly after half-past seven on Sunday with news that the Whistler was dead. How did he know? Because one of the police on the inquiry had telephoned home to let his wife know it was all right for their daughter to go alone to a party that night and the wife had telephoned her brother Harry Upjohn who kept the Crown and Anchor outside Cromer and Harry, who was a friend of his, had rung him. He remembered exactly what he had said to Theresa Blaney.

'Tell your dad they've found the Whistler's body. He's dead. Suicide. Killed himself at Easthaven. No need to worry now.'

He had phoned the Blaneys because he knew that Ryan liked his pints at nights but hadn't dared to leave the children while the Whistler was at large. Blaney hadn't come in that evening but that didn't really signify. With Miss Mair he had left the message on her answering machine in much the same terms. He hadn't telephoned Mrs Dennison because he thought she would be on her way to Norwich with the Copleys.

Rickards said: 'But you did ring her later?'

It was Mrs Jago who explained. 'That was after I reminded him. I was at half-past six Evensong and afterwards I went home with Sadie Sparks to settle arrangements for the autumn jumble sale. She found a note from Charlie to say that he'd been called out on two urgent jobs, taking the Copleys to Norwich and then fetching a couple from Ipswich. So when I got back I told

George that Mrs Dennison hadn't driven the Copleys to the train and that he ought to phone her straight away to tell her about the Whistler. I mean, she'd be more likely to get a good night's rest knowing he was dead than wondering if he was lurking in the rectory bushes. So George rang.'

Jago said: 'It was close on 9.15 by then, I reckon. I would have telephoned later anyway expecting she'd be back by half-past nine.'

Rickards said: 'And Mrs Dennison answered the phone?'

'Not then she didn't. But I tried again about thirty minutes later and got her then.'

Rickards asked: 'So you didn't tell any of them that the body had been found at the Balmoral Hotel?'

'Didn't know, did I? All I was told by Harry Upjohn was that the Whistler had been found and that he was dead. I dare say the police kept it quiet, where exactly he was found I mean. You wouldn't want a lot of morbid sightseers round the place. Nor would the hotel manager, come to that.'

'And early this morning you rang round again to say that Miss Robarts had been murdered. How did you discover that?'

'Saw the police cars passing, didn't I? So I got on my bike and went up to the gate. Your chaps had left it open so I shut it again and waited. When they came back I opened the gate for them and asked what was up.'

Rickards said: 'You seem to have an extraordinary talent for extracting information from the police.'

'Well, I know some of them, don't I? The local chaps, anyway. They drink in the Hero. The driver of the first car through wouldn't say anything. Nor would the driver of the mortuary van. But when the third car came through and stopped while I opened and shut the gate again I asked who was dead and they told me. I mean, I know a mortuary van when I see one.'

'Who exactly told you?' asked Oliphant belligerently. George Jago turned on him his bright and innocent comedian's gaze.

'Couldn't say, could I? One policeman is much like another. Someone told me.'

'So you rang round early this morning? Why then? Why wait?'

'Because it was after midnight by then. Folk like a bit of news but they like their sleep more. But I rang Ryan Blaney first thing today.'

'Why him?'

'Why not? When you've got news it's human nature to pass it on to an interested party.'

Oliphant said: 'And he was certainly an interested party. Must have come as something of a relief.'

'Might have done, might not. I didn't speak to him. I told Theresa.'

Oliphant said: 'So you didn't speak to Mr Blaney either when you rang on Sunday or this morning. Bit odd, wasn't it?'

'Depends how you look at it. The first time he was in his painting shed. He doesn't like being called to the phone when he's working. No point, anyway. I told Theresa and she told him.'

Rickards said: 'How do you know she told him?'

'Because she said so when I rang this morning. Why shouldn't she tell him?'

'But you can't know for certain that she did?'

Mrs Jago said suddenly: 'And you can't know for certain that she didn't. What does it matter, anyway? He knows now. We all do. We know about the Whistler and we know about Miss Robarts. And maybe if you'd caught the Whistler a year ago Miss Robarts would still be alive.'

Oliphant asked quickly: 'What do you mean by that, Mrs Jago?'

'What they call a copycat murder, isn't it? That's the talk in the village, anyway, apart from those who still think the Whistler did it and you've got your times all wrong. And old Humphrey, of course, who thinks it was the Whistler's ghost still on the job.'

Rickards said: 'We're interested in a portrait of Miss Robarts which was painted recently by Mr Blaney. Have either of you seen it? Did he talk about it?'

Mrs Jago said: 'Of course we've seen it. Had it hanging in the bar, didn't we? And I knew that it would bring bad luck. It was an evil picture if ever I saw one.'

Jago turned to his wife and explained with patient emphasis: 'I don't see how you can say a picture is evil, Doris, not a picture.

Things can't be evil. An inanimate object is neither good nor evil. Evil is what is done by people.'

'And what is thought by people, George, and that picture came out of evil thoughts, so I say that picture was evil.'

She spoke firmly but with no trace of obstinacy or resentment. Obviously this was the kind of marital argument, conducted without acrimony, and with scrupulous fairness, which they both relished. For a few minutes their attention was solely on each other.

Jago went on: 'Granted it wasn't the kind of picture you'd want to hang on your sitting-room wall.'

'Or in the bar, come to that. Pity you ever did, George.'

'Right enough. Still I reckon it didn't give anyone any ideas they didn't have already. And you can't say that it was evil, not a picture, Doris.'

'All right, suppose you get an instrument of torture, something used by the Gestapo.' Mrs Jago looked round the bar as if among its clutter she might reasonably expect to find an example. 'I'd say that thing was evil. I wouldn't give it house room.'

'You could say it was used for an evil purpose, Doris, that's different.'

Rickards asked: 'Why exactly did you hang the portrait in the bar?'

'Because he asked me, that's why. I usually find room for one or two of his small watercolours and sometimes he sells them and sometimes not. I always tell him they've got to be seascapes. I mean, it's all the Admiral here, isn't it, it's all nautical. But he was dead keen on having this up and I said I'd keep it for a week. He brought it down on his bike on Monday the twelfth.'

'In the hope of selling it?'

'Oh, it wasn't for sale, not that picture wasn't. He made that very plain.'

Oliphant said: 'So what was the point of putting it up?'

'That's what I said.' Jago turned triumphantly to the sergeant as if recognizing a fellow expert in logic. ' "What's the point in putting it up if you don't want to sell it?" I said. "Let them look at it," he said. "I want them to see it. I want the whole world to see it." A bit optimistic, I thought. After all, we're not the National Gallery.'

'More like the National Maritime Museum really,' said Doris surprisingly and beamed at them happily.

'Where did you find room for it?'

'On that wall opposite the door. Took down the two pictures of the Battle of the Nile, didn't I?'

'And how many people did see it in those seven days?'

'You're asking me how many customers I had. I mean, if they came in they saw it. Couldn't hardly miss it, could they? Doris wanted to take it down but I promised I'd keep it up until the Monday, so I did. Glad when he came and took it away, though. Like I said, it's all commemorative here. It's all the Admiral. It didn't seem to go with the décor. It wasn't here long. He said he'd call for it on the morning of the nineteenth and he did.'

'Did anyone from the headland or the power station see it?'

'Those who came in. The Local Hero isn't really their regular local. Most of them want to get away from the place at the end of the day and who's to blame them? I mean, living over the shop is all right, but not that shop.'

'Was there much talk about it? Did anyone ask where he kept it, for example?'

'Not to me. I reckon most of them knew where he kept it. I mean, he talked a bit about his painting shed. And if he had wanted to sell, he wouldn't have got any offers. I'll tell you someone who did see it, though. Hilary Robarts.'

'When was this?'

'The evening after he brought it in, about seven o'clock. She used to come in here from time to time. Never drank much, just a couple of dry sherries. Took them over to the seat by the fire.'

'Alone?'

'Usually she was. Once or twice she had Dr Mair with her. But she was alone that Tuesday.'

'What did she do when she saw the picture?'

'Stood and looked at it. The pub was pretty full at the time and everyone fell silent. You know how it is. They were all watching. I couldn't see her face because her back was to me. Then she walked over to the bar and said: "I've changed my mind about drinking here. Obviously you don't welcome customers from Larksoken." Then she went out. Well, I welcome customers from anywhere if they can hold their drink and don't ask for credit, but I didn't reckon she'd be much loss.'

'So she wasn't particularly popular on the headland?'

'I don't know about the headland. She wasn't particularly popular in this pub.'

Doris Jago said: 'Scheming she was to turn the Blaneys out of Scudder's Cottage. And him a widower trying to bring up four kids. Where did she think he was going to go? He gets family allowance and other bits of welfare help but that isn't going to find him another cottage. But I'm sorry she's dead, of course. I mean you have to be, don't you? It's not a nice thing to happen to anybody. We'll be sending a wreath from the Local Hero.'

'Was that the last time you saw her?'

Mrs Jago said: 'The last time George did. I saw her on the headland on Sunday. Must have been only a few hours before she died. I said to George, maybe I was the last person to see her alive, well, me and Neil Pascoe and Amy. You don't think at the time, do you? We can't see into the future, nor wouldn't want to. Sometimes I look at that power station and wonder if we'll all end up dead on the beach.'

Oliphant asked how she came to be on the headland.

'Delivering the church magazine, wasn't I? I always do on the last Sunday afternoon in the month. Collect them after morning service then take them round after dinner. Lunch to you, maybe, we call it dinner.'

Rickards had called the main meal dinner all his life and still did despite his mother-in-law's unceasing campaign to raise his social status. Her midday meal was luncheon and her evening meal dinner even if it consisted, as it often did, of sardines on toast. He wondered what they had eaten today. He said: 'I didn't realize that people on the headland were churchgoers, other than the Copleys, of course.'

'And Mrs Dennison. Very regular she is. I can't say the others actually come to church, well, not to say actually attend, not to the services, but they do take the parish magazine.' Mrs Jago's tone suggested that there were depths of irreligion to which even the headlanders would hardly sink. She added: 'All except the Blaneys, of course. Well, they wouldn't, being RC. At least she was RC, poor dear, and the children are of course. I mean they have to be, don't they? I don't think Ryan's anything. He's an artist. I never delivered to Scudder's Cottage even when his wife was alive. Anyway RCs don't have parish magazines.'

George Jago said: 'I wouldn't say that, Doris. I wouldn't go that far. They might.'

'We've lived here for four years, George, and Father McKee is in the bar often enough and I've never seen one.'

'Well, you wouldn't, would you?'

'I might have, George, if there was one to see. They're different from us. No Harvest Festival and no parish magazines.'

Her husband explained patiently: 'They're different because they have different dogmas. It's all to do with dogma, Doris, it's nothing to do with Harvest Festival and parish magazines.'

'I know it's to do with dogma. The Pope tells them that the blessed Virgin Mary ascended into Heaven and they all have to believe it. I know all about dogma.'

Before Jago could open his mouth to dispute this claim to infallibility Rickards said quickly: 'So you delivered the magazines to the headlanders on Sunday afternoon. When precisely?'

'Well, I reckon I started off at about three, or maybe a bit after. We have a latish dinner on Sundays and we didn't get started on the spotted-dick pudding much before 2.30. And then George loaded the dishwasher and I got ready to go. Say 3.15, if you want to be particular.'

Jago said: 'You were well gone by 3.15, Doris. I'd say it was nearer 3.10.'

Oliphant said impatiently: 'I don't think five minutes matters either way.'

George Jago turned on him a glance of nicely judged surprise and mild rebuke. 'They might. They could be crucial. I'd say five minutes in a murder investigation could be crucial.'

Mrs Jago added her reproof: 'One minute could be crucial if that was the actual minute she died. Crucial for her, anyway. I don't see how you can say they don't matter.'

Rickards thought it was time to intervene: 'I agree that five minutes could be important, Mr Jago, but hardly these five minutes. Perhaps your wife would tell us exactly what she did and saw.'

'Well, I got on my bicycle. George always offers to drive me but he has enough driving in the week and I don't like to bother him to get out the car. Not Sundays. Not after roast beef and spotted dick.'

'It'd be no trouble, Doris. I've told you that. No trouble.'

'I know, George. Haven't I just said you'd be willing enough? I like the exercise and I'm always back before dark.' She turned to Rickards and explained: 'George never liked me to be out after dark, not with the Whistler around.'

Oliphant said: 'So you left between 3.10 and 3.15 and cycled off over the headland.'

'With the church magazines in the basket, same as usual. First I went to the caravan. I always go to the caravan first. It's a bit tricky now with Neil Pascoe.'

'How is it tricky, Mrs Jago?'

'Well, he's asked us more than once to put out his magazine – *Nuclear Newsletter* he calls it – in the bar for people to buy or maybe read for free. But George and I have always set our faces against it. I mean, we get some of the staff from Larksoken in the pub and it's not nice, is it, to be faced with a paper saying that what you're doing is wicked and ought to be put a stop to. Not when all you want is a quiet drink. Not everybody in Lydsett agrees with what he's doing. You can't deny that Larksoken Power Station has brought more business into the village, and jobs too. And you've got to trust people, haven't you? I mean, if Dr Mair says nuclear power is safe, then it probably is. Then again, you can't help wondering, can you?'

Rickards said patiently: 'But Mr Pascoe took the church magazine?'

'Well, it's only ten pence and I suppose he likes to know what's going on in the parish. When he first arrived on the headland – two years ago it was now – I called on him and asked if he'd like to take the magazine. He seemed a bit surprised but he said he would and paid his ten pence and he's had it ever since. If he doesn't want it he's only got to say so.'

Rickards asked: 'And what happened at the caravan?'

'I saw Hilary Robarts, same as I said. I gave Neil the magazine and collected the money and was having a bit of a chat with him inside the caravan when she drove up in that red Golf of hers. Amy was outside with the kid, bringing in some of his clothes from a washing line they'd rigged up there. When he saw the car Neil got out of the caravan and went over and stood by Amy. Miss Robarts got out of the car and they both stood looking at her, not speaking, just standing side by side watching her. It wasn't much of a welcoming committee, but then what would you expect? Then, when Miss Robarts got within six yards or so of them Timmy trotted over to her and grabbed at her slacks. He's a friendly little beggar and he didn't mean any harm. You know how kids are. But he'd been mucking about in that muddy patch under the tap and started smearing the stuff all over her trousers. She pushed him away none too gently. The kid fell flat on his bum and started bawling, and then all hell was let loose.'

Oliphant asked: 'What was said?'

'Now that I can't exactly remember. There were a lot of words used which you don't expect to hear on a Sunday. Some beginning with f and some beginning with c. Use your imagination.'

Rickards said: 'Were any threats made?'

'Depends what you mean by threats. There was a lot of shouting and screaming. Not Neil. He was just standing there looking so white I thought he was going to faint. It was Amy who was making the most noise. Anyone would think Miss Robarts had gone for the kid with a knife. I can't remember the half of it. Ask Neil Pascoe. Miss Robarts didn't seem to notice that I was there. Ask Amy and Neil. They'll tell you.'

Rickards said: 'You tell me too. It's helpful to get different people's views of an incident. You get a more accurate picture that way.'

Jago interposed: 'More accurate? Different maybe. It'd only be more accurate if they were all telling the truth.'

For a moment Rickards feared that Mrs Jago was prepared to challenge the assertion with another demonstration of semantics. He said: 'Well, I'm sure that you're telling the truth, Mrs Jago. That's why we're starting with you. Can you remember what was actually said?'

'I think Miss Robarts said that she had called to say that she was thinking of dropping her legal action but that now she would bloody well go ahead with it and she hoped it would ruin them both. "You and your whore." Charming wasn't it?'

'She used those precise words?'

'And a good few others which I can't exactly remember.'

'What I mean is, Mrs Jago, Miss Robarts was the one making the threats?'

For the first time Mrs Jago seemed uneasy, then she said: 'Well she always was the one making threats, wasn't she? Neil Pascoe wasn't suing her.'

'What happened next?'

'Nothing. Miss Robarts got into the car and drove away. Amy lugged the kid into the caravan and slammed the door. Neil looked so miserable I thought he'd burst out crying, so I thought I'd say something to cheer him up.'

'What was that, Mrs Jago?'

'I said she was a vicious evil-minded bitch and one day someone would do her in.'

Jago said: 'Not very nice, Doris. Not on a Sunday.'

Doris Jago said complacently: 'Not very nice any day of the week, but I wasn't far wrong, was I?'

Rickards asked: 'What happened then, Mrs Jago?'

'I got on with delivering the magazines, didn't I? First of all I went to the Old Rectory. I don't usually call there because the Copleys and Mrs Dennison are usually at morning service and collect their own magazines, but they weren't there yesterday and I was a bit worried. Thought something might be wrong. But it was just that they were too busy packing to attend. The Copleys were off to stay with their daughter in Wiltshire. Nice for them, I thought, and it'll give Mrs Dennison a bit of a rest. She offered me a cup of tea but I said I wouldn't wait because I could see she was busy getting on with their high tea. But I did sit in the kitchen with her for five minutes and had a bit of a chat. She said that some of the staff at Larksoken had given some very nice children's clothes for the jumble which might fit the Blaney twins and she wondered whether Ryan Blaney would be interested. She'd price them up and then he could have his choice before they were taken off for the sale. We've done that once before but we have to manage it very tactfully. If Ryan thought we were offering charity he wouldn't take the clothes. But it isn't a charity, is it? It's in aid of church funds. I see him when he comes into the pub and Mrs Dennison thought that the suggestion might come better from me.'

'And after calling at the Old Rectory?'

'Then I went on to Martyr's Cottage. Miss Mair has a bill enclosed with the magazine every six months so I never bother to collect the ten pence. Sometimes she's busy and sometimes she just isn't there so I usually just put the magazine through the letter box.'

'Did you see whether she was at home on Sunday?'

'I never saw skin nor hide of her. Then I went on to the last cottage where Hilary Robarts lived. She'd got home by then, of course. I could see the red Golf outside the garage door. But I don't usually knock with her either. She isn't the kind of woman who'd welcome you in for five minutes' chat and a cuppa.'

Oliphant said: 'So you didn't see her?'

'I'd already seen her, hadn't I? If you're asking whether I saw her again the answer is no, I didn't. But I heard her.'

Mrs Jago paused for effect. Rickards asked: 'How do you mean you heard her, Mrs Jago?'

'I heard her through the letter box, didn't I, when I was pushing the magazine through? And a fine old argument she was having with somebody. I'd say it was a real row. The second of the day for her. Or, maybe, the third.'

Oliphant asked: 'What do you mean by that, Mrs Jago?'

'Just wondered, that's all. It struck me when she arrived at the caravan she was pretty wrought up. High colour. Edgy. You know.'

'You could tell that just by looking at her from the caravan door?'

'That's right. Call it a gift.'

Rickards asked: 'Could you tell whether she was speaking to a man or a woman?'

'Could be either. I only heard the one voice and that was hers. But she had someone in with her for certain, unless she was shouting at herself.'

'What time would this be, Mrs Jago?'

'About four, I reckon, or a little after. Say I got to the caravan at twenty-five past three and away by twenty-five to four. Then there was the quarter of an hour at the Old Rectory which would bring me up to five to four, and then the ride across the headland. It must have been soon after four.'

'And after that you went home?'

'That's right. And I was back here soon after half-past four, wasn't I, George?'

Her husband said: 'You might have been, dear. And then again you might not. I was asleep.'

Ten minutes later Rickards and Oliphant left.

George and Doris watched the police car until it turned the corner of the road and went out of sight.

Doris said: 'I can't say I took to that sergeant.'

'I can't say I took to either of them.'

'You don't think I was wrong, George, telling them about the quarrel?'

'Had no option, did you? This is murder, Doris, and you were one of the last people to see her alive. Anyway, they'll probably get it, or some of it from Neil Pascoe. No point in keeping back what the police will find out in the end. And you only spoke the truth.'

'I wouldn't say that, George, not the whole truth. I may have toned it down a bit. But I didn't tell them any lies.'

For a moment they contemplated this nice distinction in silence. Then Doris said: 'That mud which Timmy smeared on Miss Robarts's trousers, it came from the patch under the outside tap. Been like that for weeks. Be funny, wouldn't it, if Hilary Robarts was murdered because Neil Pascoe couldn't fix a new washer?'

George said: 'Not funny, Doris. I wouldn't exactly say that it was funny.'

32

Jonathan Reeves's parents had moved from their small terraced house in south London to a flat in a modern block overlooking the sea just outside Cromer. His appointment at the power station had coincided with his father's retirement and the idea had been that they would return to a place that they had known and liked on past holidays and, as his mother had said, 'to provide a home for you until the right girl comes along'. His father had worked for fifty years in the carpet department of a large store in Clapham, starting at fifteen straight from school and rising eventually to be head of the department. The firm let him have carpets at less than cost price; the off-cuts, sometimes large enough for a small room, he got for nothing, so that from childhood Jonathan had never known a room at home which wasn't carpeted from wall to wall.

Sometimes it seemed that their thick-pile wool and nylon had absorbed and deadened not only their footsteps. His mother's calm response to any event was either 'very nice', equally appropriate to an enjoyable dinner, a royal engagement or birth, or a spectacular sunrise, or 'Terrible, terrible, isn't it? You wonder sometimes what the world's coming to', which covered events as diverse as Kennedy's assassination, a particularly gruesome murder, children abused or violated, or an IRA bomb. But she didn't wonder what the world was coming to. Wonder was an emotion long since stifled by Axminster, mohair, underfelt. It seemed to him that they lived together in amity because their emotions, debilitated by under-use or undernourishment, couldn't cope with anything as robust as a row. At the first sign of it his mother would say 'Don't raise your voice, dear, I don't like rows.' Disagreement, never intense, was expressed in peevish resentment which died through lack of energy to keep it going.

He got on well enough with his sister Jennifer, eight years his senior but now married to a local authority officer in Ipswich. Once, watching her bending over the ironing board, her features set in their familiar mask of slightly resentful concentration, he had been tempted to say, 'Speak to me. Tell me what you think, about death, about evil, about what we're doing here.' But her reply was predictable. 'I know what I'm doing here. Ironing Dad's shirts.'

To her acquaintances and to those she might have called friends, his mother would always speak of her husband as Mr Reeves. 'Mr Reeves is very highly thought of by Mr Wainwright.' 'Of course, you could say that Mr Reeves *is* the carpet department of Hobbs and Wainwright.' The store represented those aspirations, traditions and orthodoxies that others found in their profession, in their school, regiment or religion. Mr Wainwright senior was headmaster, colonel, their high priest; their occasional Sunday attendances at the local United Reform Chapel merely a gesture to a lesser God. And they were never regular worshippers. Jonathan suspected that this was deliberate. People might want to get to know them, involve them in mothers' meetings, whist drives, Sunday-school outings, might even want to visit. On the Friday of his first week at secondary school the form bully had said, 'Reeves's dad is shopwalker at Hobbs and Wainwright. He sold my mum a rug last week,' and had minced across the room, hands obsequiously clasped. 'I know madam will find that mixture extremely hardwearing. It's a very popular line.' The laughter had been sycophantic but uneasy and the teasing, for lack of popular support, had quickly died. Most of their fathers had even less prestigious jobs.

Sometimes he thought: We can't be as ordinary, as dull as we seem, and wondered if it were some defect in himself which diminished them all so that he invested them with his own inadequacy, his own pessimism. Sometimes, too, he would take from the bureau drawer the family photograph album which seemed to document their ordinariness: his parents stiffly posed against the rail of Cromer promenade and at Whipsnade Zoo, himself ridiculous in cap and gown at his degree ceremony. Only one held any real interest for him, the sepia studio photograph of his great-grandfather in the First World War, perched sideways on an artificial wall with, beside him, a huge aspidistra in a Benares jar. He would gaze intensely across seventy-four years at that gentle-faced vulnerable boy who looked, in the ill-fitting, high-buttoned serge and the grotesquely over-large cap more like an orphaned poor-law child than a soldier. He must have been under twenty when it was taken. And he had survived Passchendaele, the Ypres Salient, and had been discharged wounded and gassed early in 1918 with strength enough at least to father a son, but for little else. That life, he told himself, could not have been ordinary. His great-grandfather had survived four years of horror with courage, endurance and a stoical acceptance of what his God or luck had dealt him.

But if not ordinary, the life seemed now of absolutely no importance to anyone. It had preserved a family, that was all. And how much did that matter? But now it struck him that his father's life had held a not-dissimilar stoicism. You couldn't, perhaps, equate fifty years with Hobbs and Wainwright with four years in France, but both had required that same dignified and stoical acceptance. He wished that he could talk to his father about his great-grandfather, about his father's early life. But it never seemed possible and he knew that what held him back was less an inhibiting shyness than the fear that, even if he broke through this strange barrier of reticence and inarticulateness, there would be nothing there. And yet surely it hadn't always been like that. He remembered the Christmas of 1968 when his father had bought him his first science book, *The Wonder Book of Science for Children*. On Christmas morning they had sat for hours together, slowly turning the pages while his father first read and then explained. He still had the book. He still occasionally looked at the diagrams. 'How television works', 'What happens when we are X-rayed', 'Newton and the apple', 'The marvel of modern ships'. And his father had said, 'I would have liked to have been a scientist if things had been different.' It was the only time in his life that his father had given any indication that there could have been for him, for them, a fuller, a different life. But things had not been different and now he knew that they never would be. He thought, 'We need, all of us, to be in control of our lives, and we shrink them until they're small and mean enough so that we can feel in control.'

Only once had the routine of their predictable days been interrupted by an event which was unexpected, dramatic. Shortly after his sixteenth birthday his father had taken the family Morris and had disappeared. Three days later he was found, sitting in the car on the top of Beachy Head, looking out to sea. It had been called a nervous breakdown due to overwork and Mr Wainwright had given him two weeks' holiday. His father had never explained what had happened, colluding in the official view that it had been a temporary amnesia. Neither of his parents had ever referred to it again.

The flat was on the fourth and top floor of a rectangular

modern block. The sitting room at the front had a glass door giving on to a narrow balcony sufficient to hold two chairs. The kitchen was small but had a flap which could be lifted to provide a table just large enough for the three of them to eat. There were only two bedrooms, his parents' at the front and his own, much smaller, giving a view of the car park, the row of breeze-block garages and the town. The sitting room had a wall-mounted gas fire to augment the background central heating, and after they had moved in his parents had surrounded this with a false mantelshelf on which his mother could display the small treasures brought from the Clapham home. He remembered the morning when they had viewed the flat, his mother stepping out on to the balcony and saying, 'Look, Father, it's just like being on the deck of a liner', and she had turned almost with animation as if remembering that store of old movie magazines she kept, the pictures of befurred film stars on the gangplanks, the ship festooned with streamers and flags, hearing in imagination the hoots of the pilot boat, the band playing on the quay. And indeed his parents had, from the start, seen the flat as a glamorous change from their small terraced house. In summer they would move the two easy chairs so that they faced the window and the sea. In winter they reversed them and huddled round the gas fire. But neither the winter gales, nor the uncomfortable heat when summer beat on the glass, ever drew from either of them a word of regret for the old life.

They had sold their car when his father retired and the single-car garage was used to house Jonathan's second-hand Ford Fiesta. He garaged it and swung back the door. Locking it he thought how very private the flats were. Nearly all of them were occupied by retired couples whose routine seemed to be to walk during the morning, meet their friends for afternoon tea and to be home before seven. By the time he returned from work the block was quiet and the rear curtains drawn. He wondered if Caroline had guessed or had known just how private his comings and goings could be. Outside the flat he hesitated for a moment, key in hand, wishing he could postpone the moment of meeting. But any longer wait would seem unnatural; they must have been listening for the lift.

His mother almost ran towards him.

'It's terrible, isn't it? That poor girl. Dad and I heard it on the local radio. But at least they found the Whistler. That's one worry over. He'll not go on killing again after her.'

He said: 'They think that he died before Miss Robarts did, so that it may not have been the Whistler.'

'But of course it was the Whistler. She died in the same way, didn't she? Who else would it be?'

'That's what the police are trying to find out. They've been at the station all morning. They didn't get round to seeing me until nearly twelve.'

'What did they want to see you for? They can't think you had anything to do with it?'

'Of course not, Mother. They're interviewing everyone, everyone who knew her, that is. Anyway, I have an alibi.'

'An alibi? What alibi? Why would you want an alibi?'

'I don't want one, but as it happens I have one. I went to supper last night with a girl from the station.'

Immediately her face brightened, pleasure at the news momentarily eclipsing the horror of the murder. She said: 'Who invited you then, Jonathan?'

'A girl at the station. I told you.'

'Well, I know it's a girl. What kind of girl? Why don't you bring her home? You know that this is your home just as much as it is Dad's and mine. You can always bring your friends here. Why not ask her to tea next Saturday or Sunday? I'd have everything very nice, your granny's best tea service, I wouldn't let you down.'

Torn with a dreadful pity he said: 'Perhaps I will one day, Mum. It's a bit early yet.'

'I don't see how it can be too early to meet your friends. It's as well you were with her if they're looking for alibis. What time did you get home, then?'

'About quarter to eleven.'

'Well, that's not so very late. You look tired. It must have been a shock for everyone at Larksoken, a girl you knew, Administrative Officer, too, so it said on the radio.'

Jonathan said: 'Yes, it has been a shock. I suppose that's why I don't feel very hungry. I'd like to wait a little bit before supper.'

'It's all ready, Jonathan. Lamb chops. They're half cooked already. I've only got to slip them under the grill. And the vegetables are cooked. It's only going to spoil.'

'All right. I won't be more than five minutes.'

He hung his jacket in the hall, then went into his own room and lay on the bed, staring at the ceiling. The thought of food nauseated him but he had said five minutes and if he lay there much longer she would be knocking at the door. She always knocked, but very gently, two distinct, discreet taps, like an assignation. What, he wondered, did she fear she might find him doing if she came in unannounced? He made himself sit up and swung his legs over the side of the bed but was immediately seized by nausea and a weakness which made him fear for a moment that he was actually going to faint. But he recognized it for what it was; a mixture of tiredness, fear and sheer misery.

And yet so far it hadn't been too bad. There had been three of them, Chief Inspector Rickards, a thickset serious-faced young man who had been introduced as Detective-Sergeant Oliphant and a younger man in the corner apparently taking notes whom no one had bothered to introduce. The small interviewing room attached to the medical physics department had been set aside for them, and they had been sitting side by side at a small table, both in plain clothes. The room, as always, smelt faintly of disinfectant. He had never understood why since no clinical procedures were carried out there. Two white coats still hung behind the door and someone had left a tray of test tubes on top of the filing cabinet, adding to the air of inadvertence and amateurism. It had all been very low-key, very matter-of-fact. He felt that he was being processed, one of the dozens who had known her or claimed to have known her and who had passed through this or a similar door to answer the same questions. Almost he expected them to ask him to roll up his sleeve and to feel the prick of a needle. He knew that the probing, if there were to be probing, would come later. But he had been surprised at his own initial lack of fear. He had somehow assumed that the police were endowed with an almost supernatural power to sniff out lying, that he would walk into that room bearing an all too visible load of guilt, prevarication and conspiracy to defeat the ends of justice.

At their request he gave his name and address. The sergeant wrote it down. Then he said almost wearily: 'If you could tell us, please, where you were yesterday between six and 10.30.'

He remembered thinking, Why six and 10.30? She had been found on the beach. She liked to swim most nights just after the nine o'clock news; everyone knew that, at least, everyone who knew her. And the news on Sunday was at 9.10. And then he remembered that they would know exactly when she had been found. There wouldn't have been time yet for the autopsy report. Perhaps they were still uncertain about the time of death or were playing it safe. Six to 10.30. But nine, or shortly after, was surely the relevant time. He was surprised that he could work it out so clearly.

He said: 'I was at home with my parents until after dinner, after the one o'clock meal I mean. Then I drove over to spend the evening with my girlfriend Miss Caroline Amphlett. I was with her until just after 10.30. She lives in a bungalow outside Holt. She's PA to the Director, Dr Mair.'

'We know where she lives, sir. And we know who she is. Did anyone see you arrive or leave?'

'I don't think so. The bungalow is very isolated and there weren't many cars on the road. I think someone in the flats may have seen me leave.'

'And you spent the evening doing what?'

The officer in the corner wasn't writing now, only looking, but he didn't seem curious, not even interested, just slightly bored.

'Caroline cooked supper and I helped. She had some home-made soup already made and heated that. We had mushroom omelettes, fruit, cheese, wine. After dinner we chatted. Then we went to bed and made love.'

'I don't think we need go into the more intimate parts of the evening, sir. How long have you and Miss Amphlett been friends?'

'About three months.'

'And when was this evening together planned?'

'A few days before. I can't remember exactly when.'

'And when did you get home, sir?'

'Just after 10.45.' He added, 'I've no witnesses to that, I'm afraid. My parents were away for the night visiting my married sister at Ipswich.'

'Did you know they would be away when you and Miss Amphlett planned your evening together?'

'Yes. They always visit my sister on the last Sunday of the month. But it wouldn't have made any difference. I mean, I'm twenty-eight. I live with them but I don't have to give them an account of my movements.'

The sergeant looked at him and said: 'Free, white and twenty-eight,' as if he were noting it down. He had blushed and thought, That was a mistake. Don't try to be clever, don't explain, just answer their questions.

The Chief Inspector said: 'Thank you, sir, that will be all for now.'

As he reached the door he heard Rickards's voice.

'She wasn't very nice to you, was she, Miss Robarts, about that local radio programme you took part in, *My religion and my job*? Did you hear it, Sergeant?'

The sergeant said stolidly: 'No, sir, I didn't hear it. Can't think how I came to miss it. Very fascinating, I'm sure.'

He turned and faced them. He said: 'She wasn't very kind about it. I'm a Christian. You don't expect it always to be easy.'

Rickards said: '"Blessed are ye when men revile and persecute you for the gospel's sake." A bit of persecution, was there? Oh well, things could be worse. At least you don't get thrown to the lions any more.'

The sergeant seemed to think that it was very funny.

He wondered, for the first time, how they could have known about Hilary's mild persecution of him over the programme. For some reason his brief, rather pathetic notoriety, his affirmation of faith, had outraged her. Someone at the station must have mentioned it to the police. After all, they had interviewed plenty of people before they got round to him.

But surely it was over now. He had given the police his alibi, his and hers, and there was no reason why they should be questioned again. He must put the whole thing out of his mind. But he knew that this wouldn't be possible. And now, remembering Caroline's story, he was struck with its inconsistencies. Why had she chosen to park the car on an isolated part of the road, down a cart track under the trees? Why had she chosen to drive with Remus to the headland when there were plenty of walks nearer home? He could have understood it if she had wanted to let the dog run on the beach and splash into the sea, but according to her they hadn't gone down to the beach. And what proof was there that she hadn't reached the cliffs until ten o'clock, half an hour after Hilary Robarts was thought to have died?

Then there was that story about her mother. He found that he just didn't believe it, hadn't believed it when she had first told him, and he believed it even less now. But that, surely, was something he might be able to check. There were private detectives, firms in London who could carry out this kind of inquiry. The thought both appalled and excited him. The idea that he might actually get in touch with those kind of people, might pay them money to spy on her, astounded him by its audacity. It wasn't something she would expect him to do, that anyone would expect him to do: but why shouldn't he? He had enough money to pay. There was nothing shameful in the inquiry. But first he must find out her date of birth. That shouldn't be difficult. He knew Shirley Coles, the junior clerk in the establishment division. Sometimes he even thought that she liked him. She wouldn't let him see Caroline's personal file but she might be willing to look up a harmless piece of information. He could say that he wanted to give Caroline a birthday present and had a feeling that the date was getting close. Then, with her name and date of birth, surely her parents could be traced. It should be possible to know whether her mother was alive, where she was living, her financial circumstances. There would be a copy of the London yellow pages in the library where private detective firms would be listed. He didn't want to do it by letter, but he could telephone with a preliminary inquiry. If necessary he could take a day's leave and go up to London. He thought: I've got to know. If this is a lie, then everything is a lie; the walk on the cliffs, everything she said to me, even her love.

He heard the two knocks on the door. To his horror he found that he was crying, not noisily but with a silent welling forth of tears which no effort could control. He called out, 'I'm coming. I'm coming.' Then he went over to the washbasin and began bathing his face. Looking up, he saw himself in the mirror. It seemed to him that fear and tiredness and a sickness of spirit which lay too deep for healing had stripped away all his pathetic pretences, that the face which had at least been ordinary, familiar, had become as disgusting to him as it must be to her. He stared at his image and saw it through her eyes; the dull brown hair with the clinging specks of scurf which daily shampooing seemed only to exacerbate, the eyes red-rimmed, a little too close together, the damp pale forehead on which the acne pustules stood out like the stigma of sexual shame.

He thought: She doesn't love me and she has never loved me. She chose me for two reasons; because she knew I loved her and because she thought I was too stupid to discover the truth. But I'm not stupid and I shall discover it. And he would begin with the smallest lie, the one about her mother. And what of his own lies, the lie to his parents, the false alibi to the police? And that greatest lie of all. 'I'm a Christian. You don't expect it always to be easy.' He wasn't a Christian any more and perhaps he never had been. His conversion had been no more than the need to be accepted, taken seriously, befriended by that little coterie of earnest proselytizers who had at least valued him for himself. But it wasn't true. None of it was true. In one day he had learned that the two most important things in his life, his religion and his love, were delusions.

The two knocks on the door were more insistent this time. His mother called: 'Jonathan, are you all right? The chops are getting overcooked.'

'It's all right, Mother. I'm coming.'

But it took another minute of vigorous splashing before his face looked normal and it was safe to open the door and join them for supper.

BOOK FIVE

33

Jonathan Reeves waited until he saw Mrs Simpson leave her office for coffee before going into the establishment office where the personnel files were kept. All the personnel records had, he knew, been computerized but the original files were still in existence, guarded by Mrs Simpson as if they were repositories of dangerous and actionable information. She was nearing the end of her service and had never come to terms with computer records. For her the only reality was set down in black and white between the manila folders of an official file. Her assistant, Shirley Coles, was a newly appointed junior, a pretty eighteen-year-old who lived in the village. She had early been instructed in the importance of the Director and the heads of departments but hadn't yet assimilated the more subtle law which permeates any organization and which defines those whose wishes are to be taken seriously whatever their grade and those who can be safely ignored. She was a pleasant child, anxious to please and responsive to friendliness.

Jonathan said: 'I'm almost sure that her birthday is early next month. I know that the personnel records are confidential, but it's only her date of birth. If you could have a look and let me know.'

He knew that he sounded gauche and nervous but that helped; she knew what it was to feel gauche and nervous. He added: 'Only the date of birth. Honestly. And I won't tell anyone how I found out. She did tell me but I've forgotten.'

'I'm not supposed to, Mr Reeves.'

'I know, but there isn't any other way that I can find out. She doesn't live at home so I can't ask her mother. I really would hate her to think I'd forgotten.'

'Couldn't you come back when Mrs Simpson is here? I expect she'd tell you. I'm not supposed to open files when she's away.'

'I could ask her, I know, but I'd rather not. You know how she is. I'm afraid she'd laugh at me. About Caroline. I thought you'd understand. Where is she, Mrs Simpson?'

'Having her coffee break. She always takes twenty minutes. But you'd better stand by the door and let me know if anyone's coming.'

But he stood instead at the side of the cabinet and watched while she went over to the security cupboard with its combination lock and began twirling the dial. He said: 'Can the police see these personnel records if they ask?'

'Oh no, Mr Reeves, that wouldn't be right. No one sees them except Dr Mair and Mrs Simpson. They're confidential. The police did see Miss Robarts's file, though. Dr Mair asked for it first thing on Monday morning, even before the police arrived. It was the first thing he rang for as soon as he got into his office. Mrs Simpson took it in to him personally. But that's different. She's dead. There isn't anything private when you're dead.'

'No,' he said. 'Nothing is private once you're dead.' And he had a sudden picture of himself in that small rented house in Romford, helping his mother clear out his grandfather's things after the old man's heart attack; the greasy clothes, the smell, the larder with its store of baked beans on which he chiefly lived, the uncovered saucers of stale and mouldy food, those shameful magazines which he had discovered at the bottom of a drawer and which, scarlet-faced, his mother had snatched from him. No, there wasn't anything left private once you were dead.

She said, her back to him, 'Awful, isn't it, the murder? You can't sort of realize it. Not someone you actually knew. It's made a lot of extra work for us in Estabs. The police wanted a list of all the staff with their addresses. And everyone's had a form asking where they were on Sunday evening and who they were with. Well, you know. You've had one. We all have.'

The combination lock needed precision. Her first effort had been unsuccessful and now she was carefully turning the dial again. Oh God, he thought, why can't she get on with it? But now, at last, the door swung open. He could glimpse the edge of a small metal box. She took from it a bunch of keys and, returning to the filing cabinet, quickly selected one and inserted it in the lock. The tray slid out at a touch of her fingers. Now she seemed infected with his anxiety. She gave one anxious look at the door and quickly rifled through the suspended files.

'Here it is.'

He had to stop himself from snatching it. She opened it and he saw the familiar buff-coloured form which he had himself completed when he first came to the station, her application for her present job. What he wanted was laid out before him in her careful capitals. Caroline Sophia St John Amphlett, date of birth 14 October 1957, place Aldershot, England, nationality British.

Shirley closed the file and quickly replaced it and slid back the drawer. As she locked it she said: 'There you are then. Fourteenth of October. Quite soon really. It's a good thing you checked. What will you do to celebrate? If the weather stays good you could have a picnic on the boat.'

He said, puzzled: 'What boat? We don't have a boat.'

'Caroline does. She bought Mr Hoskins's old cabin cruiser berthed at Wells-next-the-Sea. I know because he put a card in Mrs Bryson's window at Lydsett and my Uncle Ted thought he might have a look at it as it was going cheap. But when he rang, Mr Hoskins told him it had been sold to Miss Amphlett from Larksoken.'

'When was that?'

'Three weeks ago. Didn't she tell you?'

He thought: One more secret, innocent perhaps, but still strange. She had never shown the slightest interest in boats or the sea. An old cabin cruiser, going cheap. And it was autumn, hardly the best time to buy a boat.

He heard Shirley's voice. 'Sophia's rather a pretty name. Old-fashioned, but I like it. She doesn't look like a Sophia, though, does she?'

But Jonathan had seen more than her full name and the date of birth. Underneath were the names of her parents. Father, Charles Roderick St John Amphlett, deceased, army officer. Mother, Patricia Caroline Amphlett. He had brought with him a sheet of paper torn from a notebook and quickly wrote down both the date and the names. They were a bonus. He had forgotten that the application form was so detailed. Surely, with this information, a detective agency would be able to trace her mother without too great difficulty.

It was only when the keys had been replaced in the security cupboard that he could breathe freely. Now that he had gained what he wanted it seemed ungracious to hurry away. It was important to be gone before Mrs Simpson returned and Shirley was left to face the inevitable question about what he was doing there and might be forced into a lie. But he lingered a moment while she settled herself at her desk. She began threading paper clips together to make a chain.

She said: 'I feel really awful about this murder, I really do. Do you know, I was actually there on Sunday afternoon, I mean the actual place where she died. We went for a picnic so that Christopher could play on the beach. I mean Mum, Dad, Christopher and me. He's my baby brother, he's only four. We parked the car on the headland only about fifty yards from Miss Robarts's cottage, but of course we didn't see her. We didn't see anybody the whole afternoon, except Mrs Jago in the distance on her bicycle delivering the church magazines.'

Jonathan said: 'Have you told this to the police? I suppose they might be interested. I mean, they'd be interested in hearing that you hadn't actually seen anyone near her cottage.'

'Oh yes, I told them. And they were very interested. Do you know, they asked me whether Christopher had spilled any sand on the path. And he had. Wasn't that funny? I mean, it was funny they should think of it.'

Jonathan said: 'When were you there, then?'

'They asked me that as well. Not very long. Only from about half-past one to about half-past three. We actually ate our picnic in the car. Mum said it wasn't the time of year to sit around on the beach getting cold. Then we went down the path to that little cove and Christopher made a sandcastle near to the sea. He was happy enough but it wasn't warm enough for the rest of us to sit about. Mum more or less had to drag him away yelling. Dad went on to the car and we were lagging a bit behind. Mum said, "I'm not having you carrying that sand into the car, Christopher. You know your dad won't like it." So she made him tip it out. More yells from Christopher, of course. Honestly, that kid can be diabolical sometimes. Funny, isn't it? I mean, us being there on that very same afternoon.'

Jonathan said: 'Why do you think they were so interested in the sand?'

'That's what Dad wanted to know. That detective, the one who was here and interviewed me, said that they might find a footprint and want to eliminate it if it belonged to one of us. Dad reckons they must have found a footprint. A couple of young detectives, very nice they were, came to see Dad and Mum yesterday evening. They asked Dad and Mum what shoes they had been wearing and they actually asked if they could take them away. Well, they wouldn't do that, would they, if they hadn't found something?'

Jonathan said: 'It must have been a terrible worry to your dad and mum.'

'Oh no, it didn't bother them. After all, we weren't there when she died, were we? After we left the headland we drove to have tea with Gran at Hunstanton. We didn't leave until half-past nine. Far too late for Christopher, Mum said. He slept in the car all the way home, mind you. But it was funny though, wasn't it? Being there on the very day. If she'd been killed a few hours earlier we'd actually have seen the body. I don't think we'll go back to that part of the beach again. I wouldn't go there after dark for a thousand pounds. I'd be frightened I might see her ghost. Funny about the sand, though, isn't it? I mean, if they do find a footprint and it helps them to catch the murderer it will all be because of Christopher wanting to play on the beach and Mum making him spill out the sand. I mean, it was such a little thing. Mum said it reminded her of Vicar's sermon last Sunday when he preached about how even our smallest actions can have immense consequences. I didn't remember it. I mean, I like singing in the choir, but Mr Smollett's sermons are dead boring.'

So small a thing, a footprint in soft sand. And if that footprint was made in the sand spilled by Christopher from his bucket, then it was made by someone who had used that path after half-past three on Sunday afternoon.

He said: 'How many people here know about this? Have you told anyone except the police?'

'No one but you. They said that we weren't to talk and I haven't, not until now. I know Mrs Simpson was curious why I asked to see Chief Inspector Rickards. She kept saying that she couldn't see what I could tell them and that I wasn't to waste police time trying to make myself important. I suppose she was worried thinking I'd tell them about the row she and Miss Robarts had when Dr Gledhill's personal file was missing and Dr Mair had it all the time. But you won't tell, will you? Not even Miss Amphlett?'

'No,' he promised. 'I won't tell. Not even her.'

34

There was a surprising number of detective agencies in the yellow pages and apparently very little to choose between them. He chose one of the largest and wrote down the London telephone number. It wouldn't do to telephone from the power station and he didn't want to wait until he got home where there would be even less privacy. He was anxious, too, to ring as soon as possible. His plan was to lunch at a local pub and find a public call box.

The morning seemed interminable but at twelve o'clock he said that he was taking an early lunch hour and left, checking first that he had sufficient small coins. The nearest kiosk was, he knew, in the village close to the general store. It was a public position but he told himself that there was no need for particular secrecy.

His call was quickly answered by a woman. He had prepared what he would say and she seemed to find nothing strange in the request. But it became apparent that it wouldn't be as easy as he had hoped. Yes, she said, the agency could certainly hope to trace an individual from the information provided but there was no fixed charge. Everything depended on the difficulty and how long it took. Until his request had been formally received it was impossible even to give an estimate. The cost might be as little as £200 or as much as £400. She suggested that he should write in immediately, setting out all the information in his possession and stating clearly what he required. The letter should be accompanied by a down payment of £100. They would certainly deal with it as a matter of urgency, but until the request was received they could give no assurance of how long it would take. He thanked her, said that he would write, and put down the receiver, glad that he hadn't given her his name. Somehow he had imagined that they would take the information down over the telephone, tell him what the cost would be, promise him a quick result. It was all too formal, too expensive, too slow. He wondered whether to try another agency, then told himself that in this highly competitive field they were unlikely to give him any more encouraging news.

By the time he had got back to the power station and parked his car he had almost persuaded himself not to proceed. And then it occurred to him that he might make his own inquiries. The name was unusual enough; there might be an Amphlett in the London telephone directory and if not in London it might be worth trying some of the larger cities. And her father had been a soldier. Perhaps there was an army directory – wasn't it called the Army List? – which he could consult. It would be worth doing a little research before committing himself to expenditure he might not be able to meet, and the thought of writing to a detective agency, of actually putting his request down on paper, discouraged him. He began to feel like a conspirator, an unfamiliar role which both excited and ministered to some part of his nature which he hadn't previously known existed. He would work alone and if he were unsuccessful it would be time to think again.

And the first step was remarkably straightforward, so simple that he blushed at his folly at not having thought of it earlier. Back in the library he consulted the London telephone directory. There was a P. C. Amphlett with an address in Pont Street, SW1. He stared at it for a moment then with trembling fingers took out his notebook and jotted down the telephone number. The initials were those of Caroline's mother, but the entry bore no prefix. The subscriber could easily be a man. It could be a coincidence. And the name Pont Street meant nothing to him although he didn't think that SW1 could be a poor area of London. But would she have told him a lie which could be detected merely by consulting the telephone directory? Only if she were so confident of her dominance, of his enslavement to her, so certain of his inadequacy and stupidity that she hadn't needed to care. She had wanted that alibi and he had given it. And if this were a lie, if he visited Pont Street and discovered that her mother wasn't living in poverty, what else that she had told him had been true? When exactly had she been on the headland and for what purpose? But these were suspicions which he knew he could not seriously entertain. The idea that Caroline had killed Hilary Robarts was ridiculous. But why hadn't she been willing to tell the police the truth?

But he knew now what his next move would be. On the way home he would telephone the Pont Street number and ask for Caroline. That at least should prove whether or not it was her mother's address. And if it was then he would take a day's leave or wait until Saturday, make an excuse to have a day in London and check for himself.

The afternoon dragged on endlessly and it was difficult to keep his mind on his work. He was worried, too, in case Caroline should appear, should suggest that he go home with her. But she seemed to be avoiding him and he was grateful. He left ten minutes early, making the excuse of a headache, and within twenty minutes was back at the telephone kiosk in Lydsett. The number rang for almost half a minute and he had nearly given up hope when it was answered. A woman's voice slowly and distinctly spoke the number. He had decided to assume a Scottish accent. He knew himself to be quite a good mimic and his maternal grandmother had been a Scot. There would be no difficulty in making it convincing. He said: 'Is Miss Caroline Amphlett at home, please?'

There was a long silence, then the woman said repressively: 'Who is that speaking?'

'My name is John McLean. We're old friends.'

'Indeed, Mr McLean. Then how strange that I don't know you and that you, apparently, don't know that Miss Amphlett no longer lives here.'

'Then could you give me her address, please?'

Again there was a silence. Then the voice said: 'I hardly think I would care to do that, Mr McLean. But if you wish to leave a message I will see that it reaches her.'

He asked: 'Is that her mother speaking?'

The voice laughed. It was not an agreeable laugh. Then she said: 'No, I'm not her mother. This is Miss Beasley, the house-keeper, speaking. But did you really need to ask?'

And then it occurred to him that there could be two Caroline Amphletts, two mothers with the same initials. The chance was surely remote, but it would be as well to make sure. He said: 'Does Caroline still work at Larksoken Power Station?'

And this time there could be no mistake. Her voice was harsh with dislike as she answered. 'If you know that, Mr McLean, why bother to ring me.'

And the telephone receiver was firmly replaced.

35

It was after 10.30 on the Tuesday night when Rickards came for the second time to Larksoken Mill. He had telephoned his intention shortly after six o'clock and had made it clear that the visit, although late, was official; there were facts he wanted to check and a question he needed to ask. Earlier in the day Dalgliesh had called in at the incident room at Hoveton and made a statement describing the finding of the body. Rickards hadn't been there, but Oliphant, obviously on his way out, had stayed to receive him and had briefly filled him in on the state of the investigation, not unwillingly but with a certain formality which suggested that he was under instructions. And Rickards himself, as he dragged off his jacket and seated himself in the same high-backed chair to the right of the fire, seemed a little chastened. He was wearing a dark blue, pin-striped suit which, for all its over-careful tailoring, had the slightly seedy and rejected air of a suit relegated to second-best. But it still looked odd and inappropriately citified on his gangling limbs, particularly here on the headland, giving him the air of a man dressed for an informal wedding or a job interview from which he had little hope of success. The thinly veiled antagonism, the bitterness of failure after the death of the Whistler, and even the restless energy of Sunday night had left him. Dalgliesh wondered whether he had spoken to the Chief Constable and received advice. If so, he could guess what it had been. It was much the same as he himself would have given.

'It's irritating that he's on your patch, but he's one of the

Met's senior detectives, the Commissioner's blue-eyed boy. And he knows these people. He was at the Mair dinner party. He found the body. He's got useful information. All right, he's a professional, he's not going to withhold it, but you'll get it more easily and make life more agreeable for both of you if you stop treating him like a rival, or worse, a suspect.'

Handing Rickards his whisky, Dalgliesh inquired after his wife.

'She's fine, fine.' But there was something forced in his tone.

Dalgliesh said: 'I suppose now the Whistler's dead, she'll be coming home.'

'You'd think so, wouldn't you? I'd like it, she'd like it, but there's the little problem of Sue's ma. She doesn't want her ewe-lamb mixed up with any unpleasantness, particularly murder, and particularly just now.'

Dalgliesh said: 'It's difficult to isolate yourself from unpleasantness, even murder, if you marry a police officer.'

'She never intended Sue to marry a police officer.'

Dalgliesh was surprised at the bitterness in his voice. Again, he was uncomfortably aware that he was being asked for some kind of assurance which he, of all men, was least competent to give. While he was searching for the anodyne phrase he glanced again at Rickards's face, at the look of weariness, almost of defeat, at the lines which the fitful light of the wood fire made even more cavernous, and took refuge in practicality.

He asked: 'Have you eaten?'

'Oh, I'll get myself something from the fridge when I get back.'

'There's the remains of a cassoulet, if you'd like it. It won't take a moment to heat up.'

'Wouldn't say no, Mr Dalgliesh.'

He ate the cassoulet from a tray on his lap, voraciously, as if it was his first meal for days, and afterwards mopped up the sauce with a crust of bread. Only once did he look up from his plate to ask: 'Did you cook this, Mr Dalgliesh?'

'If you live alone you have to learn at least simple cooking if you're not prepared to be always dependent on someone else for one of the essentials of life.'

'And that wouldn't suit you, would it? Dependent on someone else for an essential of life?'

But he spoke without bitterness and carried the tray and the empty plate back into the kitchen with a smile. A second later Dalgliesh heard the splash of running water. Rickards was washing up his plate.

He must have been hungrier than he had realized. Dalgliesh knew how mistakenly easy it was, when working a sixteen-hour day, to suppose that one could function effectively on a diet of coffee and snatched sandwiches. Returning from the kitchen, Rickards leaned back in his chair with a small grunt of contentment. The colour had returned to his face and when he spoke his voice was strong again.

'Her dad was Peter Robarts. Remember him?'

'No, should I?'

'No reason. Nor did I, but I've had time to look him up. He made a packet after the war in which, incidentally, he served with some distinction. One of those chaps with an eye for the main chance, which in his case was plastics. It must have been quite a time for the wide boys, the 1950s and 60s. She was his only child. He made his fortune quickly and he lost it as fast. The usual reasons; extravagance, ostentatious generosity, women, throwing his money around as if he were printing it, thinking his luck would hold, whatever the odds. He was lucky not to end up inside. The fraud squad had put together a nice little case against him and were within days of making an arrest when he had his coronary. Slumped forward into his lunch plate at Simpson's as dead as the duck he was eating. It must have been difficult for her; daddy's little girl one day, nothing too good, and then near-disgrace, death, poverty.'

Dalgliesh said: 'Relative poverty, but that, of course, is what poverty is. You've been busy.'

'Some, but not much, we got from Mair, some we had to grub around for. The City of London police have been helpful. I've been speaking to Wood Street. I used to tell myself that nothing about the victim was irrelevant but I'm beginning to wonder if much of this grubbing about isn't a waste of time.'

Dalgliesh said: 'It's the only safe way to work. The victim dies because she is uniquely herself.'

'"And once you comprehend the life, you comprehend the

death." Old Blanco White – remember him? – used to drum that into us when I was a young DC. And what do you get in the end? A jumble of facts like an upturned waste-paper basket. They don't really add up to a person. And with this victim the pickings are small. She travelled light. There was little worth finding in that cottage, no diary, no letters except one to her solicitor making an appointment for next weekend telling him she expected to be married. We've seen him, of course. He doesn't know the name of the man and nor, apparently, does anyone else, including Mair. We found no other papers of importance except a copy of her will. And there's nothing exciting about that. She left everything she had to Alex Mair in two lines of bald lawyer's prose. But I can't see Mair killing her for twelve thousand pounds on NatWest's special reserve account and a practically derelict cottage with a sitting tenant. Apart from the will and that one letter, only the usual bank statements, receipted bills, the place obsessively tidy. You could imagine she knew she was going to die and had tidied away her life. No sign of a recent search, incidentally. If there was something in the cottage the murderer wanted, and he smashed that window to get it, he covered his tracks pretty effectively.'

Dalgliesh said: 'If he did have to smash the window to get in then he probably wasn't Dr Mair. Mair knew that the key was in the locket. He could have taken it, used it and put it back. There would be an additional risk of leaving evidence at the scene, and some murderers dislike returning to the body. Others, of course, feel a compulsion to do so. But if Mair did take the key, he'd have had to put it back whatever the risk. An empty locket would have pointed directly to him.'

Rickards said: 'Cyril Alexander Mair, but he's dropped the Cyril. Probably thinks Sir Alexander Mair will sound better than Sir Cyril. What's wrong with Cyril? My grandfather was called Cyril. I've got a prejudice against people who don't use their proper names. She was his mistress, incidentally.'

'Did he tell you?'

'More or less had to, didn't he? They were very discreet but one or two of the senior staff at the station must have known, known or suspected it, anyway. He's too intelligent to keep back information he knows we're bound to discover sooner or later. His story is that the affair was over, a natural end by common consent. He expects to move to London; she wanted to stay here. Well, she more or less had to unless she gave up her job, and she was a career woman, the job was important. His story is that what they felt for each other wasn't robust enough to be sustained by occasional weekend meetings – his words not mine. You'd think that the whole affair was a matter of convenience. While he was here he needed a woman, she needed a man. The goods have to be handy. No point if you're a hundred miles apart. Rather like buying meat. He's moving to London, she decided to stay. Find another butcher.'

Dalgliesh remembered that Rickards had always been slightly censorious about sex. He could hardly have been a detective for twenty years without encountering adultery and fornication in their various guises, apart from the more bizarre and horrifying manifestations of human sexuality beside which adultery and fornication were comfortingly normal. But this didn't mean that he liked them. He had taken his oath as a police constable and kept it. He had made his marriage vows in church and no doubt intended to keep them. And in a job where irregular hours, drink, macho camaraderie and the propinquity of women police officers made marriages vulnerable his was known to be solid. He was too experienced and basically too fair to allow himself to be prejudiced, but in one respect at least Mair was unlucky in the detective assigned to the case.

Rickards said: 'Her secretary, Katie Flack, had just given notice. Found her too demanding, apparently. There was a recent row over the girl's taking more than her allotted lunch hour. And one of her staff, Brian Taylor, admits that he found her impossible to work for and had asked for a transfer. Admirably frank about it all. He can afford to be. He was at a friend's stag party at the Maid's Head in Norwich with at least ten witnesses from eight o'clock onwards. And the girl hasn't anything to worry about, either. She spent the evening watching TV with her family.'

Dalgliesh asked: 'Just the family?'

'No. Luckily for her the neighbours called in just before nine to discuss the dresses for their daughter's wedding. She's to be a bridesmaid. Lemon dresses with bouquets of small white and yellow chrysanthemums. Very tasteful. We got a full description. I suppose she thought it added to the verisimilitude of the alibi. Anyway, they were neither of them serious suspects. These days if you don't like your boss you pack in the job. Both of them were shocked, of course, and slightly defensive. They probably felt she'd got herself killed on purpose to put them in the wrong. Neither of them pretended that they had liked her. But there was something stronger than dislike about this killing. And this may surprise you, Mr Dalgliesh. Robarts wasn't particularly unpopular with the senior staff. They respect efficiency and she was efficient. Besides, her responsibilities didn't directly impinge on theirs. It was her job to see that the station was efficiently administered so that the scientific and technical staff could do their job most effectively. Apparently that's what she did. They answered my questions without fuss but they weren't particularly forthcoming. There's a kind of camaraderie about the place. I suppose if you feel yourself constantly under criticism or attack it makes for a certain wariness in dealing with outsiders. Only one of them said he actually disliked her, Miles Lessingham. But he has produced an alibi of a kind. He claims to have been on his boat at the time of death. And he made no secret of his feelings. He didn't want to eat with her or drink with her or spend his spare time with her or go to bed with her. But, as he pointed out, he feels that about a number of people and hasn't found any impulse to murder them.' He paused for a moment, then said, 'Dr Mair showed you round the power station on Friday morning, didn't he?'

Dalgliesh asked: 'Did he tell you that?'

'Dr Mair didn't tell me anything he didn't actually have to tell me. No, it came out when we were talking to one of the junior staff, a local girl who works in the establishment department. Chatty little thing. I got a lot of useful stuff out of her one way or another. I was wondering if anything happened on your visit which could be relevant.'

Dalgliesh resisted the temptation to reply that if there had been he would have said so before now. He replied: 'It was an interesting visit and the place rather impressive. Dr Mair attempted to explain to me the difference between the thermal reactor and the new pressurized water reactor. Most of the talk was technical except when he spoke briefly about poetry. Miles Lessingham showed me the high fuelling machine from which Toby Gledhill plunged to his death. It did strike me that Gledhill's suicide could be relevant but I don't see how. It was obviously distressing to Lessingham, and not only because he witnessed it. There was a rather cryptic exchange at the Mairs' dinner party between him and Hilary Robarts.'

Rickards crouched forward, his huge hand cradling the whisky glass. Without looking up, he said: 'The Mair dinner party. I reckon that cosy little gathering – if it was cosy – is at the nub of this case. And there's something I wanted to ask you. That's really why I'm here. That child, Theresa Blaney, exactly how much of the conversation about the latest Whistler victim did she overhear?'

It was the question Dalgliesh had been expecting. What surprised him was how long it had taken Rickards to ask it.

He said carefully: 'Some of it, undoubtedly. You know that, I've told you already. I couldn't say how long she'd been standing behind the dining-room door before I noticed her or how much of the conversation she actually heard.'

'Can you remember what stage in his account Lessingham had reached at the time you saw Theresa?'

'I can't be certain. I think he was describing the body, exactly what he saw when he returned with his torch.'

'So she could have heard about the cut on the forehead and the pubic hair.'

'But would she have told her father about the hair? She had a devotedly religious mother, an RC. I don't really know the child but I imagine that she's unusually modest. Would a gently nurtured, modest girl tell that to any man, even to her father?'

'Gently nurtured? Modest? You're sixty years out of date. Spend half an hour in any secondary-school playground and you'll hear things that'll curl your hair. Today's kids will say anything to anyone.'

'Not that child.'

'All right, but she could have told her dad about the L-shaped cut and he could have guessed about the hair. Damn it, everyone knew that the Whistler's murders must have had a sexual connotation. He didn't rape them, but that wasn't how he got his kicks. You don't need to be Krafft – what's his name?'

'Krafft-Ebing.'

'Sounds like a cheese. You don't need to be Krafft-Ebing, you don't even need to be sexually sophisticated, to guess what kind of hair the Whistler helped himself to.'

Dalgliesh said: 'But this is important, isn't it, if you're casting Blaney as chief suspect? Would he, or anyone else, kill that way if he wasn't certain about the Whistler's method? He could only hope to pin it on the Whistler by getting all the details right. If you can't prove that Theresa told her father both about the hair and the L-shaped cut your case is considerably weakened. I would doubt whether you had one. Besides, I thought that Oliphant said that Blaney had an alibi both from Miss Mair, who said he was drunk and at home by 9.45, and from his daughter. Wasn't her story that she went to bed at 8.15 and came down just before nine o'clock to get herself a drink of water?'

'That's what she said, Mr Dalgliesh. But I'll tell you this: that child would confirm any story that her dad chose to tell. And the timing is suspiciously accurate. Robarts dies at 9.20 or as near as damn it. Theresa Blaney goes to bed at 8.15 and conveniently needs a drink of water forty-five minutes later. I wish you could have seen her, and seen that cottage. But of course you have. Two WPCs from the juvenile bureau were with me and they treated her as tenderly as a babe in arms. Not that she needed it. We all sat round the fire in a cosy little circle and she held the kid in her lap. Ever tried questioning a child to discover if her dad's a murderer while she's sitting there gazing at you with those huge reproachful eyes and nursing a baby? I suggested that she hand the kid over to one of the WPCs but as soon as she tried to take him he immediately started up a howling. Wouldn't let his dad take him either. You'd think that Theresa and he had arranged it between them. And Ryan Blaney was there too, of course, throughout the interview. You can't question a child without the parent being present if the parent wants to be. My God, when I arrest someone for this murder, and I shall, Mr Dalgliesh, this time I shall, I hope it doesn't have to be Ryan Blaney. Those kids have lost enough already. But he's got the strongest motive of all, and he hated Robarts. I don't think he could conceal that hatred if he tried, and he didn't even attempt to try. And it's not only that she was trying to force him out of Scudder's Cottage. It goes deeper than that. I don't know what's at the root of it. Something to do with his wife, maybe. But I'll find out. He left the kids in the cottage and walked out with us to the cars. The last thing he said was: "She was an evil bitch and I'm glad she's dead. But I didn't kill her, and you can't prove I did."

'And I know the objections. Jago says he telephoned at 7.30 to let him know the Whistler was dead. He spoke to Theresa and the kid says she told her dad. No reason why she shouldn't tell him. I think we take it that she did. He wouldn't have left the kids alone in that cottage with the Whistler alive and on the prowl. No responsible father would, and it's generally admitted he's a responsible father. We've got the local authority's word for that, by the way. A fortnight ago they sent a social worker just to check that everything was all right. And I'll tell you who instigated that, Mr Dalgliesh. Now, this is interesting. It was Robarts.'

'Did she make any specific allegations?'

'None. Her story was that she had to visit from time to time to discuss repairs and so on, and that she was concerned at the weight of responsibility he was carrying and thought he could do with some help. Talked about seeing Theresa lugging heavy shopping home with the twins tagging along, sometimes when Theresa should have been at school. Phoned the local authority to send a social worker along. The social worker satisfied herself, apparently, that things were going as well as could be expected. The twins are already attending a playgroup and she offered additional services including a home help, but she didn't find Blaney either welcoming or co-operative. Don't know that I blame him. I wouldn't want the welfare on my back.'

'Does Blaney know that Hilary Robarts instigated the visit?'

'The local authority didn't tell him; it isn't their policy. And I don't see how he could have found out. But if he did find out, it considerably strengthens his motive, doesn't it? That visit could have been the last straw.'

Dalgliesh said: 'But would he have killed in that way? Logically, the knowledge that the Whistler was dead negatives the method.'

'Not necessarily, Mr Dalgliesh. Suppose it's a double-bluff. Suppose he's saying in effect, "Look, I can prove I knew the Whistler was dead. Whoever killed Hilary Robarts didn't know. So why aren't you looking for someone who hadn't been told that the Whistler's body had been found?" And by God, Mr Dalgliesh, there's another possibility. Suppose he knew that the Whistler was dead but thought that it was very recent. I asked Theresa precisely what George Jago had said to her. She remembered accurately, anyway Jago confirmed it. Apparently he said, "Tell your dad the Whistler is dead. Killed himself. Just now, over at Easthaven." But no mention of the hotel, nor of when the Whistler booked in. Jago didn't know any of that. The message he'd got from his mate at the Crown and Anchor was pretty garbled. So Blaney could have assumed that the body was found in open country just five miles down the coast. He can kill with impunity. Everyone, including the police, will assume that the Whistler has claimed his last victim then done away with himself. My God, Mr Dalgliesh, that's neat.'

Dalgliesh privately thought that it was more neat than convincing. He said: 'So you're assuming that the smashed portrait isn't directly connected with the murder. I can't see Blaney destroying his own work.'

'Why not? From what I saw of it, it wasn't anything special.'

'I think it was to him.'

'The portrait is a puzzle, I'll grant you that. And that's not the only difficulty. Someone had a drink with Robarts before she took that last swim, someone she let into the cottage, someone she knew. There were those two glasses on the draining board and, in my book, that means two people were drinking. She wouldn't have invited Blaney to Thyme Cottage and if he turned up I doubt if she would have let him in, drunk or sober.'

Dalgliesh said: 'But if you believe Miss Mair, your case against Blaney collapses anyway. She claims to have seen him at Scudder's Cottage at 9.45, or shortly afterwards, and he was then half drunk. All right, he could have feigned his drunkenness; that wouldn't present much difficulty. What he couldn't do was to kill Hilary Robarts at about 9.20 and get home by 9.45, not without the use of a car or van which he didn't have.'

Rickards said: 'Or a bicycle.'

'It would need fast pedalling. We know that she died after her swim, not before. Her hair was still damp at the roots when I found her. So you're probably safe enough in putting the time of death at between 9.15 and 9.30. And he couldn't have taken the bicycle with him and ridden back along the shore. The tide was high; he'd have been riding over the shingle which would be more difficult than the road. There's only one part of the shore where you get a stretch of sand at high tide and that's the small cove where Hilary Robarts swam. And if he had been on the road Miss Mair must have seen him. She's given him an alibi which I don't think you'll be able to break.'

Rickards said: 'But he hasn't given her one, has he? Her story is that she was alone in Martyr's Cottage until she left just after 9.30 to collect the portrait. She and that housekeeper at the Old Rectory, Mrs Dennison, are the only ones who were at the Mairs' dinner party who made no attempt to produce an alibi. And she has a motive. Hilary Robarts was her brother's mistress. I know he tells us it was over, but we've only his word for that. Suppose they'd planned to marry when he goes to London. She's devoted her life to her brother. Unmarried. No other outlet for her emotions. Why give way to another woman just when Mair is about to achieve his ambition?'

Dalgliesh thought that this was an altogether too facile explanation of a relationship which, even on his brief acquaintance, had seemed more complicated. He said: 'She's a successful professional writer. I imagine that success provides its own form of emotional fulfilment, assuming she needs it. She seemed to me very much her own woman.'

'I thought she wrote cookery books. Is that what you call being a successful professional writer?'

'Alice Mair's books are highly regarded and extremely lucrative. We share the same publisher. If he had to make a choice between us, he'd probably prefer to lose me.'

'So you think the marriage might almost be a relief, release her from responsibilities? Let another woman cook and care for him for a change?'

'Why should he need any woman to care for him? It's dangerous to theorize about people and their emotions, but I doubt whether she feels that kind of domestic, quasi-maternal responsibility or whether he either needs or wants it.'

'How do you see it then, the relationship? They live together, after all, most of the time anyway. She's fond of him, that seems to be generally accepted.'

'They'd hardly live together if they weren't, if you can call it living together. She's away a great deal, I understand, researching her books, and he has a London flat. How can someone who's only met them together across the table at a dinner party get to the heart of their relationship? I should have thought that there was loyalty, trust, mutual respect. Ask them.'

'But not jealousy, of him or his mistress?'

'If there is, she's clever at concealing it.'

'All right, Mr Dalgliesh, take another scenario. Suppose he was tired of Robarts, suppose she's pressing him to marry her, wants to quit the job, move to London with him. Suppose she's making herself a nuisance. Wouldn't Alice Mair feel like doing something about that?'

'Like devising and carrying out a singularly ingenious murder to relieve her brother of a temporary embarrassment? Isn't that carrying sisterly devotion to unreasonable lengths?'

'Ah, but they aren't temporary embarrassments, are they, these determined women? Think. How many men do you know who've been forced into marriages they didn't really want because the woman's will was stronger than theirs? Or because they couldn't stand all the fuss, the tears, recriminations, the emotional blackmail?'

Dalgliesh said: 'She could hardly blackmail him with the relationship itself. Neither was married; they weren't deceiving anyone; they weren't causing public scandal. And I can't see anyone, man or woman, coercing Alex Mair into something he didn't want to do. I know it's dangerous to make facile judgements, although that's what we've been doing for the last five minutes, but he seems to me a man who lives his life on his own terms and probably always has.'

'Which might make him vicious if someone tried to stop him.'

'So now you're casting him as murderer?'

'I'm casting him as a strong suspect.'

Dalgliesh asked: 'What about that couple at the caravan? Is there any evidence that they knew about the Whistler's methods?'

'None that we could discover, but how certain can you be? The man, Neil Pascoe, gets about in that van of his, drinks in local pubs. He could have heard some talk. Not every policeman on the case has necessarily been discreet. We've kept the details out of the papers but that doesn't mean that there hasn't been talk. He's got an alibi of sorts. He took the van just south of Norwich to talk to a chap there who'd written to him expressing interest in PANUP, that anti-nuclear organization of his. Had some hopes, apparently, of getting a group started there. I sent a couple of DCs to see the chap. He says they were together until just after 8.20 when Pascoe started for home – said he was starting for home, anyway. The girl he lives with, Amy Camm, says he got back to the caravan by nine and they were together for the rest of the evening. My guess is that he got back a bit later. In that van he must have been pushing it a bit to get from beyond Norwich to Larksoken in forty minutes. And he's got a motive, one of the strongest. If Hilary Robarts had gone ahead with her libel action it could have ruined him. And it's in Camm's interests to support the alibi. She's got herself very cosily fixed up with the kid in that caravan. I'll tell you something else, Mr Dalgliesh, they had a dog once. The lead is still hanging inside the caravan.'

'But if one or both of them used it to strangle Robarts, would it be?'

'People might have seen it. They might have thought it would have been more suspicious to destroy or hide it than to leave it there. We took it away, of course, but it was little more than a formality. Robarts's skin was unbroken. There'll be no physical traces. And if we do manage to get prints, they'll be hers and his. We shall go on checking the alibis, obviously. Every blasted employee at that station, and there are over five hundred of them. You'd never believe that, would you? You go in the place and hardly set sight on a soul. They seem to move through the countryside as invisibly as the energy they're generating. Most of them live at Cromer or Norwich. They want to be near schools and shops, presumably. Only a handful choose to live near the station. Most of the Sunday day shift were home well before ten and virtuously watching the telly or out with their friends. We shall check on them whether or not they had anything to do with Robarts at work. But it's only a formality. I know where to look for my suspects, the guests at that dinner party. Due to Lessingham's inability to keep his mouth shut they were told two crucial facts; that the hair stuffed into her mouth was pubic hair and the mark on the forehead was an L. So that narrows the field very conveniently. Alex Mair, Alice Mair, Margaret Dennison, Lessingham himself, and, assuming that Theresa Blaney reported the conversation to her father, you can add Blaney. All right, I may not be able to break his alibi, his or Mair's, but I shall have a damn good try.'

Ten minutes later Rickards got to his feet and said it was time to get home. Dalgliesh walked with him to his car. The cloud level was low, the earth and sky subsumed in the same obliterating darkness in which the cold glitter of the power station seemed to have moved closer, and there lay over the sea a pale blue luminosity, like the faint semblance of a newly discovered Milky Way. Even to feel the ground strike hard beneath their feet was disorientating in this blackness and for a few seconds both men hesitated as if the ten yards to the car, gleaming like some floating spacecraft in the light spilling from the open door, was an odyssey over dangerous and insubstantial ground. Above them the sails of the mill gleamed white and silent, potent with latent power. For a moment Dalgliesh had the illusion that they were about to begin slowly turning.

Rickards said: 'Everything on this headland is contrast. After I left Pascoe's caravan this morning I stood on those low sandy cliffs and looked south. There was nothing but an old fishing smack, a coiled rope, an upturned box, that awful sea. It must have looked like that for near on a thousand years. And then I faced north and saw that bloody great power station. There it is, glittering away. And I'm seeing it under the shadow of the windmill. Does it work, by the way? The mill, I mean.'

Dalgliesh said: 'I'm told so. The sails turn but it doesn't grind. The original millstones are in the lower chamber. Occasionally I have a wish to see the sails slowly turning, but I resist. I'm not sure, once started, whether I could stop them. It would be irritating to hear them creaking away all night.'

They had reached the car but Rickards, pausing with his hand on the door, seemed reluctant to get in. He said: 'We've moved a long way, haven't we, between this mill and the power station? What is it? Four miles of headland and three hundred years of progress. And then I think of those two bodies in the morgue and wonder if we've progressed at all. Dad would have talked about original sin. He was a lay preacher, was Dad. He had it all worked out.'

So had mine, come to that, thought Dalgliesh. He said: 'Lucky Dad.' There was a moment's silence broken by the sound of the telephone, its insistent peal clearly heard through the open door. Dalgliesh said: 'You'd better wait a moment. It could be for you.'

It was. Oliphant's voice asked if Chief Inspector Rickards was there. He wasn't at his home and Dalgliesh's number was one of those which he'd left.

The call was brief. Less than a minute later Rickards joined him at the open door. The slight melancholy of the last few minutes had fallen away and his step was buoyant.

'It could have waited until tomorrow but Oliphant wanted me to know. This could be the breakthrough we've needed. There's been a call from the lab. They must have been working on it non-stop. Oliphant told you, I imagine, that we found a footprint.'

'He did mention it. On the right-hand side of the path in soft sand. He didn't give any details.'

And Dalgliesh, punctilious in not discussing a case with a junior officer in the absence of Rickards, hadn't asked.

'We've just got confirmation. It's the sole of a Bumble trainer, the right foot. Size ten. The pattern on the sole is unique, apparently, and they have a yellow bee on each heel. You must have seen them.' Then, when Dalgliesh didn't reply, he said: 'For God's sake, Mr Dalgliesh, don't tell me that you own a pair. That's a complication I can do without.'

'No, I don't own them. Bumbles are too fashionable for me. But I've seen a pair recently and here on the headland.'

'On whose feet?'

'They weren't on any feet.' He thought for a moment, then said: 'I remember now. Last Wednesday morning, the day after I arrived, I took some of my aunt's clothes, including two pairs of her shoes, to the Old Rectory for the church jumble. They keep a couple of tea chests in an old scullery there where people can leave things they don't want. The back door was open as it usually is in daylight so I didn't bother to knock. There was a pair of Bumbles among the other shoes. Or, more accurately, I saw the heel of one shoe. I imagine the other was there but I didn't see it.'

'On top of the chest?'

'No, about a third down. I think they were in a transparent plastic bag. As I say, I didn't see the whole pair but I did glimpse one heel with the unmistakable yellow bee. It's possible that they were Toby Gledhill's. Lessingham mentioned that he was wearing Bumbles when he killed himself.'

'And you left the trainers there. You see the importance of what you're saying, Mr Dalgliesh?'

'Yes, I see the importance of what I'm saying and yes, I left the shoe there. I was donating jumble, not stealing it.'

Rickards said: 'If there was a pair, and common sense suggests that there was, anyone could have taken them. And if they're no longer in the chest, it looks as though somebody did.' He glanced at the luminous dial of his watch and said: 'Eleven forty-five. What time do you suppose Mrs Dennison goes to bed?'

Dalgliesh said firmly: 'Earlier than this, I imagine. And she'd hardly go to bed without bolting the back door. So if someone did take them and they're still missing, they can't be returned tonight.'

They had reached the car. Rickards, with his hand on the door, didn't reply but gazed out over the headland as if in thought. His excitement, carefully controlled and unspoken, was as palpable as if he had banged his fists against the car bonnet. Then he unlocked the door and slipped inside. The headlights cut into the darkness like searchlights.

As he wound down the window to say a final goodnight, Dalgliesh said: 'There's something I ought perhaps to mention about Meg Dennison. I don't know whether you remember, but she was the teacher at the centre of that race row in inner London. I imagine that she's had about as much interrogation as she can take. That means the interview might not be easy for you.'

He had thought carefully before he spoke, knowing that it might be a mistake. It was a mistake. The warning, however carefully phrased, had sparked off that latent antagonism of which he was uneasily aware in all his dealings with Rickards.

Rickards said: 'What you mean, Mr Dalgliesh, is that it might not be easy for her. I've already spoken to the lady and I know something about her past. It took a lot of courage to stand up for her principles as she did. Some might say a lot of obstinacy. A woman who is capable of that has guts enough for anything, wouldn't you say?'

36

Dalgliesh watched the car lights until Rickards reached the coastal road and turned right, then locked the door and began a desultory tidying-up before bed. Looking back over the evening he recognized that he had been reluctant to talk to Rickards at length about his Friday morning visit to Larksoken Power Station and less than open about his reactions, perhaps because they had been more complex and the place itself more impressive than he had expected. He had been asked to arrive by 8.45 since Mair wanted to escort him personally and had to leave for a luncheon appointment in London. At the beginning of the visit he had asked: 'How much do you know about nuclear power?'

'Very little. Perhaps it might be wiser to assume that I know nothing.'

'In that case we'd better begin with the usual preamble about sources of radiation, and what is meant by nuclear power, nuclear energy and atomic energy, before we begin our tour of the plant. I've asked Miles Lessingham as Operations Superintendent to join us.'

It was the beginning of an extraordinary two hours. Dalgliesh, escorted by his two mentors, was garbed in protective clothing, divested of it, checked for radioactivity, subjected to an almost constant stream of facts and figures. He was aware, even coming as an outsider, that the station was run with exceptional efficiency, that a quietly competent and respected authority was in control. Alex Mair, ostensibly there to escort a man afforded the status of a distinguished visitor, was never uninvolved, always quietly watchful, obviously in charge. And the staff Dalgliesh met impressed him with their dedication as they patiently explained their jobs in terms which an intelligent layman could understand. He sensed beneath their professionalism a commitment to nuclear power amounting in some cases to a controlled enthusiasm combined with a defensiveness which was probably natural given the public's ambivalence about nuclear energy. When one of the engineers said: 'It's a dangerous technology but we need it and we can manage it', he heard, not the arrogance of scientific certainty but a reverence for the element which they controlled, almost the love-hate relationship of a sailor for the sea which was both a respected enemy and his natural habitat. If the tour had been designed to reassure, then it had to some extent succeeded. If nuclear power was safe in any hands then it would be safe in these. But how safe, and for how long?

He had stood in the great turbine hall, ears pulsating, while Mair produced his facts and figures about pressures, voltages and breaking capacity; had stood, garbed in protective clothing, and looked down where the spent elements lay like sinister fishes underwater in the fuel cooling pond for a hundred days before being dispatched to Sellafield for reprocessing; had walked to the edge of the sea to look at the cooling water plant and condensers. But the most interesting part of the visit had been in the reactor house. Mair, summoned by a bleep from his intercom, had temporarily left them and Dalgliesh was alone with Lessingham. They had stood on a high walkway looking down at the black charge floors of the two reactors. To one side of the reactor was one of the two immense fuelling machines. Remembering Toby Gledhill, Dalgliesh glanced at his companion. Lessingham's face was taut and so white that Dalgliesh feared that he was about to faint. Then he spoke almost like an automaton, reciting a lesson learned by rote.

'There are 26,488 fuel elements in each reactor and they're charged by the fuelling machinery over a period of five to ten years. Each of the fuelling machines is approximately 23 feet high and weighs 115 tons. It can hold 14 fuel elements as well as the other components which are necessary for the refuelling cycle. The pressure vessel is heavily shielded, with cast-iron and densified wood. What you see mounted on top of the machine is the hoist unit for lifting the fuel elements. There is also a connecting unit which couples the machine to the reactor and a television camera which allows viewing of the operations above the magazine.'

He broke off and, looking at him, Dalgliesh saw that the hands gripping the rail in front of him were shaking. Neither spoke. The spasm lasted less than ten seconds. Then Lessingham said: 'Shock is an odd phenomenon. I dreamed of watching Toby fall for weeks afterwards. Then the dream suddenly stopped. I thought I'd be able to look down at the reactor charge floor and put the image out of my mind. Most of the time I can. After all, I work here, this is my place. But the dream still recurs and sometimes, like now, I can see him lying there so clearly that it could be a hallucination.'

Dalgliesh felt that nothing he could say would be other than banal. Lessingham went on: 'I got to him first. He was lying prone but I couldn't turn him over. I couldn't make myself touch him. But I didn't need to. I knew that he was dead. He looked very small, disjointed, a rag doll. All I was aware of were those ridiculous symbols of a yellow bee on the heels of his trainers. Christ, was I glad to get rid of those bloody shoes.'

So Gledhill hadn't been wearing protective clothing. The impulse to suicide hadn't been completely spontaneous.

Dalgliesh said: 'He must have been a good climber.'

'Oh yes, Toby could climb. That was the least of his talents.'

And then, without a perceptible change in his voice, he

continued with the description of the reactor and the procedure for loading new fuel into the reactor core. Five minutes later, Mair rejoined them. On their way back to his office at the end of the tour he had suddenly asked: 'Have you heard of Richard Feynman?'

'The American physicist? I saw a television programme about him a few months ago, otherwise the name wouldn't have meant anything to me.'

'Feynman said: "Far more marvellous is the truth than any artist of the past imagined. Why do poets of the present not speak of it?" You're a poet, but this place, the power it generates, the beauty of the engineering, the sheer magnificence of it, it doesn't particularly interest you, does it? You or any other poet?'

'It interests me. That doesn't mean that I can make poetry out of it.'

'No, your subjects are more predictable, aren't they? How does it go?

> Twenty per cent to God and to His saints,
> Twenty per cent to nature and her proxies.
> And all the rest devoted to the plaints
> Of guys pursued by or pursuing doxies.'

Dalgliesh said: 'The percentage for God and His saints is down but I'd agree that the doxies are more than holding their own.'

'And that poor devil out there, the Norfolk Whistler, he's not poetic either presumably.'

'He's human. That makes him a fit subject for poetry.'

'But not one you'd choose?'

Dalgliesh could have replied that a poet doesn't choose his subject, it chooses him. But one reason for escaping to Norfolk had been to avoid discussions about poetry and even if he had enjoyed talking about his writing, it wouldn't have been with Alex Mair. But he had been surprised how little he had resented the questions. It was difficult to like the man, impossible not to respect him. And if he had murdered Hilary Robarts then Rickards was faced with a formidable opponent.

As he raked out the last ashes of the fire he remembered again with extraordinary clarity that moment when he had stood with Lessingham and looked down at the dark charge floor of the reactor beneath which that potent and mysterious power was silently working away. He wondered how long it would be before Rickards asked himself why precisely the murderer had chosen that particular pair of shoes.

37

Rickards knew that Dalgliesh was right; it would have been an unwarranted intrusion to call on Mrs Dennison so late at night. But he couldn't drive past the Old Rectory without slowing down and glancing to see if there was any sign of life. There was none; the house stood dark and silent behind the wind-torn bushes. Entering his own darkened house he felt a sudden overwhelming tiredness. But there was paperwork to be got through before he could go to bed, including his final report on the Whistler inquiry; awkward questions to be answered, a defence to be argued which would stand a chance of rebutting the charges, private and public, of police incompetence, poor supervision, too much reliance on technology and not enough good old-fashioned detection. And that was before he could begin scrutinizing the latest reports on the Robarts murder.

It was nearly four o'clock before he tore off his clothes and slumped face downwards on to the bed. Sometime during the night he must have been aware that he was cold for he awoke to find himself under the bedclothes and, stretching out his hand to the bedside lamp, saw with dismay that he had slept through the alarm and that it was almost eight o'clock. Instantly awake, he threw back the bedclothes and stumbled over to peer at himself in the glass of his wife's dressing table. The dressing table, kidney-shaped, was trimmed with pink and white flowered voile, the pretty matching set of ring stand and tray still neatly in place, a stuffed doll which Susie had won at a fair as a child hanging from the side of the glass. Only her jars of make-up were missing and their absence suddenly struck him as poignantly as if she were dead and they had been disposed of with the unimportant detritus of a life. What, he wondered, bending low to look more closely into the glass, had anything in this pink and white, utterly feminine bedroom, to do with that gaunt face, that rough, masculine torso? He experienced again what he had felt initially when they first moved in a month after the honeymoon, that nothing in the house was truly his. When he was a young DC he would have been amazed had anyone told him that he would achieve such a house, a gravel sweep of drive, its own half acre of garden, a drawing room and separate dining room, each with its carefully chosen suite of furniture which still smelt pristine new, reminding him every time he entered of the Oxford Street department store in which it had been chosen. But with Susie away he was again as ill at ease in it as if he were a barely tolerated and despised guest.

Dragging on his dressing gown, he opened the door of the small room at the south of the house which was to be the nursery. The cot was in pale lemon and white, matching the curtains. The changing table with its lower shelf for baby paraphernalia, its hanging bag for clean nappies, stood against the wall. The wallpaper was a riot of rabbits and leaping lambs. It was impossible to believe that any child of his would one day be sleeping here.

And it wasn't only the house which rejected him. With Susie absent it was sometimes difficult even to believe in the reality of his marriage. He had met her on a cultural cruise to Greece on which he had booked as an alternative to the usual solitary walking holiday. She had been one of the few younger women on the ship, travelling with her mother, the widow of a dentist. He realized now that it was Susie who had made the running, who had determined on the marriage, who had chosen him long before he had thought of choosing her. But the realization when it came was flattering rather than disturbing and, after all, he hadn't been unwilling. He had reached that time of life when he would occasionally indulge in an idealized picture of a wife waiting at home, domestic comfort, someone to return to at the end of the day, a child who would be his stake in the future, someone to work for.

And she had married him despite the opposition from her mother who at first had seemed to collude in the enterprise, perhaps reminding herself that Susie was twenty-eight and time was not on her side, but who, once the engagement had been secured, had made it plain that her only child could have done better, and had embarked on a policy of ostentatiously making the best of it while undertaking a vigorous campaign of his social re-education. But even she hadn't been able to find fault with the house. It had cost him all his savings and the mortgage was the largest his income could support but it stood as a solid symbol of the two things which mattered most to him, his marriage and his job.

Susie had been trained as a secretary but had seemed glad to give it up. If she had wanted to carry on working he would have supported her as he would in any interest she cared to take up. But he preferred her to be happily satisfied with the house and the garden, to find her waiting for him when he returned at the end of the day. It was not the kind of marriage that was currently fashionable, nor the kind that most couples could afford; but it was his kind of marriage and he was grateful that it was hers.

He hadn't been in love with her at the time of the marriage, he knew that now. He would, indeed, have said that he hardly knew the meaning of the word since it had certainly nothing to do with the half-shameful affairs, the humiliations of his earlier experiences with women. And yet not only poets and writers, the whole world used the word, seeming to know by instinct if not by direct experience exactly what it meant. Sometimes he felt uniquely disadvantaged, excluded from a universal birthright as a man might be who had been born without a sense of taste or smell. And when, three months after the honeymoon, he had fallen in love with Susie it had seemed like the revelation of something known but never experienced, as blinded eyes might suddenly open to the reality of light and colour and form. It was one night when, for the first time, she had found joy in his lovemaking and, half crying, half laughing, had clung to him whispering incoherent endearments. Tightening his arms about her he had known in what seemed a moment of amazed recognition that this was love. That moment of affirmation had been both a fulfilment and a promise, not the end of searching but the beginning of discovery. It left no room for doubts; his love, once acknowledged, seemed to him indestructible. Their marriage might have its moments of shared unhappiness and anxiety but it could never be less than it was at this moment. Was it really possible, he thought now, that it could be seriously threatened if not destroyed by its first serious test, her decision to give in to her mother's calculated mixture of bullying and entreaty and leave him when their first child was about to be born? When the baby was first placed in her arms he wanted to be there. Now he might not even be told when she went into labour. The picture which persistently haunted his imagination, before he fell asleep and at waking, of his mother-in-law standing triumphantly in the labour ward with his child in her arms deepened his dislike of her almost to paranoia.

To the right of the dressing table was one of their wedding photographs in a silver-plated frame, taken after a marriage ceremony which could have been specifically designed to empha-size the social differences between the two families. Susie was leaning a little towards him, her peaked, vulnerable face looking younger than her twenty-eight years, the fair head with its chaplet of flowers barely reaching his shoulder. The flowers had been artificial, rosebuds and lilies of the valley but, in memory as on the day, there rose from them a transitory sweetness. Her face, gravely smiling, revealed nothing, not even what the whole white mystique surely symbolized; this is what I worked for, what I want, what I've achieved. He was looking straight at the camera stolidly enduring what had after all been the last of the seemingly endless photographs taken outside the church. The family group had at last been released. Here were Susie and himself, legally yoked, an accepted pair. The photographic session had, it seemed in retrospect, been the most important part of the ceremony, the service merely a preliminary to this complicated arranging and rearranging of incongruously garbed strangers according to some hierarchy not wholly understood by him but of which the hector-ing photographer was obviously master. He heard again his mother-in-law's voice: 'Yes, a bit of a rough diamond, I'm afraid, but he's really very able. Chief constable material, I'm told.'

Well, he wasn't chief constable material and she had known it, but at least she hadn't been able to criticize the house which he had provided for her only child.

It was an early hour to telephone and he knew that his mother-in-law, who was a late riser, would make the most of the first grievance of the day. But if he didn't speak to Susie now it might well be late at night before he had another opportunity. For a moment he stood looking down at the bedside telephone, unwilling to stretch out his hand. If things had been different, if it hadn't been for this new murder, he could have got in the Rover, driven north to York and brought her home. Face to face with him she might have found the strength to resist her mother. Now she would have to travel alone, or with Mrs Cartwright if her mother insisted on accompanying her. Well, he would put up with her if she insisted on coming and it might be better for Susie than facing the long train journey alone. But he wanted her home; he wanted her here in this house.

The ringing tone seemed to last for an inordinate time and it was his mother-in-law who answered, enunciating the number with weary resignation as if this had been the twentieth call of the morning.

He said: 'This is Terry, Mrs Cartwright. Is Susie awake?'

He had never called her mother. That was a nonsense which he had not been able to get his tongue round and, to do her justice, she had never suggested it.

'Well, she will be now, won't she? Not very considerate, Terry, to ring before nine. Susie isn't sleeping very well just now and she needs her lie-in. And she was trying to get you all last evening. Hold on.'

And then, at least a minute later, came the small, tentative: 'Terry?'

'Are you all right, darling?'

'Yes, everything's fine. Mummy took me to Dr Maine yesterday. He used to look after me when I was a child. He's keeping an eye on me and he says that everything's going on very well. He's booked me a bed in the local hospital just in case.'

So she's even got that fixed up, he thought bitterly, and for a moment the treacherous thought lodged in his mind that the two of them might have planned it together, that this was what Susie wanted. He said: 'I'm sorry I couldn't spend longer on the phone yesterday. Things got pretty hectic. But I wanted you to know that the Whistler was dead.'

'It's been in all the papers, Terry. It's wonderful news. Are you all right? Are you feeding yourself properly?'

'Fine. I'm fine. Tired, but I'm OK. Look, darling, this new murder, it's different. We haven't got another serial murderer on the loose. The danger's over now. I'm afraid there's no chance I can get away to fetch you, but I could meet you at Norwich. Do you think you could make it today? There's a fast train at two minutes past three. If your mother would like to come, stay until after the baby is born, well that's all right, of course.'

It wasn't all right, but it was a small price to pay.

'Hold on, Terry. Mummy wants to talk to you.'

Then, after another long delay, he heard her mother's voice.

'Susie is staying here, Terry.'

'The Whistler is dead, Mrs Cartwright. The danger's over.'

'I know that the Whistler's dead. But you've had another murder down there, haven't you? There's still a killer at large and you're the man who's hunting him. This baby is due in less than two weeks and what Susie needs now is to get away from murder and death. Her health has to be my first consideration. What she needs is a little cosseting and kindness.'

'She's had that here, Mrs Cartwright.'

'I dare say you did your best, but you're never there, are you? Susie rang you four times last night. She really needed to talk to you, Terry, and you weren't there. It isn't good enough, not now it isn't. Out half the night catching murderers or not catching them. I know that's your job but it's hardly fair on Susie. I want my grandchild born safely. A girl's place is with her mother at a time like this.'

'I thought that a wife's place was with her husband.'

Oh, God, he thought, that I should ever hear myself speaking those words. A wave of utter misery swept over him compounded of self-disgust, anger and despair. He thought, If she doesn't come today she'll never come. The baby will be born in York and her mother will hold him in her arms before I do. She'll get her clutches into both of them, now and for ever. He knew how strong was that bond between widow and only child. There wasn't a day when Susie didn't telephone her mother, sometimes more than once. He knew with what difficulty and patience he had begun to wean her away from that obsessive maternal embrace. Now he had given Mrs Cartwright another weapon. He heard the triumph in her voice.

'Don't you talk to me about a wife's place, Terry. You'll be talking about Susie's duty next. And what about your duty to her? You've told her you can't get away to fetch her and I'm certainly not having my grandchild born on a British Rail train. Susie is staying here until this latest murder is solved and you can find time to fetch her.'

And then he was cut off. Slowly he replaced the receiver and stood waiting. Perhaps Susie would ring back. He could, of course, ring again but he knew with a sick hopelessness that there would be no use. She wasn't going to come. And then the telephone rang. He snatched up the receiver and said eagerly: 'Hello? Hello?'

But it was only Sergeant Oliphant ringing from the incident room at Hoveton, an early call letting him know that Oliphant had either been up all night or had snatched even less sleep than he. His own four hours now seemed an indulgence.

'The Chief Constable's trying to get you, sir. I told his PA there'd be no point in ringing home. You'd be on your way here by now.'

'I shall be on my way in five minutes. Not to Hoveton but to the Old Rectory at Larksoken. Mr Dalgliesh has given us a strong lead on the Bumble trainers. Meet me outside the rectory in three quarters of an hour. And you'd better ring Mrs Dennison now. Tell her to keep the back door locked and not to admit anyone to the house until we come. Don't alarm her; just say that there are one or two questions we have to put to her and we'd rather she spoke to us this morning before she talked to anyone else.'

If Oliphant was excited at the news he managed to conceal it. He said: 'You haven't forgotten that PR have fixed a press conference for ten, sir? Bill Starling from the local radio has been on to me but I told him he'll have to wait until then. And I think the CC wants to know if we're going to release the approximate time of death.'

And the Chief Constable wasn't the only one. It had been

useful to fudge the approximate time of the murder, to avoid stating categorically that this couldn't have been the work of the Whistler. But sooner or later they would have to come clean and once the post-mortem report was to hand, it would be difficult to parry the media's insistent questions. He said: 'We shan't release any forensic information until we get the written report of the autopsy.'

'We've got that now, sir. Doc Maitland-Brown dropped it in about twenty minutes ago on his way to the hospital. He was sorry he couldn't wait to see you.'

I'll bet he was, thought Rickards. Nothing, of course, would have been said; Dr Maitland-Brown didn't gossip with junior police officers. But there must have been a cosy atmosphere of mutual self-congratulation in the incident room on their joint early start to the day. He said: 'There's no reason why he should have waited. All the stuff we need from him will be in the report. Better open it now, give me the gist.'

He heard the receiver being placed down on the desk. There was a silence of less than a minute, then Oliphant spoke: 'No sign of recent sexual activity. She wasn't raped. Seems she was an exceptionally healthy woman until someone slung a ligature round her neck and strangled her. He can be a bit more precise about the time of death now he's seen the stomach contents, but he hasn't changed his first estimate. Between 8.30 and 9.45, but if we want to make it 9.20 he won't object. And she wasn't pregnant, sir.'

'All right, Sergeant. I'll be with you outside the Old Rectory in about forty-five minutes.'

But he was damned if he was going to face a heavy day without breakfast. Quickly he peeled a couple of rashers from the packet in the refrigerator and placed them under the grill, turning it to full power, then switched on the kettle and reached for a mug. Time for one mug of strong coffee, then he'd put the rashers between two hunks of bread and eat them in the car.

Forty minutes later, driving through Lydsett, he thought about the previous evening. He hadn't suggested to Adam Dalgliesh that he should come with the police to the Old Rectory. It wasn't necessary; his information had been precise and specific, and it hardly needed a Commander of the Metropolitan Police to point out a tea chest of discarded shoes. But there was another reason. He had been happy enough to drink Dalgliesh's whisky, eat his stew, or whatever it was he had called it, to discuss the salient points of the investigation. What else, after all, had they in common except their jobs? But that certainly didn't mean that he wanted Dalgliesh present while he was actually doing it. He had been glad the previous evening to call at the mill, grateful that he hadn't to return to an empty house, had sat companionably by the wood fire and had felt, by the end of the evening, at least comfortably at ease. But once away from Dalgliesh's physical presence, the old uncertainties returned as they had with such disconcerting force at the deathbed of the Whistler. He knew he would never be totally at one with the man and he knew why. He had only to think of the incident now and the old resentment would come flooding back. And yet it had happened nearly twelve years ago and he doubted whether Dalgliesh even remembered it. That, of course, was the greater part of the injury, that words which had remained in his memory for years, which at the time had humiliated him and almost destroyed his confidence as a detective, could be so easily spoken and apparently so quickly forgotten.

The place was a small top room in a narrow warren of a house behind the Edgware Road, the victim a fifty-year-old prostitute. She had been dead for over a week when they found her and the stink in the cluttered, airless hovel had been so disgusting that he had had to press his handkerchief against his mouth to hold back the vomit. One of the DCs had been less successful. He had rushed to throw open the window and might have made it if the pane hadn't been grimed fast. He himself had been unable to swallow, as if his own spittle had become contaminated. The handkerchief held against his mouth was soaked with saliva. She had been lying naked among the bottles, the pills, the half-eaten food, an obscene putrefying lump of flesh only a foot from the brimming chamber pot which she hadn't in the end been able to reach. But that had been the least of the stench in the room. After the pathologist had left he had turned to the nearest PC and said: 'For God's sake, can't we get this thing out of here?'

And then he had heard Dalgliesh's voice from the doorway like a whiplash. 'Sergeant, the word is "body". Or, if you prefer, there's "cadaver", "corpse", "victim", even "deceased" if you must. What you are looking at was a woman. She was not a thing when she was alive and she is not a thing now.'

He could still react physically to the memory of it, feel the tightening of the stomach muscles, the hot surge of anger. He shouldn't have let it pass, of course, not a public rebuke like that, not in front of the DCs. He should have looked the arrogant bastard in the face and spoken the truth, even if it had cost him his stripes.

'But she isn't a woman now is she, sir? She's not a human being any more, is she? So if she isn't human, what is she?'

It had been the unfairness that had rankled. There were a dozen of his colleagues who would have merited that cold rebuke, but not he. He had never at any time since his promotion to the CID seen the victim as an unimportant lump of flesh, never taken a prurient, half-shameful pleasure in the sight of a naked body, had rarely seen even the most degraded, most disgusting of victims without some pity and often with pain. His words had been totally out of character, torn from him out of hopelessness, tiredness after a nineteen-hour day, out of uncontrollable physical disgust. It was bad luck that they should have been overheard by Dalgliesh, a DCI whose cold sarcasm could be more devastating than another officer's bawled obscenities. They had continued working together for another six months. Nothing further had been said. Apparently Dalgliesh had found his work satisfactory; at least there hadn't been any further criticism. There hadn't been any praise, either. He had been scrupulously correct to his superior officer; Dalgliesh had acted as if the incident had never taken place. If he later regretted his words he had never said so. Perhaps he would have been amazed to know how bitterly, almost obsessively, they had been resented. But now, for the first time, Rickards wondered whether Dalgliesh too might not have been under strain, driven by his own compulsions, finding relief in the bitterness of words. After all, hadn't he at the time recently lost his wife and newborn child? But what had that to do with a dead prostitute in a London whorehouse? And he should have known better. That was the nub of it. He should have known his man. It seemed to Rickards that to remember the incident for so long and with such anger was almost paranoid. But the thought of Dalgliesh on his patch had brought it all back. Worse things had happened to him, more serious criticisms accepted and forgotten. But this he couldn't forget. Sitting by the wood fire in Larksoken Mill, drinking Dalgliesh's whisky, nearly equal in rank, secure on his own patch, it had seemed to him that the past might be put aside. But he knew now that it couldn't. Without that memory he and Adam Dalgliesh might have become friends. Now he respected him, admired him, valued his opinion, could even feel at ease with him. But he told himself that he could never like him.

38

Oliphant was waiting outside the Old Rectory, not sitting in the car but lolling cross-legged against the bonnet and reading a tabloid newspaper. The impression given and no doubt intended was that he had been wasting time there for the past ten minutes. As the car approached he straightened up and handed over the paper. He said: 'They've gone to town a bit, sir. Only to be expected, I suppose.'

The story hadn't made the front page but was spread over the two centre pages with black headlines and a screamer: 'Not again!' The byline was the paper's crime correspondent. Rickards read:

I have today learned that Neville Potter, the man now identified as the Whistler, who killed himself in the Balmoral Hotel at Easthaven on Sunday, had been interviewed by the police early in their inquiry and eliminated. The question is, why? The police knew the type of man they were looking for. A loner. Probably unmarried or divorced. Unsociable. A man with a car and a job that took him out at night. Neville Potter was just such a man. If he had been caught when he was first interviewed the lives of four innocent women could have been saved. Have we learned nothing from the Yorkshire Ripper fiasco?

Rickards said: 'The usual predictable nonsense. Female murder victims are either prostitutes who presumably deserve what they get or innocent women.'

Walking up the drive to the Old Rectory he quickly scanned the rest of the article. Its argument was that the police relied too much on computers, on mechanical aids, fast cars, technology. It was time to get back to the bobby on the beat. What use was feeding interminable data into a computer when an ordinary DC wasn't competent to spot an obvious suspect? The article was no more acceptable to Rickards because it expressed some of his own views.

He threw it back at Oliphant and said: 'What are they suggesting, that we could have trapped the Whistler by stationing a uniformed bobby on the beat at every country road intersection? You told Mrs Dennison that we were coming and asked her to keep out visitors?'

'She sounded none too pleased, sir. Said the only visitors who were likely to call were the headlanders and what reason could she give for turning away her friends. No one has called so far, at least not at the front door.'

'And you checked on the back door?'

'You said to wait outside for you, sir. I haven't been round the back.'

It was hardly a promising beginning. But if Oliphant, with his usual tactlessness, had managed to antagonize Mrs Dennison she showed no sign of displeasure on opening the door but welcomed them in with grave courtesy. Rickards thought again how attractive she was with a gentle old-fashioned prettiness which he supposed people used to call the English rose type when English rose prettiness was in fashion. Even her clothes had an air of anachronistic gentility, not the ubiquitous trousers but a grey pleated skirt and a matching cardigan over a blue blouse with a single row of pearls. But despite her apparent composure she was very pale, the carefully applied pink lipstick almost garish against the bloodless skin, and he saw that her shoulders were rigid under the thin wool.

She said: 'Won't you come into the drawing room, Chief Inspector, and explain what this is all about? And I expect you and your sergeant would like some coffee.'

'It's good of you, Mrs Dennison, but I'm afraid we haven't the time. I hope we won't have to keep you for long. We're looking for a pair of shoes, Bumble trainers, which we have reason to believe may be in your jumble box. Could we see it please?'

She gave them one quick glance then, without speaking, led them through a door at the rear of the hall and down a short passage leading to another door which was bolted. She reached up to the bolt which slid easily and they found themselves in a second and shorter passage, stone-flagged, facing a formidably stout back door which was also bolted at the top and bottom. There was a room on either side. The door on the right stood open.

Mrs Dennison led them in. She said: 'We keep the jumble here As I told Sergeant Oliphant when he telephoned, the back door was double-locked at five last evening and has remained bolted. During the daytime I usually open it so that anyone who has jumble can come in and leave it without bothering to knock.'

Oliphant said: 'Which means they could help themselves to the stuff as well as leave it. Aren't you afraid of theft?'

'This is Larksoken, Sergeant, not London.'

The room, stone-flagged, brick-walled and with a single high window, must originally have been either a pantry or perhaps a store room. Its present use was immediately apparent. Against the wall were two tea chests, the left one about three-quarters full of shoes and the right containing a jumble of belts, bags and men's ties knotted together. Next to the door were two long shelves. On one stood an assortment of bric-à-brac; cups and saucers, fairings, small statuettes, saucers and plates, a portable radio, a bedside lamp with a cracked and grubby shade. The second shelf held a row of old and rather tattered books, most of them paperbacks. A row of hooks had been screwed into the lower shelf on which hung hangers holding a variety of better-quality clothes; men's suits, jackets, women's dresses and children's clothes, some of them already priced on small scraps of paper pinned to the hem. Oliphant stood for no more than a couple of seconds surveying the room, and then turned his attention to the box of shoes. It took less than a minute of rummaging to confirm that the Bumbles weren't there, but he began a systematic search, watched by Rickards and Mrs Dennison. Each pair, most tied together by the laces, was taken out and placed on one side until the box was empty and then as methodically replaced. Rickards took a right-foot Bumble trainer from his brief case and handed it to Mrs Dennison.

'The shoes we are looking for are like this. Can you remember if a pair were ever in the jumble box and, if so, who brought them in?'

She said at once: 'I didn't realize they were called Bumbles but, yes, there was a pair like this in the box. Mr Miles Lessingham from the power station brought them in. He was asked to dispose of the clothes of the young man who killed himself at Larksoken. Two of the suits hanging up here also belonged to Toby Gledhill.'

'When did Mr Lessingham bring in the shoes, Mrs Dennison?'

'I can't remember exactly. I think it was late afternoon a week or so after Mr Gledhill died, sometime towards the end of last month. But you'd have to ask him, Chief Inspector. He may remember more precisely.'

'And he brought them to the front door?'

'Oh yes. He said he wouldn't stay to tea but he did have a word in the drawing room with Mrs Copley. Then he brought the suitcase of clothes out here with me and we unpacked them together. I put the shoes in a plastic bag.'

'And when did you last see them?'

'I can't possibly remember that, Chief Inspector. I don't come out here very often except occasionally to price up some of the clothes. And when I do I don't necessarily look in the shoe box.'

'Not even to see what's been brought in?'

'Yes, I do that from time to time, but I don't make any kind of regular inspection.'

'They're very distinctive shoes, Mrs Dennison.'

'I know that, and if I'd rummaged about in the box recently I must have seen them or even noticed that they were missing. But I didn't. I'm afraid I can't possibly say when they were taken.'

'How many people know about the system here?'

'Most of the headlanders know, and any staff at Larksoken Power Station who regularly donate jumble. They usually come by car, of course, on their way home and sometimes, like Mr Lessingham, ring at the front door. Occasionally I take the bags from them at the door or they may say that they'll drop them in at the back. We don't actually hold the jumble sale here, that takes place in the village hall in Lydsett in October. But this is a convenient collecting place for the headland and for the power station, and then Mr Sparks or Mr Jago from the Local Hero comes in a van and loads it up a day or two before the sale.'

'But I see you price up some of the stuff here.'

'Not all of it, Chief Inspector. It's just that occasionally we know of people who might like some of the items and who buy them before the sale.'

The admission seemed to embarrass her. Rickards wondered whether the Copleys might not benefit in this way. He knew about jumble sales. His ma had helped with the annual one at the Chapel. The helpers expected to get the pick of the goods; that was their perk. And why not? He said: 'You mean that anyone local wanting clothes, maybe for his kids, would know that he could buy them here?'

She flushed. He could see that the suggestion and perhaps his choice of pronoun had embarrassed her. She said: 'Lydsett people usually wait until the main sale. After all, it wouldn't be worth-while, people coming in from the village just to see what we're collecting. But sometimes I sell to people on the headland. After all, the jumble is given in aid of the church. There's no reason why it shouldn't be sold in advance if someone local happens to want it. Naturally they pay the proper price.'

'And who has from time to time wanted it, Mrs Dennison?'

'Mr Blaney has occasionally bought clothes for the children. One of Mr Gledhill's tweed jackets fitted Mr Copley so Mrs Copley paid for that. And Neil Pascoe called in about a fortnight ago to see if we had anything suitable for Timmy.'

Oliphant asked: 'Was that before or after Mr Lessingham brought in the trainers?'

'I can't remember, Sergeant. You'd better ask him. We neither of us looked in the shoe box. Mr Pascoe was interested in warm jumpers for Timmy. He paid for two. There's a tin with the money on a shelf in the kitchen.'

'So people don't just help themselves and leave the cash?'

'Oh no, Chief Inspector. No one would dream of doing that.'

'And what about the belts? Would you be able to say whether one of the belts or straps is missing?'

She said with a sudden spurt of impatience: 'How could I possibly do that? Look for yourself. This box is literally a jumble; straps, belts, old handbags, scarves. How could I possibly say if anything is missing or when it was taken?'

Oliphant said: 'Would it surprise you to be told that we have a witness who saw the trainers in this box last Wednesday morning?'

Oliphant could make the simplest and most innocuous question sound like an accusation. But his crudeness, sometimes bordering on insolence, was usually carefully judged and Rickards seldom attempted to discipline it knowing that it had its uses. It had, after all, been Oliphant who had got close to shaking Alex Mair's composure. But now he should perhaps have remembered that he was talking to an ex-schoolmistress. Mrs Dennison turned on him the mildly reproving look more appropriate to a delinquent child.

'I don't think you can have been listening carefully to what I've been saying, Sergeant. I have no idea when the shoes were taken. That being so, how could it surprise me to learn when they were last seen?' She turned to Rickards: 'If we're going to discuss this further, wouldn't it be more comfortable for all of us in the drawing room than standing about here?'

Rickards hoped that it might at least be warmer.

She led them across the hall into a room at the front of the house which faced south over the lumpy lawn and the tangle of laurels, rhododendrons and wind-stunted bushes which effectively screened the road. The room was large and barely warmer than the one they had left, as if even the strongest autumn sun had been unable to penetrate the mullioned windows and the heavy drapes of the velvet curtains. And the air was a little stuffy, smelling of polish, pot-pourri and faintly of rich food as if still redolent with long-eaten Victorian afternoon teas. Rickards almost expected to hear the rustle of a crinoline.

Mrs Dennison didn't switch on the light and Rickards felt that he could hardly ask her. In the gloom he had an impression of solid mahogany furniture, side tables laden with photographs, of comfortably upholstered armchairs in shabby covers and of so many pictures in ornate frames that the room had the air of an oppressive and rarely visited provincial gallery. Mrs Dennison seemed aware of the cold if not of the gloom. She stooped to plug in a two-bar electric fire to the right of the huge carved grate then seated herself with her back towards the window, and gestured Rickards and Oliphant to the sofa on which they sat side by side solidly upright on stiff, unyielding cushions. She sat quietly waiting, her hands folded in her lap. The room with its weight of dark mahogany, its air of ponderous respectability diminished her and it seemed to Rickards that she gleamed like a pale and insubstantial wraith dwarfed by the huge arms of the chair. He wondered about her life on the headland and in this remote and surely unmanageable house, wondered what she had been seeking when she fled to this wind-scoured coast and whether she had found it.

He asked: 'When was it decided that the Reverend and Mrs Copley should go to stay with their daughter?'

'Last Friday, after Christine Baldwin was murdered. She'd been very anxious about them for some time and pressing them to leave, but it was the fact that the last murder was so very close that persuaded them. I was to drive them to Norwich to catch the 8.30 on Sunday evening.'

'Was that generally known?'

'It was talked about, I expect. You could say it was generally known in as far as there are people here to know it. Mr Copley had to make arrangements for the services he normally takes. I told Mrs Bryson at the stores that I would only be needing half a pint of milk a day instead of the normal two and a half pints. Yes, you could say it was generally known.'

'And why didn't you drive them to Norwich as arranged?'

'Because the car broke down while they were finishing the packing. I thought I'd explained that already. At about half-past six I went to get it out of the garage and drove it to the front door. It was all right then but when I finally got them into it at 7.15 and we were ready to go it wouldn't start. So I rang Mr

Sparks at Lydsett Garage and arranged for him to take them in his taxi.'

'Without you?'

Before she could answer Oliphant got to his feet, walked over to a standard lamp close to his chair and, without a word, switched it on. The strong light flowed down on her. For a moment Rickards thought that she was about to protest. She half rose from the chair, then sat down again and went on as if nothing had happened.

'I felt bad about that. I would have been much happier to have seen them on the train, but Mr Sparks could only take the job if he could go straight on to Ipswich where he had to pick up a fare. But he promised he wouldn't leave them until he'd seen them into the carriage. And, of course, they're not children, they're perfectly capable of getting out at Liverpool Street. It's the terminus, after all; and their daughter was meeting them.'

Why, Rickards wondered, was she so defensive? She could hardly suppose herself a serious suspect. And yet, why not? He had known less likely murderers. He could see fear in the dozen small signs which no experienced policeman could miss; the tremble of the hands which she tried to control when his glance fell on them, the nervous tic at the corner of the eye, the inability to sit still one moment followed by an unnatural, controlled stillness the next, the note of strain in the voice, the way in which she was resolutely meeting his eyes with a look compounded of defiance and endurance. Taken singly each was a sign of natural stress; together they added up to something close to terror. He had resented Adam Dalgliesh's warning the previous night. It had been uncomfortably close to teaching him his job. But perhaps he had been right. Perhaps he was facing a woman who had suffered more aggressive interrogations than she could take. But he had his job to do.

He said: 'You phoned for the taxi straight away? You didn't try to find out what was wrong with the car?'

'There was no time to fuss about under the bonnet. I'm not a mechanic anyway. I've never been particularly good with a car. It was lucky that I found out in time that it wouldn't go, and even luckier that Mr Sparks could oblige. He came at once. Mr and Mrs Copley were getting very agitated. Their daughter was expecting them; all the arrangements had been made. It was important to catch the train.'

'Where was the car normally kept, Mrs Dennison?'

'I thought I told you that, Chief Inspector. In the garage.'

'Locked?'

'There's a padlock. Quite a small one. I don't suppose it's very secure if someone really wanted to break it, but no one has ever tried. It was locked when I went for the car.'

'Three-quarters of an hour before you needed to leave.'

'Yes. I don't understand what you're getting at. Is that significant?'

'I'm just curious, Mrs Dennison. Why so much time?'

'Have you ever had to load a car with the luggage required by two elderly people leaving for an indefinite stay? I had been helping Mrs Copley with the final part of her packing. I wasn't needed for a minute or so and it seemed a good opportunity to get the car out.'

'And while it stood there in front of the house, was it continually under your eye?'

'Of course not. I was busy checking that the Copleys had everything that they needed, going over the things I needed to do while they were away, parish business, a few telephone calls.'

'Where was this happening?'

'In Mr Copley's study. Mrs Copley was in her bedroom.'

'And the car was unattended in the drive?'

'Are you suggesting that someone sabotaged it?'

'Well, that would be a little fanciful, wouldn't it? What gave you that idea?'

'You did, Chief Inspector. It wouldn't otherwise have occurred to me. And I agree, it's fanciful.'

'And when, at 9.45, Mr Jago rang from the Local Hero to tell you that the Whistler's body had been found, what did you do then?'

'There was nothing I could do. There was no way of stopping the Copleys; they were over an hour into their journey. I rang their daughter at her London club and managed to catch her before she set out for Liverpool Street. She said that she'd made all her arrangements so that they might as well stay for a week since they were on their way. Actually, they're coming home tomorrow afternoon. Mrs Duncan-Smith has been called to help nurse a sick friend.'

Rickards said: 'One of my officers has seen Mr Sparks. He was anxious to reassure you that the Copleys were safely on their way. He rang you as soon as convenient for him but could get no reply. That was at about 9.15, about the same time as Mr Jago first tried to get through to you.'

'I must have been in the garden. It was a beautiful moonlit night and I was restless. I needed to get out of the house.'

'Even with the Whistler, as you thought, still at large?'

'Strangely enough, Chief Inspector, I've never been very frightened of the Whistler. The threat always seemed remote, a little unreal.'

'You went no further than the garden?'

She looked at him straight in the eyes. 'I went no further than the garden.'

'Yet you didn't hear the telephone?'

'It is a large garden.'

'But it was a quiet night, Mrs Dennison.'

She didn't reply.

He asked: 'And when did you come in from wandering alone in the dark?'

'I wouldn't describe a stroll around the garden as wandering alone after dark. I suppose I was out for about half an hour. I had been back about five minutes when Mr Jago rang.'

'And when did you hear about the Robarts murder, Mrs Dennison? Obviously it wasn't news to you when we met at Martyr's Cottage.'

'I thought you already knew that, Chief Inspector. Miss Mair telephoned me shortly after seven on Monday morning. She herself knew when her brother returned late on Sunday night after seeing the body but she didn't want to disturb me at midnight, particularly with such distressing news.'

Oliphant asked: 'And was it distressing news, madam? You hardly knew Miss Robarts. Why should it be so distressing?'

Mrs Dennison gave him a long look, then turned away. She

said: 'If you really have to ask that question, Sergeant, are you sure you're in the right job?'

Rickards rose to go. She came with him to the front door. As they were leaving she turned to him and said with sudden urgency: 'Chief Inspector, I'm not stupid. All these questions about the shoes. Obviously you've found a print at the scene and you think it could have been made by the murderer. But surely Bumbles aren't uncommon. Anyone could have been wearing them. The fact that Toby Gledhill's pair are missing could be simply coincidence. They weren't necessarily taken with evil purpose. Anyone needing a pair of trainers could have stolen them.'

Oliphant looked at her. 'Oh, I don't think so, madam, do you? As you said yourself only half an hour ago, this is Larksoken, not London.' And he smiled his thick-lipped, self-satisfied smile.

39

Rickards wanted to see Lessingham at once but the press conference called for ten meant that the interview had to be postponed and, to complicate matters further, a telephone call to Larksoken Power Station revealed that Lessingham had taken a day's leave but had left a message saying he could be reached at his cottage outside Blakeney. Luckily he was at home and, without explanation, Oliphant made an appointment for midday.

They were less than five minutes late and it was the more frustrating, therefore, to find when they arrived at the low-built wood and brick cottage set back on the coastal road a mile to the north of the village that he wasn't at home. A note in pencil was tacked to the front door.

'Anyone wanting me, try the *Heron*, berthed at Blakeney quay. That includes the police.'

'Bloody cheek!' complained Oliphant. As if unwilling to believe that any suspect could be as wilfully uncooperative, he tried the door, peered in at the window, then disappeared round the back. Returning he said: 'Ramshackle. Could do with a lick of paint. Funny place to choose to live. These marshes are pretty dreary in winter. You'd think he'd want a bit of life around him.'

Rickards privately agreed that it was an odd place for Lessingham to choose. His cottage looked as if it had once been a pair, now converted into a single dwelling, and, although agreeably proportioned with a certain melancholy charm, it looked at first sight unoccupied and neglected. Lessingham was a senior engineer after all, or technician, he couldn't for the moment remember which. Anyway, he hardly lived here because he was poor.

He said: 'He probably wants to be close to his boat. There's not much choice of harbour on this coast. It was either there or Wells-next-the-Sea.'

As they got back into the car, Oliphant gazed back at the cottage resentfully as if it were concealing behind the peeling paint some secret which a few vigorous kicks on the door might persuade it to divulge. Fastening his seat belt, he grumbled: 'And when we get to the quay I suppose there'll be a notice telling us to try the pub.'

But Lessingham was where he said he'd be. Ten minutes later they came up to him, sitting on an upturned crate on the deserted quay, an outboard motor in front of him. Berthed beside him was a thirty-foot sailing boat with a central cabin. It was obvious that he hadn't yet started to work. A relatively clean rag drooped from fingers which seemed too listless to hold it and he was regarding the engine as if it posed an intractable problem. He looked up as they stood over him and Rickards was shocked at the change in him. In only two days he seemed to have aged ten years. He was barefoot and wore a faded dark blue guernsey over knee-length denim shorts fashionably tattered at the edges. But this informal garb seemed only to emphasize his urban pallor, the skin taut over the wide cheekbones, the smudges like bruises under the deep-set eyes. He was a part-time sailor after all, thought Rickards. Extraordinary that even this bad summer hadn't produced more than a biscuit-coloured tan.

Lessingham didn't get up, but said without preamble: 'You were lucky to catch me when you rang. A day's leave is too good to waste indoors, particularly now. I thought we could talk here as well as anywhere.'

Rickards said: 'Not altogether. Somewhere more private would be better.'

'This is private enough. The locals can recognize the police when they see them. Of course if you want me to make a formal statement or were thinking of arresting me, I'd prefer the police station. I like to keep my house and my boat uncontaminated.' He added: 'I mean uncontaminated by disagreeable sensations.'

Oliphant said stolidly: 'Why do you suppose we would want to arrest you? Arrest you for what exactly?' He added: 'sir', and made the word sound like a threat.

Rickards felt a spurt of irritation. It was like the man not to miss an easy opening but this childish preliminary sparring would hardly smooth the interrogation. Lessingham looked at Oliphant, seriously considering whether the question needed a reply.

'God knows. I suppose you could think of something if you put your minds to it.' Then, seeming to realize for the first time that they were having to stand, he got up. 'All right, better come on board.'

Rickards wasn't a sailor, but it seemed to him that the boat, all wood, was old. The cabin, which they had to crouch low to enter, had a narrow mahogany table down the whole length and a bench on either side. Lessingham seated himself opposite them and they regarded each other across two feet of polished wood, their faces so close that Rickards felt he could smell his companions, a masculine amalgam of sweat, warm wool, beer and Oliphant's aftershave, as if all three were claustrophobically caged animals. It could hardly have been a more unsuitable place in which to conduct an interview, and he wondered whether Adam Dalgliesh would have engineered things better and despised himself for the thought. He was aware of Oliphant's great bulk beside him, their thighs touching, Oliphant's unnaturally warm, and had to resist an impulse to edge further away.

He said: 'Is this your boat, sir? The one you were sailing last Sunday night?'

'Not sailing, Chief Inspector, for much of the time; there wasn't enough wind. But yes, this is my boat and this is the one I was on last Sunday.'

'You seem to have damaged the hull. There's a long fresh-looking scratch on the starboard side.'

'Clever of you to notice. I scraped the water tower offshore from the power station. Careless of me. I've sailed these waters often enough. If you'd come a couple of hours later it would have been repainted.'

'And do you still say that you were never at any time within sight of the beach where Miss Robarts took her last swim?'

'You asked me that question when you saw me on Monday. It depends what you mean by "in sight of". I could have seen the beach through my binoculars if I'd happened to look, but I can confirm that I never got to within half a mile of it and that I didn't land. Since I could hardly murder her without landing, that seems to me conclusive. But I don't suppose you've come all this way just to hear me repeat my alibi.'

Reaching down with difficulty, Oliphant dragged his grip on to the seat beside him, took out a pair of Bumble trainers and placed them on the table neatly, side by side. Rickards watched Lessingham's face. He controlled himself immediately but he hadn't been able to disguise the shock of recognition in the eyes, the tensing of the muscles around the mouth. The pair of trainers, pristine, new, grey and white, with the small bumblebee on each heel, seemed to dominate the cabin. Having placed them there, Oliphant ignored them.

He said: 'But you were south of the water towers at the power station. The scratch is on the starboard side. You must have been travelling north, sir, when you got that scrape.'

'I turned for home when I was about fifty yards beyond the towers. I'd planned to make the power station the limit of the journey.'

Rickards said: 'These trainers, sir, have you seen a pair like these?'

'Of course. They're Bumbles. Not everyone can afford them but most people have seen them.'

'Have you seen them worn by anyone who worked at Larksoken?'

'Yes, Toby Gledhill had a pair. After he killed himself his parents asked me if I'd clear out his clothes. There weren't very many. Toby travelled light, but I suppose there were a couple of suits, the usual trousers and jackets and half a dozen pairs of shoes. The trainers were among them. Actually, they were almost new. He bought them about ten days before he died. He only wore them once.'

'And what did you do with them, sir?'

'I bundled up all the clothes and took them to the Old Rectory for the next church jumble sale. The Copleys have a small room at the back of the house where people can leave their junk. From time to time Dr Mair puts a notice on the notice board asking people to donate anything they don't want. It's part of the policy of being part of the community, all one happy family on the headland. We may not always go to church but we show goodwill by bestowing on the righteous our cast-off clothes.'

'When did you take Mr Gledhill's clothes to the Old Rectory?'

'I can't remember exactly, but I think it was a fortnight after he died. Just before the weekend I think. Probably on Friday the twenty-sixth of August. Mrs Dennison may remember. I doubt whether it's worth asking Mrs Copley, although I did see her.'

'So you handed them over to Mrs Dennison?'

'That's right. Actually, the back door of the rectory is usually kept open during daylight hours and people can walk in and drop anything they want to leave. But I thought on this occasion that it would be better to hand the things over formally. I wasn't entirely sure they'd be welcome. Some people are superstitious about buying the clothes of the recently dead. And it seemed, well, inappropriate just to drop them.'

'What happened at the Old Rectory?'

'Nothing very much. Mrs Dennison opened the door and showed me into the drawing room. Mrs Copley was there and I explained why I had called. She produced the usual meaningless platitudes about Toby's death and Mrs Dennison asked me if I would like tea. I declined and followed her through the hall to the room at the back where they store the jumble. There's a large tea chest there which holds the shoes. The pairs are just tied by the laces and thrown in. I had Toby's clothes in a suitcase and Mrs Dennison and I unpacked it together. She said that the suits were really too good for the jumble sale and asked if I'd mind if she sold them separately, provided, of course, the money went to church funds. She thought she might get a better price. I had a feeling that she was wondering whether Mr Copley might not use one of the jackets. I said she could do what she liked with them.'

'And what happened to the trainers? Were they put into the tea chest with the rest of the shoes?'

'Yes, but in a plastic bag. Mrs Dennison said they were in too good a condition to be thrown in with the others and get dirty. She went off and returned with the bag. She seemed to be uncertain what to do with the suits so I said I'd leave the suitcase. It was Toby's after all. It could be sold at the jumble sale with the rest of the things. Ashes to ashes, dust to dust, jumble to jumble. I was glad to see the end of it.'

Rickards said: 'I read about Dr Gledhill's suicide, of course. It must have been particularly distressing for you who actually saw it happen. He was described as a young man of brilliant promise.'

'He was a creative scientist. Mair will confirm that if you're interested one way or the other. Of course, all good science is creative whatever the humanities try to tell you, but there are scientists who have this special vision, genius as opposed to talent, inspiration as well as the necessary patient conscientiousness. Someone, I forget who, described it rather well. Most of us edge forward, painfully advancing, yard by yard; they parachute behind enemy lines. He was young, only twenty-four. He could have become anything.'

Rickards thought, anything or nothing, like most of these young geniuses. Early death usually conferred a brief vicarious immortality. He'd never known a young DCI, accidentally killed, who wasn't at once proclaimed a potential Chief Constable. He asked: 'What exactly was he doing at the power station, what was his job?'

'Working with Mair on his PWR safety studies. Briefly, it's to do with the behaviour of the core in abnormal conditions. Toby never discussed it with me, probably because he knew I couldn't understand the complicated computer codes. I'm just a poor bloody engineer. Mair is due to publish the study before he leaves for his rumoured new job, no doubt under both their names and with a suitable acknowledgement to his collaborator. All that will last of Toby is his name under Mair's on a scientific paper.'

He sounded utterly weary and, looking towards the open door, made a half movement as if to get up, out of the claustrophobic little cabin and into the air. Then he said, his eyes still on the door: 'It's no use trying to explain Toby to you, you wouldn't understand. It would be a waste of your time and mine.'

'You seem very sure of that, Mr Lessingham.'

'I am sure, very sure. I can't explain why without being offensive. So why don't we keep it simple, stick to the facts. Look, he was an exceptional person. He was clever, he was kind, he was beautiful. If you find one of these qualities in a human being, you're lucky, if you find all three then you get someone rather special. I was in love with him. He knew because I told him. He wasn't in love with me and he wasn't gay. Not that it's any business of yours. I'm telling you because it was a fact and you're supposed to deal in facts, and because if you're determined to be interested in Toby you may as well get him right. And there's another reason. You're obviously grubbing about for all the dirt you can find. I'd rather you had facts from me than rumours from other people.'

Rickards said: 'So you didn't have a sexual relationship.'

Suddenly the air was rent with a wild screeching and there was a beating of white wings against the porthole. Outside someone must be feeding the seagulls.

Lessingham started up as if the sound was alien to him. Then he collapsed back in his seat and said with more weariness than anger: 'What the hell has that to do with Hilary Robarts's murder?'

'Possibly nothing at all, in which case the information will be kept private. But at this stage it's for me to decide what may or may not be relevant.'

'We spent one night together two weeks before he died. As I said, he was kind. It was the first and the last time.'

'Is that generally known?'

'We didn't broadcast it over local radio or write to the local paper or put up a notice in the staff canteen. Of course it wasn't generally known, why the hell should it be?'

'Would it have mattered if it had been? Would either of you have cared?'

'Yes, I would, we both would. I would care in the way you would care if your sex life was sniggered about in public. Of course we would have cared. After he died, it ceased to matter as far as I was concerned. There's this to be said for the death of a friend, it frees you from so much you thought was important.'

Frees you for what? thought Rickards. For murder, that iconoclastic act of protest and defiance, that single step across an unmarked, undefended frontier which, once taken, sets a man apart for ever from the rest of his kind? But he decided to defer the obvious question.

Instead he asked: 'What sort of family had he?' The question sounded innocuous and banal, as if they were casually discussing a common acquaintance.

'He had a father and a mother. That sort of family. What other sort is there?'

But Rickards had resolved on patience. It was not a ploy that came easily to him, but he could recognize pain when its taut and naked sinews were thrust so close to his face. He said mildly: 'I mean what sort of background did he come from? Had he brothers or sisters?'

'His father is a country parson. His mother is a country parson's wife. He was an only child. His death nearly destroyed them. If we could have made it look like an accident we would have. If lying could have helped, I would have lied. Why the hell didn't he drown himself? That way there would at least have been room for doubt. Is that what you meant by background?'

'It's helping to fill in the picture.' He paused and then, almost casually, asked the seminal question. 'Did Hilary Robarts know that you and Tobias Gledhill had spent a night together?'

'Whatever possible relevance . . .? All right, it's your job to do the scavenging. I know the system. You trawl up everything you can get your nets to and then throw away what you don't want. In the process you learn a lot of secrets you've no particular right to know and cause a lot of pain. Do you enjoy that? Is that what gives you your kicks?'

'Just answer the question, sir.'

'Yes, Hilary knew. She found out by one of those coincidences which seem a one in a million chance when they happen but which aren't really so remarkable or unusual in real life. She drove past my house when Toby and I were leaving just after 7.30 in the morning. She had taken a day's leave, apparently, and must have left home early to drive off somewhere. It's no use asking me where because I don't know. I suppose, like most other people, she has friends she visits from time to time. I mean, someone somewhere must have liked her.'

'Did she ever speak about the encounter, to you or to anyone else you know?'

'She didn't make it public property. I think she regarded it as too valuable a piece of information to cast before the swine. She liked power, and this was certainly power of a kind. As she drove past, she slowed down almost to walking pace and stared straight into my eyes. I can remember that look: amusement, changing to contempt, then triumph. We understood each other all right. But she never subsequently spoke a word to me.'

'Did she talk about it to Mr Gledhill?'

'Oh yes, she spoke to Toby all right. That's the reason he killed himself.'

'How do you know that she spoke to him? Did he tell you?'

'No.'

'You're suggesting that she blackmailed him?'

'I'm suggesting that he was unhappy, muddled, uncertain about every aspect of his life, his research, his future, his sexuality. I know that she attracted him sexually. He wanted her. She was one of those dominant, physically powerful women who do attract sensitive men like Toby. I think she knew that and she used it. I don't know when she got hold of him or what she said to him, but I'm bloody sure that he'd be alive now if it weren't for Hilary Robarts. And if that gives me a motive for her murder, you're damned right. But I didn't kill her and, that being so, you won't find any evidence that I did. Part of me, a very small part, is actually sorry that she's dead. I didn't like her and I don't think she was a happy woman, or even a particularly useful one. But she was healthy and intelligent and she was young. Death ought to be for the old, the sick and the tired. What I feel is a touch of *lachrymae rerum*. Even the death of an enemy diminishes us apparently, or so, in certain moods, it seems. But that doesn't mean I'd want her alive again. But it's possible I'm prejudiced, perhaps even unjust. When Toby was happy, no one was more joyous. When he was miserable he went down into his private hell. Perhaps she could reach him there, could help him. I know I couldn't. It's difficult to comfort a friend when you suspect that he sees it as a ploy to get him into your bed.'

Rickards said: 'You've been remarkably frank in suggesting a motive for yourself. But you haven't given us a single piece of concrete evidence to support your allegation that Hilary Robarts was in any way responsible for Toby Gledhill's death.'

Lessingham looked straight into his eyes and seemed to be considering, then he said: 'I've gone so far, I may as well tell you the rest. He spoke to me when he passed me on his way to death. He said, "Tell Hilary she doesn't have to worry any more. I've made my choice." The next time I saw him he was climbing the fuelling machine. He balanced on it for a second, then dived down on top of the reactor. He meant me to see him die, and I saw him die.'

Oliphant said: 'A symbolic sacrifice.'

'To the terrifying god of nuclear fission? I thought one of you might say that, Sergeant. That was the vulgar reaction. It's altogether too crude and histrionic. All he wanted, for God's sake, was the quickest way to break his neck.' He paused, seemed to consider, then went on: 'Suicide is an extraordinary phenomenon. The result is irrevocable. Extinction. The end of all choice. But the precipitating action often seems so commonplace. A minor setback, momentary depression, the state of the weather, even a poor dinner. Would Toby have died if he'd spent the previous night with me instead of alone? If he was alone.'

'Are you saying that he wasn't?'

'There was no evidence either way and now there will never be. But then the inquest was remarkable for the lack of evidence about anything. There were three witnesses, myself and two others, to the way he died. No one was near him, no one could have pushed him, it couldn't have been an accident. There was no evidence from me or anyone else about his state of mind. You could say that it was a scientifically conducted inquest. It stuck to the facts.'

Oliphant said quietly: 'And where do you think he spent the night before he died?'

'With her.'

'On what evidence?'

'None that would stand up in a court. Only that I rang him three times between nine and midnight and he didn't reply.'

'And you didn't tell that to the police or the coroner?'

'On the contrary. I was asked when I'd last seen him. That was in the canteen on the day before he died. I mentioned my telephone call, but no one regarded it as important. Why should they? What did it prove? He could have been out walking. He could have decided not to answer the phone. There was no mystery about how he died. And now, if you don't mind, I'd like to get out of here and on with cleaning that bloody engine.'

They walked in silence back to the car. Rickards said: 'Arrogant bastard, isn't he? He made his view brutally plain. No point in trying to explain anything to the police. He can't say why without being offensive. You bet he can't. We're too thick, ignorant and insensitive to understand that a research scientist isn't necessarily an unimaginative technocrat, that you can be sorry a woman is dead without necessarily wishing her alive again, and that a sexually attractive boy might actually be prepared to go to bed with either sex.'

Oliphant said: 'He could have done it if he used the engine at full power. He'd have had to come ashore north of where she bathed and kept to the tide line, or we'd have seen his footprints. It was a thorough search, sir, at least a mile north and south. We identified Mr Dalgliesh's prints but, otherwise, the upper beach was clean.'

'Oh yes, he'd have kept pretty clear of the killing ground. But he could have beached the inflatable dinghy on shingle without much problem. There are stretches which are practically all pebbled, or with narrow strips of sand which he could leap over.'

'What about the old beach defences, the hunks of concrete? It would be difficult to come close to shore anywhere north within easy walking distance without risking the boat.'

'He has risked the boat recently, hasn't he? There's this scrape along the bow. He can't prove that he made it on the water towers. Cool about it, too, wasn't he? Calmly admitted that if we'd been an hour later he'd have repaired it. Not that repainting would have done him much good, the evidence would still be there. All right, so he manages to manoeuvre the boat as close in shore as he can, say, a hundred yards north of where she was found, makes his way along the shingle and into the trees and waits quietly in their shadow. Or he could have loaded the folding bicycle into the dinghy and landed at a safer distance. He couldn't cycle along the beach at high tide, but he'd have been safe enough on the coast road if he cycled without a light. He gets back to the boat and berths her again at Blakeney, just catching the high tide. No trouble about the knife or the shoes, he drops them overboard. We'll get the boat examined, with his consent, of course, and I want a single-handed chap to make that journey. If we've got an experienced sailor among our chaps, use him. If not, get someone local and accompany him. We've got to time it to the minute. And we'd better make inquiries of the crab fishermen down Cromer way. Someone may have been out that night and seen his boat.'

Oliphant said: 'Obliging of him, sir, to hand us his motive on a plate.'

'So obliging that I can't help wondering whether it isn't a smokescreen for something he didn't tell us.'

But as Rickards fastened his seat belt another possibility occurred to him. Lessingham had said nothing about his relationship with Toby Gledhill until he had been questioned about the Bumble trainers. He must know – how could he fail to? – that these linked the murder even more strongly to the headlanders and, in particular, to the Old Rectory. Was his new openness with the police less a compulsion to confide than a deliberate ploy to divert suspicion from another suspect? And if so, which of the suspects, Rickards wondered, was most likely to evoke this eccentric act of chivalry?

40

On Thursday morning Dalgliesh drove to Lydsett to shop at the village store. His aunt had shopped locally for most of her main provisions and he continued the practice, partly he knew to assuage a nagging guilt about having a second home, however temporary. The villagers did not on the whole resent weekenders despite the fact that their cottages remained empty for most of the year and their contribution to village life was minimal, but preferred them not to arrive with their car boots loaded with provisions from Harrods or Fortnum and Mason.

And patronizing the Brysons in their corner shop entailed no particular sacrifice. It was an unpretentious village store with a clanging bell on the door which, as the sepia photographs of the Victorian village showed, had hardly altered externally in the last 120 years. Inside, however, the last four years had seen more changes than in the whole of its history. Whether because of the growth of holiday homes or the more sophisticated tastes of the villagers, it now offered fresh pasta, a variety of French as well as English cheeses, the more expensive brands of jams, marmalade and mustard, and a well-stocked delicatessen, while a notice proclaimed that fresh croissants were delivered daily.

As he drew up in the side street, Dalgliesh had to manoeuvre past an old and heavily built bicycle with a large wicker basket which was propped against the kerb, and as he entered he saw that Ryan Blaney was just completing his purchases. Mrs Bryson was ringing up and bagging three brown loaves, packets of sugar, cartons of milk and an assortment of tins. Blaney gave Dalgliesh a glance from his bloodshot eyes, a curt nod, and was gone. He was still without his van, thought Dalgliesh, watching him load his basket with the contents of one carrier and hang the other two on the handlebars. Mrs Bryson turned on Dalgliesh her welcoming smile but did not comment. She was too prudent a shopkeeper to get a reputation as a gossip or to become too openly involved in local controversies, but it seemed to Dalgliesh that the air was heavy with her unspoken sympathy for Blaney and he felt obscurely that, as a policeman, she held him partly responsible although he was unsure precisely why and for what. Rickards or his men must have questioned the villagers about the headlanders, Ryan Blaney in particular. Perhaps they had been less than tactful.

Five minutes later he stopped to open the gate barring entry to the headland. On the other side a tramp was sitting on the bank which separated the narrow road from the reed-enclosed dyke. He was bearded and wearing a checked tweed cap beneath which two neat plaits of strong grey hair bound with a rubber band fell almost to his shoulders. He was eating an apple, slicing it with a short-handled knife and throwing the sections into his mouth. His long legs, clad in thick corduroy trousers, were stretched out widely in front of him almost as if he were deliberately displaying a pair of black, white and grey trainers, their obvious newness in stark contrast to the rest of his clothes. Dalgliesh closed the gate then walked over to him and looked down into a pair of bright and intelligent eyes set in a drawn and weatherbeaten face. If this was a tramp, the keenness of that first glance, his air of confident self-sufficiency and the cleanliness of his white rather delicate hands made him an unusual one. But he was surely too encumbered to be a casual hiker. His khaki coat looked like army surplus and was bound with a wide leather belt from which was suspended by string an enamel mug, a small saucepan and a frying pan. A small, but tightly packed backpack lay on the verge beside him.

Dalgliesh said: 'Good morning. I'm sorry if I seem impertinent, but where did you get those shoes?'

The voice that answered him was educated, a little pedantic, a voice, he thought, that might have once belonged to a schoolmaster.

'You are not, I hope, about to claim ownership. I shall regret it if our acquaintanceship, although no doubt destined to be brief, should begin with a dispute about property.'

'No, they're not mine. I was wondering how long they've been yours.'

The man finished his apple. He threw the core over his shoulder into the ditch, cleaned the blade of his clasp knife on the grass, and pushed it with care deep into his pocket. He said: 'May I ask if this inquiry arrives from – forgive me – an inordinate and reprehensible curiosity, an unnatural suspicion of a fellow mortal, or a desire to purchase a similar pair for yourself. If the last, I am afraid I am unable to help you.'

'None of these things. But the inquiry is important. I'm not being either presumptuous or suspicious.'

'Nor, sir, are you being particularly candid or explicit. My name, incidentally, is Jonah.'

'Mine is Adam Dalgliesh.'

'Then, Adam Dalgliesh, give me one good reason why I should answer your question and you shall have an answer.'

Dalgliesh paused for a moment. There was, he supposed, a theoretical possibility that here before him was the murderer of Hilary Robarts, but he did not for a moment believe it. Rickards had telephoned him the previous evening to inform him that the Bumbles were no longer in the jumble chest, obviously feeling that he owed Dalgliesh this brief report. But that did not mean that the tramp had taken them, nor did it prove that the two pairs were the same. He said: 'On Sunday night a girl was strangled here on the beach. If you recently found, or were given, those shoes or were wearing them on the headland last Sunday the police will need to know. They have found a distinct footprint. It is important to identify it if only to eliminate the wearer from their inquiries.'

'Well, that at least is explicit. You talk like a policeman. I should be sorry to hear that you are one.'

'This isn't my case. But I am a policeman and I know that the local CID are looking for a pair of Bumble trainers.'

'And these, I take it, are Bumble trainers. I had thought of them as shoes.'

'They don't have a label except under the tongue. That's the firm's sales gimmick. Bumbles are supposed to be recognizable without a blatant display of the name. But if these are Bumbles there will be a yellow bee on each heel.'

Jonah didn't reply, but with a sudden vigorous movement swung both feet into the air, held them for a couple of seconds, then dropped them again.

Neither spoke for a few moments, then Jonah said: 'You are telling me that I now have on my feet the shoes of a murderer?'

'Possibly, but only possibly, these are the shoes he was wearing when the girl was killed. You see their importance?'

'I shall no doubt be made to see it, by you or another of your kind.'

'Have you heard of the Norfolk Whistler?'

'Is it a bird?'

'A mass murderer.'

'And these shoes are his?'

'He's dead. This latest killing was made to look as if he were responsible. Are you telling me you haven't even heard of him?'

'I sometimes see a newspaper when I need paper for other more earthy purposes. There are plenty to pick up from the waste bins. I seldom read them. They reinforce my conviction that the world is not for me. I seem to have missed your murdering Whistler.' He paused then added: 'What now am I expected to do? I take it that I am in your hands.'

Dalgliesh said: 'As I said, it isn't my case. I'm from the Metropolitan Police. But if you wouldn't mind coming home with me I could telephone the officer in charge. It isn't far. I live in Larksoken Mill on the headland. And if you care to exchange these trainers for a pair of my shoes, it seems the least I can offer. We're about the same height. There should be a pair to fit you.'

Jonah got to his feet with surprising agility. As they walked to the car Dalgliesh said: 'I've really no right to question you, but satisfy my curiosity. How did you come by them?'

'They were bestowed on me, inadvertently I might say, some time on Sunday night. I had arrived on the headland after dark and made my way to my usual night shelter in these parts. It's the half-buried concrete bunker near the cliff. A pillbox I think it's called. I expect you know it.'

'I know it. Not a particularly salubrious place to spend the night I should have thought.'

'I have known better certainly. But it has the advantage of privacy. The headland is off the usual route for fellow wayfarers. I usually visit once a year and stay for a day or two. The pillbox is completely weatherproof and as the slit window faces the sea I can light a small fire without fear of discovery. I push the rubbish to one side and ignore it. It is a policy I would recommend to you.'

'Did you go straight there?'

'No. As is my custom I called at the Old Rectory. The elderly couple who live there are usually very obliging in allowing me to use their tap. I wanted to fill up my water bottle. As it happens, there was no one at home. There were lights on in the lower windows but no one responded to the bell.'

'What time would this be, do you remember?'

'I have no watch and I take little account of time between sunset and sunrise. But I did notice that St Andrew's Church clock in the village showed 8.30 as I passed. I was probably at the Old Rectory by 9.15, or shortly afterwards.'

'What did you do then?'

'I knew that there was an outside tap close to the garage. I took the liberty of filling my bottle without permission. They would hardly, I think, begrudge me clean water.'

'Did you see a car?'

'There was one standing in the drive. The garage was open but, as I have said, I saw no human beings. I then went straight to the shelter. I was by then exceedingly tired. I drank some of the water, ate a crust of bread and some cheese and fell asleep. The shoes were thrown in through the door of the bunker some time during the night.'

Dalgliesh said: 'Thrown in rather than placed?'

'I imagine so. Anyone who actually entered the bunker must have seen me. It is surely more likely that they were thrown in. There is a wayside pulpit at a church in Ipswich. Last week it said: "God gives every bird his worm, but He does not throw it into the nest." On this occasion apparently He did.'

'And they hit you without waking you? They're heavy shoes.'

'As I have said, you talk like a policeman. I had walked twenty miles on the Sunday. I have an easy conscience and I sleep sound. If they had fallen on my face I have no doubt they would have wakened me. As it was, I found them next morning when I woke up.'

'Neatly placed?'

'Not at all. What happened was that I woke and turned over from my left side on to my back. I felt something hard beneath me and lit a match. The lump was one of the shoes. The other I found near my foot.'

'They weren't tied together?'

'Had they been tied, my dear sir, it would hardly have been

possible for me to find one near the small of my back and the other at my feet.'

'And you weren't curious? After all, the trainers were practically new, hardly the kind of shoe anyone would chuck away.'

'Naturally I was curious. But unlike members of your profession I am not obsessed by the need to find explanations. It did not occur to me that I had a responsibility to find the owner or take the shoes in to the nearest police station. I doubt whether they would have thanked me for my trouble. I took gratefully what fate or God had provided. My old shoes were nearing the end of their usefulness. You will find them in the pillbox.'

'And you put on these.'

'Not immediately. They were too damp. I waited until they were dry.'

'Damp in parts or all over?'

'Damp all over. Someone had washed them very thoroughly, probably by holding them under a tap.'

'Or by walking into the sea.'

'I smelt them. It was not sea water.'

'Could you tell?'

'My dear sir, I have the use of my senses. My nose is particularly keen. I can tell the difference between sea and tap water. I can tell you what county I'm in by the smell of the earth.'

They had turned left at the crossroads, and the soaring white sails of the windmill were in sight. They sat in companionable silence for a few moments.

Then Jonah said: 'You have, perhaps, a right to know what manner of man you are inviting under your roof. I am, sir, a modern remittance man. I know that, originally, my kind were banished to the colonies but they are a little more discriminating now and, in any case, banishment from the smells and colours of the English countryside would not have suited me. My brother, a model of civil rectitude and a prominent member of his local community, transfers one thousand pounds per annum from his bank account into mine, providing I never embarrass him by intruding on his presence. The interdict, I may say, extends to the town of which he is mayor but, since he and his fellow planners have long destroyed whatever character it once possessed, I have deleted it from my itinerary without regret. He is indefatigable in good works and you could say that I am among the recipients of his charity. He has been honoured by Her Majesty. An OBE, merely, but he has, I am sure, hope of higher things.'

Dalgliesh said: 'Your brother seems to be getting off rather lightly.'

'You yourself would willingly pay more to ensure my perpetual absence?'

'Not at all. It's just that I assume that the one thousand pounds is to enable you to keep yourself and I was wondering how you managed to do it. One thousand pounds as an annual bribe could be considered generous; as a living allowance it's surely inadequate.'

'To do him justice, my brother would willingly make an annual increase in line with the Retail Price Index. He has an almost obsessive sense of bureaucratic propriety. But I have told him that twenty pounds a week is more than adequate. I have no house, no rent, no rates, no heating, no lighting, no telephone, no car. I pollute neither my own body nor the environment. A man who cannot feed himself on nearly three pounds a day must either be lacking in initiative or be the slave of inordinate desires. An Indian peasant would regard it as luxury.'

'An Indian peasant would have less problem in keeping warm. The winters must be trying.'

'A hard winter is, indeed, a discipline in endurance. Not that I complain. I am always healthiest in winter. And matches are cheap. I have never learned those boy scout tricks with a magnifying glass and rubbed sticks. Happily I know half a dozen farmers who are willing to let me sleep in their barns. They know that I don't smoke, that I am tidy, that I shall be gone by the morning. But one should never trespass on kindness. Human kindness is like a defective tap, the first gush may be impressive but the stream soon dries up. I have my annual routine and that, too, reassures them. In a farmhouse twenty miles north of here they will be saying soon, "Isn't this the time of year that Jonah drops in?" They greet me with relief rather than tolerance. If I am still alive then so are they. And I never beg. An offer to pay is far more efficacious. "Could you sell me a couple of eggs and half a pint of milk", spoken at the farm door – provided the cash is proffered – will usually produce six eggs and a full pint. Not necessarily of the freshest, but one must not expect too much of human generosity.'

Dalgliesh said: 'What about books?'

'Ah there, sir, you have hit on a difficulty. Classics I can read in public libraries, although it is sometimes a little irritating to have to break off when it is time to move on. Otherwise I rely on second-hand paperbacks from market stalls. One or two stall-holders allow you to exchange the book or get your money back at the second visit. It is a remarkably cheap form of public lending library. As for clothes, there are jumble sales, Oxfam and those useful shops that deal in army surplus. I save from my allowance for a new ex-army winter coat every three years.'

Dalgliesh said: 'How long have you been living this life?'

'Nearly twenty years now, sir. Most tramps are pitiful because they are the slaves of their own passions, usually drink. A man who is free of all human desires except to eat, sleep and walk is truly free.'

Dalgliesh said: 'Not entirely. You have a bank account apparently, and you rely on that thousand pounds.'

'True. You think I would be freer if I didn't take it?'

'More independent, perhaps. You might have to work.'

'I cannot work, to beg I am ashamed. Luckily the Lord has tempered the wind to his shorn lamb. I should be sorry to do my brother out of the satisfaction of his benevolence. True, I have a bank account to receive my annual subsidy and to that extent I conform. But since my income depends on my separation from my brother it would hardly be possible to receive the money personally and my cheque book and accompanying plastic card have a most gratifying effect on the police when, as occasionally happens, they take a presumptuous interest in my doings. I had no idea that a plastic card was such a guarantee of respectability.'

Dalgliesh asked: 'No luxuries? No other needs? Drink? Women?'

'If by women you mean sex then the answer is no. I am escaping, sir, from drink and sex.'

'Then you are on the run from something. I could argue that a man on the run is never entirely free.'

'And I could ask you, sir, from what you are escaping on this isolated headland. If from the violence of your job you have been singularly unlucky.'

'And now that same violence has touched your life. I'm sorry.'

'You needn't be. A man who lives with nature is used to violence and is companionable with death. There is more violence in an English hedgerow than in the meanest streets of a great city.'

When they reached the mill Dalgliesh telephoned Rickards. He wasn't at the incident room but Oliphant was and said that he would immediately drive over. Then Dalgliesh took Jonah upstairs to look over the half-dozen pairs of shoes he had with him at the mill. There was no problem over fit but Jonah tried them all on and examined each shoe minutely before making his choice. Dalgliesh was tempted to say that a life of simplicity and self-abnegation hadn't spoilt his guest's eye for good leather. He saw, with some regret, his favourite and most expensive pair chosen.

Jonah walked up and down the bedroom looking down at his feet with complacency. He said: 'I seem to have the best of the bargain. The Bumbles came at an opportune time but they were hardly suitable for serious walking and I intended to replace them as opportunity offered. The rules of the road are few and simple but they are imperative. I commend them to you. Keep your bowels open; bath once a week; wear wool or cotton next to the skin and leather on the feet.'

Fifteen minutes later his guest was ensconced in an armchair, a mug of coffee in hand, still regarding his feet with satisfaction. Oliphant was prompt in arriving. Apart from his driver he was alone. He came into the sitting room bringing with him an aura of masculine menace and authority. Even before Dalgliesh had made the introduction he said to Jonah: 'You must have known you'd no right to those trainers. They're new. Ever heard of stealing by finding?'

Dalgliesh said: 'A moment, Sergeant.' Drawing Oliphant aside he said in a low voice: 'You'll treat Mr Jonah with courtesy.'

And before Oliphant could protest, he added, 'All right, I'll save you the trouble of saying it. This isn't my case. But he is a guest in my house. If your men had searched the headland more thoroughly on Monday all three of us might have been saved some embarrassment.'

'He has to be a serious suspect, sir. He's got the shoes.'

Dalgliesh said: 'He also has a knife and he admits to having been on the headland on Sunday night. Treat him as a serious suspect by all means if you can find a motive or proof that he knew how the Whistler killed or even knew that he existed. But why not listen to his story before you jump to conclusions about his guilt?'

Oliphant said: 'Guilty or not, Mr Dalgliesh, he's an important witness. I don't see how we can allow him to go wandering off.'

'And I don't see how, legally, you can prevent him. But that's your problem, Sergeant.'

A few minutes later Oliphant was leading Jonah towards the car. Dalgliesh went out to see him off. Before climbing in at the back, Jonah turned to him.

'It was an ill day for me when I met you, Adam Dalgliesh.'

'But a good day, perhaps, for justice.'

'Oh, justice. Is that the business you're in? I think you may have left it rather late. This planet earth is hurtling now to its destruction. That concrete bastion on the edge of a polluted sea may bring about the final darkness. If not it will be by some other folly of man. There comes a time when every scientist, even God, has to write off an experiment. Ah, I see a certain relief on your face. You are thinking, So he is mad after all, this peculiar tramp. I need no longer take him seriously.'

Dalgliesh said: 'My mind agrees with you. My genes are more optimistic.'

'You know it. We all know it. How else can one explain the modern sickness of man. And when the final darkness falls I shall die as I have lived, in the nearest dry ditch.' And then he gave a singularly sweet smile and added: 'Wearing your shoes, Adam Dalgliesh.'

41

The encounter with Jonah had left Dalgliesh curiously restless. There were plenty of jobs to be done in the mill but he felt disinclined to tackle any of them. His instinct was to get into the Jaguar and drive very fast and very far. But he had tried that expedient too often to have any faith in its efficacy. The mill would still be standing when he returned, the problems still unsolved. He had no difficulty in recognizing the basis of his discontent; the frustrating involvement with a case which would never be his yet from which it was impossible to distance himself. He remembered some words of Rickards spoken before they had finally parted on the night of the murder.

'You may not want to be involved, Mr Dalgliesh, but you are involved. You may wish that you had never been near the body, but you were there.'

He seemed to remember using much the same words to a suspect in one of his own cases. He was beginning to understand why they had been so ill received. On an impulse he unlocked the mill and climbed up the ladders to the top storey. Here, he suspected, his aunt had found her peace. Perhaps some of that lost contentment might seep into him. But any hope of being left undisturbed was due to be frustrated.

As he looked over the headland from the southern window a bicycle came into sight. At first it was too distant to see who was riding but then he recognized Neil Pascoe. They had never spoken but, like all the headlanders, they knew each other by sight. Pascoe seemed to be cycling with a ponderous determination, his head low over the handlebars, his shoulders working. But as he came close to the mill he suddenly stopped, put both feet on the ground, stared towards the mill as if seeing it for the first time, then dismounted and began wheeling the bicycle over the rough scrubland.

For one second Dalgliesh was tempted to pretend that he wasn't home. Then he realized that the Jaguar was parked at the side of the mill and that it was possible that Pascoe in that long stare had glimpsed his face at the window. Whatever the purpose of this visit it looked as if it were one he couldn't avoid. He moved over to the window above the door, opened it and called down: 'Are you looking for me?'

The question was rhetorical. Who else would Pascoe expect to find at Larksoken Mill? Looking down at the upturned face, the thin jutting beard, Dalgliesh saw him curiously diminished and foreshortened, a vulnerable rather pathetic figure clutching his bicycle as if for protection.

Pascoe shouted up against the wind: 'Could I talk to you?'

An honest reply would have been 'If you must', but it was not one that Dalgliesh felt he could shout down against the noise of the wind without sounding ungracious. He mouthed 'I'll be down.'

Pascoe propped the machine against the wall of the mill and followed him into the sitting room.

He said: 'We haven't actually met but I expect you've heard of me. I'm Neil Pascoe from the caravan. I'm sorry if I'm butting in when you want some peace.' He sounded as embarrassed as a door-to-door salesman trying to reassure a prospective customer that he wasn't a con man.

Dalgliesh was tempted to say, 'I might want some peace but it doesn't look as if I'm likely to get it.' He asked: 'Coffee?'

Pascoe gave the predictable reply: 'If it isn't too much trouble.'

'No trouble. I was thinking of making it.'

Pascoe followed him into the kitchen and stood leaning against the door post in an unconvincing assumption of ease as Dalgliesh ground the coffee beans and put on the kettle. It struck him that he had spent a considerable time since his arrival at the mill providing food and drink for uninvited visitors. When the grinding had ceased, Pascoe said almost truculently: 'I need to talk to you.'

'If it's about the murder then you ought to be speaking to Chief Inspector Rickards not me. This isn't my case.'

'But you found the body.'

'That might in certain circumstances make me a suspect. But it doesn't give me the right to interfere professionally in another officer's case outside my own force area. I'm not the investigating officer. But you know that, you're not stupid.'

Pascoe kept his eyes on the bubbling liquid. He said: 'I didn't expect you to be particularly pleased to see me. I wouldn't have come if there were anyone else I could talk to. There are things I can't discuss with Amy.'

'As long as you remember whom you are talking to.'

'A policeman. It's like the priesthood, is it? Never off duty. Once a priest always a priest.'

'It isn't in the least like the priesthood. No guarantee of confidentiality in the confessional and no absolution. That's what I'm trying to tell you.'

They said nothing else until the coffee had been poured into the two mugs and carried by Dalgliesh into the sitting room. They sat, one each side of the fireplace. Pascoe took his mug but seemed uncertain what to do with it. He sat twisting it in his hands, looking down at the coffee, making no attempt to drink. After a moment he said: 'It's about Toby Gledhill, the boy – well, he was a boy really – who killed himself at the power station.'

Dalgliesh said: 'I've heard about Toby Gledhill.'

'Then I expect you know how he died. He hurled himself down on top of the reactor and broke his neck. That was on Friday the twelfth of August. Two days before, on the Wednesday, he came to see me at about eight o'clock in the evening. I was on my own in the caravan, Amy had taken the van into Norwich to shop and said she wanted to see a film and would be back late. I was looking after Timmy. Then there was this knock and there he stood. I knew him, of course. At least, I knew who he was. I'd seen him on one or two of those open days at the power station. I usually make time to go to those. They can't stop me, and it gives me an opportunity of putting one or two awkward questions, countering their propaganda. And I think he was present at some of the meetings of the new pressurized water reactor inquiry. But, of course, I'd never really met him. I couldn't think what he wanted of me, but I invited him in and offered him a beer. I'd lit the stove because there were a lot of Timmy's clothes which needed drying so the caravan was very hot and rather damp. When I remember that night I seem to see him through a haze of steam. After the beer he asked if we couldn't go out. He seemed restless as if he found the caravan claustrophobic and he asked more than once when Amy was expected back. So I lifted Timmy out of his cot and put him into the backpack and we set off to walk north along the shore. It was when we had got as far as the abbey ruins that he told me what he'd come to say. He came out with it quite baldly, without any preamble. He'd come to the conclusion that nuclear power was too dangerous to use and that, until we've solved the problem of radioactive waste, we ought not to build any more nuclear power stations. There was one rather odd expression he used. He said: "It's not only dangerous, it's corrupting."'

Dalgliesh asked: 'Did he say why he'd come to this conclusion?'

'I think it had been building up for quite a few months, and Chernobyl had probably brought it to a head. He said that something else had recently happened that had helped to make up his mind. He didn't say what but he promised he would tell me when he'd had more time to think. I asked him if he was merely going to give up his job and opt out or whether he was prepared to help us. He said he thought that he had to help. It wouldn't be enough just to resign his job. It was difficult for him and I could see just how difficult. He admired and liked his colleagues. He said they were dedicated scientists and very intelligent men who believed in what they were doing. It was just that he couldn't believe any more. He hadn't thought about the way ahead, not very clearly anyway. He was like I am now; he just needed to talk it through. I suppose I seemed to be the natural person. He knew about PANUP of course.' He looked up at Dalgliesh and said rather naïvely: 'That stands for People Against Nuclear Power. When the proposal was put forward for the new reactor here I formed a little local group to oppose it. I mean a group of ordinary concerned local residents, not the more powerful national protest bodies. It hasn't been easy. Most people try to pretend that the power station isn't really there. And of course quite a number welcome it because it does bring in some employment, new customers for the shops and pubs. Most of the opposition to the new reactor wasn't local, anyway, it was people from CND, Friends of the Earth and Greenpeace. Of course we welcomed them. They're the ones with the heavy guns. But I thought it important to get something going locally and I suppose I'm not really a joiner. I like to do my own thing.'

Dalgliesh said: 'And Gledhill would have been quite a catch for you.' The words were almost brutal in their implication.

Pascoe flushed then looked him in the eyes. 'There was that too. I suppose I realized it at the time. I wasn't entirely disinterested. I mean, I did know how important it would be if he came over. But I was, well, flattered I suppose that he'd come first to me. PANUP hasn't made much impact, really. Even the initials were a mistake. I wanted something that people would easily remember, but PANUP – a bit of a laugh. I can guess what you're thinking, that I might have done more good for the cause by joining an existing pressure group instead of ministering to my own ego. You'd be right.'

Dalgliesh asked: 'Did Gledhill say whether he'd spoken to anyone at the station?'

'He said that he hadn't, not yet. I think that was what he most dreaded. He particularly hated the thought of telling Miles Lessingham. While we walked along the beach with Timmy half asleep bumping on my back he felt free to talk and I think he found it a release. He told me that Lessingham was in love with him. He wasn't gay himself but he was ambivalent. But he did tremendously admire Lessingham and felt that in some way he was letting him down. He gave the impression that everything was a muddle, his feelings about atomic power, his personal life, his career, everything.'

Suddenly Pascoe seemed to realize that he was holding his coffee mug and, lowering his head, began to drink from it with great slurps, like a man desperate with thirst. When the mug was drained he put it down on the floor and wiped his mouth with his hand.

He said: 'It was a warm night after a rainy day, the night of the new moon. Funny how I remember that. We were walking just above the tide mark on the shingle. And then, suddenly, there she was, Hilary Robarts, splashing out of the foam. She was only wearing the bottom half of her bikini and she stood there for a moment with the water running off her hair, glistening in that eerie light which seems to come off the sea on a starry night. Then she came slowly up the beach towards us. I suppose we stood there almost as if mesmerized. She had lit a small fire of brushwood on the shingle and the three of us moved towards it. She picked up her towel but didn't wrap it round her. She looked – well, she looked marvellous, the drops of water glistening on her skin and that locket thing she wears resting between her breasts. I know it sounds ridiculous and, well, corny, but she looked like some goddess risen from the sea. She took absolutely no notice of me but she looked at Toby. She said: "Nice to see you, Toby. Why not come down to the cottage for a drink and a meal?" Such ordinary words. Harmless sounding words. But they weren't.

'I don't think he could resist her. I don't suppose I would have been able to either. Not at that moment. And I knew exactly what she was doing, and so did she. She was asking him to make a choice. On my side nothing but trouble, a lost job, personal anguish, possibly even disgrace. And on hers security, professional success, the respect of peers, colleagues. And love. I think she was offering him love. I knew what would happen in the cottage if he went with her and he knew too. But he went. He didn't even say goodnight to me. She slung her towel over her shoulder and turned her back on us as if absolutely confident that he would follow her. And he did follow her. And two days later, on Friday the twelfth of August, he killed himself. I don't know what she said to him. No one will know now. But after that meeting I think he just couldn't take any more. It was not what she threatened him with, or even if she threatened him at all. But if it hadn't been for that meeting on the beach I think he'd be alive now. She killed him.'

Dalgliesh said: 'None of this came out at the inquest?'

'No, none. There was no reason why it should. I wasn't called as a witness. It was all handled very discreetly. Alex Mair was anxious that there shouldn't be any publicity. As you've probably noticed, there hardly ever is when something goes wrong at an atomic power station. They all become experts at the cover-up.'

'And why are you telling me this?'

'I want to be sure that this is something Rickards needs to be told. But I suppose I'm really telling you because I need to share it with someone. I'm not sure why I picked on you. Sorry.'

A true, if hardly kind, reply would have been: 'You picked on me in the hope that I'd undertake to pass it on to Rickards and save you the responsibility.' Instead Dalgliesh said: 'You realize, of course, that this is information Chief Inspector Rickards should have.'

'But is it? That's what I want to be sure of. I suppose it's the usual fear when dealing with the police. What use are they going to make of it? Are they going to get the wrong idea? Could it point to someone who could be innocent? I suppose you have to have confidence in the integrity of the police, you wouldn't go on being a detective if you hadn't. But the rest of us know that things can go wrong, that the innocent can be harried, the guilty get off, that the police aren't always as scrupulous as they pretend to be. I'm not asking you to tell him for me, I'm not that childish. But I don't really see how it's relevant. Both of them are dead. I can't see how telling Rickards about that meeting can help to catch Miss Robarts's killer. And it can't bring either of them back to life.'

Dalgliesh refilled Pascoe's mug. Then he said: 'Of course it's relevant. You're suggesting that Hilary Robarts might have black-mailed Gledhill into staying in his job. If she could do it to one person she could do it to another. Anything about Miss Robarts could be relevant to her death. And don't worry too much about innocent suspects. I'm not going to pretend that the innocent don't suffer in a murder investigation. Of course they do. No one even remotely touched by murder goes unscathed. But Chief Inspector Rickards isn't a fool and he's an honest man. He's only going to use what is relevant to his inquiry and it's for him to decide what is relevant and what isn't.'

'I suppose that's the reassurance I wanted to hear. All right, I'll tell him.'

He suddenly jerked himself up from the chair as if anxious to be gone and, with only a final word of goodbye, mounted his bicycle and pedalled furiously down the path, bending himself against the wind. Dalgliesh took the two mugs back into the kitchen thoughtfully. That verbal picture of Hilary Robarts rising like a glistening goddess from the waves had been remarkably vivid. But one detail had been wrong. Pascoe had spoken of the key locket resting between her breasts. He remembered Mair's words as he stood looking down at the body. 'That locket round her neck. I gave it to her on August the twenty-ninth for her birthday.' On Wednesday 10 August Hilary Robarts couldn't have been wearing it. Pascoe had undoubtedly seen Hilary Robarts walking out of the sea with the locket resting between her naked breasts; but it couldn't have been on 10 August.

BOOK SIX

Saturday 1 October to Thursday 6 October

42

Jonathan had decided to wait until Saturday to visit London and continue his inquiries. His mother was less likely to question him about a trip on Saturday to visit the Science Museum, while taking a day's leave always provoked inquiries about where he was going and why. But he thought it prudent to spend half an hour in the museum before setting off to Pont Street and it was after three o'clock before he was outside the block of flats. One fact was immediately apparent: no one who lived in this building and employed a housekeeper could possibly be poor. The house was part of an imposing Victorian terrace, half stone, half brick, with pillars each side of the gleaming black door and ornate glass, like green bottle tops, in the two ground-floor windows. The door was open and he could see a square hall tiled with black and white marble, the lower balustrade of an ornate wrought-iron staircase, and the door of a golden cage lift. To the right was a porter's desk with a uniformed man on duty. Anxious not to be seen loitering he walked quickly on considering his next move.

In one sense none was necessary except to find his way to the nearest tube station, return to Liverpool Street and take the first train to Norwich. He had done what he had set out to do; he knew now that Caroline had lied to him. He told himself that he should be feeling shocked and distressed, both at her lie and at his own duplicity in discovering it. He had thought himself in love with her. He was in love with her. For the past year there had been hardly an hour in which she had been absent from his thoughts. That blonde, remote, self-contained beauty had obsessed him. Like a schoolboy he had waited at the corners of corridors where she might pass, had welcomed his bed because he could lie undisturbed and indulge his secret erotic fantasies, would wake wondering where and how they might next meet. Surely neither the physical act of possession nor the discovery of deceit could destroy love. So why was this confirmation of her deception almost agreeable, even pleasant? He should be devastated; instead he was filled with a satisfaction close to triumph. She had lied, almost carelessly, confident that he was too much in love, too enthralled, too stupid even to question her story. But now, with the discovery of the truth, the balance of power in their relationship had subtly shifted. He wasn't sure yet what use he would make of the information. He had found the energy and courage to act but whether he would have the courage to confront her with his knowledge was another matter.

He walked quickly to the end of Pont Street, his eyes on the paving stones, then turned and retraced his steps trying to make sense of his turbulent emotions, so tangled that they seemed to jostle each other for dominance: relief, regret, disgust, triumph. And it had been so easy. Every dreaded obstacle from contacting the detective agency to finding an excuse for this day in London had been surmounted with greater ease than he could believe possible. So why not chance one further step? Why not make absolutely sure? He knew the name of the housekeeper, Miss Beasley. He could ask to see her, say that he had met Caroline a year or two ago, in Paris perhaps, had lost her address, wanted to get in touch. If he kept his story simple, resisted the temptation to embroider, there was no possible danger. He knew that Caroline had taken her summer holiday in France in 1986, the year, he too, had been there. It was one of the facts that had come up in conversation on their early dates together, innocuous chat about travel and paintings, the attempt to find some common ground, a shared interest. Well, at least he had been in Paris. He had seen the Louvre. He could say that that was where they had met.

He would need a false name, of course. His father's Christian name would do. Percival. Charles Percival. It was better to choose something slightly unusual; a too common name would sound obviously false. He would say that he lived in Nottingham. He had been at the university there and knew the town. Somehow being able to picture those familiar streets made the fantasy believable. He needed to root his lies in a semblance of truth. He could say that he worked at the hospital there, a laboratory technician. If there were any other questions he could parry them. But why should there be any other questions?

He made himself walk with confidence into the hall. Only a day ago he would have found difficulty in meeting the porter's eyes. Now, filled with the self-assurance of success, he said: 'I want to visit Miss Beasley in flat three. Would you say that I'm a friend of Miss Caroline Amphlett.'

The porter left the reception desk and went into his office to telephone. Jonathan thought, What's to prevent me just going up the stairs and knocking at the door? Then he realized that the porter would immediately telephone Miss Beasley and warn her not to let him in. There was security of a kind, but it wasn't particularly tight.

Within half a minute the man was back. He said: 'That's all right, sir. You can go up. It's on the first floor.'

He didn't bother to take the lift. The double mahogany door with its numeral of polished brass, its two security locks and central spyhole was at the front of the house. He smoothed back his hair then rang the bell and made himself stare at the peephole with an assumption of ease. He could hear nothing from inside the flat and the heavy door seemed as he waited to grow into an intimidating barricade which only a presumptuous fool would attempt to breach. For a second, picturing that single eyeball scrutinizing him through the peephole, he had to fight an impulse to flee. But then there was the faint clink of a chain, the sound of a lock turning, and the door was opened.

Since his decision to call at the flat he had been too preoccupied with fabricating his story to give much conscious thought to Miss Beasley. The word housekeeper had conjured up a soberly dressed, middle-aged woman, at worst a little condescending and intimidating, at best deferential, chatty, eager to help. The reality was so bizarre that he gave a perceptible start of surprise, then blushed at his own betrayal. She was short and very thin with straight red-gold hair, white at the roots and obviously dyed, falling in a gleaming helmet to her shoulders. Her pale green eyes were immense and shallowly set, the lower lids inverted and bloodshot so that the eyeballs seemed to be swimming in an open wound.

Her skin was very white and creped with innumerable small lines except over the jutting cheekbones where it was stretched as fine as paper. In contrast to the skin's unpainted fragility her mouth was a thin gash of garish crimson. She was wearing high-heeled slippers and a kimono and was carrying a small, almost hairless dog with bulging eyes, its thin neck encircled with a jewelled collar. For a few seconds she stood silently regarding him, the dog pressed against her cheek.

Jonathan, his carefully husbanded confidence rapidly draining, said: 'I'm sorry to trouble you. It's just that I'm a friend of Miss Caroline Amphlett and I'm trying to trace her.'

'Well, you won't find her here.' The voice, which he recognized, was unexpected from so frail a woman, deep and husky, and not unattractive.

He said, 'I'm sorry if I've got the wrong Amphlett. You see, Caroline did give me her address two years ago but I've lost it, so I tried the telephone directory.'

'I didn't say that you'd got the wrong Amphlett, only that you won't find her here. But as you look harmless enough and are obviously unarmed you had better come in. One cannot be too careful in these violent times, but Baggott is very reliable. Very few impostors get past Baggott. Are you an impostor, Mr . . .?'

'Percival. Charles Percival.'

'You must excuse my *déshabillé*, Mr Percival, but I do not normally expect afternoon visitors.'

He followed her across a square hall and through double doors into what was obviously the drawing room. She pointed imperiously to a sofa set in front of the fireplace. It was uncomfortably low and as soft-cushioned as a bed, each drop end festooned with thick tasselled cords. Moving slowly as if deliberately taking her time, she placed herself opposite to him in an elegant high-winged chair, settled the dog on her lap and gazed down on him with the fixed unsmiling intensity of an inquisitor. He knew that he must look as gauche and ungainly as he felt, his thighs enclosed in the softness of the cushion, his sharp knees almost touching his chin. The dog, as naked as if it had been skinned and shivering perpetually like a creature demented with cold, turned first on him and then up at her its pleading exophthalmic eyes. The leather collar, with its great dollops of red and blue stones, lay heavily on the animal's frail neck.

Jonathan resisted the temptation to look round at the room but it seemed that every feature had entered his consciousness; the marble fireplace with above it a full-length oil painting of a Victorian army officer, a pale arrogant face with one lock of blond hair falling almost to the cheek, which bore an uncanny resemblance to Caroline; the four carved chairs with embroidered seats set against the wall; the pale, polished floor with its wrinkled carpets; the drum-shaped table in the centre of the room and the side tables with their photographs in silver frames. There was a strong smell of paint and turpentine. Somewhere in the flat a room was being decorated.

After a moment's silent scrutiny the woman spoke. 'So you're a friend of Caroline's. You surprise me, Mr . . . Mr . . . I'm afraid I have already forgotten your name.'

He said firmly: 'Percival. Charles Percival.'

'Mine is Miss Oriole Beasley. I am the housekeeper here. As I said, you surprise me, Mr Percival. But if you say you are Caroline's friend, naturally I accept your word.'

'Perhaps I shouldn't say friend. I only met her once, in Paris in 1986. We went round the Louvre together. But I would like to see her again. She did give me her address, but I lost it.'

'How careless. So you waited two years and then decided to trace her. Why now, Mr Percival? You have managed, apparently, to control your impatience for two years.'

He knew how he must look and sound to her; unconfident, shy, ill at ease. But that, surely, was what she would expect from a man gauche enough to believe that he could revive a dead and fleeting passion. He said: 'It's just that I'm in London for a few days. I work in Nottingham. I'm a technician at the hospital there. I don't often get the chance to come south. It was an impulse really, trying to trace Caroline.'

'As you see, she's not here. She has not, in fact, lived in this house since she was seventeen, and as I am only the housekeeper it is hardly my place to hand out information about the family's whereabouts to casual inquirers. Would you describe yourself as a casual inquirer, Mr Percival?'

Jonathan said: 'Perhaps it seems like that. It's just that I found the name in the telephone directory and thought it was worth a try. Of course she might not want to see me again.'

'I should imagine that is more than likely. And, of course, you have some identification, something to confirm that you are Mr Charles Percival of Nottingham.'

Jonathan said: 'Not really, I'm afraid. I didn't think . . .'

'Not even a credit card or a driving licence? You seem to have come singularly unprepared, Mr Percival.'

Something in the deep, arrogantly upper-class voice, the mixture of insolence and contempt, stung him into defiance. He said: 'I'm not from the gas board. I don't see why I need to identify myself. It was just a simple inquiry. I was hoping to see her, or perhaps Mrs Amphlett. I'm sorry if I've offended you.'

'You haven't offended me. If I were easily offended I wouldn't work for Mrs Amphlett. But I'm afraid you can't see her. Mrs Amphlett goes to Italy in late September and then flies to Spain for the winter. I'm surprised Caroline didn't tell you. In her absence I look after the flat. Mrs Amphlett dislikes the melancholy of autumn and the cold of winter. A wealthy woman need suffer neither. I'm sure you are perfectly well aware of that, Mr Percival.'

And here, at last, was the opening he needed. He made himself look into those terrible bleeding eyes and said: 'I thought Caroline told me that her mother was poor, that she'd lost all her money investing in Peter Robarts's plastics company.'

The effect of his words was extraordinary. She flushed scarlet, the mottled stain travelling like a rash from her neck to her forehead. It seemed a long time before she could bring herself to speak, but when she did her voice was perfectly under control.

'Either you wilfully misunderstood, Mr Percival, or your memory is as unreliable for financial facts as it is for addresses. Caroline could have told you nothing of the sort. Her mother inherited a fortune from her grandfather when she was twenty-one and has never lost a penny of it. It was my small capital – ten thousand pounds, in case you are interested – which was unwisely invested in the schemes of that plausible rogue. But Caroline would hardly confide that small personal tragedy to a stranger.'

He could think of nothing to say, could find no credible explanation, no excuse. He had the proof he wanted; Caroline had lied. He should have been filled with triumph that his suspicions had been justified, his small enterprise crowned with success. Instead, he was swept with a momentary but overwhelming depression and a conviction which seemed to him as frightening as it was irrational, that the proof of Caroline's perfidy had been bought at a terrible price.

There was a silence in which she continued to regard him, but did not speak. Then she suddenly asked: 'What did you think of Caroline? Obviously she made an impression on you or you wouldn't be wishing to renew the acquaintance. And no doubt she has been in your mind during the last two years.'

'I think – I thought she was very lovely.'

'Yes, isn't she? I'm glad you feel that. I was her nurse, her nanny, if one must use that ridiculous expression. You could say that I brought her up. Does that surprise you? I'm hardly the popular idea of a nanny. Warm lap, aproned bosom, *Winnie the Pooh, The Wind in the Willows*, prayers at bedtime, eat up your crusts or your hair won't curl. But I had my methods. Mrs Amphlett accompanied the Brigadier on his overseas postings and we stayed here together, just the two of us. Mrs Amphlett believed that a child should have stability provided she was not required to provide it. Of course, if Caroline had been a son it would have been different. The Amphletts have never valued daughters. Caroline did have a brother but he was killed in a friend's car when he was fifteen. Caroline was with them but survived almost without a scratch. I don't think her parents ever forgave her. They could never look at her without making it plain that the wrong child had been killed.'

Jonathan thought: I don't want to hear this, I don't want to listen. He said: 'She never told me that she had a brother. But she did mention you.'

'Did she indeed? She talked about me to you. Now you do surprise me, Mr Percival. Forgive me, but you are the last person I should have expected her to talk to about me.'

He thought: She knows; not the truth, but she knows that I'm not Charles Percival from Nottingham. And it seemed to him, meeting those extraordinary eyes in which the mixture of suspicion and contempt was unmistakable that she was allied to Caroline in a female conspiracy in which he had from the first been a hapless and despised victim. The knowledge fuelled his anger and gave him strength. But he said nothing.

After a moment, she went on: 'Mrs Amphlett kept me on after Caroline left home, even after the Brigadier passed on. But passed on is hardly an appropriate euphemism for a soldier. Perhaps I should say was called to higher service, recalled to the Colours, promoted to glory. Or is that the Salvation Army? I have a feeling that it's only the Salvation Army who get promoted to glory.'

He said: 'Caroline did tell me that her father was a professional soldier.'

'She has never been a very confiding girl but you seem to have gained her confidence, Mr Percival. So now I call myself a housekeeper rather than a nanny. My employer finds plenty to keep me occupied even when she isn't here. It would never do for Maxie and me to live here on board wages and enjoy ourselves in London, would it, Maxie? No indeed. A little skilled sewing. Private letters to be posted on. Bills to be paid. Her jewels to be taken to be cleaned. The flat to be redecorated. Mrs Amphlett particularly dislikes the smell of paint. And, of course, Maxie has to be exercised daily. He never thrives in kennels, do you, my treasure? I wonder what will happen to me when Maxie is promoted to glory?'

There was nothing he could say to that, nor, apparently, did she expect him to. After a moment's silence, during which she lifted the dog's paw and rubbed it gently against her face, she said: 'Caroline's old friends seem very anxious to get in touch with her all of a sudden. Someone telephoned to ask for her only on Tuesday. Or was it Wednesday? But perhaps that was you, Mr Percival?'

'No,' he said, and was amazed at the ease with which he could lie. 'No, I didn't telephone. I thought it better just to take my chance and call.'

'But you knew who to ask for. You knew my name. You gave it to Baggott.'

But she wasn't going to catch him like that. He said: 'I remembered it. As I said, Caroline did talk about you.'

'It might have been sensible to telephone first. I could have explained that she wasn't here, saved you time. How odd that it didn't occur to you. But that other friend didn't sound like you. Quite a different voice. Scottish, I think. If you will excuse my saying so, Mr Percival, your voice is without either character or distinction.'

Jonathan said: 'If you don't feel you can give me Caroline's address, perhaps I'd better go. I'm sorry if I came at an inconvenient time.'

'Why not write a letter to her, Mr Percival? I can let you have the writing paper. I don't think it would be right to give you her address but you can be confident that I will post on any communication that you care to trust to me.'

'She isn't in London, then?'

'No, she hasn't lived in London for over three years and she hasn't lived here since she was seventeen. But I do know where she is. We keep in touch. Your letter will be safe with me.'

He thought: This is an obvious trap. But she can't make me write. There must be nothing in my handwriting. Caroline would recognize it even if I tried to disguise it. He said: 'I think I'd rather write later when I've more time to think what to say. If I post it to this address then you can send it on.'

'I will do that with pleasure, Mr Percival. And now, I expect, you will want to be on your way. Your visit may have been less productive than you hoped, but I expect you have learned what you came to learn.'

But she didn't move and for a moment he felt himself trapped, immobilized as if the disagreeably soft and yielding cushions held him in a vice. He half expected her to leap up and bar his way to the door, to denounce him as an impostor, to keep him locked in the flat while she telephoned the police or the porter. What then would he do: attempt to seize the keys by force and make his escape, wait for the police and try to bluff his way to freedom? But the momentary panic subsided. She got to her feet and led the way to the door and, without speaking, held it open. She did not close it and he was aware that she was standing there, the dog shivering in her arms, both of them watching him leave. At the head of the stairs he turned to smile a final goodbye. What he then saw made him stand for a second immobile before he almost ran down the stairs and through the hall to the open door. He had never in all his life seen such concentrated hatred on a human face.

43

The whole enterprise had been more of a strain than Jonathan could have believed possible, and by the time he reached Liverpool Street he was very tired. The station was in the process of being rebuilt – improved, as the large displays designed to reassure and encourage proclaimed – and had become a clanging and confusing maze of temporary walkways and direction signs in which it was difficult actually to find the trains. Taking a false turn he found himself in a glossily floored piazza and felt momentarily as disorientated as if he were in a foreign capital. His arrival that morning had been less confusing, but now even the station reinforced his sense of having ventured both physically and emotionally on to alien ground.

Once the journey had started he leaned back, his eyes closed, and tried to make sense of the day and of his conflicting emotions. But instead, and almost immediately, he fell asleep and didn't stir into consciousness until the train was drawing into Norwich station. But the sleep had done him good. He strode towards the castle car park filled with renewed energy and optimism. He knew what he would do; drive at once to the bungalow, and confront Caroline with the evidence and ask her why she had lied. He couldn't go on seeing her and pretend not to know. They were lovers; they should be able to trust each other. If she was worried or frightened he was there to reassure and comfort her. He knew that she couldn't have murdered Hilary. The very thought was profanation. But she wouldn't have lied unless she was frightened. Something was dreadfully wrong. He would persuade her to go to the police, explain why she had lied and persuaded him to lie. They would go together, confess together. He didn't ask himself whether she would want to see him or even whether, late on a Saturday, she would be at home. All he knew was that the matter between them had to be settled now. There was a rightness and inevitability about his decision and he felt, too, a small surge of power. She had thought him a gullible and ineffectual fool. Well, he would show her that she was wrong. From now on there would be a subtle change in their relationship; she would have a more confident, less malleable lover.

Forty minutes later he was driving through the darkness across flat, undistinguished country towards the bungalow. Slowing down as it came into sight on his left, he was struck afresh by how remote and unattractive it was and wondered again why, with so many villages closer to Larksoken, with the attractions of Norwich and the coast, she should have rented this forbidding, almost sinister little box of crude red brick. And the very word bungalow seemed to him ridiculous, evoking a picture of suburban ribbon development, of cosy respectability, of old people who could no longer manage stairs. Caroline should live in a tower with a wide view of the sea.

And then he saw her. The silver Golf came out from the drive very fast and accelerated eastward. She was wearing what looked like a woollen cap pulled down over her yellow hair but he knew her immediately. He didn't know whether she had recognized him or the Fiesta, but instinctively he braked and let her get almost out of sight before he followed. And, waiting in the quietness of that flat landscape, he could hear Remus barking hysterically.

He was surprised how easy it was to keep her in sight. Sometimes another car passing him would obscure his view of the silver Golf and occasionally, when she slowed for traffic lights or because they had reached a village, he had quickly to reduce speed in case she realized that he was on her tail. They passed through Lydsett village and she took the right turn across the headland. By now he feared that she must have recognized him, must know that she was being followed, but she went on apparently uncaring. When she had negotiated the gate he waited until she was out of sight over the ridge before following, then stopped, put out the car lights and went a little way on foot. He saw that she was picking someone up; a slim girl with spiked yellow hair, orange at the tips, was briefly illuminated in the headlights. The car turned north along the coast road, inland at the power station, then north again. Forty minutes later their destination was known, the quay at Wells-next-the-Sea.

He parked the Fiesta beside the Golf and followed them, keeping Caroline's blue and white cap in sight. They walked quickly, apparently unspeaking and neither of them looked back. At the quay he momentarily lost them and then he saw that they were getting on a boat. And now was his chance; he had to speak to Caroline. He almost ran towards them. They were already on board. It was a small craft, no more than fifteen feet long with a low central cabin and an outboard motor. Both girls were standing in the cockpit. As he came up Caroline turned to him. 'What the hell do you think you're doing?'

'I want to talk to you. I've been following you since you left the bungalow.'

'I know that, you fool. You've been in my mirror practically the whole way. If I'd wanted to throw you off it wouldn't have been difficult. You should give up this cloak-and-dagger business. It doesn't suit you and you're no good at it.'

But there was no anger in her voice, only a kind of irritated weariness. He said: 'Caroline, I have to talk to you.'

'Then wait until tomorrow. Or stay where you are if you must. We'll be back in an hour.'

'But where are you going? What are you doing?'

'For Christ's sake, what do you think I'm doing? This is a boat, my boat. Out there is the sea. Amy and I are planning a short trip.'

Amy, he thought, Amy who? But Caroline didn't introduce her. He said weakly: 'But it's so late. It's dark and it's getting misty.'

'So it's dark and misty. This is October. Look, Jonathan, why don't you mind your own business and get off home to mother.'

She was busying herself in the cockpit. He leaned over and clutched the side of the boat, feeling the gentle rock of the tide. He said: 'Caroline, please talk to me! Don't go. I love you.'

'I doubt it.'

Both of them seemed to have forgotten Amy. He said desperately: 'I know that you lied about your mother being ruined by Hilary's father. That wasn't true, any of it. Look, if you're in trouble I want to help. We've got to talk. I can't go on like this.'

'I'm not in trouble, and if I were you'd be the last person I'd turn to. And take your hands off my boat.'

He said, as if it were the most important thing between them: 'Your boat? You never told me you had a boat.'

'There are a great many things that I didn't tell you.'

And then, suddenly, he knew. There was no longer room for doubt. 'So it wasn't real was it, any of it? You don't love me, you never did love me.'

'Love, love, love. Stop bleating the word, Jonathan. Look, go home. Stand in front of your glass and take a good long look at yourself. How could you ever have supposed that it was real? This is real, Amy and me. She is why I stay at Larksoken and I am why she stays. Now you know.'

'You used me.' He knew that he sounded like a querulous child.

'Yes, I used you. We used each other. When we went to bed I was using you and you were using me. That's what sex is. And, if you want to know, it was bloody hard work and it made me sick.'

Even in the throes of his misery and humiliation he could sense an urgency in her that had nothing to do with him. The cruelty was deliberate but it had no passion in it. It would have been more bearable if it had. His presence was merely an irritating but minor intrusion into more important preoccupations. Now the end of the rope had whipped clear of the bollard. She had started the engine and the boat was edging away from the quay. And for the first time he really noticed the other girl. She hadn't spoken since he arrived. She stood silently beside Caroline in the cockpit, unsmiling, shivering slightly, and somehow vulnerable, and he thought he saw on her childish face a look of puzzled compassion before his tears began to sting and the boat and its occupants became an amorphous blur. He waited until they were almost out of sight moving on the dark water, and then he made another decision. He would find a pub, have a beer and some food and be there when they returned. They couldn't be away long or they would miss the tide. And he had to know the truth. He couldn't spend another night in this uncertainty. He stood on the quay staring out to sea as if the little boat with its two occupants was still in sight, then turned away and dragged his feet towards the nearest pub.

44

The throb of the engine, unnaturally loud, shook the quiet air. Amy half expected doors to open, people to come running down to the quay, to hear protesting voices calling after them. Caroline made a movement and the noise died in a gentle murmur. The boat gently moved away from the quay. Amy said angrily: 'Who is he? Who is that creep?'

'Just a man from Larksoken. His name's Jonathan Reeves. He's unimportant.'

'Why did you tell him lies? Why did you tell him lies about us? We're not lovers.'

'Because it was necessary. What does it matter anyway? It isn't important.'

'It's important to me. Look at me, Caroline. I'm talking to you.'

But still Caroline didn't meet her eyes. She said calmly: 'Wait until we get clear of the harbour. There's something I have to tell you, but I want to get into deep water and I need to concentrate. Get up to the prow and keep a lookout.'

Amy stood for a moment irresolute, and then she obeyed, working her way carefully along the narrow deck, clutching the rim of the low cabin roof. She wasn't sure she liked the hold that Caroline apparently had over her. It was nothing to do with the money, which was paid irregularly and anonymously into her post office account or left hidden in the abbey ruins. It wasn't even the excitement and the secret sense of power which she gained from being part of a conspiracy. Perhaps after that first meeting in the pub at Islington which had led to her recruitment to Operation Birdcall she had subconsciously made a decision to give her loyalty and obedience and, now that the test had come, she was unable to shake off that unspoken allegiance.

Looking back she could see that the lights in the harbour were growing fainter, the windows becoming little squares of light and then pinpricks. The engine stuttered into greater life and, standing on the prow, she could feel the great power of the North Sea beneath her, the hiss of the parting water, see the unbroken waves smooth and black as oil emerging out of the mist, could feel the boat lifting, shuddering, and then settling. After ten minutes of watching she left her post and made her way back to the cockpit. She said: 'Look, we're well away from land now. What's going on? Did you have to tell him that? I know I'm supposed to keep away from people at Larksoken, but I'll find him, and I'll tell him the truth.'

Caroline was still standing motionless at the tiller, looking straight ahead. In her left hand she held a compass. She said: 'We won't be going back. That's what I have to tell you.'

Before Amy could even open her mouth she said: 'Look, don't start getting hysterical and don't argue. You're entitled to an explanation and if you keep quiet you'll get it. I've no option now; you have to know the truth, or some of the truth.'

'What truth? What are you talking about? And why aren't we going back? You said we'd only be gone about an hour. You said we were going out to meet some comrades offshore and get some new instructions. I left a note for Neil saying I wouldn't be long. I've got to get back to Timmy.'

But still Caroline didn't look at her. She said: 'We're not going back because we can't. When I recruited you from that London squat I didn't tell you the truth. It wasn't in your interest and I didn't know how far I could trust you. And I didn't know the whole truth myself, only as much as I needed to know. That's the way the operation works. Operation Birdcall is nothing to do with taking over Larksoken in the cause of animal rights. It's nothing to do with animals. It's nothing to do with threatened whales and sick seals and tormented laboratory animals and abandoned dogs and all the other spurious miseries you agonize about. It's to do with something far more important. It's to do with human beings and their future. It's to do with the way we organize our world.'

She was speaking very low and with an extraordinary intensity. Amy said above the noise of the engine: 'I can't hear you! I can't hear you properly. Turn off that engine!'

'Not yet. We've still a long way to go. We're meeting them at a precise spot. We have to sail south-east then take a bearing on the power station offshore structures and the Happisburgh light: I hope this mist doesn't thicken.'

'Who? Who are we meeting?'

'I don't know their names and I don't know their place in the organization. As I said, we are all of us told only as much as we actually need to know. My instructions were that if Operation Birdcall was blown I was to ring a number and activate the emergency procedure for getting me out. That's why I bought this boat and made sure it was always ready. I was told precisely where they'll pick us up. Then they'll get us into Germany, provide false papers, a new identity, incorporate us into the organization, find us a job.'

'Not for me they bloody well won't!' Amy looked at Caroline with horror. 'They're terrorists, aren't they? And you're one too. You're a bloody terrorist!'

Caroline said calmly: 'And what else are the agents of capital-ism? What are the armies, the police, the courts? What are the industrialists, the multinational corporations who hold down three-quarters of the world's population and keep them poor and hungry? Don't use words you don't understand.'

'I understand that word. And don't you patronize me. You crazy or something? What were you planning, for Christ's sakes, to sabotage the reactor, release all that radioactivity, worse than Chernobyl, kill everyone on the headland, Timmy and Neil, Smudge and Whisky?'

'We wouldn't need to sabotage the reactors or release any radioactivity. The threat would be sufficient once we'd taken over the power stations.'

'The stations? How many? Where?'

'One here, one in France, one in Germany. The action would be co-ordinated and it would be sufficient. It's not what we could do when we had taken them over, it's what people would think we could do. War is out of date and unnecessary. We don't need armies. All we need are a few trained, intelligent and dedicated comrades with the necessary skills. What you call terrorism can change the world, and it's more cost-effective in human life than the militaristic industry of death which my father made his career. They've only one thing in common. A soldier, in the end, has to be prepared to die for his cause. Well, so are we.'

Amy cried: 'It can't happen! Governments won't let it happen!'

'It is happening and they can't stop it. They aren't united enough and they haven't the will. This is just the beginning.'

Amy looked at her. She said: 'Stop this boat. I'm getting off.'

'And swim ashore? You'd either drown or freeze to death. And in this mist.'

Amy hadn't noticed the thickening mist. One moment it seemed to her that she could see the distant lights of the shore, like stars, almost she could see the blackness of the slopping waves, could peer ahead. But now, slowly and inexorably, there was a clammy wetness. She cried: 'Oh God, take me back. You've got to get me off. Get me off. I want Timmy. I want Neil.'

'I can't do that, Amy. Look, if you don't want to be part of all this just say so when the boat arrives. They'll put you ashore somewhere. It won't be on this coast necessarily, but somewhere. We don't want reluctant recruits. There would be enough trouble as it is fitting you up with a new identity. But if you didn't want to be part of it, didn't want to be committed, why did you kill Hilary Robarts? D'you think we wanted a murder investigation centred on Larksoken, police attention, Rickards actually on the site, every suspect's past scrutinized, nothing left private? And if Rickards had arrested you, how sure could I be that you wouldn't crack, tell him about Operation Birdcall, turn Queen's evidence?'

Amy cried: 'Are you crazy? I'm on this boat with a bloody crazy woman. I didn't kill her.'

'Then who did? Pascoe? That's almost as dangerous.'

'How could he? He was on his way back from Norwich. We lied to Rickards about the time but he was back at the caravan by 9.15 and we were there together all the evening with Timmy. And all that business about the Whistler cutting her forehead, the hair, we never knew any of that. I thought you killed her.'

'Why should I?'

'Because she discovered Operation Birdcall. Isn't that why you're running, because you've got no option?'

'You're right that I've got no option. But it's not because of Robarts. She didn't find out. How could she? But someone did. It isn't only the Hilary Robarts murder. They've started checking up on me, the security services. Somehow they've got a lead, probably from one of the German cells or from a mole in the IRA.'

'How do you know? You could be running away for nothing.'

'There are too many coincidences. That last postcard you hid in the abbey ruins. I told you it was put back the wrong way. Someone had read it.'

'Anyone could have found it. And the message wouldn't have meant anything. It never meant anything to me.'

'Found it in late September when the picnic season's well over? Found it and carefully put it back? And that wasn't all. They've checked on my mother's flat. She has a housekeeper who used to be my nanny. She rang to let me know earlier today. I didn't wait after that. I sent the signal to say I was getting out.'

On their starboard side the occasional lights of the shore were blurred by the mist but still visible. And the throb of the engine sounded less intrusive now, almost a gentle companionable hum. Or perhaps, thought Amy, she had got used to it. But it seemed extraordinary to be moving so quietly and steadily through the darkness, hearing Caroline's voice saying unbelievable things, talking about terrorism and flight and betrayal as calmly as if she were discussing the details of a picnic. And Amy needed to hear, needed to know. She found herself saying: 'Where did you meet them, these people you're working for?'

'In Germany when I was seventeen. My nanny was ill and I had to spend the summer holiday with my parents. My father was stationed there. He didn't take much notice of me, but someone else did.'

'But that was years ago.'

'They know how to wait and so do I.'

'And this nanny-housekeeper, is she a member of Birdcall too?'

'She knows nothing, absolutely nothing. She's the last person I'd choose. She's a silly old fool who's hardly worth her bed and board, but my mother finds a use for her, and so do I. She hates my mother, and I've told her that Mummy is checking on my life and to let me know at once if there are any telephone calls for me or any visitors. It helps make her life with Mummy tolerable. It makes her feel important, helps her to believe that I care about her, that I love her.'

'Do you? Do you love her?'

'I did once. A child has to love someone. I grew out of it and I grew out of her. Well, there was a call and there was a visitor. On Tuesday a Scot, or someone pretending to be a Scot rang. And today a visitor came.'

'What sort of visitor?'

'A young man who said he'd met me in France. It was a lie. He was an impostor. He was from MI5. Who else could have sent him?'

'But you can't be sure. Not sure enough to send that signal, leave everything, put yourself in their mercy.'

'I can. Look, who else could it have been? There were three separate incidents, the postcard, the telephone call, the visitor. What else should I wait for? The security services kicking down my door?'

'What was he like, this man?'

'Young. Nervous. Not very attractive. Not particularly convincing either. Even Nanny didn't believe him.'

'Funny kind of MI5 officer. Couldn't they do better than that?'

'He was supposed to be someone I'd met in France who fancied me and wanted to see me again and had steeled himself actually to call at the flat. Of course he appeared young and nervous. That's the kind of man they'd send. They'd hardly choose a seasoned forty-year-old veteran from Curzon Street. They know how to select the right man for the job. That's their business. He was the right man, all right. Perhaps he wasn't even meant to be convincing. Perhaps they were trying to scare me, get me to react, flush me out.'

'Well, you have reacted, haven't you? But if you're wrong, wrong about it all, what will they do, the people you work for? You've blown Operation Birdcall by running away.'

'This operation has been aborted but the future won't be jeopardized. My instructions were to telephone if there was firm evidence that we'd been discovered. And there was. And that's not all. My telephone is being bugged.'

'You can't possibly tell that.'

'I can't tell it for certain, but I know.'

Suddenly Amy cried: 'What did you do about Remus? Did you feed him, leave him water?'

'Of course not. This has to look like an accident. They've got to believe that we're lesbian lovers who went for an evening boat trip and were drowned. They've got to believe that we only intended to be away for a couple of hours. He gets fed at seven. They've got to find him hungry and thirsty.'

'But they might not start looking for you until Monday! He'll be frantic, barking and whining. There's no one close to hear. You bloody bitch!'

Suddenly she flew at Caroline, screaming obscenities, clawing at her face. But the girl was too strong for her. Hands gripped her wrists like steel bands and she found herself hurled back against the boards. Through the tears of rage and self-pity she whispered: 'But why? Why?'

'For a cause worth dying for. There aren't many of those.'

'Nothing's worth dying for, except maybe another person, someone you love. I'd die for Timmy.'

'That's not a cause, that's sentimentality.'

'And if I want to die for a cause I'll bloody well choose it myself. And it won't be for terrorism. It won't be for bastards who put bombs in pubs and blow up my friends and don't give a damn about ordinary people, because we're not important, are we?'

Caroline said: 'You must have suspected something. You're not educated but you're not stupid, either. I wouldn't have chosen you if I couldn't be sure of that. You never questioned me and you wouldn't have got an answer if you had, but you couldn't have thought that we were going to all that trouble for frightened kittens or butchered seal pups.'

Had she thought that? Amy wondered. Perhaps the truth was that she had believed in the intention but never that it would actually be carried out. She hadn't doubted their will, only their ability. And in the meantime it had been fun to be part of the conspiracy. She had enjoyed the excitement, the knowledge that she had a secret from Neil, the half-simulated *frisson* of fear as she left the caravan after dark to plant the postcards in the ruins of the abbey. She had hidden behind a broken breakwater almost laughing aloud that night when she had nearly been caught by Mrs Dennison and Mr Dalgliesh. And the money had been useful, too; generous payment for so small a task. And there had been the dream, the picture of a flag whose design was as yet unknown, but which they would raise over the power station and which would command respect, obedience, instant response. They would be saying to the whole world, 'Stop it. Stop it now.' They would be speaking for the captive zoo animals, the threatened whales, the polluted, sick seals, the tormented laboratory animals, the terrified beasts driven into the abattoirs to the smell of blood and their own death, the hens crowded together, unable even to peck, for the whole of the abused and exploited animal world. But it had been only a dream. This was reality; the insubstantial boards under her feet, the dark suffocating mist, the oily waves slapping against their frail craft. The reality was death, there was no other. Everything in her life, from the moment she had met Caroline in that Islington pub and they had walked back to the squat together, had led to this moment of truth, this terror.

She moaned: 'I want Timmy. What about my baby? I want my baby.'

'You won't have to leave him, not permanently. They'll find a way of reuniting you.'

'Don't be daft. What sort of life would he have with a terrorist gang? They'll write him off like they write off everyone else.'

Caroline said: 'What about your parents? Won't they take him? Can't they look after him?'

'Are you crazy? I ran away from home because my stepfather knocked Ma about. When he started on me I walked out. Do you think I'd let him have Timmy, him or her?'

Her mother had seemed to like the violence, or at least had liked what came after it. Those two years before she ran away had taught Amy one lesson; have sex only with men who want you more than you want them.

Caroline asked: 'What about Pascoe? Are you sure he knows nothing?'

'Of course he doesn't. We weren't even lovers. He didn't want me and I didn't want him.'

But there was someone she had wanted, and she had a sudden vivid memory of lying with Alex in the dunes, the smell of sea and sand and sweat, his grave ironic face. Well, she wasn't going to tell Caroline about Alex. She had one secret of her own. She would keep it.

She thought of the curious paths by which she had come to this moment in time, to this place. Perhaps if she drowned her whole life would flash before her as it was said to do, everything experienced, understood, made sense of in that final annihilating moment. But now she saw the past as a series of coloured slides, clicking in quick succession, an image briefly received, an emotion barely experienced before it disappeared. Suddenly she was shivering violently. She said: 'I'm cold.'

'I said to come with warm clothes and nothing else. That jumper isn't enough.'

'These are the only warm clothes I've got.'

'On the headland? What do you wear in winter?'

'Sometimes Neil lends me his greatcoat. We share. Whichever one of us goes out gets the coat. We were thinking we might get one for me from the Old Rectory jumble.'

Caroline took off her jacket. She said: 'Here, put this round you.'

'No, that's yours. I don't want it.'

'Put it on.'

'I said I don't want it.'

But like a child she let Caroline push her arms into the sleeves, stood obediently while the jacket was fastened. Then she crouched down, almost wedging herself under the narrow seat which ran round the boat, shutting out the horror of those silently advancing waves. It seemed to Amy that she felt for the first time and with every nerve the inexorable power of the sea. She saw in imagination her pale and lifeless body plummeting through the miles of wet darkness to the sea bed, to the skeletons of long-drowned sailors where the uncaring creatures swam between the ribs of ancient ships. And the mist, less thick now but mysteriously more frightening, had become a living thing, gently swirling and soundlessly breathing, stealing her own breath so that she found herself panting, insinuating its damp horror into every pore. It seemed impossible to believe that somewhere there was land, lighted windows behind the drawn curtains, light spilling from the doors of pubs, laughing voices, people sitting in warmth and safety. She saw the caravan as she had seen it so often, returning from Norwich after dark, a sturdy rectangle of wood which seemed rooted to the headland defying the gales and the sea, the warm glow from its windows, the twist of smoke rising from the stack. She thought of Timmy and Neil. How long would Neil wait until he called the police? He wasn't one to act in a hurry. After all, she wasn't a child, she had a right to leave. He might do nothing until morning, and perhaps even then he would wait. But it wouldn't matter. There was nothing the police could do. No one except that desolate figure on the quay knew where they were and if he raised the alarm it would be too late. It was useless to believe even in the reality of the terrorists. They were marooned here in black dampness. They would circle and circle until the fuel ran out and then drift out to sea until a coaster ran them down.

She no longer had any sense of passing time. The rhythmic throbbing of the engine had lulled her, not into peace but into a dulled acquiescence in which she was aware only of the wood hard against her back, of Caroline standing intent and motionless in the cockpit.

The engine died. For a few seconds the silence was absolute. Then, as the boat gently lurched, Amy heard the creak of wood, the slap of water. She breathed a suffocating wetness, felt its cold seeping through the jacket, into her bones. It seemed impossible that anyone could find them in this bleak expanse of water and emptiness and she had ceased to care whether they did.

Caroline said: 'This is the place. This is where they're going to meet us. We'll just have to circle here until they come.'

Amy heard the engine again, but this time it was an almost imperceptible throb. And suddenly she knew. There was no conscious process of reasoning, only a blinding and terrifying certainty which burst upon her with the clarity of a vision. There was a second in which her heart froze, leapt and its strong drumming powered her body into life. She almost sprang to her feet. 'They're not going to put me ashore, are they? They're going to kill me. You know it. You've known it all along. You've brought me here to be killed.'

Caroline's eyes were fixed on the two lights, the intermittent flash from the lighthouse, the glitter from the offshore structures. She said coldly: 'Don't be hysterical.'

'They can't risk letting me go. I know too much. And you said yourself that I wouldn't be much use to them. Look, you've got to help me. Tell them how useful I was, make believe I'm worth keeping. If I can only get ashore, somehow I'll make a break for it. But I have to have a chance. Caroline, you've got me into this. You must help me. I have to get ashore. Listen to me! Listen to me, Caroline! We've got to talk.'

'You are talking. And what you're saying is ludicrous.'

'Is it? Is it, Caroline?'

She knew now that she mustn't plead. She wanted to throw herself at Caroline's feet and scream: 'Look at me. I'm human. I'm a woman. I want to live. My child needs me. I'm not much of a mother but I'm the only one he has. Help me.' But she knew with an instinctive wisdom born of desperation that abject pleading, clutching hands, sobs, whining entreaties, would only repel. She was speaking for her life. She had to stay calm, to rely on reason. She had somehow to find the right words. She said: 'It isn't only me, it's you too. This could be a choice of life or death for both of us. They won't want you either. You were only useful to them while you worked at Larksoken, while you could pass on to them details of how the place was run, who was on duty and when. Now you're a liability, the same as me. There's no difference. What kind of work can you do for them that will make it worthwhile supporting you, setting you up with a new identity? They can't find you a job in another power station. And if MI5 are really on to you they'll still be looking. They might not believe so easily in the accident, not if our bodies aren't washed up. And our bodies won't be washed up, will they? Not unless they kill us and that's what they're planning to do. What are two more bodies to them? Why meet us here? Why so far? They could have picked us up much closer to land. They could have got us out by air if they'd really needed us. Caroline, go back. It isn't too late. You could tell the people you work for that it wasn't safe to come, the mist was too thick. They'll find another way to get you out if you want to go. I won't talk, I wouldn't dare. I promise you with my life. We can go back now and it will just have been two friends who took a boat trip and came back safely. It's my life, Caroline, and it could be yours. You gave me your jacket. I'm asking for my life.'

She didn't touch Caroline. She knew that the wrong gesture, perhaps any gesture, could be fatal. But she knew, too, that the silent figure staring rigidly ahead was at the moment of decision. And, gazing at that carved intent face, Amy realized for the first time in her life that she was utterly alone. Even her lovers, seen now as a passing procession of strained beseeching faces and grasping exploring hands, had been only casual strangers giving her the fleeting illusion that a life could be shared. And she had never known Caroline, could never know her, never begin to understand what in her past, perhaps in her childhood, had led to this dangerous conspiracy, this moment of decision. They were physically so close that each could hear, could almost smell, the other's breath. But each was alone, as much alone as if this wide sea held no other craft, no other living soul. They might be fated to die together, but each could suffer only her own death as each had lived only her own life. And there was nothing left to say. She had pleaded her cause and the words were all spent. Now she waited in the darkness and the silence to know whether she would live or die.

It seemed to her that even time had stopped. Caroline put out her hand and switched off the engine. In the eerie silence Amy could hear, like a low insistent pounding, the beating of her heart. And then Caroline spoke. Her voice was calm, reflective, as if Amy had posed her a difficult problem which needed thought to solve.

'We have to get away from the meeting place. We haven't enough power to outrun them if they find us and give chase. Our only hope is to put out all the lights, get away from this place and lie silent hoping they won't find us in the mist.'

'Can't we get back to the harbour?'

'There isn't time. It's over ten miles and they'll have a powerful engine. If they find us they'll be on to us in seconds. The mist is our only chance.'

And then they heard, blunted by the fog but clearly, the sound of an approaching boat. Instinctively they moved closer together in the cockpit and waited, not daring even to whisper. Each knew that their only chance now lay in silence, the mist, the hope that their small craft would be undetected. But the engine noise increased and became a regular, directionless, vibrating throb. And then, when they had thought that the boat would loom out of the darkness and be on them, the noise grew no louder and Amy guessed that they were being slowly circled. Then suddenly she screamed. The searchlight cut through the mist and shone full on their faces. The light dazzled so that she could see nothing but its own giant cone in which the particles of mist swam like motes of silver light. A rough, foreign voice called: 'Is that the *Lark* out of Wells harbour?'

There was a moment's silence and then Amy heard Caroline's voice. It was clear and loud but to Amy's ears it signalled a high note of fear. 'No. We're a party of four friends from Yarmouth, but we'll probably put in at Wells. We're all right. No help needed, thank you.'

But the searchlight didn't move. The boat was held as if suspended between sea and sky in a blaze of light. The seconds passed. Nothing more was said. Then the light was switched off and they heard again the sound of the retreating engines. For a minute, still waiting, still frightened to speak, they shared a common desperate hope that the ruse had worked. And then they knew. The light held them again. And now the engines were roaring and the boat came straight at them out of the mist with only time for Caroline to place an icy cheek against Amy's. She said: 'I'm sorry. I'm sorry.'

And then the great hull towered above them. Amy heard the crack as the wood splintered and the boat leapt out of the water. She felt herself hurled through an eternity of wet darkness and then falling endlessly falling, spread-eagled in space and time. Then there was the smack of the sea and a coldness so icy that for a few seconds she felt nothing. She came back to consciousness as she surfaced, gasping and fighting for breath, no more aware of the cold, feeling only the agony of a metal band crushing her chest, terror, and the desperate fight to keep her head above water, to survive. Something hard scraped against her face, then floated free. She thrashed out with flailing arms and fastened on a plank of wood from the boat. It offered at least a chance. She rested her arms on it and felt the blessed release of strain. And now she was capable of rational thought. The plank might support her until morning light and the fog lifted. But she would be dead of cold and exhaustion long before then. Somehow to swim ashore was her only hope, but which way lay the shore? If the mist lifted she would be able to see the lights, perhaps even the light of the caravan. Neil would be there waving to her. But that was silly. The caravan was miles away. Neil would be desperately worried by now. And she had never finished those envelopes. Timmy might be crying for her. She had to get back to Timmy.

But in the end the sea was merciful. The cold that numbed her arms so that she could no longer hold on to the plank numbed also her mind. She was slipping into unconsciousness when the searchlight again found her. She was beyond thought, beyond fear when the boat turned and came driving at full power into her body. And then there was silence and darkness and a single plank of wood gently bobbing where the sea was stained red.

45

It was after eight before Rickards got home on Saturday night but this was still earlier than usual and, for the first time in weeks, he was able to feel that an evening stretched ahead with its choices; a leisurely meal, television, radio, a gentle undemanding catching-up with household chores, telephoning Susie, an early bed. But he was restless. Faced with a few hours of leisure he was uncertain what to do with them. For a moment he wondered whether to go out for a solitary restaurant meal, but the effort of choosing, the expense, even the bother of booking seemed disproportionate to any possible pleasure. He showered and changed as if the steaming water were a ritual cleansing away of his job, of murder and failure, which might give the evening before him some meaning, some pleasure. Then he opened a tin of baked beans, grilled four sausages and a couple of tomatoes and carried his tray into the sitting room to eat while watching television.

At 9.20 he switched off the set and, for a few minutes, sat immobile with the tray still on his lap. He thought that he must look like one of those modern paintings, *Man with a Tray*, a stiff figure immobilized in an ordinary setting made unordinary, even sinister. As he sat, trying to summon the energy even to wash up, the familiar depression settled on him, the sense that he was a stranger in his own house. He had felt more at home in that fire-lit, stone-walled room at Larksoken Mill, drinking Dalgliesh's whisky, than he did here in his own sitting room in his familiar, tightly upholstered chair, eating his own food. And it wasn't only the absence of Susie, the heavily pregnant ghost in the opposite chair. He found himself comparing the two rooms, seeking a clue to his different responses to a deepening dejection of which the sitting room seemed partly a symbol, partly a cause. It wasn't only that the mill had a real wood fire, hissing and spitting real sparks and smelling of autumn, while his was synthetic, nor that Dalgliesh's furniture was old, polished by centuries of use, arranged purely for convenience not for show, not even that the paintings were real oils, genuine watercolours, or that the whole room had been put together with no apparent sense that anything in it was particularly highly regarded for its own sake. Above all, he decided, the difference surely lay in the books, the two walls covered with shelves holding books of every age and description, books for use, for pleasure in the reading and the handling. His own small collection, and Susie's, was in the bedroom. Susie had decreed that the books were too diverse, too tattered to be worthy of a place in what she called the lounge, and there weren't many of them. In recent years he had had so little time for reading; a collection of modern adventure novels in paperback, four volumes of a book club to which, for a couple of years, he had belonged, a few hardback travel books, police manuals, Susie's school prizes for neatness and needlework. But a child should be brought up with books. He had read somewhere that it was the best possible beginning to life, to be surrounded with books, to have parents who encouraged reading. Perhaps they could fit shelves each side of the fireplace and make a start. Dickens: he had enjoyed Dickens at school; Shakespeare, of course, and the major English poets. His daughter – neither he nor Susie doubted that the baby would be a girl – would learn to love poetry.

But all that would have to wait. He could at least make a start with the housework. The room's air of dull pretentiousness was partly due, he realized, to dirt. It looked like an uncleaned hotel room in which no one took pride because no guest was expected and those few who came wouldn't care. He realized now that he should have kept on Mrs Adcock who came in to clean for three hours every Wednesday. But she had only worked for them in the last two months of Susie's pregnancy. He had hardly met her and he disliked the thought of handing over house keys to a comparative stranger, more from his love of privacy than from any lack of trust. So, despite Susie's misgivings, he had paid Mrs Adcock a retainer and had said that he could cope. Now he added his supper things to a load of crockery in the dishwasher and took a duster from those neatly folded in the drawer. Dust lay heavy on every surface. In the sitting room he drew the duster along the window sill and saw with wonder the black line of grimed dirt.

He moved next to the hall. The cyclamen on the table beside the telephone had unaccountably wilted despite his hurried daily watering, perhaps because of it. He was standing, duster in hand, wondering whether to throw it out or whether rescue was possible, when his ears caught the crunch of wheels on the gravel. He opened the door, then flung it wide with such force that it swung back and the latch clicked. Then he was at the taxi door, gently receiving the swollen figure into his arms.

'My darling, oh my darling, why didn't you ring?'

She leaned against him. He saw with compassion the white transparent skin, the smudges under her eyes. He seemed to feel even beneath the thick tweed of her coat the stirring of his child.

'I didn't wait. Mummy had only gone up the road to see Mrs Blenkinsop. I just had time to ring for a taxi and leave her a note. I had to come. You're not cross?'

'Oh, my love, my darling. Are you all right?'

'Only tired.' She laughed. 'Darling, you've let the door close. You'll have to use my key.'

He took her handbag from her, rummaged for the key and her purse, paid the driver who had placed her one case by the door. His hands were shaking so that he could hardly fit the key in the lock. He half lifted her over the threshold and lowered her on to the hall chair.

'Sit there a moment, darling, while I see to the case.'

'Terry, the cyclamen is dead. You've overwatered it.'

'No, I haven't. It died missing you.'

She laughed. The sound was strong, a happy, contented peal. He wanted to lift her up into his arms and shout aloud. Suddenly serious, she said: 'Has Mummy phoned?'

'Not yet, but she will.'

And then, as if on cue, the telephone rang. He snatched it up. This time, awaiting the sound of his mother-in-law's voice he was totally without fear, without anxiety. By that one magnificent, affirming action Susie had placed them both forever beyond her mother's destructive reach. He felt that he had been lifted out of misery as if by a huge wave and set for ever with his feet firmly on a rock. There was a second in which he saw Susie's look of anxiety, so acute that it was a spasm of pain, and then she got clumsily to her feet and leaned against him, slipping her hand into his. But the caller wasn't Mrs Cartwright.

Oliphant said: 'Jonathan Reeves has rung headquarters, sir, and they've put him on to me. He says that Caroline Amphlett and Amy Camm have gone boating together. They've been gone three hours now and the mist is getting thicker.'

'Then why did he ring the police? He should have got on to the coast guard.'

'I've already done that, sir. That wasn't really why he phoned. He and Amphlett didn't spend last Sunday evening together. She was on the headland. He wanted to tell us that Amphlett lied. So did he.'

'I don't suppose they're the only ones. We'll pull them in first thing tomorrow morning and hear their explanations. I've no doubt she'll come up with one.'

Oliphant said stolidly: 'But why should she lie if she's got nothing to hide? And it isn't just the false alibi. Reeves says that their love affair was only pretence, that she only pretended to care for him to cover up her lesbian affair with Camm. I reckon the two women were in it together, sir. Amphlett must have known that Robarts swam at night. All the staff at Larksoken knew that. And she worked closely with Mair, none closer. She's his PA. He could have told her all the details of that dinner party, how the Whistler operated. There'd be no problem in getting hold of the Bumbles. Camm knew about the jumble box even if Amphlett didn't. Her kid had clothes from it.'

Rickards said: 'There'd be no trouble in getting hold of the shoes. There might be trouble in wearing them. Neither woman is tall.'

Oliphant dismissed what he probably felt was a puerile objection. He said: 'But they would have had no time to try them on. Better to grab a pair too large than too small, a soft shoe rather than unyielding leather. And Camm's got a motive, sir. A double motive. She threatened Robarts after her kid was pushed over. We've got Mrs Jago's evidence of their quarrel. And if Camm wanted to stay on in the caravan, close to her lover, it was important to put a stop to Robarts's libel action against Pascoe. And Camm almost certainly knew exactly where Robarts took her nightly swim. If Amphlett didn't tell her, Pascoe probably did. He admitted to us that he used to sneak out occasionally to spy on her. Dirty-minded little devil. And there's another thing. Camm has a dog lead, remember. So has Amphlett, come to that. Reeves said that she was exercising her dog on the headland Sunday night.'

'There were no paw marks at the scene, Sergeant. Don't let's get too excited. She might have been at the scene, but the dog wasn't.'

'Kept in the car, sir. Maybe she didn't have him with her but I reckon she used the lead. There's another thing. Those two wine-glasses in Thyme Cottage. I reckon Caroline Amphlett was with Robarts before she went for that last swim. She's Mair's PA. Robarts would have let her in without question. It all adds up, sir. It's a watertight case, sir.'

Rickards thought that it was as watertight as a sieve. But Oliphant was right. There was a case, even if there wasn't as yet a scintilla of proof. He mustn't let his feelings about the man cloud his judgement. And one fact was depressingly obvious. If he arrested another suspect this theory, for all the lack of firm evidence, would be a gift to any defence counsel.

He said: 'Ingenious, but it's totally circumstantial. Anyway, it can wait until tomorrow. There's nothing we can do tonight.'

'We ought to see Reeves, sir. He may change his story before morning.'

'You see him. And let me know when Camm and Amphlett get back. I'll see you at Hoveton at eight. We'll pull them in then. And I don't want them questioned, either of them, until I see them tomorrow. Is that understood?'

'Yes, sir. Goodnight, sir.'

When he had replaced the receiver, Susie said: 'If you think you ought to go, darling, don't worry about me. I'll be all right now I'm home.'

'It's not urgent. Oliphant can cope. He likes being in charge. Let's make him a happy Jumbo.'

'But I don't want to be a trouble to you, darling. Mummy thought that life would be better for you with me away.'

He turned and took her in his arms. He felt his own tears warm on her face. He said: 'Life is never better for me when you're away.'

46

The bodies were washed up two days later two miles south of Hunstanton, or enough of them to make identification certain. On the Monday morning a retired tax officer, exercising his Dalmatian dog on the beach, saw the animal sniffing round what looked like a white slab of lard entwined with seaweed, rolling and gliding at the edge of the tide. As he drew close the object was sucked back by the receding wave then taken up by the next surge and flung at his feet and he found himself gazing in incredulous horror at the torso of a woman neatly severed at the waist. For a second he stood petrified, staring down as the tide boiled in the empty socket of the left eye and swayed the flattened breasts. Then he turned away and was violently sick before shambling like a drunkard up the shingle of the beach, dragging the dog by its collar.

The body of Caroline Amphlett, unmutilated, was washed up on the same tide together with planks from the boat and part of the roof of the cabin. They were found by Daft Billy, a harmless and amiable beachcomber, on one of his regular sorties. It was the wood which first caught his eye and he dragged the planks ashore with squeals of glee. Then, his prize secure, he turned his puzzled attention to the drowned girl. It was not the first body he had found in forty years of beachcombing and he knew what he must do, who he must tell. First he placed his hands under the arms and pulled the body out of the reach of the tide. Then, moaning softly, as if mourning his clumsiness, her lack of response, he knelt beside her and, pulling off his jacket, spread it over the torn rags of her shirt and slacks.

'Comfy?' he asked. 'Comfy?'

Then, putting out his hand he carefully moved the strands of hair out of her eyes and, rocking himself gently, began crooning to her as he might to a child.

47

Dalgliesh made three visits on foot to the caravan after lunch on Thursday but on no occasion was Neil Pascoe at home. He was unwilling to telephone to check whether the man had returned. He could think of no valid excuse for wanting to see him and it seemed best to make the visit part of a walk, as if the decision to call at the caravan were merely an impulse. In one sense he supposed it could be a visit of condolence but he had only known Amy Camm by sight and that excuse seemed to him dishonest as well as unconvincing. Shortly after five o'clock, when the light was beginning to fade, he tried again. This time the door of the caravan was wide open but there was no sign of Pascoe. While he stood hesitating a billow of smoke rose from above the edge of the cliff, followed by a brief flash of flame, and the air was suddenly filled with the acrid smell of bonfire.

From the edge of the cliff he looked down on an extraordinary scene. Pascoe had built a fireplace of large stones and chunks of concrete and had lit a fire of brushwood on to which he was emptying papers, box files, cartons, bottles and what looked like an assortment of clothes. The pile awaiting burning was caged down against the strengthening wind by the bars of Timmy's cot; that too, no doubt, destined for the flames. A soiled mattress lay curled to one side like a makeshift and ineffectual windbreak. Pascoe, wearing only a pair of grubby shorts, was working like a demented demon, his eyes white saucers in his blackened face, his arms and naked chest glistening with sweat. As Dalgliesh slithered down the sandy slope of the cliff and moved up to the fire he nodded a brief acknowledgement of his presence, then began dragging a small, scuffed suitcase from under the cot bars with desperate haste. Then he sprang up and balanced himself on the wide rim of the fireplace, his legs wide apart. In the ruddy glow of the flames his whole body gleamed, seeming for a moment transparent as if it were lit from within, and the great dollops of sweat ran from his shoulders like blood. With a shout he swung the case high over the fire and wrenched it open. The baby clothes fell in a brightly coloured shower and the flames leapt like living tongues to snatch at the woollen garments in mid-air, spinning them into briefly burning torches before they fell blackened into the heart of the fire. Pascoe stood for a moment breathing heavily, then sprang down with a cry half exultant, half despairing. Dalgliesh could understand and partly shared his exultation in this tumultuous juxtaposition of wind, fire and water. With each gust the tongues of flame roared and hissed so that he saw through a shimmering haze of heat the veins of the tumbling waves stained as if with blood. As Pascoe emptied into the fire yet another box file of papers the charred fragments rose and danced like frantic birds, blew gently against Dalgliesh's face and settled over the dry stones of the upper shingle like a black contagion. He could feel his eyes prickling with the smoke.

He called out: 'Aren't you polluting the beach?'

Pascoe turned to him and spoke for the first time, shouting above the roar of the fire. 'What does it matter? We're polluting the whole bloody planet.'

Dalgliesh shouted back: 'Shove some shingle on it and leave it until tomorrow. It's too windy for a bonfire this evening.'

He had expected Pascoe to ignore him, but to his surprise the words seemed to recall his companion to reality. The exultation and vigour seemed to drain out of him. He looked at the fire and said dully: 'I suppose you're right.'

There was a spade and a rusty shovel down by the pile of rubbish. Together the two men scooped up a mixture of shingle and sand and flung it on to the flames. When the last red tongue had died with an angry hiss Pascoe turned and began scrunching his way up the beach towards the cliff. Dalgliesh followed. The question he had half feared – Are you here on purpose? Why do you want to see me? – was unspoken and apparently unthought.

In the caravan Pascoe kicked the door shut and slumped down at the table. He said: 'Want a beer? Or there's tea. I'm out of coffee.'

'Nothing, thanks.'

Dalgliesh sat and watched as Pascoe groped his way over to the refrigerator. Returning to the table, he wrenched open the seal, threw back his head and poured the beer down his throat in an almost continuous stream. Then he slumped forward silent, still clutching the tin. Neither spoke and it seemed to Dalgliesh that his companion hardly knew that he was still there. It was dark in the caravan and Pascoe's face across the two feet of wood was an indistinguishable oval in which the whites of the eyes gleamed unnaturally bright. Then he stumbled to his feet, murmuring something about matches, and a few seconds later there was a scrape and hiss and his hands stretched towards the oil lamp on the table. In its strengthening glow his face, beneath the dirt and smudges of smoke, looked drained and haggard, the eyes dulled with pain. The wind was shaking the caravan, not roughly but with a regular gentle sway as if it were being rocked by an unseen hand. The sliding door of the end compartment was open and Dalgliesh could see, on the narrow bed, a pile of female clothes topped with a jumble of tubes, jars and bottles. Apart from this, the caravan looked tidy but denuded, less a home than a temporary, ill-equipped refuge, but holding still the unmistakable milky and faecal smell of a child. The absence of Timmy and his dead mother filled the caravan as it did both their minds.

After minutes of silence Pascoe looked up at him: 'I was burning all my PANUP records out there with the rest of the rubbish. You probably guessed. It was never any use. I was only using PANUP to pander to my own need to feel important. You more or less said so that time I called at the mill.'

'Did I? I hadn't any right to. What will you do now?'

'Go to London and look for a job. The university won't extend my grant for a further year. I don't blame them. I'd prefer to go back to the north-east but I suppose London offers me more hope.'

'What sort of job?'

'Any job. I don't give a damn what I do as long as it makes money for me and is no possible use to anyone else.'

Dalgliesh asked: 'What happened to Timmy?'

'The local authority took him. They got a Place of Safety Order or something of the sort. A couple of social workers came for him yesterday. Decent enough women, but he didn't want to go with them. They had to tear him screaming from my arms. What sort of a society does that to its children?'

Dalgliesh said: 'I don't suppose they had any choice. They have to make long-term plans for his future. After all, he couldn't have stayed here indefinitely with you.'

'Why not? I cared for him for over a year. And at least I would have had something out of all this mess.'

Dalgliesh asked: 'Have they traced Amy's family?'

'They haven't had much time, have they? And when they do I don't expect they'll tell me. Timmy lived here for over a year but I'm of less account than the grandparents he never saw and who probably don't give a damn about him.'

He was still holding the empty beer can. Twisting it slowly in his hands he said: 'What really gets to me is the deception. I thought she cared. Oh, not about me, but about what I was trying to do. It was all pretence. She was using me, using this place to be near Caroline.'

Dalgliesh said: 'But they can't have seen very much of each other.'

'How do I know? When I wasn't here she probably sneaked out to meet her lover. Timmy must have spent hours alone. She didn't even care for him. The cats were more important than Timmy. Mrs Jago has taken them now. They'll be all right. Sometimes on Sunday afternoons she used to go out blatantly telling me that she was off to meet her lover in the sand dunes. I thought it was a joke, I needed to believe that. And all the time she and Caroline were out there together making love, laughing at me.'

Dalgliesh said: 'You've only got Reeves's evidence to suggest they were lovers. Caroline could have been lying to him.'

'No. No, she wasn't lying. I know that. They used us both, Reeves and me. Amy wasn't – well, she wasn't undersexed. We lived here together for over a year. On the second night she – well, she did offer to come to my bed. But it was just her way of paying for board and lodging. It wouldn't have been right then for either of us. But after a time I suppose I began to hope. I mean, living here together, I suppose I grew fond of her. But she never really wanted me to be near her. And when she came in from those Sunday walks I knew. I pretended to myself that I didn't but I knew. She looked exultant. She was shining with happiness.'

Dalgliesh said: 'Look, is it really so important to you, the affair with Caroline, even if it is true? What you had here together, the affection, friendship, comradeship, caring for Timmy, does all that go for nothing because she found her sexual life outside the walls of this caravan?'

Pascoe said bitterly: 'Forget and forgive? You make it sound so easy.'

'I don't suppose you can forget, or perhaps even want to. But I can't see why you have to use the word forgive. She never promised more than she gave.'

'You despise me, don't you?'

Dalgliesh thought how unattractive it was, the self-absorption of the deeply unhappy. But there were questions he still had to ask. He said: 'And she left nothing, no papers, no records, no diary, nothing to say what she was doing on the headland?'

'Nothing. And I know what she was doing here, why she came. She came to be near Caroline.'

'Did she have any money? Even if you fed her she must have had something of her own.'

'She always had some cash but I don't know how she got it. She never said and I didn't like to ask. I know she didn't draw any welfare payments. She said she didn't want the DHSS snooping round here to check whether we were sleeping together. I didn't blame her. Nor did I.'

'And she got no post.'

'She got postcards from time to time. Pretty regularly really. So she must have had friends in London. I don't know what she did with them. Threw them away I suppose. There's nothing in the caravan but her clothes and make-up and I'm going to burn those next. After that there'll be nothing left to show that she was ever here.'

Dalgliesh asked: 'And the murder. Do you think that Caroline Amphlett killed Robarts?'

'Perhaps. I don't care. It doesn't matter any more. If she didn't, Rickards will make her a scapegoat, her and Amy together.'

'But you can't really believe that Amy connived at murder?'

Pascoe looked at Dalgliesh with the frustration and anger of an uncomprehending child. 'I don't know! Look, I really never knew her. That's what I'm telling you. I don't know! And now that Timmy's gone I don't really care. And I'm in such a muddle, anger at what she did to me, at what she was, and grief that she's dead. I didn't think you could be angry and grieving at the same time. I ought to be mourning her but all I can feel is this terrible anger.'

'Oh yes,' said Dalgliesh. 'You can feel anger and grief together. That's the commonest reaction to bereavement.'

Suddenly Pascoe began crying. The empty beer can rattled against the table and he bent his head low over it, his shoulders shaking. Women, thought Dalgliesh, are better at coping with grief than we are. He had seen them so many times, the women police officers moving unconsciously to take the grieving mother, the lost child, in their arms. Some men were good at it too, of course. Rickards had been in the old days. He himself was good with the words, but then words were his trade. What he found difficult was what came so spontaneously to the truly generous at heart, the willingness to touch and be touched. He thought: I'm here on false pretences. If I were not, perhaps I, too, could feel adequate.

He said: 'I think the wind is less strong than it was. Why don't we finish the burning and clear up that mess on the beach?'

It was over an hour before Dalgliesh was ready to set off for the mill. As he said goodbye to Pascoe at the door of the caravan a blue Fiesta with a young man at its wheel came bumping over the grass.

Pascoe said: 'Jonathan Reeves. He was engaged to Caroline Amphlett, or thought he was. She fooled him like Amy fooled me. He's been round once or twice to chat. We thought we might walk to the Local Hero for a game of bar billiards.'

It was not, thought Dalgliesh, an agreeable picture, the two men, bound by a common grievance, consoling each other for the perfidy of their women with beer and bar billiards. But Pascoe seemed to want to introduce Reeves and he found himself grasping a surprisingly firm hand and making his formal condolences.

Jonathan Reeves said: 'I still can't believe it, but I suppose people always say that after a sudden death. And I can't help feeling that it was my fault. I should have stopped them.'

Dalgliesh said: 'They were adult women. Presumably they knew what they were doing. Short of physically dragging them off the boat, which would hardly have been practicable, I don't see how you could have stopped them.'

Reeves reiterated obstinately: 'I should have stopped them.' Then he added: 'I keep having this dream, well, nightmare really. She's standing at the side of my bed with the child in her arms and saying to me, "It's all your fault. All your fault."'

Pascoe said: 'Caroline comes with Timmy?'

Reeves looked at him as if surprised that he could be so obtuse. He said: 'Not Caroline. It's Amy who comes. Amy, whom I never met, standing there with water streaming from her hair, holding the child in her arms and telling me that it's all my fault.'

48

Just over an hour later Dalgliesh had left the headland and was driving west along the A1151. After twenty minutes he turned south along a narrow country road. Darkness had fallen and the low scudding clouds, torn by wind, moved like a tattered blanket over the moon and the high stars. He drove fast and unhesitatingly, hardly aware of the tug and howl of the wind. He had taken this route only once before, early that same morning, but he had no need to consult the map; he knew where he was going. On either side of the low hedges stretched the black, unbroken fields. The lights of the car silvered an occasional distorted tree flailing in the wind, briefly illuminated as if with a searchlight the blank face of an isolated farm cottage, picked out the pin-bright eyes of a night animal before it scuttled to safety. The drive was not long, less than fifty minutes, but, staring straight ahead and shifting the gear lever as if he were an automaton, he felt for a moment disorientated as if he had driven through the bleak darkness of this flat, secretive landscape for interminable hours.

The brick-built, early-Victorian villa stood on the outskirts of a village. The gate to the gravel drive lay open and he drove slowly between the tossing laurels and the high, creaking boughs of the beech trees and manoeuvred the Jaguar between the three cars already discreetly parked at the side of the house. The two rows of windows in the front were dark and the single bulb which illuminated the fanlight seemed to Dalgliesh less a welcoming sign of occupation than a private signal, a sinister indication of secret life. He did not need to ring. Ears had been alert for the approaching car and the door was opened just as he reached it by the same stocky, cheerful-faced janitor who had greeted him on his first summons earlier that morning. Now, as then, he was wearing blue overalls so sprucely well cut that they looked like a uniform. Dalgliesh wondered what was his precise role; driver, guard, general factotum? Or had he, perhaps, a more specialized and sinister function?

He said: 'They're in the library, sir. I'll bring in the coffee. Will you be wanting sandwiches, sir? There's some beef left or I could put up a bit of cheese.'

Dalgliesh said: 'Just the coffee, thank you.'

They were waiting for him in the same small room at the back of the house. The walls were panelled in pale wood and there was only one window, a square bay heavily curtained with faded blue velvet. Despite its name the function of the room was unclear. Admittedly the wall opposite the window was lined with bookshelves, but they held only half a dozen leather-bound volumes and piles of old periodicals which looked as if they were Sunday colour supplements. The room had an oddly disturbing air of being both makeshift yet not devoid of comfort, a staging post in which the temporary occupants were attempting to make themselves at home. Ranged round the ornate marble fireplace were six assorted armchairs, most of them leather and each with a small wine table. The opposite end of the room was occupied by a modern dining table in plain wood with six chairs. This morning it had held the remains of breakfast and the air had been oppressively heavy with the smell of bacon and eggs. But the debris had been cleared and replaced by a tray of bottles and glasses. Looking at the variety provided, Dalgliesh thought that they had been doing themselves rather well. The loaded tray gave the place the air of a temporary hospitality room in which little else was hospitable. The air struck him as rather chill. In the grate an ornamental fan of paper rustled with each moan of the wind in the chimney and the two-bar electric fire which stood in the fender was barely adequate, even for so meanly proportioned and cluttered a room.

Three pairs of eyes turned on him as he entered. Clifford Sowerby was standing against the fireplace in exactly the same pose as when Dalgliesh had last seen him. He looked, in his formal suit and immaculate linen, as fresh as he had at nine o'clock that morning. Now, as then, he dominated the room. He was a solid-fleshed, conventionally handsome man with the assurance and controlled benevolence of a headmaster or a successful banker. No customer need fear to enter his office, provided his account was well in credit. Meeting him for only the second time Dalgliesh felt again an instinctive and seemingly irrational unease. The man was both ruthless and dangerous and yet, in their hours apart, he had been unable accurately to recall either his face or his voice.

The same could not be said for Bill Harding. He stood over six foot tall and, with his pale freckled face and thatch of red hair, had obviously decided that anonymity was impossible and that he might as well opt for eccentricity. He was wearing a checked suit in heavy tweed with a spotted tie. Raising himself with some difficulty out of the low chair he ambled over to the drinks and, when Dalgliesh said he'd wait for coffee, stood holding the whisky bottle as if unsure what to do with it. But there was one addition since the morning. Alex Mair, whisky glass in hand, stood against the bookcase as if interested in the assortment of leather-bound volumes and piled periodicals. He turned as Dalgliesh entered and gave him a long, considering look, then nodded briefly. He was easily the most personable and the most intelligent of the three waiting men but something, confidence or energy, seemed to have drained out of him and he had the diminished, precariously contained look of a man in physical pain.

Sowerby said, his heavily lidded eyes amused: 'You've singed your hair, Adam. You smell as if you've been raking a bonfire.'

'I have.'

Mair didn't move but Sowerby and Harding seated themselves each side of the fire. Dalgliesh took a chair between them. They waited until coffee had arrived and he had a cup in hand. Sowerby was leaning back in his chair and looking up at the ceiling and seemed to be prepared to wait all night.

It was Bill Harding who said: 'Well, Adam?'

Putting down his cup, Dalgliesh described what exactly had happened since his arrival at the caravan. He had total verbal recall. He had made no notes, nor was it necessary. At the end of his account he said: 'So you can relax. Pascoe believes what will, I imagine, become the official line, that the two girls were lovers, went for an unwise boat trip together and were accidentally run down in the fog. I don't think he'll make any trouble for you or for anyone else. His capacity for troublemaking seems to be over.'

Sowerby said: 'And Camm left nothing incriminating in the caravan?'

'I doubt very much whether there was anything to leave. Pascoe said that he read one or two of the postcards when they arrived but they were mostly the usual meaningless phrases, tourist's chat. Camm apparently destroyed them. And he, with my help, has destroyed the detritus of her life on the headland. I helped him carry the last of her clothes and make-up down to the fire. While he was busy burning it I had a chance to return and make a fairly thorough search. There was nothing there.'

Sowerby said formally: 'It was good of you to do this for us, Adam. Obviously as Rickards isn't in the picture as far as our interest is concerned we could hardly rely on him. And you, of course, had an advantage he lacked. Pascoe would see you more as a friend than a policeman. That's obvious from his previous visit to Larksoken Mill. For some reason he trusts you.'

Dalgliesh said: 'You explained all that this morning. The request you made then seemed to me to be reasonable in the circumstances. I'm neither naïve nor ambivalent about terrorism. You asked me to do something and I've done it. I still think you should put Rickards in the picture, but that's your business. And you've got your answer. If Camm were involved with Amphlett she didn't confide in Pascoe and he has no suspicions of either woman. He believes that Camm only stayed with him to be near her lover. Pascoe, for all his liberal ideas, is as ready as the next man to believe that a woman who doesn't persist in wanting to go to bed with him must be either frigid or a lesbian.'

Sowerby permitted himself a wry smile. He said: 'While you were playing Ariel to his Prospero on the beach I suppose he didn't confess to killing Robarts. It's of small importance, but one has a natural curiosity.'

'My brief was to talk to him about Amy Camm, but he did mention the murder. I don't think he really believes that Amy helped to kill Robarts, but he doesn't really care whether the two girls did or did not. Are you satisfied yourselves that they did?'

Sowerby said: 'We don't have to be. It's Rickards who has to be satisfied and I imagine that he is. Incidentally, have you seen or spoken to him today?'

'He telephoned briefly about midday, principally, I think, to tell me that his wife has come home. For some reason he thought I'd be interested. As far as the murder is concerned, he seems to be coming round to the view that Camm and Amphlett were in it together.'

Harding said: 'And he's probably right.'

Dalgliesh asked: 'On what evidence? And since he's not allowed to know that one of them at least is a suspected terrorist, where's the motive?'

Harding said impatiently: 'Come off it, Adam, what real evidence does he expect to get? And since when was motive the first consideration? Anyway, they had a motive, at least Camm did. She hated Robarts. There's one witness at least to a physical fight between them on the Sunday afternoon of the murder. And Camm was fiercely protective of Pascoe and connected to that pressure group he started. That libel action would have ruined him and put PANUP out of business for ever. It's precarious enough as it is. Camm wanted Robarts dead and Amphlett killed her. That will be the general belief locally and Rickards will go along with it. To do him justice, he probably believes it.'

Dalgliesh said: 'Camm fiercely protective of Pascoe? Who says so? That's supposition not evidence.'

'But he's got some evidence, hasn't he? Circumstantial evidence, admittedly, but that's all he's likely to get now. Amphlett knew that Robarts went swimming at night; practically everyone at the power station knew that. She concocted a false alibi. Camm had access, like anyone else, to the jumble room at the Old Rectory. And Pascoe now admits that it could have been 9.15 when he got back from Norwich. All right, the timing is tight but it's not impossible if Robarts swam earlier than usual. It adds up to a reasonable case. Not one which would have justified arresting them if they were still living, but enough to make it difficult to get a conviction against anyone else.'

Dalgliesh said: 'Would Amy Camm have left the child?'

'Why not? He was probably asleep, and if he wasn't and started yelling, who would hear? You're not suggesting, Adam, that she was a good mother, for God's sake? She left him at the end, didn't she? Permanently, as it happens, although that may not have been intentional. If you ask me, that kid had a pretty low priority with his mother.'

Dalgliesh said: 'So you're postulating a mother who is so outraged by a minor assault on her child that she avenges it with murder, and that same mother leaves him alone in a caravan while she goes sailing with her girlfriend. Wouldn't Rickards find that difficult to reconcile?'

Sowerby said, with a touch of impatience: 'God knows how Rickards reconciles anything. Luckily we're not required to ask him. Anyway, Adam, we know of a positive motive. Robarts could have suspected Amphlett. After all she was Acting Administrative Officer. She was intelligent, conscientious – over-conscientious, didn't you say, Mair?'

They all looked towards the silent figure standing against the bookcase. Mair turned to face them. He said quietly: 'Yes, she was conscientious. But I doubt whether she was conscientious enough to detect a conspiracy which had eluded me.' He turned back to his contemplation of the books.

There was a moment's embarrassed silence which was broken by Bill Harding. He said briskly, as if Mair hadn't spoken: 'So who was better placed to smell out a spot of treason? Rickards may have no firm evidence and an inadequate motive, but essentially he'll probably get it right.'

Dalgliesh got to his feet and walked over to the table. He said: 'It would suit you to get the case closed, I see that. But if I were the investigating officer the file would stay open.'

Sowerby said wryly: 'Obviously. Then let us be grateful that you aren't. But you'll keep your doubts to yourself, Adam? That doesn't need saying.'

'Then why say it?'

He placed his coffee cup back on the table. He was aware of Sowerby and Harding watching his every move as if he were a suspect who might suddenly make a break for it. Returning to his chair he said: 'And how will Rickards or anyone else explain the boat trip?'

It was still Harding who answered: 'He doesn't have to. They were lovers, for God's sake. They fancied a sea trip. It was Amphlett's boat after all. She left her car on the quay perfectly openly. She took nothing with her and neither did Amy. She left a note to Pascoe saying she'd be back in about an hour. In Rickards's eyes and everyone else's that adds up to an unfortunate accident. And who is to say that it wasn't? We were nowhere near close enough to have scared Amphlett into making a run for it; not yet.'

'And your people have found nothing at the house?'

Harding looked at Sowerby. It was a question they preferred not to answer and one which should not have been asked. After a pause, Sowerby answered: 'Clean. No radio, no documents, no evidence of trade craft. If Amphlett did intend to do a bunk, she cleaned up efficiently before she left.'

Bill Harding said: 'OK, if she did panic and was getting out, the only mystery is why so precipitous? If she killed Robarts and thought that the police were getting close, that might have tipped the balance. But they weren't getting close. It could, of course, have been a genuine boat trip, and a genuine accident. Or, their own side could have killed them both. Once the Larksoken plan was obsolete they were expendable. What were the comrades going to do with them, for God's sake? Fit them out with new personalities, new papers, infiltrate them into a power station in Germany? They were hardly worth the trouble, I should have thought.'

Dalgliesh said: 'Is there any evidence that it was an accident? Has any ship reported bow damage in the fog, a possible collision?'

Sowerby said: 'None so far. I doubt whether there will be. But if Amphlett really was part of the organization we suspect recruited her, they'd have no compunction in providing a couple of involuntary martyrs for the cause. What sort of people did she think she was dealing with? The fog would have helped them, but they could have run down the boat without the fog. Or, for that matter, taken them off and killed them elsewhere. But to fake an accident was the sensible course particularly given the bonus of the fog. I'd have done it that way myself.' And he would, thought Dalgliesh. He would have done it without compunction.

Harding turned to Mair. He said: 'You never had the least suspicion of her?'

'You asked me that before. None. I was surprised – a little irritated even – that she preferred not to stay as my PA when I got the new job, and even more surprised at the reason. Jonathan Reeves was hardly the man I thought she'd have chosen.'

Sowerby said: 'But it was clever. An ineffectual man, one she could dominate. Not too intelligent. Already in love with her. She could have chucked him whenever she chose and he wouldn't have the wit to know why. And why should you suspect? Sexual attraction is irrational anyway.'

There was a pause, then he added: 'Did you ever see her, the other girl, Amy? I'm told that she did visit the power station on one of those open days but I don't suppose you'd remember her.'

Mair's face was like a white mask. He said: 'I did see her once, I think. Blonde dyed hair, a chubby, rather pretty face. She was carrying the child. What will happen to him, incidentally? Or is it a she?'

Sowerby said: 'Taken into care, I suppose, unless they can trace the father or the grandparents. He'll probably end up fostered or adopted. I wonder what the hell his mother thought she was doing.'

Harding spoke with sudden vehemence: 'Do they think? Ever? No faith, no stability, no family affection, no loyalty. They're blown like paper with every wind. Then when they do find something to believe in, something to give them the illusion that they're important, what do they choose? Violence, anarchy, hatred, murder.'

Sowerby looked at him, surprised and a little amused. Then he said: 'Ideas some of them think worth dying for. In that, of course, lies the problem.'

'Only because they want to die. If you can't cope with living look for an excuse, a cause you can kid yourself is worth dying for and indulge your death wish. With luck you can take a dozen or so poor sods with you, people who can cope with living, who don't want to die. And there's always the ultimate self-deception, the final arrogance. Martyrdom. Lonely and inadequate fools all over the world will clench their fists and shout your name and carry placards with your picture and start looking round themselves for someone to bomb and shoot and maim. And that girl, Amphlett. She hadn't even the excuse of poverty. Dad a senior army officer, security, a good education, privilege, money. She'd had it all.'

It was Sowerby who replied. He said: 'We know what she had. What we can't know is what she didn't have.'

Harding ignored him. 'And what did they expect to do with Larksoken if they did take it over? They wouldn't have lasted for more than half an hour. They'd have needed experts, programmers.'

Mair said: 'I think you can take it they knew what and who they'd need and had planned how they could get them.'

'Into the country? How?'

'By boat, perhaps.'

Sowerby looked at him and then said a little impatiently: 'They didn't do it. They couldn't have done it. And it's our job to see that they never can do it.'

There was a moment's silence, then Mair said: 'I suppose Amphlett was the dominant partner. I wonder what arguments or what inducements she used. The girl – Amy – struck me as an instinctive creature, not likely to die for a political theory. But that is obviously a superficial judgement. I only saw her once.'

Sowerby said: 'Without knowing them we can't be sure who was the dominant partner. But I'd say it was almost certainly Amphlett. Nothing is known or suspected about Camm. She was probably recruited as a runner. Amphlett must have had a contact in the organization, must have met him occasionally if only to receive instructions. But they'd be careful never to get in touch directly. Camm probably received the coded messages setting out time and place for the next meeting and passed them on. As for her reasons, she found life unsatisfactory no doubt.'

Bill Harding lunged over to the table and poured himself a large whisky. His voice was thick as if he were drunk. 'Life has always been unsatisfactory for most people for most of the time. The world isn't designed for our satisfaction. That's no reason for trying to pull it down about our ears.'

Sowerby smiled his sly superior smile. He said easily: 'Perhaps they thought that's what we're doing.'

Fifteen minutes later, Dalgliesh left with Mair. As they stood unlocking their cars he looked back and saw that the janitor was still waiting at the open door.

Mair said: 'Making sure that we actually leave the premises. What extraordinary people they are! I wonder how they got on to Caroline. There seemed no point in asking as they made it obvious that they had no intention of saying.'

'No, they wouldn't say. Almost certainly they got a tip-off from the security services in Germany.'

'And this house. How on earth do they find these places?

D'you suppose that they own it, borrow it, rent it or just break into it?'

Dalgliesh said: 'It probably belongs to one of their own officers, retired, I imagine. He, or she, lets them have a spare key for such an occasional use.'

'And now they'll be packing up, I suppose. Dusting down the furniture, checking for fingerprints, finishing up the food, turning off the power. And in an hour no one will know that they were ever there. The perfect temporary tenants. They've got one thing wrong, though. There wasn't a physical relationship between Amy and Caroline. That's nonsense.'

He spoke with such extraordinary strength and conviction, almost with outrage, that Dalgliesh wondered for a moment whether Caroline Amphlett had been more than his PA. Mair must surely have sensed what his companion was thinking but he neither explained nor denied. Dalgliesh said: 'I haven't congratulated you yet on your new job.'

Mair had slipped into his seat and turned on the engine. But the car door was still open and the silent warder at the door still waited patiently.

He said: 'Thank you. These tragedies at Larksoken have taken away some of the immediate satisfaction, but it's still the most important job I'm ever likely to hold.' Then, as Dalgliesh turned away, he said: 'So you think we still have a killer alive on the headland.'

'Don't you?'

But Mair didn't reply. Instead he asked: 'If you were Rickards, what would you do now?'

'I'd concentrate on trying to find out whether Blaney or Theresa left Scudder's Cottage that Sunday night. If either of them did, then I think my case would be complete. It isn't one that I'd be able to prove, but it would stand up in logic and I think that it would be the truth.'

49

Dalgliesh drove first out of the drive but Mair, accelerating sharply, overtook him on the first stretch of straight road and remained ahead. The thought of following the Jaguar all the way back to Larksoken was, for some reason, intolerable. But there was no danger of it; Dalgliesh even drove like a policeman, inside, if only just inside, the speed limit. And by the time they reached the main road Mair could no longer see the lights of the Jaguar in his mirror. He drove almost automatically, eyes fixed ahead, hardly aware of the black shapes of the tossing trees as they rushed past like an accelerated film, of the cat's-eyes unfolding in an unbroken stream of light. He was expecting a clear road on the headland and, cresting a low ridge, saw almost too late the lights of an ambulance. Violently twisting the wheel, he bumped off the road and braked on the grass verge, then sat there listening to the silence. It seemed to him that emotions which for the last three hours he had rigorously suppressed were buffeting him as the wind buffeted the car. He had to discipline his thoughts, to arrange and make sense of these astonishing feelings which horrified him by their violence and irrationality. Was it possible that he could feel relief at her death, at a danger averted, a possible embarrassment prevented, and yet, at the same time, be torn as if his sinews were being wrenched apart by a pain and regret so overwhelming that it could only be grief? He had to control himself from beating his head against the wheel of the car. She had been so uninhibited, so gallant, so entertaining. And she had kept faith with him. He hadn't been in touch with her since their last meeting on the Sunday afternoon of the murder and she had made no attempt to contact him by letter or telephone. They had agreed that the affair must end and that each would keep silent. She had kept her part of the bargain, as he had known she would. And now she was dead. He spoke her name aloud, 'Amy, Amy, Amy.' Suddenly he gave a gasp which tore at the muscles of his chest as if he were in the first throes of a heart attack and felt the blessed releasing tears flow down his face. He hadn't cried since he was a boy and even now, as the tears ran like rain and he tasted their surprising saltiness on his lips, he told himself that these minutes of emotion were good and therapeutic. He owed them to her and, once over, the tribute of grief paid, he would be able to put her out of his mind as he had planned to put her out of his heart. It was only thirty minutes later, when switching on the engine, that he gave thought to the ambulance and wondered which of the few inhabitants of the headland was being rushed to hospital.

50

As the two ambulance men wheeled the stretcher down the garden path the wind tore at the corner of the red blanket and billowed it into an arc. The straps held it down but Blaney almost flung himself across Theresa's body as if desperately shielding her from something more threatening than the wind. He shuffled crab-like down the path beside her, half bent, his hand holding hers under the blanket. It felt hot and moist and very small and it seemed to him that he was aware of every delicate bone. He wanted to whisper reassurance but terror had dried his throat and when he tried to speak his jaw jabbered as if palsied. And he had no comfort to give. There was a too-recent memory of another ambulance, another stretcher, another journey. He hardly dared look at Theresa in case he saw on her face what he had seen on her mother's; that look of pale, remote acceptance which meant that she was already moving away from him, from all the mundane affairs of life, even from his love, into a shadow land where he could neither follow nor was welcome. He tried to find reassurance in the memory of Dr Entwhistle's robust voice.

'She'll be all right. It's appendicitis. We'll get her to hospital straight away. They'll operate tonight and with luck she'll be back with you in a few days. Not to do the housework mind; we'll discuss all that later. Now, let's get to the telephone. And stop panicking, man. People don't die of appendicitis.'

But they did die. They died under the anaesthetic, they died because peritonitis intervened, they died because the surgeon made a mistake. He had read of these cases. He was without hope.

As the stretcher was gently lifted and slid with easy expertise into the ambulance he turned and looked back at Scudder's Cottage. He hated it now, hated what it had done to him, what it had made him do. Like him, it was accursed. Mrs Jago was standing at the door holding Anthony in her unpractised arms with a twin standing silently on each side. He had telephoned the Local Hero for help and George Jago had driven her over immediately to stay with the children until he returned. There had been no one else to ask. He had telephoned Alice Mair at Martyr's Cottage but all he had got was the answerphone. Mrs Jago lifted Anthony's hand and waved it in a gesture of goodbye, then bent to speak to the twins. Obediently they too waved. He climbed into the ambulance and the doors were firmly shut.

The ambulance bumped and gently swayed up the lane, then accelerated as it reached the narrow headland road to Lydsett. Suddenly it swerved and he was almost thrown from his seat. The paramedic sitting opposite him cursed.

'Some bloody fool going too fast.'

But he didn't reply. He sat very close to Theresa, his hand still in hers, and found himself praying as if he could batten on the ears of the God he hadn't believed in since he was seventeen. 'Don't let her die. Don't punish her because of me. I'll believe. I'll do anything. I can change, be different. Punish me but not her. Oh God, let her live.'

And suddenly he was standing again in that dreadful little churchyard, hearing the drone of Father McKee's voice, with Theresa at his side, her hand still cold in his. The earth was covered with synthetic grass but there was one mound left bare and he saw again the newly sliced gold of the soil. He hadn't known that Norfolk earth could be so rich a colour. A white flower had fallen from one of the wreaths, a small, tortured, unrecognized bud with a pin through the wrapped stalk and he was seized with an almost uncontrollable compulsion to pick it up before it was shovelled with the earth into the grave, to take it home, put it in water and let it die in peace. He had to hold himself tautly upright to prevent himself bending to retrieve it. But he hadn't dared, and it had been left there to be smothered and obliterated under the first clods.

He heard Theresa whisper and bent so low to listen that he could smell her breath. 'Daddy, am I going to die?'

'No. No.'

He almost shouted the word, a howled defiance of death, and was aware of the paramedic half rising to his feet. He said

quietly: 'You heard what Dr Entwhistle said. It's just appendicitis.'

'I want to see Father McKee.'

'Tomorrow. After the operation. I'll tell him. He'll visit you. I
won't forget. I promise. Now lie still.'

'Daddy, I want him now, before the operation. There's something I have to tell him.'

'Tell him tomorrow.'

'Can I tell you? I have to tell someone now.'

He said almost fiercely: 'Tomorrow, Theresa. Leave it till
tomorrow.' And then, appalled by his selfishness, he whispered:
'Tell me, darling, if you must,' and closed his eyes so that she
should not see the horror, the hopelessness.

She whispered: 'That night Miss Robarts died. I crept out to
the abbey ruins. I saw her running into the sea. Daddy, I was
there.'

He said hoarsely: 'It doesn't matter. You don't have to tell me
any more.'

'But I want to tell. I ought to have told you before. Please, Daddy.'

He put his other hand over hers. He said: 'Tell me.'

'There was someone else there, too. I saw her walking over the
headland towards the sea. It was Mrs Dennison.'

Relief flowed through him, wave after wave, like a warm
cleansing summer sea. After a moment's silence he heard her
voice again: 'Daddy, are you going to tell anyone, the police?'

'No,' he said. 'I'm glad you've told me but it isn't important.
It doesn't mean anything. She was just taking a walk in the
moonlight. I'm not going to tell.'

'Not even about me being on the headland that night?'

'No,' he said firmly, 'not even that. Not yet, anyway. But we'll
talk about it, what we ought to do, after the operation.'

And for the first time he could believe that there would be a
time for them after the operation.

51

Mr Copley's study was at the back of the Old Rectory, looking
out over the unkempt lawn and the three rows of wind-crippled

bushes which the Copleys called the shrubbery. It was the only room in the rectory which Meg would not dream of entering without first knocking and it was accepted as his private place as if he were still in charge of a parish and needing a quiet sanctum to prepare his weekly sermon or counsel those parishioners who sought his advice. It was here that each day he read Morning Prayer and Evensong, his only congregation his wife and Meg, whose low feminine voices would make the responses and read alternate verses of the psalms. On her first day with them he had said gently but without embarrassment: 'I say the two main offices every day in my study, but please don't feel that you need to attend unless you wish to.'

She had chosen to attend, at first from politeness but later because this daily ritual, the beautiful, half-forgotten cadences, seducing her into belief, gave a welcome shape to the day. And the study itself, of all the rooms in the solidly ugly but comfortable house, seemed to represent an inviolable security, a great rock in a weary land against which all the rancorous, intrusive memories of school, the petty irritations of daily living, even the horror of the Whistler and the menace of the power station beat in vain. She doubted whether it had greatly changed since the first Victorian rector had taken possession. One wall was lined with books, a theological library which she thought Mr Copley now rarely consulted. The old mahogany desk was usually bare and Meg suspected that he spent most of his time in the easy chair which looked out over the garden. Three walls were covered with pictures; the rowing eight of his university days with ridiculously small caps above the grave moustached young faces; the ordinands of his theological college; insipid watercolours in golden mounts, the record by some Victorian ancestor of his grand tour etchings of Norwich Cathedral, the nave at Winchester, the great octagon of Ely. To one side of the ornate Victorian fireplace was a single crucifix. It seemed to Meg to be very old and probably valuable but she had never liked to ask. The body of Christ was a young man's body, stretched taut in its last agony, the open mouth seeming to shout in triumph or defiance at the God who had deserted him. Nothing else in the study was powerful or disturbing; furniture, objects, pictures all spoke of order, of certainty, of hope. Now, as she knocked and listened for Mr Copley's gentle 'Come in', it occurred to her that she was seeking comfort as much from the room itself as from its occupant.

He was sitting in the armchair, a book in his lap, and made to get up with awkward stiffness as she entered. She said: 'Please don't get up. I wonder if I could talk to you privately for a few minutes.'

She saw at once the flare of anxiety in the faded blue eyes and thought, He's afraid I'm going to give notice. She added quickly but with gentle firmness: 'As a priest. I wish to consult you as a priest.'

He laid down his book. She saw that it was one he and his wife had chosen the previous Friday from the travelling library, the newest H. R. F. Keating. Both he and Dorothy Copley enjoyed detective stories and she was always slightly irritated that husband and wife took it for granted that he should always have first read. This inopportune reminder of his mild domestic selfishness assumed for a moment a disproportionate importance and she wondered why she had ever thought he could be of help. Yet was it right to criticize him for the marital priorities which Dorothy Copley had herself laid down and gently enforced over fifty-three years? She told herself, I am consulting the priest not the man. I wouldn't ask a plumber how he treated his wife and children before letting him loose on the leaking tank.

He gestured towards a second easy chair and she drew it up opposite him. He marked his page with his leather bookmark with careful deliberation and laid down the novel as reverently as if it were a book of devotions, folding both hands over it. It seemed to her that he had drawn himself together and was leaning slightly forward, head to one side, as if he were in the confessional. She had nothing to confess to him, only a question which in its stark simplicity seemed to her to go to the very heart of her orthodox, self-affirming but not unquestioning Christian faith. She said: 'If we are faced with a decision, a dilemma, how do we know what is right?'

She thought she detected in his gentle face an easing of tension as if grateful that the question was less onerous than he had feared. But he took his time before he replied.

'Our conscience will tell us if we will listen.'

'The still, small voice, like the voice of God?'

'Not *like*, Meg. Conscience *is* the voice of God, of the indwelling Holy Spirit. In the collect for Whit Sunday we do indeed pray that we may have a right judgement in all things.'

She said with gentle persistence: 'But how can we be sure that what we're hearing isn't our own voice, our own subconscious desires? The message we listen for so carefully must be mediated through our own experience, our personality, our heredity, our inner needs. Can we ever break free of the devices and desires of our own hearts? Might not our conscience be telling us what we most want to hear?'

'I haven't found it so. Conscience has usually directed me against my own desires.'

'Or what at the time you thought were your own desires.'

But this was pressing him too hard. He sat quietly, blinking rapidly as if seeking inspiration in old sermons, old homilies, familiar texts. There was a moment's pause and then he said: 'I have found it helpful to think of conscience as an instrument, a stringed instrument perhaps. The message is in the music, but if we don't keep it in repair and use it constantly in regular and disciplined practice we get only an imperfect response.'

She remembered that he had been an amateur violinist. His hands were too rheumatic now to hold the instrument, but it still lay in its case on top of the bureau in the corner. The metaphor might mean something to him but for her it was meaningless.

She said: 'But even if my conscience tells me what is right, I mean right according to the moral law or even the law of the country, that doesn't necessarily mean the end of responsibility. Suppose if I obey it, do what conscience tells me, I cause harm, even danger to someone else.'

'We must do what we know is right and leave the consequences to God.'

'But any human decision has to take account of the probable consequences; that is surely what decision means. How can we separate cause from effect?'

He said: 'Would it be helpful if you told me what is troubling you, that is if you feel you can?'

'It isn't my secret to tell, but I can give an example. Suppose I know that someone is regularly stealing, from his employer. If I expose him he'll be sacked, his marriage will be at risk, his wife and children injured. I might feel that the shop or firm could afford to lose a few pounds each week rather than cause all that hurt to innocent people.'

He was silent for a moment, then said: 'Conscience might tell you to speak to the thief rather than to his employer. Explain that you know, persuade him to stop. Of course the money would have to be returned. I can see that that might present a practical difficulty.'

She watched as he wrestled with the difficulty for a moment, brow creased, conjuring up the mythical thieving husband and father, clothing the moral problem in living flesh. She said: 'But what if he won't or can't stop his stealing?'

'Can't? If stealing is an irresistible compulsion then, of course, he needs medical help. Yes, certainly, that would have to be tried, although I'm never very sanguine about the success of psychotherapy.'

'Won't, then, or promises to stop and then goes on stealing.'

'You must still do what your conscience tells you is right. We cannot always judge the consequences. In the case you have postulated, to let the stealing go on unchecked is to connive at dishonesty. Once you have discovered what is happening you can't pretend not to know, you can't abdicate responsibility. Knowledge always brings responsibility; that is as true for Alex Mair at Larksoken Power Station as it is in this study. You said that the children would be injured if you told; they are being injured already by their father's dishonesty and so is the wife who benefits from it. Then there are the other staff to consider: perhaps they might be wrongly suspected. The dishonesty, if undetected, could well get worse so that at the end the wife and children would be in deeper trouble than if it were stopped now. That is why it is safer if we concentrate on doing what is right and leave the consequences to God.'

She wanted to say, 'Even if we're not sure any longer if He exists? Even if that seems only another way of evading the personal responsibility which you have just told me we can't and

shouldn't evade?' But she saw with compunction that he was
suddenly looking tired and she didn't miss the quick glance down
at his book.

He wanted to get back to Inspector Ghote, Keating's gentle
Indian detective who, despite his uncertainties, would get there
in the end because this was fiction; problems could be solved, evil
overcome, justice vindicated, and death itself only a mystery
which would be solved in the final chapter. He was a very old
man. It was unfair to bother him. She wanted to put her hand on
his sleeve and tell him that it was all right, he mustn't worry.
Instead she got up and, using for the first time the name that
came naturally to her, spoke the comforting lie.

'Thank you, Father, you have been very helpful. It's plainer to
me now. I shall know what to do.'

52

Every turn and hazard of the overgrown garden path leading to
the gate which gave access to the headland was so familiar to
Meg that she hardly needed to follow the jerking moon of her
torch's beam and the wind, always capricious at Larksoken,
seemed to have abated the worst of its fury. But when she
reached a slight ridge and the light at the door of Martyr's
Cottage came in sight, it renewed its strength and came swooping
down on her as if it would pluck her from the earth and send her
whirling back to the shelter and peace of the rectory. She didn't
give battle but leaned against it, her head bent, her shoulder bag
bumping at her side, clutching her scarf to her head with both
hands until the fury passed and she could again stand upright.
The sky, too, was turbulent, the stars bright but very high, the
moon reeling frantically between the shredded clouds like a
blown lantern of frail paper. Fighting her way towards Martyr's
Cottage, Meg felt as if the whole headland was whirling in chaos
about her so that she could no longer tell whether the roaring in
her ears was the wind, her blood or the crashing sea. When at
last, breathless, she reached the oak door she thought for the first
time about Alex Mair and wondered what she would do if he
were at home. It struck her as strange that the possibility hadn't

previously occurred to her. And she knew that she couldn't face him, not now, not yet. But it was Alice who answered her ring. Meg asked: 'Are you alone?'

'Yes, I'm alone. Alex is at Larksoken. Come in, Meg.'

Meg took off and hung up her coat and headscarf in the hall and followed Alice to the kitchen. She had obviously been occupied in correcting her proofs. Now she reseated herself at her desk, swivelled round and looked gravely at Meg as she took her usual fireside chair. For a few moments neither spoke. Alice was wearing a long brown skirt of fine wool with a blouse high-buttoned to the chin and over it a sleeveless, pleated shift in narrow stripes of brown and fawn which reached almost to the floor. It gave her a hieratic dignity, an almost sacerdotal look of composed authority which was yet one of total comfort and ease. A small fire of logs was burning in the hearth, filling the room with a pungent autumnal smell, and the wind, muted by thick sixteenth-century walls, sighed and moaned companionably in the chimney. From time to time it gushed down and the logs flared into hissing life. The clothes, the firelight, the smell of burning wood overlaying the subtler smell of herbs and warm bread were familiar to Meg from their many quiet evenings together and they were dear to her. But tonight was dreadfully different. After tonight the kitchen might never be home to her again.

She asked: 'Am I interrupting?'

'Obviously, but that doesn't mean that I don't welcome interruption.'

Meg bent to extract a large brown envelope from her shoulder bag.

'I've brought back the first fifty pages of proofs. I've done what you asked, read the text and checked for printing errors only.'

Alice took the envelope and, without glancing at it, placed it on the desk. She said: 'That's what I wanted. I'm so obsessed with the accuracy of the recipes that errors in the text sometimes slip through. I hope it wasn't too much of a chore.'

'No, I enjoyed it, Alice. It reminded me of Elizabeth David.'

'Not too much, I hope. She's so marvellous that I'm always afraid of being overinfluenced by her.'

There was a silence. Meg thought: We're talking as if the dialogue has been scripted for us, not as strangers exactly, but as people who are careful of their words because the space between them is loaded with dangerous thoughts. How well do I really know her? What has she ever told me about herself? Just a few details of her life with her father, snatches of information, a few phrases dropped into our conversations like a falling match, briefly illuminating the contours of a vast unexplored terrain. I've confided almost everything about myself, my childhood, the racial trouble at the school, Martin's death. But has it ever been an equal friendship? She knows more about me than any other living creature. All I really know about Alice is that she's a good cook.

She was aware of her friend's steady, almost quizzical look. Alice said: 'But you didn't fight your way in this wind just to bring back fifty pages of proofs.'

'I have to talk to you.'

'You are talking to me.'

Meg held Alice's own unflinching gaze. She said: 'Those two girls, Caroline and Amy, people are saying that they killed Hilary Robarts. Is that what you believe?'

'No. Why do you ask?'

'Nor do I believe it. Do you suppose the police will try to pin it on them?'

Alice's voice was cool. 'I shouldn't think so. Isn't that rather a dramatic idea? And why should they? Chief Inspector Rickards strikes me as an honest and conscientious officer, if not particularly intelligent.'

'Well, it's convenient for them, isn't it? Two suspects dead. The case closed. No more deaths.'

'Were they suspects? You seem to be more in Rickards's confidence than I am.'

'They didn't have alibis. The man at Larksoken Caroline was supposed to be engaged to – Jonathan Reeves, isn't it? – apparently he's confessed that they weren't together that night. Caroline forced him to lie. Most of the staff at Larksoken know that now. And it's all over the village, of course. George Jago rang to tell me.'

'So they didn't have alibis. Nor did other people – you, for example. Not having an alibi isn't proof of guilt. Nor did I, incidentally. I was at home all that evening but I doubt whether I could prove it.'

And this at last was the moment which had filled Meg's thoughts since the murder, the moment of truth which she had dreaded. She said through dry unyielding lips: 'But you weren't at home, were you? You told Chief Inspector Rickards that you were when I was here sitting in this kitchen on the Monday morning, but it wasn't true.'

There was a moment's silence. Then Alice said calmly: 'Is that what you've come to say?'

'I know that it can be explained. It's ridiculous even to ask. It's just that I've had it on my mind for so long. And you are my friend. A friend should be able to ask. There should be honesty, confidence, trust.'

'Ask what? Do you have to talk like a marriage guidance counsellor?'

'Ask why you told the police you were here at nine. You weren't. I was. After the Copleys left I had a sudden need to see you. I tried the telephone but got only the answerphone. I didn't leave a message; there was no point. I walked down. The cottage was empty. The light was on in the sitting room and the kitchen and the door was locked. I called out for you. The record player was on, very loud. The cottage was filled with triumphant music. But there was no one here.'

Alice sat in silence for a moment. Then she said calmly: 'I went for a walk to enjoy the moonlight. I didn't expect a casual caller. There are never casual callers except you, and I thought that you were in Norwich. But I took the obvious precaution against an intruder, I locked the door. How did you get in?'

'With your key. You can't have forgotten, Alice. You gave me a key a year ago. I've had it ever since.'

Alice looked at her and Meg saw in her face the dawning of memory, chagrin, even, before she turned briefly away, the beginning of a rueful smile. She said: 'But I had forgotten; completely. How extraordinary! It might not have worried me, even if I had remembered. After all, I thought you were in

Norwich. But I didn't remember. We've got so many keys to the cottage, some here, some in London. But you never reminded me that you had one.'

'I did once, early on, and you told me to keep it. Like a fool I thought that the key meant something: trust, friendship, a sign that Martyr's Cottage was always open to me. You told me that I might one day need to use it.'

And now Alice did laugh aloud. She said: 'And you did need to use it. How ironic. But it isn't like you to come in uninvited, not while I wasn't here. You never have before.'

'But I didn't know you weren't here. The lights were on and I rang and I could hear the music. When I rang the third time and you still didn't come I was afraid that you might be ill, unable to summon help. So I unlocked the door. I walked into a surge of wonderful sound. I recognized it, Mozart's Symphony in G minor. It was Martin's favourite. What an extraordinary tape to choose.'

'I didn't choose it. I just turned on the player. What do you think I should have chosen? A requiem mass to mark the passing of a soul I don't believe in?'

Meg went on as if she hadn't heard: 'I walked through to the kitchen. The light was on here too. It was the first time I'd been in this room on my own. And suddenly I felt like a stranger. I felt that nothing in it had anything to do with me. I felt that I had no right here. That's why I went away without leaving you any message.'

Alice said sadly: 'You were quite right. You had no right here. And you needed to see me so badly that you walked alone over the headland before you knew that the Whistler was dead?'

'I didn't walk in fear. The headland is so deserted. There's nowhere anyone can lurk, and I knew when I reached Martyr's Cottage I'd be with you.'

'No, you're not easily frightened are you? Are you frightened now?'

'Not of you but of myself. I'm frightened of what I'm thinking.'

'So the cottage was empty. What else is there? Obviously there is something else.'

Meg said: 'That message on your answerphone; if you'd really received it at ten past eight you would have telephoned Norwich station and left a message for me to ring back. You knew how much the Copleys disliked the thought of going to their daughter. No one else on the headland knew that. The Copleys never spoke of it and nor did I, not to anyone except you. You would have rung, Alice. There could have been an announcement over the station loudspeaker and I could have driven them home. You would have thought of that.'

Alice said: 'One lie to Rickards which could have been a matter of convenience, a wish to avoid trouble, and one instance of insensitive neglect. Is that all?'

'The knife. The middle knife in your block. It wasn't here. It meant nothing at the time, of course, but the block looked odd. I was so used to seeing the five carefully graded knives, each in its sheath. It's back now. It was back when I called in on the Monday after the murder. But it wasn't here on the Sunday night.'

She wanted to cry out: 'You can't be going to use it! Alice, don't use it!' Instead she made herself go on, trying to keep her voice calm, trying not to plead for reassurance, understanding.

'And next morning, when you telephoned to say that Hilary was dead, I didn't say anything about my visit. I didn't know what to believe. It wasn't that I suspected you; that would have been impossible for me, it still is. But I needed time to think. It was late morning before I could bring myself to come to you.'

'And then you found me here with Chief Inspector Rickards and heard me lying. And you saw that the knife was back in the block. But you didn't speak then and you haven't spoken since, not even, I presume, to Adam Dalgliesh.'

It was a shrewd thrust. Meg said: 'I've told no one, how could I? Not until we'd spoken. I knew that you must have had what seemed to you a good reason for lying.'

'And then, I suppose, slowly, perhaps unwillingly, you began to realize what that reason might be?'

'I didn't think you'd murdered Hilary. It sounds fantastic, ludicrous even to speak those words, to think of suspecting you. But the knife was missing and you weren't there. You did lie and I couldn't understand why. I still can't. I wonder who it is you're shielding. And sometimes – forgive me, Alice – sometimes I wonder whether you were there when he killed her, kept guard, stood there watching, might even have helped him by cutting off her hair.'

Alice sat so still that the long-fingered hands resting in her lap, the folds of her shift, might have been carved in stone. She said: 'I didn't help anyone – and no one helped me. There were only two people on that beach, Hilary Robarts and I. I planned it alone and I did it alone.'

For a moment they sat in silence. Meg felt a great coldness. She heard the words and she knew that they were true. Had she, perhaps, always known? She thought: I shall never be with her in this kitchen again, never again find the peace and security which I found in this room. And there fell into her mind an incongruous memory; herself sitting quietly in the same chair and watching while Alice made short pastry; sieving the flour on to a marble slab, adding the squares of soft butter, breaking in the egg, her long fingers delicately dabbling the mixture, drawing in the flour, lightly forming the glistening ball of dough. She said: 'They were your hands. Your hands tightening the belt round her throat, your hands cutting off her hair, your hands slicing that L into her forehead. You planned it alone and you did it alone.'

Alice said: 'It took courage, but perhaps less than you would imagine. And she died very quickly, very easily. We shall be lucky to go with so little pain. She hadn't even time to feel terror. She had an easier death than most of us can look forward to. And as for what followed, that didn't matter. Not to her. Not even much to me. She was dead. It's what you do to the living that takes the strong emotions, courage, hatred and love.'

She was silent for a moment, then she said: 'In your eagerness to prove me a murderess, don't confuse suspicion with proof. You can't prove any of this. All right, you say the knife was missing, but that's only your word against mine. And if it was missing, I could say that I went for a short walk on the headland and the murderer saw his chance.'

'And put it back afterwards? He wouldn't even know that it was there.'

'Of course he would. Everyone knows that I'm a cook, and a cook has sharp knives. And why shouldn't he put it back?'

'But how would he get in? The door was locked.'

'There's only your word for that. I shall say that I left it open. People on the headland usually do.'

Meg wanted to cry out: 'Don't, Alice. Don't begin planning more lies. Let there at least be truth between us.' She said: 'And the portrait, the smashed window, was that you too?'

'Of course.'

'But why? Why all that complication?'

'Because it was necessary. While I was waiting for Hilary to come out of the sea I glimpsed Theresa Blaney. She suddenly appeared on the very edge of the cliff by the abbey ruins. She was only there for a moment and then she disappeared. But I saw her. She was unmistakable in the moonlight.'

'But if she didn't see you, if she wasn't there when you . . . when Hilary died . . .'

'Don't you see? It meant that her father wouldn't have an alibi. She has always struck me as a truthful child and she has had a strict religious upbringing. Once she told the police that she was out on the headland that night Ryan would be in terrible danger. And even if she had sense enough to lie, for how long could she keep it up? The police would be gentle questioning her. Rickards isn't a brute. But a truthful child would find it difficult to lie convincingly. When I got back here after the murder I played back the messages on the answerphone. It occurred to me that Alex might change his plans and telephone. And it was then, too late, that I got George Jago's message. I knew that the murder could no longer be pinned on the Whistler. I had to give Ryan Blaney an alibi. So I tried to ring him to say that I'd collect the picture. When I couldn't get through I knew I had to call at Scudder's Cottage and as quickly as possible.'

'You could just have collected the portrait, knocked at the door to say what you'd done, seen him then. That would be proof enough that he was at home.'

'But it would have looked too deliberate, too contrived. Ryan had made it plain that he didn't want to be disturbed, that I was merely to collect the portrait. He made that very clear. And Adam Dalgliesh was with me when he said it. Not any casual caller, but Scotland Yard's most intelligent detective. No, I had to have a valid excuse to knock and speak to Ryan.'

'So you put the portrait in the boot of your car and told him that it wasn't in the shed?' It seemed to Meg extraordinary that horror could briefly be subsumed by curiosity, by the need to know. They might have been discussing complicated arrangements for a picnic.

Alice said: 'Exactly. He was hardly likely to think that it was I who had taken it only a minute earlier. It was convenient, of course, that he was half drunk. Not as drunk as I described to Rickards, but obviously incapable of killing Robarts and getting back to Scudder's Cottage by a quarter to ten.'

'Not even in the van or on his bicycle?'

'The van was out of commission and he couldn't have stayed on the bicycle. Besides, I would have passed him cycling home. My evidence meant that Ryan would be safe even if Theresa confessed that she'd left the cottage. After I left him I drove back over a deserted headland. I stopped briefly below the pillbox and threw the shoes inside. I had no way of burning them except on an open fire where I had burned the paper and string from the wrapped portrait, but I had an idea that burning rubber could leave some trace and a persistent smell. I didn't expect the police to search for them because I didn't believe they would find a print. But even if they did there would be nothing to link those particular shoes with the murder. I washed them thoroughly under the outside tap before I disposed of them. Ideally I could have returned them to the jumble box but I daren't wait and that night I knew that, with you gone to Norwich, the back door would be locked.'

'And then you threw the picture through Hilary's window?'

'I had to get rid of it somehow. That way it looked like a deliberate act of vandalism and hatred and there were plenty of possible suspects for that, not all of them on the headland. It complicated matters even further and it was one more piece of evidence to help Ryan. No one would believe that he would deliberately destroy his own work. But it had a double purpose: I wanted to get into Thyme Cottage. I smashed enough of the window to get through.'

'But that was terribly dangerous. You might have cut yourself, got a sliver of glass on your shoes. And they were your own shoes then; you had disposed of the Bumbles.'

'I examined the soles very thoroughly. And I was particularly careful where I trod. She had left the downstairs lights on so I didn't have to use my torch.'

'But why? What were you looking for? What did you hope to find?'

'Nothing. I wanted to get rid of the belt. I curled it very carefully and put it in the drawer in her bedroom among her other belts, stockings, handkerchiefs, socks.'

'But if the police examined it, it wouldn't have her prints on it.'

'Nor would it have mine. I was still wearing my gloves. Anyway why should they examine it? One would assume that the murderer had used his own belt and had taken it away again. The least likely hiding place for the killer to choose would be the victim's own cottage. That's why I chose it. And even if they did decide to examine every belt and dog lead on the headland I doubt whether they'd get any useful prints from half an inch of leather which dozens of hands must have touched.'

Meg said bitterly: 'You took a lot of trouble to give Ryan an alibi. What about the other innocent suspects? They were all at risk, they still are. Didn't you think of them?'

'I only cared about one other, Alex, and he had the best alibi of all. He would go through security to get into the station and again when he left.'

Meg said: 'I was thinking of Neil Pascoe, Amy, Miles Lessingham, even myself.'

'None of you is a parent responsible for four motherless children. I thought it very unlikely that Lessingham wouldn't be able to provide an alibi and if he couldn't there was no real evidence against him. How could there be? He didn't do it. But I have a feeling that he guesses who did. Lessingham isn't a fool. But even if he knows, he'll never tell. Neil Pascoe and Amy could give each other an alibi and you, my dear Meg, do you really see yourself as a serious suspect?'

'I felt like one. When Rickards was questioning me it was like being back in that staffroom at school, facing those cold accusing faces, knowing I'd already been judged and found guilty, wondering if perhaps I wasn't guilty.'

'The possible distress of innocent suspects, even you, was very low on my list of priorities.'

'And now you'll let them blame the murder on Caroline and Amy, both dead and both innocent?'

'Innocent? Of that, of course. Perhaps you're right and the police will find it convenient to assume they did it, one of them or together in collusion. From Rickards's point of view it's better to have two dead suspects than no arrest. And it can't hurt them now. The dead are beyond harm, the harm they do and the harm that is done to them.'

'But it's wrong and it's unjust.'

'Meg, they are dead. Dead. It can't matter. Injustice is a word and they have passed beyond the power of words. They don't exist. And life is unjust. If you feel called upon to do something about injustice concentrate on injustice to the living. Alex had a right to that job.'

'And Hilary Robarts, hadn't she a right to life? I know that she wasn't likeable, nor even very happy. There's no immediate family to mourn, apparently. She doesn't leave young children. But you've taken from her what no one can ever give back. She didn't deserve to die. Perhaps none of us do, not like that. We don't even hang the Whistler now. We've learned something since Tyburn, since Agnes Poley's burning. Nothing Hilary Robarts did deserved death.'

'I'm not arguing that she deserved to die. It doesn't matter whether she was happy, or childless, or even much use to anyone but herself. What I'm saying is that I wanted her dead.'

'That seems to me so evil that it's beyond my understanding. Alice, what you did was a dreadful sin.'

Alice laughed. The sound was so full-throated, almost happy, as if the amusement were genuine. 'Meg, you continue to astonish me. You use words which are no longer in the general vocabulary, not even in the Church's, so I'm told. The implications of that simple little word are outside my comprehension. But if you want to see this in theological terms, then think of Dietrich Bonhoeffer. He wrote: "We have at times to be willing to be guilty." Well, I'm willing to be guilty.'

'To be guilty, yes. But not to feel guilt. That must make it easier.'

'Oh, but I do feel it. I've been made to feel guilty from childhood. And if at the heart of your being you feel that you've no right even to exist, then one more cause of guilt hardly matters.'

Meg thought, I shall never be able to unlearn, never forget what's happening here this evening. But I have to know the whole of it. Even the most painful knowledge is better than half-knowledge. She said: 'That night I came here to tell you the Copleys were going to their daughter . . .'

Alice said: 'On the Friday after the dinner party. Thirteen days ago.'

'Is that all? It seems in a different dimension of time. You asked me to come and have supper with you when I got back from Norwich. Was that planned as part of your alibi? Did you use even me?'

Alice looked at her. She said: 'Yes. I'm sorry. You would have been here about half-past nine, just time for me to get back and be ready with a hot meal in the oven.'

'Which you would have cooked earlier in the evening. Safe enough with Alex at the power station, out of the way.'

'That's what I planned. When you declined I didn't press it. That would have looked suspicious later, too like trying to establish an alibi. Besides, you wouldn't have been persuaded to change your mind, would you? You never do. But the very fact of the invitation would have helped. A woman wouldn't normally invite a friend to even an informal supper if she's simultaneously planning a murder.'

'And if I had accepted, if I had turned up here at half-past nine, that would have been awkward, wouldn't it, given your later change of plan? You wouldn't have been able to drive over to Scudder's Cottage to give Ryan Blaney his alibi. And you would have been left in possession of the shoes and the belt.'

'The shoes would have been the greatest problem. I didn't think they'd ever be connected with the crime but I needed to get rid of them before next morning. I couldn't possibly explain my possession of them. I would probably have washed them and hidden them away, hoping for a chance to get them back to the jumble box the next day. Though I would have to have found a way of giving Ryan his alibi. Probably I would have told you that I couldn't get through by telephone and that we ought to drive over at once to tell him that the Whistler was dead. But it's all academic. I didn't worry. You said you wouldn't come and I knew you wouldn't.'

'But I did. Not to supper. But I came.'

'Yes. Why did you, Meg?'

'A feeling of depression after a heavy day, hating seeing the Copleys go, the need to see you. I wasn't looking for a meal. I had an early supper and then walked over the headland.'

But there was something else she needed to ask. She said: 'You knew that Hilary swam after watching the beginning of the main news. I suppose most people knew that who knew that she liked swimming at night. And you were taking trouble to see that Ryan had his alibi for 9.15 or shortly after. But suppose the body hadn't been discovered until the next day? Surely she wouldn't normally be missed until she didn't turn up at the power station on Monday morning, and then they would telephone to see if she were ill. It might even have been Monday evening before anybody made any inquiries. She could have swum in the morning and not at night.'

'The pathologist can usually estimate the time of death with reasonable accuracy. And I knew she'd be found that night. I knew that Alex had promised to visit her when he got back from the power station. He was on his way to the cottage when he met Adam Dalgliesh. And now, I think, you know it all, except for the Bumble trainers. I came through the back gardens at the Old Rectory late on Sunday afternoon. I knew that the back door would be open and it was the time when you would be having high tea. I had a bag with me with a few items of jumble in case I was seen. But I wasn't seen. I took soft shoes, easy to wear, a pair that looked roughly my size. And I took one of the belts.'

But there was one more question to ask, the most important of all. Meg said: 'But why? Alice, I have to know. Why?'

'That's a dangerous question, Meg. Are you sure you really want the answer?'

'I need the answer, need to try to understand.'

'Isn't it enough that she was determined to marry Alex and I was determined that she shouldn't?'

'That isn't why you killed her. It can't be. There was something more than that, there had to be.'

'Yes, there was. I suppose you have a right to know. She was blackmailing Alex. She could have stopped him getting that job, or, if he had got it, could have made it impossible for him to function successfully. She had the power to destroy his whole career. Toby Gledhill had told her that Alex had deliberately held up publishing the result of their research because it might have prejudiced the success of the inquiry into Larksoken's second reactor. They discovered that some of the assumptions made in generating the mathematical models were more critical than had been thought. People opposing the building of the new PWR at Larksoken could have exploited it to cause delay, whip up fresh hysteria.'

'You mean that he deliberately falsified the results?'

'That's something he's incapable of doing. All he did was to delay publishing the experiment. He'll publish it within the next month or two. But that's the kind of information which, once it got into the press, would have done irreparable harm. Toby was almost prepared to hand it over to Neil Pascoe but Hilary dissuaded him. It was far too valuable for that. She meant to use it to persuade Alex to marry her. She faced him with the knowledge when he walked home with her after the dinner party and late that night, he told me. I knew then what I had to do. The only way he might have been able to buy her off was by promoting her from Acting Administrator to Administrative Officer of Larksoken, and that was almost as impossible for him as deliberately falsifying a scientific result.'

'You mean he might actually have married her?'

'He might have been forced to. But how safe would he have been even then? She could have held that knowledge over his head until the end of his life. And what would that life have been, tied to a woman who had blackmailed him into marriage, a woman he didn't want, whom he could neither respect nor love?'

And then she said in a voice so low that Meg only just heard it, 'I owed Alex a death.'

Meg said: 'But how could you be sure, sure enough to kill her? Couldn't you have talked to her, persuaded her, reasoned with her?'

'I did talk to her. I went to see her on that Sunday afternoon. It was I who was with her when Mrs Jago arrived with the church magazine. You could say that I went to give her a chance of life. I couldn't murder her without making sure that it was necessary. That meant doing what I'd never done before, talking to her about Alex, trying to persuade her that the marriage wouldn't be in either of their interests, to let him go. I could have saved myself the humiliation. There was no argument, she was beyond that. She was no longer even rational. Part of the time she railed at me like a woman possessed.'

Meg said: 'And your brother, did he know about the visit?'

'He knows nothing. I didn't tell him at the time and I haven't told him since. But he told me what he planned; to promise her marriage and then, when the job was secure, to renege. It would have been disastrous. He never understood the woman he was dealing with, the passion, the desperation. She was a rich man's only child, alternately overindulged or neglected, trying all her life to compete with her father, taught that what you want is yours by right if you've only got the courage to fight for it and take it. And she had courage. She was obsessed by him, by her need for him, above all by her need for a child. She said that he owed her a child. Did he think she was like one of his reactors, tameable, that he could let down into that turbulence the equivalent of his rods of boron-steel and control the force which he'd let loose? When I left her that afternoon I knew I had no choice. Sunday was the deadline. He had arranged to call at Thyme Cottage on his way home from the power station. It was fortunate for him that I got to her first.

'Perhaps the worst part of all was waiting for him to come home that night. I daren't ring the power station. I couldn't be sure that he would be alone in his office or in the computer room, and I had never before telephoned him to ask when he would be home. I sat there and waited for nearly three hours. I expected that it would be Alex who would find the body. When he discovered that she wasn't in the cottage the natural move would be to check at the beach. He would find the body, telephone the police from the car and ring home to tell me. When he didn't I began to fantasize that she wasn't really dead, that somehow

I'd bungled it. I pictured him desperately working on her, giving her the kiss of life, saw her eyes slowly open. I turned off the lights and moved to the sitting room to watch the road. But it wasn't an ambulance that arrived, it was the police cars, the paraphernalia of murder. And still Alex didn't come.'

Meg asked: 'And when he did?'

'We hardly spoke. I'd gone to bed; I knew I must do what I would normally have done, not waited up for him. He came to my room to tell me that Hilary was dead and how she had died. I asked "The Whistler?" and he answered, "The police think not. The Whistler was dead before she was killed." Then he left me. I don't think either of us could have borne to be together, the air heavy with our unspoken thoughts. But I did what I had to do, and it was worth it. The job is his. And they won't take it away from him, not after it's been confirmed. They can't sack him because his sister is a murderess.'

'But if they found out why you did it?'

'They won't. Only two people know that and I wouldn't have told you if I couldn't trust you. On a less elevated level, I doubt if they'd believe you in the absence of confirmation from another witness; and Toby Gledhill and Hilary Robarts, the only two who could give it, are dead.' After a minute's silence, she said: 'You would have done the same for Martin.'

'Oh no, no.'

'Not as I did. I can't see you managing to use physical force. But when he drowned, if you could have stood on that river bank and had the power to choose which one should die and which live, would you have hesitated?'

'No, of course not. But that would have been different. I wouldn't have planned a drowning, wouldn't have wanted it.'

'Or if you were told that millions of people would live more safely if Alex got a job which he is uniquely capable of filling but at the cost of one woman's life, would you hesitate then? That was the choice which faced me. Don't evade it, Meg. I didn't.'

'But murder, how could it solve anything? It never has.'

Alice said with sudden passion: 'Oh, but it can, and it does. You read history, don't you? Surely you know that.'

Meg felt exhausted with weariness and pain. She wanted the

talking to stop. But it couldn't. There was still too much to be said. She asked: 'What are you going to do?'

'That depends on you.'

But out of horror and disbelief Meg had found courage. And she had found more than courage: authority. She said: 'Oh no, it doesn't. This isn't a responsibility I asked for and I don't want it.'

'But you can't evade it. You know what you know. Call Chief Inspector Rickards now. You can use this telephone.' When Meg made no move to use it she said: 'Surely you aren't going to do an E. M. Forster on me. If I had a choice between betraying my country and my friend I hope I would have the guts to betray my country.'

Meg said: 'That is one of those clever remarks that, when you analyse them, either mean nothing or mean something rather silly.'

Alice said: 'Remember, whatever you choose to do, you can't bring her back. You've got a number of options, but that isn't one. It's very satisfying to the human ego to discover the truth; ask Adam Dalgliesh. It's even more satisfying to human vanity to imagine you can avenge the innocent, restore the past, vindicate the right. But you can't. The dead stay dead. All you can do is to hurt the living in the name of justice or retribution or revenge. If that gives you any pleasure, then do it, but don't imagine that there's virtue in it. Whatever you decide, I know that you won't go back on it. I can believe you and I can trust you.'

Looking at Alice's face Meg saw that the look bent on her was serious, ironic, challenging; but it was not pleading. Alice said: 'Do you want some time to consider?'

'No. There's no point in having time. I know now what I have to do. I have to tell. But I'd rather you did.'

'Then give me until tomorrow. Once I've spoken there'll be no more privacy. There are things I need to do here. The proofs, affairs to arrange. And I should like twelve hours of freedom. If you can give me that I'll be grateful. I haven't the right to ask for more, but I am asking for that.'

Meg said: 'But when you confess you'll have to give them a motive, a reason, something they can believe in.'

'Oh, they'll believe it all right. Jealousy, hatred, the resentment of an ageing virgin for a woman who looked as she did, lived as she did. I'll say that she wanted to marry him, take him from me after all I've done for him. They'll see me as a neurotic, meno-pausal woman gone temporarily off her head. Unnatural affection. Suppressed sexuality. That's how men talk about women like me. That's the kind of motive that makes sense to a man like Rickards. I'll give it to him.'

'Even if it means you end up in Broadmoor? Alice, could you bear it?'

'Well, that's a possibility, isn't it? It's either that or prison. This was a carefully planned murder. Even the cleverest counsel won't be able to make it look like a sudden, unpremeditated act. And I doubt whether there's much to choose between Broadmoor and prison when it comes to the food.'

It seemed to Meg that nothing ever again would be certain. Not only had her inner world been shattered but the familiar objects of the external world no longer had reality. Alice's roll-top desk, the kitchen table, the high-backed cane chairs, the rows of gleaming pans, the stoves all seemed insubstantial, as if they would disappear at her touch. She was aware that the kitchen round which her eyes ranged was now empty. Alice had left. She leaned back, faint, and closed her eyes and then, opening them, she was aware of Alice's face bending low over hers, immense, almost moon-like. She was handing Meg a tumbler. She said: 'It's whisky. Drink this, you need it.'

'No, Alice, I can't. I can't really. You know I hate whisky, it makes me sick.'

'This won't make you sick. There are times when whisky is the only possible remedy. This is one of them. Drink it, Meg.'

She felt her knees tremble, and simultaneously the tears started like burning spurts of pain and began flowing unchecked, a salt stream over her cheeks, her mouth. She thought, This can't be happening. This can't be true. But that was how she had felt when Miss Mortimer, calling her from her class, had gently seated her in the chair opposite to her in the Head's private sitting room and had broken the news of Martin's death. The unthinkable had to be thought, the unbelievable believed. Words still meant what they had always meant; murder, death, grief, pain. She could see Miss Mortimer's mouth moving, the odd, disconnected phrases floating out, like balloons in a cartoon, noticing again how she must have wiped off her lipstick before the interview. Perhaps she had thought that only naked lips could give such appalling news. She saw again those restless blobs of flesh, noticed again that the top button on Miss Mortimer's cardigan was hanging loose on a single thread and heard herself say, actually say, 'Miss Mortimer, you're going to lose a button.'

She clasped her fingers round the glass. It seemed to her to have grown immensely large and heavy as a rock and the smell of the whisky almost turned her stomach. But she had no power to resist. She lifted it slowly to her mouth. She was aware of Alice's face still very close, of Alice's eyes watching her. She took the first small sip, and was about to throw back her head and gulp it down, when, firmly but gently, the glass was taken out of her hands, and she heard Alice's voice: 'You're quite right, Meg, it was never your drink. I'll make coffee for both of us then walk with you back to the Old Rectory.'

Fifteen minutes later Meg helped wash up the coffee cups as if this was the end of an ordinary evening. Then they set out together to walk over the headland. The wind was at their back and it seemed to Meg that they almost flew through the air, their feet hardly touching the turf, as if they were witches. At the door of the rectory Alice asked: 'What will you do tonight, Meg. Pray for me?'

'I shall pray for both of us.'

'As long as you don't expect me to repent. I'm not religious, as you know, and I don't understand that word unless, as I suppose, it means regret that something we've done has turned out less well for us than we hoped. On that definition I have little to repent of except ill luck that you, my dear Meg, are an incompetent car mechanic.'

And then, as if on impulse, she grasped Meg's arms. The grip was so fierce that it hurt. Meg thought for a moment that Alice was going to kiss her but her hold loosened and her hands fell. She said a curt goodbye and turned away.

Putting her key in the lock and pushing the door open, Meg

looked back, but Alice had disappeared into the darkness and the wild sobbing, which for an incredible moment she thought was a woman weeping, was only the wind.

53

Dalgliesh had just finished sorting the last of his aunt's papers when the telephone rang. It was Rickards. His voice, strong, high with euphoria, came over the line as clearly as if his presence filled the room. His wife had given birth to a daughter an hour earlier. He was ringing from the hospital. His wife was fine. The baby was wonderful. He only had a few minutes. They were carrying out some nursing procedure or other and then he'd be able to get back to Susie.

'She's got home just in time, Mr Dalgliesh. Lucky, wasn't it? And the midwife says she's hardly known such a quick labour for a first pregnancy. Only six hours. Seven and a half pounds, just a nice weight. And we wanted a girl. We're calling her Stella Louise. Louise is after Susie's mother. We may as well make the old trout happy.'

Replacing the receiver after warm congratulations which he suspected Rickards felt were hardly adequate, Dalgliesh wondered why he had been honoured with such early news and concluded that Rickards, possessed by joy, was ringing everyone who might have an interest, filling in the minutes before he was allowed back to his wife's bedside. His last words were: 'I can't tell you what it feels like, Mr Dalgliesh.'

But Dalgliesh could remember what it had felt like. He paused for a moment, the receiver still warm under his hand, and faced reactions which seemed to him over-complicated for such ordinary and expected news, recognizing with distaste that part of what he was feeling was envy. Was it, he wondered, his coming to the headland, the sense there of man's transitory but continuing life, the everlasting cycle of birth and death, or was it the death of Jane Dalgliesh, his last living relative, that made him for a moment wish so keenly that he too had a living child?

Neither he nor Rickards had spoken about the murder. Rickards would no doubt have felt it an almost indecent intrusion into his private, almost sacrosanct, rapture. And there was, after all, little more to be said. Rickards had made it plain that he considered the case closed. Amy Camm and her lover were both dead and it was unlikely now that their guilt would ever be proved. And the case against them was admittedly imperfect. Rickards still had no evidence that either woman had known details of the Whistler killings. But that, apparently, now assumed less importance in the police mind. Someone could have talked. Scraps of information picked up by Camm in the Local Hero could have been pieced together. Robarts herself could have told Amphlett and what they hadn't learned they could have guessed. The case might officially be classified as unsolved but Rickards had now persuaded himself that Amphlett, helped by her lover Camm, had killed Hilary Robarts. Dalgliesh, when they had briefly met on the previous evening, had felt it right to put another view and had argued it calmly and logically, and Rickards had turned his own arguments against him.

'She's her own woman. You said so yourself. She's got her own life, a profession. Why the hell should she care who he marries? She didn't try to stop him when he married before. And it's not as if he needs protection. Can you imagine Alex Mair doing anything he doesn't want to do? He's the sort of man who'll die at his own convenience, not God's.'

Dalgliesh had said: 'The absence of motive is the weakest part of the case. And I admit there isn't a single piece of forensic or other physical evidence. But Alice Mair fulfils all the criteria. She knew how the Whistler killed; she knew where Robarts would be shortly after nine o'clock; she has no alibi; she knew where she could find those trainers and she is tall enough to wear them; she had an opportunity of throwing them into the bunker on her way back from Scudder's Cottage. But there's something else, isn't there? I think this crime was committed by someone who didn't know that the Whistler was dead when she did the murder and did know shortly afterwards.'

'It's ingenious, Mr Dalgliesh.'

Dalgliesh was tempted to say that it wasn't ingenious, merely logical. Rickards would feel obliged to question Alice Mair again, but he would get nowhere. And it wasn't his case. Within two days he would be back in London. Any more dirty work which MI5 wanted done they would have to do themselves. He had already interfered more than was strictly justified and certainly more than he had found agreeable. He told himself that it would be dishonest to blame either Rickards or the murderer for the fact that most of the decisions he had come to the headland to make were still undecided.

That unexpected spurt of envy had induced a mild self-disgust which wasn't helped by the discovery that he had left the book he was currently reading, A. N. Wilson's biography of Tolstoy, in the room at the top of the tower. It was providing satisfaction and consolation of which at the present he felt particularly in need. Shutting the front door of the mill firmly against the wind, he fought his way round the curve of the tower, switched on the lights and climbed up to the top storey. Outside, the wind whooped and screamed like a pack of demented demons but here, in this small domed cell it was extraordinarily quiet. The tower had stood for over 150 years. It had resisted far worse gales. On an impulse he opened the eastward window and let the wind rush in like a wild cleansing force. It was then that he saw, over the flint wall which bounded the patio at Martyr's Cottage, a light in the kitchen window. It was no ordinary light. As he watched, it flickered, then died, flickered again, and then strengthened into a ruddy glow. He had seen that kind of light before and knew what it meant. Martyr's Cottage was on fire.

He almost slid down the two ladders linking the mill floors and, dashing into the sitting room, paused only to telephone for the fire brigade and ambulance, grateful that he hadn't yet garaged the car. Seconds later he was hurtling at top speed across the rough grass of the headland. The Jaguar rocked to a stop and he rushed to the front door. It was locked. For a second he considered battering it open with the Jaguar. But the frame was solid sixteenth-century oak and valuable seconds could be lost in futile manoeuvring and accelerating. Racing to the side he sprang at the wall, grasped the top, swung his body over and dropped on to the rear patio. It took only a second to check that the back door, too, was bolted top and bottom. He had no doubt who was inside; he would have to get her out through the window. He tore off his jacket and wrapped it round his right arm while, at the same time, turning on full the outside tap and drenching his head and upper body. The icy water dripped from him as he flexed his elbow and crashed it against the glass. But the pane was thick, designed to keep out the winter gales. He had to stand on the sill, supporting himself by the window frame, and kick violently and repeatedly before the glass crashed inwards and the flames leap⁺ at him.

Inside the window was a double sink. He rolled over it and, gasping in the smoke, dropped to his knees and began to crawl towards her. She was lying between the stove and the table, the long body rigid as an effigy. Her hair and clothes were alight and she lay there staring upwards, bathed in tongues of fire. But her face was as yet untouched and the open eyes seemed to gaze at him with such an intensity of half-crazed endurance that there flashed into his mind unbidden the image of Agnes Poley so that the blazing tables and chairs were the crackling faggots of her agonizing martyrdom, and he smelled above the acrid smoke the dreadful stink of burning flesh.

He tugged at Alice Mair's body but it was awkwardly wedged and the edge of the burning table had fallen across her legs. Somehow he had to buy a few seconds of time. He staggered coughing through the smoke to the sink, turned both taps full on and, seizing a pan, he filled it and threw water over the flames again and again. A small area of fire hissed and began to die. Kicking away the burning debris, he managed to lift her over his shoulder then stumbled to the door. But the bolts, almost too hot to touch, were jammed fast. He would have to get her out through the broken window. Gasping with the effort, he pushed the dead weight forward over the sink. But the rigid body caught on the taps and it took an eternity of agonizing time before he was able to free her, shove her forward to the window and at last see her tip forward out of sight. He gasped in the fresh air and, grasping the edge of the sink, tried to raise himself. But suddenly his legs had no strength. He felt them buckle and had to rest his arms on the sink edge to prevent himself from falling back into the strengthening fire. Until this minute he had been unaware of pain, but now it clawed and bit at his legs and back as if he were being savaged by a pack of dogs. He couldn't stretch his head to reach the running taps but he cupped his hands and threw the water against his face as if this cool benison could assuage the agony in his legs. And suddenly he was visited with an almost overwhelming temptation to let go, to fall back into the fire rather than make the impossible effort to escape. It was only a second's folly but it spurred him to a last desperate attempt. He seized the taps, one with each hand, and slowly and painfully lifted himself across the sink. And now his knees had a purchase on the hard edge and he could thrust himself forward to the windows. Smoke billowed around him and the great tongues of flame roared at his back. His ears hurt with the roaring. It filled the headland and he no longer knew whether he was hearing fire, wind or the sea. Then he made the last effort and felt himself falling on to the softness of her body. He rolled away from her. She was no longer burning. Her clothes had been burnt away and now clung like blackened rags to what was left of the flesh. He managed to get to his feet and half crawled, half stumbled towards the outside tap. He reached it just before he lost consciousness and the last thing he heard was the hiss as the stream of water quenched his burning clothes.

A minute later he opened his eyes. The stones were hard against his burnt back and when he tried to move the spasm of agony made him cry aloud. He had never known such pain. But a face, pale as the moon, was bending over him and he recognized Meg Dennison. He thought of that blackened thing by the window and managed to say: 'Don't look. Don't look.'

But she answered gently: 'She's dead. And it's all right, I had to look.'

And then he ceased to know her. His mind, disorientated, was in another place, another time. And suddenly, among the crowd of gaping spectators, the soldiers with their pikes guarding the scaffold, there was Rickards saying: 'But she isn't a thing, Mr Dalgliesh. She's a woman.' He closed his eyes. Meg's arms enclosed him. He turned his face and pressed it into her jacket, biting the wool so that he would not disgrace himself by groaning aloud. And then he felt her cool hands on his face.

She said: 'The ambulance is coming. I can hear it. Lie still, my dear. It's going to be all right.'

The last sound he heard was the clanging of the fire engine's bell as he let himself slide again into unconsciousness.

It was mid-January before Adam Dalgliesh came again to Larksoken Mill, a sunny day of such warmth that the headland lay
bathed in the bright translucence of a premature spring. Meg
had arranged to meet him at the mill in the afternoon to say
goodbye and, passing through the rear garden gate to walk across
the headland, she saw that the first snowdrops were already in
bloom and squatted to gaze with pure pleasure at their delicate
green and white heads trembling in the breeze. The turf of the
headland was springy to her feet and, in the far distance, a flock
of seagulls wheeled and swooped like a shower of white petals.

The Jaguar stood outside the mill and through the open door a
swathe of sunlight lay over the denuded room. Dalgliesh was on
his knees packing the last of his aunt's books into tea chests. The
pictures, already wrapped, were propped against the wall. Meg
knelt beside him and began to help by passing him the corded
volumes. She said: 'How are your legs and back?'

'A little stiff and the scars still itch occasionally. But they seem
fine.'

'No more pain?'

'No more pain.'

They worked for a few minutes in companionable silence.
Then Meg said: 'I know you don't want to be told this, but we're
all grateful for what you are doing for the Blaneys. The rent
you're charging for the mill is derisory and Ryan knows it.'

Dalgliesh said: 'I'm doing him no favours. I wanted a local
family to live here and he was the obvious choice. It isn't
everyone's house, after all. If he's worried about the size of the
rent he can regard himself as a caretaker. You could argue that I
should be paying him.'

'Not many men looking for a caretaker would choose an

eccentric artist with four children. But this place will be just right for them; two bathrooms, a proper kitchen and the tower for Ryan to paint in. Theresa is transformed. She's been so much stronger since her operation and now she looks radiant with happiness. She called in at the Old Rectory yesterday to tell us all about it and how she's been measuring up the rooms and planning where they'll put the furniture. It's much more suitable for them than Scudder's Cottage even if Alex hadn't wanted to sell and get rid of it for good. I can't blame him. Did you know that he's selling Martyr's Cottage, too? Now that he's so busy with the new job I think he wants to cut himself off from the headland and its memories. I suppose that's natural. And I don't think you know about Jonathan Reeves. He's engaged to a young girl from the power station, Shirley Coles. And Mrs Jago has had a letter from Neil Pascoe. After a couple of false starts he's got a temporary job as a social worker in Camden. She says he seems happy enough. And there's good news about Timmy, at least I suppose it's good news. The police have traced Amy's mother. She and her common-law husband don't want Timmy so he's being placed for adoption. He'll go to a couple who'll give him love and security.'

And then she stopped, afraid that she was prattling on, that he might not be interested in all this local gossip. But there was one question that had been in her mind for the last three months which she needed to ask, and which only he could answer. She watched for a moment in silence as the long sensitive hands fitted the corded books expertly into the case, then said: 'Does Alex accept that his sister killed Hilary? I've never liked to ask Inspector Rickards and he wouldn't tell me if I did. And I can't possibly ask Alex. We've never discussed Alice or the murder since her death. At the funeral we hardly spoke.'

But she knew that Rickards would have confided in Adam Dalgliesh. He said: 'I don't think Alex Mair is a man to deceive himself about uncomfortable facts. He must know the truth. But that doesn't mean that he'll admit it to the police. Officially he accepts their view that the murderess is dead but that it's now impossible to prove whether that murderess was Amy Camm, Caroline Amphlett or Alice Mair. The difficulty is that there still isn't a single piece of concrete evidence to connect Miss Mair with Hilary Robarts's death and certainly not enough circumstantial evidence posthumously to brand her as the killer. If she had lived and withdrawn her confession to you I doubt whether Rickards would have been justified even in making an arrest. The open verdict at the inquest means that even the suicide theory is unproved. The fire investigator's report confirms that the fire was caused by the overturn of a pan of boiling fat, probably while she was cooking, perhaps trying out a new recipe.'

Meg said bitterly: 'And it all rests on my story, doesn't it? The not-very-likely tale told by a woman who has made trouble before and who has a history of mental breakdown. That came out clearly when I was being questioned. Inspector Rickards seemed obsessed with the relationship, whether I had a grudge against Alice, whether we had quarrelled. By the time he had finished I didn't know whether he saw me as a malicious liar or her accomplice.'

Even three and a half months after the death it was difficult to think of those long interrogations without the familiar destructive mixture of pain, fear and anger. She had been made to tell her story over and over again under those sharp and sceptical eyes. And she could understand why he had been so reluctant to believe her. She had never found it easy to lie convincingly and he had known that she was lying. But why? he had asked. What reason did Alice Mair give for the murder? What was her motive? Her brother couldn't be forced to marry Hilary Robarts. And it's not as if he hadn't been married before. His ex-wife is alive and well, so what made this marriage so impossible for her? And she hadn't told him, except to reiterate obstinately that Alice had wanted to prevent it. She had promised not to tell, and she never would, not even to Adam Dalgliesh, who was the only man who might possibly have been able to make her. She guessed that he knew that too, but that he would never ask. Once when she was visiting him in hospital she had suddenly said: 'You know, don't you?'

And he had replied: 'No, I don't know, but I can guess. Blackmail isn't an uncommon motive for murder.'

But he had asked no questions, and for that she was grateful. She knew now that Alice had told her the truth only because she had planned that Meg wouldn't be alive the next day to reveal it. She had meant them to die together. But in the end she had drawn back. The whisky, almost certainly drugged with her sleeping tablets, had been gently but firmly taken from her hand. In the end Alice had kept faith with their friendship and she would keep faith with her friend. Alice had said that she owed her brother a death. Meg had pondered on those words but could still find no real meaning in them. But if Alice had owed Alex a death she, for her part, owed Alice her loyalty and her silence. She said: 'I'm hoping to buy Martyr's Cottage when the repairs are finished. I have some capital from the sale of the London house and the promise of a small mortgage which is all I'll need. I thought I could let it in summer to help with the expenses. And then, when the Copleys no longer need me, I could move in and live there. I'd like the thought that it would be waiting for me.'

If he was surprised that she should want to return to a place with such traumatic memories, he didn't say so. As if she had a need to explain Meg went on: 'Terrible things have happened in the past to people living on this headland, not only to Agnes Poley, to Hilary, to Alice, to Amy and Caroline. But I still feel at home here. I still feel that this is my place. I still feel that I want to be part of it. And if there are ghosts at Martyr's Cottage, they will be friendly spirits.'

He said: 'It's a stony soil in which to put down roots.'

'Perhaps that's the kind of soil my roots need.'

An hour later she had said her last goodbye. The truth lay between them, unspoken, and now he was leaving and she might never see him again. She realized with a smile of happy surprise that she was a little in love with him. But it didn't matter. It was as devoid of pain as it was of hope. When she reached a low ridge on the headland she turned and looked north at the power station, the generator and symbol of the potent and mysterious power which she could never separate from the image of that curiously beautiful mushroom cloud, symbol too of the intellectual and spiritual arrogance which had led Alice to murder, and it seemed to her for a second that she heard the echo of the last warning siren screaming its terrible message over the headland. And evil didn't end with the death of one evildoer. Somewhere at this moment a new Whistler could be planning his dreadful revenge against a world in which he had never been at home. But that was in the unforeseeable future and the fear had no reality. Reality was here, in a single moment of sunlit time, in the shivering grasses of the headland, the sparkling sea layered in blue and purple to the horizon and winged with a single sail, the broken arches of the abbey in which the flints struck gold from the mellowing sun, the great sails of the mill, motionless and silent, the taste of the sea-salted air. Here the past and the present fused and her own life, with its trivial devices and desires, seemed only an insignificant moment in the long history of the headland. And then she smiled at these portentous imaginings and, turning to wave a final goodbye to the tall figure still standing at the mill door, she strode out resolutely for home. The Copleys would be waiting for their afternoon tea.